THE BEAT GOES ON

Also by Ian Rankin

The Inspector Malcolm Fox Series
The Complaints
The Impossible Dead

The Detective Inspector Rebus Series
Knots & Crosses
Hide & Seek
Tooth & Nail (previously published as *Wolfman*)
A Good Hanging and Other Stories
Strip Jack
The Black Book
Mortal Causes
Let It Bleed
Black & Blue
The Hanging Garden
Death Is Not the End (a novella)
Dead Souls
Set in Darkness
The Falls
Resurrection Men
A Question of Blood
Fleshmarket Alley
The Naming of the Dead
Exit Music
Standing in Another Man's Grave
Saints of the Shadow Bible

Other Novels
Witch Hunt
Blood Hunt
Bleeding Hearts
Watchman
Doors Open
Dark Entries (graphic novel)

THE BEAT GOES ON
THE COMPLETE REBUS STORIES

IAN
RANKIN

LITTLE, BROWN AND COMPANY

NEW YORK BOSTON LONDON

Little, Brown and Company
Hachette Book Group
1290 Avenue of the Americas, New York, NY 10104
littlebrown.com

First United States Edition, August 2015
Originally published in Great Britain by Orion Publishing Group Ltd., October 2014

Little, Brown and Company is a division of Hachette Book Group, Inc. The Little, Brown name and logo are trademarks of Hachette Book Group, Inc.

The publisher is not responsible for websites (or their content) that are not owned by the publisher.

The Hachette Speakers Bureau provides a wide range of authors for speaking events. To find out more, go to hachettespeakersbureau.com or call (866) 376-6591.

ISBN 978-0-316-29683-0
Library of Congress Control Number: 2015940040

10 9 8 7 6 5 4 3 2 1

RRD-C

Printed in the United States of America

CONTENTS

A few words about these stories.

'Dead and Buried', which opens this collection, is one of the most recent stories I've written. We've placed it at the very start because it takes place in the mid-1980s, when Rebus was learning the ropes at Summerhall police station (as featured in my novel *Saints of the Shadow Bible*). There then follow the twelve stories from my collection *A Good Hanging and Other Stories*. These were written to comprise a chronological year in Rebus's life, so 'Playback' is set in March, 'A Good Hanging' in August (while the Festival Fringe is in full swing – as it were), and 'Auld Lang Syne' in December. After this come seven stories from *Beggars Banquet* along with the novella 'Death Is Not the End' (part of which ended up 'cannibalised' in my novel *Dead Souls*). Additionally, we've included six uncollected stories – these were mostly written for magazines and newspapers, sometimes for the Christmas edition, which is why the festive season crops up. Then there are two brand new stories – 'The Passenger' and 'A Three-Pint Problem'. The final story in the collection, 'The Very Last Drop', is set immediately after Rebus's retirement at the end of *Exit Music* and was written to be read aloud at a charity night at Edinburgh's Caledonian Brewery – you'll see why when you reach it.

I hope you get as much fun reading these stories as I had writing them.

Ian Rankin

PS: After the first edition of this book appeared, we found an old story lurking in the files – 'My Shopping Day'. It is included here, as is a new story, 'Cinders', written for Christmas 2014.

THE BEAT GOES ON

Dead and Buried

'Colder than an ex-wife's kiss,' Detective Inspector Stefan Gilmour muttered, shuffling his feet and rubbing his hands.

'I wouldn't know,' Rebus replied. His own hands were pushed deep into the pockets of his coat. It was 3 p.m. on a winter afternoon, and the lights in the prison yard had already been switched on. Faces sometimes appeared at the barred windows, accompanied by curious looks and gestures. The mechanical digger was making slow progress, workmen with pickaxes standing ready.

'I keep forgetting you're still married,' Gilmour commented. 'That'll be for the sake of your daughter, eh?'

Rebus glowered at him, but Gilmour was focusing his attention on the unmarked grave. They were in an unused corner of the grounds of HMP Saughton, close by its high sheer walls. The guards who had brought them to the spot had vanished indoors again sharpish. In place of a hearse, the undertaker had provided a pale blue van pockmarked with rust. It carried a cheap, plain coffin, since nobody reckoned much would remain of the original. Twenty years back Joseph Blay had been hanged not fifty yards away, one of the last men to be executed in Scotland. Rebus had been shown the hanging shed on a previous visit to the prison. It was still, he'd been informed, in full working order should capital punishment make a comeback.

The digger scraped at the ground again, and this time threw up some long splinters of wood. One of the workmen gestured for the driver to lift the arm away, before climbing into the hole, accompanied – with some apparent reluctance – by his younger colleague. As they worked with their pickaxes, more of the coffin was revealed, some sections intact. There was no smell at all, not that Rebus could pick up. The first he saw of Joseph Blay was a shank of hair with the skull below. The fresh coffin had been produced from the back of the van. Nobody was here to loiter. Blay wore a dark suit. Rebus didn't know what he'd expected from the exhumation: worms emerging from eye sockets maybe, or the stench of putrefaction. He had been steeling himself all morning, forgoing breakfast and lunch so there'd be nothing for him to bring up. But all he was looking at was a skeleton in a cheap suit, resembling the prop from some medical students' prank.

'Afternoon, Joe,' Gilmour said, giving a little salute.

After a few more minutes, the workmen were ready to lift the body. Blay's trousers and suit jacket seemed stuck to the ground beneath, but eventually came free. The remains were treated with neither great reverence nor any disrespect. The deceased was a job, and that job would be carried out with brisk efficiency before any of the living participants froze to death.

'What's that?' Rebus asked, nodding towards the hole. Gilmour narrowed his eyes, then clambered into the trench, crouching to pick up a pocket watch on a chain.

'Probably in his jacket,' he said, offering his free hand to Rebus so he could be helped back up. The lid had already been placed on the new coffin and it was being loaded into the van.

'Where will he end up?' Rebus asked.

Gilmour shrugged. 'Nowhere worse than this,' he offered, returning the sombre stare of one of the old lags at a second-storey window.

'Hard to disagree,' Rebus said. The digger's engine had started up again. There was a hole to be refilled.

At a pub near Haymarket Station, Gilmour ordered Irish coffees. The coffee was instant and the cream UHT, but with an extra slug of Grouse in each mug it might just do the job. There was no fire as such, but radiator pipes hissed away under the row of bench seats, so they sat side by side and slurped. Rebus had lit a cigarette and could feel his whole face tingling as he began to thaw.

'Remind me,' he said eventually. 'What the hell just happened?'

'It's how they did it back then,' Gilmour obliged. 'When you were hanged, you went to a grave inside the prison grounds. Joseph Blay killed a man who owed him money. Went to his house and stabbed him. Found guilty and sentenced to the scaffold.'

'And this was in '63?'

Gilmour nodded. 'Twenty years back. Charlie Cruikshank was in charge of the case. He's dead now, too – heart attack a couple of years ago.'

'I've heard of him.'

'Taught me everything I know. Man was a legend in the Edinburgh Police.'

'Did he attend the execution?'

Gilmour nodded again. 'He always did. When he used to talk about them, you could tell he thought we'd made a big mistake doing away with them. Not that he thought it was a deterrent. I've not met many killers who paused beforehand to consider the consequences.'

'So for him it was what? A vengeance sort of thing.'

'Well, it stopped them getting into any more bother, didn't it? And saved all of us the cost of their upkeep in the nick.'

'I suppose.'

Gilmour drained his glass and told Rebus it was his round.

'Same again?'

'Aye, but without the coffee and the cream,' Gilmour responded with a wink.

When Rebus returned from the bar with their whiskies, he saw that Gilmour was playing with the pocket watch, trying to prise it open.

'I thought you handed it over,' Rebus commented.

'You think he'll miss it?'

'All the same ...'

'Hell's teeth, John, it's not like it's worth anything. Case looks like pewter. Here, you have a go.' He handed the watch to Rebus and went to ask the barman for a knife. The timepiece had very little weight to it and no markings that Rebus could see. He worked at it with his thumbnail without success. Meantime, the barman had offered up a small screwdriver. Gilmour took back the watch and eventually got it open. The glass was opaque, the face discoloured and water damaged. The hands had stopped at quarter past six.

'No inscription,' Gilmour said.

'Must have had sentimental value at least,' Rebus offered. 'For him to be buried with it. His dad's maybe, or even his granddad's?'

Gilmour rubbed his thumb across the glass, turning the watch in his hand. Then he got busy with the screwdriver again, until the mechanism came free from its casing. An inch-long cardboard rectangle was stuck there. It came apart in the process, adhering to both the workings of the watch and the inner case. If there had been any writing on it, the words had long faded.

'What do you reckon?' Gilmour asked.

'Is there something I'm not seeing here, Stefan?' Rebus asked in return.

'You're the detective, John.' Gilmour placed the watch on the table between them. 'You tell me.'

*

The watch sat on Gilmour's desk at Summerhall police station for the rest of the week. The old building felt like it might not survive till spring. Two of the windows in the CID office wouldn't shut properly, and strips of newspaper had been stuffed into the gaps. An unlagged water pipe in the roof space had burst a fortnight back, bringing down part of the ceiling in a storeroom. Rebus had only been stationed there for a month and a half, but the mood of the place had managed to seep into his bones. He felt he was still being tested by his new colleagues, and that somehow the pocket watch was part of it. DS Dod Blantyre had offered to have it looked at by a watchmaker of his acquaintance, but Gilmour had shaken his head. There was a photo one day in the *Scotsman*, showing the construction work at HMP Saughton. New workshops were being built – the reason for Joseph Blay's exhumation. It still wasn't clear to Rebus why Gilmour had taken him there – or even why Gilmour himself had felt the need to be present. He hadn't joined the force until '65, two years after Blay's execution. When Rebus found himself alone in the office with Dod Blantyre, he asked if Blantyre had known Charlie Cruikshank.

'Oh aye,' Blantyre said with a chuckle. 'Some boy, Charlie.'

'He seems to have taken Stefan under his wing.'

Blantyre nodded. 'They were close,' he agreed. 'But then Charlie wasn't someone you wanted to get on the wrong side of.'

'Did he work at Summerhall?'

Blantyre shook his head. 'Leith – that was Stefan's first posting. Pair of them used to go to watch Hearts play. And here's the thing: Stefan grew up supporting *Hibs*. Could never admit as much to Charlie though. Had to keep gritting his teeth and joining in whenever a goal was scored.'

'Would it have meant a falling out between them if Cruikshank had found out?'

'You planning on writing Stefan's biography, John? What's with all the questions anyway?'

'Just curious.'

'I tend to find that's a dangerous trait in CID. You might want to get shot of it.' There was an edge to Blantyre's voice. For the rest of the afternoon, Rebus could feel the man's eyes on him, the mood lightening only when, at quarter past five, Stefan Gilmour announced that he could hear the siren call of the local bar. As the group left Summerhall, however, Rebus realised he had left his pools coupon in the office.

'I'll catch you up,' he said.

The coupon was in his desk drawer, filled out and ready to be handed in at the pub. He'd often asked himself what he would do if he ever did get a big win. Retire to warmer climes? He doubted his wife would want to give up her job. Nor, for that matter, would he. Pausing by Gilmour's desk, he scooped up the watch and turned it in his hand, the chain dangling. It was easier to open now, the mechanism sliding onto his palm. But it still wasn't about to tell him anything.

'Sixty-three?' the clerk said. 'That counts as recent history.'

The man was bald and cadaverous, his glasses horn-rimmed and greasy. The warehouse in Granton was his fiefdom, and he obviously knew every inch of it.

'How far back do records go?' Rebus inquired.

'I've got some dating from the 1940s – they're not complete sets though.'

'You sound disappointed.'

The man peered at him, then gestured towards a desk. 'You can wait here while I fetch what you need.'

'Thanks.' Rebus sat down and, seeing an ashtray, decided to get a cigarette lit. It was nine in the morning and he'd warned the office he had a dentist's appointment. Running his tongue around his mouth, he realised he really should make an appointment, having cancelled the last one. It was five minutes before the clerk returned. He placed a manila folder in front of Rebus, then produced a note-book from his pocket.

'Just need to sign you in,' he said. 'Warrant card, please.'

Rebus handed it over and watched as the man began to enter his details onto a page.

'You always do that?' Rebus asked.

'It's important to keep a record.'

'Anyone else requested this file recently?'

The clerk offered a thin smile. 'I wondered if you'd twig.'

'I'm guessing it was a DI called Gilmour.'

The clerk nodded. 'Just three weeks back. Our hanged man is suddenly a popular figure ...'

Frazer Spence was the only one in the office when Rebus returned to Summerhall.

'Must have been quite a procedure,' he said.

'What do you mean?'

Spence patted his cheek with a finger. 'The dentist. I'm usually in and out in half an hour.'

'That's because you brush your teeth.'

'Twice a day,' Spence confirmed.

'How's your bike, by the way?' Spence had come off his motorcycle the previous weekend.

'Garage says it'll take a week or so.'

'You need to be more careful on that thing.'

Spence just shrugged. 'Hit a patch of oil. Could have happened to anyone.'

'Still, sliding along a road on your backside at fifty miles an hour – maybe a lesson there, eh?'

'My leathers bore the brunt.'

'All the same.' Rebus paused and looked around the office. 'Where are the others?'

'Meeting one of Stefan's snitches. He might have something on the hold-up at that jeweller's on George Street.'

'Bit of progress would be welcome.'

'Definitely.'

Rebus was standing next to Gilmour's desk. The watch was no longer sitting there, so he opened the drawer. It lay on top of a stack of betting slips. Rebus lifted it out and slipped it into his pocket. 'I'm off out again,' he told Spence.

'So what do I tell Stefan when he gets back?'

'Tell him he's not the only cop in town with informants to keep sweet.'

'So which pub can he find you in if he needs you?'

Rebus pressed a finger to his lips and gave a wink.

'What's on your mind, John?'

It was mid-evening. A park bench next to Bruntsfield Links. Rebus had been waiting twenty minutes for Stefan Gilmour to arrive. Gilmour sat down, hands in coat pockets, legs splayed. Rebus had just stubbed a cigarette out under his heel and was resisting the urge to light another.

'I've not been at Summerhall as long as the rest of you,' Rebus began.

'You're still one of the Saints though.'

'All the same, I keep wondering if I'm still on probation.' Rebus held the watch out towards Gilmour.

'I knew you'd taken it,' his boss said with a smile. 'So what did you do with it?'

'The forensics lab. They've got some kind of camera there hooked up to a computer.'

Gilmour shook his head slowly. 'Isn't technology amazing?'

'Getting better all the time,' Rebus agreed. 'But sometimes the old ways work, too. Your name's on the list at the storage unit in Granton – three weeks ago, you pulled the file on Joseph Blay. This was after news broke that his remains would have to be moved.'

'True enough.'

'Your old mentor's doing?'

Gilmour was staring out across the links. The street-lamps were lit and a haar was encroaching from the coast. 'Charlie Cruikshank told me to keep an eye on Blay. At the time, I'd no idea what he meant – Blay was long dead.'

'But you kept to your word.'

'I usually do.'

'Did you expect something to turn up in the coffin?'

Gilmour offered a shrug. 'I'd really no idea. Poring over the case-notes didn't offer any clues.'

'Until after the body was dug up,' Rebus said.

Gilmour half-turned towards him. 'On you go then, hot-shot. The stage is all yours.'

'The evidence against Blay was flimsy. Yes, he was owed money by Jim Chivers, but he was by no means the only enemy Chivers had. You could have filled the courtroom with them. Blay's finger-prints were found in the victim's home, but then he'd been a regular visitor, so they couldn't be said to be conclusive. Added to which, the knife was never found and there didn't seem to be any traces of blood on Blay's clothes or shoes. His story was that he'd spent the evening of the stabbing at the flicks in Morningside, seeing *The Man Who Shot Liberty Valance*. Problem was, no one could verify it. Staff at the picture house knew him for a regular but weren't able to say which shows he'd been to. He hadn't gone with anyone or spoken to anyone – took the bus home straight after, and again, no driver would admit to seeing him. One thing I *did* glean was that there was history between Blay and your old boss. Cruikshank had tried a few times to put Blay away and had always fallen short.'

'We all end up with at least one of those.'

'If we stay in the job long enough,' Rebus agreed.

'Having second thoughts, John? That would be a pity. Seems to me you're shaping up to be a good detective.'

'Meaning what?'

'Meaning someone who goes the extra mile. Someone who's conscientious.' Gilmour paused. 'And someone with a clear sense of good guys and bad.'

'You could have gone to Saughton alone. That would have been the safe move. But instead you took me. You needed to see what I'd do, how I'd react.'

'I had no idea there'd be anything worth a reaction.'

'But there was.' Rebus nodded towards the pocket watch, still resting in Gilmour's hand.

'It's just a keepsake, John.'

'A keepsake with a little scrap of cardboard hidden inside. You know what they told me at the forensics lab? They told me it's a cinema ticket, one of those old-fashioned stubs they used to give you. They can't make out any of the details. My guess is, the date and time would have been legible at one time, maybe even the title of the film.'

'You're thinking *Liberty Valance*?'

'Seems to fit the bill. A tiny bit of evidence that would have helped Joseph Blay's case. Probably emptied out his pockets when he was arrested, and Charlie Cruikshank palmed it. Knew he couldn't have it being found. So Blay's found guilty and Cruikshank is there to watch him hanged. He still has the ticket stub so he hides it inside the watch, just because he can. That's why he needed you to keep an eye on Joseph Blay – because that stub could have proved a man's innocence. Your boss was content to see someone go to the scaffold, no matter whether they'd committed the crime or not.'

'We can't know that, John. Who's to say how that stub ended up where it did?'

'You know I'm right though.'

'Good luck proving it.'

Rebus shook his head. 'We both know I can't do that.'

'But do you *want* to do it? See, being a cop isn't just about getting to the truth – it's knowing what to do with it when you arrive. Making judgement calls, some of them at a moment's notice.'

'That's not what Cruikshank did though, is it?'

'Maybe it is. He knows Blay's guilty. That ticket could have come from anywhere – Blay could have picked it up off the pavement or from the floor of a bus. Charlie took it out of circulation so as not to confuse the jury.'

'He wanted a guilty verdict at all costs.'

'He didn't want a guilty man to get off, John. That's the story here.'

'And you'd do the exact same thing, Stefan? That's what your old mentor taught you?'

'He gave his whole life to the job, John, heart and soul.' Gilmour rose to his feet and stood in front of Rebus. He held out the pocket watch. 'Do you want this?' he asked.

'What would I do with it?'

'You'd take it to The Complaints, lay out your version of events.'

'And what good would that do?' Rebus stared at the watch, then averted his gaze and shook his head. Gilmour waited a few more beats, then stuffed the watch into his coat.

'That's us then,' he said, reaching out his hand. 'Welcome to the Saints of the Shadow Bible, John.'

After only a moment's hesitation, Rebus stood up and returned the handshake.

Playback

It was the perfect murder.

Perfect, that is, so far as the Lothian and Borders Police were concerned. The murderer had telephoned in to confess, had then panicked and attempted to flee, only to be caught leaving the scene of the crime. End of story.

Except that now he was pleading innocence. Pleading, yelling and screaming it. And this worried Detective Inspector John Rebus, worried him all the way from his office to the four-storey tenement in Leith's trendy dockside area. The tenements here were much as they were in any working-class area of Edinburgh, except that they boasted colour-splashed roller blinds or Chinese-style bamboo affairs at their windows, and their grimy stone façades had been power-cleaned, their doors now boasting intruder-proof intercoms. A far cry from the greasy Venetian blinds and kicked-in passage-ways of the tenements in Easter Road or Gorgie, or even in nearby parts of Leith itself, the parts the developers were ignoring as yet.

The victim had worked as a legal secretary, this much Rebus knew. She had been twenty-four years old. Her name was Moira Bitter. Rebus smiled at that. It was a guilty smile, but at this hour of the morning any smile he could raise was something of a miracle.

He parked in front of the tenement, guided by a uniformed officer who had recognised the badly dented front bumper of Rebus's car. It was rumoured that the dent had come from knocking down too many old ladies, and who was Rebus to deny it? It was the stuff of legend and it gave him prominence in the fearful eyes of the younger recruits.

A curtain twitched in one of the ground-floor windows and Rebus caught a glimpse of an elderly lady. Every tenement, it seemed, tarted up or not, boasted its elderly lady. Living alone, with one dog or four cats for company, she was her building's eyes and ears. As Rebus entered the hallway, a door opened and the old lady stuck out her head.

'He was going to run for it,' she whispered. 'But the bobby caught him. I saw it. Is the young lass dead? Is that it?' Her lips were pursed in keen horror. Rebus smiled at her but said nothing. She would know soon enough. Already she seemed to know as much as he did himself. That was the trouble with living in a city the size of a town, a town with a village mentality.

He climbed the four flights of stairs slowly, listening all the while to the report of the constable who was leading him inexorably towards the corpse of Moira Bitter. They spoke in an undertone: stairwell walls had ears.

'The call came at about 5 a.m., sir,' explained PC MacManus. 'The caller gave his name as John MacFarlane and said he'd just murdered his girlfriend. He sounded distressed by all accounts, and I was radioed to investigate. As I arrived, a man was running down the stairs. He seemed in a state of shock.'

'Shock?'

'Sort of disorientated, sir.'

'Did he say anything?' asked Rebus.

'Yes, sir, he told me, "Thank God you're here. Moira's dead." I then asked him to accompany me upstairs to the flat in question, called in for assistance, and the gentleman was arrested.'

Rebus nodded. MacManus was a model of efficiency, not a word out of place, the tone just right. Everything by rote and without the interference of too much thought. He would go far as a uniformed officer, but Rebus doubted the young man would ever make CID. When they reached the fourth floor, Rebus paused for breath then walked into the flat.

The hall's pastel colour scheme extended to the living-room and bedroom. Mute colours, subtle and warming. There was nothing subtle about the blood though. The blood was copious. Moira Bitter lay sprawled across her bed, her chest a riot of colour. She was wearing apple-green pyjamas, and her hair was silky blonde. The police pathologist was examining her head.

'She's been dead about three hours,' he informed Rebus. 'Stabbed three or four times with a small sharp instrument, which, for the sake of convenience, I'm going to term a knife. I'll examine her properly later on.'

Rebus nodded and turned to MacManus, whose face had a sickly grey tinge to it.

'Your first time?' Rebus asked. The constable nodded slowly. 'Never mind,' Rebus continued. 'You never get used to it anyway. Come on.'

He led the constable out of the room and back into the small hallway. 'This man we've arrested, what did you say his name was?'

'John MacFarlane, sir,' said the constable, taking deep breaths. 'He's the deceased's boyfriend apparently.'

'You said he seemed in a state of shock. Was there anything else you noticed?'

The constable frowned, thinking. 'Such as, sir?' he said at last.

'Blood,' said Rebus coolly. 'You can't stab someone in the heat of the moment without getting blood on you.'

MacManus said nothing. Definitely not CID material and perhaps realising it for the very first time. Rebus turned from him and entered the living-room. It was almost neurotically tidy. Magazines and newspapers in their rack beside the sofa. A chrome and glass coffee table bearing nothing more than a clean ashtray and a paperback romance. It could have come straight from an Ideal Home exhibition. No family photographs, no clutter. This was the lair of an individualist. No ties with the past, a present ransacked wholesale from Habitat and Next. There was no evidence of a struggle. No evidence of an encounter of any kind: no glasses or coffee cups. The killer had not loitered, or else had been very tidy about his business.

Rebus went into the kitchen. It, too, was tidy. Cups and plates stacked for drying beside the empty sink. On the draining-board were knives, forks, teaspoons. No murder weapon. There were spots of water in the sink and on the draining-board itself, yet the cutlery and crockery were dry. Rebus found a dishtowel hanging up behind the door and felt it. It was damp. He examined it more closely. There was a small smudge on it. Perhaps gravy or chocolate. Or blood. Someone had dried something recently, but what?

He went to the cutlery drawer and opened it. Inside, amidst the various implements was a short-bladed chopping knife with a heavy black handle. A quality knife, sharp and gleaming. The other items in the drawer were bone dry, but this chopping knife's wooden handle was damp to the touch. Rebus was in no doubt: he had found his murder weapon.

Clever of MacFarlane though to have cleaned and put away the knife. A cool and calm action. Moira Bitter had been dead three hours. The call to the police station had come an hour ago. What had MacFarlane done during the intervening two hours? Cleaned the flat? Washed and dried the dishes? Rebus looked in the kitchen's swing-bin, but found no other clues, no broken ornaments, nothing that might hint at a struggle. And if there had been no struggle, if the murderer had gained access to the tenement and to Moira Bitter's flat without forcing an entry ... if all this were true, Moira had known her killer.

Rebus toured the rest of the flat, but found no other clues. Beside the telephone in the hall stood an answering machine. He played the tape, and heard Moira Bitter's voice.

'Hello, this is Moira. I'm out, I'm in the bath, or I'm otherwise engaged.' (A giggle.) 'Leave a message and I'll get back to you, unless you sound boring.'

There was only one message. Rebus listened to it, then wound back the tape and listened again.

'Hello, Moira, it's John. I got your message. I'm coming over. Hope you're not "otherwise engaged". Love you.'

John MacFarlane: Rebus didn't doubt the identity of the caller. Moira sounded fresh and fancy-free in her message. But did MacFarlane's response hint at jealousy? Perhaps she *had* been otherwise engaged when he'd arrived. He lost his temper, blind rage, a knife lying handy. Rebus had seen it before. Most victims knew their attackers. If that were not the case, the police wouldn't solve so many crimes. It was a blunt fact. You double bolted your door against the psychopath with the chainsaw, only to be stabbed in the back by your lover, husband, son or neighbour.

John MacFarlane was as guilty as hell. They would find blood on his clothes, even if he'd tried cleaning it off. He had stabbed his girlfriend, then calmed down and called in to report the crime, but had grown frightened at the end and had attempted to flee.

The only question left in Rebus's mind was the why? The why and those missing two hours.

Edinburgh through the night. The occasional taxi rippling across setts and lone shadowy figures slouching home with hands in pockets, shoulders hunched. During the night hours, the sick and the old died peacefully, either at home or in some hospital ward. Two in the morning until four: the dead hours. And then some died horribly, with terror in their eyes. The taxis still rumbled past, the night people kept moving. Rebus let his car idle at traffic lights, missing the change to green, only coming to his senses as amber turned red again. Glasgow Rangers were coming to town on Saturday. There would be casual violence. Rebus felt comfortable with the thought. The worst football hooligan could probably not have stabbed with the same ferocity as Moira Bitter's killer. Rebus lowered his eyebrows. He was rousing himself to fury, keen for confrontation. Confrontation with the murderer himself.

*

John MacFarlane was crying as he was led into the interrogation room, where Rebus had made himself look comfortable, cigarette in one hand, coffee in the other. Rebus had expected a lot of things, but not tears.

'Would you like something to drink?' he asked. MacFarlane shook his head. He had slumped into the chair on the other side of the desk, his shoulders sagging, head bowed, and the sobs still coming from his throat. He mumbled something.

'I didn't catch that,' said Rebus.

'I said I didn't do it,' MacFarlane answered quietly. 'How could I do it? I love Moira.'

Rebus noted the present tense. He gestured towards the tape machine on the desk. 'Do you have any objections to my making a recording of this interview?' MacFarlane shook his head again. Rebus switched on the machine. He flicked ash from his cigarette onto the floor, sipped his coffee, and waited. Eventually, MacFarlane looked up. His eyes were stinging red. Rebus stared hard into those eyes, but still said nothing. MacFarlane seemed to be calming. Seemed, too, to know what was expected of him. He asked for a cigarette, was given one, and started to speak.

'I'd been out in my car. Just driving, thinking.'

Rebus interrupted him. 'What time was this?'

'Well,' said MacFarlane, 'ever since I left work, I suppose. I'm an architect. There's a competition on just now to design a new art gallery and museum complex in Stirling. Our partnership's going in for it. We were discussing ideas most of the day, you know, brainstorming.' He looked up at Rebus again, and Rebus nodded. Brainstorm: now there was an interesting word.

'And after work,' MacFarlane continued, 'I was so fired up I just felt like driving. Going over the different options and plans in my head. Working out which was strongest—'

He broke off, realising perhaps that he was talking in a rush, without thought or caution. He swallowed and inhaled some smoke. Rebus was studying MacFarlane's clothes. Expensive leather brogues, brown corduroy trousers, a thick white cotton shirt, the kind cricketers wore, open at the neck, a tailor-made tweed jacket. MacFarlane's 3-Series BMW was parked in the police garage, being searched. His pockets had been emptied, a Liberty print tie confiscated in case he had ideas about hanging himself. His brogues, too, were without their laces, these having been confiscated along with the tie. Rebus had gone through the belongings. A wallet, not exactly bulging with money but containing a fair spread of credit cards. There were more cards, too, in MacFarlane's personal organiser.

Rebus flipped through the diary pages, then turned to the sections for notes and for addresses. MacFarlane seemed to lead a busy but quite normal social life.

Rebus studied him now, across the expanse of the old table. MacFarlane was well-built, handsome if you liked that sort of thing. He looked strong, but not brutish. Probably he would make the local news headlines as 'Secretary's Yuppie Killer'. Rebus stubbed out his cigarette.

'We know you did it, John. That's not in dispute. We just want to know why.'

MacFarlane's voice was brittle with emotion. 'I swear I didn't, I swear.'

'You're going to have to do better than that.' Rebus paused again. Tears were dripping onto MacFarlane's corduroys. 'Go on with your story,' he said.

MacFarlane shrugged. 'That's about it,' he said, wiping his nose with the sleeve of his shirt.

Rebus prompted him. 'You didn't stop off anywhere for petrol or a meal or anything like that?' He sounded sceptical. MacFarlane shook his head.

'No, I just drove until my head was clear. I went all the way to the Forth Road Bridge. Turned off and went into Queensferry. Got out of the car to have a look at the water. Threw a few stones in for luck.' He smiled at the irony. 'Then drove round the coast road and back into Edinburgh.'

'Nobody saw you? You didn't speak to anyone?'

'Not that I can remember.'

'And you didn't get hungry?' Rebus sounded entirely unconvinced.

'We'd had a business lunch with a client. We took him to The Eyrie. After lunch there, I seldom need to eat until the next morning.'

The Eyrie was Edinburgh's most expensive restaurant. You didn't go there to eat, you went there to spend money. Rebus was feeling peckish himself. The canteen did a fine bacon buttie.

'When did you last see Miss Bitter alive?'

At the word 'alive', MacFarlane shivered. It took him a long time to answer. Rebus watched the tape revolving. 'Yesterday morning,' MacFarlane said at last. 'She stayed the night at my flat.'

'How long have you known her?'

'About a year. But I only started going out with her a couple of months ago.'

'Oh? And how did you know her before that?'

MacFarlane paused. 'She was Kenneth's girlfriend,' he said at last.

'Kenneth being—'

MacFarlane's cheeks reddened before he spoke. 'My best friend,' he said. 'Kenneth was my best friend. You could say I stole her from him. These things happen, don't they?'

Rebus raised an eyebrow. 'Do they?' he said. MacFarlane bowed his head again.

'Can I have a coffee?' he asked quietly. Rebus nodded, then lit another cigarette.

MacFarlane sipped the coffee, holding it in both hands like a ship-wreck survivor. Rebus rubbed his nose and stretched, feeling tired. He checked his watch. Eight in the morning. What a life. He had eaten two bacon rolls and a string of rind curled across the plate in front of him. MacFarlane had refused food, but finished the first cup of coffee in two gulps and gratefully accepted a second.

'So,' Rebus said, 'you drove back into town.'

'That's right.' MacFarlane took another sip of coffee. 'I don't know why, but I decided to check my answering machine for calls.'

'You mean when you got home?'

MacFarlane shook his head. 'No, from the car. I called home from my car-phone and got the answering machine to play back any messages.'

Rebus was impressed. 'That's clever,' he said.

MacFarlane smiled again, but the smile soon vanished. 'One of the messages was from Moira,' he said. 'She wanted to see me.'

'At that hour?' MacFarlane shrugged. 'Did she say why she wanted to see you?'

'No. She sounded ... strange.'

'Strange?'

'A bit ... I don't know, distant maybe.'

'Did you get the feeling she was on her own when she called?'

'I've no idea.'

'Did you call her back?'

'Yes. Her answering machine was on. I left a message.'

'Would you say you're the jealous type, Mr MacFarlane?'

'What?' MacFarlane sounded surprised by the question. He seemed to give it serious thought. 'No more so than the next man,' he said at last.

'Why would anyone want to kill her?'

MacFarlane stared at the table, shaking his head slowly.

'Go on,' said Rebus, sighing, growing impatient. 'You were saying how you got her message.'

'Well, I went straight to her flat. It was late, but I knew if she was asleep I could always let myself in.'

'Oh?' Rebus was interested. 'How?'

'I had a spare key,' MacFarlane explained.

Rebus got up from his chair and walked to the far wall and back, deep in thought.

'I don't suppose,' he said, 'you've got any idea *when* Moira made that call?'

MacFarlane shook his head. 'But the machine will have logged it,' he said. Rebus was more impressed than ever. Technology was a wonderful thing. What's more, he was impressed by MacFarlane. If the man was a murderer, then he was a very good one, for he had fooled Rebus into thinking him innocent. It was crazy. There was nothing to point to him not being guilty. But all the same, a feeling was a feeling, and Rebus most definitely had a feeling.

'I want to see that machine,' he said. 'And I want to hear the message on it. I want to hear Moira's last words.'

It was interesting how the simplest cases could become so complex. There was still no doubt in the minds of those around Rebus – his superiors and those below him – that John MacFarlane was guilty of murder. They had all the proof they needed, every last bit of it circumstantial.

MacFarlane's car was clean: no bloodstained clothes stashed in the boot. There were no prints on the chopping-knife, though MacFarlane's prints were found elsewhere in the flat, not surprising given that he'd visited that night, as well as on many a previous one. No prints either on the kitchen sink and taps, though the murderer had washed a bloody knife. Rebus thought that curious. And as for motive: jealousy, a falling-out, a past indiscretion discovered. The CID had seen them all.

Murder by stabbing was confirmed and the time of death narrowed down to a quarter of an hour either side of three in the morning. MacFarlane claimed that at that time he was driving towards Edinburgh, but had no witnesses to corroborate the claim. There was no blood to be found on MacFarlane's clothing, but, as Rebus himself knew, that didn't mean the man wasn't a killer.

More interesting, however, was that MacFarlane denied making the call to the police. Yet someone – in fact, whoever murdered Moira Bitter – *had* made it. And more interesting even than this was the telephone answering machine.

Rebus went to MacFarlane's flat in Liberton to investigate. The traffic was busy coming into town, but quiet heading out. Liberton was one of Edinburgh's many anonymous middle-class districts, substantial houses, small shops, a busy thoroughfare. It looked innocuous at midnight, and was even safer by day.

What MacFarlane had termed a 'flat' comprised, in fact, the top two storeys of a vast, detached house. Rebus roamed the building, not sure if he was looking for anything in particular. He found little. MacFarlane led a rigorous and regimented life and had the home to accommodate such a lifestyle. One room had been turned into a makeshift gymnasium, with weightlifting equipment and the like. There was an office for business use, a study for private use. The main bedroom was decidedly masculine in taste, though a framed painting of a naked woman had been removed from one wall and tucked behind a chair. Rebus thought he detected Moira Bitter's influence at work.

In the wardrobe were a few pieces of her clothing and a pair of her shoes. A snapshot of her had been framed and placed on MacFarlane's bedside table. Rebus studied the photograph for a long time, then sighed and left the bedroom, closing the door after him. Who knew when John MacFarlane would see his home again?

The answering machine was in the living-room. Rebus played the tape of the previous night's calls. Moira Bitter's voice was clipped and confident, her message to the point: 'Hello.' Then a pause. 'I need to see you. Come round as soon as you get this message. Love you.'

MacFarlane had told Rebus that the display unit on the machine showed time of call. Moira's call registered at 3.50 a.m., about forty-five minutes after her death. There was room for some discrepancy, but not three-quarters of an hour's worth. Rebus scratched his chin and pondered. He played the tape again. 'Hello.' Then the pause. 'I need to see you.' He stopped the tape and played it again, this time with the volume up and his ear close to the machine. That pause was curious and the sound quality on the tape was poor. He rewound and listened to another call from the same evening. The quality was better, the voice much clearer. Then he listened to Moira again. Were these recording machines infallible? Of course not. The time displayed could have been tampered with. The recording itself could be a fake. After all, whose word did he have that this *was* the voice of Moira Bitter? Only John MacFarlane's. But John MacFarlane had been caught leaving the scene of a murder. And now Rebus was being presented with a sort of an alibi for the man. Yes, the tape could well be a fake, used by MacFarlane to substantiate his story, but stupidly not put into use until after the time of death. Still, from what Rebus had heard from Moira's own answering machine, the voice was certainly similar to her own. The lab boys could sort it out with their clever machines. One technician in particular owed him a rather large favour.

Rebus shook his head. This still wasn't making much sense. He played the tape again and again.

'Hello.' Pause. 'I need to see you.'

'Hello.' Pause. 'I need to see you.'

'Hello.' Pause. 'I need—'

And suddenly it became a little clearer in his mind. He ejected the tape and slipped it into his jacket pocket, then picked up the telephone and called the station. He asked to speak to Detective Constable Brian Holmes. The voice, when it came on the line, was tired but amused.

'Don't tell me,' Holmes said, 'let me guess. You want me to drop everything and run an errand for you.'

'You must be psychic, Brian. Two errands really. Firstly, last night's calls. Get the recording of them and search for one from John MacFarlane, claiming he'd just killed his girlfriend. Make a copy of it and wait there for me. I've got another tape for you, and I want them both taken to the lab. Warn them you're coming—'

'And tell them it's priority, I know. It's *always* priority. They'll say what they always say: give us four days.'

'Not this time,' Rebus said. 'Ask for Bill Costain and tell him Rebus is collecting on his favour. He's to shelve what he's doing. I want a result today, not next week.'

'What's the favour you're collecting on?'

'I caught him smoking dope in the lab toilets last month.'

Holmes laughed. 'The world's going to pot,' he said. Rebus groaned at the joke and put down the receiver. He needed to speak with John MacFarlane again. Not about lovers this time, but about friends.

Rebus rang the doorbell a third time and at last heard a voice from within.

'Jesus, hold on! I'm coming.'

The man who answered the door was tall, thin, with wire-framed glasses perched on his nose. He peered at Rebus and ran his fingers through his hair.

'Mr Thomson?' Rebus asked. 'Kenneth Thomson?'

'Yes,' said the man, 'that's right.'

Rebus flipped open his ID. 'Detective Inspector John Rebus,' he said by way of introduction. 'May I come in?'

Kenneth Thomson held open the door. 'Please do,' he said. 'Will a cheque be all right?'

'A cheque?'

'I take it you're here about the parking tickets,' said Thomson. 'I'd have got round to them eventually, believe me. It's just that I've been hellish busy, and what with one thing and another ...'

'No, sir,' said Rebus, his smile as cold as a church pew, 'nothing to do with parking fines.'

'Oh?' Thomson pushed his glasses back up his nose and looked at Rebus. 'Then what's the problem?'

'It's about Miss Moira Bitter,' said Rebus.

'Moira? What about her?'

'She's dead, sir.'

Rebus had followed Thomson into a cluttered room overflowing with bundles of magazines and newspapers. A hi-fi sat in one corner, and covering the wall next to it were shelves filled with cassette tapes. These had an orderly look to them, as though they had been indexed, each tape's spine carrying an identifying number.

Thomson, who had been clearing a chair for Rebus to sit on, froze at the detective's words.

'Dead?' he gasped. 'How?'

'She was murdered, sir. We think John MacFarlane did it.'

'John?' Thomson's face was quizzical, then sceptical, then resigned. 'But why?'

'We don't know that yet, sir. I thought you might be able to help.'

'Of course I'll help if I can. Sit down, please.'

Rebus perched on the chair, while Thomson pushed aside some newspapers and settled himself on the sofa.

'You're a writer, I believe,' said Rebus.

Thomson nodded distractedly. 'Yes,' he said. 'Freelance journalism, food and drink, travel, that sort of thing. Plus the occasional commission to write a book. That's what I'm doing now, actually. Writing a book.'

'Oh? I like books myself. What's it about?'

'Don't laugh,' said Thomson, 'but it's a history of the haggis.'

'The haggis?' Rebus couldn't disguise a smile in his voice, warmer this time: the church pew had been given a cushion. He cleared his throat noisily, glancing around the room, noting the piles of books leaning precariously against walls, the files and folders and newsprint cuttings. 'You must do a lot of research,' he said appreciatively.

'Sometimes,' said Thomson. Then he shook his head. 'I still can't believe it. About Moira, I mean. About John.'

Rebus took out his notebook, more for effect than anything else. 'You were Miss Bitter's lover for a while,' he stated.

'That's right, Inspector.'

'But then she went off with Mr MacFarlane.'

'Right again.' A hint of bitterness had crept into Thomson's voice. 'I was very angry at the time, but I got over it.'

'Did you still see Miss Bitter?'

'No.'

'What about Mr MacFarlane?'

'No again. We spoke on the telephone a couple of times. It always seemed to end in a shouting match. We used to be like, well, it's a cliché, I suppose, but we used to be like brothers.'

'Yes,' said Rebus, 'so Mr MacFarlane told me.'

'Oh?' Thomson sounded interested. 'What else did he say?'

'Not much really.' Rebus rose from his perch and went to the window, holding aside the net curtain to stare out onto the street below. 'He said you'd known each other for years.'

'Since school,' Thomson added.

Rebus nodded. 'And he said you drove a black Ford Escort. That'll be it down there, parked across the street?'

Thomson came to the window. 'Yes,' he agreed, uncertainly, 'that's it. But I don't see what—'

'I noticed it as I was parking my own car,' Rebus continued, brushing past Thomson's interruption. He let the curtain fall and turned back into the room. 'I noticed you've got a car alarm. I suppose you must get a lot of burglaries around here.'

'It's not the most salubrious part of town,' Thomson said. 'Not all writers are like Jeffrey Archer.'

'Did money have anything to do with it?' Rebus asked. Thomson paused.

'With what, Inspector?'

'With Miss Bitter leaving you for Mr MacFarlane. He's not short of a bob or two, is he?'

Thomson's voice rose perceptibly. 'Look, I really can't see what this has to do with—'

'Your car was broken into a few months ago, wasn't it?' Rebus was examining a pile of magazines on the floor now. 'I saw the report. They stole your radio and your car phone.'

'Yes.'

'I notice you've replaced the car phone.' He glanced up at Thomson, smiled, and continued browsing.

'Of course,' said Thomson. He seemed confused now, unable to fathom where the conversation was leading.

'A journalist would need a car phone, wouldn't he?' Rebus observed. 'So people could keep in touch, contact him at any time. Is that right?'

'Absolutely right, Inspector.'

Rebus threw the magazine back onto the pile and nodded slowly. 'Great things, car phones.' He walked over towards Thomson's desk. It was a small flat. This room obviously served a double purpose as study and living-room. Not that Thomson entertained many visitors. He was too aggressive for many people, too secretive for others. So John MacFarlane had said.

On the desk there was more clutter, though in some appearance of organisation. There was also a neat word processor, and beside it a telephone. And next to the telephone sat an answering machine.

'Yes,' Rebus repeated. 'You need to be in contact.' Rebus smiled towards Thomson. 'Communication, that's the secret. And I'll tell you something else about journalists.'

'What?' Unable to comprehend Rebus's direction, Thomson's tone had become that of someone bored with a conversation. He shoved his hands deep into his pockets.

'Journalists are hoarders.' Rebus made this sound like some great wisdom. His eyes took in the room again. 'I mean, near-pathological hoarders. They can't bear to throw things away, because they never know when something might become useful. Am I right?'

Thomson shrugged.

'Yes,' said Rebus, 'I bet I am. Look at these cassettes, for example.' He went to where the rows of tapes were neatly displayed. 'What are they? Interviews, that sort of thing?'

'Mostly, yes,' Thomson agreed.

'And you still keep them, even though they're years old?'

Thomson shrugged again. 'So I'm a hoarder.'

But Rebus had noticed something on the top shelf, some brown cardboard boxes. He reached up and lifted one down. Inside were more tapes, marked with months and years. But these tapes were smaller. Rebus gestured with the box towards Thomson, his eyes seeking an explanation.

Thomson smiled uneasily. 'Answering machine messages,' he said.

'You keep these, too?' Rebus sounded amazed.

'Well,' Thomson said, 'someone may agree to something over the phone, an interview or something, then deny it later. I need them as records of promises made.'

Rebus nodded, understanding now. He replaced the brown box on its shelf. He still had his back to Thomson when the telephone rang, a sharp electronic sound.

'Sorry,' Thomson apologised, going to answer it.

'Not at all.'

Thomson picked up the receiver. 'Hello?' He listened, then frowned. 'Of course,' he said finally, holding the receiver out towards Rebus. 'It's for you, Inspector.'

Rebus raised a surprised eyebrow and accepted the receiver. It was, as he had known it would be, Detective Constable Holmes.

'Okay,' Holmes said. 'Costain no longer owes you that favour. He's listened to both tapes. He hasn't run all the necessary tests yet, but he's pretty convinced.'

'Go on.' Rebus was looking at Thomson, who was sitting, hands clasping knees, on the arm of the chair.

'The call we received last night,' said Holmes, 'the one from John MacFarlane admitting to the murder of Moira Bitter, originated from a portable telephone.'

'Interesting,' said Rebus, his eyes on Thomson. 'And what about the other one?'

'Well, the tape you gave me seems to be twice-removed.'

'What does that mean?'

'It means,' said Holmes, 'that according to Costain it's not just a recording, it's the recording of a recording.' Rebus nodded, satisfied.

'Okay, thanks, Brian.' He put down the receiver.

'Good news or bad?' Thomson asked.

'A bit of both,' answered Rebus thoughtfully. Thomson had risen to his feet.

'I feel like a drink, Inspector. Can I get you one?'

'It's a bit early for me, I'm afraid,' Rebus said, looking at his watch. It was eleven o'clock: opening time. 'All right,' he said, 'just a small one.'

'The whisky's in the kitchen,' Thomson explained. 'I'll just be a moment.'

'Fine, sir, fine.'

Rebus listened as Thomson left the room and headed off towards the kitchen. He stood beside the desk, thinking through what he now knew. Then, hearing Thomson returning from the kitchen, floor-boards bending beneath his weight, he picked up the waste-paper basket from below the desk, and, as Thomson entered the room, proceeded to empty the contents in a heap on the sofa.

Thomson stood in the doorway, a glass of whisky in each hand, dumbstruck. 'What on earth are you doing?' he spluttered at last. But Rebus ignored him and started to pick through the now strewn contents of the bin, talking as he searched.

'It was pretty close to being fool-proof, Mr Thomson. Let me explain. The killer went to Moira Bitter's flat and talked her into letting him in despite the late hour. He murdered her quite callously, let's make no mistake about that. I've never seen so much premeditation in a case before. He cleaned the knife and returned it to its drawer. He was wearing gloves, of course, knowing John MacFarlane's fingerprints would be all over the flat, and he cleaned the knife precisely to disguise the fact that he *had* worn gloves. MacFarlane, you see, had not.'

Thomson took a gulp from one glass, but otherwise seemed rooted to the spot. His eyes had become vacant, as though picturing Rebus's story in his mind.

'MacFarlane,' Rebus continued, still rummaging, 'was summoned to Moira's flat. The message did come from her. He knew her voice well enough not to be fooled by someone else's voice. The killer sat outside Moira's flat, sat waiting for MacFarlane to arrive. Then the killer made one last call, this one to the police, in the guise of an hysterical MacFarlane. We know this last call was made on a car phone. The lab boys are very clever that way. The police are hoarders, too, you see, Mr Thomson. We make recordings of emergency calls made to us. It won't be hard to voice-print that call and try to match it to John MacFarlane. But it won't be John MacFarlane, will it?' Rebus paused for effect. 'It'll be you.'

Thomson gave a thin smile, but his grip on the two glasses had grown less steady, and whisky was dribbling from the angled lip of one of them.

'Ah-ha.' Rebus had found what he was looking for in the contents of the bin. With a pleased-as-punch grin on his unshaven, sleepless face, he pinched forefinger and thumb together and lifted them for his own and Thomson's inspection. He was holding a tiny sliver of brown recording tape.

'You see,' he continued, 'the killer had to lure MacFarlane to the murder scene. Having killed Moira, he went to his car, as I've said. There he had his portable telephone and a cassette recorder. He was a hoarder. He had kept all his answering machine tapes, including messages left by Moira at the height of their affair. He found the message he needed and he spliced it. He played this message to John MacFarlane's answering machine. All he had to do after that was wait. The message MacFarlane received was "Hello. I need to see you." There was a pause after the "hello". And that pause was where the splice was made in the tape, excising this.' Rebus looked at the sliver of tape. 'The one word "Kenneth". "Hello, Kenneth, I need to see you." It was Moira Bitter talking to you, Mr Thomson, talking to you a long time ago.'

Thomson hurled both glasses at once, so that they arrowed in towards Rebus, who ducked. The glasses collided above his head, shards raining down on him. Thomson had reached the front door, had hauled it open even, before Rebus was on him, lunging, pushing the younger man forwards through the doorway and onto the tenement landing. Thomson's head hit the metal rails with a muted chime and he let out a single moan before collapsing. Rebus shook himself free of glass, feeling one or two tiny pieces nick him as he brushed a hand across his face. He brought a hand to his nose and inhaled deeply. His father had always said whisky would put hairs on his chest. Rebus wondered if the same miracle might be effected on his temples and the crown of his head ...

It had been the perfect murder.

Well, almost. But Kenneth Thomson had reckoned without Rebus's ability actually to believe someone innocent despite the evidence against him. The case against John MacFarlane had been overwhelming. Yet Rebus, feeling it to be wrong, had been forced to invent other scenarios, other motives and other means to the fairly chilling end. It wasn't enough that Moira had died – died at the hands of someone she knew. MacFarlane had to be implicated in her murder. The killer had been out to tag them both. But it was Moira the killer hated, hated because she had broken a friendship as well as a heart.

Rebus stood on the steps of the police station. Thomson was in a cell somewhere below his feet, somewhere below ground level. Confessing to everything. He would go to jail, while John MacFarlane, perhaps not realising his luck, had already been freed.

The streets were busy now. Lunchtime traffic, the reliable noises of the everyday. The sun was even managing to burst from its slumber. All of which reminded Rebus that his day was over. Time, all in all he felt, for a short visit home, a shower and a change of clothes, and, God and the Devil willing, some sleep.

The Dean Curse

The locals in Barnton knew him either as 'the Brigadier' or as 'that Army type who bought the West Lodge'. West Lodge was a huge but until recently neglected detached house set in a walled acre and a half of grounds and copses. Most locals were relieved that its high walls hid it from general view, the house itself being too angular, too gothic for modern tastes. Certainly, it was very large for the needs of a widower and his unsmiling daughter. Mrs MacLennan, who cleaned for the Brigadier, was pumped for information by curious neighbours, but could say only that Brigadier-General Dean had had some renovations done, that most of the house was habitable, that one room had become a library, another a billiard-room, another a study, another a makeshift gymnasium and so on. The listeners would drink this in deeply, yet it was never enough. What about the daughter? What about the Brigadier's background? What happened to his wife?

Shopkeepers too were asked for their thoughts. The Brigadier drove a sporty open-topped car which would pull in noisily to the side of the road to allow him to pop into this or that shop for a few things, including, each day at the same time, a bottle of something or other from the smarter of the two off-licences.

The grocer, Bob Sladden, reckoned that Brigadier-General Dean had been born nearby, even that he had lived for a few childhood years in West Lodge and so had retired there because of its carefree connections. But Miss Dalrymple, who at ninety-three was as old as anyone in that part of Barnton, could not recall any family named Dean living at West Lodge. Could not, indeed, recall any Deans ever living in this 'neck' of Barnton, with the exception of Sam Dean. But when pressed about Sam Dean, she merely shook her head and said, 'He was no good, that one, and got what he deserved. The Great War saw to him.' Then she would nod slowly, thoughtfully, and nobody would be any further forward.

Speculation grew wilder as no new facts came to light, and in

The Claymore public bar one afternoon, a bar never patronised by the Brigadier (and who'd ever heard of an Army man not liking his drink?), a young out-of-work plasterer named Willie Barr came up with a fresh proposition.

'Maybe Dean isn't his real name.'

But everyone around the pool table laughed at that and Willie just shrugged, readying to play his next shot. 'Well,' he said, 'real name or not, I wouldn't climb over that daughter of his to get to any of you lot.'

Then he played a double off the cushion, but missed. Missed not because the shot was difficult or he'd had too many pints of Snakebite, but because his cue arm jerked at the noise of the explosion.

It was a fancy car all right, a Jaguar XJS convertible, its bodywork a startling red. Nobody in Barnton could mistake it for anyone else's car. Besides, everyone was used to it revving to its loud roadside halt, was used to its contented ticking-over while the Brigadier did his shopping. Some complained – though never to his face – about the noise, about the fumes from the exhaust. They couldn't say why he never switched off the ignition. He always seemed to want to be ready for a quick getaway. On this particular afternoon, the getaway was quicker even than usual, a squeal of tyres as the car jerked out into the road and sped past the shops. Its driver seemed ready actually to disregard the red stop light at the busy junction. He never got the chance. There was a ball of flames where the car had been and the heart-stopping sound of the explosion. Twisted metal flew into the air, then down again, wounding passers-by, burning skin. Shop windows blew in, shards of fine glass finding soft targets. The traffic lights turned to green, but nothing moved in the street.

For a moment, there was a silence punctuated only by the arrival on terra firma of bits of speedometer, headlamp, even steering-wheel. Then the screaming started, as people realised they'd been wounded. More curdling still though were the silences, the dumb horrified faces of people who would never forget this moment, whose shock would disturb each wakeful night.

And then there was a man, standing in a doorway, the doorway of what had been the wine merchant's. He carried a bottle with him, carefully wrapped in green paper, and his mouth was open in surprise. He dropped the bottle with a crash when he realised his car was not where he had left it, realising that the roaring he had heard and thought he recognised was that of his own car being driven away. At his feet, he saw one of his driving gloves lying on the pavement in front of him. It was still smouldering. Only five minutes before, it had been lying on the leather of his passenger seat. The wine merchant was standing beside him now, pale and shaking, looking in dire need of a drink. The Brigadier nodded towards the carcass of his sleek red Jaguar.

'That should have been me,' he said. Then: 'Do you mind if I use your telephone?'

John Rebus threw *The Dain Curse* up in the air, sending it spinning towards his living-room ceiling. Gravity caught up with it just short of the ceiling and pulled it down hard, so that it landed open against the uncarpeted floor. It was a cheap copy, bought secondhand and previously much read. But not by Rebus; he'd got as far as the beginning of the third section, 'Quesada', before giving up, before tossing what many regard as Hammett's finest novel into the air. Its pages fell away from the spine as it landed, scattering chapters. Rebus growled. The telephone had, as though prompted by the book's demise, started ringing. Softly, insistently. Rebus picked up the apparatus and studied it. It was six o'clock on the evening of his first rest-day in what seemed like months. Who would be phoning him? Pleasure or business? And which would he prefer it to be? He put the receiver to his ear.

'Yes?' His voice was non-committal.

'DI Rebus?' It was work then. Rebus grunted a response. 'DC Coupar here, sir. The Chief thought you'd be interested.' There was a pause for effect. 'A bomb's just gone off in Barnton.'

Rebus stared at the sheets of print lying all around him. He asked the Detective Constable to repeat the message.

'A bomb, sir. In Barnton.'

'What? A World War Two leftover you mean?'

'No, sir. Nothing like that. Nothing like that at all.'

There was a line of poetry in Rebus's head as he drove out towards one of Edinburgh's many quiet middle-class districts, the sort of place where nothing happened, the sort of place where crime was measured in a yearly attempted break-in or the theft of a bicycle. That was Barnton. The line of poetry hadn't been written about Barnton. It had been written about Slough.

It's my own fault, Rebus was thinking, for being disgusted at how far-fetched that Hammett book was. Entertaining, yes, but you could strain credulity only so far, and Dashiell Hammett had taken that strain like the anchor-man on a tug-o'-war team, pulling with all his might. Coincidence after coincidence, plot after plot, corpse following corpse like something off an assembly line.

Far-fetched, definitely. But then what was Rebus to make of his telephone call? He'd checked: it wasn't 1st April. But then he wouldn't put it past Brian Holmes or one of his other colleagues to pull a stunt on him just because he was having a day off, just because he'd carped on about it for the previous few days. Yes, this had Holmes' fingerprints all over it. Except for one thing.

The radio reports. The police frequency was full of it; and when Rebus switched on his car radio to the local commercial channel, the news was there, too. Reports of an explosion in Barnton, not far from the roundabout. It is thought a car has exploded. No further details, though there are thought to be many casualties. Rebus shook his head and drove, thinking of the poem again, thinking of anything that would stop him focussing on the truth of the news. A car bomb? *A car bomb?* In Belfast, yes, maybe even on occasion in London. But here in Edinburgh? Rebus blamed himself. If only he hadn't cursed Dashiell Hammett, if only he hadn't sneered at his book, at its exaggerations and its melodramas, if only ... Then none of this would have happened.

But of course it would. It had.

The road had been blocked off. The ambulances had left with their cargo. Onlookers stood four deep behind the orange and white tape of the hastily erected cordon. There was just the one question: how many dead? The answer seemed to be: just the one. The driver of the car. An Army bomb disposal unit had materialised from somewhere and, for want of anything else to do, was checking the shops either side of the street. A line of policemen, aided so far as Rebus could judge by more Army personnel, was moving slowly up the road, mostly on hands and knees, in what an outsider might regard as some bizarre slow-motion race. They carried with them polythene bags, into which they dropped anything they found. The whole scene was one of brilliantly organised confusion and it didn't take Rebus longer than a couple of minutes to detect the mastermind behind it all – Superintendent 'Farmer' Watson. 'Farmer' only behind his back, of course, and a nickname which matched both his north-of-Scotland background and his at times agricultural methods. Rebus decided to skirt around his superior officer and glean what he could from the various less senior officers present.

He had come to Barnton with a set of preconceptions and it took time for these to be corrected. For example, he'd premised that the person in the car, the as-yet-unidentified deceased, would be the car's owner and that this person would have been the target of the bomb attack (the evidence all around most certainly pointed to a bomb, rather than spontaneous combustion, say, or any other more likely explanation). Either that or the car might be stolen or borrowed, and the driver some sort of terrorist, blown apart by his own device before he could leave it at its intended destination. There were certainly Army installations around Edinburgh: barracks, armouries, listening posts. Across the Forth lay what was left of Rosyth naval dockyard, as well as the underground installation at Pitreavie. There were targets. Bomb meant terrorist meant target. That was how it always was.

But not this time. This time there was an important difference. The apparent target escaped, by dint of leaving his car for a couple of minutes to nip into a shop. But while he was in the shop someone had tried to steal his car, and that person was now drying into the tarmac beneath the knees of the crawling policemen. This much Rebus learned before Superintendent Watson caught sight of him, caught sight of him smiling wryly at the car thief's luck. It wasn't every day you got the chance to steal a Jaguar XJS ... but what a day to pick.

'Inspector!' Farmer Watson beckoned for Rebus to join him, which Rebus, ironing out his smile, did.

Before Watson could start filling him in on what he already knew, Rebus himself spoke.

'Who was the target, sir?'

'A man called Dean.' Meaningful pause. 'Brigadier-General Dean, retired.'

Rebus nodded. 'I thought there were a lot of Tommies about.'

'We'll be working with the Army on this one, John. That's how it's done, apparently. And then there's Scotland Yard, too. Their anti-terrorist people.'

'Too many cooks if you ask me, sir.'

Watson nodded. 'Still, these buggers are supposed to be special-ised.'

'And we're only good for solving the odd drunk driving or domes-tic, eh, sir?'

The two men shared a smile at this. Rebus nodded towards the wreck of the car. 'Any idea who was behind the wheel?'

Watson shook his head. 'Not yet. And not much to go on either. We may have to wait till a mum or girlfriend reports him missing.'

'Not even a description?'

'None of the passers-by is fit to be questioned. Not yet anyway.'

'So what about Brigadier-General Whassisname?'

'Dean.'

'Yes. Where is he?'

'He's at home. A doctor's been to take a look at him, but he seems all right. A bit shocked.'

'A bit? Someone rips the arse out of his car and he's a *bit* shocked?' Rebus sounded doubtful. Watson's eyes were fixed on the advancing line of debris collectors.

'I get the feeling he's seen worse.' He turned to Rebus. 'Why don't you have a word with him, John? See what you think.'

Rebus nodded slowly. 'Aye, why not,' he said. 'Anything for a laugh, eh, sir?'

Watson seemed stuck for a reply, and by the time he'd formed one Rebus had wandered back through the cordon, hands in trouser pockets, looking for all the world like a man out for a stroll on a balmy summer's evening. Only then did the Superintendent remember that this was Rebus's day off. He wondered if it had been such a bright idea to send him off to talk to Brigadier-General Dean. Then he smiled, recalling that he had brought John Rebus out here precisely because something didn't quite feel right. If he could feel it, Rebus would feel it too, and would burrow deep to find its source – as deep as necessary and, perhaps, deeper than was seemly for a Superintendent to go.

Yes, there were times when even Detective Inspector John Rebus came in useful.

It was a big house. Rebus would go further. It was bigger than the last hotel he'd stayed in, though of a similar style: closer to Hammer Films than *House and Garden*. A hotel in Scarborough it had been; three days of lust with a divorced school-dinner lady. School-dinner ladies hadn't been like that in Rebus's day ... or maybe he just hadn't been paying attention.

He paid attention now. Paid attention as an Army uniform opened the door of West Lodge to him. He'd already had to talk his way past a mixed guard on the gate – an apologetic PC and two uncompromising squaddies. That was why he'd started thinking back to Scarborough – to stop himself punching those squaddies in their square-chinned faces. The closer he came to Brigadier-General Dean, the more aggressive and unlovely the soldiers seemed. The two on the gate were like lambs compared to the one on the main door of the house, yet he in his turn was meekness itself compared to the one who led Rebus into a well-appointed living-room and told him to wait.

Rebus hated the Army – with good reason. He had seen the soldier's lot from the inside and it had left him with a resentment so huge that to call it a 'chip on the shoulder' was to do it an injustice. Chip? Right now it felt like a whole transport cafe! There was only one thing for it. Rebus made for the sideboard, sniffed the contents of the decanter sitting there and poured himself an inch of whisky. He was draining the contents of the glass into his mouth when the door opened.

Rebus had brought too many preconceptions with him today. Brigadier-Generals were squat, ruddy-faced men, with stiff moustaches and VSOP noses, a few silvered wisps of Brylcreemed hair and maybe even a walking stick. They retired in their seventies and babbled of campaigns over dinner.

Not so Brigadier-General Dean. He looked to be in his mid- to late-fifties. He stood over six feet tall, had a youthful face and vigorous dark hair. He was slim too, with no sign of a retirement gut or a port drinker's red-veined cheeks. He looked twice as fit as Rebus felt and for a moment the policeman actually caught himself straightening his back and squaring his shoulders.

'Good idea,' said Dean, joining Rebus at the sideboard. 'Mind if I join you?' His voice was soft, blurred at the edges, the voice of an educated man, a civilised man. Rebus tried hard to imagine Dean giving orders to a troop of hairy-fisted Tommies. Tried, but failed.

'Detective Inspector Rebus,' he said by way of introduction. 'Sorry to bother you like this, sir, but there are a few questions—'

Dean nodded, finishing his own drink and offering to replenish Rebus's.

'Why not?' agreed Rebus. Funny thing though: he could swear this whisky wasn't whisky at all but whiskey – Irish whiskey. Softer than the Scottish stuff, lacking an edge.

Rebus sat on the sofa, Dean on a well-used armchair. The Brigadier-General offered a toast of *slainte* before starting on his second drink, then exhaled noisily.

'Had to happen sooner or later, I suppose,' he said.

'Oh?'

Dean nodded slowly. 'I worked in Ulster for a time. Quite a long time. I suppose I was fairly high up in the tree there. I always knew I was a target. The Army knew, too, of course, but what can you do? You can't put bodyguards on every soldier who's been involved in the conflict, can you?'

'I suppose not, sir. But I assume you took precautions?'

Dean shrugged. 'I'm not in *Who's Who* and I've got an unlisted telephone number. I don't even use my rank much, to be honest.'

'But some of your mail might be addressed to Brigadier-General Dean?'

A wry smile. 'Who gave you that impression?'

'What impression, sir?'

'The impression of rank. I'm not a Brigadier-General. I retired with the rank of Major.'

'But the—'

'The what? The locals? Yes, I can see how gossip might lead to exaggeration. You know how it is in a place like this, Inspector. An incomer who keeps himself to himself. A military air. They put two and two together then multiply it by ten.'

Rebus nodded thoughtfully. 'I see.' Trust Watson to be wrong even in the fundamentals. 'But the point I was trying to make about your mail still stands, sir. What I'm wondering, you see, is how they found you.'

Dean smiled quietly. 'The IRA are quite sophisticated these days, Inspector. For all I know, they could have hacked into a computer, bribed someone in the know, or maybe it was just a fluke, sheer chance.' He shrugged. 'I suppose we'll have to think of moving somewhere else now, starting all over again. Poor Jacqueline.'

'Jacqueline being?'

'My daughter. She's upstairs, terribly upset. She's due to start university in October. It's her I feel sorry for.'

Rebus looked sympathetic. He felt sympathetic. One thing about Army life and police life – both could have a devastating effect on your personal life.

'And your wife, sir?'

'Dead, Inspector. Several years ago.' Dean examined his now empty glass. He looked his years now, looked like someone who needed a rest. But there was something other about him, something cool and hard. Rebus had met all types in the Army – and since. Veneers could no longer fool him, and behind Major Dean's sophisticated veneer he could glimpse something other, something from the man's past. Dean hadn't just been a good soldier. At one time he'd been lethal.

'Do you have any thoughts on how they might have found you, sir?'

'Not really.' Dean closed his eyes for a second. There was resignation in his voice. 'What matters is that they *did* find me.' His eyes met Rebus's. 'And they can find me again.'

Rebus shifted in his seat. Christ, what a thought. What a, well, time-bomb. To always be watching, always expecting, always fearing. And not just for yourself.

'I'd like to talk to Jacqueline, sir. It may be that she'll have some inkling as to how they were able to—'

But Dean was shaking his head. 'Not just now, Inspector. Not yet. I don't want her – well, you understand. Besides, I'd imagine that this will all be out of your hands by tomorrow. I believe some people from the Anti-Terrorist Branch are on their way up here. Between them and the Army ... well, as I say, it'll be out of your hands.'

Rebus felt himself prickling anew. But Dean was right, wasn't he? Why strain yourself when tomorrow it would be someone else's weight? Rebus pursed his lips, nodded, and stood up.

'I'll see you to the door,' said the Major, taking the empty glass from Rebus's hand.

As they passed into the hallway, Rebus caught a glimpse of a young woman – Jacqueline Dean presumably. She had been hovering by the telephone-table at the foot of the staircase, but was now starting up the stairs themselves, her hand thin and white on the bannister. Dean, too, watched her go. He half-smiled, half-shrugged at Rebus.

'She's upset,' he explained unnecessarily. But she hadn't looked upset to Rebus. She had looked like she was moping.

The next morning, Rebus went back to Barnton. Wooden boards had been placed over some of the shop windows, but otherwise there were few signs of yesterday's drama. The guards on the gate to West Lodge had been replaced by beefy plainclothes men with London accents. They carried portable radios, but otherwise might have been bouncers, debt collectors or bailiffs. They radioed the house. Rebus couldn't help thinking that a shout might have done the job for them, but they were in love with technology; you could see that by the way they held their radio-sets. He'd seen soldiers holding a new gun the same way.

'The guvnor's coming down to see you,' one of the men said at last. Rebus kicked his heels for a full minute before the man arrived.

'What do you want?'

'Detective Inspector Rebus. I talked with Major Dean yesterday and—'

The man snapped. 'Who told you his rank?'

'Major Dean himself. I just wondered if I might—'

'Yes, well there's no need for that, Inspector. We're in charge now. Of course you'll be kept informed.'

The man turned and walked back through the gates with a steady, determined stride. The guards were smirking as they closed the gates behind their 'guvnor'. Rebus felt like a snubbed schoolboy, left out of the football game. Sides had been chosen and there he stood, unwanted. He could smell London on these men, that cocky superiority of a self-chosen elite. What did they call themselves? C13 or somesuch, the Anti-Terrorist Branch. Closely linked to Special Branch, and everyone knew the trade name for Special Branch – Smug Bastards.

The man had been a little younger than Rebus, well-groomed and accountant-like. More intelligent, for sure, than the gorillas on the gate, but probably well able to handle himself. A neat pistol might well have been hidden under the arm of his close-fitting suit. None of that mattered. What mattered was that the captain was leaving Rebus out of his team. It rankled; and when something rankled, it rankled hard.

Rebus had walked half a dozen paces away from the gates when he half-turned and stuck his tongue out at the guards. Then, satisfied with this conclusion to his morning's labours, he decided to make his own inquiries. It was eleven-thirty. If you want to find out about someone, reasoned a thirsty Rebus, visit his local.

The reasoning, in this case, proved false: Dean had never been near The Claymore.

'The daughter came in though,' commented one young man. There weren't many people in the pub at this early stage of the day, save a few retired gentlemen who were in conversation with three or four reporters. The barman, too, was busy telling his life story to a young female hack, or rather, into her tape recorder. This made getting served difficult, despite the absence of a lunchtime scrum. The young man had solved this problem, however, reaching behind the bar to refill his glass with a mixture of cider and lager, leaving money on the bartop.

'Oh?' Rebus nodded towards the three-quarters full glass. 'Have another?'

'When this one's finished I will.' He drank greedily, by which time the barman had finished with his confessions – much (judging by her face) to the relief of the reporter. 'Pint of Snakebite, Paul,' called the young man. When the drink was before him, he told Rebus that his name was Willie Barr and that he was unemployed.

'You said you saw the daughter in here?' Rebus was anxious to have his questions answered before the alcohol took effect on Barr.

'That's right. She came in pretty regularly.'

'By herself?'

'No, always with some guy.'

'One in particular, you mean?'

But Willie Barr laughed, shaking his head. 'A different one every time. She's getting a bit of a name for herself. And,' he raised his voice for the barman's benefit, 'she's not even eighteen, I'd say.'

'Were they local lads?'

'None I recognised. Never really spoke to them.' Rebus swirled his glass, creating a foamy head out of nothing.

'Any Irish accents among them?'

'In here?' Barr laughed. 'Not in here. Christ, no. Actually, she hasn't been in for a few weeks, now that I think of it. Maybe her father put a stop to it, eh? I mean, how would it look in the Sunday papers? Brigadier's daughter slumming it in Barnton.'

Rebus smiled. 'It's not exactly a slum though, is it?'

'True enough, but her boyfriends ... I mean, there was more of the car mechanic than the estate agent about them. Know what I mean?' He winked. 'Not that a bit of rough ever hurt *her* kind, eh?' Then he laughed again and suggested a game or two of pool, a pound a game or a fiver if the detective were a betting man.

But Rebus shook his head. He thought he knew now why Willie Barr was drinking so much: he was flush. And the reason he was flush was that he'd been telling his story to the papers – for a price. *Brigadier's Daughter Slumming It.* Yes, he'd been telling tales all right, but there was little chance of them reaching their intended audience. The Powers That Be would see to that.

Barr was helping himself to another pint as Rebus made to leave the premises.

It was late in the afternoon when Rebus received his visitor, the Anti-Terrorist accountant.

'A Mr Matthews to see you,' the Desk Sergeant had informed Rebus, and 'Matthews' he remained, giving no hint of rank or proof of identity. He had come, he said, to 'have it out' with Rebus.

'What were you doing in The Claymore?'

'Having a drink.'

'You were asking questions. I've already told you, Inspector Rebus, we can't have—'

'I know, I know.' Rebus raised his hands in a show of surrender. 'But the more furtive you lot are, the more interested I become.'

Matthews stared silently at Rebus. Rebus knew that the man

was weighing up his options. One, of course, was to go to Farmer Watson and have Rebus warned off. But if Matthews were as canny as he looked, he would know this might have the opposite effect from that intended. Another option was to talk to Rebus, to ask him what he wanted to know.

'What do you want to know?' Matthews said at last.

'I want to know about Dean.'

Matthews sat back in his chair. 'In strictest confidence?' Rebus nodded. 'I've never been known as a clipe.'

'A clipe?'

'Someone who tells tales,' Rebus explained. Matthews was thoughtful.

'Very well then,' he said. 'For a start, Dean is an alias, a very necessary one. During his time in the Army Major Dean worked in Intelligence, mostly in West Germany but also for a time in Ulster. His work in both spheres was very important, crucially important. I don't need to go into details. His last posting was West Germany. His wife was killed in a terrorist attack, almost certainly IRA. We don't think they had targeted her specifically. She was just in the wrong place with the wrong number plates.'

'A car bomb?'

'No, a bullet. Through the windscreen, point-blank. Major Dean asked to be ... he was invalided out. It seemed best. We provided him with a change of identity, of course.'

'I thought he looked a bit young to be retired. And the daughter, how did she take it?'

'She was never told the full details, not that I'm aware of. She was in boarding school in England.' Matthews paused. 'It was for the best.'

Rebus nodded. 'Of course, nobody'd argue with that. But why did – Dean – choose to live in Barnton?'

Matthews rubbed his left eyebrow, then pushed his spectacles back up his sharply sloping nose. 'Something to do with an aunt of his,' he said. 'He spent holidays there as a boy. His father was Army, too, posted here, there and everywhere. Never the most stable upbringing. I think Dean had happy memories of Barnton.'

Rebus shifted in his seat. He couldn't know how long Matthews would stay, how long he would continue to answer Rebus's questions. And there were so many questions.

'What about the bomb?'

'Looks like the IRA, all right. Standard fare for them, all the hallmarks. It's still being examined, of course, but we're pretty sure.'

'And the deceased?'

'No clues yet. I suppose he'll be reported missing sooner or later. We'll leave that side of things to you.'

'Gosh, thanks.' Rebus waited for his sarcasm to penetrate, then, quickly: 'How does Dean get on with his daughter?'

Matthews was caught off-guard by the question. He blinked twice, three times, then glanced at his wristwatch.

'All right, I suppose,' he said at last, making show of scratching a mark from his cuff. 'I can't see what ... Look, Inspector, as I say, we'll keep you fully informed. But meantime—'

'Keep out of your hair?'

'If you want to put it like that.' Matthews stood up. 'Now I really must be getting back—'

'To London?'

Matthews smiled at the eagerness in Rebus's voice. 'To Barnton. Don't worry, Inspector, the more *you* keep out of *my* hair, the quicker I can get out of yours. Fair enough?' He shot a hand out towards Rebus, who returned the almost painful grip.

'Fair enough,' said Rebus. He ushered Matthews from the room and closed the door again, then returned to his seat. He slouched as best he could in the hard, uncomfortable chair and put his feet up on the desk, examining his scuffed shoes. He tried to feel like Sam Spade, but failed. His legs soon began to ache and he slid them from the surface of the desk. The coincidences in Dashiell Hammett had nothing on the coincidence of someone nicking a car seconds before it exploded. Someone must have been watching, ready to detonate the device. But if they were watching, how come they didn't spot that Dean, the intended victim, wasn't the one to drive off?

Either there was more to this than met the eye, or else there was less. Rebus was wary – very wary. He'd already made far too many prejudgements, had already been proved wrong too many times. Keep an open mind, that was the secret. An open mind and an inquiring one. He nodded his head slowly, his eyes on the door.

'Fair enough,' he said quietly. 'I'll keep out of your hair, Mr Matthews, but that doesn't necessarily mean I'm leaving the barber's.'

The Claymore might not have been Barnton's most salubrious establishment, but it was as Princes Street's Caledonian Hotel in comparison with the places Rebus visited that evening. He began with the merely seedy bars, the ones where each quiet voice seemed to contain a lifetime's resentment, and then moved downwards, one rung of the ladder at a time. It was slow work; the bars tended to be in a ring around Edinburgh, sometimes on the outskirts or in the distant housing schemes, sometimes nearer the centre than most of the population would dare to think.

Rebus hadn't made many friends in his adult life, but he had his network of contacts and he was as proud of it as any grandparent would be of their extended family. They were like cousins, these contacts; mostly they knew each other, at least by reputation, but Rebus never spoke to one about another, so that the extent of the chain could only be guessed at. There were those of his colleagues who, in Major Dean's words, added two and two, then multiplied by ten. John Rebus, it was reckoned, had as big a net of 'snitches' as any copper on the force bar none.

It took four hours and an outlay of over forty pounds before Rebus started to catch a glimpse of a result. His basic question, though couched in vague and imprecise terms, was simple: have any car thieves vanished off the face of the earth since yesterday?

One name was uttered by three very different people in three distinct parts of the city: Brian Cant. The name meant little to Rebus.

'It wouldn't,' he was told. 'Brian only shifted across here from the west a year or so ago. He's got form from when he was a nipper, but he's grown smart since then. When the Glasgow cops started sniffing, he moved operations.' The detective listened, nodded, drank a watered-down whisky, and said little. Brian Cant grew from a name into a description, from a description into a personality. But there was something more.

'You're not the only one interested in him,' Rebus was told in a bar in Gorgie. 'Somebody else was asking questions a wee while back. Remember Jackie Hanson?'

'He used to be CID, didn't he?'

'That's right, but not any more ...'

Not just any old banger for Brian Cant: he specialised in 'quality motors'. Rebus eventually got an address: a third-floor tenement flat near Powderhall race-track. A young man answered the door. His name was Jim Cant, Brian's younger brother. Rebus saw that Jim was scared, nervous. He chipped away at the brother quickly, explaining that he was there because he thought Brian might be dead. That he knew all about Cant's business, but that he wasn't interested in pursuing this side of things, except insofar as it might shed light on the death. It took a little more of this, then the brother opened up.

'He said he had a customer interested in a car,' Jim Cant explained. 'An Irishman, he said.'

'How did he know the man was Irish?'

'Must have been the voice. I don't think they met. Maybe they did. The man was interested in a specific car.'

'A red Jaguar?'

'Yeah, convertible. Nice cars. The Irishman even knew where there was one. It seemed a cinch, that's what Brian kept saying. A cinch.'

'He didn't think it would be hard to steal?'

'Five seconds' work, that's what he kept saying. I thought it sounded too easy. I told him so.' He bent over in his chair, grabbing at his knees and sinking his head between them. 'Ach, Brian, what the hell have you done?'

Rebus tried to comfort the young man as best he could with brandy and tea. He drank a mug of tea himself, wandering through the flat, his mind thrumming. Was he blowing things up out of all proportion? Maybe. He'd made mistakes before, not so much errors of judgement as errors of jumping the gun. But there was something about all of this ... Something.

'Do you have a photo of Brian?' he asked as he was leaving. 'A recent one would be best.' Jim Cant handed him a holiday snap.

'We went to Crete last summer,' he explained. 'It was magic.' Then, holding the door open for Rebus: 'Don't I have to identify him or something?'

Rebus thought of the scrapings which were all that remained of what may or may not have been Brian Cant. He shook his head. 'I'll let you know,' he said. 'If we need you, we'll let you know.'

The next day was Sunday, day of rest. Rebus rested in his car, parked fifty yards or so along the road from the gates to West Lodge. He put his radio on, folded his arms and sank down into the driver's seat. This was more like it. The Hollywood private eye on a stakeout. Only in the movies, a stakeout could be whittled away to a few minutes' footage. Here, it was measured in a slow ticking of seconds ... minutes ... quarter hours.

Eventually, the gates opened and a figure hurried out, fairly trotting along the pavement as though released from bondage. Jacqueline Dean was wearing a denim jacket, short black skirt and thick black tights. A beret sat awkwardly on her cropped dark hair and she pressed the palm of her hand to it from time to time to stop it sliding off altogether. Rebus locked his car before following her. He kept to the other side of the road, wary not so much from fear that she might spot him but because C13 might have put a tail on her, too.

She stopped at the local newsagent's first and came out heavy-laden with Sunday papers. Rebus, making to cross the road, a Sunday-morning stroller, studied her face. What was the expression he'd thought of the first time he'd seen her? Yes, *moping*. There was still something of that in her liquid eyes, the dark shadows beneath. She was making for the corner shop now. Doubtless she would appear with rolls or bacon or butter or milk. All the things Rebus seemed to find himself short of on a Sunday, no matter how hard he planned.

He felt in his jacket pockets, but found nothing of comfort there, just the photograph of Brian Cant. The window of the corner shop, untouched by the blast, contained a dozen or so personal ads, felt-tipped onto plain white postcards. He glanced at these, and past them, through the window itself to where Jacqueline was making her purchases. Milk and rolls: elementary, my dear Conan Doyle. Waiting for her change, she half-turned her head towards the window. Rebus concentrated on the postcards. 'Candy, Masseuse' vied for attention with 'Pram and carry-cot for sale', 'Babysitting considered', and 'Lada, seldom used'. Rebus was smiling, almost despite himself, when the door of the shop tinkled open.

'Jacqueline?' he said. She turned towards him. He was holding open his ID. 'Mind if I have a word, Miss Dean?'

Major Dean was pouring himself a glass of Irish whiskey when the drawing-room door opened.

'Mind if I come in?' Rebus's words were directed not at Dean but at Matthews, who was seated in a chair by the window, one leg crossed over the other, hands gripping the arm-rests. He looked like a nervous businessman on an airplane, trying not to let his neighbour see his fear.

'Inspector Rebus,' he said tonelessly. 'I thought I could feel my scalp tingle.'

Rebus was already in the room. He closed the door behind him. Dean gestured with the decanter, but Rebus shook his head.

'How did you get in?' Matthews asked.

'Miss Dean was good enough to escort me through the gate. You've changed the guard detail again. She told them I was a friend of the family.'

Matthews nodded. 'And are you, Inspector? Are you a friend of the family?'

'That depends on what you mean by friendship.'

Dean had seated himself on the edge of his chair, steadying the glass with both hands. He didn't seem quite the figure he had been on the day of the explosion. A reaction, Rebus didn't doubt. There had been a quiet euphoria on the day; now came the aftershock.

'Where's Jacqui?' Dean asked, having paused with the glass to his lips.

'Upstairs,' Rebus explained. 'I thought it would be better if she didn't hear this.'

Matthews' fingers plucked at the arm-rests. 'How much does she know?'

'Not much. Not yet. Maybe she'll work it out for herself.'

'So, Inspector, we come to the reason why you're here.'

'I'm here,' Rebus began, 'as part of a murder inquiry. I thought that's why you were here, too, Mr Matthews. Maybe I'm wrong. Maybe you're here to cover up rather than bring to light.'

Matthews' smile was momentary. But he said nothing.

'I didn't go looking for the culprits,' Rebus went on. 'As you said, Mr Matthews, that was *your* department. But I did wonder who the victim was. The accidental victim, as I thought. A young car thief called Brian Cant, that would be my guess. He stole cars to order. A client asked him for a red open-top Jag, even told him where he might find one. The client told him about Major Dean. Very specifically about Major Dean, right down to the fact that every day he'd nip into the wine-shop on the main street.' Rebus turned to Dean. 'A bottle of Irish a day, is it, sir?'

Dean merely shrugged and drained his glass.

'Anyway, that's what your daughter told me. So all Brian Cant had to do was wait near the wine-shop. You'd get out of your car, leave it running, and while you were in the shop he could drive the car away. Only it bothered me that the client – Cant's brother tells me he spoke with an Irish accent – knew so much, making it easy for Cant. What was stopping this person from stealing the car himself?'

'And the answer came to you?' Matthews suggested, his voice thick with irony.

Rebus chose to avoid his tone. He was still watching Dean. 'Not straight away, not even then. But when I came to the house, I couldn't help noticing that Miss Dean seemed a bit strange. Like she was waiting for a phone call from someone and that someone had let her down. It's easy to be specific now, but at the time it just struck me as odd. I asked her about it this morning and she admitted it's because she's been jilted. A man she'd been seeing, and seeing regularly, had suddenly stopped calling. I asked her about him, but she couldn't be very helpful. They never went to his flat, for example. He drove a flashy car and had plenty of money, but she was vague about what he did for a living.'

Rebus took a photograph from his pocket and tossed it into Dean's lap. Dean froze, as though it were some hair-trigger grenade.

'I showed her a photograph of Brian Cant. Yes, that was the name of her boyfriend – Brian Cant. So you see, it was small wonder she hadn't heard from him.'

Matthews rose from the chair and stood before the window itself, but nothing he saw there seemed to please him, so he turned back into the room. Dean had found the courage to lift the photograph from his leg and place it on the floor. He got up too, and made for the decanter.

'For Christ's sake,' Matthews hissed, but Dean poured regardless.

Rebus's voice was level. 'I always thought it was a bit of a coincidence, the car being stolen only seconds before exploding. But then the IRA use remote control devices, don't they? So that someone in the vicinity could have triggered the bomb any time they liked. No need for all these long-term timers and what have you. I was in the SAS once myself.'

Matthews raised an eyebrow. 'Nobody told me that,' he said, sounding impressed for the first time.

'So much for Intelligence, eh?' Rebus answered. 'Speaking of which, you told me that Major Dean here was in Intelligence. I think I'd go further. Covert operations, that sort of thing? Counter-intelligence, subversion?'

'Now you're speculating, Inspector.'

Rebus shrugged. 'It doesn't really matter. What matters is that someone had been spying on Brian Cant, an ex-policeman called Jackie Hanson. He's a private detective these days. He won't say anything about his clients, of course, but I think I can put two and two together without multiplying the result. He was working for you, Major Dean, because you were interested in Brian Cant. Jacqueline was serious about him, wasn't she? So much so that she might have forsaken university. She tells me they were even talking of moving in together. You didn't want her to leave. When you found out what Cant did for a ... a living, I suppose you'd call it, you came up with a plan.' Rebus was enjoying himself now, but tried to keep the pleasure out of his voice.

'You contacted Cant,' he went on, 'putting on an Irish accent. Your Irish accent is probably pretty good, isn't it, Major? It would need to be, working in counter-intelligence. You told him all about a car – your car. You offered him a lot of money if he'd steal it for you and you told him precisely when and where he might find it. Cant was greedy. He didn't think twice.' Rebus noticed that he was sitting very comfortably in his own chair, whereas Dean looked ... the word that sprang to mind was 'rogue'. Matthews, too, was sparking internally, though his surface was all metal sheen, cold bodywork.

'You'd know how to make a bomb, that goes without saying. Wouldn't you, Major? Know thine enemy and all that. Like I say, I was in the SAS myself. What's more, you'd know how to make an IRA device, or one that looked like the work of the IRA. The remote was in your pocket. You went into the shop, bought your whiskey, and when you heard the car being driven off, you simply pressed the button.'

'Jacqueline.' Dean's voice was little more than a whisper. 'Jacqueline.' He rose to his feet, walked softly to the door and left the room. He appeared to have heard little or nothing of Rebus's speech. Rebus felt a pang of disappointment and looked towards Matthews, who merely shrugged.

'You cannot, of course, prove any of this, Inspector.'

'If I put my mind to it I can.'

'Oh, I've no doubt, no doubt.' Matthews paused. 'But will you?'

'He's mad, you've got to see that.'

'Mad? Well, he's unstable. Ever since his wife ...'

'No reason for him to murder Brian Cant.' Rebus helped himself to a whisky now, his legs curiously shaky. 'How long have you known?'

Matthews shrugged again. 'He tried a similar trick in Germany, apparently. It didn't work that time. So what do we do now? Arrest him? He'd be unfit to plead.'

'However it happens,' Rebus said, 'he's got to be made safe.'

'Absolutely.' Matthews was nodding agreement. He came to the sideboard. 'A hospital, somewhere he can be treated. He was a good soldier in his day. I've read his record. A good soldier. Don't worry, Inspector Rebus, he'll be "made safe" as you put it. He'll be taken care of.' A hand landed on Rebus's forearm. 'Trust me.'

Rebus trusted Matthews – about as far as he could spit into a Lothian Road headwind. He had a word with a reporter friend, but the man wouldn't touch the story. He passed Rebus on to an investigative journalist who did some ferreting, but there was little or nothing to be found. Rebus didn't know Dean's real name. He didn't know Matthews' first name or rank or even, to be honest, that he had been C13 at all. He might have been Army, or have inhabited that indefinite smear of operations somewhere between Army, Secret Service and Special Branch.

By the next day, Dean and his daughter had left West Lodge and a fortnight later it appeared in the window of an estate agent on George Street. The asking price seemed surprisingly low, if your tastes veered towards *The Munsters*. But the house would stay in the window for a long time to come.

Dean haunted Rebus's dreams for a few nights, no more. But how did you make safe a man like that? The Army had designed a weapon and that weapon had become misadjusted, its sights all wrong. You could dismantle a weapon. You could dismantle a man, too, come to that. But each and every piece was still as lethal as the whole. Rebus put aside fiction, put aside Hammett and the rest and of an evening read psychology books instead. But then they too, in their way, were fiction, weren't they? And so, too, in time became the case that was not a case of the man who had never been.

Being Frank

It wasn't easy, being Frank.

That's what everybody called him, when they weren't calling him a dirty old tramp or a scrounger or a layabout. Frank, they called him. Only the people at the hostel and at the Social Security bothered with his full name: Francis Rossetti Hyslop. Rossetti, he seemed to remember, not after the painter but after his sister the poet, Christina. Most often, a person – a person in authority – would read that name from the piece of paper they were holding and then look up at Frank, not quite in disbelief, but certainly wondering how he'd come so low.

He couldn't tell them that he was climbing higher all the time. That he preferred to live out of doors. That his face was weather-beaten, not dirty. That a plastic bag was a convenient place to keep his possessions. He just nodded and shuffled his feet instead, the shuffle which had become his trademark.

'Here he comes,' his companions would cry. 'Here comes The Shuffler!' Alias Frank, alias Francis Rossetti Hyslop.

He spent much of the spring and autumn in Edinburgh. Some said he was mad, leaving in the summer months. That, after all, was when the pickings were richest. But he didn't like to bother the tourists, and besides, summer was for travelling. He usually walked north, through Fife and into Kinross or Perthshire, setting up camp by the side of a loch or up in the hills. And when he got bored, he'd move on. He was seldom moved on by gamekeepers or the police. Some of them he knew of old, of course. But others he encountered seemed to regard him more and more as some rare species, or, as one had actually said, a 'national monument'.

It was true, of course. Tramp meant to walk and that's what tramps used to do. The term 'gentleman of the road' used to be accurate. But the tramp was being replaced by the beggar: young, fit men who didn't move from the city and who were unrelenting in their search for spare change. That had never been Frank's way. He had his regulars of course, and often he only had to sit on a bench in The Meadows, a huge grassy plain bordered by tree-lined paths, and wait for the money to appear in his lap.

That's where he was when he heard the two men talking. It was a bright day, a lunchtime and there were few spaces to be had on the meagre supply of Meadows' benches. Frank was sitting on one, arms folded, eyes closed, his legs stretched out in front of him with one foot crossed over the other. His three carrier bags were on the ground beside him, and his hat lay across his legs – not because he was hot especially, but because you never knew who might drop a coin in while you were dozing, or pretending to doze.

Maybe his was the only bench free. Maybe that's why the men sat down beside him. Well, 'beside him' was an exaggeration. They squeezed themselves onto the furthest edge of the bench, as far from him as possible. They couldn't be comfortable, squashed up like that and the thought brought a moment's smile to Frank's face.

But then they started to talk, not in a whisper but with voices lowered. The wind, though, swept every word into Frank's right ear. He tried not to tense as he listened, but it was difficult. Tried not to move, but his nerves were jangling.

'It's war,' one said. 'A council of war.'

War? He remembered reading in a newspaper recently about terrorists. Threats. A politician had said something about vigilance. Or was it vigilantes? A council of war: it sounded ominous. Maybe they were teasing him, trying to scare him from the bench so that they could have it for themselves. But he didn't think so. They were speaking in undertones; they didn't think he could hear. Or maybe they simply knew that it didn't matter whether an old tramp heard them or not. Who would believe him?

This was especially true in Frank's case. Frank believed that there was a worldwide conspiracy. He didn't know who was behind it, but he could see its tentacles stretching out across the globe. Everything was connected, that was the secret. Wars were connected by arms manufacturers, the same arms manufacturers who made the guns used in robberies, who made the guns used by crazy people in America when they went on the rampage in a shopping-centre or hamburger restaurant. So already you had a connection between hamburgers and dictators. Start from there and the thing just grew and grew.

And because Frank had worked this out, he wondered from time to time if *they* were after him. The dictators, the arms industry, or maybe even the people who made the buns for the hamburger chains. Because he *knew*. He wasn't crazy; he was sure of that.

'If I was,' he told one of his regulars, 'I wouldn't wonder if I was or not, would I?'

And she'd nodded, agreeing with him. She was a student at the university. A lot of students became regulars. They lived in Tollcross, Marchmont, Morningside, and had to pass through The Meadows on their way to the university buildings in George Square. She was studying psychology, and she told Frank something.

'You've got what they call an active fantasy life.'

Yes, he knew that. He made up lots of things, told himself stories. They whiled away the time. He pretended he'd been an RAF pilot, a spy, minor royalty, a slave-trader in Africa, a poet in Paris. But he *knew* he was making all these stories up, just as he knew that there really was a conspiracy.

And these two men were part of it.

'Rhodes,' one of them was saying now.

A council of war in Rhodes. So there was a Greek connection, too. Well, that made sense. He remembered stories about the generals and their junta. The terrorists were using Greece as their base. And Edinburgh was called the 'Athens of the north'. Yes! Of course! That's why they were basing themselves in Edinburgh too. A symbolic gesture. Had to be.

But who would believe him? That was the problem, being Frank. He'd told so many stories in the past, given the police so much information about the conspiracy, that now they just laughed at him and sent him on his way. Some of them thought he was looking for a night in the cells and once or twice they'd even obliged, despite his protests.

No, he didn't want to spend another night locked up. There was only one thing for it. He'd follow the men and see what he could find. Then he'd wait until tomorrow. They were talking about tomorrow, too, as if it was the start of their campaign. Well, tomorrow was Sunday and with a bit of luck if Frank hung around The Meadows, he'd bump into another of his regulars, one who might know exactly what to do.

Sunday morning was damp, blustery. Not the sort of day for a constitutional. This was fine by John Rebus: it meant there'd be fewer people about on Bruntsfield Links. Fewer men chipping golf-balls towards his head with a wavering cry of 'Fore!' Talk about crazy golf! He knew the Links had been used for this purpose for years and years, but all the same there were so many paths cutting through that it was a miracle no one had been killed.

He walked one circuit of the Links, then headed as usual across Melville Drive and into The Meadows. Sometimes he'd stop to watch a kickabout. Other times, he kept his head down and just walked, hoping for inspiration. Sunday was too close to Monday for his liking and Monday always meant a backlog of work. Thinking about it never did any good, of course, but he found himself thinking of little else.

'Mr Rebus!'

But then The Meadows offered other distractions, too.

'Mr Rebus!'

'Hello, Frank.'

'Sit yourself down.'

Rebus lowered himself onto the bench. 'You look excited about something.'

Frank nodded briskly. Though he was seated, he shuffled his feet on the earth, making little dance movements. Then he looked around him, as though seeking interlopers.

Oh no, thought Rebus, here we go again.

'War,' Frank whispered. 'I heard two men talking about it.'

Rebus sighed. Talking to Frank was like reading one of the Sunday rags – except sometimes the stories *he* told were more believable. Today didn't sound like one of those days.

'Talking about war? Which war?'

'Terrorism, Mr Rebus. Has to be. They've had a council of war at Rhodes. That's in Greece.'

'They were Greek, were they?'

Frank wrinkled his face. 'I don't think so. I can give you a description of them though. They were both wearing suits. One was short and bald, the other one was young, taller, with black hair.'

'You don't often see international terrorists wearing suits these days, do you?' Rebus commented. Actually, he thought to himself, that's a lie: they're becoming more smartly dressed all the time.

In any case, Frank had an answer ready. 'Need a disguise though, don't they? I followed them.'

'Did you?' A kickabout was starting nearby. Rebus concentrated on the kick-off. He liked Frank, but there were times ...

'They went to a bed and breakfast near the Links.'

'Did they now?' Rebus nodded slowly.

'And they said it was starting *today*. Today, Mr Rebus.'

'They don't hang about, do they? Anything else?'

Frank frowned, thinking. 'Something about lavatories, or laboratories. Must have been laboratories, mustn't it? And money, they talked about that. Money they needed to set it up. That's about it.'

'Well, thanks for letting me know, Frank. I'll keep my ears open, see if I can hear any whispers. But listen, don't go following people in future. It could be dangerous, understand?'

Frank appeared to consider this. 'I see what you mean,' he said at last, 'but I'm tougher than I look, Mr Rebus.'

Rebus was standing now. 'Well, I'd better be getting along.' He slipped his hands into his pockets. The right hand emerged again holding a pound note. 'Here you go, Frank.' He began to hand the money over, then withdrew it again. Frank knew what was coming and grinned.

'Just one question,' Rebus said, as he always did. 'Where do you go in the winter?'

It was a question a lot of his cronies asked him. 'Thought you were dead,' they'd say each spring as he came walking back into their lives. His reply to Rebus was the same as ever: 'Ah, that would be telling, Mr Rebus. That's *my* secret.'

The money passed from one hand to the other and Rebus sauntered off towards Jawbone Walk, kicking a stone in front of him. Jawbone because of the whale's jawbone which made an arch at one end of the path. Frank knew that. Frank knew lots of things. But he knew, too, that Rebus hadn't believed him. Well, more fool him. For over a year now they'd played this little game: where did Frank go in the winter? Frank wasn't sure himself why he didn't just say, I go to my sister's place in Dunbar. Maybe because it was the truth. Maybe because it *was* a secret.

Rebus looked to him like a man with secrets, too. Maybe one day Rebus would set out for a walk and never return home, would just keep on walking the way Frank himself had done. What was it the girl student had said?

'Sometimes I think we're *all* gentlemen of the road. It's just that most of us haven't got the courage to take that first step.'

Nonsense: that first step was the easiest. It was the hundredth, the thousandth, the millionth that was hard. But not as hard as going back, never as hard as that.

Rebus had counted the steps up to his second-floor flat many, many times. It always added up to the same number. So how come with the passing years there seemed to be more? Maybe it was the height of each step that was changing. Own up, John. For once, own up: it's *you* that's changing. You're growing older and stiffer. You never used to pause on the first-floor landing, never used to linger outside

Mrs Cochrane's door, breathing in that smell unique to blackcurrant bushes and cat-pee.

How could one cat produce that amount of odour? Rebus had seen it many a time: a fat, smug-looking creature with hard eyes. He'd caught it on his own landing, turning guiltily to look at him before sprinting for the next floor up. But it was inside Mrs Cochrane's door just now. He could hear it mewling, clawing at the carpet, desperate to be outside. He wondered. Maybe Mrs Cochrane was ill? He'd noticed that recently her brass nameplate had become tarnished. She wasn't bothering to polish it any more. How old was she anyway? She seemed to have come with the tenement, almost as if they'd constructed the thing around her. Mr and Mrs Costello on the top floor had been here nigh-on twenty-five years, but they said she'd been here when they arrived. Same brass nameplate on her door. Different cat, of course, and a husband, too. Well, he'd been dead by the time Rebus and his wife – now ex-wife – had moved here, what, was it ten years ago now?

Getting old, John. Getting old. He clamped his left hand onto the bannister and somehow managed the last flight of steps to his door.

He started a crossword in one of the newspapers, put some jazz on the hi-fi, drank a pot of tea. Just another Sunday. Day of rest. But he kept catching glimpses of the week ahead. No good. He made another pot of tea and this time added a dollop of J&B to the mixture in his mug. Better. And then, naturally, the doorbell rang.

Jehovah's Witnesses. Well, Rebus had an answer ready for them. A friend in the know had said that Roman Catholics are taught how to counter the persuasive arguments of the JWs. Just tell them you're a Catholic and they'll go away.

'I'm Catholic,' he said. They didn't go away. There were two of them, dressed in dark suits. The younger one stood a little behind the older one. This didn't matter, since he was a good foot taller than his elder. He was holding a briefcase. The chief, however, held only a piece of paper. He was frowning, glancing towards this. He looked at Rebus, sizing him up, then back to the paper. He didn't appear to have heard what Rebus said.

'I'm Catholic,' Rebus repeated, but hollowly.

The man shook his head. Maybe they were foreign missionaries, come to convert the heathen. He consulted his scrap of paper again.

'I think this is the wrong address,' he said. 'There isn't a Mr Bakewell here?'

'Bakewell?' Rebus started to relax. A simple mistake; they weren't JWs. They weren't salesmen or cowboy builders or tinkers. Simply, they'd got the wrong flat. 'No,' he said. 'No Mr Bakewell here. And his tart's not here either.'

Oh, they laughed at that. Laughed louder than Rebus had expected. They were still laughing as they made their apologies and started back downstairs. Rebus watched them until they were out of sight. He'd stopped laughing almost before they'd begun. He checked that his keys were in his pocket, then slammed shut his door – but with himself still out on the landing.

Their footsteps sent sibilant echoes up towards the skylight. What was it about them? If pressed, he couldn't have said. There was just *something*. The way the smaller, older man had seemed to weigh him up in a moment, then mentioned Bakewell. The way the younger man had laughed so heartily, as if it were such a release. A release of what? Tension, obviously.

The footsteps had stopped. Outside Mrs Cochrane's door. Yes, that was the ting-ting-ting of her antiquated doorbell, the kind you pulled, tightening and releasing the spring on a bell inside the door. The door which was now being pulled open. The older man spoke.

'Mrs Cochrane?' Well, they'd got that name right. But then it was on her nameplate, wasn't it? *Anyone* could have guessed at it.

'Aye.' Mrs Cochrane, Rebus knew, was not unique in making this sound not only questioning but like a whole sentence. Yes, I'm Mrs Cochrane, and who might you be and what do you want?

'Councillor Waugh.'

Councillor! No, no, there was no problem: Rebus had paid his Poll Tax, always put his bin-bags out the night before, never earlier. They might be after Bakewell, but Rebus was in the clear.

'It's about the roadworks.'

'Roadworks?' echoed Mrs Cochrane.

Roadworks? thought Rebus.

'Yes, roadworks. Digging up the roads. You made a complaint about the roads. I've come to talk to you about it.'

'Roadworks? Here, you mean?'

He was patient, Rebus had to grant him that. 'That's right, Mrs Cochrane. The road outside.'

There was a bit more of this, then they all went indoors to talk over Mrs Cochrane's grievances. Rebus opened his own door and went in, too. Then, realising, he slapped his hand against his head. These were the two men Shuffling Frank had been talking about! Of course they were, only Frank had misheard: council of war was Councillor Waugh; Rhodes was roads. What else had Frank said? Something about money: well, that might be the money for the repairs. That it was all planned to start on Sunday: and here they were, on Sunday, ready to talk to the residents about roadworks.

What roadworks? The road outside was clear, and Rebus hadn't heard any gossip concerning work about to start. Something else Frank had heard them say. Lavatories or laboratories. Of course, his own cherished conspiracy theory had made him plump for 'laboratories', but what if he'd misheard again? Where did lavatories fit into the scheme? And if, as seemed certain, these were the two men, what was a local councillor doing staying at a bed and breakfast? Maybe he owned it, of course. Maybe it was run by his wife.

Rebus was a couple of paces further down his hall when it hit him. He stopped dead. Slow, John, slow. Blame the whisky, maybe. And Jesus, wasn't it so obvious when you thought of it? He went back to his door opened it quietly, and slipped out onto the landing.

There was no such thing as silent movement on an Edinburgh stairwell. The sound of shoe on stone, a sound like sandpaper at work, was magnified and distorted, bouncing off the walls upwards and downwards. Rebus slipped off his shoes and left them on his landing, then started downstairs. He listened outside Mrs Cochrane's door. Muffled voices from the living-room. The layout of her flat was the same as Rebus's own: a long hallway off which were half a dozen doors, the last of which – actually around a corner – led to the living-room. He crouched down and pushed open the letterbox. The cat was just inside the door and it swiped at him with its paw. He let the hinge fall back.

Then he tried the doorhandle, which turned. The door opened. The cat swept past him and down the stairs. Rebus began to feel that the odds were going his way. The door was open just wide enough to allow him to squeeze inside. Open it an inch or two further, he knew, and it creaked with the almightiest groan. He tiptoed into the hallway. Councillor Waugh's voice boomed from the living-room.

'Bowel trouble. Terrible in a man so young.'

Yes, he'd no doubt be explaining why his assistant was taking so long in the lavatory: that was the excuse they always made. Well, either that or a drink of water. Rebus passed the toilet. The door wasn't locked and the tiny closet was empty. He pushed open the next door along – Mrs Cochrane's bedroom. The young man was closing the wardrobe doors.

'Well,' said Rebus, 'I hope you didn't think *that* was the toilet.'

The man jerked around. Rebus filled the doorway. There was no way past him; the only way to get out was to go through him, and that's what the man tried, charging at the doorway, head low. Rebus stood back a little, giving himself room and time, and brought his knee up hard, aiming for the bridge of the nose but finding mouth instead. Well, it was an imprecise science, wasn't it? The man flew backwards like a discarded ragdoll and fell onto the bed. Flat out, to Rebus's satisfaction.

They'd heard the noise of course, and the 'councillor' was already on his way. But he, too, would need to get past Rebus to reach the front door. He stopped short. Rebus nodded slowly.

'Very wise,' he said. 'Your colleague's going to need some new teeth when he wakes up. I'm a police officer by the way. And you, "councillor", are under arrest.'

'Arresting the councillor?' This from Mrs Cochrane, who had appeared in the hall.

'He's no more a councillor than I am, Mrs Cochrane. He's a con-man. His partner's been raking through your bedroom.'

'What?' She went to look.

'Bakewell,' Rebus said, smiling. They would try the same ruse at every door where they didn't fancy their chances. Sorry, wrong address, and on to the next potential sucker until they found someone old enough or gullible enough. Rebus was trying to remember if Mrs Cochrane had a telephone. Yes, there was one in her living-room, wasn't there? He gestured to his prisoner.

'Let's go back into the living-room,' he said. Rebus could call the station from there ...

Mrs Cochrane was back beside him. 'Blood on my good quilt,' she muttered. Then she saw that Rebus was in his stocking-soles. 'You'll get chilblains, son,' she said. 'Mark my words. You should take better care of yourself. Living on your own like that. You need somebody to look after you. Mark my words. He told me he was a councillor. Would you credit it? And me been wanting to talk to them for ages about the dogs' mess on the Links.'

'Hello, Shuffler.'

'Mr Rebus! Day off is it? Don't usually see you around here during the week.'

Frank was back on his bench, a newspaper spread out on his lap. One of yesterday's papers. It contained a story about some black magic conspiracy in the United States. Wealthy people, it was reckoned, influential people, taking part in orgies and rituals. Yes, and the arms manufacturers would be there, too. That's how they got to know the politicians and the bankers. It all connected.

'No, I'm off to work in a minute. Just thought I'd stop by. Here.' He was holding out a ten-pound note. Frank looked at it suspiciously, moved his hand towards it, and took it. What? Didn't Rebus even want to ask him the question?

'You were right,' Rebus was saying. 'What you told me about those two men, dead right. Well, nearly dead right. Keep your ears open, Frank. And in future, I'll try to keep *my* ears open when you talk to me.'

And then he turned and was walking away, back across the grass towards Marchmont. Frank stared at the money. Ten pounds. Enough to finance another long walk. He needed a long walk to clear his head. Now that they'd had the council of war at Rhodes, the laboratories would be making potions for satanic rituals. They'd put the politicians in a trance, and ... No, no, it didn't bear thinking about.

'Mr Rebus!' he called. 'Mr Rebus! I go to my sister's! She lives in Dunbar! That's where I go in the winter!'

But if the distant figure heard him, it made no sign. Just kept on walking. Frank shuffled his feet. Ten pounds would buy a transistor radio, or a pair of shoes, a jacket, or a new hat, maybe a little camping stove. That was the problem with having money: you ended up with decisions to make. And if you bought anything, where would you put it? He'd need either to ditch something, or to start on another carrier-bag.

That was the problem, being Frank.

Concrete Evidence

'It's amazing what you find in these old buildings,' said the contractor, a middle-aged man in safety helmet and overalls. Beneath the overalls lurked a shirt and tie, the marks of his station. He was the chief, the gaffer. Nothing surprised him any more, not even unearthing a skeleton.

'Do you know,' he went on, 'in my time, I've found everything from ancient coins to a pocket-watch. How old do you reckon he is then?'

'We're not even sure it *is* a he, not yet. Give us a chance, Mr Beesford.'

'Well, when can we start work again?'

'Later on today.'

'Must be gey old though, eh?'

'How do you make that out?'

'Well, it's got no clothes on, has it? They've perished. Takes time for that to happen, plenty of time ...'

Rebus had to concede, the man had a point. Yet the concrete floor beneath which the bones had been found ... *it* didn't look so old, did it? Rebus cast an eye over the cellar again. It was situated a storey or so beneath road-level, in the basement of an old building off the Cowgate. Rebus was often in the Cowgate; the mortuary was just up the road. He knew that the older buildings here were a veritable warren, long narrow tunnels ran here, there and, it seemed, everywhere, semi-cylindrical in shape and just about high enough to stand up in. This present building was being given the full works – gutted, new drainage system, rewiring. They were taking out the floor in the cellar to lay new drains and also because there seemed to be damp – certainly there was a fousty smell to the place – and its cause needed to be found.

They were expecting to find old drains, open drains perhaps. Maybe even a trickle of a stream, something which would lead to damp. Instead, their pneumatic drills found what remained of a corpse, perhaps hundreds of years old. Except, of course, for that concrete floor. It couldn't be more than fifty or sixty years old, could it? Would clothing deteriorate to a visible nothing in so short a time? Perhaps the damp could do that. Rebus found the cellar oppressive. The smell, the shadowy lighting provided by portable lamps, the dust.

But the photographers were finished, and so was the pathologist, Dr Curt. He didn't have too much to report at this stage, except to comment that he preferred it when skeletons were kept in cupboards, not confined to the cellar. They'd take the bones away, along with samples of the earth and rubble around the find, and they'd see what they would see.

'Archaeology's not really my line,' the doctor added. 'It may take me some time to bone up on it.' And he smiled his usual smile.

It took several days for the telephone call to come. Rebus picked up the receiver.

'Hello?'

'Inspector Rebus? Dr Curt here. About our emaciated friend.'

'Yes?'

'Male, five feet ten inches tall, probably been down there between thirty and thirty-five years. His left leg was broken at some time, long before he died. It healed nicely. But the little finger on his left hand had been dislocated and it did *not* heal so well. I'd say it was crooked all his adult life. Perfect for afternoon tea in Morningside.'

'Yes?' Rebus knew damned well Curt was leading up to something. He knew, too, that Curt was not a man to be hurried.

'Tests on the soil and gravel around the skeleton show traces of human tissue, but no fibres or anything which might have been clothing. No shoes, socks, underpants, nothing. Altogether, I'd say he was buried there in the altogether.'

'But did he die there?'

'Can't say.'

'All right, what did he die *of*?'

There was an almost palpable smile in Curt's voice. 'Inspector, I thought you'd never ask. Blow to the skull, a blow of considerable force to the back of the head. Murder, I'd say. Yes, definitely murder.'

There were, of course, ways of tracing the dead, of coming to a near-infallible identification. But the older the crime, the less likely this outcome became. Dental records, for example. They just weren't *kept* in the 50s and 60s the way they are today. A dentist practising then would most probably be playing near-full-time golf by now. And the record of a patient who hadn't been in for his check-up since 1960? Discarded, most probably. Besides, as Dr Curt pointed out, the man's teeth had seen little serious work, a few fillings, a single extraction.

The same went for medical records, which didn't stop Rebus from checking. A broken left leg, a dislocated left pinkie. Maybe some aged doctor would recall? But then again, maybe not. Almost certainly not. The local papers and radio were interested, which was a bonus. They were given what information the police had, but no memories seemed to be jogged as a result.

Curt had said he was no archaeologist; well, Rebus was no historian either. He knew other cases – contemporary cases – were yammering for his attention. The files stacked up on his desk were evidence enough of that. He'd give this one a few days, a few hours of his time. When the dead ends started to cluster around him, he'd drop it and head back for the here and now.

Who owned the building back in the 1950s? That was easy enough to discover: a wine importer and merchant. Pretty much a one-man operation, Hillbeith Vintners had held the premises from 1948 until 1967. And yes, there was a Mr Hillbeith, retired from the trade and living over in Burntisland, with a house gazing out across silver sands to the grey North Sea.

He still had a cellar, and insisted that Rebus have a 'wee taste' from it. Rebus got the idea that Mr Hillbeith liked visitors – a socially acceptable excuse for a drink. He took his time in the cellar (there must have been over 500 bottles in there) and emerged with cobwebs hanging from his cardigan, holding a dusty bottle of something nice. This he opened and sat on the mantelpiece. It would be half an hour or so yet at the very least before they could usefully have a glass.

Mr Hillbeith was, he told Rebus, seventy-four. He'd been in the wine trade for nearly half a century and had 'never regretted a day, not a day, nor even an hour'. Lucky you, Rebus thought to himself.

'Do you remember having that new floor laid in the cellar, Mr Hillbeith?'

'Oh, yes. That particular cellar was going to be for best claret. It was just the right temperature, you see, and there was no vibration from passing buses and the like. But it was damp, had been ever since I'd moved in. So I got a building firm to take a look. They suggested a new floor and some other alterations. It all seemed fairly straightforward and their charges seemed reasonable, so I told them to go ahead.'

'And when was this, sir?'

'1960. The spring of that year. There you are, I've got a great memory where business matters are concerned.' His small eyes beamed at Rebus through the thick lenses of their glasses. 'I can even tell you how much the work cost me ... and it was a pretty penny at the time. All for nothing, as it turned out. The cellar was still damp, and there was always that *smell* in it, a very unwholesome smell. I couldn't take a chance with the claret, so it became the general stock-room, empty bottles and glasses, packing-cases, that sort of thing.'

'Do you happen to recall, Mr Hillbeith, was the smell there *before* the new floor was put in?'

'Well, certainly there was *a* smell there before the floor was laid, but the smell afterwards was different somehow.' He rose and fetched two crystal glasses from the china cabinet, inspecting them for dust. 'There's a lot of nonsense talked about wine, Inspector. About decanting, the type of glasses you must use and so on. Decanting can help, of course, but I prefer the feel of the bottle. The bottle, after all, is part of the wine, isn't it?' He handed an empty glass to Rebus. 'We'll wait a few minutes yet.'

Rebus swallowed drily. It had been a long drive. 'Do you recall the name of the firm, sir, the one that did the work?'

Hillbeith laughed. 'How could I forget? Abbot & Ford, they were called. I mean, you just don't forget a name like that, do you? Abbot & Ford. You see, it sounds like Abbotsford, doesn't it? A small firm they were, mind. But you may know one of them, Alexander Abbot.'

'Of Abbot Building?'

'The same. He went on to make quite a name for himself, didn't he? Quite a fortune. Built up quite a company, too, but he started out small like most of us do.'

'How small, would you say?'

'Oh, small, small. Just a few men.' He rose and stretched an arm towards the mantelpiece. 'I think this should be ready to taste, Inspector. If you'll hold out your glass—'

Hillbeith poured slowly, deliberately, checking that no lees escaped into the glass. He poured another slow, generous measure for himself. The wine was reddish-brown. 'Robe and disc not too promising,' he muttered to himself. He gave his glass a shake and studied it. 'Legs not promising either.' He sighed. 'Oh dear.' Finally, Hillbeith sniffed the glass anxiously, then took a swig.

'Cheers,' said Rebus, indulging in a mouthful. A mouthful of vinegar. He managed to swallow, then saw Hillbeith spit back into the glass.

'Oxidisation,' the old man said, sounding cruelly tricked. 'It happens. I'd best check a few more bottles to assess the damage. Will you stay, Inspector?' Hillbeith sounded keen.

'Sorry, sir,' said Rebus, ready with his get-out clause. 'I'm still on duty.'

Alexander Abbot, aged fifty-five, still saw himself as the force behind the Abbot Building Company. There might be a dozen executives working furiously beneath him, but the company had grown from *his* energy and from *his* fury. He was Chairman, and a busy man too. He made this plain to Rebus at their meeting in the executive offices of ABC. The office spoke of business confidence, but then in Rebus's experience this meant little in itself. Often, the more dire straits a company was in, the healthier it tried to look. Still, Alexander Abbot seemed happy enough with life.

'In a recession,' he explained, lighting an overlong cigar, 'you trim your workforce pronto. You stick with regular clients, good payers, and don't take on too much work from clients you don't know. They're the ones who're likely to welch on you or go bust, leaving nothing but bills. Young businesses ... they're always hit hardest in a recession, no back-up you see. Then, when the recession's over for another few years, you dust yourself off and go touting for business again, re-hiring the men you laid off. That's where we've always had the edge over Jack Kirkwall.'

Kirkwall Construction was ABC's main competitor in the Lowlands, when it came to medium-sized contracts. Doubtless Kirkwall was the larger company. It, too, was run by a 'self-made' man, Jack Kirkwall. A larger-than-life figure. There was, Rebus quickly realised, little love lost between the two rivals.

The very mention of Kirkwall's name seemed to have dampened Alexander Abbot's spirits. He chewed on his cigar like it was a debtor's finger.

'You started small though, didn't you, sir?'

'Oh aye, they don't come much smaller. We were a pimple on the bum of the construction industry at one time.' He gestured to the walls of his office. 'Not that you'd guess it, eh?'

Rebus nodded. 'You were still a small firm back in 1960, weren't you?'

'1960. Let's think. We were just starting out. It wasn't ABC then, of course. Let's see. I think I got a loan from my dad in 1957, went into partnership with a chap called Hugh Ford, another self-employed builder. Yes, that's right. 1960, it was Abbot & Ford. Of course it was.'

'Do you happen to remember working at a wine merchant's in the Cowgate?'

'When?'

'The spring of 1960.'

'A wine merchant's?' Abbot furrowed his brow. 'Should be able to remember that. Long time ago, mind. A wine merchant's?'

'You were laying a new floor in one of his cellars, amongst other work. Hillbeith Vintners.'

'Oh, aye, Hillbeith, it's coming back now. I remember him. Little funny chap with glasses. Gave us a case of wine when the job was finished. Nice of him, but the wine was a bit off as I remember.'

'How many men were working on the job?'

Abbot exhaled noisily. 'Now you're asking. It was over thirty years ago, Inspector.'

'I appreciate that, sir. Would there be any records?'

Abbot shook his head. 'There might have been up to about ten years ago, but when we moved into this place a lot of the older stuff got chucked out. I regret it now. It'd be nice to have a display of stuff from the old days, something we could set up in the reception. But no, all the Abbot & Ford stuff got dumped.'

'So you don't remember how many men were on that particular job? Is there anyone else I could talk to, someone who might—'

'We were small back then, I can tell you that. Mostly using casual labour and part-timers. A job that size, I wouldn't think we'd be using more than three or four men, if that.'

'You don't recall anyone going missing? Not turning up for work, that sort of thing?'

Abbot bristled. 'I'm a stickler for time-keeping, Inspector. If anyone had done a bunk, I'd remember, I'm pretty sure of that. Besides, we were careful about who we took on. No lazy buggers, nobody who'd do a runner halfway through a job.'

Rebus sighed. Here was one of the dead ends. He rose to his feet. 'Well, thanks anyway, Mr Abbot. It was good of you to find time to see me.' The two men shook hands, Abbot rising to his feet.

'Not at all, Inspector. Wish I could help you with your little mystery. I like a good detective story myself.' They were almost at the door now.

'Oh,' said Rebus, 'just one last thing. Where could I find your old partner Mr Ford?'

Abbot's face lost its animation. His voice was suddenly that of an old man. 'Hugh died, Inspector. A boating accident. He was drowned. Hell of a thing to happen. Hell of a thing.'

Two dead ends.

Mr Hillbeith's telephone call came later that day, while Rebus was ploughing through the transcript of an interview with a rapist. His head felt full of foul-smelling glue, his stomach acid with caffeine.

'Is that Inspector Rebus?'

'Yes, hello, Mr Hillbeith. What can I do for you?' Rebus pinched the bridge of his nose and screwed shut his eyes.

'I was thinking all last night about that skeleton.'

'Yes?' In between bottles of wine, Rebus didn't doubt.

'Well, I was trying to think back to when the work was being done. It might not be much, but I definitely recall that there were four people involved. Mr Abbot and Mr Ford worked on it pretty much full-time, and there were two other men, one of them a teenager, the other in his forties. They worked on a more casual basis.'

'You don't recall their names?'

'No, only that the teenager had a nickname. Everyone called him by that. I don't think I ever knew his real name.'

'Well, thanks anyway, Mr Hillbeith. I'll get back to Mr Abbot and see if what you've told me jogs his memory.'

'Oh, you've spoken to him then?'

'This morning. No progress to report. I didn't realise Mr Ford had died.'

'Ah, well, that's the other thing.'

'What is?'

'Poor Mr Ford. Sailing accident, wasn't it?'

'That's right.'

'Only I remember that, too. You see, that accident happened just after they'd finished the job. They kept talking about how they were going to take a few days off and go fishing. Mr Abbot said it would be their first holiday in years.'

Rebus's eyes were open now. 'How soon was this after they'd finished your floor?'

'Well, directly after, I suppose.'

'Do you remember Mr Ford?'

'Well, he was very quiet. Mr Abbot did all the talking, really. A very quiet man. A hard worker though, I got that impression.'

'Did you notice anything about his hands? A misshapen pinkie?'

'Sorry, Inspector, it *was* a long time ago.'

Rebus appreciated that. 'Of course it was, Mr Hillbeith. You've been a great help. Thank you.'

He put down the receiver. A long time ago, yes, but still murder, still calculated and cold-blooded murder. Well, a path had opened in front of him. Not much of a path perhaps, a bit overgrown and treacherous. Nevertheless ... Best foot forward, John. Best foot forward.

Of course, he kept telling himself, he was still ruling possibilities out rather than ruling them in, which was why he wanted to know a little more about the boating accident. He didn't want to get the information from Alexander Abbot.

Instead, the morning after Hillbeith's phone-call, Rebus went to the National Library of Scotland on George IV Bridge. The doorman let him through the turnstile and he climbed an imposing staircase to the reading room. The woman on the desk filled in a one-day reader's card for him, and showed him how to use the computer. There were two banks of computers, being used by people to find the books they needed. Rebus had to go into the reading room and find an empty chair, note its number and put this on his slip when he'd decided which volume he required. Then he went to his chair and sat, waiting.

There were two floors to the reading room, both enveloped by shelves of reference books. The people working at the long desks downstairs seemed bleary. Just another morning's graft for them; but Rebus found it all fascinating. One person worked with a card index in front of him, to which he referred frequently. Another seemed asleep, head resting on arms. Pens scratched across countless sheets of paper. A few souls, lost for inspiration, merely chewed on their pens and stared at the others around them, as Rebus was doing.

Eventually, his volume was brought to him. It was a bound edition of the *Scotsman*, containing every issue for the months from January to June, 1960. Two thick leather buckles kept the volume closed. Rebus unbuckled these and began to turn the pages.

He knew what he was looking for, and pretty well where to find it, but that didn't stop him browsing through football reports and front page headlines. 1960. He'd been busy trying to lose his virginity and supporting Hearts. Yes, a long time ago.

The story hadn't quite made the front page. Instead, there were two paragraphs on page three. 'Drowning Off Lower Largo.' The victim, Mr Hugh Ford, was described as being twenty-six years of age (a year older than the survivor, Mr Alex Abbot) and a resident of Duddingston, Edinburgh. The men, on a short fishing-holiday, had taken a boat out early in the morning, a boat hired from a local man, Mr John Thomson. There was a squall, and the boat capsized. Mr Abbot, a fair swimmer, had made it back to the shore. Mr Ford, a poor swimmer, had not. Mr Ford was further described as a 'bachelor, a quiet man, shy according to Mr Abbot, who was still under observation at the Victoria Hospital, Kirkcaldy'. There was a little more, but not much. Apparently, Ford's parents were dead, but he had a sister, Mrs Isabel Hammond, somewhere out in Australia.

Why hadn't Abbot mentioned any of this? Maybe he wanted to forget. Maybe it still gave him the occasional bad dream. And of course he would have forgotten all about the Hillbeith contract precisely because this tragedy happened so soon afterwards. So soon. Just the one line of print really bothered Rebus; just that one sentence niggled.

'Mr Ford's body has still not been recovered.'

Records might get lost in time, but not by Fife Police. They sent on what they had, much of it written in fading ink on fragile paper, some of it typed – badly. The two friends and colleagues, Abbot and Ford, had set out on Friday evening to the Fishing-Net Hotel in Largo, arriving late. As arranged, they'd set out early next morning on a boat they'd hired from a local man, John Thomson. The accident had taken place only an hour or so after setting out. The boat was recovered. It had been overturned, but of Ford there was no sign. Inquiries were made. Mr Ford's belongings were taken back to Edinburgh by Mr Abbot, after the latter was released from hospital, having sustained a bump to the head when the boat went over. He was also suffering from shock and exhaustion. Mr Ford's sister, Mrs Isabel Hammond, was never traced.

They had investigated a little further. The business run jointly by Messrs Abbot and Ford now became Mr Abbot's. The case-notes contained a good amount of information and suspicion – between the lines, as it were. Oh yes, they'd investigated Alexander Abbot, but there had been no evidence. They'd searched for the body, had found none. Without a body, they were left with only their suspicions and their nagging doubts.

'Yes,' Rebus said quietly to himself, 'but what if you were looking for the body in the wrong place?' The wrong place at the wrong time. The work on the cellar had ended on Friday afternoon and by Saturday morning Hugh Ford had ceased to exist.

The path Rebus was on had become less overgrown, but it was still rock-strewn and dangerous, still a potential dead-end.

*

The Fishing-Net Hotel was still in existence, though apparently much changed from its 1960 incarnation. The present owners told Rebus to arrive in time for lunch if he could and it would be on the house. Largo was north of Burntisland but on the same coastline. Alexander Selkirk, the original of Defoe's *Robinson Crusoe*, had a connection with the fishing village. There was a small statue of him somewhere which Rebus had been shown as a boy (but only after much hunting, he recalled). Largo was picturesque, but then so were most, if not all, of the coastal villages in Fife's 'East Neuk'. But it was not yet quite the height of the tourist season and the customers taking lunch at the Fishing-Net Hotel were businessmen and locals.

It was a good lunch, as picturesque as its surroundings but with a bit more flavour. And afterwards, the owner, an Englishman for whom life in Largo was a long-held dream come true, offered to show Rebus round, including 'the very room your Mr Ford stayed in the night before he died'.

'How can you be sure?'

'I looked in the register.'

Rebus managed not to look too surprised. The hotel had changed hands so often since 1960, he despaired of finding anyone who would remember the events of that weekend.

'The register?'

'Yes, we were left a lot of old stuff when we bought this place. The store-rooms were choc-a-bloc. Old ledgers and what have you going back to the 1920s and '30s. It was easy enough to find 1960.'

Rebus stopped in his tracks. 'Never mind showing me Mr Ford's room, would you mind letting me see that register?'

He sat at a desk in the manager's office with the register open in front of him, while Mr Summerson's finger stabbed the line. 'There you are, Inspector, H. Ford. Signed in at 11.50 p.m., address given as Duddingston. Room number seven.'

It wasn't so much a signature as a blurred scrawl and above it, on a separate line, was Alexander Abbot's own more flowing signature.

'Bit late to arrive, wasn't it?' commented Rebus.

'Agreed.'

'I don't suppose there's anyone working here nowadays who worked in the hotel back then?'

Summerson laughed quietly. 'People do retire in this country, Inspector.'

'Of course, I just wondered.' He remembered the newspaper story. 'What about John Thomson? Does the name mean anything to you?'

'Old Jock? Jock Thomson? The fisherman?'

'Probably.'

'Oh, yes, he's still about. You'll almost certainly find him down by the dockside or else in the Harbour Tavern.'

'Thanks. I'd like to take this register with me if I may?'

Jock Thomson sucked on his pipe and nodded. He looked the archetype of the 'old salt', from his baggy cord trousers to his chiselled face and silvery beard. The only departure from the norm was, perhaps, the Perrier water in front of him on a table in the Harbour Tavern.

'I like the fizz,' he explained after ordering it, 'and besides, my doctor's told me to keep off the alcohol. Total abstinence, he said, total abstinence. Either the booze goes, Jock, or the pipe does. No contest.'

And he sucked greedily on the pipe. Then complained when his drink arrived without 'the wee slice of lemon'. Rebus returned to the bar to fulfil his mission.

'Oh aye,' said Thomson, 'remember it like it was yesterday. Only there's not much to remember, is there?'

'Why do you say that?'

'Two inexperienced laddies go out in a boat. Boat tips. End of story.'

'Was the weather going to be bad that morning?'

'Not particularly. But there *was* a squall blew up. Blew up and blew out in a matter of minutes. Long enough though.'

'How did the two men seem?'

'How do you mean?'

'Well, were they looking forward to the trip?'

'Don't know, I never saw them. The younger one, Abbot was it? He phoned to book a boat from me, said they'd be going out early, six or thereabouts. I told him he was daft, but he said there was no need for me to be on the dockside, if I'd just have the boat ready and tell him which one it was. And that's what I did. By the time I woke up that morning, he was swimming for the shore and his pal was food for the fish.'

'So you never actually saw Mr Ford?'

'No, and I only saw the lad Abbot afterwards, when the ambulance was taking him away.'

It was fitting into place almost too easily now. And Rebus thought, sometimes these things are only visible with hindsight, from a space of years. 'I don't suppose,' he ventured, 'you know anyone who worked at the hotel back then?'

'Owner's moved on,' said Thomson, 'who knows where to. It might be that Janice Dryman worked there then. Can't recall if she did.'

'Where could I find her?'

Thomson peered at the clock behind the bar. 'Hang around here ten minutes or so, you'll bump into her. She usually comes in of an afternoon. Meantime, I'll have another of these if you're buying.'

Thomson pushed his empty glass over to Rebus. Rebus, most definitely, was buying.

Miss Dryman – 'never married, never really saw the point' – was in her early fifties. She worked in a gift-shop in town and after her stint finished usually nipped into the Tavern for a soft drink and 'a bit of gossip'. Rebus asked what she would like to drink.

'Lemonade, please,' she said, 'with a drop of whisky in it.' And she laughed with Jock Thomson, as though this were an old and cherished joke between them. Rebus, not used to playing the part of straight-man, headed yet again for the bar.

'Oh yes,' she said, her lips poised above the glass. 'I was working there at the time all right. Chambermaid and general dogsbody, that was me.'

'You wouldn't see them arrive though?'

Miss Dryman looked as though she had some secret to impart. '*Nobody* saw them arrive, I know that for a fact. Mrs Dennis who ran the place back then, she said she'd be buggered if she'd wait up half the night for a couple of fishermen. They knew what rooms they were in and their keys were left at reception.'

'What about the front door?'

'Left unlocked, I suppose. The world was a safer place back then.'

'Aye, you're right there,' added Jock Thomson, sucking on his sliver of lemon.

'And Mr Abbot and Mr Ford knew this was the arrangement?'

'I suppose so. Otherwise it wouldn't have worked, would it?'

So Abbot knew there'd be nobody around at the hotel, not if he left it late enough before arriving.

'And what about in the morning?'

'Mrs Dennis said they were up and out before she knew anything about it. She was annoyed because she'd already cooked the kippers for their breakfast before she realised.'

So nobody saw them in the morning either. In fact ...

'In fact,' said Rebus, 'nobody saw Mr Ford at all. Nobody at the hotel, not you, Mr Thomson, nobody.' Both drinkers conceded this.

'I saw his stuff though,' said Miss Dryman.

'What stuff?'

'In his room, his clothes and stuff. That morning. I didn't know anything about the accident and I went in to clean.'

'The bed had been slept in?'

'Looked like it. Sheets all rumpled. And his suitcase was on the floor, only half unpacked. Not that there was much *to* unpack.'

'Oh?'

'A single change of clothes, I'd say. I remember them because they seemed mucky, you know, not fresh. Not the sort of stuff *I'd* take on holiday with me.'

'What? Like he'd been working in them?'

She considered this. 'Maybe.'

'No point wearing clean clothes for fishing,' Thomson added. But Rebus wasn't listening.

Ford's clothes, the clothes he had been working in while laying the floor. It made sense. Abbot bludgeoned him, stripped him and covered his body in fresh cement. He'd taken the clothes away with him and put them in a case, opening it in the hotel room, ruffling the sheets. Simple, but effective. Effective these past thirty years. The motive? A falling out perhaps, or simple greed. It was a small company, but growing, and perhaps Abbot hadn't wanted to share. Rebus placed a five-pound note on the table.

'To cover the next couple of rounds,' he said, getting to his feet. 'I'd better be off. Some of us are still on duty.'

There were things to be done. He had to speak to his superior, Chief Inspector Lauderdale. And that was for starters. Maybe Ford's Australian sister could be traced this time round. There had to be someone out there who could acknowledge that Ford had suffered from a broken leg in his youth, and that he had a crooked finger. So far, Rebus could think of only one person – Alexander Abbot. Somehow, he didn't think Abbot could be relied on to tell the truth, the whole truth.

Then there was the hotel register. The forensics lab could ply their cunning trade on it. Perhaps they'd be able to say for certain that Ford's signature was merely a bad rendition of Abbot's. But again, he needed a sample of Ford's handwriting in order to substantiate that the signature was not genuine. Who did he know who might possess such a document? Only Alexander Abbot. Or Mr Hillbeith, but Mr Hillbeith had not been able to help.

'No, Inspector, as I told you, it was Mr Abbot who handled all the paperwork, all that side of things. If there is an invoice or a receipt, it will be in his hand, not Mr Ford's. I don't recall ever seeing Mr Ford writing anything.'

No through road.

Chief Inspector Lauderdale was not wholly sympathetic. So far all Rebus had to offer were more suppositions to add to those of the Fife Police at the time. There was no proof that Alexander Abbot had killed his partner. No proof that the skeleton was Hugh Ford. Moreover, there wasn't even much in the way of circumstantial evidence. They could bring in Abbot for questioning, but all he had to do was plead innocence. He could afford a good lawyer; and even bad lawyers weren't stupid enough to let the police probe too deeply.

'We need proof, John,' said Lauderdale, 'concrete evidence. The simplest proof would be that hotel signature. If we prove it's not Ford's, then we have Abbot at that hotel, Abbot in the boat and Abbot shouting that his friend has drowned, *all* without Ford having been there. That's what we need. The rest of it, as it stands, is rubbish. You know that.'

Yes, Rebus knew. He didn't doubt that, given an hour alone with Abbot in a darkened alley, he'd have his confession. But it didn't work like that. It worked through the law. Besides, Abbot's heart might not be too healthy. BUSINESSMAN, 55, DIES UNDER QUESTIONING. No, it had to be done some other way.

The problem was, there *was* no other way. Alexander Abbot was getting away with murder. Or was he? Why did his story have to be false? Why did the body have to be Hugh Ford's? The answer was: because the whole thing seemed to fit. Only, the last piece of the jigsaw had been lost under some sofa or chair a long time ago, so long ago now that it might remain missing for ever.

He didn't know why he did it. If in doubt, retrace your steps ... something like that. Maybe he just liked the atmosphere. Whatever, Rebus found himself back in the National Library, waiting at his desk for the servitor to bring him his bound volume of old news. He mouthed the words of 'Yesterday's Papers' to himself as he waited. Then, when the volume appeared, he unbuckled it with ease and pulled open the pages. He read past the April editions, read through into May and June. Football results, headlines – and what was this? A snippet of business news, barely a filler at the bottom right-hand corner of a page. About how the Kirkwall Construction Company was swallowing up a couple of smaller competitors in Fife and Midlothian.

'The 1960s will be a decade of revolution in the building industry,' said Managing Director Mr Jack Kirkwall, 'and Kirkwall Construction aims to meet that challenge through growth and quality. The bigger we are, the better we are. These acquisitions strengthen the company, and they're good news for the workforce, too.'

It was the kind of sentiment which had lasted into the 1980s. Jack Kirkwall, Alexander Abbot's bitter rival. Now there was a man Rebus ought to meet . . .

The meeting, however, had to be postponed until the following week. Kirkwall was in hospital for a minor operation.

'I'm at that age, Inspector,' he told Rebus when they finally met, 'when things go wrong and need treatment or replacing. Just like any bit of well-used machinery.'

And he laughed, though the laughter, to Rebus's ears, had a hollow centre. Kirkwall looked older than his sixty-two years, his skin saggy, complexion wan. They were in his living-room, from where, these days, he did most of his work.

'Since I turned sixty, I've only really wandered into the company headquarters for the occasional meeting. I leave the daily chores to my son, Peter. He seems to be managing.' The laughter this time was self-mocking.

Rebus had suggested a further postponement of the meeting, but when Jack Kirkwall knew that the subject was to be Alexander Abbot, he was adamant that they should go ahead.

'Is he in trouble then?'

'He might be,' Rebus admitted. Some of the colour seemed to reappear in Kirkwall's cheeks and he relaxed a little further into his reclining leather chair. Rebus didn't want to give Kirkwall the story. Kirkwall and Abbot were still business rivals, after all. Still, it seemed, enemies. Given the story, Kirkwall might try some underhand tactic, some rumour in the media, and if it got out that the story originally came from a police inspector, well. Hello, being sued and goodbye, pension.

No, Rebus didn't want that. Yet he did want to know whether Kirkwall knew anything, knew of any reason why Abbot might wish, might *need* to kill Ford.

'Go on, Inspector.'

'It goes back quite a way, sir. 1960, to be precise. Your firm was at that time in the process of expansion.'

'Correct.'

'What did you know about Abbot & Ford?'

Kirkwall brushed the palm of one hand over the knuckles of the other. 'Just that they were growing, too. Of course, they were younger than us, much smaller than us. ABC still is much smaller than us. But they were cocky, they were winning some contracts ahead of us. I had my eye on them.'

'Did you know Mr Ford at all?'

'Oh yes. Really, he was the cleverer of the two men. I've never had much respect for Abbot. But Hugh Ford was quiet, hardworking. Abbot was the one who did the shouting and got the firm noticed.'

'Did Mr Ford have a crooked finger?'

Kirkwall seemed bemused by the question. 'I've no idea,' he said at last. 'I never actually met the man, I merely knew *about* him. Why? Is it important?'

Rebus felt at last that his meandering, narrowing path had come to the lip of a chasm. Nothing for it but to turn back.

'Well,' he said, 'it would have clarified something.'

'You know, Inspector, my company *was* interested in taking Abbot & Ford under our wing.'

'Oh?'

'But then with the accident, that tragic accident. Well, Abbot took control and he wasn't at all interested in any offer we had to make. Downright rude, in fact. Yes, I've always thought that it was such a *lucky* accident so far as Abbot was concerned.'

'How do you mean, sir?'

'I mean, Inspector, that Hugh Ford was on our side. He wanted to sell up. But Abbot was against it.'

So, Rebus had his motive. Well, what did it matter? He was still lacking that concrete evidence Lauderdale demanded.

'... Would it show up from his handwriting?'

Rebus had missed what Kirkwall had been saying. 'I'm sorry, sir, I didn't catch that.'

'I said, Inspector, if Hugh Ford had a crooked finger, would it show from his handwriting?'

'Handwriting?'

'Because I had his agreement to the takeover. He'd written to me personally to tell me. Had gone behind Abbot's back, I suppose. I bet Alex Abbot was mad as hell when he found out about that.' Kirkwall's smile was vibrant now. 'I always thought that accident was a bit too lucky where Abbot was concerned. A bit too neat. No proof though. There was never any proof.'

'Do you still have the letter?'

'What?'

'The letter from Mr Ford, do you still have it?'

Rebus was tingling now, and Kirkwall caught his excitement. 'I never throw anything away, Inspector. Oh yes, I've got it. It'll be upstairs.'

'Can I see it? I mean, can I see it now?'

'If you like,' Kirkwall made to stand up, but paused. '*Is* Alex Abbot in trouble, Inspector?'

'If you've still got that letter from Hugh Ford, then, yes, sir, I'd say Mr Abbot could be in very grave trouble indeed.'

'Inspector, you've made an old man very happy.'

It was the letter against Alex Abbot's word, of course, and he denied everything. But there was enough now for a trial. The entry in the hotel, while it was *possibly* the work of Alexander Abbot was *certainly* not the work of the man who had written the letter to Jack Kirkwall. A search warrant gave the police the powers to look through Abbot's home and the ABC headquarters. A contract, drawn up between Abbot and Ford when the two men had gone into partnership, was discovered to be held in a solicitor's safe. The signature matched that on the letter to Jack Kirkwall. Kirkwall himself appeared in court to give evidence. He seemed to Rebus a different man altogether from the person he'd met previously: sprightly, keening, enjoying life to the full.

From the dock, Alexander Abbot looked on almost reproachfully, as if this were just one more business trick in a life full of them. Life, too, was the sentence of the judge.

Seeing Things

To be honest, if you were going to see Christ anywhere in Edinburgh, the Hermitage was perfect.

Or, to give it its full title, the Hermitage of Braid, named after the Braid Burn which trickled through the narrow, bushy wilderness between Blackford Hill and Braid Hills Road. Across this road, the Hermitage became a golf course, its undulations cultivated and well-trodden, but on sunny weekend afternoons, the Hermitage itself was as wild a place as your imagination wished it to be. Children ran in and out of the trees or threw sticks into the burn. Lovers could be seen hand-in-hand as they tackled the tricky descent from Blackford Hill. Dogs ran sniffing to stump and post, watched, perhaps, by punks seated atop an outcrop. Can would be tipped to mouth, the foam savoured. Picnic parties would debate the spot most sheltered from the breeze.

It was sometimes hard to believe that the place was in Edinburgh, that the main entrance to the Hermitage was just off the busy Comiston Road at the southern reach of Morningside. The protesters – such as they were – had held vigil at these gates for a couple of days, singing songs and handing out their 'No Popery' pamphlets. Occasionally a megaphone would appear, so that they could deliver their rant. A seller of religious nick-nacks and candles had set up his pitch across the road from the protesters, and at a canny distance along the road from them. The megaphone was most often directed towards him, there being no other visible target.

A rant was occurring as Inspector John Rebus arrived. Would the day of judgement be like this, he wondered, accepting a leaflet. Would the loudest voices belong to the saved? *Megaphones will be provided*, he thought to himself as he passed through the gates. He studied the leaflet. No Popery, indeed.

'Why ever not?' And so asking, he crumpled the paper and tossed it into the nearest wastepaper-bin. The voice followed him as though it had a mission and he was it.

'There must be NO idolatry! There is but ONE God and it is HE ye should worship! Do not turn YOUR face to graven IMAGES! The Good Book is the ONLY truth ye NEED!'

Rave on ...

They were a minority of course, far outweighed by the curious who came to see. But they in their turn looked as though they might be outnumbered very soon by the shrine-builders. Rebus liked to think of himself as a Christian, albeit with too many questions and doubts to ally himself with either side, Catholic or Protestant. He could not escape the fact that he had been born a Protestant; but his mother, a religious woman, had died young, and his father had been indifferent.

Rebus hadn't even been aware of any difference between Catholic and Protestant until he'd started school. His pre-school-days best friend was a Catholic, a boy called Miles Skelly. Come their first day at school, the boys had been split up, sent to schools on different sides of town. Parted like this daily, they soon grew to have new friends and stopped playing together.

That had been Rebus's first lesson in 'the divide'. But he had nothing against Catholics. The Protestant community might call them 'left-footers', but Rebus himself kicked a ball with his left foot. He did, however, mistrust the shrine mentality. It made him uneasy: statues which wept or bled or moved. Sudden visions of the Virgin Mary. A face imprinted on a shroud.

A faith should be just that, Rebus reasoned. And if you held belief, what need had you of miracles, especially ones that seemed more the province of the Magic Circle than of the divine? So the closer he came to the spot itself, the shakier became his legs. There was a tangle of undergrowth, and in front of it a stunted tree. Around this tree had been arranged candles, small statues, photographs, written prayers, flowers, all in the last two or three days. It was quite a transformation. A knot of people knelt nearby, but at a respectful distance. Their heads were bowed in prayer. Others sat, arms out behind them, supporting themselves on the grass. They wore beatific smiles, as though they could hear or see something Rebus couldn't. He listened hard, but heard only whispers of prayer, the distant barking of dogs. He looked, but saw only a tree, though it had to be admitted that the sunlight seemed to catch it in a particularly striking way, picking it out from the undergrowth behind it.

There was a rustling from beyond the tree itself. Rebus moved around the congregation – there was no other word for the gathering – towards the undergrowth, where several police cadets were on their hands and knees, not in worship this time but searching the ground.

'Anything?'

One of the figures straightened up, pressing his fingers into his spine as he exhaled. Rebus could hear the vertebrae crackling.

'Nothing, sir, not a blasted thing.'

'Language, Holmes, language. Remember, this is a holy site.'

Detective Constable Brian Holmes managed a wry smile. He'd been smiling a lot this morning. For once he'd been put in charge and it didn't matter to him that he was in a damp copse, or that he was in charge of a shower of disgruntled cadets, or that he had twigs in his hair. He was in charge. Not even John Rebus could take that away from him.

Except that he could. And did.

'All right,' Rebus said, 'that's enough. We'll have to make do with what we've got. Or rather, what the lab boys have got.'

The cadets rose mercifully to their feet. One or two brushed white chalky powder from their knees, others scraped at dirt and grass stains. 'Well done, lads,' Rebus admitted. 'Not very exciting, I know, but that's what police work is all about. So if you're joining for thrills and spills, think again.'

That should have been *my* speech, Holmes thought to himself as the cadets grinned at Rebus's words. They would agree with anything he said, anything he did. He was an Inspector. He was *the* Inspector Rebus. Holmes felt himself losing height and density, becoming like a patch of low mist or a particularly innocuous shadow. Rebus was in charge now. The cadets had all but forgotten their former leader. They had eyes for only one man, and that man was ordering them to go and drink some tea.

'What's up, Brian?'

Holmes, watching the cadets shuffle away, realised Rebus was speaking to him. 'Sorry?'

'You look like you've found a tanner and lost a shilling.'

Holmes shrugged. 'I suppose I'm thinking about how I could have had one-and-six. No news yet on the blood?'

'Just that it's every bit as messianic as yours and mine.'

'What a surprise.'

Rebus nodded towards the clearing. 'Try telling them that. They'll have an answer for you.'

'I know. I've already been ticked off for desecration. You know they've started posting an all-night guard?'

'What for?'

'In case the Wee Frees chop down the tree and run away with it.'

They stared at one another, then burst out laughing. Hands quickly went to mouths to stifle the sound. Desecration upon desecration.

'Come on,' said Rebus, 'you look like you could do with a cuppa yourself. My treat.'

'Now that *is* a miracle,' said Holmes, following his superior out of the trees. A tall, muscled man was approaching. He wore denims and a white T-shirt. A large wooden cross swung from his neck, around which was also tied a red kerchief. His beard was as thick and black as his hair.

'Are you police officers?'

'Yes,' Rebus said.

'Then I think you should know, they're trying to steal the tree.'

'Steal it, sir?'

'Yes, steal it. We've got to keep watch twenty-four hours. Last night, one of them had a knife, but there were too many of us, thank God.'

'And you are?'

'Steven Byrne.' He paused. 'Father Steven Byrne.'

Rebus paused too, digesting this new information. 'Well, Father, would you recognise this man again? The one with the knife?'

'Yes, probably.'

'Well, we could go down to the station and have a look at some photographs.'

Father Byrne seemed to be appraising Rebus. Acknowledging that he was being taken seriously, he nodded slowly. 'Thank you, I don't think that'll be necessary. But I thought you ought to know. Things might turn nasty.'

Rebus bit back a comment about turning the other cheek. 'Not if we can help it,' he said instead. 'If you see the man again, Father, let us know straight away. Don't try anything on your own.'

Father Byrne looked around him. 'There aren't so many telephones around here.' His eyes were twinkling with humour. An attractive man, thought Rebus. Even a touch charismatic.

'Well,' he said, 'we'll try to make sure a patrol car comes by and checks on things. How would that be?'

Father Byrne nodded. Rebus made to move away. 'Bless you,' he heard the man saying. Rebus kept walking, but for some reason his cheeks had turned deep red. But it was right and proper, after all, wasn't it? Right that he should be blessed.

'Blessed are the peacemakers,' he quoted, as the megaphone came back into range.

The story was a simple one. Three girls had been in the Hermitage one late afternoon. School over, they'd decided to cut through the park, climb Blackford Hill and come down the other side towards their homes. A long way round for a short-cut, as Rebus had put it at the time.

They were sensible girls, from good Catholic homes. They were fifteen and all had future plans that included university and a career as well as marriage. They didn't seem inclined to fantasy or exaggeration. They stuck to the same story throughout. They'd been about thirty yards or so from the tree when they'd seen a man. One second he wasn't there, the next he was. Dressed in white and with a glow all around him. Long wavy dark hair and a beard. A very pale face, they were definite about that. He leaned with one hand against the tree, the other to his side. His right side – again, all three concurred on this. Then he took the hand away, and they saw that there was blood on his side. A dark red patch. They gasped. They looked to each other for confirmation that they'd seen what they had seen. When they looked again, the figure had vanished.

They ran to their separate homes, but over dinner the story came out in each of the three households. Disbelieved, perhaps, for a moment. But then why would the girls lie? The parents got together and went to the Hermitage. They were shown the place, the tree. There was no sign of anyone. But then one of the mothers shrieked before crossing herself.

'Look at that!' she cried. 'Just look at it!'

It was a smeared red mark, still wet on the bark of the tree. Blood.

The parents went to the police and the police made an initial search of the area, but in the meantime, the neighbour of one of the families telephoned a friend who was a stringer on a Sunday newspaper. The paper ran the story of the 'Hermitage Vision' and the thing began to grow. The blood, it was said, hadn't dried. And this was true, though as Rebus knew it could well have something to do with the reaction of blood and bark. Footprints were found, but so many and so varied that it was impossible to say when they'd been made or by whom. The parents, for example, had searched the area thoroughly, destroying a lot of potential evidence. There were no bloodstains on the ground. No patients with side wounds had been treated in any of the city's hospitals or by any doctor.

The description of the figure was vague: tallish, thinnish, the long hair and beard of course – but was the hair brown or black? The girls couldn't be sure. Dressed in white – 'like a gown', one of them remembered later. But by then the story had become public property; how far would that distort her memories of the evening? And as for the glow. Well, Rebus had seen how the sun hit that particular spot. Imagine a lowish sun, creeping towards evening. That would explain the glow – to a rational man.

But then the zealous – of both sides – appeared. The believers and the doubters, carrying candles or toting megaphones. It was a quiet time for news: the media loved it. The girls photographed well. When they appeared on TV, the trickle of visitors to the site became a flood. Coach-loads headed north from Wales and England. Organised parties were arriving from Ireland. A Parisian magazine had picked up on the mystery; so, it was rumoured, had a Bible-thumping cable channel from the USA.

Rebus wanted to raise his hands and turn back the tide. Instead of which that tide rolled straight over him. Superintendent Watson wanted answers.

'I don't like all this hocus-pocus,' he said, with Presbyterian assuredness and an Aberdonian lilt. 'I want something tangible. I want an explanation, one I can *believe*. Understood?'

Understood. Rebus understood it; so did Chief Inspector Lauderdale. Chief Inspector Lauderdale understood that *he* wanted Rebus to do something about it. Rebus understood that hands were being washed; that his alone were to work on the case. If in doubt, delegate. That was where Brian Holmes and his cadets entered the picture. Having found no new clues – no clues *period* – Rebus decided to back off. Media interest was already dying. Some local historian would now and again come up with a 'fact' or a 'theory' and these would revive the story for a while – the hermit who'd lived in the Hermitage, executed for witchcraft in 1714 and said still to haunt the place, that sort of thing, but it couldn't last. It was like poking at embers without feeding them. A momentary glow, no more. When the media interest died, so would that of the fringe lunatics. There had already been copycat 'visions' in Cornwall, Caerphilly and East Croydon. The Doubting Thomases were appearing. What's more, the blood had gone, washed away in an overnight deluge which also extinguished the candles around the tree.

A recurrence of the 'vision' was needed if the thing were not to die. Rebus prayed each night for a quick and merciful release. It didn't come. Instead there was a 4 a.m. phone call.

'This better be worth it.'

'It is.'

'Go on then.'

'How soon can you get to the Hermitage?'

Rebus sat up in bed. 'Talk to me.'

'They've found a body. Well, that's putting it a bit strongly. Let's say they've found a trunk.'

*

A trunk it was, and not the sort you stuck travel labels on either.

'Dear God in heaven,' Rebus whispered, staring at the thing. 'Who found it?'

Holmes didn't look too good himself. 'One of the tree people,' he said. 'Wandered over here looking for a place to do his number twos. Had a torch with him. Found this. I think you could say he's in a state of shock. Apparently, so are his trousers.'

'I can't say I blame them.' A generator hummed in the background, providing juice for the three tall halogen lamps which lit the clearing. Some uniformed officers were cordoning off the area with strips of orange tape. 'So nobody's touched it?'

'Nobody's been near it.'

Rebus nodded, satisfied. 'Better keep it that way till forensics get here. Where the hell's the pathologist?'

Holmes nodded over Rebus's shoulder. 'Speak of the devil,' he said.

Rebus turned. Two men in sombre Crombie-style coats were walking briskly towards the scene. One carried a black surgeon's bag, the other had his hands firmly in his pockets, protection from the chill air. The halogen had fooled a few of the local birds, who were chirping their hearts out. But morning wasn't far away.

Chief Inspector Lauderdale nodded curtly towards Rebus, reckoning this greeting enough under the circumstances. The pathologist, Dr Curt, was, however (and despite his name), as voluble as ever.

'Top of the morning to you, Inspector.' Rebus, knowing Dr Curt of old, waited for the inevitable joke. The doctor obliged, gesturing towards the body. 'Not often I get a trunk call these days.'

Rebus, as was expected of him, groaned. The doctor beamed. Rebus knew what came next: the corny newspaper headlines. Again, Dr Curt obliged. 'Corpse in the coppice baffles cops,' he mused brightly, donning overshoes and coveralls before making for the corpse itself.

Chief Inspector Lauderdale looked stunned. He shuffled closer to Rebus. 'Is he always like this?'

'Always.'

The doctor had crouched down to inspect the body. He asked for the position of the lamps to be changed, then started his examination. But there was time for a last twist of the head towards Rebus.

'I'm afraid we're too late,' Dr Curt called out. 'Poor chap's dead.'

Chuckling to himself, he set to work, bringing a tape-recorder out of his case and mumbling into it from time to time.

Lauderdale watched for a minute. It was about fifty-nine seconds too long. He turned to Rebus again. 'What can you tell me?'

'About Dr Curt? Or about the deceased?'

'About the deceased.'

Rebus pushed his fingers through his hair, scratching at the scalp. He was mentally listing the bad puns still available to Dr Curt – he got legless, he's out of 'arm's way, lost his head, hadn't paid his bills so got cut off, was for the chop anyway, had no bleeding right, worked as a hack, take a butcher's at him ...

'Inspector?'

Rebus started. 'What?'

Lauderdale stared at him hard.

'Oh,' Rebus said, remembering. 'Well, he's naked of course. And they haven't severed *every* limb, so we know for sure that it *is* a he. Nothing else yet, sir. Come first light, we'll search the area for the missing appendages. One thing I'm pretty sure of, he wasn't butchered here.'

'Oh?'

'No blood, sir. Not that I can see.'

'Gentlemen!' It was Curt, calling to them, waving his arm for them to join him. They, too, had to slip on the elastic shoes, like ill-fitting polythene bags, and the coveralls. The forensics people would want to cover every inch of the ground around the victim's body. It didn't do to leave erroneous 'clues' like fibres from your jacket or a dropped coin.

'What is it, Doctor?'

'First, let me tell you that he's male, aged anywhere between thirty-five and fifty. Either dissolute thirty-five or a fairly well-preserved fifty. Stocky, too, unless the legs are in ridiculous proportion to the trunk. I can give a better guesstimate once we've had him on the slab.' His smile seemed directed at Lauderdale especially. 'Been dead a day or more. He was brought here in this condition, of course.'

'Of course,' said Lauderdale. 'No blood.'

The doctor nodded, still smiling. 'But there's something else. Look here.' He pointed to what was left of the right shoulder. 'Do you see this damage?' He circled the shoulder with his finger. They had to bend closer to see what he was talking about. The shoulder had been attacked with a knife, like someone had tried to peel it. It all looked clumsy and amateurish compared to the other neat examples.

'A tattoo,' Rebus said. 'Got to be.'

'Quite right, Inspector. They've tried removing it. *After* they dumped the trunk here. They must have spotted that there was still part of the tattoo left, enough to help us identify the victim.

So ...' He moved his finger from the shoulder stump to the ground beneath it. Rebus could just make out the shreds of skin.

'We can piece it back together,' Rebus stated.

'Of course we can!' The doctor stood up. 'They must think we're stupid. They go to all this trouble, then leave something like that.' He shook his head slowly. Rebus held his breath, waiting. The doctor's face brightened. 'It's years since I last did a jigsaw,' he said, opening his bag, placing his things back in it, and closing it with a loud snap. 'An open and shut case,' he said, moving back towards the cordon.

After he'd gone, off to his slab to await delivery of the body, Lauderdale lingered to see that everything was running smoothly. It was, as Rebus assured him. Lauderdale then bid him goodnight. Rebus didn't think anyone had ever 'bid' him goodnight before; wasn't sure anyone had *ever* bid anyone goodnight, outside of books and plays. It was especially strange to be bid goodnight at dawn. He could swear there was a cock crowing in the distance, but who in Morningside would keep chickens?

He looked for Holmes and found him over beside the tree-dwellers. Overnight, a guard-duty worked in shifts, two or three people at a time for two hours at a stretch. Holmes was chatting, seeming casual. He shifted his weight from foot to foot, as though cramp or cold were seeping through his socks.

Hadn't a leg to stand on: that was another one Dr Curt could have used.

'You seem very cheerful this morning, Inspector. But then each morning is a cause for celebration in itself.' Intent on Holmes, Rebus hadn't noticed the other figure who, like him, was making his way towards the tree. Dressed in jeans, tartan shirt and lumber jacket, but with the same wooden cross. It was Father Byrne. Sky-blue eyes, piercing eyes, the pupils like tiny points of ink. The smile spreading from the lips and mouth towards the eyes and cheeks. The man's very beard seemed to take part in the process.

'I don't know about cheerful, Father Byrne—'

'Please, call me Steven.'

'Well, as I was saying, I don't know about cheerful. You know there was a murder last night?'

Now the eyes opened wide. 'A murder? Here?'

'Well, not strictly speaking, no. But the body was dumped here. We'll need to talk to anyone who was here yesterday. They may have seen something.'

Holmes waved a notebook. 'I've already collected some names and addresses.'

'Good lad. Have there been any more threats, Father?'

'Threats?'

'You remember, the man with the knife.'

'No, not that I know of.'

'Well, I really would like you to come down to the station and see if you can pick him out from some photographs.'

'Now?'

'Sometime today.' Rebus paused. 'At your convenience.'

Father Byrne caught the meaning of the pause. 'Well, of course. If you think it will help. I'll come this morning. But you don't think ...? Surely not.'

Rebus shrugged. 'Probably just a coincidence, Father. But you have to admit, it *is* quite a coincidence. Someone comes down here with a knife. Some days later, a body appears not three hundred yards away. Yes, coincidence.' That pause again. 'Wouldn't you say?'

But Father Byrne didn't seem to have an answer for that.

No, it was no coincidence, Rebus was sure of that. Fine, if you were going to dump a body the Hermitage was as good a spot as any. But not in a clearing, where it would be stumbled upon sooner rather than later. And not so close to the famous tree, where, as everyone knew, people were to be found round-the-clock, making dumping a body nearby a risky procedure. Too risky. There had to be a reason. There had to be some meaning. Some message.

Yes, some *message*.

And wasn't three hundred yards a long way to go for number twos? Well, that one was cleared up quickly. The man admitted that he hadn't gone off alone. He'd gone with his girlfriend. After finding the body, the man had sent her home. Partly because she was in shock; partly to avoid any 'slur on her character'. Father Byrne passed this news on to Rebus when he came to the station to look through the mug-shots – without success.

A new sort of tourist now visited the Hermitage, to view a new kind of 'shrine'. They wanted to see the spot where the trunk had been discovered. Locals still brought their dogs, and lovers still followed the route of the burn; but they wore fixed looks on their faces, as though unwilling to accept that the Hermitage, *their* Hermitage, had become something else, something they never believed it could be.

Rebus, meantime, played with a jigsaw. The tattoo was coming together, though it was a slow business. Errors were made. And one error, once made, led to more pieces being placed incorrectly, until the whole thing had to be broken up and started again. Blue was the predominant colour, along with some patches of red. The dark, inked lines tended to be straight. It looked like a professional job. Tattoo parlours were visited, but the description given was too vague as yet. Rebus showed yet another configuration of the pieces to Brian Holmes: it was the fifth such photograph in a week. The lab had provided their own dotted outline of how they thought the design might continue. Holmes nodded.

'It's a Kandinsky,' he said. 'Or one of his followers. Solid bars of colour. Yes, definitely a Kandinsky.'

Rebus was amazed. 'You mean Kandinsky did this tattoo?'

Holmes looked up from the photograph, grinned sheepishly. 'Sorry, I was making a joke. Or trying to. Kandinsky was a painter.'

'Oh,' Rebus sounded disappointed. 'Yes,' he said, 'yes, of course he was. Right.'

Feeling guilty at having raised his superior's hopes, Holmes concentrated all the harder on the photo. 'Could be a swastika,' he offered. 'Those lines ...'

'Yes.' Rebus turned the photograph towards him, then slapped a hand against it. 'No!' Holmes flinched. 'No, Brian, not a swastika ... a Union Jack! It's a bloody Union Jack!'

Once the lab had the design in front of them, it was a straight-forward job of following it in their reconstruction. Not just a Union Jack, though, as they found. A Union Jack with the letters UFF slurred across it, and a machine gun half-hidden behind the letters.

'Ulster Freedom Fighters,' Rebus murmured. 'Right, let's get back to those tattoo parlours.'

A CID officer in Musselburgh came up with the break. A tat-tooist there thought he recognised the design as the work of Tam Finlayson, but Finlayson had retired from the business some years ago, and tracing him was hard work. Rebus even feared for a moment that the man might be dead and buried. He wasn't. He was living with his daughter and son-in-law in Brighton.

A Brighton detective visited the address and telephoned Edinburgh with details. Shown the photograph, Finlayson had flinched, then had taken, as the daughter put it, 'one of his turns'. Pills were administered and finally Finlayson was in a state to talk. But he was scared, there was no doubt of that. Reassured, though, by the information that the tattoo belonged to a corpse, the tattooist owned up. Yes, it was his work. He'd done it maybe fifteen years before. And the customer? A young man called Philips. Rab Philips. Not a terrorist, just a tearaway looking for a cause.

'Rab Philips?' Rebus stared at his telephone. '*The* Rab Philips?'

Who else? A dim, small-time villain who'd spent enough time in prison, that university of life, to become a clever small-time villain. And who had grown, matured, if you like, into a big-game player. Well, not quite Premier League, but not Sunday kickabout either. He'd certainly been keeping himself to himself these past couple of years. No gossip on the street about him; no dirt; no news at all really.

Well, there was news now. Pubs and clubs were visited, drinks bought, occasionally an arm twisted and the information began to trickle in. Philips's home was searched, his wife questioned. Her story was that he'd told her he was going to London for a few days on a business trip. Rebus nodded calmly and handed her a photograph.

'Is that Rab's tattoo?'

She went pale. Then she went into hysterics.

Meanwhile, Philips's cronies and 'associates' had been rounded up and questioned. One or two were released and picked up again, released and picked up. The message was clear: CID thought they knew more than they were telling and unless they told what they knew, this process would go on indefinitely. They were nervous, of course, and who could blame them? They couldn't know who would now take over their ex-boss's terrain. There were people out there with grudges and knives. The longer they hung about in police stations, the more of a liability they would appear.

They told what they knew, or as much as CID needed to know. That was fine by Rebus. Rab Philips, they said, had started shifting drugs. Nothing serious, mostly cannabis, but in hefty quantities. Edinburgh CID had done much to clear up the hard drug problem in the city, mainly by clearing out the dealers. New dealers would always appear, but they were small-fry. Rab Philips, though, had been so quiet for so long that he was not a suspect. And besides, the drugs were merely passing through Edinburgh; they weren't staying there. Boats would land them on the Fife coast or further north. They would be brought to Edinburgh and from there transferred south. To England. Which meant, in effect, to London. Rebus probed for an Ulster connection, but nobody had anything to tell him.

'So who are the drugs going to in London?'

Again, nobody knew. Or nobody was saying. Rebus sat at his desk, another jigsaw to work on now, but this time in his head – a jigsaw of facts and possibilities. Yes, he should have known from the start. Dismemberment equals gangland. A betrayal, a double-cross. And the penalty for same. Rebus reached for his telephone again and this time put in a call to London.

'Inspector George Flight, please.'

Trust Flight to make it all seem so easy. Rebus gave him the description and an hour later Flight came back with a name. Rebus added some details and Flight went visiting. This time, the phone call came to Rebus's flat. It was late evening and he was lying half-asleep in his chair, the telephone waiting on his lap.

Flight was in good humour. 'I'm glad you told me about the wound,' he said. 'I asked him a few questions, noticed he was a bit stiff. As he stood up to show me out, I slapped him on his right side. I made it seem sort of playful. You know, not malicious like.' He chuckled. 'You should have seen him, John. Doubled over like a bloody pen-knife. It started bleeding again, of course. The silly sod hadn't had it seen to. I wouldn't wonder if it's gone septic or something.'

'When did he get back from Edinburgh?'

'Couple of days ago. Think we can nail him?'

'Maybe. We could do with some evidence though. But I think I can do something about that.'

As Rebus explained to Brian Holmes, it had been more than a 'hunch'. A hunch was, as Dr Curt himself might put it, a stab in the dark. Rebus had a little more light to work by. He told the story as they drove through early-morning Edinburgh towards the Hermitage. The three girls had seen a man appearing from the trees. A wounded man. It seemed clear now that he'd been stabbed in some skirmish nearer to, or by the side of, Braid Hills Road. A switch of drugs from one car to another. An attempted double-cross. He'd been wounded and had fled down the hill into the Hermitage itself, coming into the clearing at the same time as the girls, making himself scarce when he saw them.

Because, of course, he had something to hide: his wound. He had patched himself up, but had stuck around Edinburgh, looking for revenge. Rab Philips had been grabbed, dismembered and his body dumped in the Hermitage as a message to Philips's gang. The message was: you don't mess with London.

Then the wounded villain had finally headed back south. But he was the antithesis of Philips; he wore flashy clothes. 'Probably a white coat,' Rebus had told George Flight. 'White trousers. He's got long hair and a beard.'

Flight had bettered the description. 'It's a white trench-coat,' he'd said. 'And yellow trousers, would you believe. A real old ex-hippy this one.' His name was Shaun McLafferty. 'Everyone on the street knows Shaun,' Flight went on. 'I didn't know he'd started pushing dope though. Mind you, he'd try anything, that one.'

McLafferty. 'He wouldn't,' Rebus asked, 'be Irish by any chance?'

'London Irish,' said Flight. 'I wouldn't be surprised if the IRA was creaming ten per cent off his profits. Maybe more. After all, he either pays up or they take over. It happens.'

Maybe it was as simple as that then. An argument over 'the divide'. An IRA supporter finding himself doing business with a UFF tattoo. The kind of mix old Molotov himself would have appreciated.

'So,' Brian Holmes said, having digested all this, 'Inspector Flight paid a visit to McLafferty?'

Rebus nodded. 'And he was wounded in his right side. Stab wound, according to George.'

'So why,' Holmes said, 'are we here?'

They had parked the car just outside the gates and were now walking into the Hermitage.

'Because,' Rebus said, 'we still lack evidence.'

'What evidence?'

But Rebus wasn't saying; perhaps because he didn't know the answer himself. They were approaching the tree. There was no sign of the once ubiquitous guard, but a familiar figure was kneeling before the tree.

'Morning, Father.'

Father Byrne looked up. 'Good morning, Inspector. You too, Constable.'

Rebus looked around him. 'All alone?'

Byrne nodded. 'Enthusiasm seems to have waned, Inspector. No more megaphones, or coach parties, or cameras.'

'You sound relieved.'

'Believe me, I am.' Father Byrne held out his arms. 'I much prefer it like this, don't you?'

Rebus was obliged to nod his agreement. 'Anyway,' he said, 'we think we can explain what the girls saw.'

Father Byrne merely shrugged.

'No more guard-duties?' Rebus asked.

'The men stopped bothering us.'

Rebus nodded thoughtfully. His eyes were on the tree. 'It wasn't you they were after, Father. It was the tree. But not for the reason you think. Brian, give me a hand, will you?'

A literal hand. Rebus wanted Holmes to form a stirrup from his hands, so that Rebus could place a foot on them and be hoisted up into the tree. Holmes steadied himself against the tree and complied,

not without a silent groan. It was feasible that Rebus weighed a
good three and a half stones more than him. Still, ours is not to
reason why ... and *heave!*

Rebus scrabbled with his hands, finding knot-holes, moss, but
nothing else, nothing hidden. He peered upwards, seeking any fis-
sure in the bark, any cranny. Nothing.

'All right, Brian.'

Gratefully, Holmes lowered Rebus groundwards. 'Anything?'

Rebus shook his head. He was gnawing his bottom lip.

'Are you going to tell me what we're looking for?'

'McLafferty had something else to hide from the girls, something
on top of the fact that he'd been stabbed. Let's think.' McLafferty
had come through the copse, the undergrowth, had rested for a
second against the tree, fled back through the copse.

'Chalk!' Rebus thumped the tree with his fist.

'Pardon?'

'Chalk! That morning I came to check on you. When the cadets
got up, their knees had white, powdery chalk on them.'

'Yes?'

'Well look!' Rebus led Holmes into the copse. 'There's no white
rock here. No bits of chalky stone. That wasn't bloody chalk.' He
fell to his knees and began to burrow furiously, raking his hands
through the earth.

The girls' parents had messed up the ground, making the white
powder inconspicuous. Enough to mark a trouser-knee, but hardly
noticeable otherwise. Certainly, nothing a cadet would bother with.
And besides, they'd been looking for something *on* the ground, not
below it.

'Ah!' He paused, probed a spot with his fingers, then began to
dig around it. 'Look,' he said, 'just the one packet and it's burst.
That's what it was. Must have burst when McLafferty was burying
it. Better call for forensics, Brian. His blood and his prints will be
all over it.'

'Right, sir.' Stunned, Brian Holmes sprinted from the clearing,
then stopped and turned back. 'Keys,' he explained. Rebus fished
his car-keys from his pocket and tossed them to him. Father Byrne,
who had been a spectator throughout, came a little closer.

'Heroin, Father. Either that or cocaine. Bigger profits than cannabis, you see. It all comes down to money in the end. They were
doing a deal. McLafferty got himself stabbed. He was holding a
packet when it happened. Got away somehow, ran down here before
he had time to think. He knew he'd better get rid of the stuff, so
he buried it. The men who were bothering you, McLafferty's men,

it was *this* they were after. Then they got Rab Philips instead and went home satisfied. If it wasn't for your all-night vigil, they'd've had this stuff too.'

Rebus paused, aware that he couldn't be making much sense to the priest. Father Byrne seemed to read his mind and smiled.

'For a minute there, Inspector,' he said, 'I thought you were speaking in tongues.'

Rebus grinned, too, feeling breathless. With McLafferty's prints on the bag, they would have the evidence they needed. 'Sorry you didn't get your miracle,' he said.

Father Byrne's smile broadened. 'Miracles happen every day, Inspector. I don't need to have them invented for me.'

They turned to watch as Holmes came wandering back towards them. But his eyes were concentrating on an area to the left of them. 'They're on their way,' he said, handing Rebus's keys back to him.

'Fine.'

'Who was that by the way?'

'Who?'

'The other man.' Holmes looked from Rebus to Byrne back to Rebus again. 'The other man,' he repeated. 'The one who was standing here with you. When I was coming back, he was ...' He was pointing now, back towards the gate, then over towards the left of the tree. But his voice died away.

'No, never mind,' he said. 'I thought ... I just, no never mind. I must be—'

'Seeing things?' Father Byrne suggested, his fingers just touching the wooden cross around his neck.

'That's right, yes. Yes, seeing things.'

Ghosts, thought Rebus. Spirits of the wood. Rab Philips maybe, or the Hermitage Witch. My God, those two would have a lot to talk about, wouldn't they?

A Good Hanging

I

It was quite some time since a scaffold had been seen in Parliament Square. Quite some time since Edinburgh had witnessed a hanging, too, though digging deeper into history the sight might have been common enough. Detective Inspector John Rebus recalled hearing some saloon-bar story of how criminals, sentenced to hang, would be given the chance to run the distance of the Royal Mile from Parliament Square to Holyrood, a baying crowd hot on their heels. If the criminal reached the Royal Park before he was caught, he would be allowed to remain there, wandering in safety so long as he did not step outside the boundary of the park itself. True or not, the tale conjured up the wonderful image of rogues and vagabonds trapped within the confines of Arthur's Seat, Salisbury Crags and Whinny Hill. Frankly, Rebus would have preferred the noose.

'It's got to be a prank gone wrong, hasn't it?'

A prank. Edinburgh was full of pranks at this time of year. It was Festival time, when young people, theatrical people, flooded into the city with their enthusiasm and their energy. You couldn't walk ten paces without someone pressing a handbill upon you or begging you to visit their production. These were the 'Fringe lunatics' as Rebus had not very originally, but to his own satisfaction, termed them. They came for two or three or four weeks, mostly from London and they squeezed into damp sleeping-bags on bedsit floors throughout the city, going home much paler, much more tired and almost always the poorer. It was not unusual for the unlucky Fringe shows, those given a venue on the outskirts, those with no review to boast of, starved of publicity and inspiration, for those unfortunate shows to play to single-figure audiences, if not to an audience of a single figure.

Rebus didn't like Festival time. The streets became clogged, there seemed a despair about all the artistic fervour and, of course, the crime rate rose. Pickpockets loved the festival. Burglars found easy pickings in the overpopulated, underprotected bedsits. And, finding their local pub taken over by the 'Sassenachs', the natives were inclined to throw the occasional punch or bottle or chair. Which was why Rebus avoided the city centre during the Festival, skirting around it in his car, using alleyways and half-forgotten routes. Which was why he was so annoyed at having been called here today, to Parliament Square, the heart of the Fringe, to witness a hanging.

'Got to be a prank,' he repeated to Detective Constable Brian Holmes. The two men were standing in front of a scaffold, upon which hung the gently swaying body of a young man. The body swayed due to the fresh breeze which was sweeping up the Royal Mile from the direction of Holyrood Park. Rebus thought of the ghosts of the royal park's inmates. Was the wind of their making? 'A publicity stunt gone wrong,' he mused.

'Apparently not, sir,' Holmes said. He'd been having a few words with the workmen who were trying to erect a curtain of sorts around the spectacle so as to hide it from the view of the hundreds of inquisitive tourists who had gathered noisily outside the police cordon. Holmes now consulted his notebook, while Rebus, hands in pockets, strolled around the scaffold. It was of fairly ramshackle construction, which hadn't stopped it doing its job.

'The body was discovered at four-fifty this morning. We don't think it had been here long. A patrol car passed this way at around four and they didn't see anything.'

'That doesn't mean much,' Rebus interrupted in a mutter.

Holmes ignored the remark. 'The deceased belonged to a Fringe group called Ample Reading Time. They come from the University of Reading, thus the name.'

'It also makes the acronym ART,' Rebus commented.

'Yes, sir,' said Holmes. His tone told the senior officer that Holmes had already worked this out for himself. Rebus wriggled a little, as though trying to keep warm. In fact, he had a summer cold.

'How did we discover his identity?' They were in front of the hanging man now, standing only four or so feet below him. Early twenties, Rebus surmised. A shock of black curly hair.

'The scaffold has a venue number pinned to it,' Holmes was saying. 'A student hall of residence just up the road.'

'And that's where the ART show's playing?'

'Yes, sir.' Holmes consulted the bulky Fringe programme which he had been holding behind his notebook. 'It's a play of sorts called "Scenes from a Hanging".' The two men exchanged a look at this.

'The blurb,' Holmes continued, consulting the company's entry near the front of the programme, 'promises "thrills, spills and a live hanging on stage".'

'A live hanging, eh? Well, you can't say they didn't deliver. So, he takes the scaffold from the venue, wheels it out here – I notice it's on wheels, presumably to make it easier to trundle on and off the stage – and in the middle of the night he hangs himself, without anyone hearing anything or seeing anything.' Rebus sounded sceptical.

'Well,' said Holmes, 'be honest, sir.' He was pointing towards and beyond the crowd of onlookers. 'Does anything look suspicious in Edinburgh at this time of year?'

Rebus followed the direction of the finger and saw that a twelve-foot-high man was enjoying a grandstand view of the spectacle, while somewhere to his right someone was juggling three saucepans high into the air. The stilt-man walked towards the pans, grabbed one from mid-air and set it on his head, waving down to the crowd before moving off. Rebus sighed.

'I suppose you're right, Brian. Just this once you may be right.'

A young DC approached, holding a folded piece of paper towards them. 'We found this in his trousers back-pocket.'

'Ah,' said Rebus, 'the suicide note.' He plucked the sheet from the DC's outstretched hand and read it aloud.

'"Pity it wasn't *Twelfth Night*".'

Holmes peered at the line of type. 'Is that it?'

'Short but sweet,' said Rebus. '*Twelfth Night*. A play by Shakespeare and the end of the Christmas season. I wonder which one he means?' Rebus refolded the note and slipped it into his pocket. 'But is it a suicide note or not? It could just be a bog-standard note, a reminder or whatever, couldn't it? I still think this is a stunt gone wrong.' He paused to cough. He was standing beside the cobblestone inset of the Heart of Midlothian, and like many a Scot before him, he spat for luck into the centre of the heart-shaped stones. Holmes looked away and found himself gazing into the dead man's dulled eyes. He turned back as Rebus was fumbling with a handkerchief.

'Maybe,' Rebus was saying between blows, 'we should have a word with the rest of the cast. I don't suppose they'll have much to keep them occupied.' He gestured towards the scaffold. 'Not until they get back their prop. Besides, we've got a job to do, haven't we?'

II

'Well, I say we keep going!' the voice yelled. 'We've got an important piece of work here, a play people should *see*. If anything, David's death will bring audiences *in*. We shouldn't be pushing them away. We shouldn't be packing our bags and crawling back south.'

'You sick bastard.'

Rebus and Holmes entered the makeshift auditorium as the speaker of these last three words threw himself forwards and landed a solid punch against the side of the speech-maker's face. His glasses flew from his nose and slid along the floor, stopping an inch or two short of Rebus's scuffed leather shoes. He stooped, picked up the spectacles and moved forward.

The room was of a size, and had an atmosphere, that would have suited a monastery's dining-hall. It was long and narrow, with a stage constructed along its narrow face and short rows of chairs extending back into the gloom. What windows there were had been blacked-out and the hall's only natural light came from the open door through which Rebus had just stepped, to the front left of the stage itself.

There were five of them in the room, four men and a woman. All looked to be in their mid- to late-twenties. Rebus handed over the glasses.

'Not a bad right-hook that,' he said to the attacker, who was looking with some amazement at his own hand, as though hardly believing it capable of such an action. 'I'm Inspector Rebus, this is Detective Constable Holmes. And you are?'

They introduced themselves in turn. Sitting on the stage was Pam, who acted. Beside her was Peter Collins, who also acted. On a chair in front of the stage, legs and arms crossed and having obviously enjoyed tremendously the one-sided bout he had just witnessed, sat Marty Jones.

'I don't act,' he said loudly. 'I just design the set, build the bloody thing, make all the props and work the lights and the music during the play.'

'So it's your scaffold then?' commented Rebus. Marty Jones looked less confident.

'Yes,' he said. 'I made it a bit too bloody well, didn't I?'

'We could just as easily blame the rope manufacturer, Mr Jones,' Rebus said quietly. His eyes moved to the man with the spectacles, who was nursing a bruised jaw.

'Charles Collins,' the man said sulkily. He looked towards where Peter Collins sat on the stage. 'No relation. I'm the director. I also wrote "Scenes from a Hanging".'

Rebus nodded. 'How have the reviews been?'

Marty Jones snorted.

'Not great,' Charles Collins admitted. 'We've only had four,' he went on, knowing if he didn't say it someone else would. 'They weren't exactly complimentary.'

Marty Jones snorted again. Stiffening his chin, as though to take another punch, Collins ignored him.

'And the audiences?' Rebus asked, interested.

'Lousy.' This from Pam, swinging her legs in front of her as though such news was not only quite acceptable, but somehow humorous as well.

'Average, I'd say,' Charles Collins corrected. 'Going by what other companies have been telling me.'

'That's the problem with staging a new play, isn't it?' Rebus said knowledgeably, while Holmes stared at him. Rebus was standing in the midst of the group now, as though giving them a preproduction pep talk. 'Trying to get audiences to watch new work is always a problem. They prefer the classics.'

'That's right,' Charles Collins agreed enthusiastically. 'That's what I've been telling—' with a general nod in everyone's direction, 'them. The classics are "safe". That's why we need to challenge people.'

'To excite them,' Rebus continued, 'to shock them even. Isn't that right, Mr Collins? To give them a spectacle?'

Charles Collins seemed to see where Rebus's line, devious though it was, was leading. He shook his head.

'Well, they got a spectacle all right,' Rebus went on, all enthusiasm gone from his voice. 'Thanks to Mr Jones's scaffold, the people got a shock. Someone was hanged. I think his name's David, isn't it?'

'That's right.' This from the attacker. 'David Caulfield.' He looked towards the writer/director. 'Supposedly a friend of ours. Someone we've known for three years. Someone we never thought could ...'

'And you are?' Rebus was brisk. He didn't want anyone breaking down just yet, not while there were still questions that needed answers.

'Hugh Clay.' The young man smiled bitterly. 'David always said it sounded like "ukulele".'

'And you're an actor?'

Hugh Clay nodded.

'And so was David Caulfield?'

Another nod. 'I mean, we're not really professionals. We're students. That's all. Students with pretensions.'

Something about Hugh Clay's voice, its tone and its slow rhythms, had made the room darken, so that everyone seemed less animated, more reflective, remembering at last that David Caulfield was truly dead.

'And what do you think happened to him, Hugh? I mean, how do you think he died?'

Clay seemed puzzled by the question. 'He killed himself, didn't he?'

'Did he?' Rebus shrugged. 'We don't know for certain. The pathologist's report may give us a better idea.' Rebus turned to Marty Jones, who was looking less confident all the time. 'Mr Jones, could David have operated the scaffold by himself?'

'That's the way I designed it,' Jones replied. 'I mean, David worked it himself every night. During the hanging scene.'

Rebus pondered this. 'And could someone else have worked the mechanism?'

Jones nodded. 'No problem. The neck noose we used was a dummy. The real noose was attached around David's chest, under his arms. He held a cord behind him and at the right moment he pulled the cord, the trapdoor opened and he fell about a yard. It looked pretty bloody realistic. He had to wear padding under his arms to stop bruising.' He glanced at Charles Collins. 'It was the best bit of the show.'

'But,' said Rebus, 'the scaffold could easily be rejigged to work properly?'

Jones nodded. 'All you'd need is a bit of rope. There's plenty lying around backstage.'

'And then you could hang yourself? Really hang yourself?'

Jones nodded again.

'Or someone could hang you,' said Pam, her eyes wide, voice soft with horror.

Rebus smiled towards her, but seemed to be thinking about something else. In fact, he wasn't thinking of anything in particular: he was letting them stew in the silence, letting their minds and imaginations work in whatever way they would.

At last, he turned to Charles Collins. 'Do you think David killed himself?'

Collins shrugged. 'What else?'

'Any particular reason why he would commit suicide?'

'Well,' Collins looked towards the rest of the company. 'The show,' he said. 'The reviews weren't very complimentary about David's performance.'

'Tell me a little about the play.'

Collins tried not to sound keen as he spoke. Tried, Rebus noticed, but failed. 'It took me most of this year to write,' he said. 'What we have is a prisoner in a South American country, tried and found guilty, sentenced to death. The play opens with him standing on the scaffold, the noose around his neck. Scenes from his life are played out around him, while his own scenes are made up of soliloquies dealing with the larger questions. What I'm asking the audience to do is to ask themselves the same questions he's asking himself on the scaffold. Only the answers are perhaps more urgent, more important for him, because they're the last things he'll ever know.'

Rebus broke in. The whole thing sounded dreadful. 'And David would be on stage the entire time?' Collins nodded. 'And how long was that?'

'Anywhere between two hours and two and a half—' with a glance towards the stage, 'depending on the cast.'

'Meaning?'

'Sometimes lines were forgotten, or a scene went missing.' (Peter and Pam smiled in shared complicity.) 'Or the pace just went.'

'"Never have I prayed so ardently for a death to take place", as one of the reviews put it,' Hugh Clay supplied. 'It was a problem of the play. It didn't have anything to do with David.'

Charles Collins looked ready to protest. Rebus stepped in. 'But David's mentions weren't exactly kind?' he hinted.

'No,' Clay admitted. 'They said he lacked the necessary *gravitas* whatever that means.'

'"Too big a part for too small an actor",' interrupted Marty Jones, quoting again.

'Bad notices then,' said Rebus. 'And David Caulfield took them to heart?'

'David took everything to heart,' explained Hugh Clay. 'That was part of the problem.'

'The other part being that the notices were true,' sniped Charles Collins. But Clay seemed prepared for this.

'"Overwritten and messily directed by Charles Collins",' he quoted. Another fight seemed to be on the cards. Rebus blew his nose noisily.

'So,' he said. 'Notices were bad, audiences were poor. And you didn't decide to remedy this situation by staging a little publicity stunt? A stunt that just happened – nobody's fault necessarily – to go wrong?'

There were shakes of the head, eyes looked to other eyes, seemingly innocent of any such plans.

'Besides,' said Marty Jones, 'you couldn't hang yourself accidentally on that scaffold. You either had to mean to do it yourself, or else someone had to do it for you.'

More silence. An impasse seemed to have been reached. Rebus collapsed noisily into a chair. 'All things considered,' he said with a sigh, 'you might have been better off sticking to *Twelfth Night*.'

'That's funny,' Pam said.

'What is?'

'That's the play we did last year,' she explained. 'It went down very well, didn't it?' She had turned to Peter Collins, who nodded agreement.

'We got some good reviews for that,' he said. 'David was a brilliant Malvolio. He kept the cuttings pinned to his bedroom wall, didn't he, Hugh?'

Hugh Clay nodded. Rebus had the distinct feeling that Peter Collins was trying to imply something, perhaps that Hugh Clay had seen more of David Caulfield's bedroom walls than was strictly necessary.

He fumbled in his pocket, extracting the note from below the handkerchief. Brian Holmes, he noticed, was staying very much in the wings, like the minor character in a minor scene. 'We found a note in David's pocket,' Rebus said without preamble. 'Maybe your success last year explains it.' He read it out to them. Charles Collins nodded.

'Yes, that sounds like David all right. Harking back to past glories.'

'You think that's what it means?' Rebus asked conversationally.

Collins nodded. 'You should know, Inspector, that actors are conceited. The greater the actor, the greater the ego. And David was, I admit, on occasion a very gifted actor.' He was speechifying again, but Rebus let him go on. Perhaps it was the only way a director could communicate with his cast.

'It would be just like David to get depressed, suicidal even, by bad notices, and just like him to decide to stage as showy an exit as he could, something to hit the headlines. I happen to think he succeeded splendidly.'

No one seemed about to contradict him on this, not even David Caulfield's stalwart defender, Hugh Clay. It was Pam who spoke, tears in her eyes at last.

'I only feel sorry for Marie,' she said.

Charles Collins nodded. 'Yes, Marie's come into her own in "Scenes from a Hanging".'

'She means,' Hugh Clay said through gritted teeth, 'she feels sorry for Marie because Marie's lost David, not because Marie can no longer act in your bloody awful play.'

Rebus felt momentary bemusement, but tried not to show it. Marty Jones, however, had seen all.

'The other member of ART,' he explained to Rebus. 'She's back at the flat. She wanted to be left on her own for a bit.'

'She's pretty upset,' Peter Collins agreed.

Rebus nodded slowly. 'She and David were ...?'

'Engaged,' Pam said, the tears falling now, Peter Collins's arm snaking around her shoulders. 'They were going to be married after the Fringe was finished.'

Rebus stole a glance towards Holmes, who raised his eyebrows in reply. Just like every good melodrama, the raised eyebrows said. A twist at the end of every bloody act.

III

The flat the group had rented, at what seemed to Rebus considerable expense, was a dowdy but spacious second-floor affair on Morrison Street, just off Lothian Road. Rebus had been to the block before, during the investigation of a housebreaking. That had been years ago, but the only difference in the tenement seemed to be the installation of a communal intercom at the main door. Rebus ignored the entry-phone and pushed at the heavy outside door. As he had guessed, it was unlocked anyway.

'Bloody students,' had been one of Rebus's few voiced comments during the short, curving drive down the back of the Castle towards the Usher Hall and Lothian Road. But then Holmes, driving, had been a student, too, hadn't he? So Rebus had not expanded on his theme. Now they climbed the steep winding stairwell until they arrived at the second floor. Marty Jones had told them that the name on the door was BLACK. Having robbed the students of an unreasonable rent (though no doubt the going rate), Mr and Mrs Black had departed for a month-long holiday on the proceeds. Rebus had borrowed a key from Jones and used it to let Holmes and himself in. The hall was long, narrow and darker than the stairwell. Off it were three bedrooms, a bathroom, a kitchen and the living-room. A young woman, not quite out of her teens, came out of the kitchen carrying a mug of coffee. She was wearing a long baggy T-shirt and nothing else, and there was a sleepy, tousled look to her, accompanying the red streakiness of her eyes.

'Oh,' she said, startled. Rebus was quick to respond.

'Inspector Rebus, miss. This is Detective Constable Holmes. One of your friends lent us a key. Could we have a word?'

'About David?' Her eyes were huge, doe-like, her face small and round. Her hair was short and fair, the body slender and brittle. Even in grief – perhaps especially in grief – she was mightily attractive, and Holmes raised his eyebrows again as she led them into the living-room.

Two sleeping bags lay on the floor, along with paperback books, an alarm clock, mugs of tea. Off the living-room was a box-room, a large walk-in cupboard. These were often used by students to make an extra room in a temporary flat and light coming from the half-open door told Rebus that this was still its function. Marie went into the room and switched off the light, before joining the two policemen.

'It's Pam's room,' she explained. 'She said I could lie down there. I didn't want to sleep in our ... in my room.'

'Of course,' Rebus said, all understanding and sympathy.

'Of course,' Holmes repeated. She signalled for them to sit, so they did, sinking into a sofa the consistency of marshmallow. Rebus feared he wouldn't be able to rise again without help and struggled to keep himself upright. Marie meantime had settled, legs beneath her, with enviable poise on the room's only chair. She placed her mug on the floor, then had a thought.

'Would you like ...?'

A shake of the head from both men. It struck Rebus that there was something about her voice. Holmes beat him to it.

'Are you French?'

She smiled a pale smile, then nodded towards the Detective Constable. 'From Bordeaux. Do you know it?'

'Only by the reputation of its wine.'

Rebus blew his nose again, though pulling the hankie from his pocket had been a struggle. Holmes took the hint and closed his mouth. 'Now then, Miss ...?' Rebus began.

'Hivert, Marie Hivert.'

Rebus nodded slowly, playing with the hankie rather than trying to replace it in his pocket. 'We're told that you were engaged to Mr Caulfield.'

Her voice was almost a whisper. 'Yes. Not officially, you understand. But there was – a promise.'

'I see. And when was this promise made?'

'Oh, I'm not sure exactly. March, April. Yes, early April I think. Springtime.'

'And how were things between David and yourself?' She seemed not quite to understand. 'I mean,' said Rebus, 'how did David seem to you?'

She shrugged. 'David was David. He could be—' she raised her eyes to the ceiling, seeking words, 'impossible, nervous, exciting, foul-tempered.' She smiled. 'But mostly exciting.'

'Not suicidal?'

She gave this serious thought. 'Oh yes, I suppose,' she admitted. 'Suicidal, just as actors can be. He took criticism to heart. He was a perfectionist.'

'How long had you known him?'

'Two years. I met him through the theatre group.'

'And you fell in love?'

She smiled again. 'Not at first. There was a certain ... competitiveness between us, you might say. It helped our acting. I'm not sure it helped our relationship altogether. But we survived.' Realising what she had said, she grew silent, her eyes dimming. A hand went to her forehead as, head bowed, she tried to collect herself.

'I'm sorry,' she said, collapsing into sobs. Holmes raised his eyebrows: someone should be here with her. Rebus shrugged back: she can handle it on her own. Holmes's eyebrows remained raised: can she? Rebus looked back at the tiny figure, engulfed by the armchair. Could actors always tell the real world from the illusory?

We survived. It was an interesting phrase to have used. But then she was an interesting young woman.

She went to the bathroom to splash water on her face and while she was gone Rebus took the opportunity to rise awkwardly to his feet. He looked back at the sofa.

'Bloody thing,' he said. Holmes just smiled.

When she returned, composed once more, Rebus asked if David Caulfield might have left a note somewhere. She shrugged. He asked if she minded them having a quick look round. She shook her head. So, never men to refuse a gift, Rebus and Holmes began looking.

The set-up was fairly straightforward. Pam slept in the box-room, while Marty Jones and Hugh Clay had sleeping-bags on the living-room floor. Marie and David Caulfield had shared the largest of the three bedrooms, with Charles and Peter Collins having a single room each. Charles Collins's room was obsessively tidy, its narrow single bed made up for the night and on the quilt an acting-copy of 'Scenes from a Hanging', covered in marginalia and with several long speeches, all Caulfield's, seemingly excised. A pencil lay on the typescript, evidence that Charles Collins was taking the critics' view to heart himself and attempting to shorten the play as best he could.

Peter Collins's room was much more to Rebus's personal taste, though Holmes wrinkled his nose at the used underwear underfoot, the contents of the hastily unpacked rucksack scattered over every surface. Beside the unmade bed, next to an overflowing ashtray, lay another copy of the play. Rebus flipped through it. Closing it, his attention was caught by some doodlings on the inside cover. Crude heart shapes had been constructed around the words 'I love Edinburgh'. His smile was quickly erased when Holmes held the ashtray towards him.

'Not exactly Silk Cut,' Holmes was saying. Rebus looked. The butts in the ashtrays were made up of cigarette papers wrapped around curled strips of cardboard. They were called 'roaches' by those who smoked dope, though he couldn't remember why. He made a tutting sound.

'And what were we doing in here when we found these?' he asked. Holmes nodded, knowing the truth: they probably couldn't charge Peter Collins even if they'd wanted to, since there was no reason for their being in his room. *We were looking for someone else's suicide note* probably wouldn't impress a latter-day jury.

The double room shared by Marie Hivert and David Caulfield was messiest of all. Marie helped them sift through a few of Caulfield's things. His diary proved a dead end, since he had started it faithfully on 1st January but the entries ceased on 8th January. Rebus, having tried keeping a diary himself, knew the feeling.

But in the back of the diary were newspaper clippings, detailing Caulfield's triumph in the previous year's *Twelfth Night*. Marie, too, had come in for some praise as Viola, but the glory had been Malvolio's. She wept again a little as she read through the reviews. Holmes said that he'd make another cup of coffee. Did he want her to fetch Pam from the theatre? She shook her head. She'd be all right. She promised she would.

While Marie sat on the bed and Holmes filled the kettle, Rebus wandered back into the living-room. He peered into the box-room, but saw little there to interest him. Finally, he came back to the sleeping-bags on the floor. Marie was coming back into the room as he bent to pick up the paperback book from beside one sleeping-bag. It was Tom Wolfe's *Bonfire of the Vanities*. Rebus had a hardback copy at home, still unopened. Something fell from the back of the book, a piece of card. Rebus retrieved it from the floor. It was a photograph of Marie, standing on the Castle ramparts with the Scott

Monument behind her. The wind blew her hair fiercely against her face and she was attempting to sweep the hair out of her eyes as she grinned towards the camera. Rebus handed the picture to her.

'Your hair was longer then,' he said.

She smiled and nodded, her eyes still moist. 'Yes,' she said. 'That was in June. We came to look at the venue.'

He waved the book at her. 'Who's the Tom Wolfe fan?'

'Oh,' she said, 'it's doing the rounds. I think Marty's reading it just now.' Rebus flipped through the book again, his eyes lingering a moment on the inside cover. 'Tom Wolfe's had quite a career,' he said before placing the book, face down as it had been, beside the sleeping-bag. He pointed towards the photograph. 'Shall I put it back?' But she shook her head.

'It was David's,' she said. 'I think I'd like to keep it.'

Rebus smiled an avuncular smile. 'Of course,' he said. Then he remembered something. 'David's parents. Have you been in touch at all?'

She shook her head, horror growing within her. 'Oh God,' she said, 'they'll be devastated. David was very close to his mother and father.'

'Well,' said Rebus, 'give me the details and I'll phone them when I get back to the station.'

She frowned. 'But I don't … No, sorry,' she said, 'all I know is that they live in Croydon.'

'Well, never mind,' said Rebus, knowing, in fact, that the parents had already been notified, but interested that Caulfield's apparent fiancée should know their address only vaguely. If David Caulfield had been so close to his mother and father, wouldn't they have been told of the engagement? And once told, wouldn't they have wanted to meet Marie? Rebus's knowledge of English geography wasn't exactly Mastermind material, but he was fairly sure that Reading and Croydon weren't at what you would call opposite ends of the country.

Interesting, all very interesting. Holmes came in carrying three mugs of coffee, but Rebus shook his head, suddenly the brisk senior officer.

'No time for that, Holmes,' he said. 'There's plenty of work waiting for us back at the station.' Then, to Marie: 'Take care of yourself, Miss Hivert. If there's anything we can do, don't hesitate.'

Her smile was winning. 'Thank you, Inspector.' She turned to Holmes, taking a mug from him. 'And thank you, too, constable,' she said. The look on Holmes's face kept Rebus grinning all the way back to the station.

IV

There the grin promptly vanished. There was a message marked URGENT from the police pathologist asking Rebus to call him. Rebus pressed the seven digits on his new-fangled telephone. The thing had a twenty-number memory and somewhere in that memory was the single-digit number that would connect him with the pathologist, but Rebus could never remember which number was which and he kept losing the sheet of paper with all the memory numbers on it.

'It's four,' Holmes reminded him, just as he'd come to the end of dialling. He was throwing Holmes a kind of half-scowl when the pathologist himself answered.

'Oh, yes, Rebus. Hello there. It's about this hanging victim of yours. I've had a look at him. Manual strangulation, I'd say.'

'Yes?' Rebus, his thoughts on Marie Hivert, was waiting for some punch-line.

'I don't think you understand me, Inspector. *Manual* strangulation. From the Latin *manus*, meaning the hand. From the deep body temperature, I'd say he died between midnight and two in the morning. He was strung up on that contraption some time thereafter. Bruising around the throat is definitely consistent with thumb-pressure especially.'

'You mean someone strangled him?' Rebus said, really for Holmes's benefit.

'I *think* that's what I've been telling you, yes. If I find out anything more, I'll let you know.'

'Are the forensics people with you?'

'I've contacted the lab. They're sending someone over with some bags, but to be honest, we started off on this one thinking it was simple suicide. We may have inadvertently destroyed the tinier scraps of evidence.'

'Not to worry,' Rebus said, a father-confessor now, easing guilt. 'Just get what you can.'

He put down the receiver and stared at his Detective Constable. Or, rather, stared *through* him. Holmes knew that there were times for talking and times for silence, and that this fell into the latter category. It took Rebus a full minute to snap out of his reverie.

'Well I'll be buggered,' he said. 'We've been talking with a murderer this morning, Brian. A cold-blooded one at that. And we didn't even know it. I wonder whatever happened to the famous police "nose" for a villain. Any idea?'

Holmes frowned. 'About what happened to the famous police "nose"?'

'No,' cried Rebus, exasperated. 'I mean, any idea who did it?'

Holmes shrugged, then brought the Fringe programme back out from where it had been rolled up in his jacket pocket. He started turning pages. 'I think,' he said, 'there's an Agatha Christie playing somewhere. Maybe we could get a few ideas?'

Rebus's eyes lit up. He snatched the programme from Holmes's hands. 'Never mind Agatha Christie,' he said, starting through the programme himself. 'What we want is Shakespeare.'

'What, *Macbeth*? *Hamlet*? *King Lear*?'

'No, not a tragedy, a good comedy, something to cheer the soul. Ah, here we go.' He stabbed the open page with his finger. '*Twelfth Night*. That's the play for us, Brian. That's the very play for us.'

The problem, really, in the end was: which *Twelfth Night*? There were three on offer, plus another at the Festival proper. One of the Fringe versions offered an update to gangster Chicago, another played with an all-female cast and the third boasted futuristic stage-design. But Rebus wanted traditional fare, and so opted for the Festival performance. There was just one hitch: it was a complete sell-out.

Not that Rebus considered this a hitch. He waited while Holmes called his girlfriend, Nell Stapleton, and apologised to her about some evening engagement he was breaking, then the two men drove to the Lyceum, tucked in behind the Usher Hall so as to be almost invisible to the naked eye.

'There's a five o'clock performance,' Rebus explained. 'We should just make it.' They did. There was a slight hold-up while Rebus explained to the house manager that this really was police business and not some last-minute culture beano, and a place was found for them in a dusty corner to the rear of the stalls. The lights were dimming as they entered.

'I haven't been to a play in years,' Rebus said to Holmes, excited at the prospect. Holmes, bemused, smiled back, but his superior's eyes were already on the stage, where the curtain was rising, a guitar was playing and a man in pale pink tights lay across an ornate bench, looking as cheesed off with life as Holmes himself felt. Why did Rebus always have to work from instinct, and always alone, never letting anyone in on whatever he knew or thought he knew? Was it because he was afraid of failure? Holmes suspected it was. If you kept your ideas to yourself, you couldn't be proved wrong. Well, Holmes had his own ideas about this case, though he was damned if he'd let Rebus in on them.

'If music be the food of love ...' came the voice from the stage. And that was another thing – Holmes was starving. It was odds-on the back few rows would soon find his growling stomach competition for the noises from the stage.

'Will you go hunt, my lord?'

'What, Curio?'

'The hart.'

'Why, so I do, the noblest that I have ...'

Holmes sneaked a glance towards Rebus. To say the older man's attention was rapt would have been understating the case. He'd give it until the end of Act One, then sneak out to the nearest chip shop. Leave Rebus to his Shakespeare; Holmes was a nationalist when it came to literature. A pity Hugh MacDiarmid had never written a play.

In fact, Holmes went for a wander, up and down Lothian Road as far as the Caledonian Hotel to the north and Tollcross to the south. Lothian Road was Edinburgh's fast-food centre and the variety on offer brought with it indecision. Pizza, burgers, kebabs, Chinese, baked potatoes, more burgers, more pizza and the once-ubiquitous fish and chip shop (more often now an offshoot of a kebab or burger restaurant). Undecided, he grew hungrier, and stopped for a pint of lager in a noisy barn of a pub before finally settling for a fish supper, naming himself a nationalist in cuisine as well as in writing.

By the time he returned to the theatre, the players were coming out to take their applause. Rebus was clapping as loudly as anyone, enjoyment evident on his face. But when the curtain came down, he turned and dragged Holmes from the auditorium, back into the foyer and out onto the street.

'Fish and chips, eh?' he said. 'Now there's an idea.'

'How did you know?'

'I can smell the vinegar coming off your hands. Where's the chippie?'

Holmes nodded in the direction of Tollcross. They started walking. 'So did you learn anything?' Holmes asked. 'From the play, I mean?'

Rebus smiled. 'More than I'd hoped for, Brian. If you'd been paying attention, you'd have noticed it, too. The only speech that mattered was way back in Act One. A speech made by the Fool, whose name is Feste. I wonder who played Feste in ART's production last year? Actually, I think I can guess. Come on then, where's this chip shop? A man could starve to death on Lothian Road looking for something even remotely edible.'

'It's just off Tollcross. It's nothing very special.'

'So long as it fills me up, Brian. We've got a long evening ahead of us.'

'Oh?'

Rebus nodded vigorously. 'Hunting the heart, Brian.' He winked towards the younger man. 'Hunting the heart.'

V

The door of the Morrison Street flat was opened by Peter Collins. He looked surprised to see them.

'Don't worry, Peter,' Rebus said, pushing past him into the hall. 'We're not here to put the cuffs on you for possession.' He sniffed the air in the hall, then tutted. 'Already? At this rate you'll be stoned before *News at Ten*.'

Peter blushed.

'All right if we come in?' Rebus asked, already sauntering down the hall towards the living-room. Holmes followed him indoors, smiling an apology. Peter closed the door behind them.

'They're mostly out,' Peter called.

'So I see,' said Rebus, in the living-room now. 'Hello, Marie, how are you feeling?'

'Hello again, Inspector. I'm a little better.' She was dressed, and seated primly on the chair, hands resting on her knees. Rebus looked towards the sofa, but thought better of sitting down. Instead he rested himself on the sofa's fairly rigid arm. 'I see you're all getting ready to go.' He nodded towards the two rucksacks parked against the living-room wall. The sleeping-bags from the floor had been folded away, as had books and alarm clocks.

'Why bother to stay?' Peter said. He flopped onto the sofa and pushed a hand through his hair. 'We thought we'd drive down through the night. Be back in Reading by dawn with any luck.'

Rebus nodded at this. 'So the show does *not* go on?'

'It'd be a bit bloody heartless, don't you think?' This from Peter Collins, with a glance towards Marie.

'Of course,' Rebus agreed. Holmes had stationed himself between the living-room door and the rucksacks. 'So where is everyone?'

Marie answered. 'Pam and Marty have gone for a last walk around.'

'And Charles is almost certainly off getting drunk somewhere,' added Collins. 'Rueing his failed show.'

'And Hugh?' asked Rebus. Collins shrugged.

'I think,' Marie said, 'Hugh went off to get drunk, too.'

'But for different reasons, no doubt,' Rebus speculated.

'He was David's best friend,' she answered quietly.

Rebus nodded thoughtfully. 'Actually, we just bumped into him – literally.'

'Who?' asked Peter.

'Mr Clay. He seems to be in the middle of a pub crawl the length of Lothian Road. We were coming out of a chip shop and came across him weaving his way to the next watering-hole.'

'Oh?' Collins didn't sound particularly interested.

'I told him where the best pubs in this neighbourhood are. He didn't seem to know.'

'That was good of you,' Collins said, voice heavy with irony.

'Nice of them all to leave you alone, isn't it though?'

The question hung in the air. At last, Marie spoke. 'What do you mean?'

But Rebus shifted on his perch and left the comment at that. 'No,' he said instead, 'only I thought Mr Clay might have had a better idea of the pubs, seeing how he was here last year, and then again in June to look at the venue. But of course, as he was good enough to explain, he *wasn't* here in June. There were exams. Some people had to study harder than others. Only three of you came to Edinburgh in June.' Rebus raised a finger shiny with chip-fat. 'Pam, who has what I'd call a definite crush on you, Peter.' Collins smiled at this, but weakly. Rebus raised a second and then third finger. 'And you two. Just the three of you. That, I presume, is where it started.'

'What?' The blood had drained from Marie's face, making her somehow more beautiful than ever. Rebus shifted again, seeming to ignore her question.

'It doesn't really matter who took that photo of you, the one I found in *Bonfire of the Vanities*.' He was staring at her quite evenly now. 'What matters is that it was there. And on the inside cover someone had drawn a couple of hearts, very similar to some I happened to see on Peter's copy of the play. It matters that on his copy of the play, Peter has also written the words "I love Edinburgh".' Peter Collins was ready to protest, but Rebus studiously ignored him, keeping his eyes on Marie's, fixing her, so that there might only have been the two of them in the room.

'You told me,' he continued, 'that you'd come to Edinburgh to check on the venue. I took that "you" to mean all of you, but Hugh Clay has put me right on that. You came without David, who was too busy studying to make the trip. And you told me something else earlier. You said your relationship with him had "survived". Survived what? I asked myself afterwards. The answer seems pretty straightforward. Survived a brief fling, a fling that started in Edinburgh and lasted the summer.'

Now, only now, did he turn to Peter Collins. 'Isn't that right, Peter?'

Collins, his face mottled with anger, made to rise.

'Sit down,' Rebus ordered, standing himself. He walked towards the fireplace, turned and faced Collins, who looked to be disappearing into the sofa, reducing in size with the passing moments. 'You love Edinburgh,' he went on, 'because that's where your little fling with Marie started. Fair enough, these things are never anyone's fault, are they? You managed to keep it fairly secret. The Tom Wolfe book belongs to you, though, and that photo you'd kept in it – maybe forgetting it was there – that photo might have been a giveaway, but then again it could all be very innocent, couldn't it?

'But it's hard to keep something like that so secret when you're part of a very small group. There were sixteen of you in ART last year; that might have made it manageable. But not when there were only seven of you. I'm not sure who else knows about it. But I am sure that David Caulfield found out.' Rebus didn't need to turn round to know that Marie was sobbing again. He kept staring at Peter Collins. 'He found out, and last night, late and backstage, perhaps drunk, the two of you had a fight. Quite dramatic in its way, isn't it? Fighting over the heroine and all that. But during the fight you just happened to strangle the life out of David Caulfield.' He paused, waiting for a denial which didn't come.

'Perhaps,' he continued, 'Marie wanted to go to the police. I don't know. But if she did, you persuaded her not to. Instead, you came up with something more dramatic. You'd make it look like suicide. And by God, what a suicide, the kind that David himself might just have attempted.' Rebus had been moving forward without seeming to, so that now he stood directly over Peter Collins.

'Yes,' he went on, 'very dramatic. But the note was a mistake. It was a bit too clever, you see. You thought everyone would take it as a reference to David's success in last year's production, but you knew yourself that there was a double meaning in it. I've just been to see *Twelfth Night*. Bloody good it was, too. You played Feste last year, didn't you, Peter? There's one speech of his ... how does it go?' Rebus seemed to be trying to remember. 'Ah yes: "Many a good hanging prevents a bad marriage." Yes, that's it. And that's when I knew for sure.'

Peter Collins was smiling thinly. He gazed past Rebus towards Marie, his eyes full and liquid. His voice when he spoke was tender. '"Many a good hanging prevents a bad marriage; and for turning away, let summer bear it out."'

'That's right,' Rebus said, nodding eagerly. 'Summer bore it out, all right. A summer fling. That's all. Not worth killing someone for, was it, Peter? But that didn't stop you. And the hanging was so apt, so neat. When you recalled the Fool's quote, you couldn't resist putting that note in David's pocket.' Rebus was shaking his head. 'More fool you, Mr Collins. More fool you.'

Brian Holmes went home from the police station that night in sombre mood. The traffic was slow, too, with theatre-goers threading in and out between the near-stationary cars. He rolled down the driver's-side window, trying to make the interior less stuffy, less choked, and instead let in exhaust fumes and balmy late-evening air. Why did Rebus have to be such a clever bugger so much of the time? He seemed always to go into a case at an odd angle, like someone cutting a paper shape which, apparently random, could then be folded to make an origami sculpture, intricate and recognisable.

'Too clever for his own good,' he said to himself. But what he meant was that his superior was too clever for Holmes's own good. How was he expected to shine, to be noticed, to push forwards towards promotion, when it was always Rebus who, two steps ahead, came up with the answers? He remembered a boy at school who had always beaten Holmes in every subject save History. Yet Holmes had gone to university; the boy to work on his father's farm. Things could change, couldn't they? Though all he seemed to be learning from Rebus was how to keep your thoughts to yourself, how to be devious, how to, well, how to *act*. Though all this were true, he would still be the best understudy he possibly could be. One day, Rebus wouldn't be there to come up with the answers, or – occasion even more to be relished – would be unable to find the answers. And when that time came, Holmes would be ready to take the stage. He felt ready right now, but then he supposed every understudy must feel that way.

A flybill was thrown through his window by a smiling teenage girl. He heard her pass down the line of cars, yelling 'Come and see our show!' as she went. The small yellow sheet of paper fluttered onto the passenger seat and stayed there, face up, to haunt Holmes all the way back to Nell. Growing sombre again, it occurred to him how different things might have been if only Priestley had called the play *A Detective Constable Calls* instead.

Tit for Tat

Before he'd arrived in Edinburgh in 1970, Inspector John Rebus had fixed in his mind an image of tenement life. Tenements were things out of the Gorbals in the early years of the century, places of poverty and despair, safe havens for vermin and disease. They were the enforced homes of the poorest of the working class, a class almost without a class, a sub-class. Though tenements rose high into the air, they might as well have been dug deep into the ground. They were society's replacement for the cave.

Of course, in the 1960s the planners had come up with something even more outrageous – the tower-block. Even cities with plenty of spare land started to construct these space-saving horrors. Perhaps the moral rehabilitation of the tenement had something to do with this new contender. Nowadays, a tenement might contain the whole of society in microcosm – the genteel spinster on the ground floor, the bachelor accountant one floor above, then the barkeeper, and above the barkeeper, always it seemed right at the top of the house, the students. This mix was feasible only because the top two floors contained flats rented out by absentee landlords. Some of these landlords might own upwards of one hundred separate flats – as was spectacularly the case in Glasgow, where the figure was even rumoured, in one or two particulars, to rise into four figures.

But in Edinburgh, things were different. In Edinburgh, the New Town planners of the nineteenth century had come up with streets of fashionable houses, all of them, to Rebus's latter-day eyes, looking like tenements. Some prosperous areas of the city, such as Marchmont where Rebus himself lived, boasted almost nothing *but* tenements. And with the price of housing what it was, even the meaner streets were seeing a kind of renaissance, stone-blasted clean by new owner-occupiers who kept the cooking-range in the living-room as an 'original feature'.

The streets around Easter Road were as good an example as any. The knock-on effect had reached Easter Road late. People had to decide first that they couldn't afford Stockbridge, then that they couldn't quite afford any of the New Town or its immediate surroundings, and at last they might arrive in Easter Road, not by chance but somehow through fate. Soon, an enterprising soul saw his or her opportunity and opened a delicatessen or a slightly upmarket café, much to the bemusement of the 'locals'. These were quiet, accepting people for the most part, people who liked to see the tenement buildings being restored even if they couldn't understand why anyone would pay good money for bottled French water. (After all, you were always told to steer clear of the water on foreign holidays, weren't you?)

Despite this, the occasional Alfa Romeo or Golf GTi might find itself scratched maliciously, as might a too-clean 2CV or a coveted Morris Minor. But arson? Attempted murder? Well, that was a bit more serious. That was a very serious turn of events indeed. The trick was one perfected by racists in mixed areas. You poured petrol through the letter-box of a flat, then you set light to a rag and dropped it through the letter-box, igniting the hall carpet and ensuring that escape from the resulting fire was made difficult if not impossible. Of course, the noise, the smell of petrol meant that usually someone inside the flat was alerted early on, and mostly these fires did not spread. But sometimes ... sometimes.

'His name's John Brodie, sir,' the police constable informed Rebus as they stood in the hospital corridor. 'Age thirty-four. Works for an insurance company in their accounts department.'

None of which came as news to Rebus. He had been to the second-floor flat, just off Easter Road, reeking of soot and water now; an unpleasant clean-up ahead. The fire had spread quickly along the hall. Some jackets and coats hanging from a coat-stand had caught light and sent the flames licking along the walls and ceiling. Brodie, asleep in bed (it all happened around one in the morning) had been wakened by the fire. He'd dialled 999, then had tried putting the fire out himself, with a fair degree of success. A rug from the living-room had proved useful in snuffing out the progress of the fire along the hall and some pans of water had dampened things down. But there was a price to pay – burns to his arms and hands and face, and smoke inhalation. Neighbours, alerted by the smoke, had broken down the door just as the fire engine was arriving. CID, brought to the scene by a police constable's suspicions, had spoken with some of the neighbours. A quiet man, Mr Brodie, they said. A decent man. He'd only moved in a few months before. Worked for an insurance company. Nobody thought he smoked, but they seemed to assume he'd left a cigarette burning somewhere.

'Careless that. Even supposing we *do* live in Auld Reekie.' And the first-floor occupier had chuckled to himself, until his wife yelped from their flat that there was water coming in through the ceiling. The man looked helpless and furious.

'Insurance should cover it,' Rebus commented, pouring oil on troubled ... no, not the best image that. The husband went off to investigate further and the other tenement dwellers began slouching off to bed, leaving Rebus to head into the burnt-out hallway itself.

But even without the Fire Officer, the cause of the fire had been plain to Rebus. Chillingly plain. The smell of petrol was everywhere.

He took a look round the rest of the flat. The kitchen was tiny, but boasted a large sash-window looking down onto back gardens and across to the back of the tenement over the way. The bathroom was smaller still, but kept very neat. No ring of grime around the bath, no strewn towels or underpants, nothing steeping in the sink. A very tidy bachelor was Mr Brodie. The living-room, too, was uncluttered. A series of framed prints more or less covered one wall. Detailed paintings of birds. Rebus glanced at one or two: willow warbler, bearded tit. The rooms would need to be redecorated, of course, otherwise the charred smell would always be there. Insurance would probably cover it. Brodie was an insurance man, wasn't he? He'd know. Maybe he'd even squeeze a cheque out of the company without too much haggling.

Finally, Rebus went into the bedroom. Messier here, mostly as a result of the hurriedly flung-back bedclothes. Pyjama bottoms lying crumpled on the bed itself. Slippers and a used mug sitting on the floor beside the bed, and in one corner, next to the small wardrobe, a tripod atop which was fixed a good make of SLR camera. On the floor against the wall was a large-format book, *Better Zoom Pictures*, with a photograph of an osprey on the front. Probably one of the Loch Garten ospreys, thought Rebus. He'd taken his daughter there a couple of times in the past. Tourists, plenty of them, he had seen, but ospreys were there none.

If anyone had asked him what he thought most odd about the flat, he would have answered: there's no television set. What did Mr Brodie do for company then of an evening?

For no real reason, Rebus bent down and peered beneath the bed itself, and was rewarded with a pile of magazines. He pulled one out. Soft porn, a 'readers' wives' special. He pushed it back into place. The tidy bachelor's required bedtime companion. And, partly, an answer to his earlier question.

He left the flat and sought out one or two of the still wakeful neighbours. No one had seen or heard anything. Access to the tenement itself was easy; you just pushed open the communal front door, the lock of which had broken recently and was waiting to be fixed.

'Any reason,' Rebus asked, 'why anyone would bear Mr Brodie a grudge?'

That gave them pause. No smouldering cigarette then, but arson. But there were shakes of rumpled heads. No reason. A very quiet man. Kept himself to himself. Worked in insurance. Always stopped for a chat if you met him on the stairs. Always cleaned the stairs promptly when his turn came, not like some they could mention. Probably paid his rent promptly, too. Tea was being provided in the kitchen of one of the first-floor flats, where the 'Auld Reekie' wag was being consoled.

'I only painted that ceiling three months back. Do you know how much textured paint costs?'

Soon enough everyone found the answer. The man's wife looked bored. She smiled towards the tea-party's hostess.

'Wasn't that first fireman dishy?' she said.

'Which one?'

'The one with the blue eyes. The one who told us not to worry. He could give me a fireman's lift anytime.'

The hostess snorted into her tea. Rebus made his excuses and left.

Rebus had dealt with racist arson attacks before. He'd even come across 'anti-yuppie' attacks, usually in the form of graffiti on cars or the outside walls of property. A warehouse conversion in Leith had been sprayed with the slogan HOUSES FOR THE NEEDY, NOT THE GREEDY. The attack on Brodie seemed more personal, but it was worth considering all the possible motives. He was crossing things off from a list in his mind as he drove to the hospital. Once there, he talked to the police constable in the corridor and, after nodding his head a few times, he entered the ward where John Brodie had been 'made comfortable'. Despite the hour, Brodie was far from asleep. He was propped up against a pillow, his arms lying out in front of him on top of the sheets. Thick creamy white cotton pads and delicate-looking bandages predominated. Part of his hair had been shaved away, so that burns to the scalp could be treated. He had no eyebrows, and only remnants of eyelashes. His face was round and shiny; easy to imagine it breaking into a chuckle, but probably not tonight.

Rebus picked a chair out from a pile against the far wall and sat down, only then introducing himself.

Brodie's voice was shaky. 'I know who did it.'

'Oh?' Rebus kept his voice low, in deference to the sleeping bodies around him. This was not quite how he'd expected the conversation to begin.

Brodie swallowed. 'I know who did it and I know *why* she did it. But I don't want to press charges.'

Rebus wasn't about to say that this decision was not up to Brodie himself. He didn't want the man clamming up. He wanted jaw-jaw. He nodded as if in agreement. 'Is there anything I can get you?' he said, inviting further confessions, as though from one friend to another.

'She must be a bit cracked,' Brodie went on, as though Rebus hadn't spoken at all. 'I told the police that at the time. She's doolally, I said. Must be. Well, this proves it, doesn't it?'

'You think she needs help?'

'Maybe. Probably.' He seemed deep in thought for a moment. 'Yes, almost certainly. I mean, it's going a bit far, isn't it? Even if you think you've got grounds. But she didn't have grounds. The police *told* her that.'

'But they didn't manage to convince her.'

'That's right.'

Rebus thought he was playing this fairly well. Obviously, Brodie was in shock. Maybe he was even babbling a bit, but as long as he was kept talking, Rebus would be able to piece together whatever the story was that he was trying to tell. There was a wheezy, dry laugh from the bed.

Brodie's eyes twinkled. 'You don't know what I'm talking about, do you?' Rebus was obliged to shake his head. 'Of course you don't. Well, I'll have a sip of water and then I'll tell you.'

And he did.

The morning was bright but grey: 'sunshine and showers', the weatherman would term it. It wasn't quite autumn yet. The too-short summer might yet have some surprises. Rebus waited in his room – his desk located not too far from the radiator – until the two police constables could be found. They were uneasy when they came in, until he reassured them. Yes, as requested, they had brought their notebooks with them. And yes, they remembered the incident very well indeed.

'It started with anonymous phone calls,' one of them began. 'They seemed to be genuine enough. Miss Hooper told us about one of them in particular. Her phone rings. Man on the other end identifies himself as a police inspector and tells her there's an anonymous caller who's going through the Edinburgh directory trying number after number. He says her number might come up soon, but the police have put a trace on her line. So can she keep the man talking for as long as possible.'

'Oh yes.' Really, Rebus didn't need to hear the rest. But he listened patiently to the constable's story.

'Later on that day, a man did ring. He asked her some very personal questions and she kept him talking. Afterwards, she rang the police station to see if they'd caught him. Only, of course, the name the so-called inspector had given wasn't known to the station. It was the anonymous caller himself, setting her up.'

Rebus shook his head slowly. It was old, but clever. 'So she complained about anonymous calls?'

'Yes, sir. But then the calls stopped. So that didn't seem too bad. No need for an operator to intercept or a change of number or anything.'

'How did Miss Hooper seem at the time?'

The constable shrugged and turned to his colleague, who now spoke. 'A bit nervy, sir. But that was understandable, wasn't it? A very nice lady, I'd say. Not married. I don't think she even had a boyfriend.' He turned his head towards his colleague. 'Didn't she say something like that, Jim?'

'I think so, yes.'

'So then what happened?' asked Rebus.

'A few weeks later, this would be just over a week ago, we had another call from Miss Hooper. She said a man in the tenement across the back from her was a peeping Tom. She'd seen him at a window, aiming his binoculars towards her building. More particularly, she thought, towards her own flat. We investigated and spoke to Mr Brodie. He appeared quite concerned about the allegations. He showed us the binoculars and admitted using them to watch from his kitchen window. But he assured us that he was bird-watching.' The other constable smiled at this. '"Bird-watching," he said.'

'Ornithology,' said Rebus.

'That's right, sir. He said he was very interested in birds, a bird-fancier sort of thing.' Another smile. They were obviously hoping Rebus would come to enjoy the joke with them. They were wrong, though they didn't seem to sense this just yet.

'Go on,' he said simply.

'Well, sir, there did seem to be a lot of pictures of birds in his flat.'

'You mean the prints in the living-room?'

'That's right, sir, pictures of an ornithological nature.'

Now the other constable interrupted. 'You won't believe it, sir. He said he was watching the tenement and the garden because he'd seen some. ...' pause for effect ... 'bearded tits.'

Now both the young constables were grinning.

'I'm glad you find your job so amusing,' Rebus said. 'Because I don't think frightening phone calls, peeping Toms and arson attacks are material for jokes!'

The grins disappeared.

'Get on with it,' Rebus demanded. The constables looked at one another.

'Not much more to tell, sir,' said the one called Jim. 'The gentleman, Mr Brodie, seemed genuine enough. But he promised to be a bit more careful in future. Like I say, he seemed genuinely concerned. We informed Miss Hooper of our findings. She didn't seem entirely convinced.'

'Obviously not,' said Rebus, but he did not go on to clarify. Instead, he dismissed the two officers and sat back in his chair. Brodie suspected Hooper of the arson attack, not, it would appear, without reason. What was more, Brodie had said he couldn't think of any other enemies he might have made. Either that or he wasn't about to tell Rebus about them. Rebus leaned back in his chair and rested his arm along the radiator, enjoying its warmth. The next person to speak to, naturally, was Miss Hooper herself. Another day, another tenement.

'Bearded tits,' Rebus said to himself. This time, he allowed himself a smile.

'It's your lucky day,' Miss Hooper told him. 'Normally I don't come home for lunch, but today I just felt like it.'

Lucky indeed. Rebus had knocked on the door of Miss Hooper's first-floor flat but received no answer. Eventually, another door on the landing had opened, revealing a woman in her late forties, stern of face and form.

'She's not in,' the woman had stated, unnecessarily.

'Any idea when she'll be back?'

'Who are you then?'

'Police.'

The woman pursed her lips. The nameplate above her doorbell, to the left of the door itself, read McKAY. 'She works till four o'clock. She's a schoolteacher. You'll catch her at school if you want her.'

'Thank you. Mrs McKay, is it?'

'It is.'

'Could I have a word?'

'What about?'

By now, Rebus was standing at Mrs McKay's front door. Past her, he caught sight of a dark entrance hall strewn with bits and pieces of machinery, enough to make up most, but not quite all, of a motorbike.

'About Miss Hooper,' he said.

'What about her?'

No, she was not about to let him in. He could hear her television blaring. Lunchtime game-show applause. The resonant voice of the questionmaster. Master of the question.

'Have you known her long?'

'Ever since she moved in. Three, four years. Aye, four years.' She had folded her arms now, and was resting one shoulder against the door-jamb. 'What's the problem?'

'I suppose you must know her quite well, living on the same landing?'

'Well enough. She comes in for a cuppa now and again.' She paused, making it quite clear to Rebus that this was not an honour *he* was about to receive.

'Have you heard about the fire?'

'Fire?'

'Across the back.' Rebus gestured in some vague direction with his head.

'Oh aye. The fire engine woke me right enough. Nobody hurt though, was there?'

'What makes you say that?'

She shuffled now, unfolding her arms so one hand could rub at another. 'Just ... what I heard.'

'A man was injured, quite seriously. He's in hospital.'

'Oh.'

And then the main door opened and closed. Sound of feet on stone echoing upwards.

'Oh, here's Miss Hooper now,' said Mrs McKay. Said with relief, Rebus thought to himself. Said with relief ...

Miss Hooper let him in and immediately switched on the kettle. She hoped he wouldn't mind if she made herself a sandwich? And would he care for one himself? Cheese and pickle or peanut butter and apple? No, on second thoughts, she'd make some of both, and he could choose for himself.

A teacher? Rebus could believe it. There was something in her tone, in the way she seemed to have to utter all of her thoughts aloud, and in the way she asked questions and then answered them herself. He could see her standing in her classroom, asking her questions and surrounded by silence.

Alison Hooper was in her early thirties. Small and slim, almost schoolboyish. Short straight brown hair. Tiny earrings hooked into tiny ears. She taught in a primary school only ten minutes' walk from her flat. The flat itself was scattered with books and magazines, from many of which had been cut illustrations, clearly intended to find their way into her classroom. Mobiles hung from her living-room ceiling: some flying pigs, an alphabet, teddy bears waving from aeroplanes. There were colourful rugs on her walls, but no rugs at all on the stripped floor. She had a breathy, nervous way with her and an endearing twitch to her nose. Rebus followed her into the kitchen and watched her open a loaf of brown sliced bread.

'I usually take a packed lunch with me, but I slept in this morning and didn't have time to make it. I could have eaten in the canteen, of course, but I just felt like coming home. Your lucky day, Inspector.'

'You had trouble sleeping last night then?'

'Well, yes. There was a fire in the tenement across the back.' She pointed through her window with a buttery knife. 'Over there. I heard sirens and the fire-engine's motor kept rumbling away, so I couldn't for the life of me get back to sleep.'

Rebus went across to the window and looked out. John Brodie's tenement stared back at him. It could have been any tenement anywhere in the city. Same configuration of windows and drainpipes, same railing-enclosed drying-green. He angled his head further to look into the back garden of Alison Hooper's tenement. Movement there. What was it? A teenager working on his motorbike. The motorbike standing on the drying-green, and all the tools and bits and pieces lying on a piece of plastic which had been spread out for the purpose. The nearby garden shed stood with its door propped open by a wooden stretcher. Through the doorway Rebus could see yet more motorbike spares and some oil cans.

'The fire last night,' he said, 'it was in a flat occupied by Mr John Brodie.'

'Oh!' she said, her knife-hand pausing above the bread. 'The peeping Tom?' Then she swallowed, not slow on the uptake. 'That's why you're here then.'

'Yes. Mr Brodie gave us your name, Miss Hooper. He thought perhaps—'

'Well, he's right.'

'Oh?'

'I mean, I do have a grudge. I do think he's a pervert. Not that I seem able to convince the police of that.' Her voice was growing shriller. She stared at the slices of bread in a fixed, unblinking way. 'No, the police don't seem to think there's a problem. But I know. I've talked to the other residents. We *all* know.' Then she relaxed, smiled at the bread. She slapped some peanut butter onto one slice. Her voice was calm. 'I do have a grudge, Inspector, but I did not set fire to that man's flat. I'm even pleased that he wasn't injured.'

'Who says he wasn't?'

'What?'

'He's in hospital.'

'Is he? I thought someone said there'd been no—'

'Who said?'

She shrugged. 'I don't know. One of the other teachers. Maybe they'd heard something on the radio. I don't know. Tea or coffee?'

'Whatever you're having.'

She made two mugs of decaffeinated instant. 'Let's go through to the living-room,' she said.

There, she gave him the story of the phone calls, and the story of the man with the binoculars.

'Bird-watching my eye,' she said. 'He was looking into people's windows.'

'Hard to tell, surely.'

She twitched her nose. 'Looking into people's windows,' she repeated.

'Did anyone else see him?'

'He stopped after I complained. But who knows? I mean, it's easy enough to see someone during the day. But at night, in that room of his with the lights turned off. He could sit there all night watching us. Who would know?'

'You say you spoke to the other residents?'

'Yes.'

'All of them?'

'One or two. That's enough, word gets round.'

I'll bet, thought Rebus. And he had another thought, which really was just a word: tenementality. He ate the spicy sandwich and the sickly sandwich quickly, drained his mug and said he'd leave her to finish her lunch in peace. ('Finish your piece in peace,' he'd nearly said, but hadn't, just in case she didn't get the joke.) He walked downstairs, but instead of making along the passage to the front door, turned right and headed towards the tenement's back door.

Outside, the biker was fitting a bulb to his brake-light. He took the new bulb from a plastic box and tossed the empty box onto the sheet of plastic.

'Mind if I take that?' asked Rebus. The youth looked round at him, saw where he was pointing, then shrugged and returned to his work. There was a small cassette recorder playing on the grass beside him. Heavy Metal. The batteries were low and the sound was tortuous.

'Can if you like,' he said.

'Thanks.' Rebus lifted the box by its edges and slipped it into his jacket pocket. 'I use them to keep my flies in.'

The biker turned and grinned.

'Fishing flies,' Rebus explained, smiling himself. 'It's just perfect for keeping my fishing flies in.'

'No flies on you, eh?' said the youth.

Rebus laughed. 'Are you Mrs McKay's son?' he asked.

'That's right.' The bulb was fitted, the casing was being screwed back into place.

'I'd test that before you put the casing on. Just in case it's a dud. You'd only have to take it apart again.'

The boy looked round again. 'No flies on you,' he repeated. He took the casing off again.

'I've just been up seeing your mum.'

'Oh aye?' The tone told Rebus that the boy's parents were either separated, or else the father was dead. You're her latest, are you? the tone implied. Mum's latest fancy-man.

'She was telling me about the fire.'

The boy examined the casing closely. 'Fire?'

'Last night. Have you noticed any of your petrol-cans disappearing? Or maybe one's got less in than you thought?'

Now, the red see-through casing might have been a gem under a microscope. But the boy was saying nothing.

'My name's Rebus, by the way, Inspector Rebus.'

Rebus had a little courtroom conversation with himself on the way back to the station.

And did the suspect drop anything when you revealed your identity to him?

Yes, he dropped his jaw.

Dropped his jaw?

That's right. He looked like a hairless ape with a bad case of acne. And he lost his nut.

Lost his nut?

A nut he'd been holding. It fell into the grass. He was still looking for it when I left.

What about the plastic box, Inspector, the one in which the new brake-light bulb had been residing? Did he ask for it back?

I didn't give him the chance. It's my intention *never* to give a sucker an even chance.

Back at the station, comfortable in his chair, the desk solid and reliable in front of him, the heater solid and reliable behind, Rebus thought about fire, the easy assassin. You didn't need to get your hands on a gun. Didn't even need to buy a knife. Acid, poison, again, difficult to find. But fire ... fire was everywhere. A disposable lighter, a box of matches. Strike a match and you had fire. Warming, nourishing, dangerous fire. Rebus lit a cigarette, the better to help him think. There wouldn't be any news from the lab for some time yet. Some time. Something was niggling. Something he'd heard. What was it? A saying came to mind: prompt payment will be appreciated. You used to get that on the bottom of invoices. Prompt payment.

Probably pays his rent promptly, too.

Well, well. Now there was a thing. Owner-occupier. Not every owner *did* occupy, and not every occupier was an owner. Rebus recalled that Detective Sergeant Hendry of Dunfermline CID was a keen bird-watcher. Once or twice, on courses or at conferences, he'd collared Rebus and bored him with tales of the latest sighting of the Duddingston bittern or the Kilconquhar red-head smew. Like all hobbyists, Hendry was keen to have others share his enthusiasm. Like all anti-hobbyists, Rebus would yawn with more irony than was necessary.

Still, it was worth a phone-call.

'I'll have to call you back, John,' said a busy DS Hendry. 'It's not the sort of thing I could tell you offhand. Give me your number at home and I'll ring you tonight. I didn't know you were interested.'

'I'm not, believe me.'

But his words went unheeded. 'I saw siskins and twite earlier in the year.'

'Really?' said Rebus. 'I've never been one for country and western music. Siskins and twite, eh? They've been around for years.'

By the following morning, he had everything he needed. He arrived as Mrs McKay and her son were eating a late breakfast. The television was on, providing the noise necessary to their lives. Rebus had come accompanied by two other officers, so that there could be no doubting he meant business. Gerry McKay's jaw dropped again as Rebus began to speak. The tale itself was quickly told. John Brodie's front door had been examined, the metal letterbox checked for fingerprints. Some good, if oily, prints had been found, and these matched those found on the plastic box Rebus had taken from Gerry McKay. There could be no doubting that Gerry McKay had pushed open John Brodie's letterbox. If Gerry would accompany the officers to the station.

'Mum!' McKay was on his feet, yelling, panicky. 'Mum, tell them! Tell them!'

Mrs McKay had a face as dark as ketchup. Rebus was glad he had brought the other officers. Her voice trembled when she spoke. 'It wasn't Gerry's idea,' she said. 'It was mine. If there's anyone you want to talk to about it, it should be me. It was my idea. Only, I knew Gerry'd be faster getting in and out of the stairwell. That's all. He's got nothing to do with it.' She paused, her face turning even nastier. 'Besides, that wee shite deserved all he got. Dirty, evil little runt of a man. You didn't see the state Alison was in. Such a nice wee girl, wouldn't say boo to a goose, and to be got into a state like that. I couldn't let him get away with it, hell. And if it were up to you lot, he'd have gotten off scot-free, wouldn't he? It's nothing to do with Gerry.'

'It'll be taken into account at the trial,' Rebus said quietly.

John Brodie looked not to have moved since Rebus had left him. His arms still lay on the top of the bed-cover, and he was still propped up against a pillow.

'Inspector Rebus,' he said. 'Back again.'

'Back again,' said Rebus, placing a chair by the bed and seating himself. 'The doctor says you're doing fine.'

'Yes,' said Brodie.

'Anything I can get you?' Brodie shook his head. 'No? Juice? A bit of fruit maybe? How about something to read? I notice you like girlie mags. I saw one in your flat. I could get you a few of those if you like.' Rebus winked. 'Readers' wives, eh? Amateurs. That's your style. All those blurry Polaroid shots, heads cut off. That's what you like, eh, John?'

But John Brodie was saying nothing. He was looking at his arms. Rebus drew the chair closer to the bed. Brodie flinched, but could not move.

'*Panurus biarmicus*,' Rebus hissed. Now Brodie looked blankly at him. Rebus repeated the words. Still Brodie looked blank. 'Go on,' Rebus chided, 'take a guess.'

'I don't know what you're talking about.'

'No?' Rebus was wide-eyed. 'Curious that. Sounds like the name of a disease, doesn't it? Maybe you know it better as the bearded tit.'

'Oh.' Brodie smiled shyly, and nodded. 'Yes, the bearded tit.'

Rebus smiled too, but coldly. 'You didn't know, you didn't have a clue. Shall I tell you something about the bearded tit? No, better yet, Mr Brodie, you tell *me* something about it.' He sat back and folded his arms expectantly.

'What?'

'Go on.'

'Look, what's all this about?'

'It's quite simple, you see.' Rebus sat forward again. 'The bearded tit isn't commonly found in Scotland. I got that from an expert. Not commonly found, that's what he said. More than that, its habitat – and I'm quoting here – is "extensive and secluded reed-beds". Do you see what I'm getting at? You'd hardly call Easter Road a reed-bed, would you?'

Brodie raised his head a little, his thin lips very straight and wide. He was thinking, but he wasn't talking.

'You see what I'm getting at, don't you? You told those two constables that you were watching bearded tits from your window. But that's just not true. It couldn't possibly be true. You said the name of the first bird that came into your head, and it came into your head because there was a drawing on your living-room wall. I saw it myself. But it's not you that's the bird-watcher, John. It's your landlord and landlady. You rented the place furnished and you haven't changed anything. It's their drawings on the wall. They got in touch about the insurance, you see. Wondering whether the fire was accidental. They saw a bit about it in the newspaper. They could appreciate that they hadn't heard from you, what with you being in hospital and all, but they wanted to sort out the insurance. So I was able to ask them about the birds on the wall. *Their* birds, John, not yours. It was quick thinking of you to come up with the story. It even fooled those two PCs. It might have fooled me. That book about zoom photography, even that had a picture of birds on the front.' He paused. 'But you're a peeper, John, that's all. That's what you are, a nasty little voyeur. Miss Hooper was right all the time.'

'Was it her who—?'

'You'll find out soon enough.'

'It's all lies, you know. Hearsay, circumstantial. You've no proof.'

'What about the photos?'

'What photos?'

Rebus sighed. 'Come on, John. All that gear in your bedroom. Tripod, camera, zoom lenses. Photographing birds, were you? I'd be interested to see the results. Because it wasn't just binoculars, was it? You took piccies, too. In your wardrobe, are they?' Rebus checked his watch. 'With luck I'll have the search warrant inside the hour. Then I intend to take a good look round your flat, John. I intend taking a *very* good look.'

'There's nothing there.' He was shaking now, his arms moving painfully in their gauze bandages. 'Nothing. You've no right. Someone tried to kill ... No right. They tried to kill me.'

Rebus was willing to concede a point. 'Certainly they tried to scare you. We'll see what the courts decide.' He rose to his feet. Brodie was still twittering on. Twit, twit, twit. It would be a while before he'd be able to use a camera again.

'Do you want to know something else, John?' Rebus said, unable to resist one of his parting shots. 'Something about the bearded tit? It's classified as a *babbler*.' He smiled a smile of warm sunshine. 'A babbler!' he repeated. 'Looks to me like you're a bit of a babbler yourself. Well,' he picked up the chair and pretended to be considering something, 'at any rate, I'd certainly classify you as a tit.'

He returned that evening to his own tenement and his roaring gas fire. But there was a surprise awaiting him on the doorhandle of his flat. A reminder from Mrs Cochrane downstairs. A reminder that it was his week for washing the stairs and that he hadn't done it yet and it was nearly the end of the week and when was he going to do it? Rebus sent a roar into the stairwell before slamming shut the door behind him. It was only a moment before other doors started to open, faces peering out, and another Edinburgh tenement conversation began, multi-storeyed, undertone and echoing.

Not Provan

How badly did Detective Inspector John Rebus want to nail Willie Provan? Oh, badly, very badly indeed. Rebus visualised it as a full-scale crucifixion, each nail going in slowly, the way Willie liked to put the boot and the fist slowly, methodically, into the victims of his violence.

Rebus had first encountered Willie Provan five years before, as a schoolkid spiralling out of control. Both parents dead, Willie had been left in the charge of a dotty and near-deaf aunt. He had taken charge of her house, had held wild parties there, parties to which the police were eventually, habitually called by neighbours at the end of their tether.

Entering the house had been like stepping into an amateur production of *Caligula*: naked, under-aged couples so drunk or drugged they could not complete the act which so interested them; emptied tins of solvent, polythene bags encrusted with the dregs of the stuff. A whiff of something animal, something less-than-human in the air. And, in a small back room upstairs, the aunt, locked in and sitting up in her bed, a cold cup of tea and a half-eaten sandwich on the table beside her.

By the time he left school, Willie was already a legend. Four years on the dole had benefited him little. But he had learned cunning, and so far the police had been unable to put him away. He remained a thorn in Rebus's side. Today, Rebus felt someone might just come along and pluck that thorn out.

He sat in the public gallery and watched the court proceedings. Near him were a few of Willie Provan's friends, members of his gang. They called themselves the Tiny Alice, or T-Alice. No one knew why. Rebus glanced over towards them. Sleeves rolled up, sporting tattoos and unshaven grins. They were the city's sons, the product of an Edinburgh upbringing, but they seemed to belong to another culture, another civilisation entirely, reared on Schwarzenegger videos and bummed cigarettes. Rebus shivered, feeling he understood them better than he liked to admit.

The case against Provan was solid and satisfying. On a cup-tie evening several months ago, a football fan had been heading towards the Heart of Midlothian ground. He was late, his train from Fife having been behind time. He was an away supporter and he was on his own in Gorgie.

An arm snaked around his neck, yanked him into a tenement stairwell, and there Willie Provan had kicked and punched him into hospitalisation. For what reason? Rebus could guess. It had nothing to do with football, nothing with football hooliganism. Provan pretended a love of Hearts, but had never, to Rebus's knowledge, attended a game. Nor could he name more than two or three players in the current team's line-up.

Nevertheless, Gorgie was his patch, his territory. He had spotted an invader and had summarily executed him, in his own terms. But his luck had run out. A woman had heard some sounds from the stairwell and had opened her door to investigate. Provan saw her and ran off. But she had given the police a good description and had later identified Provan as the attacker. Moreover, a little while after the attack, a constable, off duty and happening to pass Tynecastle Park, had spotted a young man, apparently disorientated. He had approached the man and asked him if he was all right, but at that point some members of T-Alice had appeared from their local pub, directly opposite the Hearts ground and had taken the man inside.

The constable thought little of it, until he heard about the assault and was given a description of the attacker. The description matched that of the disorientated man, and that man turned out to be Willie Provan. With Provan's previous record, this time he would go down, Rebus was sure of that. So he sat and he watched and he listened.

He watched the jurors, too. They winced, perceptibly as they were told of the injuries to the victim, injuries which still, several months on, kept him in hospital, unable to walk and with respiratory difficulties to boot. To boot. Ha! Rebus let a short-lived smile wrinkle his face. Yes, the jury would convict. But Rebus was most interested in one juror in particular, an intense young man who was taking copious notes, sending intelligent written questions to the judge, studying photographs and diagrams with enthusiasm. The model juror, ready to see that justice was done and all was fair and proper. At one point, the young man looked up and caught Rebus watching him. After that, he gave Rebus some of his attention, but still scribbled his notes and checked and rechecked what he had written.

The other jurors were solemn, looked bored even. Passive spectators at a one-horse race. Guilty. Probably by the end of the day. Rebus would sit it out. The prosecution had finished its case, and the defence case had already begun. The usual stuff when an obviously guilty party pleaded not guilty: trying to catch out prosecution witnesses, instilling mistrust, trying to persuade the jury that things were not as cut and dried as they seemed, that there was probable cause for doubt. Rebus sat back and let it wash over him. Provan would go down.

Then came the iceberg, ripping open the bow of Rebus's confidence.

The defence counsel had called the off-duty constable, the one who had spotted Provan outside the Hearts ground. The constable was young, with a bad case of post-juvenile acne. He tried to stand to attention as the questions were put to him, but when flustered would raise a hand towards his scarred cheeks. Rebus remembered his own first time on the witness stand. A Glasgow music hall stage could not have been more terrifying.

'And what time do you say it was when you first saw the accused?' The defence counsel had a slight Irish brogue, and his eyes were dark from want of sleep. His cheap ballpoint pen had burst, leaving black stains across his hands. Rebus felt a little sorry for him.

'I'm not sure, sir.'

'You're not sure?' The words came slowly. The inference was: this copper is a bit thick, isn't he? How can you the jury trust him? For the counsel was staring at the jury as he spoke and this seemed to unnerve the constable further. A hand rubbed against a cheek.

'Roughly then,' continued the defence counsel. 'Roughly what time was it?'

'Sometime between seven-thirty and eight, sir.'

The counsel nodded, flipping through a sheaf of notes. 'And what did you say to the accused?' As the constable was about to reply, the counsel interrupted, still with his face towards the jury. 'I say "the accused" because there's no disagreement that the person the constable saw outside the football ground was my client.' He paused. 'So constable, what did you say?'

'"Are you all right?" Something like that.'

Rebus glanced towards where Provan sat in the dock. Provan was looking terribly confident. His clear blue eyes were sparkling and he sat forwards in his chair, keen to catch the dialogue going on before him. For the first time, Rebus felt an uneasy stab: the thorn again, niggling him. What was going on?

'You asked him if he was all right.' It was a statement. The counsel paused again. Now the prosecution counsel was frowning: he too was puzzled by this line of questioning. Rebus felt his hands forming into fists.

'You asked him if he was all right, and he replied? What exactly *did* he reply?'

'I couldn't really make it out, sir.'

'Why was that? Were his words slurred perhaps?'

The constable shrugged. 'A little, maybe.'

'A little? Mmm.' The counsel looked at his notes again. 'What about the noise from the stadium?'

'Sir?'

'You were directly outside the ground. There was a cup-tie being played in front of thousands of spectators. It was noisy, wasn't it?'

'Yes, sir,' agreed the constable.

'In fact, it was *very* noisy, wasn't it, Constable Davidson? It was *extraordinarily* noisy. That was why you couldn't hear my client's reply. Isn't that the case?'

The constable shrugged again, not sure where any of this was leading, happy enough to agree with the defence. 'Yes, sir,' he said.

'In fact, as you approached my client, you may remember that there was a sudden upsurge in the noise from the ground.'

The constable nodded, seeming to remember. 'That's right, yes. I think a goal had just been scored.'

'Indeed, a goal had been scored. Just after you had first spotted my client, as you were walking towards him. A goal was scored, the noise was terrific. You shouted your question to my client, and he replied, but his words were drowned out by the noise from the ground. His friends saw him from the Goatfell public house and came to his aid, leading him inside. The noise was still very great, even then. They were shouting to you to let you know they would take care of him. Isn't that right?'

Now, the counsel turned to the constable, fixing him with his dark eyes.

'Yes, sir.'

The counsel nodded, seeming satisfied. Willie Provan, too, looked satisfied. Rebus's nerves were jangling. He was reminded of a song lyric: *there's something happening here, but you don't know what it is.* Something was most definitely happening here, and Rebus didn't like it. The defence counsel spoke again.

'Do you know what the score was that night?'

'No, sir.'

'It was one–nil. The home team won by a single goal, the single goal you heard from outside the ground. A single goal scored—'

picking up the notes for effect, turning again to face the jury, 'in the fifteenth minute of the game, a game that kicked off ... when? Do you happen to recall?'

The constable knew now, knew where this was leading. His voice when he spoke had lost a little of its life. 'It was a seven-thirty kick-off.'

'That's right, it was. So you see, Police Constable Davidson, it was seven forty-five when you saw my client outside the ground. I don't think you would contest that now, would you? And yet we heard Mrs McClintock say that it was twenty to eight when she heard a noise on her stairwell and went to her door. She was quite specific because she looked at her clock before she went to the door. Her call to the police was timed at seven forty-two, just two minutes later.'

Rebus didn't need to hear any more, tried to shut his ears to it. The tenement where the assault had taken place was over a mile from Tynecastle Park and the Goatfell pub. To have been where he was when the constable had approached him, Provan would have had to run, in effect, a four-minute mile. Rebus doubted he was capable of it, doubted everything now. But looking at Provan he could *see* the little prick was guilty. He was as guilty as hell and he was about to get away scot bloody free. Rebus's knuckles were white, his teeth were gritted. Provan looked up at him and smiled. The thorn was in Rebus's side again, working away relentlessly, bleeding the policeman to death.

It couldn't be true. It just couldn't. The trial wasn't over yet. Things had been strung out over the afternoon, the prosecution clearly flustered and playing for time, wondering what tactic to try next, what question to ask. He had lasted the afternoon and court had been adjourned after the summings up. It was all to do with time, as the defence counsel contended. The prosecution tried to negate the time factor and rely instead on the one and only witness. He asked: can we be certain a goal had been scored at that precise moment when PC Davidson approached the accused? Is it not better to trust the identification of the witness, Mrs McClintock, who had actually disturbed the attacker in the course of the assault? And so on. But Rebus knew the case was doomed. There was too much doubt now, way too much. Not guilty, or maybe that Scots get-out clause of 'not proven', whatever. If only the victim had caught a glimpse of Provan, if only. If, if, if. The jury would assemble again tomorrow at ten-thirty, retire to their room and emerge before lunch with a decision which would make Provan a free man. Rebus shook his head.

He was sitting in his car, not up to driving. Just sitting there, the key in the ignition, trying to think things through. But going around in circles, no clear direction, his mind filled with Provan's smile, a smile he would happily tear from that face. Illegal thoughts coursed through his head, ways of fixing Provan, ways of putting him inside. But no: it had to be clean, it had to be *right*. Justification was only part of the process; justice demanded more.

At last, he gave an audible growl, the sound of a caged animal, and turned the ignition, starting the car, heading nowhere in particular. At home he would only brood. A pub might be an idea. There were a few pubs, their clientele almost silent, where a man might drink in solitude and quiet. A kind of a wake for The Law. Damn it, no, he knew where he was headed. Tried not to know, but knew all the same. He was driving towards Gorgie, driving deep into Willie Provan's territory, into the gangland ruled by Tiny Alice. He was heading into the Wild West End of Edinburgh.

The streets were narrow, tenements rising on either side. A cold October wind was blowing, forcing people to angle their walk into the wind, giving them the jack-knife look of a Lowry painting. They were all coming home from work. It was dark, the headlamps of cars and buses like torches in a cave. Gorgie always seemed dark. Even on a summer's day it seemed dark. It had something to do with the narrowness of the streets and the height of the tenements; they seemed like trees in the Amazon, blocking out the light to the pallid vegetation beneath.

Rebus found Cooper Road and parked on the opposite side of the street from number 42. He switched off his engine and wondered what to do now. He was treading dangerously: not the physical danger of the T-Alice, but the more enveloping danger of involvement in a case. If he spoke with Mrs McClintock and the defence counsel were to learn of it, Rebus might be in serious trouble. He wasn't even sure he should be in the vicinity of the crime. Should he turn back? No. Provan was going to get off anyway, whether because of an unconvinced jury or a procedural technicality. Besides, Rebus wasn't getting involved. He was just in the area, that was all.

He was about to get out of the car when he saw a man dressed in duffel coat and jeans shuffle towards the door of number 42 and stop there, studying it. The man pushed at the door and it opened. He looked around before entering the stairwell, and Rebus recognised with a start the intent face of the keen juror from Provan's trial.

Now *this* might be trouble. This might be very bad indeed. What the hell was the juror doing here anyway? The answer seemed simple enough: he was becoming involved, the same as Rebus.

Because he, too, could not believe Provan's luck. But what was he doing at number 42? Was he going to talk to Mrs McClintock? If so, he faced certain disqualification from the jury. Indeed, it was Rebus's duty as a police officer, having seen the juror enter that stairwell, to report this fact to the court officials.

Rebus gnawed at his bottom lip. He could go in and warn the juror, of course, but then he, a policeman, would be guilty of approaching a juror on the very evening prior to a judgment. That could mean more than a slapped wrist and a few choice words from the Chief Super. That could mean the end of his career.

Suddenly, Rebus's mind was made up for him. The door of the tenement was heaved open and out ran the juror, an eye on his watch as he turned left and sprinted towards Gorgie Road. Rebus smiled with relief and shook his head.

'You little bugger,' he murmured in appreciation. The juror was timing the whole thing. It was all a matter of time, so the defence had said, and the juror wanted to time things for himself. Rebus started the car and drove off, following behind the juror until the young man discovered a short cut and headed off down an alleyway. Unable to follow, Rebus fed into the traffic on the main road and found himself in the rush hour jams, heading west out of town. It didn't matter: he knew the juror's destination.

Turning down a sidestreet, Rebus rounded a bend and came immediately upon Tynecastle Park. The Goatfell was ahead of him on the other side of the street. Rebus stopped the car on some double yellow lines by the stadium side of the road. Opposite the Goatfell, the juror was doubled over on the pavement, hands pressing into his sides, exhausted after the run and trying to regain his breath. Rebus examined his watch. Eight minutes since the juror had started off from the tenement. The only witness placed the attack at seven-forty, absolutely certain in her mind that this had been the time. The goal had been scored at seven forty-five. Perhaps Mrs McClintock's clock had been wrong? It could be that simple, couldn't it? But they'd have a hell of a job proving it in court, and no jury would convict on the possibility of a dodgy clock.

Besides, her call to the police had been logged, hadn't it? There was no room for manoeuvre on the time, unless ... Rebus tapped his fingers against the steering wheel. The juror had recovered some of his equilibrium, and was now staring at the Goatfell. *Don't do it, son*, Rebus intoned mentally. *Don't.*

The juror looked both ways as he crossed the road and, once across, he looked both ways again before pushing open the door of the Goatfell and letting it rattle shut behind him. Rebus groaned and screwed shut his eyes.

'Stupid little ...' He pulled the keys from the ignition, and leaned across the passenger seat to lock the passenger side door. You couldn't be too careful around these parts. He stared at his radio. He could call for back-up, *should* call for back-up, but that would involve explanations. No, he was in this one alone.

He opened his own door and swivelled out of his seat, closing the door after him. Pausing to lock the door, he hesitated. After all, you never knew when a quick getaway might be needed. He left the door unlocked. Then, having taken three steps in the direction of the Goatfell, he stopped again and returned to the car, this time unlocking the passenger-side door, too.

You can't afford to get involved, John, he told himself. But his feet kept moving forwards. The front of the Goatfell was uninviting, its bottom half a composition of large purple and black tiles, some missing, the others cracked and chipped and covered in graffiti. The top half was constructed from glass panels, some frosted, some bottle glass. From the fact that there seemed no rhyme or reason to the pattern of these different panels, Rebus guessed that many a fight or thrown stone had seen most of the original panels replaced over time with whatever was available and cheap. He stopped for a moment at the solid wooden door, considering his madness, his folly. Then he pushed open the door and went inside.

The interior was, if anything, less prepossessing than the exterior. Red stubbled linoleum, plastic chairs and long wooden benches, a pool table, its green baize torn in several places. The lone gaming machine coughed up a few coins for an unshaven man who looked as though he had spent most of his adult life battling with it. At one small table sat three thick-set men and a dozing greyhound. Behind the pool table, three more men, younger, shuffling, were arguing over selections from the jukebox. And at the bar stood a solitary figure – the juror – being served with a half pint of lager by the raw-faced barman.

Rebus went to the far end of the bar, as far from the juror as he could get and, keeping his face towards the optics, waited to be served.

'What'll it be?' The barman's question was not unfriendly.

'Half of special and a Bell's,' replied Rebus. This was his gambit in any potentially rough pub. He could think of no good reason why; somehow it just seemed like the right order. He remembered the roughest drinking den he'd ever encountered, deep in a Niddrie housing scheme. He'd given his order and the barman asked, in all seriousness, whether he wanted the two drinks in the same glass. That had shaken Rebus, and he hadn't lingered.

Served with two glasses this evening, one foaming, the other a generous measure of amber, he thanked the barman with a nod and the exact money. But the barman was already turning away, walking back to the conversation he had been having at the other end of the bar before Rebus had walked in, the conversation he'd been having with the juror.

'Aye, that was some game all right. Pity you missed it.' 'Well,' explained the juror, 'what with being away for so long. I've kind of lost touch with their fortunes.'

'Fortune had nothing to do with that night. Cracker of a goal. I must've seen it on the telly a dozen times. Should have been goal of the season.'

The juror sighed. 'Wish I'd been here to see it.'

'Where did you say you'd been again?'

'Europe mostly. Working. I'm only back for a few weeks, then I'm off again.'

Rebus had to admit that the juror made a convincing actor. Of course, there might be a grain of truth in his story, but Rebus doubted it. All the same, good actor or no, he was digging too deep too soon into the barman's memory of that night.

'When did you say the goal was scored?'

'Eh?' The barman seemed puzzled.

'How far into the game,' explained the juror.

'I don't know. Fifteen, twenty minutes, something like that. What difference does it make?'

'Oh, nothing, no, no difference. I was just wondering.'

But the barman was frowning, suspicious now. Rebus felt his grip on the whisky glass tightening.

There's no need for this, son. I know the answer now. It was you that led me to it, but I know now. Just drink your drink and let's get out of here.

Then, as the question and answer session between the juror and barman began again, Rebus glanced into a mirror and his heart dipped fast. The three young men had turned from the wall-mounted jukebox and were now in the process of starting a game of pool. Rebus recognised one of them from the public gallery. Tattoos. Tattoos had sat in the public gallery most of the morning and a little of the afternoon. He seemed not to have recognised Rebus. More to the point, he had not yet recognised the juror – but he would. Rebus had no doubt in his mind about that. Tattoos had spent a long portion of the day staring at fifteen faces, fifteen individuals who, collectively, could put his good friend Willie Provan away for a stretch. Tattoos would recognise the juror, and God alone could tell what would happen then.

God was in a funny mood. Tattoos, standing back while one of the other two T-Alice members played a thunderous break-shot, glanced towards the bar and saw the juror. Perhaps because Rebus was much further away, and partly hidden from view by the juror, Tattoos gave him no heed. But his eyes narrowed as he spotted the juror and Rebus could feel the young man trying to remember where he'd seen the drinker at the bar before. Where and when. Not too long ago. But not to speak to; just a face, a face in a crowd. On a bus? No. In a shop? No. But just a short time ago.

A grunt from one of the other players told Tattoos it was his turn. He lifted a cue from against the wall and bent low over the table, potting an easy ball. Meantime, Rebus had missed the low-voiced conversation between the juror and the barman. From the look on the juror's face, however, it was clear he had discovered something of import: the same 'something' Rebus had deduced while sitting in his car. Keen to leave now that he had his answer, the juror finished his drink.

Tattoos was walking around the table to his next shot. He looked again towards the bar, then towards the table. Then towards the bar again. Rebus, watching this in the wall mirror, saw Tattoos's jaw visibly drop open. Damn him, he had finally placed the juror. He placed his cue on the table and started slowly towards the bar. Rebus felt the tide rising around him. Here he was, where he shouldn't be, following a jury member on the eve of a retiral for verdict and now said juror was about to be approached by a friend of the accused.

For 'approached' read 'nobbled', or at the very least 'scared off'.

There was nothing for it. Rebus finished off the whisky and pushed the half pint away.

Tattoos had reached his quarry, who was just turning to go. Tattoos pointed an unnecessary finger.

'It's you, isn't it? You're on my pal's case. One of the jury. Christ, it *is* you.' Tattoos sounded as though he would have been less surprised to have encountered the entire Celtic team supping in his local. He grabbed hold of the juror's shoulder. 'Come on, I want a wee word.'

The juror's face, once red from running, had drained of all colour. Tattoos was hauling him towards the pub door.

'Easy, Dobbs!' called the barman.

'Not your concern, shite-face!' Tattoos, aka Dobbs, growled, tugging the door open and propelling the juror through it, out onto the street.

The bar fell quiet again. The dog, who had awakened at the noise, rested its head back on its paws. The pool game continued. A record came on the jukebox.

'Turn it up a bit!' yelled one of the pool players. 'I can hardly hear it!'

Rebus nodded to the barman in a gesture of farewell. Then he, too, made for the door.

Outside, he knew he must act quickly. At any sign of trouble, members of T-Alice would crawl out of the woodwork like so many termites. Tattoos had pinned the juror to a shop-front window between the Goatfell and Rebus's car. Rebus's attention was drawn from the conflict to the car itself. Its doors were open! He could see two kids playing inside it, crawling over its interior, pretending they were at the wheel of a racing car. Rebus hissed and moved forwards. He was almost passing Tattoos and the juror when he yelled:

'Get out of my bloody car!'

Even Tattoos turned at this and as he did so Rebus hammered a clenched fist into his nose. It had to be fast: Rebus didn't want Tattoos to be able ever to identify him. The sound of the nose flattening was dull and unmistakable. Tattoos let go of the juror and held his hands to his face. Rebus hit him again, this time in proper boxing fashion, knuckles against the side of the jaw. Tattoos fell against the glass shop-front and sank to the pavement.

It was Rebus's turn to grab the juror's shoulder, marching him towards the car with no words of explanation. The juror went quietly, glancing back just the once towards the prone body.

Seeing Rebus approach, brimstone in his eyes, the two boys ran from the car. Rebus watched them go, committing their faces to memory. Future Willie Provans.

'Get in,' he said to the juror, shoving him towards the passenger side. They both shut the car doors after them. Rebus's police radio was missing, and wires protruded from beneath the dashboard, evidence of an attempted hot-wiring. Rebus was relieved the attempt hadn't worked. Otherwise he would be trapped in Gorgie, surrounded by hostile natives. It didn't bear thinking about.

The car started first time and Rebus revved it hard as he drove off, never looking back.

'I know you,' said the juror. 'You were in the public gallery, too.'

'That's right.'

The juror grew quiet. 'You're not one of ...?'

'I want to see Willie Provan behind bars. That's all you need to know, and I don't want to know anything about you. I just want you to go home, go back to court tomorrow, and do your duty.'

'But I know how he—'

'So do I.' Rebus stopped at a red traffic light and checked in the mirror. No one was following. He turned to the juror. 'It was a cup-tie, a big crowd,' he said. 'And ever since Hillsborough, the football bosses and the police have been careful about big crowds.'

'That's right.' The juror was bursting to come out with it first. 'So they held up the game for ten minutes to let everybody in. The barman told me.'

Rebus nodded. The game had been a seven-thirty kick-off all right, but that intended kick-off time had been delayed. The goal, scored fifteen minutes into the game, had been scored at seven fifty-five, *not* seven forty-five, giving Provan plenty of time to make the one-mile trip from Cooper Road to the Goatfell. The truth would have come out eventually, but it might have taken a little time. The situation, however, was still dangerous. The light turned green, and Rebus moved off.

'So you think Provan is guilty?' he asked the juror.

'I know he is. It's obvious.'

Rebus nodded. 'He could still get away with it.'

'How?'

'If,' Rebus explained carefully, 'it comes to light that you and I have been doing a little snooping. You'll be thrown off the jury. It could go to a retrial, or some technicality might arise which would see Provan go free. We can't let that happen, can we?'

Rebus heard his own words. They sounded calm. Yet inside him the adrenalin was racing and his fist was pleasantly sore from use.

'No,' answered the juror, as Rebus had hoped he would.

'So,' continued Rebus, 'what I propose is that I have a quiet word with the prosecution counsel. Let's let him stand up in court and come out with the solution. That way no problems or technicalities arise. You just stay quiet and let the process work through.'

The juror seemed disheartened. This was his feat, after all, his sleuthing had turned things around. And for what?

'There's no glory in it, I'm afraid,' said Rebus. 'But at least you'll have the satisfaction of knowing Provan is inside, not out there, waiting to pick off another victim.' Rebus nodded through the windscreen and the juror stared at the city streets, thinking it over.

'Okay,' he said at last. 'Yes, you're right.'

'So we keep it quiet?'

'We keep it quiet,' the juror agreed. Rebus nodded slowly. This might shape up all right after all. The whisky was warming his veins. A quiet word to the prosecution, maybe by way of a typed and anonymous note, something that would keep Rebus out of the case. It was a pity he couldn't be in court tomorrow for the revelation. But the last thing he wanted was to encounter a broken-nosed Tattoos. A pity though; he wanted to see Provan's face and he wanted to catch Provan's eyes and he wanted to give him a great big pitiless smile.

'You can stop here,' said the juror, waking Rebus from his reverie. They were approaching Princes Street. 'I just live down Queens—'

'Don't tell me,' Rebus said abruptly. The juror looked at him.

'Technicalities?' he ventured. Rebus smiled and nodded. He pulled the car over to the side of the road. The juror opened his door, got out, but then bent down into the car again.

'I don't even know who you are,' he said.

'That's right,' said Rebus, reaching across and pulling shut the door. 'You don't.'

He drove off into the Edinburgh evening. No thorn jabbed him now. By tomorrow there would be another. And then he'd have to report the theft of his radio. There would be smiles at that, smiles and, behind his back if not to his face, laughter.

John Rebus could laugh, too.

Sunday

Where was that light coming from? Bright, hot light. Knives in the night. Last night, was it? No, the night before. Just another Friday in Edinburgh. A drug haul at a dance hall. A few of the dealers trying to run for it. Rebus cornering one. The man, sweating, teeth bared, turning before Rebus's eyes into an animal, something wild, predatory, scared. And cornered. The glint of a knife ...

But that was Friday, the night before last. So this was Sunday. Yes! Sunday morning. (Afternoon, maybe.) Rebus opened his eyes and squinted into the sunshine, streaming through his uncurtained window. No, not sunshine. His bedside lamp. Must have been on all night. He had come to bed drunk last night, drunk and tired. Had forgotten to close the curtains. And now warming light, birds resting on the window-ledge. He stared into a small black eye, then checked his watch. Ten past eight. Morning then, not afternoon. Early morning.

His head was the consistency of syrup, his limbs stiff. He'd been fit as a young man; not fitness daft, but fit all the same. But one day he had just stopped caring. He dressed quickly, then checked and found that he was running out of clean shirts, clean pants, clean socks. Today's chore then: doing the laundry. Ever since his wife had left him, he had taken his dirty washing to a public laundrette at the top of Marchmont Road, where a service wash cost very little and the manageress always used to fold his clean clothes away very neatly, a smile on her scrupulous lips. But in a fit of madness one Saturday afternoon, he had walked calmly into an electrical shop and purchased a washer/dryer for the flat.

He pressed the dirty bundle into the machine and found he was down to one last half-scoop of washing powder. What the hell, it would have to do. There were various buttons and controls on the machine's fascia, but he only ever used one programme: Number 5 (40 degrees), full load, with ten minutes' tumble dry at the end. The results were satisfactory, if never perfect. He switched the machine on, donned his shoes and left the flat, double-locking the door behind him.

His car, parked directly outside the main entrance to the tenement, scowled at him. *I need a wash, pal.* It was true, but Rebus shook his head. Not today, today was his day off, the only day this week. Some other time, some other free time. Who was he kidding? He'd drive into a car wash one afternoon between calls. His car could like it or lump it.

The corner shop was open. Rebus had seldom seen it closed. He bought ground coffee, rolls, milk, margarine, a packet of bacon. The bacon, through its plastic wrapping, had an oily, multicoloured look to it, but its sell-by date seemed reasonable. Pigs: very intelligent creatures. How could one intelligent creature eat another? Guilty conscience, John? It must be Sunday. Presbyterian guilt, Calvinist guilt. *Mea culpa*, he thought to himself, taking the bacon to the checkout till. Then he turned back and bought some washing powder, too.

Back in the flat, the washing machine was churning away. He put Coleman Hawkins on the hi-fi (not too loud; it was only quarter to nine). Soon the church bells would start ringing, calling the faithful. Rebus would not answer. He had given up churchgoing. Any day but Sunday he might have gone. But Sunday, Sunday was the only day off he had. He remembered his mother, taking him with her to church every Sunday while his father stayed at home in bed with tea and the paper. Then one Sunday, when he was twelve or thirteen, his mother had said he could choose: go with her or stay with his father. He stayed and saw his little brother's jealous eyes glance at him, desperate to be of an age where he would be given the same choice.

Ah me, John, Sunday morning. Rubbedy-rrub of the washing machine, the coffee's aroma wafting up from the filter. (Getting short on filters, but no panic: he only used them on Sunday.) He went into the bathroom. Suddenly, staring at the bath itself, he felt an overwhelming urge to steep himself in hot water. Wednesdays and Saturdays: those were his usual days for a bath. Go on, break the rules. He turned on the hot tap, but it was a mere trickle. Damn! the washing machine was being fed all the flat's hot water. Oh well. Bath later. Coffee now.

At five past nine, the Sunday papers thudded through the letterbox. *Sunday Post, Mail,* and *Scotland on Sunday.* He seldom read them, but they helped the day pass. Not that he got bored on a Sunday. It was the day of rest, so he rested. A nice lazy day. He refilled his coffee mug, went back into the bathroom and walked over to the toilet to examine a roughly circular patch on the wall beside it, a couple of feet up from floor level. The patch was slightly discoloured and he touched it with the palm of his hand. Yes, it was damp. He had first noticed the patch a week ago. Damp, slightly damp. He couldn't think why. There was no dampness anywhere else, no apparent source of the damp. Curious, he had peeled away the paper from the patch, had scratched at the plaster wall. But no answer had emerged. He shook his head. That would irritate him for the rest of the day. As before, he went to the bedroom and returned with an electric hairdryer and an extension flex. He plugged the hairdryer into the flex, and rested the dryer on the toilet seat, aimed towards the patch, then switched on the hairdryer and tested that it was hitting the spot. That would dry things out a bit, but he knew the patch would return.

Washing machine rumbling. Hairdryer whirring. Coleman Hawkins in the living-room. He went into the living-room. Could do with a tidy, couldn't it? Hoover, dust. Car sitting outside waiting to be washed. Everything could wait. There were the papers to be read. There they were on the table, just next to his briefcase. The briefcase full of documents for his attention, half-completed case-notes, reminders of appointments, all the rubbish he hadn't found time for during the week at the station. All the so-important paperwork, without which his life would be milk and honey. Some toast perhaps? Yes, he would eat some toast.

He checked his watch: ten past eleven. He had switched off the hairdryer, but left it sitting on the toilet, the extension lead snaking across the floor to the wall-socket in the hall. The washing machine was silent, spent. One more cup of coffee left in the pot. He had flicked through the papers, looking for the interesting, the unusual. Same old stories: court cases, weekend crime, sport. There was even a paragraph on Friday night's action. He skipped that, but remembered all the same. Bright knife's flat edge, caught in the lamplight. Sour damp smell in the alleyway. Feet standing in something soft. Don't look down, look at him, look straight at him, the cornered animal. Look at him, talk to him with your eyes, try to calm him, or quell him.

There were birds on the window sill, chirping, wanting some crumbled up crusts of bread, but he had no bread worth the name left in the flat; just fresh rolls, too soft to be thrown out. Ach, he'd never eat six rolls though, would he? One or two would go stale and then he'd give them to the birds. So why not give them some in advance, while the rolls are soft and sweet?

In the kitchen he prepared the broken pieces of bread on a plate, then took it to the birds on the window-ledge. Hell: what about lunch? Sunday afternoon lunch. In the freezer compartment, he found a steak. How long would it take to defrost? Damn! he meant to pick up the microwave during the week. The shop had called him to say they'd fixed the fault. He was supposed to have collected it on Friday, but he'd been too busy. So: defrost in a low oven. And wine. Yes, open a bottle. He could always drink just one or two glasses, then keep the rest of the bottle for some other occasion. Last Christmas, a friend had given him a vacuum-tube. It was supposed to keep wine fresh after opening. Where had he put it? In the cupboard beside the wine: that would make sense. But there was no gadget to be found.

He chose a not-bad bottle, bought from a reliable wine merchant in Marchmont and stood it on the table in the living-room. Beside his briefcase. Let the sediment settle. That's what Sunday was all about, wasn't it? Maybe he could try one of the crosswords. It was ages since he'd done a crossword. A glass of wine and a crossword while he waited for the meat to thaw. Sediment wouldn't be settled yet, but what the hell. He opened the bottle and poured an inch into his glass. Glanced at his watch again. It was half past eleven. A bit early to be drinking. Cheers.

You could break the rules on a Sunday, couldn't you?

Christ, what a week it had been at work. Everything from a senile rapist to a runaway blind boy. A shotgun robbery at a bookmaker's shop and an apparently accidental drowning at the docks. Drunk, the victim had been. Dead drunk. Fished about a bottle of whisky and a recently dismembered kebab from his stomach. Annual crime figures for the Lothians were released: murder slightly up on the previous year, sexual assaults well up, burglaries up, street crime down a little, motoring offences significantly reduced. The clear-up rate for housebreakings in some parts of Edinburgh was standing at less than five per cent. Rebus was not exactly a fascist, not quite a totalitarian, but he knew that given wider powers of entry and search, that final figure could be higher. There were high-rise blocks where a flat on the twelfth floor would be broken into time after time. Was someone climbing twelve flights to break in? Of course not: someone in the block was responsible, but without the powers of immediate and indiscriminate search, they'd never find the culprit.

And that was the tip of the whole polluted iceberg. Maniacs were put back on the streets by institutions unable or unwilling to cope. Rebus had never seen so many beggars in Edinburgh as in this past year. Teenagers (and younger) up to grandparents, dossing, cadging the occasional quid or cigarette. Christ, it depressed him to think of it almost as much as it did to pretend he could ignore it. He stalked through to the kitchen and felt the steak. It was still solid at its core. He lifted the nearly dry clothes out of the machine and draped them over the cold radiators throughout the flat. More music on the hi-fi. Art Pepper this time, a little louder, the hour being respectable. Not that the neighbours ever complained. Sometimes he could see in their eyes that they wanted to complain – complain about his noise, his irregular comings and goings, the way he revved his car or coughed his way up the stairwell. They wanted to complain, but they daren't, for fear that he would somehow 'stitch them up' or would prove not to be amenable to some favour they might ask one day. They all watched the TV police dramas and thought they must know their neighbour pretty well. Rebus shook his head and poured more wine: two inches deep in the glass this time. They knew nothing about him. Nothing. He didn't have a TV, hated all the game shows and the cop shows and the news programmes. Not having a TV had set him apart from his colleagues at the station: he found he had little to discuss with them of a morning. His mornings were quieter and saner for it.

He checked the damp patch in the bathroom again, letting his hand rest against it for half a minute. Mmm: it still wasn't completely dry. But then maybe his hands were damp from the washing he had been carrying. What the hell. Back in the bedroom, he picked up some books from the floor and stacked them against a wall, beside other columns of paperbacks and hardbacks, read and unread. One day he would get time to read them. They were like contraband: he couldn't stop himself buying them, but then he never really did anything with them once he'd bought them. The buying was the thing, that sense of ownership. Perhaps somewhere in Britain someone had exactly the same collection of books as him, but he doubted it. The range was too eclectic, everything from secondhand rugby yearbooks to dense philosophical works. Meaningless, really; without pattern. So much of his working life was spent to a pattern, a modus operandi. A series of rules for the possible (not probable) solving of crimes. One of the rules would have it that he get through the briefcase full of work before Monday morning and, preferably, while still sober.

Bell. Bell?

Bell. Someone at his front door. Jesus, on a *Sunday*? Not on a Sunday, please, God. The wrong door: they'd got the wrong door. Give them a minute and they would realise their mistake. Bell again. Bloody hell's bells. Right then, he would answer it.

He pulled the door open slowly, peering around it. Detective Constable Brian Holmes was standing on the tenement landing.

'Brian?'

'Hello, sir. Hope you don't mind. I was in the neighbourhood and thought I'd ... you know.'

Rebus held open the door. 'Come in.'

He led Holmes through the hall, stepping over the electric flex. Holmes stared at the flex, an alarmed look on his face.

'Don't worry,' said Rebus, pausing at the threshold of the living-room. 'I'm not going to jump in the bath with an electric fire. Just drying out a damp patch.'

'Oh.' Holmes sounded unconvinced. 'Right.'

'Sit down,' said Rebus. 'I've just opened a bottle of wine. Would you like some?'

'Bit early for me,' Holmes said, glancing towards Rebus's glass.

'Well, coffee then. I think there's still some in the pot.'

'No thanks, I'm fine.'

They were both seated, Rebus in his usual chair, Holmes perched on the edge of the sofa. Rebus knew why the younger officer was here, but he was damned if he would make it easy for him.

'In the neighbourhood you say?'

'That's right. I was at a party last night in Mayfield. Afterwards, I stopped the night.'

'Oh?'

Holmes smiled. 'No such luck, I slept on the sofa.'

'It's still off with Nell then?'

'I don't know. Sometimes she ... let's change the subject.'

He flipped one of the newspapers over so that he could study the back page. 'Did you see the boxing last night?'

'I don't have a television.'

Holmes looked around the room, then smiled again. 'Neither you do. I hadn't noticed.'

'I'll bear that in mind when you come up for promotion, Constable.' Rebus took a large gulp of wine, watching Holmes over the rim of the glass. Holmes was looking less comfortable by the second.

'Any plans for the day?'

'Such as?'

Holmes shrugged. 'I don't know. I thought maybe you had a Sunday routine. You know: clean the car, that sort of thing.'

Rebus nodded towards the briefcase on the table. 'Paperwork. That'll keep me busy most of the day.'

Holmes nodded, flicking through the paper until he came, as Rebus knew he would, to the piece about the nightclub bust.

'It's at the bottom of the page,' Rebus said. 'But then you know that, don't you? You've already seen it.' He rose from his chair sharply and walked to the hi-fi, turning the record over. Alto sax bloomed from the speakers. Holmes still hadn't said anything. He was pretending to read the paper, but his eyes weren't moving. Rebus returned to his seat.

'Was there really a party, Brian?'

'Yes.' Holmes paused. 'No.'

'And you weren't just passing?'

'No. I wanted to see how you were.'

'And how am I?'

'You look fine.'

'That's because I *am* fine.'

'Are you sure?'

'Perfectly.'

Holmes sighed and threw aside the paper. 'I'm glad to hear it. I was worried, John. We were all a bit shaken up.'

'I've killed someone before, Brian. It wasn't the first time.'

'Yes, but Christ, I mean ...' Holmes got up and walked to the window, looking down on the street. A nice quiet street in a quiet part of town. Net curtains and trim front gardens, the gardens of professional people, lawful people, people who smiled at you in shops or chatted in a bus queue.

But Rebus's mind flashed again to the dark alleyway, a distant streetlamp, the cornered drug dealer. He had thrown packets from his pockets onto the ground as he had run. Like sowing seed.

Small polythene bags of drugs soft and hard. Sowing them in the soft mud, every year a new crop.

Then the blinding light. The flat steel of a knife. Not a huge knife, but how big did a knife need to be? An inch of blade would be enough. Anything more was excess. It was a very excessive knife indeed, curved, serrated edge, a commando special. The kind you could buy from a camping shop. The kind *anybody* could buy from a camping shop. A serious knife for outdoor pursuits. Rebus had the idea they called them 'survival' knives.

The man – not much more than a boy in reality, eighteen or nineteen – had not hesitated. He slid the knife out from the waistband of his trousers. He lunged, one swipe, two swipes. Rebus wasn't fit, but his reactions were fast. On the third swipe, he snapped out a hand and caught the wrist, twisting it all the way. The knife fell to the ground. The dealer cried out in pain and dropped to one knee. No words had passed between the two men. There was no real need for words.

But then Rebus had realised that his opponent was not on his knees as a sign of defeat. He was scrabbling around for the knife and found it with his free hand. Rebus let go of the dead wrist and pinned the man's left arm to his body, but the arm was strong and the blade sheared through Rebus's trousers, cutting a red line up across his thigh. Rebus brought his knee up hard into his adversary's crotch and felt the body go limp. He repeated the action, but the dealer wasn't giving up. The knife was rising again. Rebus grabbed the wrist with one hand, the other going for the man's throat. Then he felt himself being spun and pushed hard up against the wall of the alley. The wall was damp, smelling of mould. He pressed a thumb deep into the dealer's larynx, still wrestling with the knife. His knee thudded into the man's groin again. And then, as the strength in the knife-arm eased momentarily, Rebus yanked the wrist and pushed.

Pushed hard, driving the dealer across the alley and against the other wall. Where the man gasped, gurgled, eyes bulging. Rebus stood back and released his grasp on the wrist, the wrist which held the knife, buried up to the hilt in the young man's stomach.

'Oh shit,' he whispered. 'Oh shit, oh shit, oh shit.'

The dealer was staring in surprise at the handle of the knife. His hand fell away from it, but the knife itself stayed put. He shuffled forward, walking past Rebus, who could only stand and watch, making for the entrance to the alleyway. The tip of the knife was protruding through the back of the dealer's jacket. He made it to the mouth of the alley before falling to his knees.

'Sir?'

'Mmm?' Rebus looked up and saw that Holmes was studying him from the window. 'What is it, Brian?'

'Are you okay?'

'I told you, I'm fine.' Rebus tipped the last of the wine down his throat and placed the glass on the floor, trying to control the trembling in his hand.

'It's just that ... well, I've never—'

'You've never killed anyone.'

'That's right,' Holmes came back to the sofa. 'I haven't.' He sat down, hands pressed between his knees, leaning slightly forwards as he spoke. 'What does it feel like?'

'Feel like?' Rebus smiled with half his mouth. 'It doesn't feel like anything. I don't even think about it. That's the best way.'

Holmes nodded slowly. Rebus was thinking: *get to the point.* And then Holmes came to the point.

'Did you mean to do it?' he asked.

Rebus had no hesitation. 'It was an accident. I didn't know it had happened until it did happen. We got into a clinch and somehow the knife ended up where it ended up. That's all. That's what I told them back at the station and that's what I'll tell any inquiry they shove at me. It was an accident.'

'Yes,' said Holmes quietly, nodding. 'That's what I thought.'

Accidents will happen, won't they?

Like burning the steak. Like finishing the bottle when you'd meant to have just a couple of glasses. Like punching a dent in the bathroom wall. Accidents happened and most of them happened in the home.

Holmes refused the offer of lunch and left. Rebus sat in the chair for a while, just listening to jazz, forgetting all about the steak. He only remembered it when he went to open another bottle of wine. The corkscrew had found its way back into the cutlery drawer, and he plucked out a knife by mistake. A small sharp-bladed knife with a wooden handle. He kept this knife for steaks especially.

It was good of Holmes to look in, no matter what the motive. And it was good of him not to stay, too. Rebus needed to be alone, needed time and space enough to think. He had told Holmes he never thought about it, never thought about death. That was a lie; he thought about it all the time. This weekend he was replaying Friday night, going over the scene time and time again in his head. Trying to answer the question Holmes himself had asked: was it an accident? But every time Rebus went through it, the answer became more and more vague. The hand was holding the knife, and then Rebus was angling that hand away from himself, propelling the hand and the body behind it backward into the wall of the alley. Angling the hand ... That was the vital moment. When he grabbed the wrist so that the knife was pointing towards the dealer, what had been going through his mind then? The thought that he was saving himself? Or that he was about to kill the dealer?

Rebus shook his head. It was no clearer now than it had been at the time. The media had chalked it up yesterday as self-defence and the internal inquiry would come to the same conclusion. Could he have disarmed the young man? Probably. Would the man have killed Rebus, given the chance? Certainly. Had he lived, would he have become Prime Minister, or fascist dictator, or Messiah? Would he have seen the error of his ways, or would he have gone on dispensing the only thing he had to sell? What about his parents, his family, his friends who had known him at school, who had known

him as a child: what would they be thinking now? Were the photograph albums and the paper hankies out? Pictures of the dealer
as a boy, dressed up as a cowboy on his birthday, pictures of him
splashing in the bath as a baby. Memories of someone John Rebus
had never known.

He shook his head again. Thinking about it would do no good,
but it was the only way to deal with it. And yes, he felt guilty. He
felt soiled and defeated and bad. But he would stop feeling bad, and
then eventually he would stop feeling anything at all. He had killed
before; it might be he would kill again. You never knew until the
moment itself.

And sometimes even then, you still didn't know, and would continue not to know. Holmes mentioned Mayfield. Rebus knew of a
church in Mayfield with an evening service on a Sunday. A church
with a restrained congregation and a minister not overly keen on
prying into one's affairs. Maybe he would go there later. Meantime,
he felt like a walk. He would walk through The Meadows and back
across Bruntsfield Links, with a diversion towards the ice-cream
shop near Tollcross. Maybe he'd bump into his friend Frank.

For this was Sunday, his day off, and he could do whatever he
liked, couldn't he? After all, Sunday was a day for breaking the
rules. It was the only day he could afford.

Auld Lang Syne

Places Detective Inspector John Rebus did not want to be at midnight on Hogmanay: number one, the Tron in Edinburgh.

Which was perhaps, Rebus decided, why he found himself at five minutes to midnight pushing his way through the crowds which thronged the area of the Royal Mile outside the Tron Kirk. It was a bitter night, a night filled with the fumes of beer and whisky, of foam licking into the sky as another can was opened, of badly sung songs and arms around necks and stooped, drunken proclamations of undying love, proclamations which would be forgotten by morning.

Rebus had been here before, of course. He had been here the previous Hogmanay, ready to root out the eventual troublemakers, to break up fights and crunch across the shattered glass covering the setts. The best and worst of the Scots came out as another New Year approached: the togetherness, the sharpness, the hugging of life, the inability to know when to stop, so that the hug became a smothering stranglehold. These people were drowning in a sea of sentiment and sham. *Flower of Scotland* was struck up by a lone voice for the thousandth time, and for the thousandth time a few more voices joined in, all falling away at the end of the first chorus.

'Gawn yirsel there, big man.'

Rebus looked around him. The usual contingent of uniformed officers was going through the annual ritual of having hands shaken by a public suddenly keen to make friends. It was the WPCs Rebus felt sorry for, as another slobbering kiss slapped into the cheek of a young female officer. The police of Edinburgh knew their duty: they always offered one sacrificial lamb to appease the multitude. There was actually an orderly queue standing in front of the WPC waiting to kiss her. She smiled and blushed. Rebus shivered and turned away. Four minutes to midnight. His nerves were like struck chords. He hated crowds. Hated drunken crowds more. Hated the fact that another year was coming to an end. He began to push through the crowd with a little more force than was necessary.

People Detective Inspector John Rebus would rather not be with at midnight on Hogmanay: number one, detectives from Glasgow CID.

He smiled and nodded towards one of them. The man was standing just inside a bus shelter, removed from the general scrum of the road itself. On top of the shelter, a Mohican in black leather did a tribal dance, a bottle of strong lager gripped in one hand. A police constable shouted for the youth to climb down from the shelter. The punk took no notice. The man in the bus shelter smiled back at John Rebus. He's not waiting for a bus, Rebus thought to himself, he's waiting for a bust.

Things Detective Inspector John Rebus would rather not be doing at midnight on Hogmanay: number one, working.

So he found himself working, and as the crowd swept him up again, he thought of Dante's *Inferno*. Three minutes to midnight. Three minutes away from hell. The Scots, pagan at their core, had always celebrated New Year rather than Christmas. Back when Rebus was a boy, Christmases were muted. New Year was the time for celebration, for first-footing, black bun, Madeira cake, coal wrapped in silver foil, stovies during the night and steak pie the following afternoon. Ritual after ritual. Now he found himself observing another ritual, another set of procedures. A meeting was about to take place. An exchange would be made: a bag filled with money for a parcel full of dope. A consignment of heroin had entered Scotland via a west coast fishing village. The CID in Glasgow had been tipped off, but failed to intercept the package. The trail had gone cold for several days, until an informant came up with the vital information. The dope was in Edinburgh. It was about to be handed on to an east coast dealer. The dealer was known to Edinburgh CID, but they'd never been able to pin a major possession charge on him. They wanted him badly. So did the west coast CID.

'It's to be a joint operation,' Rebus's boss had informed him, with no trace of irony on his humourless face. So now here he was, mingling with the crowds, just as another dozen or so undercover officers were doing. The men about to make the exchange did not trust one another. One of them had decided upon the Tron as a public enough place to make the deal. With so many people around, a double-cross was less likely to occur. The Tron at midnight on Hogmanay: a place of delirium and riot. No one would notice a discreet switch of cases, money for dope, dope for money. It was perfect.

Rebus, pushing against the crowd again, saw the money-man

for the very first time. He recognised him from photographs. Alan Lyons, 'Nal' to his friends. He was twenty-seven years old, drove a Porsche 911 and lived in a detached house on the riverside just outside Haddington. He had been one of Rab Philips's men until Philips's demise. Now he was out on his own. He listed his occupation as 'entrepreneur'. He was sewerage.

Lyons was resting his back against a shop window. He smoked a cigarette and gave the passers-by a look that said he was not in the mood for handshakes and conversation. A glance told Rebus that two of the Glasgow crew were keeping a close watch on Lyons, so he did not linger. His interest now was in the missing link, the man with the package. Where was he? A countdown was being chanted all around him. A few people reckoned the New Year was less than ten seconds away; others, checking their watches, said there was a minute left. By Rebus's own watch, they were already into the New Year by a good thirty seconds. Then, without warning, the clock chimes rang and a great cheer went up. People were shaking hands, hugging, kissing. Rebus could do nothing but join in.

'Happy New Year.'

'Happy New Year, pal.'

'Best of luck, eh?'

'Happy New Year.'

'All the best.'

'Happy New Year.'

Rebus shook a Masonic hand, and looked up into a face he recognised. He returned the compliment – 'Happy New Year' – and the man smiled and moved on, hand already outstretched to another well-wisher, another stranger. But this man had been no stranger to Rebus. Where the hell did he know him from? The crowd had rearranged itself, shielding the man from view. Rebus concentrated on the memory of the face. He had known it younger, less jowly, but with darker eyes. He could hear the voice: a thick Fife accent. The hands were like shovels, miner's hands. But this man was no miner.

He had his radio with him, but trapped as he was in the midst of noise there was no point trying to contact the others on the surveillance. He wanted to tell them something. He wanted to tell them he was going to follow the mystery man. Always supposing, that was, he could find him again in the crowd.

And then he remembered: Jackie Crawford. Dear God, it was Jackie Crawford!

People Rebus did not want to shake hands with as the old year became the new: number one, Jackie 'Trigger' Crawford.

Rebus had put Crawford behind bars four years ago for armed

robbery and wounding. The sentence imposed by the judge had been a generous stretch of ten years. Crawford had headed north from court in a well-guarded van. He had not gained the nickname 'Trigger' for his quiet and homely outlook on life. The man was a headcase of the first order, gun happy and trigger happy. He'd taken part in a series of bank and building society robberies; short, violent visits to High Streets across the Lowlands. That nobody had been killed owed more to strengthened glass and luck than to Crawford's philanthropy. He'd been sent away for ten, he was out after four. What was going on? Surely, the man could not be out and walking the streets *legally*? He had to have broken out, or at the very least cut loose from some day-release scheme. And wasn't it a coincidence that he should bump into Rebus, that he should be here in the Tron at a time when the police were waiting for some mysterious drug pedaller?

Rebus believed in coincidence, but this was stretching things a bit too far. Jackie Crawford was somewhere in this crowd, somewhere shaking hands with people whom, a scant four years before, he might have been terrorising with a sawn-off shotgun. Rebus had to do something, whether Crawford was the 'other man' or not. He began squeezing through the crowd again, this time ignoring proffered hands and greetings. He moved on his toes, craning his head over the heads of the revellers, seeking the square-jawed, wiry-haired head of his prey. He was trying to recall whether there was some tradition in Scotland that ghosts from your past came to haunt you at midnight on Hogmanay. He thought not. Besides, Crawford was no ghost. His hands had been meaty and warm, his thumb pressing speculatively against Rebus's knuckles. The eyes which had glanced momentarily into Rebus's eyes had been clear and blue, but uninterested.

Had Crawford recognised his old adversary? Rebus couldn't be sure. There had been no sign of recognition, no raising of eyebrows or opening of the mouth. Just three mumbled words before moving on to the next hand. Was Crawford drunk? Most probably: few sane and sober individuals visited the Tron on this night of all nights. Good: a drunken Crawford would have been unlikely to recognise him. Yet the voice had been quiet and unslurred, the eyes focussed. Crawford had not seemed drunk, had not acted drunk. Sober as a judge, in fact. This, too, worried Rebus.

But then, *everything* worried him this evening. He couldn't afford any slip-ups from the operation's Edinburgh contingent. It would give too much ammo to the Glasgow faction: there was a certain competitive spirit between the two forces. For 'competitive spirit' read 'loathing'. Each would want to claim any arrest as *its* victory; and each would blame any foul-up on the other.

This had been explained to him very clearly by Chief Inspector Lauderdale.

'But surely, sir,' Rebus had replied, 'catching these men is what's most important.'

'Rubbish, John,' Lauderdale had replied. 'What's important is that we don't look like arseholes in front of McLeish and his men.'

Which, of course, Rebus had already known: he just liked winding his superior up a little the better to watch him perform. Superintendent Michael McLeish was an outspoken and devout Catholic, and Rebus's chief did not like Catholics. But Rebus hated bigots, and so he wound up Lauderdale whenever he could and had a name for him behind his back: the Clockwork Orangeman.

The crowd was thinning out as Rebus headed away from the Tron and uphill towards the castle. He was, he knew, moving away from the surveillance and should inform his fellow officers of the fact, but if his hunch was right, he was also following the man behind the whole deal. Suddenly he caught sight of Crawford, who seemed to be moving purposefully out of the crowd, heading onto the pavement and giving a half-turn of his head, knowing he was being followed.

So he had recognised Rebus, and now had seen him hurrying after him. The policeman exhaled noisily and pushed his way through the outer ring of the celebrations. His arms ached, as though he had been swimming against a strong current, but now that he was safely out of the water, he saw that Crawford had vanished. He looked along the row of shops, separated each from the other by narrow, darkened closes. Up those closes were the entrances to flats, courtyards surrounded by university halls of residence, and many steep and worn steps leading from the High Street down to Cockburn Street. Rebus had to choose one of them. If he hesitated, or chose wrongly, Crawford would make good his escape. He ran to the first alley and, glancing down it, listening for footsteps, decided to move on. At the second close, he chose not to waste any more time and ran in, passing dimly-lit doorways festooned with graffiti, dank walls and frozen cobbles. Until, launching himself down a flight of steps into almost absolute darkness, he stumbled. He flailed for a hand-rail to stop him from falling, and found his arm grabbed by a powerful hand, saving him.

Crawford was standing against the side of the alley, on a platform between flights of steps. Rebus sucked in air, trying to calm himself. There was a sound in his ears like the aftermath of an explosion.

'Thanks,' he spluttered.

'You were following me.' The voice was effortlessly calm.

'Was I?' It was a lame retort and Crawford knew it. He chuckled. 'Yes, Mr Rebus, you were. You must have gotten a bit of a shock.'

Rebus nodded. 'A bit, yes, after all these years, Jackie.'

'I'm surprised you recognised me. People tell me I've changed.'

'Not that much.' Rebus glanced down at his arm, which was still in Crawford's vice-like grip. The grip relaxed and fell away. 'Sorry.'

Rebus was surprised at the apology, but tried not to let it show. He was busy covertly studying Crawford's body, looking for any bulge big enough to be a package or a gun.

'So what were you doing back there?' he asked, not particularly interested in the answer, but certainly interested in the time it might buy him.

Crawford seemed amused. 'Bringing in the New Year, of course. What else would I be doing?'

It was a fair question, but Rebus chose not to answer it. 'When did you get out?'

'A month back.' Crawford could sense Rebus's suspicion. 'It's legit. Honest to God, Sergeant, as He is my witness. I haven't done a runner or anything.'

'You ran from *me*. And it's Inspector now, by the way.'

Crawford smiled again. 'Congratulations.'

'Why did you run?'

'Was I running?'

'You know you were.'

'The reason I was running was because the last person I wanted to see tonight of all nights was you, Inspector Rebus. You spoilt it for me.'

Rebus frowned. He was *looking* at Trigger Crawford, but felt he was talking to somebody else, someone calmer and less dangerous, someone, well, *ordinary*. He was confused, but still suspicious. 'Spoilt what exactly?'

'My New Year resolution. I came here to make peace with the world.'

It was Rebus's turn to smile, though not kindly. 'Make peace, eh?'

'That's right.'

'No more guns? No more armed robberies?'

Crawford was shaking his head slowly. Then he held open his coat. 'No more shooters, Inspector. That's a promise. You see, I've made my own peace.'

Peace or piece? Rebus couldn't be sure. He was reaching into his own jacket pocket, from which he produced a police radio. Crawford looked on the level. He even sounded on the level, but facts had to be verified. So he called in and asked for a check to be made on John Crawford, nickname 'Trigger'. Crawford smiled shyly at the mention of that name. Rebus held onto the radio, waiting for the computer to do its stuff, waiting for the station to respond.

'It's been a long time since anyone called me Trigger,' Crawford said. 'Quite some time.'

'How come they released you after four?'

'A bit less than four, actually,' corrected Crawford. 'They released me because I was no longer a threat to society. You'll find that hard to believe. In fact, you'll find it *impossible* to believe. That's not my fault, it's yours. You think men like me can never go straight. But we can. You see, something happened to me in prison. I found Jesus Christ.'

Rebus knew the look on his face was a picture, and it caused Crawford to smile again, still shyly. He looked down at the tips of his shoes.

'That's right, Inspector. I became a Christian. It wasn't any kind of blinding light. It took a while. I got bored inside and I started reading books. One day I picked up the Bible and just opened it at random. What I read there seemed to make sense. It was the Good News Bible, written in plain English. I read bits and pieces, just flicked through it. Then I went to one of the Sunday services, mainly because there were a few things I couldn't understand and I wanted to ask the minister about them. And he helped me a bit. That's how it started. It changed my life.'

Rebus could think of nothing to say. He thought of himself as a Christian, too, a sceptical Christian, a little like Crawford himself perhaps. Full of questions that needed answering. No, this couldn't be right. He was *nothing* like Crawford. Nothing at all like him. Crawford was an animal; his kind never changed. Did they? Just because he had never met a 'changed man', did that mean such a thing did not exist? After all, he'd never met the Queen or the Prime Minister either. The radio crackled to life in his hand.

'Rebus here,' he said, and then listened.

It was all true. The details from Crawford's file were being read to him. Model prisoner. Bible class. Recommended for early release. Personal tragedy.

'Personal tragedy?' Rebus looked at Crawford.

'Ach, my son died. He was only in his twenties.'

Rebus, having heard enough, had already switched off the radio. 'I'm sorry,' he said. Crawford just shrugged, shrugged shoulders beneath which were tucked no hidden shotguns, and slipped his hands into his pockets, pockets where no pistols lurked. But Rebus held out a hand towards him.

'Happy New Year,' he said.

Crawford stared at the hand, then brought out his own right hand. The two men shook warmly, their grips firm.

'Happy New Year,' said Crawford. Then he glanced back up the close. 'Look, Inspector, if it's all right with you I think I'll go back up the Tron. It was daft of me to run away in the first place. There are plenty of hands up there I've not shaken yet.'

Rebus nodded slowly. He understood now. For Crawford, the New Year was something special, a new start in more ways than one. Not everyone was given that chance.

'Aye,' he said. 'On you go.'

Crawford had climbed three steps before he paused. 'Incidentally,' he called, 'what were *you* doing at the Tron?'

'What else would I be doing there on New Year?' replied Rebus. 'I was working.'

'No rest for the wicked, eh?' said Crawford, climbing the slope back up to the High Street.

Rebus watched until Crawford disappeared into the gloom. He knew he should follow him. After all, he *was* still working. He was sure now that Crawford had been speaking the truth, that he had nothing to do with the drug deal. Their meeting had been coincidence, nothing more. But who would have believed it? Trigger Crawford a 'model prisoner'. And they said mankind no longer lived in an age of miracles.

Rebus climbed slowly. There seemed more people than ever on the High Street. He guessed things would be at their busiest around half past midnight, with the streets emptying quickly after that. If the deal was going to go through, it would take place before that time. He recognised one of the Glasgow detectives heading towards him. As he spotted Rebus, the detective half-raised his arms.

'Where have you been? We thought you'd buggered off home.'

'Nothing happening then?'

The detective sighed. 'No, nothing at all. Lyons looks a bit impatient. I don't think he's going to give it much longer himself.'

'I thought your informant was air-tight?'

'As a rule. Maybe this will be the exception.' The detective smiled, seemingly used to such disappointments in his life. Rebus had noticed earlier that the young man possessed badly chewed fingernails and even the skin around the nails was torn and raw-looking. A stressed young man. In a few years he would be overweight and then would become heart attack material. Rebus knew that he himself was heart attack material: h.a.m., they called it back at the station. You were lean (meaning fit) or you were ham. Rebus was decidedly the latter.

'So anyway, where were you?'

'I bumped into an old friend. Well, to be precise an old adversary. Jackie Crawford.'

'Jackie Crawford? You mean Trigger Crawford?' The young detective was rifling through his memory files. 'Oh yes, I heard he was out.'

'Did you? Nobody bothered to tell me.'

'Yes, something about his son dying. Drug overdose. All the fire went out of Crawford after that. Turned into a Bible basher.'

They were walking back towards the crowd. Back towards where Alan Lyons waited for a suitcase full of heroin. Rebus stopped dead in his tracks.

'Drugs? Did you say his son died from drugs?'

The detective nodded. 'The big H. It wasn't too far from my patch. Somewhere in Partick.'

'Did Crawford's son live in Glasgow then?'

'No, he was just visiting. He stayed here in Edinburgh.' The detective was not as slow as some. He knew what Rebus was thinking. 'Christ, you don't mean ...?'

And then they were both running, pushing their way through the crowd, and the detective from Glasgow was shouting into his radio, but there was noise all around him, yelling and cheering and singing, smothering his words. Their progress was becoming slower. It was like moving through water chest-high. Rebus's legs felt useless and sore and there was a line of sweat trickling down his spine. Crawford's son had died from heroin, heroin purchased most probably in Edinburgh, and the man behind most of the heroin deals in Edinburgh was waiting somewhere up ahead. Coincidence? He had never really believed in coincidences, not really. They were convenient excuses for shrugging off the unthinkable.

What had Crawford said? Something about coming here tonight to make peace. Well, there were ways and ways of making peace, weren't there? 'If any mischief should follow, then thou shalt give life for life.' That was from Exodus. A dangerous book, the Bible. It could be made to say anything, its meaning in the mind of the beholder.

What was going through Jackie Crawford's mind? Rebus dreaded to think. There was a commotion up ahead, the crowd forming itself into a tight semi-circle around a shop-front. Rebus squeezed his way to the front.

'Police,' he shouted. 'Let me through, please.'

Grudgingly, the mass of bodies parted just enough for him to make progress. Finally he found himself at the front, staring at the slumped body of Alan Lyons. A long smear ran down the shop window to where he lay and his chest was stained dark red. One of the Glasgow officers was trying unsuccessfully to stem the flow of blood, using his own rolled-up coat, now sopping wet. Other officers were keeping back the crowd. Rebus caught snatches of what they were saying.

'Looked like he was going to shake hands.'

'Looked like he was hugging him.'

'Then the knife ...'

'Pulled out a knife.'

'Stabbed him twice before we could do anything.'

'Couldn't do anything.'

A siren had started nearby, inching closer. There were always ambulances on standby near the Tron on Hogmanay. Beside Lyons, still gripped in his left hand, was the bag containing the money for the deal.

'Will he be all right?' Rebus said to nobody in particular, which was just as well since nobody answered. He was remembering back a month to another dealer, another knife ... Then he saw Crawford. He was being restrained on the edge of the crowd by two more plainclothes men. One held his arms behind him while the other frisked him for weapons. On the pavement between where Crawford stood and Alan Lyons lay dying or dead there was a fairly ordinary looking knife, small enough to conceal in a sock or a waistband, but enough for the job required. More than an inch of blade was excess. The other detective was beside Rebus.

'Aw, Christ,' he said. But Rebus was staring at Crawford and Crawford was staring back, and in that moment they understood one another well enough. 'I don't suppose,' the detective was saying, 'we'll be seeing the party with the merchandise. Always supposing he was going to turn up in any event.'

'I'm not so sure about that,' answered Rebus, turning his gaze from Crawford. 'Ask yourself this: how did Crawford know Lyons would be in the High Street tonight?' The detective did not answer. Behind them, the crowd was pressing closer for a look at the body and then making noises of revulsion before opening another can of lager or half-bottle of vodka. The ambulance was still a good fifty yards away. Rebus nodded towards Crawford.

'He knows where the stuff is, but he's probably dumped it some-where. Somewhere nobody can ever touch it. It was just bait, that's all. Just bait.'

And as bait it had worked. Hook, line and bloody sinker. Lyons had swallowed it, while Rebus, equally fooled, had swallowed something else. He felt it sticking in his throat like something cancerous, something no amount of coughing would dislodge. He glanced towards the prone body again and smiled involuntarily. A headline had come to mind, one that would never be used.

LYONS FED TO THE CHRISTIAN.

Someone was being noisily sick somewhere behind him. A bottle shattered against a wall. The loudest voices in the crowd were growing irritable and hard-edged. In fifteen minutes or so, they would cease to be revellers and would be transformed into troublemakers. A woman shrieked from one of the many darkened closes. The look on Jackie Crawford's face was one of calm and righteous triumph. He offered no resistance to the officers. He had known they were watching Lyons, had known he might kill Lyons but he would never get away. And still he had driven home the knife. What else was he to do with his freedom?'

The night was young and so was the year. Rebus held out his hand towards the detective.

'Happy New Year,' he said. 'And many more of them.'

The young man stared at him blankly. 'Don't think you're blaming us for this,' he said. 'This was your fault. You let Crawford go. It's Edinburgh's balls-up, not ours.'

Rebus shrugged and let his arm fall to his side. Then he started to walk along the pavement, moving further and further from the scene. The ambulance moved past him. Someone slapped him on the back and offered a hand. From a distance, the young detective was watching him retreat.

'Away to hell,' said Rebus quietly, not sure for whom the message was intended.

The Gentlemen's Club

It was the most elegant of all Edinburgh's elegant Georgian circuses, a perfect circle in design and construction, the houses themselves as yet untouched by the private contractors who might one day renovate and remove, producing a dozen tiny flats from each.

A perfect circle surrounding some private gardens, the gardens a wash of colour despite the January chill: violet, pink, red, green and orange. A tasteful display, though. No flower was allowed to be too vibrant, too bright, too inelegant.

The gate to the gardens was locked, of course. The keyholders paid a substantial fee each year for the privilege of that lock. Everyone else could look, could peer through the railings as he was doing now, but entrance was forbidden. Well, that was Edinburgh for you, a closed circle within a closed circle.

He stood there, enjoying the subtle smells in the air now that the flurry of snowflakes had stopped. Then he shifted his attention to the houses, huge three- and four-storey statements of the architect's confidence. He found himself staring at one particular house, the one outside which the white police Sierra was parked. It was too ripe a day to be spoiled, but duty was duty. Taking a final deep breath, he turned from the garden railings and walked towards number 16, with its heavy closed curtains but its front door ajar.

Once inside, having introduced himself, John Rebus had to climb three large flights of stairs to 'the children's floor', as his guide termed it. She was slender and middle-aged and dressed from head to toe in grey. The house was quiet, only one or two shafts of sunlight penetrating its gloom. The woman walked near-silently and quickly, while Rebus tugged on the bannister, breathing hard.

It wasn't that he was unfit, but somehow all the oxygen seemed to have been pumped out of the house.

Arriving at last at the third floor, the woman passed three firmly closed doors before stopping at a fourth. This one was open, and inside Rebus could make out the gleaming tiles of a large bathroom and the shuffling, insect-like figures of Detective Constable Brian Holmes and the police pathologist, not the lugubrious Dr Curt but the one everybody called – though not to his face, never to his face – Dr Crippen. He turned to his guide.

'Thank you, Mrs McKenzie.' But she had already averted her eyes and was making back for the safety of the stairs. She was a brave one though, to bring him all the way up here in the first place. And now there was nothing for it but to enter the room. 'Hello, Doctor.'

'Inspector Rebus, good morning. Not a pretty sight, is it?'

Rebus forced himself to look. There was not much water in the bath, and what water there was had been dyed a rich ruby colour by the girl's blood. She was undressed and as white as a statue. She had been very young, sixteen or seventeen, her body not yet quite fully formed. A late developer.

Her arms lay peacefully by her sides, wrists turned upwards to reveal the clean incisions. Holmes used a pair of tweezers to hold up a single razor blade for Rebus's inspection. Rebus winced and shook his head.

'What a waste,' he said. He had a daughter himself, not much older than this girl. His wife had taken their daughter with her when she left him. Years ago now. He'd lost touch, the way you do sometimes with family, though you keep in contact with friends.

He was moving around the bath, committing the scene to memory. The air seemed to glow, but the glow was already fading.

'Yes,' said Holmes. 'It's a sin.'

'Suicide, of course,' Rebus commented after a silence. The pathologist nodded, but did not speak. They were not usually so awkward around a corpse, these three men. Each thought he had seen the worst, the most brutal, the most callous. Each had anecdotes to relate which would make strangers shudder and screw shut their eyes. But this, this was different. Something had been taken quietly, deliberately and ruinously from the world.

'The question,' Rebus said, for the sake of filling the void, 'is why.'

Why indeed. Here he was, standing in a bathroom bigger than his own living-room, surrounded by powders and scents, thick towels, soaps and sponges. But here was this gruesome and unnecessary death. There had to be a reason for it. Silly, stupid child. What had she been playing at? Mute anger turned to frustration, and he almost staggered as he made his way out to the landing.

There had to be a reason. And he was just in the mood now to track it down.

*

'I've told you already,' said Thomas McKenzie irritably, 'she was the happiest girl in Christendom. No, we didn't spoil her, and no, we never forbade her seeing anyone. There is no reason in the world, Inspector, why Suzanne should have done what she did. It just doesn't make sense.'

McKenzie broke down again, burying his face in his hands. Rebus loathed himself, yet the questions had to be asked.

'Did she,' he began, 'did she have a boyfriend, Mr McKenzie?'

McKenzie got up from his chair, walked to the sideboard and poured himself another whisky. He motioned to Rebus who, still cradling a crystal inch of the stuff, shook his head. Mrs McKenzie was upstairs resting. She had been given a sedative by her doctor, an old friend of the family who had seemed in need of similar treatment himself.

But Thomas McKenzie had not needed anything. He was sticking to the old remedies, sloshing a fresh measure of malt into his glass.

'No,' he said, 'no boyfriends. They've never really been Suzanne's style.'

Though he would not be travelling to his office today, McKenzie had still dressed himself in a dark blue suit and tie. The drawing-room in which Rebus sat had about it the air of a commercial office, not at all homely or lived-in. He couldn't imagine growing up in such a place.

'What about school?' he asked.

'What do you mean?'

'I mean, was she happy there?'

'Very.' McKenzie sat down with his drink. 'She gets good reports, good grades. She ... she *was* going to the University in October.'

Rebus watched him gulp at the whisky. Thomas McKenzie was a tough man, tough enough to make his million young and then canny enough not to lose it. He was forty-four now, but looked younger. Rebus had no idea how many shops McKenzie now owned, how many company directorships he held along with all his other holdings and interests. He was new money trying to look like old money, making his home in Stockbridge, convenient for Princes Street, rather than further out in bungalow land.

'What was she going to study?' Rebus stared past McKenzie towards where a family portrait sat on a long, polished sideboard. No family snapshot, but posed, a sitting for a professional photographer. Daughter gleaming in the centre, sandwiched by grinning parents. A mock-up cloudscape behind them, the clouds pearl-coloured, the sky blue.

'Law,' said McKenzie. 'She had a head on her shoulders.'

Yes, a head of mousy-brown hair. And her father had found her early in the morning, already cold. McKenzie hadn't panicked. He'd made the phone calls before waking his wife and telling her. He always rose first, always went straight to the bathroom. He had remained calm, most probably from shock. But there was a stiffness to McKenzie, too, Rebus noticed. He wondered what it would take really to rouse the man.

Something niggled. Suzanne had gone to the bathroom, run some water into the bath, lain down in it, and slashed her wrists. Fine, Rebus could accept that. Maybe she had expected to be found and rescued. Most failed suicides were cries for help, weren't they? If you *really* wanted to kill yourself, you went somewhere quiet and secret, where you couldn't possibly be found in time. Suzanne hadn't done that. She had almost certainly expected her father to find her in time. Her timing had been a little awry.

Moreover, she must have known her father always rose before her mother, and therefore that he would be the first to find her. This notion interested Rebus, though no one around him seemed curious about it.

'What about friends at school,' Rebus went on. 'Did Suzanne have many friends?'

'Oh yes, lots.'

'Anyone in particular?'

McKenzie was about to answer when the door opened and his wife walked in, pale from her drugged sleep.

'What time is it?' she asked, shuffling forwards.

'It's eleven, Shona,' her husband said, rising to meet her. 'You've only been asleep half an hour.' They embraced one another, her arms tight around his body. Rebus felt like an intruder on their grief, but the questions still had to be asked.

'You were about to tell me about Suzanne's friends, Mr McKenzie.'

Husband and wife sat down together on the sofa, hands clasped.

'Well,' said McKenzie, 'there were lots of them, weren't there, Shona?'

'Yes,' said his wife. She really was an attractive woman. Her face had the same smooth sheen as her daughter's. She was the sort of woman men would instinctively feel protective towards, whether protection was needed or not. 'But I always liked Hazel best,' she went on.

McKenzie turned to Rebus and explained. 'Hazel Frazer, daughter of Sir Jimmy Frazer, the banker. A peach of a girl. A real peach.' He paused, staring at his wife, and then began, softly, with dignity, to cry. She rested his head against her shoulder and stroked his hair, talking softly to him. Rebus averted his eyes and drank his whisky. Then bit his bottom lip, deep in thought. In matters of suicide, just who was the victim, who the culprit?

Suzanne's room was a cold and comfortless affair. No posters on the walls, no teenage clutter or signs of an independent mind. There was a writing-pad on the dressing table, but it was blank. A crumpled ball of paper sat in the bottom of an otherwise empty bin beside the wardrobe. Rebus carefully unfolded the sheet. Written on it, in a fairly steady hand, was a message: 'Told you I would.'

Rebus studied the sentence. Told whom? Her parents seemed to have no inkling their daughter was suicidal, yet the note had been meant for someone. And having written it, why had she discarded it? He turned it over. The other side, though blank was slightly tacky. Rebus sniffed the paper, but could find no smell to identify the stickiness. He carefully folded the paper and slipped it into his pocket.

In the top drawer of the dressing-table was a leather-bound diary. But Suzanne had been no diarist. Instead of the expected teenage outpourings, Rebus found only one-line reminders, every Tuesday for the past six months or so, 'The Gentlemen's Club – 4.00'. Curiouser and curiouser. The last entry was for the previous week, with nothing in the rest of the diary save blank pages.

The Gentlemen's Club – what on earth could she have meant? Rebus knew of several clubs in Edinburgh, dowdy remnants of a former age, but none was called simply The Gentlemen's Club. The diary went into his pocket along with the note.

Thomas McKenzie saw him to the door. The tie around his neck was hanging loosely now and his voice was sweet with whisky.

'Just two last questions before I go,' Rebus said.

'Yes?' said McKenzie, sighing.

'Do you belong to a club?'

McKenzie seemed taken aback, but shrugged. 'Several, actually. The Strathspey Health Club. The Forth Golf Club. And Finlay's as was.'

'Finlay's Gentlemen's Club?'

'Yes, that's right. But it's called Thomson's now.'

Rebus nodded. 'Final question,' he said. 'What did Suzanne do on Tuesdays at four?'

'Nothing special. I think she had some drama group at school.'

'Thank you, Mr McKenzie. Sorry to have troubled you. Goodbye.'

'Goodbye, Inspector.'

Rebus stood on the top step, breathing in lungfuls of fresh air. Too much of a good thing could be stifling. He wondered if Suzanne McKenzie had felt stifled. He still wondered why she had died. And, knowing her father would be the first to find her, why had she lain down *naked* in the bath? Rebus had seen suicides before – lots of them – but whether they chose the bathroom or the bedroom, they were always clothed.

'Naked I came,' he thought to himself, remembering the passage from the Book of Job, 'and naked shall return.'

On his way to Hawthornden School for Girls, Rebus received a message from Detective Constable Holmes, who had returned to the station.

'Go ahead,' said Rebus. The radio crackled. The sky overhead was the colour of a bruise, the static in the air playing havoc with the radio's reception.

'I've just run McKenzie's name through the computer,' said Holmes, 'and come up with something you might be interested in.'

Rebus smiled. Holmes was as thorough as any airport sniffer dog. 'Well?' he said. 'Are you going to tell me, or do I have to buy the paperback?'

There was a hurt pause before Holmes began to speak and Rebus remembered how sensitive to criticism the younger man could be. 'It seems,' Holmes said at last, 'that Mr McKenzie was arrested several months back for loitering outside a school.'

'Oh? Which school?'

'Murrayfield Comprehensive. He wasn't charged, but it's on record that he was taken to Murrayfield police station and questioned.'

'That *is* interesting. I'll talk to you later.' Rebus terminated the call. The rain had started to fall in heavy drops. He picked up the radio again and asked to be put through to Murrayfield police station. His luck was in. A colleague there remembered the whole incident.

'We kept it quiet, of course,' the Inspector told Rebus. 'And McKenzie swore he'd just stopped there to call into his office. But the teachers at the school were adamant he'd parked there before, during the lunch-break. It's not the most refined area of town after all, is it? A Daimler does tend to stand out from the crowd around there, especially when there isn't a bride in the back of it.'

'I take your point,' said Rebus, smiling. 'Anything else?'

'Yes, one of the kids told a teacher he'd seen someone get into McKenzie's Daimler once, but we couldn't find any evidence of that.'

'Vivid imaginations, these kids,' Rebus agreed. This was all his colleague could tell him, but it was enough to muddy the water. Had Suzanne discovered her father's secret and, ashamed, killed herself? Or perhaps her schoolfriends had found out and teased her about it? If McKenzie liked kids, there might even be a tang of incest about the whole thing. That would at least go some way towards explaining Suzanne's nudity: she wasn't putting on show anything her father hadn't seen before. But what about The Gentlemen's Club? Where did it fit in? At Hawthornden School, Rebus hoped he might find some answers.

It was the sort of school fathers sent their daughters to so that they might learn the arts of femininity and ruthlessness. The headmistress, as imposing a character as the school building itself, fed Rebus on cakes and tea before leading him to Suzanne's form mistress, a Miss Selkirk, who had prepared more tea for him in her little private room.

Yes, she told him, Suzanne had been a very popular girl and news of her death came as quite a shock. She had run around with Hazel Frazer, the banker's daughter. A very vivacious girl, Hazel, head of school this year, though Suzanne hadn't been far behind in the running. A competitive pair, their marks for maths, English, languages almost identical. Suzanne the better at sciences; Hazel the better at economics and accounts. Splendid girls, the pair of them.

Biting into his fourth or fifth cake, Rebus nodded again. These women were all so commanding that he had begun to feel like a schoolboy himself. He sat with knees primly together, smiling, asking his questions almost apologetically.

'I don't suppose,' he said, 'the name The Gentlemen's Club means anything to you?'

Miss Selkirk thought hard. 'Is it,' she said at last, 'the name of a discotheque?'

Rebus smiled. 'I don't think so. Why do you ask?'

'Well, it's just that I do seem to recall having heard it before from one of the girls, quite recently, but only in passing.'

Rebus looked disappointed.

'I am sorry, Inspector.' She tapped her skull. 'This old head of mine isn't what it used to be.'

'That's quite all right,' said Rebus quietly. 'One last thing, do you happen to know who takes the school's drama classes?'

'Ah,' said Miss Selkirk, 'that's young Miss Phillips, the English teacher.'

Miss Phillips, who insisted that Rebus call her Jilly, was not only young but also very attractive. Waves of long auburn hair fell over her shoulders and down her back. Her eyes were dark and moist with recently shed tears. Rebus felt more awkward than ever.

'I believe,' he said, 'that you run the school's drama group.'

'That's right.' Her voice was fragile as porcelain.

'And Suzanne was in the group?'

'Yes. She was due to play Celia in our production of *As You Like It*.'

'Oh?'

'That's Shakespeare, you know.'

'Yes,' said Rebus, 'I do know.'

They were talking in the corridor, just outside her classroom, and through the panes of glass in the door, Rebus could see a class of fairly mature girls, healthy and from well-ordered homes, whispering together and giggling. Odd that, considering they'd just lost a friend.

'Celia,' he said, 'is Duke Frederick's daughter, isn't she?'

'I'm impressed, Inspector.'

'It's not my favourite Shakespeare play,' Rebus explained, 'but I remember seeing it at the Festival a few years back. Celia has a friend, doesn't she?'

'That's right, Rosalind.'

'So who was going to play Rosalind?'

'Hazel Frazer.'

Rebus nodded slowly at this. It made sense. 'Is Hazel in your classroom at the moment?'

'Yes, she's the one with the long black hair. Do you see her?'

Oh yes, Rebus could see her. She sat, calm and imperturbable, at the still centre of a sea of admirers. The other girls giggled and whispered around her, hoping to catch her attention or a few words of praise, while she sat oblivious to it all.

'Yes,' he said, 'I see her.'

'Would you care to speak with her, Inspector?'

He knew Hazel was aware of him, even though she averted her eyes from the door. Indeed, he knew precisely *because* she refused to look, while the other girls glanced towards the corridor from time to time, interested in this interruption to their classwork. Interested and curious. Hazel pretended to be neither, which in itself interested Rebus.

'No,' he said to Jilly Phillips, 'not just now. She's probably upset, and it wouldn't do much good for me to go asking her questions under the circumstances. There was one thing, though.'

'Yes, Inspector?'

'This after-school drama group of yours, the one that meets on Tuesdays, it doesn't happen to have a nickname, does it?'

'Not that I know of.' Jilly Phillips furrowed her brow. 'But, Inspector?'

'Yes?'

'You're under some kind of misapprehension. The drama group meets on Fridays, not Tuesdays. And we meet before lunch.'

Rebus drove out of the school grounds and parked by the side of the busy main road. The drama group met during school hours, so what had Suzanne done on Tuesdays after school, while her parents thought she was there? At least, McKenzie had said he'd thought that's what she'd done on Tuesdays. Suppose he'd been lying? Then what?

A maroon-coloured bus roared past Rebus's car. A 135, on its way to Princes Street. He started up the car again and followed it along its route, all the time thinking through the details of Suzanne's suicide. Until suddenly, with blinding clarity, he saw the truth of the thing, and bit his bottom lip fiercely, wondering just what on earth he could – should – do about it.

Well, the longer he thought about doing something, the harder it would become to do it. So he called Holmes and asked him for a large favour, before driving over to the house owned by Sir Jimmy Frazer.

Frazer was not just part of the Edinburgh establishment – in many ways he *was* that establishment. Born and educated in the city, he had won hard-earned respect, friendship and awe on his way to the top. The nineteenth-century walled house in which his family made its home was part of his story. It had been about to be bought by a company, an English company, and knocked down to make way for a new apartment block. There were public protests about this act of vandalism and in had stepped Sir Jimmy Frazer, purchasing the house and making it his own.

That had been years ago, but it was a story still heard told by hard men to other hard men in watering holes throughout the city. Rebus examined the house as he drove in through the open gates. It was an ugly near-Gothic invention, mock turrets and spires, hard, cold and uninviting. A maid answered the door. Rebus introduced himself and was ushered into a large drawing-room, where Sir Jimmy's wife, tall and dark haired like her daughter, waited.

'I'm sorry to trouble you, Lady—' Rebus was cut short by an imperious hand, but an open smile.

'Just Deborah, please.' And she motioned for Rebus to sit.

'Thank you,' he said. 'I'm sorry to trouble you, but—'

'Yes, your call *was* intriguing, Inspector. Of course, I'll do what I can. It's a tragedy, poor Suzanne.'

'You knew her then?'

'Of course. Why ever shouldn't we know her? She visited practically every Tuesday.'

'Oh?' Rebus had suspected as much, but was keen to learn more.

'After school,' Lady Deborah continued. 'Hazel and Suzanne and a few other chums would come back here. They didn't stay late.'

'But what exactly did they do?'

She laughed. 'I've no idea. What do girls of that age do? Play records? Talk about boys? Try to defer growing up?' She gave a wry smile, perhaps thinking of her own past. Rebus checked his wristwatch casually. Five to four. He had a few minutes yet.

'Did they,' he asked, 'confine themselves to your daughter's room?'

'More or less. Not her bedroom, of course. There's an old playroom upstairs. Hazel uses that as a kind of den.'

Rebus nodded. 'May I see it?'

Lady Deborah seemed puzzled. 'I suppose so, though I can't see—'

'It would help,' Rebus interrupted, 'to give me an overall picture of Suzanne. I'm trying to work out the kind of girl she was.'

'Of course,' said Lady Deborah, though she sounded unconvinced.

Rebus was shown to a small, cluttered room at the end of a long corridor. Inside, the curtains were closed. Lady Deborah switched on the lights.

'Hazel won't allow the maid in here,' Lady Deborah explained, apologising for the untidiness. '*Secrets*, I suppose,' she whispered.

Rebus did not doubt it. There were two small sofas, piles of pop and teenage magazines scattered on the floor, an ashtray full of dog-ends (which Lady Deborah pointedly chose to ignore), a stereo against one wall and a desk against another, on which sat a personal computer, its screen switched on but blank.

'She always forgets to turn that thing off,' said Lady Deborah. Rebus could hear the telephone ringing downstairs. The maid answered it and then called up to Lady Deborah.

'Oh dear. Please excuse me, Inspector.'

Rebus smiled and bowed slightly as she left. His watch said four o'clock. As prearranged, it would be Holmes on the phone. Rebus had told him to pretend to be anybody, to say *any*thing, so long as he kept Lady Deborah occupied for five minutes. Holmes had suggested he be a journalist seeking some quotes for a magazine feature. Rebus smiled now. Yes, there was probably vanity enough in Lady Deborah to keep her talking with a reporter for at least five minutes, maybe more.

Still, he couldn't waste time. He had expected to have to do a lot of searching, but the computer seemed the obvious place to start. There were floppy discs stored in a plastic box beside the monitor. He flipped through them until he came to one labelled GC DISC. There could be no doubt. He slipped the disc into the computer and watched as the display came up. He had found the records of The Gentlemen's Club.

He read quickly. Not that there was much to read. Members must attend every week, at four o'clock on Tuesday. Members must wear a tie. (Rebus looked quickly in a drawer of the desk and found five ties. He recognised them as belonging to various clubs in the city: the Strathspey, the Forth Golf Club, Finlay's Club. Stolen from the girls' fathers of course, and worn to meetings of a secret little clique, itself a parody of the clubs their fathers frequented.)

In a file named 'Exploits of the Gentlemen's Club', Rebus found lists of petty thefts, acts of so-called daring, and lies. Members had stolen from city centre shops, had carried out practical jokes against teachers and pupils alike, had been, in short, malicious.

There were many exploits attributed to Suzanne, including lying to her parents about what she did on Tuesday after school. Twenty-eight exploits in all. Hazel Frazer's list totalled thirty at the bottom, yet Rebus could count only twenty-nine entries on the screen. And in a separate file, the agenda for a meeting yet to be held, was a single item, recorded as 'New Business: can suicide be termed an exploit of the Gentlemen's Club?'

Rebus heard steps behind him. He turned, but it was not Lady Deborah. It was Hazel Frazer. Her eyes looked past him to the screen, firstly in fear and disbelief, then in scorn.

'Hello, Hazel.'

'You're the policeman,' she said in a level tone. 'I saw you at the school.'

'That's right.' Rebus studied her as she came into the room. She was a cool one, all right. That was Hawthornden for you, breeding strong, cold women, each one her father's daughter. 'Are you jealous of her?'

'Of whom? Suzanne?' Hazel smiled cruelly. 'Why should I be?'

'Because,' answered Rebus, 'Suzanne's is the ultimate exploit. For once, she beat you.'

'You think that's why she did it?' Hazel sounded smug. When Rebus shook his head, a little of her confidence seeped away.

'I know why she did it, Hazel. She did it because she found out about you and her father. She found out because you told her. I notice it's too much of a secret for you to put on your computer, but you've added it to the list, haven't you? As an exploit. I expect you were having an argument, bragging, being competitive. And it just slipped out. You told Suzanne you were her father's lover.'

Her cheeks were becoming a deep strawberry red, while her lips drained of colour. But she wasn't about to speak, so Rebus went on at her.

'You met him at lunchtime. You couldn't meet near Hawthornden. That would be too risky. So you'd take a bus to Murrayfield. It's only ten minutes ride away. He'd be waiting in his car. You told Suzanne and she couldn't bear to know. So she killed herself.' Rebus was becoming angry. 'And all you can be bothered to do is write about her on your files and wonder whether suicide is an "exploit".' His voice had risen and he hardly registered the fact that Lady Deborah was standing in the doorway, looking on in disbelief.

'No!' yelled Hazel. 'She did it first! She slept with Daddy months ago! So I did it back to her. *That's* what she couldn't live with! That's why she—'

Then it happened. Hazel's shoulders fell forward and, eyes closed, she began to cry, silently at first, but then loudly. Her mother ran to comfort her and told Rebus to leave. Couldn't he see what the girl was going through? He'd pay, she told him. He'd pay for upsetting her daughter. But she was crying too, crying like Hazel, mother and child. Rebus could think of nothing to say, so he left.

Descending the stairs, he tried not to think about what he had just unleashed. Two families broken now instead of one, and to what end? Merely to prove, as he had always known anyway, that a pretty face was no mirror of the soul and that the spirit of competition still flourished in Scotland's well-respected education system. He dug his hands deep into his jacket pockets, felt something there and drew out Suzanne's note. The crumpled note, found discarded in her bin, sticky on one side. He stopped halfway down the stairs, staring at the note without really seeing it. He was visualising something else, something almost too horrible, too unbelievable.

Yet he believed it.

Thomas McKenzie was surprised to see him. Mrs McKenzie had, he said, gone to stay with a sister on the other side of the city. The body had been taken away, of course, and the bathroom cleaned. McKenzie was without jacket and tie and had rolled up his shirt-sleeves. He wore half-moon glasses and carried a pen with him as he opened the door to Rebus.

In the drawing-room, there were signs that McKenzie had been working. Papers were strewn across a writing desk, a briefcase open on the floor. A calculator sat on the chair, as did a telephone.

'I'm sorry to disturb you again, sir,' Rebus said, taking in the scene. McKenzie had sobered up since the morning. He looked like a businessman rather than a grieving father.

McKenzie seemed to realise that the scene before Rebus created a strange impression.

'Keeping busy,' he said. 'Keeping the mind occupied, you know. Life can't stop because ...' He fell silent.

'Quite, sir,' Rebus said, seating himself on the sofa. He reached into his pocket. 'I thought you might like this.' He held the paper towards McKenzie, who took it from him and glanced at it. Rebus stared hard at him, and McKenzie twitched, attempting to hand back the note.

'No, sir,' said Rebus, 'you keep it.'

'Why?'

'It will always remind you,' said Rebus, his voice cold and level, 'that you could have saved your daughter.'

McKenzie was aghast. 'What do you mean?'

'I mean,' said Rebus, his voice still lacking emotion, 'that Suzanne wasn't intending to kill herself, not really. It was just something to attract your attention, to shock you into ... I don't know, action I suppose, a *re*action of some kind.'

McKenzie positioned himself slowly so that he rested on the armrest of one of the upholstered chairs.

'Yes,' Rebus went on, 'a reaction. That's as good a way of putting it as any. Suzanne knew what time you got up every morning. She wasn't stupid. She timed the slashing of her wrists so that you would find her while there was still time to save her. She also had a sense of the dramatic, didn't she? So she stuck her little note to the bathroom door. You saw the note and you went into the bathroom. And she wasn't dead, was she?'

McKenzie had screwed shut his eyes. His mouth was open, the teeth gritted in remembrance.

'She wasn't dead,' Rebus continued, 'not quite. And you knew damned well why she'd done it. Because she'd warned you she would. She had told you she would. Unless you stopped seeing Hazel, unless you owned up to her mother. Perhaps she had a lot of demands, Mr McKenzie. You never really got on with her anyway, did you? You didn't know what to do. Help her, or leave her to die? You hesitated. You waited.'

Rebus had risen from his seat now. His voice had risen, too. The tears were streaming down McKenzie's face, his whole body shuddering. But Rebus was relentless.

'You walked around a bit, you walked into her room. You threw her note into the waste-bin. And eventually, *eventually* you reached for a telephone and made the calls.'

'It was already too late,' McKenzie bawled. 'Nobody could have saved her.'

'They could have tried!' Rebus was yelling now, yelling close to McKenzie's own twisted face. '*You* could have tried, but you didn't. You wanted to keep your secret. Well by God your secret's out.' The last words were hissed and with them Rebus felt his fury ebb. He turned and started to walk away.

'What are you going to do?' McKenzie moaned.

'What can I do?' Rebus answered quietly. 'I'm not going to do anything, Mr McKenzie. I'm just going to leave you to get on with the rest of your life.' He paused. 'Enjoy it,' he said, closing the doors of the drawing-room behind him.

He stood on the steps of the house, trembling, his heart pounding. In a suicide, who was to blame, who the victim? He still couldn't answer the question. He doubted he ever would. His watch told him it was five minutes to five. He knew the pub near the circus, a quiet bar frequented by thinkers and amateur philosophers, a place where nothing happened and the measures were generous. He felt like having one drink, maybe two at most. He would raise his glass and make a silent toast: to the lassies.

Monstrous Trumpet

John Rebus went down onto his knees.

'I'm begging you,' he said, 'don't do this to me, please.'

But Chief Inspector Lauderdale just laughed, thinking Rebus was clowning about as per usual. 'Come on, John,' he said. 'It'll be just like Interpol.'

Rebus got back to his feet. 'No it won't,' he said. 'It'll be like a bloody escort service. Besides, I can't speak French.'

'Apparently he speaks perfect English, this Monsieur ...' Lauderdale made a show of consulting the letter in front of him on his desk.

'Don't say it again, sir, please.'

'Monsieur Cluzeau.' Rebus winced. 'Yes,' Lauderdale continued, enjoying Rebus's discomfort, 'Monsieur Cluzeau. A fine name for a member of the *gendarmerie*, don't you think?'

'It's a stunt,' Rebus pleaded. 'It's got to be. DC Holmes or one of the other lads ...'

But Lauderdale would not budge. 'It's been verified by the Chief Super,' he said. 'I'm sorry about this, John, but I thought you'd be pleased.'

'*Pleased?*'

'Yes. Pleased. You know, showing a bit of Scots hospitality.'

'Since when did the CID job description encompass "tourist guide"?'

Lauderdale had had enough of this: Rebus had even stopped calling him 'sir'. 'Since, Inspector, I ordered you to do it.'

'But why *me*?'

Lauderdale shrugged. 'Why not you?' He sighed, opened a drawer of his desk and dropped the letter into it. 'Look, it's only a day, two at most. Just do it, eh? Now if you don't mind, Inspector, I've got rather a lot to do.'

But the fight had gone out of Rebus anyway. His voice was calm, resigned. 'When does he get here?'

Again, there was a pause while that missing 'sir' hung motionless in the air between them. Well, thought Lauderdale, the sod deserves this. 'He's already here.'

'What?'

'I mean, he's in Edinburgh. The letter took a bit of a time to get here.'

'You mean it sat in someone's office for a bit of time.'

'Well, whatever the delay, he's here. And he's coming to the station this afternoon.'

Rebus glanced at his watch. It was eleven-fifty. He groaned.

'*Late* afternoon, I'd imagine,' said Lauderdale, trying to soften the blow now that Rebus was heading for the canvas. This had been a bit of a mess all round. He'd only just received final confirmation himself that Monsieur Cluzeau was on his way. 'I mean,' he said, 'the French like to take a long lunch, don't they? Notorious for it. So I don't suppose he'll be here till after three.'

'Fine, he can take us as he finds us. What am I supposed to do with him anyway?'

Lauderdale tried to retain his composure: *just say it once, damn you! Just once so I know that you recognise me for what I am!* He cleared his throat. 'He wants to see how we work. So show him. As long as he can report back to his own people that we're courteous, efficient, diligent, scrupulous, and that we always get our man, well, I'll be happy.'

'Right you are, sir,' said Rebus, opening the door, making ready to leave Lauderdale's newly refurbished office. Lauderdale sat in a daze: *he'd said it! Rebus had actually ended a sentence with 'sir'!*

'That should be easy enough,' he was saying now. 'Oh, and I might as well track down Lord Lucan and catch the Loch Ness monster while I'm at it. I'm sure to have a spare five minutes.'

Rebus closed the door after him with such ferocity that Lauderdale feared for the glass-framed paintings on his walls. But glass was more resilient than it looked. And so was John Rebus.

Cluzeau had to be an arse-licker, hell-bent on promotion. What other reason could there be? The story was that he was coming over for the Scotland–France encounter at Murrayfield. Fair enough, Edinburgh filled with Frenchmen once every two years for a week-end in February, well-behaved if boisterous rugby fans whose main pleasure seemed to be dancing in saloon bars with ice-buckets on their heads.

Nothing out of the ordinary there. But imagine a Frenchman who, having decided to take a large chunk of his annual leave so as to coincide with the international season, then has another idea: while in Scotland he'll invite himself to spend a day with the local police force. His letter to his own chief requesting an introduction so impresses the chief that *he* writes to the Chief Constable. By now, the damage is done, and the boulder starts to bounce down the hillside – Chief Constable to Chief Super, Chief Super to Super, Super to Chief Inspector – and Chief Inspector to Mr Muggins, aka John Rebus.

Thank you and *bonne nuit*. Ha! There, he did remember a bit of French after all. Rhona, his wife, had done one of those teach-yourself French courses, all tapes and repeating phrases. It had driven Rebus bonkers, but some of it had stuck. And all of it in preparation for a long weekend in Paris, a weekend which hadn't come off because Rebus had been drawn into a murder inquiry. Little wonder she'd left him in the end.

Bonne nuit. Bonjour. That was another word. *Bonsoir.* What about *Bon accord*? Was that French, too? Bo'ness sounded French. Hadn't Bonnie Prince Charlie been French? And dear God, what was he going to do with the Frenchman?

There was only one answer: get busy. The busier he was, the less time there would be for small-talk, xenophobia and falling-out. With the brain and the body occupied, there would be less temptation to mention Onion Johnnies, frogs'-legs, the war, French letters, French kissing and *French and Saunders*. Oh dear God, what had he done to deserve this?

His phone buzzed.

'*Oui?*' said Rebus, smirking now because he remembered how often he'd managed to get away with not calling Lauderdale 'sir'.

'Eh?'

'Just practising, Bob.'

'You must be bloody psychic then. There's a French gentleman down here says he's got an appointment.'

'What? Already?' Rebus checked his watch again. It was two minutes past twelve. Christ, like sitting in a dentist's waiting-room and being called ahead of your turn. Would he really look like Peter Sellers? What if he didn't speak English?

'John?'

'Sorry, Bob, what?'

'What do you want me to tell him?'

'Tell him I'll be right down.' Right down in the dumps, he thought to himself, letting the receiver drop like a stone.

There was only one person in the large, dingy reception. He wore a biker's leather jacket and had a spider's-web tattoo creeping up out of his soiled T-shirt and across his throat. Rebus stopped in his tracks. But then he saw another figure, over to his left against the wall. This man was studying various Wanted and Missing posters. He was tall, thin, and wore an immaculate dark blue suit with a tightly-knotted red silk tie. His shoes looked brand new, as did his haircut.

Their eyes met, forcing Rebus into a smile. He was suddenly aware of his own rumpled chain-store suit, his scuffed brogues, the shirt with a button missing on one cuff.

'Inspector Rebus?' The man was coming forward, hand held out.

'That's right.' They shook. He was wearing after-shave too, not too strong but certainly noticeable. He had the bearing of someone much further up the ladder, yet Rebus had been told they were of similar ranks. Having said which, there was no way Rebus was going to say 'Inspector Cluzeau' out loud. It would be too ... too ...

'For you.'

Rebus saw that he was being handed a plastic carrier-bag. He looked inside. A litre of duty-free malt, a box of chocolates and a small tin of something. He lifted out the chocolates.

'Escargots,' Cluzeau explained. 'But made from chocolate.'

Rebus studied the picture on the box. Yes, chocolates in the shape of snails. And as for the tin ...

'Foie gras. It is a pâté made from fatted goose liver. A local delicacy. You spread it on your toast.'

'Sounds delicious,' Rebus said, with just a trace of irony. In fact, he was overwhelmed. None of this stuff looked as though it came cheap, meat paste or no. 'Thank you.'

The Frenchman shrugged. He had the kind of face which, shaved twice a day, still sported a five o'clock shadow. Hirsute: that was the word. What was that joke again, the one that ended with someone asking 'Hirsute?' and the guy replying 'No, the suit's mine, but the knickers are hers'? Hairy wrists, too, on one of which sat a thin gold wristwatch. He was tapping this with his finger.

'I am not too early, I hope.'

'What?' It was Rebus's curse to remember the endings of jokes but never their beginnings. 'No, no. You're all right. I was just, er, hold on a second, will you?'

'Sure.'

Rebus walked over to the reception desk, behind which stood the omnipresent Bob Leach. Bob nodded towards the bag.

'Not a bad haul,' he said.

Rebus kept his voice low, but not so low, he hoped, as to arouse Cluzeau's suspicions. 'Thing is, Bob, I wasn't expecting him for a few hours yet. What the hell am I going to do with him? I don't suppose you've got any calls?'

'Nothing you'd be interested in, John.' Leach examined the pad in front of him. 'Couple of car smashes. Couple of break-ins. Oh, and the art gallery.'

'Art gallery?'

'I think young Brian's on that one. Some exhibition down the High Street. One of the pieces seems to have walked.'

Well, it wasn't too far away, and it *was* a tourist spot. St Giles. John Knox's House. Holyrood.

'The very dab,' said Rebus. 'That'll do us nicely. Give me the address, will you?'

Leach scribbled onto a pad of paper and tore off the sheet, handing it across the counter.

'Thanks, Bob.'

Leach was nodding towards the bag. Not only omnipresent, thought Rebus, but omniscrounging too. 'What else did you get apart from the whisky?'

Rebus bent towards him and hissed: 'Meat paste and snails!'

Bob Leach looked disheartened. 'Bloody French,' he said. 'You'd think he'd bring you something decent.'

Rebus didn't bother with back-street shortcuts as they drove towards the Royal Mile. He gave Cluzeau the full tour. But the French policeman seemed more interested in Rebus than in the streets of his city.

'I was here before,' he explained. 'Two years ago, for the rugby.'

'Do they play a lot of rugby down your way then?'

'Oh yes. It is not so much a game, more a love affair.'

Rebus assumed Cluzeau would be Parisian. He was not. Parisians, he said, were – his phrase – 'cold fish'. And in any case the city was not representative of the real France. The countryside – that was the real France, and especially the countryside of the south-west. Cluzeau was from Périgueux. He had been born there and now lived and worked there. He was married, with four children. And yes, he carried a family photo in his wallet. The wallet itself he carried inside a black leather pouch, almost like a clutch-purse. The pouch also contained identity documents, passport, chequebook, diary, a small English–French dictionary. No wonder he looked good in a suit: no bulges in the pockets, no wear on the material.

Rebus handed back the photograph.

'Very nice,' he said.

'And you, Inspector?'

So it was Rebus's turn to tell his tale. Born in Fife. Out of school and into the Army. Paras eventually and from there to the SAS. Breakdown and recovery. Then the police. Wife, now ex-wife, and one daughter living with her mother in London. Cluzeau, Rebus realised, had a canny way of asking questions, making them sound more like statements. So that instead of answering, you were merely acknowledging what he already seemed to know. He'd remember that for future use.

'And now we are going where?'

'The High Street. You might know it better as the Royal Mile.'

'I've walked along it, yes. You say separated, not divorced?'

'That's right.'

'Then there is a chance ...?'

'What? Of us getting back together? No, no chance of that.'

This elicited another huge shrug from Cluzeau. 'It was another man ...?'

'No, just *this* man.'

'Ah. In my part of France we have many crimes of passion. And here in Edinburgh?'

Rebus gave a wry grin. 'Where there's no passion ...'

The Frenchman seemed to make hard work of understanding this.

'French policemen carry guns, don't they?' Rebus asked, filling the silence.

'Not on vacation.'

'I'm glad to hear it.'

'Yes, we have guns. But it is not like in America. We have respect for guns. They are a way of life in the country. Every Frenchman is a hunter at heart.'

Rebus signalled, and drew in to the roadside. 'Scotsmen, too,' he said, opening his door. 'And right now I'm going to hunt down a sandwich. This cafe does the best boiled ham in Edinburgh.'

Cluzeau looked dubious. 'The famous Scottish cuisine,' he murmured, unfastening his seatbelt.

They ate as they drove – ham for Rebus, salami for Cluzeau – and soon enough arrived outside the Heggarty Gallery. In fact, they arrived outside a wools and knitwear shop, which occupied the street-level. The gallery itself was up a winding stairwell, the steps worn and treacherous. They walked in through an unprepossessing door and found themselves in the midst of an argument. Fifteen or so women were crowded around Detective Constable Brian Holmes.

'You can't keep us here, you know!'

'Look, ladies—'

'Patronising pig.'

'Look, I need to get names and addresses first.'

'Well, go on then, what are you waiting for?'

'Bloody cheek, like we're criminals or something.'

'Maybe he wants to strip-search us.'

'Chance would be a fine thing.' There was some laughter at this.

Holmes had caught sight of Rebus and the look of relief on his face told Rebus all he needed to know. On a trellis table against one wall stood a couple of dozen wine bottles, mostly empty, and jugs of orange juice and water, mostly still full. Cluzeau lifted a bottle and wrinkled his nose. He sniffed the neck and the nose wrinkled even further.

The poster on the gallery door had announced an exhibition of paintings and sculpture by Serena Davies. The exhibition was entitled 'Hard Knox' and today was its opening. By the look of the drinks table, a preview had been taking place. Free wine all round, glasses replenished. And now a squabble, which might be about to turn ugly.

Rebus filled his lungs. 'Excuse me!' he cried. The faces turned from Brian Holmes and settled on him. 'I'm Inspector Rebus. Now, with a bit of luck we'll have you all out of here in five minutes. Please bear with us until then. I notice there's still some drink left. If you'll fill your glasses and maybe have a last look round, by the time you finish you should be able to leave. Now, I just need a word with my colleague.'

Gratefully, Holmes squeezed his way out of the scrum and came towards Rebus.

'You've got thirty seconds to fill me in,' Rebus said.

Holmes took a couple of deep breaths. 'A sculpture in bronze, male figure. It was sitting in the middle of one of the rooms. Preview opens. Somebody starts yelling that it's disappeared. The artist goes up the wall. She won't let anybody in or out, because if somebody's nicked it, that somebody's still in the gallery.'

'And that's the state of play? Nobody in or out since it went missing?'

Holmes nodded. 'Of course, as I tried telling her, they could have high-tailed it *before* she barricaded everyone else in.' Holmes was looking at the man who had come to stand beside Rebus. 'Can we help you, sir?'

'Oh,' said Rebus. 'You haven't been introduced. This is ...' But no, he still couldn't make himself say the name. Instead, he nodded towards Holmes. 'This is Detective Constable Holmes.' Then, as Cluzeau shook hands with Holmes: 'The inspector here has come over from France to see how we do things in Edinburgh.' Rebus turned to Cluzeau. 'Did you catch what Brian was saying? Only I know his accent's a bit thick.'

'I understood perfectly.' He turned to Holmes. 'Inspector Rebus forgot to say, but my name is Cluzeau.' Somehow it didn't sound so funny when spoken by a native. 'How big is the statue? Do we know what it looks like?'

'There's a picture of it in the catalogue.' Holmes took the small glossy booklet from his pocket and handed it to Cluzeau. 'That's it at the top of the page.'

While Cluzeau studied this, Holmes caught Rebus's eye, then nodded down to the Frenchman's pouch.

'Nice handbag.'

Rebus gave him a warning look, then glanced at the catalogue. His eyes opened wide. 'Good Christ!'

Cluzeau read from the catalogue. '"Monstrous Trumpet. Bronze and multi-media. Sixteen—" what do these marks mean?'

'Inches.'

'Thank you. "Sixteen inches. Three thousand five hundred pounds." *C'est cher*. It's expensive.'

'I'll say,' said Rebus. 'You could buy a car for that.' Well, he thought, you could certainly buy *my* car for that.

'It is an interesting piece, don't you think?'

'Interesting?' Rebus studied the small photograph of the statue called 'Monstrous Trumpet'. A nude male, his face exaggeratedly spiteful, was sticking out his tongue, except that it wasn't a tongue, it was a penis. And where that particular organ should have been, there was what looked like a piece of sticking-plaster. Because of the angle of the photo, it was just possible to discern something protruding from the statue's backside. Rebus guessed it was meant to be a tongue.

'Yes,' said Cluzeau, 'I should very much like to meet the artist.'

'Doesn't look as though you've got any choice,' said Holmes, seeming to retreat though in fact he didn't move. 'Here she comes.'

She had just come into the room, of that Rebus was certain. If she'd been there before, he'd have noticed her. And even if he hadn't Cluzeau certainly would have. She was just over six feet tall, dressed in long flowing white skirt, black boots, puffy white blouse and a red satin waistcoat. Her eye make-up was jet black, matching her long straight hair, and her wrists fairly jangled with bangles and bracelets. She addressed Holmes.

'No sign of it. I've had a thorough look.' She turned towards Rebus and Cluzeau. Holmes started making the introductions.

'This is Inspector Rebus, and Inspector Cl ...' he stumbled to a halt. Yes, thought Rebus, it's a problem, isn't it, Brian? But Cluzeau appeared not to have noticed. He was squeezing Serena Davies's hand.

'Pleased to meet you.'

She looked him up and down without embarrassment, gave a cool smile, and passed to Rebus. 'Well, thank goodness the grown-ups are here at last.' Brian Holmes reddened furiously. 'I hope we didn't interrupt your lunch, Inspector. Come on, I'll show you where the piece was.'

And with that she turned and left. Some of the women offered either condolences over her loss, or else praise for what works remained, and Serena Davies gave a weak smile, a smile which said: I'm coping, but don't ask me how.

Rebus touched Holmes's shoulder. 'Get the names and addresses, eh, Brian?' He made to follow the artist, but couldn't resist a parting shot. 'You've got your crayons with you, have you?'

'And my marbles,' Holmes retorted. By God, thought Rebus, he's learning fast. But then, he had a good teacher, hadn't he?

'Magnificent creature,' Cluzeau hissed into his ear as they passed through the room. A few of the women glanced towards the Frenchman. I'm making him look too good, Rebus thought. Pity I had to be wearing this old suit today.

The small galleries through which they passed comprised a maze, an artful configuration of angles and doorways which made more of the space than there actually was. As to the works on display, well, Rebus couldn't be sure, of course, but there seemed an awful lot of violence in them, violence acted out upon a particular part of the masculine anatomy. Even the Frenchman was quiet as they passed red splashes of colour, twisted statues, great dollops of paint. There was one apparent calm centre, an extremely large and detailed drawing of the vulva. Cluzeau paused for a moment.

'I like this,' he said. Rebus nodded towards a red circular sticker attached to the wall beside the portrait.

'Already sold.'

Cluzeau tapped the relevant page of the catalogue. 'Yes, for one thousand five hundred pounds.'

'In here!' the artist's voice commanded. 'When you've stopped gawping.' She was in the next room of the gallery, standing by the now empty pedestal. The sign beneath it showed no red blob. No sale. 'It was right here.' The room was about fifteen feet by ten, in the corner of the gallery: only one doorway and no windows. Rebus looked up at the ceiling, but saw only strip lighting. No trapdoors.

'And there were people in here when it happened?'

Serena Davies nodded. 'Three or four of the guests. Ginny Elyot, Margaret Grieve, Helena Mitchison and I think Lesley Jameson.'

'Jameson?' Rebus knew two Jamesons in Edinburgh, one a doctor and the other ...

'Tom Jameson's daughter,' the artist concluded.

The other a newspaper editor called Tom Jameson. 'And who was it raised the alarm?' Rebus asked.

'That was Ginny. She came out of the room shouting that the statue had vanished. We all rushed into the room. Sure enough.' She slapped a hand down on the pedestal.

'Time, then,' Rebus mused, 'for someone to sneak away while everyone else was occupied?'

But the artist shook her mane of hair. 'I've already told you, there's nobody missing. Everyone who was here *is* here. In fact, I think there are a couple more bodies now than there were at the time.'

'Oh?'

'Moira Fowler was late. As usual. She arrived a couple of minutes after I'd barred the door.'

'You let her in?'

'Of course. I wasn't worried about letting people *in*.'

'You said "a couple of bodies"?'

'That's right. Maureen Beck was in the loo. Bladder trouble, poor thing. Maybe I should have hung a couple of paintings in there.'

Cluzeau frowned at this. Rebus decided to help him. 'The toilets being where exactly?'

'Next flight up. A complete pain really. The gallery shares them with the shop downstairs. Crammed full of cardboard boxes and knitting patterns.'

Rebus nodded. The Frenchman coughed, preparing to speak. 'So,' he said, 'you have to leave the gallery actually to use the ... loo?'

Serena Davies nodded. 'You're French,' she stated. Cluzeau gave a little bow. 'I should have guessed from the *pochette*. You'd never find a Scotsman carrying one of those.'

Cluzeau seemed prepared for this point. 'But the sporran serves the same purpose.'

'I suppose it does,' the artist admitted, 'but its primary function is as a signifier.' She looked to both men. Both men looked puzzled. 'It's hairy and it hangs around your groin,' she explained.

Rebus stayed silent, but pursed his lips. Cluzeau nodded to himself, frowning.

'Maybe,' said Rebus, 'you could explain your exhibition to us, *Ms* Davies?'

'Well, it's a comment on Knox of course.'

'Knocks?' asked Cluzeau.

'John Knox,' Rebus explained. 'We passed by his old house a little way back.'

'John Knox,' she went on, principally for the Frenchman's benefit, but perhaps too, she thought, for that of the Scotsman, 'was a Scottish preacher, a follower of Calvin. He was also a misogynist, hence the title of one of his works – *The First Blast of the Trumpet Against the Monstrous Regiment of Women.*'

'He didn't mean all women,' Rebus felt obliged to add. Serena Davies straightened her spine like a snake rising up before its kill.

'But he did,' she said, 'by association. And, also by association, these works are a comment on *all* Scotsmen. And all men.'

Cluzeau could feel an argument beginning. Arguments, to his knowledge, were always counter-productive even when enjoyable. 'I think I see,' he said. 'And your exhibition responds to this man's work. Yes.' He tapped the catalogue. '"Monstrous Trumpet" is a pun then?'

Serena Davies shrugged, but seemed pacified. 'You could call it that. I'm saying that Knox talked with one part of his anatomy – *not* his brain.'

'And,' added Rebus, 'that at the same time he talked out of his arse?'

'Yes,' she said.

Cluzeau was chuckling. He was still chuckling when he asked: 'And who could have reason for stealing your work?'

The mane rippled again. 'I've absolutely no idea.'

'But you suspect one of your guests,' Cluzeau continued. 'Of course you do: you have already stated that there was no one else here. You were among friends, yet one of them is the Janus figure, yes?'

She nodded slowly. 'Much as I hate to admit it.'

Rebus had taken the catalogue from Cluzeau and seemed to be studying it. But he'd listened to every word. He tapped the missing statue's photo.

'Do you work from life?'

'Mostly, yes, but not for "Monstrous Trumpet".'

'It's a sort of ... ideal figure then?'

She smiled at this. 'Hardly ideal, Inspector. But in that it comes from up here—' she tapped her head, 'from an idea rather than from life, yes, I suppose it is.'

'Does that go for the face, too?' Rebus persisted. 'It seems so life-like.'

She accepted the compliment, studying the photo with him. 'It's not any one man's face,' she said. 'At most it's a composite of men I know.' Then she shrugged. 'Maybe.'

Rebus handed the catalogue to Cluzeau. 'Did you search anyone?' he asked the artist.

'I asked them to open their bags. Not very subtle of me, but I was – *am* – distraught.'

'And did they?'

'Oh yes. Pointless really, there were only two or three bags big enough to hide the statue in.'

'But they were empty?'

She sighed, pinching the bridge of her nose between two fingers. The bracelets were shunted from wrist to elbow. 'Utterly empty,' she said. 'Just as I feel.'

'Was the piece insured?'

She shook her head again, her forehead lowered. A portrait of dejection, Rebus thought. Lifelike, yet not quite real. He noticed too that, now her eyes were averted, the Frenchman was appraising her. He caught Rebus watching him and raised his eyebrows, then shrugged, then made a gesture with his hands. Yes, thought Rebus, I know what you mean. Only don't let *her* catch you thinking what I know you're thinking.

And, he supposed, what he was thinking too.

'I think we'd better go through,' he said. 'The other women will be getting impatient.'

'Let them!' she cried.

'Actually,' said Rebus, 'perhaps you could go ahead of us? Warn them that we may be keeping them a bit longer than we thought.'

She brightened at the news, then sneered. 'You mean you want me to do your dirty work for you?'

Rebus shrugged innocently. 'I just wanted a moment to discuss the case with my colleague.'

'Oh,' she said. Then nodded: 'Yes, of course. Discuss away. I'll tell them they've to stay put.'

'Thank you,' said Rebus, but she'd already left the room.

Cluzeau whistled silently. 'What a creature!'

It was meant as praise, of course, and Rebus nodded assent. 'So what do you think?'

'Think?'

'About the theft.'

'Ah.' Cluzeau scraped at his chin with his fingers. 'A crime of passion,' he said at last and with confidence.

'How do you work that out?'

Cluzeau gave another of his shrugs. 'The process of elimination. We eliminate money: there are more expensive pieces here and besides, a common thief would burgle the premises when they were empty, no?'

Rebus nodded, enjoying this, so like his own train of thought was it. 'Go on.'

'I do not think this piece is so precious that a collector would have it stolen. It is not insured, so there is no reason for the artist herself to have it stolen. It seems logical that someone invited to the exhibition stole it. So we come to the figure of the Janus. Someone the artist herself knows. Why should such a person – a supposed friend – steal this work?' He paused before answering his own question. 'Jealousy. Revenge, *et voilà*, the crime of passion.'

Rebus applauded silently. 'Bravo. But there are thirty-odd suspects out there and no sign of the statue.'

'Ah, I did not say I could solve the crime; all I offer is the "why".'

'Then follow me,' Rebus said, 'and we'll encounter the "who" and the "how" together.'

In the main gallery, Serena Davies was in furious conversation with one knot of women. Brian Holmes was trying to take names and addresses from another group. A third group stood, bored and disconsolate, by the drinks table, and a fourth group stood beside a bright red gash of a painting, glancing at it from time to time and talking among themselves.

Most of the women in the room either carried clutch-purses tucked safely under their arms, or else let neat shoulder-bags swing effortlessly by their sides. But there were a few larger bags and these had been left in a group of their own between the drinks table and another smaller table on which sat a small pile of catalogues and a visitors' book. Rebus walked across to this spot and studied the bags. There was one large straw shopping-bag, apparently containing only a cashmere cardigan and a folded copy of the *Guardian*. There was one department store plastic carrier-bag, containing an umbrella, a bunch of bananas, a fat paperback and a copy of the *Guardian*. There was one canvas shopping-bag, containing an empty crisp packet, a copy of the *Scotsman* and a copy of the *Guardian*.

All this Rebus could see just by standing over the bags. He reached down and picked up the carrier-bag.

'Can I ask whose bag this is?' he said loudly.

'It's mine.'

A young woman stepped forward from the drinks table, starting to blush furiously.

'Follow me, please,' said Rebus, walking off to the next room along. Cluzeau followed and so, seconds later, did the owner of the bag, her eyes terrified.

'Just a couple of questions, that's all,' Rebus said, trying to put her at ease. The main gallery was hushed; he knew people would be straining to hear the conversation. Brian Holmes was repeating an address to himself as he jotted it down.

Rebus felt a little bit like an executioner, walking up to the bags, picking them up in turn and wandering off with the owner towards the awaiting guillotine. The owner of the carrier-bag was Trish Poole, wife of a psychology lecturer at the university. Rebus had met Dr Poole before, and told her so, trying to help her relax a little. It turned out that a lot of the women present today were either academics in their own right, or else were the wives of academics. This latter group included not only Trish Poole, but also Rebecca Eiser, wife of the distinguished Professor of English Literature. Listening to Trish Poole tell him this, Rebus shivered and could feel his face turn pale. But that had been a long time ago.

After Trish Poole had returned for a whispered confab with her group, Rebus tried the canvas bag. This belonged to Margaret Grieve, a writer and, as she said herself, 'one of Serena's closest friends'. Rebus didn't doubt this, and asked if she was married. No, she was not, but she did have a 'significant other'. She smiled broadly as she said this. Rebus smiled back. She'd been in the room with the statue when it was noticed to be missing? Yes, she had. Not that she'd seen anything. She'd been intent on the paintings. So much so that she couldn't be sure whether the statue had been in the room when she'd entered, or whether it had already gone. She thought perhaps it had already gone.

Dismissed by Rebus, she returned to her group in front of the red gash and they too began whispering. An elegant older woman came forward from the same group.

'The last bag is mine,' she said haughtily, her vowels pure Morningside. Perhaps she'd been Jean Brodie's elocution mistress; but no, she wasn't even quite Maggie Smith's age, though to Rebus there were similarities enough between the two women.

Cluzeau seemed quietly cowed by this grand example of Scottish womanhood. He stood at a distance, giving her vowels the necessary room in which to perform. And, Rebus noticed, he clutched his pouch close to his groin, as though it were a lucky charm. Maybe that's what sporrans were?

'I'm Maureen Beck,' she informed them loudly. There would be no hiding *this* conversation from the waggling ears.

Maureen Beck told Rebus that she was married to the architect

Robert Beck and seemed surprised when this name meant nothing to the policeman. She decided then that she disliked Rebus and turned to Cluzeau, answering to his smiling countenance every time Rebus asked her a question. She was in the loo at the time, yes, and returned to pandemonium. She'd only been out of the room a couple of minutes, and hadn't seen anyone ...

'Not even *Ms* Fowler?' Rebus asked. 'I believe she was late to arrive?'

'Yes, but that was a minute or two *after* I came back in.'

Rebus nodded thoughtfully. There was a teasing piece of ham wedged between two of his back teeth and he pushed it with his tongue. A woman put her head around the partition.

'Look, Inspector, some of us have got appointments this afternoon. Isn't there at least a telephone we can use?'

It was a good point. Who was in charge of the gallery itself? The gallery director, it turned out, was a timid little woman who had burrowed into the quietest of the groups. She was only running the place for the real owner, who was on a well-deserved holiday in Paris. (Cluzeau rolled his eyes at this. 'No one,' he said with a shudder, 'deserves such torture.') There was a cramped office, and in it an old Bakelite telephone. If the women could leave twenty pence for each call. A line started to form outside the office. ('Ah, how you love queuing!') Mrs Beck, meantime, had returned to her group. Rebus followed her, and was introduced to Ginny Elyot, who had raised the alarm, and to Moira Fowler the latecomer.

Ginny Elyot kept patting her short auburn hair as though searching it for misplaced artworks. A nervous habit, Rebus reasoned. Cluzeau quickly became the centre of attention, with even the distant and unpunctual Moira becoming involved in the interrogation. Rebus sidled away and touched Brian Holmes's arm.

'That's all the addresses noted, sir.'

'Well done, Brian. Look, slip upstairs, will you? Give the loo a recce.'

'What am I looking for exactly – suspiciously shaped bundles of four-ply?'

Rebus actually laughed. 'We should be so lucky. But yes, you never know what you might find. And check any windows, too. There might be a drainpipe.'

'Okay.'

As Holmes left, a small hand touched Rebus's arm. A girl in her late-teens, eyes gleaming behind studious spectacles, jerked her head towards the gallery's first partitioned room. Rebus followed her. She was so small, and spoke so quietly, he actually had to grasp hands to knees and bend forward to listen.

'I want the story.'

'Pardon?'

'I want the story for my dad's paper.'

Rebus looked at her. His voice too was a dramatic whisper. 'You're Lesley Jameson?'

She nodded.

'I see. Well, as far as I'm concerned the story's yours. But we haven't *got* a story yet.'

She looked around her, then dropped her voice even lower. 'You've seen her.'

'Who?'

'Serena, of course. She's ravishing, isn't she?' Rebus tried to look non-committal. 'She's terribly attractive to men.' This time he attempted a Gallic shrug. He wondered if it looked as stupid as it felt. Her voice died away almost completely, reducing Rebus to lip-reading. 'She has loads of men after her. Including Margaret's.'

'Ah,' said Rebus, 'right.' He nodded, too. So Margaret Grieve's boyfriend was ...

The lips made more movements: 'He's Serena's lover.'

Yes, well, now things began to make more sense. Maybe the Frenchman was right: a crime of passion. The one thing missing thus far had been the passion itself; but no longer. And it was curious, when he came to think of it, how Margaret Grieve had said she couldn't recall whether the statue had been in the room or not. It wasn't the sort of thing you could miss, was it? Not for a bunch of samey paintings of pink bulges and grey curving masses. The newspapers in her bag would have concealed the statue quite nicely, too. There was just one problem.

Cluzeau's head appeared around the partition. 'Ah! Here you are. I'm sorry if I interrupt—'

But Lesley Jameson was already making for the main room. Cluzeau watched her go, then turned to Rebus.

'Charming women.' He sighed. 'But all of them either married or else with lovers. And one of them, of course, is the thief.'

'Oh?' Rebus sounded surprised. 'You mean one of the women you've just been talking with?'

'Of course.' Now he, too, lowered his voice. 'The statue left the gallery in a bag. You could not simply hide it under your dress, could you? But I don't think a plastic bag would have been strong enough for this task. So, we have a choice between Madame Beck and Mademoiselle Grieve.'

'Grieve's boyfriend has been carrying on with our artist.'

Cluzeau digested this. But he too knew there was a problem. 'She did not leave the gallery. She was shut in with the others.' Rebus nodded. 'So there has to have been an accomplice. I think I'd better have another word with Lesley Jameson.'

But Brian Holmes had appeared. He exhaled noisily. 'Thank Christ for that,' he said. 'For a minute there I thought you'd buggered off and left me.'

Rebus grinned. 'That might not have been such a bad idea. How was the loo?'

'Well, I didn't find any solid evidence,' Holmes replied with a straight face. 'No skeins of wool tied to the plumbing and hanging out of the windows for a burglar to shimmy down.'

'But there is a window?'

'A small one in the cubicle itself. I stood on the seat and had a squint out. A two-storey drop to a sort of back yard, nothing in it but a rusting Renault Five and a skip full of cardboard boxes.'

'Go down and take a look at that skip.'

'I thought you might say that.'

'And take a look at the Renault,' ordered Cluzeau, his face set. 'I cannot believe a French car would rust. Perhaps you are mistaken and it is a Mini Cooper, no?'

Holmes, who prided himself on knowing a bit about cars, was ready to argue, then saw the smile spread across the Frenchman's face. He smiled, too.

'Just as well you've got a sense of humour,' he said. 'You'll need it after the match on Saturday.'

'And you will need your Scottish stoicism.'

'Save it for the half-time entertainment, eh?' said Rebus, but with good enough humour. 'The sooner we get this wrapped up, the more time we'll have left for sightseeing.'

Cluzeau seemed about to argue, but Rebus held up a hand. 'Believe me,' he said, 'you'll want to see these sights. Only the locals know the *very* best pubs in Edinburgh.'

Holmes went to investigate the skip and Rebus spoke in whispers with Lesley Jameson – when he wasn't fending off demands from the detainees. What had seemed to most of them something unusual and thrilling at first, a story to be repeated across the dining-table, had now become merely tiresome. Though they had asked to make phone calls, Rebus couldn't help overhearing some of those conversations. They weren't warning of a late arrival or cancelling an appointment: they were spreading the news.

'Look, Inspector, I'm really tired of being kept here.'

Rebus turned from Lesley Jameson to the talker. His voice lacked emotion. 'You're not being kept here.'

'What?'

'Who said you were? Only *Ms* Davies as I understand. You're free to leave whenever you want.'

There was hesitation at this. To leave and taste freedom again? Or to stay, so as not to miss anything? Muttered dialogues took place and eventually one or two of the guests did leave. They simply walked out, closing the door behind them.

'Does that mean we can go?'

Rebus nodded. Another woman left, then another, then a couple.

'I hope you're not thinking of kicking me out,' Lesley Jameson warned. She wanted desperately to be a journalist, and to do it the hard way, *sans* nepotism. Rebus shook his head.

'Just keep talking,' he said.

Cluzeau was in conversation with Serena Davies. When Rebus approached them, she was studying the Frenchman's strong-looking hands. Rebus waved his own nail-bitten paw around the gallery.

'Do you,' he asked, 'have any trouble getting people to pose for all these paintings?'

She shook her head. 'No, not really. It's funny you should ask, Monsieur Cluzeau was just saying—'

'Yes, I'll bet he was. But Monsieur Cluzeau—' testing the words, not finding them risible any more, 'has a wife and family.'

Serena Davies laughed; a deep growl which seemed to run all the way up and down the Frenchman's spine. At last, she let go his hand. 'I thought we were talking about modelling, Inspector.'

'We were,' said Rebus drily, 'but I'm not sure Mrs Cluzeau would see it like that ...'

'Inspector ...?' It was Maureen Beck. 'Everyone seems to be leaving. Do I take it we're free to go?'

Rebus was suddenly businesslike. 'No,' he said. 'I'd like you to stay behind a little longer.' He glanced towards the group – Ginny Elyot, Moira Fowler, Margaret Grieve – 'all of you, please. This won't take long.'

'That's what my husband says,' commented Moira Fowler, raising a glass of water to her lips. She placed a tablet on her tongue and washed it down.

Rebus looked to Lesley Jameson, then winked. 'Fasten your seatbelt,' he told her. 'It's going to be a bumpy ride.'

The gallery was now fast emptying and Holmes, having battled against the tide on the stairwell, entered the room on unsteady legs, his eyes seeking out Rebus.

'Jeez!' he cried. 'I thought you'd decided to bugger off after all. What's up? Where's everyone going?'

'Anything in the skip?' But Holmes shrugged: nothing. 'I've sent everyone home,' Rebus explained.

'Everyone except us,' Maureen Beck said sniffily.

'Well,' said Rebus, facing the four women, 'that's because nobody but *you* knows anything about the statue.'

The women themselves said nothing at this, but Cluzeau gave a small gasp – perhaps to save them the trouble. Serena Davies, however, had replaced her growl with a lump of ice.

'You mean one of *them* stole my work?'

Rebus shook his head. 'No, that's not what I mean. One person couldn't have done it. There had to be an accomplice.' He nodded towards Moira Fowler. '*Ms* Fowler, why don't you take DC Holmes down to your car? He can carry the statue back upstairs.'

'Moira!' Another change of tone, this time from ice to fire. For a second, Rebus thought Serena Davies might be about to make a lunge at the thief. Perhaps Moira Fowler thought so too, for she moved without further prompting towards the door.

'Okay,' she said, 'if you like.'

Holmes watched her pass him on her way to the stairwell.

'Go on then, Brian,' ordered Rebus. Holmes seemed undecided. He knew he was going to miss the story. What's more, he didn't fancy lugging the bloody thing up a flight of stairs.

'*Vite!*' cried Rebus, another word of French suddenly coming back to him. Holmes moved on tired legs towards the door. Up the stairs, down the stairs, up the stairs. It would, he couldn't help thinking, make good training for the Scottish pack.

Serena Davies had put her hand to her brow. Clank-a-clank-clank went the bracelets. 'I can't believe it of Moira. Such treachery.'

'Hah!' This from Ginny Elyot, her eyes burning. 'Treachery? You're a good one to speak. Getting Jim to "model" for you. Neither of you telling her about it. What the hell do you think she thought when she found out?'

Jim being, as Rebus knew from Lesley, Moira Fowler's husband. He kept his eyes on Ginny.

'And you, too, *Ms* Elyot. How did you feel when you found out about ... David, is it?'

She nodded. Her hand went towards her hair again, but she caught herself, and gripped one hand in the other. 'Yes, David,' she said quietly. 'That statue's got David's eyes, his hair.' She wasn't looking at Rebus. He didn't feel she was even replying to his question.

She was remembering.

'And Gerry's nose and jawline. I'd recognise them anywhere.'

This from Margaret Grieve, she of the significant other. 'But Gerry can't keep secrets, not from me.'

Maureen Beck, who had been nodding throughout, never taking her moist eyes off the artist, was next. Her husband too, Robert, the architect, had modelled for Serena Davies. On the quiet, of course. It had to be on the quiet: no knowing what passions might be aroused otherwise. Even in a city like Edinburgh, even in women as seemingly self-possessed and cool-headed as these. Perhaps it had all been very innocent. Perhaps.

'He's got Robert's figure,' Maureen Beck was saying. 'Down to the scar on his chest from that riding accident.'

A crime of passion, just as Cluzeau had predicted. And after Rebus telling him that there was no such thing as passion in the city. But there was; and there were secrets too. Locked within these paintings, fine so long as they were abstract, so long as they weren't modelled from life. But for all that 'Monstrous Trumpet' was, in Serena Davies's words, a 'composite', its creation still cut deep. For each of the four women, there was something recognisable there, something modelled from life, from husband or lover. Something which burned and humiliated.

Unable to stand the thought of public display, of visitors walking into the gallery and saying 'Good God, doesn't that statue look like ...?' Unable to face the thought of this, and of the ridicule (the detailed penis, the tongue, and that sticking-plaster) they had come together with a plan. A clumsy, almost unworkable plan, but the only plan they had.

The statue had gone into Margaret Grieve's roomy bag, at which point Ginny Elyot had raised the alarm – hysterically so, attracting all the guests towards that one room, unaware as they pressed forwards that they were passing Margaret Grieve discreetly moving the other way. The bag had been passed to Maureen Beck, who had then slipped upstairs to the toilet. She had opened the window and dropped the statue down into the skip, from where Moira Fowler had retrieved it, carrying it out to her own car. Beck had returned, to find Serena Davies stopping people from leaving; a minute or two later, Moira Fowler had arrived.

She now walked in, followed by a red-faced Holmes, the statue cradled in his arms. Serena Davies, however, appeared not to notice. She had her eyes trained on the parquet floor and, again, she was being studied by Cluzeau. 'What a creature,' he had said of her. What a creature indeed. The four thieves would certainly be in accord in calling her 'creature'.

Who knows, thought Rebus, they might even be in *bon accord*.

The artist was neither temperamental nor stupid enough to insist on pressing charges and she bent to Rebus's suggestion that the piece be withdrawn from the show. The pressure thereafter was on Lesley Jameson not to release the story to her father's paper. Female solidarity won in the end, but it was a narrow victory.

Not much female solidarity elsewhere, thought Rebus. He made up a few mock headlines, the sort that would have pleased Dr Curt. Feminist Artist's Roll Models; Serena's Harem of Husbands; The Anti-Knox Knocking Shop. All as he sat squeezed into a corner of the Sutherland Bar. Somewhere along the route, Cluzeau – now insisting that Rebus call him Jean-Pierre – had found half a dozen French fans, in town for the rugby and already in their cups. Then a couple of the Scottish fans had tagged along too and now there were about a dozen of them, standing at the bar and singing French rugby songs. Any minute now someone would tip an ice-bucket onto their heads. He prayed it wouldn't be Brian Holmes, who, shirt-tail out and tie hanging loose, was singing as lustily as anyone, despite the language barrier – or even, perhaps, because of it.

Childish, of course. But then that was men for you. Simple pleasures and simple crimes. Male revenge was simple almost to the point of being infantile: you went up to the bastard and you stuck your fist into his face or kneed him in the nuts. But the revenge of the female. Ah, that was recondite stuff. He wondered if it was finished now, or would Serena Davies face more plots, plots more subtle, or better executed, or more savage? He didn't really want to think about it. Didn't want to think about the hate in the four women's voices, or the gleam in their eyes. He drank to forget. That was why men joined the Foreign Legion too, wasn't it? To forget. Or was it?

He was buggered if he could remember. But something else niggled too. The women had laid claim to a lover's jawline, a husband's figure. But whose, he couldn't help wondering, was the penis?

Someone was tugging at his arm, pulling him up. The glasses flew from the table and suddenly he was being hugged by Jean-Pierre.

'John, my friend, John, tell me who this man Peter Zealous is that everyone is talking to me about?'

'It's Sellers,' Rebus corrected. To tell or not to tell? He opened his mouth. There was the machine-gun sound of things spilling onto the bar behind him. Small, solid things. Next thing he knew, it was dark and his head was very cold and very wet.

'I'll get you for this, Brian,' he said, removing the ice-bucket from his head. 'So help me I will.'

My Shopping Day

Two things about being a good-looking guy who dresses well: one, you tend to get noticed; two, nobody thinks you capable of a naughty deed. In my line of work – necessarily peripatetic – there's a trade-off between the two. I'm hoping people will be looking at my face and not my hands. And I'm hoping they'll wander off in blissful ignorance afterwards.

I'm a pickpocket, only the term has lost its meaning – fine for Oliver Twist, but not for the 1990s. We're dippers, lifters. I specialise in handbags, shopping-bags, carriers. I'm not a weight-lifter or a big dipper – a little but often, that's me. I saw a stage act once, he could have your wristwatch off your hand, the belt off your trousers, and you wouldn't notice. He'd have your wallet, your glasses, your wife, your kids, and you'd take a look around and be naked and shivering in a dark alley.

He was that good. I'm not. But I look better than he did; I take care of myself. I went backstage after the show and he was pouring whisky into a glass that wasn't too clean. I got him to go through a couple of moves, thinking I could maybe incorporate them into *my* act, but nothing came of it. I asked him why, when he could make a fortune in train stations, airports and cinema foyers, he was wasting his time on the stage of a working-men's club in Leven. He said the problem was he needed to show off. He had this gift, and he couldn't keep it quiet. He knew damned well that if he lifted a wallet, he'd want the victim to know about it.

Theatrical types, I've met a few.

I'm a bit of an actor myself of course; have to be. My face is smiling, giving a come-on, and my mouth is saying all this 'pardon-me-all-my-fault' stuff, but my mind is on what my hands are doing, slipping in and out of bags and baskets, palming the purse or the wallet or whatever of value happens to be lying there in plain view or just beyond. I wear expensive aftershave – not that cloying crap you see shagged to death on TV just before Christmas – and when

I get close they get a good waft of it. It all helps to keep them occupied – preoccupied – during the performance. That was one lesson
the old stooge in Leven taught me: preoccupation. Persuade them
they're part of a certain scenario and they'll go along with it. Simple
really.

I frequent the big supermarkets and shopping centres. I see
young women kicking their heels and holding clipboards, ready to
collar some brain-fried shopper into taking part in their 'consumer
survey'. Right, only what they're really doing is easing you into a
pitch for double glazing, new kitchen, conservatory. And people
keep taking the bait. I want to scream at them: come *on*! Wakey-
wakey! But what use would it do? A trawl up and down those aisles
and your head is mush.

I know shopping centres don't want you doing it, but just walk
in some day and position yourself on the safe side of the check-outs.
Now stand there and watch the show. Watch a shopper breeze into
the shop with head held high, trolley buzzing. Then watch them at
the check-out, watch them as they leave. Their skin's turned grey,
eyes dark. They frown, their jaw moves, there's almost drool there
at the corners. Shoulders slumped, head sagging. These people have
been beaten, pummelled. They've been hijacked, gagged, throttled,
stymied, shaken and stirred. On the way home, they'll be argu-
mentative, downright rude, and once home they'll collapse, fight
with spouse and kids, maybe have a little weep in the privacy of the
toilet. And inside their head will be some shocking refrain, something they can't seem to shrug off without the aid of hard drink.
It'll be some synthesised, sanitised, la-la-la singalong hit from the
'60s or '70s. The music they shopped to, music you don't so much
hear as ingest. While you're standing at the check-out, watching the
sorry parade, you might want to try *listening* to that music. Believe
me, it's hard to do: the music doesn't want you to listen to it. It
wants you to feel it, which is a different thing altogether.

Okay, so you're thinking: the best time to lift those purses and
wallets is when the shoppers come stumbling out with their trolleys laden, right? Wrong: I take them *inside* the shop, while their
minds are at the same time filling with junk and jangling with a
mental shopping list. They're seeing novelties they didn't know
they needed – chocolate-flavoured pasta; canned caffeine with a
free colour-change straw – and almost forgetting washing-up liquid
and the kids' dinner. Boom: that's when I bump into them. That's
when I brush against their cheap coats as I lean past for that perfect
tomato towards the back of the display. That's when I half-turn my
head, give them the smile, and say something about how crowded

the shop is today. Caught a little off-guard, they're open to the full effect: dental work, jawline, groomed hair, expensive clothes, sweetened breath and aftershave. My blue eyes sparkle with the same drops TV presenters use. The hand I've reached past their own wears a Breitling wristwatch, all bells and whistles and 2k of Swiss whatever. I'm working now. See, I don't just have to hold this woman – nearly always a woman – in thrall; I have at the same time to hide what my other hand is doing from other shoppers in the vicinity, some of whom, attracted to the show, will be watching me, watching her, and thinking they'd like to be over by the tomatoes right now instead.

It can take ten or fifteen minutes to size up the punter. They need to be a certain type – that goes without saying – and there has to be something worth nicking from them. I have to make sure nobody knows I'm shadowing them as I pass down the aisles with my handbasket (one or two items in it which I'll ditch later: I don't want to be standing in a check-out queue while my victim finds out she's missing cash and credit cards). So many variables, it's a juggling act really. And I have to be a good psychologist. And I have to get away.

So you can see, it's not easy money when all's said and done.

But it beats clerical work, no?

Edinburgh had produced a good haul that Saturday. I'd hit three edge-of-town superstores. Saturday afternoons in those places are like hell on earth. Plus, they're either shrewd or tight-fisted on the east coast: no really easy pickings. They keep their money close to them and are suspicious of any stranger – *any* stranger. I blame those market researchers; you never know who's going to turn out to be one. Best-looking man I've ever seen came to my door one night with the old clipboard and pen. Turned out he was trying to sell carpets. Looked like he was wearing one, too.

And in the morning, just to show I'm not a bad bloke, I'd rejected a wallet which had been held out to me on a plate. There was a blind guy in the first shopping centre, walking the marbled and mirrored halls with confidence and a guide-dog. The guide-dog was a beauty of a Labrador: I love dogs, always have done. It was early in the day and I was just limbering up, sizing the place and its level of security. So I asked the old guy if I could pat his dog, gave me a chance to take a surreptitious look around. Gorgeous dog it was, come-hither eyes, all that. Nice and solid with a good coat. Liked to be stroked, too. So me and the old guy got talking. He was wearing some tatty old tweed jacket with greasy elbows – mind, I can see that smartness of appearance is problematical when you're blind. Anyway, the jacket was all baggy and worn, and when it swung open as the man leaned down to stroke his Lab, I saw his wallet inside, swinging from a loose pocket. And I could have had it, but he was blind for Christ's sake, and maybe I just wasn't ready. So I'd decided to leave it alone and guess what? He leaned a bit further down and the bloody thing slipped out onto the floor. He didn't seem to have heard it, too busy murmuring sweet nothings to the dog, whose name was 'Sabre'. I picked up the wallet, gave its contents a once-over. Sabre's eyes were on me, but he wasn't saying anything. Seemed like he was on my side.

'You dropped this,' I told the old fellow, wedging the wallet into his hand.

Temptation is a terrible thing though ...

Anyway, afternoon shift over, I'd returned to my car and driven it to the furthest corner of the car park to count my haul. I always choose the quietest corner, usually round by the loading bays. Saturday afternoons these aren't usually in use, unless someone's bought a bed or a bike and has driven round to load it into the car. Today, there was a transit van parked nearby, but nobody was in it, and when I looked around I didn't see anyone. So I spread the stuff on the passenger seat and got to work.

There was a guy I knew once called Playtex, partnered him a couple of times. He was called Playtex because he could lift and separate – as in lift people's money and separate them from it. Anyway, his advice was to get away from the scene pronto. But then one day while driving out of the car park, he smacked into a disabled car. There was a cop car nearby, and of course Playtex didn't just have cash and plastic in his own car, he had the purses and wallets too, spread all over the place after the impact.

Now me, I like to take my time, not panic. Go through everything then and there, that way I can ditch the unnecessaries as soon as possible. The purses and wallets go into a bottle bank if there is one: stick them in a bin and they might be found too soon. ID cards, photo-cards, that sort of thing – same place. Cash and credit cards, cash cards, stuff like that I keep, plus any little things like stamps. These days, of course, nobody's supposed to carry cash, but you'd be surprised. First thing a lot of people do before they start their shopping is visit the bank or the machine: they might need cash for a restaurant, a cup of coffee or a double gin, a taxi home, the TV papers ... I get a lot of nice fresh tens and twenties. The plastic I offload to a guy I meet three times a week in a pub in Glasgow. It's a hassle, meeting him this often, but he says we have to 'strike while the iron is hot'. In other words, he needs the cards before they get too old. Some people, so he tells me, will wait up to a week before reporting missing cards, on the chance that they might turn up. Or they simply won't notice they're missing. But all the same, he needs them pronto, so he can maximise their shelf-life. He can use cash cards too, though I don't know how. He bypasses the code or something; works a couple of times then you throw the card away or the machine swallows it.

I'd made not too bad a showing that afternoon. The bottle bank was about ten yards away, so I got out of the car and walked over to it, pushing the leatherware inside. I could smell sour wine and beer slops, and knew I'd be drinking better than either that evening.

I was just getting back into my car when I heard the squeal. It was coming from the transit. I heard it again. There was no one in the front of the van, so the sound had to be coming from the back. No windows, so I couldn't be sure. But yes: the whole van rocked suddenly and I heard a thudding sound. Then a voice – definitely a voice this time – a man's, hissing something that sounded very much like, 'You won't do that again, you bitch!'

I got back into my car and just sat there, hands resting on the steering-wheel. Then I put my window down. I didn't hear anything else. The van was white mostly, but with a black roof. It looked like a respray. The front grille was crimson and the wing-mirror nearest me was missing. There was a partition behind the seats, blocking off the back. I licked my lips, wondering what was happening in there, wondering what to do about it. This last was easy to answer: nothing. Get the hell away from there and forget about it. I started my engine and slipped into first, crawling from the scene.

I'd got as far as the bottle bank when, eyes on the rearview, I saw the transit's back doors swing open. I couldn't see inside: the van had been backed close to a wall. I watched a man jump down and slam the doors shut. He wiped his mouth with the back of his hand, then put his wrist to his mouth and sucked on it. He was over six feet, black T-shirt, black denims and a black leather waistcoat. He looked in his forties, long hair thinning badly. When he looked up, he saw my car and seemed interested in it. I started off again, hoping he'd think I'd been paying a visit to the bottle bank – which, after all, was the truth.

I circled the car park, but ignored the arrows to the exit, instead coming back round to where, from a safe distance, I could again see the transit. The man was moving now, walking towards the super-store's front entrance. He had an awkward, gangling gait, arms swinging low. He reminded me of a guy I'd known years back who'd been the roadie with a third-rate rock band. Same straggly brown hair and overdone sideburns, same sleepless eyes. It wasn't him, it just looked like him.

He disappeared through the automatic doors. I stared towards the van. From this distance, I couldn't see any movement, couldn't hear anything. But I knew there was someone in there, a woman. I didn't like to think about what she was doing there. Had he locked the doors after him? I could hare over there and maybe let her out ...

If he didn't come back out and find me there. He'd seen me by the bottle bank. Maybe he was standing in the shop doorway, waiting for me to make a move. A car was moving slowly towards the bottle bank. It was a shiny black BMW, tinted windows. It didn't stop at the bottle bank; it made for the van, stopped dead in front of it.

Christ, now what?

A man got out. He wore a cream-coloured suit, well-cut, and a pink polo shirt, plus sunglasses – and I'd bet they were Ray-Bans. His hair was light brown, neatly trimmed, and his jaw made chewing motions. He walked to the back of the transit and, without hesitating, pulled open the doors and jumped in. The doors closed after him.

I sat there frowning, conjuring innocent scenarios. The only one that seemed even remotely feasible was that the roadie-lookalike was a pimp, the BMW a punter, and the woman in the back a prossie. But in all honesty I didn't believe that, not for one minute.

Then the doors of the superstore opened and this time it was a security guard who came out, two-way held to his mouth. He seemed to be scanning the car park. I knew the score: he wasn't looking for anyone in a transit van. Chances were, he was looking for *me*. This time, I followed the exit arrows.

I was staying in a bed & breakfast, nicely anonymous on the Dalkeith Road. The front garden had been paved over to create three parking spaces, but mine was the only car there. It was out of season. I'd been asked if I was in town on business, and had answered that I was, the proprietor not seeming to notice that the weekend was a funny time to be conducting business.

There was a bathroom along the hall, and I soaked in a bath for half an hour, eyes closed. My jacket hung from a hook on the back of the door, its inside pocket padded with cash. The plastic was in a brown A4 envelope – sealed – beneath my car's passenger seat. Hotel and B&B rooms were public property. You never knew who'd come traipsing through, or how curious they'd be, so I preferred to keep the stuff in my locked car. The car itself was not worth stealing, not even worth breaking into. There was a yawning gap where a radio should be, and the upholstery was torn and frayed. There were times when it paid not to be showy.

I was reasoning with myself: there was nothing you could do; it would have been too risky; what if there'd been some innocent explanation? Do you want to see yourself in the clink? There was nothing you could do.

I kept coming back to that, trying to convince myself. *You won't do that again, you bitch!* And he'd come out of the van wiping his mouth and sucking his wrist. Had he tried something and she'd bitten him? The squeal I'd heard had been the sound of someone in pain. Maybe the man. Maybe her.

Probably her.

The bath was cold before I got out.

That evening, I tried eating Indian, but couldn't summon up an appetite. Instead I drove through the city, wishing I had a radio, something that might take my mind off things. A radio would have been cheap at the price.

I found myself back at the 'retail park'. It looked different at night, eerie, otherworldly. The interiors of the buildings were well-lit, so you could see a lot of merchandise, only no one was buying.

The car park was empty, sodium lights overhead deterring ne'er-do-wells. But I drove into the car park anyway. These places used private security firms, but they'd be tucked up inside the stores, and probably wouldn't venture out except in the direst emergency. I saw that there was a single car parked in the car park, a nice-looking Volvo, surrounded by a sea of spaces and the occasional island of metal trolleys. But there was no transit van. I stopped my car in front of where it had been, and, headlights full-beam, got out to examine the ground.

I didn't know what I was doing, what I was looking for. Clues? Clues to what? Something that might put my mind at rest perhaps, but I wasn't sure what would do that. There was nothing, of course, not the least sign that any vehicle had ever been there. Just a wad of gum lying next to the wall. I remembered the man in the BMW had been chewing something; this was probably his. Could I take it to the police? Look at this valuable piece of evidence, officers! Can you test the saliva for DNA? Will it lead you to a house of slaughter, an evil trade in sex-slaves?

Thank you, sir, and could we have your name and profession ...?

What was I doing? There had been a noise from a van. A man had yelled something and come out of the van. Another man had gone into the van. So what? I would be leaving town the following day.

By tomorrow night, it would all be forgotten. I got back into my car and reversed from the scene.

But as I passed the solitary Volvo, I slowed, then stopped. If someone had been in that van against their will, then maybe they'd been abducted. Abducted from where? From this very car park perhaps. Which meant their car would still be here, unclaimed at the end of the day.

I got out of my car once more and walked around the Volvo. Could have been dumped by joy-riders of course, except how many joy-riders opted for Volvos? Again, I didn't know what I was looking for. I glanced around, saw nobody, and took a closer look at the car. No keys in the ignition. Something lying on the passenger seat. What was it? Looked like a letter. I tried to read the name on the envelope, but couldn't. Then I did something crazy – I tried the driver's door. And it wasn't locked. It opened with a soft click, no alarm. An unlocked Volvo: now I knew something was wrong. I took out the envelope and held it under lamplight. There was a man's name on it – Mr Roger Masson – but no address.

The woman's husband? The car didn't seem about to yield any other clues. I heard a lorry revving, and closed the door to the Volvo, heading back to my own car. I was behind the steering-wheel before the lorry came into view. It seemed to be collecting rubbish from one of the other shops. I was driving out of the car park before I realised I still had the envelope in my hand.

I stopped at a pub on Corstorphine Road and asked for the phone book. Saturday night: the place was mobbed. Plenty of good-looking young women, a few giving me interested looks as I stood at the bar. Under normal circumstances, I'd have stayed for a drink, flashed around a bit of money. Maybe I'd have found someone for the night. But tonight, all I wanted was an address. Roger Masson: Barnton Avenue West. Back in my car I checked my A-Z, found the street, and drove there.

Ask me why. Go on, do it. I couldn't give you an answer now, couldn't have done then. It just seemed ... it seemed a thing to do; maybe not *the* thing to do – certainly not the *sensible* thing to do – but a thing to do. And I did it.

Big houses next to a golf course. Very big houses actually, de-tached, modern, big gardens. Very nice, and completely silent. It wasn't the sort of street where you'd nip next door for the loan of some coffee: you'd phone the stuff in instead. I stopped the car at the bottom of the drive. The gates were open, and I could see the house clearly. There were lights on inside. Someone walked across a window: a man. He looked worried. He was holding a portable phone to his ear. He held it away from his ear and broke the connection, then rubbed at his forehead. A very worried man. He let his shoulders slump. It was hard to tell from a distance, but he looked in his fifties, if well-preserved. Nice greying hair, open-necked shirt. He seemed to be staring into space, but I realised finally that he wasn't. He was looking out of the window.

He was looking at me.

He turned and walked from the room. The anxious husband, wondering where his wife was. What could I tell him? Nothing. All he'd done was satisfy me that something was wrong. And now that I'd seen his home, I had the feeling that maybe the reason why Mrs Masson had taken her Volvo to the shops this afternoon and not come back was that she'd been unavoidably detained.

By kidnappers.

I watched the front door open, and Masson come running out. He didn't have anything but socks on his feet, and consequently ran on tiptoe down the gravel drive.

'Hey, you!' he was shouting. 'I want to talk to you!'

I started the car and moved off.

'Wait a minute! Help, somebody! Help!'

I tore away from there like I had something to fear. Up onto Queensferry Road and back towards town, missing at least one red light in the process and decidedly ignoring the speed limit.

Which is why the cops caught me.

Flashing blue lights in my rearview, and headlamps flicking to full-beam to tell me to pull over. So what else could I do? I pulled over, easing two wheels up onto the pavement to make room for passing traffic – ever the courteous driver.

I can wing this, I thought. I've not been drinking, and I've no unpaid fines. I can wing this.

'Step out of the car, please, sir.'

I stepped out of the car. There were two of them, uniformed, one – the elder – talking to me, the other walking around the car like I was planning to sell it.

'Something wrong, officers?' The elder blinked at me like I'd been watching too many films.

'Does a red light mean "go faster"?' he asked, while his partner smirked. I tried a shy grin.

'It was on me before I saw it."

'Been drinking this evening, sir?'

'Not a drop.' The younger cop was peering in through the front passenger window. I was all too aware of the plastic in the envelope under the seat. But the envelope was *sealed:* they couldn't open it even if they found it, not without reasonable suspicion. That might not stop them opening it, of course, but at least my lawyer would have a stick to beat them with.

'No?'

I shook my head, breathed out hard, remembered I'd tried eating a curry.

'Was that a madras or a vindaloo?' the older cop asked, not bothering to wait for an answer. His car had a computer on board; a lot of them do these days. Depends where you are; whether the regional force has had enough money in the kitty. He could go and put my licence plate through his machine: it would come up clean. Never buy a dodgy car.

'Just wait there,' the youngster said, going to join his partner. So I stood by my car, arms folded, trying not to look guilty as a parade of motorists slowed to watch. The old guy was on his radio. I had a sudden thought: Masson has called a 999 with my description. Would he do that? No telling what a man will do when he's desperate. The cops were looking at me through their windscreen, maybe trying to sweat me, get me to run for it. No way, not with the envelope under the passenger seat.

So I stood and waited, and at last they came back, both of them.

'We'd like you to come down the station,' the elder said.

'What? Am I being arrested?'

'Just a routine matter.'

'For not stopping at a red light?'

'Routine, sir. If you'll come with us.'

I tried to look disgruntled, appalled – it wasn't hard. 'What about my car?'

'My colleague will drive it, sir. If you'll come with me ...'

I sat mute in the passenger seat all the way to the cop shop.

Police stations are not designed to make you feel like the driven snow, even if the worst thing you've done in your life is try peeping at your sister while she was in the bath. They are like black holes. Once you're in there, to the outside world you've ceased to exist, and the outside world itself ceases to have meaning for you.

That can be frightening. It can loosen tongues. Suddenly you remember about your sister, and blurt it out, dredging up a memory from ten or twenty years ago. You'd tell them anything, these quiet listeners, these stone faces. You'd tell them you once waded through her underwear drawer too, even if this were a downright lie.

I don't have a sister. I wasn't about to tell them anything.

The CID office was big and needed a lick of paint. There were large cracks snaking across the ceiling towards the flickering lengths of centred strip-lighting. There were six desks, big old bulky things, like school surplus from the Billy Bunter era. And there were detectives, wearing suits and ties and looking like they couldn't wait to knock off. I was seated in front of one of the tables. There was no one sitting across from me. I'd been asked if I wanted a cup of coffee. I'd declined. They didn't want to breath-test me, that much was clear. Nothing else was.

Then the detective came and sat down, pulling his chair in inch by inch till he was happy with the arrangement. He lined three ballpoint pens in a row in front of him. There was a clean pad of paper below the pens.

'Do you know why we've asked you here, Mr ...' He looked at a slip of paper in his paw. 'Mr Croft?'

He was not especially tall, but had bulk and confidence. His temples were turning grey; the rest of his hair looked like it would follow soon enough. His eyes were dark, sceptical. He watched me shake my head, then searched his in-tray, at last pulling out a sheet of paper.

'"Six feet one or two",' he read, '"dark hair, well-groomed, well-dressed, blue eyes, squarish face, good teeth. A nice manner".' He looked up. 'Sound familiar, Mr Croft?'

'I might know a few women like that.'

He allowed a smile. 'It could be you, Mr Croft.'

'Could be a lot of people, Sergeant.'

'It's Inspector. Inspector Rebus.'

'Look,' I sat forward, 'what is this all about?'

'It's about someone lifting purses out of bags, Mr Croft.'

'Ridiculous.' I half-laughed. 'Good God, where's this supposed to have happened?'

'All over the city. You live here, Mr Croft?'

'Visiting.'

'When did you arrive?'

'Yesterday evening.'

The detective nodded to himself. 'Two women came up with this description, Mr Croft. Two women in two different supermarkets, two different areas of the city.'

'I did go to *one* supermarket this afternoon.'

'Which one?'

I shrugged. 'Cameron Toil, was that it? Somewhere near my hotel.'

'Foot of Dalkeith Road?'

I nodded.

'What did you want?'

'Razors, deodorant ...' I lowered my voice. 'Contraceptives.'

He ignored my man-to-man admission. 'Got the receipt by any chance?'

I laughed again. 'Threw it away.'

'What line of work are you in?'

'I'm a photographer.' I am too: there's an SLR in the boot of my car. One thing about travelling around the country, I get to take some wonderful photographs. Twice now I've won my camera club's annual prize.

'For a company?'

I shook my head. 'Freelance. I can show you my portfolio.'

'Don't be disgusting,' someone called from across the room. The Inspector smiled at that, and I smiled, too. We were beginning to get along just fine.

'There's been some sort of mistake,' I said. 'Check my hotel room, my car.' I gave him my most honest look, dewy eyes and all.

'Why were you in such a rush?'

'Sorry?'

'On Queensferry Road.'

'I wasn't in any hurry. But when that road's quiet ... you can build up a head of steam without noticing.'

'Lucky you,' the same voice called.

'So you've no objections to us searching your hotel room or your car?'

'None.'

He nodded again. 'So where's the stuff stashed?'

Bluff! my brain yelled. I stared him out, made sure my smile wasn't wavering. 'Look, Inspector ...'

Someone had answered a phone. Now they called across the room. 'John, someone called Masson for you.'

My heart dropped like a stone.

The Inspector picked up his receiver, pushed a button, and leaned back in his chair. 'Mr Masson? What can I do for you, sir?' The way he spoke, I knew this Masson had clout to spare. Rebus's face hardened as he listened. 'What?' He began writing on his notepad. For the moment, I'd been forgotten. 'A pet? When was this?' He listened some more, scribbling furiously. 'Why didn't you come to us straight away? What make of car?' His writing was appalling, but I read the words 'Volvo' and 'car park'. 'And there was no note? Where's your wife now? Can I speak to her, please, sir?'

He put his hand over the mouthpiece. 'Be with you in a minute.'

I nodded, feeling like my head might actually fall off. Mrs Masson was coming to the phone! Her husband was bringing her! So she hadn't been in the van. She was nothing to do with it. What had he said about a pet and a note ...? My hand went to my jacket pocket. The envelope was still there.

'Mrs Masson?' Rebus said now. 'How are you? Yes, must be terrible. They were supposed to leave a note? Have you seen these men?' He listened, started scribbling again. 'You've only spoken to one man? But he spoke in the plural? Well, it might be important, Mrs Masson. When was this?' He began writing again. I could feel sweat trickling down my back. 'No, it's serious all right, I just wish you'd come to us right at the start. I'd like to come out there and see you.' He listened again, scribbled – by now the top sheet of the pad looked like a blackboard at the end of a school day. When he put the receiver down he did so slowly, still writing. Then he got up abruptly and went to talk with someone at the far end of the room.

I slipped my hand into my pocket and felt the envelope. It hadn't been stuck down. I felt inside. Sure enough there was a sheet of paper there. I eased it out, my face blank, unfolded it on my knee and read the pencilled capitals.

£2,000 TO GET THE BITCH BACK. GET MONEY READY, WE'LL CALL.

The squeal I'd heard had been human, but it had been the roadie's voice. He'd just been bitten by Mrs Masson's pet dog: *You won't do that again, you bitch!* Maybe he'd muzzled her, tied her up, knocked her cold. Maybe he'd done worse. If there's one thing I abhor more than the cruelty we inflict on each other, it's cruelty inflicted on animals.

Especially dogs.

It was as clear as day now. Mrs Masson had been instructed to leave her car in the car park, and to return some time later, when she'd find a ransom note on the passenger seat. Only I'd chanced by and lifted the bloody note. So now she didn't know what was expected of her and was going up the wall. And her husband, driven by this, had at last called the police – perhaps against her wishes. All she wanted was her dog back. Meantime, I had the note *and* a description of the dognappers. I had more than any of them.

And I was stuck here.

Rebus came back and tore the sheet from his pad, folded it into his pocket. By now the other note was safe in my pocket. He looked at me for a long time, as if trying to place me. I went dewy-eyed again.

'I've got your licence plate, your name and your address,' he said quietly. 'I've got everything I need – for the moment. I'll want to talk to you again tomorrow. Be here at ten-thirty, understood?'

Two choices: stick with innocent bewilderment, or nod. I nodded. Not that I'd be here tomorrow morning: I'd be packed and gone by midnight.

He gave me another long stare. 'Your car's outside, get the keys from the desk.' He moved away, but paused and turned. 'See you tomorrow, Mr Croft.' He made it sound like a threat

It didn't bother me, I knew I was off and running. That was the only sensible course, I kept telling myself. And I believed it, too.

I sat in my car, hands trembling as they ran over the steering-wheel. I didn't know whether to laugh or cry. In the end, I think I did both simultaneously. I leaned down and felt beneath the passenger seat. The envelope was still there. Everyone deserves a lucky break, I thought, starting the engine.

I'd go back to the B&B, pack my things, and never come back.

Wouldn't that be a callous ending?

But as I drove, I thought of the two men and wondered what kind of dog Mrs Masson owned: something small and snapping, or a big, hearty beast fit for walks across the golf course? I hoped for the latter, for something like the blind man's Labrador. I heard the squeal again. It could have been a dog squealing. And the thump I'd heard: had the roadie smashed its head? My hands tightened on the steering-wheel and, first pub I saw, I pulled over and went looking for another phone book.

This time I had a whisky – a good-sized one. Well, they weren't going to stop me twice in the same night, were they? And I needed the courage. I looked up Masson's address and took down his telephone number. I couldn't call from the bar: too noisy. But there was a box fifty yards along the road, and I used that. A man answered, Masson himself I presumed.

'Inspector Rebus, please."

I heard the man say 'someone for you' as he handed the phone over. 'Hello?'

'Just listen. You're looking for two men.' I gave my descriptions, eyes squeezed shut as I tried to make them as accurate and telling as I could. Then I described the van and the BMW. 'And they want two grand. They'll probably be phoning later.'

Rebus had listened to this in silence. Now he spoke.

'Mr Croft, is that you?'

This time my heart sank like something altogether more massive than a mere stone. A block of city granite maybe.

'Was it your car Mr Masson saw?' Rebus went on.

I licked dry lips. 'Yes,' I said.

'Are you mixed up in this?'

'Only as a ... well, I saw the van. I thought I heard something. I was worried, so I went back tonight.'

'You found the note?' He sounded amused.

'Yes.'

'Why didn't you come forward?' He caught himself. 'No, stupid question. Thanks for your call.'

'Do you still want me at the station tomorrow?'

'Were you planning on coming?'

'It doesn't really fit with my schedule.'

'Get out of the city, Mr Croft. Don't ever come back.'

'Inspector, one question – what breed is she?'

There was a pause while the detective checked. 'Persian Blue,' he said at last.

'What?'

'Persian Blue.'

'But that's a cat.'

'Sorry?'

'A cat.'

'That's right.'

'I *hate* cats!'

I slammed the phone down, went back to the B&B and packed my suitcase in a blind fury. I had paid till noon Sunday, so there was no problem. I just left my key behind, got back into the car and drove.

I was heading down Dalkeith Road, making for the city by-pass, when I saw the van. I blinked, shook my head, but it was definitely the van. I knew not only from the black roof, the missing wing-mirror, but because it was being shadowed by a black BMW. They were going around a roundabout as I approached it. I watched them turn off, then followed. Cameron Toll Shopping Precinct. They were driving into the car park, the only vehicles around at that time of night. I switched off my lights and hung back, watching as they came to a stop.

The roadie got out of the van, and was joined by Mr Smooth, who checked his watch. There was a wall-mounted telephone close by. The roadie opened the back of the van and got in. After checking his watch again, rocking on the balls of his feet, Mr Smooth got in too, closing the doors after him. I kept my lights off and lifted my foot from the brake, rolling down the slight incline towards them, keeping going until my front bumper touched their rear. My car's a big old Merc, same axle-height as a transit. They felt the impact and tried opening the doors, only they were jammed shut by my radiator grille. I got out and jumped up onto my bonnet, my face close to the inch-wide gap in the transit's rear doors.

'A female cat isn't called a bitch!' I screamed at them.

I might have screamed it more than once actually, before getting down and going to the telephone.

Talk Show

Lowland Radio was a young but successful station broadcasting to lowland Scotland. It was said that the station owed its success to two very different personalities. One was the DJ on the midmorning slot, an abrasive and aggressive Shetland Islander, called Hamish MacDiarmid. MacDiarmid hosted a phone-in, supposedly concerning the day's headlines, but in fact these were of relatively minor importance. People did not listen to the phone-in for opinion and comment: they listened for the attacks MacDiarmid made on just about every caller. There were occasional fierce interchanges, interchanges the DJ nearly always won by dint of severing the connection with anyone more intelligent, better informed, or more rational than himself.

Rebus knew that there were men in his own station who would try to take a break between ten-forty-five and eleven-fifteen just to listen. The people who phoned the show knew what they'd get, of course: that was part of the fun. Rebus wondered if they were masochists, but in fact he knew they probably saw themselves as challengers. If they could best MacDiarmid, they would have 'won'. And so MacDiarmid himself became like some raging bull, entering the ring every morning for another joust with the picadors. So far he'd been goaded but not wounded, but who knew how long the luck would last ...?

The other 'personality' – always supposing personality could be applied to someone so ethereal – was Penny Cook, the softly spoken, seductive voice on the station's late-night slot. Five nights a week, on her show *What's Cookin'*, she offered a mix of sedative music, soothing talk, and calming advice to those who took part in her own phone-in segment. These were very different people from those who chose to confront Hamish MacDiarmid. They were quietly worried about their lives, insecure, timid; they had home problems, work problems, personal problems. They were the kind of people, Rebus mused, who got sand kicked in their faces. MacDiarmid's callers, on the other hand, were probably the ones doing the kicking ...

Perhaps it said something about the lowlands of Scotland that Penny Cook's show was said to be the more popular of the two. Again, people at the station talked about it with the fervour usually reserved for TV programmes.

'Did you hear yon guy with the bend in his tackle ...?'

'That woman who said her husband didn't satisfy her ...'

'I felt sorry for that hooker though, wantin' out o' the game ...'

And so on. Rebus had listened to the show himself a few times, slumped on his chair after closing-time. But never for more than a few minutes; like a bedtime story, a few minutes of Penny Cook sent John Rebus straight to the land of Nod. He'd wondered what she looked like. Husky, comfortable, come-to-bed: the picture of her he'd built up was all images, but none of them exactly physical. Sometimes she sounded blonde and tiny, sometimes statuesque with flowing raven hair. His picture of Hamish MacDiarmid was much more vivid: bright red beard, caber-tossing biceps and a kilt.

Well, the truth would out. Rebus stood in the cramped reception area of Lowland Radio and waited for the girl on the switchboard to finish her call. On the wall behind her, a sign said WELCOME:. That colon was important. This seemed to be Lowland Radio's way of greeting the personalities who'd come to the station, perhaps to give interviews. Today, below the WELCOME:, written in felt tip were the names JEZ JENKS and CANDY BARR. Neither name meant anything to Rebus, though they probably would to his daughter. The receptionist had finished her call.

'Have you come for some stickers?'

'Stickers?'

'Car-stickers,' she explained. 'Only we're all out of them. Just temporary, we'll be getting more next week if you'd like to call back.'

'No, thanks anyway. I'm Inspector Rebus. I think Miss Cook's expecting me.'

'Oh, sorry.' The receptionist giggled. 'I'll see if she's around. It was Inspector ...?'

'Rebus.'

She scribbled the name on a pad and returned to her switchboard. 'An Inspector Reeves to see you, Penny ...'

Rebus turned to another wall and cast an eye over Lowland Radio's small display of awards. Well, there was stiff competition these days, he supposed. And not much advertising revenue to go round. Another local station had countered the challenge posed by Hamish MacDiarmid, hiring what they called 'The Ranter', an anonymous individual who dished out insult upon insult to anyone foolish enough to call his show.

It all seemed a long way from the Light Programme, a long way from glowing valves and Home Counties diction. Was it true that the BBC announcers used to wear dinner jackets? DJs in DJs, Rebus thought to himself and laughed.

'I'm glad somebody's cheerful.' It was Penny Cook's voice; she was standing right behind him. Slowly he turned to be confronted by a buxom lady in her early forties – only a year or two younger than Rebus himself. She had permed light brown hair and wore round glasses – the kind popularised by John Lennon on one hand and the NHS on the other.

'I know, I know,' she said. 'I'm never what people expect.' She held out a hand, which Rebus shook. Not only did Penny Cook sound unthreatening, she *looked* unthreatening.

All the more mysterious then that someone, some anonymous caller, should be threatening her life ...

They walked down a corridor towards a sturdy-looking door, to the side of which had been attached a push-button array.

'Security,' she said, pressing four digits before pulling open the door. 'You never know what a lunatic might do given access to the airwaves.'

'On the contrary,' said Rebus, 'I've heard Hamish MacDiarmid.'

She laughed. He didn't think he'd heard her laugh before. 'Is Penny Cook your real name?' he asked, thinking the ice sufficiently broken between them.

'Afraid so. I was born in Nairn. To be honest, I don't think my parents had heard of Penicuik. They just liked the name Penelope.'

They were passing studios and offices. Loudspeakers placed in the ceiling of the corridor relayed the station's afternoon show.

'Ever been inside a radio station before, Inspector?'

'No, never.'

'I'll show you around if you like.'

'If you can spare the time ...'

'No problem.' They were approaching one studio outside which a middle-aged man was in quiet conversation with a spiky-headed teenager. The teenager looked sullen and in need of a wash. Rebus wondered if he were the man's son. If so, a lesson in parental control was definitely needed.

'Hi, Norman,' Penny Cook said in passing. The man smiled towards her. The teenager remained sullen: a controlled pose,

Rebus decided. Further along, having passed through another combination-lock door, Penny herself cleared things up.

'Norman's one of our producers.'

'And the kid with him?'

'Kid?' She smiled wryly. 'That was Jez Jenks, the singer with Leftover Lunch. He probably makes more a day than you and I make in a good year.'

Rebus couldn't remember ever having a 'good year' – the curse of the honest copper. A question came to him.

'And Candy Barr?'

She laughed at this. 'I thought my own name took some beating. Mind you, I don't suppose it's her real name. She's an actress or a comedienne or something. From across the water, of course.'

'Doesn't sound like an Irish name,' Rebus said as Penny Cook held open her office door.

'I wouldn't make jokes around here, Inspector,' she said. 'You'll probably find yourself being signed up for a spot on one of our shows.'

'The Laughing Policeman?' Rebus suggested. But then they were in the office, the door was closed, and the atmosphere cooled appropriately. This was business, after all. Serious business. She sat at her desk. Rebus sat down on the chair across from her.

'Do you want a coffee or anything, Inspector?'

'No thanks. So, when did these calls start, Miss Cook?'

'About a month ago. The first time he tried it, he actually got through to me on-air. That takes some doing. The calls are filtered through two people before they get to me. Efficient people, too. They can usually tell a crank caller from the real thing.'

'How does the system work? Somebody calls in ... then what?'

'Sue or David takes the call. They ask a few questions. Basically, they want to know the person's name, and what it is they want to talk to me about. Then they take a telephone number, tell the caller to stay by his or her telephone, and if we want to put the person on-air, they phone the caller back and prepare them.'

'Fairly rigorous then.'

'Oh yes. And even supposing the odd crank does get through, we've got a three-second delay on them when they're on-air. If they start cussing or raving, we cut the call before it goes out over the ether.'

'And is that what happened with this guy?'

'Pretty much.' She shook a cassette box at him. 'I've got the tape here. Do you want to hear?'

'Please.'

She started to load a cassette player on the ledge behind her. There were no windows in the office. From the number of steps they'd descended to get there, Rebus reckoned this whole floor of the building was located beneath ground-level.

'So you got a phone number for this guy?'

'Only it turned out to be a phone box in some housing scheme. We didn't know that at the time. We never usually take calls from phone boxes. But it was one of those ones that use the phone cards. No beeps, so nobody could tell.' She had loaded the tape to her satisfaction, but was now waiting for it to rewind. 'After he tried getting through again, we phoned his number. It rang and rang, and then some old girl picked it up. She explained where the box was. That was when we knew he'd tricked us.' The tape thumped to a stop. She hit the play button, and sat down again. There was a hiss as the tape began, and then her voice filled the room. She smiled in embarrassment, as if to say: yes, it's a pose, this husky, sultry, late-night me. But it's a living ...

'And now we've got Peter on line one. Peter, you're through to Penny Cook. How are things with you this evening?'

'Not so good, Penny.'

She interrupted the tape for a moment: 'This is where we cut him off.'

The man's voice had been sleepy, almost tranquillised. Now it erupted. 'I know what you're up to! I know what's going on!' The tape went dead. She leaned back in her chair and switched off the machine.

'It makes me shiver every time I hear it. That anger ... such a sudden change in the voice. Brr.' She reached into her drawer and brought out cigarettes and a lighter. Rebus accepted a cigarette from her.

'Thanks,' he said. Then: 'The name'll be false, of course, but did he give a surname?'

'A surname, an address, even a profession. He said he lived in Edinburgh, but we looked up the street name in the *A to Z* and it doesn't exist. From now on, we check that addresses are real before we call back. His surname was Gemmell. He even spelt it out for Sue. She couldn't believe he was a crank, he sounded so genuine.'

'What did he tell her his problem was?'

'Drinking too much ... how it was affecting his work. I like that sort of problem. The advice is straightforward, and it can be helping a lot of people too scared to phone in.'

'What did he say his job was?'

'Bank executive. He gave Sue the bank's name and everything, and he kept saying it wasn't to be broadcast.' She smiled, shook her head. 'I mean, this nut really was *good*.'

Rebus nodded. 'He seems to have known the set-up pretty well.'

'You mean he got to the safe without triggering any of the alarms?' She smiled still. 'Oh yes, he's a real pro.'

'And the calls have persisted?'

'Most nights. We've got him tagged now though. He's tried using different accents ... dialects ... always a different name and job. But he hasn't managed to beat the system again. When he knows he's been found out, he does that whole routine again. "I know what you've done." Blah, blah. We put the phone down on him before he can get started.'

'And what *have* you done, Miss Cook?'

'Absolutely nothing, Inspector. Not that I know of.'

Rebus nodded slowly. 'Can I hear the tape again?'

'Sure.' She wound it back, and they listened together. Then she excused herself – 'to powder my nose' – and Rebus listened twice more. When she returned, she was carrying two plastic beakers of coffee.

'Thought I might tempt you,' she said. 'Milk, no sugar ... I hope that's all right.'

'Thank you, yes, that's just the job.'

'So, Inspector, what do you think?'

He sipped the lukewarm liquid. 'I think,' he said, 'you've got an anonymous phone-caller.'

She raised her cup, as though to toast him. 'God bless CID,' she said. 'What would we do without you?'

'The problem is that he's probably mobile, not sticking to the same telephone kiosk every time. That's supposing he's as clever as he seems. We can get BT to put a trace on him, but for that you'd have to keep him talking. Or, if he gives his number, we can trace him from that. But it takes time.'

'And meanwhile he could be slipping off into the night?'

'I'm afraid so. Still, apart from continuing to fend him off and hoping he gets fed up, I can't see what else can be done. You don't recognise the voice? Someone from your past ... an ex-lover ... someone with a grudge?'

'I don't make enemies, Inspector.'

Looking at her, listening to her voice, he found that easy to believe. Maybe not personal enemies ...

'What about the other radio stations? They can't be too thrilled about your ratings.'

Her laughter was loud. 'You think they've put out a contract on me, is that it?'

Rebus smiled and shrugged. 'Just a thought. But yours *is* the most popular show Lowland has got, isn't it?'

'I think I'm still just about ahead of Hamish, yes. But then Hamish's show is just ... well, Hamish. My show's all about the people themselves, the ones who call in. Human interest, you could say.'

'And there's plenty of interest.'

'Suffering is always interesting, isn't it? It appeals to the voyeur. We *do* get our fair share of crank calls. Maybe that's why. All those lonely, slightly deranged people out there ... listening to me. Me, pretending I've got all the answers.' Her smile this time was rueful. 'The calls recently have been getting ... I don't know whether to say "better" or "worse". Worse problems, better radio.'

'Better for your ratings, you mean?'

'Most advertisers ignore the late-night slots. That's common knowledge. Not a big enough audience. But it's never been a problem on my show. We did slip back for a little while, but the figures picked up again. Up and up and up ... Don't ask me what sort of listeners we're attracting. I leave all that to market research.'

Rebus finished his coffee and clasped both knees, preparing to rise. 'I'd like to take the tape with me, is that possible?'

'Sure.' She ejected the tape.

'And I'd like to have a word with ... Sue, is it?'

She checked her watch. 'Sue, yes, but she won't be in for a few hours yet. Night shift, you see. Only us poor disc jockeys have to be here twenty-four hours. I exaggerate, but it feels like it sometimes.' She patted a tray on the ledge beside the cassette player. The tray was filled with correspondence. 'Besides, I have my fan mail to deal with.'

Rebus nodded, glanced at the cassette tape he was now holding. 'Let me have a think about this, Miss Cook. I'll see what we can do.'

'OK, Inspector.'

'Sorry I can't be more constructive. You were quite right to contact us.'

'I didn't suppose there was much you could—'

'We don't know that yet. As I say, give me a little time to think about it.'

She rose from her chair. 'I'll see you out. This place is a maze, and we can't have you stumbling in on the *Afternoon Show*, can we? You might end up doing your Laughing Policeman routine after all ...'

*

As they were walking down the long, hushed corridor, Rebus saw two men in conversation at the bottom of the stairwell. One was a beefy, hearty-looking man with a mass of rumpled hair and a good growth of beard. His cheeks seemed veined with blood. The other man proved a significant contrast, small and thin with slicked-back hair. He wore a grey suit and white shirt, the latter offset by a bright red paisley-patterned tie.

'Ah,' said Penny Cook quietly, 'a chance to kill two birds. Come on, let me introduce you to Gordon Prentice – he's the station chief – and to the infamous Hamish MacDiarmid.'

Well, Rebus had no trouble deciding which man was which. Except that, when Penny did make the introductions, he was proved utterly wrong. The bearded man pumped his hand.

'I hope you're going to be able to help, Inspector. There are some sick minds out there.' This was Gordon Prentice. He wore baggy brown cords and an open-necked shirt from which protruded tufts of wiry hair. Hamish MacDiarmid's hand, when Rebus took it, was limp and cool, like something lifted from a larder. No matter how hard he tried, Rebus couldn't match this ... for want of a better word, *yuppie* ... couldn't match him to the combative voice. But then MacDiarmid spoke.

'Sick minds is right, and stupid minds too. I don't know which is worse, a deranged audience or an educationally subnormal one.' He turned to Penny Cook. 'Maybe you got the better bargain, Penelope.' He turned back to Prentice. So that's what a sneer looks like, Rebus thought. But MacDiarmid was speaking again. 'Gordon, how about letting Penny and me swap shows for a day? She could sit there agreeing with every bigoted caller I get, and I could get stuck in about her social cripples. What do you think?'

Prentice chuckled and placed a hand on the shoulder of both his star DJs. 'I'll give it some thought, Hamish. Penny might not be too thrilled though. I think she has a soft spot for her "cripples".'

Penny Cook certainly didn't look 'too thrilled' by the time Rebus and she were out of earshot.

'Those two,' she hissed. 'Sometimes they act like I'm not even there! Men ...' She glanced towards Rebus. 'Present company excluded, of course.'

'I'll take that as a compliment.'

'I shouldn't be so hard on Gordon actually. I know I joke about being here twenty-four hours a day, but I really think he *does* spend all day and all night at the station. He's here from early morning, but each night he comes into the studio to listen to a bit of my show. Beyond the call of duty, wouldn't you say?'

Rebus merely shrugged.

'I bet,' she went on, 'when you saw them you thought it was Hamish with the beard.'

Rebus nodded. She giggled. 'Everybody does,' she said. 'Nobody's what they seem in this place. I'll let you into a secret. The station doesn't keep any publicity shots of Hamish. They're afraid it would hurt his image if everyone found out he looks like a wimp.'

'He's certainly not *quite* what I expected.'

She gave him an ambiguous look. 'No, well, *you're* not quite what *I* was expecting either.' There was a moment's stillness between them, broken only by some coffee commercial being broadcast from the ceiling: '. . . but Camelot Coffee is no myth, and mmm . . . it tastes *so* good.' They smiled at one another and walked on.

Driving back into Edinburgh, Rebus listened, despite himself, to the drivel on Lowland Radio. Advertising was tight, he knew that. Maybe that was why he seemed to hear the same dozen or so adverts over and over again. Lots of air-time to fill and so few advertisers to fill it . . .

'. . . and mmm . . . it tastes *so* good.'

That particular advert was beginning to get to him. It careered around in his head, even when it wasn't being broadcast. The actor's voice was so . . . what was the word? It was like being force-fed a tablespoon of honey. Cloying, sickly, altogether too much.

'Was Camelot a myth or is it real? Arthur and Guinevere, Merlin and Lancelot. A dream, or—'

Rebus switched off the radio. 'It's only a jar of bloody coffee,' he told his radio set. Yes, he thought, a jar of coffee . . . and mmm . . . it tastes *so* good. Come to think of it, he needed coffee for the flat. He'd stop off at the corner shop, and whatever he bought it wouldn't be Camelot.

But, as a promotional gimmick, there was a fifty-pence refund on Camelot, so Rebus did buy it, and sat at home that evening drinking the vile stuff and listening to Penny Cook's tape. Tomorrow evening, he was thinking, he might go along to the station to catch her show live. He had an excuse after all: he wanted to speak with Sue, the telephonist. That was the excuse; the truth was that he was intrigued by Penny Cook herself.

You're not quite what I was expecting.

Was he reading too much into that one sentence? Maybe he was. Well, put it another way then: he had a *duty* to return to Lowland Radio, a duty to talk to Sue. He wound the tape back for the umpteenth time. That ferocious voice. Sue had been surprised by its ferocity, hadn't she? The man had seemed so quiet, so polite in their initial conversation. Rebus was stuck. Maybe the caller *would* simply get fed up. When it was a question of someone's home being called, there were steps you could take: have someone intercept all calls, change the person's number and keep it ex-directory. But Penny Cook needed her number to be public. She couldn't hide, except behind the wall provided by Sue and David.

Then he had an idea. It wasn't much of an idea, but it was better than nothing. Bill Costain at the Forensic Science Lab was keen on sound recording, tape recorders, all that sort of stuff. Maybe he could do something with Mr Anonymous. Yes, he'd call him first thing tomorrow. He sipped his coffee, then squirmed.

'Tastes more like camel than Camelot,' he muttered, hitting the play button.

The morning was bright and clear, but Bill Costain was dull and overcast.

'I was playing in a darts match last night,' he explained. 'We won for a change. The amount of drink we put away, you'd think Scotland had just done the Grand Slam.'

'Never mind,' said Rebus, handing over the cassette tape. 'I've brought you something soothing ...'

'Soothing' wasn't the word Costain himself used after listening to the tape. But he enjoyed a challenge, and the challenge Rebus had laid down was to tell him anything at all about the voice. He listened several times to the tape, and put it through some sort of analyser, the voice becoming a series of peaks and troughs.

Costain scratched his head. 'There's too big a difference between the voice at the beginning and the voice when hysterical.'

'How do you mean?' Costain always seemed able to baffle Rebus.

'The hysterical voice is so much higher than the voice at the beginning. It's hardly ... natural.'

'Meaning?'

'I'd say one of them's a put-on. Probably the initial voice. He's disguising his normal tone, speaking in a lower register than usual.'

'So can we get back to his *real* voice?'

'You mean can we retrieve it? Yes, but the lab isn't the best place for that. A friend of mine has a recording studio out Morningside way. I'll give him a bell ...'

They were in luck. The studio's facilities were not in use that morning. Rebus drove them to Morningside and then sat back as Costain and his friend got busy at the mixing console. They slowed the hysteric part of the tape; then managed somehow to take the pitch of the voice down several tones. It began to sound more than slightly unnatural, like a Dalek or something electronic. But then they started to build it back up again, until Rebus was listening to a slow, almost lifeless vocal over the studio's huge monitor speakers.

'I ... know ... what ... you've ... done.'

Yes, there was life there now, almost a hint of personality. After this, they switched to the caller's first utterance – 'Not so good, Penny' – and played around with it, heightening the pitch slightly, even speeding it up a bit.

'That's about as good as it gets,' Costain said at last.

'It's brilliant, Bill, thanks. Can I get a copy?'

Having dropped Costain back at the lab, Rebus wormed his way back through the lunchtime traffic to Great London Road police station. He played this new tape several times, then switched from tape to radio. Christ, he'd forgotten: it was still tuned to Lowland.

'... and mmm ... it tastes *so* good.'

Rebus fairly growled as he reached for the off button. But the damage, the delirious, wonderful damage, had already been done ...

The wine bar was on the corner of Hanover Street and Queen Street. It was a typical Edinburgh affair in that though it might have started with wine, quiche and salad in mind, it had reverted to beer – albeit mainly of the 'designer' variety – and pies. Always supposing you could call something filled with chickpeas and spices a 'pie'. Still, it had an IPA pump, and that was good enough for Rebus. The place had just finished its lunchtime peak, and tables were still cluttered with plates, glasses and condiments. Having paid over the odds for his drink, Rebus felt the barman owed him a favour. He gave the young man a name. The barman nodded towards a table near the window. The table's sole occupant looked just out of his teens. He flicked a lock of hair back from his forehead and gazed out of the window. There was a newspaper folded into quarters on his knee. He tapped his teeth with a ballpoint, mulling over some crossword clue.

Without asking, Rebus sat down opposite him. 'It whiles away the time,' he said. The tooth-tapper seemed still intent on the window.

Maybe he could see his reflection there. The modern Narcissus. Another flick of the hair.

'If you got a haircut, you wouldn't need to keep doing that.'

This achieved a smile. Maybe he thought Rebus was trying to chat him up. Well, after all, this was known as an actors' bar, wasn't it? Half a glass of orange juice sat on the table, the ubiquitous ice-cube having melted away to a sliver.

'Aye,' Rebus mused, 'passes the time.'

This time the eyes turned from the window and were on him. Rebus leaned forward across the table. When he spoke, he spoke quietly, confidently.

'I know what you've done,' he said, not sure even as he said it whether he were quoting or speaking for himself.

The lock of hair fell forward and stayed there. A frozen second, then another, and the man rose quickly to his feet, the chair tipping back. But Rebus, still seated, had grabbed at an arm and held it fast.

'Let go of me!'

'Sit down.'

'I said let go!'

'And I said sit down!' Rebus pulled him back on to his chair. 'That's better. We've got a lot to talk about, you and me. We can do it here or down at the station, and by "station" I don't mean Scotrail. OK?'

The head was bowed, the careful hair now almost completely dishevelled. It was that easy ... Rebus found the tiniest grain of pity. 'Do you want something else to drink?' The head shook from side to side. 'Not even a cup of coffee?'

Now the head looked up at him.

'I saw the film once,' Rebus went on. 'Bloody awful it was, but not half as bad as the coffee. Give me Richard Harris's singing any day.'

Now, finally, the head grinned. 'That's better,' said Rebus. 'Come on, son. It's time, if you'll pardon the expression, to spill the beans.'

The beans spilled ...

Rebus was there that night for *What's Cookin'*. It surprised him that Penny Cook herself, who sounded so calm on the air, was, before the programme, a complete bundle of nerves. She slipped a small yellow tablet on to her tongue and washed it down with a beaker of water.

'Don't ask,' she said, cutting off the obvious question. Sue and David were stationed by their telephones in the production room;

which was separated from Penny's studio by a large glass window. Her producer did his best to calm things down. Though not yet out of his thirties, he looked to be an old pro at this. Rebus wondered if he shouldn't have his own counselling show ...

Rebus chatted with Sue for ten minutes or so, and watched as the production team went through its paces. Really, it was a two-man operation – producer and engineer. There was a last-minute panic when Penny's microphone started to play up, but the engineer was swift to replace it. By five minutes to eleven, the hysteria seemed over. Everyone was calm now, or was so tense it didn't show. Like troops just before a battle, Rebus was thinking. Penny had a couple of questions about the running order of the night's musical pieces. She held a conversation with her producer, communicating via mikes and headphones, but looking at one another through the window.

Then she turned her eyes towards Rebus, winked at him, and crossed her fingers. He crossed his fingers back at her.

'Two minutes everyone ...'

At the top of the hour there was news, and straight after the news ...

A tape played. The show's theme music. Penny leaned towards her microphone, which hung like an anglepoise over her desk. The music faded.

'Hello again. This is Penny Cook, and this is *What's Cookin'*. I'll be with you until three o'clock, so if you've got a problem, I'm just a phone call away. And if you want to ring me the number as ever is ...'

It was extraordinary, and Rebus could only marvel at it. Her eyes were closed, and she looked so brittle that a shiver might turn her to powder. Yet that voice ... so controlled ... no, not controlled; rather, it was as though it were apart from her, as though it possessed a life of its own, a personality ... Rebus looked at the studio clock. Four hours of this, five nights a week? All in all, he thought, he'd rather be a policeman.

The show was running like clockwork. Calls were taken by the two operators, details scribbled down. There was discussion with the producer about suitable candidates, and during the musical interludes or the commercials – '... and mmm ... it tastes *so* good' – the producer would relay details about the callers to Penny.

'Let's go with that one,' she might say. Or: 'I can't deal with that, not tonight.' Usually, her word was the last, though the producer might demur.

'I don't know, it's quite a while since we covered adultery ...' Rebus watched. Rebus listened. But most of all, Rebus waited ...

'OK, Penny,' the producer told her, 'it's line two next. His name's Michael.'

She nodded. 'Can somebody get me a coffee?'

'Sure.'

'And next,' she said, 'I think we've got Michael on line two. Hello, Michael?'

It was quarter to midnight. As usual, the door of the production room opened and Gordon Prentice stepped into the room. He had nods and smiles for everyone, and seemed especially pleased to see Rebus.

'Inspector,' he said shaking Rebus's hand. 'I see you take your work seriously, coming here at this hour.' He patted the producer's shoulder. 'How's the show tonight?'

'Been a bit tame so far, but this looks interesting.'

Penny's eyes were on the dimly lit production room. But her voice was all for Michael.

'And what do you do for a living, Michael?'

The caller's voice crackled out of the loudspeakers. 'I'm an actor, Penny.'

'Really? And are you working just now?'

'No, I'm what we call "resting".'

'Ah well, they say there's no rest for the wicked. I suppose that must mean you *haven't* been wicked.'

Gordon Prentice, running his fingers through his beard, smiled at this, turning to Rebus to see how he was enjoying himself. Rebus smiled back.

'On the contrary,' the voice was saying. 'I've been really quite wicked. And I'm ashamed of it.'

'And what is it you're so ashamed of, Michael?'

'I've been telephoning you anonymously, Penny. Threatening you. I'm sorry. You see, I thought you knew about it. But the policeman tells me you don't. I'm sorry.'

Prentice wasn't smiling now. His eyes had opened wide in disbelief.

'Knew about what, Michael?' Her eyes were staring at the window. Light bounced off her spectacles, sending flashes like laser beams into the production room.

'Knew about the fix. When the ratings were going down, the station head, Gordon Prentice, started rigging the shows, yours and Hamish MacDiarmid's. MacDiarmid might even be in on it.'

'What do you mean, rigging?'

'Kill it!' shouted Prentice. 'Kill transmission! He's raving mad! Cut the line someone. Here, I'll do it—'

But Rebus had come up behind Prentice and now locked his own arms around Prentice's. 'I think you'd better listen,' he warned.

'Out of work actors,' Michael was saying, the way he'd told Rebus earlier in the day. 'Prentice put together a ... you could call it a cast, I suppose. Half a dozen people. They phone in using different voices, always with a controversial point to make or some nice juicy problem. One of them told me at a party one night. I didn't believe her until I started listening for myself. An actor can tell that sort of thing, when a voice isn't quite right, when something's an act rather than for real.'

Prentice was struggling, but couldn't break Rebus's hold. 'Lies!' he yelled. 'Complete rubbish! Let go of me, you—'

Penny Cook's eyes were on Prentice now, and on no one but Prentice.

'So what you're saying, Michael, if I understand you, is that Gordon Prentice is rigging our phone-ins so as to boost audience figures?'

'That's right.'

'Michael, thank you for your call.'

It was Rebus who spoke, and he spoke to the producer.

'That'll do.'

The producer nodded through the glass to Penny Cook, then flipped a switch. Music could be heard over the loudspeakers. The producer started to fade the piece out. Penny spoke into her microphone.

'A slightly longer musical interlude there, but I hope you enjoyed it. We'll be going back to your calls very shortly, but first we've got some commercials.'

She slipped off her glasses and rubbed the bridge of her nose.

'A private performance,' Rebus explained to Prentice. 'For our benefit only. The listeners were hearing something else.' Rebus felt Prentice's body soften, the shoulders slump. He was caught, and knew it for sure. Rebus relaxed his hold on the man: he wouldn't try anything now.

The Camelot Coffee ad was playing. It had been easy really. Recognising the voice on the commercial as that of the phone caller, Rebus had contacted the ad agency involved, who had given him the name and address of the actor concerned: Michael Barrie, presently resting and to be found most days in a certain city-centre wine bar ...

Barrie knew he was in trouble, but Rebus was sure it could be smoothed out. But as for Gordon Prentice ... ah, that was different altogether.

'The station's ruined!' he wailed. 'You must know that!' He pleaded with the producer, the engineer, but especially with the hate-filled eyes of Penny Cook who, behind glass, could not even hear him. 'Once this gets out, you'll *all* be out of a job! All of you! That's why I—'

'Back on in five seconds, Penny,' said the producer, as though it was just another night on *What's Cookin'*. Penny Cook nodded, resting her glasses back on her nose. The stuffing looked to have been knocked out of her. With one final baleful glance towards Prentice, she turned to her microphone.

'Welcome back. A change of direction now, because I'd like to say a few words to you about the head of Lowland Radio, Gordon Prentice. I hope you'll bear with me for a minute or two. It shouldn't take much longer than that ...'

It didn't, but what she said was tabloid news by morning, and Lowland Radio's licence was withdrawn not long after that. Rebus went back to Radio Three for when he was driving, and no radio at all in his flat. Hamish MacDiarmid, as far as he could ascertain, went back to a croft somewhere, but Penny Cook stuck around, going freelance and doing some journalism as well as the odd radio programme.

It was very late one night when the knock came at Rebus's door. He opened it to find Penny standing there. She pretended surprise at seeing him.

'Oh, hello,' she said. 'I didn't know you lived here. Only, I've run out of coffee and I was wondering ...'

Laughing, Rebus led her inside. 'I can let you have the best part of a jar of Camelot,' he said. 'Or alternatively we could get drunk and go to bed ...'

They got drunk.

Trip Trap

Blame it on patience.

Patience, coincidence, or fate. Whatever, Grace Gallagher came downstairs that morning and found herself sitting at the dining table with a cup of strong brown tea (there was just enough milk in the fridge for one other cup), staring at the pack of cards. She sucked cigarette smoke into her lungs, feeling her heart beat the faster for it. This cigarette she enjoyed. George did not allow her to smoke in his presence, and in his presence she was for the best part of each and every day. The smoke upset him, he said. It tasted his mouth, so that food took on a funny flavour. It irritated his nostrils, made him sneeze and cough. Made him giddy. George had written the book on hypochondria.

So the house became a no-smoking zone when George was up and about. Which was precisely why Grace relished this small moment by herself, a moment lasting from seven fifteen until seven forty-five. For the forty years of their married life, Grace had always managed to wake up thirty clear minutes before her husband. She would sit at the table with a cigarette and tea until his feet forced a creak from the bedroom floorboard on his side of the bed. That floorboard had creaked from the day they'd moved into 26 Gillan Drive, thirty-odd years ago. George had promised to fix it; now he wasn't even fit to fix himself tea and toast.

Grace finished the cigarette and stared at the pack of cards. They'd played whist and rummy the previous evening, playing for stakes of a penny a game. And she'd lost as usual. George hated losing, defeat bringing on a sulk which could last the whole of the following day, so to make her life a little easier Grace now allowed him to win, purposely throwing away useful cards, frittering her trumps. George would sometimes notice and mock her for her stupidity. But more often he just clapped his hands together after another win, his puffy fingers stroking the winnings from the table top.

Grace now found herself opening the pack, shuffling, and laying out the cards for a hand of patience, a hand which she won without effort. She shuffled again, played again, won again. This, it seemed, was her morning. She tried a third game, and again the cards fell right, until four neat piles stared back at her, black on red on black on red, all the way from king to ace. She was halfway through a fourth hand, and confident of success, when the floorboard creaked, her name was called, and the day – her real day – began. She made tea (that was the end of the milk) and toast, and took it to George in bed. He'd been to the bathroom, and slipped slowly back between the sheets.

'Leg's giving me gyp today,' he said. Grace was silent, having no new replies to add to this statement. She placed his tray on the bed and pulled open the curtains. The room was stuffy, but even in summer he didn't like the windows open. He blamed the pollution, the acid rain, the exhaust fumes. They played merry hell with his lungs, making him wheezy, breathless. Grace peered out on to the street. Across the road, houses just like hers seemed already to be wilting from the day's ordinariness. Yet inside her, despite everything, despite the sour smell of the room, the heavy breath of her unshaven husband, the slurping of tea, the grey heat of the morning, Grace could feel something extraordinary. Hadn't she won at patience? Won time and time again? Paths seemed to be opening up in front of her.

'I'll go fetch you your paper,' she said.

George Gallagher liked to study racing form. He would pore over the newspaper, sneering at the tipsters' choices, and would come up with a 'super yankee' – five horses which, should they all romp home as winners, would make them their fortune. Grace would take his betting slip to the bookie's on the High Street, would hand across the stake money – less than £1.50 per day – and would go home to listen on the radio as horse after horse failed in its mission, the tipsters' choices meantime bringing in a fair return. But George had what he called 'inside knowledge', and besides, the tipsters were all crooked, weren't they? You couldn't trust them. Grace was a bloody fool if she thought she could. Often a choice of George's would come in second or third, but despite her efforts he refused to back any horse each way. All or nothing, that's what he wanted.

'You never win big by betting that way.'

Grace's smile was like a nail file: *we never win at all.*

George wondered sometimes why it took his wife so long to fetch the paper. After all, the shop was ten minutes' walk away at most, yet Grace would usually be out of the house for the best part of an hour. But there was always the story of a neighbour met, gossip exchanged, a queue in the shop, or the paper not having arrived, entailing a longer walk to the newsagent's further down the road ...

In fact, Grace took the newspaper to Lossie Park, where, weather permitting, she sat on one of the benches and, taking a ballpoint pen (free with a woman's magazine, refilled twice since) from her handbag, proceeded to attempt the newspaper's crossword. At first, she'd filled in the 'quick' clues, but had grown more confident with the years so that she now did the 'cryptic', often finishing it, sometimes failing for want of one or two answers, which she would ponder over the rest of the day. George, his eyes fixed on the sports pages, never noticed that she'd been busy at the crossword. He got his news, so he said, from the TV and the radio, though in fact Grace had noticed that he normally slept through the television news, and seldom listened to the radio.

If the weather was dreich, Grace would sit on a sheltered bench, where one day a year or so back she had been joined by a gentleman of similar years (which was to say, eight or nine years younger than George). He was a local, a widower, and his name was Jim Malcolm. They talked, but spent most of the time just watching the park itself, studying mothers with prams, boys with their dogs, games of football, lovers' tiffs, and, even at that early hour, the occasional drunk. Every day they met at one bench or another, seeming to happen upon one another by accident, never seeing one another at any other time of the day, or any other location, other than those truly accidental meetings in a shop or on the pavement.

And then, a few weeks back, springtime, standing in the butcher's shop, Grace had overheard the news of Jim Malcolm's death. When her turn came to be served, Grace asked for half a pound of steak mince, instead of the usual 'economy' stuff. The butcher raised an eyebrow.

'Something to celebrate, Mrs Gallagher?'

'Not really,' Grace had said quietly. That night, George had eaten the expensive mince without comment.

Today she completed the crossword in record time. It wasn't that the clues seemed easier than usual; it was more that her brain seemed to be working faster than ever before, catching that inference or this anagram. Anything, she decided, was possible on a day like this. Simply anything. The sun was appearing from behind a bank of cloud. She closed the newspaper, folded it into her bag alongside the pen, and stood up. She'd been in the park barely ten minutes. If she returned home so quickly, George might ask questions. So instead she walked a slow circuit of the playing fields, her thoughts on patience, and crosswords and creaking floorboards, and much more besides.

Blame it on Patience.

Detective Inspector John Rebus had known Dr Patience Aitken for several years, and not once during their working relationship had he been able to refuse her a favour. Patience seemed to Rebus the kind of woman his parents, if still alive, would have been trying to marry him off to, were he still single. Which, in a sense, he was, being divorced. On finding he *was* divorced, Patience had invited Rebus round to her surprisingly large house for what she had called 'dinner'. Halfway through a home-baked fruit pie, Patience had admitted to Rebus that she was wearing no underwear. Homely but smouldering: that was Patience. Who could deny such a woman a favour? Not John Rebus. And so it was that he found himself this evening standing on the doorstep of 26 Gillan Drive, and about to intrude on private grief.

Not that there was anything very private about a death, not in this part of Scotland, or in any part of Scotland come to that. Curtains twitched at neighbouring windows, people spoke in lowered voices across the divide of a garden fence, and fewer televisions than usual blared out the ubiquitous advertising jingles and even more ubiquitous game show applause.

Gillan Drive was part of an anonymous working-class district on the south-eastern outskirts of Edinburgh. The district had fallen on hard times, but there was still the smell of pride in the air. Gardens were kept tidy, the tiny lawns clipped like army haircuts, and the cars parked tight against the kerbs were old – W and X registrations predominated – but polished, showing no signs of rust. Rebus took it all in in a moment. In a neighbourhood like this, grief was for sharing. Everybody wanted their cut. Still something stopped him lifting the door knocker and letting it fall. Patience Aitken had been vague, wary, ambivalent: that was why she was asking him for a favour, and not for his professional help.

'I mean,' she had said over the telephone, 'I've been treating George Gallagher on and off – more *on* than off – for years. I think about the only complaints I've ever not known him to think he had are beri-beri and elephantiasis, and then only because you never read about them in the "Doc's Page" of the *Sunday Post*.'

Rebus smiled. GPs throughout Scotland feared their Monday morning surgeries, when people would suddenly appear in droves suffering from complaints read about the previous morning in the *Post*. No wonder people called the paper an 'institution' ...

'And all the while,' Patience Aitken was saying, 'Grace has been by his bedside. Always patient with him, always looking after him. The woman's been an angel.'

'So what's the problem?' Rebus nursed not only the telephone, but a headache and a mug of black coffee as well. (Black coffee because he was dieting; a headache for not unconnected reasons.)

'The problem is that George fell downstairs this morning. He's dead.'

'I'm sorry to hear it.'

There was a silence at the other end of the line.

'I take it,' Rebus said, 'that you don't share my feelings.'

'George Gallagher was a cantankerous old man, grown from a bitter younger man and most probably a fairly unsociable teenager. I don't think I ever heard him utter a civil word, never mind a "please" or a "thank you".'

'Fine,' said Rebus, 'so let's celebrate his demise.'

Silence again.

Rebus sighed and rubbed his temples. 'Out with it,' he ordered.

'He's supposed to have fallen downstairs,' Patience Aitken explained. 'He did go downstairs in the afternoon, sometimes to watch racing on the telly, sometimes just to stare at a different set of walls from the bedroom. But he fell at around eleven o'clock, which is a bit early for him ...'

'And you think he was pushed?' Rebus tried not to sound cynical. Her reply was blunt. 'Yes, I do.'

'By this angel who's managed to put up with him all these years?'

'That's right.'

'OK, Doc, so point me to the medical evidence.'

'Well, it's a narrow staircase, pretty steep, about eleven or twelve steps, say. If you weighed around thirteen stone, and happened to slip at the top, you'd sort of be bounced off the sides as you fell, wouldn't you?'

'Perhaps.'

'And you'd try to grab hold of something to stop your fall. There's a banister on one wall. They were waiting for the council to come and fit an extra banister on the other wall.'

'So you'd reach out to grab something, fair enough.' Rebus drained the sour black coffee and studied the pile of work in his in-tray.

'Well, you'd have bruising, wouldn't you?' said Patience Aitken. 'Grazes on your elbows or knees, there'd be marks where you'd clawed at the walls.'

Rebus knew that she was surmising, but could not disagree thus far. 'Go on,' he said.

'George Gallagher only has significant marks on his head, where he hit the floor at the bottom of the stairs, breaking his neck in the process. No real bruising or grazing to the body, no marks on the wall as far as I can see.'

'So you're saying he flew from the top landing with a fair bit of momentum, and the first thing he touched was the ground?'

'That's how it looks. Unless I'm imagining it.'

'So he either jumped, or he was pushed?'

'Yes.' She paused again. 'I know it sounds tenuous, John. And Christ knows I don't want to accuse Grace of anything ...'

Rebus picked up a ballpoint pen from beside the telephone and scrabbled on the surface of his desk until he found the back of an envelope upon which to write.

'You're only doing your job, Patience,' he said. 'Give me the address and I'll go pay my respects.'

The door of 26 Gillan Drive opened slowly, and a man peered out at Rebus, then ushered him quickly inside, laying a soft hand on his arm.

'In ye come, son. In ye come. The women are in the living-room. The kitchen's through here.' He nodded his head, then led Rebus through a narrow hallway past a closed door, from behind which came tearful sounds, towards a half-open door at the back of the house. Rebus had not even glanced at the stairs as they'd passed them, the stairs which had faced him at the open front door of the house. The kitchen door was now opened from within, and Rebus saw that seven or eight men had squeezed into the tiny back room. There were stale smells of cooking fat and soup, stew and fruit cake, but above them wafted a more recent smell: whisky.

'Here ye are, son.' Someone was handing him a tumbler with a good inch of amber liquid in it. Everyone else had just such a glass nestling in their hand. They all shuffled from one foot to another, awkward, hardly daring to speak. They had nodded at Rebus's entrance, but now gave him little heed. Glasses were replenished. Rebus noticed the Co-op price label on the bottle.

'You've just moved into Cashman Street, haven't you?' someone was asking someone else.

'Aye, that's right. A couple of months ago. The wife used to meet Mrs Gallagher at the shops, so we thought we'd drop in.'

'See this estate, son, it was miners' rows once upon a time. It used to be that you lived here and died here. But these days there's that much coming and going ...'

The conversation continued at the level of a murmur. Rebus was standing with his back to the sink's draining board, next to the back door. A figure appeared in front of him.

'Have another drop, son.' And the inch in his glass rose to an inch and a half. Rebus looked around him in vain, seeking out a relative of the deceased. But these men looked like neighbours, like the sons of neighbours, the male half of the community's heart. Their wives, sisters, mothers would be in the living-room with Grace Gallagher. Closed curtains blocking out any light from what was left of the day: handkerchiefs and sweet sherry. The bereaved in an armchair, with someone else perched on an arm of the chair, offering a pat of the hand and well-meant words. Rebus had seen it all, seen it as a child with his own mother, and as a young man with his father, seen it with aunts and uncles, with the parents of friends and more recently with friends themselves. He wasn't so young now. The odd contemporary was already falling victim to the Big C or an unexpected heart attack. Today was the last day of April. Two days ago, he'd gone to Fife and laid flowers on his father's grave. Whether it was an act of remembrance or of simple contrition, he couldn't have said ...

His guide pulled him back to the present. 'Her daughter-in-law's already here. Came over from Falkirk this afternoon.'

Rebus nodded, trying to look wise. 'And the son?'

Eyes looked at him. 'Dead these past ten years. Don't you know that?'

There was suspicion now, and Rebus knew that he had either to reveal himself as a policeman, or else become more disingenuous still. These people, authentically mourning the loss of someone they had known, had taken him as a mourner too, had brought him in here to share with them, to be part of the remembering group.

'I'm just a friend of a friend,' he explained. 'They asked me to look in.'

It looked from his guide's face, however, as though an interrogation might be about to begin. But then somebody else spoke.

'Terrible crash it was. What was the name of the town again?'

'Methil. He'd been working on building a rig there.'

'That's right,' said the guide knowledgeably. 'Pay night it was. They'd been out for a few drinks, like. On their way to the dancing. Next thing ...'

'Aye, terrible smash it was. The lad in the back seat had to have both legs taken off.'

Well, thought Rebus, I bet he didn't go to any more hops. Then he winced, trying to forgive himself for thinking such a thing. His guide saw the wince and laid the hand back on his arm.

'All right, son, all right.' And they were all looking at him again, perhaps expecting tears. Rebus was growing red in the face.

'I'll just ...' he said, motioning towards the ceiling with his head.

'You know where it is?'

Rebus nodded. He'd seen all there was to see downstairs, and so knew the bathroom must lie upstairs, and upstairs was where he was heading. He closed the kitchen door behind him and breathed deeply. There was sweat beneath his shirt, and the headache was reasserting itself. That'll teach you, Rebus, it was saying. That'll teach you for taking a sip of whisky. That'll teach you for making cheap jokes to yourself. Take all the aspirin you like. They'll dissolve your stomach lining before they dissolve me.

Rebus called his headache two seven-letter words before beginning to climb the stairs.

He gave careful scrutiny to each stair as he climbed, and to the walls either side of each stair. The carpet itself was fairly new, with a thickish pile. The wallpaper was old, and showed a hunting scene, horse-riders and dogs with a fox panting and worried in the distance. As Patience Aitken had said, there were no scrapes or claw-marks on the paper itself. What's more, there were no loose edges of carpet. The whole thing had been tacked down with a professional's skill. Nothing for George Gallagher to trip over, no threads or untacked sections; and no smooth threadbare patches for him to slip on.

He gave special attention to where the upstairs landing met the stairs. George Gallagher probably fell from here, from this height. Further down the stairs, his chances of survival would have been much greater. Yes, it was a steep and narrow staircase all right. A trip and a tumble would certainly have caused bruising. Immediate death at the foot of the stairs would doubtless have arrested much of the bruising, the blood stilling in the veins and arteries, but bruising there would have been. The post-mortem would be specific; so far Rebus was trading on speculation, and well he knew it.

Four doors led off the landing: a large cupboard (what Rebus as a child would have called a 'press'), filled with sheets, blankets, two ancient suitcases, a black-and-white television lying on its side; a musty spare bedroom, its single bed made up ready for the visitor who never came; the bathroom, with a battery-operated razor lying on the cistern, never to be used again by its owner; and the bedroom. Nothing interested Rebus in either the spare bedroom or the bathroom, so he slipped into the main bedroom, closing the door behind him, then opening it again, since to be discovered behind a closed door would be so much more suspicious than to be found inside an open one.

The sheets, blanket and quilt had been pulled back from the bed, and three pillows had been placed on their ends against the headboard so that one person could sit up in bed. He'd seen a breakfast tray in the kitchen, still boasting the remnants of a morning meal: cups, toast crumbs on a greasy plate, an old coffee jar now holding the remains of some home-made jam. Beside the bed stood a walking-frame. Patience Aitken had said that George Gallagher usually wouldn't walk half a dozen steps without his walking-frame (a Zimmer she'd called it, but to Rebus Zimmer was the German for 'room'...). Of course, if Grace were helping him, he could walk without it, leaning on her the way he'd lean his weight on a stick. Rebus visualised Grace Gallagher coaxing her husband from his bed, telling him he wouldn't be needing his walking-frame, she'd help him down the stairs. He could lean on her ...

On the bed rested a newspaper, dotted with tacky spots of jam. It was today's paper, and it was open at the racing pages. A blue pen had been used to ring some of the runners – Gypsy Pearl, Gazumpin, Lot's Wife, Castle Mallet, Blondie – five in total, enough for a super yankee. The blue pen was sitting on a bedside table, beside a glass half filled with water, some tablets (the label made out to Mr G. Gallagher), a pair of reading spectacles in their case, and a paperback cowboy novel – large print – borrowed from the local library. Rebus sat on the edge of the bed and flipped through the newspaper. His eyes came to rest on a particular page, the letters and cartoons page. At bottom right was a crossword, a completed crossword at that. The pen used to fill in the squares seemed different to that used for the racing form further on in the paper, and the hand seemed different too: more delicate, more feminine. Thin faint marks rather than the robust lines used to circle the day's favoured horses. Rebus enjoyed the occasional crossword, and, impressed to find this one completed, was more impressed to find that the answers were those to the cryptic clues rather than the quick clues most people favoured. He began to read, until at some point in his reading his brow furrowed, and he blinked a couple of times before closing the paper, folding it twice, and rolling it into his jacket pocket. A second or two's reflection later, he rose from the bed and walked slowly to the bedroom door, out on to the landing where, taking careful hold of the banister, he started downstairs.

*

He stood in the kitchen with his whisky, pondering the situation. Faces came and went. A man would finish his drink with a sigh or a clearing of the throat.

'Ay well,' he'd say, 'I suppose I'd better ...' And with these words, and a bow of the head, he would move out of the kitchen, timidly opening the living-room door so as to say a few words to the widow before leaving. Rebus heard Grace Gallagher's voice, a high, wavering howl: 'Thanks for coming. It was good of you. Cheerio.'

The women came and went, too. Sandwiches appeared from somewhere and were shared out in the kitchen. Tongue, corned beef, salmon paste. White 'half-pan' bread sliced in halves. Despite his diet, Rebus ate his fill, saying nothing. Though he only half knew it, he was biding his time, not wishing to create a disturbance. He waited as the kitchen emptied. Once or twice someone had attempted to engage him in conversation, thinking they knew him from a neighbouring street or from the public bar of the local. Rebus just shook his head, the friend of a friend, and the enquiries usually ended there.

Even his guide left, again patting Rebus's arm and giving him a nod and a wink. It was a day for universal gestures, so Rebus winked back. Then, the kitchen vacant now, muggy with the smell of cheap cigarettes, whisky and body odour, Rebus rinsed out his glass and stood it end-up on the draining board. He walked into the hallway, paused, then knocked and pushed open the living-room door.

As he had suspected, Grace Gallagher, as frail-looking as he'd thought, dabbing behind her fifties-style spectacles, was seated in an armchair. On the arm of the chair sat a woman in her forties, heavy-bodied but not without presence. The other chairs were vacant. Teacups sat on a dining table, alongside an unfinished plate of sandwiches, empty sherry glasses, the bottle itself, and, curiously, a pack of playing cards, laid out as though someone had broken off halfway through a game of patience.

Opposite the television set sat another sunken armchair, looking as if it had not been sat in this whole afternoon. Rebus could guess why: the deceased's chair, the throne to his tiny kingdom. He smiled towards the two women. Grace Gallagher only half looked towards him.

'Thanks for dropping by,' she said, her voice slightly revived from earlier. 'It was good of you. Cheerio.'

'Actually, Mrs Gallagher,' said Rebus, stepping into the room, 'I'm a police officer, Detective Inspector Rebus. Dr Aitken asked me to look in.'

'Oh.' Grace Gallagher looked at him now. Pretty eyes sinking into crinkly white skin. A dab of natural colour on each cheek. Her silvery hair hadn't seen a perm in quite a while, but someone had combed it, perhaps to enable her to face the rigours of the afternoon. The daughter-in-law – or so Rebus supposed the woman on the arm of the chair to be – was rising.

'Would you like me to ...?'

Rebus nodded towards her. 'I don't think this'll take long. Just routine really, when there's been an accident.' He looked at Grace, then at the daughter-in-law. 'Maybe if you could go into the kitchen for five minutes or so?'

She nodded keenly, perhaps a little too keenly. Rebus hadn't seen her all evening, and so supposed she'd felt duty bound to stay cooped up in here with her mother-in-law. She seemed to relish the prospect of movement.

'I'll pop the kettle on,' she said, brushing past Rebus. He watched the door close, waited as she padded down the short hallway, listened until he heard water running, the sounds of dishes being tidied. Then he turned back to Grace Gallagher, took a deep breath, and walked over towards her, dragging a stiff-backed dining chair with him. This he sat on, only a foot or two from her. He could feel her growing uneasy. She writhed a little in the armchair, then tried to disguise the reaction by reaching for another paper hankie from a box on the floor beside her.

'This must be a very difficult time for you, Mrs Gallagher,' Rebus began. He wanted to keep things short and clear cut. He had no evidence, had nothing to play with but a little bit of psychology and the woman's own state of mind. It might not be enough; he wasn't sure whether or not he *wanted* it to be enough. He found himself shifting on the chair. His arm touched the newspaper in his pocket. It felt like a talisman.

'Dr Aitken told me,' he continued, 'that you'd looked after your husband for quite a few years. It can't have been easy.'

'I'd be lying if I said that it was.'

Rebus tried to find the requisite amount of iron in her words. Tried but failed.

'Yes,' he said, 'I believe your husband was, well, a bit *difficult* at times.'

'I won't deny that either. He could be a real bugger when he wanted to.' She smiled, as if in memory of the fact. 'But I'll miss him. Aye, I'll miss him.'

'I'm sure you will, Mrs Gallagher.'

He looked at her, and her eyes fixed on to his, challenging him.

He cleared his throat again. 'There's something I'm not absolutely sure about, concerning the accident. I wonder if maybe you can help me?'

'I can try.'

Rebus smiled his appreciation. 'It's just this,' he said. 'Eleven o'clock was a bit early for your husband to be coming downstairs. What's more, he seemed to be trying to come down without his walking-frame, which is still beside the bed.' Rebus's voice was becoming firmer, his conviction growing. 'What's more, he seems to have fallen with a fair amount of force.'

She interrupted him with a snap. 'How do you mean?'

'I mean he fell straight down the stairs. He didn't just slip and fall, or stumble and roll down them. He went flying off the top step and didn't hit anything till he hit the ground.' Her eyes were filling again. Hating himself, Rebus pressed on. 'He didn't fall, Mrs Gallagher. He was helped to the top of the stairs, and then he was helped down them with a push in the back, a pretty vigorous push at that.' His voice grew less severe, less judgemental. 'I'm not saying you meant to kill him. Maybe you just wanted him hospitalised, so you could have a rest from looking after him. Was that it?'

She was blowing her nose, her small shoulders squeezed inwards towards a brittle neck. The shoulders twitched with sobs. 'I don't know what you're talking about. You think I ... How could you? Why would you say anything like that? No, I don't believe you. Get out of my house.' But there was no power to any of her words, no real enthusiasm for the fight. Rebus reached into his pocket and brought out the newspaper.

'I notice you do crosswords, Mrs Gallagher.'

She glanced up at him, startled by this twist in the conversation. 'What?'

He motioned with the paper. 'I like crosswords myself. That's why I was interested when I saw you'd completed today's puzzle. Very impressive. When did you do that?'

'This morning,' she said through another handkerchief. 'In the park. I always do the crossword after I've bought the paper. Then I bring it home so George can look at his horses.'

Rebus nodded, and studied the crossword again. 'You must have been preoccupied with something this morning then,' he said. 'What do you mean?'

'It's quite an easy one, really. I mean, easy for someone who does crosswords like this and finishes them. Where is it now?' Rebus seemed to be searching the grid. 'Yes,' he said. 'Nineteen across. You've got the down solutions, so that means the answer to nineteen across must be something R something P. Now, what's the clue?' He looked for it, found it. 'Here it is, Mrs Gallagher. "Perhaps deadly in part." Four letters. Something R something P. Something deadly. Or deadly in part. And you've put TRIP. 'What were you thinking about, I wonder? I mean, when you wrote that? I wonder what your mind was on?'

'But it's the right answer,' said Grace Gallagher, her face creasing in puzzlement. Rebus was shaking his head.

'No,' he said. 'I don't think so. I think the "in part" means the letters of "part" make up the word you want. The answer's TRAP, Mrs Gallagher. "Perhaps deadly in part": TRAP. Do you see? But you were thinking of something else when you filled in the answer. You were thinking about how if your husband tripped down the stairs you might be rid of him. Isn't that right, Grace?'

She was silent for a moment, the silence broken only by the ticking of the mantelpiece clock and the clank of dishes being washed in the kitchen. Then she spoke, quite calmly.

'Myra's a good lass. It was terrible when Billy died. She's been like a daughter to me ever since.' Another pause, then her eyes met Rebus's again. He was thinking of his own mother, of how old she'd be today had she lived. Much the same age as this woman in front of him. He took another deep breath, but stayed silent, waiting.

'You know, son,' she said, 'if you look after an invalid, people think you're a martyr. I was a martyr all right, but only because I put up with him for forty years.' Her eyes strayed to the empty armchair, and focused on it as though her husband were sitting there and hearing the truth for the very first time. 'He was a sweet talker back then, and he had all the right moves. None of that once Billy came along. None of that ever again.' Her voice, which had been growing softer, now began hardening again. 'They shut the pit, so he got work at the bottle factory. Then they shut that, and all he could get was part-time chalking up the winners at the bookie's. A man gets gey bitter, Inspector. But he didn't have to take it out on me, did he?' She moved her eyes from the chair to Rebus. 'Will they lock me up?' She didn't sound particularly interested in his answer.

'That's not for me to say, Grace. Juries decide that sort of thing.'

She smiled. 'I thought I'd done the crossword in record time. Trust me to get one wrong.' And she shook her head slowly, the smile falling from her face as the tears came again, and her mouth opened in a near-silent bawl.

The door swung open, the daughter-in-law entering with a tray full of crockery.

'There now,' she called. 'We can all have a nice cup of—' She saw the look on Grace Gallagher's face, and she froze.

'What have you done?' she cried accusingly. Rebus stood up.

'Mrs Gallagher,' he said to her, 'I'm afraid I've got a bit of bad news ...'

She had known of course. The daughter-in-law had known. Not that Grace had said anything, but there had been a special bond between them. Myra's parting words to Rebus's retreating back had been a vicious 'That bugger deserved all he got!' Net curtains had twitched; faces had appeared at darkened windows. Her words had echoed along the street and up into the smoky night air.

Maybe she was right at that. Rebus couldn't judge. All he could be was fair. So why was it that he felt so guilty? So ashamed? He could have shrugged it off, could have reported back to Patience that there was no substance to her fears. Grace Gallagher had suffered; would continue to suffer. Wasn't that enough? OK, so the law demanded more, but without Rebus there was no case, was there?

He felt right, felt vindicated, and at the same time felt a complete and utter bastard. More than that, he felt as though he'd just sentenced his own mother. He stopped at a late-night store and stocked up on beer and cigarettes. As an afterthought, he bought six assorted packets of crisps and a couple of bars of chocolate. This was no time to diet. Back home, he could conduct his own post-mortem, could hold his own private wake. On his way out of the shop, he bought the final edition of the evening paper, and was reminded that this was 30 April. Tomorrow morning, before dawn, crowds of people would climb up Arthur's Seat and, at the hill's summit, would celebrate the rising of the sun and the coming of May. Some would dab their faces with dew, the old story being that it would make them more beautiful, more handsome. What exactly was it they were celebrating, all the hungover students and the druids and the curious? Rebus wasn't sure any more. Perhaps he had never known in the first place.

Later that night, much later, as he lay along his sofa, the hi-fi blaring some jazz music from the sixties, his eye caught the day's racing results on the paper's back page. Gypsy Pearl had come home first at three-to-one. In the very next race, Gazumpin had won at seven-to-two on. Two races further on, Lot's Wife had triumphed at a starting price of eight-to-one. At another meeting, Castle Mallet had won the two thirty. Two-to-one joint favourite. That left only Blondie. Rebus tried to focus his eyes, and finally found the horse, its name misprinted to read 'Bloodie'. Though three-to-one favourite, it had come home third in a field of thirteen.

Rebus stared at the misspelling, wondering what had been going through the typist's mind when he or she had made that one small but no doubt meaningful slip ...

Castle Dangerous

Sir Walter Scott was dead.

He'd been found at the top of his namesake's monument in Princes Street Gardens, dead of a heart attack and with a new and powerful pair of binoculars hanging around his slender, mottled neck.

Sir Walter had been one of Edinburgh's most revered QCs until his retirement a year ago. Detective Inspector John Rebus, climbing the hundreds (surely it must be hundreds) of spiralling steps up to the top of the Scott Monument, paused for a moment to recall one or two of his run-ins with Sir Walter, both in and out of the courtrooms on the Royal Mile. He had been a formidable character, shrewd, devious and subtle. Law to him had been a challenge rather than an obligation. To John Rebus, it was just a day's work.

Rebus ached as he reached the last incline. The steps here were narrower than ever, the spiral tighter. Room for one person only, really. At the height of its summer popularity, with a throng of tourists squeezing through it like toothpaste from a tube, Rebus reckoned the Scott Monument might be very scary indeed.

He breathed hard and loud, bursting through the small doorway at the top, and stood there for a moment, catching his breath. The panorama before him was, quite simply, the best view in Edinburgh. The castle close behind him, the New Town spread out in front of him, sloping down towards the Firth of Forth, with Fife, Rebus's birthplace, visible in the distance. Calton Hill ... Leith ... Arthur's Seat ... and round to the castle again. It was breathtaking, or would have been had the breath not already been taken from him by the climb.

The parapet upon which he stood was incredibly narrow; again, there was hardly room enough to squeeze past someone. How crowded did it get in the summer? Dangerously crowded? It seemed dangerously crowded just now, with only four people up here. He looked over the edge upon the sheer drop to the gardens below, where a massing of tourists, growing restless at being barred from the monument, stared up at him. Rebus shivered.

Not that it was cold. It was early June. Spring was finally late-blooming into summer, but that cold wind never left the city, that wind which never seemed to be warmed by the sun. It bit into Rebus now, reminding him that he lived in a northern climate. He looked down and saw Sir Walter's slumped body, reminding him why he was here.

'I thought we were going to have another corpse on our hands there for a minute.' The speaker was Detective Sergeant Brian Holmes. He had been in conversation with the police doctor, who himself was crouching over the corpse.

'Just getting my breath back,' Rebus explained.

'You should take up squash.'

'It's squashed enough up here.' The wind was nipping Rebus's ears. He began to wish he hadn't had that haircut at the weekend. 'What have we got?'

'Heart attack. The doctor reckons he was due for one anyway. A climb like that in an excited state. One of the witnesses says he just doubled over. Didn't cry out, didn't seem in pain ...'

'Old mortality, eh?' Rebus looked wistfully at the corpse. 'But why do you say he was excited?'

Holmes grinned. 'Think I'd bring you up here for the good of your health? Here.' He handed a polythene bag to Rebus. Inside the bag was a badly typed note. 'It was found in the binocular case.'

Rebus read the note through its clear polythene window: GO TO TOP OF SCOTT MONUMENT. TUESDAY MIDDAY. I'LL BE THERE. LOOK FOR THE GUN.

'The gun?' Rebus asked, frowning.

There was a sudden explosion. Rebus started, but Holmes just looked at his watch, then corrected its hands. One o'clock. The noise had come from the blank charge fired every day from the castle walls at precisely one o'clock.

'The gun,' Rebus repeated, except now it was a statement. Sir Walter's binoculars were lying beside him. Rebus lifted them – 'He wouldn't mind, would he?' – and fixed them on the castle. Tourists could be seen walking around. Some peered over the walls. A few fixed their own binoculars on Rebus. One, an elderly Asian, grinned and waved. Rebus lowered the binoculars. He examined them. 'These look brand new.'

'Bought for the purpose, I'd say, sir.'

'But what exactly *was* the purpose, Brian? What was he supposed to be looking at?' Rebus waited for an answer. None was forthcoming. 'Whatever it was,' Rebus went on, 'it as good as killed him. I suggest we take a look for ourselves.'

'Where, sir?'

Rebus nodded towards the castle. 'Over there, Brian. Come on.'

'Er, Inspector ...?' Rebus looked towards the doctor, who was upright now, but pointing downwards with one finger. 'How are we going to get him down?'

Rebus stared at Sir Walter. Yes, he could see the problem. It would be hard graft taking him all the way back down the spiral stairs. What's more, damage to the body would be unavoidable. He supposed they could always use a winch and lower him straight to the ground ... Well, it was a job for ambulancemen or undertakers, not the police. Rebus patted the doctor's shoulder.

'You're in charge, Doc,' he said, exiting through the door before the doctor could summon up a protest. Holmes shrugged apologetically, smiled, and followed Rebus into the dark. The doctor looked at the body, then over the edge, then back to the body again. He reached into his pocket for a mint, popped it into his mouth, and began to crunch on it. Then he, too, made for the door.

Splendour was falling on the castle walls. Wrong poet, Rebus mused, but right image. He tried to recall if he'd ever read any Scott, but drew a blank. He thought he might have picked up *Waverley* once. As a colleague at the time had said, 'Imagine calling a book after the station.' Rebus hadn't bothered to explain; and hadn't read the book either, or if he had it had left no impression ...

He stood now on the ramparts, looking across to the Gothic exaggeration of the Scott Monument. A cannon was almost immediately behind him. Anyone wanting to be seen from the top of the monument would probably have been standing right on this spot. People did not linger here though. They might wander along the walls, take a few photographs, or pose for a few, but they would not stand in the one spot for longer than a minute or two.

Which meant, of course, that if someone *had* been standing here longer, they would be conspicuous. The problem was twofold: first, conspicuous to whom? Everyone else would be in motion, would not notice that someone was lingering. Second, all the potential witnesses would by now have gone their separate ways, in tour buses or on foot, down the Royal Mile or on to Princes Street, along George the Fourth Bridge to look at Greyfriars Bobby ... The people milling around just now represented a fresh intake, new water flowing down the same old stream.

Someone wanted to be seen by Sir Walter, and Sir Walter wanted to see him – hence the binoculars. No conversation was needed, just the sighting. Why? Rebus couldn't think of a single reason. He turned away from the wall and saw Holmes approaching. Meeting his eyes, Holmes shrugged his shoulders.

'I've talked to the guards on the gate. They don't remember seeing anyone suspicious. As one of them said, "All these bloody tourists look the same to me."'

Rebus smiled at this, but then someone was tugging at his sleeve, a small handbagged woman with sunglasses and thick lipstick.

'Sorry, could I ask you to move over a bit?' Her accent was American, her voice a nasal sing-song. 'Lawrence wants a picture of me with that gorgeous skyline behind me.'

Rebus smiled at her, even made a slight bow, and moved a couple of yards out of the way, Holmes following suit.

'Thanks!' Lawrence called from behind his camera, freeing a hand so that he could wave it towards them. Rebus noticed that the man wore a yellow sticker on his chest. He looked back to the woman, now posing like the film star she so clearly wasn't, and saw that she too had a badge, her name – Diana – felt-tipped beneath some package company's logo.

'I wonder ...' Rebus said quietly.

'Sir?'

'Maybe you were asking the wrong question at the gate, Brian. Yes, the right idea but the wrong question. Come on, let's go back and ask again. We'll see how eagle-eyed our friends really are.'

They passed the photographer – his badge called him Larry rather than Lawrence – just as the shutter clicked.

'Great,' he said to nobody in particular. 'Just one more, sweetheart.' As he wound the film, Rebus paused and stood beside him, then made a square from the thumb and forefinger of both hands and peered through it towards the woman Diana, as though assessing the composition of the picture. Larry caught the gesture.

'You a professional?' he asked, his tone just short of awe.

'Only in a manner of speaking, Larry,' said Rebus, turning away again. Holmes was left standing there, staring at the photographer. He wondered whether to shrug and smile again, as he had done with the doctor. What the hell. He shrugged. He smiled. And he followed Rebus towards the gate.

Rebus went alone to the home of Sir Walter Scott, just off the Corstorphine Road near the zoo. As he stepped out of his car, he could have sworn he detected a faint wafting of animal dung. There was another car in the driveway, one which, with a sinking heart, he recognised. As he walked up to the front door of the house, he saw that the curtains were closed in the upstairs windows, while downstairs, painted wooden shutters had been pulled across to block out the daylight.

The door was opened by Superintendent 'Farmer' Watson.

'I thought that was your car, sir,' Rebus said as Watson ushered him into the hall. When he spoke, the superintendent's voice was a whispered growl.

'He's still up there, you know.'

'Who?'

'Sir Walter, of course!' Flecks of saliva burst from the corners of Watson's mouth. Rebus thought it judicious to show not even the mildest amusement.

'I left the doctor in charge.'

'Dr Jameson couldn't organise a brewery visit. What the hell did you think you were doing?'

'I had ... *have* an investigation on my hands, sir. I thought I could be more usefully employed than playing undertaker.'

'He's stiff now, you know,' Watson said, his anger having diminished. He didn't exactly know why it was that he could never stay angry with Rebus; there was something about the man. 'They don't think they can get him down the stairs. They've tried twice, but he got stuck both times.'

Rebus pursed his lips, the only way he could prevent them spreading into a wide grin. Watson saw this and saw, too, that the situation was not without a trace of humour.

'Is that why you're here, sir? Placating the widow?'

'No, I'm here on a personal level. Sir Walter and Lady Scott were friends of mine. That is, Sir Walter was, and Lady Scott still is.'

Rebus nodded slowly. Christ, he was thinking, the poor bugger's only been dead a couple of hours and here's old Farmer Watson already trying to ... But no, surely not. Watson was many things, but not callous, not like that. Rebus rebuked himself silently, and in so doing missed most of what Watson was saying.

'—in here.'

And a door from the hallway was being opened. Rebus was being shown into a spacious living-room – or were they called drawing-rooms in houses like this? Walking across to where Lady Scott sat by the fireside was like walking across a dance hall.

'This is Inspector Rebus,' Watson was saying. 'One of my men.'

Lady Scott looked up from her handkerchief. 'How do you do?'

She offered him a delicate hand, which he lightly touched with his own, in place of his usual firm handshake. Lady Scott was in her mid fifties, a well-preserved monument of neat lines and precise movements. Rebus had seen her accompanying her husband to various functions in the city, had come across her photograph in the paper when he had received his knighthood. He saw, too, from the corner of his eye, the way Watson looked at her, a mixture of pity and something more than pity, as though he wanted at the same time to pat her hand and hug her to him.

Who would want Sir Walter dead? That was, in a sense, what he had come here to ask. Still the question itself was valid. Rebus could think of adversaries – those Scott had crossed in his professional life, those he had helped put behind bars, those, perhaps, who resented everything from his title to the bright blue socks that had become something of a trademark after he admitted on a radio show that he wore no other colour on his feet ...

'Lady Scott, I'm sorry to intrude on you at a time like this. I know it's difficult, but there are a couple of questions ...'

'Please, ask your questions.' She gestured for him to sit on the sofa – the sofa on which Farmer Watson had already made himself comfortable. Rebus sat down awkwardly. This whole business was awkward. He knew the chess player's motto: if in doubt, play a pawn. Or as the Scots themselves would say, ca' canny. But that had never been his style, and he couldn't change now. As ever, he decided to sacrifice his queen.

'We found a note in Sir Walter's binocular case.'

'He didn't own a pair of binoculars.' Her voice was firm.

'He probably bought them this morning. Did he say where he was going?'

'No, just out. I was upstairs. He called that he was "popping out for an hour or two", and that was all.'

'What note?' This from Watson. What note indeed. Rebus wondered why Lady Scott hadn't asked the same thing.

'A typed note, telling Sir Walter to be at the top of the Scott Monument at midday.' Rebus paused, his attention wholly on Sir Walter's widow. 'There have been others, haven't there? Other notes?'

She nodded slowly. 'Yes. I found them by accident. I wasn't prying, I'm not like that. I was in Walter's office – he always called it that, his "office", never his study – looking for something, an old newspaper I think. Yes, there was an article I wanted to reread, and I'd searched high and low for the blessed paper. I was looking in Walter's office, and I found some ... letters.' She wrinkled her nose.

'He'd kept them quiet from me. Well, I suppose he had his reasons. I never said anything to him about finding them.' She smiled ruefully. 'I used to think sometimes that the unsaid was what kept our marriage alive. That may seem cruel. Now he's gone, I wish we'd told one another more ...'

She dabbed at a liquid eye with the corner of her handkerchief, wrapped as it was around one finger, her free hand twisting and twisting the corners. To Rebus, it looked as if she were using it as a tourniquet.

'Do you know where these other notes are?' he asked.

'I don't know. Walter may have moved them.'

'Shall we see?'

The office was untidy in the best legal tradition: any available flat surface, including the carpet, seemed to be fair game for stacks of brown folders tied with ribbon, huge bulging manilla envelopes, magazines and newspapers, books and learned journals. Two walls consisted entirely of bookcases, from floor to near the ornate but flaking ceiling. One bookcase, glass-fronted, contained what Rebus reckoned must be the collected works of the other Sir Walter Scott. The glass doors looked as though they hadn't been opened in a decade; the books themselves might never have been read. Still, it was a nice touch – to have one's study so thoroughly infiltrated by one's namesake.

'Ah, they're still here.' Lady Scott had slid a concertina-style folder out from beneath a pile of similar such files. 'Shall we take them back through to the morning-room?' She looked around her. 'I don't like it in here ... not now.'

Her Edinburgh accent, with its drawn vowels, had turned 'morning' into 'mourning'. Either that, thought Rebus, or she'd said 'mourning-room' in the first place. He would have liked to have stayed a little longer in Sir Walter's office, but was compelled to follow. Back in her chair, Lady Scott untied the ribbon around the file and let it fall open. The file itself was made up of a dozen or more compartments, but only one seemed to contain any paperwork. She pulled out the letters and handed them to Watson, who glanced through them wordlessly before handing them to Rebus.

Sir Walter had taken each note from its envelope, but had paper-clipped the envelopes to the backs of their respective notes. So Rebus was able to ascertain that the notes had been posted between three weeks and one week ago, and all bore a central London postmark. He read the three notes slowly to himself, then reread them. The first came quickly to its point.

I ENCLOSE A LETTER. THERE ARE PLENTY MORE

WHERE IT CAME FROM. YOU WILL HEAR FROM ME
AGAIN.

The second fleshed out the blackmail.

I HAVE ELEVEN MORE LETTERS. IF YOU'D LIKE
THEM BACK, THEY WILL COST £2,000. GET THE MONEY.

The third, posted a week ago, finalised things.

PUT THE MONEY IN A CARRIER BAG. GO TO THE
CAFE ROYAL AT 9 P.M. FRIDAY. STAND AT THE BAR
AND HAVE A DRINK. LEAVE THE BAG THERE AND GO
MAKE A PHONE CALL. SPEND TWO MINUTES AWAY
FROM THE BAR. WHEN YOU COME BACK, THE LETTERS
WILL BE THERE.

Rebus looked up at Lady Scott. 'Did he pay?'

'I've really no idea.'

'But you could check?'

'If you like, yes.'

Rebus nodded. 'I'd like to be sure.' The first note said that a
letter was enclosed, obviously a letter concerning Sir Walter – but
what kind of letter? Of the letter itself there was no sign. Twelve apparently incriminating or embarrassing letters for £2,000. A small
price to pay for someone of Sir Walter's position in society. What's
more, it seemed to Rebus a small price to *ask*. And if the exchange
had taken place as arranged, what was the point of the last note,
the one found in Sir Walter's binocular case? Yes, that was a point.

'Did you see the mail this morning, Lady Scott?'

'I was first to the door, yes.'

'And was there an envelope like these others?'

'I'm sure there wasn't.'

Rebus nodded. 'Yes, if there had been, I think Sir Walter would
have kept it, judging by these.' He shook the notes – all with envelopes attached.

'Meaning, John?' Superintendent Watson sounded puzzled. To
Rebus's ears, it was his natural voice.

'Meaning,' he explained, 'that the last note, the one we found on
Sir Walter, was as it arrived at the house. No envelope. It must have
been pushed through the letterbox. I'd say sometime yesterday or
this morning. The blackmail started in London, but the blackmailer
came up here for the payoff. And he or she is still here – or was until
midday. Now, I'm not so certain. If Sir Walter paid the money' – he
nodded towards Lady Scott – 'and I *would* like you to check on that,
please, today if possible. *If*, as I say, Sir Walter paid, *if* he got the
letters back, then what was this morning's little game all about?'

Watson nodded, arms folded, looking down into his lap as though seeking answers. Rebus doubted they'd be found so close to home. He rose to his feet.

'We could do with finding those letters, too. Perhaps, Lady Scott, you might have another look in your husband's ... office.'

She nodded slowly. 'I should tell you, Inspector, that I'm not sure I *want* to find them.'

'I can understand that. But it would help us track down the blackmailer.'

Her voice was as low as the light in the room. 'Yes, of course.'

'And in the meantime, John?' Watson tried to sound like a man in charge of something. But there was a pleading edge to his voice.

'Meantime,' said Rebus, 'I'll be at the Castellain Hotel. The number will be in the book. You can always have me paged.'

Watson gave Rebus one of his dark looks, the kind that said: I don't know what you're up to, but I can't let anyone else know that I *don't* know. Then he nodded and almost smiled.

'Of course,' he said. 'Yes, off you go. I may stay on a little longer ...' He looked to Lady Scott for her assent. But she was busy with the handkerchief again, twisting and twisting and twisting ...

The Castellain Hotel, a minute's walk from Princes Street, was a chaos of tourists. The large pot-planted lobby looked as though it was on someone's tour itinerary, with one large organised party about to leave, milling about as their luggage was taken out to the waiting bus by hard-pressed porters. At the same time, another party was arriving, the holiday company's representative conspicuous by being the only person who looked like he knew what was going on.

Seeing that a group was about to leave, Rebus panicked. But their lapel badges assured him that they were part of the Seascape Tours package. He walked up to the reception desk and waited while a harassed young woman in a tartan two-piece tried to take two telephone calls at the same time. She showed no little skill in the operation, and all the time she was talking her eyes were on the scrum of guests in front of her. Finally, she found a moment and a welcoming smile for him. Funny how at this time of year there were so many smiles to be found in Edinburgh ...

'Yes, sir?'

'Detective Inspector Rebus,' he announced. 'I'd like a word with the Grebe Tours rep if she's around.'

'She's a he,' the receptionist explained. 'I think he might be in his room, hold on and I'll check.' She had picked up the telephone. 'Nothing wrong, is there?'

'No, nothing, just want a word, that's all.'

Her call was answered quickly. 'Hello, Tony? There's a gentleman in reception to see you.' Pause. 'Fine, I'll tell him. 'Bye.' She put down the receiver. 'He'll be down in a minute.'

Rebus nodded his thanks and, as she answered another telephone call, moved back into the reception hall, dodging the bags and the worried owners of the bags. There was something thrilling about holidaymakers. They were like children at a party. But at the same time there was something depressing, too, about the herd mentality. Rebus had never been on a package holiday in his life. He mistrusted the production-line cheerfulness of the reps and the guides. A walk along a deserted beach: now *that* was a holiday. Finding a pleasant out-of-the-way pub ... playing pinball so ruthlessly that the machine 'tilted' ... wasn't he due for a holiday himself?

Not that he would take one: the loneliness could be a cage as well as a release. But he would never, he hoped, be as caged as these people around him. He looked for a Grebe Tours badge on any passing lapel or chest, but saw none. The Edinburgh Castle gatekeepers had been eagle-eyed all right, or one of them had. He'd recalled not only that a Grebe Tours bus had pulled in to the car park at around half past eleven that morning, but also that the rep had mentioned where the tour party was staying – the Castellain Hotel.

A small, balding man came out of the lift and fairly trotted to the reception desk, then, when the receptionist pointed towards Rebus, trotted over towards him, too. Did these reps take pills? potions? laughing gas? How the hell did they manage to keep it up?

'Tony Bell at your service,' the small man said. They shook hands. Rebus noticed that Tony Bell was growing old. He had a swelling paunch and was a little breathless after his jog. He ran a hand over his babylike head and kept grinning.

'Detective Inspector Rebus.' The grin subsided. In fact, most of Tony Bell's face seemed to subside.

'Oh Jesus,' he said, 'what is it? A mugger, pickpocket, what? Is somebody hurt? Which hospital?'

Rebus raised a hand. 'No need to panic,' he reassured him. 'Your charges are all quite safe.'

'Thank Christ for that.' The grin returned. Bell nodded towards a door, above which was printed the legend Dining-Room and Bar. 'Fancy a drink?'

'Anything to get out of this war zone,' Rebus said.

'You should see the bar after dinner,' said Tony Bell, leading the way, 'now *that's* a war zone ...'

As Bell explained, the Grebe Tours party had a free afternoon. He checked his watch and told Rebus that they would probably start returning to the hotel fairly soon. There was a meeting arranged for before dinner, when the next day's itinerary would be discussed. Rebus told the rep what he wanted, and Bell himself suggested he stay put for the meeting. Yes, Rebus agreed, that seemed sensible, and meantime would Tony like another drink?

This particular Grebe Tours party was American. They'd flown in almost a month ago for what Bell called the 'Full British Tour' – Canterbury, Salisbury, Stonehenge, London, Stratford, York, the Lake District, Trossachs, Highlands, and Edinburgh.

'This is just about the last stop,' he said. 'For which relief much thanks, I can tell you. They're nice people mind, I'm not saying they're not, but ... demanding. Yes, that's what it is. If a Brit doesn't quite understand what's been said to him, or if something isn't *quite* right, or whatever, they tend to keep their gobs shut. But Americans ...' He rolled his eyeballs. 'Americans,' he repeated, as though it explained all.

It did. Less than an hour later, Rebus was addressing a packed, seated crowd of forty American tourists in a room off the large dining-room. He had barely given them his rank when a hand shot into the air.

'Er ... yes?'

The elderly woman stood up. 'Sir, are you from Scotland Yard?'

Rebus shook his head. 'Scotland Yard's in London.'

She was still standing. 'Now why is that?' she asked. Rebus had no answer to this, but someone else suggested that it was because that part of London was called Scotland Yard. Yes, but why was it called Scotland Yard in the first place? The woman had sat down now, but all around her was discussion and conjecture. Rebus looked towards Tony Bell, who rose from his own seat and succeeded in quietening things down.

Eventually, Rebus was able to make his point. 'We're interested', he said, 'in a visitor to Edinburgh Castle this morning. You may have seen someone while you were there, someone standing by the walls, looking towards the Scott Monument. He or she might have been standing there for some time. If that means something to anybody, I'd like you to tell me about it. At the same time, it's possible that those of you who took photographs of your visit may have by chance snapped the person we're looking for. If any of you have cameras, I'd like to see the photos you took this morning.'

He was in luck. Nobody remembered seeing anyone suspicious – they were too busy looking at the sights. But two photographers had used polaroids, and another had taken his film into a same-day processor at lunchtime and so had the glossy photographs with him. Rebus studied these while Tony Bell went over the next day's arrangements with the group. The polaroid photos were badly taken, often blurry, with people in the background reduced to matchstick men. But the same-day photos were excellent, sharply focused 35 mm jobs. As the tour party left the room, en route for dinner, Tony Bell came over to where Rebus was sitting and asked the question he knew he himself would be asked more than once over dinner.

'Any joy?'

'Maybe,' Rebus admitted. 'These two people keep cropping up.' He spread five photographs out in front of him. In two, a middle-aged woman was caught in the background, staring out over the wall she was leaning on. Leaning on, or hiding behind? In another two, a man in his late twenties or early thirties stood in similar pose, but with a more upright stance. In one photo, they could both be seen half turning with smiles on their faces towards the camera.

'No.' Tony Bell was shaking his head. 'They might look like wanted criminals, but they're in our party. I think Mrs Eglinton was sitting in the back row near the door, beside her husband. You probably didn't see her. But Shaw Berkely was in the second row, over to one side. I'm surprised you didn't see him. Actually, I take that back. He has this gift of being innocuous. Never asks questions or complains. Mind you, I think he's seen most of this before.'

'Oh?' Rebus was gathering the photos together.

'He told me he'd been to Britain before on holiday.'

'And there's nothing between him and—?' Rebus was pointing to the photograph of the man and woman together.

'Him and Mrs Eglinton?' Bell seemed genuinely amused. 'I don't know – maybe. She certainly mothers him a bit.'

Rebus was still studying the print. 'Is he the youngest person on the tour?'

'By about ten years. Sad story really. His mother died, and after the funeral he said he just had to get away. Went into the travel agent's and we were offering a reduction for late bookings.'

'His father's dead too, then?'

'That's right. I got his life story one night late in the bar. On a tour, I get everyone's story sooner or later.'

Rebus flipped through the sheaf of photos a final time. Nothing new presented itself to him. 'And you were at the castle between about half past eleven and quarter to one?'

'Just as I told you.'

'Oh well.' Rebus sighed. 'I don't think—'

'Inspector?' It was the receptionist, her head peering around the door. 'There's a call for you.'

It was Superintendent Watson. He was concise, factual. 'Withdrew five hundred pounds from each of four accounts, all on the same day, and in plenty of time for the rendezvous at the Café Royal.'

'So presumably he paid up.'

'But did he get the letters back?'

'Mmm. Has Lady Scott had a look for them?'

'Yes, we've been through the study – not thoroughly, there's too much stuff in there for that. But we've had a look.' That 'we' sounded comfortable, sounded as though Watson had already got his feet under the table. 'So what now, John?'

'I'm coming over, if you've no objection, sir. With respect, I'd like a look at Sir Walter's office for myself ...'

He went in search of Tony Bell, just so he could say thanks and goodbye. But he wasn't in the musty conference room, and he wasn't in the dining-room. He was in the bar, standing with one foot on the bar rail as he shared a joke with the woman he had called Mrs Eglinton. Rebus did not interrupt, but he did wink at the phone-bound receptionist as he passed her, then pushed his way out of the Castellain Hotel's double doors just as the wheezing of a bus's air brakes signalled the arrival of yet more human cargo.

There was no overhead lighting in Sir Walter Scott's study, but there were numerous floor lamps, desk lamps, and anglepoises. Rebus switched on as many as worked. Most were antiquated, with wiring to match, but there was one newish anglepoise attached to the bookcase, pointing inwards towards the collection of Scott's writings. There was a comfortable chair beside this lamp, and an ashtray on the floor between chair and bookcase.

When Watson put his head around the door, Rebus was seated in this chair, elbows resting on his knees, and chin resting between the cupped palms of both hands.

'Margaret – that is, Lady Scott – she wondered if you wanted anything.'

'I want those letters.'

'I think she meant something feasible – like tea or coffee.'

Rebus shook his head. 'Maybe later, sir.'

Watson nodded, made to retreat, then thought of something. 'They got him down in the end. Had to use a winch. Not very digni-fied, but what can you do? I just hope the papers don't print any pictures.'

'Why don't you have a word with the editors, just to be on the safe side?'

'I might just do that, John.' Watson nodded. 'Yes, I might just do that.'

Alone again, Rebus rose from his chair and opened the glass doors of the bookcase. The position of chair, ashtray and lamp was interesting. It was as though Sir Walter had been reading volumes from these shelves, from his namesake's collected works. Rebus ran a finger over the spines. A few he had heard of; the vast majority he had not. One was titled *Castle Dangerous*. He smiled grimly at that. Dangerous, all right; or in Sir Walter's case, quite lethal. He angled the light farther into the bookcase. The dust on a row of books had been disturbed. Rebus pushed with one finger against the spine of a volume, and the book slid a good two inches back until it rested against the solid wall behind the bookcase. Two uniform inches of space for the whole of this row. Rebus reached a hand down behind the row of books and ran it along the shelf. He met resistance, and drew the hand out again, now clutching a sheaf of papers. Sir Walter had probably thought it as good a hiding place as any – a poor testament to Scott the novelist's powers of attraction. Rebus sat down in the chair again, brought the anglepoise closer, and began to sift through what he'd found.

There were, indeed, twelve letters, ornately fountain-penned promises of love with honour, of passion until doomsday. As with all such youthful nonsense, there was a lot of poetry and classical imagery. Rebus imagined it was standard private boys' school stuff, even today. But these letters had been written half a century ago, sent from one schoolboy to another a year younger than himself. The younger boy was Sir Walter, and from the correspondence it was clear that Sir Walter's feelings for the writer had been every bit as inflamed as those of the writer himself.

Ah, the writer. Rebus tried to remember if he was still an MP. He had the feeling he had either lost his seat, or else had retired. Maybe he was still on the go; Rebus paid little attention to politics. His attitude had always been: don't vote, it only encourages them. So, here was the presumed scandal. Hardly a scandal, but just about enough to cause embarrassment. At worst a humiliation. But then Rebus was beginning to suspect that humiliation, not financial profit, was the price exacted here.

And not even necessarily public humiliation, merely the private knowledge that someone knew of these letters, that someone had possessed them. Then the final taunt, the taunt Sir Walter could not resist: come to the Scott Monument, look across to the castle, and you will see who has been tormenting you these past weeks. You will know.

But now that same taunt was working on Rebus. He knew so much, yet in effect he knew nothing at all. He now possessed the 'what', but not the 'who'. And what should he do with the old love letters? Lady Scott had said she wasn't sure she wanted to find them. He could take them away with him – destroy them. Or he could hand them over to her, tell her what they were. It would be up to her either to destroy them unread or to discover this silly secret. He could always say: It's all right, it's nothing really ... Mind you, some of the sentences were ambiguous enough to disturb, weren't they? Rebus read again. 'When you scored 50 n.o. and afterwards we showered ...' 'When you stroke me like that ...' 'After rugger practice ...'

Ach. He got up and opened the bookcase again. He would replace them. Let time deal with them; he could not. But in placing his hand back down behind the line of books, he brushed against something else, not paper but stiff card. He hadn't noticed it before because it seemed stuck to the wall. He peeled it carefully away and brought it into the light. It was a photograph, black and white, ten inches by eight and mounted on card. A man and woman on an esplanade, arm in arm, posing for the photographer. The man looked a little pensive, trying to smile but not sure he actually wanted to be caught like this. The woman seemed to wrap both her arms round one of his, restraining him; and she was laughing, thrilled by this moment, thrilled to be with him.

The man was Sir Walter. A Sir Walter twenty years older than the schoolboy of the love letters, mid thirties perhaps. And the woman? Rebus stared long and hard at the woman. Put the photograph down and paced the study, touching things, peering through the shutters. He was thinking and not thinking. He had seen the woman before somewhere ... but where? She was not Lady Scott, of that he was certain. But he'd seen her recently, seen that face ... that face.

And then he knew. Oh yes, he knew.

He telephoned the Castellain, half listening as the story was given to him. Taken ill suddenly ... poorly ... decided to go home ... airport ... flying to London and catching a connection tonight ... Was there a problem? Well, of course there was a problem, but no one at the hotel could help with it, not now. The blackmail over, Rebus himself had inadvertently caused the blackmailer to flee. He had gone to the hotel hoping – such a slim hope – for help, not realising that one of the Grebe Tours party was his quarry. Once again, he had sacrificed his queen too early in the game.

He telephoned Edinburgh Airport, only to be told that the flight had already taken off. He asked to be rerouted to Security, and asked them for the name of the security chief at Heathrow. He was calling Heathrow when Watson appeared in the hall.

'Making quite a few calls, aren't you, John? Not personal, I hope.'

Rebus ignored his superior as his call was connected. 'Mr Masterson in Security, please,' he said. And then: 'Yes, it is urgent. I'll hold.' He turned to Watson at last. 'Oh, it's personal all right, sir. But it's nothing to do with me. I'll tell you all about it in a minute. Then we can decide what to tell Lady Scott. Actually, seeing as you're a friend of the family and all, *you* can tell her. That'd be best, wouldn't it, sir? There are some things only your friends can tell you, after all, aren't there?'

He was through to Heathrow Security, and turned away from Watson the better to talk with Masterson. The superintendent stood there, dimly aware that Rebus was going to force him to tell Margaret something she would probably rather not hear. He wondered if she would ever again have time for the person who would tell her … And he cursed John Rebus, who was so good at digging yet never seemed to soil his own hands. It was a gift, a terrible, destructive gift. Watson, a staunch believer in the Christian God, doubted Rebus's gift had come down from on high. No, not from on high.

The phone call was ending. Rebus put down the receiver and nodded towards Sir Walter's study.

'If you'll step into the office, sir,' he said, 'there's something I'd like to show you …'

Shaw Berkely was arrested at Heathrow, and, despite protestations regarding his health and cries for consular aid, was escorted back to Edinburgh, where Rebus was waiting, brisk and definitive, in Interview Room A of Great London Road police station.

Berkely's mother had died two months before. She had never told him the truth about his birth, spinning instead some story about his father being dead. But in sorting through his mother's papers, Shaw discovered the truth – several truths, in fact. His mother had been in love with Walter Scott, had become pregnant by him, but had been, as she herself put it in her journal, 'discarded' in favour of the 'better marriage' provided by Margaret Winton-Addams.

Shaw's mother accepted some money from Scott and fled to the United States, where she had a younger sister. Shaw grew up believing his father dead. The revelation not only that he was alive, but that he had prospered in society after having caused Shaw's mother misery and torment, led to a son's rage. But it was impotent rage, Shaw thought, until he came across the love letters. His mother must at some point have stolen them from Scott, or at least had come out of the relationship in possession of them. Shaw decided on a teasing revenge, knowing Scott would deduce that any blackmailer in possession of the letters was probably also well informed about his affair and the bastard son.

He used the tour party as an elaborate cover (and also, he admitted, because it was a cheap travel option). He brought with him to Britain not only the letters, but also the series of typed notes. The irony was that he had been to Edinburgh before, had studied there for three months as part of some exchange with his American college. He knew now why his mother, though proud of the scholarship, had been against his going. For three months he had lived in his father's city, yet hadn't known it.

He sent the notes from London – the travel party's base for much of its stay in England. The exchange – letters for cash – had gone ahead in the Café Royal, the bar having been a haunt of his student days. But he had known his final note, delivered by hand, would tempt Sir Walter, would lead him to the top of the Scott Monument. No, he said, he hadn't just wanted Sir Walter to see him, to see the son he had never known. Shaw had much of the money on him, stuffed into a money belt around his waist. The intention had been to release wads of money, Sir Walter's money, down on to Princes Street Gardens.

'I didn't mean for him to die ... I just wanted him to know how I felt about him ... I don't know. But Jesus' – he grinned – 'I still wish I'd let fly with all that loot.'

Rebus shuddered to think of the ramifications. Stampede in Princes Street! Hundreds dead in lunchtime spree! Biggest *scoo-root* ever! No, best not to think about it. Instead, he made for the Café Royal himself. It was late morning, the day after Berkely's arrest. The pub was quiet as yet, but Rebus was surprised to see Dr Jameson standing at the bar, fortifying himself with what looked suspiciously like a double whisky. Remembering how he had left the doctor in the lurch regarding Sir Walter's body, Rebus grinned broadly and offered a healthy slap on the back.

'Morning, Doc, fancy seeing you in here.' Rebus leaned his elbows on the bar. 'We mustn't be keeping you busy enough.' He paused. There was a twinkle in his eye as he spoke. 'Here, let me get you a stiff one ...' And he laughed so hard even the waiters from the Oyster Bar came to investigate. But all they saw was a tall, well-built man leaning against a much smaller, more timid man, and saying as he raised his glass: 'Here's to mortality, to old mortality!'

So all in all it was just another day in the Café Royal.

In the Frame

Inspector John Rebus placed the letters on his desk.

There were three of them. Small, plain white envelopes, locally franked, the same name and address printed on each in a careful hand. The name was K. Leighton. Rebus looked up from the envelopes to the man sitting on the other side of the desk. He was in his forties, frail-looking and restless. He had started talking the moment he'd entered Rebus's office, and didn't seem inclined to stop.

'The first one arrived on Tuesday, last Tuesday. A crank, I thought, some sort of malicious joke. Not that I could think of anyone who might do that sort of thing.' He shifted in his seat. 'My neighbours over the back from me ... well, we don't always see eye to eye, but they wouldn't resort to this.' His eyes glanced up towards Rebus for a second. 'Would they?'

'You tell me, Mr Leighton.'

As soon as he'd said this, Rebus regretted the choice of words. Undoubtedly, Kenneth Leighton *would* tell him. Rebus opened the first envelope's flap, extracted the sheet of writing-paper and unfolded it. He did the same with the second and third letters and laid all three before him.

'If it had been only the one,' Kenneth Leighton was saying, 'I wouldn't have minded, but it doesn't look as though they're going to stop. Tuesday, then Thursday, then Saturday. I spent all weekend worrying about what to do ...'

'You did the right thing, Mr Leighton.'

Leighton wriggled pleasurably. 'Well, they always say you should go to the police. Not that I think there's anything serious. I mean, *I've* not got anything to hide. My life's an open book ...'

An open book and an unexciting one, Rebus would imagine. He tried to shut out Leighton's voice and concentrated instead on the first letter.

Mr Leighton,
We've got photos you wouldn't want your wife to see, believe us.
Think about it. We'll be in touch.

Then the second:

Mr Leighton,
£2,000 for the photos. That seems fair, doesn't it? You really
wouldn't want your wife to see them. Get the money. We'll be in
touch.

And the third:

Mr Leighton,
We'll be sending one reprint to show we mean business. You'd
better get to it before your wife does. There are plenty more copies.

Rebus looked up, and caught Leighton staring at him. Leighton immediately looked away. Rebus had the feeling that if he stood behind the man and said 'boo' quite softly in his ear, Leighton would melt all down the chair. He looked like the sort of person who might make an enemy of his neighbours, complaining too strenuously about a noisy party or a family row. He looked like a crank.

'You haven't received the photo yet?'

Leighton shook his head. 'I'd have brought it along, wouldn't I?'

'And you've no idea what sort of photo it might be?'

'None at all. The last time somebody took my picture was at my niece's wedding.'

'And when was that?'

'Three years ago. You see what I'm saying, Inspector? This doesn't make any sense.'

'It must make sense to at least one person, Mr Leighton.' Rebus nodded towards the letters.

They had been written in blue ball-point, the same pen which had been used to address the envelopes. A cheap blue ball-point, leaving smears and blots of ink. It was anything but professional-looking. The whole thing looked like a joke. Since when did blackmailers use their own handwriting? Anyone with a rudimentary education in films, TV cop shows and thriller novels knew that you used a typewriter or letters cut out of newspapers, or whatever; anything that would produce a dramatic effect. These letters were too personal to look dramatic. Polite, too: that use of 'Mr Leighton' at the start of each one. A particular word caught Rebus's attention and held it. But then Leighton said something interesting.

'I don't even have a wife, not now.'

'You're not married?'

'I was. Divorced six years ago. Six years and one month.'

'And where's your wife now, Mr Leighton?'

'Remarried, lives in Glenrothes. I got an invite to the wedding, but I didn't go. Can't remember what I sent them for a present ...' Leighton was lost in thought for a moment, then collected himself. 'So you see, if these letters are written by someone I know, how come they *don't* know I'm divorced?'

It was a good question. Rebus considered it for a full five seconds. Then he came to his conclusion.

'Let's leave it for now, Mr Leighton,' he said. 'There's not much we can do till this photo arrives ... *if* it arrives.'

Leighton looked numb, watching Rebus fold the letters and replace them in their envelopes. Rebus wasn't sure what the man had expected. Fingerprints lifted from the envelopes by forensic experts? A tell-tale fibre leading to an arrest? Handwriting identi-fied ... saliva from the stamps and the envelope-flaps checked ... psychologists analysing the wording of the messages themselves, coming up with a profile of the blackmailer? It was all good stuff, but not on a wet Monday morning in Edinburgh. Not with CID's case-load and budget restrictions.

'Is that it?'

Rebus shrugged. That was it. We're only human, Mr Leighton. For a moment, Rebus thought he'd actually voiced his thoughts. He had not. Leighton still sat there, pale and disappointed, his mouth set like the bottom line of a balance sheet.

'Sorry,' said Rebus, rising.

'I've just remembered,' said Leighton.

'What?'

'Six wine glasses, that's what I gave them. Caithness glass they were too.'

'Very nice I'm sure,' said Rebus, stifling a post-weekend yawn as he opened the office door.

But Rebus was certainly intrigued.

No wife these past six years, and the last photograph of Leighton dated back three years to a family wedding. Where was the material for blackmail? Where the motive? Means, motive and opportunity. Means: a photograph, apparently. Motive: unknown. Opportunity

... Leighton was a nobody, a middle-aged civil servant. He earned enough, but not enough to make him blackmail material. He had confided to Rebus that he barely had £2,000 in his building society account.

'Hardly enough to cover their demand,' he had said, as though he were considering actually paying off the blackmailers, even though he had nothing to hide, nothing to fear. Just to get them off his back? Or because he *did* have something to hide? Most people did, if it came to it. The guilty secret or two (or more, many more) stored away just below the level of consciousness, the way suitcases were stored under beds. Rebus wondered if he himself were blackmail material. He smiled: was the Pope a Catholic? Was the Chief Constable a Mason? Leighton's words came back to him: *Hardly enough to cover their demand.* What sort of civil servant was Leighton anyway? Rebus sought out the day-time telephone number Leighton had left along with his home address and phone number. Seven digits, followed by a three-figure extension number. He punched the seven digits on his receiver, waited, and heard a switchboard operator say, 'Good afternoon, Inland Revenue.' Rebus replaced the receiver with a guilty silence.

On Tuesday morning, Leighton phoned the station. Rebus got in first.

'You didn't tell me you were a taxman, Mr Leighton.'

'What?'

'A taxman.'

'What does it matter?'

What did it matter? How many enemies could one taxman make? Rebus swallowed back the question. He could always use a friend in Her Majesty's Inland Revenue, for personal as well as strictly professional use ...

'I know what you're thinking,' Leighton was saying, though Rebus doubted it. 'And it's true that I work in the Collector's office, sending out the demands. But my name's never on the demands. The Inspector of Taxes might be mentioned by name, but I'm a lowly cog, Inspector.'

'Even so, you must write to people sometimes. There might be somebody out there with a grudge.'

'I've given it some thought, Inspector. It was my *first* thought. But in any case I don't deal with Edinburgh.'

'Oh?'

'I deal with south London.'

Rebus noted that, phoning from his place of work, Leighton was less nervous-sounding. He sounded cool, detached. He sounded like a tax collector. South London: but the letters had local postmarks – another theory sealed under cover and posted into eternity, no return address.

'The reason I'm calling,' Leighton was saying, 'is that I had another letter this morning.'

'With a photo?'

'Yes, there's a photo.'

'And?'

'It's difficult to explain. I could come to the station at lunchtime.'

'Don't bother yourself, Mr Leighton. I'll come to the tax office. All part of the service.'

Rebus was thinking of back-handers, gifts from grateful members of the public, all the pubs where he could be sure of a free drink, chip shops that wouldn't charge for a feed, all the times he'd helped out for a favour, the way those favours accumulated and were paid off ... Tax forms asked you about tips received. Rebus always left the box blank. Had he always been accurate about amounts of bank interest? More crucially, several months ago he had started renting his flat to three students while he lived rent-free with Dr Patience Aitken. He had no intention of declaring ... well, maybe he would. It helped to know a friendly taxman, someone who might soon owe him a favour.

'That's very good of you, Inspector,' Leighton was saying.

'Not at all, sir.'

'Only it all seems to have been a mistake anyway.'

'A mistake?'

'You'll see when I show you the photograph.'

Rebus saw.

He saw a man and a woman. In the foreground was a coffee table, spread with bottles and glasses and cans, an ashtray full to overflowing. Behind this, a sofa, and on the sofa a man and a woman. Lying along the sofa, hugging one another. The photographer had caught them like this, their faces just beginning to turn towards the camera, grinning and flushed with that familiar mix of alcohol and passion. Rebus had been to these sorts of party, parties where the alcohol was necessary before there could be any passion. Behind the couple, two men stood in animated conversation. It was a good clear photo, the work of a 35 mm camera with either a decent flash-gun or else no necessity for one.

'And here's the letter,' said Leighton. They were seated on an uncomfortable, spongy sofa in the tax office's reception area. Rebus had been hoping for a sniff behind the scenes, but Leighton worked in an open-plan office with less privacy even than the reception area. Few members of the public ever visited the building, and the receptionist was at the other end of the hallway. Staff wandered through on their way to the coffee machine or the snack dispenser, the toilets or the post-room, but otherwise this was as quiet as it got.

'A bit longer than the others,' Leighton said, handing the letter over.

Mr Leighton,
Here is the photo. We have plenty more, plus negatives. Cheap at
£2,000 the lot, and your wife will never know. The money should
be in fives and tens, nothing bigger. Put it in a William Low's
carrier-bag and go to Greyfriars Kirkyard on Friday at 3 p.m.
Leave the bag behind Greyfriars Bobby's gravestone. Walk away.
Photos and negatives will be sent to you.

'Not exactly the quietest spot for a handover,' Rebus mused. Although the actual statue of Greyfriars Bobby, sited just outside the kirkyard, was more popular with tourists, the gravestone was a popular enough stop-off. The idea of leaving a bagful of money there surreptitiously was almost laughable. But at least now the extortion was serious. A time and place had been mentioned as well as a sum, a sum to be left in a Willie Low's bag. Rebus more than ever doubted the blackmailer's professionalism.

'You see what I mean?' Leighton said. 'I can only think that if it isn't a joke, then it's a case of mistaken identity.'

True enough, Leighton wasn't any of the three men in the photo, not by any stretch of the will or imagination. Rebus concentrated on the woman. She was small, heavy, somehow managing to fit into a dress two sizes too small for her. It was black and short, rumpled most of the way to her bum, with plenty of cleavage at the other end. She also wore black tights and black patent-leather shoes. But somehow Rebus didn't think he was looking at a funeral.

'I don't suppose', he said, 'this is your wife?'

Leighton actually laughed, the sound of paper shredding.

'Thought not,' Rebus said quietly. He turned his attention to the man on the sofa, the man whose arms were trapped beneath the weight of the smirking woman. There was something about that face, that hairstyle. Then it hit Rebus, and things started to make a little more sense.

'I didn't recognise him at first,' he said, thinking out loud.

'You mean you know him?'

Rebus nodded slowly. 'Only I've never seen him smile before, that's what threw me.' He studied the photo again, then stabbed it with a finger. The tip of his finger was resting on the face of one of the other men, the two behind the sofa. 'And I know him,' he said. 'I can place him now.' Leighton looked impressed. Rebus moved his finger on to the recumbent woman. 'What's more, I know her too. I know her quite well.'

Leighton didn't look impressed now, he looked startled, perhaps even disbelieving.

'Three out of four,' Rebus said. 'Not a bad score, eh?' Leighton didn't answer, so Rebus smiled reassuringly. 'Don't you worry, sir. I'll take care of this. You won't be bothered any more.'

'Well ... thank you, Inspector.'

Rebus got to his feet. 'All part of the service, Mr Leighton. Who knows, maybe *you'll* be able to help *me* one of these days ...'

Rebus sat at his desk, reading the file. Then, when he was satisfied, he tapped into the computer and checked some details regarding a man who was doing a decent stretch in Peterhead jail. When he'd finished, there was a broad grin on his face, an event unusual enough in itself to send DC Siobhan Clarke sauntering over in Rebus's direction, trying not to get too close (fear of being hooked), but close enough to register interest. Before she knew it, Rebus was reeling her in anyway.

'Get your coat,' he said.

She angled her head back towards her desk. 'But I'm in the middle of—'

'You're in the middle of *my* catchment, Siobhan. Now fetch your coat.'

Never be nosy, and always keep your head down: somehow Siobhan Clarke hadn't yet learned those two golden rules of the easy life. Not that anything was easy when John Rebus was in the office. Which was precisely why she liked working near him.

'Where are we going?' she said.

Rebus told her on the way. He also handed the file to her so she could read it through.

'Not guilty,' she said at last.

'And I'm Robbie Coltrane,' said Rebus. They were both talking about a case from a few months before. A veteran hard man had been charged with the attempted armed hold-up of a security van. There had been evidence as to his guilt – just about enough evidence – and his alibi had been shaky. He'd told police of having spent the day in question in a bar near his mother's home in Muirhouse, probably the city's most notorious housing scheme. Plenty of witnesses came forward to agree that he had been there all day. These witnesses boasted names like Tam the Bam, Big Shug, the Screwdriver, and Wild Eck. The look of them in the witness-box, police reasoned, would be enough to convince the jury of the defendant's guilt. But there had been one other witness ...

'Miss June Redwood,' quoted DC Clarke, rereading the case-notes.

'Yes,' said Rebus, 'Miss June Redwood.'

An innocent, dressed in a solemn two-piece as she gave her evidence at the trial. She was a social worker, caring for the most desperate in Edinburgh's most desperate area. Needing to make a phone call, and sensing she'd have no luck with Muirhouse's few public kiosks, she had walked into the Castle Arms, probably the first female the regulars had seen in the saloon bar since the land-lord's wife had walked out on him fifteen years before. She'd asked to use the phone, and a man had wandered over to her from a table and, with a wink, had asked if she'd like a drink. She'd refused. She could see he'd had a few – more than a few. His table had the look of a lengthy session about it – empty pint glasses placed one in-side another to form a leaning tower, ashtray brimming with butts and empty packets, the newspaper's racing page heavily marked in biro.

Miss Redwood had given a quietly detailed account, at odds with the loud, confident lies of the other defence witnesses. And she was sure that she'd walked into the bar at 3 p.m., five minutes before the attack on the security van took place. The prosecution counsel had tried his best, gaining from the social worker the acknowledgement that she knew the accused's mother through her work, though the old woman was not actually her client. The prosecutor had stared out at the fifteen jury members, attempting without success to plant doubt in their minds. June Redwood was a rock-solid witness. Solid enough to turn a golden prosecution case into a verdict of 'not guilty'. The accused had walked free. Close, as the fairground say-ing went, but definitely no goldfish.

Rebus had been in court for the verdict, and had left with a shrug and a low growl. A security guard lay in hospital suffering from shotgun wounds. Now the case would have to be looked at again, if not by Rebus then by some other poor bugger who would go through the same old steps, knowing damned fine who the main suspect was, and knowing that he was walking the streets and drinking in pubs, and chuckling at his luck.

Except that it wasn't luck: it was planning, as Rebus now knew.

DC Clarke finished her second reading of the file. 'I suppose you checked on Redwood at the time?'

'Of course we did. Not married, no boyfriends. No proof – not even the faintest rumour – that she knew Keith.'

Clarke looked at the photo. 'And this is her?'

'It's her, and it's him – Keith Leyton.'

'And it was sent to ...?'

'It was addressed to a Mr K. Leighton. They didn't get the spelling right. I checked in the phone book. Keith Leyton's ex-directory. Either that or he doesn't have a phone. But our little tax collector is in there under K. Leighton.'

'And they sent the letters to him by mistake?'

'They must know Keith Leyton hangs out in Muirhouse. His mum lives in Muirhouse Crescent.'

'Where does Kenneth Leighton live?'

Rebus grinned at the windscreen. 'Muir*wood* Crescent – only it's not in Muirhouse, it's in Currie.'

Siobhan Clarke smiled too. 'I don't believe it,' she said.

Rebus shrugged. 'It happens. They looked in the phone book, thought the address looked right, and started sending the letters.'

'So they've been trying to blackmail a criminal ...'

'And instead they've found a taxman.' Now Rebus laughed outright. 'They must be mad, naïve, or built like a hydro-electric station. If they'd *really* tried this bampot caper on with Leyton, he'd have dug a fresh grave or two in Greyfriars for them. I'll give them one thing, though.'

'What's that?'

'They know about Keith's wife.'

'His wife?'

Rebus nodded. 'She lives near the mum. Big woman. Jealous. That's why Keith would keep any girlfriend secret – that's why he'd *want* to keep her a secret. The blackmailers must have thought that gave them a chance that he'd cough up.'

Rebus stopped the car. He had parked outside a block of flats in Oxgangs. The block was one of three, each one shaped like a capital H lying on its face. Caerketton Court: Rebus had once had a fling with a school-dinner lady who lived on the second floor ...

'I checked with June Redwood's office,' he said. 'She's off sick.' He craned his neck out of the window. 'Tenth floor apparently, let's hope the lift's working.' He turned to Siobhan. 'Otherwise we'll have to resort to the telephone.'

The lift was working, though barely. Rebus and Siobhan ignored the wrapped paper parcel in one corner. Neither liked to think what it might contain. Still, Rebus was impressed that he could hold his breath for as long as the lift took to crackle its way up ten flights. The tenth floor seemed all draughts and high-pitched winds. The building had a perceptible sway, not quite like being at sea. Rebus pushed the bell of June Redwood's flat and waited. He pushed again. Siobhan was standing with her arms folded around her, shuffling her feet.

'I'd hate to see you on a football terrace in January,' said Rebus.

There was a sound from inside the door, then the door itself was opened by a woman with unwashed hair, a tissue to her nose, and wrapped in a thick dressing-gown.

'Hello there, Miss Redwood,' said Rebus brightly. 'Remember me?' Then he held up the photograph. 'Doubtless you remember him too. Can we come in?'

They went in. As they sat in the untidy living-room, it crossed Siobhan Clarke's mind that they had no way of proving *when* the photo was taken. And without that, they had nothing. Say the party had taken place after the trial – it could well be that Leyton and June Redwood had met then. In fact, it made sense. After his release, Leyton probably *would* want to throw a party, and he would certainly want to invite the woman who had been his saviour. She hoped Rebus had thought of this. She hoped he wasn't going to go too far ... as usual.

'I don't understand,' said June Redwood, wiping her nose again.

'Come on, June,' said Rebus. 'Here's the proof. You and Keith together in a clinch. The man you claimed at his trial was a complete stranger. Do you often get this comfortable with strangers?'

This earned a thin smile from June Redwood.

'If so,' Rebus continued, 'you must invite me to one of your parties.'

Siobhan Clarke swallowed hard. Yes, the Inspector was going to go too far. Had she ever doubted it?

'You'd be lucky,' said the social worker.

'It's been known,' said Rebus. He relaxed into his chair. 'Doesn't take a lot of working out, does it?' he went on. 'You must have met Keith through his mum. You became ... friends, let's call it. I don't know what his wife will call it.' Blood started to tinge June

Redwood's neck. 'You look better already,' said Rebus. 'At least I've put a bit of colour in your cheeks. You met Keith, started going out with him. It had to be kept secret though. The only thing Keith Leyton fears is *Mrs* Keith Leyton.'

'Her name's Joyce,' said Redwood.

Rebus nodded. 'So it is.'

'I could know that from the trial,' she snapped. 'I wouldn't have to know him to know that.'

Rebus nodded again. 'Except that you were a witness, June. You weren't in court when Joyce Leyton was mentioned.'

Her face now looked as though she'd been lying out too long in the non-existent sun. But she had a trump card left. 'That photo could have been taken any time.'

Siobhan held her breath: yes, this was the crunch. Rebus seemed to realise it too. 'You're right there,' he said. 'Any time at all ... up to a month before Keith's trial.'

The room was quiet for a moment. The wind found a gap somewhere and rustled a spider-plant near the window, whistling as though through well-spaced teeth.

'What?' said June Redwood. Rebus held the photograph up again.

'The man behind you, the one with long hair and the tattoo. Ugly-looking loon. He's called Mick McKelvin. It must have been some party, June, when bruisers like Keith and Mick were invited. They're not exactly your cocktail crowd. They think a canapé's something you throw over a stolen car to keep it hidden.' Rebus smiled at his own joke. Well, someone had to.

'What are you getting at?'

'Mick went inside four weeks before Keith's trial. He's serving three years in Peterhead. Persistent B and E. So you see, there's no way this party could have taken place *after* Keith's trial. Not unless Peterhead's security has got a bit lax. No, it had to be before, meaning you *had* to know him before the trial. Know what that means?' Rebus sat forward. June Redwood wasn't wiping her nose with the tissue now; she was hiding behind it, and looking frightened. 'It means you stood in the witness-box and you lied, just like Keith told you to. Serious trouble, June. You might end up with your own social worker, or even a prison visitor.' Rebus's voice had dropped in volume, as though June and he were having an intimate tête-à-tête over a candlelit dinner. 'So I really think you'd better help us, and you can start by talking about the party. Let's start with the photograph, eh?'

'The photo?' June Redwood looked ready to weep.

'The photo,' Rebus echoed. 'Who took it? Did he take any other pics of the two of you? After all, at the moment you're looking at a jail sentence, but if any photos like this one get to Joyce Leyton, you might end up collecting signatures.' Rebus waited for a moment, until he saw that June didn't get it. 'On your plaster casts,' he explained.

'Blackmail?' said Rab Mitchell.

He was sitting in the interview room, and he was nervous. Rebus stood against one wall, arms folded, examining the scuffed toes of his black Dr Martens. He'd only bought them three weeks ago. They were hardly broken in – the tough leather heel-pieces had rubbed his ankles into raw blisters – and already he'd managed to scuff the toes. He knew how he'd done it too: kicking stones as he'd come out of June Redwood's block of flats. Kicking stones for joy. That would teach him not to be exuberant in future. It wasn't good for your shoes.

'Blackmail?' Mitchell repeated.

'Good echo in here,' Rebus said to Siobhan Clarke, who was standing by the door. Rebus liked having Siobhan in on these interviews. She made people nervous. Hard men, brutal men, they would swear and fume for a moment before remembering that a young woman was present. A lot of the time, she discomfited them, and that gave Rebus an extra edge. But Mitchell, known to his associates as 'Roscoe' (for no known reason), would have been nervous anyway. A man with a proud sixty-a-day habit, he had been stopped from lighting up by a tutting John Rebus.

'No smoking, Roscoe, not in here.'

'What?'

'This is a non-smoker.'

'What the f— what are you blethering about?'

'Just what I say, Roscoe. No smoking.'

Five minutes later, Rebus had taken Roscoe's cigarettes from where they lay on the table, and had used Roscoe's Scottish Bluebell matches to light one, which he inhaled with great delight.

'Non-smoker!' Roscoe Mitchell fairly yelped. 'You said so yourself!' He was bouncing like a kid on the padded seat. Rebus exhaled again.

'Did I? Yes, so I did. Oh well ...' Rebus took a third and final puff from the cigarette, then stubbed it out underfoot, leaving the longest, most extravagant stub Roscoe had obviously ever seen in his life. He stared at it with open mouth, then closed his mouth tight and turned his eyes to Rebus.

'What is it you want?' he said.

'Blackmail,' said John Rebus.

'Blackmail?'

'Good echo in here.'

'Blackmail? What the hell do you mean?'

'Photos,' said Rebus calmly. 'You took them at a party four months ago.'

'Whose party?'

'Matt Bennett's.'

Roscoe nodded. Rebus had placed the cigarettes back on the table. Roscoe couldn't take his eyes off them. He picked up the box of matches and toyed with it. 'I remember it,' he said. A faint smile. 'Brilliant party.' He managed to stretch the word 'brilliant' out to four distinct syllables. So it really had been a good party.

'You took some snaps?'

'You're right. I'd just got a new camera.'

'I won't ask where from.'

'I've got a receipt.' Roscoe nodded to himself. 'I remember now. The film was no good.'

'How do you mean?'

'I put it in for developing, but none of the pictures came out. Not one. They reckoned I'd not put the film in the right way, or opened the case or something. The negatives were all blank. They showed me them.'

'They?'

'At the shop. I got a consolation free film.'

Some consolation, thought Rebus. Some swap, to be more accurate. He placed the photo on the table. Roscoe stared at it, then picked it up the better to examine it.

'How the—?' Remembering there was a woman present, Roscoe swallowed the rest of the question.

'Here,' said Rebus, pushing the pack of cigarettes in his direction. 'You look like you need one of these.'

Rebus sent Siobhan Clarke and DS Brian Holmes to pick up Keith Leyton. He also advised them to take along a back-up. You never could tell with a nutter like Leyton. Plenty of back-up, just to be on the safe side. It wasn't just Leyton after all; there might be Joyce to deal with too.

Meantime, Rebus drove to Tollcross, parked just across from the traffic lights, tight in at a bus stop, and, watched by a frowning queue, made a dash for the photographic shop's doorway. It was chucking it down, no question. The queue had squeezed itself so tightly under the metal awning of the bus shelter that vice might have been able to bring them up on a charge of public indecency. Rebus shook water from his hair and pushed open the shop's door.

Inside it was light and warm. He shook himself again and approached the counter. A young man beamed at him.

'Yes, sir?'

'I wonder if you can help,' said Rebus. 'I've got a film needs developing, only I want it done in an hour. Is that possible?'

'No problem, sir. Is it colour?'

'Yes.'

'That's fine then. We do our own processing.'

Rebus nodded and reached into his pocket. The man had already begun filling in details on a form. He printed the letters very neatly, Rebus noticed with pleasure.

'That's good,' said Rebus, bringing out the photo. 'In that case, you must have developed this.'

The man went very still and very pale.

'Don't worry, son, I'm not from Keith Leyton. In fact, Keith Leyton doesn't know anything about you, which is just as well for you.'

The young man rested the pen on the form. He couldn't take his eyes off the photograph.

'Better shut up shop now,' said Rebus. 'You're coming down to the station. You can bring the rest of the photos with you. Oh, and I'd wear a cagoule, it's not exactly fair, is it?'

'Not exactly.'

'And take a tip from me, son. Next time you think of blackmailing someone, make sure you get the right person, eh?' Rebus tucked the photo back into his pocket. 'Plus, if you'll take my advice, don't use words like "reprint" in your blackmail notes. Nobody says reprint except people like you.' Rebus wrinkled his nose. 'It just makes it too easy for us, you see.'

'Thanks for the warning,' the man said coolly.

'All part of the service,' said Rebus with a smile. The clue had actually escaped him throughout. Not that he'd be admitting as much to Kenneth Leighton. No, he would tell the story as though he'd been Sherlock Holmes and Philip Marlowe rolled into one. Doubtless Leighton would be impressed. And one day, when Rebus was needing a favour from the taxman, he would know he could put Kenneth Leighton in the frame.

Facing the Music

An unmarked police car.

Interesting phrase, that. Inspector John Rebus's car, punch-drunk and weather-beaten, scarred and mauled, would still merit description as 'unmarked', despite the copious evidence to the contrary. Oily-handed mechanics stifled grins whenever he waddled into a forecourt. Garage proprietors adjusted the thick gold rings on their fingers and reached for the calculator.

Still, there were times when the old war-horse came in handy. It might or might not be 'unmarked'; unremarkable it certainly was. Even the most cynical law-breaker would hardly expect CID to spend their time sitting around in a breaker's-yard special. Rebus's car was a must for undercover work, the only problem coming if the villains decided to make a run for it. Then, even the most elderly and infirm could outpace it.

'But it's a stayer,' Rebus would say in mitigation.

He sat now, the driving-seat so used to his shape that it formed a mould around him, stroking the steering-wheel with his hands. There was a loud sigh from the passenger seat, and Detective Sergeant Brian Holmes repeated his question.

'Why have we stopped?'

Rebus looked around him. They were parked by the side of Queensferry Street, only a couple of hundred yards from Princes Street's west end. It was early afternoon, overcast but dry. The gusts of wind blowing in from the Firth of Forth were probably keeping the rain away. The corner of Princes Street, where Fraser's department store and the Caledonian Hotel tried to outstare one another, caught the winds and whipped them against unsuspecting shoppers, who could be seen, dazed and numb, making their way afterwards along Queensferry Street, in search of coffee and shortcake. Rebus gave the pedestrians a look of pity. Holmes sighed again. He could murder a pot of tea and some fruit scones with butter.

'Do you know, Brian,' Rebus began, 'in all the years I've been in Edinburgh, I've never been called to any sort of a crime on this street.' He slapped the steering-wheel for emphasis. 'Not once.'

'Maybe they should put up a plaque,' suggested Holmes.

Rebus almost smiled. 'Maybe they should.'

'Is that why we're sitting here? You want to break your duck?' Holmes glanced into the tea-shop window, then away again quickly licking dry lips. 'It might take a while, you know,' he said.

'It might, Brian. But then again ...'

Rebus tapped out a tattoo on the steering-wheel. Holmes was beginning to regret his own enthusiasm. Hadn't Rebus tried to deter him from coming out for this drive? Not that they'd driven much. But anything, Holmes reasoned, was better than catching up on paperwork. Well, just about anything.

'What's the longest time you've been on a stake-out?' he asked, making conversation.

'A week,' said Rebus. 'Protection racket run from a pub down near Powderhall. It was a joint operation with Trading Standards. We spent five days pretending to be on the broo, playing pool all day.'

'Did you get a result?'

'We beat them at pool,' Rebus said.

There was a yell from a shop doorway, just as a young man was sprinting across the road in front of their car. The young man was carrying a black metal box. The person who'd called out did so again.

'Stop him! Thief! Stop him!'

The man in the shop doorway was waving, pointing towards the sprinter. Holmes looked towards Rebus, seemed about to say something, but decided against it. 'Come on then!' he said.

Rebus started the car's engine, signalled, and moved out into the traffic. Holmes was focusing through the windscreen. 'I can see him. Put your foot down!'

'"Put your foot down, *sir*",' Rebus said calmly. 'Don't worry, Brian.'

'Hell, he's turning into Randolph Place.'

Rebus signalled again, brought the car across the oncoming traffic, and turned into the dead end that was Randolph Place. Only, while it was a dead end for cars, there were pedestrian passages either side of West Register House. The young man, carrying the narrow box under his arm, turned into one of the passages. Rebus pulled to a halt. Holmes had the car door open before it had stopped, and leapt out, ready to follow on foot.

'Cut him off!' he yelled, meaning for Rebus to drive back on to Queensferry Street, around Hope Street and into Charlotte Square, where the passage emerged.

'"Cut him off, *sir*",' mouthed Rebus.

He did a careful three-point turn, and just as carefully moved back out into traffic held to a crawl by traffic lights. By the time he reached Charlotte Square and the front of West Register House, Holmes was shrugging his shoulders and flapping his arms. Rebus pulled to a stop beside him.

'Did you see him?' Holmes asked, getting into the car.

'No.'

'Where have you been anyway?'

'A red light.'

Holmes looked at him as though he were mad. Since when had Inspector John Rebus stopped for a red light? 'Well, I've lost him anyway.'

'Not your fault, Brian.'

Holmes looked at him again. 'Right,' he agreed. 'So, back to the shop? What was it anyway?'

'Hi-fi shop, I think.'

Holmes nodded as Rebus moved off again into the traffic. Yes, the box had the look of a piece of hi-fi, some slim rack component. They'd find out at the shop. But instead of doing a circuit of Charlotte Square to take them back into Queensferry Street, Rebus signalled along George Street. Holmes, still catching his breath, looked around disbelieving.

'Where are we going?'

'I thought you were fed up with Queensferry Street. We're going back to the station.'

'*What?*'

'Back to the station.'

'But what about—?'

'Relax, Brian. You've got to learn not to fret so much.'

Holmes examined his superior's face. 'You're up to something,' he said at last.

Rebus turned and smiled. 'Took you long enough,' he said.

But whatever it was, Rebus wasn't telling. Back at the station, he went straight to the main desk.

'Any robberies, Alec?'

The desk officer had a few. The most recent was a snatch at a specialist hi-fi shop.

'We'll take that,' said Rebus. The desk officer blinked.

'It's not much, sir. Just a single item, thief did a runner.'

'Nevertheless, Alec,' said Rebus. 'A crime has been committed, and it's our duty to investigate it.' He turned to head back out to the car.

'Is he all right?' Alec asked Holmes.

Holmes was beginning to wonder, but decided to go along for the ride anyway.

'A cassette deck,' the proprietor explained. 'Nice model, too. Not top of the range, but nice. Top-of-the-range stuff isn't kept out on the shop floor. We keep it in the demonstration rooms.'

Holmes was looking at the shelf where the cassette deck had rested. There were other decks either side of the gap, more expensive decks at that.

'Why would he choose that one?' Holmes asked.

'Eh?'

'Well, it's not the dearest, is it? And it's not even the closest to the door.'

The dealer shrugged. 'Kids these days, who can tell?' His thick hair was still tousled from where he had stood in the Queensferry Street wind-tunnel, yelling against the elements as passers-by stared at him.

'I take it you've got insurance, Mr Wardle?' The question came from Rebus, who was standing in front of a row of loudspeakers.

'Christ yes, and it costs enough.' Wardle shrugged. 'Look, it's okay. I know how it works. Points system, right? Anything under a four-point crime, and you lads don't bother. You just fill out the forms so I can claim from the insurance. What does this rate? One point? Two at the most?'

Rebus blinked, perhaps stunned by the use of the word 'lads' in connection with him.

'You've got the serial number, Mr Wardle,' he said at last. 'That'll give us a start. Then a description of the thief – that's more than we usually get in cases of shop-snatching. Meantime, you might move your stock a bit further back from the door and think about a common chain or circuit alarm so they can't be taken off their shelves. Okay?'

Wardle nodded.

'And be thankful,' mused Rebus. 'After all, it could've been worse. It could have been a ram-raider.' He picked up a CD case from where it sat on top of a machine: Mantovani and his Orchestra. 'Or even a critic,' said Rebus.

*

Back at the station, Holmes sat fuming like a readying volcano. Or at least like a tin of something flammable left for too long in the sun.

Whatever Rebus was up to, as per usual he wasn't saying. It infuriated Holmes. Now Rebus was off at a meeting in the Chief Super's office: nothing very important, just routine ... like the snatch at the hi-fi shop.

Holmes played the scene through in his mind. The stationary car, causing an obstruction to the already slow movement of traffic. Then Wardle's cry, and the youth running across the road, jinking between cars. The youth had half turned, giving Holmes a moment's view of a cheek speckled with acne, cropped spiky hair. A skinny runt of a sixteen-year-old in faded jeans and trainers. Pale blue windcheater with a lumberjack shirt hanging loose below its hemline.

And carrying a hi-fi component that was neither the easiest piece in the shop to steal, nor the dearest. Wardle had seemed relaxed about the whole affair. The insurance would cover it. An insurance scam: was that it? Was Rebus working on some insurance diddle on the q.t., maybe as a favour to some investigator from the Pru? Holmes hated the way his superior worked, like a greedy if talented footballer hogging the ball, dribbling past man after man, getting himself trapped beside the by-line but still refusing to pass the ball. Holmes had known a boy at school like that. One day, fed up, Holmes had scythed the smart-arse down, even though they'd been on the same side ...

Rebus had known the theft would take place. Therefore, he'd been tipped off. Therefore, the thief had been set up. There was just one big *but* to the whole theory – Rebus had let the thief get away. It didn't make sense. It didn't make any sense at all.

'Right,' Holmes said, nodding to himself. 'Right you are, sir.' And with that, he went off to find the young offender files.

That evening, just after six, Rebus thought that since he was in the area anyway, he'd drop into Mr Wardle's home and report the lack of progress on the case. It might be that, time having passed, Wardle would remember something else about the snatch, some crucial detail. The description he'd been able to give of the thief had been next to useless. It was almost as though he didn't want the hassle, didn't want the thief caught. Well, maybe Rebus could jog his memory.

The radio came to life. It was a message from DS Holmes. And when Rebus heard it, he snarled and turned the car back around towards the city centre.

It was lucky for Holmes, so Rebus said, that the traffic had been heavy, the fifteen-minute journey back into town being time enough for him to calm down. They were in the CID room. Holmes was seated at his desk, hands clasped behind his head. Rebus was standing over him, breathing hard. On the desk sat a matt-black cassette deck.

'Serial numbers match,' Holmes said, 'just in case you were wondering.'

Rebus couldn't quite sound disinterested. 'How did you find him?'

With his hands still behind his head, Holmes managed a shrug. 'He was on file, sir. I just sat there flipping through them till I spotted him. That acne of his is as good as a tattoo. James Iain Bankhead, known to his friends as Jib. According to the file, you've arrested him a couple of times yourself in the past.'

'Jib Bankhead?' said Rebus, as though trying to place the name. 'Yes, rings a bell.'

'I'd have thought it'd ring a whole fire station, sir. You last arrested him three months ago.' Holmes made a show of consulting the file on his desk. 'Funny, you not recognising him ...' Holmes kept his eyes on the file.

'I must be getting old,' Rebus said.

Holmes looked up. 'So what now, sir?'

'Where is he?'

'Interview Room B.'

'Let him stay there then. Can't do any harm. Has he said anything?'

'Not a word. Mind you, he *did* seem surprised when I paid him a visit.'

'But he kept his mouth shut?'

Holmes nodded. 'So what now?' he repeated.

'Now,' said Rebus, 'you come along with me, Brian. I'll tell you all about it on the way ...'

Wardle lived in a flat carved from a detached turn-of-the-century house on the south-east outskirts of the city. Rebus pressed the bell on the wall to the side of the substantial main door. After a moment, there was the muffled sound of footsteps, three clicks as locks were undone, and the door opened from within.

'Good evening, Mr Wardle,' said Rebus. 'I see you're security-conscious at home at least.' Rebus was nodding towards the door, with its three separate keyholes, spy-hole and security chain.

'You can't be too—' Wardle broke off as he saw what Brian Holmes was carrying. 'The deck!'

'Good as new,' said Rebus, 'apart from a few fingerprints.' Wardle opened the door wide. 'Come in, come in.'

They entered a narrow entrance hall which led to a flight of stairs. Obviously the ground floor of the house did not belong to Wardle. He was dressed much as he had been in the shop: denims too young for his years, an open-necked shirt louder than a Wee Free sermon, and brown moccasins.

'I can't believe it,' he said, leading them towards the stairs. 'I really can't. But you could have brought it round to the shop ...'

'Well, sir, we were going to be passing anyway.' Rebus closed the door, noting the steel plate on its inner face. The door-surround too was reinforced with metal plates. Wardle turned and noticed Rebus's interest.

'Wait till you see the hi-fi, Inspector. It'll all become clear.' They could already hear the music. The bass was vibrating each step of the stairs.

'You must have sympathetic neighbours,' Rebus remarked.

'She's ninety-two,' said Wardle. 'Deaf as a post. I went round to explain to her about the hi-fi just after I moved in. She couldn't hear a word I was saying.'

They were at the top of the stairs now, where a smaller hallway led into a huge open-plan living-room and kitchen. A sofa and two chairs had been pushed hard back against one wall, and there was nothing but space between them and the opposite wall, where the hi-fi system sat, with large floor-standing speakers either side of it. One rack comprised half a dozen black boxes, boasting nothing to Rebus's eye but a single red light.

'Amplifiers,' Wardle explained, turning down the music.

'What, all of them?'

'Pre-amp and power supply, plus an amp for each driver.' Holmes had rested the cassette deck on the floor, but Wardle moved it away immediately.

'Spoils the sound,' he said, 'if there's an extra piece of gear in the room.'

Holmes and Rebus stared at one another. Wardle was in his element now. 'Want to hear something? What's your taste?'

'Rolling Stones?' Rebus asked.

'*Sticky Fingers, Exile, Let It Bleed?*'

'That last one,' said Rebus.

Wardle went over to where a twenty-foot row of LPs was standing against the wall beneath the window.

'I thought those went out with the Ark,' said Holmes.

Wardle smiled. 'You mean with the CD. No, vinyl's still the best. Sit down.' He went over to the turntable and took off the LP he'd been playing. Rebus and Holmes sat. Holmes looked to Rebus, who nodded. Holmes got up again.

'Actually, could I use your loo?' he asked.

'First right out on the landing,' said Wardle. Holmes left the room. 'Any particular track, Inspector?'

'"Gimme Shelter",' stated Rebus. Wardle nodded agreement, set the needle on the disc, rose to his feet, and turned up the volume. 'Something to drink?' he asked. The room exploded into a wall of sound. Rebus had heard the phrase 'wall of sound' before. Well, here he was with his nose pressed against it.

'A whisky, please,' he yelled. Wardle tipped his head towards the hall. 'Same for him.' Wardle nodded and went off towards the kitchen area. Pinned to the sofa as he was, Rebus looked around the room. He had eyes for everything but the hi-fi. Not that there was much to see. A small coffee table whose surface seemed to be covered with arcana to do with the hi-fi system, cleaning-brushes and such like. There were some nice-looking prints on the wall. Actually, one looked like a real painting rather than a print: the surface of a swimming-pool, someone moving through the depths. But no TV, no shelves, no books, no knick-knacks, no family photos. Rebus knew Wardle was divorced. He also knew Wardle drove a Y-registered Porsche 911. He knew quite a lot about Wardle, but not yet enough ...

A healthy glass of whisky was handed to him. Wardle placed another on the floor for Holmes, then returned to the kitchen and came back with a glass for himself. He sat down next to Rebus.

'What do you think?'

'Fantastic,' Rebus called back.

Wardle grinned.

'How much would this lot cost me?' Rebus asked, hoping Wardle wouldn't notice how long Holmes had been out of the room.

'About twenty-five K.'

'You're joking. My flat didn't cost that.'

Wardle just laughed. But he was glancing towards the living-room door. He looked as though he might be about to say something, when the door opened and Holmes came in, rubbing his hands as though drying them off. He smiled, sat, and toasted Wardle with his glass. Wardle went over to the amplifier to turn down the volume. Holmes nodded towards Rebus. Rebus toasted no one in particular and finished his drink. The volume dipped.

'What was that?' Holmes asked.

'*Let It Bleed.*'

'I thought my ears would.'

Wardle laughed. He seemed to be in a particularly good mood. Maybe it was because of the cassette deck.

'Listen,' he said, 'how the hell did you get that deck back so quickly?'

Holmes was about to say something, but Rebus beat him to it. 'It was abandoned.'

'Abandoned?'

'At the bottom of a flight of stairs on Queen Street,' Rebus went on. He had risen to his feet. Holmes took the hint and, eyes twisted shut, gulped down his whisky. 'So you see, sir, we were just lucky, that's all. Just lucky.'

'Well, thanks again,' said Wardle. 'If you ever want some hi-fi, drop into the shop. I'm sure a discount might be arranged.'

'We'll bear that in mind, sir,' said Rebus. 'Just don't expect me to put my flat on the market ...'

Back at the station, Rebus first of all had Jib released, then went to his office, where he spread the files out across his desk, while Holmes pulled over a chair. Then they both sat, reading aloud from lists. The lists were of stolen goods, high-quality stuff stolen in the dead of night by real professionals. The hauls – highly selective hauls – came from five addresses, the homes of well-paid middle-class people, people with things well worth the stealing.

Five robberies, all at dead of night, alarm systems disconnected. Art objects had been taken, antiques, in one case an entire collection of rare European stamps. The housebreakings had occurred at more or less monthly intervals, and all within a twenty-mile radius of central Edinburgh. The connection between them? Rebus had explained it to Holmes on their way to Wardle's flat.

'Nobody could see *any* connection, apart from the fact that the five victims worked in the west end. The Chief Super asked me to take a look. Guess what I found? They'd all had smart new hi-fi systems installed. Up to six months before the break-ins. Systems bought from Queensferry Audio and installed by Mr Wardle.'

'So he'd know what was in each house?' Holmes had said.

'And he'd be able to give the alarm system a look-over while he was there, too.'

'Could just be coincidence.'

'I know.'

Oh yes, Rebus knew. He knew he had only the hunch, the coincidence. He had no proof, no evidence of any kind. Certainly nothing that would gain him a search warrant, as the Chief Super had been good enough to confirm, knowing damned well that Rebus would take it further anyway. Not that this concerned the Chief Super, so long as Rebus worked alone, and didn't tell his superiors what he was up to. That way, it was Rebus's neck in the noose, Rebus's pension on the line.

Rebus guessed his only hope was that Wardle had kept some of the stolen pieces, that some of the stuff was still on his premises. He'd already had a young DC go into Queensferry Audio posing as a would-be buyer. The DC had gone in four times in all, once to buy some tapes, then to look at hi-fi, then to spend an hour in one of the demo rooms, and finally just for a friendly chat ... He'd reported back to Rebus that the place was clean. No signs of any stolen merchandise, no locked rooms or cupboards ...

So then Rebus had persuaded a uniformed constable to pose as a Neighbourhood Watch supervisor. He had visited Wardle at home, not getting past the downstairs hallway. But he'd been able to report that the place was 'like Fort Knox, metal door and all'. Rebus had had experience of steel-reinforced doors: they were favoured by drug dealers, so that when police came calling with a sledgehammer for invitation, the dealers would have time enough to flush everything away.

But a hi-fi dealer with a steel door ... Well, that was a new one. True, twenty-five grand's worth of hi-fi was an investment worth protecting. But there were limits. Not that Rebus suspected Wardle of actually doing the breaking and entering himself. No, he just passed the information on to the men Rebus really wanted, the gang. But Wardle was the only means of getting at them ...

Finally, in desperation, Rebus had turned to Jib. And Jib had done what he was told, meaning Rebus now owed him a large favour. It was all highly irregular; unlawful, if it came to it. If anyone found out ... well, Rebus would be making the acquaintance of his local broo office. Which was why, as he explained to Holmes, he'd been keeping so quiet about it.

The plan was simple. Jib would run off with something, anything, watched by Rebus to make sure nothing went wrong – such as a daring citizen's arrest by one or more passers-by. Later, Rebus would turn up at the shop to investigate the theft. Then later still, he would arrive at Wardle's flat, ostensibly to report the lack of progress. If a further visit was needed, the cassette deck would be found. But now he had Holmes's help, so one visit only should suffice, one man keeping Wardle busy while the other sniffed around the rooms in the flat.

They sat now, poring over the lists, trying to match what Holmes had seen in Wardle's two bedrooms with what had been reported stolen from the five luxury homes.

'Carriage clock,' read Rebus, 'nineteenth-century Japanese cigar box, seventeenth-century prints of Edinburgh by James Gordon, a Swarbreck lithograph ...'

Holmes shook his head at the mention of each, then read from one of his own lists. 'Ladies' and gents' Longines watches, a Hockney print, Cartier pen, first-edition set of the Waverley novels, Ming vase, Dresden pieces ...' He looked up. 'Would you believe, there's even a case of champagne.' He looked down again and read: 'Louis Roederer Cristal 1985. Value put at six hundred pounds. That's a hundred quid a bottle.'

'Bet you're glad you're a lager man,' said Rebus. He sighed. 'Does none of this mean anything to you, Brian?'

Holmes shook his head. 'Nothing like any of this in either of the bedrooms.'

Rebus cursed under his breath. 'Hold on,' he said. 'What about that print?'

'Which one? The Hockney?'

'Yes, have we got a photo of it?'

'Just this,' said Holmes, extracting from the file a page torn from an art gallery's catalogue. He handed it to Rebus, who studied the picture. 'Why?'

'Why?' echoed Rebus. 'Because you sat with this painting in front of your nose on Wardle's living-room wall. I thought it was a real painting, but this is it all right.' He tapped the sheet of paper. 'It says here the print's limited to fifty impressions. What number is the stolen one?'

Holmes looked down the list. 'Forty-four.'

'Right,' said Rebus. 'That should be easy enough to confirm.' He checked his watch. 'What time are you expected home?'

Holmes was shaking his head. 'Never mind that. If you're going back to Wardle's flat, I'm coming too.'

'Come on then.'

It was only as they were leaving the office that Holmes thought to ask: 'What if it isn't the same number on the print?'

'Then we'll just have to face the music,' said Rebus.

But as it turned out, the only one facing the music was Wardle, and he sang beautifully. A pity, Rebus mused later, that he hadn't arranged for a discount on a new hi-fi system first. He'd just have to wait for Queensferry Audio's closing-down sale ...

Window of Opportunity

Bernie Few's jailbreaks were an art.

And over the years he had honed his art. His escapes from prison, his shrugging off of guards and prison officers, his vanishing acts were the stuff of lights-out stories in jails the length and breadth of Scotland. He was called 'The Grease-Man', 'The Blink', and many other names, including the obvious 'Houdini' and the not-so-obvious 'Claude' (Claude Rains having starred as the original *Invisible Man*).

Bernie Few was beautiful. As a petty thief he was hopeless, but after capture he started to show his real prowess. He wasn't made for being a housebreaker; but he surely did shine as a jailbreaker. He'd stuffed himself into rubbish bags and mail sacks, taken the place of a corpse from one prison hospital, squeezed his wiry frame out of impossibly small windows (sometimes buttering his naked torso in preparation), and crammed himself into ventilation shafts and heating ducts.

But Bernie Few had a problem. Once he'd scaled the high walls, waded through sewers, sprinted from the prison bus, or cracked his guard across the head, once he'd done all this and was outside again, breathing free air and melting into the crowd ... his movements were like clockwork. All his ingenuity seemed to be exhausted. The prison psychologists put it differently. They said he wanted to be caught, really. It was a game to him.

But to Detective Inspector John Rebus, it was more than a game. It was a chance for a drink.

Bernie would do three things. One, he'd go throw a rock through his ex-wife's living-room window. Two, he'd stand in the middle of Princes Street telling everyone to go to hell (and other places besides). And three, he'd get drunk in Scott's Bar. These days, option one was difficult for Bernie, since his ex-wife had not only moved without leaving a forwarding address but had, at Rebus's suggestion, gone to live on the eleventh floor of an Oxgangs tower block.

No more rocks through the living-room window, unless Bernie was handy with ropes and crampons.

Rebus preferred to wait for Bernie in Scott's Bar, where they refused to water down either the whisky or the language. Scott's was a villain's pub, one of the ropiest in Edinburgh. Rebus recognised half the faces in the place, even on a dull Wednesday afternoon. Bail faces, appeal faces. They recognised him, too, but there wasn't going to be any trouble. Every one of them knew why he was here. He hoisted himself on to a barstool and lit a cigarette. The TV was on, showing a satellite sports channel. Cricket, some test between England and the West Indies. It is a popular fallacy that the Scots don't watch cricket. Edinburgh pub drinkers will watch *anything*, especially if England are involved, more especially if England are odds on to get a drubbing. Scott's, as depressing a watering hole as you could ever imagine, had transported itself to the Caribbean for the occasion.

Then the door to the toilets opened with a nerve-jarring squeal, and a man loped out. He was tall and skinny, loose-limbed, hair falling over his eyes. He had a hand on his fly, just checking prior to departure, and his eyes were on the floor.

'See youse then,' he said to nobody, opening the front door to leave. Nobody responded. The door stayed open longer than it should. Someone else was coming in. Eyes flashed from the TV for a moment. Rebus finished his drink and rose from the stool. He knew the man who'd just left the bar. He knew him well. He knew, too, that what had just happened was impossible.

The new customer, a small man with a handful of coins, had a voice hoarse from shouting as he croakily ordered a pint. The barman didn't move. Instead, he looked to Rebus, who was looking at Bernie Few.

Then Bernie Few looked at Rebus.

'Been down to Princes Street, Bernie?' Rebus asked.

Bernie Few sighed and rubbed his tired face. 'Time for a short one, Mr Rebus?'

Rebus nodded. He could do with another himself anyway. He had a couple of things on his mind, neither of them Bernie Few.

Police officers love and hate surveillance operations in more or less equal measure. There's the tedium, but even that beats being tied to a CID desk. Often on a stakeout there's a good spirit, plus there's that adrenal rush when something eventually happens.

The present surveillance was based in a second-floor tenement flat, the owners having been packed off to a seaside caravan for a fortnight. If the operation needed longer than a fortnight, they'd be sent to stay with relations.

The watchers worked in two-man teams and twelve-hour shifts. They were watching the second-floor flat of the tenement across the road. They were keeping tabs on a bandit called Ribs Mackay. He was called Ribs because he was so skinny. He had a heroin habit, and paid for it by pushing drugs. Only he'd never been caught at it, a state of affairs Edinburgh CID were keen to rectify.

The problem was, since the surveillance had begun, Ribs had been keeping his head down. He stayed in the flat, nipping out only on brief sorties to the corner shop. He'd buy beer, vodka, milk, cigarettes, sometimes breakfast cereal or a jar of peanut butter, and he'd always top off his purchases with half a dozen bars of chocolate. That was about it. There had to be more, but there wasn't any more. Any day now, the operation would be declared dead in the water.

They tried to keep the flat clean, but you couldn't help a bit of untidiness. You couldn't help nosy neighbours either: everyone on the stairwell wondered who the strangers in the Tully residence were. Some asked questions. Some didn't need to be told. Rebus met an old man on the stairs. He was hauling a bag of shopping up to the third floor, stopping for a breather at each step.

'Help you with that?' Rebus offered.

'I can manage.'

'It wouldn't be any bother.'

'I said I can manage.'

Rebus shrugged. 'Suit yourself.' Then he climbed to the landing and gave the recognised knock on the door of the Tullys' flat.

DC Jamphlar opened the door a crack, saw Rebus, and pulled it all the way open. Rebus nipped inside.

'Here,' he said, handing over a paper bag, 'doughrings.'

'Thank you, sir,' said Jamphlar.

In the cramped living-room, DC Connaught was sitting on a dining chair at the net curtain, peering through the net and out of the window. Rebus joined him for a moment. Ribs Mackay's window was grimy, but you could see through the grime into an ordinary-looking living-room. Not that Ribs came to the window much. Connaught wasn't concentrating on the window. He was ranging between the second-floor window and the ground-floor door. If Ribs left the flat, Jamphlar went haring after him, while Connaught followed Ribs's progress from the window and reported via radio to his colleague.

Initially, there'd been one man in the flat and one in a car at street level. But the man at street level hadn't been needed, and looked suspicious anyway. The street was no main thoroughfare, but a conduit between Clerk Street and Buccleuch Street. There were a few shops at road level, but they carried the look of permanent closure.

Connaught glanced up from the window. 'Afternoon, sir. What brings you here?'

'Any sign of him?' Rebus said.

'Not so much as a tweet.'

'I reckon I know why that is. Your bird's already flown.'

'No chance,' said Jamphlar, biting into a doughring.

'I saw him half an hour ago in Scott's Bar. That's a fair hike from here.'

'Must've been his double.'

But Rebus shook his head. 'When was the last time you saw him?'

Jamphlar checked the notebook. 'We haven't seen him this shift. But this morning Cooper and Sneddon watched him go to the corner shop and come back. That was seven-fifteen.'

'And you come on at eight?'

'Yes, sir.'

'And you haven't seen him since?'

'There's someone in there,' Connaught persisted. 'I've seen movement.'

Rebus spoke slowly. 'But you haven't seen Ribs Mackay, and I have. He's out on the street, doing whatever he does.' He leaned closer to Connaught. 'Come on, son, what is it? Been skiving off? Half an hour down the pub, a bit of a thirst-quencher? Catching some kip on the sofa? Looks comfortable, that sofa.'

Jamphlar was trying to swallow a mouthful of dough which had become suddenly dry. 'We've been doing our job!' he said, spraying crumbs.

Connaught just stared at Rebus with burning eyes. Rebus believed those eyes.

'All right,' he conceded, 'so there's another explanation. A back exit, a convenient drainpipe.'

'The back door's been bricked up,' Connaught said stiffly. 'There's a drainpipe, but Ribs couldn't manage down it.'

'How do you know?'

'I know.' Connaught stared out through the curtain.

'Something else then. Maybe he's using a disguise.'

Jamphlar, still chewing, flicked through the notebook. 'Everyone who comes out and goes in is checked off.'

'He's a druggie,' said Connaught. 'He's not bright enough to fool us.'

'Well, son, that's just what he's doing. You're watching an empty flat.'

'TV's just come on,' said Connaught. Rebus looked out through the curtain. Sure enough, he could see the animated screen. 'I hate this programme,' Connaught muttered. 'I wish he'd change the channel.'

'Maybe he can't,' said Rebus, making for the door.

He returned to the surveillance that evening, taking someone with him. There'd been a bit of difficulty, getting things arranged. Nobody was keen for him to walk out of the station with Bernie Few. But Rebus would assume full responsibility.

'Damned right you will,' said his boss, signing the form.

Jamphlar and Connaught were off, Cooper and Sneddon were on.

'What's this I hear?' Cooper said, opening the door to Rebus and his companion.

'About Ribs?'

'No,' said Cooper, 'about you bringing the day shift a selection of patisseries.'

'Come and take a look,' Sneddon called. Rebus walked over to the window. The light was on in Ribs's living-room, and the blinds weren't shut. Ribs had opened the window and was looking down on to the night-time street, enjoying a cigarette. 'See?' Sneddon said.

'I see,' said Rebus. Then he turned to Bernie Few. 'Come over here, Bernie.' Few came shuffling over to the window, and Rebus explained the whole thing to him. Bernie thought about it, rasping a hand over his chin, then asked the same questions Rebus had earlier asked Jamphlar and Connaught. Then he thought about it some more, staring out through the curtain.

'You keep an eye on the second-floor window?' he asked Cooper.

'That's right.'

'And the main door?'

'Yes.'

'You ever think of looking anywhere else?'

Cooper didn't get it. Neither did Sneddon.

'Go on, Bernie,' said Rebus.

'Look at the top floor,' Bernie Few suggested. Rebus looked. He saw a cracked and begrimed window, covered with ragged bits of cardboard. 'Think anyone lives there?' Bernie asked.

'What are you saying?'

'I think he's done a proper switch on you. Turned the tables, like.' He smiled. 'You're not watching Ribs Mackay. *He's* watching *you*.'

Rebus nodded, quick to get it. 'The change of shifts.' Bernie was nodding too. 'There's that minute or two when one shift's going off and the other's coming on.'

'A window of opportunity,' Bernie agreed. 'He watches, sees the new shift arrive, and skips downstairs and out the door.'

'And twelve hours later,' said Rebus, 'he waits in the street till he sees the next shift clocking on. Then he nips back in.'

Sneddon was shaking his head. 'But the lights, the telly ...'

'Timer switches,' Bernie Few answered casually. 'You think you see people moving about in there. Maybe you do, but not Ribs. Could just be shadows, a breeze blowing the curtains.'

Sneddon frowned. 'Who *are* you?'

'An expert witness,' Rebus said, patting Bernie Few's shoulder. Then he turned to Sneddon. 'I'm going over there. Keep an eye on Bernie here. And I *mean* keep an eye on him. As in, don't let him out of your sight.'

Sneddon blinked, then stared at Bernie. 'You're Buttery Bernie.' Bernie shrugged, accepting the nickname. Rebus was already leaving.

He went to the bar at the street's far corner and ordered a whisky. He sluiced his mouth out with the stuff, so that it would be heavy on his breath, then came out of the bar and weaved his way towards Ribs Mackay's tenement, just another soak trying to find his way home. He tugged his jacket over to one side, and undid a couple of buttons on his shirt. He could do this act. Sometimes he did it too well. He got drunk on the method.

He pushed open the tenement door and was in a dimly lit hall-way, with worn stone steps curving up. He grasped the banister and started to climb. He didn't even pause at the second floor, but he could hear music from behind Ribs's door. And he saw the door was reinforced, just the kind dealers fitted. It gave them those vital extra seconds when the drug squad came calling, sledgehammers and axes their invitations. Seconds were all you needed to flush evidence away, or to swallow it. These days, prior to a house raid, the drugs squad opened up the sewers and had a man stationed there, ready for the flush ...

On the top-floor landing, Rebus paused for breath. The door facing him looked hard done by, scarred and chipped and beaten. The nameplate had been hauled off, leaving deep screw holes in the wood. Rebus knocked on the door, ready with excuses and his drunk's head-down stance. He waited, but there was no answer.

He listened, then put his eyes to the letterbox. Darkness. He tried the door handle. It turned, and the door swung inwards. When he thought about it, an unlocked door made sense. Ribs would need to come and go in a hurry, and locks took time.

Rebus stepped quietly into the short hallway. Some of the interior doors were open, bringing with them chinks of streetlight. The place smelt musty and damp, and it was cold. There was no furniture, and the wallpaper had peeled from the walls. Long strips now lay in wrinkled piles, like an old woman's stockings come to rest at her ankles. Rebus walked on tiptoe. He didn't know how good the floors were, and he didn't want anyone below to hear him. He didn't want Ribs Mackay to hear him.

He went into the living-room. It was identical in shape to the surveillance living-room. There were newspapers on the floor, a carpet rolled up against one wall. Tufts of carpet lay scattered across the floor. Mice had obviously been taking bits for nesting. Rebus went to the window. There was a small gap where two pieces of cardboard didn't quite meet. Through this gap he had a good view of the surveillance flat. And though the lights were off, the streetlight illuminated the net curtain, so that anyone behind the curtain who moved became a shadow puppet. Someone, Sneddon or Cooper or Bernie Few, was moving just now.

'You clever little runt,' Rebus whispered. Then he picked something up off the floor. It was a single-lens reflex camera, with telephoto lens attached. Not the sort of thing you found lying in abandoned flats. He picked it up and focused on the window across the street. There was absolutely no doubt in his mind now. It was so simple. Ribs sneaked up here, watched the surveillance through the telephoto while they thought they were watching him, and at eight o'clock walked smartly out of the tenement and went about his business.

'You're as good as gold, Bernie,' said Rebus. Then he put the camera back just the way he'd found it and tiptoed back through the flat.

'Where is he?'

Stupid question, considering. Sneddon just shrugged. 'He had to use the bathroom.'

'Of course he did,' said Rebus.

Sneddon led him through to the bathroom. It had a small window high on one wall. The window was open. It led not to the outside, but merely back into the hall near the flat's stairwell door.

'He was in here a while, so I came looking. Banged on the door, no answer, managed to force the thing open, but he wasn't here.' Sneddon's face and neck were red with embarrassment; or maybe it was just the exercise. 'I ran downstairs, but there was no sign of him.'

'I don't believe he could have squeezed out of that window,' Rebus said sceptically. 'Not even Bernie Few.' The window was about twelve inches by nine. It could be reached by standing on the rim of the bath, but the walls were white tile, and Rebus couldn't see any signs of scuff marks. He looked at the toilet. Its lid was down, but didn't sit level with the pan. Rebus lifted the lid and found himself staring at towels, several of them, stuffed down into the pan.

'What the ...?' Sneddon couldn't believe his eyes. But Rebus could. He opened the small airing cupboard beneath the sink. It was empty. A shelf had been lifted out and placed upright in the back of the cupboard. There was just about room inside to make for a hiding place. Rebus smiled at the disbelieving Sneddon.

'He waited till you'd gone downstairs.'

'Then what?' said Sneddon. 'You mean he's still in the flat?'

Rebus wondered. 'No,' he said at last, shaking his head. 'But think of what he just told us, about how Ribs was tricking us.'

He led Sneddon out of the flat, but instead of heading down, he climbed up a further flight to the top floor. Set into the ceiling was a skylight, and it too was open.

'A walk across the rooftops,' said Rebus.

Sneddon just shook his head. 'Sorry, sir,' he offered.

'Never mind,' said Rebus, knowing, however, that his boss would.

At seven next morning, Ribs Mackay left his flat and walked jauntily to the corner shop, followed by Sneddon. Then he walked back again, enjoying a cigarette, not a care in the world. He'd shown himself to the surveillance team, and now they had something to tell the new shift, something to occupy them during the changeover.

As usual the changeover happened at eight. And exactly a minute after Jamphlar and Connaught entered the tenement, the door across the street opened and Ribs Mackay flew out.

Rebus and Sneddon, snug in Rebus's car, watched him go. Then Sneddon got out to follow him. He didn't look back at Rebus, but he did wave an acknowledgement that his superior had been right. Rebus hoped Sneddon was better as a tail than he was as a watcher. He hoped they'd catch Ribs with the stuff on him, dealing it out perhaps, or taking delivery from his own supplier. That was the plan. That had been the plan throughout.

He started the ignition and drove out on to Buccleuch Street. Scott's Bar was an early opener, and John Rebus had an appointment there.

He owed Bernie Few a drink.

Death is Not the End

I

Is loss redeemed by memory? Or does memory merely swell the sense of loss, becoming the enemy? The language of loss is the language of memory: remembrance, memorial, momento. People leave our lives all the time: some we met only briefly, others we'd known since birth. They leave us memories – which become skewed through time – and little more.

The silent dance continued. Couples writhed and shuffled, threw back their heads or ran hands through their hair, eyes darting around the dance floor, seeking out future partners maybe, or past loves to make jealous. The TV monitor gave a greasy look to everything.

No sound, just pictures, the tape cutting from dance floor to main bar to second bar to toilet hallway, then entrance foyer, exterior front and exterior back. Exterior back was a puddled alley, full of rubbish bins and a Merc belonging to the club's owner. Rebus had heard about the alley: a punter had been knifed there the previous summer. Mr Merc had complained about the bloody smear on his passenger-side window. The victim had lived.

The club was called Gaitanos, nobody knew why. The owner just said it sounded American and a bit jazzy. The larger part of the clientele had decided on the nickname 'Guisers', and that was what you heard in the pubs on a Friday and Saturday night – 'Going down Guisers later?' The young men would be dressed smart-casual, the women scented from heaven and all stations south. They left the pubs around ten or half past – that's when it would be starting to get lively at Guisers.

Rebus was seated in a small uncomfortable chair which itself sat in a stuffy dimly lit room. The other chair was filled by an audio-visual technician, armed with two remotes. His occasional belches – of which he seemed blissfully ignorant – bespoke a recent snack of spring onion crisps and Irn-Bru.

'I'm really only interested in the main bar, foyer and out front,' Rebus said.

'I could edit them down to another tape, but we'd lose definition. The recording's duff enough as it is.' The technician scratched inside the sagging armpit of his black T-shirt.

Rebus leaned forward a little, pointing at the screen. 'Coming up now.' They waited. The view jumped from back alley to dance floor. 'Any second.' Another cut: main bar, punters queuing three deep. The technician didn't need to be told, and froze the picture. It wasn't so much black and white as sepia, the colour of dead photographs. Interior light, the audio-visual wizard had explained. He was adjusting the tracking now, and moving the action along one frame at a time. Rebus moved in on the screen, bending so one knee rested on the floor. His finger was touching a face. He took out the assortment of photos from his pocket and held them against the screen.

'It's him,' he said. 'I was pretty sure before. You can't go in a bit closer?'

'For now, this is as good as it gets. I can work on it later, stick it on the computer. The problem is the source material, to wit: one shitty security video.'

Rebus sat back on his chair. 'All right,' he said. 'Let's run forward at half-speed.'

The camera stayed with the main bar for another fifteen seconds, then switched to the second bar and all points on the compass. When it returned to the main bar, the crush of drinkers seemed not to have moved. Unbidden, the technician froze the tape again.

'He's not there,' Rebus said. Again he approached the screen, touched it with his finger. 'He should be there.'

'Next to the sex goddess.' The technician belched again.

Yes. Spun silver hair, almost like a cloud of candy-floss, dark eyes and lips. While those around her were either intent on catching the eyes of the bar staff or on the dance floor, she was looking off to one side. There were no shoulders to her dress.

'Let's check the foyer,' Rebus said.

Twenty seconds later, there showed a steady stream entering the club, but no one leaving. Exterior front showed a queue awaiting admittance by the brace of bouncers, and a few passers-by.

'In the toilet maybe,' the technician suggested. But Rebus had studied the tape a dozen times already, and though he watched just once more he knew he wouldn't see the young man again, not at the bar, not on the dance floor, and not back around the table where his mates were waiting – with increasing disbelief and impatience – for him to get his round in.

The young man's name was Damon Mee and, according to the timer running at the bottom right-hand corner of the screen, he had vanished from the world sometime between 11.44 and 11.45 p.m. on Friday 22 April.

'Where is this place anyway? I don't recognise it.'

'Kirkcaldy,' Rebus said.

The technician looked at him. 'How come it ended up here?'

Good question, Rebus thought, but not one he was about to answer. 'Go back to that bar shot,' he said. 'Take it nice and slow again.'

The technician aimed his right-hand remote. 'Yes, sir, Mr DeMille,' he said.

April meant still not quite spring in Edinburgh. A few sunny days to be sure, buds getting twitchy, wondering if winter had been paid the ransom. But there was snow still hanging in a sky the colour of chicken bones. Office talk: how Rangers were going to retain the championship; why Hearts and Hibs would never win it – was it finally time for the two local sides to become friends, form one team which might – *might* – stand half a chance? As someone said, their rivalry was part and parcel of the city's make-up. Hard to imagine Rangers and Celtic thinking of marriage in the same way, or even of a quick poke on the back stairs.

After years of following football only on pub televisions and in the back of the daily tabloid, Rebus was starting to go to matches again. DC Siobhan Clarke was to blame, coaxing him to a Hibs game one dreary afternoon. The men on the green sward weren't half as interesting as the spectators, who proved by turns sharp-witted, vulgar, perceptive and incorrigible. Siobhan had taken him to her usual spot. Those in the vicinity seemed to know her pretty well. It was a good-humoured afternoon, even if Rebus couldn't have said who scored the eventual three goals. But Hibs had won: the final-whistle hug from Siobhan was proof of that.

It was interesting to Rebus that, for all the barriers around the ground, this was a place where shields were dropped. After a while, it felt like one of the safest places he'd ever been. He re-called fixtures his father had taken him to in the fifties and early sixties – Cowdenbeath home games, and a crowd numbered in the hundreds; getting there necessitated a change of buses, Rebus and his younger brother fighting over who could hold the roll of tickets. Their mother was dead by then and their father was trying to carry on much as before, like they might not notice she was missing. Those Saturday trips to the football were supposed to fill a gap. You saw a lot of fathers and sons on the terraces but not many mothers, and that in itself was reminder enough. There was a boy of Rebus's age who stood near them. Rebus had walked over to him one day and blurted out the truth.

'I don't have a mum at home.'

The boy had stared at him, saying nothing.

Ever since, football had reminded him of those days and of his mother. He stood on the terraces alone these days and followed the game mostly – movements which could be graceful as ballet or as jagged as free association – but sometimes found that he'd drifted elsewhere, to a place not at all unpleasant, and all the time surrounded by a community of bodies and wills.

'I'll tell you how to beat Rangers,' he said now, addressing the whole office.

'How?' Siobhan Clarke offered.

'Clone Stevie Scoular half a dozen times.'

There were murmurs of agreement, and then the Farmer put his head around the door.

'John, my office.'

The Farmer – Chief Superintendent Watson to his face – was pouring a mug of coffee from his machine when Rebus knocked at the open door.

'Sit down, John.' Rebus sat. The Farmer motioned with an empty mug, but he turned down the offer and waited for his boss to get to his chair and the point both.

'My birthday's coming up,' the Farmer said. This was a new one on Rebus, who kept quiet. 'I'd like a present.'

'Not just a card this year then?'

'What I want, John, is Topper Hamilton.'

Rebus let that sink in. 'I thought Topper was Mr Clean these days?'

'Not in my books.' The Farmer cupped his hands around his coffee mug. 'He got a fright last time and, granted, he's been keeping a low profile, but we both know the best villains have got little or no profile at all.'

'So what's he been up to?'

'I heard a story he's the sleeping partner in a couple of clubs and casinos. I also hear he bought a taxi firm from Big Ger Cafferty when Big Ger went into Barlinnie.'

Rebus was thinking back three years to their big push against Topper Hamilton: they'd set up surveillance, used a bit of pressure here and there, got a few people to talk. In the end, it hadn't so much amounted to a hill of beans as to a fart in an empty can. The procurator fiscal had decided not to proceed to trial. But then God or Fate, call it what you like, had provided a spin to the story. Not a plague of boils or anything for Topper Hamilton, but a nasty little cancer which had given him more grief than the whole of the Lothian and Borders Police. He'd been in and out of hospital, endured chemo and the whole works, and had emerged a more slender figure in every sense.

The Farmer – who'd once settled an office argument by reeling off the books in both Old and New Testaments – wasn't yet content that God and life had done their worst to Topper, or that retribution had been meted out in some mysterious divine way. He wanted Topper in court, even if they had to wheel him there on a trolley.

It was a personal thing.

'Last time I looked,' Rebus said now, 'it wasn't illegal to invest in a casino.'

'It is if your name hasn't come up during the vetting procedure. Think Topper could get a gaming licence?'

'Fair point. But I still don't see—'

'Something else I heard. You've got a snitch works as a croupier.'

'So?'

'Same casino Topper has a finger in.'

Rebus saw it all and started shaking his head. 'I made him a promise. He'll tell me about punters, but nothing on the management.'

'And you'd rather keep that promise than give me a birthday present?'

'A relationship like that ... it's eggshells.'

The Farmer's eyes narrowed. 'You think ours isn't? Talk to him, John. Get him to do some ferreting.'

'I could lose a good snitch.'

'Plenty more bigmouths out there.' The Farmer watched Rebus get to his feet. 'I was looking for you earlier. You were in the video room.'

'A missing person.'

'Suspicious?'

Rebus shrugged. 'Could be. He went up to the bar for a round of drinks, never came back.'

'We've all done that in our time.'

'His parents are worried.'

'How old is he?'

'Twenty-three.'

The Farmer thought about it. 'Then what's the problem?'

II

The problem was the past. A week before, he'd received a phone call from a ghost.

'Inspector John Rebus, please.'

'Speaking.'

'Oh, hello there. You probably won't remember me.' A short laugh. 'That used to be a bit of a joke at school.'

Rebus, immune to every kind of phone call, had this pegged a crank. 'Why's that?' he asked, wondering which punchline he was walking into.

'Because it's my name: Mee.' The caller spelt it for him. 'Brian Mee.'

Inside Rebus's head, a fuzzy photograph took sudden shape – a mouth full of prominent teeth, freckled nose and cheeks, a kitchen-stool haircut. 'Barney Mee?' he said.

More laughter on the line. 'Aye, they used to call me Barney. I'm not sure I ever knew why.'

Rebus could have told him: after Barney Rubble in *The Flintstones*. He could have added, because you were a dense wee bastard. But instead he asked how this ghost from his past was doing.

'No' bad, no' bad.' The laugh again; Rebus recognised it now as a sign of nerves.

'So what can I do for you, Brian?'

'Well, me and Janis, we thought ... Well, it was my mum's idea actually. She knew your dad. Both my mum and dad knew him, only my dad passed away, like. They all used to drink at the Goth.'

'Are you still in Bowhill?'

'Never quite escaped. Ach, it's all right really. I work in Glenrothes though. Lucky to have a job these days, eh? Mind, you've done well for yourself, Johnny. Do you still get called that?'

'I prefer John.'

'I remember you hated it when anyone called you Jock.' Another wheezing laugh. The photo was even sharper now, bordered with a white edge the way photos always were in the past. A decent footballer, a bit of a terrier, the hair reddish-brown. Dragging his satchel along the ground until the stitching rubbed away. Always with some huge hard sweet in his mouth, crunching down on it, his nose running. And one incident: he'd lifted some nude mags from under his dad's side of the bed and brought them to the toilets next to the Miners' Institute, there to be pored over like textbooks. Afterwards, half a dozen twelve-year-old boys had looked at each other, minds fizzing with questions.

'So what can I do for you, Brian?'

'Like I say, it was my mum's idea. Only, she remembered you were in the police in Edinburgh – saw your name in the paper a while back – and she thought you could maybe help.'

'With what?'

'Our son. I mean, mine and Janis's. He's called Damon.'

'What's he done?' Rebus thought: something minor, and way outside his territory anyway.

'He's vanished.'

'Run away?'

'More like in a puff of smoke. He was in this club with his pals, see, and he went—'

'Have you tried calling the police?' Rebus caught himself. 'I mean Fife Constabulary.'

'Oh aye.' Mee sounded dismissive. 'They asked a few questions, like, sniffed around a bit, then said there was nothing they could do. Damon's twenty-three. They say he's got a right to bugger off if he wants.'

'They've got a point. People run away all the time, Brian. Girl trouble maybe.'

'He was engaged.'

'Maybe he got scared?'

'Helen's a lovely girl. Never a raised voice between them.'

'Did he leave a note?'

'Nothing. I went through this with the police. He didn't take any clothes or anything. He didn't have any reason to go.'

'So you think something's happened to him?'

'I know what those buggers are thinking. They say we should give him another week or so to come back, or at least get in touch, but I know they'll only start doing something about it when the body turns up.'

Again, Rebus could have confirmed that this was only sensible. Again, he knew Mee wouldn't want to hear it.

'The thing is, Brian,' he said, 'I work in Edinburgh. Fife's not my patch. I mean, I can make a couple of phone calls, but it's hard to know what else to do.'

The voice was close to despair. 'Well, if you could just do *some-thing*. Like, anything. We'd be very grateful. It would put our minds at rest.' A pause. 'My mum always speaks well of your dad. He's remembered in this town.'

And buried there, too, Rebus thought. He picked up a pen. 'Give me your phone number, Brian.' And, almost an afterthought, 'Better give me the address, too.'

That evening, he drove north out of Edinburgh, paid his toll at the Forth Bridge, and crossed into Fife. It wasn't as if he never went there – he had a brother in Kirkcaldy. But though they spoke on the phone every month or so, there were seldom visits. He couldn't think of any other family he still had in Fife. The place liked to call itself 'the Kingdom' and there were those who would agree that it was another country, a place with its own linguistic and cultural currency. For such a small place it seemed almost endlessly complex – had seemed that way to Rebus even when he was growing up. To outsiders the place meant coastal scenery and St Andrew's, or a stretch of motorway between Edinburgh and Dundee, but the west-central Fife of Rebus's childhood had been very different, ruled by coal mines and linoleum, dockyards and chemical plants, an indus-trial landscape shaped by basic needs, and producing people who were wary and inward-looking with the blackest humour you'd ever find.

They'd built new roads since Rebus's last visit, and knocked down a few more landmarks, but the place didn't feel so very different from thirty-odd years before. It wasn't such a great span of time after all, except in human terms; maybe not even then. Entering Cardenden – Bowhill had disappeared from road signs in the 1960s, even if locals still knew it as a village distinct from its neighbour – Rebus slowed to see if the memories would turn out sweet or sour. Then he caught sight of a Chinese takeaway and thought: both, of course.

Brian and Janis Mee's house was easy enough to find: they were standing by the gate waiting for him. Rebus had been born in a prefab but brought up in a house just like the one he now parked in front of. Brian Mee practically opened the car door for him, and was trying to shake his hand while Rebus was still emerging from his seat.

'Let the man catch his breath!' Janis Mee snapped. She was still standing by the gate, arms folded. 'How have you been, Johnny?'

And Rebus realised that Brian Mee had married Janis Playfair, the only girl in his long and trouble-strewn life who'd ever managed to knock him unconscious.

The narrow, low-ceilinged living-room was full to bursting – not just Rebus and Janis and Brian, but Brian's mother and Mr and Mrs Playfair. Introductions had to be made, and Rebus guided to 'the seat by the fire'. The room was overheated. A pot of tea was produced, and on the table by Rebus's armchair sat enough slices of cake to feed a football crowd.

'He's a brainy one,' Janis's mother said, handing Rebus a framed photo of Damon Mee. 'Plenty of certificates from school. Works hard. Saving up to get married. The date's set for next August.'

The photo showed a smiling imp, not long out of school. 'Have you got anything more recent?'

Janis handed him a packet of snapshots. 'From last summer.'

Rebus went through them slowly. It saved having to look at the faces around him. He felt like a doctor, expected to produce an immediate diagnosis and remedy. The photos showed a man in his early twenties, still retaining the impish smile but recognisably older. Not careworn exactly, but with something behind the eyes, some disenchantment with adulthood. A few of the photos showed Damon's parents.

'We all went together,' Brian explained. 'Janis's mum and dad, my mum, Helen and her parents.'

Beaches, a big white hotel, poolside games. 'Where is it?'

'Lanzarote,' Janis said, handing him his tea. In a few of the pictures she was wearing a bikini – good body for her age, or any age come to that. He tried not to linger.

'Can I keep a couple of the close-ups?' he asked. Janis looked at him. 'Of Damon.' She nodded and he put the other photos back in their packet.

'We're really grateful,' someone said. Janis's mum? Brian's? Rebus couldn't tell.

'Does Helen live locally?'

'Practically round the corner.'

'I'd like to talk to her.'

'I'll give her a bell,' Brian Mee said, leaping to his feet.

'Damon had been drinking in some club?'

'Guisers,' Janis said, handing round cigarettes. 'It's in Kirkcaldy.'

'On the Prom?'

She shook her head, looking just the same as she had that night of the school dance ... shaking her head, telling him so far and no further. 'In the town. It used to be a department store.'

'It's really called Gaitanos,' Mr Playfair said. Rebus remembered him, too. He was an old man now.

'Where does Damon work?' Careful to stick to the present tense.

Brian Mee came back into the room. 'Same place I do. I managed to get him a job in packaging. He's been learning the ropes; it'll be management soon.'

Working-class nepotism; jobs handed down from father to son. Rebus was surprised it still existed.

'Helen'll be here in a minute,' Brian added.

'Are you not eating any cake, Inspector?' said Mrs Playfair.

Helen Cousins hadn't been able to add much to Rebus's picture of Damon, and hadn't been there the night he'd vanished. But she'd introduced him to someone who had, Andy Peters. Andy had been part of the group at Gaitanos. There'd been four of them. They'd been in the same year at school and still met up once or twice a week, sometimes to watch Raith Rovers if the weather was decent and the mood took them, other times for an evening session in a pub or club. It was only their third or fourth visit to Guisers.

Rebus thought of paying the club a visit, but knew he should talk to the local cops first, and decided that it could all wait until morning. He knew he was jumping through hoops. He didn't expect to find anything the locals had missed. At best, he could reassure the family that everything possible had been done.

Next morning he made a few phone calls from his office, trying to find someone who could be bothered to answer some casual questions from an Edinburgh colleague. He had one ally – Detective Sergeant Hendry at Dunfermline CID – but only reached him at the third attempt. He asked Hendry for a favour, then put the phone down and got back to his own work. But it was hard to concentrate. He kept thinking about Bowhill and about Janis Mee, née Playfair. Which led him – eventually – guiltily – to thoughts of Damon. Younger runaways tended to take the same route: by bus or train or hitching, and to London, Newcastle, Edinburgh or Glasgow. There were organisations who would keep an eye open for runaways, and even if they wouldn't always reveal their whereabouts to the anxious families, at least they could confirm that someone was alive and unharmed.

But a twenty-three-year-old, someone a bit cannier and with money to hand ... could be anywhere. No destination was too distant – he owned a passport, and it hadn't turned up. Rebus knew, too, that Damon had a current account at the local bank, complete with cashcard, and an interest-bearing account with a building society in Kirkcaldy. The bank might be worth trying. Rebus picked up the telephone again.

The manager at first insisted that he'd need something in writing, but relented when Rebus promised to fax him later. Rebus held while the manager went off to check, and had doodled half a village, complete with stream, parkland and school, by the time the man came back.

'The most recent withdrawal was from a cash machine in Kirkcaldy. One hundred pounds on the twenty-second.'

'What time?'

'I've no way of knowing.'

'No other withdrawals since then?'

'No.'

'How up-to-date is that information?'

'Very. Of course a cheque – especially if post-dated – would take longer to show up.'

'Could you keep tabs on that account, let me know if anyone starts using it again?'

'I could, but I'd need it in writing, and I might also need Head Office approval.'

'Well, see what you can do, Mr Brayne.'

'It's Bain,' the bank manager said coldly, putting down the phone.

DS Hendry didn't get back to him until late afternoon.

'Gaitanos,' Hendry said. 'I don't know the place personally. Locals call it Guisers. It's a pretty choice establishment. Two stabbings last year, one inside the club itself, the other in the back alley where the owner parks his Merc. Local residents are always girning about the noise when the place lets out.'

'What's the owner's name?'

'Charles Mackenzie, nicknamed "Charmer". He seems to be clean. A couple of uniforms talked to him about Damon Mee, but there was nothing to tell. Know how many missing persons there are every year? They're not exactly a white-hot priority. God knows there are times I've felt like doing a runner myself.'

'Haven't we all? Did the woolly suits talk to anyone else at the club?'

'Such as?'

'Bar staff, punters.'

'No. Someone did take a look at the security video for the night Damon was there, but they didn't see anything.'

'Where's the video now?'

'Back with its rightful owner.'

'Am I going to be stepping on toes if I ask to see it?'

'I think I can cover you. I know you said this was personal, John, but why the interest?'

'I'm not sure I can explain.' There were words – community, history, memory – but Rebus didn't think they'd be enough.

'They mustn't be working you hard enough over there.'

'Just the twenty-four hours every day.'

III

Matty Paine could tell a few stories. He'd worked his way round the world as a croupier. Cruise liners he'd worked on, and in Nevada. He'd spent a couple of years in London, dealing out cards and spinning the wheel for some of the wealthiest in the land, faces you'd recognise from the TV and the papers. Moguls, royalty, stars – Matty had seen them all. But his best story – the one people sometimes disbelieved – was about the time he'd been recruited to work in a casino in Beirut. This was at the height of the civil war, bomb sites and rubble, smoke and charred buildings, refugees and regular bursts of small-arms fire. And amazingly, in the midst of it all (or, to be fair, on the edge of it all), a casino. Not exactly legal. Run from a hotel basement with torchlight when the generator failed and not much in the way of refreshments, but with no shortage of punters – cash bets, dollars only – and a management team of three who prowled the place like Dobermanns, since there was no surveillance and no other way to check that the games were being played honestly. One of them had stood next to Matty for a full forty minutes one session, making him sweat despite the air-conditioning. He'd reminded Matty of the gaffers casinos employed to check on apprentices. He knew the gaffers were there to protect *him* as much as the punters – there were professional gamblers out there who'd psych out a trainee, watch them for hours, whole nights and weeks, looking for the flaw that would give them an edge over the house. Like, when you were starting out, you didn't always vary the force with which you span the wheel, or sent the ball rolling, and if they could suss it, they'd get a pretty good idea which quadrant the ball was going to stop in. Good croupiers were immune to this. A really good croupier – one of a very select, very highly thought of group – could master the wheel and get the ball to land pretty well where *they* wanted.

Of course, this might be against the interests of the house, too. And in the end, that's why the checkers were out there, patrolling the tables. They were looking out for the house. In the end it all came down to the house.

And when things had got a wee bit too hot in London, Matty had come home, meaning Edinburgh, though really he was from Gullane – perhaps the only boy ever to be raised there and not show the slightest interest in golf. His father had played – his mother too, come to that. Maybe she still did; he didn't keep in touch. There had been an awkward moment at the casino when a neighbour from Gullane days, an old business friend of his father's, had turned up, a bit the worse for wear and in tow with three other middle-aged punters. The neighbour had glanced towards Matty from time to time, but had eventually shaken his head, unable to place the face.

'Does he know you?' one of the all-seeing gaffers had asked quietly, seeking out some scam against the house.

Matty had shaken his head. 'A neighbour from when I was growing up.' That was all; just a ghost from the past. He supposed his mother *was* still alive. He could probably find out by opening the phone book. But he wasn't that interested.

'Place your bets, please, ladies and gentlemen.'

Different houses had different styles. You either did your spiel in English or French. House rules changed, too. Matty's strengths were roulette and blackjack, but really he was happy in charge of any sort of game – most houses liked that he was flexible, it meant there was less chance of him trying some scam. It was the one-note wonders who tried small, stupid diddles. His latest employers seemed fairly laid back. They ran a clean casino which boasted only the very occasional high roller. Most of the punters were business people, well enough heeled but canny with it. You got husbands and wives coming in, proof of a relaxed atmosphere. There were younger punters too – a lot of those were Asians, mainly Chinese. The money they changed, according to the cashier, had a funny feel and smell to it.

'That's because they keep it in their underwear,' the day boss had told her.

The Asians ... whatever they were ... sometimes worked in local restaurants; you could smell the kitchen on their crumpled jackets and shirts. Fierce gamblers, no game was ever played quickly enough for their liking. They'd slap their chips down like they were in a playground betting game. And they talked a lot, almost never in English. The gaffers didn't like that, never could tell what they might be scheming. But their money was good, they seldom caused trouble, and they lost a percentage same as everyone else.

'Daft bastards,' the night manager said. 'Know what they do with a big win? Go bung it on the gee-gees. Where's the sense in that?'

Where indeed? No point giving your money to a bookmaker when the casino would happily take it instead.

It wasn't really on for croupiers to be friends with the clients, but sometimes it happened. And it couldn't very well not happen with Matty and Stevie Scoular, since they'd been in the same year at school. Not that they'd known one another well. Stevie had been the football genius, also more than fair at the hundred and two hundred metres, swimming and basketball. Matty, on the other hand, had skived off games whenever possible, forgetting to bring his kit or getting his mum to write him notes. He was good at a couple of subjects – maths and woodwork – but never sat beside Stevie in class. They even lived at opposite ends of the town.

At playtime and lunchtime, Matty ran a card game – three-card brag mostly, sometimes pontoon – playing for dinner money, pocket money, sweets and comics. A few of the cards were nicked at the corners, but the other players didn't seem to notice and Matty got a reputation as 'lucky'. He'd take bets on horse races too, sometimes passing the bets on to an older boy who wouldn't be turned away by the local bookmaker. Often though, Matty would simply pocket the money and if someone's horse happened to win, he'd say he couldn't get the bets on in time and hand back the stake.

He couldn't tell you exactly when it was that Stevie had started spending less breaktime dribbling past half a dozen despairing pairs of legs and more hanging around the edges of the card school. Thing about three-card brag, it doesn't take long to pick it up and even a moron can have a stab at playing. Soon enough, Stevie was losing his dinner money with the rest of them, and Matty's pockets were about bursting with loose change. Eventually, Stevie had seemed to see sense, drifted away from the game and back to keepie-up and dribbling. But he'd been hooked, no doubt about it. Maybe only for a few weeks, but a lot of those lunchtimes had been spent cadging sweets and apple cores, the better to stave off hunger.

Even then, Matty had thought he'd be seeing Stevie again. It had just taken the best part of a decade, that was all.

When Stevie Scoular walked into the casino, people looked his way. It was the done thing. He was a sharp dresser, young, usually accompanied by women who looked like models. When Stevie had first walked into the Morvena, Matty's heart had sunk. They hadn't seen one another since school and here Stevie was, local boy made good, a hero, picture in the papers and plenty of money in the bank. Here was a schoolboy dream made flesh. And what was Matty? He had stories he could tell but that was about it. So he'd been hoping Stevie wouldn't grace his table, or if he did that he wouldn't recognise him. But Stevie had seen him, seemed to know him straight off and come bouncing up.

'Matty!'

'Hello there, Stevie.'

It was flattering really. Stevie hadn't become big-headed or anything. He took the whole thing – the way his life had gone – as a bit of a joke really. He'd made Matty promise to meet him for a drink when his shift was over. All through their conversation, Matty had been aware of gaffers hovering and when Stevie wandered off to another table one of them muttered in Matty's ear and another croupier took over from him.

He hadn't been in the plush back office that often, just for the initial interview and to discuss a couple of big losses on his table. The casino's owner, Mr Mandelson, was watching a football match on Sky Sports. He was well-built, mid-forties, his face pockmarked from childhood acne. His hair was black, slicked back from the forehead, long at the collar. He always seemed to know what he was about.

'How's the table tonight?' he asked.

'Look, Mr Mandelson, I know we're not supposed to be too friendly with the punters, but Stevie and me were at school together. Haven't clapped eyes on one another since – not till tonight.'

'Easy, Matty, easy.' Mandelson motioned for him to sit down. 'Something to drink?' A smile. 'No alcohol on shift, mind.'

'Ehh ... a Coke maybe.'

'Help yourself.'

There was a fridge in the far corner, stocked with white wine, champagne and soft drinks. A couple of the female croupiers said Mandelson had tried it on with them, plying them with booze. But he didn't seem upset by a refusal: they still had their jobs. There were seven female croupiers all told, and only two had spoken to Matty about it. It made him wonder about the other five.

He took a Coke and sat down again.

'So, you and Stevie Scoular, eh?'

'I haven't seen him in here before.'

'I think he only recently found out about the place. He's been in a few times, dropped some hefty bets.' Mandelson was staring at him. 'You and Stevie, eh?'

'Look, if you're worried, just take me off whatever table he's playing.'

'Nothing like that, Matty.' Mandelson's face broke into a grin. 'It's nice to have a friend, eh? Nice to meet up again after all these years. Don't you worry about anything. Stevie's the King of Edinburgh. As long as he keeps scoring goals, we're all his subjects.' He paused. 'Nice to know someone who knows the King, almost makes me feel like royalty myself. On you go now, Matty.'

Matty got up, leaving the Coke unopened.

'And don't you go upsetting that young man. We don't want to put him off his game, do we?'

IV

It had taken a couple of days to get the tape from Gaitanos. At first, they thought they'd wiped it, and then they'd sent the wrong day's recording. But at last Rebus had the right tape and had watched it at home half a dozen times before deciding he could use someone who knew what he was doing ... and a video machine that would freeze-frame without the screen looking like a technical problem.

Now he'd seen all there was to see. He'd watched a young man cease to exist. Of course, Hendry was right, a lot of people disappeared every year. Sometimes they turned up again – dead or alive – and sometimes they didn't. What did it have to do with Rebus, beyond the promise to a family that he'd make sure the Fife police hadn't missed something? Maybe the pull wasn't Damon Mee, but Bowhill itself; and maybe even then, the Bowhill of his past rather than the town as it stood today.

He was working the Damon Mee case in his free time, which, since he was on day shift at St Leonard's, meant the evenings. He'd checked again with the bank – no money had been withdrawn from any machines since the twenty-second – and with Damon's building society. No money had been withdrawn from that account either. Even this wasn't unknown in the case of a runaway; sometimes they wanted to shed their whole history, which meant ditching their identity and everything that went with it. Rebus had passed a description of Matty to hostels and drop-in centres in Edinburgh, and faxed the same description to similar centres in Glasgow, Newcastle, Aberdeen and London. He'd also faxed details to the National Missing Persons Bureau in London. He checked with a colleague who knew about 'MisPers' that he'd done about all he could.

'Not far off it,' she confirmed. 'It's like looking for a needle in a haystack without knowing which field to start with.'

'How big a problem is it?'

She puffed out her cheeks. 'Last figures I saw were for the whole of Britain. I think there are around 25,000 a year. Those are the *reported* MisPers. You can add a few thousand for the ones nobody notices. There's a nice distinction actually: if nobody knows you're missing, are you really missing?'

Afterwards, Rebus telephoned Janis Mee and told her she might think about running up some flyers and putting them up in positions of prominence in nearby towns, maybe even handing them out to Saturday shoppers or evening drinkers in Kirkcaldy. A photo of Damon, a brief physical description, and what he was wearing the night he left. She said she'd already thought of doing so, but that it made his disappearance seem so final. Then she broke down and cried and John Rebus, thirty-odd miles away, asked if she wanted him to 'drop by'.

'I'll be all right,' she said.

'Sure?'

'Well ...'

Rebus reasoned that he was going to go to Fife anyway. He had to drop the tape back to Gaitanos, and wanted to see the club when it was lively. He'd take the photos of Damon with him and show them around. He'd ask about the candyfloss blonde. The technician who had worked with the videotape had transferred a still to his computer and managed to boost the quality. Rebus had some hard copies in his pocket. Maybe other people who'd been queuing at the bar would remember something.

Maybe.

His first stop, however, was the cemetery. He didn't have any flowers to put on his parents' grave, but he crouched beside it, fingers touching the grass. The inscription was simple, just names and dates really, and underneath, 'Not Dead, But at Rest in the Arms of the Lord'. He wasn't sure whose idea that had been, not his certainly. The headstone's carved lettering was inlaid with gold, but it had already faded from his mother's name. He touched the surface of the marble, expecting it to be cold, but finding a residual warmth there. A blackbird nearby was trying to worry food from the ground. Rebus wished it luck.

By the time he reached Janis's, Brian was home from work. Rebus told them what he'd done so far, after which Brian nodded, apologised, and said he had a Burns Club meeting. The two men shook hands. When the door closed, Janis and Rebus exchanged a look and then a smile.

'I see that bruise finally faded,' she said.

Rebus rubbed his right cheek. 'It was a hell of a punch.'

'Funny how strong you can get when you're angry.'

'Sorry.'

She laughed. 'Bit late to apologise.'

'It was just ...'

'It was everything,' she said. 'Summer holidays coming up, all of us leaving school, you going off to join the army. The last school dance before all of that. That's what it was.' She paused. 'Do you know what happened to Mitch?' She watched Rebus shake his head. 'Last I heard,' she said, 'he was living somewhere down south. The two of you used to be so close.'

'Yes.'

She laughed again. 'Johnny, it was a long time ago, don't look so solemn.' She paused. 'I've sometimes wondered ... ach, not for years, but just now and then I used to wonder what would have happened ...'

'If you hadn't punched me?'

She nodded. 'If we'd stayed together. Well, you can't turn the clock back, eh?'

'Would the world be any better if we could?'

She stared at the window, not really seeing it. 'Damon would still be here,' she said quietly. A tear escaped her eye, and she fussed for a handkerchief in her pocket. Rebus got up and made towards her. Then the front door opened, and he retreated.

'My mum,' Janis smiled. 'She usually pops in around this time. It's like a railway station around here, hard to find any privacy.'

Then Mrs Playfair walked into the living-room.

'Hello, Inspector, thought that was your car. Is there any news?'

'I'm afraid not,' Rebus said. Janis got to her feet and hugged her mother, the crying starting afresh.

'There there, pet,' Mrs Playfair said quietly. 'There there.'

Rebus walked past the two of them without saying a word.

*

It was still early when he reached Gaitanos. He had a word with one of the bouncers, who was keeping warm in the lobby until things started getting busy, and the man lumbered off to fetch Charles Mackenzie, *aka* Charmer. It seemed strange to Rebus: here he was, standing in the very foyer he'd stared at for so long on the video monitor. The camera was high up in one corner with nothing to show whether it was working. Rebus gave it a wave anyway. If he disappeared tonight, it could be his farewell to the world.

'Inspector Rebus.' They'd spoken on the phone. The man who came forward to shake Rebus's hand stood about five feet four and was as thin as a cocktail glass. Rebus placed him in his mid-fifties. He wore a powder-blue suit and an open-necked white shirt with suntan and gold jewellery beneath. His hair was silver and thinning, but as well-cut as the suit. 'Come through to the office.'

Rebus followed Mackenzie down a carpeted corridor to a gloss-black door with a sign on it saying 'Private'. There was no door handle. Mackenzie unlocked the door and motioned for Rebus to go in.

'After you, sir,' Rebus said. You never knew what could be waiting behind a locked door.

What greeted Rebus this time was an office which seemed to double as a broom-cupboard. Mops and a vacuum cleaner rested against one wall. A bank of screens spread across three filing cabinets showed what was happening inside and outside the club. Unlike the video Rebus had watched, these screens each showed a certain location.

'Are these recording?' Rebus asked. Mackenzie shook his head.

'We've got a roaming monitor, and that's the only recording we get. But this way, if we spot trouble anywhere, we can watch it unfold.'

'Like that knifing in the alley?'

'Messed up my Mercedes.'

'So I heard. Is that when you called the police? When your car stopped being a bystander?'

Mackenzie laughed and wagged a finger, but didn't answer. Rebus couldn't see where he'd earned his nickname. The guy had all the charm of sandpaper.

'I brought back your video.' Rebus placed it on the desk.

'All right to record over it now?'

'I suppose so.' Rebus handed over the computer-enhanced photograph. 'The missing person is slightly right of centre, second row.'

'Is that his doll?'

'Do you know her?'

'Wish I did.'

'You haven't seen her before.'

'She doesn't look the sort I'd forget.'

Rebus took back the picture. 'Mind if I show this around?'

'The place is practically empty.'

'I thought I might stick around.'

Mackenzie frowned and studied the backs of his hands. 'Well, you know, it's not that I don't want to help or anything ...'

'But?'

'Well, it's hardly conducive to a party atmosphere, is it? That's our slogan – "The best party of your life, every night!" – and I don't think a police officer mooching around asking questions is going to add to the ambience.'

'I quite understand, Mr Mackenzie. I was being thoughtless.' Mackenzie lifted his hands, palms towards Rebus: no problem, the hands were saying.

'And you're quite right,' Rebus continued. 'In fact, I'd be a lot quicker if I had some assistance – say, a dozen uniforms. That way, I wouldn't be "mooching around" for nearly so long. In fact, let's make it a couple of dozen. We'll be in and out, quick as a virgin's first poke. Mind if I use your phone?'

'Whoah, wait a minute. Look, all I was saying was ... Look, how much do you want?'

'Sorry, sir?'

Mackenzie reached into a desk drawer, lifted out a brick of twenties, pulled about five notes free. 'Will this do it?'

Rebus sat back. 'Am I to understand you're trying to offer me a cash incentive to leave the premises?'

'Whatever. Just slope off, eh?'

Rebus stood up. 'To me, Mr Mackenzie, that's an open invitation to stay.'

So he stayed.

The looks he got from staff made him feel like a football fan trapped on the opposition's turf. The way they all shook their heads as soon as he held up the photo, he knew word had gone around. He had a little more luck with the punters. A couple of lads had seen the woman before.

'Last week, was it?' one asked the other. 'Maybe the week before.'

'Not long ago anyway,' the other agreed. 'Cracker, isn't she?'

'Has she been in since?'

'Haven't seen her. Just that one night. Didn't quite get the nerve up to ask for a dance.'

'Was she with anyone?'

'No idea.'

They didn't recognise Damon Mee though. They said they never paid much attention to blokes.

'We're not that way inclined, sweetie.'

The place was still only half full, but the bass was loud enough to make Rebus feel queasy. He managed to order an orange juice at the bar and just sat there, looking at the photo. The woman interested him. The way her head was angled, the way her mouth was open, she could have been saying something to Damon. A minute later, he was gone. Had she said she'd meet him somewhere? Had something happened at that meeting? He'd shown the photo to Damon's mates from that night. They remembered seeing her, but swore Damon hadn't introduced himself.

'She seemed sort of cold,' one of them had said. 'You know, like she wanted to be left alone.'

Rebus had studied the video again, watched her progress towards the bar, showing no apparent interest in Damon's leaving. But then she'd turned and started pushing her way back through the throng, no drink to show for her long wait.

At midnight exactly, she'd left the nightclub. The final shot was of her turning left along the pavement, watched by a few people who were waiting to get in. And now Charles Mackenzie wanted to give Rebus money.

At three quid for an orange juice, maybe he should have taken it.

If the place had been heaving, maybe he wouldn't have noticed them.

He was finishing his second drink and trying not to feel like a leper in a children's ward when he recognised one of the doormen. There was another man with him, tall and fat and pale. His idea of clubbing was probably the connection of baseball bat to skull. The bouncer was pointing Rebus out to him. Here we go, Rebus thought. They've brought in the professionals. The fat man said something to the bouncer, and they both retreated to the foyer, leaving Rebus with an empty glass and only one good reason to order another drink.

Get it over with, he thought, sliding from his bar stool and walking around the dance floor. There was always the fire exit, but it led on to the alley and, if they were waiting for him there, the only witness would be Mackenzie's Mercedes. He wanted things kept as public as possible. The street outside would be busy, no shortage of onlookers and possible good Samaritans. Or at the very least, someone to call for an ambulance.

He paused in the foyer and saw that the bouncer was back at his post on the front door. No sign of the fat man. Then he glanced along the corridor towards Mackenzie's office, and saw the fat man planted outside the door. He had his arms folded in front of him and wasn't going anywhere.

Rebus walked outside. The air had seldom tasted so good. He tried to calm himself with a few deep breaths. There was a car parked at the kerbside, a gold-coloured Rolls-Royce, with nobody in the driver's seat. Rebus wasn't the only one admiring the car, but he was probably alone in memorising its number plate.

He moved his own car to where he could see the Roller, then sat tight. Half an hour later, the fat man emerged, looking to left and right. He walked to the car, unlocked it and held open the back door. Only now did another figure emerge from the club. Rebus caught a swishing full-length black coat, sleek hair and chiselled face. The man slipped into the car, and the fat man closed the door and squeezed in behind the steering wheel.

Like them or not, you had to admire Rollers. They carried tonnage.

V

Back in Edinburgh he parked his car and sat in it, smoking his eleventh cigarette of the day. He sometimes played this game with himself – I'll have one more tonight, and deduct one from tomorrow's allowance. Or he would argue that any cigarette after midnight came from the next day's stash. He'd lost count along the way, but reckoned by now he should be going whole days without a ciggie to balance the books. Well, when it came down to it, ten cigarettes a day or twelve, thirteen, fourteen – what difference did it make?

The street he was parked on was quiet. Residential for the most part with big houses. There was a basement bar on the corner, but it did mostly lunchtime business from the offices on neighbouring streets. By ten, the place was usually locked up. Taxis rippled past him and the occasional drunk, hands in pockets, would weave slowly homewards. A few of the taxis stopped just in front of him and disgorged their fares, who would then climb half a dozen steps and push open the door to the Morvena Casino. Rebus had never been inside the place. He placed the occasional bet on the horses, but that was about it. Gave up doing the football pools. He bought a National Lottery ticket when opportunity arose, but often didn't get round to checking the numbers. He had half a dozen tickets lying around, any one of which could be his fortune. He quite liked the notion that he might have won a million and not know it; preferred it, in fact, to the idea of actually having the million in his bank account. What would he do with a million pounds? Same as he'd do with fifty thou – self-destruct.

Only faster.

Janis had asked him about Mitch – Roy Mitchell, Rebus's best friend at school. The more time Rebus had spent with her, the less he'd seen of Mitch. They'd been going to join the army together, hoping they might get the same regiment. Until Mitch lost his eye. That had been the end of that. The army hadn't wanted him any more. Rebus had headed off, sent Mitch a couple of letters, but by the time his first leave came, Mitch had already left Bowhill. Rebus had stopped writing after that ...

When the Morvena's door opened next, it was so eight or nine young people could leave. The shift changeover. Three of them turned one way, the rest another. Rebus watched the group of three. At the first set of lights, two kept going and one crossed the road and took a left. Rebus started his engine and followed. When the lights turned green, he signalled left and sounded his horn, then pulled the car over and wound down his window.

'Mr Rebus,' the young man said.

'Hello, Matty. Let's go for a drive.'

Officers from other cities, people Rebus met from time to time, would remark on how cushy he had it in Edinburgh. Such a beautiful place, and prosperous. So little crime. They thought to be dangerous a city had to look dangerous. London, Manchester, Liverpool – these places were dangerous in their eyes. Not Edinburgh, not this sleepy walking-tour with its monuments and museums. Tourism aside, the lifeblood of the city was its commerce, and Edinburgh's commerce – banking, insurance and the like – was discreet. The city hid its secrets well, and its vices too. Potentially troublesome elements had been moved to the sprawling council estates which ringed the capital, and any crimes committed behind the thick stone walls of the city centre's tenements and houses were often muffled by those same walls. Which was why every good detective needed his contacts.

Rebus took them on a circuit – Canonmills to Ferry Road, back up to Comely Bank and through Stockbridge into the New Town again. And they talked.

'I know we had a sort of gentleman's agreement, Matty,' Rebus said.

'But I'm about to find out you're no gentleman?'

Rebus smiled. 'You're ahead of me.'

'I wondered how long it would take.' Matty paused, stared through the windscreen. 'You know I'll say no.'

'Will you?'

'I said at the start, no ratting on anyone I work with or work for. Just the punters.'

'Not even many of them. It's not like I've been milking you, Matty. I'll bet you've dozens of stories you haven't told me.'

'I work tables, Mr Rebus. People don't place a bet and then start yacking about some job they've pulled or some scam they're running.'

'No, but they meet friends. They have a drink, get mellow. It's a relaxing place, so I've heard. And maybe then they talk.'

'I've not held anything back.'

'Matty, Matty.' Rebus shook his head. 'It's funny, I was just thinking tonight about that night we met. Do you remember?'

How could he forget? A couple of drinks after work, a car borrowed from a friend who was away on holiday. Matty hadn't been back long. Driving through the town was great, especially with a buzz on. Streets glistening after the rain. Late night, mostly taxis for company. He just drove and drove and, as the streets grew quieter, he pushed the accelerator a bit further, caught a string of green lights, then saw one turning red. He didn't know how good the tyres were, imagined braking hard and skidding in the wet. Fuck it, he put his foot down.

Just missed the cyclist. The guy was coming through on green and had to twist his front wheel hard to avoid contact, then teetered and fell on to the road. Matty's foot eased off the accelerator, thought about the brake, then went back on the accelerator again.

That's when he saw the cop car. And thought: I can't afford this.

They'd breathalysed him and taken him to St Leonard's, where he'd sat around and let the machinery chew him up. Would it come to a trial? Would there be a report in the papers? How could he keep his name from getting around? He'd worked himself up into a right state by the time Detective Inspector John Rebus had sat down across from him.

'I can't afford this,' Matty had blurted out.

'Sorry?'

He'd swallowed and tried to find a story. 'I work in a casino. Any black mark against me, they'll boot me out. Look, if it's a question of compensation or anything ... like, I'll buy him a new bike.'

Rebus had picked up a sheet of paper. 'Drunk driving ... in a borrowed car you weren't insured to drive ... running a red light ... leaving the scene of an accident ...' Rebus had shaken his head, read the sheet through one more time and then put it down, and looked up at Matty. 'What casino did you say you work for?'

Later, he'd given Matty two business cards, both with his phone number. 'The first one's for you to tear up in disgust,' he'd said. 'The other one's to keep. Have we got a deal?'

'Look, Mr Rebus,' Matty said now, as the car stopped for lights on Raeburn Place, 'I'm doing the best I can.'

'I want to know what's happening behind the scenes at the Morvena.'

'I wouldn't know.'

'Anything at all, it doesn't matter how small it seems. Any stories, gossip, anything overheard. Ever seen the owner entertain people in his office? Maybe open the place for a private party? Names, faces, anything at all. Put your mind to it, Matty. Just put your mind to it.'

'They'd skin me alive.'

'Who's they?'

Matty swallowed. 'Mr Mandelson.'

'He's the owner, right?'

'Right.'

'On paper at least. What I need to know is who might be pulling his strings.'

'I can't see anyone pulling his strings.'

'You'd be surprised. Hard bastard, is he?'

'I'd say so.'

'Given you grief?' Matty shook his head. 'Do you see much of him?'

'Not much,' Matty said. Not, he might have added, until recently at any rate.

Rebus dropped him at the foot of Broughton Street, headed back up to Leith Walk and along York Place on to Queen Street. He passed the casino again and slowed, a frown on his face. At the next set of lights, he did a U-turn so he could be sure. Yes, it was the Roller from Gaitanos, no doubt about it.

Parked outside the Morvena.

VI

'Mind if I join you?'

Rebus was eating breakfast in the canteen and wishing there was more caffeine in the coffee, or more coffee in the coffee come to that. He nodded to the empty chair and Siobhan sat down.

'Heavy night?' she said.

'Believe it or not, I was on orange juice.'

She bit into her muffin, washing it down with milk. 'Harry tells me you had him working a tape.'

'Harry?'

'Our video wizard. He said it was a missing person. News to me.'

'It's not official. The son of an old schoolfriend of mine.'

'Standing at a bar one minute and gone the next?' Rebus looked at her and she smiled. 'Harry's a great one for gossip.'

'I'm working on it in my own time.'

'Need any help?'

'Handy with a crystal ball, are you?' But Rebus dug into his pocket and brought out the still from the video. 'That's Damon there,' he said, pointing.

'Who's that with him?'

'I wish I knew. She's not with him. I don't know who she is.'

'You've asked around?'

'I was at the club last night. A few punters remembered her.'

'Male punters?' She waited till Rebus nodded. 'You were asking the wrong sex. Any man would have given her the once-over, but only superficially. A woman, on the other hand, would have seen her as competition. Have you never noticed women in nightclubs? They've got eyes like lasers. Plus, what if she visited the loo?'

Rebus was interested now. 'What if she did?'

'*That's* where women talk. Maybe someone spoke to her, maybe she said something back. Ears would have been listening.' Siobhan stared at the photo. 'Funny, it's almost like she's got an aura.'

'How do you mean?'

'Like she's shining.'

'Interior light.'

'Exactly.'

'No, that's what your friend Harry said. It's the interior lighting that gives that effect.'

'Maybe he didn't know what he was saying.'

'I'm not sure I know what *you're* saying.'

'Some religions believe in spirit guides. They're supposed to lead you to the next world.'

'You mean this one's not the end?'

She smiled. 'Depends on your religion.'

'Well, it's plenty enough for me.' He looked at the photo again. 'I was sort of joking, you know, about her being a spirit guide.'

'I know.'

He met with Helen Cousins that night. They spoke over a drink in the Auld Hoose. Rebus hadn't been in the place in quarter of a century, and there'd been changes. They'd installed a pool table.

'You weren't invited along that night?' Rebus asked her.

She shook her head. She was twenty, three years younger than Damon. The fingers of her right hand played with her engagement ring, rolling it, sliding it off over the knuckle and then back down again. She had short, lifeless brown hair, dark, tired eyes, and acne around her mouth.

'I was out with the girls. See, that was how we played it. One night a week the boys would go off on their own, and we'd go somewhere else. Then another night we'd all get together.'

'Do you know anyone who was at Gaitanos that night? Apart from Damon and his pals?'

She chewed her bottom lip while considering. The ring came off her finger and bounced once before hitting the floor. She stooped to pick it up.

'It's always doing that.'

'You better watch it, you're going to lose it.'

She pushed the ring back on. 'Yes,' she said, 'Corinne and Jacky were there.'

'Corinne and Jacky?' She nodded. 'Where can I find them?'

A phone call brought them to the Auld Hoose. Rebus got in the round: Bacardi and Coke for Corinne, Bacardi and blackcurrant for Jacky, a second vodka and orange for Helen and another bottle of no-alcohol lager for himself. He eyed the optics behind the bar. His mean little drink was costing more than a whisky. Something was telling him to indulge in a Teacher's. Maybe it's my spirit guide, he thought, dismissing the idea.

Corinne had long black hair crimped with curling tongs. Her pal Jacky was tiny, with dyed platinum hair. When he got back to the table, they were in a huddle, exchanging gossip. Rebus took out the photograph again.

'Look,' Corinne said, 'there's Damon.' So they all had a good look. Then Rebus touched his finger to the strapless aura.

'Remember her?'

Helen prickled visibly. 'Who is she?'

'Yeah, she was there,' Jacky said.

'Was she with anyone?'

'Didn't see her up dancing.'

'Isn't that why people go to clubs?'

'Well, it's one reason.' All three broke into a giggle.

'You didn't speak to her?'

'No.'

'Not even in the toilets?'

'I saw her in there,' Corinne said. 'She was doing her eyes.'

'Did she say anything?'

'She seemed sort of ... stuck-up.'

'Snobby,' Jacky agreed.

Rebus tried to think of another question and couldn't. They ignored him for a while as they exchanged news. It was like they hadn't seen each other in a year. At one point, Helen got up to use the toilet. Rebus expected the other two to accompany her, but only Corinne did so. He sat with Jacky for a moment, then, for want of anything else to say, asked her what she thought of Damon. He meant about Damon disappearing, but she didn't take it that way.

'Ach, he's all right.'

'Just all right?'

'Well, you know, Damon's heart's in the right place, but he's a bit thick. A bit slow, I mean.'

'Really?' The impression Rebus had received from Damon's family had been of a genius-in-waiting. He suddenly realised just how superficial his own portrait of Damon was. Siobhan's words should have been a warning – so far he'd heard only one side of Damon. 'Helen likes him though?'

'I suppose so.'

'They're engaged.'

'It happens, doesn't it? I've got friends who got engaged just so they could throw a party.' She looked around the bar, then leaned towards him. 'They used to have some mega arguments.'

'What about?'

'Jealousy, I suppose. She'd see him notice someone, or he'd say she'd been letting some guy chat her up. Just the usual.' She turned the photo around so it faced her. 'She looks like a dream, doesn't she? I remember she was dressed to kill. Made the rest of us spit.'

'But you'd never seen her before?'

Jacky shook her head. No, no one seemed to have seen her before, nobody knew who she was. Unlikely then that she was local.

'Were there any buses in that night?'

'That doesn't happen at Gaitanos,' she told him. 'It's not "in" enough any more. There's a new place in Dunfermline. That gets the busloads.' Jacky tapped the photo. 'You think she's gone off with Damon?'

Rebus looked at her and saw behind the eyeliner to a sharp intelligence. 'It's possible,' he said quietly.

'I don't think so,' she said. 'She wouldn't be interested, and he wouldn't have had the guts.'

On his way home, Rebus dropped into St Leonard's. The amount he was paying in bridge tolls, he was thinking about a season ticket. There was a fax on his desk. He'd been promised it in the afternoon, but there'd been a delay. It identified the owner of the Rolls-Royce as a Mr Richard Mandelson, with an address in Juniper Green. Mr Mandelson had no criminal record outstanding, whether for motoring offences or anything else. Rebus tried to imagine some poor parking warden trying to give the Roller a ticket with the fat man behind the wheel. There were a few more facts about Mr Mandelson, including last known occupation.

Casino manager.

VII

Matty and Stevie Scoular saw one another socially now. Stevie would sometimes phone and invite Matty to some party or dinner, or just for a drink. At the same time as Matty was flattered, he did wonder what Stevie's angle was, had even come out and asked him.

'I mean,' he'd said, 'I'm just a toe-rag from the school playground, and you ... well, you're SuperStevie, you're the king.'

'Aye, if you believe the papers.' Stevie had finished his drink – Perrier, he had a game the next day. 'I don't know, Matty, maybe it's that I miss all that.'

'All what?'

'Schooldays. It was a laugh back then, wasn't it?'

Matty had frowned, not really remembering. 'But the life you've got now, Stevie, man. People would kill for it.'

And Stevie had nodded, looking suddenly sad.

Another time, a couple of kids had asked Stevie for his autograph, then had turned and asked Matty for his, thinking that whoever he was, he had to be somebody. Stevie had laughed at that, said something about it being a lesson in humility. Again, Matty didn't get it. There were times when Stevie seemed to be on a different planet. Maybe it was understandable, the pressure he was under. Stevie seemed to remember a lot more about school than Matty did: teachers' names, the lot. They talked about Gullane, too, what a boring place to grow up. Sometimes they didn't talk much at all. Just took out a couple of dolls: Stevie would always bring one along for Matty. She wouldn't be quite as gorgeous as Stevie's, but that was all right. Matty could understand that. He was soaking it all up, enjoying it while it lasted. He had half an idea that Stevie and him would be best friends for life, and another that Stevie would dump him soon and find some other distraction. He thought Stevie needed him right now much more than *he* needed Stevie. So he soaked up what he could, started filing the stories away for future use, tweaking them here and there ...

Tonight they took in a couple of bars, a bit of a drive in Stevie's Beamer: he preferred BMWs to Porsches, more space for passengers. They ended up at a club, but didn't stay long. Stevie had a game the next day. He was always very conscientious that way: Perrier and early nights. Stevie dropped Matty off outside his flat, sounding the horn as he roared away. Matty hadn't spotted the other car, but he heard a door opening, looked across the road and recognised Malibu straight off. Malibu was Mr Mandelson's driver. He'd eased himself out of the Roller and was holding open the back door while looking over to Matty.

So Matty crossed the street. As he did so, he walked into Malibu's shadow, cast by the sodium street lamp. At that moment, though he didn't know what was about to happen, he realised he was lost.

'Get in, Matty.'

The voice, of course, was Mandelson's. Matty got into the car and Malibu closed the door after him, then kept guard outside. They weren't going anywhere.

'Ever been in a Roller before, Matty?'

'I don't think so.'

'You'd remember if you had. I could have had one years back, but only by buying secondhand. I wanted to wait until I had the cash for a nice new one. That leather smell – you don't get it with any other car.' Mandelson lit a cigar. The windows were closed and the car started filling with sour smoke. 'Know how I came to afford a brand new Roller, Matty?'

'Hard work?' Matty's mouth was dry. Cars, he thought: Rebus's, Stevie's, and now this one. Plus, of course, the one he'd borrowed that night, the one that had brought him to this.

'Don't be stupid. My dad worked thirty years in a shop, six days a week and he still couldn't have made the down-payment. Faith, Matty, that's the key. You have to believe in yourself, and some-times you have to trust other people – strangers some of them, or people you don't like, people it's hard to trust. That's the gamble life's making with you, and if you place your bet, sometimes you get lucky. Except it's not luck – not entirely. See, there are odds, like in every game, and that's where judgement comes in. I like to think I'm a good judge of character.'

Only now did Mandelson turn to look at him. There seemed to Matty to be nothing behind the eyes, nothing at all.

'Yes, sir,' he said, for want of anything better.

'That was Stevie dropped you off, eh?' Matty nodded. 'Now, your man Stevie, he's got something else, something we haven't discussed yet. He's got a gift. He's had to work, of course, but the thing was there to begin with. Don't ask me where it came from or why it should have been given to him in particular – that's one for the philosophers, and I don't claim to be a philosopher. What I am is a businessman ... and a gambler. Only I don't bet on nags or dogs or a turn of the cards, I bet on people. I'm betting on you, Matty.'

'Me?'

Mandelson nodded, barely visible inside the cloud of smoke. 'I want you to talk to Stevie on my behalf. I want you to get him to do me a favour.'

Matty rubbed his forehead with his fingers. He knew what was coming but didn't want to hear it.

'I saw a recent interview,' Mandelson went on, 'where he told the reporter he always gave a hundred and ten per cent. All I want is to knock maybe twenty per cent off for next Saturday's game. You know what I'm saying?'

Next Saturday ... An away tie at Kirkcaldy. Stevie expected to run rings around the Raith Rovers defence.

'He won't do it,' Matty said. 'Come to that, neither will I.'

'No?' Mandelson laughed. A hand landed on Matty's thigh. 'You fucked up in London, son. They knew you'd end up taking a croupier's job somewhere else, it's the only thing you know how to do. So they phoned around, and eventually they phoned *me*. I told them I'd never heard of you. That can change, Matty. Want me to talk to them again?'

'I'd tell them you lied to them the first time.'

Mandelson shrugged. 'I can live with that. But what do you think they'll do to *you*, Matty? They were pretty angry about whatever scheme it was you pulled. I'd say they were furious.'

Matty felt like he was going to heave. He was sweating, his lungs toxic. 'He won't do it,' he said again.

'Be persuasive, Matty. You're his friend. Remind him that his tab's up to three and a half. All he has to do is ease off for one game, and the tab's history. And Matty, I'll know if you've talked to him or not, so no games, eh? Or you might find yourself with no place left to hide.'

VIII

Rebus searched his flat, but came up with only half a dozen snapshots: two of his ex-wife Rhona, posing with Samantha, their daughter, back when Sammy was seven or eight; two further shots of Sammy in her teens; one showing his father as a young man, kissing the woman who would become Rebus's mother; and a final photograph, a family grouping, showing uncles, aunts and cousins whose names Rebus didn't know. There were other photographs, of course – at least, there had been – but not here, not in the flat. He guessed Rhona still kept some, maybe his brother Michael had the others. But they could be anywhere. Rebus hadn't thought of himself as the kind to spend long nights with the family album, using it as a crutch to memory, always with the fear that remembrance would yield to sentiment.

If I died tonight, he thought, what would I bequeath to the world? Looking around, the answer was: nothing. The thought scared him, and worst of all it made him want a drink, and not just one drink but a dozen.

Instead of which, he drove north back into Fife. It had been overcast all day, and the evening was warm. He didn't know what he was doing, knew he had precious little to say to either of Damon's parents, and yet that's where he ended up. He'd had the destination in mind all along.

Brian Mee answered the door, wearing a smart suit and just finishing knotting his tie.

'Sorry, Brian,' Rebus said. 'Are you off out?'

'In ten minutes. Come in anyway. Is it Damon?'

Rebus shook his head and saw the tension in Brian's face turn to relief. Yes, a visit in person wouldn't be good news, would it? Good news had to be given immediately by telephone, not by a knock at the door. Rebus should have realised; he'd been the bearer of bad news often enough in his time.

'Sorry, Brian,' he repeated. They were in the hallway. Janis's voice came from above, asking who it was.

'It's Johnny,' her husband called back. Then to Rebus, 'It's all right to call you that?'

'Of course. It's my name, isn't it?' He could have added: again, after all this time. He looked at Brian, remembering the way they'd sometimes mistreated him at school: not that 'Barney' had seemed to mind, but who could tell for sure? And then that night of the last school dance ... Brian had been there for Mitch. Brian had been there; Rebus had not. He'd been too busy losing Janis, and losing consciousness.

She was coming downstairs now. 'I'll be back in a sec,' Brian said, heading up past her.

'You look terrific,' Rebus told her. The blue dress was well-chosen, her make-up highlighting all the right features of her busy face. She managed a smile.

'No news?'

'Sorry,' he said again. 'Just thought I'd see how you are.'

'Oh, we're pining away.' Another smile, tinged by shame this time. 'It's a dinner–dance, we bought the tickets months back. It's for the Jolly Beggars.'

'Nobody expects you to sit at home every night, Janis.'

'But all the same ...' Her cheeks grew flushed and her eyes sought his. 'We're not going to find him, are we?'

'Not easily. Our best bet's that he'll get in touch.'

'If he can,' she said quietly.

'Come on, Janis.' He put his hands on her shoulders, like they were strangers and about to dance. 'You might hear from him tomorrow, or it might take months.'

'And meantime life goes on, eh?'

'Something like that.'

She smiled again, blinking back tears. 'Why don't you come with us, John?'

Rebus dropped his hands from her shoulders. 'I haven't danced in years.'

'So you'd be rusty.'

'Thanks, Janis, but not tonight.'

'Know something? I bet they play the same records we used to dance to at school.'

It was his turn to smile. Brian was coming back downstairs, patting his hair into place.

'You'd be welcome to join us, Johnny,' he said.

'I've another appointment, Brian. Maybe next time, eh?'

'Let's make that a promise.'

They went out to their cars together. Janis pecked him on the cheek, Brian shook his hand. He watched them drive off then headed to the cemetery.

It was dark, and the gates were locked, so Rebus sat in his car and smoked a cigarette. He thought about his parents and the rest of his family and remembered stories about Bowhill, stories which seemed inextricable from family history: mining tragedies; a girl found drowned in the River Ore; a holiday car crash which had erased an entire family. Then there was Johnny Thomson, Celtic goalkeeper, injured during an 'Old Firm' match. He was in his early twenties when he died, and was buried behind those gates, not far from Rebus's parents. *Not Dead, But at Rest in the Arms of the Lord.*

The Lord had to be a bodybuilder.

From family he turned to friends and tried recalling a dozen names to put to faces he remembered from schooldays. Other friends: people he'd known in the army, the SAS. All the people he'd dealt with during his career in the police. Villains he'd put away, some who'd slipped through his fingers. People he'd interviewed, suspected, questioned, broken the worst kind of news to. Acquaintances from the Oxford Bar and all the other pubs where he'd ever been a regular. Local shopkeepers. Jesus, the list was endless. All these people who'd played a part in his life, in shaping who he was and how he acted, how he felt about things. All of them, out there somewhere and nowhere, gathered together only inside his head. And chief among them tonight, Brian and Janis.

That night of the school dance ... It was true he'd been drunk – elated. He'd felt he could *do* anything, *be* anything. Because he'd come to a decision that day – he wouldn't join the army, he'd stay in Bowhill with Janis, apply for a job at the dockyard. His dad had told him not to be so stupid – 'short-sighted' was the word he'd used. But what did parents know about their children's desires? So he'd drunk some beer and headed off to the dance, his thoughts only of Janis. Tonight he'd tell her. And Mitch, of course. He'd have to tell Mitch, tell him he'd be heading into the army alone. But Mitch wouldn't mind, he'd understand, as best friends had to.

But while Rebus had been outside with Janis, his friend Mitch was being cornered by four teenagers who considered themselves his enemies. This was their last chance for revenge, and they'd gone in hard, kicking and punching. Four against one ... until Barney had waded in, shrugging off blows, and dragged Mitch to safety. But one kick had done the damage, dislodging a retina. Mitch's vision stayed fuzzy in that eye for a few days, then disappeared. And where had Rebus been? Out cold on the concrete by the bike sheds.

And why had he never thanked Barney Mee?

He blinked now and sniffed, wondering if he was coming down with a cold. He'd had this idea when he came back to Bowhill that the place would seem beyond redemption, that he'd be able to tell himself it had lost its sense of community, become just another town for him to pass through. Maybe he'd wanted to put it behind him. Well, it hadn't worked. He got out of the car and looked around. The street was dead. He reached up and hauled himself over the iron railings and walked a circuit of the cemetery for an hour or so, and felt strangely at peace.

IX

'So what's the panic, Matty?'

After a home draw with Rangers, Stevie was ready for a night on the town. One–one, and of course he'd scored his team's only goal. The reporters would be busy filing their copy, saying for the umpteenth time that he was his side's hero, that without him they were a very ordinary team indeed. Rangers had known that: Stevie's marker had been out for blood, sliding studs-first into tackles which Stevie had done his damnedest to avoid. He'd come out of the game with a couple of fresh bruises and grazes, a nick on one knee but, to his manager's all too palpable relief, fit to play again midweek.

'I said what's the panic?'

Matty had worried himself sleepless. He knew he had several options. Speak to Stevie, that was one of them. Another was not to speak to him, but tell Mandelson he had. Then it would be down to whether or not Mandelson believed him. Option three: do a runner; only Mandelson was right about that – he was running out of places to hide. With *two* casino bosses out for his blood, how could he ever pick up another croupier's job?

If he spoke with Stevie, he'd lose a new-found friend. But to stay silent ... well, there was very little percentage in it. So here he was in Stevie's flat, having demanded to see him. In the corner, a TV was replaying a tape of the afternoon's match. There was no commentary, just the sounds of the terraces and the dug-outs.

'No panic,' he said now, playing for time.

Stevie stared at him. 'You all right? Want a drink or something?'

'Maybe a vodka.'

'Anything in it?'

'I'll take it as it comes.'

Stevie poured him a drink. Matty had been here half an hour now, and they still hadn't talked. The telephone had hardly stopped: reporters' questions, family and friends offering congratulations. Stevie had shrugged off the superlatives.

Matty took the drink, swallowed it, wondering if he could still walk away. Then he remembered Malibu, and saw shadows falling.

'Thing is, Stevie,' he said. 'You know my boss at the Morvena, Mr Mandelson?'

'I owe him money, of course I know him.'

'He says we could do something about that.'

'What? My tab?' Stevie was checking himself in the mirror, having changed into his on-the-town clothes. 'I don't get it,' he said.

Well, Stevie, Matty thought, it was nice knowing you, pal. 'All you have to do is ease off next Saturday.'

Stevie frowned and turned from the mirror. 'Away to Raith?' He came and sat down opposite Matty. 'He told you to tell me?' He waited till Matty nodded. 'That bastard. What's in it for him?'

Matty wriggled on the leather sofa. 'I've been thinking about it. Raith are going through a bad patch, but you know yourself that if you're taken out of the equation ...'

'Then they'd be up against not very much. My boss has told everybody to get the ball to me. If they spend the whole game doing that and I don't do anything with it ...'

Matty nodded. 'What I think is, the odds will be on you scoring. Nobody'll be expecting Raith to put one in the net.'

'So Mandelson's cash will be on a goalless draw?'

'And he'll get odds, spread a lot of small bets around ...'

'Bastard,' Stevie said again. 'How did he get you into this, Matty?'

Matty shifted again. 'Something I did in London.'

'Secrets, eh? Hard things to keep.' Stevie got up, went to the mirror again, and just stood there, hands by his sides, staring into it. There was no emotion in his voice when he spoke.

'Tell him he can fuck himself.'

Matty had to choke out the words. 'You sure that's the message?'

'Cheerio, Matty.'

Matty rose shakily to his feet. 'What am I going to do?'

'Cheerio, Matty.'

Stevie was as still as a statue as Matty walked to the door and let himself out.

Mandelson sat at his desk, playing with a Cartier pen he'd taken from a punter that day. The man was overdue on a payment. The pen was by way of a gift.

'So?' he asked Matty.

Matty sat on the chair and licked his lips. There was no offer of a drink today; this was just business. Malibu stood by the door. Matty took a deep breath – the last act of a drowning man.

'It's on,' he said.

Mandelson looked up at him. 'Stevie went for it?'

'Eventually,' Matty said.

'You're sure?'

'As sure as I can be.'

'Well, that better be watertight, or you might find yourself going for a swim with heavy legs. Know what I mean?'

Matty held the dark gaze and nodded.

Mandelson glanced towards Malibu, both of them were smiling. Then he picked up the telephone. 'You know, Matty,' he said, pushing numbers. 'I'm doing you a favour. You're doing *yourself* a favour.' He listened to the receiver. 'Mr Hamilton, please.' Then, to Matty, 'See, what you're doing here is saving your job. I overstretched myself, Matty. I wouldn't like that to get around, but I'm trusting you. If this comes off – and it better – then you've earned that trust.' He tapped the receiver. 'It wasn't all my own money either. But this will keep the Morvena alive and kicking.' He motioned for Matty to leave. Malibu tapped his shoulder as an incentive.

'Topper?' Mandelson was saying as Matty left the room. 'It's locked up. How much are you in for?'

Matty bided his time and waited till his shift was over. He walked out of the smart New Town building like a latterday Lazarus, and found the nearest payphone, then had to fumble through all the rubbish in his pockets, stuff that must have meant something once upon a time, until he found the card.

The card with a phone number on it.

*

The following Saturday, Stevie Scoular scored his team's only goal in their 1–0 win over Raith Rovers, and Mandelson sat alone in his office, his eyes on the Teletext results.

His hand rested on the telephone receiver. He was expecting a call from Topper Hamilton. He couldn't seem to stop blinking, like there was a grain of sand in either eye. He buzzed the reception desk, told them to tell Malibu he was wanted. Mandelson didn't know how much time he had, but he knew he would make it count. A word with Stevie Scoular, see if Matty really *had* put the proposition to him. Then Matty himself ... Matty was a definite, no matter what. Matty was about to be put out of the game.

The knock at the door had to be Malibu. Mandelson barked for him to come in. But when the door opened, two strangers sauntered in like they owned the place. Mandelson sat back in his chair, hands on the desk. He was almost relieved when they introduced themselves as police officers.

'I'm Detective Inspector Rebus,' the younger one said, 'this is Chief Superintendent Watson.'

'And you've come about the Benevolent Fund, right?'

Rebus sat down unasked, his eyes drifting to the TV screen and the results posted there. 'Looks like you just lost a packet. I'm sorry to hear it. Did Topper take a beating, too?'

Mandelson made fists of his hands. 'That wee bastard!'

Rebus was shaking his head. 'Matty did his best, only there was something he didn't know. Seems you didn't know either. Topper will be doubly disappointed.'

'What?'

Farmer Watson, still standing, provided the answer. 'Ever heard of Big Ger Cafferty?'

Mandelson nodded. 'He's been in Barlinnie a while.'

'Used to be the biggest gangster on the east coast. Probably still is. And he's a fan of Stevie's, gets videotapes of all his games. He almost sends him love letters.'

Mandelson frowned. 'So?'

'So Stevie's covered,' Rebus said. 'Try fucking with him, you're asking Big Ger to bend over. Your little proposal has probably already made it back to Cafferty.'

Mandelson swallowed and felt suddenly dry-mouthed.

'There was no way Stevie was going to throw that game,' Rebus said quietly.

'Matty ...' Mandelson choked the sentence off.

'Told you it was fixed? He was scared turdless, what else was he going to say? But Matty's *mine*. You don't touch him.'

'Not that you'd get the chance,' the Farmer added. 'Not with Topper *and* Cafferty after your blood. Malibu will be a big help, the way he took off five minutes ago in the Roller.' Watson walked up to the desk, looming over Mandelson like a mountain. 'You've got two choices, son. You can talk, or you can run.'

'You've got nothing.'

'I saw you that night at Gaitanos,' Rebus said. 'If you're going to lay out big bets, where better than Fife? Optimistic Raith fans might have bet on a goalless draw. You got Charmer Mackenzie to place the bets locally, spreading them around. That way it looked less suspicious.'

Which was why Mackenzie had wanted Rebus out of there, whatever the price: he'd been about to do some business ...

'Besides,' Rebus continued, 'when it comes down to it, what choice do you have?'

'You either talk to us ...' the Farmer said.

'Or you disappear. People do it all the time.'

And it never stops, Rebus could have added. Because it's part of the dance – shifting partners, people you shared the floor with, it all changed. And it only ended when you disappeared from the hall.

And sometimes ... sometimes, it didn't even end there.

'All right,' Mandelson said at last, the way they'd known he would, all colour gone from his face, his voice hollow, 'what do you want to know?'

'Let's start with Topper Hamilton,' the Farmer said, sounding like a kid unwrapping his birthday present.

It was Wednesday morning when Rebus got the phone call from a Mr Bain. It took him a moment to place the name: Damon's bank manager.

'Yes, Mr Bain, what can I do for you?'

'Damon Mee, Inspector. You wanted us to keep an eye on any transactions.'

Rebus leaned forward in his chair. 'That's right.'

'There've been two withdrawals from cash machines, both in central London.'

Rebus grabbed a pen. 'Where exactly?'

'Tottenham Court Road was three days ago: fifty pounds. Next day, it was Finsbury Park, same amount.'

Fifty pounds a day: enough to live on, enough to pay for a cheap bed and breakfast and two extra meals.

'How much is left in the account, Mr Bain?'

'A little under six hundred pounds.'

Enough for twelve days. There were several ways it could go. Damon could get himself a job. Or when the money ran out he could try begging. Or he could return home. Rebus thanked Bain and telephoned Janis.

'John,' she said, 'we got a postcard this morning.'

A postcard saying Damon was in London and doing fine. A post-card of apology for any fright he'd given them. A postcard saying he needed some time to 'get my head straight'. A postcard which ended 'See you soon.' The picture on the front was of a pair of breasts painted with Union Jacks.

'Brian thinks we should go down there,' Janis said. 'Try to find him.'

Rebus thought of how many B&Bs there'd be in Finsbury Park. 'You might just chase him away,' he warned. 'He's doing OK, Janis.'

'But why did he do it, John? I mean, is it something *we* did?'

New questions and fears had replaced the old ones. Rebus didn't know what to tell her. He wasn't family and couldn't begin to answer her question. Didn't *want* to begin to answer it.

'He's doing OK,' he repeated. 'Just give him some time.'

She was crying now, softly. He imagined her with head bowed, hair falling over the telephone receiver.

'We did everything, John. You can't know how much we've given him. We always put ourselves second, never a minute's thought for anything but him ...'

'Janis ...' he began.

She took a deep breath. 'Will you come and see me, John?'

Rebus looked around the office, eyes resting eventually on his own desk and the paperwork stacked there.

'I can't, Janis. I'd like to, but I just can't. See, it's not as if I ...'

He didn't know how he was going to finish the sentence, but it didn't matter. She'd put her phone down. He sat back in his chair and remembered dancing with her, how brittle her body had seemed. But that had been half a lifetime ago. They'd made so many choices since. It was time to let the past go. Siobhan Clarke was at her desk. She was looking at him. Then she mimed the drinking of a cup of coffee, and he nodded and got to his feet.

Did a little dance as he shuffled towards her.

No Sanity Clause

It was all Edgar Allan Poe's fault. Either that or the Scottish Parliament. Joey Briggs was spending most of his days in the run-up to Christmas sheltering from Edinburgh's biting December winds. He'd been walking up George IV Bridge one day and had watched a down-and-out slouching into the Central Library. Joey had hesitated. He wasn't a down-and-out, not yet anyway. Maybe he would be soon, if Scully Aitchison MSP got his way, but for now Joey had a bedsit and a trickle of state cash. Thing was, nothing made you miss money more than Christmas. The shop windows displayed their magnetic pull. There were queues at the cash machines. Kids tugged on their parents' sleeves, ready with something new to add to the present list. Boyfriends were out buying gold, while families piled the food trolley high.

And then there was Joey, nine weeks out of prison and nobody to call his friend. He knew there was nothing waiting for him back in his home town. His wife had taken the children and tiptoed out of his life. Joey's sister had written to him in prison with the news. So, eleven months on, Joey had walked through the gates of Saughton Jail and taken the first bus into the city centre, purchased an evening paper and started the hunt for somewhere to live.

The bedsit was fine. It was one of four in a tenement basement just off South Clerk Street, sharing a kitchen and bathroom. The other men worked, didn't say much. Joey's room had a gas fire with a coin-meter beside it, too expensive to keep it going all day. He'd tried sitting in the kitchen with the stove lit, until the landlord had caught him. Then he'd tried steeping in the bath, topping up the hot. But the water always seemed to run cold after half a tub.

'You could try getting a job,' the landlord had said.

Not so easy with a prison record. Most of the jobs were for security and nightwatch. Joey didn't think he'd get very far there.

Following the tramp into the library was one of his better ideas. The uniform behind the desk gave him a look, but didn't say anything. Joey wandered the stacks, picked out a book and sat himself down. And that was that. He became a regular, the staff acknowledged him with a nod and sometimes even a smile. He kept himself presentable, didn't fall asleep the way some of the old guys did. He read for much of the day, alternating between fiction, biographies and textbooks. He read up on local history, plumbing and Winston Churchill, Nigel Tranter's novels and National Trust gardens. He knew the library would close over Christmas, didn't know what he'd do without it. He never borrowed books, because he was afraid they'd have him on some blacklist: convicted housebreaker and petty thief, not to be trusted with loan material.

He dreamt of spending Christmas in one of the town's posh hotels, looking out across Princes Street Gardens to the Castle. He'd order room service and watch TV. He'd take as many baths as he liked. They'd clean his clothes for him and return them to the room. He dreamt of the presents he'd buy himself: a big radio with a CD player, some new shirts and pairs of shoes; and books. Plenty of books.

The dream became almost real to him, so that he found himself nodding off in the library, coming to as his head hit the page he'd been reading. Then he'd have to concentrate, only to find himself drifting into a warm sleep again.

Until he met Edgar Allan Poe.

It was a book of poems and short stories, among them 'The Purloined Letter'. Joey loved that, thought it was really clever the way you could hide something by putting it right in front of people. Something that didn't look out of place, people would just ignore it. There'd been a guy in Saughton, doing time for fraud. He'd told Joey: 'Three things: a suit, a haircut and an expensive watch. If you've got those, it's amazing what you can get away with.' He'd meant that clients had trusted him, because they'd seen something they were comfortable with, something they expected to see. What they hadn't seen was what was right in front of their noses, to wit: a shark, someone who was going to take a big bite out of their savings.

As Joey's eyes flitted back over Poe's story, he started to get an idea. He started to get what he thought was a very good idea indeed. Problem was, he needed what the fraudster had called 'the start-up', meaning some cash. He happened to look across to where one of the old tramps was slumped on a chair, the newspaper in front of him unopened. Joey looked around: nobody was watching. The place was dead: who had time to go to the library when Christmas was around the corner? Joey walked over to the old guy, slipped a hand into his coat pocket. Felt coins and notes, bunched his fingers around them. He glanced down at the newspaper. There was a story about Scully Aitchison's campaign. Aitchison was the MSP who wanted all offenders put on a central register, open to public inspection. He said law-abiding folk had the right to know if their neighbour was a thief or a murderer – as if stealing was the same as killing somebody! There was a small photo of Aitchison, too, beaming that self-satisfied smile, his glasses glinting. If Aitchison got his way, Joey would never get out of the rut.

Not unless his plan paid off.

John Rebus saw his girlfriend kissing Santa Claus. There was a German Market in Princes Street Gardens. That was where Rebus was to meet Jean. He hadn't expected to find her in a clinch with a man dressed in a red suit, black boots and snowy-white beard. Santa broke away and moved off, just as Rebus was approaching. German folk songs were blaring out. There was a startled look on Jean's face.

'What was that all about?' he asked.

'I don't know.' She was watching the retreating figure. 'I think maybe he's just had too much festive spirit. He came up and grabbed me.' Rebus made to follow, but Jean stopped him. 'Come on, John. Season of goodwill and all that.'

'It's assault, Jean.'

She laughed, regaining her composure. 'You're going to take St Nicholas down the station and put him in the cells?' She rubbed his arm. 'Let's forget it, eh? The fun starts in ten minutes.'

Rebus wasn't too sure that the evening was going to be 'fun'. He spent every day bogged down in crimes and tragedies. He wasn't sure that a 'mystery dinner' was going to offer much relief. It had been Jean's idea. There was a hotel just across the road. You all went in for dinner, were handed envelopes telling you which character you'd be playing. A body was discovered, and then you all turned detective.

'It'll be fun,' Jean insisted, leading him out of the gardens. She had three shopping bags with her. He wondered if any of them were for him. She'd asked for a list of his Christmas wants, but so far all he'd come up with were a couple of CDs by String Driven Thing.

As they entered the hotel, they saw that the mystery evening was being held on the mezzanine floor. Most of the guests had already gathered and were enjoying glasses of cava. Rebus asked in vain for a beer.

'Cava's included in the price,' the waitress told him. A man dressed in Victorian costume was checking names and handing out carrier bags.

'Inside,' he told Jean and Rebus, 'you'll find instructions, a secret clue that only you know, your name, and an item of clothing.'

'Oh,' Jean said, 'I'm Little Nell.' She fixed a bonnet to her head. 'Who are you, John?'

'Mr Bumble.' Rebus produced his name-tag and a yellow woollen scarf, which Jean insisted on tying around his neck.

'It's a Dickensian theme, specially for Christmas,' the host revealed, before moving off to confront his other victims. Everyone looked a bit embarrassed, but most were trying for enthusiasm. Rebus didn't doubt that a couple of glasses of wine over dinner would loosen a few Edinburgh stays. There were a couple of faces he recognised. One was a journalist, her arm around her boyfriend's waist. The other was a man who appeared to be with his wife. He had one of those looks to him, the kind that says you should know him. She was blonde and petite and about a decade younger than her husband.

'Isn't that an MSP?' Jean whispered.

'His name's Scully Aitchison,' Rebus told her.

Jean was reading her information sheet. 'The victim tonight is a certain Ebenezer Scrooge,' she said.

'And did you kill him?'

She thumped his arm. Rebus smiled, but his eyes were on the MSP. Aitchison's face was bright red. Rebus guessed he'd been drinking since lunchtime. His voice boomed across the floor, broadcasting the news that he and Catriona had booked a room for the night, so they wouldn't have to drive back to the constituency.

They were all mingling on the mezzanine landing. The room where they'd dine was just off to the right, its doors still closed. Guests were starting to ask each other which characters they were playing. As one elderly lady – Miss Havisham on her name-tag – came over to ask Jean about Little Nell, Rebus saw a red-suited man appear at the top of the stairs. Santa carried what looked like a half-empty sack. He started making his way across the floor, but was stopped by Aitchison.

'*J'accuse!*' the MSP bawled. 'You killed Scrooge because of his inhumanity to his fellow man!' Aitchison's wife came to the rescue, dragging her husband away, but Santa's eyes seemed to follow them. As he made to pass Rebus, Rebus fixed him with a stare.

'Jean,' he asked, 'is he the same one ...?'

She only caught the back of Santa's head. 'They all look alike to me,' she said.

Santa was on his way to the next flight of stairs. Rebus watched him leave, then turned back to the other guests, all of them now tricked out in odd items of clothing. No wonder Santa had looked like he'd stumbled into an asylum. Rebus was reminded of a Marx Brothers line, Groucho trying to get Chico's name on a contract, telling him to sign the sanity clause.

But, as Chico said, everyone knew there was no such thing as Sanity Clause.

Joey jimmied open his third room of the night. The Santa suit had worked a treat. Okay, so it was hot and uncomfortable, and the beard was itching his neck, but it worked! He'd breezed through reception and up the stairs. So far, as he'd worked the corridors all he'd had were a few jokey comments. No one from security asking him who he was. No guests becoming suspicious. He fitted right in, and he was right under their noses.

God bless Edgar Allan Poe.

The woman in the fancy dress shop had even thrown in a sack, saying he'd be wanting to fill it. How true: in the first bedroom, he'd dumped out the crumpled sheets of old newspaper and started filling the sack – clothes, jewellery, the contents of the mini-bar. Same with the second room: a tap on the door to make sure no one was home, then the chisel into the lock and hey presto. Thing was, there wasn't much in the rooms. A notice in the wardrobe told clients to lock all valuables in the hotel safe at reception. Still, he had a few nice things: camera, credit cards, bracelet and necklace. Sweat was running into his eyes, but he couldn't afford to shed his disguise. He was starting to have crazy thoughts: take a good long soak; ring down for room service; find a room that hadn't been taken and settle in for the duration. In the third room, he sat on the bed, feeling dizzy. There was a briefcase open beside him, just lots of paperwork. His stomach growled, and he remembered that his last meal had been a Mars Bar supper the previous day. He broke open a jar of salted peanuts, switched the TV on while he ate. As he put the empty jar down, he happened to glance at the contents of the briefcase. 'Parliamentary briefing ... Law and Justice Sub-Committee ...' He saw a list of names on the top sheet. One of them was coloured with a yellow marker.

Scully Aitchison.

The drunk man downstairs ... That was where Joey knew him from! He leapt to his feet, trying to think. He could stay here and give the MSP a good hiding. He could ... He picked up the room-service menu, called down and ordered smoked salmon, a steak, a bottle each of best red wine and malt whisky. Then heard himself saying those sweetest words: 'Put it on my room, will you?'

Then he settled back to wait. Flipped through the paperwork again. An envelope slipped out. Card inside, and a letter inside the card.

Dear Scully, it began. *I hope it isn't all my fault, this idea of yours for a register of offenders ...*

'I haven't a clue,' said Rebus.

Nor did he. Dinner was over, the actor playing Scrooge was flat out on the mezzanine floor, and Rebus was as far away from solving the crime as ever. Thankfully, a bar had been opened up, and he spent most of his time perched on a high stool, pretending to read the background notes while taking sips of beer. Jean had hooked up with Miss Havisham, while Aitchison's wife was slumped in one of the armchairs, drawing on a cigarette. The MSP himself was playing ringmaster, and had twice confronted Rebus, calling for him to reveal himself as the villain.

'Innocent, m'lud,' was all Rebus had said.

'We think it's Magwitch,' Jean said, suddenly breathless by Rebus's side, her bonnet at a jaunty angle. 'He and Scrooge knew one another in prison.'

'I didn't know Scrooge served time,' Rebus said.

'That's because you're not asking questions.'

'I don't need to; I've got you to tell me. That's what makes a good detective.'

He watched her march away. Four of the diners had encircled the poor man playing Magwitch. Rebus had harboured suspicions, too ... but now he was thinking of jail time, and how it affected those serving it. It gave them a certain look, a look they brought back into the world on their release. The same look he'd seen in Santa's eyes.

And here was Santa now, coming back down the stairs, his sack slung over one shoulder. Crossing the mezzanine floor as if seeking someone out. Then finding them: Scully Aitchison. Rebus rose from his stool and wandered over.

'Have you been good this year?' Santa was asking Aitchison.

'No worse than anyone else,' the MSP smirked.

'Sure about that?' Santa's eyes narrowed.

'I wouldn't lie to Father Christmas.'

'What about this plan of yours, the offender register?'

Aitchison blinked a couple of times. 'What about it?'

Santa held a piece of paper aloft, his voice rising. 'Your own nephew's serving time for fraud. Managed to keep that quiet, haven't you?'

Aitchison stared at the letter. 'Where in hell ...? How ...?'

The journalist stepped forward. 'Mind if I take a look?'

Santa handed over the letter, then pulled off his hat and beard. Started heading for the stairs down. Rebus blocked his way.

'Time to hand out the presents,' he said quietly. Joey looked at him and understood immediately, slid the sack from his shoulder. Rebus took it. 'Now on you go.'

'You're not arresting me?'

'Who'd feed Dancer and Prancer?' Rebus asked.

His stomach full of steak and wine, a bottle of malt in the capacious pocket of his costume, Joey smiled his way back towards the outside world.

Tell Me Who to Kill

Saturday afternoon, John Rebus left the Oxford Bar after the foot-ball results and decided that he would try walking home. The day was clear, the sun just above the horizon, casting ridiculously long shadows. It would grow chilly later, maybe even frost overnight, but for now it was crisp and bright – perfect for a walk. He had limited himself to three pints of IPA, a corned beef roll and a pie. He carried a large bag with him – shopping for clothes his excuse for a trip into the city centre, a trip he'd known would end at the Ox. Edinburgh on a Saturday meant day-trippers, weekend warriors, but they tended to stick to Princes Street. George Street had been quieter, Rebus's tally finally comprising two shirts and a pair of trousers. He'd gone up a waist size in the previous six months, which was reason enough to cut back on the beer, and for opting to walk home.

He knew his only real problem would be The Mound. The steep slope connected Princes Street to the Lawnmarket, having been created from the digging out of the New Town's foundations. It posed a serious climb. He'd known a fellow cop – a uniformed sergeant – who'd cycled up The Mound every day on his way to work, right up until the day he'd retired. For Rebus, it had often proved problematical, even on foot. But he would give it a go, and if he failed, well, there was a bus stop he could beat a retreat to, or taxis he could flag down. Plenty of cabs about at this time of day, ferrying spent shoppers home to the suburbs, or bringing revellers into town at the start of another raucous evening. Rebus avoided the city centre on Saturday nights, unless duty called. The place took on an aggressive edge, violence spilling on to the streets from the clubs on Lothian Road and the bars in the Grassmarket. Better to stay at home with a carry-out and pretend your world wasn't changing for the worse.

A crowd had gathered at the foot of Castle Street. Rebus noticed that an ambulance, blue lights blinking, was parked in front of a stationary double-decker bus. Walking into the middle of the scene, Rebus overheard muttered exchanges of information.

'Just walked out ...'

'... right into its path ...'

'Wasn't looking ...'

'Not the first time I've seen ...'

'These bus drivers think they own the roads, though ...'

The victim was being carried into the ambulance. It didn't look good for him. One glance at the paramedics' faces told Rebus as much. There was blood on the roadway. The bus driver was sitting in the open doorway of his vehicle, head in his hands. There were still passengers on the bus, reluctant to admit that they would need to transfer, loaded down with shopping and unable to think beyond their own concerns. Two uniformed officers were taking statements, the witnesses only too happy to fulfil their roles in the drama. One of the uniforms looked at Rebus and gave a nod of recognition.

'Afternoon, DI Rebus.'

Rebus just nodded back. There was nothing for him to do here, no part he could usefully play. He made to cross the road, but noticed something lying there, untouched by the slow crawl of curious traffic. He stooped and picked it up. It was a mobile phone. The injured pedestrian must have been holding it, maybe even using it. Which would explain why he hadn't been paying attention. Rebus turned his head towards the ambulance, but it was already moving away, not bothering to add a siren to its flashing lights: another bad sign, a sign that the medics in the back either didn't want or didn't feel the need of it. There was either severe trauma, or else the victim was already dead. Rebus glanced down at the phone. It was unscathed, looked almost brand new. Strange to think such a thing could survive where its owner might not. He pressed it to his ear, but the line wasn't open. Then he looked at it again, noting that there were words on its display screen. Looked like a text message.

TELL ME WHO TO KILL.

Rebus blinked, narrowed his eyes. He was back on the pavement.

TELL ME WHO TO KILL.

He scrolled up and down the message, but there wasn't any more to it than those five words. Along the top ran the number of the caller; looked like another mobile phone. Plus time of call: 16.31. Rebus walked over to the uniformed officer, the one who'd spoken to him.

'Larry,' he said, 'where was the ambulance headed?'

'Western General,' the uniform said. 'Guy's skull's split open, be lucky to make it.'

'Do we know what happened?'

'He walked straight out into the road, by the look of it. Can't really blame the driver ...'

Rebus nodded slowly and walked over to the bus driver, crouched down in front of him. The man was in his fifties, head shaved but with a thick silvery beard. His hands shook as he lifted them away from his eyes.

'Couldn't stop in time,' he explained, voice quavering. 'He was right there ...' His eyes widened as he played the scene again. Shaking his head slowly. 'No way I could've stopped ...'

'He wasn't looking where he was going,' Rebus said softly.

'That's right.'

'Busy on his phone, maybe?'

The driver nodded. 'Staring at it, aye ... Some people haven't got the sense they were born with. Not that I'm ... I mean, I don't want to speak ill or anything.'

'Wasn't your fault,' Rebus agreed, patting the man's shoulder.

'Colleague of mine, same thing happened not six months past. Hasn't worked since.' He held up his hands to examine them.

'He was too busy looking at his phone,' Rebus said. 'That's the whole story. Reading a message, maybe?'

'Maybe,' the driver agreed. 'Doing something anyway, something more important than looking where he was bloody well going ...'

'Not your fault,' Rebus repeated, rising to his feet. He walked to the back of the bus, stepped out into the road, and waved down the first taxi he saw.

Rebus sat in the waiting area of the Western General Hospital. When a dazed-looking woman was led in by a nurse and asked if she wanted a cup of tea, he got to his feet. The woman sat herself down, twisting the handles of her shoulder bag in both hands, as if wringing the life out of them. She'd shaken her head, mumbled something to the nurse, who was now retreating.

'As soon as we know anything,' were the nurse's parting words.

Rebus sat down next to the woman. She was in her early thirties, blonde hair cut in a pageboy style. What make-up she had applied to her eyes that morning had been smudged by tears, giving her a haunted look. Rebus cleared his throat, but she still seemed unaware of his close presence.

'Excuse me,' he said. 'I'm Detective Inspector Rebus.' He opened his ID; she looked at it, then stared down at the floor again. 'Has your husband just been in an accident?'

'He's in surgery,' she said.

Rebus had been told as much at the front desk. 'I'm sorry,' he said. 'I don't even know his name.'

'Carl,' she said. 'Carl Guthrie.'

'And you're his wife?'

She nodded. 'Frances.'

'Must be quite a shock, Frances.'

'Yes.'

'Sure you don't want that tea?'

She shook her head, looked up into his face for the first time. 'Do you know what happened?'

'Seems he was starting to cross Princes Street and didn't see the bus coming.'

She squeezed shut her eyes, tears glinting in her lashes. 'How is that possible?'

Rebus shrugged. 'Maybe he had something on his mind,' he said quietly. 'When was the last time you spoke to him?'

'Breakfast this morning. I was planning to go shopping.'

'What about Carl?'

'I thought he was working. He's a physiotherapist, sports injuries mostly. He has his own practice in Corstorphine. He gets some work from the Bupa hospital at Murrayfield.'

'And a few rugby players too, I'd guess.'

Frances Guthrie was dabbing at her eyes with a tissue. 'How could he get hit by a bus?' She looked up at the ceiling, blinking back tears.

'Do you know what he was doing in town?'

She shook her head.

'This was found lying in the road,' Rebus said, holding up the phone. 'There's a text message displayed. You see what it says?'

She peered at the screen, then frowned. 'What does it mean?'

'I don't know,' Rebus admitted. 'Do you recognise the caller's number?'

She shook her head, then reached out a hand and took the phone from Rebus, turning it in her palm. 'This isn't Carl's.'

'What?'

'This isn't Carl's phone. Someone else must have dropped it.'

Rebus stared at her. 'You're sure?'

She handed the phone back, nodding. 'Carl's is a silver flip-top sort of thing.'

Rebus studied the one-piece black Samsung. 'Then whose is it?' he asked, more to himself than to her. She answered anyway.

'What does it matter?'

'It matters.'

'But it's a joke, surely.' She nodded at the screen. 'Someone's idea of a practical joke.'

'Maybe,' Rebus said.

The same nurse was walking towards them, accompanied by a surgeon in green scrubs. Neither of them had to say anything. Frances Guthrie was already keening as the surgeon began his speech.

'I'm so sorry, Mrs Guthrie ... we did everything we could.'

Frances Guthrie leaned in towards Rebus, her face against his shoulder. He put his arm around her, feeling it was the least he could do.

Carl Guthrie's effects had been placed in a large cardboard box. His blood-soaked clothes were protected by a clear polythene bag. Rebus lifted them out. The pockets had been emptied. Watch, wallet, small change, keys. And a silver flip-top mobile phone. Rebus checked its screen. The battery was low, and there were no messages. He told the nurse that he wanted to take it with him. She shrugged and made him sign a docket to that effect. He flipped through the wallet, finding banknotes, credit cards, and a few of Carl Guthrie's business cards, giving an address in Corstorphine, plus office and mobile numbers. Rebus took out his own phone and punched in the latter. The silver telephone trilled as it rang. He cancelled the call, then nodded to the nurse to let her know he was finished. The docket was placed in the box, along with the polythene bag. Rebus pocketed all three phones.

The police lab at Howdenhall wasn't officially open at weekends, but Rebus knew that someone was usually there, trying to clear a backlog, or just because they'd nothing better to do. He got lucky. Ray Duff was one of the better technicians. He sighed when Rebus walked in.

'I'm up to my eyes,' he complained, turning away to walk back down the corridor.

'Yes, but you'll like this,' Rebus said, holding out the mobile. Duff stopped and turned, stared at it, then ran his fingers through an unruly mop of hair.

'I really am up to my eyes ...'

Rebus shrugged, arm still stretched out. Duff sighed again and took the phone from him.

'Discovered at the scene of an accident,' Rebus explained. Duff had found a pair of spectacles in one of the pockets of his white lab coat and was putting them on. 'My guess is that the victim had just received the text message, and was transfixed by it.'

'And walked out in front of a car?'

'Bus actually. Thing is, the phone doesn't belong to the victim.' Rebus produced the silver flip-top. 'This is his.'

'So whose is this?' Duff peered at Rebus over the top of his glasses. 'That's what you're wondering.' He was walking again, heading for his own cubicle, Rebus following.

'Right.'

'And also who the caller was.'

'Right again.'

'We could just phone them.'

'We could.' They'd reached Duff's workstation. Each surface was a clutter of wires, machines and paperwork. Duff rubbed his bottom lip against his teeth. 'Battery's getting low,' he said, as the phone uttered a brief chirrup.

'Any chance you can recharge it?'

'I can if you like, but we don't really need it.'

'We don't?'

The technician shook his head. 'The important stuff's on the chip.' He tapped the back of the phone. 'We can transfer it ...' He grew thoughtful again. 'Of course, that would mean accessing the code number, so we're probably better off hanging on to it as it is.' He reached down into a cupboard and produced half a dozen mains adaptors. 'One of these should do the trick.'

Soon the phone was plugged in and charging. Meantime, Duff had worked his magic on the keypad, producing the phone number. Rebus punched it into his own phone, and the black mobile trilled.

'Bingo,' Duff said with a smile. 'Now all we do is call the service provider ...' He left the cubicle and returned a couple of minutes later with a sheet of numbers. 'I hope you didn't touch anything,' he said, waving a hand around his domain.

'I wouldn't dare.' Rebus leaned against a workbench as Duff made the call, identified himself, and reeled off the mobile phone number. He placed his hand over the mouthpiece.

'It'll take a minute,' he told Rebus.

'Can anyone get this sort of information?' Rebus asked. 'I mean, what's to stop Joe Public calling up and saying they're a cop?'

Duff smiled. 'Caller recognition. They've got a screen their end. IDs the caller number as Lothian and Borders Police Forensic Branch.'

'Clever,' Rebus admitted. Duff just shrugged. 'So how about the other number? The one belonging to whoever sent that message.'

Duff held up a finger, indicating that he was listening to the person at the other end of the line. He looked around him, finding a scrap of paper. Rebus provided the pen, and he started writing.

'That's great, thanks,' he said finally. Then: 'Mind if I try you with something else? It's a mobile number ...' He proceeded to reel off the number on the message screen, then, with his hand again muffling the mouthpiece, he handed the scrap of paper to Rebus.

'Name and address of the phone's owner.'

Rebus looked. The owner's name was William Smith, the address a street in the New Town. 'What about the text sender?' he asked.

'She's checking.' Duff removed his hand from the mouthpiece, listening intently. Then he started shaking his head. 'Not one of yours, eh? Don't suppose you can tell from the number just who is the service provider?' He listened again. 'Well, thanks anyway.' He put down the receiver.

'No luck?' Rebus guessed. Duff shrugged.

'Just means we have to do it the hard way' He picked up the sheet of telephone numbers. 'Maybe nine or ten calls at the most.'

'Can I leave it with you, Ray?'

Duff stretched his arms wide. 'What else was I going to be doing at half past six of a Saturday?'

Rebus smiled. 'You and me both, Ray.'

'What do you reckon we're dealing with? A hit man?'

'I don't know.'

'But if it is ... then Mr Smith would be his employer, making him someone you might not want to mess about with.'

'I'm touched by your concern, Ray.'

Duff smiled. 'Can I take it you're headed over to that address any-way?'

'Not too many gangsters living in the New Town, Ray.'

'Not that we know of,' Duff corrected him. 'Maybe after this, we'll know better ...'

The streets were full of maroon-scarved Hearts fans, celebrating a rare victory. Bouncers had appeared at the doors of most of the city-centre watering holes: an unnecessary expense in daylight, but indispensable by night. There were queues outside the fast-food restaurants, diners tossing their empty cartons on to the pavement. Rebus kept eyes front as he drove. He was in his own car now, having stopped home long enough for a mug of coffee and two paracetamol. He guessed that a breath test might just about catch him, but felt OK to drive nonetheless.

The New Town, when he reached it, was quiet. Few bars here, and the area was a dead end of sorts, unlikely to be soiled by the city-centre drinkers. As usual, parking was a problem. Rebus did one circuit, then left his car on a double yellow line, right next to a set of traffic lights. Doubled back on himself until he reached the tenement. There was an entryphone, a list of residents printed beside it. But no mention of anyone called Smith. He ran a finger down the column of names. One space was blank. It belonged to Flat 3. He pushed the button and waited. Nothing. Pushed it again, then started pressing various bells, waiting for someone to respond. Eventually the tiny loudspeaker grille crackled into life.

'Hello?'

'I'm a police officer. Any chance of speaking to you for a minute?'

'What's the problem?'

'No problem. It's just a couple of questions concerning one of your neighbours ...'

There was silence, then a buzzing sound as the door unlocked itself. Rebus pushed it open and stepped into the stairwell. A door on the ground floor was open, a man standing there. Rebus had his ID open. The man was in his twenties, with cropped hair and Buddy Holly spectacles. A dishtowel was draped over one shoulder.

'Do you know anyone called William Smith?' Rebus asked.

'Smith?' The man narrowed his eyes, shook his head slowly.

'I think he lives here.'

'What does he look like?'

'I'm not sure.'

The man stared at him, then shrugged. 'People come and go. Sometimes they move on before you get to know their names.'

'But you've been here a while?'

'Almost a year. Some of the neighbours I know to say hello to, but I don't always know their names.' He smiled apologetically. Yes, that was Edinburgh for you: people kept themselves to themselves, didn't want anyone getting too close. A mixture of shyness and mistrust.

'Flat 3 doesn't seem to have a name beside it,' Rebus said, nodding back towards the main door.

The man shrugged again.

'I'm just going to go up and take a look,' Rebus said.

'Be my guest. You know where I am if you need me.'

'Thanks for your help.' Rebus started climbing the stairs. The shared space was well maintained, the steps clean, smelling of disinfectant mixed with something else, a perfume of sorts. There were ornate tiles on the walls. Flats 2 and 3 were on the first floor.

There was a buzzer to the right of Flat 3, a typed label attached to it. Rebus bent down for a closer look. The words had faded but were readable: *LT Lettings*. While he was down there, he decided he might as well take a look through the letter box. All he could see was an unlit hallway. He straightened up and pressed the bell for Flat 2. Nobody was home. He took out one of his business cards and a ballpoint pen, scribbled the words *Please call me* on the back, and pushed the card through the door of Flat 2. He thought for a moment, but decided against doing the same for Flat 3.

Back downstairs again, he knocked on the door of the young man with the dishtowel. Smiled as it was opened.

'Sorry to bother you again, but do you think I could take a look at your phone book ...?'

Rebus went back to his car and made the call from there. An answering machine played its message, informing him that LT Lettings was closed until ten o'clock on Monday morning, but that any tenant with an emergency should call another number. He jotted it down and called. The person who answered sounded like he was stuck in traffic. Rebus explained who he was.

'I need to ask about one of your properties.'

'I'm not the person you need to speak to. I just mend things.'

'What sorts of things?'

'Some tenants aren't too fussy, know what I mean? Place isn't their own, they treat it like shit.'

'Until you turn up and sort them out?'

The man laughed. 'I put things right, if that's what you mean.'

'And that's all you do?'

'Look, I'm not sure where you're going with this ... It's my boss you need to speak to. Lennox Tripp.'

'OK, give me his number.'

'Office is shut till Monday.'

'His home number, I meant.'

'I'm not sure he'd thank me for that.'

'This is a police matter. And it's urgent.'

Rebus waited for the man to speak, then jotted down the eventual reply. 'And your name is ...?'

'Frank Empson.'

Rebus jotted this down too. 'Well, thanks for your help, Mr Empson. You heading for a night out?'

'Absolutely, Inspector. Just as soon as I've fixed the heating in one flat and unblocked the toilet in another.'

Rebus thought for a moment. 'Ever had cause to visit Gilby Street?'

'In the New Town?'

'Number 26, Flat 3.'

'I moved some furniture in, but that was months back.'

'Never seen the person who lives there?'

'Nope.'

'Well, thanks again ...' Rebus cut the call, punched in the number for Lennox Tripp. The phone was answered on the fifth ring. Rebus asked if he was speaking to Lennox Tripp.

'Yes.' The voice hesitant.

'My name's John Rebus. I'm a detective inspector with Lothian and Borders Police.'

'What seems to be the problem?' The voice more confident now, an educated drawl.

'One of your tenants, Mr Tripp, 26 Gilby Street.'

'Yes?'

'I need to know what you know ...'

Rebus was smoking his second cigarette when Tripp arrived, driving a silver Mercedes. He double-parked outside number 26, using a remote to set the locks and alarm.

'Won't be long, will we?' he asked, turning to glance at his car as he shook Rebus's hand. Rebus flicked the half-smoked cigarette on to the road.

'Wouldn't imagine so,' he said.

Lennox Tripp was about Rebus's age – mid fifties – but had worn considerably better. His face was tanned, hair groomed, clothes casual but classy. He stepped up to the door and let them in with a key. As they climbed the stairs, he said his piece.

'Only reason William Smith sticks in my head is that he pays cash for the let. A wad of twenties in an envelope, delivered to the office on time each month. This is his seventh month.'

'You must have met him, though.'

Tripp nodded. 'Showed him the place myself.'

'Can you describe him?'

Tripp shrugged. 'White, tallish ... nothing much to distinguish him.'

'Hair?'

Tripp smiled. 'Almost certainly.' Then, as if to apologise for the glib comeback: 'It was six months ago, Inspector.'

'And that's the only time you've seen him?'

Tripp nodded. 'I'd have called him a model tenant ...'

'A model tenant who pays cash? You don't find that a mite suspicious?'

Tripp shrugged again. 'I try not to pry, Inspector.' They were at the door to Flat 3. Tripp unlocked it and motioned for Rebus to precede him inside.

'Was it rented furnished?' Rebus asked, walking into the living room.

'Yes.' Tripp took a look around. 'Doesn't look like he's added much.'

'Not even a TV,' Rebus commented, walking into the kitchen. He opened the fridge. There was a bottle of white wine inside, open and with the cork pushed back into its neck. Nothing else: no butter, milk ... nothing. Two tumblers drying on the draining board the only signs that anyone had been here in recent memory.

There was just the one bedroom. The bedclothes were mostly on the floor. Tripp bent to pick them up, draping them over the mattress. Rebus opened the wardrobe, exposing a dark blue suit hanging there. Nothing in any of the pockets. In one drawer: underpants, socks, a single black T-shirt. The other drawers were empty.

'Looks like he's moved on,' Tripp commented.

'Or has something against possessions,' Rebus added. He looked around. 'No phone?'

Tripp shook his head. 'There's a wall socket. If a tenant wants to sign up with BT or whoever, they're welcome to.'

'Too much trouble for Mr Smith, apparently.'

'Well, a lot of people use mobiles these days, don't they?'

'They do indeed, Mr Tripp.' Rebus rubbed a thumb and forefinger over his temples. 'I'm assuming Smith provided you with some references?'

'I'd assume he did.'

'You don't remember?'

'Not offhand.'

'Would you have any records?'

'Yes, but it's by no means certain ...'

Rebus stared at the man. 'You'd rent one of your flats to someone who couldn't prove who they were?'

Tripp raised an eyebrow by way of apology.

'Cash upfront, I'm guessing,' Rebus hissed.

'Cash does have its merits.'

'I hope your tax returns are in good order.'

Tripp was brought up short. 'Is that some kind of threat, Inspector?'

Rebus feigned a look that was between surprise and disappointment. 'Why would I do a thing like that, Mr Tripp?'

'I wasn't meaning to suggest ...'

'I would hope not. But I'll tell you what.' Rebus laid a hand on the man's shoulder. 'We'll call it quits once we've been to your office and checked those files ...'

There was precious little in the file relating to Flat 3, 26 Gilby Street – just a signed copy of the lease agreement. No references of any kind. Smith had put his occupation down as 'market analyst' and his date of birth as 13 January 1970.

'Did you ask him what a market analyst does?'

Tripp nodded. 'I think he said he worked for one of the insurance companies, something to do with making sure their portfolios didn't lose money.'

'You don't recall which company?'

Tripp said he didn't.

In the end, Rebus managed a grudging 'thank you', headed out to his car, and drove home. Ray Duff hadn't called, which meant he hadn't made any progress, and Rebus doubted he would be working Sunday. He poured himself a whisky, stuck John Martyn on the hi-fi, and slumped into his chair. A couple of tracks passed without him really hearing them. He slid his hand into his pocket and came out with both phones, the silver and the black. For the first time, he checked the silver flip-top, finding messages from Frances Guthrie to her husband. There was an address book, probably listing clients and friends. He laid this phone aside and concentrated on the black one. There was nothing in its memory: no phone numbers stored, no messages. Just that one text: *TELL ME WHO TO KILL*. And the number of the caller.

Rebus got up and poured himself another drink, then took a deep breath and pushed the buttons, calling the sender of the text message. The ringing tone sounded tremulous. He was still holding his breath, but after twenty rings he gave up. No one was about to answer. He decided to send a text instead, but couldn't think what words to use.

Hello, are you a hired killer?

Who do you think I want you to kill?

Please hand yourself in to your nearest police station ...

He smiled to himself, decided it could wait. Only half past nine, the night stretching ahead of him. He surfed all five TV channels, went into the kitchen to make some coffee, and found that he'd run out of milk. Decided on a walk to the corner shop. There was a video store almost next door to it. Maybe he'd rent a film, something to take his mind off the message. Decided, he grabbed his keys, slipped his jacket back on.

The grocer was about to close, but he knew Rebus's face and asked him to be quick. Rebus settled for a packet of sausages, a box of eggs and a carton of milk. Then added a four-pack of lager. Settled up with the grocer and carried his purchases to the video store. He was inside before he remembered that he'd forgotten to bring his membership card; thought the assistant would probably let him rent something anyway. After all, if William Smith could rent a flat in the New Town, surely Rebus could rent a three-quid video.

He was even prepared to pay cash.

But as he stared at the rack of new releases, he found himself blinking and shaking his head. Then he reached out a hand and lifted down the empty video box. He approached the desk with it.

'When did this come out?' he asked.

'Last week.' The assistant was in his teens, but a good judge of Hollywood's gold dust and dross. His eyes had gone heavy-lidded, letting Rebus know this film was the latter. 'Rich guy's having an affair, hires an assassin. Only the assassin falls for the wife and tops the mistress instead. Rich guy takes the fall, breaks out of jail with revenge in mind.'

'So I don't need to watch it now?'

The assistant shrugged. 'That's all in the first fifteen minutes. I'm not telling you anything they don't give away on the back of the box.'

Rebus turned the box over and saw that this was largely true. 'I should never have doubted you,' he said.

'It got terrible reviews, which is why they end up quoting from an obscure radio station on the front.'

Rebus nodded, turning the box over in his hands. Then he held it out towards the assistant. 'I'll take it.'

'Don't say I didn't warn you.' The assistant turned and found a copy of the film in a plain box. 'Got your card?'

'Left it in the flat.'

'Surname's Rebus, right? Address in Arden Street.' Rebus nodded. 'Then I suppose it's OK, this one time.'

'Thanks.'

The assistant shrugged. 'It's not like I'm doing you a favour, letting you walk out with that film.'

'Even so ... you have to admit, it's got a pretty good title.'

'Maybe.' The assistant studied the box for *Tell Me Who to Kill*, but seemed far from convinced.

Rebus had finished all four cans of lager by the time the closing credits rolled. He reckoned he must have dozed off for a few minutes in the middle, but didn't think this had affected his viewing pleasure. There were a couple of big names in the main roles, but they too tended towards drowsiness. It was as if cast, crew and writers had all needed a decent night's sleep.

Rebus rewound the tape, ejected it, and held it in his hand. So it was a film title. That was all the text message had meant. Maybe someone had been choosing a film for Saturday night. Maybe Carl Guthrie had found the phone lying on the pavement. William Smith had dropped it, and Guthrie had found it. Then someone, maybe Smith's girlfriend, had texted the title of the film they'd be watching later on, and Guthrie had opened the message, hoping to find some clue to the identity of the phone's owner.

And he'd walked out under a bus.

TELL ME WHO TO KILL.

Which meant Rebus had wasted half a day. Half a day that could have been better spent ... well, spent differently, anyway. And the film had been preposterous: the assistant's summary had only just scratched the surface. Starting off with a surfeit of twists, there'd been nowhere for the film to go but layer on more twists, deceits, mixed identities, and conspiracies. Rebus could not have been more insulted if the guy had woken up at the end and it had all been a dream.

He went into the kitchen to make some coffee. The place still held the aroma of the fry-up he'd amassed before sitting down to watch the video. Over the sound of the boiling kettle, he heard his phone ringing. Went back through to the living room and picked it up.

'Got a name for you, sorry it took so long.'

'Ray? Is that you?' Rebus checked his watch: not far short of midnight. 'Tell me you're not still at work.'

'Called a halt hours ago, but I just got a text message from my friend who was doing some cross-checking for me.'

'He works odder hours than even we do.'

'He's an insomniac, works a lot from home.'

'So I shouldn't ask where he got this information?'

'You can ask, but I couldn't possibly tell you.'

'And what is it I'm getting?'

'The text message came from a phone registered to Alexis Ojiwa. I've got an address in Haddington.'

'Might as well give it to me.' Rebus picked up a pen, but something in his voice had alerted Ray Duff.

'Do I get the feeling you no longer need any of this?'

'Maybe not, Ray.' Rebus explained about the film.

'Well, I can't say I've ever heard of it.'

'It was news to me too,' Rebus didn't mind admitting.

'But for the record, I do know Alexis Ojiwa.'

'You do?'

'I take it you don't follow football.'

'I watch the results.'

'Then you'll know that Hearts put four past Aberdeen this afternoon.'

'Four–one, final score.'

'And two of them were scored by Alexis Ojiwa ...'

Rebus's mobile woke him an hour earlier than he'd have liked. He blinked at the sunshine streaming through his uncurtained windows and grabbed at the phone, dropping it once before getting it to his ear.

'Yes?' he rasped.

'I'm sorry, is this too early? I thought maybe it was urgent.'

'Who is this?'

'Am I speaking to DI Rebus?'

'Yes.'

'My name's Richard Hawkins. You put your card through my door.'

'Did I?'

Rebus heard a soft chuckle. 'Maybe I should call back later ...'

'No, wait a sec. You live at Gilby Street?'

'Flat 2, yes.'

'Right, right.' Rebus sat up, ran his free hand through his hair. 'Thanks for getting back to me.'

'Not at all.'

'It was about your neighbour, actually.'

'Will Smith?'

'What?'

Another chuckle. 'When he introduced himself, we had a laugh about that coincidence. Really it was down to me. He called himself "William", and it just clicked: Will Smith, same as the actor.'

'Right.' Rebus was trying to gather himself. 'So you've met Mr Smith, talked to him?'

'Just a couple of times. Passing on the stairs ... He's never around much.'

'Not much sign of his flat being lived in, either.'

'I wouldn't know, never been inside. Must have something going for him, though.'

'Why do you say that?'

'Absolute cracker of a girlfriend.'

'Really?'

'Just saw her the once, but you always know when she's around.'

'Why's that?'

'Her perfume. It fills the stairwell. Smelled it last night, actually ...'

Yes, Rebus had smelt it too. He moistened his lips, feeling sourness at the corners of his mouth. 'Mr Hawkins, can you describe William Smith to me?'

Hawkins could, and did.

Rebus turned up unannounced at Alexis Ojiwa's, reckoning the player would be resting after the rigours of the previous day. The house was an unassuming detached bungalow with a red Mazda sports car parked in the driveway. It was on a modern estate, a couple of neighbours washing their cars, watching Rebus with the intensity of men for whom his arrival was an event of sorts, something they could dissect with their wives over the carving of the afternoon sirloin. Rebus rang the doorbell and waited. A woman answered. She seemed surprised to see him.

He showed his ID as he introduced himself. 'Mind if I come in for a minute?'

'What's happened?'

'Nothing. I just have a question for Mr Ojiwa.'

She left the door standing open and walked back through the hall and into an L-shaped living area, calling out: 'Cops are here to put the cuffs on you, baby.' Rebus closed the door and followed her. She stepped out through French windows into the back garden, where a tiny, bare-chested man stood, nursing a drink that looked like puréed fruit. Alexis Ojiwa was wiry, with thick-veined arms and a tight chest. Rebus tried not to think about what the neighbours thought. Scotland was still some way short of being a beacon of multiculturalism, and Ojiwa, like his partner, was black. Not just coffee-coloured, but as black as ebony. Still, probably the only question that would count in most local minds was whether he was Protestant black or Catholic black.

Rebus held out a hand to shake, and introduced himself again.

'What's the problem, officer?'

'I didn't catch your wife's name.'

'It's Cecily.'

Rebus nodded. 'This is going to sound strange, but it's about your mobile phone.'

'My phone?' Ojiwa's face creased in puzzlement. Then he looked to Cecily, and back again at Rebus. 'What about my phone?'

'You do have a mobile phone, sir?'

'I do, yes.'

'But I'm guessing you wouldn't have used it yesterday afternoon? Specifically not at 16.31. I think you were still on the pitch at that time, am I right?'

'That's right.'

'Then someone else used your phone to send this message.' Rebus held up William Smith's mobile so Ojiwa could read the text. Cecily came forward so she could read it too. Her husband stared at her.

'What's this all about?'

'I don't know, baby.'

'You sent this?' His eyes had widened. She shook her head.

'Am I to assume that you had your husband's phone with you yesterday, Mrs Ojiwa?' Rebus asked.

'I was shopping in town all day ... I didn't make any calls.'

'What the hell is this?' It appeared that the footballer had a short fuse, and Rebus had touched a match to it.

'I'm sure there's a reasonable explanation, sir,' Rebus said, raising his hands to try to calm Ojiwa.

'You go spending all my money, and now this!' Ojiwa shook the phone at his wife.

'I didn't do it!' She was yelling too now, loud enough to be heard by the car-polishers. Then she dived inside, producing a silver mobile phone from her bag. 'Here it is,' she said, brandishing the phone. 'Check it, check and see if I sent any messages. I was shopping all day!'

'Maybe someone could have borrowed it?' Rebus suggested.

'I don't see how,' she said, shaking her head. 'Why would anyone want to do that, send a message like that?'

Ojiwa had slumped on to a garden bench, head in hands. Rebus got the feeling that theirs was a relationship stoked by melodrama. He seated himself on the bench next to the footballer.

'Can I ask you something, Mr Ojiwa?'

'What now?'

'I was just wondering if you've ever needed physio?'

Ojiwa looked up. 'Course I need physio! You think I'm Captain Superman or something?' He slapped his hands against his thighs.

If anything, Rebus's voice grew quieter as he began his next question. 'Then does the name Carl Guthrie mean anything to you ...?'

'You've not committed any crime.'

These were Rebus's first words to Frances Guthrie when she opened her door to him. The interior of her house was dark, the curtains closed. The house itself was large and detached and sited in half an acre of grounds in the city's Ravelston area. Physios either earned more than Rebus had counted on, or else there was family money involved.

Frances Guthrie was wearing black slacks and a loose, low-cut black top. Mourning casual, Rebus might have termed it. Her eyes were red-rimmed, and the area around her nose looked raw.

'Mind if I come in?' he asked. It wasn't really a question. He was already making to pass the widow. Hands in pockets, he walked down the hallway and into the sitting room. Stood there and waited for her to join him. She did so slowly, perching on the arm of the red leather sofa. He repeated his opening words, expecting that she would say something, but all she did was stare at him, wide-eyed, maybe a little scared.

He made a tour of the room. The windows were large, and even when curtained there was enough light to see by. He stopped by the fireplace and folded his arms.

'Here's the way I see it. You were out shopping with your friend Cecily. You got to know her when Carl was treating her husband. The pair of you were in Harvey Nichols. Cecily was in the changing room, leaving her bag with you. That's when you got hold of her phone and sent the message.' He paused to watch the effect his words were having. Frances Guthrie had lowered her head, staring down at her hands.

'It was a video you'd watched recently. I'm guessing Carl watched it too. A film about a man who cheats on his wife. And Carl had been cheating on you, hadn't he? You wanted to let him know you knew, so you sent a text to his other phone, the one registered to his fake name – William Smith.' Smith's neighbour had given Rebus a good description of the man, chiming with accident victim Carl Guthrie. 'You'd done some detective work of your own, found out about the phone, the flat in town ... the other woman.' The one whose perfume had lingered in the stairwell. Saturday afternoon: Carl Guthrie heading home after an assignation, leaving behind only two glasses and an unfinished bottle of wine.

Frances Guthrie's head jerked up. She took a deep breath, almost a gulp.

'Why use Cecily's phone?' Rebus asked quietly.

She shook her head, not blinking. Then: 'I never wanted this ... Not this ...'

'You weren't to know what would happen.'

'I just wanted to do something.' She looked up at him, wanting him to understand. He nodded slowly. 'What ... what do I do now?'

Rebus slipped his hands back into his pockets. 'Learn to live with yourself, I suppose.'

That afternoon, he was back at the Oxford Bar, nursing a drink and thinking about love, about how it could make you do things you couldn't explain. All the passions – love and hate and everything in between – they all made people act in ways that would seem inexplicable to a visitor from another planet. The barman asked him if he was ready for another, but Rebus shook his head.

'How's the weekend been treating you?' the barman asked.

'Same as always,' Rebus replied. It was one of those little lies that went some way towards making life appear that bit less complicated.

'Seen any good films lately?'

Rebus smiled, stared down into his glass. 'Watched one last night,' he said. 'Let me tell you about it ...'

Saint Nicked

The man dressed as Santa Claus took to his heels and ran, arms held out to stop the branches scratching his face. It was night, but the moon had appeared from its hiding place behind the clouds. The man's shadow stretched in front of him, snared by the car's headlights. He dodged left, deeper into the woods, hoping he would soon outrun the bright beams. There was laughter at his back, the laughter of men who were not yet pursuing him, men who knew his flight was doomed.

'Come back, Santa! Where do you think you're going?'

'You're not exactly in camouflage! Got Rudolph tied to a tree, ready for a quick getaway?'

More laughter, then the first voice again: 'Here we come, ready or not ...'

He didn't pause to look back. His red jacket was heavy, its thick lining padding out a frame that was stocky to begin with. Funny thing was, he'd been stick thin until his thirties. Made up for it since, though. Chips, chocolate and beer. He knew he could ditch the costume, but that would leave a trail for them to follow. They were right: no way was he going to outrun them. He was already down to a light trot, a stitch developing in his side. The baggy red trousers kept snagging on low branches and bracken. When he paused at last, catching his breath, he heard whistling. '*Jingle Bells*', it sounded like. The light over to his right was wavering: his pursuers had brought torches. He could hear their boots crunching over the ground. They weren't running. Their steps were steady and purposeful. He started moving again. His plan: to get away. There was a road junction somewhere not far off. Maybe a passing car would save him. The sweat was icy on his neck, steam rising from his body, reminding him of the last horse home in the 2.30.

'You're going to get a kick in the fairy lights for this!' one of the voices called out.

'There won't be enough of you left to fill a Christmas stocking!' yelled the other.

They were still a hundred, maybe two hundred yards behind him. He started picking his way over the ground, trying to muffle any sound. Something scratched his face. He wiped a thumb across his cheek, feeling the prickle of blood. The stitch was getting worse. His heart was pounding in his ears, so loud he feared they would hear it. As the pain grew worse, he remembered someone telling him once that the secret to beating a stitch was touching your toes. He paused, bent down, but his hands didn't even make it to his knees. He fell into a crouch instead, resting his forehead against cold bark. There was a piney smell in the air, like those air fresheners you could get for the car. His clenched fists were pushing against the frozen ground. There was something jagged there beneath his knuckles: a thin slice of stone. He prised it from the earth, held it as he would a weapon. But it wasn't a weapon, and never would be. Instead, he had an idea, and started working its edge against the tree trunk.

The movement behind him had stopped, torchlight scanning the night. For the moment, they had lost him. He couldn't make out what they were saying: they were either too far away, or keeping their voices low. If they stayed where they were, they would hear him scratching. Sure enough, the beam from at least one torch was arcing towards him. He had a sudden, ludicrous image from films he'd devoured as a kid: he was escaping from Colditz; he'd tunnelled out and now the searchlights were tracking him, the Nazis in pursuit. *The Great Escape:* that was the one they'd always shown at Christmas. He wondered if it would be shown this year, and whether he'd be around to see it.

'Is that you, Santa?' The voice was closer. But he'd finished now, and was back on his feet, moving away from the light, sweat stinging his eyes. It was the smoking that had taken its toll. Time was, he wasn't a bad athlete. At school he'd sometimes come runner-up in races. OK, so that had been forty years ago, but were his pursuers any fitter? Maybe they would be tiring, thinking of giving up. Was he worth all this effort to them, when the snug warmth of the BMW was waiting?

Of course! The BMW! He could circle back, nick the car from beneath their noses. If only he could keep going. But his sides were burning, his legs buckling. And the truth was, he didn't even know which direction he was headed. He'd been doing anything but run in a straight line. The car could be anywhere. Chances were he was heading further into the middle of nowhere. Even if he got away, he might end up freezing to death on the hills. There were pockets of habitation out here; he'd spotted the lights during the drive south. But they were within shouting distance of the roadside, and he felt suddenly he was a long way from any road. He was an achingly long way from home.

He knew now that he would give them what they wanted, but only on his terms. It had to be on his terms, not theirs. And he didn't want a kicking. Didn't deserve it. He'd done everything just the way he'd been told ... well, almost everything.

His head felt light, but his body was a dead weight. It was like wading through waist-deep water, and he was slowing again. Did he want to escape, to end up alone in this wilderness? The sky was darkening again, clouds closing over the land. Sleet might be on its way. How could it be that he was floating and drowning both at the same time?

And falling to his knees.

Stretching out, as if on crisp sheets. His eyes closing ...

And then the glare of the searchlights. The guards with their torches. Hands pulling at him, grabbing him by the hair. The silver wig came away. He'd forgotten he'd been wearing it.

'Sleeping on the job, Santa?'

They had him now, both of them. He didn't care. He didn't feel well enough to care.

'Tell us where it is.'

'I ...' His chest was ablaze, as if he'd fallen asleep too close to the fire. He started pulling at the front of his costume, trying to shed it.

'Just tell us where it is.'

'I ...' He knew that if he told them, they might leave him here. Or punish him. He knew he had to play for time. Blood pounded in his ears, deafening him.

'No more fun and games.'

'Scratched it,' he blurted out.

'What's that?'

He tried to swallow. 'Scratched it on a tree.'

'Which tree?'

'I'll ... show you.'

They were trying to pull him to his feet, but he was too heavy, altogether too large for them. Which was how he'd broken away from them in the first place.

'Just tell us!'

He tried shaking his head. 'Show you.'

They dropped him then, arguing with one another.

'He's having us on,' the taller one said.

The stocky one shrugged. 'Tells us or shows us, what's the difference?'

'Difference is ...' But the tall one didn't seem to have an answer. He sniffed instead. 'He's caused us enough grief as it is.'

'Agreed, which is why I want this over with.'

'So why don't I persuade him?' The tall man slapped his torch against the palm of his hand.

'What do you say, Santa?' The stocky one shone his own torch against Santa's face. The eyes were open, but staring. The face seemed to be going slack. The stocky man knelt down.

'Don't tell me ...' the tall man groaned.

'Looks like.' The stocky man made a few checks, and stood up again. 'Heart gave out.'

'Don't tell me ...'

'I just did tell you.'

'So what do we do now?'

The stocky man waved his torch around. 'Said he'd scratched the answer on one of the trees. Can't be too far. Let's start looking ...'

But after twenty minutes, they'd found nothing. They reconvened at Santa's cooling body. 'So what now?'

'We'll come back in the morning. The tree's not going anywhere. Plenty of daylight tomorrow.'

'And him?' The torch picked out the prone figure.

'What about him?'

'We can't just leave him. Think about it ...'

The stocky man nodded. 'You're right. Can't have the kids finding out Santa's not around any more.' He tucked his torch under his arm. 'You take the feet ...'

Detective Inspector John Rebus was in a bad place, doing a bad thing, at his least favourite time of year.

Which is to say that he was Christmas shopping in Glasgow. It had been his girlfriend's idea: everyone, she'd explained, knew that Glasgow boasted better shops than Edinburgh. Which was why he found himself traipsing around busy stores on the last Saturday before Christmas, carrying more and more bags as Jean consulted the neatly typed list she'd brought with her. Each purchase had been selected carefully beforehand, something Rebus was forced to admire. He, after all, shopped from what some would call instinct and others desperation. What he couldn't work out was why the process took so long: even though Jean knew what she was looking for, and where to find it, they still spent half an hour in each shop.

Sometimes – when she was buying something for him – he had to stand outside, shuffling his chilled toes and trying not to look like a man with an impatient wait ahead of him.

It was when they stopped for lunch that Jean, noticing his slumped shoulders, patted his cheek.

'A good impersonation of the condemned man,' she told him. 'You're not exactly entering into the spirit.'

'I'm not the festive sort.'

'I'm beginning to realise.' She smiled. 'The words "retail" and "therapy" don't coincide in your world, do they? Maybe we should go our separate ways this afternoon.'

Rebus nodded slowly. 'That would let me buy a few things for you – without you knowing.'

She studied him, seeing through the lie. 'Consider yourself off the hook,' she said. 'Do you want to meet up later?'

Rebus nodded again. 'Give me a bell when you're finished.'

They parted outside the restaurant, Jean pecking his cheek. Rebus watched her go. Fifty yards down Buchanan Street, she disappeared into an arcade of small, expensive-looking shops. Rebus let his nose guide him to the Horseshoe Bar, where he sat at a corner table, nursing a first and then a second whisky, perusing a newspaper. Thursday's theft from the First Minister's residence in Edinburgh was still causing plenty of amusement. Rebus had already heard two hardened Glaswegian accents joking about it at the bar:

'Looks like Christmas came early, eh?'

'Only Santa was the one on the receiving end ...'

It was all grist to the mill, and rightly so. Doubtless Rebus would have laughed had a man dressed as Father Christmas walked into a reception in Glasgow and wandered out again with a priceless necklace tucked beneath his costume. No ordinary piece of jewellery, but once the property of Mary, Queen of Scots, brought into the light just one day each year so it could be shown off at a party. With the First Minister of the recently devolved Scottish Parliament as victim, Rebus's police station had been a hive of activity, which was why he intended enjoying what was left of today.

Finishing his drink, he asked at the bar for a Yellow Pages, jotting down the addresses of local record shops. He was going to find a small gift for himself, a rarity or some new album, something he could play on the big day. Something to take his mind off Christmas. The third shop he tried was a second-hand record specialist, and Rebus was its only customer. The proprietor had frizzy greying hair tied in a ponytail, and was wearing a Frank Zappa T-shirt that had shrunk in the wash at some point in the 1970s. As Rebus consulted the racks, the man asked if he was looking for anything in particular.

'I'll know it when I see it,' Rebus told him. On an overcast day, it was easy enough to start a conversation. Five minutes in, Rebus realised he knew the man from somewhere. He pointed a finger. 'You were in a band yourself once.'

The man grinned, showing gaps between his teeth. 'That's some memory you've got.'

'You played bass for the Parachute Game.' The man held up his hands in surrender. 'Ted Handsome?' Rebus guessed, eyes narrowed in concentration.

The man nodded. 'The name's Hanson, actually. Ted Hanson.'

'I had a couple of your albums.'

'Almost as many as we made.'

Rebus nodded slowly. The Parachute Game had appeared on the Scottish scene in the mid seventies, supporting headliners such as Nazareth and Alex Harvey. Then things had gone quiet.

'Your singer did a runner, didn't he?'

Hanson shrugged. 'Bad timing.'

Rebus remembered: the band had crept into the lower reaches of the Top 30 with a single from their second album. Their first headlining tour was looming. And then their singer had walked out. Jack ... no, Jake, that was it.

'Jake Wheeler,' he said out loud.

'Poor Jake,' Ted Hanson said. He was thoughtful for a moment, then checked his watch. 'You look like a drinking man, am I right?'

'You've got a good eye.'

'Then I reckon this could be my early-closing day.'

Rebus didn't like to say, but he got the feeling Ted had a few of those each week.

They hit a couple of bars, talking music, bands from the 'old days'. Hanson had a fund of stories. He'd started the shop with stock ransacked from his own collection.

'And my flat still looks like a vinyl museum.'

'I'd like to see that,' Rebus said with a smile. So they jumped in a taxi, heading for Hillhead. Rebus called Jean on his mobile, said he might be late getting back to Edinburgh. She sounded tired and unbothered. Hanson's Victorian tenement flat was as promised. Albums lay slumped against every wall. Boxes of them sat on tables, singles spilling from home-made shelves that had warped under the weight.

'A little piece of heaven,' Rebus said.

'Try telling that to my ex-wife.' Hanson handed him a can of beer.

They spent a couple of hours on the sofa, staring into the space between the loudspeakers and listening to a shared musical heritage. Finally, Rebus plucked up the courage to ask about Jake Wheeler.

'You must have been gutted when he walked out.'

'He had his reasons.'

'What were they?'

Hanson offered a shrug. 'Come to think of it, he never said.'

'There were rumours about drugs ...'

'Rock stars and drugs? Surely not.'

'A good way to meet some very bad people.' Rebus knew of these rumours too: gangsters, dealers. But Hanson just shrugged again.

'He never resurfaced?' Rebus asked.

Hanson shook his head. Then he smiled. 'You said you had a couple of our albums, John ...' He sprang to his feet, rummaged in a box by the door. 'Bet this isn't one of them.' He held out the album to Rebus.

'I did own it once upon a time,' Rebus mused, recognising the cover. *The Oldest Tree,* recorded by the remaining trio after Wheeler had walked out. 'Lost it at a party, week after I'd bought it.' Examining the cover – swirly late-hippy pencil drawings of dells and hills, a broad oak tree at the centre – Rebus remembered something. 'You drew this?'

Hanson nodded. 'I had more than a few pretensions back then.'

'It's good.' Rebus studied the drawing. 'I mean it.'

Hanson sat down again. 'Back at the shop, you said you were after something special. Could this be it?'

Rebus smiled. 'Could be. How much do you want?'

'Compliments of the season.'

Rebus raised an eyebrow. 'I couldn't ...'

'Yes you could. It's not like it's worth anything.'

'Well, OK then, thanks. Maybe I can do you a favour some day in return.'

'How's that then?'

Rebus had lifted a business card out of his wallet. He handed it over. 'I'm in CID, Ted. Never know when you might need a friend ...'

Studying the record sleeve again, Rebus failed to notice the look of fear and panic that flitted across his new friend's face.

Sunday morning, Neil Bryant woke up and knew something was wrong. He was the stockier of the two men who'd spent much of the previous evening chasing an overweight, unfit Santa to his death. He was also supposed to be the brains of the outfit, which was why he was so annoyed. He was annoyed because he'd asked Malky Bunker – his tall, skinny partner in crime – to wake him up. It was past ten, and still no sign of Malky. So much for his dawn wake-up call. He phoned Malky and gave him a good roasting.

Twenty minutes later, the BMW pulled up at Bryant's door. Malky's hair was tousled, face creased from sleep. He was yawning.

'You got rid of the deceased?' Bryant asked. Malky nodded. Good enough: the fewer details Bryant knew, the better. They drove out of Glasgow, heading east and south. Different route from last night, and a map neither of them knew how to read.

'Be easier if we drove into Edinburgh and out again,' Malky suggested.

'We're late as it is,' Bryant snapped. The thing was, as you headed towards the Border country, it all started to look the same. Plenty of forests and crossroads. It was early afternoon before they started to recognise a few landmarks. Passing a couple of flatbed trucks, Bryant sensed they were getting warm.

'Working on a Sunday,' Malky commented, glancing out at another truck.

'Run-up to Christmas,' Bryant explained. Then his heart sank as he saw what the trucks were carrying.

'This has got to be it,' Malky was saying.

'Aye,' Bryant agreed, voice toneless.

Malky was parking the car, only now realising that the forest they'd run through the previous night was not a forest. It had been denuded by chainsaws, half its trees missing. Not a forest: a plantation. A fresh consignment of Christmas firs, heading north to Edinburgh.

The two men looked at one another, then sprinted from the car. There were still trees left, plenty of them. Maybe, if they were lucky … maybe Santa's tree would still be there.

Two hours and countless arguments later, they were back in the car, heater going full blast. The foreman had threatened to call the police. They'd threatened violence if he did.

'They're all the same,' he'd shouted, meaning the trees.

'Just call us particular,' Bryant had snarled back.

'What are we going to do?' Malky asked now. 'We go back there without the necklace, our goose is well and truly stuffed.'

Bryant looked at him, then got out of the car, marching towards the nervous-looking foreman.

'Where are they headed?' he demanded.

'The trees?' The foreman watched Bryant nod. 'Edinburgh,' he said.

'Where in Edinburgh?'

'All over.' The foreman shrugged. 'Probably be sold within the day.'

'Addresses,' Bryant said, his face inches away from the older man's. 'I need addresses.'

Rebus and Jean ate Sunday lunch at a hotel in Portobello, surrounded by families pulling crackers and wearing lopsided paper crowns.

'Basic training for the big day,' Rebus commented, excusing himself from the table as his mobile started ringing. It was his boss, Detective Chief Superintendent Gill Templer.

'Enjoying a lazy Sunday?' she enquired.

'Up until now.'

'We're looking at fences, John.' Meaning people who might be able to shift an item as hot as the necklace. 'You know Sash Hooper, don't you? Wondered if you might pay him a visit.'

'Today?'

'Sooner the better.'

Rebus glanced back in Jean's direction. She was stirring her coffee, no room for dessert. Rebus had promised to go and buy a Christmas tree.

'Fine,' he said into the mouthpiece. 'So where can I find Sash?'

'Skating on thin ice, as usual,' Gill Templer said.

Ever the entrepreneur, Sash – real name Sacha, courtesy of a mother with a thing for French crooners – had opened an outdoor skating rink on Leith Links.

'Just trying to make an honest dollar,' he told Rebus, as they walked around the rinks perimeter. 'Licences in place and everything.' He watched two teenagers as they shuffled across the slushy ice, the rink's only customers. Then he stared accusingly at the sun, cursing its liquefying powers. Music blared from a faulty loudspeaker: Abba, 'Dancing Queen'.

'No interest in stolen antiquities, then?'

'All in the past, Mr Rebus.' Hooper was a big man, with clenched fists. What was left of his hair was jet black, tightly curled. His thick moustache was black too. He wore sunglasses, through which Rebus could just make out his small, greedy eyes.

'And if someone came to you with an offer ...'

'The three wise men could knock on my door tonight, Mr Rebus, and I'd give them the brush-off.' Hooper shrugged a show of innocence.

Rebus looked all around. 'Not rushed off your feet, are you?'

'The day's young. Besides, Kiddie Wonderland's doing all right.' He nodded at the double-decker bus decorated with fake snow and tinsel. Mums and young children were lining up for entry. Rebus had passed the bus when he'd first arrived. It promised 'A visit you'll never forget – one gift per child.' 'Santa's *grotto on wheels,*' had been Hooper's explanation, rubbing his hands together. The interior looked to have been decorated with white cotton and sheets of coloured crêpe paper. The queuing parents appeared dubious, but Kiddie Wonderland was the only show in Leith. Still, to Rebus's mind, there was something missing.

'No Santa,' he said, nodding towards the bus.

'Soon as you're gone there will be.' Hooper patted his own stomach.

Rebus stared at him. 'You realise some of these kids could be traumatised for life?' Hooper didn't reply. 'Let me know if Christmas brings you anything nice, Sash.'

Hooper was rehearsing his *ho, ho, ho*s as Rebus walked back to the car.

He knew that there was a place off Dalkeith Road that sold Christmas trees. It was a derelict builders' yard, empty all year round except for the run-up to 25 December. When he arrived, two men were doing a good impression of taking the place apart, studying each tree before dismissing it, while the proprietor watched bemused, arms folded. One of the men shook his head at the other, and the pair stormed out.

'I got a call half an hour back,' the proprietor told Rebus. 'They did the same thing to a friend of mine.'

'Takes all sorts,' Rebus said. But he watched the men get into their rusty BMW and drive off. The elder and shorter of the two – his face was familiar. Rebus frowned in concentration, bought the first five-foot fir offered to him, and took it out to his car. It stretched from boot to passenger seat. He still couldn't put a name to the face, and it bothered him all the way to St Leonards police station, where he made his report to Gill Templer.

'Could do with clearing this one up, John,' she said.

Rebus nodded. She would have the brass on her back, because the First Minister was on theirs.

'We can but try, Gill,' he offered, making to leave. He was driving out of the car park when he saw a face he recognised, and this time the name came easily. It was Ted Hanson. Rebus stopped and wound down his window. 'This is a surprise, Ted.'

'I was in town, thought I'd look you up.' Hanson looked cold.

'How did you find me?'

'Asked a policeman,' Hanson said with a smile. 'Any chance of a cuppa?'

They were only five minutes from Rebus's tenement flat. He made two mugs of instant coffee while Hanson flicked through his record collection.

'A pale imitation of yours, Ted,' Rebus apologised.

'A lot of the same albums.' Hanson waved a copy of Wishbone Ash's *Argus*. 'Great cover.'

'It's not the same with CDs, is it?'

Hanson wrinkled his nose. 'Nothing like.'

Rebus handed over the coffee and sat down. 'What are you doing here, Ted?' he asked.

'Just wanted to get out of the shop – out of Glasgow.' Hanson blew across the surface of the mug, then took a sip. 'Sorry, John. Got any sugar?'

'I'll fetch some.' Rebus got to his feet again.

'Mind if I use your loo meantime?'

'Be my guest.' Rebus pointed the way, then retreated to the kitchen. Music was playing in the living room: the Incredible String Band. Rebus returned and placed the sugar beside Hanson's mug. Something was going on. He had a few questions for his new friend. After a couple of minutes, he walked back into the hall, knocked on the bathroom door. No answer. He turned the handle. There was no one inside. Ted Hanson had done a runner.

'Curiouser and curiouser,' Rebus muttered to himself. He looked down on to the street from his living room window: no sign of anyone. Then he stared at his record collection. It took him a couple of minutes to work out what was missing.

The last Parachute Game album, the one Hanson himself had given him. Rebus sat in his chair, thinking hard. Then he called Jean.

'Not found a tree yet?' she asked.

'It's on its way, Jean. Could you do me a favour?'

'What?'

'Something I'd like for Christmas ...'

Christmas itself was fine. He'd no complaints about Christmas. There was the slow run-up to Hogmanay, Gill Templer growing less festive as the necklace failed to turn up. New Year's Day, Rebus nursed his accessory of choice: a thumping head. He managed to forgo any resolutions, apart from the usual one to stop drinking.

His Christmas present finally arrived on 4 January, having been posted in Austin, Texas, on 24 December. Jean handed it over, having taken the trouble to wrap it in second-hand paper.

'You shouldn't have,' he said. Then he kissed her, and took the album home for a listen. The lyrics were on the inside of the gatefold sleeve. The songs tended to the elegiac, each seeming to refer to Jake Wheeler. Ted Hanson had taken over vocal duties, and though he didn't make too bad a fist of it, Rebus could see why the band had folded. Without Wheeler, there was something missing, something irreplaceable. Listening to the title track, Rebus studied the drawing on the front of the sleeve – Ted Hanson's drawing. An old oak tree with the initials JW carved on it, enclosed in a heart, pierced by an arrow that wasn't quite an arrow. Holding the sleeve to the light, Rebus saw that it was a syringe.

And there beneath the oldest tree, Hanson sang, *you took your last farewell of me* … But was it the bassist talking, or something else? Rebus rubbed a hand across his forehead and concentrated on other songs, other lyrics. Then he turned back to the sleeve. So detailed, it couldn't just be imagined. It had to be a real place. He picked up his phone, called Jean's number. She worked at the museum. There were things she could find out.

Such as the location of Scotland's oldest tree.

On the morning of the sixth, he let the office know he'd be late.

'That's got to be a record-breaker: the five-day hangover.'

Rebus didn't bother arguing. Instead, he drove to Glasgow, parking on the street outside Ted Hanson's shop. Hanson was just opening up; he looked tired and in need of a shave.

'Amazing what you can find on the internet these days,' Rebus said. Hanson turned, saw what Rebus was holding: a near-mint copy of *The Oldest Tree*. 'Here's what I think,' Rebus went on, taking a step forward. 'I think Jake's dead. Maybe natural causes, maybe not. Rock stars have a way of hanging around with the wrong people. They get into situations.' He tapped the album sleeve. 'I know where this is now. Is that where he's buried?'

The ghost of a smile passed across Hanson's face. 'That's what you think?'

'It's why you had to get the album back from me, once you knew what I did for a living.'

Hanson bowed his head. 'You're right.' Then he looked up again, eyes gleaming. 'That's exactly why I had to get the album back.'

He paused, seemed to take a deep breath. 'But you're wrong. You couldn't be more wrong.'

Rebus frowned, thinking he'd misheard.

'I'll show you,' Hanson said. 'And by the way, happy new year.'

The drive took them over an hour, north out of Glasgow, the scenery stretching, rising, becoming wilderness. They passed lochs and mountains, the sky a vast, bruised skein.

'All your detective work,' Hanson said, slouched in the passenger seat, 'did you notice where the album was recorded?' Rebus shook his head. Hanson just nodded, then told him to pull over. They were on a stretch of road that would fill with camper vans in the summer, but for now it seemed desolate. Below them lay a valley, and across the valley a farmhouse. Hanson pointed towards it. 'Owned by our producer at the time. We set up all the gear, did the album in under a month. Braepath Farm, it was called back then.'

Rebus had spotted something. On the hillside behind the farmhouse, the tree from the album sleeve. The tree Jean had told him was the oldest in Scotland: the Braepath Oak. And behind it, a small stone bothy, little more than a shelter for shepherds, outside which a man was splitting logs, watched by his sheepdog.

'Jake fell apart,' Hanson was saying, voice low. 'Maybe it was the company he was keeping, or the industry we were supposed to be part of. He just wanted to be left alone. I promised him I'd respect that. The drawing ... it was a way of showing he'd always be part of the band, whatever happened.' He paused, clearing his throat. Rebus watched the distant figure as it picked up the kindling, taking it indoors. Long-haired, ragged-clothed: too far away to really be sure, but Rebus knew all the same.

'He's been out here ever since?' he asked.

Hanson nodded. His eyes glistened.

'And you've never ...?'

'He knows where I am if he wants me.' He angled his head. 'So now you know, John. Up to you what you do about it.'

Rebus nodded, put the car into gear and started a three-point turn.

'Know what I'd like, Ted?' he said. 'I'd like you to sign that album for me. Will you do that?'

'With pleasure,' Hanson said with a smile.

*

Back at St Leonards, Rebus was passing the front desk when he saw the duty sergeant emerging from the comms room, shaking his head in disbelief. 'I'm not that late,' Rebus said.

'It's not that, John. It's Mother Hubbard.'

Now Rebus knew: Edwina Hubbard from down the road. Two or three times a week she would call to report some imagined mischief.

'What is it this time?' Rebus asked. 'The peeping postmen or the disappearing dustbins?'

'Christmas trees,' the sergeant said. 'Being collected and taken away.'

'And did you explain to her that it happens every year, courtesy of our caring, sharing council?'

The sergeant nodded. 'Thing is, she says they're early. And using a double-decker bus.'

'A bus?' Rebus laughed. 'Firs, please.'

The sergeant laughed too, turning to retreat into the comms room. 'It gets better,' he said. 'The bus is covered in Christmas decorations.'

Rebus was still laughing as he climbed the stairs. After the morning he'd had, he needed something to cheer him up. Then he froze. A Christmas bus ... Kiddie Wonderland. Collecting Christmas trees ... Two men running around Edinburgh, looking for a tree ... The name flashed from brain to mouth.

'Neil Bryant!' Rebus took the stairs two at a time, sat down at a computer and typed in Bryant's name. Ex-bouncer, convictions for violence. Clever with it. The other man, the taller one, had looked like bouncer material too. And hadn't Sash Hooper run a nightclub a few years back? Sash ... ready to take an unlikely turn as Santa on the bus.

'Santa,' Rebus hissed. Then he was back downstairs and in the comms room, grabbing the sergeant's arm.

'The bus with the trees,' he said. 'Where did she see it?'

Rink.

The bus was full of trees, both decks. But finally they'd found one with that single word scratched on its trunk.

Rink.

The way Bryant had explained it to Sash Hooper, they needed the bus so they could collect as many trees as possible, as quickly as possible. Eventually Hooper had seen the wisdom of the plan. He had got a buyer for the necklace, but the sale had to be quick.

Rink.

Well it didn't take a genius, did it? They'd turned the bus round and headed for Leith Links. The costume had been Bryant's idea too, when he'd heard that the First Minister was throwing a party. Send someone in there dressed as Santa, they could walk out with anything they liked. He'd gone to Sash with the idea, and Sash had suggested Benny Welsh, a pretty good housebreaker in his time, now down on his luck. Benny had been good as gold – until he'd found out how much the necklace was worth. After which he'd tried upping out. Wasn't going to hand it over until they had a deal.

Three of them now – Sash, Malky and Bryant – slipping and sliding across the ice. Looking for the telltale dark patch, finding it. Benny had cut himself a hole, stuffed the necklace in, then poured in some water, letting it freeze over again. Sash had his penknife out. It took a while, the day darkening around them.

'Give me the knife,' Malky said, chipping away with it.

'Watch the blade doesn't snap,' Sash Hooper warned, as if the knife were somehow more precious than the necklace. Eventually all three men clambered to their feet, Hooper holding the necklace, examining it. A string of shimmering diamonds, embracing a vast blood-red ruby. He actually gasped. They came off the ice and back on to solid earth. They were almost in the shadow of the bus before they noticed Rebus. And he wasn't alone.

Two uniforms could be seen through the upper-deck windows. Two more were downstairs. Another was outside, circling the bus.

'Nice little stocking-filler,' Rebus said, motioning towards the necklace.

'You got a warrant?' Hooper asked.

'Do I look as if I need one?'

'You can't just go trampling all over my bus. That's private property.' Hooper was attempting to slide the necklace into his pocket.

Malky tugged at Bryant's sleeve. His eyes had widened. They were on the policeman who'd been circling the bus, the policeman who was now turning the handle that would open the vehicle's luggage compartment. Bryant saw his friend's look, and his own mouth dropped open in dismay.

'Malky, for the love of God, tell me you didn't ...'

Hooper was still concentrating on protesting his innocence. He knew this was the most important speech he would ever make. He felt that if he could just get the words right, then maybe ...

'DI Rebus,' the constable was saying. 'Something here you should take a look at ...'

And Hooper shifted his gaze and saw what everyone else was

seeing. Benny Welsh, still dressed in the telltale red suit, lying at peace on the floor of the luggage bay.

Rebus turned to face the three men.

'I'm guessing that means you're Saint Nicked,' he said.

Atonement

'They're dropping like flies.'

The man collapsed into another fit of coughing, doubling over in the tattered armchair. Rebus looked around him, but no one in the large, overheated room was paying the slightest attention. Some were watching a daytime nature programme, others dozing or staring out of the window. It was a large sash window – three windows actually, forming a bay. The paintwork looked new. Rebus thought he could smell fresh paint, its aroma not quite exhausted. There were other smells, too: the remains of a fish lunch; talcum powder and perfume; perished rubber. The redecorating did not stretch as far as the cornices and ceiling. The cornicing was elaborate, the design almost Celtic. The ceiling was pale green, a few veined cracks radiating from the central light fitting.

At one time, this would have been a fine private home, enjoyed by a bank manager and his growing family. Edinburgh had no shortage of these detached Victorian mansions. Some had been divided into flats, of course. Others were business HQs, or owned by large institutions and charities. Renshaw House, however, had become a care home for the elderly, which meant that the man in the armchair must be elderly. His name was Ken Flatley. When Rebus had first joined the police, Flatley had been a mentor of sorts. Not that the word 'mentor' would ever have been used between them: Rebus was a detective, Ken Flatley the uniform who manned the police station's front desk. All the same, the older man had looked at the younger and understood – understood that tips and hints would be appreciated.

This had been in the early 1970s, the era of boot boys and pub rock: Rod Stewart in his tartan scarf, and Elton John telling teenagers that it was all right to fight on a Saturday night. One such altercation had put Ken Flatley behind the desk: suedeheads clashing after a football derby, Flatley between them quickly becoming their shared target, leaving him with a limp. He used a walking frame these days. His thick brown hair had never gone grey, so that strangers sometimes mistook it for a wig. The face below the low fringe was creased but resolute. Take away the walking frame, Rebus reckoned, and his friend would seem younger than himself.

They had lost touch for a number of years, reunited briefly at the funeral of Flatley's wife Irma. But when Rebus had learned that Flatley had sold the bungalow in Prestonfield and moved to a nursing home, he'd arranged to visit. That first meeting had not started well, Ken asserting that he needed no pity.

'I'm not here for that,' Rebus had told him.

'What then?'

'Maybe I'm just on the lookout,' Rebus had replied, scanning the room. Flatley had caught his meaning and laughed.

'Aye, not too long till you'll be joining me.'

It was a thought Rebus had been pushing away ever since. After all, he was in his late fifties, maybe only fifteen years younger than Flatley. And he lived alone. If anything happened ... if his faculties started to fail or went into reverse ... He had no family nearby, and though he would try to cope, try to do everything for himself, there was always the possibility that he would not succeed. When he had first married and moved into the tenement flat where he still lived, there'd been a man on the top floor who'd lived alone. Rebus had always been slightly wary of this man, especially when his daughter Sammy had been young; hadn't even bothered to attend the neighbour's funeral. And yet now ... now there were students and young couples in his tenement, and he himself had become the oldest inhabitant.

'Dropping like flies,' Flatley repeated, clutching the arms of the chair. It was his own chair, one of the few possessions he'd been allowed to bring with him from home. Much of the rest had been disposed of at auction, a daughter in Bristol taking only a few mementoes – photograph albums and some bone china. Asked if he had thought of going to stay nearer his daughter, Flatley had shaken his head vigorously.

'Got her own life now,' he'd insisted.

Now Rebus watched him as he wiped the back of one tremulous hand across his mouth. 'How do you mean?' he asked.

His friend leaned forward, inviting Rebus to do the same, until their heads were inches apart.

'Faces in here,' Flatley muttered, 'they don't last long.'

Rebus nodded as if he understood, but Flatley gave him the same hard gaze he'd given the young detective whenever Rebus had made some tiro's error.

'I don't mean they just get old and peg it.' He nodded towards an empty chair by the fireplace. 'Mrs Edwards used to sit there. Sprightly, she was, when she came in here. Family said she couldn't cope – what they meant was, *they* couldn't cope. So in she comes and lights the place up ... until last week. Ambulance came for her, and three days later they tell us she's dead.'

'Ken ...'

'She's not the only one, John.' Flatley's voice was insistent, knowing the objection Rebus had been about to make. 'Dot Parker took ill one day, died the next. Same with Manny Lehrer.'

'You're saying they're being bumped off, one by one?'

'It's no joke, John.'

Rebus's smile faded. 'No, I'm sure it's not. So what are we talking about here?'

'I'm not sure ... There was something in the paper recently about staff in care homes letting people die.'

'Benign neglect?'

'I don't think "benign" enters into it.'

'Are you saying they don't feed you?'

'Oh, they feed us all right ... after a fashion.'

'What then?'

'You hear about it all the time, don't you? Nurses who're secretly poisoning their patients.'

'Ken ...' The tone of warning had returned to Rebus's voice. Flatley just stared at him and Rebus sighed, sitting back in his chair. 'What is it you want me to do?'

'I just thought someone should ...' The words trailed off.

'You know, when someone dies unexpectedly, even if they're old, there's an autopsy.'

'What if it's not unexpected, though? They've been ill or frail ... a pathologist is going to find what he expects to find. He's not going to be as thorough as with a corpse with a knife in its back.'

Rebus held his hands up, palms towards his tormentor. He glanced around him, but no one seemed to have heard the outburst. 'If it will help put your mind at rest,' he said, 'let me see what I can do.'

Some of the tension left Flatley's face. He shifted his gaze floorwards. 'Why do you keep coming here, John?'

'Maybe I'm a fan of conspiracy theories.'

'I'm serious.' Flatley fixed him with a stare. 'I mean, it's good to have a visitor now and then ... I just don't see what you get out of it.'

'Could be I've got a guilty conscience, Ken. All those years I never kept in touch.'

'We have to share the dock then – I'm as guilty as you are.'

Rebus patted his friend's leg. 'Let me do some digging, see if someone really is doing a bit of drastic bed-clearing.' He got to his feet. 'And if I don't find anything, will your mind be at rest?'

'My mind gets too much bloody rest these days,' Flatley snorted.

Rebus nodded slowly: maybe that's the trouble, he thought to himself ...

'What exactly is it we're being accused of, Inspector?'

Donald Morrison sat back in his black leather office chair. Rebus was seated at the other side of the desk. Diplomacy had never been his strong point, but all the same, he felt he'd presented the case fairly. Morrison, however, the owner of Renshaw House, was riled. Rebus could tell this because of the way the blood had risen to the man's cheeks.

'As I said, sir, I'm not here in any official capacity ...'

'But you *are* a police officer?' Morrison waited for Rebus to nod agreement. 'And you're here to visit someone who was also a policeman.' He forced the beginnings of a smile. 'It seems Mr Flatley is finding it hard to give up his old job.'

Morrison rose from his chair and turned to face the window – a replica of the one in the communal sitting room. He clasped his hands behind his back and stared out at the expanse of mown lawn, broken only by a sundial at its centre. There were benches around its periphery, shaded by mature trees. He was broad-shouldered, had probably played rugby in his younger days. His hair was greying at the ears and temples, thinning on top. There were horizontal creases above the vents of his suit jacket.

'He's free to leave, you know,' he said, patting one hand against the other. 'Our waiting list is substantial.'

'Of people wanting to leave?'

Morrison turned back to Rebus, tried out another smile on him. 'Wanting to get in, Inspector. Time was, there were plenty of care homes, but not any more. So if Mr Flatley really isn't happy here ...'

'Nobody's saying he's unhappy. He's just worried.'

'Of course he is.' Morrison pulled out his chair and sat down again. 'He's surrounded by people who are not exactly in the first flush of youth. I'm afraid it's part and parcel of the way of things, Inspector. People don't come here to get younger and flourish – I only wish that were the case.' He gave a slight shrug. 'Mrs Edwards and Mrs Parker ... Mr Lehrer ... they were in their eighties, and hardly in the most robust health to begin with.'

'Ken's description of Mrs Edwards was "sprightly".'

Morrison pondered this. 'He saw what he wanted to see.'

'You're saying he fancied her?'

'Age doesn't always blinker the heart.'

'And that's why her death has hit him so hard?'

Morrison gave another shrug. 'Do you think you can put Mr Flatley's mind at rest, Inspector?'

'I can try.'

Morrison bowed his head a little, satisfied at this outcome. 'Mortality is sometimes a difficult concept even for the elderly.'

'I don't think it's the concept that's bothering Ken.'

'You're right, of course.' Morrison had risen, indicating that the meeting was at its end. 'It may not help that he doesn't get many visitors.'

'His daughter lives in England.'

'He must have friends ... ex-colleagues like yourself?'

'I'm not sure he wants them to see him in a care home.'

Morrison chose not to see this as a further slight. Instead he nodded slowly. 'Self-reliance ... it's something we see a lot of: people too proud to ask for help, even when it's needed.' He held out his hand for Rebus to shake. Rebus took it.

'Just out of curiosity,' he asked, 'what did they die of?'

Morrison's face darkened a little, the blood threatening to return to his cheeks. 'Old age, Inspector, nothing more than that.'

'Ken seemed to think they were taken to hospital.'

'Yes?'

'So they all died in hospital?'

'That's right. When a patron weakens dangerously, we're duty-bound to seek medical attention for them.'

'And I'm sure you do so conscientiously.'

'We'd be closed down otherwise.' Morrison reached out to open the door. 'I wish I could feel that I've allayed your concerns, Inspector.'

'I don't have any concerns, Mr Morrison. Thanks for your time.' Rebus was on the other side of the threshold when he stopped and turned. 'I parked my car next to a silver Merc. Is it yours, by any chance?'

'It's mine.' Morrison seemed to be waiting for something more, but Rebus just nodded thoughtfully. 'Nice motor,' he said, turning to leave.

Flatley was waiting for him at the main door. It stood open, letting some much-needed air into the place. Flatley was leaning heavily against his walking frame, but straightened up when he saw Rebus.

'Keeping tabs on me, Ken?' Rebus asked.

'Just contemplating a nice long stroll.'

'Anywhere in mind?'

'Nearest pub's in Marchmont.'

'That's a good half-mile. Maybe I'll join you.'

Flatley's mouth twitched. He looked down at the metal frame against which he leaned. 'Maybe another time, eh? Did you get any joy from the commandant?'

'You're not a fan?'

Flatley wrinkled his nose. 'He's in it for the money, same as the rest of them.'

'I think there's probably better money out there somewhere.'

'Maybe so, but something tells me he's not giving himself the same minimum wage the rest of the staff have to swallow.'

'Steady, Ken, you're choking the life out of that thing.'

Flatley followed Rebus's gaze to the frame's rubber hand-grips, then smiled and relaxed his knuckles a little. 'Did you ask him about the body count?'

'I did.'

'Mention my name at all?'

'Hard not to.'

'So that's me on half-rations.'

'No hardship – you don't like the food anyway. I'll bring you a couple of pies next time I visit.'

There was silence between them, punctuated only by the sounds of the TV set in the room opposite.

'You think I'm turning gaga, John?' Flatley's eyes bored into Rebus's.

'No.'

'Maybe I am at that.'

'Maybe you could leave here ... try making do with a home help.'

'My home's not there any more.'

'Then you've got to make the best of it.' Rebus hated himself for saying the words. They sounded hollow, clichéd. *Make do ... mustn't grumble ...* He felt his old mentor deserved more.

There was sudden movement behind them. An elderly man, stick-thin and with a pale, skeletal face, was shambling in their direction, eyes wide at the sight of the open door.

'Oh Christ, it's—' The rest of the sentence went unfinished as Ken Flatley was barged aside by the old man. He stumbled into the wall, dislodging a framed painting. The frame fell apart as it hit the parquet floor, Flatley sliding down after it. A care assistant's head appeared around a doorway.

'Mr Waters!' she called. But by this time, Mr Waters was through the door. Rebus, crouching to help Ken Flatley back to his feet, saw the man waddle down the wheelchair ramp outside the entrance to Renshaw House.

'Mr Waters!' the woman called again. She was striding down the hall now, drying her hands on the front of her sky-blue uniform. Flatley was nodding that he was all right. Rebus made sure his friend had a good grip on his walking frame, then turned his attention to the fleeing man. Waters was wearing neither shoes nor socks. His upper body was covered only by a white cotton vest, accentuating his thinness. His trousers had slipped down far enough to reveal that he was wearing some sort of incontinence pad beneath.

'Need a hand?' Rebus asked the assistant as she passed him.

'I'll manage,' she muttered.

'She won't,' Ken Flatley said, jerking his head to let Rebus know he should follow her. Waters's gait was that of a walker in the Olympics. He seemed to take what weight he had on the balls of his feet, and his arms were pumping, elbows jutting out to either side. He was heading in a straight line across the lawn, towards an eight-foot stone wall. There was dew on the grass, and the care worker's rubber soles went from under her. There was a banana-skin inevitability to her slow, graceless fall. She snatched at a wrenched ankle and let out a roar that brought Mr Waters to a halt. He turned, arms dropping to his sides. Rebus leaned down to help the woman up.

'Any damage?' he asked her.

'Just twisted it.'

An arm around her waist, he brought her to her feet. Mr Waters was standing directly in front of them.

'I can't remember,' he said, voice high-pitched, false teeth missing.

'Remember what?' the woman asked angrily.

'Where the body's buried.'

'Not that again.' She gave a loud hiss. 'There's nobody dead, Mr Waters,' she told him, as if explaining something to a stubborn child.

'She buried the body. I'm not what you think I am.'

'We know who you are, Mr Waters. Your name's Lionel.' She turned to Rebus and rolled her eyes. His fingers were around the bare flesh of her arm. She eased away from him slightly, and he let her go.

'My treasure's all gone ... The fishing boat ... the castle ... all gone.'

'That's right, Mr Waters, all gone.' She was talking to the man but her eyes were on Rebus, and she was shaking her head slowly, to let him know this was a regular exchange. 'Now let's get you back to the house.'

'I need to see Colin, to tell him I'm sorry. You believe me, don't you?'

'Of course I do.'

But Waters wasn't looking at her. Rebus was his focus. The old man's eyes narrowed, as if trying to place the face. 'Nobody believes me,' he stated.

'You're a bloody nutcase, Waters!' The voice was Ken Flatley's. He was standing in the doorway, while a carer started tidying up the picture frame. 'About time they sectioned you again!' A hand patted Flatley's shoulder, and he turned towards his comforter: Donald Morrison.

Rebus insisted on accompanying the care assistant back to Lionel Waters's bedroom. As she gave the old man a blue tablet and a glass of water, Rebus looked around. The room was bare. He got the feeling all the furnishings belonged to Renshaw House itself. Waters was seated on a chair by his bedside. A tattered magazine was lying open on the bed, showing a half-finished word puzzle.

'What's your name?' Rebus asked the assistant.

'Annie.'

'Sure that ankle's OK?'

'I'll manage.' She was tucking a tartan travel rug around Waters's legs.

'I'd say you've probably got a good case for a day or two on the sick.'

'Maybe so.'

'But you'll manage?'

She turned to him. Her eyes were a deep hazel. 'It's tough enough working here; one goes sick, that just makes it tougher.'

'You're short-staffed?'

'Lousy wages for back-breaking work ... what do you think?'

'I think I couldn't do it.' His eyes shifted over the walls. 'He didn't bring much with him, did he?'

Annie turned her attention to Waters. He was mumbling, but his eyes had gone glassy, the lids drooping. 'Poor sod was in a mental institution before this. Locked away since his twenties. Never really right in the head, according to the family. Eventually they couldn't cope. He was aggressive, you see.'

'And he killed someone called Colin?'

She smiled at the mistake. 'Colin's his brother. Colin Waters?' Her eyes were on Rebus's again.

'The car dealer?'

'Biggest on the east coast – isn't that what the advert says?'

Rebus nodded slowly. 'He comes from a rich family, then. They're paying for this place?'

'I suppose so.' Waters's eyes had closed now. Annie motioned with her head for Rebus to leave. Out in the corridor, she left the door ajar a few inches. The unconscious figure of Lionel Waters could be seen through the gap.

'Why did they let him out of the other place?' *The other place* – because Rebus didn't know what the current term was for a nuthouse, a loony bin, an asylum.

'Said he no longer posed a threat. If you ask me, it's been a long time since he did. All he wants to do is run away.'

'To see his treasure.'

She wrinkled her nose. 'Aye, right.'

'And to tell Colin he's sorry ... sorry for what?'

'Sorry he killed him.' She started walking down the corridor, trying hard not to limp. 'He thinks he killed his brother.'

'But Colin must have visited?'

'A few times, yes.'

'Only a few?'

She stopped again, turned to face him. 'How would you feel if every time your brother saw you, he thought you were a ghost?'

Rebus could think of no reply, so gave a shrug. Satisfied with this, she went a few more paces, then stopped at a swing door, ready with her palm against its surface.

'Thanks for your help,' she said.

'My name's John.'

She nodded at this information. 'You're a friend of Mr Flatley. Did he tell you his theory?'

'He thinks people are dying.'

'And what do you think, John?'

'I think you get lousy pay for back-breaking work.'

'And?' Her face was almost breaking into a smile.

'And you do the best you can for your patrons.'

She nodded slowly, pushed open the door and disappeared through it into what seemed to be the kitchen.

*

The painting had been removed from the entrance hall. There was no sign of either Ken Flatley or Donald Morrison. Outside, Morrison's Merc had gone from the car park. As Rebus manoeuvred his own rusting Saab down the driveway, slowing for the speed bumps, each one a potential nail in his car's coffin, he had to pull on to the verge so that a delivery van could pass him. His eyes sought the driver's, expecting some gesture of thanks at the show of courtesy, but the man stared resolutely ahead. The side of the white transit bore the legend 'Pakenham Fresh Fleshing'. Rebus stayed on the verge and watched in his rear-view as the van rattled towards its destination. He knew the driver from somewhere; seemed to recognise the face. It was the jawline, the set of the mouth. Maybe from a butcher's shop, but he didn't know the name Pakenham. All the same, he was reminded that he needed something for dinner. Steak pie maybe, and a tin of marrowfat peas. Or he could always eat out, provided he could find a dinner partner. He thought again of Annie and those deep hazel eyes. Shame she wore a wedding ring. His mobile started ringing. He fished it out of his pocket and checked the display, then held it to his ear.

'How do you fancy dinner tonight, my treat?'

'And will there be any solids involved?' a voice replied.

'Some,' he promised, knowing that Detective Sergeant Siobhan Clarke had already taken the bait.

Diners in the Oxford Bar needed no menu. There was the Cambridge Bar further along Young Street if you really wanted a meal. The Ox, on the other hand, served pies and bridies (until they ran out), and filled rolls – corned beef and beetroot a speciality. Snacks consisted of crisps, nuts and pork scratchings.

'Yummy,' Siobhan Clarke said.

'We can hit a chip shop later if you're not replete,' Rebus responded, placing her vodka and lemonade on the table. She'd settled for a ham and tomato roll. The barman had gone to some lengths to also supply a crusty jar of French mustard. Rebus pulled out a chair and settled himself. Two inches were already missing from his pint of IPA. A macaroni cheese pie sat on the plate before him. 'It was the last hot thing they had,' he explained now.

'I can imagine.'

He took a bite and shrugged. Siobhan spread mustard thinly across the roll, and closed it up again. 'How was Ken?' she asked, lifting it to her mouth.

'He says the inmates are dropping like flies – his exact words.'

'Meaning?'

'Meaning a few of his fellow codgers have caught the last train.'

'Isn't that what happens when you get old?'

Rebus nodded his agreement. 'Something else happened while I was out there.'

Siobhan ate in silence as Rebus told her the story of Lionel Waters. By the end of it, he'd finished his first pint. He raised the empty glass. She shook her head, letting him know she didn't yet need a refill.

'I mean it's your shout,' he said. When she made to get up, he beat her to it. 'Only kidding: you're my guest, remember?'

By the time he returned from the bar, she had finished her roll and was swirling the ice cubes in what was left of her drink.

'I bought my car from Waters Motors,' she told him.

'So did half the city.'

'I'd never heard about a brother, though.'

'Me neither.'

'He's lucky he wasn't lobotomised – they used to do that, you know.'

'You mean they don't any more?'

She saw that he was teasing. 'John F. Kennedy's sister ... I was reading about her only the other day.'

'He had a sister?'

'She died recently. Locked up for sixty years ...'

'And given a lobotomy?'

'That's right.'

'Well, we don't do that any more.'

They sat in silence for a moment, concentrating on their drinks. Siobhan was first to speak. 'What is it?' she asked.

'How do you mean?'

'Something's bugging you. I hope it's not gold fever.'

'What are you talking about?'

'Tales of hidden treasure.' She widened her eyes theatrically. 'They've sent many a man mad before you.'

'Sod off, Siobhan.'

She laughed. 'But there *is* something, isn't there?'

'It's what he said when he was standing in front of me.'

'What?'

'"I'm not what you think I am". He said "what" rather than "who".'

Siobhan snapped her fingers. 'They've swapped places! Lionel is Colin and vice versa – that's how it would work in a film.'

'I'm warning you ...' Rebus stared into his beer. 'And he said "she" – "she buried the body". He wanted to say sorry to his brother.'

Siobhan leaned across the table. 'We're not psychiatrists, John.'

'I know that.'

'We're *detectives*.'

'That's right.' He looked up at her. 'You're absolutely right.'

His tone alerted her. She sat back again, hands resting around her empty glass. 'What are you going to do?'

'For now, I'm going to get you a refill.' He pushed himself to his feet.

'And after?'

'You said it yourself, Shiv: I'm a detective.'

'You're going to see the car man, aren't you?'

A smile flitted across Rebus's face. 'If nothing else, maybe he'll do me a trade-in on the Saab ...'

The main Edinburgh showroom for Waters Motors was just off Calder Road. Rebus headed there next morning, the rush-hour traffic numbing his senses, so that he happily accepted the secretary's offer of caffeine.

'Instant OK?' she asked apologetically.

'Instant's fine.' Colin Waters had yet to arrive from his home in Linlithgow, but that didn't bother Rebus. He had a call to make: to the Scottish Criminal Records Office. During part of the crawl here, he'd stared at the blacked-out windows of the van in front, and this had triggered a memory – a name, which in turn had brought another name into play. He gave both to his SCRO colleague, along with his mobile phone number.

'How soon till you call me?' he asked. He was seated on the showroom's mezzanine level, its smoked-glass walls giving a view of the business area below. The cars on display gleamed. Their very tyres sparkled, picked out by well-positioned halogen bulbs suspended from the ceiling. The salesmen were young and wore commission-bought suits, which made it easy to spot the most successful ones. When the revolving door spat out a newcomer, those who had been sitting leaped to their feet, eyes seeking an acknowledgement from the elderly man in the sagging jacket and slacks.

Colin Waters.

He was in his seventies, much the same age as his brother, but there the similarity ended. Colin Waters was about a foot shorter than Lionel, and boasted a thick head of hair and a face grown pink and round from indulgence. Ignoring the greetings from those around him, he started climbing the open-sided glass staircase, a busy man with a crowded schedule ahead. He glanced at Rebus as he passed him, perhaps mistaking him for a rep of some kind. He closed the office door after him, and Rebus thought he could hear the muffled conversation that followed. When the door opened again, Colin Waters gestured with a crooking of his finger. Rebus thought about staying put – just to see how the man would react – but decided against it. He followed Waters into the office, accepted the mug from the secretary, and watched her leave, closing the door quietly behind her.

There were two desks: one for the secretary, one for her boss. Rebus decided that the proximity had to be for one of two reasons: either Waters liked looking at her, or else he didn't want to miss anything going on around him. Waters was gesturing again, this time for Rebus to sit, but Rebus stayed standing. There was a full-height glass wall here, again looking down on to the sales floor. Rebus pretended to be watching from it, mug cupped in front of him.

'Elaine says you're a police officer,' Waters barked, landing heavily on his own leather-upholstered chair and pulling it in towards his desk.

'That's right, sir. CID.'

'You wouldn't tell her what it's about. All very mysterious.'

'Not really, sir. Just didn't think you'd want me discussing family matters in front of the staff.' When Rebus turned his head, the blood was draining from Waters's face.

'Lionel?' he gasped.

'Don't worry, sir, your brother's fine.' Rebus decided finally to sit down.

'Then what's ... Not Martha?'

'Martha?'

'My sister.' Waters caught himself. 'Obviously not, since you don't know who I'm talking about.'

Rebus was remembering Lionel's words: *she buried the body.* 'Actually, sir, it is about your brother. I happened to be at Renshaw House yesterday, and had to help the staff restrain him. Seems he wanted to walk out of there, so he could find you and say sorry.'

'Oh Christ.' Waters bowed his head, pinching the skin at the bridge of his nose.

'You know he thinks he killed you?'

Colin Waters nodded. 'Right from when he was a kid, we knew there was something that wasn't right about him. He was a lot of fun, though ... boisterous, you know?' He seemed to expect some response, so Rebus produced a slow nod. 'But he never seemed to

have any sense of when he was taking things too far. He'd bite …
lash out … even at strangers on the street. Our parents decided he
needed to be kept home, at least for as long as they were able.' He
took a deep breath. 'Martha and I … we tried to pretend he was
just like anybody else.' He broke off, flicked at something invisible
on the arm of his jacket. 'Special needs is the term these days; back
then, the local children had other ways of putting it. Keeping Lionel
at home became problematic.'

'It couldn't have been easy,' Rebus acknowledged. Waters gave
the briefest of smiles.

'We were wrestling one day,' he said. 'Middle of July – teenagers,
the pair of us – out on the lawn. Lionel loved to wrestle … probably
fell on me a bit too solidly – he was well built in those days.'

'What happened?'

'I think I passed out. When I came to, he was up to high doh …
reckoned he'd done me in. We couldn't make him see sense.'

'By "we" you mean …?'

'Martha and me. She's younger than us. The way he was carrying
on, it scared the hell out of her – roaring like a wild beast, almost
foaming at the mouth. As far as Lionel was concerned, I was a
ghost …'

Waters paused, lost in memory. His fingers had stretched out to
touch a photo frame on his desk. Rebus could see only the back of it.

'Is that …?' He pointed to the frame.

'This is afterwards. Me and Martha.'

'Do you mind if I take a look?'

Waters's shoulder twitched as he turned the photo round. It was
black and white, and showed Colin Waters still not quite out of
his teens. His sister looked four or five years younger, breasts just
beginning to appear, hair still held in pigtails. They were seated on
the staircase of what appeared to be a grand house – probably not
dissimilar to Renshaw House. They were peering through the iron
banisters. There was a painting on the wall behind them. Neither
looked particularly happy, and the photographer had failed to get
their faces in sharp focus. There was a ghostly quality to the whole.
Rebus couldn't help wondering why the photo was so important. To
him, it seemed a daily reminder of something lost: the hopes and
dreams of youth.

'Interesting painting,' he said, as Waters turned the photo back
towards himself.

'It's still in the family.'

'Is it a loch or a river?'

'I think the artist invented it, whatever it is. Not too many cliff-top castles in Scotland.'

'Not that I know of.' Rebus made to rise to his feet, Waters following suit.

'I'm still not sure why you came, Inspector,' he commented.

'Me neither,' Rebus told him. Then he slid his hands into his pockets. 'Your brother just seemed so confused and lonely. I take it a visit from you would upset him?'

Waters shrugged. 'I'm a ghost, remember.'

'And your sister? Does she see him much?'

Waters shook his head. 'It upsets her too much to see him like that.' He gestured with an expansive right arm. 'Now, if there's nothing else ...'

'I appreciate your time, sir.' Rebus didn't bother mentioning the Saab; reckoned it would do him another year.

He decided that a further visit to Renshaw House was in order, but first drove towards his home in Marchmont, stopping at the local butcher's shop. He was a known face here, and as with a good barman, the butcher knew what his regulars liked.

'Steak pie, Mr Rebus?' he was asking as Rebus walked over the threshold.

'No thanks, Andy.'

'Couple of nice pork chops, then?'

Rebus shook his head. There was sawdust on the floor – for show rather than anything else. Andy wore a striped apron and a straw boater. Photos on the white-tiled wall showed his father in the selfsame get-up. Rebus was struck again by what the photo on Waters's desk must have meant to the car dealer.

'Just a question actually, Andy,' he said.

'Is this me becoming a police informer? The Huggy Bear of Edinburgh?'

Rebus answered the laugh with a smile of his own. He'd never seen the butcher at rest. Even now, with no order to fill, Andy was sorting the display of various hams and sausages. 'I was wondering if you knew about a butcher called Pakenham.'

'Pakenham?'

Rebus spelled it for him. 'They'd be local, I think. "Fresh Fleshing" is what it says on their van.'

'Have they got a shop?'

'I've only seen the van. It was delivering to an old folk's home'

Andy pursed his lips.

'What is it?' Rebus asked.

'Well, it's not always top-grade, is it?'

'Cheap cuts, you mean?'

'Cheapest possible.' Andy held his hands up. 'I'm not saying they're all like that ...'

'But some are?' Rebus nodded to himself. 'Got a phone book, Andy?'

The butcher fetched one from the back of the shop. Rebus checked, but there was no Pakenham Fresh Fleshing.

'Thanks, Andy,' he said, handing it back.

'Sorry I can't be more help. More Yogi Bear than Huggy, eh?'

'Actually, you've been a big help. And maybe I will take one of those steak pies.'

'Family size, as usual?'

'As usual,' Rebus confirmed. He would drop it home before his visit to Renshaw House.

He rang the bell and waited. It was late afternoon now, the sun low in the sky. The detached villa sat on Minto Street, a busy thoroughfare on the city's south side. The house had a faded elegance, its stonework blackened by time and traffic. Most of the houses around it had become bed and breakfasts, but not this one. The name on the unpolished brass door plate was Waters, the letters picked out in verdigris. The sister, it seemed, had never married.

She opened the door herself. No pigtails now, the hair grey and thin, scraped back from the forehead and tucked behind both ears. Her eyes were sunken, as were her cheeks. Colin Waters, it seemed, had stolen all the heartiest genes from his parents.

'Martha Waters?' Rebus said, realising that he was pitching his voice a little louder than was probably necessary – she was only ten or so years older than him.

'Yes?'

He held open his warrant card. 'I'm from the police, Miss Waters. Do you mind if I come in?'

She said nothing, her mouth forming a crumpled O. But she held the door open so he could pass into the hall. It wasn't the same one as in the photograph. The banisters were wooden, darkly varnished. The only natural light came from a window on the upstairs landing. The carpet was ornate but as worn as its owner. She closed the door, adding to the pervasive gloom. Rebus noted an alarm panel on the wall beside the umbrella stand. The panel looked new, with a digital display. A sensor blinked in the far corner of the ceiling.

'Would you care for a cup of tea?' She spoke quietly, pronouncing each syllable. She had yet to ask him why he was here.

'Is there somewhere we can sit, Miss Waters?'

She shuffled in her carpet slippers towards another door, opening it to reveal what she would probably call the parlour. It was like stepping back in time: antimacassars on the sofas, an empty three-tiered cake stand on a large embroidered doily. Little ornaments and knick-knacks covered every surface. A grandfather clock had ceased to work some time back, frozen for ever at one minute to twelve.

'Did you say you wanted tea?' she enquired.

'No thanks.' Rebus had strode over to the fireplace, admiring the large painting framed above the mantel. A bus sped past outside, causing some of the ornaments to rattle. Martha Waters sat herself down. Before his arrival, she'd been listening to the radio: a classical station, the sound barely audible. Nothing much wrong with her hearing, then ... or she was just saving batteries.

'This is a grand painting,' Rebus told her.

'I used to like it,' she said. 'I hardly see it any more.'

Rebus nodded his understanding. Nothing wrong with her eyes either; she meant something else entirely.

'Who's it by?' he asked.

'My brother says it's a Gainsborough.'

'Explains the alarm system ... I take it Colin had that fitted?'

'Do you know about art?'

Rebus shook his head. 'But I know the name. It must be quite old, then.'

'Seventeen eighties.'

'As old as that? And worth a bit, I dare say?'

'Six figures, so Colin tells me.'

Rebus shook his head again, this time in apparent wonder. 'I saw that photograph of it. You know the one I mean?' He turned to her. 'Colin keeps it on his office desk. It stares back at him every working day.'

Her eyes seemed to regain their focus. 'What is it you want here?'

'Me?' He shrugged. 'I just wanted to see it in the flesh. I thought maybe you'd've sold it or something.'

'We could never sell it.'

'Not even after what you went through to get it?'

'I don't know what you mean.'

'I think you do, Miss Waters. I think it's been your little secret all these long years. I've just come from Renshaw House, had a nice long chat with Lionel.'

At the mention of her brother's name, Martha stiffened, clasping her hands on her lap in front of her.

'All those crazy stories he tells ... about his treasure and how he killed his brother ... and how *you* buried him. He keeps rambling about a boat and a castle.' Rebus pointed to the painting. 'And there they are: a castle on a hilltop, fishing boat on the water below it – Lionel's treasure. My bet is, he loved that painting and your parents had decided he could have it. Maybe they were going to will it to him, I don't know. But Colin wanted it, didn't he? And you, young as you were, you wanted it too. Two greedy little kids.' Rebus was standing in front of her now. He crouched so that she couldn't escape his eyes. 'Two brothers having a wrestle. Colin told me Lionel loved to wrestle, but Lionel says he never did: the wrestling was Colin's idea.' Rebus paused for effect. 'And then one of them's not moving, and he's covered in blood. What was it, Martha – ketchup? Paint? Whatever it was, it did the trick, sent Lionel over the edge. Especially when you told him you'd buried Colin.' Rebus stayed in a crouch, but Martha's eyes had drifted to the painting.

'We could never sell it, not after that. We never meant ...' She broke off, took a deep breath. 'We didn't stop to think.'

'You were just a girl, Martha. How were you supposed to know it wasn't a game, some sort of joke? But Colin was that bit older than you ... old enough to know exactly what he was doing. More than half a century Lionel's been kept shut up.'

'It would have happened anyway,' she said in a whisper, a tear trickling from one eye. 'We couldn't have coped. He was driving our parents demented ... nice as ninepence one minute, flying off the handle the next. Schizophrenic, the doctors said. He was turning us into pariahs.'

'You mean the local kids called him names?'

'Not just Lionel ... all of us. We were "the weird ones", "the loonies".' She wiped a hand across her face. 'Do you know how much he's cost us? All the family money, soaked up by care for Lionel.'

'Soaked up by guilt, if you ask me. That's why neither of you could let the painting go.' He rose to his feet. 'All these years ...' He let the words hang in the dusty air. His whole body felt dried out by this house, as if the life were being drained from him.

'What will happen to us?' she asked, her voice trembling.

'Lionel's not going to be in that home much longer – nobody is. So you'll offer him a room here, with his painting above his bed. And if you die before him, you'll make sure the painting goes to him.'

She looked up. 'That's all?'

Rebus offered a shrug. 'Anything you've just told me, Colin will deny – he's got too much to lose. I'd be delighted to see the pair of you in court, but I don't think that will happen. I could dig into your parents' wills, any changes in them, see if the painting was to be Lionel's at any stage, but I'm not sure I'd get anywhere. So … yes, Miss Waters, that's all.' He started to walk towards the door, but paused.

'You *could* own up, of course, tell Lionel what the two of you did. But I wouldn't, if I were you. It might be too much for him. So don't think of letting Colin near him … and pray Lionel stays in good health, because if I hear otherwise … well, I might have to do that digging after all.'

The Suruchi restaurant was Rebus's idea – and his treat.

'Felt I short-changed you last night,' he explained to Siobhan.

After ordering their starters and main courses, they snapped off pieces of poppadom from a central shared plate, dipping them in chutney and biting down on them.

And Rebus told his story.

'Amazing,' she said as he finished. He was drinking lager for a change, while she stuck to mineral water. 'But you're not going to explain it all to Lionel?'

'Even if I got through to him, would it change anything?'

'His whole life's been …' She couldn't quite find the right words.

'How does that old song go? "If I could turn back time …" If I could, believe me, I would.'

'It would be handy,' she conceded. 'We'd solve the crimes before they were ever committed.'

'Didn't do Tom Cruise much good in that film.' Their waiter had appeared at the table to clear away the empty plate. Siobhan brushed crumbs from her lap. 'Something else I did today,' Rebus was adding.

'What?'

'Solved Ken Flatley's little mystery.'

She looked at him. 'Who's been a busy boy then?'

He shrugged. 'Easy enough once I remembered the face driving the meat van. Belongs to a guy called Bernie Cable. I arrested him once at Ingliston Market.'

'A Trading Standards bust?'

Rebus nodded. 'Cable was selling dodgy meat from a van.'

'Is this something I should be hearing prior to dinner?'

'Chicken breasts past their sell-by … that sort of stuff.'

'And now he's selling meat to care homes?'

'Until today he was. I've been on to Environmental Health ... the council ... Trading Standards.'

'You *have* been busy.'

'That's not the half of it. When I asked the Records Office to look up Cable, I gave them Donald Morrison's name too.'

'That suspicious mind of yours.' Siobhan leaned back as a clean plate was placed before her. Another waiter stood ready with orders of pakora and kebab.

'It was the way Morrison addressed me,' Rebus explained. 'He kept calling me "Inspector", even though I'd made it clear I wasn't there in any official capacity.'

'And that got your antennae clicking?'

'Made me think I might not be the first cop he'd ever had dealings with.'

'And?'

'And his name's not really Morrison – that's one of his many aliases. Real name's Charles Kirkup. He's been done for fraud.'

'You reckon he was in cahoots with Cable?'

'I contacted the hospital about those poor old sods who died. Food poisoning didn't show up on the original autopsies, but they're going to check again. It's like Ken said: the pathologists aren't always so rigorous when the corpse was on its last legs anyway.'

'So he was right, after a fashion?'

Rebus nodded.

'And you've told the council this?' Another nod. 'So now he'll be closed down?'

'Bound to be.'

'And where will Ken go?'

'I told him you had a spare room.' Rebus bit into a kebab.

'I've got a better idea,' Siobhan said, spooning sauce over her pakora. 'Colin Waters will know an investment when he sees one. He could keep the place open, maybe just promote one of the staff to manage it.'

Rebus saw those hazel eyes again. 'And why would he do that?'

'You could tell him there's a Gainsborough resting on it,' Siobhan said coyly. 'And after all, if he owns Renshaw House, he won't have to pay for Lionel's care any more. I'm sure you could get Martha to argue your case for you.'

Rebus was thoughtful. 'Maybe I could at that.'

'Atonement, I think it's called.'

'Whatever it's called, I'll drink to it,' Rebus said, raising his glass.

Not Just Another Saturday

It had taken Rebus longer than usual to get to the barber's shop on Rose Street. He'd known about the Make Poverty History march, of course; just hadn't reckoned with the barriers going up so early. Melville Drive had been filling with buses from all over: church congregations from Derbyshire; anti-nuclear pensioners; African drummers; Fair Trade and Christian Aid and Water Aid and Farm Aid ... everything but the one thing Rebus needed – Lucozade. He'd only drunk four pints the previous night, but one of them must have been bad.

There was a stage erected on the Meadows, along with tents and vans preparing to sell food to the hungry masses. Someone was doling out Palestinian flags. The *Sunday Mail* had provided placards saying 'Drop the Debt'. People were dropping the placards instead, then tearing off the newspaper's name before picking them up again. Maybe they were southerners, confusing the Scottish paper with its near-namesake. Rebus was handed a plastic carrier bag. Inside he found a Help the Aged T-shirt. First kid he saw, he passed the bag along. He knew George IV Bridge would be impossible, so headed for South Bridge instead, feeling like a salmon swimming against the prevailing current. Families passed him, the kids with their faces painted. People were smiling in the sun, ready to be seen if not heard. At Fettes HQ, the High Hiedyins had guessed 175,000, but to Rebus it looked likely there'd be more: 200, maybe 250. A quarter of a million people, more than half the city's population. Scale it up, it became four million on the streets of London. Maybe that was why everyone was smiling. They had no need to shout. Their very presence would be louder than that.

Teams of uniforms milled around. Rebus didn't recognise any of them. Their accents were foreign. One sported Metropolitan Police insignia; others were from Cardiff, Liverpool, Middlesbrough ... every bit as varied as the marchers. Rebus didn't stop to say hello. He looked the way he felt: like a civilian. When the cops bothered to meet his eyes, he saw no recognition there. Just mistrust, mixed with controlled adrenalin. They'd been warned to expect trouble. Looked to Rebus as though a few of them might even welcome it. A couple of police motorbikes were controlling traffic on Buccleuch Street, making sure drivers followed the diversions. Not much for them to do, the roads unnaturally quiet for a Saturday. But then this wasn't just another Saturday. He did a double-take when he saw what was written on the back of one yellow protective jacket: London Transport Police. Nice overtime, but he couldn't help feeling the officer would be more use on his own patch, chasing muggers and fare-dodgers. More diversions, more police checkpoints. Some of his colleagues were loving it, looking forward to the whole week. They'd get to tear around the city like they owned it. Courts and cells had been cleared, ready for action. Everyone was poised.

'You'll have to go back that way, sir,' a uniform was explaining now, as Rebus tried to squeeze through the gap between one metal crash barrier and a tenement wall. The accent was English.

Rebus made show of looking back in the direction the man was pointing.

'You mean, cut along the Meadows, through the hordes and the coaches, and take a right at Tollcross, then make a sudden stop at the first barricade on Lothian Road, where I'll be politely told to "go back that way, sir"?'

The officer's eyes narrowed. When Rebus moved a hand towards his inside pocket, he even took a step back.

'Easy, pal, easy,' Rebus said, bringing out his warrant card. 'We're supposed to be on the same side.'

The officer studied the ID for longer than Rebus felt necessary. 'CID,' he said, handing it back. 'Something going down?' He hauled at the barrier, giving Rebus more room.

'Could be a close shave,' Rebus answered, heading on his way.

A close shave it was. Barber's shop on Rose Street. An occasional Saturday treat: hot towels, unguents, the works. Even a splash of cologne afterwards. They didn't use cut-throat razors these days: fear of hep B and HIV. Little disposable blades instead. Still gave a good shave, even though Rebus missed the sliding of the cut-throat against the leather strap. As a kid, he'd watched his father get a regular wet shave, the barber winking at him as he honed the gleaming blade.

'Might call it a day,' the barber told Rebus now. 'Most of my bookings have cancelled.'

'Wimps,' Rebus said.

'Half the shops on Princes Street are shut. Some with the boards up. That fellow Geldof, he wants a million marchers.'

'He won't get them,' Rebus said. 'Man runs a decent concert, but that's about it. He'll get his moment in the sun, shake hands with George W even, and that'll be about it.'

The barber snorted. 'We're maybe cynical old buggers, John.'

'I marched in the sixties.'

'But not now?'

Rebus just shrugged. It was different then, he wanted to say. But he wasn't sure that was true. *He* was different then; no doubt about that. He'd always assumed ideals were for the young, but the people he'd seen heading for the march ... they'd been all ages. Probably all backgrounds and creeds, too. The sun was out, and forty miles up the road at Gleneagles, eight men would sit down to make decisions affecting the whole planet. Not that there was any pressure. Edinburgh's own Chief Constable would be there too, shuffling around in the background, usurped by spooks and Special Branch, bodyguards and Marines. Jack McConnell kept saying how great it was for Scotland, putting the place on the map. Rebus wondered how close Jack would get to the real power; suspected he'd be little more than a meeter and greeter, positioned front-of-house while the real work went on elsewhere.

'Off to the Ox?' the barber said.

'As per,' Rebus acknowledged. A wee Saturday afternoon session: racing on TV and a filled roll to feed the soul. The Live Eight concert would be on later. He'd probably watch The Who and Pink Floyd – especially the Floyd; had to see it with his own eyes. If Dave Gilmour let Roger Waters back on stage with him, anything was possible ... maybe even world peace, an end to hunger and a cure for global warming.

'Might shut up shop and follow you,' the barber said.

'I'll wait,' Rebus offered. The man nodded and began to sweep up. Rebus stepped outside for a cigarette, watching through the window as towels were dumped in a laundry bag, cutters cleaned, the basin rinsed. There was something comforting in observing a person's routine. It was a ritual that placed a full stop at the end of a working day, and it showed pride, too. Combs and clippers went into a little leather pouch, which was rolled up and tied shut. They'd go home with the barber: his talisman.

At last he turned off the lights and switched on the alarm, locking the door behind him. He looked up at the sky. Rebus nodded to let him know he could hear it too: a cacophony of chants, whistles and drums in the near distance. The march had reached Princes Street.

'Fancy a quick look-see?' the barber asked.

'Sure,' Rebus said.

They walked down together. More barricades separated the slow parade from bemused shoppers. Policemen stood with arms folded, legs slightly parted. This was ritual, too. Rebus didn't doubt there'd be troublemakers dotted about the place. Something like this would be a magnet for the city's tearaways, never mind the international brotherhood of anarchists. But right now it all looked as innocuous as a cavalcade.

'Think anyone's listening?' the barber asked. But Rebus couldn't answer that. He noticed that the windows of the shops behind them were covered with protective boards.

'Even the Ann Summers shop,' the barber said with a laugh. 'Can you see the good folk of Edinburgh looting a few bits of cheeky lingerie?'

Rebus shook his head. 'It's the Basque separatists they're afraid of,' he said, lighting another cigarette.

Just for a moment, as he smoked and watched the march, there was the temptation to join in, to add another particle to the mass. But he knew he lacked the passion and the faith. He could try comforting himself with the thought that it wouldn't change anything. The rules of the game were well established, the cards already dealt. But doing nothing wouldn't change anything either. In the end it was the barber who broke the spell, offering up a shrug of his own, that most Scottish of gestures. As if synchronised, the two men turned away from the march.

They wouldn't have let you smoke anyway, Rebus told himself. But he knew he would spend the rest of the day wondering. Wondering, and maybe even regretting.

Penalty Claus

They even had a name for themselves: the Holly and Ivy Gang.

It was Debby's idea. 'They're our aliases.'

Her mother, Liz, wasn't so sure. 'Why do we need aliases? And which one am I?'

'You're Ivy.'

Liz snorted at this. 'Why can't I be Holly?'

'The name's just something they can use about us on the news.'

'But that's my whole point – we're good at this, and that means we don't get anywhere *near* the news.'

'But just in case ...'

'Besides which, there's only the two of us, so we're not technically a "gang".'

'Bandits, then. The Holly and Ivy Bandits ...'

Liz was in the electric wheelchair. Debby was on a hard plastic seat next to her. They were at a table in a fast-food restaurant on Princes Street. Debby's chair was bolted to the floor, meaning she couldn't get comfortable. They were having a bit of a rest. Edinburgh wasn't a place they knew well. They'd come by train, booking off-peak to make it worthwhile. Liz had her head screwed on about such things. No point making money on the day if your outgoings added up to more.

'Harsh economic realities,' she'd explained, nodding slowly at her own wisdom.

Debby was in her early twenties, Liz her mid forties. They lived in a scheme on the outskirts of Glasgow. Glasgow's shopping streets had given them their first taste of success, three years back. The run-up to Christmas, that was their season. They'd get want-lists from friends and would always say, 'We'll see what we can do.' But the lists had to be specific: electrical goods were usually too bulky and well guarded. Clothes and perfumes were what it came down to. Dresses and tops; posh underwear; Paris brands. Liz in the wheelchair, shopping bags hooked over its handles, a travel rug on her lap. Debby light-fingered and shrewd, eyes in the back of her head.

There'd be security staff, but they could be blindsided or distracted. CCTV wasn't always the all-seeing eye. The clothes would carry security tags, but that was where the wheelchair came in. Exiting each shop, Liz would get a bit clumsy and barge into the alarm rail, setting it off. There'd be apologies from Debby as she helped her mother manoeuvre the chair past the obstacle. The staff would be helpful, might even say that the security measures were a pain. No one, so far, had ever stopped them and asked for a rummage.

There was a big 'but', though. It wasn't the sort of stunt you could pull time and again. If you went back to the same shop and set the alarm off a second time, there'd be a bit more suspicion. So they'd moved the operation from Glasgow to Dundee last year, and now it was Edinburgh's turn. Princes Street: big names ... department stores and fashion chains ... easy pickings. They'd already done three shops, and after the burger and fizzy drink would try at least two more.

'Need the loo?' Debby asked. Her mother shook her head. The stuff they'd lifted so far, Debby had gone into Princes Street Gardens with it and found a hiding place in a clump of bushes. Always a worry: you never knew if it would be waiting for you at the day's end. But you couldn't risk the tags setting off alarms as you entered other shops – a lesson learned after their very first attempt. Besides, they needed the shopping bags on the back of the wheelchair nice and empty, the travel rug unbulging.

Their next port of call was all of twenty yards further along the street. Liz had felt it worth pointing out that Princes Street was good for wheelchairs: ramped pavements, helpful pedestrians. Waverley Station had been more of a challenge, sunk as it was beneath street level. All the same, the day was shaping up. They'd even discussed going further afield next time – Carlisle or Newcastle or Aberdeen. Debby wasn't sure about England: 'we'd stand out a mile with these accents'. But her mother had added that maybe they didn't need to wait a whole year. Their friends were always after clothes and make-up and other bits and pieces.

'This operation could go global,' was the seed she planted in her daughter's head.

Their chosen shop turned out to be less than brilliant. The better stuff was kept under glass. The available accessories looked cheap because they were cheap. It was a question of weighing up the risks. The guard was in a uniform of sorts and prowled the floor like he was pacing a cage, just waiting to pounce. The music was too loud for Liz's taste. The place was packed with customers, too. There was a sort of ideal midway point: you didn't want it to be dead, but neither did you want too many pairs of eyes on you. That was one thing about the wheelchair: it drew attention. You had to be careful.

On their way to the exit, Liz did some clumsy reversing. The alarm rang out, the red light on the sensor flashing. Debby started to chide her and the security guard came over. She told him she was sorry.

'One too many sherries,' she explained. 'Lucky there's nobody with a breathalyser.'

'It happens,' the guard said with a smile. He was resetting the alarm as Liz trundled the chair out through the doors. Her way was blocked by a pair of legs. She looked up and saw that the man had his arms folded. He was smiling too, but she sensed there was nothing friendly about it.

'Aw, no,' was all she said.

'So who does the wheelchair belong to?'

Liz and Debby were seated in one of the interview rooms at Gayfield Square police station. Detective Inspector John Rebus was standing, arms folded again.

'It was my gran's,' Debby answered.

Rebus nodded slowly. Even he – though he would never admit as much – had been surprised when Liz Doherty had opted for a patrol car over a van with a ramp at the back. She had risen from the wheelchair with what might have passed for a sheepish look and walked to the car unaided.

'And where's your gran now?' he asked.

'Buried her four years back. Nobody ever came for the wheelchair ...'

Liz asked for a cup of tea. Rebus told her she'd get one in a minute.

'Before that,' he said, 'I need you to tell me where the rest of the stuff is.'

The silence was broken by Debby. 'What stuff?'

Rebus made a tutting sound, as though disappointed in her. He dragged the empty chair out from under the table and sat down so he was facing both women.

'You're not as smart as you think you are. Store detectives tend to share gossip about their day. They'd start telling each other about the clumsy woman in the wheelchair. Glasgow two years back and Dundee last. So you might say alarm bells were ringing across the country. First shop you were in today, they got on the phone. You'd done two more by the time I could get to the scene. We've got CCTV going back three years. It was just a matter of time ...'

'Don't know what you're talking about,' Liz muttered.

Rebus tutted again. 'Christmas in the cells for the pair of you. Is there a Mr Doherty?'

'Aye,' from the mother. A shake of the head from the daughter.

'Best tell him he'll be doing his own cooking.'

'Couldn't boil an egg,' Debby blurted out. Then, turning towards her mother, 'And he's *not* Mr Doherty. He's just a fat guy you brought home one night.'

'That's enough from you,' her mother snapped back.

Rebus let them bicker for a few more minutes, biding his time by checking messages on his phone. Debby kept looking at the device greedily. Her own mobile had been taken from her at the booking desk. Half an hour had passed, and she was suffering the texting DTs.

'What did we ever do without these?' Rebus asked out loud, twisting the knife.

'So when do we get out?' Liz Doherty was fixing him with a look.

'When the process says you can,' Rebus assured her. 'But I'm still waiting to hear where the rest of the stuff is. Hidden up a lane somewhere? Or how about Princes Street Gardens? Me, I'd probably say the Gardens. Edinburgh's not your turf. Laziest option's probably the one you went for.' He turned his attention back to his phone's screen.

'Am I warm?' he asked into the silence. 'Toasty warm,' he decided.

He gave it a couple more minutes, then got up, stretched, and left the room. Liz Doherty was reminding him about the tea as he closed the door on her. He went to the machine and got one for himself, then took it outside so he could smoke a cigarette. He had half a mind to phone his colleague, Siobhan Clarke. She was on a surveillance operation and hadn't replied to the dozen or so mischievous texts he'd sent her over the course of the past twenty-four hours. It was mid afternoon, but dark and damp in the car park. A metal No Smoking notice on the brick wall had seen so many butts stubbed out on it that its message had been all but obliterated. Rebus stood next to it and tried not to think about Christmas. He would be on his own, because that was how he liked it. There were a couple of pubs he could visit on the day itself. He'd buy himself something decent for dinner, and a better-than-usual bottle of malt. Maybe a few CDs and a DVD box-set. Sorted. Then, mid evening would come the phone call or the door buzzer. Siobhan Clarke, feeling sorry for him and maybe a little for herself, though she would never admit it.

She'd want them to watch a soppy comedy, or go for a stroll through the silent streets. He had already considered his options, but felt he couldn't let her down, couldn't scurry out of town for the day or unplug his phone.

'Humbug,' he said, stabbing the remains of his cigarette against the sign.

Back indoors, a couple of officers were discussing the bag-snatcher. He'd gone and done it again, the little sod. His targets were the elderly and infirm, walking frames and wheelchairs a speciality. There'd be a handbag hanging from one or the other, and he'd have his hand in and out of it in a flash, hurtling from the scene with bus passes, purses and keepsakes, none of which ever turned up, meaning he was either dumping them intelligently or else keeping them as trophies. Description: denims and a dark hooded top. The local evening paper had been having a go at the police for their inability to stop him, interviewing victims and potential targets.

Shopping centres were what he liked. The Gyle, Waverley, Cameron Toll.

'Got to be the St James Centre one of these days,' one of the officers was saying. Yes, that was Rebus's feeling, too. The St James Centre, sited at the east end of Princes Street. Plenty of exits. All on one level, meaning it was popular with the walking frames and wheelchairs.

Walking frames and wheelchairs ...

Rebus ran a finger from his chin to his Adam's apple, then made his way back to the interview room.

There had obviously been a bit of a falling-out. The daughter was up on her feet, standing in one corner with her back to the room. The mother had decided to turn away from her in her chair. Rebus cleared his throat.

'All out of tea,' he said. 'But I've brought something else instead.'

Both women turned their heads towards him. Both asked the same question: 'What?'

'A deal,' Rebus said, retaking his seat and motioning for Debby Doherty to do the same.

Siobhan Clarke had another two hours left of her shift. She was seated in an unmarked car alongside a detective constable called Ronnie Wilson. The small talk had run out of steam almost before it had begun. Ronnie had no interest in football or music. He built models – galleons and racing cars and the like. There were blobs of glue on the tips of his fingers, which he took delight in picking clean.

And he had a cold, a persistent sniffle. Siobhan had tried the radio, but he only seemed to like the classical station, and then proceeded to hum along to the first three tunes, causing Siobhan to switch the sound off. There was a faint aroma in the car: the cheese and onion sandwich Wilson had brought with him from home; the chive and sour cream crisps he'd bought from a petrol station. Every now and then he would attempt to dislodge a morsel from between his teeth with his tongue or a fingernail, making sucking noises throughout.

They were parked in a suburban street. It was lined with cars and vans, meaning they stood out less. They were sixty yards shy of John Kerr's bungalow. The family was at home – wife Selina and teenage son and daughter. Everyone but John Kerr himself. Kerr had gone on the run from prison two days ago. He'd been done for fraud, tax evasion and a dozen or so further money-related crimes, but all without landing his employer in it with him. Kerr was the accounting brain behind Morris Gerald Cafferty's operation. Cafferty had more or less run Edinburgh these past several decades. If money was to be made from anything illegal, you'd usually find his name linked to it somewhere. But despite a lengthy court appearance and a slew of questions and inferences, Kerr had kept his trap shut. Then, on a community work placement to the west of the city, he'd simply walked off the job and not come back.

Siobhan had the files with her. They took up half the back seat, and every now and then she would reach for one and flick through it. Kerr had been sentenced to two and a half years, but with good behaviour and incentives would serve only nine or ten months. A model prisoner, it said in the report. Helping inmates on a literacy programme; working in the library; keeping himself to himself. Of course, no one was going to have a pop at him – he was protected by his employer's reputation. So why did he do a runner? As far as anyone could see, the answer had to be Christmas. He wasn't due to be released until March. There were photos in one of the folders. Kerr playing Santa Claus at an old people's home; Kerr – again dressed as Santa – donating a Christmas tree to a city hospice; Kerr with a sack of toys as he arrived at a special needs school ...

Siobhan stared through the windscreen. The bungalow was unassuming. The car in the driveway was a five-year-old mid-range Jaguar. The wife worked behind the desk at a health centre. The kids went to a private school, but that was far from unusual in Edinburgh. It didn't appear to be a lavish lifestyle for a man who'd had two million pounds in his various accounts at the time of his arrest. Siobhan studied his photograph again. Kerr was fifty, short and overweight. That was why they were guessing he'd use the front door. An eight-foot-high fence went around the rest of the property, disguised by leylandii. Nobody could envisage Kerr shinning his way into his garden. He would use front gate, path and door.

Because of Christmas. Because Christmas obviously meant something to him. Siobhan had already asked Wilson what plans he had for the big day. He was travelling to see his parents, who lived in Peterhead. He'd catch up with old pals from school. Boxing Day would see a schedule of visits to members of what seemed to be a hugely extended family. Siobhan just had her mum and dad, and they were in England. She could surprise them, turn up out of the blue, but she knew she wouldn't. She had to visit Rebus, make sure he wasn't sinking. Keep his spirits up. He would miss her if she didn't.

She looked at the clock on the dashboard. An hour and forty minutes till the changeover. She felt muzzy from inactivity. She'd taken a couple of breaks, walking around the block. Christmas trees in most of the windows, lights sparkling. One householder had gone a bit further, adding an outdoor display: reindeer and sleigh on the roof; a waterfall effect cascading down the walls and past the windows; polystyrene snowman next to the front step. Her own decorations hadn't been put up yet. They were still in their box in the hall cupboard. She was wondering whether it was worth going to all the trouble when no one would see them but her.

Wilson was whistling through his teeth. Sounded vaguely like a carol. There was a newspaper on his lap, crossword and other puzzles completed. He was drumming his fingers against the newsprint. Ten seconds he'd been at it, and she was already irritated. But he stopped and jerked his head around as the car's back door flew open. Files and folders were shoved aside. Someone had climbed in and was slamming the door shut again. Siobhan looked in the rear-view mirror.

'Evening,' she said. Then, for Wilson's benefit: 'Don't panic. He's with us. DC Wilson, meet DI Rebus.'

Wilson had had a shock and was slow to recover. He stretched out a trembling hand, which Rebus met with his own.

'Smells like a chip shop in here,' Rebus stated.

'My fault,' Wilson owned up.

'Don't apologise, son. I'm quite liking it.'

'What brings you here?' Siobhan asked.

'You never got back to me.' Rebus was trying to sound aggrieved.

Siobhan's eyes met his in the mirror. 'No, I didn't,' she said. 'So you thought you'd come and gloat in person?'

'Who's gloating? Nice warm car. Bit of a chinwag and a read of the papers ... not a bad way to spend a shift. Some of us are out there on the front line.'

Siobhan's face creased into a smile.

'I haven't heard any reports,' Wilson said in all seriousness.

'Princes Street's a war zone, son. Those Christmas shoppers are like something out of a video game.' Rebus made show of peering in the direction of the bungalow. 'No sign of Al Capone? Do we think he's armed and dangerous?' He had opened one of the files. He knew about John Kerr, knew all about him. Cafferty had been top of Rebus's hit list for most of his professional life. He was picking up the photos Siobhan had been looking at, the Christmas shots.

'I doubt he'll be armed,' Wilson said into the silence, having given the matter some thought. Rebus and Siobhan shared a look. 'Nothing in his profile suggests violent tendencies.'

'Violent tendencies?' Rebus was nodding slowly. He patted Wilson on the shoulder. 'With insights like that, son, you're headed to the top. Wouldn't you agree, DS Clarke? Young officers like Wilson here are the future of the force.'

Siobhan Clarke managed the slightest of nods. Wilson looked as if his name had just been announced at school prize-giving.

'Let me ask you this,' Rebus went on. He had Wilson's full attention now. 'What makes you think Kerr'll come back here? Won't he know we're waiting for him to do just that?'

'No sign of the family shipping out elsewhere for Christmas,' Siobhan felt obliged to respond.

Rebus was shaking his head. 'They don't need to. But tell me this ...' She saw that he was holding up one of the photos of Kerr dressed as Santa Claus. 'Where's St Nick going to go when his sledge lands in our fair city?'

'Rooftops?' Wilson guessed. 'Chimneys?' He even looked out towards the bungalow, as if scanning the skies above it.

Siobhan kept silent. Rebus would tell them eventually. Tell them what he'd gleaned in two minutes that they'd been unable to work out over the past two days. But instead he posed a further question.

'Where do *all* the jolly Santas go?'

And then, for the first time, Siobhan knew the answer.

Two in the afternoon, a couple of hours of daylight left, and Princes Street Gardens was filling up. The Festival of Santas drew locals as well as tourists to watch a couple of hundred Father Christmases running for charity. Some participants were changing into their costumes; others had arrived suited and bearded. As usual, there were some flourishes: a tartan suit instead of the archetypal red; a long blue beard in place of white … It was a well-organised event. Each runner had raised money by sponsorship. They'd registered beforehand and were given numbers to attach to their costumes, just like any other athlete. Registration was a bonus for Siobhan: made it easy to check the alphabetised list of runners to ensure there was no one called John Kerr on it.

'Could be using an alias,' Wilson had proposed.

But it was much more likely he would just turn up, hoping to blend in with the other runners. Except he wouldn't quite blend in. He'd be the Santa with no number on his back.

'Bit of a long shot?' Wilson had suggested.

No, not really; just annoying that Rebus had thought of it first. A chance for Kerr to spend time with his family without the fear of being apprehended as he entered his home. Siobhan rubbed her hands together, trying to put some feeling back into them. She and Wilson had watched the taxi pull to a stop outside the bungalow. They'd watched Selina Kerr and her son and daughter come out of the house. They had stayed a couple of cars back from the cab as it headed for the city centre.

'Bingo,' Siobhan had said as the cab signalled to a stop on Princes Street.

But then there had been a slight glitch. The son, Francis, had begun a conversation on the pavement with his mother. She had seemed to remonstrate with him. He'd touched her arm, as if to reassure her, then had turned and walked away, sticking his hands into the front of his jacket. His mother had called after him, then rolled her eyes.

'Should we split up?' Wilson had suggested to Siobhan. 'I'll tail him, you stay with mother and daughter?'

Siobhan had shaken her head.

'What if he's off to see his dad?'

'He's not. I think that's what's got his mum narked.'

As Francis Kerr melted into the crowd of shoppers, Selina Kerr and daughter Andrea crossed the street towards the Gardens. They weren't the only ones, of course. Probably a thousand or more spectators would be on hand to watch the runners. But Siobhan and Wilson had no trouble keeping them in view, thanks to Andrea's bright-pink knee-length coat and matching bobble hat.

'Not exactly subtle,' was Rebus's comment when they caught up with him. He was finishing a mug of glühwein from the German market, and a garlicky sausage smell was wafting up from his fingers.

'Getting in the spirit?' Siobhan asked.

'Always.' He smacked his lips and glanced towards mother and daughter. 'Was I right or was I right?'

'Well, they're here,' Siobhan commented. 'But that could just be family tradition.'

'Aye, right.' Rebus took out his mobile phone and checked the screen.

'We keeping you from something?' Siobhan asked.

'Bit of business elsewhere,' Rebus stated. People were milling around. Some had started taking photographs of the Santas, or of the glowering Castle Rock, acting as background scenery to this performance. A DJ had been installed on the Ross Bandstand and was playing the usual favourites, between which he doled out instructions to the runners and interviewed a few of them. One Santa had run from Dundee to Edinburgh, collecting money all the way. There was a cheer from the crowd and a round of applause.

'They don't seem to be on the lookout for anyone,' Wilson commented, watching the mother and daughter.

'Don't seem that excited either,' Siobhan added.

'This was probably Kerr's idea,' Rebus suggested. 'They'd much rather be meeting him in the Harvey Nicks café, but Kerr needs his wee annual dressing-up fix.' He paused. 'Where's the son?'

'Francis came as far as Princes Street,' Siobhan explained, 'but then went his own way.'

Rebus watched Selina Kerr check the time and then turn to peer in the direction of the gates. She said something to her daughter, who glanced in the same direction, gave a shrug, then did some texting on her phone.

'Can we get any closer?' Wilson asked.

'If Kerr sees us, we lose him,' Siobhan cautioned.

'Always supposing he's coming. What if he's meeting them one at a time? The son comes back and the daughter heads off?'

'It's a fair point,' Rebus agreed. 'We can only wait and see.' He looked at his own phone again.

'This bit of business ...' Siobhan began. Rebus just shook his head.

'Think he'll actually do any running?' Wilson was asking.

'Not without a number. The organisers are pretty strict.'

Rebus's phone was ringing. He held it to his ear.

'Ten minutes left until the start,' the DJ was announcing. 'Get those limbs warmed up. Can't have any Santa cramps ...'

'Yes?' Rebus asked into the phone.

'We didn't get him.' It was Debby's voice. She was calling from the St James Centre. Rebus could hear noises in the background: bystanders, trying to comfort Liz.

'He got away?' Rebus guessed.

'Aye. Fast as a ferret. Maybe if you'd been here ...'

'What about security?'

'The guy's right here. Ferret shot past him. Got away with the purse.'

The purse with nothing in it. The purse sitting in a tempting position at the top of the shopping bag on the back of the wheelchair.

The bait.

The bait that had so nearly worked.

'Description?' Rebus asked.

'Same one you gave us. Just another hoodie with trackie bottoms and trainers ...'

'Hey, look,' Wilson was saying. There was a Santa standing just behind Selina Kerr and her daughter. Behind them and between them. Talking to them. Andrea Kerr spun round and gave him a hug.

'That him?' Wilson was asking.

'We tried, though,' Debby was telling Rebus. 'We did what you told us to. So the deal's still good, eh? You'll still put in a word?'

'I have to go,' Rebus told her. 'Be at the police station in an hour. I'll meet you there.'

'And you'll put in a word?'

'I'll put in a word.'

'We're the Holly and Ivy Bandits, remember ...'

Rebus slid the phone back into his pocket.

'Is it him?' Siobhan was asking. There were so many heads between them and the Kerrs, and the light was already fading.

'Got to be.' Wilson was sounding agitated, ready to barge in there.

'Is there a number on his back? Let's get a bit closer.' Siobhan was already heading off. Rebus clasped a hand around Wilson's forearm.

'Nice and slow,' he cautioned.

They took a wide curve around and behind the three figures. The three figures in animated conversation.

A young man brushed past Rebus, and the three were suddenly four. Francis Kerr had his hands stuffed in his pockets. Black hooded top ... tracksuit bottoms ... dark blue trainers ... He was sweating, breathing hard. Nodded at Santa without taking his hands from the pouch on the front of his jacket. Santa gave him a playful punch on the shoulder. Rebus decided it was time to move, Siobhan and

Wilson flanking him. The competitors were being called to the starting line.

'All right, John?' Rebus said, tugging down the elasticated beard and staring into the face of John Kerr.

'Leave him alone,' Selina Kerr snarled. 'He's not done anything.'

'Oh, but he has. He's led young Francis here astray.' Rebus nodded in the son's direction. John Kerr's brow furrowed.

'How do you mean?'

'Might not be your influence,' Rebus allowed. 'Might be your employer's. But something's rubbed off, hasn't it, Francis?' Rebus turned towards the youth. 'Private school and plenty of money ... makes me wonder why you'd take the risk.' He held out his hand. 'Still got the purse, or did you ditch it already? Bit miffed that it was empty, I dare say. But there's plenty of CCTV. Plenty of witnesses, too. Wonder what the search warrant'll turn up in your bedroom ...'

'Francis?' John Kerr's voice was shaking. 'What's he talking about?'

'Nothing,' the son muttered. His shoulders were twitching.

'Then take your hands out and show me.' When his son made show of ignoring this, Kerr took a step forward and hauled both hands out from their hiding place. The purse dropped to the ground. Selina Kerr clamped a hand to her mouth, but Andrea didn't seem surprised. Rebus thought to himself: she probably knows; maybe he told her, proud of his little secret and desperate to share.

'Well now,' Rebus said into the silence. 'There's good news as well as bad.' John Kerr stared at him. 'The bad news,' he went on, 'is that the two of you are coming with us.'

'And the good?' John Kerr asked in a voice just above a whisper.

'Courts won't be sitting until after Christmas. Means the two of you can share a cell at the station for the duration of the festivities.' He looked towards mother and daughter. 'I don't suppose a visit's out of the question either.'

There were whoops and screams from the spectators. The race had begun. Rebus glanced in Siobhan's direction.

'Don't say I never give you anything,' he told her. 'And this year,' gesturing towards Kerr's Santa outfit, 'it even comes gift-wrapped ...'

The Passenger

'She was from Edinburgh.'

'The victim?'

Siobhan Clarke shook her head and gestured towards the book Rebus was holding. 'Muriel Spark.'

It was a slim paperback, not much more than a hundred pages. Rebus had been looking at the blurb on the back. He placed the book on the bedside table where he'd found it.

'How much does a room like this cost?' he asked.

'Got to be a few hundred.' Clarke saw his look. 'Yes, that does mean per night.'

'With breakfast extra, I dare say.'

Clarke was opening the last drawer, checking it was every bit as empty as the others. The small suitcase lay on the floor under the window, unzipped and mostly unpacked. The victim had changed just the once. A toilet bag sat next to the sink in the bathroom. She had showered, made up her face, and brushed her teeth. Clothes lay rumpled on the floor next to the bed – short dress, slip, tights, underwear. A pair of black high-heeled shoes. Jewellery on the bedside table next to the book, including an expensive watch.

'Her name's Maria Stokes,' Clarke said. Rebus had picked up the woman's handbag. It had already been taken apart by the scene-of-crime team. Cash and credit cards still in her purse, meaning they were probably ruling out robbery as a motive.

'Where's she from?' Rebus asked.

'We don't know that yet. I've got someone going through her phone.'

'She didn't give an address when she checked in?'

'Not needed. Just signed her name and turned down the offer of a newspaper or wake-up call.'

'And this was Friday?'

'Friday afternoon,' Clarke confirmed. 'Do Not Disturb sign on the door, meaning it wasn't until lunchtime today that anyone bothered to knock.'

'And they knocked because ...?'

'Checkout's eleven. They needed to get the room ready. Called up from reception but of course she didn't answer. Just assumed she'd left, I suppose.'

'Maid must have got a fright.' Rebus was staring at the unmade bed. He thought Maria Stokes's outline was still there, contoured into the sheets and pillows.

'Doctor reckons she was probably killed the night she got here. Whoever did it, they were clever to put the sign on the door.'

'I suppose we're lucky she didn't pay for a week. How do you think he got in?'

'Either he had a key card, or he just knocked.'

Rebus nodded. 'Someone knocks, you'll assume it's staff. Hotel's the easiest place to walk in and out of, as long as you look like you belong.'

'We'll be asking the manager if there have been any problems.'

'Stuff going missing from rooms, you mean? Not the sort of thing they'd want to broadcast.'

'I wouldn't think so.'

Rebus was studying a card on the dressing table. 'There's a list here of all the different pillows you can request with your turndown service. Doesn't say if strangulation comes extra. What time's the autopsy?'

Clarke glanced at her watch. 'Just under an hour.'

'Staff are being questioned? CCTV?' Rebus watched her nod. 'Not much more for us to do here, then.'

'Not much,' she agreed.

He took a final look around. 'A better place to die than some, but even so ...'

'Even so,' Clarke echoed.

Maria Stokes had reverted to her own surname after the divorce. Her ex-husband's name was Peter Welburn. They had been separated for four years and divorced for one. No children.

Welburn sat in one of the small office cubicles at Gayfield Square police station. He was holding a mug of tea, focusing all his attention on it. He had just been explaining that Maria and he lived on opposite sides of Newcastle but were still friendly.

'Well, sociable, anyway. No nastiness.'

'The separation was amicable?' Clarke asked.

'We just sort of drifted apart – busy lives, usual story.'

'Where did she work?'

'She owns a graphic design business.'

'In Newcastle?' Rebus watched the man nod. 'Doing OK, is it?'

'Far as I know.' Welburn lifted one hand from the mug long enough to scratch the side of his head. He was in his late forties, a couple of years older than his ex-wife. Rebus reckoned they'd have made a good-looking couple – same sort of height and build.

'What do you do, Mr Welburn?' Clarke was asking.

'Architect – currently between projects.'

'Any support from Ms Stokes? Financially, I mean?'

The man shook his head. 'I hardly ever saw her – maybe a phone call or a text once a week.'

'But no nastiness?' Rebus asked, echoing Welburn's own words.

'No.'

'Did you know she was coming to Edinburgh?'

Another slow shake of the head.

'Did she have any friends in the city? Any connection to the place?'

'We visited a few times – years ago now. It's quick on the train. Used to book a B and B, hit a few of the pubs, maybe catch some music ...' Welburn's voice cracked as the memories took hold. He cleared his throat. 'It was terrible, seeing her like that.'

'Formal identification is always difficult on the loved ones,' Clarke offered, trying to sound sympathetic, though she had trotted out the same words so many times before.

'When was the last time you were in Edinburgh?' Rebus broke in. 'Before today, I mean?'

'Couple of years, probably.'

'And this past weekend ...?'

Welburn lifted his eyes to meet Rebus's. 'I was at home. With my girlfriend and her kid.'

Clarke lifted a hand. 'I'm sorry, but these things have to be asked.'

'Why would I want to kill Maria? It's insane.'

'Did she have anyone she was seeing? Someone she might have wanted to spend the weekend with?'

'No idea.'

'And I'm guessing no enemies that you'd know of?'

'Enemies?' Welburn's face crumpled. 'She was a sweetheart, an absolute angel. Even when we were splitting up, there wasn't any drama. We just ... got on with it.' He placed the mug on the desk and let his head fall into his hands, shoulders spasming as he sobbed.

*

'What do you reckon?' Clarke asked. She drummed her fingers on the steering wheel as she waited for the lights to change.

'Seemed genuine enough. Did the deceased take the train this time, or did she drive?'

'She didn't leave a car at the hotel. It's a five-minute walk from the station.'

'I didn't see a return ticket in her bag. Maybe her coat or jacket?'

'Don't think so.'

'Meaning she only bought a single. Does she strike you as the impetuous type?'

'We really don't know much about her.'

'Are you on to CID in Newcastle?'

Clarke nodded. 'They'll give her flat a look. See if there's a diary, or maybe something useful on her computer. You think she was meeting someone? Returning to Newcastle not uppermost in her mind?'

'Or she left in a hurry.'

'She'd taken some care packing that case. Didn't look thrown together in a panic.'

'Then we're not much further forward, are we?'

'Not much. But whoever did it, they've had three days to make themselves scarce.'

'And arrange an alibi.'

'That too,' Clarke agreed.

The general manager's name was Kate Ferguson. She met them in the airy reception and asked if anyone had offered them something to drink.

'We declined,' Clarke replied.

'Well then. This way.'

Ferguson led them to an office on the mezzanine level. Her size-able desk had been cleared of everything but a laptop computer. Two chairs awaited, both with a view of the screen.

'Two of your officers have already viewed the footage,' she said, in a tone that told them she was busy and important and wanted the whole business consigned to history.

'Just need to see for ourselves.'

'I'm sure we could have forwarded you a copy.'

Clarke offered a professional smile. 'We appreciate the hotel's cooperation.'

Realising that she had lost the skirmish, Ferguson used the mouse to start the film. Four onscreen squares, all in colour and of high quality: the outside steps, reception desk, lift and bar.

'This is her checking in,' she said. She was standing just behind the two detectives, her hand reaching between them to point to the top left square. 'Just the one overnight case, meaning she didn't need help with luggage and didn't want to be escorted to her room.'

'How long ago did she book?'

'Ten days.'

'By phone? Email?'

'It was an online booking.'

'She didn't say if it was business or pleasure?'

'She arrives dressed for business,' Clarke interrupted. 'Two-piece, neutral, flat shoes.'

The clothes that had been left in a pile on the bathroom floor, prior to her shower.

'She didn't hang anything up,' Rebus commented.

The action moved to the lift, Maria Stokes pushing the button. Then pushing it again a couple of times.

'She's in a hurry,' Clarke said.

'No calls that needed connecting to her room?' Rebus asked.

'Everyone has their own phone these days.' The general manager seemed every bit as irritated by this as by the intrusion of the police into her life.

'We're asking her service provider for a breakdown,' Clarke added for Rebus's benefit.

They watched as the lift doors opened and Maria Stokes got in. 'No cameras in the corridors?' Rebus enquired.

'No.'

'So someone could try the doors on every floor and not be spotted?'

'As I told your colleagues, that sort of thing has *never* happened here.'

'Why not?' Rebus turned to meet Ferguson's stare. 'It's a genuine question – seems to me you've left the place wide open.'

'Staff are rigorously vetted. They're also trained to tell a guest from someone who doesn't belong.'

'So what happens now?' Clarke interrupted. 'With Ms Stokes, I mean.'

Ferguson dragged the cursor along the timeline at the bottom of the screen.

'Seven twenty-three p.m.,' she said. 'As you can see, she's changed her outfit.'

Stokes was emerging from the lift, dressed in the clothes they had seen next to her bed. She looked nervous, scanning the lobby.

'A rendezvous?' Rebus offered. He watched as she made her way to the bar. She stopped at the threshold, a member of staff smiling a greeting.

'She's looking for someone, isn't she?' Clarke asked, to herself as much as anyone else.

'And not finding them,' Rebus added. Because now Stokes was shaking her head at the offer of a table. There seemed to be only two couples in the whole place. Friday night was happening elsewhere.

Back in the lobby, she stopped to talk to someone.

'That's one of our concierges,' Ferguson offered. 'Daniel. *Very* knowledgeable.'

'So what's he telling her?' Clarke asked.

'She wanted to know where to eat, where to drink.' Daniel was nodding in the direction of the bar. 'Of course,' Ferguson went on, sounding proud, 'he told her that our own bar and dining room couldn't be bettered.'

There was a little laugh from Maria Stokes, and she even touched the concierge on the arm.

'Friendly sort,' Rebus commented.

'His patter didn't seal the deal, though.' Clarke leaned in a little towards the screen, where Stokes was walking out of the hotel – the door held open by Daniel. She looked to right and left, until the obliging concierge emerged to point her in the right direction. Then off she went, slightly hesitantly, as though the height of her heels were a new and daunting experience.

'Which brings us to ...' Ferguson again used the mouse, dragging the cursor along the screen. 'Ten twenty-six.'

'So she was out and about for almost exactly three hours.' Clarke added the numbers to a small notepad. The sky was dark but the front of the hotel was brightly illuminated. The bar area was at last doing good business, and a middle-aged couple laden with luggage were checking in at the reception desk. There was no one to hold open the door for Maria Stokes, and she struggled a little. Tipsy strides across the floor to the lift, whose button she needed to press just the once, its doors sliding open immediately. A half-glance behind her as a man arrived from outside. She entered the lift and he hurried forward, squeezing in as the doors slid shut.

'Another guest?' Clarke asked.

'Or the person she was meeting?' Rebus added.

'Did she look as though she knew him?'

'Hard to say?' Rebus turned towards Ferguson. 'We need as clear a printout of his face as we can get. Then all the staff need to be shown it.'

'I assumed he was staying here,' Ferguson blurted out. 'Are you saying he could be the one who ...?' She lifted the palm of one hand to her mouth.

'As of right now, we're saying precisely nothing,' Rebus said in a warning tone. 'But we do need that printout.'

'Yes, of course. Anything while you're waiting? A tea or coffee maybe?'

'Tea would be fine,' Clarke said.

'Of course.'

'And one more thing,' Rebus said. 'Get Daniel to fetch it, please.'

'I only spoke to her that one time,' the concierge protested.

'Easy, Daniel. No one's accusing you of anything.'

They were in Ferguson's office, with the general manager on the other side of the door. Clarke was seated behind the desk and Daniel Woods opposite her, with Rebus standing off to one side, feet apart and arms folded. Woods was in his late twenties, lean and sharp-faced. His uniform consisted of charcoal waistcoat and tie, white shirt, dark trousers. Only the shoes really belonged to him, and they were scuffed and cheap.

'Actually,' Rebus broke in, '*I'm* accusing him of something.' He had Clarke's attention, while his was on the concierge. 'Faking your application, for a start. Ferguson's vetting's not as hot as she thinks. Been a while, though, hasn't it, Daniel? Since you did time, I mean.'

Woods's mouth opened but then closed again soundlessly.

'Don't know what it is that changes a man when they're put away,' Rebus ploughed on. 'But it sticks to them. Either that or I'm just receptive. Young Offenders, was it? Fighting or break-ins?'

Woods was running a finger along the edge of his gold-coloured badge, the one that identified him as Concierge. 'Drugs,' he eventually muttered.

'Wee bit of dealing? Probably grassed up by the competition. Clean since?'

'Ever since.' Woods tightened his jaw. 'So do I lose my job now or what?'

'Management hold you in high regard, Danny. I just wanted you to know how things lie, here in this room, between the three of us.'

'Right.'

'So tell us again.'

Woods took a deep breath. 'Just like I said. She looked dressed for a bit of fun, said she was after a wine bar or similar, somewhere she could maybe get a bite. She'd put on too much perfume and lipstick – trying that bit too hard. I wondered if she'd already had a drink, either that or a wee bit of powder or a tab.'

'Nothing out of the minibar,' Clarke interjected. 'No sign of drugs in her handbag.'

'Maybe it was just excitement, then. She was like one of those … cougars, is it?'

'An older woman out for a good time?'

'And a bit of male company,' Woods added with a nod.

'You didn't offer?' Rebus enquired.

'Not at all.'

'Don't tell me it hasn't happened in the past.'

'Not once.' The fixing of the jaw again. 'I mean, sometimes guests ask me to sort them out …'

'With an escort?'

Another nod. 'But I didn't get the feeling she was in the market.'

'So where did you send her?'

'The Abilene, on Market Street.'

Clarke looked to Rebus, who knew pretty much every pub in the city, but he just offered a twitch of one shoulder. 'Why there?' she asked Woods.

'It's not too raucous. They do bar food that's edible and pretty good cocktails.'

'You know anyone who works there?'

'Doddy works the door, but he wouldn't have been on duty till later.'

'What sort of crowd is it?'

'Office drones. Ties off and jackets over chairs while they work up a sweat on the dance floor. Tunes the ladies can sing along to. It can be a fun night.'

'Ms Stokes was back here by ten thirty.'

'Do we know she even went there? Plenty of other places in the vicinity.'

Clarke turned the laptop around so it was facing Woods. The CCTV footage had been paused. 'This man here,' she said, 'the one making for the lift.'

'What about him?'

'A guest?'

'Might be.'

'You don't recognise him?'

Woods shook his head. 'Has he got something to do with it?'

Clarke didn't answer. Instead she swivelled the laptop back around again.

'One way to tell if he's a guest,' Woods offered.

'What's that?'

'Keep watching. See if he leaves ...'

With Clarke supplied with another pot of tea and the fast-forward function, Rebus stepped outside for a cigarette. He'd just missed a shower and the pavement glistened, the evening crowd hurrying past, some with hair still dripping. The doorman knew he was a cop and didn't have anything to say. He was in his sixties and had the thickset build and squashed nose of a one-time boxer. Pale blue eyes sinking into puffy red-veined flesh. He held a rolled umbrella, ready for any taxi that might arrive.

Someone had died a few windows up, strangled in their bed, the last moments of their life filled with horror and terror. Rebus doubted any of the pedestrians would care. They had worries of their own and not half enough time. As he headed back inside, the doorman cleared his throat.

'Papers have been sniffing,' he said.

'Make sure they cough up for anything you give them,' Rebus advised. As reward, the door was held open for him, as if he were a regular and cherished guest, the kind that always tipped.

At reception, Rebus showed his ID and asked for the key to 407. He shared the lift with a young couple who didn't look as if they were going to make it fully clothed to their room. Rebus slid the key card into 407's lock, stepped inside and switched on the light. Everything deemed potential evidence had been removed by the forensics team since his last visit – sheets and pillowcases, Stokes's bag and belongings. But the book was still there. Maybe someone had decided that it belonged to the hotel or a previous guest. Maybe it did at that. Rebus picked it up and sniffed it. It smelled faintly of perfume. It was called *The Driver's Seat* and had obviously been turned into a film – the cover showed a heavily made-up Elizabeth Taylor. It had cost £1.25 when first published, but had been bought second-hand for twice that, according to a pencilled price on the inside cover. The author's biography was there, too: born and educated in Edinburgh ... spent time in Africa ... became a Roman Catholic ... Rebus nodded to himself when he came to the title of another of her books: *The Prime of Miss Jean Brodie*. He'd gone to see the film when it had come out. Had it been on a double bill with something else Scottish ...? *The Wicker Man*, maybe? Closing the book, he rubbed his thumb over Elizabeth Taylor's face, removing a light dusting of fingerprint powder. Then he stuck the book in his jacket pocket, went over to the chair in the corner, and sat down to think.

'Quarter past four,' Clarke said, sounding satisfied.

Rebus walked around the desk so she could show him what she'd found. The lift doors opening and the man emerging, moving briskly across the floor. No one around at all.

'There's a night manager,' Clarke explained. 'But he's in an office somewhere. If you're late back, there's a bell you can press and he'll come let you in. But if you're already in, you just push the bar on the door and you're gone.'

Which was what the visitor had done. Walking out of shot into what remained of the night, hands digging into his pockets. The other cameras showed a silent reception desk and a closed bar.

'Half past ten till quarter past four,' Rebus commented, lifting a photocopied still from next to the laptop – the general manager had provided half a dozen, all showing the clearest shot of the man. 'Doesn't take that long to throttle someone.'

'Well,' Clarke replied, as though she'd given it some thought, 'first you've got to get good and angry.' She picked up another of the photos and studied it.

'Because things aren't turning out as planned?' Rebus guessed.

'Maybe.' She stretched her spine, rolling her shoulders and neck.

'It's been a long day,' Rebus sympathised. 'Can I buy you a drink?'

'I've got to go home. Bills to open, plants to water. Need me to give you a lift?'

Rebus was shaking his head. 'I'll walk,' he said.

'Without your course deviating at any point into some pub or other?'

'Oh ye of little faith,' Rebus tutted, his smile eventually matching hers.

'Are you Doddy?'

Time was, all that was required of a bouncer was that he look scary. But these days they had to be smartly dressed too. The man giving Rebus a hard stare wasn't tall, or especially broad, but there was plenty of muscle beneath the black woollen coat and polo neck. An earpiece coiled down past his collar, and an embossed photo ID was strapped high up on one arm.

'Anything wrong, officer?'

Rebus had been about to dig his warrant card from his pocket, but smiled instead. 'Guilty as charged,' he said. The doorman shook his head when Rebus offered a cigarette. He got his own lit and blew the smoke upwards. 'Quiet tonight,' he commented.

'Usual Monday. Money's all spent.'

'That explain the half-price drinks?' Rebus nodded towards a poster to one side of the door.

'Might be an extra reduction for members of the constabulary.'

'Fruit-flavour shots, though – which rots first, the liver or the teeth?'

Doddy dredged up a thin smile. 'So that's the ice broken. Now what do you want?'

'The tourist strangled in her hotel room – I assume you've heard.'

'It was on the news.'

'Friday night around half past seven, we think she came by here.' Rebus described Maria Stokes and Doddy nodded slowly.

'I remember,' he said. 'We get a few single women coming here, but not too many.'

'Did she say anything?'

'Just asked if it cost anything to get in.'

'Did you see her come out again?'

'No.'

'Might have been just before ten thirty.'

'There was a bit of an altercation. Stag party trying to get in. Two of them could barely stand.'

'There'll be CCTV inside, yes?' As Doddy nodded, Rebus held up the photo of the man from the hotel foyer. 'Recognise him?'

'Might have seen him.'

'To talk to?'

'Don't think so.'

'Is he a regular?'

'No. Just looks familiar. Should I tell the boss you want a chat?' The doorman held up his wrist, showing Rebus the mic secreted there.

'I think so,' Rebus said.

Inside, the Abilene was a single room, a long rectangle with a dance floor at one end and a raised dining area at the other, with a shiny chrome bar separating the two. There were about thirty people in the place, only four of them dancing to piped music. Rebus didn't recognise the singer and couldn't make out the words. It was the kind of thing he only heard being pumped from cars, usually driven by young men with carburettor problems.

'Let me get you a drink,' the manager said. 'I'm guessing you're either whisky or beer.'

'An IPA, thanks,' Rebus said. The manager's name was Terry Soames. He was in his late twenties and dressed in a suit that looked made for him. Open-necked shirt and an unadorned silver chain around his throat. They perched on stools at the bar while their drinks were fetched.

'I'd like to see the footage from Friday night,' Rebus said, having explained about Maria Stokes.

'I wish I could help,' Soames apologised, sipping orange juice. 'But we record on a loop. Every forty-eight hours there's a refresh. We only store the pictures if there's been a problem.'

'There was a problem Friday night.'

Soames thought for a moment. 'The stag party? Doddy dealt with that. They didn't get in.'

'This is someone we'd like to talk to,' Rebus went on, placing the photo on the bar. 'Doddy says he's a known quantity.'

'Not to me.' Soames was peering at the face. He gestured for the barman to join them. 'Any ideas, James?'

'He's been in a few times.'

'Got a name?' Rebus asked.

The barman pursed his lips, then shook his head. 'He paid with a card, though.'

'He did?'

'I remember because the first two tries at his PIN, he got it wrong. Couple of drinks too many. He managed on the third go. We had a little joke about it.'

Rebus turned his attention to Terry Soames.

'My office,' Soames said. 'We keep the receipts in the safe ...'

Clarke was already at her desk when Rebus got into Gayfield Square next morning.

'Autopsy and forensics,' she said, gesturing towards the paperwork in front of her.

'Anything useful?'

'Plenty of prints in the room – too many, in fact. Seems housekeeping didn't do a great job with a duster.'

'How about the Do Not Disturb sign?'

'Just the victim's prints on that.'

Rebus ran a hand along his jawline. 'They sure?'

'Positive.'

'So our notion that the attacker put the sign up to stop anyone going in ...'

'May need rethinking. Victim had downed a fair few gin and tonics and eaten nothing but salted peanuts. No drugs. Signs of sexual intercourse – traces of the lubricant from a condom.'

'No condom in the room, though.'

'And no wrapper either. So the assailant either pocketed both or else flushed them. And we can't be sure if penetration was pre- or post-mortem. No signs of trauma.'

Rebus rubbed at his jaw again. 'We're saying this is all the one guy? She picks him up in a bar and takes him to her room. Instead of saying thank you, he then strangles her?'

'It's the simplest explanation, no?'

Eventually Rebus nodded.

'There are some strands of hair that don't seem to match the victim ...' Clarke was skimming the pages. 'Et cetera, et cetera.' She paused, holding up one final sheet. 'And then there's this.'

Rebus took the piece of paper from Clarke and started to read as she spoke.

'A team from Newcastle went to her flat. Everything neat and tidy, but there was stuff next to her computer, including correspondence from her GP and a couple of hospitals ...'

'Brain tumour,' Rebus muttered.

'Shelf in her bathroom stacked with strong painkillers, none of which she brought to Edinburgh – unless *he* lifted them.'

Rebus placed the sheet of paper on top of the others. 'She was dying.'

'Maybe Edinburgh was on her bucket list.'

'Maybe.'

'Ironic, though, isn't it? You head north to let your hair down. You want to feel something, so you maybe don't bother deadening the pain with drugs. And you end up meeting the one man you shouldn't.'

'Ironic, yes,' Rebus echoed, though he didn't really believe it. 'And his name's Robert Jeffries, by the way.'

'What?'

'The man who went up to her room with her. I'm in the process of getting an address.'

'You better take a seat and tell me.'

Rebus nodded his agreement. 'But can we make it quick?'

Clarke just stared at him.

'I have a book I need to read,' he explained.

*

That evening, Rebus and Clarke sat in the office, listening to the recording that had been made of their interview with Robert Jeffries. A lawyer had been present throughout, but Jeffries had made it clear that he had nothing to hide and wanted to explain.

'That's good, Mr Jeffries,' Clarke had said. 'And we appreciate your help.'

'I hate my voice,' she said to Rebus as she listened.

'Hush,' he chided her.

'I was in the Abilene,' Jeffries was saying. 'It's a nightclub on Market Street. I don't go often, but sometimes the boredom gets to me. Ever since Margaret passed away, I've found my life ... not withering away exactly. Squeezed into a box maybe. Just the telly and the computer, you know. Used to go to the football, but I lost interest. Stopped returning friends' calls. Bit pathetic really.'

Rebus's voice: 'Why the Abilene in particular?'

'I suppose it's handy for the train back to Falkirk. You can sit at the bar and sometimes people talk to you. Even if they don't, you can watch them enjoying themselves. I used to reminisce about clubs me and Margaret went to. Duran Duran was her thing. Simon Le Bon. Even in the living room, I'd come home and find her shimmying around the place.'

There was a pause. A plastic cup of water was being lifted, sipped from, placed with care back on the table. A chair creaked as the lawyer shifted slightly, trying to get more comfortable.

'I only meant to have a couple of drinks that night, but then she was standing beside me. I told her I liked her perfume. She laughed. Really nice white teeth. So then we got talking. Gin and tonic she was drinking. With a slice of lime rather than lemon, and not too much ice. After the third round, they brought us some peanuts and pretzels. She didn't like pretzels.'

Clarke: 'What did you talk about?'

'My job ... her job. She'd dumped her husband – that was the word she used, "dumped" – and found herself a nice flat near the river in Newcastle. I said I'd been through it on the train to York and London but never stopped. She said I should. "It's full of life." *She* was full of life. It was like sparks were coming off her. Deep dark eyes and a nice husky voice. A couple of times I thought she was losing interest – she would scan the room, smiles for everybody. But then she would turn her attention back to me. I was ... flattered.'

Rebus: 'Whose idea was it to leave?'

'Hers. I think she saw me glance at my watch. Horrible thing to say, but I was thinking of last trains. "You're not leaving?" she said. She sounded aghast that I might be. "It's Friday night, you need to live!" Then she mentioned her hotel and how it had a bar that would be getting lively. I honestly thought that was where we were heading.'

Another pause.

'No, I'm lying. I *hoped* that after the bar there'd be an invite to her room. I was tingling all over. Feelings I hadn't had in years. But as it turned out, the bar wasn't the destination she had in mind.'

Clarke: 'You paid for the drinks like a gentleman?'

'I nearly didn't, though. I got my PIN wrong twice.'

Rebus: 'Footage from the hotel entrance shows you a few seconds behind Ms Stokes ...'

'Yes. I thought I'd lost my phone. I stopped to check my pockets. By the time I caught up, she was already in the lift. So that was that.'

Rebus: 'But you'd come prepared? A condom, I mean?'

'That was hers. She had it in her bag.'

'You flushed it afterwards?'

'Yes.' Another pause for water. 'After I'd got dressed. We'd fallen asleep. I mean ... I was sure she was asleep. I woke up feeling awful. Pounding headache and everything.'

Clarke: 'We need you to tell us what happened, Mr Jeffries. Not just the before and the after.'

'Oh God ...'

There was a short interjection by the lawyer, but Jeffries started to make noises. Then: 'No, I *need* to say it. I need to!' Sniffling, nose-blowing, throat-clearing.

'I need you to know it wasn't me. I'm not the adventurous sort. I'd never even heard of it. I know now, though – auto-erotic asphyxiation. She said she liked it, said she wanted it. My hands around her throat while we had sex. "Squeeze tighter. Keep squeezing. Your thumbs. Harder ..." Oh Christ.' Another loud sob. 'And this look on her face, her eyes tight shut, teeth clenched. I thought she was enjoying it, getting into it. So I kept pressing down, pressing, pressing. And then I collapsed on her, rolled off, even said a few sweet nothings ... And passed out.'

Clarke: 'And when you woke up?'

'I got dressed as quietly as I could. Didn't want to wake her. I thought ... well, cold light of day and all that. She might hate herself or me.'

Rebus: 'You didn't check she was breathing?'

'She looked so peaceful. I still can't believe she was dead. It was an accident. A terrible, terrible accident ...'

Clarke: 'Why didn't you come forward, sir? Why did we have to fetch you?'

'I knew how horrible it would sound. The whole thing. And I didn't think.' A further pause. 'Just that, really – I didn't think ...'

Clarke stopped the recording and leaned back in her chair, staring across the desk at Rebus.

'You've had a chance to read it?' he asked.

She nodded and took the copy of *The Driver's Seat* from her drawer, flicking through its pages.

'It's a sort of nightmare,' she said. 'A woman travels to a strange city looking for someone to kill her. Not because she has cancer, but ... well, I'm not quite sure why. To create a sensation at the end of a mundane life?'

'Maybe.'

'The book gave Maria Stokes the idea?'

Rebus shrugged. 'The story doesn't turn out the way Maria's life did.'

'She *was* in the driving seat, though – is that what we're saying? With Robert Jeffries as her passenger – meaning we should feel sorry for him.'

'You don't sound as if you do.'

Clarke started gathering up all the loose sheets of paper on the desk, as if putting them in some sort of order were suddenly important.

'A single ticket,' Rebus said into the silence.

'Sorry?'

'She didn't buy a return because she wasn't going home. Yet she paid for three nights at the hotel – three shots at getting it right.'

'Her head was pretty messed up.'

'And she's messed up Robert Jeffries' head pretty good now too.' Rebus rose to his feet. 'Let me buy you a drink,' he said, reaching across the desk for the book.

'Anywhere but the Abilene.'

'Anywhere but the Abilene,' Rebus agreed.

Clarke placed the paperwork in a drawer, stood up and lifted her jacket from the back of her chair. She crossed to the window as she slipped it on. There was a whole city somewhere out there, waking to another night of possibility and accident, chance and fate, pity and fear.

A Three-Pint Problem

The missing man's car was found on the third day.

It was a gloss-black Bentley GT, parked in a bay two floors up at Edinburgh airport's multi-storey car park – a businessman had recognised it from the description on the news. When police arrived, they found the Bentley unlocked. No key, no parking chitty.

'So we've no idea what time it was left there,' Siobhan Clarke explained to Rebus on the way to the man's home.

'He took a flight?'

'We're checking.'

'Was the business in trouble? That's why people usually run.'

'According to the wife, things had picked up after a lean couple of years.'

'P.T. Forbes – I've been past the showroom many a time.'

'Me too. There was a red E-type in the window one time ...'

'You were tempted?'

'Until I saw the price tag. Plus: no power steering in those old models.'

'What does the P stand for, by the way?'

'Philip. The wife's name is Barbara. Twenty-six years married.'

Rebus had seen the photos of P.T. Forbes in the *Scotsman* and the *Evening News* – a head of thick silver hair, a bit of heft filling out a pinstripe suit. Always posing with one of his cars. He dealt in 'cherished' high-end automobiles, meaning second-hand but pricier than most new models.

'Was the Bentley his?' Rebus asked as Clarke slowed to a stop at a set of traffic lights. They were heading out of town down the coast, towards Musselburgh. The Forbes home was part of a small modern estate backing on to a newish golf course. Rebus reckoned the developer would have called it 'bespoke', like one of P.T. Forbes's motors.

'Not as such,' Clarke was answering. 'According to Mrs Forbes, he came home with a different car every week.'

'Must have been confusing when she came out of the supermarket looking for it.'

'She drives a Mini,' Clarke said.

The disappearance of Philip Forbes was out of character. He had left the house as usual at 9.30 on Monday morning, headed for his glass-fronted South Gyle premises. His wife hadn't begun to fret until 7 p.m. She had called her husband's right-hand man, but found him driving back from Carlisle, where he'd spent the day negotiating the purchase of an Aston Martin DB5. He in turn had called the showroom's receptionist, but she'd been at home all day with a migraine, having texted her boss to apologise.

Forbes had never replied. The showroom had remained closed all that day, mail sitting unopened on the floor.

Philip Forbes was what was known as 'a weel-kent face' in the city. He had been part of a group that had dug deep to try to keep one of the local football teams afloat, and he was photographed at plenty of charity balls and black-tie events. The local MPs and MSPs knew him, as did many councillors and the Lord Provost. Consequently, there was media interest, though no one had gone to the lengths of doorstepping the family home or setting up camp nearby.

Clarke signalled off the main road into Musselburgh and headed down a long straight lane. The modern two-storey golf club was visible in the near distance, the houses bordering it forming a wide crescent. They were constructed predominantly of brick, with feature windows, and garages big enough for three or four vehicles. Each house boasted a name rather than a number. The Forbeses lived at Heriots.

'They're all named after private schools,' Rebus pointed out as Clarke parked her car on the driveway.

Barbara Forbes was already at the door, one hand clasped in the other. She was dressed soberly, and hadn't bothered with her hair or make-up. There were tired cusps under her eyes.

'You've found the Bentley?' she said.

Clarke nodded her agreement, before identifying herself and Rebus.

'Come in,' Mrs Forbes said, backing up a couple of steps into a huge entrance hall. Polished wood underfoot, cream-coloured walls, and a wide central staircase. The space was flooded with light from a glass cupola.

'You know about the car?' Rebus was asking. 'We thought we were here to break the news ...'

'A reporter phoned me. He said it was at the airport.'

'I'm assuming your husband had no plans to fly anywhere?' Clarke enquired.

'Not that I know of.'

'Did he carry his passport with him?'

'It's kept in one of the drawers in the bedroom.'

'You've checked?'

The woman hesitated. 'I don't remember,' she finally admitted. 'Should I go and look?'

'Please,' Clarke said.

They watched her as she headed upstairs. Rebus walked across the hall to a set of double doors and opened them, entering a well-appointed living room. There was a flat-screen TV attached to one wall. French windows led to an enclosed patio beyond which stretched a professionally tended garden. Behind a further set of doors was a formal dining room. One more door and he was back in the entrance hall. Clarke had gone in the opposite direction and was emerging from the kitchen.

'Worth a look,' she informed him.

'Ditto,' he replied, gesturing over his shoulder.

The kitchen offered all mod cons, several of which Rebus failed to recognise. There was a table where he reckoned husband and wife took most of their meals. He nearly tripped over a narrow Persian rug, smoothing it back into place with the heel of his shoe. Off the kitchen was a smaller room, probably originally intended for laundry or as a walk-in pantry but converted into a home office. There were shelves crammed with paperwork, car brochures stacked on the floor, and a laptop computer on the wooden desk. It was currently in sleep mode, a green light on the side of the keyboard pulsing slowly. Rebus lifted a framed snapshot from the far corner of the desk. Voices were approaching, Clarke and Mrs Forbes entering the kitchen.

'No sign of it,' Clarke explained for Rebus's benefit.

'But why would he take a sudden notion to fly anywhere?' Barbara Forbes was asking, voice trembling a little.

'Your son?' Rebus asked, holding up the photo.

'Until five years ago,' she replied. Then, into the questioning silence: 'He took an overdose. In Thailand.'

Clarke was looking at the photo with its three smiling faces. 'I'm sorry,' she said.

'That picture was a couple of years before. Rory was twenty-two when he ...'

'Just the one child?' Rebus asked. The woman nodded. She seemed dazed, pinching the bridge of her nose and screwing shut her eyes for a moment.

'I hate to ask,' Rebus said, 'but is Rory buried here or in Thailand?'

She took a deep breath. 'We brought him home.' She suddenly saw what he was getting at. 'Why would Philip go to Thailand?'

Rebus could only shrug.

'We're checking with the airport anyway,' Clarke offered. 'Still no sign of him using his credit cards or withdrawing money?'

'It's been a few hours since I checked. I know he hasn't switched his phone on.'

'Oh?'

'He was very proud of some tracking thing he has on it. The phone's been off since Monday.' She paused. 'Should I look at the bank stuff again?'

'Might be an idea,' Clarke said. 'Maybe while I put the kettle on ...?'

Barbara Forbes went through to her husband's study and woke up the computer. Rebus followed her, placing the photo back where he'd found it.

'A terrible blow, losing your son like that,' he offered.

'Yes,' she agreed. She had taken a pair of spectacles from a pocket and was peering at the screen.

'Your husband must trust you,' Rebus added.

'In what way?'

'Allowing you to see all his finances.'

'This only lets me into our joint account.'

'He has others in his own name?'

She nodded. 'I've applied for access. Apparently it takes time. You think he's using those to fund his ... well, whatever it is he's doing or done? I mean, nobody's kidnapped him, have they?' She looked up at Rebus.

'There's no evidence of it.'

'Archie probably knows more about the company money than I do.'

'Archie being your husband's business partner?'

'Not partner, no – Archie works *for* Philip.'

'An employee, in other words. But he'd still know if Mr Forbes had dipped into the till, as it were?'

'I suppose so.'

'What about the receptionist?'

'What about her?'

'In my experience, they often know more about the place where they work than anyone else.'

'Then ask her.'

Rebus stayed silent for a moment, watching over her shoulder. 'Is this the only computer in the house?'

'We have laptops, too.'

'I'm guessing you've looked at Mr Forbes's emails?'

'Your lot told me to – there was nothing out of the ordinary.'

'How about stuff he deleted?'

'I'm sorry?'

'When you press delete, stuff doesn't just vanish.'

She was studying a list of recent transaction details. 'His cards still haven't been used,' she muttered.

'The ones you're able to check,' Rebus added.

'What were you saying about emails?'

'Even deleted ones will be stored somewhere, unless your husband really wanted them gone.'

She had closed the banking website and clicked on the email account.

'See where it says "deleted"?' Rebus reached past her so his finger nearly touched the screen. If you click on that ...'

She did so, and a long list appeared.

'I'd no idea,' she said.

Rebus's eyes were running down the items. They were mostly rubbish – offers for insurance and Canadian medicines. But one caught his attention, the one right at the top – received on the Sunday, the eve of Forbes's disappearing act. The subject line consisted of only the one word – Philip – followed by three exclamation marks. The sender was marked as Unknown.

'Can you open that?' Rebus asked.

Barbara Forbes did as she was asked, then gave a little gasp.

WE NEED TO MAKE A RUN FOR IT! THEY KNOW!!!

Nothing else. It didn't look as if Philip Forbes had replied. He had just deleted the message and followed the instruction.

'What does it mean?' Barbara Forbes's voice was shaking. Clarke was standing in the doorway, a carton of milk in her hand.

'You might want to offer Mrs Forbes something stronger,' Rebus said, gesturing towards the screen.

'It's called forensic computing,' Clarke told Rebus. They were in her car again. The laptop had spent the afternoon at the forensic science facility at Howdenhall. Now night had fallen and Rebus was holding his fifth or sixth takeaway coffee of the day.

'So just because it says "Sender Unknown ..."?'

'There's information tucked away for a lab coat to work with.'

'Like a deleted file that isn't actually deleted?'

'Exactly.'

Rebus drained the last of his drink. 'No news from the airport?'

'No record of P. T. Forbes as a passenger with any carrier.'

'But he did take his passport.'

'Airport might be a red herring. Plenty of other ways to leave the country.'

'It would help if we knew the why.'

'Fingers crossed Archie Sellers has some answers.'

They parked on a wide residential street near Inverleith Park. The houses were substantial. Archie Sellers's top-floor flat had been carved from one of them. The windows were small but gave views south across the city, the castle and Calton Hill silhouetted against the darker sky.

'Is this about Philip?' Sellers had asked when he'd answered the door. In place of an answer, Clarke had suggested they go in.

'Lovely view, Mr Sellers,' Rebus said as he stood by one of the living room's three windows. Sellers had lowered himself into a leather armchair. The room had a distinct bachelor feel to it: car magazines, a dartboard on the back of the door, untidy stacks of CDs on the floor next to a hi-fi system. 'Better than from the police station anyway.' With a smile, Rebus settled on the sofa beside Clarke.

'It was DS Rebus's opinion,' Clarke explained to Sellers, 'that Gayfield Square police station should be where we're having this little chat.'

Sellers's eyes widened a fraction. He hadn't shaved in a day or two and his collar-length hair was unruly. A generation younger than his employer, but maybe still too old for the distressed denims and Cuban-heeled boots.

'Why? What have I done?'

'How was business, Mr Sellers? Anything untoward that an audit might be about to throw up? VAT in order?'

'Things were fine.'

'Then how do you explain this?' Clarke unfolded the sheet of paper and held it up towards him, the message printed there clear to see. 'You sent this,' she stated.

'Did I?'

'We have proof that you did. Identifiers lead more or less straight back to your Hotmail account.'

'There must be a mistake.'

'Must there?' The two detectives sat side by side in silence, while Sellers twisted in his chair, looking as though it were made of drawing pins rather than cowhide. He sprang to his feet, but couldn't think what came next.

'Sit down,' Rebus ordered, glowering until Sellers obeyed.

Clarke turned the sheet of paper round again so she could recite the words. '"We need to make a run for it! They know!!!" Sent by you to Philip Forbes on Sunday afternoon at half past three. What was it the pair of you had to be scared of, Mr Sellers? And why are you still here?'

'It was a joke!' Sellers blurted out, clasping his hands around his knees.

'A joke?'

'A prank. I sent it to half a dozen people. Just to see what their reaction would be.'

'Who else got one?'

'A mate I play squash with ... couple of old school friends ... a cousin ... plus Philip and Andrea.'

'Andrea being ...?'

'She works for us.'

'On reception?'

'Reception, secretary, you name it. I was going to go into work on Tuesday and see what they said. It was supposed to be a bit of fun.' He paused. 'You don't know the story?'

'Enlighten us,' Clarke said, no emotion in her voice.

'Arthur Conan Doyle – Sherlock Holmes and all that. It was in an article I was reading about him. He sent an anonymous telegram to a few of his friends. It said something like "We've been rumbled! What will we do?"'

Sellers was grinning, with the eager-to-make-amends look of a schoolkid caught red-handed.

'And?' Rebus asked.

The grin vanished. Sellers licked his lips, eyes towards the floor. 'Apparently one of them did a runner. He was never seen again. That's what's happened, isn't it? Philip *did* have something he didn't want rumbled.'

'Any idea what that might have been?'

The man shook his head.

'Do you have a number for Andrea, Mr Sellers?'

'Andrea?'

'To verify your story.'

The man's face sagged further. 'She's going to be furious with me.' Then he thought of something. It was obvious in his eyes, in the way his spine stiffened.

'Yes?' Clarke nudged.

But Sellers shook his head.

'We'll need the other names, too,' Rebus stated. 'Your friends, your cousin ...'

'Can't I tell them myself?' Sellers begged.

Clarke eventually nodded. 'If you let us speak to them first, just so we hear it from them. After that, we'll hand the phone back to you and you can come clean.' She was gesturing towards Sellers's mobile. It was sitting on the coffee table, half hidden under the magazine he'd been reading only ten minutes ago, before his world started to go wrong.

'How funny is that joke looking now?' Rebus decided to enquire, as Sellers reached towards the phone.

They were seated in the back room of the Oxford Bar, having found a parking space right outside. That had been the deal: no convenient place to park, no stopping for a drink. Instead of which, Rebus was starting on his third pint while Clarke nursed a soda water and lime.

'I can take a taxi home if you want a proper drink,' Rebus had offered.

'And leave the car outside to be towed in the morning?'

'Right enough.'

There was an open packet of crisps in front of them, but neither had turned out to be hungry enough. The back room was midweek empty. Only four regulars in the front bar, and some European football game on the TV.

'So what have we got?' Clarke asked, playing with one of the beer mats.

'Maybe nothing at all. That email might not have anything to do with it.'

'Bit of a coincidence, though.'

'A bit, aye.' Rebus took another mouthful of beer.

'Is this your version of the three-pipe problem?' Clarke nodded towards Rebus's glass.

'The what?'

'Sherlock Holmes – when he was stuck, he smoked three pipes.'

'Not at the same time, I hope.'

She shook her head. 'And probably not tobacco either.'

'This might be the opposite.'

'Meaning?'

'Maybe we're thinking *too* hard.'

'So there's a nice simple explanation, and you're just about to provide it?'

'We should talk to Andrea.'

'The secretary?'

'You saw it, didn't you? Sellers was thinking how mad she was going to be with him ...'

'He froze for a second.'

'He did, didn't he? And someone like Andrea – working the phones, making appointments, doing the paperwork ...'

'Might know what the big bad secret was?'

Rebus was nodding slowly, his glass halfway to his mouth.

'First thing tomorrow then,' Clarke decided. 'Reckon her migraine will have gone?'

'You think that's why she stayed home Monday?' Rebus asked. His eyes were twinkling behind the pint as he tipped it towards him.

They sat in Clarke's car and watched the receptionist unlock the showroom. Through the plate-glass window they saw her walk briskly to a keypad on the wall behind her desk and disarm the alarm. Her phone was already ringing and she answered it, pushing stray locks of hair back behind one ear.

'Ten sharp,' Rebus commented, tapping his wristwatch.

'Much the same time the boss usually arrives.'

'I'd say Archie Sellers then slopes in a bit later. Not quite as dedicated.'

'Not like us.'

No, because they'd already had to brief their own boss on the case – half past eight in his office. For once he'd seemed apologetic – pressure bearing down on him from above; all those politicians who considered P.T. Forbes a friend, an ally, a contributor.

Having dealt with the call, the receptionist shrugged off her coat. Rebus judged her to be in her late twenties or early thirties. Good-looking. Seated at her desk, she suddenly seemed at a loss what to do next. She got up and walked over to one of the gleaming cars, ran a finger along its paintwork.

'Maserati,' Clarke stated.

'I knew that,' Rebus said, opening the passenger door.

'Liar,' Clarke retorted, removing the key from the ignition.

'She didn't drive,' she added as they crossed the empty forecourt.

'So I noticed.' Rebus was pushing open the showroom door, a

smile on his face. 'Nice Maserati,' he said, gesturing towards the car.

'Can I help you?'

'You're Andrea ...?'

'Mathieson,' she obliged. 'Are you the detectives I spoke with last night?'

They both opened their warrant cards for an inspection that never came. Mathieson had retreated back behind her desk, pulling the seat in.

'You don't drive?' Rebus asked.

'What makes you think that?'

'You arrived on foot.'

'Sometimes I take the bus.'

'Better for the environment, eh?'

She stared at him, unblinking. 'Is there something I can help you with?'

'Must have come as a shock,' Rebus began. He saw that Clarke was either taking a keen interest in the contents of the showroom or else pretending to, so as to give him a clear run. He took the chair opposite Andrea Mathieson. Her eyes were red-rimmed.

'Philip, you mean?'

Rebus shook his head. 'Well, that too. But I was thinking of the email.'

'Bloody Archie!' She spat out the words, causing Clarke to turn away from a sleek BMW.

'Likes to think of himself as a bit of a joker,' Rebus sympathised. 'For what it's worth, the friends he sent the message to were every bit as pissed off. He might be in the market for new drinking buddies.' He paused. 'Did you know he was going to Carlisle on the Monday?'

She eventually nodded. 'I've a good mind to slap him when I see him.'

'He sent you the email Sunday afternoon – when did you open it?'

'That night. I nearly jumped out of my clothes. Ran to the door and made sure it was locked. I was scared half to death. Your imagination starts running away with you ...'

'Same for everyone. But only Mr Forbes seemed to take any action.'

'Is that what you think happened?'

'Did you really have a migraine on the Monday?'

'What?'

'Or was it that you couldn't bring yourself to come to work? Maybe because you'd been fretting about that email all night.'

'Well, yes, maybe.'

'Who did you think had sent it?'

'I'm not sure.'

'No?'

She shook her head, without making eye contact.

'Not Archie? Not Philip Forbes?'

'I'm not sure what it is you're getting at.'

'So everything was fine between the three of you? A happy ship and all that?'

'Why wouldn't it be?'

'Business doing OK?'

Clarke had wandered over from her tour of the showroom. She had a question of her own. 'What car do you drive, Ms Mathieson?'

'A BMW Z4.'

'Oh, those are nice.' Then, as if for Rebus's benefit: 'Sporty. Two-seater. I'd have mine in red ...'

'Same as mine,' Mathieson conceded.

'They drink the fuel, though, don't they? Probably not a hit with the environmental lobby ...'

Mathieson's head collapsed into her hands. She mumbled something they struggled to make out.

'Sorry?' Clarke asked.

Mathieson lifted her face. Tears were streaming down either cheek. 'It was a present from Philip!'

'Nice of him,' Clarke said quietly.

'Is that why you've not been able to drive to work, Andrea?' Rebus asked, dropping his own voice. 'Every time you see your car, you think of him?'

'He loved me.'

Rebus and Clarke shared a look.

'You were having an affair?' Clarke enquired.

Andrea Mathieson shook her head violently. 'Not now. *Then*.'

'Then being ...?'

'Two years ago. It didn't last long – "a fling", he called it. But I knew what it really was.'

'And what was that?'

'He was still grieving for his son. After Rory died, Philip felt crushed. His wife didn't help – that whole part of his life was just dust. He could talk to me – *did* talk to me. Poured everything out. And that's when it started. Just long enough for some healing. But not a "fling". He was wrong about that.' She took in gulps of air, trying to regain some composure. Clarke offered a tissue, which she accepted with a nod of thanks.

When enough time had elapsed, Rebus threw out another question.

'So when Mr Forbes opened that email ...?'

'Yes?'

'He might have thought the affair was about to come to light?'

When Mathieson didn't answer, Clarke asked a question of her own.

'He phoned you, didn't he?'

'He tried.'

'Because the message said *we* need to flee. So if it was to do with your affair, it could only have come from you?'

'I was out early evening. He left a voicemail. I texted him back.'

'On Sunday night?'

'I'd seen the email for myself by then.'

'You must have wondered ...'

'What?'

'Well, suddenly it's not a creepy anonymous message sent out randomly. As far as you knew, only the two of you received it.'

Rebus cleared his throat. 'It had to be someone who knew you both, whether it was about the affair or not.'

'I didn't really think about it,' Mathieson admitted. 'My head was ... You're right, of course. Maybe if I'd had the chance to speak to Philip.'

'Did you think he'd come to your home on Monday?'

'I hoped he would.'

'He knew the place from back in the day?'

'Yes.'

'But instead of that, he disappeared. Andrea, do you think he's run away?'

'I don't know.'

'Is there anything that could have panicked him? Anything at all?'

'Maybe he just wanted to be free from that bloody woman.'

'His wife, you mean?'

'Who else?'

'Did she know about the affair ...?'

There was a soft tapping from the other side of the glass door. Archie Sellers stood there, attempting to look contrite.

'You bastard!' Mathieson shrieked. She was up out of her chair, marching towards confrontation, eyes suddenly steely. Sellers had already started to retreat. The Aston Martin DB5 was parked on the forecourt. He unlocked the driver's side with an old-fashioned key.

'This is all your fault!' Mathieson was yelling as she pulled open the showroom door. Rebus noticed the large welcome mat she'd had to cross. Various marques were listed on it, but what caught his eye were the runs of tape fixing it firmly to the floor.

Health and safety.

Couldn't have anyone taking a tumble.

'Should we do something?' Clarke was asking.

Sellers had gunned the engine and was reversing on to the carriageway. A white van had to brake hard, its horn rasping. Her anger spent, Mathieson's face was in her hands again, shoulders heaving.

'Maybe make her a cup of tea,' Rebus suggested.

'And then?'

'Then we pay another visit to Heriots ...'

'You again,' was all Barbara Forbes said when she opened the door.

'Sorry to trouble you,' Rebus managed.

'I suppose you want to come in.'

'You'll be wondering if there's news.'

'What?'

'Would we drive over here if there wasn't news,' Rebus explained. They were in the entrance hall by now, Clarke pushing the door closed.

'Has he been sighted, is that it?' Mrs Forbes had her back to the detectives as she headed in the direction of the kitchen. But she paused when she reached its threshold, and turned towards the living room instead.

'I'm parched,' Rebus said, holding his hand to his throat for effect. 'Water or a cup of tea wouldn't go amiss.'

'I'll make tea,' Mrs Forbes said.

'Very grateful.' Rebus even gave a small bow.

'If you'd like to wait in there.' She was gesturing towards the living room.

'Fine,' Rebus agreed.

'I might just use the ...' Clarke held up a thumb, indicating one of the closed doors behind her.

'On the left behind the stairs,' Barbara Forbes said with a sigh. Then she turned and entered the kitchen. Rebus gave Clarke the nod and made sure he was filling the kitchen doorway as she started making her way noiselessly up the stairs.

'It's very quiet out here, isn't it?' Rebus asked.

'Comparatively,' Mrs Forbes agreed, filling the kettle and switching it on. 'I did say you could wait in the—'

'You're not anxious to hear what we've learned?'

'All right then.' But rather than stop to concentrate, she got busy with mugs, teapot, sugar bowl and milk. Rebus said his piece anyway – as much of the story as she needed to hear. By the time he had finished, Clarke was back. He felt the pressure of her hand on the small of his back and turned his head. She nodded gravely. So the passport was in the drawer in the bedroom, and Barbara Forbes had lied to them.

'I've never thought much of Archie Sellers,' she was saying as she stared at the kettle, willing it to come to the boil. 'He's like an adolescent in many respects. Bloody irresponsible of him to send that message. I hope he feels a measure of guilt.'

'Interesting phrase,' Rebus said.

'What?'

'"A measure of guilt". Meaning there's more to be apportioned elsewhere.'

'I'm not sure I understand.'

'I think you do, Mrs Forbes. And if we were to go upstairs, I think we'd find your husband's passport just where he left it. You saw an opportunity to muddy the water and you took it. But that means you were trying to mislead us, and that looks bad. Almost as bad as that rug.'

'The rug?' She looked down at it.

'Not something you often see in a kitchen. On a stone floor, I mean. It's too slippy. Could lead to a nasty accident. A rug like this is more the sort of thing you'd find in a room like your husband's den. So what is it doing here?' He had placed one foot on the rug and was starting to move it.

'Don't touch that!' she implored. But Rebus had already revealed the stained surface beneath. A series of blotches and splashes of a dull rust colour.

'Will Forensics tell us that's blood, Mrs Forbes?' Rebus enquired quietly. Clarke had stepped past him to switch off the kettle, and to stand guard near the display of chef's knives. But Barbara Forbes had gone very still, one hand clasped in the other as when they'd first set eyes on her.

'So here's what I think,' Rebus intoned. 'Either you saw the original email, in which case you were maybe the one who deleted it, not knowing it would linger on the machine. Or else it was the text you saw, the one Andrea Mathieson sent to your husband's phone. Was he maybe asleep by then? Or in a different room? You'd known about the relationship but he'd promised it was in the past. Now here was proof to the contrary. She still had her talons in him, and you were furious. Furious enough to grab one of those big solid knives. Furious enough to stab at him. The blood wouldn't shift, so you covered it up as best you could in the meantime.'

Her eyes were closed but she seemed at peace – the ordeal over now that her secret was out. No tears, her breathing slow and steady.

'What happens next?' was all she said, after a few seconds of silence, a silence deeper than any Rebus could remember.

'You need to show us – show us or tell us.'

She nodded, understanding exactly.

'The Mercedes Benz in the garage,' she said quietly. 'It was the only one with a boot big enough. Anyway, I wanted to drop the Bentley at the airport; that's the one he would have taken.' She opened her eyes again and seemed to be staring into some distance far beyond the walls of her kitchen and her home.

'After Rory died,' she began. But then she decided that those three words were maybe enough. Enough to her mind, certainly.

'After Rory died,' she repeated in a whisper, closing her eyes again as if for the last time.

The Very Last Drop

'And this is where the ghost's usually seen,' the guide said. 'So I hope nobody's of a nervous disposition.' His eyes were fixed on Rebus, though there were four other people on the tour. They had wandered through the brewery in their luminous health-and-safety vests and white hard-hats, climbing up flights of steps, ducking for low doorways, and were now huddled together on what seemed to be the building's attic level. The tour itself had been a retirement present. Rebus had almost let the voucher lapse, until reminded by Siobhan Clarke, whose gift it had been.

'Ghost?' she asked now. The guide nodded slowly. His name was Albert Simms, and he'd told them to call him 'Albie' – 'not alibi, though I've provided a few in my time'. This had been said at the very start of the tour, as they'd been trying the protective helmets for size. Siobhan had made a joke of it, warning him that he was in the presence of police officers. 'Officer singular,' Rebus had almost interrupted.

Almost.

Simms was currently looking uncomfortable, eyes darting around him. 'He's usually only seen at night, our resident ghost. More often it's the creaking of the floorboards the workers hear. He paces up and down ... up and down ...' He made a sweeping gesture with his arm. The narrow walkway was flanked by rectangular stainless-steel fermentation tanks. This was where the yeast did its work. Some vats were three-quarters full, each topped with a thick layer of brown foam. Others were empty, either clean or else waiting to be sluiced and scrubbed.

'His name was Johnny Watt,' Simms went on. 'Sixty years ago he died – almost to the day.' Simms's eyes were rheumy, his face blotchy and pockmarked. He'd retired a decade back, but liked leading the tours. They kept him fit. 'Johnny was up here on his own. His job was to do the cleaning. But the fumes got him.' He pointed towards one of the busier vats. 'Take too deep a breath and you can turn dizzy.'

'He fell in?' Siobhan Clarke guessed.

'Aye,' Simms appeared to agree. 'That's the story. Banged his head and wasn't found for a while.' He slapped the rim of the nearest vat. 'They were made of stone back then, and metal-lined.' His eyes were on Rebus again. 'A fall like that can do some damage.'

There were murmurs of agreement from the other visitors.

'Two more stops,' Simms told them, clapping his hands together. 'Then it's the sample room ...'

The sample room was laid out like a rural pub, its brickwork exposed. Simms himself manned the pumps while the others removed their safety-ware. Rebus offered a brief toast to the guide before taking his first gulp.

'That was interesting,' Siobhan offered. Simms gave a nod of thanks. 'Is it really sixty years ago? Almost exactly, I mean – or do you tell all the tours that?'

'Sixty years next week,' Simms confirmed.

'Ever seen the ghost yourself, Albie?'

Simms's face tightened. 'Once or twice,' he admitted, handing her a glass and taking Rebus's empty one. 'Just out the corner of my eye.'

'And maybe after a couple of these,' Rebus added, accepting the refill. Simms gave him a stern look.

'Johnny Watt was real enough, and he doesn't seem to want to go away. Quite a character he was, too. The beer was free to employees back then, and no limits to how much you had. Legend has it Johnny Watt could sink a pint in three seconds flat and not be much slower by the tenth.' Simms paused. 'None of which seemed to stop him being a hit with the ladies.'

Clarke wrinkled her nose. 'Wouldn't have been a hit with me.'

'Different times,' Simms reminded her. 'Story goes, even the boss's daughter took a bit of a shine to him ...'

Rebus looked up from his glass, but Simms was busy handing a fresh pint to one of the other visitors. He fixed his eyes on Siobhan Clarke instead, but she was being asked something by a woman who had come on the tour with her husband of twenty years. It had been his birthday present.

'Is it the same with you and your dad?' the woman was asking Clarke. 'Did you buy him this for his birthday?'

Clarke replied with a shake of the head, then tried to hide the fact that she was smiling by taking a long sip from her glass.

'You might say she's my "companion",' Rebus explained to the woman. 'Charges by the hour.'

He was still quick on his toes; managed to dodge the beer as it splashed from Siobhan Clarke's glass ...

The next day, Rebus was back at the brewery, but this time in the boardroom. Photos lined the walls. They showed the brewery in its heyday. At that time, almost a century ago, there had been twenty other breweries in the city, and even this was half what there had been at one time. Rebus studied a posed shot of delivery men with their dray horse. It was hitched to its cart, wooden barrels stacked on their sides in a careful pyramid. The men stood with arms folded over their three-quarter-length aprons. There was no date on the photograph. The one next to it, however, was identified as 'Workers and Managers, 1947'. The faces were blurry. Rebus wondered if one of them belonged to Johnny Watt, unaware that he had less than a year left to live.

On the wall opposite, past the large, polished oval table, were portraits of twenty or so men, the brewery managers. Rebus looked at each of them in turn. The one at the end was a colour photograph. When the door opened and Rebus turned towards the sound, he saw the man from the portrait walk in.

'Douglas Cropper,' the man said, shaking Rebus's hand. He was dressed identically to his photo – dark blue suit, white shirt, burgundy tie. He was around forty and looked the type who liked sports. The tan was probably put there by nature. The hair showed only a few flecks of grey at the temples. 'My secretary tells me you're a policeman ...'

'Was a policeman,' Rebus corrected him. 'Recently retired. I might not have mentioned that to your secretary.'

'So there's no trouble, then?' Cropper had pulled out a chair and was gesturing for Rebus to sit down too.

'Cropper's a popular name,' Rebus said, nodding towards the line of photographs.

'My grandfather and my great-grandfather,' Cropper agreed, crossing one leg over the other. 'My father was the black sheep – he became a doctor.'

'In one picture,' Rebus said, 'the inscription says "workers and managers" ...'

Cropper gave a short laugh. 'I know. Makes it sound as if the managers don't do any work. I can assure you that's not the case these days.'

'Your grandfather must have been in charge of the brewery when that accident happened,' Rebus stated.

'Accident?'

'Johnny Watt.'

Cropper's eyes widened a little. 'You're interested in ghosts?'

Rebus offered a shrug, but didn't say anything. The silence lengthened until Cropper broke it.

'Businesses weren't so hot on health and safety back then, I'm afraid to say. Lack of ventilation ... and nobody partnering Mr Watt.' Cropper leaned forward. 'But I've been here the best part of twenty years, on and off, and I've never seen anything out of the ordinary.'

'You mean the ghost? But other people have?'

It was Cropper's turn to shrug. 'It's a story, that's all. A bit of shadow ... a squeaky floorboard ... Some people can't help seeing things.' He sat back again and placed his hands behind his head.

'Did your grandfather ever talk to you about it?'

'Not that I remember.'

'Was he still in charge when you started here?'

'He was.'

Rebus thought for a moment. 'What would have happened after the accident?' he asked.

'I dare say the family would have been compensated – my grandfather was always very fair. Plenty of evidence of it in the annals.'

'Annals?'

'The brewery's records are extensive.'

'Would they have anything to say about Johnny Watt?'

'No idea.'

'Could you maybe look?'

Cropper's bright blue eyes drilled into Rebus's. 'Mind explaining to me why?'

Rebus thought of Albie Simms's words: *Johnny Watt was real ... and he doesn't seem to want to go away ...* But he didn't say anything, just bided his time until Douglas Cropper sighed and began getting to his feet.

'I'll see what I can do,' Cropper conceded.

'Thank you, sir,' Rebus said.

'You're supposed to be retired,' Dr Curt said.

In the past, the two men would normally have met in the city mortuary, but Rebus had arrived at the pathologist's office at the university, where Curt maintained a full teaching load between autopsies. The desk between them was old, ornate and wooden. The wall behind Curt was lined with bookshelves, though Rebus doubted the books themselves got much use. A laptop sat on the desk, its cover closed. There was no paperwork anywhere.

'I am retired,' Rebus stated.

'Funny way of showing it ...' Curt opened a drawer and lifted out a leather-bound ledger. A page had been marked. He opened the book and turned it to face Rebus.

'Report of the post-mortem examination,' he explained. 'Written in the finest copperplate lettering by Professor William Shiels.'

'Were you ever taught by him?' Rebus asked.

'Do I really look that old?'

'Sorry.' Rebus peered at the hand-written notes. 'You've had a read?'

'Professor Shiels was a great man, John.'

'I'm not saying he wasn't.'

'Contusions ... fractured skull ... internal bleeding to the brain ... We see those injuries most days even now.'

'Drunks on a Saturday night?' Rebus guessed. Curt nodded his agreement.

'Drink and drugs. Our friend Mr Watt fell eleven feet on to an inch-thick steel floor. Unconscious from the fumes, no way to defend himself ...'

'The major damage was to the base of the skull,' Rebus commented, running a finger along the words on the page.

'We don't always fall forehead first,' Curt cautioned. Something in his tone made Rebus look up.

'What is it?' he asked.

Curt gave a twitch of the mouth. 'I did a bit of digging. Those vats give off carbon dioxide. Ventilation's an issue, same now as it was back then. There are plenty of recorded cases of brewery employees falling into the vats. It's worse if someone tries to help. They dive into the beer to rescue their friend, and come up for air ... take a deep breath and suddenly they're in as much trouble as the other fellow.'

'What a way to go ...'

'I believe one or two had to climb out and go to the toilet a couple of times prior to drowning,' Curt offered. Rebus smiled, as was expected.

'OK,' he said. 'Carbon dioxide poisoning ... but what is it you're not saying?'

'The vat our friend fell into was empty, John. Hence the injuries. He didn't drown in beer – there was no beer.'

Finally Rebus got it.

'No beer,' he said quietly, 'meaning no fermenting. No carbon dioxide.' His eyes met the pathologist's. Curt was nodding slowly.

'So what was it caused him to pass out?' Curt asked. 'Of course, he could have just tripped and fallen, but then I'd expect to see signs that he'd tried to stop his fall.'

Rebus glanced back at the ledger. 'No injuries to the hands,' he stated.

'None whatsoever,' Professor Curt agreed.

Rebus's next stop was the National Library of Scotland, where a one-day reader's pass allowed him access to a microfiche machine. A member of staff threaded the spool of film home and showed him how to wind it to the relevant pages and adjust the focus. It was a slow process – Rebus kept stopping to read various stories and sports reports, and to smile at some of the advertisements. The film contained a year's worth of *Scotsman* newspapers, the year in question being 1948. I was one year old, Rebus thought to himself. Eventually he came to news of Johnny Watt's demise. It must have been a quiet day in the office: they'd sent a journalist and a photographer. Workers had gathered in the brewery yard. They looked numbed. The manager, Mr Joseph Cropper, had been interviewed. Rebus read the piece through twice, remembering the portrait of Douglas Cropper's grandfather – stern of face and long of sideburn. Then he spooled forward through the following seven days.

There was coverage of the funeral, along with another photograph. He wondered if the horse pulling the carriage had been borrowed from the brewery. Warriston Cemetery was the destination. Watt and his family had lived in the Stockbridge area for umpteen generations. He had no wife, but three brothers and a sister, and had served a year in the army towards the end of World War Two. Rebus paused for a moment, pondering that: you survived a war, only to die in your home town three years later. Watt was twenty years old, and had only been working at the brewery for eleven months. Joseph Cropper told the reporter that the young man had been 'full of energy, a hard worker with excellent prospects'.

In the photo showing the procession into the cemetery, Cropper was central. There was a woman next to him, identified as his wife. She wore black, her eyes to the ground, her husband gripping her arm. She was skinny and slight, in contrast to the man she'd married. Rebus leaned in a little further towards the screen, then wound the film back to the previous photo. Twenty minutes later, he was still looking.

Albert Simms seemed surprised to see him.

Simms had just finished one of his brewery tours. Rebus was sitting at a table in the sample room, nursing the best part of a pint of IPA. It had been a busy tour: eight guests in all. They offered Rebus half-smiles and glances but kept their distance. Simms poured them their drinks but then seemed in a hurry for them to finish, ushering them from the room. It was five minutes before he returned. Rebus was behind the pumps, topping up his glass.

'No mention of Johnny Watt's ghost,' Rebus commented.

'No.' Simms was tidying the vests and hard-hats into a plastic storage container.

'Do you want a drink? My shout.'

Simms thought about it, then nodded. He approached the bar and eased himself on to one of the stools. There was a blue folder lying nearby, but he tried his best to ignore it.

'Always amazes me,' Rebus said, 'the way we humans hang on to things – records, I mean. Chitties and receipts and old photographs. Brewery's got quite a collection. Same goes for the libraries and the medical college.' He handed over Simms's drink. The man made no attempt to pick it up.

'Joseph Cropper's wife never had a daughter,' Rebus began to explain. 'I got that from Joseph's grandson, your current boss. He showed me the archives. So much stuff there ...' He paused. 'When Johnny Watt died, how long had you been working here, Albie?'

'Not long.'

Rebus nodded and opened the folder, showing Simms the photo from the *Scotsman*, the one of the brewery workers in the yard. He tapped a particular face. A young man, seated on a corner of the wagon, legs dangling, shoulders hunched. 'You've not really changed, you know. How old were you? Fifteen?'

'You sound as if you know.' Simms had taken the photocopy from Rebus and was studying it.

'The police keep records too, Albie. We never throw anything away. Bit of trouble in your youth – nicking stuff; fights. Brandishing a razor on one particular occasion – you did a bit of juvenile time for that. Was that when Joseph Cropper met you? He was the charitable type, according to his grandson. Liked to visit prisons, talk to the men and the juveniles. You were about to be released; he offered you a job. But there were strings attached, weren't there?'

'Were there?' Simms tossed the sheet of paper on to the bar, picked up the glass and drank from it.

'I think so,' Rebus said. 'In fact, I'd go so far as to say I know so.' He rubbed a hand down his cheek. 'Be a bugger to prove, mind, but I don't think I need to do that.'

'Why not?'

'Because you want to be caught. You're an old man now, maybe only a short while left, but it's been plaguing you. How many years is it, Albie? How long have you been seeing Johnny Watt's ghost?'

Albert Simms wiped foam from his top lip with his knuckles, but didn't say anything.

'I've been to take a look at your house,' Rebus continued. 'Nice place. Semi-detached; quiet street off Colinton Road. Didn't take much searching to come up with the transaction. You bought it new a couple of months after Johnny Watt died. No mortgage. I mean, houses were maybe more affordable back then, but on wages like yours? I've seen your pay slips, Albie – they're in the company files too. So where did the money come from?'

'Go on then – tell me.'

'Joseph Cropper didn't have a daughter. You told me he did because you knew fine well it would jar if I ever did any digging. I'd start to wonder why you told that particular lie. He had a wife, though, younger than him.' Rebus showed Simms a copy of the photo from the cemetery. 'See how her husband's keeping a grip on her? She's either about to faint or he's just letting everyone know who the boss is. To be honest, my money would be on both. You can't see her face, but there's a photo she sat for in a studio ...' He slid it from the folder.

'Very pretty, I think you'll agree. This came from Douglas Cropper, by the way. Families keep a lot of stuff too, don't they? She'd been at school with Johnny Watt. Johnny, with his eye for the ladies. Joseph Cropper couldn't have his wife causing a scandal, could he? Her in her late teens, him in his early thirties ...' Rebus leaned across the bar a little, so that his face was close to that of the man with the sagging shoulders and face.

'Could he?' he repeated.

'You can't prove anything, you said as much yourself.'

'But you wanted someone to find out. When you found out I was a cop, you zeroed in on me. You wanted to whet my appetite, because you needed to be found out, Albie. That's at the heart of this, always has been. Guilt gnawing away at you down the decades.'

'Not down the decades – just these past few years.' Simms took a deep breath. 'It was only meant to be the frighteners. I was a tough kid but I wasn't big. Johnny was big and fast, and that bit older. I just wanted him on the ground while I gave him the warning.' Simms's eyes were growing glassy.

'You hit him too hard,' Rebus commented. 'Did you push him in or did he fall?'

'He fell. Even then, I didn't know he was dead. The boss ... when he heard ...' Simms sniffed and swallowed hard. 'That was the both of us, locked together ... We couldn't tell. They were still hanging people back then.'

'They hanged a man at Perth jail in '48,' Rebus acknowledged. 'I read it in the *Scotsman*.'

Simms managed a weak smile. 'I knew you were the man, soon as I saw you. The kind who likes a mystery. Do you do crosswords?'

'Can't abide them.' Rebus paused for a mouthful of IPA. 'The money was to hush you up?'

'I told him he didn't need to – working for him, that was what I wanted. He said the money would get me a clean start anywhere in the world.' Simms shook his head slowly. 'I bought the house instead. He didn't like that, but he was stuck with it – what was he going to do?'

'The two of you never talked about it again?'

'What was there to talk about?'

'Did Cropper's wife ever suspect?'

'Why should she? Post-mortem was what we had to fear. Once they'd declared it an accident, that was that.'

Rebus sat in silence, waiting until Albert Simms made eye contact, then asked a question of his own. 'So what are we going to do, Albie?'

Albert Simms exhaled noisily. 'I suppose you'll be taking me in.'

'Can't do that,' Rebus said. 'I'm retired. It's up to you. Next natural step. I think you've already done the hard part.'

Simms thought for a moment, then nodded slowly. 'No more ghosts,' he said quietly, almost to himself, as he stared up at the ceiling of the sample room.

'Maybe, maybe not,' Rebus said.

'Been here long?' Siobhan Clarke asked as she entered the Oxford Bar.

'What else am I going to do?' Rebus replied. 'Now I'm on the scrapheap. What about you – hard day at the office?'

'Do you really want to hear about it?'

'Why not?'

'Because I know what you're like. Soon as you get a whiff of a case – mine or anyone else's – you'll want to have a go at it yourself.'

'Maybe I'm a changed man, Siobhan.'

'Aye, right.' She rolled her eyes and told the landlord she'd have a gin and tonic.

'Double?' he asked.

'Why not?' She looked at Rebus. 'Same again? Then you can make me jealous by telling me stories of your life of leisure.'

'Maybe I'll do that,' said Rebus, raising his pint glass and draining it to the very last drop.

Cinders

The Fairy Godmother was dead.

Rebus had had to fight his way through the throng of rubber-neckers outside the Theatre Royal. It was early evening, dark and drizzling, but they didn't seem to mind. He showed his warrant card to a uniformed officer at the cordon, and then again as he entered the red-carpeted foyer. The doors to the auditorium were open, the remaining audience members grumbling in that Edinburgh way as they queued to give their contact details before being allowed to leave. The curtain had been raised for the show's second act, revealing the kitchen of some grand house or castle, all fake stone walls and glowing fireplace.

'Apparently,' a voice next to Rebus announced, 'there's a bit of slapstick with Buttons as he tries baking a cake.'

'Shaving-foam in the face?' Rebus guessed.

'That sort of thing.' Detective Inspector Siobhan Clarke managed a thin smile.

The youngest members of the audience were setting up cries of protest, their annual panto treat ruined. Parents looked numbed, some of the mothers dabbing away tears.

'They know?' Rebus said.

'Second half doesn't start, police arrive – I'd say they've guessed there's no happy ending.'

'So what happened?'

'Easier if I show you.' She turned back into the foyer and pushed open a door marked Private. Stairs up, a narrow corridor, then another door, more stairs, and turns to left and right.

'Should we be leaving a trail of breadcrumbs?' Rebus inquired.

'Wrong story,' Clarke answered.

She had to knock at a final door. It was opened by a uniformed officer. They were in another corridor with doors off.

'Make-up, wardrobe, dressing rooms,' Clarke intoned.

'The business of show.' Rebus peered into some of the rooms as they passed them. Rails festooned with gaudy clothing, strip-lit mirrors, props and wigs. There were loudspeakers set into the walls, broadcasting the sounds from the auditorium. The Scene of Crime crew were bagging and tagging.

'We're not worried about contamination?' Rebus checked.

'Twenty or thirty people pass this way a dozen or more times per show. Maxtone doesn't think we'd be adding much to the mix.'

'Doug Maxtone is in charge?'

'How do you not know that?' Clarke stopped in her tracks.

'I was just passing, Siobhan.'

'Just passing?'

'Well, maybe I heard something at the station...'

'But you're not on the team?' She rolled her eyes at the stupidity of her own question. 'Of course not – Doug Maxtone's hardly in your fan club.'

'I can't understand it – we've got badges and everything.'

'This is a murder inquiry, John. You don't just walk in.'

'Yet here I am.' Rebus gave a shrug. 'So why not show me where it happened?'

She sighed as she made up her mind, then led the way. 'We can't go in, not without being suited up.'

'Understood.'

So they stood at the threshold instead. The interior seemed frozen in the moment. Vases of flowers and good luck cards. Bottles of water and blackcurrant cordial. A bowl of fruit. A small suitcase, lying open. A chair tipped over. A dark stain on the pale blue carpet.

'I smell smoke.'

'Not quite enough to set off the alarm,' Clarke said. 'A metal waste-bin.' She nodded to where it had once sat. 'Off to the lab.'

'Was she a smoker?'

'It was paper of some kind – plus sandwich wrappers and who knows what else.'

'A blow to the head, I heard.'

'Probably when she was seated, facing the mirror. She didn't have the biggest of roles – pops up with the gown and glass slippers, then the coach. Comes on again near the end – or would have.'

'So it's the interval and she's changed out of her sparkly gown and wings?' Rebus mused. 'Meaning the costume department would have been lurking.'

'We're interviewing them.'

'How long is the interval?'

'Twenty minutes.'

'Lots of people backstage?'

'Lots.'

'She would have seen them.' He nodded towards the mirror. 'She'd have seen whoever walked in.'

'Baron Hardup has the next dressing room along. Didn't hear any screams. Then again, he had the radio on, listening to some horse race.'

'And through the other wall?'

'Stairwell.'

'No security cameras?'

'Not here, no.' Clarke paused. 'Did you know her?'

'How do you mean?'

'She was on TV in the 70s and 80s. A couple of sitcoms, even a few films.'

'I saw her face on the poster outside. Didn't ring any bells.'

'And the name? Celia Jagger?' She watched Rebus shrug. 'You've not asked about the weapon.'

Rebus scanned the dressing room but came up empty. 'Enlighten me,' he said.

'The glass slipper,' Clarke said. 'The one left behind at the Ball...'

Not that it was a real glass slipper. It was Perspex or something similar. And it wasn't the one from the performance. The production kept two spares. One of these had been removed from the props department and used in the attack, its stiletto heel piercing Jagger's skull and killing her instantly.

The props department was basically a large walk-in cupboard with shelves. The door had a lock, but was always open during performances. There were storage boxes bearing the name of each character along with a list of contents. Rebus held one of the remaining slippers in his hand. It was heavier than he had anticipated. Nicely made, but scuffed from use. Not that an audience would notice, not with a spotlight making it shine.

Clarke had gone off somewhere, with a warning that he should 'keep his head down'. Some of the chaos had subsided. Fewer headless chickens as the inquiry found its rhythm. Twelve dressing rooms, three of them to accommodate the chorus (who doubled as dancers). The theatre had no orchestra pit – the music was pre-recorded. Two technicians ran everything from a couple of laptops. Everyone would be asked about their movements during the interval. Statements would have to be verified. As yet, no one seemed to be asking the most basic question of all: who would want Celia Jagger dead? Her killing was the end of a story, and for stories you went to people. Which was why Rebus placed the shoe back in the box marked Cinders, and walked towards the exit.

The sign said Stage Door, and that was where he eventually found himself. There was an antechamber of sorts, with a list of actors and crew fixed to its wall. Like clocking in to some old-fashioned factory job, when you arrived you slid a wooden slat along to show you were IN. From behind a glass partition, the man in the security booth watched Rebus.

'I like this,' Rebus said, pointing to the wall.

'It's been here almost as long as the building.'

'And what about you?'

'I used to build the sets. Everything was custom-made in those days.'

'And now?'

'Mostly from stock. Newcastle or somewhere does Cinderella one year, we'll take what we need from them the next, while our Aladdin might head to Aberdeen. We built the tram from scratch, mind.'

'The tram?'

'Director's idea – instead of a carriage. Big puff of smoke and there's an Edinburgh tram. Pretty clever really – means we don't need any horses. Couple of the stage hands use a pulley and Cinders is off to the ball.' The man's smile faded. 'How long will we be closed?'

'Hard to say.'

'Theatre can't go on without it. Same for a lot of these old places – a full house for a few months means you can afford to run the rest of the year.'

'Is that what happens?'

The guard nodded. He was in shirt-sleeves, a mug of tea on the desk next to him. CCTV screens showed the alleyway outside, empty auditorium, and front of house.

'I'm Detective Sergeant Rebus, by the way,' Rebus said.

'Willie Mearns.'

'How long have you been doing this job, Mr Mearns?'

'Fifteen years.'

'Ever since you retired from the workshop?' Making Mearns seventy-five, maybe even eighty. He looked sprightly though. Rebus reckoned the man's memory would be sharp. 'Have you been questioned yet?'

'Not formally – just asked if I'd seen anyone suspicious.'

'I'm guessing you said no.'

'Quite right.'

'And Celia Jagger – did you know her to talk to?'

'Oh aye. I had to remind her that I built the set when she appeared in a play here back in her heyday.'

'Did you use the word "heyday"?'

'I'm not that daft.'

'She had a bit of an ego then?'

'Most of them do. Don't get me wrong – they're lovely with it. But Celia was miffed she didn't get one of the big dressing rooms.'

'They all looked much the same to me.'

'A few inches can make all the difference.'

'You say she was "miffed" – is that as far as it went?'

'More or less.'

Rebus studied the man for a few seconds. 'There's a pub across the street. Do you know it?'

'I might have passed through its door on occasion.'

Rebus smiled. 'Well, tonight we've got half a dozen of Police Scotland's finest keeping watch on the Theatre Royal. I think you can maybe call it a day, Mr Mearns.'

The man made show of considering his options, then started rising to his feet. 'I'll drink to that,' he said.

The interviews were taking place at St Leonard's police station. Rebus found Clarke pacing a corridor, scanning transcripts.

'Who have we got?' he asked her.

She nodded in turn towards four doors. 'Tracy Sidwell, John Carrier, Robert Tennant, Jamie Salter.'

'So that's Cinderella, Baron Hardup, Prince Charming and Buttons.'

'You're well informed.'

'I just spent an hour in a pub with a man who likes to talk. Hardup's a bit too fond of the horses apparently. Always needing to borrow a few quid to tide him over. Meantime, Prince Charming left his wife and two kids for Cinderella – not quite a fairy tale.'

Clarke stared at him. 'Anything else?'

Rebus shrugged. 'There are whispers about Buttons and the Wicked Stepmother. Giggles and whispers behind closed dressing-room doors. Who else have we got?'

'They're waiting in the office until we're ready for them.' They walked together to the MIT suite. The Ugly Sisters – panto stalwarts Davie Clegg and Russell Gloag – had changed out of their costumes but still bore traces of make-up. They were seated alongside the show's writer/director Maurice Welsh, who was visibly trembling as he spoke with another man. Rebus guessed this would be Alan Yates, producer and owner of the Theatre Royal. Seeing the two detectives, Yates leapt to his feet. He was in his sixties and looked to have dined out for most of them.

'Any news?' he asked.

'Not yet, sir,' Clarke assured him.

'We need to offer refunds...prep an understudy. The show must – '

'Sorry to disillusion you, sir,' Rebus butted in. 'But the theatre remains a crime scene. It doesn't open again until we say so.'

'And even then, Alan,' Welsh added tiredly, 'who's going to be in the mood? I mean the audience rather than the cast. We'll have nothing but ghouls...'

'Run's finished,' Davie Clegg agreed. 'Can't sit in that dressing-room and not think of Celia.'

Yates ran a hand through what hair he had left. 'But without the panto there *is* no Theatre Royal! It's our banker!'

'Sorry, Alan.' Clegg offered a shrug of sympathy.

'Ruined,' Yates muttered, falling back on to his seat. Maurice Welsh patted his arm.

'That's all very well,' Russell Gloag piped up, 'but it doesn't tell us who killed poor Celia. And if I find out it was any one of you...'

'Actually that's our job,' Clarke informed him. She broke off as an exhausted-looking detective filled the doorway. He checked his notepad.

'Maurice Welsh?' The director stood up, looking as if a gust might topple him. 'If you'll follow me, sir.' The detective locked eyes with Clarke and shook his head: nothing to report.

Rebus gestured for Clarke to follow him into the corridor. He checked they were out of earshot. 'Where's everyone else? The crew and chorus, plus Dandini and the Stepmother?'

'One of the other offices. Otherwise they'd have been like sardines.' She studied him. 'What else did your friend in the pub tell you?'

'Bits and pieces. I'm not sure yet what they – '

'What in God's name is *he* doing here?'

They both turned in the direction of the approaching voice. DCI Doug Maxtone seemed to fill the corridor as he strode towards them.

'I was just passing,' Rebus explained slowly. 'Happened to bump into DI Clarke and she was just singing your praises.'

Maxtone ignored Rebus, his attention fixed on Clarke. He brandished a sheet of paper ripped from a pad. 'Forensics played a blinder,' he told her.

'The waste-bin?'

'Salient contents: one promotional photograph of Celia Jagger. Not quite done to a cinder...'

'And?'

'It was signed.' Maxtone checked his note. '"To my darling Ed with all my love".'

'Ed?' Clarke narrowed her eyes. 'Edwin Oakes?'

'AKA Dandini. Is he inside?' Maxtone was gesturing towards the MIT room.

'He's with the chorus and crew.'

Maxtone's face hardened. 'I've just come from there.'

Clarke's lips formed an O. 'No Dandini?' she surmised.

'They thought he must be here.'

Rebus made show of clearing his throat. 'Maybe he found the trap-door.'

'You're as useful as last year's turkey,' Maxtone snarled, before barrelling his way back along the corridor, Clarke at his heels.

Rebus stayed where he was. Then he took out his phone and a scrap of paper, reading Willie Mearns' number from it as he got busy on the keypad.

'I need everything there is to know about Edwin Oakes,' he said. As he listened, his eyes began to narrow and his brow furrow. *Curiouser and curiouser...*

The following morning, Rebus was at St Leonard's early. He went through the interview transcripts, gleaning bits and pieces. There was no love lost between the Ugly Sisters apparently – they worked together for the sake of the pay cheque, each privately confiding his loathing of the other to various stagehands. Wardrobe department, make-up, deputy stage manager...all had sung for the detectives. The show's director had a history of substance abuse, as did Prince Charming. Buttons was notoriously lazy, and had almost come to blows with both director and producer while attempting to cut back on his lines so he wouldn't have to remember them. He would also ad lib weak jokes, meaning more arguments after each and every performance.

But there was plenty of gossip about the crew, too. Assignations and affairs, minor misdemeanours and fallings-out. As the show's director had said: *it's a pressure cooker, but if you try turning the heat down sometimes the production suffers.* And in the end, it was all about the show, its run sold out weeks before opening.

'Quite the drama,' Siobhan Clarke said, reading over Rebus's shoulder. She was carrying a cardboard coffee-cup and a leather satchel. 'Maxtone not in yet?'

'Think I'd be here if he was?'

'Fair point.' She put down her things and started removing her long woollen coat. 'I meant to ask you – what are you doing for Christmas?'

'Probably not going to the panto.'

'I mean the day itself – you know you'd be welcome at mine.'

'Thanks, Siobhan, but I have my own traditions to stick to.'

'Meaning finding a pub that's open? Maybe a meal from the freezer after?'

'I'm old-fashioned that way.'

'I feel bad about us shutting down *Cinderella*.'

'We're not the villains here, remember that. Though sometimes all Doug Maxtone lacks is a moustache to twirl.' Rebus looked at his watch. 'Shouldn't have bothered taking your coat off.'

'Is the heating playing up or something?'

Rebus shook his head. 'But we're going out again.'

'We are? Why's that?'

'Because Edwin Oakes is a creature of habit,' he said, rising to his feet.

They decided on Rebus's car so Clarke could continue drinking her coffee, but as they turned out of the car park, they were blocked by a man, his arms outstretched. He wore a flapping coat and was wide-eyed and unshaven.

'Isn't that one of our Ugly Sisters?' Clarke asked.

Rebus was already out of the car. 'Mr Gloag, isn't it?' he was saying.

'I know what he told you and it's not true! Not one word of it!' There were flecks of foam at the corners of the actor's mouth.

'Just calm down.' Rebus held up the palms of both hands. 'I know everyone's a bit on edge…'

'He told you I'd slept with Celia, didn't he?'

'Are we talking about your colleague Davie Clegg?' Clarke inquired.

'Last time I work with that wretched piece of…' Gloag looked at his hands, willing them to stop shaking. 'He told you about *Earnest*? It's true, I was in the same play as her, but nothing ever happened. I mean…she flirted a bit. You know – all touchy-feely, and maybe I picked up the signals wrong.'

'You'd have been accommodating?' Rebus guessed.

'But if you think that was going to make me jealous of Ed…'

'You knew about them though?' Clarke probed.

'We all *knew*.'

'But it didn't make you angry?' Rebus asked. 'The same anger you're feeling right now?'

'I'm not angry.' Gloag tried to laugh. 'I just can't believe Davie would have said anything.'

'Rest easy then, Mr Gloag – Davie Clegg didn't tell tales.'

Gloag looked as if he'd been hit. 'Wh-what?'

'He's been winding you up, sir,' Rebus confirmed. 'Telling you he did something he didn't.'

Colour rose to Gloag's cheeks. 'That does it!' he spat. 'If he thinks we're working together again, he can bloody well whistle. That's our divorce papers right there!' He spun away, hurtling down the pavement.

'Think we should warn Clegg?' Clarke asked, getting back into the car.

'We need to be elsewhere.' Rebus started the car. After a minute of silence, he asked about Oakes.

'Shares a flat in the Grassmarket with Buttons. Though apparently they don't see much of one another.'

'Because Buttons is shacked up with the Wicked Stepmother?'

'Reading between the lines, yes. Bit awkward, with both flatmates carrying on their little liaisons. Oakes's actual home is in Glasgow but he hardly gets back there during the season.'

'Officers have been to both?'

'Camped outside through the night,' Clarke confirmed. 'We've also interviewed Prince Charming's ex-wife plus our esteemed director's partner – he's gay, by the way. And the substance abuse?' She shook her head. 'I don't buy it – he's just naturally hyper.' She peered from the window. 'Where are we headed?'

'The Meadows.'

'Is this your security guy again?'

'He's like a priest – they all tell him their story at some point.'

'Stagehands mostly knew about Oakes and Celia Jagger.' Clarke took another sip from her cup. 'I mean, they knew or they'd had an inkling. Seems she had a bit of history in that department – every production she was in, she managed an affair with someone in the cast. Doesn't seem to matter that she was old enough to be Oakes's mother – actually, maybe even his grandmother.'

'But she decides he's not the one – maybe has her eye on someone else. So he burns the photo and then whacks her over the head.'

'It's a fairly classic set-up.'

'You may be wiser than you know.'

'How so?'

'The relevant phrase is "set up".'

She stared at him as he stopped the car kerbside. They were on Melville Drive. The Meadows was an expanse of playing fields criss-crossed by paths. A lot of students used it as a route to the university. In summer, they would host barbecues and games of

Frisbee, but there was an icy wind today and the few pedestrians were well wrapped up.

'I wish you'd tell me what's in that head of yours,' Clarke complained. Rebus just winked and got out of the car. She followed him to where he had come to a halt, next to a line of trees. There was a circuit of bare earth, the grass worn away by a generation of joggers. Two young women passed them, managing to hold a conversation while they ran. From the opposite direction came an older man, headphones on, steam rising from his singlet. And then, fifty yards or so back, a figure that seemed out of place. He was dressed in cream chinos and a zip-up jacket, below which was an open-necked shirt. Yes, because Edwin Oakes hadn't felt able to return to his digs or to the theatre. He was wearing the same outfit as when he'd walked out of the police station. And Rebus guessed he hadn't slept either. Despite which, he had come for his morning run.

A creature of habit, just as Willie Mearns had said.

Rebus stepped on to the trail, blocking him. Oakes came to a stop, leaning forward to catch his breath.

'Morning, Mr Oakes,' Rebus said.

'You're the police?' Oakes guessed.

'We need you at St Leonard's, sir.'

Oakes straightened his back. 'I didn't do anything.'

'You ran away,' Clarke corrected him.

'I knew you'd think...' He broke off and shook his head. 'I just needed some time.'

'To come up with a story?'

'To *grieve*.' His eyes bored into Clarke's. 'I loved her. I mean, I knew her reputation and everything – once the show ended, we'd be history. But all the same...'

'She gave you a photo,' Rebus said. 'We found it in the waste-bin in her dressing-room.'

Oakes frowned. 'Nobody knew about that.'

'You're saying you didn't set light to it?' Clarke demanded.

'I kept it in a drawer in my own dressing-room, tucked away where it wouldn't be seen.'

'Somebody found it,' Rebus stated. He half-turned towards Clarke. 'No raised voices from behind Celia Jagger's door – someone from the crew would have heard an argument, they all seem to have pretty good ears.'

'I could never have hurt her,' Oakes was saying. 'Never in a million years.'

'Yet you did a runner.'

'I knew you'd find out about us – either that or I'd have to tell you.' Oakes rubbed at his hair. 'I've a girlfriend – sort of – back in Glasgow. Someone I'm fond of. She's got a daughter who dotes on me. It was the look on her face I couldn't stand, finding out I'd cheated on her mum...'

'You need to come back with us,' Rebus said quietly. 'We know you didn't do anything. Talking to us means taking us a step closer to finding whoever did.'

Oakes nodded slowly. Clarke's eyes were on Rebus. He knew what she was thinking: *How can we be sure?* As they escorted Oakes to the waiting car, she asked the actor when he had last seen the photo.

'A few days back. Maybe longer than that. It actually hurt me a little.'

'Why was that?'

'It's the sort of thing you hand to a fan at the stage door. I mean, the message was personal but not *that* personal. And that was actually the real message – none of this means anything except in the moment. Soon as the production ends, we go our separate ways.' Oakes angled his head back, as if to stop the tears coming.

Just as well someone usually writes your lines for you, Rebus thought, before inquiring whether Oakes had ever walked into his dressing room and found someone from the cast or crew there.

'All the time – it's an open house. I've usually got chocolate biscuits or cans of cola. Jamie's a demon for the sugar.'

'Jamie meaning Buttons?'

Oakes nodded. 'And John's always wandering in with some sure-fire bet he wants to share. They're like family...' His face darkened. 'It can't be any of them. There must be someone else.'

'Maybe so, Mr Oakes. Maybe so.' Rebus pulled a slip of paper from his pocket and handed it across for Siobhan Clarke to take.

'See if you can track down this guy,' he said. 'He's the one we probably need to talk to now.'

She read the name. 'Howard Corbyn? Who the hell is Howard Corbyn?'

'You're a detective,' Rebus told her. 'You'll work it out.'

They installed Oakes in the back of the car. But before getting in, Clarke grabbed Rebus by the arm.

'Maxtone needs to know you're the one who did this.' She gestured towards the actor.

'I don't mind you grabbing the good reviews, Siobhan.'

She narrowed her eyes. 'It's not over, is it? There's another act coming?'

Rebus nodded towards the slip of paper. 'Depends what comes from that,' he said, making his way round to the driver's seat.

*

Rebus stood alone on the stage of the Theatre Royal. A stage-hand had raised the curtain and put on a few lights. The scene was still set for the opening of the panto's second half – the kitchen of Baron Hardup's castle. Close up, the set and props looked tired, paint fading or flaking, edges chipped – not unlike the building itself. He knew that council officials had ordered expensive modifications (yet to be carried out). The roof needed repairs and the carpets were fraying or threadbare.

None of which would have mattered to each day's audience, primed with sugary snacks and drinks, pockets emptied in the purchase of glo-sticks, magic wands and glossy programmes. Each year's twelve-week panto run just about made up for nine months of loss-making. The box office next door had been handing out refunds when Rebus arrived. The apology taped over the poster for Cinderella said that the show had been cancelled 'until further notice'.

'Is there any news?' Alan Yates asked, coming on to the stage from the wings.

'Isn't that bad luck?' Rebus said. Yates looked confused. 'You entered stage left. Lighting director told me the show was cursed from the moment Celia Jagger made the mistake of entering stage left during the first rehearsal. Stage left is for villains. Goes back to the medieval mysteries or something.'

Yates forced a smile. 'Stage left is hell, stage right heaven – I know the story, but it's only actors who are superstitious that way. Theatre owners live in the real world – we're even allowed to say the word Macbeth, as long as none of the cast is in earshot.'

'You might have just jinxed yourself then, Mr Yates. You asked if there's news and there is – we've got Russell Gloag in a cell at St Leonard's.'

'Russell?' Yates sounded disbelieving.

'He gave Davie Clegg a bit of a battering – so it looks like you've lost your Ugly Sisters, too. The real world you live in isn't doing you any favours, eh?' Rebus paused. 'Bit of a blow to your ego, I dare say, when your Fairy Godmother decided on Edwin Oakes.'

Yates's face creased. 'I'm not sure I follow.'

'She played here seven years ago in *The Mousetrap*. Then again three years later in an Oscar Wilde play...'

'Yes?'

'And both times you enjoyed what Wilde might have called "a dalliance".'

Yates's face was colouring. 'We most certainly did not.'

'Oh yes, you did. Crew at the time knew it. *Everyone* knew it. So you reckoned it would be the same again this year. Must have hurt your pride to be rebuffed.' Rebus took a step closer. 'In the lane outside the stage door – the lane covered by CCTV. Willie Mearns saw you. Trying for a clinch, being pushed away. A pointed finger, a slap, a few angry words.'

'This is preposterous.' Yates made to lean against the table, but it creaked, reminding him that it was not solid. 'You're suggesting I killed Celia because she was seeing Oakes?'

'Not at all.' Rebus paused again. 'You killed her out of simple greed, more than anything. You're like Baron Hardup with a castle that's going to ruin you.' Rebus gestured to the set. 'Just the single solitary panto run each year keeping the creditors from your door. But all the renovations and improvements that need to be made... It'd be years before you saw any return. If the panto could be stopped from spinning gold, you'd have the perfect excuse to sell the place off – no one would blame you or paint you as the villain. That's why you started talking to Howard Corbyn.'

'Who?'

'Howard Corbyn,' Rebus repeated.

'I've never heard of him.'

'Is that right? Well, he's a property developer.' Rebus turned towards the auditorium and raised his voice a little. 'Aren't you, Mr Corbyn?'

He was seated in the front row of the Grand Circle, Siobhan Clarke next to him, the pair of them just about visible beyond the stage lighting. Corbyn nodded and waved, and Alan Yates swallowed a gulp. Perspiration made his face gleam.

'Willie Mearns watched the pair of you,' Rebus went on, turning towards Yates again. 'Three visits when you knew the theatre would be empty. A handshake in the lane at the end of the third. Flats, commercial use, maybe a super-pub – Mr Corbyn wasn't sure what he would do with the place, but he wanted it if the price was right. You just had to shut down *Cinderella*. A real-life tragedy would do the trick. You could get back at Celia Jagger for her snub, and maybe even put her lover in the frame – all you had to do was take that photo from his dressing-room and place it in hers – just singed enough to look the part. You think we can't lift fingerprints from a half-burned picture, Mr Yates? You'd be surprised what we can do these days with anything less than cinders.'

Yates was looking at the floor, as if willing it to reveal an escape route.

'No disappearing act for you,' Rebus warned him. 'But you might want to take one last good look around. Because you know where your reputation's going to be from now on?'

'Where?' Yates couldn't help asking, his voice cracking.

Instead of answering, Rebus looked up to where Siobhan Clarke was sitting.

'Behind you!' she called down.

'Behind you,' Rebus repeated quietly, leading Alan Yates from the stage.

Further Copyright Information

About the Author

Ian Rankin is a #1 international bestselling author. Winner of an Edgar Award and the recipient of a Gold Dagger for fiction and the Chandler-Fulbright Award, he lives in Edinburgh, Scotland, with his wife and their two sons.

The Linux® Networking Architecture

Design and Implementation of Network Protocols in the Linux Kernel

Klaus Wehrle • Frank Pählke • Hartmut Ritter
Daniel Müller • Marc Bechler

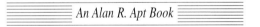

An Alan R. Apt Book

PEARSON
Prentice
Hall

Upper Saddle River, New Jersey 07458

Library of Congress Cataloging-in-Publication Data
CIP DATA AVAILABLE.

Vice President and Editorial Director, ECS: *Marcia J. Horton*
Publisher: *Alan Apt*
Associate Editor: *Toni Dianne Holm*
Editorial Assistant: *Patrick Lindner*
Vice President and Director of Production and Manufacturing, ESM: *David W. Riccardi*
Executive Managing Editor: *Vince O'Brien*
Managing Editor: *Camille Trentacoste*
Production Editor: *Irwin Zucker*
Director of Creative Services: *Paul Belfanti*
Creative Director: *Carole Anson*
Art Director and Cover Manager: *Jayne Conte*
Managing Editor, AV Management and Production: *Patricia Burns*
Art Editor: *Gregory Dulles*
Manufacturing Manager: *Trudy Pisciotti*
Manufacturing Buyer: *Lisa McDowell*
Marketing Manager: *Pamela Hersperger*
Translator: *Angelika Shafir*

© 2005 Pearson Education, Inc.
Pearson Prentice Hall
Pearson Education, Inc.
Upper Saddle River, NJ 07458

Authorized translation from the German language edition entitled *Linux Netzwerkarchitektur: Design und Implementierung von Netzwerkprotokollen im Linux-Kern* published by Addison-Wesley, an imprint of Pearson Education Deutschland GmbH, München, ©2002.

Printed in the United States of America

10 9 8 7 6 5 4 3 2 1

ISBN 0-13-177720-3

Pearson Education Ltd., *London*
Pearson Education Australia Pty. Ltd., *Sydney*
Pearson Education Singapore, Pte. Ltd.
Pearson Education North Asia Ltd., *Hong Kong*
Pearson Education Canada, Inc., *Toronto*
Pearson Educación de Mexico, S.A. de C.V.
Pearson Education—Japan, *Tokyo*
Pearson Education Malaysia, Pte. Ltd.
Pearson Education, Inc., *Upper Saddle River, New Jersey*

Contents

Preface

This book deals with the architecture of the network subsystem in the Linux kernel. The idea for this book was born at the Institute of Telematics at the University of Karlsruhe, Germany, where the Linux kernel has been used in many research projects and its network functionality is modified or enhanced, respectively, in a targeted way. For instance, new services and protocols were developed for the next-generation Internet, and their behavior was studied. In addition, existing protocols, such as the TCP transport protocol, were modified to improve their behavior and adapt them to the new situation in the Internet.

In the course of these research projects, it has been found that the Linux kernel is very suitable for studying new network functionalities, because it features a stable and extensive implementation of the TCP/IP protocol family. The freely available source code allows us to modify and enhance the functionality of protocol instances easily. In addition, the enhancement of the kernel functionality is very elegantly supported by the principle of the kernel modules. However, many studies and theses in this field showed that familiarization with the Linux network architecture, which is required before you can modify the behavior of a protocol instance, demands considerable work and time. Unfortunately, this is mainly due to the facts that the network subsystem of the Linux kernel is poorly documented and that there is no material that would explain and summarize the basic concepts.

Although there are a few books that deal with the Linux kernel architecture and introduce its basic concepts, none of these books includes a full discussion of the network implementation. This situation may be due to the following two reasons:

▧ The network subsystem in the Linux kernel is very complex. As mentioned above, it implements a large number of protocols, which is probably one good reason for the enormous success of Linux. Both [BoCe00] and [BBDK+01] mention that the description of all these protocols and their concepts would actually fill an entire book. Well, you are reading such a book now, and, as you can see, it has eventually turned out to be quite a large volume, although it describes only part of the network functionality, in addition to the basic concepts of the Linux network architecture.

▧ Operating-system developers normally deal with the classical topics of system architecture—for example, the management of memories, processes, and devices, or the synchronization of parallel activities in a system—rather than with the handling of network packets. As you go along in this book, you will surely notice that it has been written not by system developers, but by computer-science specialists and communication engineers.

While considering the facts that there was little documentation covering the Linux network architecture and that students had to familiarize themselves with it over and over again, we had the idea of creating a simple documentation of the Linux network architecture ourselves. Another wish that eventually led to the more extensive concept of this book was a stronger discussion of important communication issues: *design and implementation of network protocols in real-world systems*. Networking courses teach students the most important concepts and standards in the field of telecommunication, but the design and implementation of network functionality (mainly of network protocols) by use of computer-science concepts has enjoyed little attention in teaching efforts, despite the fact that this knowledge could have been used often within the scope of studies and theses. The authors consider the description of the implementation of the Linux network architecture and its structure, interfaces, and applied concepts a step towards strengthening the informatics component in networking classes.

The authors hope that this book will help to make the processes and structures of the Linux network architecture easier to understand, and, above all, that our readers will have fun dealing with it and perhaps learn a few things about the networking concept and its practical implementation.

The content of this book corresponds to our knowledge of the Linux network architecture. This knowledge is neither comprehensive nor exhaustive. Nevertheless, we have tried to represent the processes and structures of the Linux network architecture in a fashion as easily understandable and detailed as possible. We are thankful for all hints, suggestions for improvement, ideas, and comments, and we will try to consider them in later editions. Updated information about the Linux network architecture and this book is available online at `http://www.Linux-netzwerkarchitektur.de`.

ORGANIZATION OF THIS BOOK

Chapter 1 will deal intensively with the motivation behind Linux in general and the Linux network architecture in particular; Chapter 2 is an introduction into the basic mechanisms and components of the Linux kernel. To keep the volume of this book manageable, we will discuss only those components that are important for understanding the Linux network architecture. With regard to the other components of the Linux kernel, we refer our readers to other books (e.g., [BBDK+01]).

Chapter 3 is an introduction to the general architecture of communication systems and the functionality of protocols and protocol instances. It includes an introduction to the popular TCP/IP and ISO/OSI layering models.

Chapters 4 and 5 discuss fundamental concepts of the Linux network architecture, including the representation and management of network packets in the Linux kernel (see *Socket Buffers*—Chapter 4) and the concept of *network devices* (Chapter 5). Network devices form the links between the protocol instances on the higher layers and hide the particularities of the respective network adapters behind a uniform interface.

Chapter 6 gives an overview of the activity forms in the Linux network architecture and the flow of transmit and receive processes. In addition, this chapter introduces the interface to the higher-layer protocol instances.

Chapters 7 through 12 discuss protocols and mechanisms of the *data link layer*. More specifically, it describes the *SLIP*, *PPP*, and *PPP-over-Ethernet* protocols and how the *ATM* and *Bluetooth* network technologies are supported in Linux. Finally, we will describe how a Linux computer can be used as a *transparent bridge*.

Our discussion of the TCP/IP protocols starts with an overview of the *TCP/IP protocol family* in Chapter 13. We will begin with a brief history of the Internet, then give an overview of the different protocols within the TCP/IP protocol family. Chapter 14 will deal with the *Internet Protocol* and its mechanisms in detail. In addition, it introduces the *IP options* and the *ICMP protocol*. Chapters 15 through 23 discuss the following protocols and mechanisms on the network layer: *ARP*, *routing*, *multicasting*, *traffic control*, *firewalls*, *connection tracking*, *NAT*, *KIDS*, and *IPv6*.

Chapters 24 and 25 describe the *TCP* and *UDP* transport protocols, respectively. We will close our discussion of the kernel with an explanation of the *socket interface*, in Chapter 26, then end with a short overview of the *programming of network functionality* on the application level.

The appendix includes additional information and introduces tools facilitating your work with the Linux network architecture. The issues dealt with include the *LXR source code browser*, *debugging work in the Linux kernel*, and *tools* you can use to manage and monitor the Linux network architecture.

ADDITIONAL SOURCES OF INFORMATION

This section lists a few useful sources of information where you can find additional information about the Linux network architecture.

Magazines

- The *Linux Magazine* (`http://www.Linux-mag.com`) is probably the best-known Linux magazine. It features articles about all issues that are of interest when you deal with Linux. Of special interest is the *Kernel Corner* column, which regularly publishes articles about the architecture and implementation of components of the Linux kernel—most of them by developers themselves.

- *Linux Focus* (`http://www.linuxfocus.org`) is an online magazine publishing articles in many different languages. It also includes a *Kernel Corner*.

- The *Linux Gazette* (`http://www.linuxgazette.com`) is another online magazine dedicated to Linux.

Useful Links in the World Wide Web

▓ Linux Headquarters: `http://www.linuxhq.com`
▓ Linux Documentation Project: `http://www.linuxdoc.org`
▓ Linux Weekly News: `http://www.lwn.net`

Other Information

▓ *Howtos* include a lot of information about different Linux issues. Most deal with the configuration and installation of various Linux functionalities. Especially for the Linux kernel, there are also a few howto documents—for example, how to use locks in the kernel [Russ00b], and general information on *hacking* in the Linux kernel [Russ00c]. Of course, we should not forget to mention the networking howto, which includes a wealth of tips and information about configuring the network functionality in Linux [Drak00].
▓ The source code of the current kernels is found at `ftp.kernel.org`. There are also mirrors of this FTP server, a list of which can be found at `http://www.kernel.org/mirrors/`.
▓ Information about components and drivers of the Linux kernel are also included directly in the source code of a kernel version, in the Documentation subdirectory. In addition, the file Documentation/kernel-docs.txt includes a list of current information about the Linux kernel—for example, documentation, links, and books. (It's worth taking a look at this file!)

CONVENTIONS USED IN THIS BOOK

This book uses the following typographical conventions to emphasize various elements of the Linux kernel, source texts, and other things.

Functions

A gray bar denotes important functions. A bar describes the function name on the left and the file name (within the kernel's source-code tree) on the right.

When giving a function name in such a place and throughout the body of this book, we normally leave out the parameters, because they would take up much space and impair the readability and text flow.

In general, when introducing a function, we describe the entire parameter set and give a brief description. The variable type is normally left out. For example, the description of the function `int ip_rcv(struct sk_buff *skb, struct net_device *dev, struct packet_type *pt)` from the file `net/ipv4/ip_input.c` is denoted as follows:

`ip_rcv()`	**net/ipv4/ip_input.c**

Throughout the body of this book, we would then refer to this function as `ip_rcv()` or `ip_rcv(skb, dev, pt)`.

Variables, Function Names, Source Text Excerpts, and so on

A sans-serif font is used for excerpts from the source code, variable and function names, and other keywords referred to in the text.

Commands, Program Names, and so on

A sans-serif font is used for the names of programs and command-line tools. Parameters that should be passed unchanged are also printed in sans-serif; those parameters that have to be replaced by values are printed in *sans-serif italic*.

Direct input in the command line is often denoted by a leading shell prompt—for example,

Files, Directories, Web Links, and so on

A sans-serif font is used for files and directories. We generally give the relative path in the kernel source code for files of the Linux kernel (e.g., net/ivp4/ip_input.c). Web links are also printed in sans-serif font (e.g., http://www.Linux-netzwerkar-chitektur.de).

Other Conventions

Italic text denotes emphasis, or an introduction to a key term or concept.

ACKNOWLEDGMENTS

Many people's contributions were indispensable in the creation and production of this book. First and foremost, we would like to thank all students who studied the structure of the Linux network architecture in their papers and theses. They contributed enormously to collecting knowledge about the Linux network architecture at the Institute of Telematics:

Nasieh Abdel-Haq, Paul Burczek, Michael Conrad, Frank Dinies, Paul Hankes Drielsma, Jérôme Freilinger, Carolin Gärtner, Stefan Götz, Karsten Hahn, Artur Hecker, Tobias Hinkel, Michael Hofele, Verena Kahmann, Vera Kießling, Stefan Klett, Andreas Kramm, Jan Kratt, Eckehardt Luhm, David Metzler, Ulrich Mohr, Rainer Müller, Sven Oberländer, Vincent Oberle, Jan Oetting, Torsten Pastoors, Christian Pick, Christian Schneider, Steffen Schober, Marcus Schöller, Achim Settelmeier, Uwe Walter, and Jürgen Walzenbach.

The authors wrote this book mainly for their students.

Much appreciation is due to Professor Gerhard Krüger, who has always supported our activities, given us the freedom necessary to write this book, and assisted us with valuable advice. His support also allowed us to procure a Linux test network, which served as the basis for our research activities at the Institute of Telematics in the field of services for the next-generation Internet.

Our special thanks go to all the folks at the publishing houses who published the original German version of this book and the English translation that you are currently reading. Particularly, we would like to thank our editors, Sylvia Hasselbach and Toni

Holm. Their admirable patience helped shepherd us through this book-writing process. The English translation was done by Angelika Shafir, whom we would also like to thank in this place. We also thank all the people who read the manuscript, especially Mark Doll, Sebastian Döweling, Thomas Geulig, Thorsten Sandfuchs, Marcus Schöller, Bernhard Thurm, Uwe Walter, Anja Wehrle, Kilian Weniger, and Friederike Daenecke.

Last but not least, we gratefully acknowledge the support, encouragement, and patience of our families and friends.

KARLSRUHE • BERKELEY • BERLIN • BRAUNSCHWEIG

KLAUS WEHRLE • FRANK PÄHLKE • HARTMUT RITTER • DANIEL MÜLLER • MARC BECHLER

The Linux® Networking Architecture

The Linux Kernel

CHAPTER 1

Motivation

Digital data transmission and processing form the basis of our today's information society. Within a short time, the Internet has penetrated all areas of our daily lives, and most of us can surely not imagine everyday life without it. With its new services, it offers us ways to communicate, fascinating all social strata, but corporations and organizations also use the possibilities of the Internet as a basis for internal exchange of information and for communication and handling business with customers and partners.

The technique of the Internet has been developed during the past twenty years; the actual boom began with the introduction of the World Wide Web at the beginning of the nineties. Development has progressed since then; new protocols and standards have been integrated, improving now both the functionality and the security in the "global net."

As developments in the Internet progressed, so did the technologies of the underlying network: The first e-mails were sent over telephone lines at 1200 bits/s in the eighties, but we can now communicate over gigabit or terabit lines. In addition, new technologies for mobile communication are emerging, such as UMTS and Bluetooth.

All these technologies have one thing in common: They are integral parts of digital communication systems, allowing spatial communication and interaction of distributed applications and their users. Modern communication systems decompose these extremely complex tasks into several layers, and the instances of these layers interact via predefined protocols to supply the desired service.

Telematics[1] is a field that handles both the development and research of telecommunication systems (and their basic mechanisms) and the implementation and realization of these systems by using means of computer science. This means that, in addition to the design of communication systems and protocols, the implementation of these mechanisms is an important task within the telematics discipline. Unfortunately, many universities and academic institutions neglect this point. For example, during coverage

---

[1] *Telematics* is the subdiscipline of informatics that deals with the design and implementation of telecommunication systems by use of information technologies.

of the basics and the current standards with regard to communication protocols in detail, only very little knowledge is conveyed as to how these principles can be used (e.g., which basic principles of computer science can be used when implementing communication protocols).

With this book, the authors—who themselves teach computer-science students—attempt to contribute to promoting the computer-science component in telematics. Using the Linux operating system as an example, which the authors employ mainly for research purposes, in addition to the usual office applications (e-mail, World Wide Web, word processing, etc.), we will introduce the practical realization of communication systems and communication protocols. Essentially, the structuring of the network subsystem in the Linux kernel, the structuring of interfaces between network components, and the applied software methods will be used to show the reader various ways to implement protocols and network functionality.

In addition to its teaching use, of course, this book is also intended to address all those interested in the architecture of the network subsystem in the Linux kernel, taking a look behind the scenes at this poorly documented part of the Linux kernel. The following section discusses the Linux operating system and the reasons for its use in offices, companies, networks, and research.

1.1 THE LINUX OPERATING SYSTEM

Linux is a freely available multiuser, multitasking, multiprocessor, and multiplatform UNIX operating system. Its popularity and the number of users increase continually, making Linux an increasingly serious factor in the operating-systems market. Thanks to the freely available source code that everybody can obtain over the Internet and to the fact that everybody can participate in and contribute to the further development of the Linux system, many developers, all over the world, are constantly busy further developing this system, removing existing errors, and optimizing the system's performance.

The fact that most developers do this very time-consuming work for free in their spare time is a sign of the great fun working with Linux and mainly with the Linux kernel can be. As we progress in this book, we will try to pass some of this enthusiasm on to our readers. The large number of research projects at the University of Karlsruhe that have used, enhanced, or modified the Linux network architecture experienced a high motivation of all participating students. The reason was mainly that this offered them a way to participate in the "Linux movement."

The development of Linux was initiated by a student by the name of Linus B. Torvalds, in 1991. At that time, he worked five months on his idea of a new PC-based UNIX-like operating system, which he eventually made available for free on the Internet. It was intended to offer more functions than the Minix system designed by Andrew S. Tanenbaum, which was developed for teaching purposes only [Tane95]. With his message in the Minix newsgroup (see page 1), he set a movement in motion, the current result of which is one of the most stable and widely developed UNIX operating systems. Back then, Linus Torvalds planned only the development of a purely experimental system, but his idea further developed during the following years, so that Linux is now used successfully by many private people, corporations, and scientists alike.

Mainly, the interoperability with other systems (Apple, MS-Windows) and the ability to run on many different platforms (Intel x86, MIPS, PA-RISC, IA64, Alpha, ARM, Sparc, PowerPC, M68, S390) make Linux one of the most popular operating systems.

Not only the extensive functionality of Linux, but also the freely accessible source code of this operating system, have convinced many private people and companies to use Linux. In addition, the German government, with its program for the support of open-source software, promotes the use of freely available programs with freely available source code. The main reason for this is seen not in the low procurement cost, but in the transparency of the software used. In fact, anyone can view the source code and investigate its functionality. Above all, anyone can check what—perhaps security-relevant—functionalities or errors are contained in an application or operating system. Especially with commercial systems and applications, there are often speculations that they could convey information about the user or the installed applications to the manufacturer.

You do not have such fears with freely developed software, where such a behavior would be noticed and published quickly. Normally, several developers work concurrently on an open-source project in a distributed way over the Internet, monitoring themselves implicitly. After all, free software is not aimed at maximizing the profit of a company or its shareholders. Its goal is to develop high-quality software for everybody. Linux is a very good example showing that freely developed software is not just the hobby of a handful of freaks, but leads to serious and extremely stable applications.

The authors of this book use Linux mainly for research work in the network area. The freely available source texts allow us to implement and evaluate new theories and protocols in real-world networks. For example, Linux was used to study various modifications of the TCP transport protocol [WeRW01, Ritt01], to develop a framework for the KIDS QoS support [Wehr01b], and to develop the high-resolution UKA-APIC timer [WeRi00].

1.2   WHAT IS LINUX?

Originally, the term *Linux* described only the operating-system kernel that abstracts from the hardware of a system, offering applications a uniform interface. Over time, the term *Linux* has often come to mean the kernel (the *actual* Linux) together with the entire system environment, including the following components:

- the operating-system kernel (currently version 2.0, 2.2, or 2.4);
- the system programs (compiler, libraries, tools, etc.);
- the graphical user interface (e.g., XFree) and a window manager or an application environment (KDE, Gnome, FVWM, etc.);
- a large number of applications from all areas (editors, browsers, office applications, games, etc.).

Different components not forming part of the kernel originate largely from the GNU project of Free Software Foundation, which explains why the complete system environment is often called "GNU/Linux system." A characteristic common to the

Linux kernel and GNU programs is that they may all be freely distributed under the GNU Public License (GPL), provided that the source text is made publicly available. To the extent that enhancements or modifications have been effected to the programs, then these are automatically governed by the GNU license (i.e., their source text must also be made freely available). Since the advent of Linux, this has had the effect that the system has been further developed free from corporate policy interests and that it has been more strongly oriented to word its users' needs than are other, commercial operating systems. Anyone can participate in the development and implement new capabilities, ones based on the freely available source texts. This means that Linux is always involved in the support of international standards, and no attempt is made to enforce corporate or proprietary standards to secure a market position.

Errors made during the development of a piece of software are normally removed quickly. In addition, there is a continual effort to keep the system performing as well as possible. This has become very clear in the example of the network implementation in the last kernel version: After it had become known that the performance of Linux in the area of protocol handling on multiprocessor systems suffers from a few flaws, the network part was extensively rewritten to remove these faults. This means that Linux is an example that clearly shows the benefits of open-source projects:

- stability,
- performance, and
- security.

1.3 REASONS FOR USING LINUX

The previous section introduced the important properties and objectives of Linux as a free software project. This section will discuss a number of general properties of the Linux kernel, offering more reasons for its use:

- Linux supports *preemptive multitasking*: All processes run independently in different protected memory spaces, so that the failure of one process does not in any way impair the other processes. When a process claims too much computing time, its processor can be taken and allocated to another waiting application. Preemptive multitasking is a fundamental requirement for stable systems.
- *Multiprocessor*: Linux is one of the few operating systems supporting several processors in SMP (*Symmetric MultiProcessing*) operation. This means that several processes can be handled concurrently by different CPUs. Since kernel version 2.0, multiprocessor systems with Intel and Sparc processors are supported. Version 2.2 and the current Version 2.4 additionally improved the performance and parallelism in the Linux kernel.
- *Multiuser*: Several users can work concurrently in one system, when they are logged in over different consoles. In addition, users can work easily on several graphical user interfaces.

▓ *Multiplatform*: Linux was originally developed only for the personal computer (Intel 80386), but it runs on more than ten processor architectures today. The bandwidth of supported platforms extends from small digital personal assistants over the standard personal computer to mainframe architectures: Intel x86, MIPS, PA-RISC, IA64, Alpha, ARM, Sparc, PowerPC, M68, and so on.

▓ *Linux is a UNIX system*: It is compatible with the POSIX-1300.1 standard[2] and includes large parts of the functionality of UNIX System V and BSD. This means that you can use UNIX standard software under Linux.

▓ *Rich network functionality*: The Linux network architecture makes available an extensive choice of network protocols and functionalities in the networking area. The development of the Internet and its services is inseparably linked to UNIX systems. This is why the properties of the TCP/IP protocol family and its behavior can best be studied and controlled in a UNIX system. Other PC operating systems would be unsuitable for this, especially those with source code not publicly available.

▓ *Open source*: The source code of the entire Linux kernel is freely available and can be used according to the GNU Public License. A large number of programmers work on the further development of the Linux kernel all over the world, continually enhancing and improving it. Linux is distributed over the Internet so that each user can test the kernel and make improvements or enhancements. The development of Linux in this dimension would not have been possible without the Internet.

Formerly, users had to put up with defects in software they purchased; Linux now allows everyone to remove such defects. And it really works. An often heard criticism has been that the driver support for Linux is one of its major problems. This situation has changed dramatically during the past years. For instance, all actually available network cards are supported by Linux. In fact, we can rely to the Linux community to such an extent that there will soon be a matching driver for each new device.

▓ *Efficient network implementation*: Meanwhile, the Linux kernel makes available a well-structured implementation of the network functionality, which will be our main focus of discussion in the next 27 chapters of this book. The functions can be adapted to the special requirements of the desired system and meet the specifications of the Internet Engineering Task Force (IETF), IEE, and ISO better than many other systems.

In the creation of a new kernel, its desired functionality can be individually configured. For instance, you can enable a large number of optimization options or add specific functionalities (e.g., multicast support and various protocols). While the system is running, you can also use the Proc file system (see Section 2.8) to

---

[2]*Portable Operating System Interface based on UniX—POSIX 1300.1* defines a minimum interface that each UNIX-like operating system must offer.

change parameters—For example, various timeout values for the TCP transport protocol or configuration parameters of other protocol instances. There is even a way to use the Proc file system to enable and disable certain functions at runtime, such as packet forwarding.

- *IP Next Generation*: Since Version 2.1.38, the Linux kernel provides a stable and relatively complete implementation of the new Internet Protocol IPv6. (See Chapter 23.)

- And, finally, the best argument: *Linux is free of charge*. Everyone can download it from the Internet or buy it on CD for a few dollars, usually with a few gigabyte applications (some of them being more useful, some less) and with extensive installation instructions and free support. This means that, for very little money, you can get a high-performing, extremely stable, and easily adaptable operating system that turns a Pentium PC into a high-performing workstation, a highly reliable server, or an individually configurable Internet router.

This chapter has been a brief introduction to Linux; the next chapter will introduce the internal structure of the Linux kernel. We will then discuss the basic structure of communication systems in general and the structure of the Linux network architecture in particular.

The Kernel Structure

This chapter deals with the basic architecture of the Linux kernel and its components. It provides an overview of the most important areas of the kernel, such as the different forms of activity in the kernel, memory management, device drivers, timers, and modules. Each of these issues will be discussed briefly in this book, to give you an insight into the tasks and processes of each component. Detailed information about each of these issues is found in other books and references. A choice of corresponding sources is given in the bibliography, where we particularly recommend [RuCo01], [BBDK+01], and [BoCe00].

The goal of this chapter is to describe the framework in which the Linux network architecture operates. All areas described below offer basic functions required to offer network services in the first place. This is the reason why knowing them is an essential prerequisite for an understanding of the implementation of the Linux networking architecture.

Figure 2–1 shows the structure of the Linux kernel. The kernel can be divided into six different sections, each possessing a clearly defined functionality and offering this functionality to the other kernel components. This organization is reflected also in the kernel's source code, where each of these sections is structured in its own subtree.

Here we briefly describe these components.

▨ *Process management*: This area is responsible for creating and terminating processes and other activities of the kernel (software interrupts, tasklets, etc.). In addition, this is the area where interprocess communication (signals, pipes, etc.) takes place. The scheduler is the main component of process management. It handles all active, waiting, and blocked processes and takes care that all application processes obtain their fair share of the processor's computing time.

▨ *Memory management*: The memory of a computer is one of the most important resources. A computer's performance strongly depends on the main memory it is equipped with. In addition, memory management is responsible for allowing each process its own memory section, which has to be protected against access by other processes.

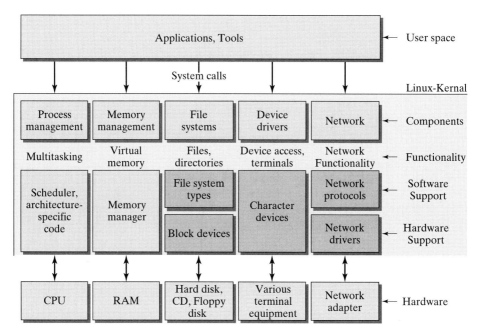

FIGURE 2–1
Structure of the Linux kernel according to [RuCo01].

■ *File systems*: In UNIX, the file system assumes a central role. In contrast to other operating systems (e.g., Windows NT), almost everything is handled over the file-system interface. For example, device drivers can be addressed as files, and the Proc file system (see Section 2.8) allows you to access data and parameters within the kernel. These two functionalities can be used very effectively and elegantly, so that they are often used for debugging purposes. (See Appendix B.)

■ *Device drivers*: Device drivers abstract from the underlying hardware in every operating system, and they allow you to access this hardware. The modular concept of Linux we will introduce in Section 2.4 offers a way to add or remove device drivers during a running operation, despite its monolithic kernel.

■ *Network*: All network operations have to be managed by the operating system, because certain network operations cannot be allocated to a specific process, such as handling an incoming packet. Incoming packets are asynchronous events. They have to be collected, identified, and forwarded before a process can handle them. This is the reason why the kernel is responsible for the handling of packets across program and network interfaces.

Within the kernel, defined interfaces are used to facilitate the design of new functionalities. For instance, there is an interface to the virtual file system, which can be used to add new file systems. The availability of more than a dozen supported file systems shows clearly that this interface was a good design decision by the Linux developers, because no other operating system provides such a large supply of supported file systems. The Linux network architecture also includes many interfaces supporting the dynamic enhancement of the wealth of protocols and network drivers.

The components shown on dark background in Figure 2–1 provide interfaces for the dynamic registration of new functionalities, so that such functionalities can be easily implemented in modules.

2.1   MONOLITHIC ARCHITECTURES AND MICROKERNELS

In contrast to current operating-system developments tending toward a microkernel architecture, the Linux operating system is based on a monolithic kernel. In microkernel architectures, such as the Mach kernel [Tane95] or the Windows NT kernel, the operating system kernel represents merely the absolute necessary minimum of functionality. Good examples are interprocess communication (IPC) and memory management (MM). Building on the microkernel, the remaining functionality of the operating system is moved to independent processes or threads, running outside the operating system kernel. They use a defined interface to communicate with the microkernel, generally via system calls.

In monolithic kernels, to which the Linux kernel belongs, the entire functionality is concentrated in one (large) kernel. In addition to the basic mechanisms known from microkernels, the Linux operating system kernel also includes device drivers, file system drivers, most instances of the network protocols, and much more. (See Figure 2–1.) Compared to microkernel architectures, the use of a monolithic kernel has both benefits and drawbacks, as we will see below.

The benefits include the fact that the entire functionality of the operating system is concentrated in the kernel, allowing the system to work more efficiently. You can access resources directly from within the kernel, so costly system calls and context changes are needed less frequently. One major drawback is that the source code for the operating system kernel can quickly become rather complex, even messy, because no defined interfaces are required within the kernel. In addition, the development of new drivers can be made more difficult by the lack of an interface definition. For example, if you install a new device, you have to retranslate the entire kernel to ensure that this device driver can be compiled with the kernel, a need avoided by microkernel architectures.

That Linux is based on a monolithic operating-system kernel is due to historical reasons. A system that had not been planned to become such a big project, at the beginning, has continually been developed further, so that it became impossible, at some point in time, to migrate to a microkernel architecture. However, since Version 2.0, Linux has made a step towards microkernel architectures. More specifically, the possibility was created of moving certain functionalities into modules, which are loaded into the kernel at runtime, from which they can be removed again.

This removed an important drawback of monolithic kernels and opened the way to loading drivers or other functionalities at runtime. In addition, modularization offers another benefit: Uniform interfaces are defined. This feature had previously been characteristic only of microkernel architectures. Linux has a number of such interfaces, allowing the kernel to be dynamically enhanced by a number of functionalities. This very flexibility and openness of its interfaces is one of the most important benefits of Linux.

TABLE 2–1   Interfaces in the Linux kernel to embed new functionalities.

Functionality	Functions for Dynamic Registration
Character devices	`(un)register_chrdev( )`
Block devices	`(un)register_blkdev( )`
Binary formats	`(un)register_binfmt( )`
File systems	`(un)register_filesystem( )`
Serial interfaces	`(un)register_serial( )`
Network adapters	`(un)register_netdev( )`
Layer-3 protocols	`dev_add_pack( ), dev_remove_pack( )`
Layer-4 protocols (TCP/IP)	`inet_add_protocol( ), inet_del_protocol( )`
Console drivers	`tty_(un)register_driver( )`
Symbol tables	`(un)register_symtab( )`
Modules	`init_module( ), cleanup_module( )`

Table 2–1 shows a selection of the most important interfaces, including the pertinent methods used to register and unregister functionalities.

Despite its modularization, Linux has preserved a major benefit of monolithic kernels: All functions implemented in modules run in protected kernel mode, which means that they do not require any context change when called from within the kernel. This can be seen as a clever combination of the benefits from both main operating-system architectures.

The following sections briefly introduce the kernel components, to better explain the Linux network architecture. You should know the structure and properties of these components to understand how the Linux network architecture works. We refer again to [RuCo01, BBDK+01, BoCe00] for an in-depth study of the Linux kernel components described below.

2.2   ACTIVITIES IN THE LINUX KERNEL

Linux is a multitasking system. This means that several application processes can be active, and several applications can be used, simultaneously. In multiprocessor systems, which have been supported since kernel Version 2.0, even several applications or their processes can be processed in parallel. However, a process is not the only form of activity you can execute in the Linux kernel.

2.2.1   Processes and System Calls

Processes are normally activities that are started to run a specific application, and they are terminated once the application is through. Creating, controlling, and destroying of processes are tasks handled by the kernel of an operating system. Processes operate exclusively in the user address space (i.e., in unprotected mode) of a processor, where they can access only the memory section allocated to them. An attempt to access memory sections of other processes or the kernel address space leads to an *exception*, which has to be dealt with by the kernel.

However, when a process wants to access devices or use a functionality of the operating-system kernel, it has to use a system call to do this. A system call causes the processor to change to the protected mode, and access to the kernel address space is a function of the system call. All devices and memory sections can be accessed in protected mode, but only with methods of the kernel.

The work of processes and system calls can be interrupted by other activities. In such a case, their current state (contents of CPU registers, MMU registers, etc.) is saved; then it is restored when the interrupted process or system call resumes its work. Processes and system calls can be stopped voluntarily or involuntarily. In the first case, they cede processing voluntarily—for example, when they wait for a system resource (external device, semaphore, etc.) and go to sleep until that resource becomes available. Involuntary cession of processing is caused by interrupts, which tell the kernel that an important action has taken place, one that the kernel should be dealing with. This could be a notification about availability of a previously busy resource.

In addition to normal processes and to processes within a system call, we distinguish between further forms of activity in the Linux kernel. These forms of activity are of decisive importance for the Linux network architecture, because the network functionality is handled in the kernel. We will explain the following forms of activity in more detail in the next sections, when we will be discussing mainly their tasks within the Linux network architecture:

- Kernel threads;
- interrupts (hardware IRQs);
- software interrupts (soft IRQs);
- tasklets; and
- bottom halves.

When thinking of the different forms of activity in the kernel (except processes in the system call and kernel threads), an important point will be the parallel execution of the respective form of activity. On the one hand, this concerns the question of whether the instance of a form of activity can be executed concurrently on several processors; on the other hand, of whether two different instances of one form of activity can be executed concurrently on several processors. Table 2–2 shows an overview of these possibilities.

Another interesting thing about the individual forms of activity is to know by what other forms of activity they can be interrupted; Table 2–3 gives an overview. This information is important mainly for protection from undesired side effects caused by concurrent or overlapping operations of two activities on a jointly used data structure. This problem and possible solutions are discussed in detail in Section 2.3. That section will introduce locking mechanisms that, though offering protection against undesired side effects, can reduce a system's performance when used too cautiously. For this reason, it is important to know when which locking mechanisms are required. Note that the possible parallelism and interruptability of different forms of activity play an important role.

TABLE 2–2   Concurrent execution of same activities on several processors.

	Same Activity	**Different Activities**
HW IRQ	—	•
Soft IRQ	•	•
Tasklet	—	•
Bottom half	—	—

TABLE 2–3   Interruption of activities by other forms of kernel activities.

	HW-IRQ	**Soft-IRQ**	**Tasklet**	**Bottom Half**
HW IRQ	+/−[1]	−	−	−
Soft IRQ	+	−	−	−
Tasklet	+	−	−	−
Bottom half	+	−	−	−
System call	+	+	+	+
Process	+	+	+	+

[1]Only slow interrupts can be interrupted by other interrupts, as we will see in Section 2.2.2.

2.2.2   Hardware Interrupts

Peripherals use hardware interrupts (often abbreviated as HW IRQs) to inform an operating system about important events (e.g., that the mouse has been moved, a key has been pressed, or a packet has arrived in the network adapter). Hardware interrupts interrupt the current activity in one of the processors and execute the pertinent interrupt-handling routine.

The handling routine for a specific interrupt can be registered at runtime by using the function request_irq(). Details about the registration and management of interrupts are described in [RuCo01]. free_irq() is used to release the handling routine of an interrupt, so that it is no longer executed.

We distinguish between two types of interrupts in the Linux kernel:

- *Fast interrupts* are characterized by the fact that they have a very short interrupt-handling routine and so interrupt the current activity only very briefly. One characteristic of fast interrupts is that all other interrupts in the local CPU are locked while it is executed, so that the interrupt-handling routine cannot be interrupted. Fast interrupts are designated by the flag SA_INTERRUPT when they are registered with request_irq().
- *Slow interrupts* can be interrupted by other interrupts during their execution. They normally have a much longer-interrupt handling routing than fast interrupts and so would claim the processor for too long. This is the reason why only the repeated execution of that interrupt is stopped when a slow interrupt is executed.

Interrupts can generally stop all other activities when they are executed. (See Table 2–3.) At the same time, various interrupts in several CPUs can be handled concurrently, but the interrupt-handling routine of a specific interrupt can be executed only in one CPU at a time.

You can call the function `in_irq()` (`include/asm/hardirq.h`) to check whether the current activity is an interrupt-handling routine (see details in [Russ00b]).

Top Halfs and Bottom Halfs   Interrupt-handling routines should be executed as soon as possible after the interrupt was triggered and interrupt the current activity only briefly. But not every task can be executed by few instructions. For example, handling of a packet arrived in a network adapter requires several thousand ticks, until the packet can be passed on to the relevant process in the user address space. Though it is triggered by an interrupt, this task cannot be done in an interrupt-handling routine.

To keep interrupt handling as short as possible, such time-consuming tasks are divided into two parts:

- The so-called *top half* runs only the most important tasks after a triggered interrupt. The top half corresponds to the interrupt-handling routine. As we will see in Chapter 6, for example, the interrupt-handling routine of a network adapter might just copy the arrived packet to the kernel, where it will be buffered in a queue pending detailed handling by the corresponding protocol instances.
- The *bottom half* runs all operations that are not time-critical and which could not be executed within the interrupt-handling routine for time reasons. The bottom half is scheduled for execution while the top half is running, and, as soon as the scheduler is called again upon completion of the interrupt, it will most likely run the bottom half (depending on the bottom half's type).

For example, if a packet arrives, then the tasks of the bottom half are run by the software interrupt `NET_RX_SOFTIRQ`. (See Chapter 6.)

The following sections introduce three possible activities that can be used as the bottom half in the interrupt-handling process.

2.2.3   Software Interrupts

Software interrupts (or soft IRQs for short) are actually a form of activity that can be scheduled for later execution rather than real interrupts. Software and hardware interrupts differ mainly in that a hardware interrupt actively interrupts another form of activity: Triggering the interrupt causes the (immediate) interruption of the running activity (but, of course, only if the triggering of interrupts is currently allowed).

In contrast, a software interrupt is scheduled for execution by an activity of the kernel and has to wait until it is called by the scheduler. Software interrupts scheduled for execution are started by the function `do_softirq()` (`kernel/softirq.c`). This means that the running activity is not interrupted when a soft IRQ is activated by `__cpu_raise_softirq()`. The corresponding handling routine is triggered when `do_softirq()` is called. This occurs currently only when a system call (in `schedule()`) or a hardware interrupt (in `do_IRQ()`) terminates.

A maximum of 32 software interrupts can be defined in the Linux kernel. Note that only four were defined in the Versions 2.4.x. This includes the soft IRQs NET_RX_SOFTIRQ and NET_TX_SOFTIRQ, which have ensured efficient protocol handling since kernel Version 2.4, and the soft IRQ TASKLET_SOFTIRQ, which is used to implement the concept of tasklets, further described later in this chapter.

Software interrupts differ clearly from the *tasklet* and *bottom half* forms of activity, as we have seen in Tables 2–2 and 2–3. The most important properties of software interrupts are the following:

▨ A software interrupt can run concurrently in several processors. This means that the handling routine has to be implemented reentrantly (e.g., with net_rx_action). If critical sections exist in a software interrupt (e.g., any global variable it accesses), then these have to be protected by locks.

▨ A software interrupt cannot interrupt itself while running on a processor.

▨ A software interrupt can be interrupted during its handling on a processor only by a hardware interrupt.

Calling in_softirq() (include/asm/softirq.h) causes a function to check immediately on whether it is currently in a software interrupt; see details in [Russ00b].

2.2.4   Tasklets

Tasklets are a combination of parallel executable (but lock-intensive) software interrupts and the old bottom halfs,[1] where we can talk neither of parallelism nor of performance. Tasklets were introduced to replace the old bottom halfs.

Tasklets have the following properties:

▨ The function tasklet_schedule(&tasklet_struct) can be used to schedule a tasklet for execution. A tasklet is run only once, even if it was scheduled for execution several times.

▨ A tasklet can run on one processor only at any given time.

▨ Different tasklets can run on several processors concurrently.

The macro DECLARE_TASKLET(name, func, data) can be used to define a new tasklet, where name denotes a name for the tasklet_struct data structure and func denotes the tasklet's handling routine. When the tasklet is to run, then the pointer data, pointing to private data, if applicable, are passed to the function func().

Tasklet_schedule() is used to schedule a tasklet for execution; tasklet_disable() can be used to stop a tasklet from running, even when it is scheduled for execution. It remains scheduled for execution or can be rescheduled. Tasklet_enable() is used to reactivate a deactivated tasklet. However, if that tasklet was not scheduled for execution, it will not run when you activate it.

---

[1]In this connection, we have to differentiate between the general concept of a bottom half that can be implemented by a tasklet (a soft IRQ) and a bottom half in the Linux kernel. In contrast, the form of activity of a bottom half is Linux-specific and denoted by sans-serif font in this text.

The following example shows how easy it is to define and activate a new tasklet:

```
#include <linux/interrupt.h>
/* Handling routine of new tasklet */
void test_func(unsigned long);
/* Data of new tasklet */
char test_data[] = "Hello, I am a test tasklet";
/* Definition of tasklet_struct structure of tasklet */
DECLARE_TASKLET (test_tasklet, test_func, (unsigned long) &test_data);
void test_func(unsigned long data)
{
        /*Do here what you think you have to do, e.g.:*/
        printk(KERN_DEBUG "%s\n", (char *) data);
}
...
/* Use an activity to activate the tasklet */
tasklet_schedule(&test_tasklet);
```

2.2.5   Bottom Halfs

Bottom halfs (BHs) had been the main form of activity in the kernel in early kernels. For example, NET_BH was responsible for handling of network protocols and sending of packets. There can be a maximum of 32 BHs, which are scheduled for execution by the mark_bh() function.

BHs are the form of activity with the smallest parallelism in the kernel, as mentioned in previous sections. The following property shows the major drawback of BHs:

  ▓ Only one bottom half can run concurrently on all processors of a system at one time.

Because BHs are inflexible and because they are to be replaced by tasklets or software interrupts in future Linux kernel versions, we will not discuss them further here. Information on BHs is found in the literature (e.g., [RuCo01], [BBDK+01] or [BoCe00]).

2.3   LOCKING—ATOMIC OPERATIONS

Several different forms of activity can operate and interrupt each other in the Linux kernel. (See Section 2.2.) In multiprocessor systems, different activities even operate in parallel. This is the reason why it is very important for the stability of the system that these operations run in parallel without undesired side effects.

As long as the activities in the Linux kernel operate independently, there will not be any problem. But as soon as several activities access the same data structures, there can be undesired effects, even in single-processor systems.

Figure 2–2 shows an example with two activities, A and B, trying to add the structures skb_a and skb_b to the list queue. At some point, activity A is interrupted by activity B. After some processing of B, A continues with its operations. Figure 2–3 shows the result of this procedure of the two activities. Structure skb_b was added to the list correctly.

```
A                                                B
  skb_a->next = queue->next;
                                                   skb_b->next = queue->next;
                                                   queue->next = skb_b;
  queue->next = skb_a;
```

FIGURE 2–2
Activity *B* interrupts activity *A* in the critical section.

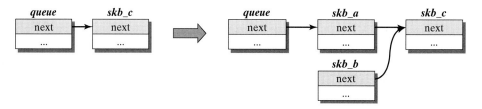

FIGURE 2–3
(Undesired) result of the unprotected operations of activities *A* and *B*.

```
A                                                B
                                                   skb_b->next = queue->next;
  skb_a->next = queue->next;
                                                   queue->next = skb_b;
  queue->next = skb_a;
```

FIGURE 2–4
Parallel operations of the activities *A* and *B* in the critical section.

Undesired results can also occur in multiprocessor systems when the two activities *A* and *B* run quasi-in-parallel on different processors, as in the example shown in Figure 2–4.

To avoid these problems when several activities operate on a common data structure (the so-called *critical section*), then these operations have to be *atomic*. Atomic means that an operation composed of several steps is executed as an undividable operation. No other instance can operate on the data structure concurrently with the atomic operation (i.e., no other activity can access a critical section that's already busy [Tan95]).

The next four sections introduce mechanisms for atomic execution of operations. These mechanisms differ mainly in the way they wait for entry into a potentially occupied critical section, which implicitly depends on the size of the critical section and the expected waiting time.

2.3.1   Bit Operations

Atomic bit operations form the basis for the locking concepts *spinlocks* and *semaphores*, described in the following subsections. Locks are used to protect critical sections, and they are normally implemented by variables, which manage the status of locks (i.e., they remember how many activities there currently are in a critical section.

This means that, first of all, the status of locking variables has to be checked and then set, before entry into a critical section. In a processor, this generally adds up to two machine commands to be executed, one after the other. However, it can now happen that a situation like the one described above can occur exactly between these two machine commands (i.e., the activity is interrupted and another activity of the kernel changes the state of variables). For this reason, atomic test and set machine commands are required to support critical sections. Modern processors support these commands and many more. (It would go beyond the scope of this book to describe each one in detail.)

Some of these atomic machine operations, as well as useful operations to manipulate single bits or integer variables, which are often useful to handle protocol headers, are listed in the following examples. Another benefit of these atomic operations is that no additional locks are required for their operations. They run in one single (very fast) machine command.

- `test_and_set_bit(nr, void *addr)` sets the bit with number `nr` in the unsigned long variables of the pointer `addr`. The previous value of the bit is returned as return value.
- `test_and_clear_bit(nr, void *addr)` deletes the specified bit and also returns that bit's previous value.
- `test_and_change_bit(nr, void *addr)` inverts bit `nr` and resets it to its original value.
- `set_bit(nr, void *addr)` sets the bit with number `nr` at address `addr`.
- `clear_bit(nr, void *addr)` deletes the specified bit.
- `change_bit(nr, void *addr)` inverts bit number `nr`.
- `test_bit(nr, void *addr)` returns the current values of the bits.

Integer Operations Operations can also be run atomically on integers. To do this, however, you have to use the `atomic_t` data type, which corresponds to the `int` data type in all supported architectures.

- `atomic_set(atomic_t *var, int i)` sets the variables to value `i`.
- `atomic_read(atomic_t *var)` reads the variables.
- `atomic_add/atomic_sub(int i, atomic_t *var)` adds or subtracts.
- `atomic_inc/atomic_dec(atomic_t *var)` adds or subtracts in increments of 1.
- `atomic_..._and_test(...)`: see *Bit Operations*.

All of these atomic operations are implemented by one single machine command. However, critical sections often cannot be reduced to one single command, but consist of several operations. Using the atomic bit or integer operations introduced in this section, you can implement locks to protect larger ranges for exclusive access. These *spinlocks* and *semaphores* are introduced in the following subsections.

2.3.2 Spinlocks

Spinlocks are also called *busy wait locks* because of the way they work. When a critical section begins and the lock—in this case the spinlock—has already been set, then the processor waits actively until the lock is removed. This means that the processor continues testing the locking variable in a continuous loop until that locking variable is released by the locking activity.

Though this wastes computing time because the processor seems to continually test the locking variable "meaninglessly," it can prove more effective to continually test the lock for a brief moment and then be able to enter the critical section upon its release rather than call the scheduler and grant the computing time to another activity. A lot of time can elapse until the waiting activity will get its turn after the lock's release. In addition, a change of activity caused by calling the scheduler could eventually take more computing time than a brief wait in the *busy wait loop*. For this reason, we observe the principle that spinlocks represent the best locking method for small critical program points (i.e., points with short locking times).

In the Linux kernel, spinlocks are implemented by the variable `spinlock_t`, which consists of one single integer locking variable. To use a spinlock, you have to create and initialize a `spinlock_t` structure, as in the following example:

```
#include <linux/spinlock.h>
spinlock_t my_spinlock = SPIN_LOCK_UNLOCKED;
/* You can also use spin_lock_init(&my_spinlock) instead of
   an assignment in the definition. */
```

You can now use a set of different functions to request, set, or release spinlocks. Each of these functions is especially suited for certain application cases. First, let's look at how we can set a spinlock:

- `spin_lock(spinlock_t *my_spinlock)` tries to set the spinlock `my_spinlock`. If it is not free, then we have to wait or test until it is released. The free spinlock is then set immediately.
- `spin_lock_irqsave(spinlock_t *my_spinlock, unsigned long flags)` works similarly to `spin_lock()`, but it additionally prevents interrupts and stores the current value of the CPU status register in the variable flags.
- `spin_lock_irq(spinlock_t *my_spinlock)` works similarly to `spin_lock_irqsave()`, but does not store the value of the CPU status register. It assumes that interrupts are already being prevented.
- Similar to `spin_lock()`, `spin_lock_bh(spinlock_t *my_spinlock)` tries to set the lock, but it prevents bottom halves (see Section 2.2.5) from running at the same time.

The following functions can be used to mark the end of the critical section, depending on the application. Each of them releases an occupied spinlock.

- `spin_unlock(spinlock_t *my_spinlock)` releases an occupied spinlock.
- `spin_unlock_irqrestore(spinlock_t *my_spinlock, unsigned long flags)` releases the specified spinlock and allows interrupts, if there were any activated interrupts when the CPU status register was saved to the variable flags; otherwise it doesn't allow interrupts.
- `spin_unlock_irq(spinlock_t *my_spinlock)` releases the specified spinlock and allows interrupts.
- `spin_unlock_bh(spinlock_t *my_spinlock)` also releases the lock and allows immediate processing of bottom halves.

The functions introduced above can be used to protect critical sections to avoid undesired side effects from parallel operations on the critical sections from occurring. The example shown in Figures 2–2 and 2–4 can be used as follows, where the use of a spinlock prevents undesired side effects:

```
#include <linux/spinlock.h>
spinlock_t my_spinlock = SPIN_LOCK_UNLOCKED;
// Activity A
spin_lock(&my_spinlock);
skb_a->next = queue->next;
queue->next = skb_a;
spin_unlock(&my_spinlock);

...
// Activity B
spin_lock(&my_spinlock);
skb_b->next = queue->next;
queue->next = skb_b;
spin_unlock(&my_spinlock);
```

The following useful functions are available to handle spinlocks, in addition to the methods used to set and release spinlocks:

- `spin_is_locked(spinlock_t *my_lock)` polls the current status of the lock, without changing it. For a set lock, a value unequal to zero is return; for a free lock, zero is returned.
- `spin_trylock(spinlock_t *my_lock)` sets the spinlock, if it is currently unoccupied; otherwise, the functions immediately returns a value unequal to zero.
- `spin_unlock_wait(spinlock_t *my_lock)` waits for the lock to be released, if the lock is occupied, but the lock is not set.

2.3.3 Read–Write Spinlocks

Spinlocks represent a simple and useful element to protect parallel operations on common data structures from undesired side effects. However, they slow down the progress of activities, because these activities have to wait *actively* for locks to be released. Active waiting is not always necessary in certain situations. For example, there are data structures with frequent read, but few write accesses. A well-known example from the Linux network architecture for this situation would be the list of registered network devices, dev_base. It is rarely changed during a system's runtime (in fact, only by registering a network device), but it is subject to many read accesses.

During accessing of such a jointly used data structure, it is absolutely necessary to use a spinlock, but reading activities do not have to be stopped when no write activity currently operates on that data structure. This is the reason why so-called *read–write spinlocks* are used. They allow several read activities to enter a critical section while there is no write activity operating on it. As soon as an activity with write intention occupies the lock, then no read activities must be in or enter the critical section until the write lock is released.

When we are adding a new net_device structure in our above example of the dev_base list, the undesired effect demonstrated in Figures 2–2 and 2–4 could occur. For this reason, we use the read–write spinlock dev_base_lock to protect our dev_base list. The data structure rwlock_t is used to implement read–write spinlocks.

The following functions are available to set and release read–write spinlocks. Note that we distinguish them according to whether the lock should be entered for read or for write purposes. Again, RW spinlock functions come in different variants with regard to how they handle interrupts and bottom halfs (..._irq(), ..._bh() etc.). We will not repeat a description of their differences here, because their behavior corresponds to the spin_lock() functions.

- read_lock...() tries to access a critical section for reading purposes. If it contains no activities or only reading activities, then the section is accessed immediately. If there is a write activity in the critical section, then we have to wait until that activity releases the lock.

- read_unlock...() leaves the critical section, which it entered for reading purposes only. If a write activity is waiting and there is no other read activity in that section, then it can access the section.

- write_lock...() tries to occupy the critical section for writing purposes. If there is already a (write or read) activity in the critical section, then the activity waits for all activities to leave that section. Subsequently, it puts an exclusive lock on the critical section.

- write_unlock...() releases the (write) lock and thus the critical section.

2.3.4   Semaphores

In addition to active locks, there is a way to avoid waiting until a critical section can be accessed when a lock is set. Instead of waiting, the activity releases the CPU by calling the scheduler. This means that the computing time can be used by other activities. This concept is known by the term *semaphore* or *mutex* in computer science.

The Linux kernel offers semaphores. However, they are not frequently used in the Linux network architecture. Therefore, instead of describing here in detail, we refer our readers to [BBDK+01].

2.4 KERNEL MODULES

We explained in Section 2.1 that monolithic operating-system kernels, including the Linux kernel, have the drawback that all functionality of the operating system is accommodated in a large kernel, making this kernel big and inflexible. To add a new functionality to the operating-system kernel, you first have to create and install a new kernel. This is a rather cumbersome task and can also be expensive, because running applications have to be interrupted and the system has to be restarted. Moreover, using an operating-system kernel that includes all possible kinds of functions, drivers, and protocols is not recommended either, because the kernel would then become huge and consume an unnecessary amount of memory. In addition, there are always new functionalities we would like to integrate into the kernel, or newer versions of existing functionalities, where errors have been removed. In fact, we can assume that the set of functions of an operating-system kernel will change over time. For this reason, monolithic kernels have to be continually updated—with the problems described above.

Linux is based on the monolithic approach, but it has used a different method to solve the problems noted, since kernel Version 2.0. Note that it does not opt for the microkernel-based approach, which also has drawbacks. The solution are *kernel modules*. These modules can be easily added to the kernel at runtime and they behave as if they had belonged to the monolithic kernel since the system started. When the functionality of a module is no longer needed, then it can simply be removed and the memory space it used is freed.

We saw in Figure 2–1 in which components of the kernel we can use modules: *device drivers, file systems, network protocols*, and *network drivers*. The use of modules is actually not limited to these components. Modules can normally be used on an individual basis. However, adding some functionality means that you need a corresponding kernel interface to inform the rest of the kernel about the new components. The interfaces of the Linux network architecture and the possibilities to expand it by new functionalities are one of the central issues of this book.

When compiled as kernel modules, new functionalities can be added as needed and removed once you don't need them anymore. (See Section 2.4.1.) This means that the principle of modularization is very similar to the flexibility of microkernels, the only difference being that Linux modules run in the kernel address space, components of microkernel systems in the user address space. More specifically, the Linux module concept combines the benefits of both operating-system variants. On the one hand, it avoids the expensive change of address spaces known from the microkernel-based approach; on the other, it lets you expand the kernel functionality individually at runtime at the same time.

The following sections take a closer look at the structure and management of kernel modules, because modules are the best and most flexible option to enhance the Linux network architecture. Unfortunately, a detailed description of kernel modules would go beyond the scope of this book; we refer mainly to [RuCo01] and [BBDK+01] instead.

2.4.1 Managing Kernel Modules

A kernel module consists of object code, which is loaded into the kernel address space at runtime, where it can be executed. When the system starts, it is not known which modules with what functionalities should be loaded, so the module has to make itself known to the respective components of the kernel. A module should also remove all references to itself when it is removed from the kernel address space. There are two methods available for these tasks, which each kernel module should implement—namely, init_module() and cleanup_module(). We will have a closer look at these methods in Section 2.4.2; first, however we need some general information about the management of kernel modules outside the kernel.

The following tools are used to manually load a module into the kernel, or remove it from the system:

- insmod Modulename.o [arguments]—This command tries to load a kernel module into the kernel address apace. In a successful case, the object code of the module is linked to the kernel; the module can now access the symbols (functions and data structures) of the kernel. Calling insmod causes the following system calls to run implicitly:

  - sys_create_module() allocates memory space to accommodate the module in the kernel address space.
  - sys_get_kernel_syms() returns the kernel's symbol table to resolve the missing references within the module to kernel symbols. (See Section 2.4.4.)
  - sys_init_module() copies the module's object code into the kernel address space and calls the module's initialization function (init_module()).

  When loading a module, we can also pass parameters (e.g., values for device names, name, interrupt lines, irq, and I/O ports, io_addr). In the module itself, these parameters should be designated by the macro MODULE_PARM(arg, type). When the module is loaded, then these parameters are simply passed by module name—for example:

  ```
  root@tux # insmod wvlan_cs eth=1 network_name="myWavelan"
  ```

- rmmod Modulename removes the specified module from the kernel address space. For this purpose, we use the system call sys_delete_module(), which, in turn, calls the module's method cleanup_module().

  The module can now be removed, if the module's reference counter is zero, which means that the module is currently not used in any point within the kernel. (See details in [RuCo01].)

- lsmod lists all currently loaded modules and their dependencies and reference counters.

- modinfo shows information about a module (e.g., its functionality, parameters, and author). This information cannot be generated automatically; it has to be set by the macros MODULE_DESCRIPTION, MODULE_AUTHOR, and so on in the module's source text.

```
# Aliases - specify your hardware
alias eth0  wvlan_cs
options wvlan_cs eth=1 network_name="MyNet" station_name="neo"

alias char-major-4          serial
alias char-major-5          serial
alias char-major-6          lp
alias char-major-9          st

alias tty-ldisc-1           slip
alias tty-ldisc-3           ppp
```

FIGURE 2–5
Configuration file of the module loader: `/etc/modules.conf`.

Loading Modules Automatically   In addition to via the command-line tools described above, kernel modules can also be loaded into the kernel automatically when needed. To enable the automatic loading of modules, the corresponding support has to be activated when creating the kernel (`CONFIG_KMOD`).

Using the tools described in the previous section to add and remove modules always requires a user's intervention—more specifically, the intervention of `root`. For security reasons, only the system administrator is authorized to load and remove kernel modules. Though this approach is secure, it is somewhat inflexible—for example, when a user requires the functionality of a module that is currently not loaded in the kernel. For this reason, a means was created for reloading modules automatically into the kernel upon demand.

Normally, the kernel generates an error message when a resource or a specific driver is not registered. You can ask for this component in advance by use of the kernel function `request_module()`. To use this function, you have to first activate the option `Kernel Module Loader` when configuring the kernel. `Request_module()` will then try to use the `modprobe` command to automatically reload the desired module (and any additionally required modules). You can select such options in the file `/etc/modules.conf`.

Figure 2–5 shows an example of the configuration file `/etc/modules.conf`. This file specifies that the network device eth0 is currently represented by the module `wvlan_cs` and that, for loading of this module, the specified parameters should be passed to this module. If `modprobe` cannot find the module, then `printk()` generates an error message. (See Appendix B.1.1.)

Though this mechanism runs automatically, it can load only those modules the administrator has specified in the configuration files, to ensure that no user can load system-critical modules. Modules loaded automatically can also be removed automatically after some time. More configuration options of the `Kernel Module Loader` and the `modprobe` tool are described on the man pages and in [RuCo01].

2.4.2   Registering and Unregistering Module Functionality

In contrast to an application that runs its tasks after its start, a module normally provides functions used by other parts of the kernel in the course of the system operation. The kernel is enhanced by a new functionality, which may be removed after its use. It is not known upon system start which functionalities will be added to the kernel by modules, so we need interfaces for a module to register its functionality. The different set, of kernel components (see Figure 2–1) have such interfaces (e.g., to register and unregister network drivers, file systems, protocols, etc.). (See Table 2–1.)

These interfaces can most easily be identified by function names. They generally begin with `register_...` and `unregister_...`, respectively. Table 2–1 showed a few examples.

The functionality of a module is registered and initialized in the module's own method `init_module()`. As described earlier, it is called directly after successful integration of the module in the kernel. `Init_module()` should run all initialization tasks, such as reserving memory, creating entries in the /proc directory, initializing data structures, registering and unregistering the functionality, and so on.

Upon successful execution of `init_module()`, the functionality of the module should be known in the kernel, and all initialization steps required for it should have run. However, if something goes wrong during the initialization, all actions done up to this point should be undone in any event. The reason is that, when `init_module()` returns with an error code, the object code of the module is removed from the kernel address space, and all attempts to access methods of the module lead to a memory access error. [RuCo01] includes several tips to solve this problem.

Appendix D shows a kernel module that adds a fictitious functionality to the kernel. In the further course of this book, we will introduce many elements of the Linux network architecture that can be implemented in the form of kernel modules (e.g., network drivers and protocols). You can use the module from Appendix D as a framework for modules you design yourself to enhance the Linux network architecture.

One of the module's own methods, `cleanup_module()`, is used to remove that module from the kernel address space. It should be used to clean up the work environment of the module (i.e., to unregister the module's functionality, free the memory it used, and remove dependencies between the module and other parts of the kernel).

Once you have called and run `cleanup_module()`, there should be no more references by the kernel or other modules to the module concerned. Otherwise, this would lead to a memory access error, causing the computer to crash.

The method `cleanup_module()` is called only if the reference counter (*use counter*) of the module is equal to zero. Otherwise, it is assumed that the module's functionality is currently needed, so that it cannot be removed. The macro `MOD_IN_USE` can be used to check the *use counters*.

A good example for the use of the reference counter is a module-based network driver. As soon as the relevant network device is opened, it is possible to access the driver's methods (and thus the module's methods) asynchronously. For this reason, the reference counter (for module-based drivers) is always incremented by the macro `MOD_INC_USE_COUNT` in the method `dev->open()`. When the network device is closed, so that driver methods can no longer be accessed, then `MOD_DEC_USE_COUNT` decrements the reference counter by one.

2.4.3   Passing Parameters When Loading a Module

We mentioned in Section 2.4.1 that parameters can be passed during loading of a kernel module. These parameters are specified either directly by `insmod` when loading or by `modprobe` in the configuration file. To be able to pass parameters to a module, you have to have previously declared these parameters in the module's source text. The following macros are available for this purpose:

▨ `MODULE_PARM(var, type)` designates the variable *var* as a parameter of the module, and a value can be assigned to this parameter during loading. It needs to be previously declared, of course. The second parameter of the macro (*type*) specifies the data type of the module parameter. The following types can be specified:

  ▷ `b:` `byte`
  ▷ `h:` `short` (two bytes)
  ▷ `i:` `integer`
  ▷ `l:` `long`
  ▷ `s:` `string` (or a pointer to a string)

  If the parameter is an array, then this can be specified as such by stating the array size before the type. For example, `1-3i` means that the parameter is an array with integer values, and between one and three values can be assigned to this array. More information about this topic are included in the header file `<linux/module.h>`.

▨ `MODULE_PARM_DESC(var, desc)` allows you to add a description (*desc*) for the parameter *var*. For example, this description is displayed when the tool `modinfo` is called. The description of a parameter should be short, but descriptive enough to make clear the task of that parameter.

In addition, the following macros can be used to output additional information, which can be called by use of the command-line tool `modinfo`. It is recommended that one use this informative option, because there could often be situations where the user of a module does not provide the source text:

▨ `MODULE_AUTHOR(name)` can be used to specify the author of a module. It is recommended to also state an e-mail address, in addition to names, for easy contact in the event that the module contains errors (and, of course, to be able to accept the large number of thank-you messages for your generous contribution to the open-source movement :-)).

▨ `MODULE_DESCRIPTION(desc)` should contain a description of the module's functionality. Ideally, you describe the basic functionality and include reference to further information (e.g., a URL).

▨ `MODULE_SUPPORTED_DEVICE(dev)` is currently not used. However, it might be used in future kernel versions to load the module automatically when the device *dev* is required.

The sample module in Appendix D shows how to use the macros described above.

2.4.4 Symbol Tables of the Kernel and Modules

Kernel modules are object code, which is added to the kernel at runtime. Once it has been embedded, the module is in the kernel address space. Before the embedding of a

```
c01e2640    register_netdevice
c01e2888    unregister_netdevice
c01e0ef8    netdev_state_change
c01ddf94    skb_clone
c01de20c    skb_copy
c01e147c    netif_rx
c01e0b40    dev_add_pack
c01e0b8c    dev_remove_pack
c01e0d78    dev_get
c01e0e94    dev_alloc
d0a03ec4    ppp_register_channel        [ppp_generic]
d0a03f98    ppp_unregister_channel      [ppp_generic]
d0a08660    ppp_crc16_table             [ppp_async]
```

FIGURE 2–6
Symbol table of the Linux kernel (excerpt).

module, however, several aspects have to be observed. As the module will probably have to call functions of the actual kernel and want to use its data structures, we first have to resolve the addresses of these functions and data structures. The Linux kernel includes a table, the ksym symbol table,[2] for this purpose. This table includes all required information. Each row of the table contains the name and memory address of a function or variable. Information about the data type or parameters is not saved to the table. Note that the programmer has to ensure correct mapping.

You can see in Figure 2–6 that a module can access only functions and data structures saved in the kernel's symbol table. Other parts of the kernel are not accessible to a module. This has the benefit that modules cooperate with the kernel exclusively over defined interfaces, as is true for the microkernel architectures described in Section 2.1.

The instruction EXPORT_SYMBOL(xxx) from the file kernel/ksyms.c adds a function or variable of the kernel to the symbol table. From then on, each module can access these variables or call functions. In addition, modules can export references to functions and variables from the module into the symbol table. The macro EXPORT_SYMBOL can be used to allow modules to export selected function and data pointers into the symbol table of the kernel. A module that does not want to export methods or variables can simply use the macro EXPORT_NO_SYMBOLS to express its wish.

A module can normally access only those symbols that are listed in the symbol table when the module loads. For this reason, a situation where two modules loaded consecutively into the kernel want to access each other's symbols may cause problems. The module loaded first cannot access the symbols of the second module, because they are not yet known. Since Linux kernel Version 2.4, however, there is a solution to this problem. This solution is called *intermodule communication* and is introduced in [RuCo01] and [BBDK+01].

---

[2]You can use the command-line call ksyms –a to view the contents of the current symbol table.

2.5 DEVICE DRIVERS

UNIX has its own way of handling physical devices. They are hidden from the user and accessible only over the file system, without limiting their functionality. For example, an application programmer can use the simple file operations `read()` and `write()` to access the driver's hardware, while the `ioctl()` command can be used to configure properties of a device.

Device drivers in the form of modules can be added or removed in Linux at any time. This offers you a comfortable tool to develop and test new functionalities. Figure 2–7 shows an excerpt from the `/dev` directory, where all devices are listed. In Linux, network adapters are not treated as normal devices and so they are not listed in the `/dev` directory. Linux has a separate interface for them. The reasons are described in [RuCo01]. Chapter 5 will discuss network devices in detail.

We can see in Figure 2–7 that the entries for device drivers differ from regular directory entries. Each entry includes two numbers used to identify the device and its driver.

■ The *major number* identifies the driver of a device. For example, Figure 2–7 shows that the PS/2 driver has major number 10 and the hard disk driver (`hdxx`) has major number 3.

The major number can be specified when you register a device driver, but it has to be unique. For drivers you think you will use less often, it is recommended that you let the kernel assign a major number. This ensures that the numbers are all unique. See details in [RuCo01].

■ The *minor number* is used to distinguish different devices used by the same driver. In Linux, a device driver can control more than one device, if the driver is designed as a reentrant driver. The minor number is then used as an additional number to distinguish the devices that driver controls. For example, the hard disk driver with major number 3 in Figure 2–7 controls three hard disks, distinguished by the minor numbers 1, 2, and 65.

Figure 2–7 also shows that the type of each driver is specified at the beginning of each row. Linux differs between two types of physical devices:

■ *Block-oriented* devices allow you optional access (i.e., an arbitrary set of blocks can be read or written consecutively without paying attention to the order in

```
brw-rw----   1 root     disk   3,    0 May 12 19:23 hda
brw-rw----   1 root     disk   3,    1 May 12 19:23 hda1
brw-rw----   1 root     disk   3,    2 May 12 19:23 hda2
brw-rw----   1 root     disk   3,   64 May 12 19:23 hdb
brw-rw----   1 root     disk   3,   65 May 12 19:23 hdb1
crw-rw----   1 root     uucp   4,   64 May 12 19:23 ttyS0
crw-rw----   1 root     uucp   4,   65 May 12 19:23 ttyS1
crw-rw-r--   1 root     root  10,    1 Sep 13 08:45 psaux
```

FIGURE 2–7
Excerpt from the /dev directory.

which you access them). To increase performance, Linux uses a cache memory to access block devices. File system can be accommodated only in block devices (hard disks, CD-ROMs, etc.), because they are required for optional or random access. Block devices are marked with a b in the /dev directory.

A block-oriented driver can be registered with the kernel function register_blkdev(). If the function was completed successfully, then the driver can be addressed by the returned major number. Release_blkdev() is used to release the device.

Character-oriented devices are normally accessed in sequential order. They can be accessed only outside of a cache. Most devices in a computer are character-oriented (e.g., printer and sound card). Character-oriented devices are marked with a c in the /dev directory. You can use register_chrdev() to register and release_chrdev() to release character-oriented devices.

The virtual file /proc/devices lists all devices currently known to the kernel. This file is used to find the major number of a driver in the user address space, in case none has been specified during the registration.

To be able to use a device that has not been registered yet, you need to first select a driver and generate an entry in the /dev directory. To create this entry, you use the command mknod /dev/*name typ major minor*, which is passed the name, the type (b or c), the major number of the driver, and the selected minor number for that device. If the command is successful, then you can now use the usual file operations (read(), write(), ioctl(), ...) to access that device.

Figure 2–8 shows how the data structure is passed when you register a character-oriented driver. A driver is addressed over a virtual file in UNIX, so these are all regular file operations. We will briefly describe here only the most important functions, to give you an overview:

owner refers to the module implemented by the driver (for a module-based driver);

lseek() sets the position pointer in a file. This function can be used for other purposes for non-file-oriented devices;

```
struct file_operations
{
        struct module      *owner;
        int                (*lssek) (file, offset, origin);
        int                (*read) (file, buffer, count, pos);
        int                (*write) (file, buffer, count, pos);
        int                (*readdir) (file, dir);
        int                (*poll) (file, poll_table);
        int                (*ioctl) (inode, file, cmd, unsigned arg);

        ...
        int                (*open) (inode, file);
        int                (*release) (inode, file);

        ...
}
```

FIGURE 2–8
File operations on a device driver.

- read() transfers data from the driver to the user address space. The driver has to have previously confirmed that the desired buffer is available in the user address space and whether this memory page is currently outsourced. Subsequently, the function copy_to_user() can be used to copy data to the user address space.

- As with to read(), write() is used to transfer data, but, in this case, from the user address space to the kernel address space (with copy_from_user()). Here again, before you can copy, you have to check the validity of the data range in the user address space. The memory range in the kernel does not have to be verified, because the kernel segment is never outsourced.

- ioctl() offers the most extensive functionality. It is used to set certain parameters of a driver or device. A constant that represents the desired command[3] and a pointer to the data to be passed with this command are passed to the ioctl() command. This can be arbitrary data. The power of this function is such that the ioctl() command could actually replace all other file operations of a driver.

- open() and close() are used to prepare (or postedit) a driver for subsequent (or completed) commands. This function must not be confused with similar functions used to configure a driver. Such tasks are normally executed by the ioctl() command. open() is called by a process to inform the driver that it wants to use the device. If a process can be made available only exclusively, then this is policed by the open() function. For this purpose, open() checks on whether another process has already *opened* that device and, if so, denies access to it.

   close() releases the device. Whether exclusive use is desired depends on the type of device.

When a device driver is accessed, certain things can happen at the interface of the device driver. For example, if you use the C library function fopen() to open a device file from the /dev directory, then the open() function of the driver is called in the kernel. If you use fprintf() to write data to the device file, then the write() function of the driver will run in the kernel. Not all operations of a driver have to be supported; only those that the driver really needs.

2.6   MEMORY MANAGEMENT IN THE KERNEL

Memory management is one of the main components in the kernel of any operating system. It supplies a virtual memory space to processes, often one much larger than the physical memory. This can be achieved by partitioning memory pages and outsourcing memory pages that are temporarily not needed to the swap memory on the hard disk. Access to an outsourced page by an application is intercepted and handled by the kernel. The page is reloaded into the physical memory and the application can access the memory without even noticing anything about insourcing and outsourcing of things.

The memory residing in the kernel cannot be outsourced because, if the memory management were to move the code to the swap memory, it would not be available later

---

[3]The commands and their constants are specified arbitrarily by the programmer, but they should be unique within the kernel. For this reason, it is recommended to use a hierarchical coding. (See [RuCo01].)

on, and the system would be blocked. For this and, of course, performance reasons, the memory of the kernel cannot be outsourced. Therefore, we will always distinguish between the *kernel address space* and the *user address space* in the rest of this book.

Virtual memory management is one of the most important and most complex components of an operating system. [Tan95] offers an overview of the theory of virtual memory management, and detailed information about its implementation in the Linux kernel is described in [BBDK+01] and [BoCe00]. Within the Linux network architecture, the structure of the virtual memory management is less interesting; it is of interest only in regard to whether memory can be reserved and released in an efficient way, as we will see in the following section. We will also introduce methods to exchange data between the kernel address space and the user address space. Section 2.6.2 ends with a brief introduction of the slab cache, representing an efficient management of equal-sized memory spaces (for example, similar to those use for socket buffers).

2.6.1 Selected Memory Management Functions

This section introduces the basic functions of memory management a programmer writing kernel components or kernel modules needs. First, we will discuss how memory spaces can be reserved and released in the kernel. Then we will introduce functions used to copy data between the kernel address space and the user address space.

Reserving and Releasing Memory in the Kernel

`kmalloc()`	**mm/slab.c**

`kmalloc(size, priority)` attempts to reserve consecutive memory space with a size of `size` bytes in the kernel's memory. This may mean that some more bytes will be reserved, because the memory is managed in the kernel in so-called *slabs*. Slabs are caches, each managing memory spaces with a specific size. (See /proc/slabinfo.) Letting a slab cache reserve memory space is clearly better performing than many other methods [Tan95].

The parameter `priority` can be used to specify options. We will briefly describe the most important options below and refer our readers to [RuCo01] for a detailed explanation of the large number of options offered by `kmalloc()`. The abbreviation GFP_ means that the function `get_free_pages()` may be used to reserve memory.

- GFP_KERNEL is normally used when the requesting activity can be interrupted during the reservation. It can also be used for processes that want to reserve memory within a system call. For activities that must not be interrupted (e.g., interrupt routines), GFP_KERNEL should not be used.
- GFP_ATOMIC is the counterpart of GFP_KERNEL and shows that the memory request should be atomic (i.e., without interrupting the activity).
- GFP_DMA shows that memory in the DMA-enabled area should be reserved. GFP_DMA can be combined with one of the two previous flags.
- [RuCo01] introduces additional options, but we will not repeat them here, as they are of lesser interest.

The return value of kmalloc() is a pointer to the successfully reserved memory space, or NULL, if no more memory is available.

kfree()	mm/slab.c

kfree(objp) released the memory space reserved at address objp. This memory space should previously have been reserved by kmalloc().

Copying Between Kernel and User Address Space   The following functions can be used to exchange data between the user address space and the kernel address space. They are defined in the file include/asm/uaccess.h.

- copy_from_user(to, from, count) copies count bytes from the address from in the user address space to the address to in the kernel address space.
- copy_to_user(to, from, count) copies count bytes from the address from in the kernel address space to the address to in the user address space.
- [RuCo01] and [BBDK+01] introduce more functions, but most of them can be implemented by copy_from/to_user().

Before the user address space is accessed, the above functions use the method access_ok() to confirm that the corresponding virtual memory page is actually residing in the physical memory. This control had to be done manually in earlier versions of the Linux kernel.

2.6.2   Memory Caches

Reserving memory spaces by calling kmalloc() can take a while, but it is the only way to reserve a memory space. However, when memory spaces of the same size are required over and over again, it is not useful to release them with kfree() after each use. Instead, they should be briefly buffered in a list and used from there when needed.

The Linux kernel allows this approach by providing *slab caches*. This means that you can create a cache with memory spaces of specific sizes, where the memory spaces no longer needed are managed until they are requested again.

Information about the current slab caches, including their use and sizes, can be polled from the proc file /proc/slabinfo. We will now introduce the methods required to build and tear down slab caches as well as functions to reserve and release memory spaces from a slab cache.

kmem_cache_create()	mm/slab.c

The function kmem_cache_create(name, size, offset, flags, ctor, dtor) is used to create a slab cache for memory spaces with sizes in size bytes. An arbitrary number of memory spaces (of equal size) can be managed in this slab cache. The parameter name should point to a string containing the name of the slab cache, which is specified in outputs in the proc directory.

Offset can be used to specify the offset of the first memory space of a memory page. Note, however, that this is normally not necessary, so it is initialized to null. The parameter `flags` can be used to specify additional options when reserving memory spaces:

- ▓ SLAB_HWCACHE_ALIGN: Aligns to the size of the first-level cache in the CPU.
- ▓ SLAB_NO_REAP: Prevents the slab cache from being reduced when the kernel needs memory.
- ▓ SLAB_CACHE_DMA: Specifies that the reserved memory spaces have to be within DMA-enabled areas.

The `ctor` and `dtor` parameters allow you to specify a constructor and a destructor for your memory spaces. They are then used to initialize or clean up, respectively, the reserved memory spaces.

The return value of the function `kmem_cache_create()` is a pointer to the management structure of the slab cache, which is of data type `kmem_cache_t`. In the Linux network architecture, slab caches can be used—for instance, for socket buffers (as in Chapter 4). The cache for socket buffers is created as follows:

```
skbuff_head_cache = kmem_cache_create("skbuff_head_cache", sizeof(struct
                    sk_buff), 0, SLAB_HWCACHE_ALIGN, skb_headerinit, NULL);
```

`kmem_cache_destroy()`	**mm/slab.c**

`kmem_cache_destroy(cachep)` releases the slab cache `cachep`. Note, however, that this call will be successful only provided that all memory spaces granted by the cache have been returned to the cache; otherwise, `kmem_cache_destroy()` will be unsuccessful.

`kmem_cache_shrink()`	**mm/slab.c**

`kmem_cache_shrink(cachep)` is called by the kernel when the kernel itself requires memory space and might may have to reduce the cache.

`kmem_cache_alloc()`	**mm/slab.c**

`kmem_cache_alloc(cachep, flags)` can be used to request a memory space from the slab cache, `cachep`. If memory space is available, then this call immediately returns a pointer to it for the caller. If the slab cache is empty, then `kmalloc()` can be used to reserve new memory space. For this call of `kmalloc()`, you can use flags to specify the options introduced in Section 2.6.1.

`kmem_cache_free()`	**mm/slab.c**

`kmem_cache_free(cachep, ptr)` frees the memory space that begins at address `ptr` and gives it back to the cache, `cachep`. Of course, this should be a memory space that had been previously reserved with `kmem_cache_alloc()`.

2.7 TIMING IN THE LINUX KERNEL

In the Linux kernel, clocks "tick" slightly different by than they do in the real world. The time does not progress continually, but in increments of 10 ms (milliseconds) each, which is called a *tick*. This means that the time virtually stands still between any two ticks. The number of ticks since the system started is recorded in a variable called jiffies in the kernel. The timer interrupt increments the jiffies variable at each interrupt. The terms *ticks* and *jiffies* are often used interchangeably.

The resolution frequency of the timer interrupt is initialized to the value of the variable HZ (include/asm/param.h), and it increments the jiffies variable every $\frac{1}{HZ} s$.[4] This length of time is absolutely sufficient for normal applications, because a higher interrupt frequency would only mean a higher load on the system due to too many unnecessary interruptions [RuCo01]. However, there are certain situations where a high timer resolution is required, especially to measure smaller time increments or for running actions at specific points in time [WeRi00]. In networks, you often find such requirements for protocol instances, for example protocol instances that have to calculate packet run times or traffic shapers that have to measure minimum time intervals in the microsecond range.

Most of these tasks require clocks with a resolution that is at least in the microsecond range. For example, to implement a traffic shaper [Tane97], you have to calculate the number of bytes that could be sent within a specific interval. For example, the jiffies time measurement with a resolution of 100 Hz is not suitable. With a rate of 2 Mbits/s, an interval of $\frac{1}{100} s$ already corresponds to a packet with a length of 2500 bytes.

To avoid this problem, most modern processors (Pentium, Alpha, etc.) have appropriate registers. They have been added to those processors mainly to allow system performance measurements and less for traffic shaping in networks. But, while they are present, their use is quite popular. In the Pentium processor and its successors (and most of its clones), this is a 64-bit-wide *TSC* (*Time Stamp Counter*) register; its content is incremented by a value of one in each processor clock. The content of this register shows the number of elapsed clock cycles since system start.

The TSC register is actually nothing more than a hardware variant of jiffies, except that its resolutions is higher by a factor of between 10^6 and 10^8. This means, for example, that you can measure intervals with an accuracy of 0.001 μs in a Pentium processor with a clock rate of 1 GHz.

Nevertheless, there is a certain inaccuracy when measuring with the TSC register, because it takes a few clocks (approx. ten) to read the register. The reason is the main memory access that occurs after the register value has been read. It can be done only in the bus frequency, which corresponds to a fraction of the CPU frequency. In addition, there could be effects in the first-level and second-level cache accesses that can easily lead to false measurements. However, the error caused by the TSC register is meaningless for normal measurements, because most of them measure only relatively big time cycles (in the 1-μs range). The command get_cycles() (defined in <asm/timex.h>) can be used to read the content of the TSC register.

---

[4]HZ depends on the architecture: In Alpha processors, HZ = 1024; HZ = 100 in most other architectures.

2.7.1 Standard Timers

In addition to measuring intervals in the microsecond range, we also need a way to run a function at a specific point in time to implement a traffic shaper [WeRi00], which sends packets at specific points in time. The resolution of such a *timer* should be at least in the 100-μs range. However, due to the fact that a PC has only *one* timer component, you can use only this one. As described above, the interrupt is triggered HZ times per second. In addition to updating `jiffies`, Linux uses the timer interrupt to run functions at specific points in time (i.e., the *timer handler*).

A *timer queue* can be used when a function of the kernel should run at a specific point in time (e.g., switching off the floppy motor). At each occurrence of a timer interrupt, the timer interrupt routine updates the `jiffies` variable and also checks the timer queue for timer handling routines, as may be present. Each `timer_list` structure within the timer queue stands for one function (timer handling routine), which is to run at a specific point in time (`expires`). The exact process of the timer resolution and of subsequent checking of the timer queue is described in [RuCo01].

The following functions are available to manage the timer queue:

- `add_timer()` adds a `timer_list` structure to the timer queue according to the time specified by expires. A `timer_list` structure represents a timer handling routine (i.e., a function to be executed). The kernel runs this function at the specified time.

  Note, however, that the timer interrupt is triggered only HZ times per second. This means that the method can run only when *expires* reaches the value of `jiffies`. Therefore, there is a small difference between time t when the function should theoretically run and the next possible value of `jiffies`. This difference can take up to $\frac{1}{HZ}s = \frac{1}{100}s$. But 10 ms is too long to allow reasonable traffic shaping.[5]

- `del_timer()` deletes a `timer_list` structure from the timer queue. The corresponding function will then no longer run.

- `init_timer()` initializes a `timer_list` structure. This function should always be called when a `timer_list` structure was created.

2.7.2 Using the APIC for High-resolution Timers

The current Linux kernel does not support any freely programmable timers with an accuracy in the microsecond range. As explained above, such high-resolution timers are required to support various functionalities (e.g., for traffic shaping in high-speed networks and to synchronize multimedia contents playback), but additional usages are conceivable. On the other hand, there is the problem that modern processors become increasingly faster, while the accuracy of timers remains at the state of the eighties for downward compatibility with vintage PCs.

---

[5]10 ms corresponds to the transmission time for approximately eighty packets of maximum length over a 100Mbps network.

There are two basic usages for high-resolution timers:

▨ *Periodic shot*: A timer with a specific interval is initialized and then periodically triggers an interrupt when this interval expires. This corresponds to the behavior of the timer interrupt in the Linux kernel, which always triggers an interrupt after 10 ms.

This type of timer is suitable for all scenarios where actions have to run frequently and normally after fixed intervals. If the accuracy of these intervals is within the range of milliseconds, then the standard timers described in the previous sections can be used.

▨ *One shot*: Exactly one action needs to run at a specific time, regardless of other events. Such an action is, for example, when you send a packet at a pre-calculated time or represent an image from a video.

Until recently, one-shot and periodic-shot timers had been available only on the basis of timer interrupts, offering an accuracy of not more than $\frac{1}{HZ}$ seconds. The timer functionality introduced next is based on the APIC component (in short *APIC timer*) to avoid the problems outlined above. The UKA-APIC timer was developed at the Institute for Telematics at the University of Karlsruhe, Germany, and can be downloaded from [ObWe01].

Technical Basis of the APIC Timer   Intel's x86 processor family originally used the *PIC 8259A Programmable Interrupt Controller* to manage triggered interrupts. It was used since the first personal computer at the beginning of the eighties and met its tasks without problem. However, multiprocessor capability needs to distribute triggered interrupts among several processors of an SMP computer. For this reason, Intel introduced the so-called *APIC (Advanced Programmable Interrupt Controller)*. More specifically, there are the following two different chips, as shown in Figure 2–9:

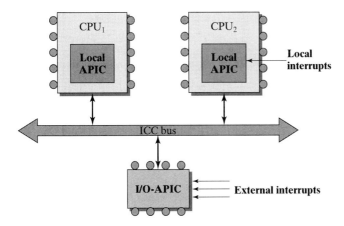

FIGURE 2–9
Use of an Advanced Programmable
Interrupt Controller (APIC) in
multiprocessor systems.

▓ The *local APIC* has been integrated in all Pentium processors (since Pentium P54C), and cooperates with the I/O APIC described below in multiprocessor systems. In addition to communicating with the I/O APIC and handling of incoming interrupts, a local APIC offers interesting possibilities, so it will be described here in more detail. Each local APIC has several 32-bit registers, an internal clock, an internal timer, 240 interrupt vectors, and two additional interrupt lines that can be used for interrupts generated locally.

▓ The *I/O APIC* is a separate component, collecting external interrupts and distributing them to the set of processors of a system. An I/O APIC is generally present only in multiprocessor systems, where such systems may indeed use more than one I/O APIC, which is supported in Linux since Version 2.4 [BoCe00]. The I/O APIC connects to the local APIC components of each installed processor over an interrupt Controller Communication Bus (ICC).

The internal timer of a local APIC is the most interesting part for the tasks discussed in this section. The internal timer works in bus-clock accuracy and can be initialized to a specific value. Subsequently, the value of the timer is decremented at each bus clock, and an interrupt is triggered when zero is reached. This means that the internal timer of the APIC component can be used to implement a high-resolution timer with almost bus-clock accuracy.

In contrast, single-processor systems do not integrate I/O components, and their local APICs are not activated when the system starts in most operating systems. In older P5 processors, you could activate the local APIC component only when the system started, and hardware manipulation was the only way to initialize it again. Since the P6 processor generation (Pentium Pro and successors), you can activate the integrated local APIC also during operation by use of software commands. This means that it can be used to implement a high-resolution timer.

Functionality of the UKA-APIC Timer   We emphasize here once more that the local APIC can be used for a freely programmable timer only in single-processor computers, because the timer of the local APIC in multiprocessor systems is used for interprocessor synchronization.

Some versions of the Linux kernel 2.3 allowed you to reactivate the local APIC component over a module. Unfortunately, this module is no longer present in the 2.4 versions. However, there is a patch [Pett01] you can use to activate the local APIC in single-processor systems at runtime. Based on an activated local APIC and its integrated timer, a high-resolution timer support was developed, featuring a programming interface similar to that of the standard timer of the Linux kernel [ObWe01, WeRi00].

The APIC timer also consists of a patch, integrating the interfaces required in the kernel and from a kernel module that manages the timers. One of the goals set when developing the APIC timer was to pack as much functionality and tasks as possible into one module to keep the understanding and maintenance simple. Unfortunately, there is no way around changes to the kernel for two reasons: First, you first have to activate the APIC component; second, there is no interface to register an interrupt handling routing for the APIC timer interrupt; `request_irq()` does not help either. For this reason, the

APIC timer handling routing, `smp_apic_timer_interrupt()`, normally used in an SMP configuration, is overwritten by another one, which allows entry into the use as a freely programmable timer (`set_apic_timer_up_handler()`). This method can be used only to set a new handling routine for the APIC timer interrupt.

The UKA APIC Timer Module The UKA APIC Timer module offers the interface required to register individual handling routines. The module consists mainly of management functions for the timer and methods to achieve as high a timer accuracy as possible.

Registered handling routines are managed in a linked list, similar to the management of the standard timer of the Linux kernel. The individual elements are structured as follows:

```
struct apic_timer_list
{
        struct apic_timer_list *next, *prev;
        unsigned long long expires;
        unsigned long data;
        void (*function)(unsigned long long, unsigned long)
};
```

- `next` and `prev` are used to link the `apic_timer_list` entries.
- The variable `expires` contains a value for the timestamp counter register, which specifies the time when the handling routine should run. Note that the TSC register operates with the processor clock and not with the bus clock (like the local APIC). The linked list is ordered by trigger points (`expires`) for performance reasons.
- `data` is a pointer that can be used to point to private data contained in the handling routine. This can be useful for reentrant functions to point to a specific instance.
- `function` is the function pointer pointing to the handling routine to be executed. Function() is called as soon as the time specified by expires is reached. The parameter `data` is also passed at this point in time.

The UKA-APIC timer module offers the following interface to the outside. The header file `uka_apic_timer.h` should be embedded to use this interface. To make things simpler for the programmer, the structure of the UKA-APIC timer interface is almost identical to the interface of the standard kernel timer:

- `init_apic_timer(struct apic_timer_list *timer)` initializes the passed structure of type `apic_timer_list`. Currently, only pointers for the linking are set to NULL.
- `add_apic_timer(struct apic_timer_list *timer)` registers a structure of type `apic_timer_list` and adds it to the linked list of the registered timers. The handling method `timer->function()` runs when the timer reaches `timer->expires`.
- `del_apic_timer(struct apic_timer_list *timer)` removes an `apic_timer_list` structure from the list of registered timers. This means that the handling routine will no longer run when the timer reaches `expires`.

▪ `mod_apic_timer(struct apic_timer_list *timer, unsigned long long expires)` modifies the time when a registered timer should run. This change can mean that the `apic_timer_list` structure may have to be put in another place within the list.

The following code fragment is a simple example to show how you can use the UKA-APIC timer. The following steps are required to register the handling routine `test_timer_handler()` so that it will run within two microseconds:

```
#include <asm/timex.h>
#include "uka_apic_timer.h"
#define SYS_CLOCK 500000000 //(500 MHz)
static struct apic_timer_list test_timer;
unsigned long long timestamp;
static struct egal_daten data1;
void test_timer_handler(unsigned long long exp, unsigned long data)
{
        /* Do here what you think you have to do :-) */
        * e.g., use hard_start_xmit to send a packet */
}
/* ... This is a routine, in which the timer is activated ... */
/* Initialize the apic_timer_list structure */
init_apic_timer(&test_timer);
/* Read the current time (status of the TSC register) */
timestamp = get_cycles();
/* Set the values... */
timer.function = (void*) &test_timer_handler;
timer.expires = timestamp + (SYS_CLOCK * (2 / 1000000));
timer.data = (unsigned long) &data1;
/* Register the timer */
add_apic_timer(&timer);
```

2.8   THE PROC FILE SYSTEM

All files in the /proc directory are virtual files. They do not exist on any memory medium, but are generated directly by the kernel upon each read access. A proc file is normally a text file showing information about specific parts of the kernel. For example, the commands lspci or apm show you information from the proc files /proc/pci und /proc/apm, respectively, and information about the current devices on the PCI bus or the state of the notebook battery.

The possibilities of the proc file system to display information on the kernel easily in the user mode are used by many system developers. Files and directories in the /proc directory can be easily implemented. In addition, you can register and unregister dynamically, so that the proc directory is often used by modules.

The files and directories in the /proc directory are essentially based on the `proc_dir_entry` structure, shown in Figure 2–10. Such a structure represents either a directory or a file. The directory *proc* is represented by the variable `proc_root`. The attributes and methods of the `proc_dir_entry` structure have the following meaning:

```
struct proc_dir_entry
{
        unsigned short              low_ino;
        unsigned short              namelen;
        const char                  *name;
        mode_t                      mode;
        nlink_t                     nlink;
        uid_t                       uid;
        gid_t                       gid;
        unsigned long               size;

        ...
        struct proc_dir_entry       *next, *parent, *subdir;
        void                        *data;
        int                         (*get_info)(buffer, start, off, count);
        int                         (*read_proc) (buffer, start, off, count, eof, data);
        int                         (*write_proc)(file, buffer, count, data);
        int                         (*readlink_proc)(proc_dir_entry, page);
        unsigned int                count;   /* use count */
        int                         deleted; /* delete flag */
};
```

FIGURE 2–10
Structure of proc_dir_entry.

- low_ino is the file's Inode number. This value is filled automatically by proc_register when the file is initialized.
- namelen specifies the length of the file or directory name, name.
- name is a pointer to the name of the file (or directory).
- mode specifies the file's mode; this value is set to S_DIR for directories.
- nlink specifies the number of links to this file (default = 1).
- uid or gid specifies the user or group ID of the file.
- size specifies the length of the file as shown when the directory is displayed.
- data is a pointer that can point to private data.
- next, parent, and subdir are pointers to link the proc directory structure.
- read_proc() runs when you read-access a proc file. The only task of this function is to fill the buffer with the file's output and return the number of written characters as result.
- write_proc() is called when you write-access the proc file.

In earlier kernel versions, a proc_dir_entry structure had to be created and initialized for each entry to be added to the proc directory. As we have seen above, many of the variables in the structure are needed only after registration.

The following functions were defined to simplify handling of proc entries.

create_proc_entry( )   **fs/prof/generic.c**

create_proc_entry(name, mode, parent) creates a file with name in the proc directory. The relative path to /proc/ can be specified in a name, or a pointer to the proc_dir_entry structure of the directory, in which the file should appear, can be set in the parameter parent. References to the /proc and /proc/net directories can be obtained from the pointers proc_root and proc_net. The parameter mode lets you pass flags for file properties of the proc file you want to create. Normally, this is filled with value 0.

As a result of this function, you obtain a pointer to the proc_dir_entry structure created. Now you can enter handling routines for read and write operations on the proc file. You can also set the pointer data to private data of a proc entry. This is necessary especially when a read or write function is used for several proc files.

The following source text is a good example to show you how a proc file, /proc/net/test, is created and initialized:

```
test_entry = create_proc_entry("test", 0600, proc_net);

test_entry->nlink = 1;
test_entry->data = (void *) &test_data;
test_entry->read_proc = test_read_proc;
test_entry->write_proc = test_write_proc;
```

remove_proc_entry( )	fs/proc/generic.c

remove_proc_entry(name, parent) removes the proc file specified in name. As with create_proc_entry(), you can either state the relative path to /proc or the proc_dir_entry structure of the directory where the file name is located.

proc_mkdir( )	fs/proc/generic.c

Though create_proc_entry() can be used to create directories in the proc directory, the kernel offers a simpler way with proc_mkdir(name, parent). The parameters name and parent can be used as in the functions described above. The result of this function is a pointer to the proc_dir_entry structure of the directory you created. The example in Appendix D shows how you can create the directory /proc/test by using this function.

create_proc_read_entry( )	include/Linux/proc_fs.h

We often want to create files in the proc directory merely to display certain information. This means that it is sufficient to register a function to handle a read access to the proc file. Though you can use create_proc_entry() and then register the read function, as in our example above, the kernel offers another function to achieve this in one step.

The function create_proc_read_entry(name, mode, base, get_info) creates the proc file name and uses the function get_info() to initialize read accesses. The parameters name, mode, and base are used as in create_proc_entry().

When there is no write access to the proc file proc/net/test and no private data has to be passed in the above example, then this function can be simplified as follows, where get_info() is the method used to handle read access to the proc file:

```
test_entry = create_proc_read_entry("test", 0600, proc_net, test_get_info);
```

`create_proc_info_entry( )`	**include/linux/proc_fs.h**

`create_proc_info_entry(name, mode, base, read_proc, data)` creates a file in the proc directory, just as `create_proc_read_entry()`$$$, but it additionally sets the parameter `data` in the `proc_dir_entry` structure. This variant is used when the read function `read_proc()` is needed more than once. Note that it has to be reentrant, and the pointer data to the private data passed corresponds to the proc file called.

This means that the above example can be replaced by the following function call:

```
test_entry = create_proc_read_entry("test", 0600, proc_net, test_read_proc,
&test_data);
```

2.9 VERSIONING

The Linux kernel is subject to constant improvement and development, and new versions (releases) are published regularly. To prevent users from getting confused and to identify stable versions, we distinguish between so-called *hacker* and *user* kernels. The version of a Linux kernel is denoted by a tuple composed of three letters, x,y,z:

▨ A *hacker kernel* is not a kernel version used by malicious people to break into highly classified computers. The very opposite is the case; in fact, a hacker kernel is the prototype of a Linux kernel under further development. Normally, new concepts and functions have been added to such a prototype and some errors of the previous version have been (hopefully) removed. Hacker kernels are in the testing phase, and faulty behavior or system failure has to be expected at any time. They mainly serve to integrate and test new drivers and functionalities.

Once a sufficient number of new drivers and technologies have been added to a hacker kernel, Linus Torvalds will proclaim a so-called *feature freeze*. This means that no new functionality can be integrated, and the only change allowed to that prototype is to remove errors. The objective is a stable user kernel. You can identify a hacker kernel by its odd y version number (e.g., 2.3.z, where z denotes the consecutive number of the kernel version). The next version (e.g., 2.3.51), will then have removed some errors of 2.3.50.

▨ *User kernels* are stable kernel versions, where you can assume that they are normally free from errors. A user kernel is denoted by an even version number, e.g., 2.2.z. Such versions are recommended to normal users, because you don't have to fear that the system might crash. For example, when version 2.3.51 is very stable and the feature freeze has already been proclaimed, then the kernel will be declared user kernel 2.4.1. New drivers and properties will then be added to hacker kernel 2.5.1.

## PART II

Architecture of Network Implementation

The Architecture
of Communication Systems

This chapter discusses basic models used to structure communication systems and architectures. The ISO/OSI reference model introduced in Section 3.1.1 failed in practice because of its complexity, especially that of its application-oriented layers. Nevertheless, it still has some fundamental significance for the logical classification of the functionality of telecommunication systems. Though it was less successful in proliferating than expected, this model offers the proposed structure of telecommunication systems in similar form in the field of telematics.

Currently, the technologies and protocols of the Internet (TCP/IP reference model; see Chapter 13) have made inroads and are considered the de facto standards. The architecture of the Internet can easily be paralleled to the ISO/OSI reference model, as far as the four lower layers are concerned. The other layers are application-specific and cannot be compared to the ISO/OSI model.

However, the architecture and protocols of the Internet also represent a platform for open systems (i.e., no proprietary solutions supported by specific manufacturers are used in the network). In addition, the development process for new protocols in the Internet by the Internet Engineering Task Force (IETF) is open for everyone and is designed so that the best and most appropriate technical proposals are accepted.

3.1 LAYER-BASED COMMUNICATION MODELS

Telecommunication systems bridge the spatial distance between distributed computers. The implementation of this task is extremely complex for a number of reasons, so it is not recommended to use a monolithic architecture, which could prove very inflexible and difficult to maintain. This is the reason why communication systems are normally developed as *layered architectures*, where each layer assumes a specific task, offering it in the form of services. The ISO/OSI reference model is probably the best known example of such a layered architecture.

To solve its task, a layer, N, must use only the services provided by the next lower layer $(N - 1)$. More specifically, layer N expands the properties of layer $N - 1$ and abstracts from its weaknesses. For this purpose, the instance of layer N communicates with the instances of the same layer on other computers. This means that the entire functionality of the communication system is available in the top layer. In contrast to a monolithic structure, layering a communication system means a more expensive implementation, but it offers invaluable benefits, such as the independent development of single partial components, easy exchange of single instances, better maintainability, and higher flexibility. Figure 3–1 shows the principles of communication in a layered system.

We can deduce two central terms for layer-oriented communication models from the current section, which will be discussed in more detail in Section 3.2:

▓ Communication between two instances of the same layer on different computers is governed by predefined rules. These rules are called *protocols*.

▓ The set of functions offered by a layer, N, to its higher-order layer $(N + 1)$, is called *its service*. The interface through which this service is offered is called *service interface*.

This means that an instance is the implementation of a communication protocol and the service provided within one layer on a computer. The theoretical basis of services and protocols are discussed in Section 3.2.

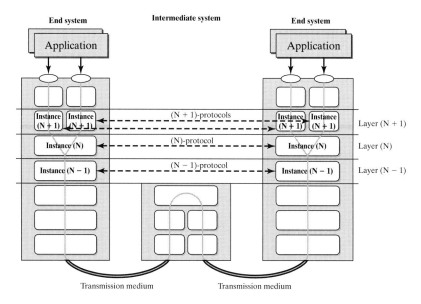

FIGURE 3–1
Communication in layered systems.

3.1.1 The ISO/OSI Reference Model

At the end of the seventies, experts observed increasingly that the interconnection of several computer networks was difficult (because of vendor-specific properties of these networks), if not impossible, so it was found hard to ensure interoperability between the large number of networks in place. This situation led to the proposal to create a uniform and standardized platform for computer-based communication networks.

Open vendor-independent communication required the definition and observance of general standards. The *ISO/OSI reference model* (in short, ISO/OSI model) proposed by the International Organization for Standardization (ISO) for *open systems communication* (OSI) [ITU-94] describes a general abstract model for communication between computer-assisted systems based on digital data. It serves as a framework for the development of communication standards to achieve open communication systems. This reference model has the character of a functional standard for other standards, i.e., it does not represent a specification for implementation, but refers merely to the mutual use of standardized methods for the exchange of data.

The ISO/OSI model consists of seven layers (see Figure 3–2), where one layer offers specific services to its higher-order layer. The ISO/OSI model does not describe a real implementation of a specific system, but merely defines the tasks of each layer. For this reason, it has become the basic model for telecommunication systems during the past decade. That's why the ISO/OSI model is often referred to as the *basic* reference model. In fact, knowledge of the ISO/OSI is normally the basis for the design and structuring of modern computer networks, although it is not a perfect model. It has certain strengths and weaknesses, as we will see later when comparing it to the more *streamlined* TCP/IP model.

The seven layers of the ISO/OSI reference model and their purposes are as follows:

▨ *Physical layer*: The physical layer handles the transmission of single bits over a physical medium. More specifically, (unstructured) bit sequences are converted to physical signals and transmitted over a physical medium (copper cables, fiber glass, wireless, etc.). The physical layer defines special coding methods, hardware connections, and media types.

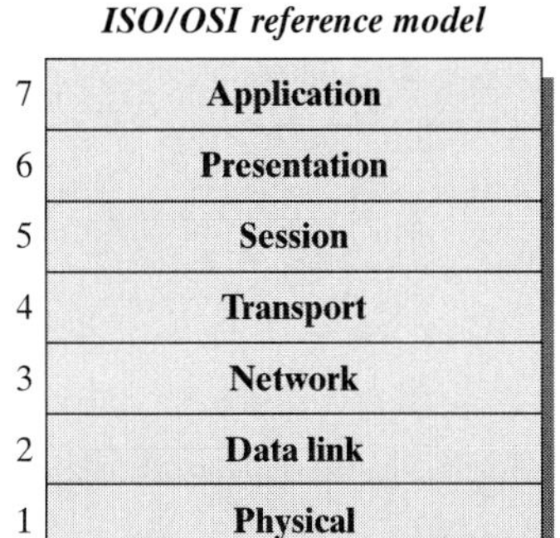

ISO/OSI reference model

7	**Application**
6	**Presentation**
5	**Session**
4	**Transport**
3	**Network**
2	**Data link**
1	**Physical**

FIGURE 3–2
The ISO/OSI basic reference model.

Data link layer: This layer specifies how data should be transmitted between two stations directly connected over a medium. The sending system organizes the data in frames and transmits them back to back. If errors occur, then the data link layer is responsible for detecting such errors and retransmitting the data frames. Moreover, the data flow between the two systems should be regulated so that the receiver does not get overloaded (flow control). Examples of data-link-layer protocols are HDLC (High-level Data Link Control), SLIP (Serial Line IP), and PPP (Point-to-Point Protocol); the latter two offer the described functions to only a limited extent.

In local networks, the data link layer often assumes the task to regulate access to a shared medium. In such cases, the data link layer is divided into the *Medium Access Control* (*MAC*) layer and the *Logical Link Control* (*LLC*) layer.

Network layer: The network layer is responsible for establishing connectivity between all systems of a telecommunication network. For this reason, the network layer deals mainly with switching and forwarding of data (e.g., routing, adapting data units to the admissible size of the respective data link layer (fragmenting), or ensuring various service qualities). Within the scope of this book, we will mainly discuss the Internet protocols Versions 4 and 6.

Transport layer: The transport layer regulates the transport of data between applications (i.e., between the sender and the receiver application). Among other things, it is responsible for addressing applications, for controlling the data flow between the end systems, and for securing both the correctness and the order of data.

Session layer: The session layer handles the structured exchange of messages over transport links. For example, it can control within a session whether the transfer of data should be concurrently in both directions or only one of the communicating partners should have the right to transmit. In the latter case, the session layer manages the right to transmit.

Presentation layer: The presentation layer regulates the presentation of transmitted data in a form independent of the communicating computer systems. Many operating systems use different forms of representation for characters (e.g., ASCII, Unicode), numbers (big-endian, little-endian), and so on. To ensure that this data can be exchanged between the systems involved, the representation layer transmits it in a standardized form (e.g., by using Abstract Syntax Notation (ASN.1) or Basic Encoding Rules (BER)).

Application layer: This layer uses specific protocols for different applications, using the lower-level layers to fulfill their tasks—for example, the application layer includes protocols for electronic mail, file transferred, and remote procedure call.

3.1.2   The TCP/IP Reference Model

The naming convention for the Internet reference model is based on the two most important Internet protocols—the Transmission Control Protocol (TCP) and the Internet Protocol (IP). The 7-layer ISO/OSI reference model described earlier was devised before internetworking was invented. Furthermore, the 7-layer reference model devotes an entire layer to session protocols, which have become much less important as

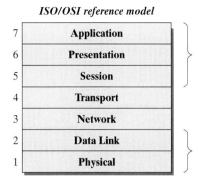

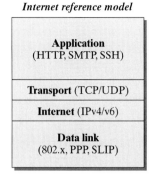

FIGURE 3–3
Comparing the ISO/OSI reference model and the TCP/IP reference model.

computer systems have changed from large mainframe systems to private worksta-tions. As a result, researchers who developed TCP/IP invented a new layering model. This section describes the new layering model briefly.

The TCP/IP layering model, which is also called Internet Reference Model, con-tains the following layers (shown in Figure 3–3):

- *Application layer*: The application layer combines all application-specific tasks (i.e., the properties of layers 5 to 7 of the ISO/OSI model). The protocols of the application layer include Telnet (for virtual terminals), FTP (file transfer), and SMTP (to transmit e-mail). More recent protocols include DNS (Domain Name System) and HTTP (Hypertext Transfer Protocol).

- *Transport layer*: As in the ISO/OSI model, the transport layer of the TCP/IP ref-erence model allows end-system applications to communicate. The TCP/IP refer-ence model defines two basic protocols for this purpose: the Transmission Control Protocol (TCP) and the User Datagram Protocol (UDP). TCP is a reli-able connection-oriented protocol and can transmit a byte stream without errors over the Internet to another computer. UDP is unreliable and connectionless, but is preferred over the more complex TCP in many situations (e.g., to transmit mul-timedia data).

- *Internet layer*: The Internet layer of the TCP/IP reference model defines the In-ternet Protocol (IP), including two auxiliary protocols, the Internet Control Mes-sage Protocol (ICMP) and the Internet Group Management Protocol (IGMP). The main purpose of the Internet layer is to forward IP packets from the sender to the receiver over the network, where routing of the packets plays an important role. The Internet Control Message Protocol (ICMP) is an integral part of each IP implementation; it serves to transmit diagnostics and error information for the Internet Protocol. The Internet Group Management Protocol (IGMP) is used to manage communication groups.

- *Interface layer*: This layer combines the two lower layers of the ISO/OSI refer-ence model. It handles network adapters and their drivers, which are used to ex-change data packets in a specific maximum length over a local area network (Ethernet, Token Ring, etc.) or over a wide area network (ISDN, ATM).

3.2   SERVICES AND PROTOCOLS

Services and *protocols* were briefly discussed in Section 3.1; they are basic elements of layered communication systems. This section describes the meaning of these two terms and the functionality of services and protocols. These two terms serve as a theoretical basis for further explanations in this book, where we will focus on services and protocols used in real-world systems.

We know from the models described in the previous sections that modern telecommunication systems consist of several layers. Each layer has different purposes (depending on the reference model) and offers services to the next higher layer. For example, the IP layer in the TCP/IP reference model offers the following services: *forwarding data units (without guarantees) from a local computer to another computer, specified by its IP address.* This service is used by the transport layer (e.g., by TCP) and expanded so that a byte stream can be transmitted free from errors and in the correct order.

We can say that a service describes the set of functions offered to the next higher layer. In addition, a service defines single service elements, used to access the entire range of services. In other words, the service definition defines the extent and type of service and the interface used to call that service. The definition of a service refers only to the interaction between two neighboring layers and the interfaces concerned. The literature describes this often as *vertical communication*. Exactly how a layer provides its service is not part of the service definition; it only deals with what an implementation has to offer the service user at the interface.

To be able to use the services of a layer, the participating systems have to overcome the spatial separation and coordinate their communication. This is achieved by use of *communication protocols*, which run by *instances* of a layer in the communicating systems. A protocol regulates the behavior of the distributed instances and defines rules for their coordination. For example, it defines messages to be exchanged between the instances to regulate distributed handling between these instances. More specifically, a layer, N, provides its service by distributed algorithms in the respective instances of layer N and by exchanging protocol messages about their coordination. (See Figure 3–1.) Coordination between the instances by protocol messages is also called *horizontal communication*. The service of the lower layer $(N - 1)$ is used to exchange protocol messages.

The specification of a service describes the behavior of a layer versus the next higher layer (*vertical communication*), but says nothing about how a service is implemented. It merely defines the format and dynamics at the interfaces to the layer that uses the service. A service is rendered by instances of a layer, which use protocols to coordinate themselves (*horizontal communication*). The protocol specification describes the syntactic and dynamic aspects of a protocol. The protocol syntax describes the format of the *protocol data units* (*PDUs*) to be exchanged and the protocol dynamics describe the behavior of the protocol. The goal of this book is to explain how all of these elements can be designed and implemented in a communication system. Using Linux as our example operating system, we will see what the interfaces between the different layers can look like and what design decisions play a role, mainly from the perspective of efficiency and correctness of the protocols. In addition, we will see how different protocols use their instances, to show the technologies used to implement network protocols.

3.2.1 Interplay of Layers, Instances, and Protocols

After our brief introduction to services and protocols in the previous sections, this section describes the horizontal and vertical processes involved when protocol instances provide a service. The description of these processes forms the basis for understanding how network protocols work, mainly the principles of horizontal and vertical communication. The terms introduced earlier will help us better classify and distinguish structures and parameters involved in the interaction of different layers at the interfaces.

Instances are the components offering services within a layer. To offer a service, the instances of a layer communicate (horizontally). This communication is realized by exchanging protocol data units (PDUs) of layer N. However, data is not exchanged directly between the two instances, but indirectly, over the next lower layer. This means that the instance of layer N uses the service of layer $(N - 1)$ to exchange a PDU with its partner instance. Figure 3–4 shows the interplay of layers and the elements involved.

▨ *Protocol Data Unit (PDU)*: A PDU is a message exchanged between two instances of a layer to coordinate their behavior. It represents the basic element of horizontal communication. A PDU consists of the following two elements:

▷ The *Protocol Control Information (PCI)* contains control information used to coordinate the two protocol instances and is also called the *packet header*. A PCI carries protocol-specific data and is created by the sending instance, depending on its state. The information is then evaluated and removed from the PDU in the receiver instance.

▷ The *Service Data Unit (SDU)* contains the payload to be transmitted at the order of the higher-level layer. The SDU of layer N normally consists of the PCI of layer $(N + 1)$ and an SDU of layer $(N + 1)$ (i.e., of the $(N + 1)$ PDU).

In certain states of a protocol, it can happen that the PDU does not contain any SDU at all (e.g., to establish a connection or in pure acknowledgment packets). In such cases, merely information needed to coordinate the protocols, but no payload, is exchanged.

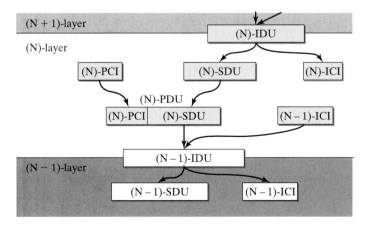

FIGURE 3–4
Data units for vertical and horizontal communication.

▧ Interface Control Information (*ICI*) is created by an instance and forwarded to the next lower layer together with a PDU (vertical communication). This information is needed by the service-rendering layer $(N - 1)$ to offer that service. For example, an ICI can contain the address of the partner instance that should receive the (N) PDU. The (N) PDU are pure payload data for layer $(N - 1)$, so that it cannot evaluate the elements of the (N) PCI included in the (N) PDU, but has to rely on the ICI contents.

▧ The *Interface Data Unit* (*IDU*) of layer $(N - 1)$ is composed of the PDU and the ICI of layer N. The IDU is delivered to layer $(N - 1)$ at the service access point and forms the basis for horizontal communication.

Note that, in the case of a vertical communication between two layers, this communication can take place only in defined *service access points* (*SAPs*), serving to distinguish different service users. SAPs are identified by service-access-point addresses, based on the rule that a service access point addresses exactly one service user. The principle of a service access point will come up often in the following chapters in connection with different environments (e.g., IP address for IP, ports for TCP, etc.).

The further course of this book will show how the dynamic aspects of a network protocol can be implemented (i.e., which programming elements there are and how they can be used in Linux. In addition, we will introduce interfaces and data structures of different instances and explain which parameters play a role as interface control information for different protocols. In this connection, we will explain that the theoretical model of a communication instance described above and the strict separation of the individual layers have to be given up if we want to achieve better performance of the entire protocol stack. When compared with a standard telecommunication work (e.g., [Tane97]), this book deals not only with the specification of protocols and their horizontal communication, but also with vertical communication and implementation aspects of different network protocols.

Managing Network Packets in the Kernel

One of the most important tasks of the network subsystem of an operating system is to process data packets according to the protocols used. In the designing of such a system, the multitude and flexibility of available methods play an important role, in addition to the performance and correctness of these protocols. Many network protocols differ a lot externally, but, when you implement them within an operating system, you can see quickly that the algorithms and operations on data packets are similar, and most of them can be reused. This chapter uses a Linux system as an example to show how data packets can be realized and what general methods are available to manipulate them.

One main reason for the flexibility and efficiency of the Linux network implementation is the architecture of the buffers that manage network packets—the so-called *socket buffers*, or *skb* for short. This central structure of the network implementation represents a packet during its entire processing lifetime in the kernel, representing one of the two basic elements of this network implementation, in addition to network devices. This means that a socket buffer corresponds to a sending or received packet.

This chapter introduces buffer management (i.e., the structure of *socket buffers*) and the operations used to manage or manipulate them. Beginning with an introduction to the sk_buff structure, we will use an example to show how an IP packet is represented in this structure and how it changes along its way across different protocols and layers. In addition, this chapter introduces functions used to manage and change the structure.

4.1   SOCKET BUFFERS

The network implementation of Linux is designed to be independent of a specific protocol. This applies both to the network and transport layer protocols (TCIP/IP, IPX/SPX, etc.) and to network adapter protocols (Ethernet, token ring, etc.). Other protocols can be added to any network layer without a need for major changes. As

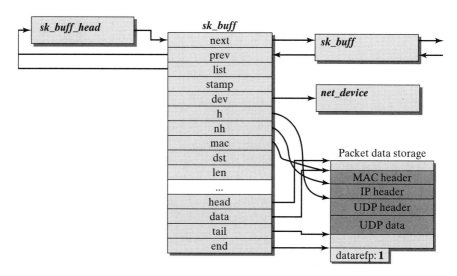

FIGURE 4–1
Structure of socket buffers (`struct sk_buff`) with packet storage locations.

mentioned before, socket buffers are data structures used to represent and manage packets in the Linux kernel.

A socket buffer consists of two parts (shown in Figure 4–1):

- *Packet data*: This storage location stores data actually transmitted over a network. In the terminology introduced in Section 3.2.1, this storage location corresponds to the protocol data unit.

- *Management data* (`struct sk_buff`): While a packet is being processed in the Linux kernel, the kernel requires additional data that are not necessarily stored in the actual packet. These mainly implementation-specific data (pointers, timers, etc.). They form part of the interface control information (ICI) exchanged between protocol instances, in addition to the parameters passed in function calls.

The socket buffer is the structure used to address and manage a packet over the entire time this packet is being processed in the kernel. When an application passes data to a socket, then the socket creates an appropriate socket buffer structure and stores the payload data address in the variables of this structure. During its travel across the layers (see Figure 4–2), packet headers of each layer are inserted in front of the payload. Sufficient space is reserved for packet headers that multiple copying of the payload behind the packet headers is avoided (in contrast to other operating systems). The payload is copied only twice: once when it transits from the user address space to the kernel address space, and a second time when the packet data is passed to the network adapter. The free storage space in front of the currently valid packet data is called *headroom*, and the storage space behind the current packet data is called *tailroom* in Linux.

When a packet is received over a network adapter, the method dev_alloc_skb() is used to request an sk_buff structure during the interrupt handling. This structure is

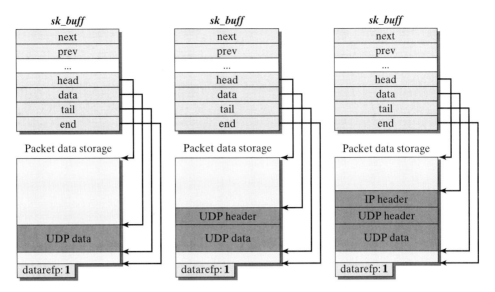

FIGURE 4–2
Changes to the packet buffers across the protocol hierarchy.

then used to store the data from the received packet. Until it is sent, the packet is always addressed over the socket buffer created.

We now explain briefly the parameters of the sk_buff structure (Figure 4–3):

▪ next, prev are used to concatenate socket buffers in queues (struct skb_queue_head). They should always be provided by special functions available to process socket buffers (skb_queue_head(), skb_dequeue_tail(), etc.) and should not be changed directly by programmers. These operations will be introduced in Section 4.1.1.

▪ list points to the queue where the socket buffer is currently located. For this reason, queues should always be of the type struct sk_buff_head, so that they can be managed by socket buffer operations. This pointer should point to null for a packet not assigned to any queue.

▪ sk points to the socket that created the packet. For a software router, the driver of the network adapters creates the socket buffer structure. This means that the packet is not assigned to a valid socket, and so the pointer points to null.

▪ stamp specifies the time when the packet arrived in the Linux system (in jiffies).

▪ dev and rx_dev are references to network devices, where dev states the current network device on which the socket buffer currently operates. Once the routing decision has been taken, dev points to the network adapter over which the packet should leave the computer. Until the output adapter for the packet is known, dev points to the input adapter. rx_dev always points to the network device that received the packet.

```
struct sk_buff
{
    struct sk_buff       *next,*prev;
    struct sk_buff_head  *list;
    struct sock          *sk;
    struct timeval       stamp;
    struct net_device    *dev, *rx_dev;

    union /* Transport layer header */
    {
        struct tcphdr    *th;
        struct udphdr    *uh;
        struct icmphdr   *icmph;
        struct igmphdr   *igmph;
        struct iphdr     *ipiph;
        struct spxhdr    *spxh;
        unsigned char    *raw;
    } h;

    union /* Network layer header */
    {
        struct iphdr     *iph;
        struct ipv6hdr   *ipv6h;
        struct arphdr    *arph;
        struct ipxhdr    *ipxh;
        unsigned char    *raw;
    } nh;

    union /* Link layer header */
    {
        struct ethhdr    *ethernet;
        unsigned char    *raw;
    } mac;

    struct dst_entry     *dst;
    char                 cb[48];
    unsigned int         len, csum;
    volatile char        used;
    unsigned char        is_clone, cloned, pkt_type, ip_summed;
    __u32                priority;
    atomic_t             users;
    unsigned short       protocol, security;
    unsigned int         truesize;
    unsigned char        *head, *data, *tail, *end;
    void                 (*destructor)(struct sk_buff *);

    ...
};
```

FIGURE 4–3

The sk_buff structure, including management data for a packet.

▪ h, nh, and mac are pointers to packet headers of the transport layer (h), the network layer (nh), and the MAC layer (mac). These pointers are set for a packet as it travels across the kernel. (See Figure 4–2.) For example, the h pointer of an IP packet is set in the function ip_rcv() to the IP protocol header (type iphdr).

▪ dst refers to an entry in the routing cache, which means that it contains either information about the packet's further trip (e.g., the adapter over which the packet is to leave the computer) or a reference to a MAC header stored in the hard header cache. (See Chapters 15 and 16a.)

▦ `cloned` indicates that a packet was cloned. Clones will be explained in detail later in this chapter. For now, it is sufficient to understand that clones are several copies of a packet and that, though several `sk_buff` structures exist for a packet, they all use one single packet data location jointly.

▦ `pkt_type` specifies the type of a packet, which can be one of the following:

  ▷ `PACKET_HOST` specifies packet a sent to the local host.
  ▷ `PACKET_BROADCAST` specifies a broadcast packet.
  ▷ `PACKET_MULTICAST` specifies a multicast packet.
  ▷ `PACKET_OTHERHOST` specifies packets not destined for the local host, but received by special modes (e.g., the promiscuous mode).
  ▷ `PACKET_OUTGOING` specifies packets leaving the computer.
  ▷ `PACKET_LOOPBACK` specifies packets sent from the local computer to itself.
  ▷ `PACKET_FASTROUTE` specifies packets fast-forwarded between special network cards (`fastroute` is not covered in this book).

▦ `len` designates the length of a packet represented by the socket buffer. This considers only data accessible to the kernel. This means that only the two MAC addresses and the type/length field are considered in an Ethernet packet. The other fields (preamble, padding, and checksum) are added later in the network adapter, which is the reason why they are not handled by the kernel.

▦ `data`, `head`, `tail`, `end`: The `data` and `tail` pointers point to currently valid packet data. Depending on the layer that currently handles the packet, these parameters specify the currently valid protocol data unit.

  `head` and `end` point to the total location that can be used for packet data. The latter storage location is slightly bigger to allow a protocol to add protocol data before or after the packet, without the need to copy the packet data. This avoids expensive copying of the packet data location. If it has to be copied in rare cases, then appropriate methods can be used to create more space for packet data.

  The space between `head` and `data` is called *headroom*; the space between `tail` and `end` is called *tailroom*.

▦ The other parameters are not discussed here, because they are of minor importance. Some of them are discussed in other chapters (e.g., `netfilter` in Section 19.3).

The pointer `datarefp` is actually not part of the `sk_buff` structure, because it is located at the end of the packet data space and not defined as a variable of a structure. (See Figure 4–1.) `datarefp` is a reference counter; it can be easily addressed and manipulated by use of the macro `skb_datarefp(skb)`.

The reference counter was arranged in this way because, during cloning of socket buffers, several `sk_buff` structures will still point to the same packet data space. If a socket buffer is released, then no other references to the packet data space should also release the packet data space. Otherwise, this would quickly lead to a huge storage hole. The only location where the number of references to packet data can be managed is the packet data space itself, because there is no list managing all clones of a packet. For this reason, and to avoid having to create another data type, we simply reserve a few more bytes than specified by the user when allocating the packet data space. Using the macro skb_datarefp, it is easy to access and test the reference counter to see whether there are other references to the packet data space, in addition to the own reference.

4.1.1 Operations on Socket Buffers

The Linux kernel offers you a number of functions to manipulate socket buffers. In general, these functions can be grouped into three categories:

- *Create, release, and duplicate socket buffers*: These functions assume the entire storage management for socket buffers and their optimization by use of socket-buffer caches.
- *Manipulate parameters and pointers* within the sk_buff structure: These mainly are operations to change the packet data space.
- *Manage socket buffer queues.*

Creating and Releasing Socket Buffers

alloc_skb()	net/core/skbuff.c

alloc_skb(size, gpf_mask) allocates memory for a socket buffer structure and the corresponding packet memory. In this case, size specifies the size of the packet data space, where this space will be increased (*aligned*) to the next 16-bit address.

In the creation of a new socket buffer, no immediate attempt is made to allocate the memory with kmalloc() for the sk_buff structure; rather, an attempt is made to reuse previously consumed sk_buff structures. Note that requesting memory in the kernel's storage management is very expensive and that, because structures of the same type always require the same size, an attempt is first made to reuse an sk_buff structure no longer required. (This approach can be thought of as simple recycling; see Section 2.6.2.)

There are two different structures that manage consumed socket buffer structures:

- First, each CPU manages a so-called skb_head_cache that stores packets no longer needed. This is a simple socket buffer queue, from which alloc_skb() takes socket buffers.
- Second, there is a central stack for consumed sk_buff structures (skbuff_head_cache).

If there are no more sk_buff structures available for the current CPU, then kmem_cache_alloc() is used to try obtaining a packet from the central socket-buffer cache (skbuff_head_cache). If this attempt fails, then kmalloc() is eventually used. gfp_mask contains flags required to reserve memory.

Using these two caches can be justified by the fact that many packets are created and released in a system (i.e., the memory of sk_buff structures is frequently released), only to be required again shortly afterwards. The two socket buffer caches were introduced to avoid this expensive releasing and reallocating of memory space by the storage management (similarly to first-level and second-level caches for CPU memory access). This means that the time required to release and reserve sk_buff structures can be shortened. When kmem_cache_alloc() is used to reserve an sk_buff structure, the function skb_header_init() is called to initialize the structure. It will be described further below.

Naturally, for the sk_buff structure, a socket buffer requires memory for the packet data. Because the size of a packet is usually different from and clearly bigger than that of an sk_buff structure, a method like the socket-buffer cache does not provide any benefit. The packet data space is reserved in the usual way (i.e., by use of kmalloc()).

The pointers head, data, tail, and end are set once memory has been reserved for the packet data. The counters user and datarefp (number of references to these socket buffer structure) are set to one. The data space for packets begins to grow from the top (data) (i.e., at that point, the socket buffer has no headroom and has tailroom of size bytes).

dev_alloc_skb()	include/linux/skbuff.h

dev_alloc_skb(length) uses the function alloc_skb() to create a socket buffer. The length of this socket buffer's packet data space is length + 16 bytes. Subsequently, skb_reserve(skb, 16) is used to move the currently valid packet data space 16 bytes backwards. This means that the packet has now a headroom of 16 bytes and a tailroom of length bytes.

skb_copy()	net/core/skbuff.c

skb_copy(skb, gfp_mask) creates a copy of the socket buffer skb, copying both the sk_buff structure and the packet data. (See Figure 4-4.) First the function uses alloc_skb() to obtain a new sk_buff structure; then it sets the attributes. Note that only protocol-specific parameters (priority, protocol, ...), the relevant network device (device), and an entry in the route cache are accepted. All pointers dealing with the concatenation of socket buffers (next, prev, sk, list) are set to null.

Memory needed for the payload of the new socket buffers is allocated by kmalloc() and copied by memcopy(). Subsequently, pointers to the new data space are set in the new sk_buff structure. The result of skb_copy() is a new socket buffer (with its own packet data space), which exists independently of the original and can be processed independently. This means that the reference counter of the created copy also shows a value of one, in contrast to a using skb_clone() to replicate a packet.

skb_copy_expand()	net/core/skbuff.c

skb_copy_expand(skb, newheadroom, newtailroom, gfp_mask) also creates a new and independent copy of the socket buffer and packet data; however, a larger

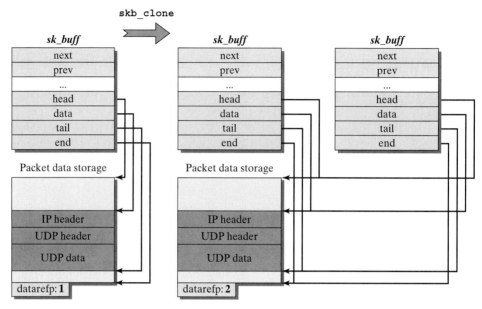

FIGURE 4–4
Copying socket buffers.

space before and after the packet data can be reserved. newheadroom and newtailroom specify the size of this space before and behind the packet data space, respectively.

skb_clone()	net/core/skbuff.c

skb_clone() also creates a new socket buffer; however, it allocates only one new sk_buff structure, and no second memory space for packet data. The pointers of the original sk_buff structure and of the new structure point to the same packet data space. There is no backward reference from the packet memory to the references sk_buff structures, so the packet memory should be read-only. Figure 4–5 shows the situation before and after skb_clone() is called. Among other things, this function is required in multicast implementation. (See Chapter 17.) This allows us to prevent the time-intensive copying of a complete packet data space when a packet is to be sent to several network devices. The memory containing packet data is not released before the variable datarefp contains a value of one (i.e., when there is only one reference to the packet data space left).

kfree_skb()	include/linux/skbuff.h

kfree_skb() does the same thing as kfree_skbmem() and is called by kfree_skb(), but it additionally tests whether the socket buffer is still in a queue (if so, an error message is output). In addition, it removes the reference from the route cache and, if present, calls a destructor() for the socket buffer. kfree_skb() should be preferred over other options because of these additional security checks.

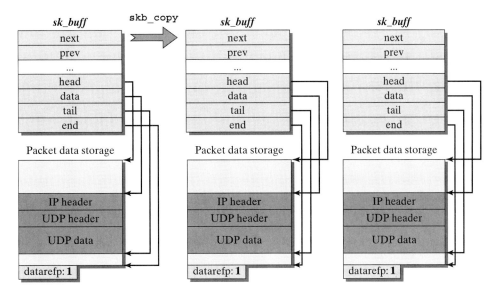

FIGURE 4–5
Cloning socket buffers.

---

dev_kfree_skb()   **include/linux/skbuff.h**

dev_kfree-skb(skb) is identical to the method kfree_skb() and is mapped to kfree_skb() by a preprocessor macro.

---

kfree_skbmem()   **include/linux/skbuff.h**

kfree_skbmem() frees a socket buffer, provided that it was not cloned and that no instance in the kernel refers to it (datrefp - 1). The variable skb_cloned is tested for null, and datarefp is tested for one. If everything is okay, kfree() first releases the packet memory. Then skb_head_to_pool() is used to insert the sk_buff structure into the socket-buffer cache of the current processor for further use. This means that the memory of the socket-buffer structure is not released for general use (kfree()), but instead is buffered for recycling.

---

skb_header_init()   **include/linux/skbuff.h**

skb_header_init() initializes some fields of the sk_buff structure with standard values. Most fields are set to null or NULL, and PACKET_HOST is registered as the packet type.

Manipulating the Packet Data Space   The following functions are declared in the include file <Linux/skbuff.h>. Most of them are defined as inline and have only little functionality; nevertheless, they are important and are used often.

skb_get()	include/linux/skbuff.h

This increments the number of user references to the sk_buff structure by one.

skb_unshare()	include/linux/skbuff.h

skb_unshared(skb) uses skb_cloned to check for whether the socket buffer is available for exclusive use. If it isn't, then a copy of skb is created and returned, so that an exclusive socket buffer is available. In the original packet, the reference counter is decremented by a value of one.

skb_put()	include/linux/skbuff.h

skb_put(skb, len) is an inline function that appends data to the end of the current data range of a packet. Though this occurs seldom, because most protocols write their PCI (Protocol Control Information) before the current protocol data unit, there are a few protocol, that require this. More specifically, skb_put() increments the pointer tail and the parameter skb-> by len. Note that skb_put() merely sets the pointers again; the caller is responsible for copying the correct data to the packet data space. The return value is the old value of skb->tail, so as to be able to add new packet data to the correct place. Before calling skb_put(), we should confirm that the *tailroom* is sufficient; otherwise, the kernel will output an error message and call skb_over_panic().

skb_push()	include/linux/skbuff.h

skb_push(skb, len) works like skb_put(), but increases the current packet data space at the beginning of the packet by len bytes. This means that the data pointer is decremented by len, and skb->len is incremented by this amount. The return value of skb_push() points to the new data space (skb->data, in this case). Again, we should first check the *headroom* size.

skb_pull()	include/linux/skbuff.h

skb_pull(skb, len) serves to truncate len bytes at the beginning of a packet. The pointer skb->data is adjusted, and the length of the packet (skb->len) is reduced accordingly—but, first, we check on whether there are still len bytes in the free part of the packet data space.

skb_tailroom()	include/linux/skbuff.h

skb_tailroom(skb) returns the bytes still free at the end of the data space. If skb_put() requests more data in this space than skb_tailroom states, then this will lead to a *kernel panic*.

skb_headroom()	include/linux/skbuff.h

skb_headroom(skb) returns (data - head). This corresponds to the amount of free bytes in the front space of the packet data memory. Exactly skb_headroom bytes can still be inserted into the packet by skb_push().

skb_realloc_headroom()	include/linux/skbuff.h

skb_realloc_headroom(skb, newheadroom) is required when the memory space between skb->data and skb->head is getting too small. This function can be used to create a new socket buffer with a *headroom* corresponding to the size newheadroom (and not one single byte more). The data part of the old socket buffer is copied into the new one, and most parameters of the sk_buff structure are taken from the old one. Only sk and list are set to NULL. skb_realloc_headroom() is implemented by calling the function skb_copy_expand().

skb_reserve()	include/linux/skbuff.h

skb_reserve(skb, len) shifts the entire current data space backwards by len bytes. This means that the total length of this space remains the same. Of course, this function is meaningful only when there are no data in the current space yet, and only if the initial occupancy of this space has to be corrected.

skb_trim()	include/linux/skbuff.h

skb_trim(skb, len) sets the current packet data space to len bytes, which means that this space now extends from the initial occupancy of data to tail - data + len. This function is normally used to truncate data at the end (i.e., we call skb_trim() with a length value smaller than the current packet size).

skb_cow()	include/linux/skbuff.h

skb_cow(skb, headroom) checks on whether the passed socket buffer has still at least headroom bytes free in the front packet data space and whether the packet is a clone. If either of the two situations is true, then skb_alloc_headroom(skb, headroom) creates and returns a new independent packet. If none of the two tests is true, then the socket buffer skb is returned. skb_cow() is used when a protocol requires an independent socket buffer with sufficient *headroom*.

4.1.2 Other Functions

skb_cloned()	include/linux/skbuff.h

skb_cloned(skb) specifies whether this socket buffer was cloned and whether the corresponding packet data space is exclusive. The reference counter datarefp is used to check this.

skb_shared()	include/linux/skbuff.h

skb_shared(skb) checks whether skb->users specifies one single user or several users for the socket buffer.

skb_over_panic(), skb_under_panic()	include/linux/skbuff.h

These functions are used as error-handling routines during an attempt to increase too small a headroom or tailroom of a socket buffer. A debug message is output after each function, and the function BUG() is called.

skb_head_to_pool()	net/core/skbuff.c

skb_head_to_pool(skb) is used to register a socket buffer structure with the socket-buffer pool of the local processor. It is organized as a simple socket-buffer queue, so this product is simply added to the front of the queue by skb_queue_head(). This means that the memory of the socket buffer is not released, but buffered for use by other network packets. This method is much more efficient than to repeatedly allocate and release the memory of a socket buffer by the more complex memory management of the kernel.

The queue skb_head_pool[smp_processor_id()].list cannot grow to an arbitrary length; it can contain a maximum of sysctl_hot_list_len. As soon as this size is reached, additional socket buffers are added to the central pool for reusable socket buffers (skbuff_head_cache).

skb_head_from_pool()	net/core/skbuff.c

This function is used to remove and return a socket buffer from the pool of used socket buffers of the current processor.

4.2   SOCKET-BUFFER QUEUES

When a packet is currently not handled by a protocol instance, it is normally managed in queues. Linux supports the management of packets in a queue structure (struct sk_buff_head) and in a number of operations on this structure. The programmer can use these functions to abstract from the actual implementation of a socket buffer and queues to easily change the underlying implementation of the queue management.

Figure 4–6 shows that the socket buffers stored in a queue are dual-concatenated in a ring structure. This dual concatenation allows quick navigation in either of the two directions. The ring structure facilitates concatenation and prevents the occurrence of NULL pointers.

A queue header consists of the following skb_queue_head structure:

```
struct sk_buff_head
{
        struct sk_buff *next;
        struct sk_buff *prev;
```

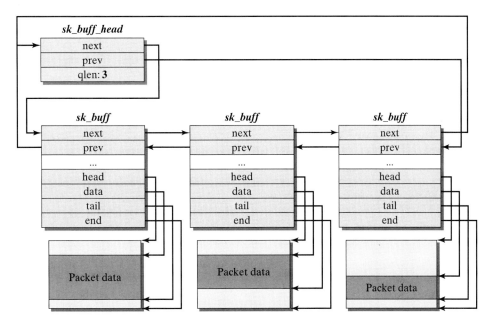

FIGURE 4–6
Packet queues in the Linux kernel.

```
        __u32 qlen;
        spinlock_t lock;
};
```

- **next** and prev are used to concatenate socket buffers; **next** points to the first and prev to the last packet in the queue.
- qlen specifies the current length of the queue in packets.
- lock is a spinlock (see Section 2.3.2) and can be used for atomic execution of operations on the queue. When a critical access occurs, if the spinlock is not free, the access will have to wait until it is released.

4.2.1 Operations on Socket-Buffer Queues

Socket-buffer queues are a powerful tool to arrange packets in Linux. The power of this functionality is complemented by a large number of methods to manage socket buffers in queues.

Most operations on socket buffers are executed during critical phases, or they can be interrupted by higher-priority operations (interrupt handling, soft-IRQ, tasklet, etc.). For this reason, packet data and pointer structures should be processed in an atomic way. Though this introduces some additional cost, because certain mechanisms (e.g., spinlocks and semaphores) have to be used to achieve save states, it is the only way to prevent inconsistent states, which could endanger the stability of the network subsystem and thus of the entire operating system. Security and stability are always more important than performance or benchmarks in Linux.

For example, a fault concatenation could be produced by consecutive nested operations on a queue. The consequence would be a memory access error and eventually a system crash (kernel panic). For this reason, (mainly) the multiprocessor capability of Linux requires atomic handling of such critical processes.

Most queue operations are defined as *inline* procedures in the *include* file `<linux/skbuff.h>`. This *inline* definition means that there are no real procedures; instead, procedures are built into the body of the calling function, similarly to macros. This reduces overhead of a function call and tolerates a slightly larger kernel. During each function call, we would otherwise have to pack the registers onto the stack and initialize the variable environment of the new function. For the smaller socket-buffer functions, this is far too costly; that's why they are declared `inline`. The role of each function is still maintained to keep the source code easy to understand and maintain.

Managing Queue Structures

`skb_queue_head_init()`	include/linux/skbuff.h

`skb_queue_head-init(list)` initializes an `skb_queue_head` structure so that it can be used as a queue. Essentially, pointers are set to the structure, and the length is set to null (i.e., `next` and `prev` in an empty queue point to the queue list and not to NULL).

`skb_queue_empty()`	include/linux/skbuff.h

`skb_queue_empty(list)` checks on whether the queue (`list`) is empty or still contains buffers. The queue length `list->qlen` is returned for the sake of simplicity. If it is null, then it is considered to be `false`; otherwise, it is `true`.

`skb_queue_len()`	include/linux/skbuff.h

`skb_queue_len(list)` returns the actual length of the specified queue, in packets.

Managing Socket Buffers in Queues   The following functions are available to manage packets in queues. These are mainly different strategies for arranging or removing socket buffers in a socket-buffer queue. When a packet is inserted into a queue, then the parameter `skb->list` of the socket-buffer structure points to this queue. Of course, a packet can always be in one queue only.

Each of the following functions exists in two different versions one with and a second without locked interrupts. This means that, when a function already disabled interrupts, we don't have to do this in queue functions. Functions without locked interrupts are marked by two leading underlines, e.g., `__skb_dequeue()`.

`skb_queue_head()`	include/linux/skbuff.h

`skb_queue_head(list, skb)` orders a packet at the header of the specified queue and increments the length of the queue, (`list->qlen`), by one.

`skb_queue_tail()`	**include/linux/skbuff.h**

`skb_queue_tail(list, skb)` appends the socket buffer `skb` to the end of the queue and increments its length, (`list->qlen`), by one.

`skb_dequeue()`	**include/linux/skbuff.h**

`skb_dequeue(list)` removes the top packet from the queue and returns a pointer to it. The length of the queue is decremented by one. If there is no packet in the queue, then the `NULL` pointer is returned.

`skb_dequeue_tail()`	**include/linux/skbuff.h**

`skb_dequeue_tail(list)` removes the last packet from a queue and returns a pointer to it. If there is no packet in the list, then `NULL` is returned.

`skb_queue_purge()`	**include/linux/skbuff.h**

`skb_queue_purge` empties the queue list: All packets are removed from the list and released by `kfree_skb()`.

`skb_insert()`	**include/linux/skbuff.h**

`skb_insert(oldskb, newskb)` orders the socket buffer `newskb` *in front* of the buffer `oldskb` in the queue. In addition, it sets the `list` pointer of the new socket buffer to the list of the next buffer and increments the queue length.

`skb_append()`	**include/linux/skbuff.h**

`skb_append(oldskb, newskb)` places the socket buffer `newskb` *behind* `oldskb` in the queue of `oldskb`. Additionally, the `list` pointer is set to the queue of the previous buffer and the queue length is incremented by one.

`skb_unlink()`	**include/linux/skbuff.h**

`skb_unlink(skb)` removes the specified socket buffer from its queue (it is not explicitly passed as parameter) and decrements the queue length. `skb_unlink()` checks explicitly for whether the list exists; the function `__skb_unlink(skb, list)` does not run this test, which means that we have to ensure that the buffer is actually in a list.

`skb_peek()`	**include/linux/skbuff.h**

`skb_peek(list)` returns a pointer to the first element of a list, if this list is not empty; otherwise, it returns `NULL`. If a socket buffer is in the queue, then only a pointer to this socket buffer is returned; the socket buffer is not removed from the queue. This is to ensure that no other activities in the kernel can remove that buffer from the queue while operations run on the socket buffer, which can lead to inconsistencies. There is no interrupt-save version of skb_peek().

skb_peek_tail()	include/linux/skbuff.h

skb_peek_tail(list) returns a pointer to the last element of a queue. If this queue is empty, then NULL is returned. Again, the buffer remains in the queue and should be protected. (See skb_peek().)

CHAPTER 5

Network Devices

Each (tele)communication over a network normally requires a physical medium, which is accessed over a network adapter (network interface). Together, the network adapter and the medium eventually allow bridging of the spatial distance, so that data can be exchanged between two or more communication systems. If we use the ISO/OSI reference model introduced in Section 3.1.1, then the tasks of a network adapter extend over layers 1 and 2a: They include all tasks dealing with data–signal–data conversion (and media access in the case of shared media). All higher-order protocol functions are handled by the protocol instances of the respective operating system.[1] This interface is characterized by the following properties:

- interfacing between specialized hardware in the network adapters and software-based protocols;
- asynchronous input and output point of the protocol stack in the operating system kernel.

In the network architecture of the Linux operating systems, this interface between software-based protocols and network adapters is implemented by the concept of *network devices*. A network-device interface primarily should meet the following requirements:

- *Abstract from the technical properties of a network adapter*: Network adapters might implement different layer-1 and layer-2 protocols and are manufactured by different vendors. This means that their configurations are individual and specific to each network adapter. For this reason, we need a piece of software for each adapter to communicate with the hardware: the *driver* of a network adapter (which is, by the way, also a protocol).

---

[1] This view is limited to software-based communication systems on PC basis. More instances are normally implemented in hardware for dedicated systems.

■ *Provide a uniform interface for access by protocol instances*: In a system like Linux, there are several protocol instances using the services of network adapters. To be consistent with the principle of layered communication systems (see Section 3.1), these instances should be implemented independently of a specific type of adapter. This means that network adapters should have a uniform interface to the higher layers.

In the Linux kernel, these two tasks are handled by the concept of network devices and are often seen as one single unit. However, it makes sense to distinguish between the two views of network devices and discuss them separately. For this reason, the following section introduces the network-device interface visible from the "top," which offers a uniform interface to the higher protocol instances for physical transmission of data. Later on, Section 5.3 will discuss the "lower" half: the adapter-specific functions that are the actual network driver. Subsequently, Chapter 6 will introduce an example describing how a packet is sent and received on the level of network devices interfacing to the higher protocols.

Not every network device in the Linux kernel represents a physical network adapter. There are network devices, such as the `loopback` network device, that offer a logical network functionality. The interface of network devices is also often used to bind protocols, such as the point-to-point protocol (PPP).

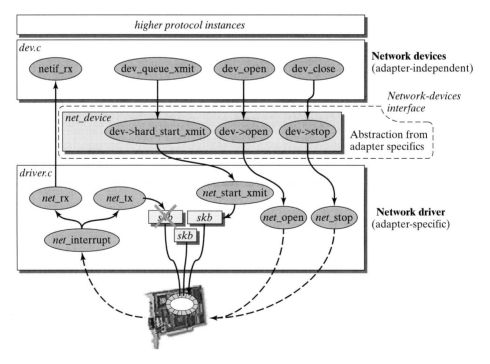

FIGURE 5–1
The structure of a network device interface.

5.1   THE net_device INTERFACE

In addition to character and block devices, network devices represent the third category of adapters in the Linux kernel [RuCo01]. This section describes the concept of network devices from the perspective of higher-layer protocols and their data structures and management.

Network adapters differ significantly from the character and block devices introduced in Section 2.5. One of their main characteristics is that they have no representation in the device file system /dev/, which means that they cannot be addressed by simple read-write operations. In addition, this is not possible because network devices work on a packet basis; a behavior comparable to character-oriented devices can be achieved only by use of complex protocols (e.g., TCP). For example, there are no such network devices as /dev/eth0 or /dev/atm1. Network devices are configured separately by the ifconfig tool on the application level. More recently, another tool available is ip, which can be used for extensive configuration of most network functions.

One of the reasons why network devices are so special is that the actions of a network adapter cannot be bound to a unique process; instead, they run in the kernel and independently of user processes [RuCo01]. For example, a hard disk is requested to pass a block to the kernel: The action is triggered by the adapter (in the case of network adapters), and the adapter has to explicitly request the kernel to pass the packet.

5.1.1   The net_device Structure

struct net_device	include/linux/netdevice.h

```
struct net_device
{
    char                 name[IFNAMSIZ];
    unsigned long        rmem_end, rmem_start, mem_end, mem_start, base_addr;
    unsigned int         irq;
    unsigned char        if_port, dma;
    unsigned long        state;
    struct net_device    *next, *next_sched;
    int                  ifindex, iflink;

    unsigned long        trans_start, last_rx;
    unsigned short       flags, gflags, mtu, type, hard_header_len;
    void                 *priv;
    struct net_device    *master;
    unsigned char        broadcast[MAX_ADDR_LEN], pad;
    unsigned char        dev_addr[MAX_ADDR_LEN], addr_len;
```

```
        struct dev_mc_list    *mc_list;
        int                   mc_count, promiscuity, allmulti;

        int                   watchdog_timeo;
        struct timer_list     watchdog_timer;

        void                  *atalk_ptr, *ip_ptr, *dn_ptr, *ip6_ptr, *ec_ptr;
        struct Qdisc          *qdisc, *qdisc_sleeping, *qdisc_list, *qdisc_ingress;
        unsigned long         tx_queue_len;

        spinlock_t            xmit_lock;
        int                   xmit_lock_owner;
        spinlock_t            queue_lock;
        atomic_t              refcnt;

        int                   features;
        int                   (*init)(struct net_device *dev);
        void                  (*uninit)(struct net_device *dev);
        void                  (*destructor)(struct net_device *dev);
        int                   (*open)(struct net_device *dev);
        int                   (*stop)(struct net_device *dev);
        int                   (*hard_start_xmit) (struct sk_buff *skb,          \
                                  struct net_device *dev);
        int                   (*hard_header) (struct sk_buff *skb,struct net_device \
                                  *dev,unsigned short type,void *daddr,void *saddr, \
                                  unsigned len);
        int                   (*rebuild_header)(struct sk_buff *skb);
        void                  (*set_multicast_list) (struct net_device *dev);
        int                   (*set_mac_address) (struct net_device *dev, void *addr);
        int                   (*do_ioctl)(struct net_device *dev, struct ifreq *ifr,\
                                  int cmd);
        int                   (*set_config)(struct net_device *dev, struct ifmap \
                                  *map);
        int                   (*hard_header_cache) (struct neighbour *neigh, struct \
                                  hh_cache *hh);
        void                  (*header_cache_update) (struct hh_cache *hh, struct   \
                                  net_device *dev, unsigned char *haddr);
        int                   (*change_mtu)(struct net_device *dev, int new_mtu);
        void                  (*tx_timeout) (struct net_device *dev);
        int                   (*hard_header_parse) (struct sk_buff *skb, unsigned  \
                                  char *haddr);
        int                   (*neigh_setup) (struct net_device *dev, struct       \
                                  neigh_parms *);
        struct net_device_stats* (*get_stats) (struct net_device *dev);
        struct iw_statistics* (*get_wireless_stats) (struct net_device *dev);

        struct module         *owner;
        struct net_bridge_port *br_port;
};
```

The net_device structure forms the basis of each network device in the Linux kernel. It contains not only information about the network adapter hardware (interrupt, ports, driver functions, etc.), but also the configuration data of the network device with regard to the higher network protocols (IP address, subnet mask, etc.).

As was mentioned at the beginning of this chapter, the net_device structure represents a general interface between higher protocol instances and the hardware used. It allows you to abstract from the network components used. For an efficient implementation of this abstraction, we once again use the concept of function pointers. For this reason, the net_device structure contains a number of function pointers, which are called by higher protocols by using their global names, and then the hardware-specific methods of the driver are called from each network device.

For example, e13_start_xmit() is used to actually call the function hard_start_xmit() for a network adapter of type 3Com/3c509.

In general, the parameters of the net_device structure can be divided into different areas, as described below.

General Fields of a Network Device   The following parameters of the net_device structure (see previous subsection) are used to manage network devices. They have no significance with regard to special layers or protocol instances.

- name is the name of the network device. In general, device types are numbered from 0 to *n* (e.g., eth0-eth4). Some network devices, such as the loopback device (lo), occur only once, which means that they have fixed names.

  When registering a network device, you can suggest a name, which should be unique. However, you can also let the system assign the eth*n* name automatically. (See init_etherdev.) The naming convention for network devices will be described in detail in Section 5.2.3.

- next is used to concatenate several net_device structures. We will see in Section 5.2 that all network devices are managed in a singly linked linear list that starts with the pointer dev_base.

- owner is a pointer to the module structure of the module created by the net_device structure of this network device.

- ifindex is a second identifier for a network device, in addition to the name. When a new network device is created, dev_get_index() assigns a new unused index to this device. This index allows you to quickly find a network device from the list of all devices, which is much faster, compared to search by name.

- iflink specifies the index of the network device used to send a packet. This is normally the index ifindex, but, for tunneling network devices, such as ipip, iflink includes the index of the network device that is eventually used to send the enveloped packet.

- state: The field dev->state contains status information about the network device and the network adapter. It was added to the kernel for the first time in version 2.3.43 and replaces the previous fields start (network adapter is open), interrupt (driver handles an adapter interrupt), and tbusy (all packet buffers are busy). These functions are now replaced by the following flags in the field state:

▷ LINK_STATE_START shows whether the network adapter was opened with dev->open() (i.e., whether it was activated and can be used). However, a LINK_STATE_START state set does not automatically mean that packets can be sent. In fact, all buffers on the adapter could be busy. (See next flag.) The flag LINK_STATE_START should have read access only, because it should be modified only by the methods used to manage network devices. The method netif_running(dev) is available to test this flag.

▷ LINK_STATE_XOFF shows whether the network adapter can accept socket buffers for transmission or its transmit buffers (which are normally organized as ring buffers) are already busy. The method netif_queue_stopped(dev) can be used to test for this state. Again, only read access to this flag should be allowed.

LINK_STATE_XOFF replaces the previous field dev->tbusy. Older drivers could take either of three different situations, which accessed the tbusy flag. The latter was replaced by the following functions, which make the programming style much easier to read:

▷ *Stopping a transmission*: When the packet buffers of a network adapter are busy, dev->tbusy = 1 was previously used to stop sending packets to the adapter. Now, there is the (inline) function netif_stop_queue(dev), which sets the LINK_STATE_XOFF flag in dev->state. This means that no packets are removed from the queue and passed to this adapter. Normally, netif_stop_queue() is called by the driver of an adapter, and then the driver is responsible for restarting the transmission. (See Section 5.3.)

▷ *Resuming a transmission*: Once a network adapter has sent a packet from the (ring) packet buffer, it can resume accepting packets from the kernel. The method netif_start_queue(dev), which deletes the LINK_STATE_XOFF flag, is used for this purpose. In general, netif_start_queue(dev) is used by the driver methods. (See Section 5.3.) This corresponds to dev->tbusy = 0 in older kernel versions.

▷ *Starting a transmission*: The method netif_start_queue(dev) is used to resume passing socket buffers to the network adapter.

▷ In addition, the method netif_wake_queue(dev) is used to resume passing packets and, at the same time, to trigger the NET_TX software interrupt, which handles the passing of packets to the network adapter.

▷ The field interrupt has no counterpart in the new kernel versions. It was previously used to prevent concurrent handling of interrupt methods. The new and SMP-improved kernels have special methods to control parallel processes. (See Section 2.3.) A driver should use these methods and manage their lock variables in its private data structures as needed.

▪ trans_start stores the time (in jiffies) when the transmission of a packet started. If, after some time, the driver still hasn't received an acknowledgment to send the packet (ack interrupt), then it can introduce appropriate actions. For these purposes, kernel versions 2.4 and higher use a timer called `watchdog_timer`.

- `last_rx` should include the time (in jiffies) when the last packet arrived.

- `priv` is a pointer to the private data of a network device or to the private data of its driver. Private data contains those variables and structures that are required to manage a network adapter. They are not stored in the `net_device` structure, but they are normally specific to an adapter.

- `qdisc` refers to a structure of the type `Qdisc`, which mirrors the serving strategy of the current network device. Chapter 18 will discuss this issue in detail.

- `refcnt` stores the number of references to this network device.

- `xmit_lock`, `xmit_lock_owner`, and `queue_lock` are used to protect against parallel handling of a transmit process or parallel access to the transmit queue. For example, `xmit_lock_owner` includes the number of the processor, which is currently in the transmit function `hard_start_xmit()`. When no processor is currently transmitting, then `xmit_lock_owner` takes the value −1.

Hardware-Specific Fields

- `rmem_end`, `rmem_start`, `mem_end`, `mem_start`: These fields specify the beginning and end of the common memory space that the network adapter and the kernel share. The location (`mem_start` − `mem_end`) designates the buffers for packets to be sent, and (`rmem_start` − `rmem_end`) designates the location for received packets. The size of the buffers indicates the amount of storage available on the card. When using `ifconfig` to initialize a network adapter, you can specify the addresses of memory locations.

- `base_addr`: The I/O basic address is also set in the driver's *probing* routine during a search for a device. `ifconfig` can be used to display and set the value. In addition, the I/O basic address can be specified when loading most of the modules and as a kernel boot parameter.

- `irq`: The number of the interrupt of a network adapter is also set during the so-called *probing phase* of the driver or by explicitly specifying it when loading the module or starting the kernel. In addition, `ifconfig` can be used to modify the interrupt number during operation.

- `dma` contains the number of the DMA (Direct Memory Access) channel, if the device supports the DMA transfer mode.

- `if_port` stores the media type of the network adapter currently used. For Ethernet, we distinguish between BNC, Twisted Pair (TP), and AUI. There are no unique constants; instead, each driver can use its own values.

Data on the Physical Layer The values of the following fields are set by the `ethersetup()` function for Ethernet cards. They are generally identical for all Ethernet-based cards, except for the `flag` field, which has to be set to match the card's capability.

There are similar functions to set standard values for token-ring and FDDI adapters (fddi_setup(), tr_setup()). These fields have to be set manually for other network types.

- hard_header_length specifies the length of the layer-2 packet header. This value is 14 for Ethernet adapters. This does not correspond to the length of the actual packet header on the physical medium, but only to the part passed to the network adapter. In general, the network adapter adds additional fields (e.g., the preamble and checksum for Ethernet).

- mtu is the *maximum transfer unit*, which specifies the maximum length of the payload of a layer-2 frame. Layer-3 protocols have to consider this value; they must not pass more octets to the network device. Ethernet has an MTU of 1500 bytes.

- tx_queue_len specifies the maximum length of the output queue of the network device. ether_setup() sets this value to 100. tx_queue_len should not be confused with the buffers of the network adapter. A network adapter normally has an additional ring buffer for 16 or 32 packets.

- type specifies the hardware type of the network adapter. The values are specified in RFC 1700 for the ARP protocol, which has to state the hardware type for address-resolution purposes. Linux defines additional constants not defined in FRC 1700. (See Figure 5–2.)

- addr_len, dev_addr[MAX_ADDR_LEN], broadcast[MAX_ADDR_LEN]: These fields contain the data of the layer-2 address. addr_len specifies the length of the layer-2 address, which is stored in the dev_addr field. The third field contains the broadcast address, which can be used to reach all computers in the local network.

- dev_mc_list points to a linear list with multicast layer-2 addresses. When the network adapter receives a packet with a destination address included in dev_mc_list,

```
ARPHRD_NETROM      0    /* NET/ROM pseudo               */
ARPHRD_ETHER       1    /* Ethernet 10Mbps              */
ARPHRD_EETHER      2    /* Experimental Ethernet        */
ARPHRD_AX25        3    /* AX.25 Level 2                */
ARPHRD_PRONET      4    /* PROnet token ring            */
ARPHRD_CHAOS       5    /* Chaosnet                     */
ARPHRD_IEEE802     6    /* IEEE 802.2 Ethernet/TR/TB    */
ARPHRD_ARCNET      7    /* ARCnet                       */
ARPHRD_APPLETLK    8    /* APPLEtalk                    */
ARPHRD_DLCI        15   /* Frame Relay DLCI             */
ARPHRD_ATM         19   /* ATM                          */

 /* Dummy types for non-ARP hardware */
ARPHRD_SLIP        256
ARPHRD_CSLIP6      259
ARPHRD_PPP         512
ARPHRD_LOOPBACK    772  /* Loopback device              */
ARPHRD_IRDA        783  /* Linux-IrDA                   */
```

FIGURE 5–2
Hardware types defined in RFC 1700 and Linux-specific constants.

then the network adapter has to pass this packet to the upper layers. The driver method set_multicast_list is used to pass the addresses of this list to the network adapter. The hardware filter of this network adapter (if present) is responsible for passing to the kernel only those packets of interest to this computer.

- mc_count contains the number of addresses in dev_mc_list.

- watchdog_timeo and watchdog_timer are used to detect problems an adapter may incur when sending packets. For this reason, the watchdog_timer is initialized when a network device starts and always called after watchdog_timeo time units (jiffies). The handling routine dev_watchdog() checks whether or not watchdog_timeo time units have passed since the last transmission of a packet (stored in trans_start). If this is the case, then there were problems in the transmission of the last packet, and the network adapter has to be checked. To check the network adapter, the driver function tx_timeout() is called. If not much time has passed since the last start of a transmission, then nothing is done, except the watchdog timer is started.

Data on the Network Layer

- ip_ptr, ip6_ptr, atalk_ptr, dn_ptr, and ec_ptr point to information of layer-3 protocols that use this network device. If the network device was configured for the Internet protocol, among others, then ip_ptr points to a structure of the type in_device, which manages information and configuration parameters of the relevant IP instance. For example, the in_device structure manages a list with IP addresses of the network device, a list with active IP multicast groups, and the parameters for the ARP protocol.

- family designates the address family of the network device. In the case of the Internet protocol (IP), this field takes the constant AF_INET.

- pa_alen specifies the length of the addresses of the protocol used. IP addresses of the class AF_INET have the length four bytes.

- pa_addr, pa_braddr, and pa_mask describe the addressing of a network device on the network layer. pa_addr contains the address of the computer or network device. pa_baddr specifies the broadcast address, and pa_mask includes the network mask. All three values are set by ifconfig when a network device is activated.

- pa_dstaddr specifies the address of the other partner in a point-to-point connection (e.g., PPP or SLIP).

- flags includes different switches. Some of them describe properties of the network device (IFF_ARP, IFF_MULTICAST,...); others output the current state (IFF_UP). Table 5–1 lists the meaning of these switches, which can be set by use of the ifconfig command.

Device-Driver Methods   As mentioned earlier, one of the tasks of the network device interface is to abstract a network device from the underlying hardware. The set of methods available for network driver functions have to be mapped to a uniform interface so

TABLE 5–1 IFF flags of a network device.

Flag	Meaning
IFF_UP	The network device is activated and can send and receive packets.
IFF_BROADCAST	The device is broadcast-enabled, and the broadcast address pa_braddr is valid.
IFF_DEBUG	This flag switches the debug mode on (currently not used by any driver).
IFF_LOOPBACK	This flag shows that this is a loopback network device.
IFF_POINTOPOINT	This is a point-to-point connection. If this switch is set, then pa_dstaddr should contain the partner's address.
IFF_NOARP	This device does not support the Address Resolution Protocol (ARP) (e.g., in point-to-point connections).
IFF_PROMISC	This flag switches the *promiscuous* mode on. This means that all packets currently received in the network adapter are forwarded to the upper layers, including those not intended for this computer. This mode is of interest for tcpdump only.
IFF_MULTICAST	This flag activates the receipt of multicast packets. ether_setup() activates this switch. A card that does not support multicast should delete this flag.
IFF_ALLMULTI	All multicast packets should be received. This is required when the computer is to work as multicast router. IFF_MULTICAST has to be set in addition.
IFF_PORTSEL	Setting of the output port is supported by the hardware.
IFF_AUTOMEDIA	Automatic selection of the output medium (*autosensing*) is enabled.
IFF_DYNAMIC	Dynamic change of the network device's address is enabled (e.g., for dialup connections).

that higher protocols can be accessed. This functionality is implemented exactly by the function pointers of the net_device structure (see above) described in this section. These pointers let you use individual functions for different instances of the net_device structure, which are eventually addressed over a common name.

Some of these functions depend on the hardware of the network adapter and have to be set in the initialization function of the network driver. The other functions are specific to the MAC protocol used by the network adapter and can be initialized by special methods (e.g., eth_setup()). A function pointer not required can be initialized to NULL.

We will next discuss the tasks of the methods of a network device. More specifically, we will describe their basic tasks from the view of the higher protocols. These methods are implemented by the network driver used. The exact implementation in general will be discussed in Section 5.3, using the skeleton network driver as an example.

- init() is used to search and initialize network devices. This method is responsible for finding and initializing a network adapter of the present type. Primarily, a net_device structure has to be created and filled with the driver-specific data of the network device or network driver. Subsequently, the network device is registered by register_netdevice(). (See Section 5.3.1.)

- uninit() is called when a network device is unregistered (unregister_netdevice()). This method can be used to execute driver-specific functions, which may be necessary when a network device is removed. The uninit() has been introduced to the net_device structure since version 2.4 and is currently not used by any driver.

- destructor() is also new in the net_device structure. This function is called when the last reference to a network device was removed (dev->refcnt) (i.e., when no protocol instances or other components in the Linux kernel point to the net_device structure). This means that you can use the destructor() function to do cleanup work (e.g., free memory or similar things). The destructor() function is currently not used by any driver.

- open() opens (activates) a named network device. During the activation, the required system resources are requested and assigned. Note that this method can open only network devices that were previously registered. Normally, dev->open() is used in the dev_open() method which, in turn, is called by the ifconfig command. Upon successful execution of open(), the network device can be used.

- stop() terminates the activity of a network adapter and frees the system resources it has used. The network device is then no longer active, but it remains in the list of registered network devices (net_devs).

- hard_start_xmit() uses a packet (in the form of a socket buffer) over the network device. If successful (i.e., the packet was delivered to the adapter), then hard_start_xmit() returns with the return value 0; otherwise, 1.

- get_stats() gets statistics and information about the network device and its activities. This information is returned in the form of a net_device_stats structure. The elements of this structure will be introduced in the course of this chapter.

- get_wireless_stats() returns additional information for wireless network adapters. This information is forwarded in a structure of the type iw_statistics. The tool iwconfig can be used to display this specific information.

- set_multicast_list() passed the list with multicast MAC addresses to the network adapter, so that the adapter can receive packets with these addresses. This list is called either when the multicast receipt for the network device is activated (IFF_MULTICAST flag) or when the list of group MAC addresses to be received has changed. (See also Section 17.4.1.)

- watchdog_timeo() deals with problems during the transmission of a packet across the network adapter (not when the socket buffer is passed to the network adapter). If no acknowledgment for the packet is received after dev->tx-timeout, then the kernel calls the method watchdog_timeo() to solve the problem.

- do_ioctl():This method is generally not used by higher protocols, because they have no generic functions. It is normally used to pass adapter-specific ioctl() commands to the network driver.
- set_config() is used to change the configuration of a network adapter at run-time. The method lets you change system parameters, such as the interrupt or the memory location of the network adapter.

The methods for a network device described above depend on the network adapter used, which means that they have to be provided by the driver, if their functionality is required. The methods described below depend less on the hardware of a network adapter, but rather on the layer-2 protocol used. For this reason, they don't necessarily have to be implemented by driver-specific methods, but can run on top of existing methods (e.g., those for Ethernet and FDDI).

- hard_header() creates a layer-2 packet header from layer-2 addresses for source and destination.
- rebuild_header() is responsible for rebuilding the layer-2 packet header before a packet is transmitted. This function was the entry point to the ARP protocol in earlier versions of the Linux kernel. The conversion to the neighbour cache (see Section 15.3.1) should create a stored layer-2 packet header, so that rebuild_header() is called only when the hard header cache contains wrong information.
- hard_header_cache() fills a layer-2 packet header in the hard header cache with passed data. This means that subsequent transmission processes can access a prepared layer-2 packet header.
- header_cache_update() changes the layer-2 destination address in a stored layer-2 packet header in the hard header cache.
- hard_header_parse() reads the layer-2 sender address from the layer-2 packet header in the packet data space of a socket buffer and copies it to the passed address, haddr.
- set_mac_address() can be used to change the layer-2 address of a network adapter, if it supports alternative MAC addresses.
- change_mtu() changes the MTU (Maximum Transfer Unit) of a network device and implements all necessary changes.

5.2   MANAGING NETWORK DEVICES

Now that we know how a network device can be represented by the net_device structure in the Linux kernel, this section discusses the management of network devices. First, we will describe how network devices can be linked, then we will introduce methods that can be used to manage and manipulate network devices. As was mentioned earlier, this section will look at network devices only from the "top"—their uniform interface for protocol instances of the higher-order layers.

All network devices in the Linux kernel are connected in a linear list (Figure 5–3). The kernel variable dev_base represents the entry point to the list of registered network

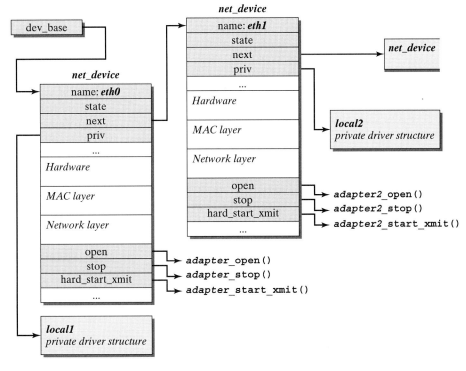

FIGURE 5–3
Linking net_device structures.

devices, pointing to the first element in the list, which, in turn, uses **next** to point to the next element. Each net_device structure represents one network device.

The proc directory (/proc/net/dev) or the (easier to read) command ifconfig -a can be used to call the list of currently registered devices. (See Appendix C.1.)

5.2.1   Registering and Unregistering Network Devices

We know from the previous section that network devices are managed in the list dev_base. This list stores all registered network devices, regardless of whether they are activated. When register_netdevice() is used to add a new device to this list, then we first have to create and initialize a net_device structure for it. This process can be done in two different ways:

- If we specified in the kernel configuration that the driver of a network device should be integrated permanently into the kernel, then there is already a net_device structure. A clever mechanism with preprocessor definitions creates different instances of the net_device structure during the translation, depending on the kernel configuration, and these instances are used for the existing network adapters when booting.

  For example, to integrate the driver of an Ethernet card into the kernel, eight net_device structures are created for Ethernet network devices, and these structures are initially not allocated to any card.

███ If the driver was translated as a kernel module, then the driver itself has to create a net_device structure for each existing network adapter. This can be done by the module itself or, for Ethernet drivers, by use of the function init_etherdev().

The list of network devices is used to store entries for those network adapters actually existing. For this reason, before an entry is added to this list, we check for whether a network adapter can be found for a driver. To check this, each of these drivers has an init() or probe() function. It is very specific to each adapter and will be described in more detail in Section 5.3. Among the exception, are logical network devices, such as loopback (lo) and PPP (ppp0), which don't have to rely on underlying hardware.

The following discussion assumes that we want to register a network device based on an Ethernet adapter. During booting of the system or loading of the driver module, the appropriate adapter was found. However, before the network device can be added to the list of known network devices (dev_base), the net_device structure should have been initialized so that the network device can actually be activated and used. The kernel has certain functions (mainly for Ethernet adapters) that facilitate the driver programmer's work.

init_netdev()	drivers/net/net_init.c

init_netdev(dev, sizeof_priv, mask, setup) initializes the most important elements from the general range of the net_device structure. (See Section 5.1.1.) First, however, we have to check on whether there is a net_device structure at all. If the value null was entered for dev in the call, then init_alloc_dev() is used to create a new net_device structure, which is also added to the list of network devices by register_netdevice() at the end of the initializing process. If the net_device structure existed already before the call, then the caller has to register it.

Subsequently, the name of the network device is verified. If the array dev->name consists of an empty string or begins with a blank, then the kernel uses the method dev_alloc_name() to allocate a name. In this case, there is an option to use the mask parameter to specify a prefix, which is extended to a valid name for a network device by the known scheme. For example, the prefix test%d produces the name test0, test1, and so on, depending on the network devices already existing with this prefix. If the prefix does not contain a formatting character (%d), then the name should be unique; otherwise, consecutive numbering is not possible, and the function will return an error. Consequently, the network device cannot be initialized.

Once a network device has a unique name, we verify that parameters for its hardware configuration have been stated when the system boots. For this purpose, the list dev_boot_setup in the method netdev_boot_setup_check() is searched for an entry with the name of the new network device. If there is such an entry, then the parameters irq, mem_start, mem_end, and base_addr are taken and added to the net_device structure of the network device.

Now the general part of the initialization of the net_device structure is completed. In the calling of init_netdev, a pointer in the setup parameter has to be passed to a function, which can be used for individual configuration. In general, the setup function handles layer-2 initialization tasks. When one is using `init_etherdev()`, reference is made to the `ether_setup()` method, which initializes the Ethernet-specific function pointers in the `net_device` structure. Finally, `init_netdev()` returns with a pointer to the network device.

`init_etherdev()`	**drivers/net/net_init.c**

`init_etherdev(dev, priv_size)` can be used by Ethernet-based network devices. The function does nothing but call `init_netdev()` with the correct parameters. Similar functions are also available for other MAC protocols (FDDI, HIPPI, etc.).

```
struct net_device *init_etherdev(struct net_device *dev, int sizeof_priv)
{
        return init_netdev(dev, sizeof_priv, "eth%d", ether_setup);
}
```

`ether_setup()`	**drivers/net/net_init.c**

`ether_setup(dev)` is called in `init_netdev()` to initialize the Ethernet-specific parameters and methods of a network device. It adds the pointers of the MAC protocol-specific functions for Ethernet adapters to the `net_device` structure (`hard_header`, `mtu`, ...). In addition, it sets the flags (`dev->flags`) of the network device to `IFF_BROADCAST|IFF|MULTICAST`.

```
dev->change_mtu          = eth_change_mtu;
dev->hard_header         = eth_header;
dev->rebuild_header      = eth_rebuild_header;
dev->set_mac_address     = eth_mac_addr;
dev->hard_header_cache   = eth_header_cache;
dev->header_cache_update = eth_header_cache_update;
dev->hard_header_parse   = eth_header_parse;
dev->type                = ARPHRD_ETHER;
dev->hard_header_len     = ETH_HLEN;
dev->mtu                 = 1500;       /* eth_mtu */
dev->addr_len            = ETH_ALEN;
dev->tx_queue_len        = 100;        /* Ethernet wants good queues */
memset(dev->broadcast,0xFF, ETH_ALEN);
dev->flags               = IFF_BROADCAST|IFF_MULTICAST;
```

`register_netdevice()`	**net/core/dev.c**

`register_netdevice(dev)` is responsible for registering the network device represented by the passed `net_device` structure with the kernel. If the function `dev->init()` exists, then the network adapter is first searched and initialized by the driver function `init()`. Subsequently, there is a check on whether a network device with the requested name is already available. If so, then `register_netdevice()`

returns an error message; otherwise, the network device is simply appended to the end of the linked list dev_base, so that it is available for general use.

In addition, the state dev->state is set to LINK_STATE_PRESENT in register_netdevice(), and dev_init_scheduler() sets the scheduling process for the new network device to the standard FIFO mechanism. This method is also used to cause the function dev_watchdog_init() to initialize the timer to detect transmission problems (dev->watchdog_timer; see Section 5.3.4). However, this timer is not started before the network adapter is activated (dev_open(); see Section 5.2.2).

Finally, the network device obtains a new number (dev->ifindex), and notifier_call_chain(&netdev_chain, NETDEV_REGISTER, dev) calls all registered methods in the notification chain netdev_chain.

unregister_netdevice()	net/core/dev.c

unregister_netdevice(dev) removes the net_device structure passed as parameter from the list of registered network devices (dev_base). If the network device is still in active state (IFF_UP), it is now closed by the driver function dev->close(). Subsequently, it is searched in the list dev_base and removed. If it is not found, then the function returns an error message.

Once the structure has been removed, unregister_netdevice() synchronizes itself to the NET-RX software interrupt by the big reader lock BR_NETPROTO_LOCK. Subsequently, the queuing discipline is released by dev_shutdown(), and all registered functions in the notification chain netdev_chain are informed about the NETDEV_UNREGISTER event. Subsequently, the destructor of the network driver is called, if it exists. Only the more recent network drivers have destructors, so we have to check periodically on whether existing references to the network device (dev->refcnt) disappeared for older drivers to be able to actually remove the network device.

5.2.2 Opening and Closing Network Devices

The previous section described how a network device is registered; the current section explains how one can be activated and deactivated. As with other device types in the Linux system, activating and deactivating is also referred to as *opening* and *closing*. To open and close a network device, the administrator can use the command ifconfig. It is used not only to activate and deactivate network devices, but also to configure them. More specifically, this command is used to set protocol-specific parameters, such as addresses and subnet masks, and to modify interface parameters for the network adapter (hardware parameters).

In addition, ifconfig can be used to change the flags of a network device. The syntax of ifconfig and its options are listed in Appendix C.1. Naturally, before a network device can be activated, it has to be registered.

Activating a Network Device   When we use ifconfig *name address* up to activate a network device, ifconfig uses the ioctl() command SIOCSIFADDR *(Socket I/O Control Set InterFace ADDRess)* to allocate the specified address to the network device *name*. The handling routine for the INET address family is devinet_ioctl.

Subsequently, the ioctl() command SIOCSIFFLAGS (*Socket I/O Control Set InterFace FLAGS*) is used to set the IFF_UP flag for the network device in the handling method dev_ifsioc(). To manipulate the flag, we use the method dev_change_flags(dev, flags), which also causes the method dev_open(dev) to be called when the IFF_UP flag is set.

dev_open()	net/core/dev.c

The function dev_open(dev) opens a network device (i.e., the network device is activated and can be used). If the network device is already active (IFF_UP), or if it has not been registered ((!netif_device_present(dev)), then the function returns an error message.

The actual initialization (i.e., the device-specific functions) is executed by the open() function of the network driver, if it exists. If this initialization is successful (i.e., no error occurred), then the net_device specific states are set as follows:

- dev->flags assumes the state IFF_UP.
- dev->state is set to LINK_START_START.
- The multicast state is activated by dev_mc_upload().
- The queue and the scheduler of the network device are activated (dev_activate(dev)). At the same time, the method dev_watchdog_up(dev) starts the timer to detect transmission problems. (See Section 5.3.4.) The timer calls the method dev_watchdog() every dev->watchdog_timeo ticks to check that the network adapter works properly.
- The notification chain netdev_chain is informed about the event NETDEV_UP.

Deactivating a Network Device   When we use the command ifconfig *name down* in dev_ifsioc to deactivate a network device, the method dev_change_flags(dev, flags) in the variable dev->flags deletes the IFF_UP flag. The general part of transferring the network device into the inactive state is done by dev_close(). The adapter-specific actions are executed in the driver method dev->stop().

dev_close()	net/core/dev.c

If the network device dev is in the IFF_UP state, then it is deactivated by dev_close(dev) in the following steps:

- All methods in the notification chain netdev_chain are informed about the upcoming deactivation of the network device (NETDEV_GOING_DOWN) and can act accordingly.
- Next, dev_deactivate(dev) removes the packet scheduler dev->qdisc, and the LINK_STATE_START bit in dev->state is deleted. In addition, dev_watchdog_down() stops the timer used to detect transmission problems.
- The driver function dev->stop() deactivates the network adapter.

■ Next, all protocols concerned are notified that the network device was stopped (`notifier_call_chain(.., NETDEV_DOWN, ..)`).

■ Finally, the reference counter that points to the `net_device` structure is decremented by one.

5.2.3 Creating and Finding Network Devices

`dev_alloc_name()`	**net/core/dev.c**

Each network device in Linux has a unique name. As mentioned earlier, network devices are not represented in the file system, in contrast to character and block devices, which means that they are not addressed by `major` and `minor` numbers. In general, network devices are named by the network type. Table 5–2 shows a few of the names currently used. In addition, devices of the same type are shown and numbered in ascending order, starting from zero (e.g., `isdn0, isdn1`, etc.).

Notice, however, that there are exceptions in allocating network adapters to a category. Linux is strongly oriented to Ethernet, and some functions in the kernel facilitate handling of Ethernet-like adapters, so some (non-Ethernet) adapters also use the category `ethn`, including some ISDN cards.

The convention used in Linux to name network devices has several benefits:

■ When one is designing applications and creating configuration scripts, it is simpler to address network devices without knowing their manufacturers and their hardware parameters (interrupt number, port number).

■ When replacing equal-type hardware, for example to upgrade an Ethernet adapter from 10 Mbit/s to 100 Mbit/s, we don't have to change the network setting; simply accessing `ethn` is sufficient.

TABLE 5–2   Naming convention for Linux network devices.

Name	Network Device Type
eth	Ethernet (802.3, Ethernet V2), 10 Mbit/s or 100 Mbit/s
tr	Token Ring (802.5)
atm	Asynchronous Transfer Mode
sl	SLIP (Serial Line Interface Protocol)
ppp	PPP (Point-to-Point Protocol)
plip	PLIP (Parallel Line Interface Protocol)
tunl	IPIP Tunnel
isdn	ISDN (Integrated Services Digital Network)
dummy	Dummy-Device
lo	Loopback-Device

dev_alloc()	net/core/dev.c

dev_alloc(name, err) reserves memory for a net_device structure. Subsequently, a name is assigned to the network device. As described in connection with init_netdev(), we can use name to specify a prefix. In both cases, the method dev_alloc_name() is used to construct the name.

The parameter err is a pointer to an integer variable, which is contained in the return value of dev_alloc_name() wherever an error occurs. If an error occurs, then dev_alloc() always returns a NULL pointer. Naturally, if the if is successful, it returns a pointer to the new net_device structure.

dev_get...()	net/core/dev.c

Various kernel components need to access a specific network device from time to time. We can search for the right net_device structure in different ways. net/core/dev.c has several functions that facilitate this search. These functions step through the linear list of network devices, starting with dev_base, and, when they find it, they return a pointer to the net_device structure we looked for:

- dev_get_by_name(name) searches for the network device specified by name.
- dev_get(name) also searches for the device specified by name.
- dev_get_by_index(ifindex) uses the index of the network device as search criterion.
- dev_getbyhwaddr(type, ha) searches for the network device by the MAC address ha and the type.

dev_load()	net/core/dev.c

When a network device is unavailable (i.e., not present in the list of registered devices), then we can use dev_load(name) to request the corresponding driver module. To request a driver module, the kernel has to support the automatic loading of modules. Also, the process in which the request for the network device originates has to have privileges to load the module (CAP_SYS_MODULE):

```
if (!dev_get(name) && capable(CAP_SYS_MODULE))
        request_module(name);
```

5.2.4 Notification Chains for State Changes

As mentioned above, network devices can be registered and removed dynamically. Also, their state can change in the course of time. For example, a network device can change its hardware address or name.

On the network-device level, a state change did not cause problems, but protocol instances in the higher layers use the services of network devices. For efficiency and simplicity reasons, these protocol instances often store references to the network devices

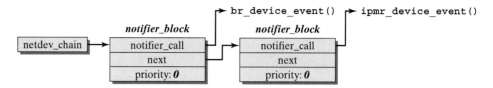

FIGURE 5–4
Notification chain for network devices.

they use. When the state of a network device changes, then these stored states become invalid. The protocol instances concerned should be notified about this fact. Unfortunately, a network device does not normally know the protocols that use its services, or what references they store.

For this reason, protocols can register themselves to be notified of state changes in network devices. This concept is called *notifier chains*; it consists of a list (`netdev_chain`) of `notifier_block` structures. Figure 5–4 shows an example of how they are structured. Each of these `notifier_block` elements includes a request for notification when the state of a network device changes:

▨ `notifier_call()` is a pointer to a handling routine, which handles the notification about a network device's state change. Each protocol instance that stores states of network devices should have such a function. For example, the method `bridge_device_event()` is used for the instance of a transparent bridge described in Chapter 12.

If a state change occurs in a network device, then all handling routines stored in the list `netdev_chain` are called, where the following arguments are passed:

▨ a pointer to the `notifier_block` structure, the handling routine of which is actually called;
▨ a pointer to the network device (`net_device`) that changed its state;
▨ the state representing the cause for this notification.

▨ `priority` specifies a priority for processing of notifications.
▨ `next` points to the next `notifier_block` element in the list and is used for concatenation.

The concept of notifier chains is used not only for network devices, but also for other states that can change. For this reason, the implementation of these notifier chains is generic and can easily be used for other purposes. For example, there is a `reboot_notifier_list` chain informing that the system is about to reboot.

In the networking area, the concept of notifier chains is used for state changes in network devices. The following list shows possible causes for notifications. Subsequently, we introduce three important functions of this concept.

▨ `NETDEV_UP` activates a network device (by `dev_open`).
▨ `NETDEV_DOWN` deactivates a network device. As a consequence of this message, all references to this network device should be removed.
▨ `NETDEV_CHANGE` informs that a network device changed its state.

- `NETDEV_REGISTER` means that a network device was registered but no instance of it has yet been opened.
- `NETDEV_UNREGISTER` informs that a network driver was removed.
- `NETDEV_CHANGEMTU` means that the MTU (Maximum Transfer Unit) changed.
- `NETDEV_CHANGEADDR` means that the hardware address of a network device changed.
- `NETDEV_CHANGENAME` means that the name of a network device changed.

When a registered handling routine is called, it can use the appropriate functions based on the type passed. For example, when a network device is deactivated (`NETDEV_DOWN`) in KIDS (see Chapter 22), the corresponding hook is deleted. The method `notifier_call_chain(&netdev_chain, `*EVENT*`, dev)`, which will be described below, is used to call the notifier chain.

`notifier_call_chain()`	**net/core/dev.c**

`notifier_call_chain(&netdev_chain, `*EVENT*`, dev)` informs all handling methods registered in the list `netdev_chain` about the *EVENT*, where the events described above can occur. `notifier_call_chain()` is very simple. The linking in the list is used to call all registered functions, one after the other. If one of the functions called returns the constant `NOTIFY_STOP_MASK`, then the notification is stopped. This is useful to prevent there being several reactions to one event. Otherwise, all registered handling routines are always informed about the event each time this function is called. The registered handling method alone decides whether the message is meaningful for it.

`register_netdevice_notifier()`	**net/core/dev.c**

`register_netdevice_notifier(nb)` is merely another representation of the method `notifier_chain_register(&netdev_chain, nb)`, which inserts the `notifier_block` structure passed to the list `netdev_chain`. The position within the list is determined by the priority.

`unregister_netdevice_notifier()`	**net/core/dev.c**

`unregister_netdevice_notifier(nb)` removes the specified `notifier_block` structure from the list `netdev_chain`. The function `notifier_chain_unregister()` is used for this purpose.

5.2.5 Transmitting Over Network Devices

`dev_queue_xmit()`	**net/core/dev.c**

`dev_queue_xmit(skb)` is used by protocol instances of the higher protocols to send a packet in the form of the socket buffer `skb` over a network device, which is specified by the parameter `skb->dev` in the socket buffer structure. Section 6.2.2 explains how a packet is transmitted in detail.

5.3 NETWORK DRIVERS

The large number of different protocols in the Linux network architecture leads to considerable differences in the implementations of drivers for different physical network adapters. As was mentioned in the section that described the `net_device` structure, the properties of different network adapters are hidden at the interface of network devices, which means that they offer a uniform view upwards.

Hiding specific functions (i.e., abstracting from the driver used) is achieved by using function pointers in the `net_device` structure. For example, a higher-layer protocol instance uses the method `hard_start_xmit()` to send an IP packet over a network device. Notice, however, that this is merely a function pointer, hiding the method `el3_start_xmit()` in the case of a 3c509 network adapter. This method takes the steps required to pass a socket buffer to the 3c509 adapter. The upper layers of the Linux network architecture don't know which driver or network adapter is actually used. The function pointer can be used to abstract from the hardware actually used and its particularities.

The following sections provide an overview of the typical structuring and implementation characteristics of the functions of a network driver, without discussing adapter-specific properties, such as manipulating the hardware registers or describing the transmit buffers. In general, these tasks depend on the hardware, so we will skip them here. Readers interested in these details can use the large number of network drivers included in the `drivers/net` directory as examples. We use the `skeleton` driver to explain how driver methods work. This is a sample driver used to show usual processes in driver methods rather than a real driver for a network adapter. For this reason, it is particularly useful for explaining the implementation characteristics of network drivers.[2]

Some of the methods listed below are not implemented by some drivers (e.g., `example_set_config()` to change system resources at runtime); others are essential, such as `example_hard_start_xmit()` to start a transmission process.

5.3.1 Initializing Network Adapters

Before a network device can be activated, we first have to find the appropriate network adapter; otherwise, it won't be added to the list of registered network devices. The `init()` function of the network driver is responsible for searching for an adapter and initializing its `net_device` structure with patching driver information. Because we search for a network adapter, this function is often called *search function*.

The argument of the `init()` method is a pointer to the initializing device `dev`. The return value of `init()` is usually 0, but a negative error code (e.g., `-ENODEV`) when no adapter was found.

`net_init()/net_probe()`	**net/core/dev.c**

The tasks of the method `dev->init(dev)` are explained in the source text of our example driver, `isa_skeleton`. There is an example driver in `drivers/net/pci_skeleton.c` for PCI network adapters, but we will not describe it here.

---

[2]At this point, we would like to thank Donald Becker, who implemented most of the network drivers for Linux, greatly contributing to the success of Linux. Donald Becker is also the author of the `skeleton` driver used here.

As was mentioned earlier, the main task of the `init()` method is to search for a matching network adapter (i.e., it has to discover the I/O port, especially of the basic address stored in `dev->base_addr`).

We distinguish between two different cases of searching for a network adapter:

- *Specifying the basic address*: In this case, the previously created `net_device` structure of the network device is passed as parameter to the `init()` method. The caller can use this structure to specify a basic address for I/O ports in advance. When no matching adapter is found in this address, then the `init()` method returns the error message -ENODEV. The basic address can be specified in either of the two following ways:

  - For modularized drivers, parameters can be passed when loading the module, including the I/O basic address (e.g., `io=0×280`). In this case, it should be transferred to the `net_device` structure of the network device in the `init_module()` method of the driver module, so that it will be considered during the search for the network adapter.
  - For drivers permanently integrated in the kernel, we can also pass parameters when the system boots; these parameters are maintained in the list `dev_boot_setup`. They are transferred to the `net_device` structure of a network device in the method `init_netdev()` (see Section 5.2) and can be used when the network adapter is initialized.

- *Searching in known basic addresses*: A network adapter generally supports a set of defined port addresses. If no basic address is specified when calling the `init()` method, then the addresses in this list can be probed one after the other. If no adapter can be found in any of these basic addresses in the list, then -ENODEV is returned.

The following source code of the `init()` method for the skeleton driver handles only the selection of basic addresses where we want to search (by the methods described above). The actual verification of a specific basic address and the initialization of the `net_device` structure takes place in the method `netcard_probe1(dev, ioaddr)`, which is actually part of the `init()` method and was implemented separately to keep the code simple and easy to understand.

```
/* The name of the card. Is used for messages and in the requests for
 * io regions, irqs and dma channels */
static const char* cardname = "netcard"

/* A zero-terminated list of I/O addresses to be probed. */
static unsigned int netcard_portlist[] __initdata =
        { 0x200, 0x240, 0x280, 0x2C0, 0x300, 0x320, 0x340, 0};

/* The number of low I/O ports used by the ethercard. */
#define IO_NUM 32
```

```
/* Information that needs to be kept for each board. */
struct net_local {
    struct net_device_stats stats;
    long open_time;          /* Useless example local info. */

        /* Tx control lock. This protects the transmit buffer ring
         * state along with the "tx full" state of the driver. This
         * means all netif_queue flow control actions are protected
         * by this lock as well. */
    spinlock_t lock;
};


/* The station (ethernet) address prefix, used for IDing the board. */
#define SA_ADDR0 0x00
#define SA_ADDR1 0x42
#define SA_ADDR2 0x65

int __init netcard_probe(struct net_device *dev) {
    int i;
    int base_addr = dev->base_addr;

    SET_MODULE_OWNER(dev);

    if (base_addr > 0x1ff)   /* Check a single specified location. */
        return netcard_probe1(dev, base_addr);
    else if (base_addr != 0) /* Don't probe at all. */
        return -ENXIO;

    for (i = 0; netcard_portlist[i]; i++) {
        int ioaddr = netcard_portlist[i];
        if (check_region(ioaddr, IO_NUM))
            continue;

        if (netcard_probe1(dev, ioaddr) == 0)
            return 0;
    }
    return -ENODEV;
}
```

Once we have selected a basic address for the network adapter in the above method, the method netcard_probe1(dev, ioaddr) tests whether the adapter we searched for is really at this basic address. For this purpose, the method has to check specific properties of the card, where access should be limited to read access on the I/O ports to ensure that no other adapters will be involved. At this point, it is still unknown whether the adapter we're searching for is really present in the basic address ioaddr.

A very simple method to identify the adapter compares the manufacturer identification with the MAC address. Each network adapter has a unique MAC address, where the first three bytes identify the manufacturer. This identification must correspond with the manufacturer code of the searched card. In any event, additional checks should be done, but they are adapter-specific and are not described in detail here.

Once we are sure that the network adapter we searched for is present in the basic address ioaddr, this address is stored in the net_device structure (dev->base_addr), and the network device is initialized. The I/O ports, starting from the basic address, are reserved by request_region(ioaddr, IO_NUM, cardname) at the end of the initialization function to ensure that no other initialization method can get write access to it.

The initialization process can be divided into the following three phases:

- If the network adapter does not support dynamic interrupt allocation, then the interrupt set by jumpers on the network adapter should be determined and reserved at this point. The kernel supports the search for the interrupt number. Calling the method autoirq_setup() makes the kernel remember interrupt lines not currently registered in a variable. Subsequently, the network adapter should be caused to trigger an interrupt. We can then use the method autoirq_report() to discover, from the previously stored and the actual interrupt vectors, which interrupt was actually active. Next, the interrupt found is reserved for the network adapter by the method request_irq(). In addition, the DMA channel is determined and reserved by request_dma().

  For modern adapters that do not necessarily require specific interrupt or DMA lines, the two system resources are allocated not at this point, but rather when the device is opened. This is necessary to avoid conflicts with other devices.

- Once system resources have been allocated (for older adapters only), memory is reserved for the private data structure of the network device dev->priv and is initialized. This data structure stores the private data of the network driver and statistic information collected during the operation of the network device (net_device_stats structure).

- Finally, the references to driver-specific methods are set in the net_device structure, so that they can be used by the higher layers and protocols. The adapter-specific methods (see also Section 5.1.1) have to be set explicitly. Methods specific to the MAC protocol used (e.g., Ethernet) can be set by special methods (e.g., ether_setup()).

If the network adapter was found and all data structures were initialized correctly, then dev->init() returns 0.

```
/* This is the real probe routine. Linux has a history of friendly device
 * probes on the ISA bus. A good device probe avoids doing writes, and
 * verifies that the correct device exists and functions.*/
static int __init netcard_probe1(struct net_device *dev,int ioaddr) {
    struct net_local *np;
    static unsigned version_printed = 0;
    int i;
```

```
    /*
     * For Ethernet adaptors the first three octets of the station address
     * contains the manufacturer's unique code. That might be a good probe
     * method. Ideally you would add additional checks.
     */
    if (inb(ioaddr + 0) != SA_ADDR0
        ||   inb(ioaddr + 1) != SA_ADDR1
        ||   inb(ioaddr + 2) != SA_ADDR2) {
        return -ENODEV;
    }

    if (net_debug && version_printed++ == 0)
        printk(KERN_DEBUG "%s", version);

    printk(KERN_INFO "%s: %s found at %#3x, ", dev->name, cardname, ioaddr);

    /* Fill in the 'dev' fields. */
    dev->base_addr = ioaddr;

    /* Retrieve and print the Ethernet address. */
    for (i = 0; i < 6; i++)
        printk(" %2.2x", dev->dev_addr[i] = inb(ioaddr + i));

#ifdef jumpered_interrupts
    /* If this board has jumpered interrupts, allocate the interrupt
     * vector now. There is no point in waiting since no other device
     * can use the interrupt, and this marks the irq as busy. Jumpered
     * interrupts are typically not reported by the boards, and we must
     * used autoIRQ to find them. */

    /* ... REMOVED for this book, details see in drivers/net/isa-skeleton.c */
#endif /* jumpered interrupt */
#ifdef jumpered_dma
    /* If we use a jumpered DMA channel, that should be probed for and
     * allocated here as well. See lance.c for an example.*/

    /* ... REMOVED for this book, details see in drivers/net/isa-skeleton.c */
#endif /* jumpered DMA */

    /* Initialize the device structure. */
    if (dev->priv == NULL) {
        dev->priv = kmalloc(sizeof(struct net_local), GFP_KERNEL);
        if (dev->priv == NULL)
            return -ENOMEM;
    }
```

```
memset(dev->priv, 0, sizeof(struct net_local));

np = (struct net_local *)dev->priv;
spin_lock_init(&np->lock);

/* Grab the region so that no one else tries to probe our ioports. */
request_region(ioaddr, IO_NUM, cardname);

dev->open = net_open;
dev->stop = net_close;
dev->hard_start_xmit = net_send_packet;
dev->get_stats = net_get_stats;
dev->set_multicast_list = &set_multicast_list;

dev->tx_timeout = &net_tx_timeout;
dev->watchdog_timeo = MY_TX_TIMEOUT;

/* Fill in the fields of the device structure with Ethernet values. */
ether_setup(dev);

return 0;
}
```

Helper Functions to Allocate System Resources

request_region(), release_region(), check_region()	**kernel/resource.c**

request_region(port, range, name) reserves a region of I/O ports, starting with the address port, and marks them as allocated. The kernel manages these reserved port ranges in a linear list. This list can be output from the proc file /proc/ioports, where name is the output name of the reserved instance.

We reserve ports to prevent a driver that searches for an adapter from accessing the ports of another device, causing that device to take an undefined or unintended state. For this reason, before port ranges are assigned, we should always use check_region() to check on whether that range is already taken. The address of the first I/O port of an adapter is stored in the variable dev->base_addr.

release_region(start, n) can be used to release allocated port ranges.

request_irq(), free_irq()	**kernel/irq.c**

request_irq(irq, handler, flags, device, dev_id) reserves and initializes the interrupt line with number irq. At the same time, the handling routine handler() is registered for this interrupt.

Similarly to what it does with I/O ports, the kernel manages a list of reserved interrupts and can output this list in the proc directory (`/proc/interrupts`). Again, the string `device` tells you who reserved this interrupt. The parameter `flags` can be used to output options when reserving an interrupt. For more information, see [RuCo01].

A reserved interrupt can be released by `free_irq(irq, dev_id)`.

`request_dma()`, `free_dma()`	**kernel/dma.c**

`request_dma(dmarr, device_id)` tries to reserve the DMA channel `dmarr`. `free_dma(dmarr)` can be used to release a reserved DMA channel.

5.3.2   Opening and Closing a Network Adapter

We know from Section 5.2 that network devices are activated and deactivated by the command `ifconfig`. More specifically, `ioctl()` calls invoke the methods `dev_open()` or `dev_close()`, where the general steps to activate and deactivate a network device are executed. The adapter-specific actions are handled in the driver methods `dev->open()` and `dev->stop()`, respectively, of the present network adapter. We use the `skeleton` sample driver to explain these steps.

`net_open()`	**drivers/net/isa_skeleton.c**

The `open()` method is responsible for initializing and activating the network adapter. At the beginning, the system resources required (interrupt, DMA channel, etc.) are requested. To make available these system resources, the kernel offers various methods you can use as helpers. These methods were introduced briefly in the previous section. System resources are reserved in the `open()` method for modern adapters, which do not have fixed values for IRQ and DMA lines. For older cards, the resources are searched for and reserved in the `init()` method. (See `init()`.)

Once a network adapter has been initialized successfully, the use counter of the module should be incremented for modularized drivers, to prevent inadvertent loading of the driver module from the kernel. We can use the macro `MOD_INC_USE_COUNT` for this purpose.

The network adapter is initialized when all system resources have been allocated successfully. Each adapter is initialized in an individual manner. Normally, a specific value is written to a hardware register (I/O port) of the adapter, which causes the adapter to initialize itself.

The transmission of packets over the network device is started by `netif_start_queue(dev)`. Finally, the value 0 is returned if the transmission was successful; otherwise, a negative error code is returned.

```
/*
 * Open/initialize the board. This is called (in the current kernel)
 * sometime after booting when the 'ifconfig' program is run.
 *
 * This routine should set everything up anew at each open, even
 * registers that "should" only need to be set once at boot, so that
```

```
 * there is non-reboot way to recover if something goes wrong.
 */
static int net_open(struct net_device *dev) {
    struct net_local *np = (struct net_local *)dev->priv;
    int ioaddr = dev->base_addr;
    /*
     * This is used if the interrupt line can turned off (shared).
     * See 3c503.c for an example of selecting the IRQ at config-time.
     */
    if (request_irq(dev->irq, &net_interrupt, 0, cardname, dev))
        return -EAGAIN;
    }
    /*
     * Always allocate the DMA channel after the IRQ, and clean up on failure.
     */
    if (request_dma(dev->dma, cardname)) {
        free_irq(dev->irq, dev);
        return -EAGAIN;
    }

    MOD_INC_USE_COUNT;

    /* Reset the hardware here. Don't forget to set the station address. */
    chipset_init(dev, 1);
    outb(0x00, ioaddr);
    np->open_time = jiffies;

    /* We are now ready to accept transmit requests from
     * the queuing layer of the networking.
     */
    netif_start_queue(dev);
    return 0;
}
```

Deactivating a Network Adapter

example_stop()	drivers/net/isa_skeleton.c

During deactivation of a network adapter, all operations done when the adapter was opened should be undone. This concerns mainly allocated system resources (interrupts, DMA channels, etc.), which should now be freed.

For modularized drivers, the use counter has to be decremented with MOD_DEC_USE_COUNT, and the network device must not accept any more packets from higher layers (netif_stop_queue). Again, the return value is either 0, if successful, or a negative error code.

```
/* The inverse routine to net_open(). */

static int net_close(struct net_device *dev) {
```

```
struct net_local *lp = (struct net_local *)dev->priv;
int ioaddr = dev->base_addr;

lp->open_time = 0;

netif_stop_queue(dev);

/* Flush the Tx and disable Rx here. */

disable_dma(dev->dma);

/* If not IRQ or DMA jumpered, free up the line. */
outw(0x00, ioaddr+0); /* Release the physical interrupt line. */

free_irq(dev->irq, dev);
free_dma(dev->dma);

/* Update the statistics here. */
MOD_DEC_USE_COUNT;

return 0;
}
```

5.3.3 Transmitting Data

Each data transmission in the Linux network architecture occurs over a network device, more specifically by use of the method hard_start_xmit() (start hardware transmission). Of course, this is a function pointer, pointing to a driver-specific transmission function, ..._start_xmit(). This method is responsible for forwarding the packet in the form of a socket buffer and starting the transmission. Before we discuss the usual steps involved in the driver method dev->hard_start_xmit() in this section, we will briefly describe the common architecture of network adapters.

A network adapter is an interface adapter that automatically transmits and receives network packets according to a defined MAC protocol (Ethernet, token ring, etc.). This means that a network adapter has an independent logic that works in parallel to the regular central processor(s). The network adapter and a system processor interact over I/O ports (hardware registers) and interrupts. When a processor wants to pass data to the network adapter, then the processor writes its data to the appropriate I/O ports and starts the desired action. When the adapter wants to pass data to the processor (e.g., a packet it received), then the adapter triggers an interrupt, and the processor uses the interrupt-handling routine of the network adapter to serve the network adapter. This shows clearly that system processors have a leading role versus interface adapters (master–slave relationship).

Transmitting Data Packets

net_start_xmit()	drivers/net/isa_skeleton.c

dev->hard_start_xmit(skb, dev) is responsible for forwarding a data packet to the network adapter so that the latter can transmit it. The packet data of the socket buffer is copied to an internal buffer location in the network adapter, and the time stamp dev->trans_start = jiffies is attached, marking the beginning of that transmission. If this copying action was successful, it is also assumed that the transmission will be successful. In this case, hard_start_xmit() has to return a value of 0. Otherwise, it should return 1, so that the kernel knows that the packet could not be sent.

When forwarding network packets between the operating system and the network adapter, we can distinguish between two different techniques:

■ Older network adapters (e.g., 3Com 3c509) have an internal buffer memory on the adapter for packets to be sent. This means that the kernel can always forward only one single packet to the adapter at a time. If a buffer is free, a packet is copied to the adapter right away and the kernel can delete the corresponding socket buffer.

■ More recent network adapters work differently. The driver manages a ring buffer consisting of 16 to 64 pointers to socket buffers. When a packet is ready to be sent, then the corresponding socket buffer is arranged within this ring, and a pointer to the packet data is passed to the network adapter. Subsequently, the socket buffer remains in the ring buffer until the network adapter, using an interrupt, has notified that the packet was transmitted. Finally, the socket buffer is removed from the ring buffer and freed.

If the transmission was successful, then the socket buffer is no longer required, and it can be freed by dev_kfree_skb(). (See Section 4.1.1.) If an error occurred during the transmission, then the socket buffer should not be touched, because the kernel will most likely try to retransmit the packet.

When the method hard_start_xmit() is called, we can assume that there is currently at least one free place in the ring buffer. Whether this is true is checked by netif_queue_stopped(dev) before the call. Once the socket buffers have been arranged within the ring buffer, which add_to_tx_ring indicates as an example, we should check for whether there are more free buffer places. If this is not the case, i.e., if the ring buffer is fully occupied, then we have to use netif_stop_queue() to prevent more packets from being forwarded to the network adapter. The network device is stopped until there will be free places in the ring buffer. The kernel is notified about this situation by an interrupt, as explained in the following section.

```
/* This will only be invoked if your driver is _not_ in XOFF state.
 * What this means is that you need not check it, and that this
 * invariant will hold if you make sure that the netif_*_queue()
 * calls are done at the proper times.
 */
static int net_send_packet(struct sk_buff *skb, struct net_device *dev) {
    struct net_local *np = (struct net_local *)dev->priv;
    int ioaddr = dev->base_addr;
    short length = ETH_ZLEN < skb->len ? skb->len : ETH_ZLEN;
    unsigned char *buf = skb->data;
```

```
    /* If some error occurs while trying to transmit this
     * packet, you should return '1' from this function.
     * In such a case you _may not_ do anything to the
     * SKB, it is still owned by the network queuing
     * layer when an error is returned. This means you
     * may not modify any SKB fields, you may not free
     * the SKB, etc.
     */

#if TX_RING
    /* This is the most common case for modern hardware.
     * The spinlock protects this code from the TX complete
     * hardware interrupt handler. Queue flow control is
     * thus managed under this lock as well.
     */
    spin_lock_irq(&np->lock);

    add_to_tx_ring(np, skb, length);
    dev->trans_start = jiffies;

    /* If we just used up the very last entry in the
     * TX ring on this device, tell the queuing
     * layer to send no more.
     */
    if (tx_full(dev))
        netif_stop_queue(dev);

    /* When the TX completion hw interrupt arrives, this
     * is when the transmit statistics are updated.
     */

    spin_unlock_irq(&np->lock);
#else
    /* This is the case for older hardware which takes
     * a single transmit buffer at a time, and it is
     * just written to the device via PIO.
     *
     * No spin locking is needed since there is no TX complete
     * event. If by chance your card does have a TX complete
     * hardware IRQ then you may need to utilize np->lock here.
     */
    hardware_send_packet(ioaddr, buf, length);
    np->stats.tx_bytes += skb->len;

    dev->trans_start = jiffies;

    /* You might need to clean up and record Tx statistics here. */
    if (inw(ioaddr) == /*RU*/81)
        np->stats.tx_aborted_errors++;
```

```
    dev_kfree_skb (skb);
#endif

    return 0;
}
```

Receiving Packets and Messages from a Network Adapter

`net_interrupt()`	**drivers/net/isa_skeleton.c**

A network adapter uses interrupts and its driver-specific interrupt-handling routine to communicate with the operating system. More specifically, the network adapter triggers an interrupt to stop the current processor operation and notify it about an event. When a network adapter uses an interrupt, we generally distinguish between three different events:

- *Receive a data packet*: The network adapter has accepted and buffered a data packet and now wants to forward this packet to the operating system.
- *Acknowledge a packet transmission*: The network adapter uses this interrupt to acknowledge that a packet previously forwarded by the operating system was sent and that there is now space available in the ring buffer. However, this acknowledgment does not mean that the receiver received the packet successfully; it merely means that the network adapter has put the packet successfully to the medium.
- *Notify an error situation*: Depending on the network adapter used, an interrupt can be used to notify the driver of error situations.

Figure 5–5 shows how the interrupt handling routine of a network driver works. First, we should set an IRQ lock to prevent the function from being executed more than once at the same time. In older versions of the Linux kernel, the flag

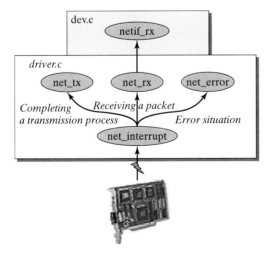

FIGURE 5–5
A network adapter uses an interrupt to send messages.

dev->interrupt was used to this end. From version 2.4 and higher, the driver should have its own lock variable.

Next, we want to know the cause of the interrupt. For this purpose, we normally read a state value from a state register, which shows whether a new packet has been received, whether a transmission was completed, and whether an error situation occurred. If a packet was received, then the driver-specific receive function net_rx() is called. If a packet transmission was fully completed, then the statistics are updated first; then netif_wake_queue(dev) (or dev->busy = 0; mark_bh(NET_BH) in earlier versions) announces the end of transmission and marks the NET_RX software interrupt for execution.

The NET_RX soft IRQ handles all incoming packets. Because it interrupts the normal work of a processor, an interrupt should complete its job quickly. Unfortunately, handling an incoming packet can be very complex, mainly because many protocols (e.g., PPP, IP, TCP, and FTP) normally participate in the process. To ensure that a processor's work is not interrupted for an excessive duration, the interrupt-handling routine carries out only those steps absolutely required to receive a packet. The more intensive part of protocol handling is done in the NET_RX software interrupt, which has a lower priority than interrupt handling.

```
static void net_interrupt(int irq, void *dev_id, struct pt_regs * regs) {
    struct net_device *dev = dev_id;
    struct net_local *np;
    int ioaddr, status;

    ioaddr = dev->base_addr;

    np = (struct net_local *)dev->priv;
    status = inw(ioaddr + 0);

    if (status & RX_INTR) {
        /* Got a packet(s). */
        net_rx(dev);
    }
#if TX_RING
    if (status & TX_INTR) {
        /* Transmit complete. */
        net_tx(dev);
        np->stats.tx_packets++;
        netif_wake_queue(dev);
    }
#endif
    if (status & COUNTERS_INTR) {
        /* Increment the appropriate 'localstats' field. */
        np->stats.tx_window_errors++;
    }
}
```

Acknowledging a Transmission Process

net_tx()	**drivers/net/isa_skeleton.c**

With more recent network adapters, the network driver manages a ring buffer of socket buffers, which should be used to transmit over the network adapter. These socket buffers remain in the ring buffer until the network adapter uses an interrupt to acknowledge their transmission. The method net_tx() shows the tasks to be executed when a network adapter acknowledges a transmission. The method net_tx() is actually part of the interrupt-handling routine and normally is implemented as a separate function only for clarity.

First, we should set a lock (normally a spinlock) to ensure that parallel access attempts cannot cause inconsistent states in data structures. Subsequently, the adapter is repeatedly asked which packets have been sent, until all sent packets have been recorded. Next, the packets are removed from the ring buffer and freed by dev_kfree_skb_irq(skb).

Finally, we should check on whether the network device has been briefly halted by a full ring buffer. At least one buffer place has now been released, so the network can be freed by netif_wake_queue(dev). To free the network device, the flag LINK_STATE_XOFF is deleted, as described in Section 5.1.1.

```
void net_tx(struct net_device *dev) {
    struct net_local *np = (struct net_local *)dev->priv;
    int entry;

    /* This protects us from concurrent execution of
     * our dev->hard_start_xmit function above.
     */
    spin_lock(&np->lock);

    entry = np->tx_old;
    while (tx_entry_is_sent(np, entry)) {
        struct sk_buff *skb = np->skbs[entry];

        np->stats.tx_bytes += skb->len;
        dev_kfree_skb_irq (skb);

        entry = next_tx_entry(np, entry);
    }
    np->tx_old = entry;

    /* If we had stopped the queue due to a "tx full"
     * condition, and space has now been made available,
     * wake up the queue.
     */
    if (netif_queue_stopped(dev) && ! tx_full(dev))
        netif_wake_queue(dev);

    spin_unlock(&np->lock);
}
```

Receiving a Data Packet   In contrast to sending a data packet, receiving a data packet from the network is an unforeseeable event for the operating system. The network adapter receives a packet in parallel to processor operations and wants to forward this packet to the kernel. In general, there are two methods to inform the kernel that a packet has arrived.

First, the system could periodically ask the network adapter whether data has been received; this is the so-called *polling principle*. One major problem of this method is the size of the time interval in which the network adapter should be asked. It this interval is too short, then unnecessary computing time is wasted, but, if it is too long, then the data exchange is unnecessarily delayed and the network adapter might be unable to buffer all incoming packets.

The second and better method uses an interrupt and an appropriate interrupt-handling routine to inform the operation system about an incoming packet. A processor of the system is briefly interrupted in its current work, accepts the packet received, and stores it in a queue. Next, the packet is further handled as soon as the processor has time. This *interrupt principle* clearly performs better than the polling principle, and it adapts itself better to the current system load. For this reason, each modern network adapter works by this principle (i.e., the receive function of the network driver is called by its interrupt-handling routine).

`net_rx()`	**drivers/net/isa_skeleton.c**

The driver method used to handle incoming packets is responsible for requesting a socket buffer and for filling the packet data space with the packet received. The method `dev_alloc_skb()` can be used to request a new socket buffer. This method attempts to get a used socket buffer from the socket-buffer cache to avoid slow memory management. Section 4.1.1 introduced the way how `dev_alloc_skb()` works.

Occasionally, more than one packet arrives. In the example discussed in this section, we use up to ten packets that are accepted by the network adapter and introduced as socket buffers to the Linux network architecture. The status of a received packet can generally be verified from specific hardware registers (i.e., whether the packet was received correctly and, if not, which error occurred). If errors occur, then these are generally collected in a `net_device_stats` structure, which is not part of the `net_device` structure; it has to be managed in the private data space (`dev->priv`) of the network device.

Once a packet has been received correctly and the packet data has been transferred to the packet data range of the socket buffer, the receiving network device **dev** is registered in the `sk_buff` structure, and the protocol type present in the packet is learned. Notice that this information cannot be carried out from the payload of the MAC packet, so it has to be learned here, before the packet is forwarded to the higher layers. For Ethernet packets, the method `eth_type_trans()` handles this task and extracts this information from the protocol field of the Ethernet frame. (See Section 6.3.1.)

Subsequently, `netif_rx(skb)` can place the socket buffers in the input queue. Finally, the statistics for the network device are updated, and the interrupt-handling routine either continues handling the next packet received or terminates the interrupt handling.

```
/* We have a good packet(s), get it/them out of the buffers. */
 static void net_rx(struct net_device *dev) {
   struct net_local *lp = (struct net_local *)dev->priv;
```

```
int ioaddr = dev->base_addr;
int boguscount = 10;

do {
    int status = inw(ioaddr);
    int pkt_len = inw(ioaddr);

    if (pkt_len == 0)        /* Read all the frames? */
        break;               /* Done for now */

    if (status & 0x40) {     /* There was an error. */
        lp->stats.rx_errors++;
        if (status & 0x20) lp->stats.rx_frame_errors++;
        if (status & 0x10) lp->stats.rx_over_errors++;
        if (status & 0x08) lp->stats.rx_crc_errors++;
        if (status & 0x04) lp->stats.rx_fifo_errors++;
    } else {
        /* Malloc up new buffer. */
        struct sk_buff *skb;

        lp->stats.rx_bytes+=pkt_len;

        skb = dev_alloc_skb(pkt_len);
        if (skb == NULL) {
            printk(KERN_NOTICE "%s: Memory squeeze, dropping packet.\n",
                    dev->name);
            lp->stats.rx_dropped++;
            break;
        }

        /* 'skb->data' points to the start of sk_buff data area. */
        memcpy(skb_put(skb,pkt_len), (void*)dev->rmem_start,
                pkt_len);
        /* or */
        insw(ioaddr, skb->data, (pkt_len + 1) >> 1);

        skb->dev = dev;
        skb->protocol = eth_type_trans(skb, dev);

        netif_rx(skb);
        dev->last_rx = jiffies;
        lp->stats.rx_packets++;
        lp->stats.rx_bytes += pkt_len;
    }
} while (-boguscount);
return;
}
```

5.3.4   Problems In Transmitting Packets

Even when a packet was passed to the network adapter, it is not yet certain whether the packet can be transmitted. The network adapter could be faulty, or the interrupt with the acknowledgment of the transmission process could have been lost. For this reason, a *watchdog timer* is used to detect errors.

During the registration of a network device (`register_netdevice()` — see Section 5.2.1), the watchdog timer `dev->watchdog_timer` is initialized in the function `dev_watchdog_init()`. The handling routine of the timer is set not to the function `dev->tx_timeout()`, but to `dev_watchdog()`. Also, the `net_device` structure of the network device is entered as the timer's private data.

When the network device is activated (`dev_open()`) at a later point in time (see Section 5.2.2), then the watchdog timer is started by the method `dev_activate()` or `dev_watchdog_up()`. The time when the timer should be triggered is set to `jiffies + dev->watchdog_timeo`. If no valid value was stated for the interval when the network device was registered, then `dev_watchdog_up()` takes 5 · HZ.

This means that the handling routine of the watchdog timer has completed all `dev->watchdog_timeo` ticks. At the same time, `dev_watchdog()` is tested to check on whether the network device is active and usable at all. And, if the transmit buffers of the network adapter are still full (`netif_queue_stopped(dev)`) and the condition (`jiffies − dev->trans_start > dev->watchdog_timeo`) is met, then there is a problem. The driver method `dev->tx_timeout()` is called to solve this problem, as is described later in this chapter.

If no problem occurred, or if the network device is not active, then the timer is registered again to be executed in `dev->watchdog_timeo` ticks.

In earlier kernel versions, the drivers of network devices were responsible themselves for implementing and managing a watchdog timer. This mechanism assumes that task now in the newer versions. This means that only the adapter-specific reset method `dev->tx_timeout()` has to be implemented.

`net_timeout()`	**drivers/net/isa_skeleton.c**

When a problem situation occurs during the transmission of data packets, then the above described watchdog timer of the network device (`dev->watchdog_timer`) detects the problem. As soon as more than `dev->watchdog_timeo` ticks have passed since the last packet start (`trans_start`), then the handling routine `dev->tx_timeout()` should take care of this problem.

This handling routine is responsible for analyzing the problem and for handling it. Often, the only way to solve the problem is to reset and reinitialize the complete hardware of the network adapter. In any event, an attempt should be made to send the packets waiting in the queue.

```
static void net_tx_timeout(struct net_device *dev) {
    struct net_local *np = (struct net_local *)dev->priv;

    printk(KERN_WARNING "%s: transmit timed out, %s?\n", dev->name,
           tx_done(dev) ? "IRQ conflict" : "network cable problem");

    /* Try to restart the adaptor. */
    chipset_init(dev, 1);

    np->stats.tx_errors++;

    /* If we have space available to accept new transmit
     * requests, wake up the queuing layer. This would
```

```
 * be the case if the chipset_init() call above just
 * flushes out the tx queue and empties it.
 *
 * If instead, the tx queue is retained then the
 * netif_wake_queue() call should be placed in the
 * TX completion interrupt handler of the driver instead
 * of here.
 */
if (!tx_full(dev))
    netif_wake_queue(dev);
}
```

5.3.5 Runtime Configuration

`example_set_config()`	**drivers/net/isa_skeleton.c**

In certain situations, it can be necessary to change the configuration of the system resources used by a network adapter at runtime—for example, when the interrupt cannot be identified automatically, or when there are conflicts with other devices. The driver method `set_config()` can be used to manipulate the configuration of system resources (i.e., interrupt, DMA, etc.) at runtime.

When the current configuration is polled on the application level, then the `irq`, `dma`, `base_addr`, `mem_start`, and `mem_end` parameters can be read directly from the `net_device` structure. However, when one of these parameters has to be changed, then we need a driver-specific method to effect the changes in the adapter. We will use the method `net_set_config()`, which allows us to change only the interrupt line, as an example to show how system resources can be changed in general.

The driver method `set_config()` is called when an application process invokes the `ioctl()` command SIOCSIFMAP (*Socket I/O Control Set InterFace MAP*). Beforehand, however, the process should have read the current configuration by use of the `ioctl()` command SIOCGIFMAP (*Socket I/O Control Get InterFace MAP*). The reason is that, when it wants to change a value, the other parameters should have the current values.

For both `ioctl()` commands, the system parameters are passed in a structure of the type `ifmap`. The `ifmap` structure has the following fields, corresponding to the fields with the same names in the `net_device` structure.

```
struct ifmap
{
    unsigned long mem_start;
    unsigned long mem_end;
    unsigned short base_addr;
    unsigned char irq;
    unsigned char dma;
    unsigned char port;
};
```

The method's return value is also used as return value for the `ioctl()` call. Drivers that don't implement `set_config()` return -EOPNOTSUPP.

```
static int net_set_config(struct net_device *dev, struct ifmap *map){

    if (dev->flags & IFF_UP)        /* no changes on running devices */
        return -EBUSY

    /* we don't allow to change the port address */
    if (map->base_addr != dev->base_addr) {
        return -EOPNOTSUPP;
    }

    /* changing the irq is o.k. */
    if (map->irq != dev->irq) {
        dev->irq = map->irq;
    }

    /* ... */
    return 0;
}
```

5.3.6   Adapter-Specific ioctl() Commands

`ioctl()` commands are extremely useful tools to start certain actions from within the user address space. Normally, executing the system call `ioctl()` in a socket causes an `ioctl()` command of a network protocol to be invoked. The corresponding symbols are defined in the file `include/linux/sockios.h` and normally relate to a specific protocol instance. However, when an `ioctl()` command of higher protocol instances cannot be processed, then the kernel forwards it to the network devices, which can then define their own commands in the driver method `do_ioctl()`.

`net_do_ioctl()`	**drivers/net/isa_skeleton.c**

The `ioctl()` implementation for sockets knows 16 additional `ioctl()` commands, which can be used by drivers. More specifically, these are the commands `SIOCDEVPRIVATE to SIOCDEVPRIVATE + 15`. When one of these commands is used, then the method `dev->do_ioctl()` of the relevant network device is invoked.

When called, `do_ioctl(dev, ifr, cmd)` gets a pointer to a structure of the type `ifreq`. This pointer (`ifr`) points to an address in the kernel address space, which contains a copy of the `ifreq` structure passed by the user. After the loopback from the `do_iotcl()` method, this structure is copied back to the user address space. This means that a network driver can then use its own `ioctl()` commands both to receive and to output data. Examples for driver-specific `ioctl()` commands include reading or writing special registers, such as the *MII* register of some modern network adapters (`eepro100`, `epic100`, etc.).

We use the following basic example to demonstrate a driver-specific `ioctl()` implementation:

```
static int net_ioctl(struct net_device *dev, struct ifreq *ifr, int cmd)
{
    struct net_local *lp = (struct net_local *)dev->priv;
    long ioaddr = dev->base->addr;
```

```
u16 *data = (u16 *)&ifr->ifr_data;
int phy = lp->phy[0] & 0x1f;

switch(cmd) {
    case SIOCDEVPRIVATE:     /* Get the address of the PHY in use */
        data[0] = phy;
    case SIOCDECPRIVATE+1: /* Special ioctl command 1 */
        special_ioctl_1();
    case SIOCDEVPRIVATE+2: /* Special ioctl command 2 */
        special_ioctl_2();

    /* ... */
    default:
        return -EOPNOTSUPP;
}
}
```

5.3.7 Statistical Information About a Network Device

In most cases, we could want to obtain statistical information about the operation of a network device or its network adapters. Detailed logging of the events can help us find and troubleshoot errors and faulty configurations easily. For this purpose, we always use the data structure `net_device_stats` in the Linux kernel.

struct net_device_stats	include/linux/netdevice.h

- `rx_packets` and `tx_packets` contain the total number of packets successfully received and transmitted, respectively, over this network device.
- `rx_errors` and `tx_errors` store the number of faulty packets received and unsuccessful transmissions, respectively. Typical receive errors are wrong checksums or wrong packet sizes. Transmit errors are mainly due to physical problems or faulty configurations.
- `rx_dropped` and `tx_dropped` give the number of incoming and outgoing packets that were dropped for various reasons (e.g., memory unavailable for packet data).
- `multicasts` shows the number of multicast packets received.

The `net_device_stats` structure has a number of additional fields you can use to specify occurring errors in more detail, such as the number of ring buffer overflows, CRC errors, and synchronization errors. The exact structure and content of the `net_device_stats` structure can be found in `<linux/netdevice.h>`. In addition, there is a separate structure (`iw_statistics`) for wireless network adapters, containing radio connection data. (See the file `include/linux/wireless.h`.)

net_get_stats()	drivers/net/isa_skeleton.c

Interestingly, there is no pointer to the `net_device_stats` structure for statistical data in the `net_device` structure. The structure for statistical data has to be accommodated in the private data space of a network driver and is invoked by the driver method `get_stats()`.

get_stats(dev)() returns a pointer to the statistical data of a network device (dev). A sample implementation might look like this:

```
/*
 * Get the current statistics.
 * This may be called with the card open or closed.
 */
static struct net_device_stats *net_get_stats(struct net_device *dev) {
    struct net_local *lp = (struct net_local *)dev->priv;
    short ioaddr = dev->base_addr;

    /* Update the statistics from the device registers. */
    lp->stats.rx_missed_errors = inw(ioaddr+1);
    return &lp->stats;
}
```

5.3.8   Multicast Support on Adapter Level

net_set_multicast_list()	drivers/net/isa_skeleton.c

A network adapter uses the MAC destination address of a data packet to decide whether it will accept or ignore it. This process runs on the network adapter, so it doesn't interfere with the central processor's work. The central processor will be interrupted in its work only if the network adapter triggers an interrupt because it wants to forward the packet to higher protocol instances. In general, a network adapter accepts only packets intended for it, to ensure that the processor is not unnecessarily interrupted. Of course, an exception to this rule is the *promiscuous* mode, where all packets are accepted for analytical purposes.

For unicast packets, it is relatively easy to see whether the computer is interested in a packet. The network adapter merely has to detect its own MAC address as the destination address contained in the layer-2 packet header. Broadcast packets are also accepted without exception. However, the situation is different when detecting the correct multicast packets. How can the card know whether the computer is interested in the data of that group? In case of doubt, the card accepts the packet and passes it on to higher protocols, which should be able to know the groups subscribed. Though this method is very expensive, because the central processor has to check each multicast packet, it is the only way for some (older) network adapters to receive the *correct* multicast packets.

A better support for multicast on the MAC level is offered by modern network adapters. Such adapters manage a list of MAC addresses from which they want to receive packets. If only the packets of a specific multicast group should be received, then the corresponding MAC group address is passed to the network adapter, which will then receive the multicast packets. Section 17.4.1 describes the connection between groups and group addresses on the MAC and IP levels.

A network device stores the list of active MAC group addresses in a list (dev->mc_list). Whenever a new address is added or the state of the network device changes, then the driver method dev->set_multicast_list transfers this list to the adapter. The accompanying example illustrates how this method works.

When the network device is in promiscuous mode, then this mode is activated on the card. If all multicast packets should be received or if the list of MAC multicast addresses is bigger than the filter memory on the adapter, then all multicast packets are received; otherwise, the desired MAC addresses are transferred to the adapter—for example, as expressed by `hardware_set_filter`.

```
/*
 * Set or clear the multicast filter for this adaptor.
 * num_addrs == -1 Promiscuous mode, receive all packets
 * num_addrs == 0 Normal mode, clear multicast list
 * num_addrs > 0 Multicast mode, receive normal and MC packets,
 * and do best-effort filtering.
 */
static void set_multicast_list(struct net_device *dev) {
    short ioaddr = dev->base_addr;
    if (dev->flags&IFF_PROMISC)
    {
        /* Enable promiscuous mode */
        outw(MULTICAST|PROMISC, ioaddr);
    }
    else if((dev->flags&IFF_ALLMULTI) || dev->mc_count > HW_MAX_ADDRS)
    {
        /* Disable promiscuous mode, use normal mode. */
        hardware_set_filter(NULL);

        outw(MULTICAST, ioaddr);
    }
    else if(dev->mc_count)
    {
        /* Walk the address list, and load the filter */
        hardware_set_filter(dev->mc_list);

        outw(MULTICAST, ioaddr);
    }
    else
        outw(0, ioaddr);
}
```

Layer I + II—Medium Access and Logical Link Layer

Introduction to the Data-Link Layer

In the following chapters, we will leave the hardware area and move on to the world of network protocols. Chapters 7 through 24 discuss the structure and implementation of network protocols in the Linux kernel.

The previous chapters introduced the most important basics of the Linux network architecture, including the general structure of communication systems and protocol instances (Chapter 3), representation of network packets in the Linux kernel (socket buffers, Chapter 4), and the abstraction of physical and logical network adapters (network devices, Chapter 5). Before we continue discussing the structure and implementation of network protocols in detail, this chapter gives a brief introduction to the structuring of the data-link layer, which represents the connecting layer between network devices and higher network protocols. Of primary interest is the background where network protocols run. Another important topic of this chapter is the interplay of different activities (hardware and software interrupts, tasklets) of the Linux network architecture.

The transition between the different activities in the data-link layer (layers 1 and 2 of the OSI model) occurs when packets are sent and received; these processes are described in detail in Sections 6.2.1 and 6.2.2. First, we will describe the path a packet takes from its arrival in a network adapter until it is handled by a protocol instance in the network layer; then we will describe how a packet is sent from the network layer until it is forwarded to the network adapter.

6.1 STRUCTURE OF THE DATA-LINK LAYER

Chapter 3 introduced two reference models where the lower layers up to the network layer were structured in a different way. In the Internet reference model (TCP/IP model) there is only the data-link layer with the network adapter, and no other instance underneath the Internet protocol (network layer). In the ISO/OSI basic reference model, there are two different layers (*physical layer* and *data-link layer*), where the data-link layer is expanded by the media-access layer (Layer 2a) when using local area networks.

This book deals mainly with the protocols of the Internet world, and one assumes that the Internet reference model would best describe the structure of the Linux network architecture. Interestingly, the classification of the ISO/OSI reference model matches the structure of communication systems in local area networks much better. When taking a closer look at the IEEE 802 standards for local area networks, which are actually always used in the Internet, and their implementation in the Linux kernel, we can clearly recognize the structuring of the ISO/OSI model.

For this reason, the following discussion assumes a structuring as shown in Figure 6–1:

- The *OSI layers 1* (physical layer) and *2a* (media-access control layer — MAC) are implemented in network adapters.

- The *logical-link control* (LLC) layer is implemented in the operating system kernel; network adapters are connected to the operating system kernel by the network devices described in Chapter 5.

6.1.1 IEEE Standard for Local Area Networks (LANs)

With its IEEE 802.x standards, the IEEE (Institute of Electrical and Electronics Engineers) found a very extensive proliferation for local area networks (LANs). The best known LAN technologies are 802.3 (CSMA/CD), 802.5 (Token Ring), and 802.11 (wireless LANs). Figure 6–1 gives a rough overview of the 802.x standards and classifies them within the ISO/OSI layer model. As mentioned above, the data-link layer is divided into a logical-link control (LLC) and a media-access control (MAC) layer for networks with jointly used media. The LLC layer hides all media-specific differences and should provide a uniform interface for protocols to the higher layers; the MAC layer reflects the differences between different transmission technologies.

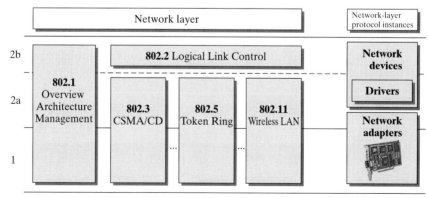

FIGURE 6–1
Standardization of layers 1 and 2 in IEEE 802 and their implementation in the Linux network architecture.

To hide the characteristics of the underlying transmission technology, the LLC layer should offer three services, regardless of this technology:

- *Unreliable datagram service* (LLC type 1): This very simple service offers no flow control or error control, so it doesn't even guarantee that data is transmitted. The removal of errors is left to the protocols of the higher layers.
- *Connection-oriented service* (LLC type 2): This service establishes a logical connection between the sender and the receiver, and it supports flow control and error control.
- *Reliable datagram service* (LLC type 3): This service combines LLC types 1 and 2—it is connectionless, but it supports both flow control and error control.

The very simple service (LLC type 1) is used mainly in local area networks, probably for its simplicity. No connection has to be established, and the higher-layer protocols offer an integrated error-handling feature (e.g., TCP in the transport layer). The protocol header of the LLC type-1 protocol consists of three fields:

- *DSAP* and *SSAP* specify the service access points in the sender and receiver. It is unclear why a protocol identification is stated for both the sender and the receiver, especially because no example is known where the two values would be different. Both fields have a width of only eight bits, so very few protocols can be defined. For this reason, the SNAP extension described below was defined.
- The *Control* field always takes the value 0x03 for LLC type 1. This corresponds to an *Unnumbered Information Frame* in the HDLC protocol, on which the LLC protocols are based.

For these reasons, the LLC layer and the relevant protocol-control information (LLC packet header) can no longer be recognized in some variants of local network protocols, because they were integrated into the packet headers of MAC PDUs. The best-known example is probably 802.3, which has the protocol control information (PCI) of the LLC layer in its protocol field.

One major drawback of this integrated solution is that many organizations and companies try to integrate their proprietary standards into a MAC PDU. To ensure that duplicate assignments of some identifications by different organizations are prevented, the IEEE invented a packet format for the LLC PDU, which allows each organization to define its own packet types. This packet format is called the SNAP extension of the LLC protocol.

In the SNAP extension, the *SSAP* and *DSAP* fields take the constant 0xAA, indicating that they expand the LLC packet header by five bytes (SNAP extension). These five bytes can be used to identify a large number of new protocols. In addition, the extension field is divided into a part for the assigning organization and another part for the actual protocol identification, to prevent conflicts in the assigning of protocol identifiers.

6.2   PROCESSES ON THE DATA-LINK LAYER

As was mentioned in the beginning of this chapter, the data-link layer forms the connecting layer between drivers or network devices and the higher world of protocol

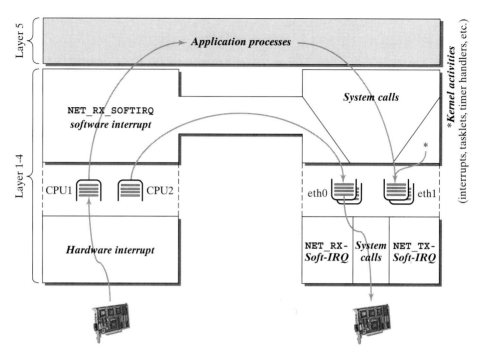

FIGURE 6–2
Activity forms in the Linux network architecture.

instances. This section gives an overview of the processes on the data-link layer. We will explain what activity forms play an important role on this layer and how the transition between them occurs. Section 6.2.1 describes the process involved when a packet arrives, and Section 6.2.2 discusses how a packet is sent. First, however, we introduce the activity forms and their tasks in the Linux network architecture.

Figure 6–2 gives an overview of the activity forms in the Linux network architecture. As compared with earlier kernel versions, Version 2.4 and up introduced significant performance improvements. Mainly, the use of software interrupts, as compared with the low-performing bottom halves, means a clear performance increase in multiprocessor systems. As shown in Figure 6–2, we can distinguish between the following activities:

- *Hardware interrupts* accept incoming data packets from the network adapters and introduce them to the Linux network architecture (per Chapter 5). To ensure that the interrupt can terminate as quickly as possible (see Section 2.2.2), incoming data packets are put immediately into the incoming queue of the processing CPU, and the hardware interrupt is terminated. The software interrupt NET_RX_SOFTIRQ is marked for execution to handle these packets further.

- The *software interrupt* NET_RX_SOFTIRQ (for short, NET_RX soft-IRQ) assumes subsequent (not time-critical) handling of incoming data packets. This includes mainly the entire handling of protocol instances on layers 2 through 4 (for packets to be delivered locally) or on layers 2 and 3 (for packets to be forwarded). This means that most of the protocol instances introduced in Chapters 7 through 25 run in the context of NET_RX soft-IRQ.

Packets incoming for an application are handled by NET_RX soft-IRQ upto the kernel boundary and then forwarded to the waiting process. At this point, the packet leaves the kernel domain.

Packets to be forwarded are put into the outgoing queue of a network device over the layer-3 protocol used (or by the bridge implementation). If the NET_RX soft-IRQ has not yet used more than one tick $(\frac{1}{Hz})$ to handle network protocols, then it tries immediately to send the next packet. If the soft-IRQ was able to send a packet successfully, it will handle it to the point where it is passed to the network adapter. (See Chapter 5 and Section 6.2.2.)

- The software interrupt NET_TX_SOFTIRQ (for short, NET_TX soft-IRQ) also sends data packets, but only provided that it was marked explicitly for this task. This case, among others, occurs when a packet cannot be sent immediately after it was put in the output queue—for example, because it has to be delayed for traffic shaping. In such a case, a timer is responsible for marking the NET_RX soft-IRQ for execution at the target transmission time (see Section 6.2.2) and transmitting the packet.

This means that the NET_TX soft-IRQ can transmit packets in parallel with other activities in the kernel. It primarily assumes the transmission of packets that had to be delayed.

- Data packets to be sent by application processes are handled by *system calls* in the kernel. In the context of a system call, a packet is handled by the corresponding protocol instances until it is put into one of the output queues of the sending network device. As with NET_RX soft-IRQ, this activity tries to pass the next packet to the network adapter immediately after the previous one.
- *Other activities of the kernel* (*tasklets, timer handling routines, etc.*) do various tasks in the Linux network architecture. However, unlike the tasks of the activities described so far, they cannot be clearly classified, because they are activated by other activities upon demand. In general, these activity forms run tasks *at a specific time* (*timer handling routines*) or at a *less specified, later time* (*tasklets*).
- *Application processes* are not activities in the operating-system kernel. Nevertheless, we mentioned them here within the interplay of activities of the kernel, because some are started by system calls and because incoming packets are forwarded to some.

As compared with earlier kernel versions, where no software interrupts were yet available, their task was executed by the net bottom half (NET_BH). Unfortunately, the NET_BH did not run on two processors in parallel, which means that it was much less performing than software interrupts, which can run in parallel on several CPUs.

The next two sections describe how packets are received and sent in the data-link layer, but details with regard to network adapters, which were introduced in Chapter 5, will be discussed only superficially.

6.2.1 Receiving a Packet

The path of each packet not generated locally in the computer begins in a network adapter or a comparable interface (e.g., the parallel port in PLIP). This port receives a packet and informs the kernel about its arrival by triggering an interrupt. The following process in the network driver was described in Chapter 5, but we will repeat it here briefly for the sake of completeness.

If the transmission was correct, then the path of a packet through the kernel begins at this point (as in Figure 6–3). Up to when the interrupt was triggered, the Linux kernel had nothing to do with the packet. This means that the interrupt-handling routine is the first activity of the kernel that handles an incoming packet.

- When it has received a packet correctly, the network adapter triggers an interrupt, which is handled by the interrupt-handling routine of the network driver. For the example driver described in Section 5.3 (`drivers/net/isa_skeleton.c`), this is the method `net_interrupt()`. As soon as the interruption was identified as an incoming packet, `net_rx()` is responsible for further handling. If the interrupt was caused not by an incoming packet, but by a message that a data transmission was completed, then `net_tx()` continues.

- `net_rx()` uses `dev_alloc_skb(pkt_len)` to obtain a socket-buffer structure and copies the incoming packet from the network adapter to its packet-data space. (See Chapter 4 and Section 5.3.) Subsequently, the pointer `skb->dev` is set

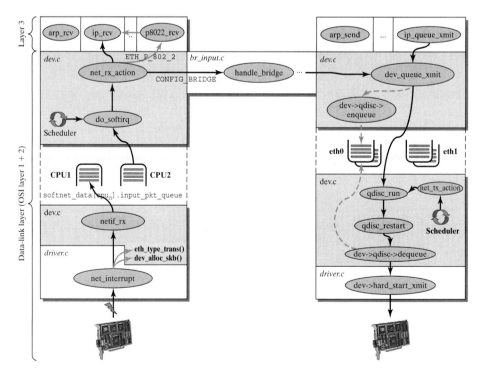

FIGURE 6–3
The path of a packet in the data-link layer of the Linux kernel.

to the receiving network device, and the type of the data contained in the layer-2 data frame is recognized. For this purpose, Ethernet drivers can use the method eth_type_trans(). There are similar methods for other MAC technologies (FDDI, token ring).

The demultiplexing process takes place in the LLC layer at this point. The exact process will be explained in Section 6.3.1.

▓ netif_rx() completes the interrupt handling. First, the current time is set in skb->time, and the socket buffer is placed in the input queue. As compared with earlier versions of the Linux kernel, there is now not only one single queue having the name "backlog"; instead, each CPU stores "its" incoming packets in the structure softnet_data[cpu].input_pkt_queue. This means that the processor that handles the interrupt always stores the packet in its queue. This mechanism was introduced to avoid kernel-wide locks of a single input queue.

Once the packet was placed in the queue, the interrupt handling is complete. As was explained in Section 2.2.2, the handling routine of a hardware interrupt should run only the operations absolutely required to ensure that other activities of the computer (software interrupts, tasklets, processes) won't be unnecessarily interrupted.

Incoming packets are further handled by the software interrupt (NET_RX_SOFTIRQ), which replaces the net bottom half (NET_BH) used in earlier versions of the Linux kernel. NET_RX_SOFTIRQ is marked for execution by __cpu_raise_softirq(cpu, NET_RX_SOFTIRQ). This mechanism is similar to bottom halfs, but the use of software interrupts allows much more parallelism and so makes possible improved performance on multiprocessor systems. (See Section 2.2.3.)

The path of a packet initially ends in the queue for incoming packets. The interrupt handling was terminated, and the kernel continued handling the interrupted activity (process, software interrupt, tasklet, etc.). When the process scheduler (schedule() in kernel/sched.c) is invoked once more after a certain interval, then it first checks for whether a software interrupt is marked for execution. This is the case here, and it uses do_softirq() to start the marked soft-IRQ. The following section assumes that this concerns the NET_RX soft-IRQ:

net_rx_action()	net/core/dev.c

net_rx_action() is the handling routine of NET_RX_SOFTIRQ. In a continuous loop (for(;;){...}), packets are fetched one after the other from the input queue of the processing CPU and passed to the protocol-handling routine, until the input queue is empty. The continuous loop is also exited when the packet-handling duration exceeds one tick (10 ms) or when budget =net_dev_max_backlog[1] packets have been

---

[1]net_dev_max_backlog specified the maximum length of the (only) input queue, backlog, in earlier versions of the Linux kernel, and was initialized with the value 300 (packets). In the new kernel versions, this is the maximum length of the input queues of the processors.

removed and processed from the queue. This prevents the protocol-handling routine from blocking the remaining activities of the computer and thereby inhibits denial-of-service attacks.

The first action in the continuous loop is to request a packet from the input queue of the CPU by the method __skb_dequeue(). If a socket buffer is found, then the reference counter of the socket buffer is first incremented in skb_bond(). Subsequently, the socket buffer is transferred to instances of the handling protocols.

First, the socket buffer is passed to all protocols registered in the list ptype_all. (See Section 6.3.) In general, no protocols are registered in this list. However, this interface is excellently suitable for inserting analytical tools.

If the computer was configured as a bridge (CONFIG_BRIDGE) and the pointer br_handle_frame_hook() was set, then the packet is passed to the method handle_bridge(). It will then be processed in the bridge instance. (See Chapter 12.)

The last action (which is generally the most common case) passed the socket buffer to all protocols registered with the protocol identifier (dev->protocol). They are managed in the hash table (ptype_base). Section 6.3 will explain the details of how layer-3 protocols are managed.

For example, the method eth_type_trans() recognizes the protocol identifier 0x0800 and stores it in dev->protocol for an IP packet. In net_rx_action(), this identifier is now mapped by the hash function to the entry of the Internet Protocol (IP) instance. Handling of the protocol is started by a call of the corresponding protocol handling routine (func()). In the case of the Internet Protocol, this is the known method ip_rcv(). If other protocol instances are registered with the identifier 0x0800, then a pointer to the socket buffer is passed to all of these protocols one after the other.

This means that the actual work with protocol instances of the Linux kernel begins at this point. In general, the protocols that start at this point are layer-3 protocols. However, this interface is also used by several other protocols that instead fit in the first two layers of the ISO/OSI basic reference model. The following section describes the inverse process (i.e., how a data packet is sent).

6.2.2   Transmitting a Packet

As is shown in Figure 6–3, the process of transmitting a packet can be handled in several activity forms of the kernel. We distinguish two main transmission processes:

- *Normal* transmission process, where an activity tries to send off ready packets and send them over the network device immediately after the placing of a packet in the output queue of that network adapter. This means that the transmission process is executed either by NET_RX soft-IRQ or as a consequence of a system call. This form of transmitting packets is discussed in the following section.

- The second type of transmission is handled by NET_TX soft-IRQ. It is marked for execution by some activity of the kernel and invoked by the scheduler at the next possible time. The NET_TX soft-IRQ is normally used when packets are to be sent outside the regular transmission process or at a specific time for certain reasons. This transmission process is introduced after the section describing the normal transmission process.

The Normal Transmission Process

`dev_queue_xmit()`	**net/core/dev.c**

`dev_queue_xmit(skb)` is used by the protocol instances of higher protocols to send a packet in the form of a socket buffer, `skb`, over a network device. The network device is specified by the parameter `skb->dev` of the socket buffer structure. (See Figure 6–4.)

First, the socket buffer is placed in the output queue of the network device. This is done by use of the method `dev->qdisc->enqueue()`. In general, packets are handled by the FIFO (First In — First Out) principle. However, it is also possible to define several queues and introduce various mechanisms for differentiated handling of packets. (See Chapters 18 and 22.)

Once the packet has been placed in the queue by the desired method (`qdisc`), further handling of packets ready to be sent is triggered. This task is handled by `qdisc_run()`.

There is one special case: that a network device has not defined methods for queue management (`dev->enqueue == NULL`). In this case, a packet is simply sent by `dev->hard_start_xmit()` right away. In general, this case concerns logical network devices, such as loopback, or tunnel network devices.

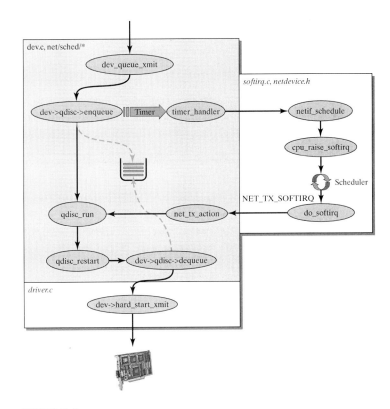

FIGURE 6–4
The process involved when sending a packet by `dev_queue_xmit()`.

`qdisc_run()`	**include/net/pkt_sched.h**

`qdisc_run(dev)` has rather little functionality. All it actually does is call `qdisc_restart()` until it returns a value greater-equal null (no more packet in the queue), or until the network device does not accept any more packets (`netif_queue_stopped(dev)`).

`qdisc_restart()`	**net/sched/sch_generic.c**

`qdisc_restart(dev)` is responsible for getting the next packet from the queue of the network device and sending it. In general, the network device has only a single queue and works by the FIFO principle. However, it is possible to define several queues and serve them by a special strategy (`qdisc`).

This means that `dev->qdisc->dequeue()` is used to request the next packet. If this request is successful, then this packet is sent by the driver method `dev->hard_start_xmit()`. (See Chapter 5.) Of course, the method also checks on whether the network device is currently able to send packets (i.e., whether `netif_queue_stopped(dev) == 0` is true).

Another problem that can potentially occur in `qdisc_restart()` is that `dev->xmit_lock` sets a lock. This spinlock is normally set when the transmission of a packet is to be started in `qdisc_restart()`. At the same time, the number of the locking CPU is registered in `dev->xmit_lock_owner`.

If this lock is set, then there are two options:

■ The locking CPU is not identical with the one discussed here, which is currently trying to set the lock `dev->xmit_lock`. This means that another CPU sends another packet concurrently over this network device. This is actually not a major problem; it merely means that the other CPU was simply a little faster. The socket buffer is placed back into the queue (`dev->qdisc->requeue()`). Finally, NET_TX_SOFTIRQ is activated in `netif_schedule()` to trigger the transmission process again.

■ If the locking CPU is identical with the CPU discussed here, then this means that a so-called *dead loop* is present: Forwarding of a packet to the network adapter was somehow interrupted in this processor, and an attempt was made to retransmit a packet. The response to this process is that the packet is dropped and everything returns immediately from `qdisc_restart()` to complete the first transmission process.

The return value of `qdisc_restart()` can take either of the following values:

■ = 0: The queue is empty.

■ > 0: The queue is not empty, but the queue discipline (`dev->qdisc`) prevents any packet from being sent (e.g., because it has not yet reached its target transmission time in active traffic shaping).

■ < 0: The queue is not empty, but the network device currently cannot accept more packets, because all transmit buffers are full.

If the packet can be forwarded successfully to a network adapter, then the kernel assumes that this transmission process is completed, and the kernel turns to the next packet (`qdisc_run()`).

Transmitting over NET_TX Soft-IRQ   The `NET_TX_SOFTIRQ` is an alternative for sending packets. It is marked for execution (`__cpu_raise_softirq()`) by the method `netif_schedule()`. `netif_schedule()` is invoked whenever a socket buffer cannot be sent over the normal transmission process, described in the previous section. This problem can have several causes:

▨ Problems occurred when a packet was forwarded to the network adapter (e.g., no free buffer spaces).

▨ The socket buffer has to be sent later, to honor special handling of packets. In the case of traffic shaping, packets might have to be delayed artificially, to maintain a specific data rate. For this purpose, a timer is used, which starts the transmission of the packet when the transmission time is reached. (See Figure 6–4.)

Now, if `NET_TX_SOFTIRQ` is marked for execution by `netif_schedule()`, it is started at the next call of the CPU scheduler.

`net_tx_action()`	**net/core/dev.c**

`net_tx_action()` is the handling routine of the `NET_TX_SOFTIRQ` software interrupt. The main task of this method is to call the method `qdisc_restart()` to start the transmission of the packets of a network device.

The benefit of using the `NET_TX_SOFTIRQ` software interrupt is that processes can be handled in parallel in the Linux network architecture. In addition to `NET_RX_SOFTIRQ`, which is responsible for the main protocol handling, the `NET_TX` soft-IRQ can also be used to increase the throughput considerably in multiprocessor computers.

6.3   MANAGING LAYER-3 PROTOCOLS

The previous section of this chapter described the path of a packet between a network adapter and the interface to higher protocol instances. This section discusses this interface in more detail. First, we will explain how new protocols can be added. Because only protocols of the network layer (IP, ARP, IPv6, IPX) are added to the Linux network architecture over this interface, it is also referred to as the interface to the network layer or layer-3 protocols in the following discussion.

In the Linux kernel, we distinguish between two types of layer-3 protocols, where the first type is used mostly for analysis purposes:

▨ A protocol receives all packets arriving at the interface to the layer-3 protocols.

▨ A protocol receives only packets with the correct protocol identifier (e.g., 0x0800 for the Internet Protocol).

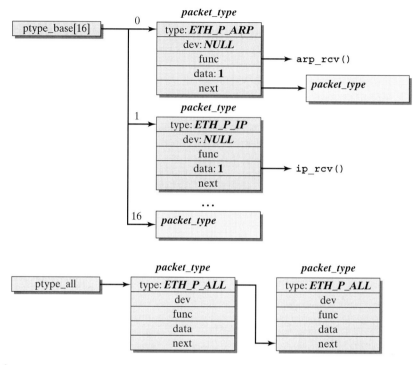

FIGURE 6–5
Managing protocols above network devices.

Figure 6–5 shows that these two types of protocols are managed in two different data structures. We can see in this figure that the two types of layer-3 protocols do not differ much. Both types are managed in a structure of the type `packet_type` and linked in different lists, depending on the above-mentioned type. The simple linked list, `ptype_all`, stores the protocols that should receive all incoming socket buffers. The hash table, `ptype_base`, manages all *normal* layer-3 protocols.

A `packet_type` structure is created and placed into the corresponding data structure for each protocol. The following parameters are required in the `packet_type` structure to define a protocol:

▪ `type`: This field specifies the protocol identifier (i.e., the constants listed in Figure 6–6). If ETH_P_ALL is stated in this field, then the protocol is added to the list `ptype_all` when it is registered, and it receives all packets. Otherwise, it receives only packets with protocol identifier type.

The identifier of a protocol has to be extracted from the packet data in the receive routine of the network driver (e.g., by the method `eth_type_trans()`, which will be introduced at the end of this chapter).

▪ `dev` can take a pointer to a network device. In that case, only the packets received on that network device are passed to the protocol. If several, but not all, network

```
/* These are the defined Ethernet Protocol ID's. */
ETH_P_LOOP      0x0060        /* Ethernet Loopback packet     */
ETH_P_IP        0x0800        /* Internet Protocol packet     */
ETH_P_X25       0x0805        /* CCITT X.25                   */
ETH_P_ARP       0x0806        /* Address Resolution packet    */
  ...
ETH_P_IPX       0x8137        /* IPX over DIX                 */
ETH_P_IPV6      0x86DD        /* IPv6                         */

/* Non DIX types. Won't clash for 1500 types. */
ETH_P_802_3     0x0001        /* Dummy type for 802.3 frames  */
ETH_P_AX25      0x0002        /* Dummy protocol id for AX.25  */
ETH_P_ALL       0x0003        /* Every packet (be careful!!!) */
ETH_P_802_2     0x0004        /* 802.2 frames                 */
ETH_P_SNAP      0x0005        /* Internal only                */
  ...
```

FIGURE 6–6
Identifiers for layer-3 protocols on the LLC layer (include/Linux/if_ether.h).

adapters should have this preference, then the protocol for each network device has to be registered separately. If dev contains a NULL pointer, which corresponds to the normal case, then the input network device does not play any role in selecting a protocol.

▪ func() is the handling routine for the protocol. This means that this is the point where the protocol's work begins. For example, the handling routine ip_rcv() is registered in the packet_type structure of the Internet Protocol. (See Chapter 14.)

▪ data can be used to point to private data of the protocol, but it is generally not used.

▪ next is used to link several packet_type structures.

The following two methods are available to manage the protocols or their packet_type structures:

dev_add_pack()	net/core/dev.c

dev_add_pack(pt) registers with the Linux network architecture the layer-3 protocol represented by the packet_type structure pt. If the field type has the value ETH_P_ALL, then the protocol is added to the list ptype_all. Otherwise, it is inserted in the appropriate row of the hash table ptype_base. From now on, all received packets with protocol identifier **type** are delivered to this protocol instance.[2]

dev_remove_pack()	net/core/dev.c

dev_remove_pack(pt) removes the protocol with the packet_type structure pt. Depending on the identifier in the type field, it is removed from the corresponding data structure.

---

[2]—provided that the protocol type is not ETH_P_ALL and the protocol was not registered for one single special network device.

6.3.1 Logical Link Control—Determining the Layer-3 Protocol Identifier

`eth_type_trans()`	**net/ethernet/eth.c**

`eth_type_trans(skb, dev)` is the second important part of the Logical Link Control (LLC) implementation in the Linux kernel, in addition to managing the network-layer protocols described in Section 6.3. Two important tasks are executed for this purpose:

- Recognize the LLC protocol type used and the protocol identifier of the layer-3 protocol from the protocol control information contained in the layer-2 data frame.
- Identify the packet type (unicast, multicast, broadcast) and check on whether the packet is addressed to the local computer.

The method `eth_type_trans()`, which can be used for all Ethernet-compatible network adapters, is called by the network driver in the packet-receive method. (See Section 5.3.) It is responsible for extracting protocol-control information of the LLC layer and handling it appropriately. For this reason, all network devices of a MAC protocol type use the same `type_trans()` method. There are similar methods for token ring and FDDI devices (`tr_type_trans()`, `fddi_type_trans()`).

In general, Ethernet networks do not use any of the LLC standards, but transmit the layer-3 protocol identifier directly in the MAC frame. The only protocol mechanism is thus demultiplexing of different layer-3 protocols. This is the reason why `eth_type_trans()` is relatively simple and easy to understand. However, you can use an LLC protocol based on IEEE 802.2.

First, `skb_pull(skb, dev->hard_header_length)` takes the layer-2 packet header from `eth_type_trans()`. Next, the type of the packet is identified and registered in `skb->pkt_type`. The following mutually exclusive types are possible:

- PACKET_BROADCAST: The packet was sent to the broadcast address of the local network and is intended for all connected computers.
- PACKET_MULTICAST: The packet was sent to a layer-2 group address, which means that it is intended for a group of computers.
- PACKET_HOST: The packet is intended for the local computer (i.e., it was sent to the layer-2 address of the receiving network adapter).
- PACKET_OTHERHOST: The packet is not intended for the local computer and was received only because the computer is in promiscuous mode.

Subsequently, the protocol identifier of the incoming packet is recognized. In local networks based on the IEEE 802 standard, there are several options, but this book considers only Ethernet-compatible networks:

- If a value in the length or protocol field of the Ethernet packet header is bigger than the maximum frame length (1536 bytes), then it is assumed that it is an 802.3-compatible Ethernet adapter. As mentioned earlier, the 802.3 protocol

LLC variant   **MAC and LLC frame formats**

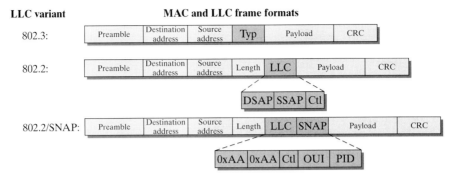

FIGURE 6–7
Variants for LLC protocol control information in Ethernet networks.

integrates the protocol-control information of the LLC layer in the protocol field of the 802.3 frame, thus sparing any need for a separate LLC packet header. This means that the field value contains the protocol identifier of the layer-3 protocol and is registered in skb->type.

▒ Older Ethernet adapters store the length of the frame rather than the protocol identifier of the layer-3 protocol in the length or protocol field. For this reason, the protocol-control information of the LLC layer has to be contained in the payload of the Ethernet frame (i.e., an explicit LLC packet header based on the 802.2 standard, SSAP and DSAP—see Figure 6–7).

eth_type_trans() does not verify the LLC-PDU any further, but returns ETH_P_802_2 as the layer-3 protocol identifier. The 802.2 LLC protocol instance is treated as a layer-3 protocol instance. (See Section 6.3.) It is also registered as a layer-3 protocol instance in the hash table ptype_base. Though this conflicts with the layer model, it allows a simpler implementation in this case, because most Ethernet adapters use the integrated LLC variant mentioned previously, and 802.2 is rather an exceptional case. Finally, the demultiplexing process to the layer-3 protocol takes place in the handling routine of the 802.2 protocol (p8022_rcv(), net/802/p8022.c).

Layer-3 protocols can register themselves with the 802.2 protocol instance by use of the method register_8022_client(). For example, the SNAP protocol extension (net/802/psnap.c) can register itself with register_8022_client(0xAA, snap_rcv). From then on, the method snap_rcv(), which links to the corresponding layer-3 protocol, is invoked for all SNAP frames.

Figure 6–7 shows a summary of the frame formats used for different LLC variants in Ethernet:

▒ 802.3: LLC-PCI, integrated in the MAC-PCI.
▒ 802.2: LLC-PDU in the MAC payload.
▒ 802.2/SNAP: SNAP extension in the LLC-PDU.

The Serial-Line Internet Protocol (SLIP)

7.1 INTRODUCTION

The packet-oriented IP protocol is used to communicate over the Internet. However, a modem can transmit only a continuous byte stream. For this reason, to establish a connection from your local PC over an analog telephone line to the worldwide Internet, we need a protocol that encapsulates network packets so that they can be transmitted over a modem connection between a local computer and a point of presence (PoP). The two endpoints of the modem connection can then communicate over IP. The point of presence itself is directly connected to the Internet and routs IP packets between the local PC and the Internet. (See Figure 7–1.)

Another possible use of such a protocol is for the IP communication of two computers over the serial V.24 interface, which is available in most PCs. This use lets you build an IP network at little cost (and very low speed) without the need to install additional interfaces, such as Ethernet cards.

RFC 1055 [Romk88] specifies the SLIP (Serial Line IP) for the V.24 task. SLIP represents an intermediate layer within the network architecture: At its upward face, packets are taken from or forwarded to the IP layer; at its downward face, data are sent to or received from a serial interface driver.

As compared with the more recent PPP protocol (see Chapter 8), SLIP is very simple, but offers a rather limited functionality:

▪ SLIP includes no mechanisms for establishment of a controlled connection: As soon as SLIP has been started on both ends, the connection is implicitly established. For this reason, no parameters, such as IP address, DNS information, or the SLIP operating mode used, can be negotiated. These parameters have to be set manually or by use of a script before SLIP is started.

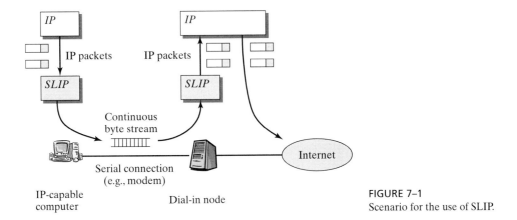

FIGURE 7–1
Scenario for the use of SLIP.

▦ SLIP serves exclusively for the transmission of Version-4 IP packets. Other network protocols (e.g., IP version 6 or X.25) are not supported.

▦ SLIP has no mechanisms to detect or correct errors; these functions have to be handled by higher network layers.

▦ In contrast to PPP, the payload in transmitted IP packets cannot be compressed. The CSLIP operating mode (described in the next bullet) allows you to compress the IP packet headers only.

In addition to the standard operating mode, SLIP supports the following modes:

▦ In *CSLIP* (Compressed SLIP), the packet headers in transmitted IP packets are compressed by the Van–Jacobson algorithm to utilize slow modem connections better.

▦ *SLIP6* uses only printable ASCII characters for data transmission. This is necessary when the underlying modem connection cannot transmit all control characters of the ASCII alphabet—for example, because the XON and XOFF control characters are used for flow control. However, a maximum payload of 6 bits per character can be transmitted in this way, and so the transmission rate drops by one-quarter.

7.1.1   Packet Detection and Character Stuffing

A serial interface or a modem connection is designed for the transmission of continuous byte sequences. To be able to send data packets of the IP protocol over such a connection, the sender has to insert special markings, which are then used by the receiver to detect the end of each packet. In SLIP, this is implemented so that the END control character (byte code 192) is inserted before and after each packet.

▦ To ensure unique detection of packet boundaries, the END character must never occur inside a packet. Of course, this constraint is undesirable, because we want to be able to transmit arbitrary data packets transparently. To maintain this *code*

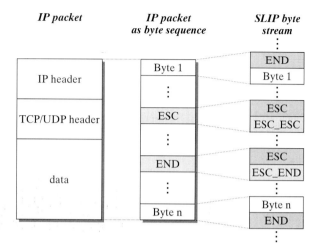

FIGURE 7–2
SLIP marks packet boundaries and uses character stuffing at the sender side.

TABLE 7–1 SLIP control characters.

Character	Byte Code
END	192
ESC	219
ESC_END	220
ESC_ESC	221

transparency, three additional control characters (ESC, ESC_END, and ESC_ESC) are used to implement a so-called *character stuffing* (shown in Figure 7–2):

▨ Each occurrence of END in packet data is replaced by the ESC ESC_END string.
▨ Each occurrence of ESC in packet data is replaced by the ESC ESC_ESC string.

The receiver can reverse character stuffing as follows to reconstruct the original IP packet:

▨ If the ESC character occurs, then the next character is ESC_ESC or ESC_END. In this case, the first ESC is deleted, and the second character is replaced by ESC or END.
▨ If the END character occurs, then this is the end of that packet, and so the packet can be forwarded to the IP layer.

Table 7–1 lists the four control characters used by SLIP and their byte codes.

7.2 SLIP IMPLEMENTATION IN THE LINUX KERNEL

Before we describe the SLIP implementation in the Linux kernel, we will first discuss the concept of TTY devices and TTY line disciplines, the better to illustrate how SLIP is implemented in Linux. Subsequently, this section will give an overview of the most

TABLE 7–2   Examples of TTY devices.

/dev Entry	Meaning
tty0–tty7	virtual consoles
pty#	pseudo-terminals—e.g., xterm window
ttyS#	serial interfaces

important functions of the SLIP implementation before we describe the steps involved in implementing SLIP in detail.

7.2.1   TTY Devices and Line Disciplines

In Linux, all devices that can act as terminals are grouped under the collective term TTY (Teletype or Terminal Type). Table 7–2 shows several examples. A TTY device is a *character device* offering special functions to control a terminal. This includes, for example, the flag for whether the terminal should produce an echo and commands to position the cursor and change color.

A TTY device can generally switch between different *TTY line disciplines*. This means that, in the Linux kernel, each system call to read (read()), write (write()), or control (ioctl()) invokes a routine specific to this line discipline. More specifically, the implementation of a TTY line discipline is inserted between the TTY device driver (*low-level driver*), which is in charge for the actual input and output, and the user process that wants to access the TTY device. (See Figure 7–3.)

One possible use for a TTY line discipline is the automatic conversion of all line ends between UNIX and Windows computers (LF versus CR/LF). In addition, TTY line disciplines offer an elegant means whereas serial interfaces can intercept and change all data transmitted over a serial interface without the need for the TTY line discipline driver to open and close the serial interface or to establish a modem dialup connection.

To register a new TTY line discipline with the Linux kernel, the driver has to first create a tty_ldisc structure (declared in <include/linux/tty_ldisc.h>) and set the

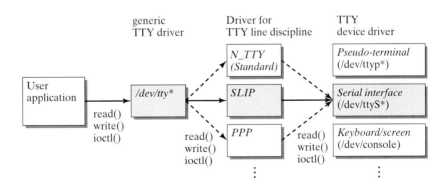

FIGURE 7–3
Interplay between TTY line disciplines and TTY device drivers.

function pointers contained in it. Subsequently, this data structure is registered by
`tty_register_ldisc()` with the kernel to make the new TTY line discipline available
for user programs.

struct tty_ldisc	include/linux/tty_ldisc.h

The `tty_ldisc` structure includes a number of function pointers, which have to be
set by the driver of the TTY line discipline. The following code briefly explains the most
important function pointers.

```
struct tty_ldisc {
        int     magic;
        char    *name;
        int     num;
        int     flags;
        /*
         * The following routines are called from above.
         */
        int     (*open)(struct tty_struct *);
        void    (*close)(struct tty_struct *);
        void    (*flush_buffer)(struct tty_struct *tty);
        ssize_t (*chars_in_buffer)(struct tty_struct *tty);
        ssize_t (*read)(struct tty_struct * tty, struct file * file,
                        unsigned char * buf, size_t nr);
        ssize_t (*write)(struct tty_struct * tty, struct file * file,
                        const unsigned char * buf, size_t nr);
        int     (*ioctl)(struct tty_struct * tty, struct file * file,
                        unsigned int cmd, unsigned long arg);
        void    (*set_termios)(struct tty_struct *tty, struct termios * old);
        unsigned int (*poll)(struct tty_struct *, struct file *,
                        struct poll_table_struct *);

        /*
         * The following routines are called from below.
         */
        void    (*receive_buf)(struct tty_struct *, const unsigned char *cp,
                        char *fp, int count);
        int     (*receive_room)(struct tty_struct *);
        void    (*write_wakeup)(struct tty_struct *);
};
```

The following functions are called from "above" (i.e., by the program or module
accessing the TTY device):

■ The function `open()` is called as soon as the TTY device switches to this line
discipline.

■ The function `close()` is called when the current TTY line discipline is deactivated.
This happens when a TTY device switches from this line discipline into another

one (where the device is first reset to the standard line discipline N_TTX by the Linux kernel) and when the TTY device itself is closed.

- The function read() is called when a program wants to read data from the TTY device.
- The function write() is called when a program wants to send data to the TTY device.
- The function ioctl() is called when a program uses the system call ioctl() to change the configuration of the TTY line discipline or of the actual TTY device, but only provided that the higher-layer generic driver for TTY devices was unable to process the ioctl() call (as is the case, for example, when the device switches to another TTY line discipline).

The following functions are called from "below" (i.e., from the actual device driver of the TTY device):

- The function receive_buf() is called when the device driver has received data and wants to forward this data to the higher-layer program (i.e., to the driver of the TTY line discipline in this case). The parameters passed include the address and length of data.
- The function receive_room() is called by the device driver to request the maximum number of bytes that the TTY line discipline can accept with receive_buf().
- The function write_wakeup() optionally can be called by the device driver as soon as it has finished sending a data block and is ready to accept more data. However, this happens only provided that it has been explicitly requested by the flag TTY_DO_WRITE_WAKEUP <linux/tty.h>.

7.2.2 General Procedure

The lifetime of a SLIP connection under Linux consists of the following phases; the sections below will explain how they are implemented in the Linux kernel:

1. *Initialize the SLIP driver*: the driver is initialized either when the system boots or when the driver module slip.o is loaded. At the same time, it registers the new TTY line discipline SLIP.
2. *Establish the connection*: A user program (e.g., dip or slattach) uses a modem connected to a serial interface (e.g., /dev/ttyS0) to dial to an Internet provider, and then switches the TTY line discipline of this serial interface to SLIP. At the same time, the SLIP operating mode (e.g., CSLIP or SLIP6) has to be set correctly.
3. *Activate and configure the network device*: Once the TTY line discipline has been switched to SLIP, a new network device is available, and the name of this device begins with "sl" (e.g., sl0). ifconfig can then be used to activate and configure this network device (e.g., by assigning valid IP addresses to both ends of the SLIP connection).
4. *Exchange data*: As soon as the network device has been configured correctly, the SLIP connection is available for sending IP packets.
5. *Deactivate the network device*: Before the SLIP connection is torn down, the network device has to be deactivated by ifconfig.

6. *Tear down the connection*: The user program (dip or slattach) separates the underlying modem connection, which causes the network device to be deregistered.

7. *Deinitialize the SLIP driver*: As soon as the driver module slip.o has been removed from the Linux kernel, it frees its memory and undoes the registration of the SLIP TTY line discipline.

7.2.3 Functions and Data Structures

The files drivers/net/slip.c and drivers/net/slip.h contain the source code for the SLIP implementation in the Linux kernel. Compression of the IP packet headers by the Van–Jacobson method (CSLIP) is implemented in drivers/net/slhc.c. However, this implementation will not be discussed in detail in what follows.

`struct slip`	**drivers/net/slip.h**

■ The SLIP driver represents each SLIP connection by a slip structure. This structure includes pointers to the net_device structure of the relevant SLIP network device and to the tty_struct structure of the underlying TTY device. (See Figure 7–4.) The slip structure includes buffer pointers and counters to send and receive data. In addition, it stores the SLIP mode (e.g., CSLIP or SLIP6). In total, the slip structure consists of the following fields:

■ tty points to a structure of the type tty_struct, which represents the TTY device allocated to this SLIP channel. This structure also includes a tty_ldisc structure with the TTY line discipline currently active (in this case, naturally, SLIP).

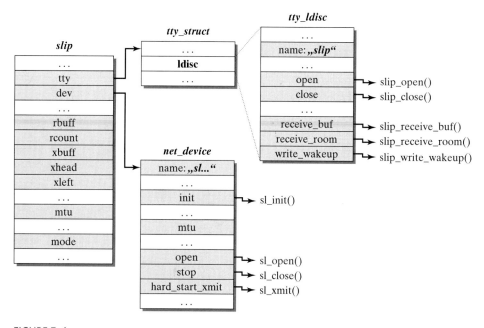

FIGURE 7–4
Important data structures of the SLIP implementation.

▓ dev points to the `net_device` structure with the data of the network device allocated to the SLIP connection.

▓ mtu is the MTU (*Maximum Transmission Unit*) of the SLIP connection, which is additionally stored in the `net_device` structure.

▓ mode specifies the active SLIP operating mode (e.g., SL_MODE_SLIP, SL_MODE_CSLIP, or SL_MODE_SLIP6).

▓ rbuff points to the receive buffer, which is used to buffer data incoming over the TTY device.

▓ rcount is the number of data bytes currently present in the receive buffer.

▓ xbuff points to the transmit buffer, which buffers data ready to be output over the TTY device.

▓ xhead points to the first character in the transmit buffer that has yet to be sent.

▓ xleft specifies the number of bytes still waiting in the transmit buffer (from xhead).

The SLIP functions can be divided into three categories: general management functions, functions to implement the SLIP TTY line discipline, and functions to implement SLIP network devices. The functions used to implement network devices can be recognized by the prefix "sl_"; the other functions have the prefix "slip_". Figure 7–5

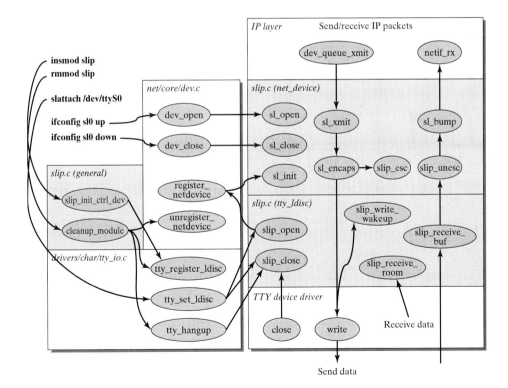

FIGURE 7–5
Functions of the SLIP implementation and their integration in the Linux kernel.

gives an overview of the functions discussed below. The following section also explains their interplay with other parts of the Linux kernel.

`slip_init_ctrl_dev( )`	**drivers/net/slip.c**

This function is called by `init_module()` when the SLIP module is loaded, and it uses the function `tty_register_ldisc()` to register the SLIP TTY line discipline with the Linux kernel.

`slip_open( )`	**drivers/net/slip.c**

This function is invoked by the function pointer `open()` in the `tty_ldisc` structure as soon as a user program wants to switch a TTY device to the SLIP line discipline. It reserves memory for the transmit and receive buffers and registers the new network device for the SLIP connection with the Linux kernel.

`sl_init( )`	**drivers/net/slip.c**

This function is invoked by the Linux kernel whenever a new network device is registered, and it does a complete initialization of the network device and the appropriate `net_device` structure.

`sl_open( )`	**drivers/net/slip.c**

This function is invoked by the function pointer `open()` of the `net_device` structure as soon as the SLIP network device is activated (e.g., by the command `ifconfig up`).

`sl_close( )`	**drivers/net/slip.c**

This function is invoked by the function pointer `stop()` of the `net_device` structure as soon as the SLIP network device is deactivated (e.g., by the command `ifconfig down`).

`slip_close( )`	**drivers/net/slip.c**

This function is invoked by the function pointer `close()` of the `tty_ldisc` structure whenever the underlying TTY device is switched from the SLIP line discipline to another line discipline.

`cleanup_module( )`	**drivers/net/slip.c**

This function is invoked whenever the SLIP module is removed. Among other things, it ensures that all buffers are freed and all SLIP network devices are deregistered. Finally, the registration of the SLIP TTY line discipline with the Linux kernel is removed by calling `tty_register_ldisc(N_SLIP, NULL)`.

`sl_xmit( )`	**drivers/net/slip.c**

This function is invoked by the IP layer, which uses the function pointer `hard_start_xmit()` of the `net_device` structure to output an IP packet over the SLIP network device. The actual work is delegated to the function `sl_encaps()`.

`sl_encaps( )`	**drivers/net/slip.c**

This function is invoked by `sl_xmit()`. As explained in section 7.1.1, it converts the IP packet into a byte sequence. Depending on the SLIP operating mode (CSLIP, etc.), other functions may be called in addition (e.g., the function `slip_esc()`). Subsequently, `sl_encaps()` invokes the function `write()` of the underlying TTY device driver, which eventually sends the byte sequence previously created over the TTY device.

`slip_esc( )`	**drivers/net/slip.c**

This function is invoked by `sl_encaps()` and does the character stuffing described in Section 7.1.1. A similar function called `slip_esc6()` exists for the SLIP operating mode SLIP6, which additionally divides the data into 6-bit blocks and converts it into printable characters.

`slip_write_wakeup( )`	**drivers/net/slip.c**

This function is invoked by the underlying TTY device driver over the function pointer `write_wakeup()` of the `tty_ldisc` structure (see Section 7.2.1) as soon as the TTY device is ready to accept more data. (See also Section 7.2.7.)

`slip_receive_room()`	**drivers/net/slip.c**

This function is invoked by the underlying TTY device driver over the function pointer `receive_room()` of the `tty_ldisc` structure and simply returns the value 65536, because the SLIP implementation can process a maximum of 65536 bytes per call of `slip_receive_buf()`.

`slip_receive_buf()`	**drivers/net/slip.c**

This function is invoked by the underlying TTY device driver over the function pointer `receive_buf()` of the `tty_ldisc` structure to transfer data from the TTY device to the SLIP driver. The function `slip_unesc()` (`slip_unesc6()`, for the SLIP6 operating mode) is invoked to convert the incoming byte stream back into IP packets.

`slip_unesc()`	**drivers/net/slip.c**

This function is invoked by `slip_receive_buf()`; it converts the incoming byte stream into IP packets, using the method described in Section 7.1.1. The function sl_bump() is invoked as soon as the END control character specifies that a complete IP packet was received. There is a corresponding function (slip_unesc6()) for the SLIP6 operating mode.

sl_bump()	drivers/net/slip.c

This function is invoked by slip_unesc() (or slip_unesc6()) as soon as a complete IP packet was reconstructed from the byte stream received. It generates a corresponding sk_buff structure and invokes the function netif_rx() to forward the packet to the IP layer.

7.2.4 Initializing the Driver and Establishing a Connection

The initialization function of the SLIP driver (slip_init_ctrl_dev()) is invoked when the SLIP driver is loaded into the Linux kernel (by the command insmod slip, by the kernel daemon, or, if the SLIP driver is permanently integrated into the Linux kernel, during booting). This initialization function registers the SLIP TTY line discipline with the Linux kernel. For this purpose, a tty_ldisc structure, sl_ldisc, is created, which contains pointers to the functions of the SLIP driver, and tty_register_ldisc (N_SLIP, &sl_ldisc) registers the new line discipline.

A modem connection is established by a user program (e.g., dip) regardless of the SLIP driver. To establish a modem connection, the dip program can call a script, which registers with the system at the other end of the line (i.e., with the PoP of the Internet provider) and also starts a SLIP implementation at that end. Subsequently, it uses the system call ioctl (tty, TCIOCSETD, N_SLIP) to switch the corresponding TTY device (e.g., /dev/ttyS0) to SLIP. Alternatively, the user program slattach can be used to switch an existing modem connection to SLIP line discipline.

The above ioctl() call causes the function tty_set_ldisc() to be invoked in the generic TTY driver; that function, in turn, invokes the routine slip_open of the SLIP driver. The latter reserves memory for a slip structure and for the transmit and receive buffers and uses the system call register_netdevice() to register a new network device, by the name of sl#, with the system kernel. A net_device structure is passed to this system call (see Section 5.1.1), and the function pointer init() in this structure points to the function sl_init().

To initialize the new network device, the Linux kernel invokes the function sl_init() immediately after the above actions. The function sl_init() initializes the net_device structure—for example, by setting the function pointers remaining in the net_device structure (including pointers to the functions sl_open(), sl_close(), and sl_xmit()).

7.2.5 Activating and Deactivating a Network Device

A user can now use the command ifconfig up to activate the new network device. This activation invokes the function sl_open() in the Linux kernel. The user program passes parameters (e.g., the IP address or the MTU) during that action. Subsequently, packets can be sent over the SLIP network device or received from that device. However, to be able to actually transmit packets, we have to set an appropriate route (either automatically, by `ifconfig`, or by another user program).

The above steps are done in reverse order to tear down a SLIP connection. More specifically, `ifconfig` is used to deactivate the network device. Any route registered for this device is now deleted automatically by the Linux kernel, so that no more data can be sent over this network device. The user can then use the command `ifconfig down` to cause the routine `sl_close()` to be invoked in the Linux kernel. This routine informs the driver that the network device was deactivated, but it doesn't free the relevant data structures just yet. Subsequently, no more data can be sent or received over this SLIP device.

7.2.6   Tearing Down a Connection and Deinitializing the Driver

The SLIP TTY line discipline might need to be terminated for several reasons: First, it is possible that a user program calls the system call `close()` or the Linux kernel calls the function `tty_hangup()` to close a serial connection. In the latter case, the Linux kernel resets the line discipline of the relevant TTY device automatically to the standard value N_TTY. Second, it can happen that the TTY device is switched to another line discipline by the function `tty_set_ldisc()`. Each of these cases invokes the routine `slip_close()` in the SLIP driver. This routine does some cleanup work (e.g., it decrements the usage counter of the SLIP module).

When the SLIP module is removed (by the command `rmmod slip`, or automatically), then the function `cleanup_module()` is invoked. First of all, this function ensures that all open SLIP connections are closed by the function `tty_hangup()` and that all SLIP network devices are removed. Subsequently, it deregisters the SLIP TTY line discipline by calling `tty_register_ldisc (N_SLIP, NULL)`. After that, the SLIP TTY line discipline is no longer known in the system, and user programs can no longer use it.

7.2.7   Transmitting IP Packets

To transmit an IP packet, the IP layer invokes the function `sl_xmit()` and passes an `sk_buff` structure to this function. This causes `sl_encaps()` to be invoked, which uses the function `slip_esc()` to do character stuffing and marks packet boundaries. (See Section 7.1.1.) Subsequently, the converted packet is in the transmit buffer, and the pointer `xbuff` in the slip structure points to this buffer.

To output data to the TTY device, `sl_encaps()` invokes the `write()` routine of the relevant device driver. This routine returns the number of bytes that can actually be transmitted in one shot. Subsequently, the `xleft` variable is set to the number of bytes still missing, and the `xhead` pointer is set to the first of these bytes.

Because the function `sl_encaps()` has set the flag TTY_DO_WRITE_WAKEUP, the TTY device driver invokes the function `slip_write_wakeup()` as soon as it has transmitted the announced number of bytes. Next, the function `slip_write_wakeup()` tries to transmit the remaining `xleft` bytes, starting from the position `xhead`. The `write()` routine of the device driver, once more, returns the number of bytes to be actually transmitted, which causes `xhead` and `xleft` to be adapted accordingly. This process is repeated until the complete IP packet has been transmitted successfully, so that `xleft` equals null.

7.2.8   Receiving IP Packets

As soon as data have arrived over the TTY device, the device driver invokes the function `slip_receive_buf()` of the SLIP driver. The maximum number of bytes passed to `slip_receive_buf` were previously polled (65536 for the SLIP driver) by the function `slip_receive_room()`.

The function `slip_receive_buf()` invokes the function `slip_unesc()` for each single buffer character, to undo the character stuffing described in Section 7.1.1 and detect the boundaries of IP packets. More specifically, for a normal character, `slip_unesc()` writes the character passed to the receive buffer, `rbuff`, and increments the counter `rcount`. If the special character ESC is detected, then it is understood that the next character (ESC_ESC or ESC_END) has to be treated appropriately.

If the END character is found, then `slip_unesc()` forwards the ready packet to `sl_bump()` and deletes the `rbuff` receive buffer by resetting `rcount` to null. The function `sl_bump()` reserves memory for an `sk_buff` structure, copies the readily reconstructed IP packet into this structure, and calls the function `netif_rx()` to pass the `sk_buff` structure to the IP layer for further processing.

The Point-to-Point Protocol (PPP)

8.1   INTRODUCTION

The Point-to-Point protocol (PPP) can be used by two computers connected directly (i.e., not over a local area network) to communicate. PPP is defined in RFC 1661 [Simp94a]. A typical application for PPP is dialing into the Internet over a modem; see Figure 8–1. In this case, it increasingly replaces the older SLIP protocol (see Chapter 7), which has proven to be not as flexible as modern applications demand.

In contrast to SLIP, PPP is *multiprotocol enabled*. In addition to IPv4, IPv6, and a large number of other network protocols, PPP also supports several subprotocols, which handle authentication and configuration tasks (e.g., negotiating important connection parameters and allocating dynamic IP addresses).

The architecture of PPP is basically designed for peer-to-peer communication. Nevertheless, in the case of a dialup connection to the Internet, the point of presence is

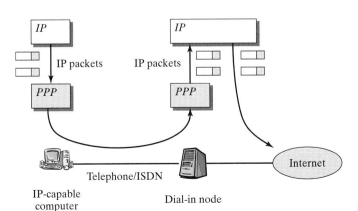

FIGURE 8–1
Scenario for the use of PPP.

often called server and the dialing computer is called client. Though the protocol allows both ends of a connection to expect that the peer authenticate itself and allocates it a dynamic IP address, this would naturally not make much sense when dialing into the Internet.

Linux distinguishes between synchronous and asynchronous PPP, depending on whether the underlying TTY device supports packet-oriented data transmission (synchronous—for example, in ISDN with HDLC as the layer-2 protocol) or it works with a continuous byte stream (asynchronous—e.g., in a modem connection).

We will discuss the asynchronous transmission over a serial interface in more detail later, because it requires more protocol functionality than synchronous PPP. The ISDN subsystem of Linux has its own, independent PPP implementation, which is not discussed here.

8.1.1   Subprotocols

Figure 8–2 shows the structure of a (synchronous) PPP packet. Synchronous PPP always processes entire frames of the lower-layer protocol, which is the reason why it is not necessary to specify the length. Asynchronous PPP additionally requires a frame detection, similar to SLIP. (See Section 7.1.1.) Section 8.3.5 describes how this frame detection is implemented in PPP.

The first 16 bits of a PPP packet specify the content encapsulated in the payload field. Table 8–1 gives an overview of the protocol numbers used. These numbers are built by the address-extension scheme of the HDLC protocol [ISO93], so that the protocols most frequently used can be encoded in one single byte. This means that all protocols have numbers where the first bit of the higher-order byte is deleted and the first bit of the lower-order byte is set (i.e., all have odd numbers). However, truncating the protocol field to 8 bits means that both communicating peers have to support this mode. Linux doesn't know this short version, and such configuration attempts of the peer are blocked off.

FIGURE 8–2
Structure of a PPP packet.

Protocol 8/16 Bit	Payload	Padding

TABLE 8–1   Protocol numbers for PPP packets.

Number	Protocol
0x0001-0x3FFF	network-layer protocols (e.g., IPv4, IPv6, IPX)
0x4001-0x7FFF	transmission of small payload amounts without network-layer protocol (low-volume traffic)
0x8001-0xBFFF	subprotocols to configure the network layer (network-control protocols—e.g., IPCP)
0xC001-0xFFFF	subprotocols to establish a PPP connection (link-layer control protocols—e.g., LCP, PAP, CHAP)

The current PPP implementation in Linux can transport four layer-3 protocols: IP, IPv6, IPX, and AppleTalk—which are exactly the protocols that the network layer can handle. The higher-layer network protocol of PPP is handled transparently, so it is easy to add new protocols.

In addition, PPP has so-called subprotocols, which are handled directly by the PPP instance, rather than by forwarding them to the network layer. The most important subprotocols are the following:

- *LCP (Link Control Protocol)*: Subprotocol to configure PPP instances.
- *PAP (Password Authentication Protocol)*: Authenticates the user by clear-text password (often used by Internet service providers).
- *CHAP (Challenge Handshake Authentication Protocol)*: Secure user authentication over a challenge-response mechanism, where the user's password is not transmitted in clear text.
- *IPCP (IP Configuration Protocol)*: Subprotocol to configure the IP layer (e.g., to allocate IP addresses once a PPP connection has been established).

8.1.2 Components of the Linux Implementation

The Linux PPP implementation is composed of four parts: a generic PPP driver, one TTY line discipline (see Section 7.2.1) each for asynchronous and synchronous TTY devices, and a user-space daemon, pppd.

Figure 8–3 gives a rough overview of how these components interact. Some of the communication channels represented in this figure are used, if at all, only during the establishment and teardown of connections; they are shown by dashed lines in the figure.

While the generic PPP driver is communicating with the network layer and one of the drivers (for asynchronous or synchronous PPP) is serving the underlying TTY device, pppd is responsible for the correct interaction of all components. It is also responsible for establishing and tearing down connections and handling the subprotocols described in Section 8.1.1.

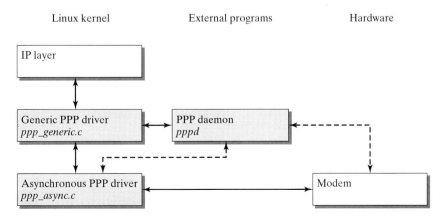

FIGURE 8–3
Interaction of the PPP components.

Each instance of pppd corresponds to exactly one PPP network device (ppp0, ppp1, etc.). This allows several independent PPP interfaces, each having its own settings. To let the PPP daemon communicate with the generic PPP driver, a special character-oriented device with *major number* PPP_MAJOR (108) is set up; normally, it is embedded under /dev/ppp in the file system.

The close interaction of all of these components makes it absolutely necessary to always use the pppd matching the Linux kernel. Otherwise, pppd will report a version conflict when the system starts.

8.2   PPP CONFIGURATION IN LINUX

PPP drivers in the Linux kernel have comparatively few configuration options. The reason is that most settings were moved to pppd, which means that they can be changed at runtime or even set separately for different devices.

It is important to note that PPP over ISDN requires different settings, which have nothing to do with the settings discussed in this section, because the ISDN subsystem includes its full PPP implementation. This applies particularly to the kernel options, but also to the pppd configuration. To be able to use PPP over ISDN, for example, it is not necessary to activate the "normal" PPP in the configuration of the Linux kernel.

8.2.1   Kernel Options

The Linux kernel version 2.2 included only one option that could be used to enable or disable the full PPP support. Version 2.3 introduced three additional setting options (shown in Table 8–2).

The payload compression by the deflate option is preferred over the BSD compression algorithm, because it is free from patents and more effective. By the way, the deflate algorithm is also used in gzip.

8.2.2   pppd—the PPP Daemon

As was mentioned before, most settings are effected by pppd. The configuration files required for these settings are normally stored in the directory /etc/ppp/. See also the manpage of pppd, *Files* section, for details.

Upon startup, pppd reads first the general configuration file options and then a device-specific configuration file (e.g., options.ppp0). In addition, there is a possibility

TABLE 8–2   PPP driver options in the Linux kernel.

Option	Meaning
CONFIG_PPP	Activates the generic PPP.
CONFIG_PPP_ASYNC	Activates the asynchronous PPP.
CONFIG_PPP_DEFLATE	Supports payload compression.
CONFIG_PPP_BSDCOMP	Supports alternative payload compression.

of adding user-specific settings in $HOME/.ppprc. These files include information about the serial interface to be used, about whether configuration requests of the peer should be accepted, and about which user name will be used to log into the peer. The following represent some important entries in the configuration file; however, they do not represent a full configuration:

```
# Options for pppd over a serial line
# /etc/ppp/options
modem                   # use the modem control lines
crtscts                 # use hardware flow control
lock                    # create lockfile to ensure exclusive access
defaultroute            # set default route to this interface
debug                   # enable connection debugging facilities
user egon
```

The user name in the last line serves as key for the entry in the pap-secrets and chap-secrets files, which include the passport of each user in a PAP or CHAP authentication. Both files have the same structure and include clear-text passwords, so the user root should have exclusive read access to these files:

```
# Secrets for authentication using PAP
# /etc/ppp/pap-secrets
# client         server     secret        IP addresses
"egon"           *          "mypassword"
"hugo"           *          "myotherpassword"
```

The structure of the underlying physical connection is left to an external program. For modem connections, this program has to deal particularly with the modem initialization, dialing of the correct phone number (perhaps from a choice of several numbers), and appropriate handling of error messages output by the modem. chat is a program especially suitable for this task; it processes a special script (the so-called *chatscript*) and is included in the pppd package. Of course, you don't need a chatscript to connect two neighboring computers over a null-modem cable.

pppd offers a way to run shell scripts after successful establishment of a connection or before a connection is torn down. The most popular scripts are ip-up and ip-down. The ip-up script is invoked as soon as an IP address was allocated to the end system. It can be used, for example, to send all waiting mails automatically. It is less well known that a number of different scripts can be invoked, in addition to ip-up and ip-down. For example, auth-up is invoked as soon as the user authentication over PPP or CHAP was successful, but before the network protocol used (e.g., IP) is initialized, and ipv6-up and ipx-up are the counterparts to ip-up for IP Version 6 and IPX, respectively. Of course, there is a corresponding "down" script to each of these "up" scripts.

8.2.3 Dial on Demand

Since Version 2.3, pppd supports the dial-on-demand mode directly (i.e., no additional program, such as diald, is required).

The dial-on-demand mode means that a PPP connection is established automatically when needed (i.e., when IP packets are ready to be output from the corresponding network device). If the connection remains idle for a specific (configurable) period, then pppd tears it down automatically. This means that the expensive telephone line is used only upon demand, and the user does not have to dial. The only drawback of this mode is that it introduces a certain delay until the connection is up.

This functionality is implemented by the state PHASE_DORMANT. (See Section 8.4.2.) pppd assumes this state before a peer dialed, if the option demand is stated in its configuration file. In this case, the generic PPP driver in the Linux kernel sends outgoing IP packets for the respective PPP device directly to pppd, which dials into the provider, rather than to the asynchronous driver.

To better control the cost, the option active-filter can be used to specify a filter to decide which network traffic is important enough to establish a connection. Detailed information about this functionality is found in the manpage of pppd in the *Options* section.

8.2.4   Automatic Callback

The automatic callback function means that the client first dials normally to a remote server. During the configuration phase, however, the client uses the PPP subprotocol *CBCP (Call Back Configuration Protocol)* to request a callback. Subsequently, the connection is torn down, and pppd terminates with return value 14. If the server is configured appropriately, then it calls back the client, so that the client and the server, in effect, switch their roles. This functionality is suitable, for example, when a company wants to assume the cost for its teleworkers dialing into company computers.

8.3   PPP IMPLEMENTATION IN THE LINUX KERNEL

As mentioned before, the PPP implementation in Linux is divided into four different tasks: three kernel modules and the pppd user space daemon. During design of this division, care was taken to move as little functionality as possible into the Linux kernel. For this reason, the kernel modules are rather simple. pppd includes 13,000 lines of code (2,100 lines alone in main.c), which means that it is four times the size of the three kernel modules (ppp_generic.c, ppp_synctty.c, and ppp_async.c) together. In the following sections, we will first discuss the generic PPP driver and then the driver for the asynchronous PPP TTY line discipline. The driver for the synchronous PPP line discipline is relatively simple, so we will not discuss it here.

8.3.1   Functions and Data Structures of the Generic PPP Driver

Figure 8–4 shows the most important data structures of the generic PPP driver. There is a separate ppp structure with general management information for each PPP device. Some important entries, particularly the transmit and receive queues, xq and rq, are in a substructure of the type ppp_file. This substructure is also found in the channel structure, which is used to manage single channels in *multilink PPP*, which will not be discussed here, for the sake of simplicity.

There is a PPP device for each network device, the net_device structure of which refers to the related ppp structure in the field priv. In addition, the PPP daemon can send

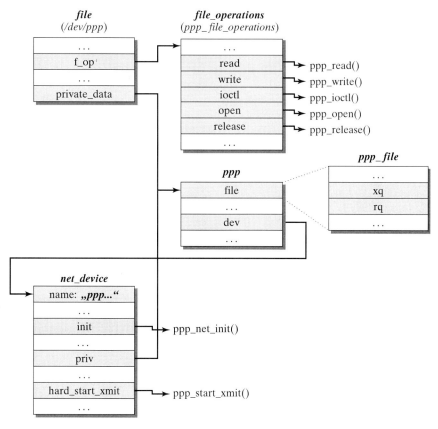

FIGURE 8–4
Important data structures of the generic PPP driver.

and receive control packets of subprotocols (see Section 8.1.1) over the device /dev/ppp.
For this purpose, it must first bind the device /dev/ppp to a specific PPP device by use of
an ioctl() call. This binding means that a pointer to the ppp structure is entered into the
field private_data of the relevant file structure.

ppp_init()	drivers/net/ppp_generic.c

This function is invoked by init_module() whenever the PPP module is loaded: It
uses the function devs_register_chrdev() to register the character-oriented device
/dev/ppp (see Section 8.1.2) with the Linux kernel.

ppp_cleanup()	drivers/net/ppp_generic.c

This function is invoked whenever the PPP module is removed. It frees all data
structures used and deregisters the device /dev/ppp.

ppp_open()	drivers/net/ppp_generic.c

This function is invoked by the function pointer open() in the file_operations structure as soon as the PPP daemon opens the device /dev/ppp.

ppp_release()	drivers/net/ppp_generic.c

This function is invoked by the function pointer release() in the file_operations structure as soon as the device /dev/ppp is closed again.

ppp_write()	drivers/net/ppp_generic.c

This function is invoked by the function pointer write() in the file_operations structure when the PPP daemon sends a PPP control packet over the device /dev/ppp. For this, a matching ppp_file structure is determined and passed to the function ppp_file_write() as the pf parameter. First, an sk_buff structure with the data to be sent is created in this function and appended to the transmit queue pf->xq by skb_queue_tail(); then it is output to the underlying network device by ppp_xmit_process().

ppp_read()	drivers/net/ppp_generic.c

This function is invoked by the function pointer read() in the file_operations structure when the PPP daemon wants to receive PPP control packets over the device /dev/ppp. As with ppp_write(), a matching ppp_file structure first is located and passed to the function ppp_file_read() as the pf parameter. In this function, add_wait_queue() first waits for packets to arrive in the receive queue pf->rq; then the incoming packets are read by skb_dequeue().

ppp_ioctl()	drivers/net/ppp_generic.c

This function is invoked by the function pointer ioctl() in the file_operations structure when the PPP daemon uses an ioctl() call for the device /dev/ppp to change various parameters of the PPP drivers in the Linux kernel.

ppp_unattached_ioctl()	drivers/net/ppp_generic.c

This function is invoked by ppp_ioctl() when the device /dev/ppp has not yet been bound to a PPP device and so (the private_data field of the related file structure has the value 0). Its tasks include the ioctl() call PPPIOCNEWUNIT, which creates a new PPP device and writes a pointer to the relevant ppp structure in the field file->private_data.

ppp_net_init()	drivers/net/ppp_generic.c

This function is invoked by the Linux kernel whenever a new PPP network device is registered. It initializes the net_device structure; in particular, the function pointers described below are set.

`ppp_start_xmit()`	**drivers/net/ppp_generic.c**

This function is invoked by the function pointer `hard_start_xmit()` in the `net_device` structure of the IP layer to output an IP packet over the PPP network device. First, the required PPP header is added, then `skb_queue_tail()` adds the complete packet to the transmit queue (similarly to the function `ppp_write()`), and finally `ppp_xmit_process()` outputs the packet to the underlying network device.

`ppp_xmit_process()`	**drivers/net/ppp_generic.c**

This function is responsible for outputting all packets waiting in the transmit queue `ppp->file.xq` to the underlying device. The auxiliary function `ppp_send_frame()`, which can optionally compress the PPP packets, is used for the actual output.

`ppp_input()`	**drivers/net/ppp_generic.c**

This function is invoked by the driver of the underlying TTY line discipline (asynchronous or synchronous) as soon as a PPP packet has been received. After a defragmenting of the packets, if necessary, the function `ppp_do_recv()` is invoked for further processing; then this function forwards the packet to `ppp_receive_frame()`.

`ppp_receive_frame()`	**drivers/net/ppp_generic.c**

This function checks for whether multilink PPP is activated and forwards an incoming PPP packet to either the function `ppp_receive_mp_frame()` (with multilink PPP) or `ppp_receive_nonmp_frame()` (without multilink PPP).

`ppp_receive_nonmp_frame()`	**drivers/net/ppp_generic.c**

When a PPP packet arrives, this function first undoes the compression, if applicable, and then checks for whether it is a data packet or a control packet of a subprotocol. (See Section 8.1.1.) If it is a control packet, then `skb_queue_tail()` adds the packet to the receive queue, where it can be read by the PPP daemon over the device /dev/ppp. If it is a data packet, then the payload is packed in an `sk_buff` structure with the correct protocol identifier and passed to the network layer by calling `netif_rx()`.

8.3.2 Functions and Data Structures of the Asynchronous PPP Driver

The asynchronous PPP module essentially supplies a new TTY line discipline (see Section 7.2.1), by the name of `N_PPP`, and representing an intermediate layer between the generic PPP driver and the driver of the underlying TTY device.

Figure 8–5 gives an overview of the most important data structures. The driver's state information is maintained in an `asynctty` structure. As in the SLIP implementation (see Section 7.2.3), there is a reference to the `tty_struct` structure of the underlying TTY device, which contains a `tty_ldisc` structure for the PPP TTY line discipline.

A `ppp_channel` structure (which will not be discussed in detail here) is used to reach both the `ppp` structure of the relevant generic PPP driver and a structure of the type `ppp_channel_ops`, which includes function pointers to, among others, the function

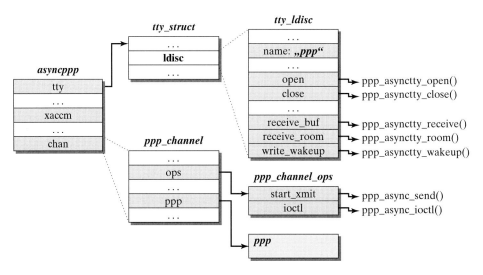

FIGURE 8–5
Important data structures of the asynchronous PPP driver.

ppp_async_send() described further below. Inversely, the ppp structure of the generic PPP driver can be used to reach the relevant ppp_channel structure (and thus the function pointers in ppp_channel_ops) over several detours (which will not be described here, to keep things simple). This is important for being able to pass outgoing packets to the function ppp_async_send() in case of asynchronous PPP.

ppp_async_init()	drivers/net/ppp_async.c

This function is invoked whenever the ppp_async.o module loads. It uses tty_register_ldisc() to register the PPP TTY line discipline with the Linux kernel.

ppp_async_cleanup()	drivers/net/ppp_async.c

This function is invoked whenever the ppp_async.o module is removed. It calls tty_register_ldisc(N_PPP, NULL) to deregister the PPP TTY line discipline.

ppp_async_send()	drivers/net/ppp_async.c

This function is invoked by the function ppp_push() of the generic PPP driver over the function pointer start_xmit() in the ppp_channel_ops structure (see Figure 8–5) as soon as a PPP packet is ready to be sent. It forwards the packet to the function ppp_async_push().

ppp_async_push()	drivers/net/ppp_async.c

This function is invoked by the function ppp_async_send() to transmit a PPP packet. The function uses the auxiliary function ppp_async_encode() to prepare the packet for asynchronous transmission and then sends it to the driver of the underlying TTY device by repeatedly calling `tty->driver.write()`.

`ppp_async_encode()`	**drivers/net/ppp_async.c**

This function uses the character stuffing described in Section 7.1.1 to transmit a PPP packet over an asynchronous device.

`ppp_async_input()`	**drivers/net/ppp_async.c**

This function is invoked by `ppp_asynctty_receive()` as soon as new data was supplied by the underlying TTY device. As with the SLIP functionality (see Section 7.1.1), it undoes character stuffing and detects the beginning and end of PPP packets. As soon as a packet has been read completely, it is forwarded to the function `process_input_packet()`.

`process_input_packet()`	**drivers/net/ppp_async.c**

This function is invoked by `ppp_async_input()` as soon as a PPP packet has been read completely. First, the packet checksum (*Frame Check Sequence—FCS*) is checked. After a number of additional checks, `ppp_input()` is called eventually, to forward the packet to the generic PPP driver.

`ppp_asynctty_open()`, `ppp_asynctty_close()`	**drivers/net/ppp_async.c**

These functions are invoked by the function pointers `open()` and `close()` of the `tty_ldisc` structure as soon as a user program switches a TTY device to the PPP line discipline or resets it to another line discipline. Essentially, an `asynctty` structure is created in `tty_asynctty_open()` for the state data of the TTY line discipline, then initialized, and finally released in `tty_asynctty_close()`.

`ppp_asynctty_read()`, `ppp_asynctty_write()`	**drivers/net/ppp_async.c**

These functions are invoked by the function pointers `read()` and `write()` of the `tty_ldisc` structure whenever a program attempts to send data to a TTY device in PPP line discipline or read from it. Its only functionality is that it returns an error message, because all inputs and outputs of the asynchronous PPP driver run over the device `/dev/ppp`.

`ppp_asynctty_room()`, `ppp_asynctty_receive()`, `ppp_asynctty_wakeup()`	**drivers/net/ppp_async.c**

These functions correspond largely to the functions `slip_receive_room()`, `slip_receive_buf()`, and `slip_write_wakeup()` of the SLIP implementation. (See Section 7.2.3). When data arrives, then `ppp_asynctty_receive()` invokes the function `ppp_async_input()` (as described earlier).

8.3.3   Initialization

When the PPP module `ppp_generic.o` is loaded, then `ppp_init()` first registers a character-oriented device with the major number 108, which is normally embedded under /dev/ppp into the system. In the next step, the module uses `ppp_async_init()` to register a new TTY line discipline (see Section 7.2.1) by the name "ppp" for the asynchronous PPP driver (`ppp_async.o`). This TTY line discipline is an intermediate layer between the device driver of the underlying device and the `ppp_async.o` module, which facilitates access to all incoming data packets. Once the /dev/tty device and the PPP TTY line discipline have been registered, the first initialization phase is completed.

The second phase is initiated by the calling of pppd. After a brief test of whether its version number matches the kernel driver version, it opens the device /dev/ppp. It then obtains a file descriptor, which is required later to communicate with the generic PPP driver; at first, however, only the reference pointer USAGE_COUNT of the PPP device is incremented.

Next, a user process has to establish a physical connection (e.g., the chat program could dial the number of a dialup server). If this action was successful, then pppd uses the system call `ioctl(tty_fd, TIOCSETD, N_PPP)` to change the TTY line discipline to N_PPP. It then uses `ioctl(ppp_dev_fd, PPPIOCNEWUNIT)` to request the generic PPP driver to create a new network device and then uses `ioctl(fd, _PPPIOCATTACH)` to bind the new network device to the underlying TTY device.

These steps complete the establishment of the actual PPP connection; now the PPP subprotocols, such as LCP, can start authenticating the user and configure higher layers. (See Section 8.4.)

8.3.4   Transmitting IP Packets

The generic PPP driver accepts packets ready for transmission over two different routes: The network layer sends payload packets over the matching network device (pppX), and the PPP daemon sends control packets over the character-oriented device /dev/ppp.

Each data packet to be sent is passed to the function `ppp_start_xmit()` by the network layer in an `sk_buff` structure. (See Section 4.1.) This function appends a 2-byte PPP header (see Figure 8–2) to the beginning of the packet and stores the packet in the transmit queue ppp->xq. Virtually the same thing happens in `ppp_write()`, the function that accepts packets from pppd.

Finally, the function `ppp_xmit_process()` is invoked in each case. It takes packets from the transmit queue and forwards them to the function `ppp_send_frame()` for further processing. Depending on the setting, the packet headers might be compressed by the Van–Jacobson method and the deflate or BSD-Compress method might be used for payload compression. After a forwarding to the function `ppp_async_send()_` of the asynchronous PPP driver (or to the corresponding function of the synchronous PPP driver), the generic PPP driver has completed its processing.

8.3.5   Detecting Frame Boundaries

Frame synchronization (*framing*) is implemented as a TTY line discipline in the asynchronous PPP driver (`drivers/net/ppp_async.c`) and follows the standard specified in [Simp94b]. Basically, this is an easily modified and streamlined *HDLC* (*High Level Data Link Control*; see [ISO93]).

Section 7.1.1 briefly explained why framing is necessary: An asynchronous TTY device (e.g., a modem connection) can process only unstructured byte streams and not full packets, so it is necessary to mark the beginning and end of a packet specially. In PPP, this is done by use of the special control character PPP_FLAG with the binary representation 01111110.

Of course, the remaining data stream should not inadvertently contain such special characters. To prevent special characters from occurring, we use *character stuffing*. This means that all payload bytes corresponding to a control character, such as PPP_FLAG, are prefixed by the character PPP_ESCAPE (binary 01111101). There are more control characters; see include/linux/ppp.defs.h for a complete list.

Framing and character stuffing are largely implemented in the function ppp_async_encode(). A bit vector in the field xaccm in the struct asyncppp structure is used to detect the characters that should have a PPP_ESCAPE prefix. Each of the 32×8 bits in this vector corresponds to one of the 256 available 8-bit characters.

The following program dump from drivers/net/ppp async.c shows how you can convert payload into a data stream:

```
#define PUT_BYTE(ap, buf, c, islcp)              do {           \
        if ((islcp && c < 0x20) || (ap->xaccm[c >> 5] & (1 << (c & 0x1f)))) {\
                *buf++ = PPP_ESCAPE;                              \
                *buf++ = c ^ 0x20;                                \
        } else                                                   \
                *buf++ = c;                                      \
} while (0)
```

In this code, islcp is a flag set only for special LCP commands, which have to work even when the bit vector ap->xaccm has not yet been initialized or has been wrongly initialized.

To protect against transmission errors, a 2-byte CRC checksum (*Frame Check Sequence—FCS*) is appended to the PPP packet before the closing end character (PPP_FLAG). If the packet was fully converted into a data stream, then the driver of the underlying TTY device, which is called by tty->driver.write(), assumes the remaining work.

8.3.6 Receiving IP Packets

Receiving PPP packets over the asynchronous PPP driver works much as does sending packets, just in opposite direction: Incoming data is first sent to the function ppp_asynctty_receive() of the asynchronous PPP driver by the driver of the underlying TTY device. Then the function ppp_async_input()_searches for frame boundaries and undoes character stuffing. The function process_input_packet() tests for whether the checksum (FCS; see Section 8.3.5) is correct. Finally, the fully restored packet is passed to the function ppp_input() of the generic PPP driver.

Next, if the packet was compressed, it is now unpacked in the function `ppp_receive_nonmp_frame()` (or, in the case of multilink PPP, `ppp_receive_mp_frame()`). On the basis of the protocol identifier in the first two bytes of the packet (see Figure 8–2), a decision is made about whether the packet should be passed to the network layer in an `sk_buff` structure or added to the receive queue `ppp->rq`, from which it can be read by pppd over the device `/dev/ppp`.

8.4   IMPLEMENTING THE PPP DAEMON

As was mentioned repeatedly in previous sections, the largest part of the implementation effort takes place in the PPP daemon, pppd. One of the reasons is that it processes all subprotocols to control the PPP connection. To maintain expandability, utmost care was taken to keep the implementation highly modular, and it has a clearly defined interface for subprotocol implementations.

8.4.1   Managing Subprotocols

`struct protent`	**pppd/pppd.h**

The core of the pppd interface for subprotocols is the `protent` structure, which is defined in the file `pppd/pppd.h`. It includes mainly entries for callback functions, which are always called whenever pppd receives a packet that it allocates to this subprotocol, given the protocol ID:

```
struct protent {
    u_short protocol;              /* PPP protocol number */
    /* Initialization procedure */
    void (*init) __P((int unit));
    /* Process a received packet */
    void (*input) __P((int unit, u_char *pkt, int len));
    /* Process a received protocol-reject */
    void (*protrej) __P((int unit));
    /* Lower layer has come up */
    void (*lowerup) __P((int unit));
    /* Lower layer has gone down */
    void (*lowerdown) __P((int unit));
    /* Open the protocol */
    void (*open) __P((int unit));
    /* Close the protocol */
    void (*close) __P((int unit, char *reason));
    /* Print a packet in readable form */
    int (*printpkt) __P((u_char *pkt, int len,
                    void (*printer) __P((void *, char *, ...)),
                    void *arg));
    /* Process a received data packet */
    void (*datainput) __P((int unit, u_char *pkt, int len));
```

```
    bool enabled_flag;          /* 0 iff protocol is disabled */
    char *name;                 /* Text name of protocol */
    char *data_name;            /* Text name of corresponding data protocol */
    option_t *options;          /* List of command-line options */
    /* Check requested options, assign defaults */
    void (*check_options) __P((void));
    /* Configure interface for demand-dial */
    int (*demand_conf) __P((int unit));
    /* Say whether to bring up link for this pkt */
    int (*active_pkt) __P((u_char *pkt, int len));
};
```

Each of the protocols known to pppd has exactly one entry in the global list struct protent protocols[].

Figure 8–6 shows a flow diagram representing a simplified procedure of how a connection is established. The function init() is executed immediately after pppd has started. Shortly after that, the function check_options() is run to handle settings, if applicable, using command-line arguments or options in /etc/ppp/options.

The function lowerup() is invoked for each subprotocol as soon as the lower layers are active. For LCP, the lower layer is the TTY device concerned; all other sub-protocols wait for LCP in turn.

Authentication per PAP or CHAP is now triggered in the function link_established() in pppd/auth.c. If the authentication can be completed suc-cessfully, then the subprotocols are informed by the function pointer open() in the protent structure, and they all can now start working. As soon as the PPP connection

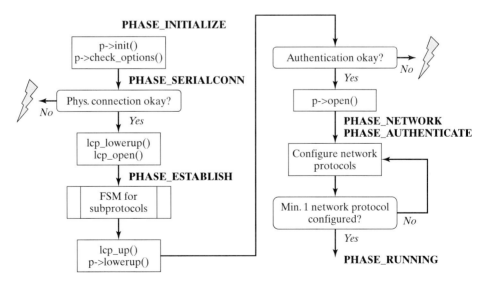

FIGURE 8–6
Procedure involved when pppd establishes a connection.

is closed again, all subprotocols are notified accordingly by the function pointer `close()`. For the authentication protocols PAP and CHAP, the value NULL each is entered for `open()` and `close()` as callback function.

8.4.2 States

The protocol logic of most subprotocols can be represented elegantly in the form of a *finite state machine* (*FSM*). To save cost and avoid errors, the PPP daemon implements a generic FSM, which handles things like state transitions and timers. It is implemented in `pppd/fsm.c` and primarily takes care that the correct callback functions are invoked at the right time. Examples for subprotocols with an implementation that accesses this generic finite state machine include LCP and IPCP.

PPP itself, and thus the PPP daemon, also know different states; however, these states have little to do with the states of subprotocols. These so-called phases are listed in Table 8–3. The PPP daemon behaves differently, depending on the state. For example, it would be fatal to admit configuration protocols for the network layer, such as IPCP, before a successful authentication.

A callback function can be invoked upon request in each of these state transitions. To this end, the callback function need only be added to the otherwise unused global variable `new_phase_hook`.

TABLE 8–3 States (phases) of the PPP daemon.

State	Meaning
PHASE_INITIALIZE	Initial state: pppd initialization.
PHASE_DORMANT	Waiting for activity (for dial-on-demand).
PHASE_SERIALCONN	Establish physical connection.
PHASE_ESTABLISH	Physical connection is up and running.
PHASE_AUTHENTICATE	Authentication in progress.
PHASE_CALLBACK	CBCP (see Section 8.2.4) is running.
PHASE_NETWORK	Network protocols are being configured.
PHASE_RUNNING	Higher layers can start working.
PHASE_TERMINATE	LCP requested connection to be torn down.
PHASE_DISCONNECT	Program to tear down connection has started.
PHASE_HOLDOFF	Wait a little before the next connection is established.
PHASE_DEAD	Connection was interrupted.

PPP over Ethernet

9.1 INTRODUCTION

Chapter 8 introduced the Point-to-Point protocol (PPP). Today, it is most frequently used in access networks that use ADSL as the access technology.

The ADSL (Asymmetric Digital Subscriber Line) access technology offers high-speed Internet access for private or commercial customers. From the technical viewpoint, this is a dedicated line (i.e., a permanent connection). Dedicated lines are normally billed on the basis of transmission volumes. In contrast, private Internet links are billed on a time basis. To enable ADSL to support time-specific billing as well, a new protocol, PPPoE, was developed. PPPoE is based on two accepted standards—PPP and Ethernet.

More specifically, an ADSL modem (NTBBA—Network Termination Point Broad-Band Access), installed behind a so-called splitter, is connected to the computer over Ethernet. This means that the computer has to be equipped with an Ethernet network card. This dedicated Ethernet line between the PC of the home user and the dialup computer of the access network operator is used to establish a PPP connection, which allows the access network operator to identify the user and bill for the usage time between the PPP dialup and the termination of that PPP session. This PPP connection can be used to exchange IP packets.

Figure 9–1 shows the resulting protocol stack. This chapter first introduces the PPPoE (PPP over Ethernet) protocol described in [MLEC+99]. Then, it introduces the implementation in the user space, which is used in kernel Versions 2.2 and 2.3. Finally, this chapter discusses the implementation in the kernel from kernel version 2.4 and up.

9.2 PPPOE SPECIFICATION IN RFC 2516

To be able to transport PPP protocol units over Ethernet, they are inserted as payload in Ethernet frames. For this purpose, two new ethertype values were defined, which show the receiver that the Ethernet frame contains PPP payload.

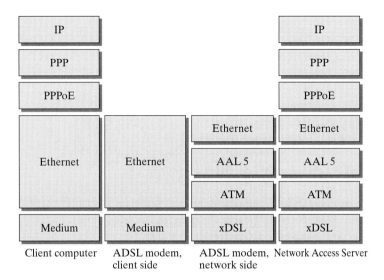

FIGURE 9–1
Protocol stack for the use of PPP over Ethernet.

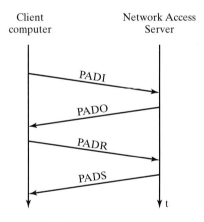

FIGURE 9–2
Typical sequence for PPPoE Active
Discovery.

The two different types serve to distinguish between two phases within PPoE: the discovery stage, and the session stage. A typical discovery stage consists of four steps, which appear as follows (in Figure 9–2): The host sends a PADI (PPPoE Active Discovery Initiation) packet to the Ethernet broadcast address to find out which access concentrators are available in the Ethernet. One (or several) of these access concentrators replies by sending a PADO (PPPoE Active Discovery Offer) packet, informing the host about the Ethernet address where an access concentrator is available, which may specify additional services. The host selects one from the available access concentrators and requests that this concentrator establish a connection by sending a PADR

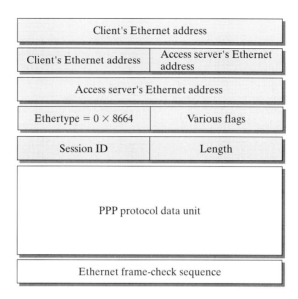

FIGURE 9–3
Protocol data unit of the PPPoE session stage.

(PPPoE Active Discovery Request) packet. The access concentrator replies by sending a PADS (PPPoE Active Discovery Session Confirmation) packet.

Subsequently, the discovery stage is left behind and the session stage begins, where PPP payload is packed transparently in Ethernet frames having ethertype value 0x8864 (in contrast to packets in the discovery stage, which have ethertype value 0x8863). Figure 9–3 shows what a PPPoE packet looks like in the session stage. The underlying Ethernet already forms frames, so PPPoE does not require character stuffing, in contrast to the asynchronous case described in Chapter 8.

The PPP protocol should generally initiate a PPPoE connection to be torn down, but there is also a PADT (PPPoE Active Discovery Terminate) packet, which can be used to terminate a PPPoE connection. Once a PADT packet has been sent or received, not even a normal PPP connection termination packet may be sent.

9.3   IMPLEMENTATION IN THE USER SPACE

The kernels of Versions 2.2 and 2.3 do not support PPPoE. Instead, another daemon is started in the user space, in addition to pppd. This daemon is called pppoed; it processes PPP packets of the Ethernet card and forwards them to pppd. pppd, and pppoed communicate over a pseudo-terminal, as shown in Figure 9–4.

FIGURE 9–4
pppd and pppoed communicate in the user space.

There are various implementations in the user space, including the Roaring Penguin implementation [Roar01], which appears to be the most elaborate. The major drawback of this approach and similar approaches is that the intermediate pseudo-terminal requires an additional transition between the kernel and the user space, which reduces the performance considerably. For this reason, we will consider only the kernel implementation available from kernel Version 2.4 in the following discussion.

9.4   IMPLEMENTATION IN THE LINUX KERNEL

Together with kernel Version 2.4, PPPoE support was integrated in the pppd daemon, and the kernel was expanded by a connection between the generic PPP driver and the Ethernet network card.

Figure 9–5 shows the interaction between these components. The PPPoE driver assumes several functions within the kernel. To the lower layer (i.e., the Ethernet card and the driver software), the PPPoE driver plays the role of a layer-3 protocol. As we will see later in more detail, incoming Ethernet packets are allocated to a protocol matching the type identifier in the Ethernet frame (e.g., the IP protocol or the PPPoE protocol for the ethertype values 0x8863 and 0x8864 mentioned earlier). Towards the higher-layer generic PPP driver, which was described in the previous chapter, the PPPoE driver behaves much as does the asynchronous PPP driver. In contrast to that driver, however, the PPPoE driver does not implement a tty operating mode.

To initiate the PPPoE discovery stage of pppd in the user space, it is additionally necessary to have the PPPoE driver and pppd communicate directly. Section 9.4.2 discusses this communication in detail.

9.4.1   Changes to the Kernel

The PPPoE driver, which is included in kernel Version 2.4 and higher in experimental form, consists of the file drivers/net/pppoe.c. In addition, there is a file called drivers/net/pppox.c, which is intended to harmonize present and future PPP implementations in the kernel. General functions that previously were used only by the

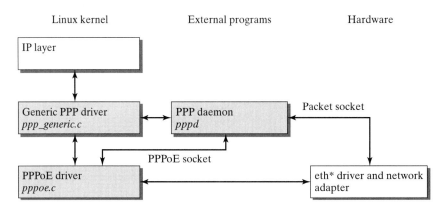

FIGURE 9–5
Communication between pppd and the PPP and PPPoE drivers.

PPPoE implementation were moved to the file pppox.c, and other PPP implementations over other networks should be available in the future.

Functions and Data Structures of the PPPoE Driver   In the first step, the PPPoE driver registers the PPPoE protocol with the kernel. This can be seen in the following piece of source text:

pppoe_init()	drivers/net/pppoe.c

```
{
Use a function from drivers/net/pppox.c to register the PPPoE protocol:
int err = register_pppox_proto(PX_PROTO_OE, &pppoe_proto);
if (err==0) {
        dev_add_pack(&pppoes_ptype);
        /*Add a packet handler
        for incoming packets of type ETH_P_PPP_SES
        (PPPoE session packets), which points to pppoe_rcv */
        dev_add_pack(&pppoed_ptype);
        /*Add a packet handler for incoming packets of type
        ETH_P_PPP_DISC (PPPoE connection setup packets), which
        points to pppoe_disc_rcv */
        register_netdevice_notifier(&pppoe_notifier);
        /*Add to netdevice notification chain */
        proc_net_create("pppoe", 0, pppoe_proc_info);
        /*Generate an entry in the proc directory */
}
return (err);
}
```

Subsequently, the PPoE driver provides functions that can be used by pppd to access the PPPoE protocol functionality over a PPPoE socket. The structure struct proto_ops pppoe_ops in driver/net/pppoe.c is used to bind the functionality of the PPPoE socket to general socket functions (e.g., connect(), sendmsg(), rcvmsg(), and bind()). Chapter 26 includes a more detailed description of how sockets are implemented in the Linux kernel.

pppoe_create()	drivers/net/pppoe.c

This function is invoked whenever a new PPPoE socket is opened. The function is exported and announced over the structure pppoe_proto and the function register_pppox_proto().

pppoe_connect()	drivers/net/pppoe.c

This function calls connect() at the PPPoE socket interface. If the call is successful, then PPPoE packets that have previously been sent or received over the specified Ethernet card can be accessed over the PPPoE socket in the application layer.

`pppoe_sendmsg()`	**drivers/net/pppoe.c**

The function `pppoe_sendmsg()` is used to pack data sent by `pppd` to the PPPoE socket into PPPoE packets and send them over the Ethernet.

`pppoe_rcvmsg()`	**drivers/net/pppoe.c**

This function serves to receive PPPoE packets over the PPPoE socket. However, only packets belonging to the discovery stage of the PPPoE protocol are processed; all other packets are instead forwarded to the generic PPP driver. Information about whether the PPPoE protocol is in the discovery stage or in the session stage is saved in `sk->state`.

Finally, once the PPPoE discovery stage is completed, incoming packets are forwarded to the generic PPP driver. (The case of PPPoE relay is not discussed here.) Various functions can be used to receive packets:

`pppoe_rcv()`	**drivers/net/pppoe.c**

This function is executed within the `NET_RX` tasklet. It handles error cases and passes packets to the function `pppoe_rcv_core()` for further processing.

`pppoe_rcv_core()`	**drivers/net/pppoe.c**

This function determines the dependency on the phase of the PPPoE protocol stored in `sk->state`, which means that an incoming packet is either forwarded to the generic PPP driver (by the function `ppp_input()`) or appended to the queue of the PPPoE socket by the function `sock_queue_rcv_skb()`, where it will be further processed by the above mentioned function `pppoe_rcvmsg()`.

`pppoe_disc_rcv()`	**drivers/net/pppoe.c**

This function is invoked whenever a packet of the PPPoE discovery stage was received (ethertype 0x8863 or `ETH_P_PPP_DISC`, as defined in `linux/if_ether.h`). However, the function `pppoe_disc_rcv()` serves only to receive PADT packets; all other packets are rejected. If an incoming packet is a PADT packet, then the PPPoE connection is disconnected and the socket is released.

`pppoe_xmit()`	**driver/net/pppoe.c**

This function is invoked by the generic PPP driver. It serves as wrapper for the function `__pppoe_xmit()`.

`_pppoe_xmit()`	**driver/net/pppoe.c**

This function is used to pack transmit data of the generic PPP driver into a PPPoE frame and send it over the specified Ethernet network card.

9.4.2   Tasks of the ppp Daemon

A data connection is established in several phases. The phase of the PPPoE discovery stage is fully handled by the ppp daemon, avoiding the pppoe driver. Special `packet sockets` are included in kernel Version 2.4 (see Chapter 26) and can be used to send or receive packets specified in RFC 2516 directly to or from the network card. If the discovery stage is successful, then the ppp daemon sets up a ppp interface in the kernel. The ppp daemon achieves this by opening a PPPoE socket and binding this socket to the PPPoE driver. Finally, the ppp daemon uses an `ioctl()` call with the parameter `PPPIOCGCHAN` (implemented in `driver/net/pppox.c`) to set the field `sk->state` to `PPPOX_BOUND`.

As was described in the previous section, this causes the PPPoE driver to forward all incoming packets to the generic PPP driver, except for the PPPOE relay case, which is not considered here, and for PADT packets, which are handled by the function `pppoe_disc_rcv()` (as already described). The ppp daemon can use different `ioctl()` calls over the PPPoE socket to change other parameters. However, the data path always leads over the generic PPP driver, from which the PPPoE driver now accepts PPP packets (data and control packets); it packs them and, eventually, passes them to the network card.

9.4.3   Configuration

To be able to use PPPoE in Linux from kernel Version 2.4 and higher, the option `PPPoverEthernet` and the option `Packet Socket` have to be activated in the kernel configuration upon compilation (via activation of the support for experimental drivers). If the PPPoE support is compiled as a module, then we additionally have to add the line "`alias net-pf-24 pppoe`" to the file `/etc/modules.conf`. This line is used to allocate the protocol with identifier 24 to the `pppoe` module. A package that integrates PPPoE extensions is available for pppd. All we have to do is to complete the file `/etc/ppp/options` by adding the line `plugin pppoe`; pppd can then be started with `pppd eth0`. [Ostr01] includes more installation instructions.

Asynchronous Transfer Mode—ATM

10.1   INTRODUCTION

Initially, the Asynchronous Transfer Mode (ATM) was introduced to provide a uniform protocol for the transmission of voice and data, offering guarantees for the required QoS (Quality of Service) parameters (such as data rate and delay) [McSp95]).

In contrast to initial expectations and forecasts, the ATM network technology has not established itself in end systems, but it is widely used in core networks. First of all, ATM offers a uniform concept to support QoS (Quality of Service) in networks; QoS was attempted much later in IP-based networks.

The ATM network technology is connection-oriented, which means that a connection has to be established before data can be transmitted. There are two types of connections: In a Permanent Virtual Connection (PVC), the connection throughout the network is established by the network management; a network management station extends the forwarding tables within the forwarding nodes between two endpoints of an ATM connection so that the ATM cells created by the endpoints are forwarded to the other endpoint. The second type of ATM connection is a Signaled Virtual Connection (SVC); in this connection type, the connection is established by the communicating end systems, which send connection requests and respond to such requests.

In ATM jargon, packets are called *cells*. In contrast to IP protocol data units, an ATM cell has a fixed size, 53 bytes: 5 bytes for the packet header, 48 bytes for the payload. The 5-byte packet header includes forwarding information, as for IP frames, which allocates a cell to a connection. The ATM network technology uses a hierarchical connection concept, which distinguishes between paths and channels. Each cell is allocated to exactly one virtual path, and to exactly one virtual channel within that path, as shown in Figure 10–1. This allocation to a path and a channel is specified in two bit fields in the cell header: an 8-bit field for the Virtual Path Identifier (VPI), and a 16-bit field for the Virtual Channel Identifier (VCI).

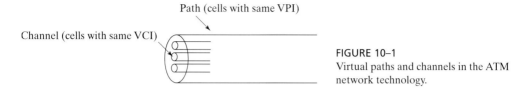

Path (cells with same VPI)

Channel (cells with same VCI)

FIGURE 10–1
Virtual paths and channels in the ATM
network technology.

10.2 IMPLEMENTING ATM IN LINUX

Figure 10–2 shows how the ATM support is structured in the Linux kernel. This implementation comprises two major parts:

- Extension of the socket interface to support the ATM protocol. We will not further discuss this part in this chapter, because the socket interface will be described in detail in Chapters 26 and 27.

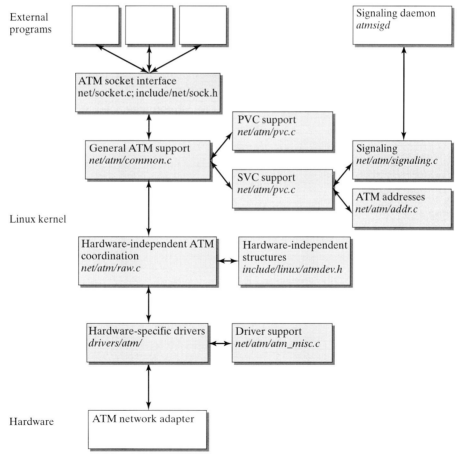

FIGURE 10–2
Structure of the ATM support in the Linux kernel.

▓ General ATM support within the operating system kernel. Various additional functions are available, depending on whether a connection is a permanent or a signaled virtual connection. This part will be described in detail below.

▓ Support of various ATM network cards. Again, this is divided into a general part, which is independent of the type of hardware used, and a part that includes the driver for the respective network card and some support functions.

The following sections begin with a description of the data transmission over a permanent virtual channel (PVC). Subsequently, we describe how the signaled virtual channel (SVC) is supported in the Linux kernel.

10.2.1 Permanent Virtual Channels

An application accesses a permanent virtual channel (PVC) over a socket. A PVC socket can take any of four states; closed, created, connected, and connecting (as shown in Figure 10–3).

First, an application creates a socket. When an application creates a socket, the following functions in the kernel are addressed:

`pvc_create()`	**net/atm/pvc.c**

In this function, the operations that belong to the protocol family PF_ATMPVC and should be available over the socket are announced. This is done by the allocation

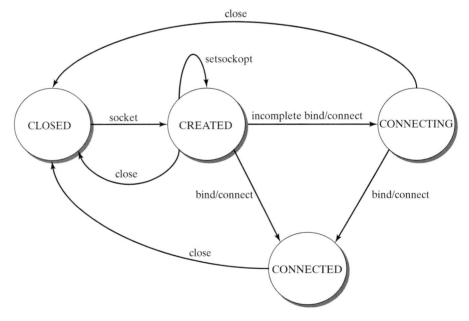

FIGURE 10–3
State transition diagram when opening a socket for a permanent virtual channel.

sock->ops = &pvc_proto_ops;. Subsequently, atm_create(sock,protocol, PF_ATMPVC) is used to create a new socket.

atm_create()	net/atm/common.c

This function handles a number of memory reservations and initializations required for an ATM socket. In particular, it initializes the structure atm_vcc specified in include/linux/atmdev.h. The following code fragment was taken from this structure:

```
struct atm_vcc {
        atm_vcc_flags_t flags;          /* VCC flags (ATM_VF_*) */
        unsigned char   family;         /* address family; 0 if unused */
        short           vpi;            /* VPI and VCI (types must be */
        int             vci;            /* equal with sockaddr) */

        unsigned long   aal_options;    /* AAL layer options */
        unsigned long   atm_options;    /* ATM layer options */
        struct atm_dev  *dev;           /* device back pointer */
        struct atm_qos  qos;            /* QOS */
        atomic_t        tx_inuse,rx_inuse; /* buffer space in use */
        void (*push)(struct atm_vcc *vcc,struct sk_buff *skb);
        void (*pop)(struct atm_vcc *vcc, struct sk_buff *skb);  /* optional */
        struct sk_buff *(*alloc_tx)(struct atm_vcc *vcc,unsigned int size);
                                        /* TX allocation routine can be */
                                        /* modified by protocol or by */
                                        /* driver. NOTE: */
                                        /* this interface will change */
        int (*send)(struct atm_vcc *vcc,struct sk_buff *skb);
        void            *dev_data;      /* per-device data */
        void            *proto_data;    /* per-protocol data */
        struct timeval  timestamp;      /* AAL timestamps */
        struct sk_buff_head recvq;      /* receive queue */
        struct k_atm_aal_stats *stats;  /* pointer to AAL stats group */
        wait_queue_head_t sleep;        /* if socket is busy */
        struct sock     *sk;            /* socket backpointer */
        struct atm_vcc  *prev,*next;
};
```

Most entries in this structure are set to null when they are created (e.g., the values for VPI and VCI, the atm_options, and the aal_options).

In the next step, the application can specify QoS parameters for the socket previously created. To this end, an application calls setsockopt() and uses the options SOL_ATM and SO_ATMQOS.

atm_do_setsockopt()	net/atm/common.c

In the function atm_do_setsockopt(), the values specified by the application are entered in the structure struct atm_qos (from include/linux/atm.h) contained in the structure `atm_vcc`. The structure `atm_qos` includes two additional structures and one value:

```
struct atm_qos {
        struct atm_trafprm txtp;      /* parameters in TX direction */
        struct atm_trafprm rxtp;      /* parameters in RX direction */
        unsigned char aal;
};
```

The structure `atm_trafprm` (also from `include/linux/atm.h`) is used to specify traffic parameters for the ATM connection. This structure includes the following entries:

```
struct atm_trafprm {
        unsigned char   traffic_class;  /* traffic class (ATM_UBR, ...) */
        int             max_pcr;        /* maximum PCR in cells per second */
        int             pcr;            /* desired PCR in cells per second */
        int             min_pcr;        /* minimum PCR in cells per second */
        int             max_cdv;        /* maximum CDV in microseconds */
        int             max_sdu;        /* maximum SDU in bytes */

        ...
        /* A number of parameters for the ABR service class follows here. */
};
```

The parameter `traffic_class` can take the following values, which are defined in `include/linux/atm.h`: ATM_NONE (no traffic class specified), ATM_UBR (UBR—Unspecified Bit Rate), ATM_CBR (CBR—Constant Bit Rate), ATM_VBR (VBR—Variable Bit Rate), ATM_ABR (ABR—Available Bit Rate), and ATM_ANYCLASS (any traffic class).

The function `atm_do_setsockopt()` is used to run a few checks on the socket status. Subsequently, the function `check_qos()` is invoked.

`check_qos()`	**net/atm/common.c**

This function merely checks on whether the parameters of the transmit and receive directions are identical or are specified for one direction only (different parameters are currently not supported); subsequently, the function `check_tp()` is invoked.

`check_tp()`	**net/atm/common.c**

This function is used to check a few combinations of QoS parameters with regard to their admissibility. If these checks run successfully, then the function `atm_do_setsockopt()` invokes the function `atm_change_qos()`, which uses the function `adjust_tp()` to run further checks. For a PVC, `vcc->dev->ops->change_qos()` is used to invoke the function supplied by the driver to change QoS parameters. For an SVC, the function `svc_change_qos()` defined in `net/atm/svc.c` is called to change QoS parameters.

| pvc_bind() | **net/atm/pvc.c** |

Next, the function `pvc_bind()` is invoked when the application wants to open the socket to send or receive data. The implementation does not distinguish between the socket calls `bind()` and `connect()`. The function `pvc_bind()` is used to initialize the address structure `struct sockaddr_atmpvc`, which is used for PVC only. The other functions are located in the file `net/atm/common.c`, because they are used both for PVC and for SVC.

| atm_connect(), atm_connect_vcc(), atm_do_connect(), atm_do_connect_dev() | **net/atm/common.c** |

These functions are used in the order shown here. First, `atm_connect()` checks the socket status. Next, the function `atm_do_connect()` or the function `atm_do_connect_dev()` is invoked, depending on whether a network interface was specified. If no network interface was specified, then `atm_do_connect()` is invoked, and the function `atm_find_dev()` available in `net/atm/resources.h` is used to search the list of ATM network cards for an interface with the matching identifier. If this search is successful, then the `open()` function supplied by the driver (over `dev->ops->open()`) is invoked, much as for the function `atm_do_connect_dev()`.

| atm_sendmsg() | **net/atm/common.c** |

The transmission of data is identical over PVC and SVC, so this functionality is maintained in the file `net/atm/common.c`. First, the function `atm_sendmsg()` waits for a transmission possibility; next, the transmit data are sent by the driver-specific transmit routine, which is addressed over `vcc->dev->ops->send()`.

| atm_recvmsg() | **net/atm/common.c** |

Like the function `atm_sendmsg()`, the function `atm_recvmsg()` is used for both PVC and SVC connections. The function waits in a loop for incoming data, which is then copied from the socket buffer into the user space by the function `copy_to_user()`.

| atm_release(), atm_release_vcc_sk() | **net/atm/common.c** |

We mention the function for orderly release of an ATM socket for the sake of completeness. This is done by the two functions, `atm_release()` and `atm_release_vcc_sk()`, which eventually use the `close()` function supplied by the driver to release all pertinent resources in the driver.

10.2.2 Signaled Virtual Channels

As with PPPoE, a large part of the connection management for the support of signaled virtual channels was moved into a daemon in the user space, as shown in Figure 10–4.

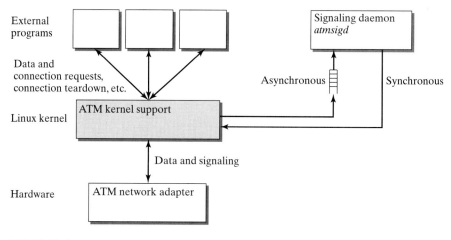

FIGURE 10–4
SVC support in Linux.

Requests to establish or tear down connections and other tasks pertaining to connection management are handled by the signaling daemon, atmsigd. More specifically, all corresponding requests, which can originate both from applications and from the network, are forwarded to the signaling daemon. Requests are put asynchronously into a message queue, from which the signaling daemon fetches messages. In most cases, the kernel performs a synchronous (i.e., blocking) wait for the daemon's response.

Many of the functions available in the file net/atm/svc.c correspond to the previously introduced functions in net/atm/pvc.c, so we will not describe them here in detail. For example, as with the function pvc_create(), the function svc_create() is initially used to announce operations that belong to the protocol family PF_ATMSVC and should be made available over the socket. Subsequently, atm_create(sock, protocol, PF_ATMSVC) creates a new socket.

svc_bind()	net/atm/svc.c

The function svc_bind(), which is normally invoked at this point of the procedure, serves as an example for the communication between the kernel and the signaling daemon. The following code fragment was taken from the source code:

```
...
sigd_enq(vcc,as_bind,NULL,NULL,&vcc->local);
add_wait_queue(&vcc->sleep,&wait);
while (vcc->reply == WAITING && sigd) {
        set_current_state(TASK_UNINTERRUPTIBLE);
        schedule();
}
remove_wait_queue(&vcc->sleep,&wait);
...
return vcc->reply;
```

First, the function `sigd_enq()` for the input queue of the signaling daemon, defined in `net/atm/signaling.c`, is passed the message type `as_bind`, together with a pointer to the structure `atm_vcc`, which belongs to the connection. Subsequently, the relevant process remains in the `TASK_UNINTERRUPTIBLE` state until the signaling daemon has fetched the message from the input queue and changed the field `vcc->reply` from WAITING to another value (say, 0 when the action was successful). This value is returned to the function `svc_bind()`.

The full set of messages that can be exchanged between the kernel and the signaling daemon is specified in the `atmsvc_msg_type` structure, stored in the file `include/linux/atmsvc.h`:

```
enum atmsvc_msg_type {
        as_catch_null,as_bind,as_connect,as_accept,as_reject,
        as_listen,as_okay,as_error,as_indicate,as_close,as_itf_notify,
        as_modify,as_identify,as_terminate };
```

The following message types are used for connection control:

▨ `as_okay`

The signaling daemon acknowledges a previous message.

▨ `as_error`

The signaling daemon reports an error.

▨ `as_close`

The kernel informs the daemon that a connection is to be closed.

▨ `as_bind`

The kernel sends this message to obtain a local address.

▨ `as_connect`

The kernel sends a request to establish a connection to the signaling daemon.

▨ `as_listen`

The kernel uses this message to notify that an endpoint was opened, where it will wait for a connection-establishment request.

▨ `as_indicate`

The kernel informs the signaling daemon that a connection-establishment request has arrived.

▨ `as_accept`

The kernel notifies the signaling daemon that it wants to accept a connection.

▨ `as_reject`

The kernel informs the signaling daemon that an incoming connection-establishment request was rejected.

The parameters for these message types are specified in the structure atmsvc_msg in the file include/linux/atmsvc.h. They include addresses and QoS parameters for SVC connections.

10.2.3 ATM Device Drivers

In contrast to Ethernet network cards, ATM network cards handle a large part of the protocol-processing work themselves. Normally, an ATM network card is responsible not only for forming ATM cells, but also for composing these cells into protocol data units for the higher ATM adaptation layer (AAL). This means that the operating system is relieved from these tasks. On the other hand, it means that ATM network cards are more expensive, because the hardware is more costly.

For ATM device drivers, we distinguish between one part that manages the physical layer (PHY driver) and another part that reserves resources and coordinates the protocol and hardware.

The structure atm_dev (in include/linux/atmdev.h) groups device-independent parameters:

```
struct atm_dev {
        const struct atmdev_ops *ops;    /* device operations; NULL if unused */
        const struct atmphy_ops *phy;    /* PHY operations, may be undefined */
                                         /* (NULL) */
        const char      *type;           /* device type name */
        int             number;          /* device index */
        struct atm_vcc  *vccs;           /* VCC table (or NULL) */
        struct atm_vcc  *last;           /* last VCC (or undefined) */
        void            *dev_data;       /* per-device data */
        void            *phy_data;       /* private PHY date */
        atm_dev_flags_t flags;           /* device flags (ATM_DF_*) */
        struct atm_dev_addr *local;      /* local ATM addresses */
        unsigned char   esi[ESI_LEN];    /* ESI ("MAC" addr) */
        struct atm_cirange ci_range;     /* VPI/VCI range */
        struct k_atm_dev_stats stats;    /* statistics */
        char            signal;          /* signal status (ATM_PHY_SIG_*) */
        int             link_rate;       /* link rate (default: OC3) */
#ifdef CONFIG_PROC_FS
        struct proc_dir_entry *proc_entry; /* proc entry */
        char *proc_name;                 /* proc entry name */
#endif
        struct atm_dev  *prev,*next;     /* linkage */
};
```

These structures are linked in a list by the pointers prev and next. The structure serves as an interface between the kernel and the driver; this is where all parameters required by the driver for further protocol handling are made available, plus those that the driver must make available to the kernel (e.g., the MAC address of the ATM card). The entries vccs and last are used to manage a list of descriptors for virtual connections, which are known to the ATM network card. The first two elements of the structure atm_dev point to the driver operations supplied by the driver over the structure atmdev_ops and to the PHY driver operations, which are available from the structure atmphy_ops. (Both structures are also defined in include/linux/atmdev.h.)

The most important operations available from the structure atmdev_ops are the following:

- open() reserves resources on the hardware for a new virtual connection; the VPI and the VCI for the connection are passed to the driver.
- The function ioctl() is used to pass ioctl() commands to the driver. If the driver does not know these commands, then it forwards them to the PHY driver.
- The function send() passes data units for transmission.
- The function phy_put() and phy_get() are used by the PHY driver to write a byte to or read one from a hardware register of the network card.

10.2.4 Further ATM Support

The support of "pure" ATM described above (i.e., the support of applications that access ATM sockets directly) was extended by the support of protocols, which convert IP packets to ATM, in a very early stage.

This support includes the following protocols:

- *Classical IP*: Classical IP [Laub94] is the simplest form for transporting IP data traffic over ATM networks. The functions included in net/atm/clip.c are used to support Classical IP.
- *LAN Emulation*: The LAN Emulation [Foru95] represents a second approach to IP over ATM, which, in contrast to Classical IP, uses signaled virtual connections rather than permanent virtual connections. The Linux kernel includes functions for this emulation in the file net/atm/lec.c.
- *MPOA*: The abbreviation "MPOA" [Hein93] stands for "Multiple Protocols over ATM" and represents a more recent approach for the support of IP over ATM. The Linux kernel includes functions for MPOA in the files net/atm/mpc.c, mpoa_caches.c, and net/atm/mpoa_proc.c for corresponding entries in the proc directory.

The functions used by all of these approaches are grouped in net/atm/ipcommon.c.

10.3 CONFIGURATION

ATM support has been part of the Linux kernel since kernel Version 2.4 and requires no additional patches; however, configuring of the kernel requires the entry "Prompt for development and/or incomplete driver" to be activated to provide selection of the desired ATM support.

The signaling daemon described above is not part of the Linux kernel; it has to be installed additionally in the user space. It can be downloaded from [BlAl01], where you will also find other utilities that complete the ATM support in Linux. The current development of the ATM support for Linux can be followed up from the mailing list available at [BlAl01].

CHAPTER 11

Bluetooth in Linux

In connection with the enormous proliferation of portable devices such as laptops, PDAs (Personal Digital Assistants), and mobile phones, it becomes increasingly important to find ways to network these devices. Wireless technologies appear to be an ideal solution to this problem, because they don't need a permanently installed infrastructure and facilitate fast establishment and tear-down of networks (so-called ad-hoc networks). In 1998, a number of manufacturers, including Ericsson, Nokia, IBM, Toshiba, and Intel, cooperated in the development of a standard for wireless communication over short distances for consumer electronics. The result of this joint effort is the Bluetooth technology, which operates in the 2.4 GHz frequency range. The Bluetooth consortium specified the radio interface and the higher protocol layers (Bluetooth *core*), plus so-called profiles (Bluetooth *profiles*), each of which defines procedures and parameters of the protocol stack for a specific application field (e.g., telephones, headsets, and file transfer). This standardization effort was intended to ensure interoperability of all Bluetooth devices. The Bluetooth specifications are available at [Group01].

The core specifications include the elements shown in Figure 11–1. The three bottom layers are implemented in the Bluetooth hardware (*firmware*). The radio interface deals with frequency bands, signal outputs, transmission channel parameters, and other mobile properties. The baseband processing includes both additional transmission-specific aspects and media-access aspects (e.g., detection of devices in the neighborhood and initialization of synchronous or asynchronous communication channels).

The higher-layer *Link Management Protocol* (LMP), which is implemented by the Link Manager, serves to exchange control data between the higher layers and the baseband processing. The Bluetooth technology is primarily designed for cellular devices, so the standard defines an audio interface on a very low layer. However, this audio interface does not play an important role for networked computers. In addition, the standard defines a protocol stack above the three layers mentioned above, which are implemented in hardware. This protocol stack normally runs in software on a client (e.g., a PDA or a laptop).

The bottom layer of this protocol stack—the optional *Host Controller Interface* (HCI)—lets you access device parameters directly, regardless of the interface to the

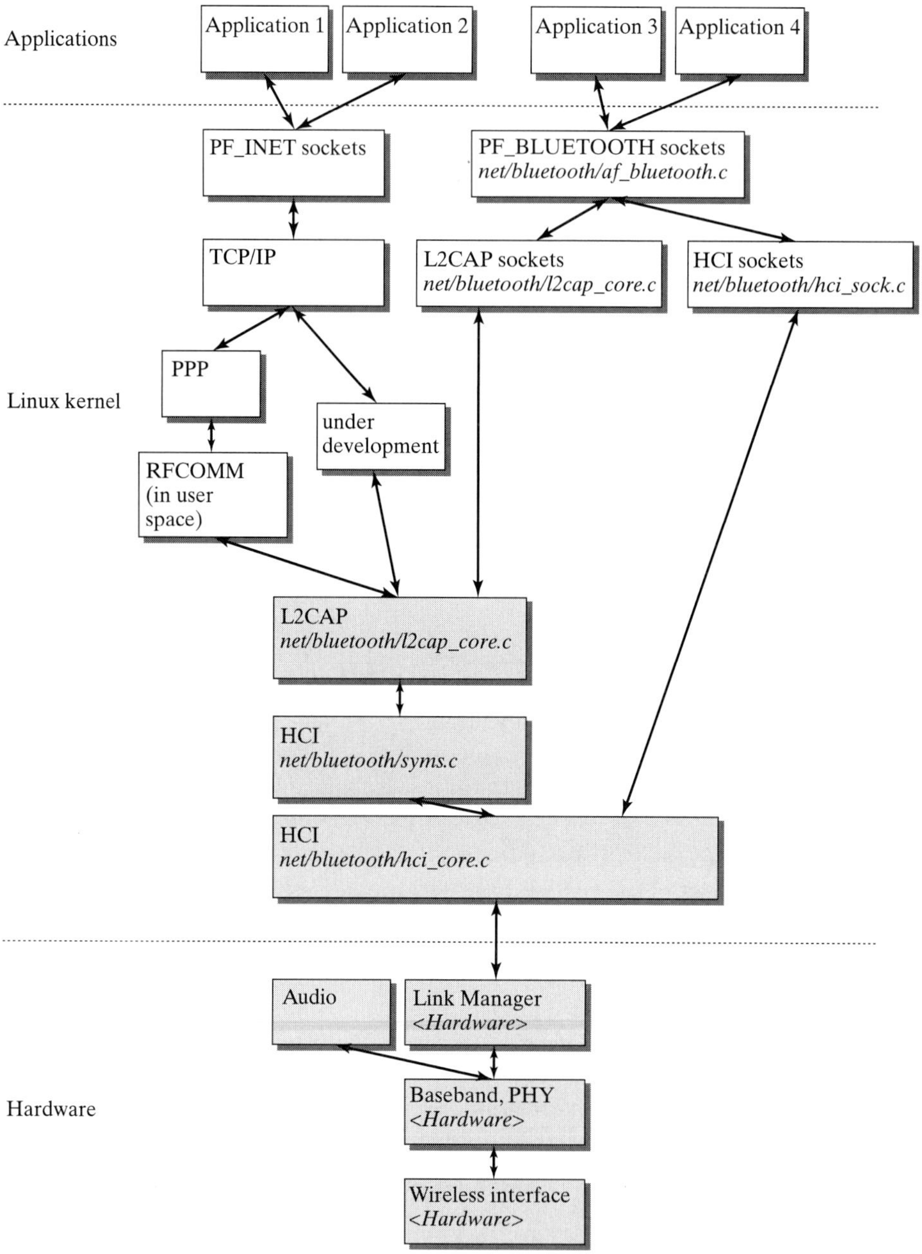

FIGURE 11–1
The Bluetooth protocol stack in the Linux kernel.

device (USB, serial interface), to change or view device parameters. However, it does not serve for data transmission over a Bluetooth device.

The *Logical Link Control and Adaptation Protocol* (L2CAP) is used for each data transmission. It represents the data-link layer of the Bluetooth protocol stack. More specifically, L2CAP is used to send higher-layer packets to the other end of the layer-2 link in another device within the Bluetooth network and to receive from this device. Notice that this is a connection-oriented layer, except for group communication. This means that, if a Bluetooth device moves into the receiving range of another Bluetooth device, then L2CAP has to establish a connection before higher layers can transmit data. This requirement makes the implementation of IP directly over L2CAP more difficult; no such implementation has yet been specified and implemented in the Linux kernel. To find an intermediate solution, the RFCOMM was specified for a virtual RS232 link over the L2CAP protocol of Bluetooth. This means that a virtual COM port is available; it can be used, for example, by PPP (see Chapter 8) to transmit data. The PPP protocol can then also support the use of the TCP/IP protocol suite.

Linux kernel Version 2.4 introduced *Bluez*, a Bluetooth implementation developed by Qualcomm. You can follow up on how Bluez is further developed at `http://sourceforge.net/projects/bluez`. In addition, there are other implementations, among them the Axis stack (`http://sourceforge.net/projects/openbt/`).

11.1   HOST CONTROLLER INTERFACE (HCI)

The Host Controller Interface (HCI) forms the interface between the software protocol stack and the Link Manager underneath it, which is implemented in the firmware of a Bluetooth device. Notice that this is a packet-oriented communication between HCI and the Link Manager rather than a device driver. The difference is that HCI does not access the register and the memory locations of a Bluetooth device directly. Instead, it sends command and data packets to the device and receives data packets and event-message packets from this device. This means that the Host Controller Interface offers a uniform interface for accessing the hardware.

11.1.1   Command Packets

There is a uniform packet format for command packets sent by HCI to the Link Manager. All packets are ordered in groups. In the command group (opcode group), we distinguish between individual commands (opcode commands). Each command packet consists of a 10-bit OCF (Opcode Command Field) and a 6-bit OGF (Opcode Group Field). There are the following command groups:

- *Link control commands* serve to establish a connection to other Bluetooth devices and to control the connection.
- *Link policy commands* serve to change parameters, which are used by the Link Manager to manage connections. For example, such commands can cause connections to switch into the hold mode.

▨ *Host controller and baseband commands* allow you to specify additional parameters for the behavior of the Link Manager (e.g., to filter event messages or to activate the flow control discussed further below).

▨ *Information parameters* offer a pure read access to values of a Bluetooth device, such as the size of the transmit buffer, the version number, and the 48-bit Bluetooth device address.

In addition to these groups, there are the following groups: *status parameters*, *testing commands*, *Bluetooth logo testing*, and *vendor-specific debug commands*.

The following sections describe how command packets can be sent within the Bluetooth implementation in the Linux kernel.

`hci_send_cnd()`	**net/bluetooth/hci_core.c**

This function is used to compose a command packet in the form of an `sk_buff` out of the passed data, the OCF and OGF values, the length, and a pointer to parameters. The function `skb_queue_tail` then appends this packet to the end of the command queue of the `struct hci_dev` of the Bluetooth device.

The structure `hci_dev` is defined in `include/net/bluetooth/hci_core.h`. In addition to the command queue, it contains queues for transmit data. In addition to a number of other parameters, it includes four function pointers, to the functions `open()`, `close()`, `flush()`, and `send()` made available by the Bluetooth device.

Finally, the function `hci_send_cmd()` invokes the function `hci_sched_cmd()`, which marks the `hdev->cmd_task` as ready to be executed. This tasklet was assigned to the device by the function `tasklet_init()` within the function call `hci_register_init()` (net/bluetooth/hci_core.c) when the HCI support was initialized. In addition, there is a `hdev->rx_task` to receive data and another `hdev->tx_task` to send data. When the tasklet `hdev->cmd_task` runs, then the function `hci_cmd_task()` is invoked. This function invokes `hci_send_frame()`.

`hci_send_frame()`	**net/bluetooth/hci_core.c**

This function serves as a central transmit function for the HCI. This function serves not only to send command packets, but also to send data packets. It uses the entry `int (*send)` from the structure `hci_dev` to invoke the transmit function of the Bluetooth device, to which it passes the `skb`.

11.1.2 Event Packets

The time it takes to process different HCI commands can be different, Bluetooth implements asynchronous communication. The results of a command are announced to HCI in the form of an event packet. In most cases, this is merely an event of the type *Command Complete*, which means that the command was successfully completed. A Bluetooth device can receive arbitrary packets by activating the tasklet `hci_rx_task` when the interrupt triggered by the incoming packet is handled. This tasklet invokes the function `hci_rx_task()`.

`hci_rx_task()`	**net/bluetooth/hci_core.c**

This function is used to distinguish an incoming packet further by type. Incoming event packets are further processed by the function `hci_event_packet()`; accordingly, the functions `hci_acldata_packet()` and `hci_scodata_packet()` are invoked for the ACL and SCO data described further below.

Event packets are further distinguished by type of event in the function `hci_event_packet()`. For example, the type *Number of Completed Packets* invokes the function `hci_num_comp_pkts_evt()`. This function evaluates the content of the event packet, which includes the number of packets actually sent per connection by the Bluetooth device. A handle negotiated between the Link Manager and HCI can be used to map the reported number of sent packets to a specific connection (an `hci_conn` structure). This is done via a hash table in the HCI layer. The counter `acl_cnt` of `struct hci_dev` is incremented by one for each acknowledged packet. Feedback on the number of packets sent serves the flow control described in the following section.

11.1.3   Data Packets

We distinguish between asynchronous connectionless (ACL) and synchronous connection-oriented (SCO) data packets. Both data types are sent when the tasklet `hdev->tx_task` becomes active, and then the function `hci_sched_acl()` (`net/bluetooth/hci_core.c`) is executed. If flow control for ACL data runs between HCI and the Link Manager, then we first have to check on whether ACL data may be sent.

Flow control is used to prevent the transmit buffer of the Bluetooth device from overflowing. This can happen, for example, when an application sends data faster than the Bluetooth device can transport it further—for instance, because the communication partner is temporarily not reachable. The initial size of the output buffer can be polled from HCI. The current size of the output buffer can be derived from event packets of the type *Number of Completed Packets*, described above. HCI assumes that the free output buffer becomes smaller with each packet it passes to the Link Manager. The actual current size can be learned only upon receipt of a new event packet.

Flow control in the Bluetooth protocol stack of the Linux kernel is handled by the function `hci_sched_acl()`. In turn, this function invokes the function `hci_low_acl_sent()`:

`hci_low_acl_sent()`	**net/bluetooth/hci_core.c**

First, this function finds out the total number, `num`, of all connections known to the specified network device. For each connection (represented by the structure `hci_conn`), the field `acl_sent` includes the number of ACL data packets sent over this connection. This field is incremented during a transmission, but decremented by the number of acknowledged packets over this connection when the described event packet *Number of Completed Packets* is received. In addition, the function `hci_low_acl_sent()` identifies the connection with the smallest number of ACL packets sent, which has to be smaller than `0xffff`. If none of the existing connections meets these conditions, then the function's return value is set to null. If there is such a connection, then the total number of acknowledged packets (acl_cnt entry in struct hci_dev) is divided by the number (num) of connections. The result is returned by the parameter quote, and the identified connection is the return value of the function. The number of acknowledged packets forms the transmit credit, which is distributed over all ready-to-send connections.

hci_sched_acl()	net/bluetooth/hci_core.c

Using the quote calculated by the function hci_low_acl_sent(), this function tries to send ACL data packets over the specified connection (by using the function hci_send_frame()). ACL data packets may be sent as long as the queue is not empty, as long as the number of ACL packets to be formed from one skb does not exceed the transmit credit of the Bluetooth device, and as long as quote is not yet null. Both quote and the transmit credit stored in the hci_dev structure are decremented by one for each packet sent. At the same time, the number of packets sent over this connection is incremented.

hci_sched_sco()	net/bluetooth/hci_core.c

Only the transmit credit for SCO packets, included in the field sco_cnt of struct hci_dev, is considered in the case of SCO data packets. There is no distribution over several connections for SCO connections. SCO data packets are simply sent until the transmit credit is used up.

11.1.4 Accessing the Host Controller Interface

The functionality of the Host Controller Interface (HCI) in Linux is available in different ways. Figure 11–1 shows that HCI can be accessed directly from the user space over a socket. This is normally a socket of the PF_BLUETOOTH socket family with protocol identifier BTPROTO_HCI und type SOCK_RAW. These sockets are created in the file net/bluetooth/hci_sock.c. The socket interface is used to supply the usual BSD socket functions. An application can use these functions to send and receive data directly over HCI from and to the network.

Alternatively, an application can use ioctl() calls to access the Bluetooth device (e.g., to open, close, or reset the device).

For higher protocol layers to be implemented in the Linux kernel, HCI functions are available over the macro EXPORT_SYMBOL. For example, the L2CAP protocol described in the next section accesses these functions, including functions to register and deregister the HCI device (hci_register_dev() and hci_unregister_dev()) and interfaces to higher protocols. For example, the functions hci_register_proto() and hci_unregister_proto() serve to register the higher-layer protocol (e.g., L2CAP) that supplies a receive function or other functions to the HCI. The function hci_register_notifier() is used by the higher-layer protocol to register itself with the notifier chain of the device. (See Chapter 5.) The function hci_connect(), which sends a command packet from HCI to the Link Manager (net/bluetooth/hci_core.c), is used to establish a connection. The counterpart of this function is the function `hci_disconnect()`. The functions `hci_send_acl()`, `hci_send_sco()`, and `hci_send_raw()` are used to transmit, and the function `hci_recv_frame()` is used to receive.

11.2   L2CAP

The Logical Link Control and Adaptation Protocol (L2CAP) handles tasks on the data-link layer in the Bluetooth protocol stack. It establishes ACL connections for the next lower layer, but does not transport pure audio data, which primarily is transported over SCO connections. In particular, the L2CAP protocol is responsible for multiplexing data streams from higher layers to an ACL connection, because there must always be at most one ACL connection at a time between two Bluetooth devices. Other important tasks include the segmenting and reassembling of data packets to be able to send and receive the much larger packets of the higher-layer protocols despite the small packet sizes of the baseband layer. L2CAP supports packet sizes of up to 64 Kbytes.

To multiplex several data streams, L2CAP uses the abstraction of the channel. Each channel is allocated to one specific protocol. There are connection-oriented channels for point-to-point communication and connectionless channels used for group communication. A simple signaling method is used to establish an L2CAP connection. The L2CAP protocol can also be accessed directly from the user space over a socket. This is normally a socket from the `PF_BLUETOOTH` socket family with protocol identifier `BTPROTO_L2CAP`.

Now, when HCI receives an ACL packet, then it is passed to the receive function `l2cap_recv_frame()`. If the channel identifier in the packet header is 0x0001, then it is a signaling packet. Subsequently, the function `l2cap_sig_channel()` is invoked; otherwise, the function `l2cap_data_channel()` is invoked.

`l2cap_sig_channel()`	**net/bluetooth/l2cap_core.c**

The type of signaling packet is recognized within this function and, depending on the type, an appropriate handling function is invoked:

```
switch (cmd.code) {
        case L2CAP_CONN_REQ:
                err = l2cap_connect_req(conn, &cmd, data);
                break;
        case L2CAP_CONN_RSP:
                err = l2cap_connect_rsp(conn, &cmd, data);
                break;
        case L2CAP_CONF_REQ:
                err = l2cap_config_req(conn, &cmd, data);
                break;
        case L2CAP_CONF_RSP:
                err = l2cap_config_rsp(conn, &cmd, data);
                break;
```

```
case L2CAP_DISCONN_REQ:
      err = l2cap_disconnect_req(conn, &cmd, data);
      break;
case L2CAP_DISCONN_RSP:
      err = l2cap_disconnect_rsp(conn, &cmd, data);
      break;
```

The following section uses the example of an incoming connection request from a remote communication partner in the Bluetooth network to describe how the L2CAP protocol implementation works.

11.2.1 Connection Establishment Phase

When a request to establish a connection arrives from a remote communication partner, then the signaling code L2CAP_CONN_REQ is detected, and the function l2cap_connect_req() is invoked.

l2cap_connect_req()	net/bluetooth/l2cap_core.c

This function first checks on whether there is a waiting socket for this connection request that matches exactly the source address of the Bluetooth device from which the connection request originates and which concurrently matches the PSM field. The PSM (Protocol/Service Multiplexer) field specifies the desired higher protocol (e.g., RFCOMM).

Such a socket has to have been previously created by an application with the command listen and the function l2cap_sock_listen(), and it has to be in blocking wait state after the function accept() was invoked. This wait state is implemented in the function l2cap_sock_accept(), which uses the function l2cap_accept_dequeue() to wait until the state sk->state switches from BT_LISTEN to BT_CONNECTED.

The function l2cap_get_sock_listen(), which searches all sockets listening to the L2CAP protocol, checks for a socket waiting for an incoming connection request. Subsequently, it ensures that there is not already a connection with the source address of the requesting Bluetooth device. Next, the pertinent sock structure is initialized. The state sk->state in BT_CONFIG and the new channel with the function l2cap_chan_add() are added to the list of channels, conn->chan_list. Subsequently, the function l2cap_send_rsp(), which, in turn, accesses the function hci_send_acl() supplied by HCI, returns a L2CAP_CONN_RSP message to acknowledge the connection request.

11.2.2 Configuration Phase

If there are no errors, then the next step walks through the configuration phase, before the connection can be used for data transmission. First, both ends send a configuration request (signaling code L2CAP_CONF_REQ). The configuration phase can be completed successfully only if the configuration request of the other end has been acknowledged and a positive acknowledgement of its own configuration request was made.

The end that received the connection request waits for a configuration request after successful completion of the connection establishment phase. When the connection request arrives, the function l2cap_sig_channel() invokes the function l2cap_config_req().

l2cap_config_req()	net/bluetooth/l2cap.core.c

This function first uses l2cap_parse_conf_req() to evaluate the configuration options of the peer and store them in the protinfo structure of the sock structure. However, the QoS option is currently not evaluated. Next, the function l2cap_build_conf_rsp() is invoked. This function uses l2cap_conf_output() to discover whether the peer's configuration options (currently only the MTU) can be accepted. The function l2cap_send_rsp() is used to return a response. Subsequently, the function l2cap_send_req() uses the function l2cap_build_conf_req() to create and send a configuration request to the other end. Currently, only the MTU is considered.

l2cap_config_rsq()	net\bluetooth/l2cap.core.c

This function handles the peer's response to the configuration request. If the peer sends a nonempty response, then the current implementation disconnects immediately. Otherwise, the configuration phase can be abandoned. The field sk->state is set to BT_CONNECTED and, starting with the function call l2cap_chan_ready() (net/bluetooth/l2cap_core.c), the function pointer sk->state_change() is used to invoke the function sock_def_wakeup() (both in net/core/sock.c), which eventually marks the process waiting at the socket as an executable process.

11.2.3 Data Transmission Phase

This section describes the data transmission.

l2cap_data_channel()	net/bluetooth/l2cap.core.c

The function l2cap_data_channel() is invoked when data packets are received. The first step is to check for whether a connection is present in the list of channels, conn->chan_list, for the SCID (Source Connection IDentification). This check is done by the function l2cap_get_chan_by_scid(). After further checks, the data packet is put into the receive queue, and the function data_ready() of the sock structure is invoked, which then informs the application that new data is ready.

Looking at things from the BSD socket interface, data is received at the socket interface over the socket call recvmsg, which is mapped to the function l2cap_sock_recvmsg(). In this respect, there are no major differences from the implementations of other protocols that also use the function skb_recv_datagram() (net/core/datagram.c). This function causes a blocking or nonblocking wait for data in the input queue sk->receive_queue.

When sending, the socket call sendmsg() invokes the function l2cap_sock_sendmsg(), which uses the function l2cap_chan_send() to prepare a packet and then uses hci_send_acl() to send it.

11.3 OTHER PROTOCOLS

The L2CAP functionality is currently available for BTPROTO_L2CAP sockets only. An interface to higher protocol layers, such as RFCOMM, or for future developments that will allow you to run TCP/IP directly over L2CAP, was not available in the Linux kernel implementation at the time of writing. However, the L2CAP sockets allow you to install these protocols in the user space. The SDP (Service Discovery Protocol) protocol is not integrated in the Linux kernel either. RFCOMM might be implemented in the kernel in the future, but this is currently not intended for SDP.

Transparent Bridges

12.1   INTRODUCTION

Local area networks (LANs) are limited both in their reach and in the number of stations that can be connected. For example, only a maximum of 30 stations per segment can be connected to Ethernet based on the *10Base2* standard; and even if you connect fewer than the maximum number of stations, but use an extremely traffic-intensive application, it can happen that the traffic in a LAN is so high that the throughput of the entire network drops rapidly.

This degradation is due mainly to the fact that local area networks are broadcast networks—when station A sends a data frame to station B, then the data packet is concurrently transported to all other stations. The bandwidth in a local area network is used only by the sending station at that time (asynchronous time division multiplexing—TDM). The more stations there are in a local area network, the smaller is the share of each single station. Depending on the network technology, a lot of additional time might be used to decide which station may send next (Medium Access Control).

For the above reasons, it is meaningful to divide a heavily loaded or very large local area network into several subnetworks. Similarly, several local area networks can be linked by single coupling elements to form one large internetwork. In this regard, the parts of the original local area network should not be split into different subnetworks (as is possible in IP), but should always represent themselves as one single (sub)network to the network layer. The two networks are connected transparently, for the network layer.

One coupling element that can link different local area networks to form one single logical LAN is called a *bridge*. A bridge connects several local area networks on the data-link layer (layer 2 in the OSI reference model) and distributes the traffic over the subnetworks. Stations that communicate often are generally grouped into one subnetwork. Grouping frequently communicating stations within the same subnetwork means that the entire network has less load to carry, because these stations can exchange traffic within their subnetwork regardless of the traffic in other subnetworks.

12.2   BASICS

As was mentioned above, a bridge is a coupling element that links several local area networks on the data link layer [BaHK94]. For this purpose, a bridge has two or more network adapters (*ports*), which are used to connect to a local area network. In contrast to a repeater, which can merely extend the distance of a LAN, and which simply forwards packets as it received them, a bridge can evaluate certain information in a packet and decide whether that packet should be forwarded.

Bridges come in different variants and with various properties, which will be briefly introduced below:

▨ *Local or remote bridges*: Local bridges connect two or more neighboring local area networks—see Figure 12–1. These local area networks are normally linked on the MAC layer.

Remote bridges connect two local area networks physically separated by another network, normally a Wide Area Network (WAN). This bridge type interconnects local area networks on the LLC layer. [BaHK94] includes a detailed description of local and remote bridges. This chapter considers only local bridges.

▨ *Translation or nontranslation bridges*: A translation bridge is capable of connecting several local area networks over different media-access protocols (e.g., Ethernet and token ring). Linux is limited in supporting this property, because there could be problems during the transition from one standard to another one. For example, 802.3 supports a limited maximum frame size of 1,500 bytes, but 802.5 supports a much bigger size. For this reason, we cannot feed large 802.5 packets into an 802.3 network.

▨ *Source-routing or transparent bridges*: Source-routing bridges represent an extension of the token-ring standard and must be used in token-ring networks only. We will not consider them any further.

In contrast, transparent bridges can be used in all 802.x networks. They mainly handle the transparent interconnection of different 802.x LANs, where the participating stations do not know that there is a bridge in the LAN. In other words, the bridge is not visible to the stations in the interconnected LANs—it is transparent. The bridge functionality under Linux corresponds exactly to the type of a transparent bridge.

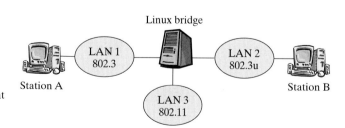

FIGURE 12–1
A Linux computer acts as a transparent bridge, connecting several local area networks.

12.2.1 Properties of Transparent Bridges

In accord with the definition in Section 12.2, a Linux system can be used to implement a *local transparent translation*[1] bridge, which can interconnect different 802.x LANs. Figure 12–1 shows an example in which the Linux computer acts as a bridge, connecting three LANs of different types: one Ethernet (IEEE 802.3), one Fast Ethernet (IEEE 802.3u), and one wireless LAN (IEEE 802.11).

When we use a translation bridge to link different 802.x LANs, then the properties of the different sets of protocols have to be adapted. For example, the bridge should consider the different access methods of the interconnected LANs; it should also consider and convert different packet formats. In addition, we have to consider that properties could be lost during the transition from one LAN type to another type. Examples include priorities or acknowledgments in 802.5 networks, which are lost in 802.3 networks, because the latter don't have anything comparable. Linux currently supports only the interconnection of local area networks that use an Ethernet-compatible frame format on MAC level.

The transparent bridge in Figure 12–1 is responsible for switching data packets between the three networks used in this example to allow the stations in these three networks to communicate. Data packets (which are also called frames on layer 2) with their destination within one local area network are not transported to the other two LANs—internetwork and intranetwork traffic is separate.

The bridge need forward only those data packets intended for another LAN. This translates into a considerable reduction of the network load, because internal traffic loads remain within the LANs and parallel communication is possible internally in each of these LANs. If a computer in one LAN wants to send data to another LAN, then only those LANs required for the transport are used. In addition, the bridge ensures that faulty data packets are filtered and prevented from being transported to the other networks. The *filtering* concept supported by bridges will be described in Section 12.2.2.

Transparent bridges are characterized mainly by the fact that they are hidden from the stations in the network. In addition, they forward frames from one LAN into another LAN independently. To both the inside and the outside, it seems like there is one large local IEEE-802-compatible network. The bridge does not consider protocols used on the network layer; you can select arbitrary protocols.

To achieve transparency, each bridge maintains a table (*forwarding database*) that stores the output line used to reach a station for each layer-2 address. We will see in Section 12.4.2 how this forwarding table is implemented in Linux.

The properties of a Linux bridge introduced above will be discussed in more detail in the next sections.

---

[1] ... however, with the limitation that the 802.x networks be compatible, mainly with regard to their maximum frame lengths. For example, 802.3 and 802.11 can easily be combined, but problems could arise when you use 802.5 LANs.

12.2.2 Forwarding Function

The main task of a bridge is its filter function to separate the traffic between local area networks from the traffic within one local area network. For this function, the bridge is not addressed explicitly; it is transparent for the communication partners. None of the computers in the local area networks knows that the bridge is present. For this reason, the bridge receives each data packet as it passes each network adapter, interprets its destination address, and uses the filter criterion to decide whether the packet should be forwarded to another LAN or not be handled. In the latter case, the addressed station is in the LAN that received the data packet. The bridge can assume that the destination station has already received the packet, so that it does not have to forward it.

As mentioned earlier, a transparent bridge uses a *forwarding table* which stores forwarding information. It also uses positive filters, which are entered as a result of the learning function. (See Section 12.2.3.) The forwarding table provides general information how each computer can be reached over the outputs. If only one LAN is connected to each bridge adapter, then the decision about the LAN on which a computer resides is obvious. If this is not the case, then the LAN and an output adapter are specified to reach the LAN of a computer (the so-called *next hop*).

The example in Figure 12–2 shows how the forwarding function of a bridge works. Station A sends a data packet to station B. Though the bridge was not addressed directly, it receives the packet and searches the forwarding table for destination address B. It finds an entry that refers to LAN2, and eventually sends the packet to this LAN. Packets addressed to computers within the same LAN are not forwarded by the bridge. (See Figure 12–3.)

If the bridge cannot find a destination address in the forwarding table (i.e., if the bridge does not know to which LAN the destination station is connected), then it sends the packet over all of its outputs, except the input port (*flooding*). Figure 12–4 shows this process. Flooding means that the bridge can reach all stations, including those with yet unknown location.

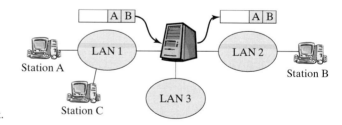

FIGURE 12–2
A transparent bridge forwards a packet.

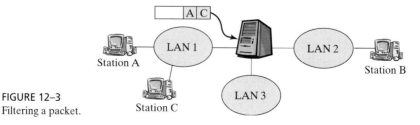

FIGURE 12–3
Filtering a packet.

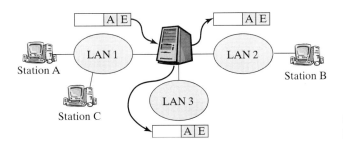

FIGURE 12–4
Forwarding a packet to all outputs.

MAC addresses are not structured hierarchically and hence cannot provide information about the LAN of a destination station, so packets would have to be sent to all outputs of a bridge in a group of interconnected LANs. Unfortunately, flooding packets when the destination network is not known shouldn't be done often. For this reason, transparent bridges have a way to learn the location or direction of an unknown station.

12.2.3 Learning Function

One major problem of transparent bridges relates to how the bridge is structured and how it maintains its forwarding table. Though the system administrator could simply use a static data configuration, this is not desirable for the following reason: A static configuration of the forwarding table cannot respond to changes in the network topology—all tables in all bridges would have to be changed manually as soon as a new station is added to one of the LANs. In addition, there would be consistency problems if one station moves from one LAN to another LAN. For this reason, transparent bridges use a learning algorithm, allowing a bridge to learn the location of an unknown station and to be able to respond to a change in location (i.e., forget the old location and learn the new one).

For this purpose, a bridge follows the entire traffic in all LANs connected to it. For each data packet sent to one LAN, the bridge stores its sender MAC address and the LAN that transported the packet in its forwarding table. The bridge assumes that the LAN that received the packet is the home network of the sending station or at least the best path to reach its home network. The method used to learn routing information by looking at the sender address and the input network is also called *backward learning* in the literature [Tane97].

Backward learning allows a bridge to learn the location of each station that sent a packet. If the bridge receives a packet for a currently unknown station, then it has to use flooding; but it is assumed that a response or acknowledgment will follow from this packet, so the destination address can be found from this reply packet. This means that flooding is normally done only once for each destination address.

To keep the entries in the forwarding table of a bridge up to date, they are extended by a time stamp (activity time). This time value states how long this entry will be valid. This activity time is updated each time that the bridge receives a packet with a sender MAC address it had previously learned. When the activity time of an entry expires, then this entry is deleted (aging mechanism). It is also assumed that the station was either disconnected from the network or no longer exists. On the other hand, if a packet with a previously unknown source address arrives, then the bridge assumes that this station is new to the network. The address of this system and the network adapter that received the packet are added to the forwarding table, and the activity time is initialized.

12.2.4 Spanning-Tree Protocol

There are often redundant connections in a large local internetwork. For example, there could be several bridges running in parallel to connect two LANs, for load-distribution and failure-safety reasons. Figure 12–5 shows an example with redundant connected networks. In this example, if station A in LAN 2 sends a packet to computer B in LAN 5, then bridge 1 floods this packet to LAN 1, and bridge 3 floods it to LANs 3 and 5. Bridge 3 learns that it can reach station A in LAN 2. In the meantime, bridge 2 receives the packet in LAN 1 and floods it to LANs 3 and 4. This means that bridge 3 receives the same packet again, only this time over a different network adapter. Using its learning function, this bridge changes that entry in the forwarding table and floods the packet to the other networks. We could continue this example endlessly to see that, with this network topology, the forwarding tables of all stations would change continuously, and packets would be duplicated and travel around in the network. The bridges have no way to recognize and destroy duplicate packets.

Transparent bridges uses the so-called spanning-tree protocol to solve this problem. This protocol should detect redundant connections in a cyclic topology and build a tree structure that does not include any more cycles. Redundant connections are made inactive and can be reactivated when needed. This means that the LAN internetwork maintains its redundancy. Special messages are used by the bridges in the internetwork to work out the tree structure and to build this structure in a decentralized way.

The spanning-tree method is known from graph theory [OTWi96]. Normally, a spanning tree with minimum total cost can be constructed with an undirected connected graph, where the edges are used as weights to allocate costs. Several algorithms have been introduced as minimum spanning tree (MST) methods to handle this task. The spanning-tree method described here and the MST method have in common that a connected graph is used to form a tree structure. However, the spanning tree in a LAN internetwork is not always the minimum spanning tree from the MST method. This is shown by the example in Figure 12–6.

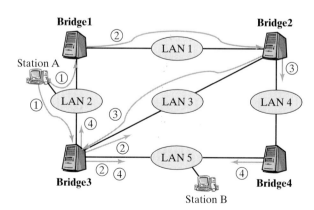

FIGURE 12–5
The effect of cycles.

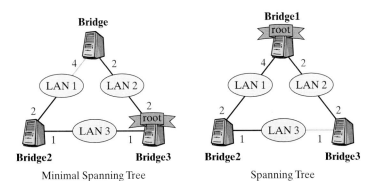

FIGURE 12–6
Spanning-tree protocol versus the MST method.

Minimal Spanning Tree   Spanning Tree

Under the spanning-tree protocol, the root of the tree topology is not determined by the least total cost; instead, the bridge with the smallest bridge identifier is selected. The reason is that the spanning-tree algorithm operates in a decentralized way—it is not calculated centrally in one station. This means that, first of all, all bridges have to agree on the bridge to be selected as the root of the tree. Subsequently, working from the root, the branches of the tree with "minimum" path cost are calculated. These minimum-cost paths do not necessarily have to correspond to the tree structure with the least total cost.

Prerequisites and Terminology   Bridges need certain parameters and values to be able to run the spanning-tree algorithm. These values are then used to manipulate the resulting spanning tree. The following parameters are required by the spanning-tree algorithm:

- Each bridge requires a unique 6-byte identifier, the *bridge ID*.
- Each network adapter (*port*) of a bridge obtains a unique identifier, the *port ID*.
- *Port cost* is assigned to each network adapter. This cost influences the structure of the tree topology, because the total cost should be minimized by the spanning-tree algorithm. For example, the port cost can reflect the load on or speed of a local area network.
- When two LANs can be reached over several paths, then a priority for each network adapter (*port priority*) can be considered when selecting a path. The spanning-tree algorithm will then select the adapter with higher priority and equal path cost.

The following are other important terms:

- *Root bridge*: This is the bridge representing the root of the tree topology.
- *Root port*: This is the port of a bridge with the least transmission cost to the root bridge.
- *Root-path cost*: This is the sum of the cost of all root ports on the path from a LAN within the internetwork to the root bridge. The objective is to find the path with the least root-path cost.

Figure 12–7 shows these terms in an example of the topology described above, where `Bridge1` is the root of the tree structure shown in Figure 12–8.

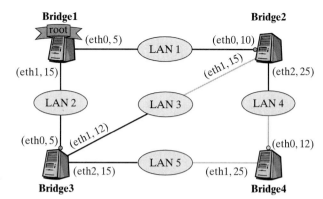

FIGURE 12–7
Topology after running the spanning-tree protocol.

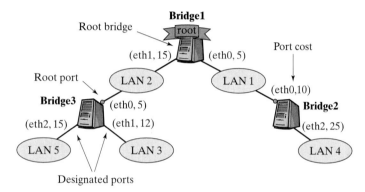

FIGURE 12–8
Tree topology of the LAN internetwork.

Special packets in the form of so-called *Bridge Protocol Data Units* (BPDUs) are exchanged to determine the root bridge and distribute path or port cost. There are two types of BPDUs:

▓ *Configuration BPDUs* are also called hello packets or configuration messages. They are used to announce the root-bridge identifier, the cost currently accumulated, and certain timer values. Section 12.4.5 will describe the format of this configuration BPDU.

▓ *Topology change notification BPDUs* (TCN BPDUs): These packets are exchanged when changes occur in the topology. This can happen when a component has failed and when the execution of the spanning-tree method causes certain network adapters of bridges to move into the blocking state.

Bridge PDUs are sent with a special group MAC address. This means that each bridge that receives such a packet can identify a bridge PDU.

Running the Spanning-Tree Algorithm   The spanning-tree algorithm is defined in IEEE standard 802.1d. It specifies the principle used to build a noncyclic topology from a partly meshed or cyclic LAN internetwork. This method operates in an absolutely decentralized way.

The spanning-tree algorithm runs in three steps:

1. *Select the root bridge*: The root bridge is the root of the tree topology we want to build. The problem is now to select one of the bridges as the root bridge. To this end, we use a principle similar to the one used in token-ring networks: The bridge with the smallest identifier (bridge ID) is selected as the root bridge.

   At the beginning, the bridges in the LAN internetwork send configuration BPDUs periodically with their own identifiers as root ID to all other bridges. When a bridge receives a BPDU, it is immediately compared with its own bridge ID. If the received root ID is smaller, then the BPDU is forwarded. In contrast, if the own bridge ID is smaller, then it is registered as the root ID and distributed to the other bridges. Eventually, the bridge with the smallest identifier becomes the root bridge.

   One major benefit of this principle is its decentralized property. This means that no central management unit is required. However, the path cost in a LAN internetwork does not play any role in determining the root bridge. This means that you won't necessarily select the best topology, such as in the Minimal Spanning Tree method.

2. *Determine the root port of each bridge*: Each bridge selects the network adapter with the smallest path cost on the path to the root bridge as its root port (root-path cost, RPC). If several paths have the same cost, then the port with the highest priority or (if no priorities are set) the port with the smallest port ID is selected as the root port.

3. *Select the designated bridge for a LAN*: When one subnetwork within the LAN internetwork is connected to several bridges, so that at least one route over each of these bridges leads to the root bridge, then one of these bridges has to be selected for traffic forwarding to the root bridge. This is the only way to create a tree topology. In a local area network, the bridge with the smallest path cost to the root bridge (the so-called *root-path cost*) is normally selected. The network adapter used to connect this designated bridge to the local area network is called the *designated port*. Consequently, there is only one single designated port for each LAN. All adapters of the root bridge are designated ports.

   All output adapters that were not selected as root ports or designated ports are locked (i.e., they take the `blocking` state). Though no payload packets will be transported over these ports, they can continue receiving BPDUs. This means that a deactivated adapter can detect a component failure and reactivate itself when needed.

Behavior When a Component Fails   When an active bridge (i.e., a root bridge or a designated bridge or an active port) fails, then this can be discovered by a message-age mechanism. To this end, each bridge manages a *max age* value. If the message age value of a BPDU (see Section 12.4.5) exceeds this value, then the spanning-tree algorithm is reactivated to check for which bridges should be active in the new topology. More specifically, bridges where network adapters change states send the topology-change notification BPDUs described above over the path to the root bridge. This means that all other bridges are informed about a change in topology, so that they can respond accordingly.

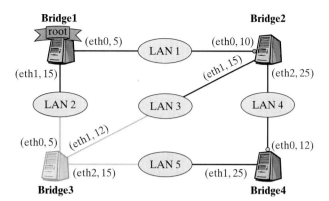

FIGURE 12–9
Topology of Figure 12–7 after bridge 3 has failed.

The message-age value of a bridge PDU is incremented after each forwarding action. If a failure or the adding of a new bridge causes a cycle, then the message-age value increases continually as the packet cycles, eventually reaching the threshold that triggers the spanning-tree algorithm (to reconfigure the LAN internetwork).

Figure 12–9 shows the topology from Figure 12–7, but with a change: Bridge 3 has failed. This means that the connection from LAN 3 to the root bridge over bridge 2 has to be restored, and LAN 5 is reached over bridge 4. The blocked ports of bridge 4, eth0 and eth1, are activated in this situation, allowing proper communication, even though bridge 3 failed.

Avoiding Temporary Loops   The decentralized operation of the spanning tree algorithm makes it possible that some bridges have not stored the globally correct information (i.e., they have only local knowledge). For this reason, the interfaces could be in a "wrong" state, causing loops that can be removed during the further procedure.

For example, if one interface is the designated port, and if no configuration message from a higher-order bridge has arrived in this bridge yet, then data packets would be forwarded on the basis of their local information. Globally, this would cause a loop and the wrong behavior described earlier.

To solve this problem, the standard includes two intermediate states between the blocking and the forwarding states. The transition from one state to another occurs when the so-called *forward delay timer* expires. In the listening state, a bridge must neither learn addresses nor forward packets. It receives configuration messages only if

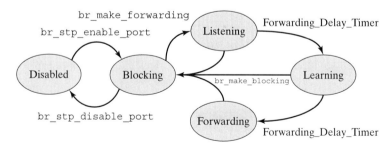

FIGURE 12–10
State automaton of a bridge port.

these messages reset the interface into the blocking state. The next state allows the bridge to enter addresses in the forwarding table (learning function); this state is called the learning state. In the forwarding state, which is reached after another expiry of the forward delay timer, data packets can be forwarded. Figure 12–10 shows the state transitions of a network adapter.

12.3   CONFIGURING A BRIDGE IN LINUX

A bridge interconnects several local area networks on the data-link layer, simulating the behavior of one large single network to the outside. To connect several local area networks in a Linux system, we need only install several network adapters in the computer. Linux also allows you to manage several bridges within one system, which can operate independently of one another. Each bridge instance has a logical name. One network adapter can always belong to exactly one bridge instance. This allows the system administrator to build virtual local networks (VLANs), which previously required expensive VLAN switches.

The following sections introduce options to configure and control Linux bridges.

12.3.1   Configuring the Kernel and the Network Adapter

To be able to use a Linux system as a bridge, the Linux kernel has to contain the bridge functionality. This is normally not the case, so we have to create a new kernel. When configuring the kernel, you should select the BRIDGING option from the Networking Options. You can integrate it into the kernel either as a module or permanently.

Once you have booted your new kernel (and loaded the module, if applicable), you can use the bridge functionality. Sometimes, you might incur problems when trying to activate several network adapters. If this happens, you can specify the boot parameters linux ether=0,0,ethx for each card when you start the system. If you use the LILO boot loader, you can also have the boot parameter passed automatically.

If the bridge functionality resides in the loaded kernel and all network adapters are activated, you can use the brctl tool to create and configure the desired bridge instances. brctl will be introduced in the next section.

12.3.2   Using the brctl Tool to Configure Linux Bridges

You can use the brctl (Bridge Control) tool to configure a bridge in Linux. This tool is part of the bridge-utils package and can be obtained from [Buyt01].

This tool can be used by the administrator to pass control commands to the bridge implementation in the kernel by using ioctl() commands. This section gives an overview of how you can use this program. [BoBu01] includes a detailed description of these commands and several examples.

The brctl tool lets you use the following commands to activate and deactivate a bridge. The commands are passed as parameters when brctl is called:

- addbr bridge: This command creates a new instance of a bridge with the identifier *bridge*.
- addif bridge device: This command adds the network adapter *device* to *bridge*. A network adapter can always belong to one bridge only.

▓ delbr bridge: This command deletes the instance of the specified bridge.

▓ delif bridge device: This command deletes the adapter *device* from *bridge*.

The following commands are available in the brctl tool to change the default parameters of a bridge:

▓ setaging bridge time: This command sets the *max age* parameter to the specified value. The topology of the LAN internetwork is recalculated when a BPDU with a larger aging time arrives.

▓ setbridgeprio bridge prio: This command sets the bridge priority, not to be confused with the port priority.

▓ setfd bridge time: This command sets the *bridge forward delay* parameter. This value is added to the *aging timer* parameter of a BPDU in each bridge.

▓ setgcint bridge time: This command sets the duration of the *garbage collection* (GC) *interval* for a bridge. Once a GC interval expires, there is a check for whether the forwarding table includes old entries. If it does, then these entries are deleted.

▓ sethello bridge time: This command is used to change the time interval in which hello packets are sent.

▓ setmaxage bridge time: This command sets the *max age* parameter. (See Section 12.2.4.)

▓ setpathcost bridge port cost: This command can be used to change the path cost for a network adapter of the specified bridge.

▓ setportprio bridge port prio: This command changes the priority of a network adapter in a bridge.

▓ stp bridge [en|dis]: This switch can be used to enable (en) or disable (dis) the spanning-tree protocol in a bridge.

12.3.3 Checking the Bridge Functionality

The following commands are included in the brctl tool to check the operation of a bridge and control its functionality:

▓ show: This command shows a list of all bridge instances currently existing in the computer.

▓ showbr bridge: This command outputs the current configuration of the specified bridge. The output for bridge 3 from the example in Figure 12–11 will be shown later.

▓ showmacs bridge: This command outputs the current filter or forwarding table, including the MAC addresses of all known stations (as shown below).

In addition, you can use the tcpdump tool to monitor the traffic in each of the interconnected LANs. To monitor LANs, you start tcpdump -i ethn and tcpdump -i ethm each in a separate window. You should see packets being forwarded in both adapters. In contrast, packets for computers in the same LAN should appear in one adapter only.

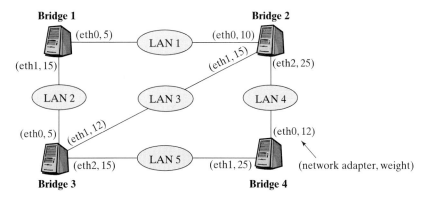

FIGURE 12–11
Redundant LAN internetwork.

12.3.4 Sample Configuration

The following example shows how you can add a bridge based on the configuration of bridge 1 from the LAN internetwork shown in Figure 12–11:

```
root@tux:   #  brctl addbr bridge1
root@tux:   #  brctl addif bridge1 eth0
root@tux:   #  brctl addif bridge1 eth1
root@tux    #  brctl setpathcost bridge1 eth0 5
root@tux    #  brctl setpathcost bridge1 eth1 15
root@tux:   #  ifconfig eth0 0.0.0.0
root@tux:   #  ifconfig eth1 0.0.0.0
root@tux:   #  ifconfig bridge1 129.13.42.100 netmask 255.255.255.0 up
```

In this example, we first create a bridge, bridge1. Subsequently, we add network adapters. The IP addresses are deleted, because the network adapters are allocated to the bridge and should actually forward or filter packets in the LAN internetwork independently of a protocol.

Nevertheless, it is possible to address the bridge (regardless of a network adapter) by using an IP address. This address is allocated to the virtual adapter, bridge1, as shown in the last command. Each bridge instance has such a virtual network device, which has the same name as its bridge instance.

The outputs of brctl showstp bridge3 and brctl showmacs bridge3 are as follows:

```
root@tux # brctl showmstp bridge 3
bridge3
    bridge id          0003.00902744822b
    designated root    0002.00902744da29
    root port          1                   path cost            10
    max age            20.00               bridge max age       20.00
    hello time         2.00                bridge hello time    2.00
    forward delay      15.00               bridge forward delay 15.00
```

aging time	300.00	gc interval	4.00
hello timer	0.00	tcn timer	0.00
topology change timer		0.00 gc timer	0.99
flags	TOPOLOGY_CHANGE		

eth0 (1)

port id	8001	state	forwarding
designated root	0002.00902744da29	path cost	5
designated bridge	0006.009027d1362b	message age timer	1.98
designated port	8002	forward delay timer	0.00
designated cost	5	hold timer	0.00
flags			

eth1 (2)

port id	8002	state	blocking
designated root	0002.00902744da29	path cost	12
designated bridge	0002.00902744da29	message age timer	1.98
designated port	8002	forward delay timer	0.00
designated cost	0	hold timer	0.00
flags			

eth2 (3)

port id	8003	state	forwarding
designated root	0002.00902744da29	path cost	15
designated bridge	0003.00902744822b	message age timer	0.00
designated port	8003	forward delay timer	0.00
designated cost	10	hold timer	0.00
flags			

root@tux # brctl showmacs bridge3

port no mac addr	is local?	aging timer	
2	00:90:27:44:82:2b	yes	0.00
1	00:90:27:72:0c:31	yes	0.00
3	00:90:27:cb:a3:cd	yes	0.00

12.4   IMPLEMENTATION

The implementation of the bridge functionality discussed here is relatively new. It has been integrated into the Linux kernel since Version 2.2.14 and 2.3.x and replaces the former and in many ways less flexible implementation. This version includes several new functions (e.g., the capability of managing several bridges in one system, and better options to configure the bridge functionality).

In addition, several details of the implementation have changed to provide more efficient handling. Among other things, the forwarding table is no longer stored in the form of an AVL tree, but in a hash table. Though AVL trees are data structures with a relatively low search cost, $O(\log n)$, hash tables are generally faster when the collision domain remains as low as possible. This means that a well-distributed hash table has the cost $O(1)$. We can assume that a Linux bridge has to store several hundred reachable systems at most, so a hash table is probably the better choice, especially considering that it is much easier to configure.

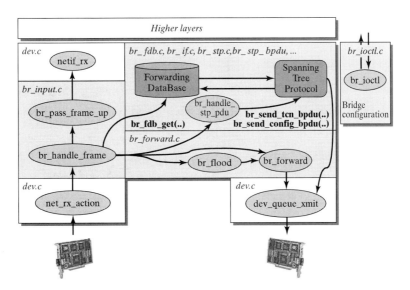

FIGURE 12–12
Integrating the bridge implementation into the Linux network architecture.

The following sections describe in more detail how you can implement the bridge functionality in Linux. We will first introduce the most important data structures and how they are linked, then discuss the algorithms and functions.

12.4.1 Architecture of the Bridge Implementation

Figure 12–12 shows the architecture of the bridge implementation in the Linux kernel. The individual components are divided, by their tasks and over several files. This makes the program text easier to understand and forces the programmer to define the interfaces between the individual components well.

12.4.2 Building and Linking Important Data Structures

The most important data structures of a Linux bridge include information about the bridges themselves and information about the network adapters (ports) allocated to them. We want to repeat here that you can use the new bridge implementation to construct several logically separated bridges in a Linux system. For example, this allows you to easily configure virtual local area networks (VLANs) that are not mutually accessible. In addition to information about the bridge and its ports, you need to store the forwarding table (filter table) for each bridge.

The forwarding table stores the IDs of each reachable station and the port used to reach that station. In addition, a transparent bridge also manages information for the spanning-tree protocol.

The file net/bridge/br_private.h defines the structures used to manage the information about bridges and their ports. Figure 12–13 shows how they are built and generally interlinked.

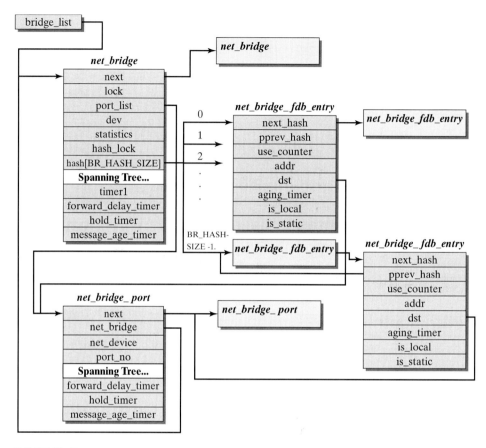

FIGURE 12–13
Structures in the Linux bridge implementation.

All bridges of a system are linked in a linear list, where the entry point is the bridge_list variable. A net_bridge structure with the following parameters is created for each bridge:

- next is used to link all net_bridge structures in a linear list. It points to the next element in the list.
- lock is a kind of mutex used to provide atomic access to important bridge structures and to prevent problems caused by concurrent access attempts.
- port_list is the entry point into a linear list that stores all ports of a bridge instance.
- dev is a pointer to the net_device structure of the virtual network adapter of a bridge.
- hash is a pointer to the hash table, which stores the stations a bridge can reach (forwarding table).

The following parameters relate to the spanning-tree algorithm and are discussed in Section 12.4.5. As mentioned earlier, the ports of a bridge are managed in a linear list, starting from the `net_bridge` structure. Each port in this list is represented by a `net_bridge_port` structure:

- `next` serves for linear linking of the ports of a bridge.
- `net_bridge` points to the `net_bridge` structure of the specified bridge. This pointer allows you to find the appropriate bridge instance quickly.
- `net_device` is a pointer to the `net_device` structure of the network adapter allocated to that port.
- `port_no` stores the port number.

More parameters also relate to the spanning-tree algorithm and are discussed in Section 12.2.4.

Using a Hash Table for Forwarding Information   The Forwarding Data Base (*fdb*), which is used for forwarding in a bridge, is stored in a hash table. The major benefit of hash tables is that they normally offer direct access to the desired data.

Each `net_bridge` structure uses the forwarding table to point to the hash vector. The preprocessor variable BR_HASH_SIZE can be used to set the number of entries. If a large number of stations is connected in a LAN internetwork, then the size of the hash vector should be selected accordingly.

If you want to check on whether a MAC address is already known to the destination station, then a more complex hash function (`br_mac_hash()`) is used to select a row of the hash vector. This row links all entries linearly with the same hash value (linear collision resolution). Figure 12–13 shows how structures are linked.

An entry in the hash table consists of a `net_bridge_fdb_entry` structure. The first two parameters of this structure serve to link a hash row. The other parameters store the MAC address of the destination station and a reference to the port used to reach that station. The variable `aging_timer` is used to delete an entry from the hash table after some time when it is no longer required.

12.4.3 The Path of a Packet Through the Kernel

This section describes the path of packets through the Linux kernel (i.e., through a transparent bridge in Linux). As with packets entering a Linux router (see Chapter 6), the network adapter receives a packet, triggers an interrupt on the network adapter, and stores the packet in an input queue. Subsequently, the function `net_rx_action()` runs the `net_rx` tasklet. This function also includes the entry point for the bridge implementation (`br_handle_frame_hook()`).

In contrast to a router implementation, the network layer is not accessed here. Instead, once a bridge is activated, the function `br_handle_frame()` is invoked, and a pointer, `br_handle_frame_hook`, points to this function. If no bridge has been activated—for instance, when the bridge functionality was created as a module—then the hook points to null. In this case, an attempt is made to forward the packet to the higher layers. If the kernel was created without bridge support, then these functions are missing, and no valuable computing time is wasted on searching for an activated bridge.

After a few checks (e.g., on whether the port was activated), the function `br_handle_frame()` decides whether the packet should be forwarded or its destination should have been in the previous LAN. It obtains this information from the function `br_fdb_get()`, which searches the forwarding table for the MAC destination address of the packet. If the packet has to be forwarded, then `br_forward()` will forward it; otherwise, it will be rejected.

But first, `br_fdb_put()` updates or creates the sender's entry in the forwarding table. As described earlier, a bridge can alternatively pass packets to the higher layers (e.g., the IP instance). For this reason, there has to have been a previous check on whether the destination station is the bridge itself. If this is the case, then the packet is further handled by `br_pass_frame_up()`, where a clone rather than the original packet is passed upwards. Other cases in which the packet has to be transported upwards are multicast packets and an adapter in *promiscuous* mode.

If the packet belongs to the spanning-tree protocol, it is passed to the function `br_stp_handle_bpdu()`. These bridge PDUs can be identified by a special MAC address.

As was mentioned earlier, a hash table within each bridge instance is used to manage the forwarding table. The spanning-tree algorithm and the relevant protocol messages (*Config BPDUs*, *TCN BPDUs*) ensure that no cycles can persist in the topology of a redundant LAN internetwork. (See Section 12.2.4). `ioctl()` commands are used to configure the bridge and set the parameters of the spanning-tree algorithm.

After this brief introduction to the architecture of the bridge implementation in Linux, the following sections describe each of the functions in more detail.

Forwarding Functions

`br_handle_frame()`	**net/bridge/br_input.c**

This function represents the entry point to the bridge implementation. All packets received by a Linux bridge travel through this function. It is invoked by the NET_RX tasklet in the function `net_rx_action()`, if the bridge functionality in the kernel was activated (CONFIG_BRIDGE).

The first step checks for whether the input port or the network adapter is deactivated (BR_PORT_DISABLED !IFF_UP); if this is the case, then the packet would be rejected. Next, the MAC header is removed from the packet, and the packet is subjected to several checks. For example, if it is a multicast packet, or if the network adapter is in *promiscuous* mode, then a clone of the packet is created and passed to the higher layers (`br_pass_frame_up()`).

Subsequently, the function checks for whether the packet is a bridge PDU. If the MAC destination address begins with the combination 01.80.C2.00.00, then the packet is treated as a special PDU of the spanning-tree protocol and is passed to the function `br_stp_handle_pdu()`.

If the packet is not a bridge PDU, then the bridge remembers its origin (or more specifically, the port on which it was received and the MAC sender address within the Ethernet frame). If the bridge is in either the BR_STATE_LEARNING or BR_STATE_FORWARDING state, it invokes the function `br_fdb_insert()` for this purpose. This action either adds a new entry to the table or renews the validity of an existing entry. If the bridge is in the BR_STATE_BLOCKING state, then the packet is rejected and the bridge does not remember its origin.

Any further handling of packets is done only in the BR_STATE_FORWARDING state. If an input port is in another state, then the packets are rejected. To be able to forward a packet, a decision has to be taken as to whether the packet should be forwarded at all and, if so, over which port. A multicast or broadcast packet is output to all ports of the bridge (br_flood()). In addition, such a packet is also passed to the higher layers.

br_fdb_get() searches the forwarding table for an entry with the specified MAC destination address. If it concerns the MAC address of an adapter of the bridge instance, then the packet is passed to the higher layers and not forwarded. If the destination is not the bridge, then the function br_forward() forwards the packet over the appropriate output port. Notice that the packet is passed to br_forward(), even if the input port was identified as the destination port, where it will eventually be verified and filtered. If no entry is found in the forwarding table, then the packet is flooded to all outputs (br_flood()).

br_forward()	net/bridge/br_forward.c

br_forward() is invoked either once by br_handle_frame() or several times by br_flood(). The purpose of this function is to output a data packet on the specified port. To this end, the function dev_queue_xmit(), described in Section 6.2.2, is used.

Beforehand, however, there are two checks (br_should_forward()). First, the output port has to be in the BR_STATE_FORWARDING state; and, second, it must not be identical with the input port of the packet. Otherwise, the packet would be transferred twice within the local area network.

br_flood()	net/bridge/br_forward.c

br_flood() is invoked by br_learn() or br_forward() when a packet should be sent to all ports, except the input port, for some reason. br_flood() simply invokes the function br_forward() for each entry in port_list of the net_bridge structure. As mentioned earlier, this function checks for the port's forwarding state and for mismatch between input and output adapters.

br_pass_frame_up()	net/bridge/br_input.c

Transparent bridges are normally invisible to the other stations in a LAN internetwork; they forward data packets on the data-link layer or filter packets. But when we use a Linux system as a bridge, we will probably want to use it also for other purposes. Consequently, the computer should be able to receive IP packets. This is possible with the bridge implementation discussed here. When the bridge receives a packet with the MAC destination address of one of its adapters, it is passed to the higher layers by br_pass_frame_up().

The packet type is set to PACKET_HOST (arrived in the destination system), and the Ethernet header is removed. Subsequently, the packet is passed to the function netif_rx(), which invokes the protocol-handling routine of the appropriate layer-3 protocol.

br_fdb_get()	net/bridge/br_fdb.c

br_fdb_get() searches the forwarding table in the hash table of the specified bridge instance for a MAC destination address passed as a parameter. It first calculates the hash value and searches the hash row to see whether there is an entry with the desired MAC address. If there is an entry, then the desired information for the MAC address is found, and a pointer to the output port used to reach that station is returned. If no entry is found, then the route to the destination station is unknown and the value **null** is returned.

12.4.4 Learning New MAC Addresses

The learning of new MAC addresses is a characteristic of a transparent bridge. It can be achieved only provided that the port is in learning or forwarding state. (See Section 12.2.4.) As was described earlier, the learning function is invoked for each data packet. The source address is added to the forwarding table. If an address already exists in the table, then the information of the net_bridge_fdb_entry structure is updated and the pointer to the entry is returned.

Functions

br_fdb_insert()	net/bridge/br_fdb.c

br_fdb_insert() includes the entire learning function of a transparent bridge. The MAC sender address is entered in the forwarding table for each incoming packet in the BR_STATE_LEARNING and BR_STATE_FORWARDING states. To this end, the hash value of the MAC address is calculated (br_mac_hash()), and the hash row is searched for the appropriate entry. If this entry is found, then both the entry for the input adapter and the aging_timer are updated. This means that the bridge will also learn when a station has moved.

If no entry can be found in the hash row, then br_fdb_insert() creates a new net_bridge_fdb_entry structure and uses hash_link() to add it to the hash row.

br_fdb_cleanup()	net/bridge/br_fdb.c

The forwarding table should be updated whenever a station is no longer active or the network has changed. Unfortunately, a bridge cannot see such an action, because it responds actively to a station's packets only by remembering the origin of a packet in the forwarding table. This means that, when a station has not sent anything for a certain period of time, then the bridge assumes that the station was deactivated or moved. For this purpose, the `gc_timer` is set in a bridge instance. This timer starts the function `br_fdb_cleanup()` periodically in a specific interval, `gc_interval`. It checks all entries in the hash table of a bridge instance and removes all entries with an aging value exceeding timeout.

12.4.5   Implementing the Spanning-Tree Protocol

This section describes how the spanning-tree protocol according to IEEE 802.1d and the relevant functions are implemented. The spanning-tree protocol is used to prevent cycles in a redundant LAN internetwork. The algorithm operates in a decentralized way: Each station has to work out the current state in the LAN internetwork from the information contained in control packets (BPDUs). For example, each bridge assumes initially that it is the root bridge, and it probably has to learn that this is not so from incoming BPDUs.

For this reason, the implementation of the spanning tree protocol is based on the fact that the currently "best" configuration is stored in each port. This means that each new incoming message is verified to see whether the information it contains is better than the information currently stored, so that the currently best configuration is accepted. By comparing the configuration message most recently received with the information available on the bridge itself, it is easy to figure out the root bridge, the root port, and the designated ports.

This also means that all steps are executed consecutively for each configuration message with better information. This means that the root bridge is not defined in all bridges to then compute the least cost for all bridges, and so on; instead, the bridges decide first on the basis of their own knowledge, and subsequently the knowledge of the immediate neighbors is added, and so on, until the configuration messages have eventually visited the entire LAN internetwork, so that the bridges can make their optimal choice for the LAN internetwork. This shows clearly that a real-world implementation does not necessarily have to correspond to the theoretical model to be efficient.

One major benefit of this implementation is that relatively few configuration messages have to be exchanged. How fast a tree structure can be built also depends on the bridges that send their configuration messages first. It is normally more beneficial when bridges with smaller identifiers or higher priorities send configuration messages earlier. However, bridges do not immediately change from the blocking into the forwarding state; they take various intermediate states where no data packets may be forwarded, so that the probability of temporary cycles is low.

The following subsections describe the important aspects of how the spanning-tree protocol is implemented.

Initialization   A bridge in the kernel is initialized by the functions `br_add_bridge()` and `new_nb()` when a bridge instance is created by the `brctl addbr ...` command. As the instructions in this command are processed, the bridge is set as the designated root bridge. When `brctl addif ...` adds ports to the bridge, then these ports are initially put into the `BR_STATE_BLOCKING` state. All timers are initially set to inactive (`br_stp_enable_port()`). Subsequently, the information currently available is verified to see the state the new port can now take.

When a bridge instance is initialized, the bridge timer is also initialized. This timer is a `timer_list` type (see Section 2.7.1); it invokes the `br_tick()` function each second. This function is used to control all timer functions of the bridge instance and the spanning-tree protocol. This means that each bridge instance uses only one single system timer. All internal time-controlled processes run over this timer. (See more information in the later subsection *Timer Handling*.)

Processing BPDUs   The function `br_handle_stp_pdu()` of `br_handle_frame()` is invoked as soon as a BPDU is received. When topology-change packets (TCN) arrive, then `br_received_tcn_bpdu()` assumes all further handling. When configuration packets (Config BPDU) arrive, then the packet content is copied into a `br_config_bpdu` structure, and some of the fields are converted into the internal representation format. For example, time values are stored in jiffies rather than in ticks. Subsequently, the BPDU is further handled by the function `br_received_config_bpdu()`.

Steps of the Spanning-Tree Algorithm   The individual steps of the spanning-tree algorithm were described in Section 12.2.4. As mentioned in that section, the spanning-tree mechanism runs for each configuration message received that changes something in the current configuration.

Whether a new configuration message has information that is better than that currently stored is a decision implemented by logic functions, as are the selection of a root port and the naming of a designated port. Notice that these actions normally use few comparisons.

`br_received_config_bpdu()`	**net/bridge/br_stp.c**

This function initially invokes `br_is_root_bridge()` to check on whether it has been the root bridge itself. Notice that the bridge does not have a global view of the LAN internetwork, as mentioned earlier. There could indeed be other bridges that classify themselves as the root bridge. This situation will change gradually as the spanning-tree algorithm runs its steps, and one bridge will eventually become the only root bridge.

When a new configuration message is better than the current information (a result of calling `br_supersedes_port_info()`), then the following things happen:

- First, the invocation of `br_record_config_information()` causes the data of the configuration BPDU to be written to the `net_bridge_port` structure.
- Next, the `br_configuration_update()` function is invoked. It selects the root ports and designated ports. This action could cause the information structures of the bridge and its ports to change.
- Subsequently, `br_port_state_selection()` recognizes the state of a port. The hello timer is stopped, if the bridge was the root bridge before the new information was stored, but now if it is no longer the root bridge. If a change to the topology is discovered in additional, then the `topology_change_timer` is stopped, the `tcn_timer` is started, and a topology-change message is sent (`br_transmit_tcn()`).

If the input port was marked as the root port, then the timeout values of the configuration BPDU are added to the `net_bridge` structure and a configuration BPDU is generated (by `br_config_bpdu_generation()`). In addition, the function `br_topology_change_acknowledged()` is invoked, if the `topoplogy_change_ack` flag was set in the configuration BPDU.

In contrast, if nothing changes in response to the configuration BPDU, then `br_reply()` is invoked, provided that the input port is the designated port. This means that a configuration message with locally stored values is sent.

`br_supersedes_port_info()`	net/bridge/br_stp.c

This function checks for whether the stored `net_bridge_port` structure changes in response to a configuration BPDU received (i.e., if the new configuration BPDU includes "better" information). This is the case in either of the following situations:

The root bridge in the BPDU has a smaller ID than the root bridge currently stored in the structure.

The two IDs are equal, but the path cost in the BPDU is less.

The path cost is equal, but the ID of the sending bridge is smaller than the ID of the bridge itself.

The IDs of the bridges match, but the port ID of the sending bridge is smaller than the ID of the input port.

The first two points in the above list are normally decisive, but if two local area networks are connected by parallel bridges, then the port ID could also play a role.

`br_record_config_information()`	net/bridge/br_stp.c

This function is invoked if the configuration message is better than the information currently stored. The root bridge ID and the cost over the path to the root bridge (RPC) are stored in the `net_bridge_port` structure as designated root and cost, respectively. The bridge sending the configuration message and its output port serve as the designated bridge and port.

The message-age timer is started with the value from the configuration message, to be able to detect potential failures of a component.

`br_record_config_timeout_values()`	net/bridge/br_stp.c

An invocation of this function causes the values for expiry of the timers to be copied from the configuration message to the information memory of the bridge. This ensures that critical timers in all bridges of the LAN internetwork have the same time-out values, which are determined by the root bridge.

br_root_selection()	net/bridge/br_stp.c

This function selects the root port of a bridge. The function iterates over all ports, starting with the smallest port number, and it checks for whether the conditions for the root port are met (br_should_become_root_port()). The port must not be a designated port, it must not have the BR_STATE_DISABLED state, and the bridge must not be the root bridge. Subsequently, the path cost to the root bridge is compared. If the costs are equal, then the information from the net_bridge_port structure is considered. Figure 12–14 shows the algorithm used for this procedure.

If the loop was fully walked through, but no root port was assigned, then the bridge itself becomes the root bridge. Finally, the selected root bridge and the root path cost (RPC) are entered in the net_bridge structure.

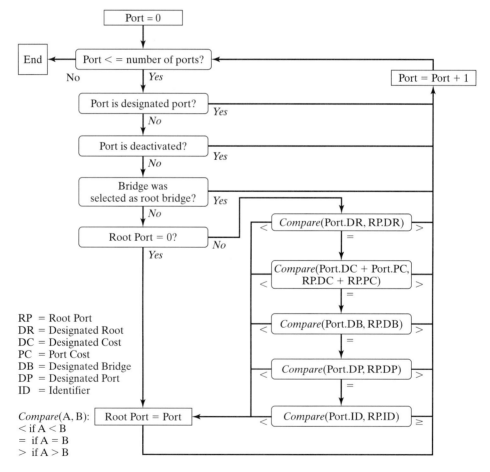

FIGURE 12–14
Selecting a root port.

| `br_designated_port_selection()` | **net/bridge/br_stp.c** |

This function also checks the ports one after the other. A port becomes the designated port if the configuration message that arrived on this port is better than the configuration message received (and stored in the `net_bridge_port` structure). The configuration message consists mainly of the root bridge ID, the path cost to the root bridge, and the bridge and port IDs, so the corresponding fields in the `net_bridge` structure and in the `net_bridge_port` structure have to be compared. Figure 12–15 shows the algorithm used to implement this condition.

| `br_become_designated_port()` | **net/bridge/br_stp.c** |

This function is invoked in `br_designated_port_selection()` for each designated port. The port in the bridge whose number is called in this function becomes the designated port. This means that the corresponding information is stored in the `net_bridge_port` structure.

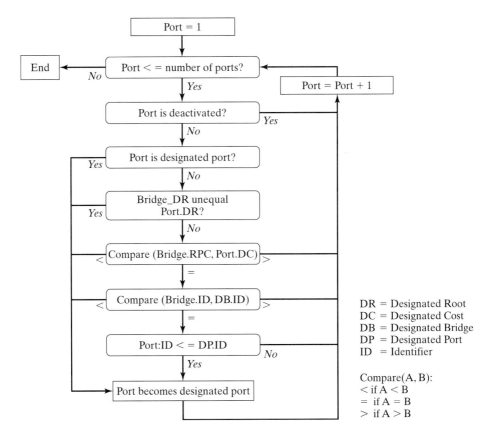

FIGURE 12–15
Selecting a designated port.

br_port_state_selection()	net/bridge/br_stp.c

The future state is determined for each port, and appropriate functions are invoked. If the port is in the BR_STATE_DISABLED state, then nothing is done. If a port is the root port or a designated port, then br_make_forwarding() is invoked to put that port in the forwarding state.

Remember that the intermediate states, BR_STATE_LISTENING und BR_STATE_LEARNING, are used first, as described in Section 12.2.4. The forward delay timer controls this procedure.

In all other cases, br_make_blocking() is invoked to put the port in the blocking state. In addition, a topology-change request is caused by br_topology_change_detection(), if the port has been in the forwarding or learning state.

br_transmit_config()	net/bridge/br_stp.c

This function initially checks whether for the hold timer is active. If so, then config_pending is set to 1, and the function returns immediately.

If the hold timer has not always been active, then a configuration BPDU with the corresponding values is filled in from the net_bridge structure; then the function br_send_config_bpdu() is invoked, and the hold timer is started. Figure 12–16 shows how a configuration message is built from the net_bridge structure.

Example—Running the Spanning-Tree Protocol   The initialization of the bridges results in the configuration shown in Figure 12–17. However, this figure shows only the most important fields in the structures. Each bridge is initialized as a root bridge. Though the interfaces are in blocking state, configuration messages are sent, because the ports are defined as designated ports.

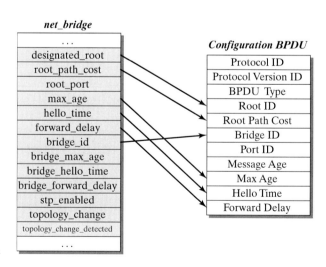

FIGURE 12–16
Example of a configuration message.

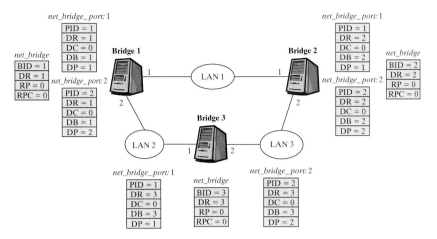

FIGURE 12–17
Initializing bridges for the spanning-tree protocol.

After the bridge initialization, configuration messages are sent over all network adapters. In this example, bridge 1 sends the first configuration message. This information is better than the information stored in the input ports of bridges 2 and 3 (in this case), so the new information is stored in the `net_bridge_port` structures of these ports. Figure 12–18 shows this procedure.

From this information, the root port is selected in bridges 2 and 3. In the example shown in Figure 12–18, port 1 is selected in both bridges, because it is the only port that stored the root bridge with the smallest ID. This selection causes the `net_bridge` structure to change, as shown in Figure 12–19.

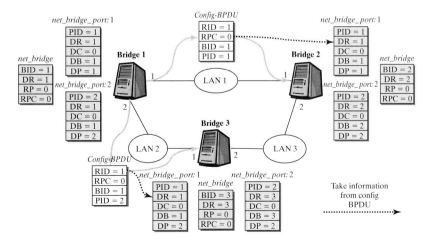

FIGURE 12–18
Storing information from a configuration message.

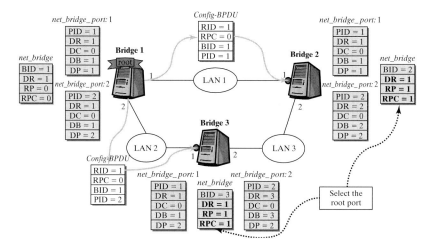

FIGURE 12–19
Selecting a root port.

The next step selects designated ports in the bridges. Port 2 is defined as the designated port in each of the two bridges, because the information about the root bridge in the `net_bridge_port` structure of this port differs from the information in the `net_bridge` structure. The selecting of designated ports changes the `net_bridge_port` structure of these ports, so the new root bridge and its path cost are entered. Figure 12–20 shows this procedure.

Two paths to the root bridge exist for LAN 3 in this example, and so there is a cycle; hence, we have to select a bridge as designated bridge for this LAN. We opt for bridge 2 as the designated bridge, because it has the smaller ID. Notice that this selection, too, depends on the order of the exchanging of configuration messages. For example, if bridge 3

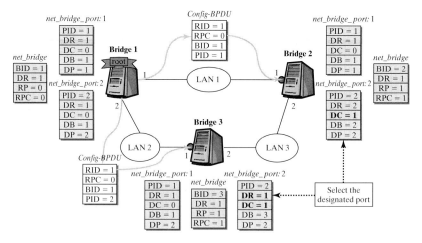

FIGURE 12–20
Selecting designated ports.

sends the first configuration message over its designated port, then bridge 2 will check for whether it is better than the stored configuration. Such would not be the case in this example, so bridge 2 would return a configuration message with its own values. The information in this message would be better than the configuration stored on port 2 in bridge 3. Consequently, this bridge would run the spanning-tree algorithm. Port 1 would remains the root port, but port 2 would no longer be a designated port and would be put into the blocking state. (See Figure 12–21.)

Timer Handling Each bridge has a function, `br_tick()`, to handle timers. This section describes the seven defined timers. To implement these timers, only one system timer of the type `timer_list` is used. This is the variable tick in each `net_bridge` structure.

The timer `tick` is invoked once every second (`expires = jiffies + HZ`) This causes the function `br_tick()` to be invoked each time. This function defines the behavior of the timers in the following list. Whether a timer has expired is checked for each timer (`br_check_timers()`). In addition, the timers are incremented. The appropriate behavior function is invoked as soon as a timer expires.

- *Hold timer*: The hold timer starts after the configuration BPDU has been sent. When it is active, no configuration BPDU can be sent over the same port. The hold timer expires when its value reaches or exceeds the stored `hold_time`. Then the function `br_transmit_config()` is invoked, if no BPDU has been sent yet. Once it has expired, the hold timer is not restarted. It is stopped explicitly when a port is disabled.

- *GC timer*: The garbage collection timer does cleanup work in the forwarding table. It checks periodically (`gc_interval`) on whether there are old entries in the forwarding table. If there are, then these entries are deleted, to respond to moving stations. In addition, this cleanup work prevents the forwarding table

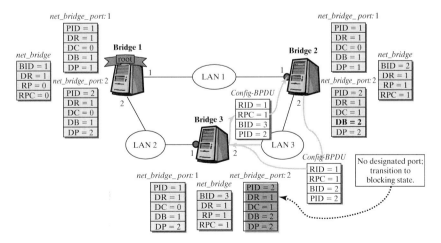

FIGURE 12–21
Configuration for LAN 3.

from filling up with entries for inactive stations. The function `br_fdb_cleanup()` is responsible for this check.

▪ *Hello timer*: The hello timer is used to send hello packets (configuration BPDUs) at regular intervals. This timer is started after the call of `br_config_bpdu_generation()`, while the spanning-tree protocol is running. It is incremented until its value has reached the stored hello time. Subsequently, `br_config_bpdu_generation()` is invoked again, and the hello timer is restarted.

▪ *TCN timer*: The TCN timer is used once a TCN BPDU has been sent. This timer causes TCN BPDUs to be sent at regular intervals until the topology change has been acknowledged. The intervals are identical to those for configuration BPDUs.

▪ *Topology-change timer*: This timer is used exclusively by the root bridge. It specifies the period for which the flags for a topology change request are set (i.e., the period during which configuration messages may be passed). The fields `topology_change_detected` and `topology_change` in the `net_bridge` structure are set to null as soon as this timer expires. This timer is not restarted.

▪ *Message-age timer*: There is one message-age timer for each network interface in each bridge. This timer is started when the values of a configuration BPDU are written to the `net_bridge_port` structure. The expiry of the message-age timer means that a component has failed. For this reason, the spanning-tree protocol is restarted, where the port with the expired timer is set to be the designated port. Subsequently, the spanning-tree algorithm runs its normal procedure.

▪ *Forward-delay timer*: The forward-delay timer is used to move the ports of a bridge from the blocking to the forwarding state. This is the reason why there is one such timer for each port. This timer specifies the time interval between two states. It is started by the function `br_make_forwarding()`, and the state of a port is set to `BR_STATE_LISTENING` in this function.

When in the `BR_STATE_LISTENING`, the port is switched to the `BR_STATE_LEARNING` state, and the forward-delay timer is restarted. When the timer expires again, then the state changes from `BR_STATE_LEARNING` to `BR_STATE_FORWARDING`. This requires the `br_topology_change_detection()` function to be invoked, if any of the ports stored this bridge is the designated bridge. Figure 12–11 shows these transitions.

Topology Changes   When a new bridge is added to the LAN internetwork, then the spanning-tree protocol (STP) runs as described above: The bridge is initialized as root bridge. If it is actually the (new) root bridge, then its configuration messages will win across all bridges in the internetwork. Otherwise, it receives configuration messages from neighboring bridges, which it will then use to configure its interfaces.

As was mentioned previously, if a bridge or an active port fails, then the message-age timer in the neighboring bridge expires. Figure 12–22 shows this procedure in an example. The port owning the expired timer is set to be the designated port. This means that the current configuration of this port is overwritten. Subsequently, the spanning-tree mechanism runs once more in this bridge.

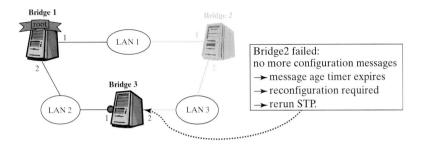

FIGURE 12–22
Example for a topology change: The message-age timer expires.

Functions Used to Display a Topology Change   As previously described, the execution of the spanning-tree protocol in a LAN internetwork could cause changes to the topology. TCN BPDUs are sent over the path to the root bridge to ensure that all bridges are informed about such a topology change. In turn, the root bridge sends then configuration BPDUs with the `topology_change` field set, and these BPDUs are transported across all paths within the tree topology.

It is interesting to note that MAC addresses are not added to the forwarding table when the topology is reconfigured. Instead, this is done exclusively by the learning function. However, the entries in the forwarding table can become invalid after a relatively short time, so packets are sent to the relevant stations over all ports so that they will eventually reach their destination.

`br_received_tcn_bpdu()`	**net/bridge/br_stp.c**

If the port that received a BPDU is a designated port, then the function `br_topology_change_detection()` is invoked. `br_topology_change_acknowledge()` is used to send a configuration message with the `topology_change_ack` field set over the input port.

`br_topology_change_detection()`	**net/bridge/br_stp.c**

If the bridge is the root of the tree topology, then the `topology_change` field in the `net_bridge` structure is set to one, and the topology-change timer is started. Unless the topology change has been detected, all other bridges use the `br_transmit_tcn()` function to send a TCN BPDU over their root ports and start their TCN timers. Finally, it is marked that the topology change was detected, to limit the number of TCN BPDUs announcing the same topology change.

`br_topology_change_acknowledged()`	**net/bridge/br_stp.c**

The marking for a topology change is reset, and the TCN timer is stopped. This function is invoked by `br_received_config_bpdu()`, if the flag `topology_change_ack` is set in the incoming configuration message.

PART IV

Network Layer

The TCP/IP Protocols

This chapter introduces the TCP/IP protocol suite, which represents the basis of the popular Internet. Chapter 3 introduced the TCP/IP reference model. The sections in this chapter and the following chapters begin with an introduction of the tasks of each of these protocols and then describe how they operate and how they are implemented in Linux.

The history of the Internet and its protocols began in 1961, when Leonard Kleinrock developed packet-switching theory at MIT. His work was based on the idea of splitting data into many small packets and sending them to the destination separately, without specifying the exact path. After initial skepticism, the principle was eventually used in a research project of ARPA (Advanced Research Projects Agency), a division of the United States Department of Defense. In 1968, ARPA granted a budget of more than half a million dollars for a heterogeneous network, which was called *ARPANET*.

In 1969, this experimental network connected the four universities of Los Angeles (UCLA), Santa Barbara (UCSB), Utah, and the Stanford Research Institute (SRI) and expanded very quickly. Later, satellite and cellular links were successfully connected to the ARPANET. In one impressive demonstration, a truck in California was connected with the next university over a radio link and used the satellite network to access a computer based in London, UK.

This system was used intensively in the years following. On the basis of the knowledge gained from this system, a second generation of protocols was developed. By 1982, a protocol suite with the two important protocols, TCP and IP, had been specified. Today, the name TCP/IP is used for the entire protocol suite. In 1983, TCP/IP became the standard protocol for the ARPANET. The TCP/IP protocols proved particularly suitable for providing a reliable connection of networks within the continually growing ARPANET. ARPA was very interested in establishing the new protocols and convinced the University of California at Berkeley to integrate the TCP/IP protocols into its widely used Berkeley UNIX operating system. They used the principle of sockets to design applications with network functionality. This helped the TCP/IP protocols to soon become very popular for the exchange of data between applications.

In the following years, the ARPANET had grown to a size that made the management of all computers IP addresses in one single file too expensive. As a consequence, the

Domain Name Service (DNS) was developed and is used to hide IP addresses behind easy-to-remember computer and domain names. Today, the Internet protocol Version 4 is the most frequently used network-layer protocol. However, it was not designed for such an enormous proliferation and has already hit its capacity limits, so a new version had to be developed. The new Internet Protocol Version 6 is also called IPv6 or IPng.

13.1 THE INTERNET PROTOCOL SUITE

Each protocol of the TCP/IP protocol suite handles certain tasks within the TCP/IP protocol stack. Figure 13–1 gives an overview of the TCP/IP protocol stack and its protocols.

- On the data-link *layer* in the Internet model, you find network adapters and their drivers. They allow you to exchange data packets having a specific maximum length within the connected LAN (Ethernet, token ring, . . .) or within a WAN (PPP over ISDN, ATM). The previous chapters introduced some protocols that also belong to the data-link layer (SLIP, PPP, ATM, Bluetooth, etc.). All adapters and protocols on this layer have the common property that they represent only *one* communication link between two IP routers (i.e., they don't support Internet routing).

- The *Address Resolution Protocol* (*ARP*) also resides on the data-link layer. Notice that there are contradictory opinions in the literature. ARP is used to map globally valid IP addresses to locally valid MAC addresses. ARP is actually not limited to IP addresses or specific physical addresses; it was designed for general use. ARP uses the broadcast capability of local area networks to find addresses. Chapter 15 describes this protocol in detail.

- The *Internet Protocol* (*IP*) forms the core of the entire architecture, because it allows all IP-enabled computers in the interconnected networks to communicate. Each computer in the Internet has to support the Internet Protocol. IP offers unreliable transport of data packets. IP uses information from routing protocols (OSPF, BGP, etc.) to forward packets to their receivers.

- The *Internet Control Message Protocol* (*ICMP*) has to be present in each IP-enabled computer; it handles the transport of error messages of the Internet Protocol. For example, ICMP sends a message back to the sender of a packet if the packet cannot

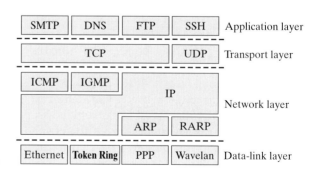

FIGURE 13–1
The protocols of the TCP/IP protocol stack.

be forwarded because routing information is missing or faulty. Section 14.4 deals with ICMP and its implementation in Linux.

- The *Internet Group Management Protocol* (*IGMP*) is responsible for managing multicast groups in local area networks. Multicast provides for efficient sending of data to a specific group of computers. IGMP allows the computers of a LAN to inform its router that they want to receive data for a certain group in the future. Chapter 17 discusses multicast in the Internet.

- The *Transmission Control Protocol* (*TCP*) is a reliable, connection-oriented and byte-stream-oriented transport-layer protocol. TCP is primarily responsible for providing a secured data transport between two applications over the unreliable service of the IP protocol. TCP is the most frequently used transport protocol in the Internet. It has a large functionality, and so its implementation is extensive. Chapter 24 discusses the TCP.

- The *User Datagram Protocol* (*UDP*) is a very simple transport protocol, providing connectionless and unreliable transport of data packets between applications in the Internet. In this context, unreliable does not mean that the data could arrive corrupted at the destination computer. It means that UDP does not offer any protocol mechanisms to guarantee that the data will arrive at the destination at all. When data arrives at the destination computer, than it can only be checked for correctness.

  As compared with TCP, UDP has the benefit that it has very little functionality and so can easily be extended. Many applications that normally transmit only small amounts of data (e.g., client/server applications) use UDP as their preferred transport protocol. Establishing a connection and reliable data transmission would be more costly than the retransmission of faulty or missing data.

- The *application layer* accommodates various standardized application protocols, which form the basis of a large number of applications:

  - The *HyperText Transfer Protocol* (*HTTP*) is currently the protocol most frequently used in the Internet application layer. It allows you to exchange data in the World Wide Web—say, by loading Web sites into your Web browser (Netscape, Mozilla, Lynx, etc.). The unprecedented success of the World Wide Web has led to the enormous proliferation of the Internet and its revolutionary growth.

  - *TELNET* is the protocol for virtual terminals. It is used to access a computer connected to the network in the form of a terminal session. Its unsecured transmission of passwords and data has caused TELNET to be increasingly replaced by the SSH (Secure Socket Shell) protocol.

  - The *File Transfer Protocol* (*FTP*) can be used to transport files from a local computer to another computer and vice versa. Like TELNET, its most important drawback is that passwords are transmitted in cleartext. FTP has increasingly been replaced by *Secure Copy* (*SCP*).

  - The *Simple Mail Transfer Protocol* (*SMTP*) is the protocol used to exchange electronic mail (e-mail) in the Internet.

▷ The *Domain Name Service* (*DNS*) translates DNS names, which are most commonly used and are easy for humans to remember (e.g., www.linux-netzwerkarchitektur.de[1]) into IP addresses. It is used mainly to convert computer names and mail-server locations into IP addresses.

▷ The *Network File System* (*NFS*) is used to allow several computers to access the same file system. The NFS service represents an extension of local file systems beyond network boundaries.

Such protocols of the application layer are not discussed in this book, because they are not part of the Linux kernel. Simple application programming is normally sufficient to emulate them. For example, there are many of HTTP protocol implementations in different WWW browsers and WWW servers. Chapter 27 explains how applications with network functionality can be programmed.

The following chapters describe each protocol of the TCP/IP protocol stack and how they are implemented in Linux. These chapters also discuss various extensions, which are related to the Internet Protocol suite, but normally not mentioned together with it. This includes mainly concepts and protocols for computer security (firewalls, NAT) and the support of specific guaranteed services within the Internet Protocol (Quality of Service (QoS) with *TC* or *KIDS*).

The Internet Protocol V4

The Internet Protocol (IP) is the central element in the TCP/IP protocol stack. It provides the basic service for all the data traffic in the Internet and other IP-based networks and was specified in RFC 791. The primary task of the Internet Protocol is to hide differences between data transmission layers and to offer a uniform presentation of different network technologies. For example, the Internet protocol can run on top of LAN technologies and SLIP (Serial Line IP) or PPP (Point-to-Point Protocol) over modem or ISDN connections. The uniform presentation of the underlying technology includes an introduction of the uniform addressing scheme (IP address family) and a mechanism to fragment large data packets, so that smaller maximum packet sizes can be transported across networks.

In general, each network technology defines a maximum size for data packets—the *Maximum Transmission Unit* (*MTU*). The MTU depends on the hardware used and the transmission technology and varies between 276 bytes and 9000 bytes. The Internet layer fragments IP datagrams, which are bigger than the MTU of the network technology used, into smaller packets (*fragments*). These fragments of a datagram are then put together into the original IP datagram in the destination computer. Section 14.2.3 explains how data packets are fragmented and reassembled.

In summary, the Internet Protocol handles the following functions:

- provides an unsecured connectionless datagram service;
- defines IP datagrams as basic units for data transmission;
- defines the IP addressing scheme;
- routes and forwards IP datagrams across interconnected networks;
- verifes the lifetime of packets;
- fragments and reassembles packets; and
- uses ICMP to output errors.

14.1   PROPERTIES OF THE INTERNET PROTOCOL

The Internet Protocol was developed with the idea of maintaining communication between two systems even when some transmission sections fail. For this reason, the Internet Protocol was developed on the basis of the principle of datagram switching, to transport IP data units, rather than on that of circuit-switching, like conventional telephone network.

The following sections describe the protocol mechanisms of the Internet Protocol. Section 14.2 will then explain how IP is implemented in the Linux kernel.

14.1.1   Routing IP Packets Across Routers

Figure 14–1 shows how the Internet is structured. Rather than being one single network, the Internet is composed of many smaller local area networks, which are connected by routers. This is the reason why it is often called the *network of networks* or *global network*. Each network connected to the Internet can be different both in size and in technology. Within one network (e.g., the network of a university), it is often meaningful to build several subnetworks. These—often independent—networks and subnetworks are connected by routers and point-to-point lines.

The interconnection of single local area networks offers a way to send data from an arbitrary computer to any other computer within the internetwork. Before it sends a packet, an Internet computer checks for whether the destination computer is in the same local area network. If this is not the case, then the data packet is forwarded to the next router. If both the sender and the receiver are in the same local area network, then the packet is delivered to the receiver directly over the physical medium. In either case, the IP layer uses the service of the data-link layer to physically transport the packet (horizontal communication—see Section 3.2).

Let's assume that, in the first case, the packet has not yet arrived in the destination computer. The router checks the destination address in the IP packet header and the information in the routing table to determine how the packet should be forwarded. Next, the packet travels from one router to the next until it eventually arrives in the destination computer. Chapter 16 discusses routing in IP networks.

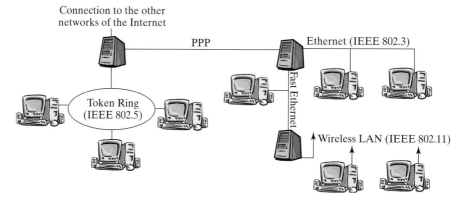

FIGURE 14–1
The structure of the global Internet.

14.1.2 The IP Packet Header

Figure 14–2 shows the format of an IP packet. The fields of the IP packet header have the properties described below.

- *Version*: This field contains the version number of the Internet Protocol used. Including the version number provides a way to use several versions of the Internet Protocol. Currently, only versions v4 and v6 are defined. In general, the two versions are not specified in the *Version* field; they are identified by their protocol identifiers on the MAC layer (0x800 for IPv4, 0x86DD for IPv6—see include/linux/if_ether.h).

- *IHL (Internet Header Length)*: This field contains the length of the packet header, because it can be longer than 20 bytes, if options are used. The length is stated in multiples of 32 bits. The smallest valid value is 5 (no options), and the highest value is 15 (corresponds to a header length of 60 bytes).

- *Codepoint*: This field was originally called *Type of Service*. Its purpose was changed to *Differentiated Services Codepoint* in RFC 2474. This field shows the forwarding behavior used [NBBB98].

- *Total length*: This value includes the entire length of the IP packet. Its 16-bit length makes the maximum size of an IP datagram 65,535 bytes. RFC 791 specifies that each IP-enabled computer should be capable of processing data packets with a size of 576 bytes. In general, however, it is possible to process packets with a bigger length. Otherwise, a packet has to be fragmented. (See Section 14.2.3.)

- *Fragment ID*: The destination computer can use this identifier, together with the sender address, to reassemble fragments of IP datagrams to reconstruct the original datagrams. All fragments of an IP datagram have the same fragment ID, which is set by the sender.

- *Flags*: An IP packet can include two flags (the third flag is currently not used): *Don't Fragment* (*DF*) and *More Fragments* (*MF*). MF is used for a fragmented packet. The DF bit means that a datagram must not be fragmented, even if this means that the packet cannot be transported any further. The MF bit shows whether more fragments follow this IP packet (i.e., the MF flag is set in all fragments of a datagram, except for the last fragment).

- *Fragment Offset*: This field specifies where in relation to the beginning of the entire datagram the present fragment has to be ordered. This information is required

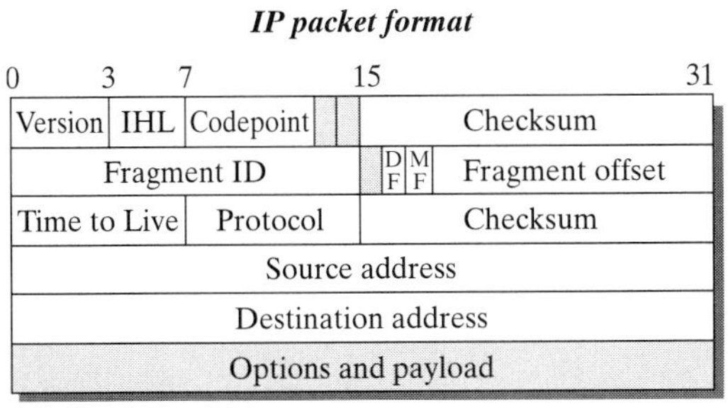

FIGURE 14–2
Packet-header format of the Internet Protocol.

to reassemble the original packet from the individual fragments in the destination computer. Since this field has a size of 13 bits, a maximum number of 8192 fragments can be created from one IP datagram. All fragments, except the last fragment, have to be a multiple of 8 bytes. This is the elementary fragment unit.

▨ *Time To Live (TTL)*: This is a counter used to limit the lifetime of IP packets. This field originally stated the maximum lifetime in seconds, but is used today to specify the maximum number of intermediate systems (routers). Each router on the path has to decrement this counter by at least one. If a longer buffering time is necessary, then the counter should be decremented by more. If the field has the value 0, then the packet has to be rejected, to keep a packet from wandering in the network forever.

▨ *Protocol*: This field includes the number of the transport protocol to which the packet should be forwarded. Numbering of protocols was defined in [RePo94] (e.g., TCP (6), UDP (17), IDMP(1), IGMP (2)).

▨ *Checksum*: This field includes the checksum over the fields of the IP packet header. The payload in the IP datagram is not checked, for efficiency reasons. In general, this check occurs within the transport protocol. The checksum has to be recomputed in each network node visited, because the IP header changes in each hop, in the TTL field. For this reason, it is important to use efficient checksums. A sender computes the 1's-complement sum of all 16-bit quantities in the header, excluding the checksum field itself, and then stores the 1's complement of the sum in the *CHECKSUM* field. A receiver computes the same 16-bit sum of values in the header, including the checksum field. If the checksum is correct, then the result is zero.

▨ *Sender and destination addresses*: These fields include the 32-bit Internet addresses of the sender and the receiver. Section 15.1.5 describes the address classes of the Internet Protocol.

▨ *Option and padding fields*: To keep the headers of datagrams small, IP defines a set of options that can be present, if needed. The header length is specified in 32-bit multiples; if options do not end on a 32-bit boundary, then *PADDING* that contains zero-bits is added to make the header a multiple of 32 bits. Section 14.3 describes all IP options.

14.1.3 Lifetime of an IP Data Packet

Faulty functions in the network can cause packets to circulate in the network rather than arriving at their destination address. These data packets consume valuable resources in the network, so they have to be destroyed by control mechanisms at some point in time.

The following method is used to destroy such packets: The TTL (*Time To Live*) field of the IP data header takes the number of routers (hops). This field is actually intended to specify the lifetime of a packet in seconds, but it is currently used to count the hops through the routers on the path. Each router reduces this value by 1, and the packet is rejected when the value 0 is reached. This prevents a packet that cannot be delivered from circulating forever. In addition, you can set a specific TTL value in the sender to limit the reach of a packet.

14.1.4 Addressing in the Internet

Three different addresses are used to reach a communication partner or an application in the Internet. These addresses identify a unique communication endpoint within the Internet and are often called *sockets*:

- The *IP address* specifies a unique computer in the Internet. Each computer in an IP network has to have a unique Internet address. Section 14.1.5 explains the structure of this address format and the set of different classes.
- The *transport protocol ID* specifies the transport protocol instance used (i.e., TCP, UDP, ICMP, etc.). The Internet Protocol uses this identifier to know which transport protocol is used.
- The *port number* identifies a unique and specific application within the TCP and UDP transport protocols (multiplexing).

The following section discusses the first part of the sockets defined above, IP addresses and their structure. The chapters dealing with the transport layer introduce and describe the TCP and UDP protocols, which are the most important transport protocols today. These chapters also explain the meaning of port numbers.

14.1.5 IP Addresses and IP Address Classes

Each network device in the Internet or in other IP-based networks has its own unique IP address. Computers connected to several networks concurrently (*multihomed hosts*) have a separate address for each network connection. These addresses are assigned by the *Internet Assigned Numbers Authority* (*IANA*) and their national representatives (e.g., *Reseau IP Europe—RIPE*). Notice that these addresses are not assigned on an individual basis, but in blocks by so-called *network classes*. If somebody needs an IP address to connect a computer to the Internet, then he or she will obtain a network address and an entire range of addresses. For this reason, each range of network addresses is managed within those addresses themselves.

Accordingly, IP addresses are structured in a hierarchy: They are divided into a *network part* and a *computer* or *host part*. Figure 14–3 shows the classes and their different network and host parts.

The network part identifies the network to which a station is connected. All computers within a network have the same network part. The computer part identifies a specified computer within a network. If a computer is connected to more than one network, then it has a separate IP address for each network.

IP addresses are 32 bits long and are normally written in dotted decimal notation (e.g., `129.13.42.117`). As was mentioned earlier, IP addresses are divided into several classes. The prefix of an IP address specifies the address class. The five classes of IP addresses are as follows:

- *Class A*: The first bit of the address is zero (i.e., the first byte is smaller than 128). The first byte is the network number, and the last three bytes identify a computer in the network. Accordingly, there are 126 class-A networks, which can manage up to 16 million computers in one network.

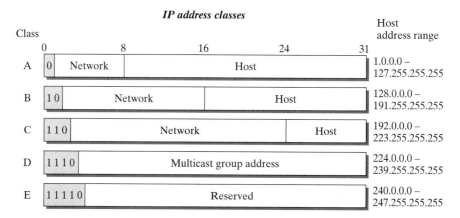

FIGURE 14–3
Address classes of the Internet Protocol.

▨ *Class B*: A value between 128 and 191 for the first byte (i.e., the first two bits are 10) identifies a class-B address. The first two bytes specify the network, and the last two bytes specify a computer in this network. This results in 16,382 class-B networks with up to 64,534 computers in any one network.

▨ *Class C*: This class uses values between 192 and 223 for the first byte (the first three bits have a value of 110). There are approximately two million class-C networks; the first three bytes are used for the network address and the last for up to 254 computers.

▨ *Class D*: Class-D addresses have a special meaning. They identify a group of computers that can be in different networks, rather than identifying a single computer or network adapter. Class-D addresses are also called *multicast addresses*. The first byte in a multicast address has a value in the range from 224 to 239; the first four bits are to 1110. When an application sends an IP packet to a class-D address, then the message is broadcast to all members of the addressed group. A special protocol, the *Internet Group Management Protocol* (*IGMP*), is used to manage such groups. Chapter 17 discusses IP multicast and IGMP.

▨ *Class E*: this last range of IP addresses, ranging from 240 to 254 in the first byte, is reserved for future use.

As mentioned earlier, IP addresses have to be unique within the Internet. For this reason, all network addresses are assigned by a central organization to ensure that all addresses are unique and visible in the Internet. However, this is not always required. Networks that do not connect to the global Internet do not need an address that is visible in the Internet. Also, it is not necessary that these addresses not be used in another private network. For this reason, address ranges were defined especially for private networks. These ranges are defined in RFC 1918. IP packets with private addresses may not be forwarded in the Internet. This means that private IP addresses can be used in an arbitrary number of nonpublic networks.

The following address ranges are reserved for use in private networks:

- The range from 10.0.0.0 to 10.255.255.254 was reserved in class A for private class-A networks.
- The range from 172.16.0.0 to 172.31.0.0 was reserved in class B for private class-B networks. This means that 16 class-B network are reserved for private use. Each of these networks can connect up to 65,534 computers.
- The range from 192.168.0.0 to 192.168.255.0, a total of 256 networks, was reserved in class C for private use. Each of these networks can connect up to 254 computers.

In addition, there are other reserved IP addresses with special meanings:

- The class-A network address 127 represents the loopback network device of a computer. IP packets to an address in the form 127.x.y.z are not output to a network adapter; they are processed locally.
- In addition to network addresses, computer addresses are also reserved for special use. The values 0 and 255 in computer addresses are reserved in all network classes.

An IP address with all bits of the computer part set to zero identifies the network itself. For example, the address 80.0.0.0 refers to the class-A network 80, and the address 128.66.0.0 refers to the class-B network 128.66.

An IP address where the computer part consists of 1-bits defines a broadcast address, which can be used to address all computers in a network.

14.2 IMPLEMENTING THE INTERNET PROTOCOL

This section explains the architecture of the IP instance in the Linux kernel. We will use the path a packet takes across the IP layer to introduce the basic properties of the Internet Protocol. We assume that this is a normal IP packet without special properties, to ensure that our explanations will be clear and easy to understand. All special functions of the Internet Protocol, such as fragmenting and reassembling, source routing, multicasting, and so on, will be described in the next chapters.

The objective of this section is to introduce the fundamental operation of the IP implementation in Linux, to be able to better understand more complex parts later on. This section also serves as an entry point into the other chapters of this book, because each packet passes the IP layer, where it can take a particular path (e.g., across a firewall or a tunnel). It is necessary to understand how the Internet Protocol is implemented in the Linux kernel to understand later chapters.

An IP packet can enter the IP instance in three different places:

- Packets arriving in a computer over a network adapter are stored in the input queue of the respective CPU, as described in Chapter 6. Once the layer-3 protocol in the data-link layer has been determined (which is ETH_PROTO_IP in this case), the packets are passed to the ip_rcv() function. The path these packets take will be described in Section 14.2.1.
- The second entry point for IP packets is at the interface to the transport protocols. These are packets used by TCP, UDP, and other protocols that use the IP protocol.

They use the `ip_queue_xmit()` function to pack a transport-layer PDU into an IP packet and send it. Other functions are available to generate IP packets at the boundary with the transport layer. These functions and the operation of `ip_queue_xmit()` will be described in Section 14.2.2.

▪ With the third option, the IP layer generates IP packets itself, on the Internet Protocol's initiative. These are mainly new multicast packets, new fragments of a large packet, and ICMP or IGMP packets that don't include a special payload. Such packets are created by specific methods (e.g., `icmp_send()`). (See Section 14.4.)

Once a packet (or socket buffer) has entered the IP layer, there are several options for how it can exit. We generally distinguish two different roles a computer can assume with regard to the Internet Protocol, where the first case is a special case of the second:

▪ *End system*: A Linux computer is normally configured as an end system—it is used as a workstation or server, assuming primarily the task of running user applications or providing application services. Also, a Web server and a network printer are nothing but end systems (with regard to the IP layer). The basic property of end systems is that they do not forward IP packets. This means that you can recognize an end system easily by the fact that it has only one network adapter. Even a system that has several network accesses can be configured as a host, if packet forwarding is disabled.

▪ *Router*: A router passes IP packets arriving in a network adapter to a second network adapter. This means that a router has several network adapters that forward packets between these interfaces. When packets arrive in a router, there are generally two options: they can deliver packets locally (i.e., deliver them to the transport layer) or they can forward them. The first case is identical with the procedure of packets arriving in an end system, where packets are always delivered locally. Consequently, a router can be thought of as a generalization of an end system, with the additional capability of forwarding packets. In contrast to end systems, generally no applications are started in routers, to ensure that packets can be forwarded as fast as possible.

Linux lets you enable and disable the packet-forwarding mechanism at runtime, provided that the forwarding support was integrated when the kernel was created. The directory `/proc/sys/net/ipv4/` includes a virtual file, `ip_forward`. You will see in Appendix B.3 that there is a way to change system settings from within the `proc` directory. If a 0 is written to this file, then packet forwarding is disabled. To activate IP packet forwarding, you can use the command `echo '1' > /proc/sys/net/ipv4/ip_forward`.

Figure 14–4 shows the path an IP packet takes across the Internet Protocol implementation in Linux. The gray ovals represent invoked functions, and the rectangles show the position of the netfilter hooks in the Internet Protocol.

The following sections describe different paths a packet can take across the IP implementation in the Linux kernel. We begin with incoming packets, which have to be either forwarded or delivered locally. The next section describes how packets are passed from the transport layer to IP.

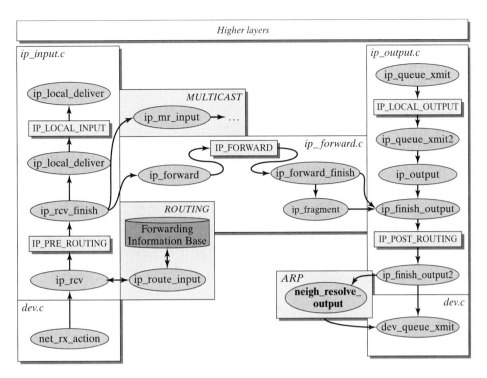

FIGURE 14-4
Architecture of the Internet Protocol implementation in Linux.

14.2.1   The Path of Incoming IP Packets

Chapter 6 introduced the path of an incoming packet up to the boundary of layer 3. Once the NET_RX tasklet has removed a packet from the input queue, netif_rx_action() chooses the appropriate layer-3 protocol. Next, the Internet Protocol is selected, and the ip_rcv() function is invoked on the basis of the identifier in the Ethernet protocol field (ETH_PROTO_IP) or from appropriate fields of other MAC transmission protocols.

ip_rcv( )	net/ipv4/ip_input.c

ip_rcv(skb, dev, pkt_type) does some work for the IP protocol. First, the function rejects packets not addressed to the local computer. For example, the promiscuous mode allows a network device to accept packets actually addressed to another computer. Such packets are filtered by the packet type (skb->pkt_type PACKET_OTHERHOST) in the lower layers.

Subsequently, the basic correctness criteria of a packet are checked:

▨ Does the packet have at least the size of an IP header?
▨ Is this IP Version 4?

     ■ Is the checksum correct?

     ■ Does the packet have a wrong length?

If the actual packet size does not match the information maintained in the socket buffer (skb->len), then the current packet data range is adapted by skb_trim(skb, iph->total_len). (See Section 4.1.) Now that the packet is correct, the netfilter hook NF_IP_PRE_ROUTING is invoked. Netfilter allows you to extend the procedure of various protocols by specific functions, if desired. Netfilter hooks always reside in strategic points of certain protocols and are used, for example, for firewall, QoS, and address-translation functions. These examples will be discussed in later chapters. A netfilter hook is invoked by a macro, and the function following the handling of the netfilter extension is passed to this macro in the form of a function pointer. If netfilter was not configured, then the macro ensures that there is a direct jump to this follow-up function. We can see in Figure 14–4 that the procedure continues with ip_rcv_finish(skb).

ip_rcv_finish( )	net/ipv4/ip_input.c

The function ip_route_input() is invoked within ip_rcv_finish(skb) to determine the route of a packet. The skb->dst pointer of the socket buffer is set to an entry in the routing cache, which stores not only the destination on the IP level, but also a pointer to an entry in the hard header cache (cache for layer-2 frame packet headers), if present. If ip_route_input() cannot find a route, then the packet is discarded.

In the next step, ip_rcv_finish() checks for whether the IP packet header includes options. If this is the case, then the options are analyzed, and an ip_options structure is created. All options set are stored in this structure in an efficient form. Section 14.3 describes how IP options are handled.

Finally in ip_rcv_finish(), the procedure of the IP protocol reaches the junction between packets addressed to the local computer and packets to be forwarded. The information about the further path of an IP packet is stored in the routing entry skb->dst. Notice that a trick often used in the Linux kernel is used here. If a switch (variable value) is used to select different functions, then we simply insert a pointer to each of these functions. This saves us an if or switch instruction for each decision of how the program should continue. In the example used here, the pointer skb->dst->input() points to the function that should be used to handle a packet further:

     ■ ip_local_deliver() is entered in the case of unicast and multicast packets that should be delivered to the local computer.

     ■ ip_forward() handles all unicast packets that should be forwarded.

     ■ ip_mr_input() is used for multicast packets that should be forwarded.

We can see from the above discussion that a packet can take different paths. The following section describes how packets to be forwarded are handled (skb->dst->input = ip_forward). Subsequently, we will see how skb->dst->input = ip_local_deliver handles packets to be delivery locally.

Forwarding Packets   If a computer has several network adapters, and if packet IP forwarding is enabled (`/proc/sys/net/ipv4/ip_forward 1`), then packets addressed to other computers are handled by the `ip_forward()` function. This function does all the work necessary for forwarding a packet. The most important task—routing—was already done in `ip_input()`, because it is necessary to be able to discover whether the packet is to be delivered locally or has to be forwarded.

`ip_forward( )`	**net/ipv4/ip_forward.c**

The primary task of `ip_forward(skb)` is to process a few conditions of the Internet Protocol (e.g., a packet's lifetime) and packet options. First, packets not marked with `pkt_type == PACKET_HOST` are deleted. Next, the reach of the packet is checked. If the value in its TTL field is 1 (before it is decremented), then the packet is deleted. RFC 791 specifies that, if such an action occurs, an ICMP packet has to be returned to the sender to inform the latter (`ICMP_TIME_EXCEEDED`).

Once a redirect message has been checked, if applicable, the socket buffer is checked to see if there is sufficient memory for the headroom. This means that the function `skb_cow(skb, headroom)` is used to check whether there is still sufficient space for the MAC header in the output network device (`out_dev->hard_header_len`). If this is not the case, then `skb_realloc_headroom()` creates sufficient space. Subsequently, the TTL field of the IP packet is decremented by one.

When the actual packet length (including the MAC header) is known, it is checked for whether it really fits into the frame format of the new output network device. If it is too long (`skb->len > mtu`), and if no fragmenting is allowed because the *Don't-Fragment* bit is set in the IP header, then the packet is discarded, and the ICMP message `ICMP_FRAG_NEEDED` is transmitted to the sender. In any case, the packet is not fragmented yet; fragmenting is delayed. The early test for such cases prevents potential *Don't-Fragment* candidates from running through the entire IP protocol-handling process, only to be dropped eventually.

`ip_forward_finish( )`	**net/ipv4/ip_forward.c**

We can see in Figure 14–4 that the `ip_forward()` function is split into two parts by a netfilter hook. Once the `NF_IP_FORWARD` hook has been processed, the procedure continues with `ip_forward_finish()`. This function has actually very little functionality (unless `FASTROUTE` is enabled). Once the IP options, if used, have been processed in `ip_forward_options()`, the `ip_send()` function is invoked to check on whether the packet has to be fragmented and to eventually do a fragmentation, if applicable. (See Section 14.2.3.)

`ip_send()`	**include/net/ip.h**

`ip_send(skb)` decides whether the packet should be passed to `ip_finish_output()` immediately or `ip_fragment()` should first adapt it to the appropriate layer-2 frame size. (See Section 14.2.3.)

---

ip_finish_output()   **net/ipv4/ip_output.c**

---

ip_finish_output(skb) initiates the last tasks of the Internet Protocol. First, the skb->dev pointer is set to the output network device dev, and the layer-2 packet type is set to ETH_P_IP. Subsequently, the netfilter hook NF_IP_POST_ROUTING is processed. The exact operation of netfilter and the set of different hooking points within the Internet Protocol are described in Section 19.3. It is common for netfilter hooks to continue with the inline function ip_finish_output2() after their invocation.

---

ip_finish_output2()   **net/ipv4/ip_output.c**

At this point, the packet leaves the Internet Protocol, and the Address Resolution Protocol (ARP) is used, if necessary. Chapter 15 describes the Address Resolution Protocol. For now, it is sufficient to understand the following:

- If the routing entry used (skb->dst) already includes a reference to the layer-2 header cache (dst->hh), then the layer-2 packet header is copied directly into the packet-data space of the socket buffer, in front of the IP packet header. The output() function used here is dev_queue_xmit(), which is invoked if the entry in the hardware header cache is valid. dev_queue_xmit() ensures that the socket buffer is sent immediately over the network device, dev.
- If there is no entry in the *hard header cache* yet, then the corresponding address-resolution routine is invoked, which is normally the function neigh_resolve_output().

The procedure described above was optimized so that a packet can pass the router quickly without special options. However, it became clear where there are junctions to the corresponding handling routines (e.g., netfilter, multicasting, ICMP, fragmenting, or IP packet options).

Delivering Packets Locally   The previous section described the route a packet travels when it has to be forwarded. If ip_route_input() is the selected route, then the packet is addressed to the local computer. In this case, branching is to ip_local_deliver() rather than to ip_forward(). This section describes the path of packets to be delivered locally.

At this point, too, instead of using a conditioned if instruction to distinguish the two options, a pointer (skb->dst->input()) is used, which points to ip_local_deliver() in this case. At the end of ip_input(), the procedure continues with the packet's local delivery.

---

ip_local_deliver()   **net/ipv4/ip_input.c**

The first (and only) task of ip_local_deliver(skb) is to reassemble fragmented packets, using ip_defrag(). Section 14.2.3 describes in detail how packets are fragmented and defragmented. For now, it is sufficient to understand that all fragments of a packet are collected over a certain period of time, until all fragments of an IP datagram have arrived, so that they can be passed upwards as a whole.

Subsequently, it is almost mandatory to call a netfilter hook (NF_IP_LOCAL_IN) when the procedure continues with the ip_local_deliver_finish() function.

ip_local_deliver_finish()	net/ipv4/ip_input.c

The packet has now reached the end of the Internet Protocol processing. It is checked to see whether the packet is intended for a *RAW-IP* socket; otherwise, the transport protocol has to be determined for further processing (*demultiplexing*).

All transport protocols are managed in the ipprot hash table on the IP layer in Linux. At the end of the IP processing, there is now a special data structure, instead of simple query sequences and simple commands. The reason lies mainly in the nature of the Internet Protocol. Unless a packet includes special options, IP processing is very simple, and so IP is efficient and easy to implement. The complexity of IP packet options normally necessitates several more complex *programming methods*.

The protocol ID of the IP header modulo (MAX_INET_PROTOS - 1) is used to calculate the hash value in the ipprot hash table. The hash table is organized so that there are no collisions. If a new transport protocol would ever have to be integrated, then the assignment in the hash table should be checked. If the corresponding transport protocol can be found, then the appropriate handling routine (*handler*) of the protocol is invoked. The following handling routines are most common:

- tcp_v4_rcv(): Transmission Control Protocol (TCP)
- udp_rcv(): User Datagram Protocol (UDP)
- icmp_rcv(): Internet Control Message Protocol (ICMP)
- igmp_rcv(): Internet Group Management Protocol (IGMP)

If no transport protocol can be found, then the packet either is passed to a *RAW* socket (if there is one) or it is dropped and an *ICMP Destination Unreachable* message is returned to the sender.

The chapters dealing with the TCP and UDP transport protocols describe how a packet is further handled in the transport layer. Chapter 17 describes IGMP packets, and ICMP packets are discussed in Section 14.4. The following section describes the path a packet takes as it passes from the transport layer to the Internet Protocol for transmission.

14.2.2 Transport-Layer Packets

Packets created locally and passed from the transport layer to the Internet Protocol are handled in a way totally separate from the procedures introduced so far. (See Figure 14–4.) First of all, there is not just one single function available to the transport layer, but several, including ip_queue_xmit() and ip_build_and_send_pkt(). Each of these functions is specialized and optimized for a specific use.

This section considers only the ip_queue_xmit() function, because this is the one normally used for data packets; ip_build_and_send_pkt() is used for SYN or ACK packets that do not transport payload.

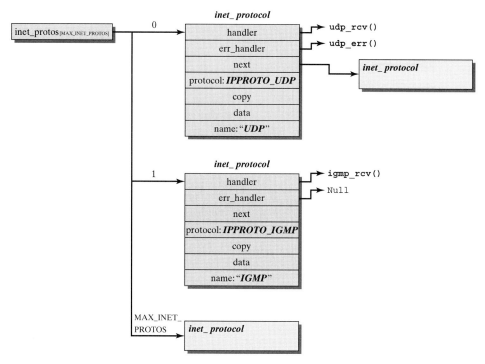

FIGURE 14–5
Hash table used to multiplex transport protocols.

`ip_queue_xmit()`	**net/ipv4/ip_output.c**

At the beginning, `ip_queue_xmit(skb)` checks for whether the socket structure `sk->dst` includes a pointer to an entry in the routing cache and, if so, whether this pointer is actually valid. The route for a packet is stored in the `skb->sk` socket structure, because all packets of a socket go to the same destination. Storing a reference means that expensive searches for routes can be avoided.

If no route is present yet (e.g., when the first packet of a socket is ready), then the `ip_route_output()` function is used to choose a route. Once this route has been entered in the routing cache, its *use counter* is incremented to ensure that the route is not inadvertently deleted as long as there is still a socket buffer referencing it.

Subsequently, the fields of the IP packet are filled (version, header length, TOS field, fragment offset, TTL, addresses, and protocol). Next, `ip_options_build()` handles options, if present, and the netfilter hook `NF_IP_LOCAL_OUTPUT` is invoked.

`ip_queue_xmit2()`	**net/ipv4/ip_output.c**

The next function, `ip_queue_xmit2(dev)` of the netfilter hook `NF_IP_LOCAL_OUTPUT`, sets the output network device as specified in the routing cache entry. Now it is necessary to check once more how much headroom is available in the socket buffer, although the buffer reservation is already complete. Also, it is necessary to learn the network device used and its MTU size. Unfortunately, it can happen that a socket buffer was created for the device `dev1` (with `mtu1`), but the route has changed in the meantime, and the packet is sent over device `dev2` with a smaller MTU. This means that, infrequently, the available headroom has to be increased. Subsequently, the packet is checked for fragmentation, and the checksum is computed (`ip_send_check(iph)`).

Subsequently, the packet created locally crosses the path for forwarding packets. The function pointer `dst->output()`, which is set during the routing process, causes the `ip_output()` function to be invoked, which executes the last steps in the Internet Protocol, primarily guiding the packet across the netfilter hook `NF_IP_POST_ROUTING`.

14.2.3 Fragmenting Packets

The Internet Protocol has to be capable of adapting the size of IP packets to the respective network type in order to be able to send IP datagrams over any type of network. Each network has a maximum packet size, which is called *Maximum Transfer Unit (MTU)*. Only packets within this size can be transported over the network. For example, if packets have to be sent over a token-ring network, they must not be larger than 4500 bytes, and 1500 bytes must not be exceeded by Ethernet packets. If the MTU of a transmission medium is smaller than the size of a packet, then the packet has to be split into smaller IP packets.

However, it is not sufficient to let the transport-layer protocols transmit smaller packets independently. The reason is that a packet can traverse several networks with a different MTU each on the way from the source host to the destination host. This means that we need a more flexible method that can create smaller packets, also in a router, on the IP layer. This method is called *fragmenting*.

Fragmenting means that the IP protocol in each IP computer (router or end system) has to be capable of splitting incoming packets, if necessary, and to transport them over a subnetwork (with a smaller MTU) all the way to the destination computer. In addition, each end system must be able to put these fragments together to rebuild the original packet. This method is called *reassembling*.

Each fragment of a split IP datagram is treated like an independent IP packet and contains a complete IP packet header. The Fragment ID field in the IP packet header can be used to identify all fragments of an IP datagram and to allocate them to their original datagram. However, the Fragment ID field alone is not a unique key to identify fragments arriving from different computers. For this reason, the following packet header fields are used additionally sender address, destination address, and protocol.

All the fragments of a datagram can take different paths to travel to the destination computer, and they may be fragmented more than once along these paths. The position of a fragment's data within the original IP datagram is marked by the Fragment Offset field. All fragments, except the last one, have the *MF (More Fragments)* bit set, which means that more fragments are to follow. Figure 14–6 shows the example of an IP datagram that has to be fragmented several times.

We will describe below how fragmenting and reassembling of IP datagrams is implemented in the Linux kernel. Remember that IP packets can be fragmented in each IP node along the path to the destination (router or end system), but can be reassembled only in the destination computer.

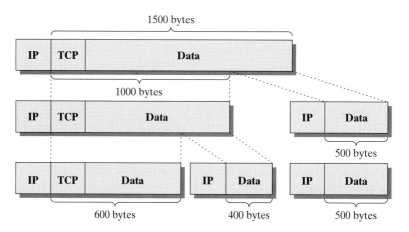

FIGURE 14–6
Fragmenting an IP datagram.

Fragmenting Large IP Datagrams

`ip_fragment()`	**net/ipv4/ip_output.c**

`ip_fragment(skb, output)` is responsible for fragmenting an IP datagram into smaller IP packets, if the IP datagram is too big to be transmitted over the network device. The size for the new—smaller—packets is selected so that they do not exceed the maximum frame length of the transmission medium.

First, the maximum packet size is computed, and then IP fragments are created in a `while` loop until the datagram has been completely divided into smaller packets. Next, `alloc_skb()` is used to create a new socket buffer for each new fragment. Initially, the IP packet header is copied from the original packet to the new one, and then the payload to be transported in this fragment is copied to the fragment. It should be mentioned once more that previously fragmented datagrams can be fragmented again in one or more routers later along the path. Subsequently, the new value for the Fragment Offset field has to be set in the new fragment. This field specifies the position of payload in the original IP datagram. Also, the *MF* bit has to be set, unless it is the last fragment. Before the `output()` function (pointer to the transmit function set in the routing process) can send the packet, the function `ip_options_fragment()` handles IP options, if present, and `ip_send_check()` computes the checksum.

Once all fragments have been created, the original packet is released by `kfree_skb()`.

Collecting and Reassembling Packets   Fragmented IP datagrams are reassembled in the end system only. To this end, the function `ip_local_deliver()` passes all fragmented IP packets to `ip_defrag()`. The fragments are then managed in the fragment cache, until either all fragments of a datagram have arrived, so that the packet can be delivered to the local machine, or the maximum wait time for the fragments of a datagram (`ipfrag_time`, ~30 seconds) has expired, which means that the datagram will be discarded. The fragment cache consists of a hash table with `ipq` structures. Each of these `ipq` structures represents a fragmented IP datagram. The individual fragments of the datagram are collected in a linked list (`fragments`). All fragments of a datagram are ordered in the same sequence as they occur in the original packet. (See Figure 14–7.)

The parameters of the `ipq` structure have the following meaning:

- `next` and `pprev` are used to link `ipq` structures in a hash row. This means that this is a doubly linked list and a linear collision resolution in the hash table.
- The `saddr`, `daddr`, `id`, and `protocol` elements are keys for the hash function and the allocation of incoming fragments to their IP datagrams.
- `last_in` stores a flag that specifies whether all fragments have arrived and whether the first and the last fragments of a datagram have arrived.
- `fragments` is a list of linked socket buffers that stores all incoming fragments in the sequence required later to reassemble the complete datagram.
- `len` specifies the length of the original IP datagram, and `meat` specifies the number of bytes already stored in the fragment cache. When `meat` reaches the value of `len`, then all fragments of the datagram have arrived, and the fragment can be reassembled.
- `lock` is used to protect against parallel operations on the `ipq` data structure.

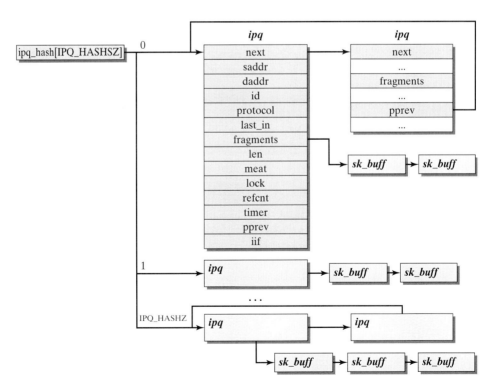

FIGURE 14–7
A fragment cache manages all incoming IP fragments.

- timer is a pointer to a `timer_list` structure. The associated timer restarts when the `IPFRAG_TIME` interval expires, and it checks for whether all fragments have arrived.
- iif contains an index to the network device and is used for ICMP replies.

The following functions are used to reassemble fragmented IP datagrams:

`ipq_unlink()`	**net/ipv4/fragment.c**

`ipq_unlink(qp)` removes the `ipq` entry from the fragment cache referenced by the `qp` pointer. The counter for arrived fragments, `ip_frag_nqueues`, is decremented by 1.

`ipq_frag_destroy()`	**net/ipv4/fragment.c**

`ip_frag_destroy(qp)` releases an `ipq` fragment list. First, `frag_kfree_skb()` releases all socket buffers of individual fragments. Subsequently, `frag_free_queue()` releases the `ipq` structure of the fragment cache.

`ip_evictor()`	**net/ipv4/ip_fragment.c**

`ip_evictor()` is invoked by `ip_defrag()` when fragmented packets use too much memory. Normally, the threshold for maximum memory in the fragment cache (`sysctl_ipfrag_high_thresh`) is 256 Kbytes. Next, all hash rows of the fragment cache are checked within this function, and entries are deleted. More specifically, `ipq` structures and their socket buffers are deleted until the bottom threshold (normally 192 Kbytes) is reached.

The two threshold values, `ipfrag_high_thresh` and `ipfrag_low_thresh`, and the maximum wait time for fragments, `ipfrag_time`, can be changed from within the proc directory (`/proc/sys/net/ipv4`).

`ip_expire()`	**net/ipv4/ip_fragment.c**

`ip_expire()` is a handling routine for the timer that starts for the fragments of an IP datagram. If this timer expires before all fragments of the packet have arrived, the entry in the fragment cache is deleted. This function does nothing, if all fragments have been received (`COMPLETE`).

If some fragments are still missing, but at least the first one is present, then an ICMP error message of the type (`ICMP_TIME_EXCEEDED/ICMP_EXC_FRAGTIME`) is sent, and then the IP datagram is discarded.

`ip_frag_create()`	**net/ipv4/ip_fragment.c**

`ip_frag_create(hash, iph)` creates a new entry in the fragment cache and uses the parameters from the IP packet header of the fragment that just arrived to initialize this entry. The new entry represents an IP datagram that could not be transmitted fully and had to be fragmented. This entry is created when the first fragment of an

IP datagram arrives and is held in the fragment cache until either the wait time for all fragments (IP_FRAG_TIME) expires or all fragments of that IP datagram have arrived.

ip_find()	net/ipv4/ip_fragment.c

ip_find(iph) searches the fragment cache for the ipq entry for an IP datagram with the iph packet header. To this end, ipqhashfn() is used to compute the hash value of this entry from the sender address, destination address, protocol ID, and fragment IP from the packet header fields. Based on these parameters, different fragmented datagrams can be distinguished, and incoming fragments can be allocated to each datagram. Collisions of several ipq structures with identical hash values are resolved linearly in a doubly linked list. (See Figure 14–7.) If ip_find() cannot find a matching entry for the iph fragment, then a new ipq entry is created in the fragment cache (ip_frag_create()).

ip_frag_queue()	net/ipv4/fragment.c

ip_frag_queue(qp, skb) orders a new fragment, as it arrives, within the queue of fragments for an IP datagram (represented by the ipq structure qp). The function checks first for whether the datagram is complete, which would mean that a new fragment is a duplicate. If this is not the case, the position (offset and end) of the fragment in the original IP datagram is computed from the Fragment Offset parameter in the IP packet header. Subsequently, the MF flag is used to check on whether this is the last fragment of a datagram (LAST_IN is set).

Subsequently, the list of received fragments (pq->fragments) is searched for the correct position, and the socket buffer is placed at this position. The meat parameter in the ipq structure of the datagram is increased by the length corresponding to the fragment just added. As mentioned earlier, the meat parameter specifies the number of bytes received for a fragmented IP datagram.

ip_frag_reasm()	net/ipv4/ip_fragment.c

This function is invoked by ip_defrag(); it reassembles all fragments of a packet (qp->len == qp->meat) arrived and treats them as a single IP datagram. First, a new socket buffer with a headroom of length qp->len is created, and the IP datagram header is initialized. Next, the IP payload of each single fragment is copied to the headroom of the new socket buffer.

ip_defrag()	net/ipv4/ip_fragment.c

The ip_defrag(skb) method is invoked in ip_local_deliver() for each IP fragment. As described in Section 14.2.1, this path of the Internet Protocol is taken only by packets to be delivered to the local machine (i.e., fragmented IP datagrams are reassembled in the destination system).

The first thing here is to check on whether there is sufficient buffer space in the fragment cache for the new fragment. If this is not the case, then ip_evictor() removes entries until the bottom threshold value, `sysctl_ipfrag_low_thresh`, is reached. Subsequently, `ip_find()` searches the fragment cache for the relevant entry. As mentioned earlier, a new `ipq` structure is created as soon as the first fragment of an IP datagram arrives.

Finally, `ip_frag_queue()` adds the new fragment to the list of present fragments. As soon as all fragments of the IP datagram have arrived, which can be checked by `pq->len == pq->meat`, reassembly of the datagram (`ip_frag_reasm()`) can start.

14.2.4   Data of the IP Instance

The primary task of an IP instance (in a router) is to forward IP packets. To this end, several network devices have to be configured for the IP instance. These network devices (*INET devices*), which are to be used by the Internet Protocol, are managed mainly by the functions stored in the file `net/ipv4/devinet.c`. We will call these network devices *IP network devices* in the further course of our discussion.

This section is aimed at briefly introducing the structure of IP network-device management. This point represents the binding member between several functions of the Internet Protocol. For example, the data structures introduced below can be used to manage IP addresses and network devices of the IP instance and active multicast groups or different IP configuration parameters (Packet forwarding permitted?, Accept redirect packets?, etc.).

The data structure `in_device` represents the starting point for IP network device management:

`struct in_device`	**include/linux/inetdevice.h**

An `in_device` structure is created for each network device that was configured for the Internet Protocol. This structure manages the configuration data for this IP network device. Figure 14–8 shows that the `net_device` structures of IP network devices have an `ip_ptr` parameter each, which references the pertaining `in_device` structure. There is no explicit list for IP network devices. The list is accessed with `dev_base`.

The file `net/ipv4/devinet.c` includes functions to manage IP network devices, including `inetdev_init()` to initialize an IP network device.

The structure and the elements of the `in_device` structure are as follows:

```
struct in_device
{
    struct net_device          *dev;
    atomic_t refcnt;
    rwlock_t lock;
    int dead;
    struct in_ifaddr *ifa_list; /* IP ifaddr chain */
    struct ip_mc_list *mc_list; /* IP multicast filter chain */
    unsigned long mr_v1_seen;
    struct neigh_parms *arp_parms;
    struct ipv4_devconf cnf;
};
```

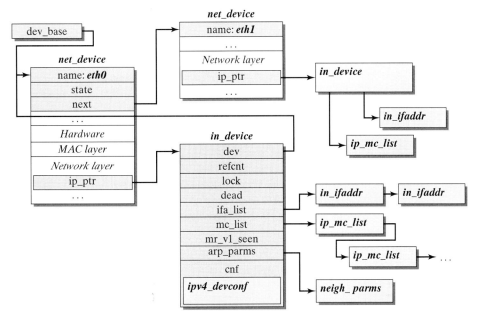

FIGURE 14–8
Data structures to manage IP network devices and their parameters.

▓ dev points to the net_device structure of the network device configured for the Internet Protocol.

▓ refcnt stores the number of references to this structure, or the number of instances currently used by this IP network device. The refcnt variable essentially is changed by the functions in_dev_get() and in_dev_put(). (Both are defined in <linux/inetdevice.h>.)

▓ lock is used to protect against errors caused by parallel manipulation in the in_device structure.

▓ dead shows whether the IP network device is still valid.

▓ ifa_list points to a list of in_ifaddr structures, which stores the IP addresses of this IP network device. This is a list, because Linux lets you allocate more than one IP address to a network device (*alias* function).

In addition to the IP address (ifa_address), the in_ifaddr structure stores other parameters (e.g., the subnet mask (ifa_mask), the broadcast address (ifa_address), etc.). The content of the in_ifaddr structure is as follows:

```
struct in_ifaddr
{
    struct in_ifaddr     *ifa_next;
    struct in_device     *ifa_dev;
    u32                  ifa_local;
    u32                  ifa_address;
```

```
        u32                     ifa_mask;
        u32                     ifa_broadcast;
        u32                     ifa_anycast;
        unsigned char           ifa_scope;
        unsigned char           ifa_flags;
        unsigned char           ifa_prefixlen;
        char                    ifa_label[IFNAMSIZ];
    };
```

▨ mc_list is a list consisting of ip_mc_list structures. Each element in this list stores information for an IP multicast group to which the IP instance is currently subscribed, and receives it over the current network device. Section 17.4.1 describes the content of the ip_mc_list structure.

▨ mr_v1_seen is used by IGMP. (See Section 17.3.)

▨ arp_parms points to a structure of the type neigh_parms, which stores the most important parameters of the ARP protocol. (See Chapter 15.)

▨ cnf points to an ipv4_devconf structure, which stores important settings for the IP instance. ipv4_devconf is described below.

---

struct ipv4_devconf   **include/linux/inetdevice.h**

The ipc4_devconf data structure can be used to activate or deactivate various properties of the IP instance for an IP network device. For this purpose, the proc directory /proc/sys/net/ipv4/conf includes a subdirectory for each IP network device, from which the properties mentioned below can be set. These properties will then be described briefly below. Appendix B discusses all proc entries for the Internet Protocol.

```
struct ipv4_devconf
{
        int             accept_redirects;
        int             send_redirects;
        int             secure_redirects;
        int             shared_media;
        int             accept_source_route;
        int             rp_filter;
        int             proxy_arp;
        int             bootp_relay;
        int             log_martians;
        int             forwarding;
        int             mc_forwarding;
        int             tag;
        int             arp_filter;
        void            *sysctl;
};
```

▨ accept_redirects accepts ICMP redirect packets.

▨ send_redirects enables the transmission of ICMP redirect packets.

- `secure_redirects` accepts ICMP redirect messages.
- `accept_source_route` accepts Source Route packets.
- `rp_filter` disables the sender IP address check.
- `proxy_arp` supports an ARP proxy.
- `log_martians` enables or disables the logging of "strange" addresses ("Martians"— see Section 16.2.2).
- `forwarding` enables this network device to forward packets.
- `mc_forwarding` enables multicast routing or forwarding over this IP network device.

14.2.5 Auxiliary Functions for the Internet Protocol

The functions introduced in the previous sections operate mainly in the data path of the Internet Protocol: They process incoming IP packets. In addition to these functions, there are other things to be done in the Internet Protocol that do not directly relate to socket buffers or IP packets. These auxiliary functions are introduced below.

Managing Transport Protocols   The Internet Protocol operates on the network layer and offers an unreliable datagram service for the transport layer. In general, the TCP and UDP protocols are used in the transport layer. However, a layer-based architectural model should also allow us to use our own protocols. The Linux network architecture allows you to do that. You can register and use new protocols on top of the IP layer. In connection with kernel modules, this represents a flexible and highly dynamic property of the Linux network architecture.

The Linux kernel includes two functions, `inet_add_protocol()` and `inet_del_protocol()`, which will be described below, to manage transport-layer protocols. Appendix F includes an example for a rudimentary transport protocol, which does nothing but output the length of incoming transport-layer PDUs.

`inet_add_protocol()`	**net/ipv4/protocol.c**

All protocols arranged immediately on top of the Internet Protocol are managed in a hash table, `inet_protos`. `inet_add_protocol(prot)` registers a new protocol for the transport layer and adds it to the `inet_protos` hash table. The required protocol information is passed in the `prot` structure of the type `inet_protocol` (as shown in Figure 14–5):

- `handler()` is a function pointer to the entry function of the transport protocol (handling routine), for example the `tcp_v4_rcv()` for TCP. The parameters passed here include the socket buffer and the length of the transport-layer PDU. Appendix F includes an example of a very simple transport protocol. All it does is output the length of a PDU.
- `err_handler()` is a handling routine for error cases. It is invoked only once in the current implementation, in the method `icmp_unreach()`.

- next is used to link `inet_protocol` structures in a hash table.
- `id` is the protocol identifier of the registered protocol. In the future, if an IP packet with this identifier in the protocol field of the IP packet header arrives, then it is passed to the `handler()` handling routine. If several protocols with the same `id` are registered, then a copy of the socket buffer is passed to each of these protocols.
- The copy bit specifies whether another protocol is registered with the same protocol ID. If a protocol with the same protocol ID is already registered when you register a new protocol, then the new protocol is also added to the hash table, and the copy bit of all previous protocols with the same ID is set to one. In this case, all protocols with the same ID get a copy of the packet.
- `data` points to private data of the protocol, if present. However, it is not used by any of the implemented protocols (TCP, UDP, ICMP, and IGMP).
- name stores the name of the protocol in a string.

The Linux kernel currently implements four protocols on the transport layer, where only TCP and UDP are actually true transport protocols. Though ICMP and IGMP also use IP to exchange data, they are normally thought of as belonging to the network layer.

`inet_del_protocol()`	**net/ipv4/protocol.c**

`inet_del_protocol(prot)` removes the protocol, together with the passed pointer to an `inet_protocol` structure, from the hash table `inet_protos`. If there is a second protocol with the same protocol ID, then the **copy** bit of this protocol is checked and deleted, if applicable.

Useful Functions

`in_ntoa()`	**net/ipv4/utils.c**

`in_ntoa(in)` converts the IP address into the dotted decimal form, which is easier to read for humans (i.e., the 32-bit address 0x810D2A75 is converted into the string 129.13.42.117).

`in_aton()`	**net/ipv4/utils.c**

`in_aton(str)` converts the string `str` into a 32-bit IP address.

14.3   IP OPTIONS

When a packet is sent to the IP layer, then it normally includes all required information in the packet's protocol header. However, there could be times when packets require additional information in the protocol header—for example, for diagnostics purposes, or if a packet's path across the Internet is specified before it is sent. For these purposes, an Option field with variable length can be added to each IP packet header. All guidelines for these IP options are described in [Post81c].

14.3.1   Standardized IP Packet Options

Figure 14–9 shows that the IP packet options are appended to the end of an IP header. The length of the Option field is variable, and the end of a packet header has to be aligned to a 32-bit boundary, so an additional *padding field* of the appropriate length is added (and set to 0 by default). In this case, "variable" also means that the packet options can be left out, if they are not required. The Option field can take one or several packet options, where an option can be given in either of two formats:

▪ One single byte describes only the option type. The length of these options is always exactly one byte.

▪ The first byte includes the option type, and the second byte contains the length of this packet option. The following bytes include the actual data of that option.

The byte stating the length of the packet option in the second case includes merely the number of data bytes. The first two bytes are not counted. The option type in the first byte is composed as follows:

Copy Flag	Option Class	Option Number

The (1-bit) *copy flag* is required for packet fragmentation. If a packet has to be fragmented, then this bit states whether this packet option has to appear in all fragments or may be set in the first fragment only.

The *option class* is represented by 2 bits. The (5-bit) *option number* shows the length of a packet option implicitly (i.e., we can see whether the next byte also belongs to this packet option or already belongs to the next packet option). Table 14–1 lists all IP packet options defined in RFC 791, including their lengths and their defined option numbers and option classes. There are four option classes in total, but only two are currently used. Option class 0 includes packet options for control and management; option class 2 includes debugging and measurement options. The option classes 1 and 3 are reserved for future IP packet-option classes.

Version	IHL	TOS	Total Length	
Identification			Flags	Fragment Offset
TTL		Protocol	Header Checksum	
Source Address				
Destination Address				
Options (optional)			Padding	
Data				

FIGURE 14–9
The IP packet header.

TABLE 14–1   Defined IP packet options.

Class	Number	Length	Name
0	0	–	End of Option List
0	1	–	No Operation
0	2	11	Security
0	3	var	Loose Source Routing
0	9	var	Strict Source Routing
0	7	var	Record Route
0	8	4	Stream ID
2	4	var	Internet Timestamp

We will discuss each of these IP packet options in the following sections.

End of Option List
Bit sequence:

```
?0000000
```

This packet option marks the end of a series of options; it is appended to the last packet option and must never be between any other pair of options. The *End-of-Option-List* packet option is superfluous if the end of the option list is aligned at a 32-bit boundary. (See Figure 14–9.) The question mark at the beginning of this bit sequence corresponds to the *copy flag*, which was described above. If fragmentation is necessary, then this option can be copied, inserted, or deleted, depending on the number of packet options in the fragments of an IP datagram. It then has to be inserted into a fragment—for example, if only a part of the original options has to be copied, and the end of the new option list no longer matches the 32-bit boundary.

No Operation
Bit sequence:

```
?0000001
```

No Operation can be between any two packet options, for example to let the second option begin at a 32-bit boundary. If fragmentation is necessary, then this option can be copied, inserted or deleted. Like the *End-of-Option List* option, this option can always be inserted into a fragment, if only some of the original options are copied and if a packet option must begin at a 32-bit boundary.

Security
Bit sequence:

10000010	00001011	Security	
Compartments		Restrictions	
Transmission Control Code			

The *Security* option is used primarily in military networks; it comprises a total of 11 bytes. The *Security* option allows end systems to send security parameters or define own (controllable) groups of communication partners, which want to exchange IP packets "in isolation" from all other traffic. The two-byte *Security* field can be used to state 16 security levels for an IP packet; of these, the original RFC 791 defines eight levels, including *Unclassified*, *Confidential*, *Restricted*, *Secret* or *Top Secret*. The other security levels are reserved for future use. As the One in the first bit (corresponding to the *Copy Flag*) of this packet option already states, this packet option has to be set in each fragment, if IP packets are fragmented.

These fields are primarily specified by the *Defense Intelligence Agency*. For this reason, the current implementation in Linux does not support the *Security* option.

Loose Source Routing
Bit sequence:

10000011	Length	Pointer	Route Data

This option is used to specify all routers an IP packet has to visit on its way across the network. In addition, it accepts data about the packet's path. The third byte includes a pointer to the address of the next router that the packet has to pass. This pointer is relative to this option—the smallest possible value is four. If the pointer points to a byte not belonging to this option according to the length byte, then the packet can be sent over an arbitrary path to the actual destination address. In contrast, if the packet has reached the address specified in the destination address field, yet the pointer still points to another valid address, then the destination address field is overwritten with this address. The pointer is incremented by the length of an IP address, 4 bytes. The consequence of this replacement strategy is that the protocol header of the IP packet maintains a constant length all the time. In contrast to the *Record Route* packet option, addresses are defined exclusively by the sender; no addresses are entered by intermediate systems.

If the packet has to be fragmented, then this packet option has to be copied to each packet fragment, because the fragments are forwarded independently of one another, which means that they can reach the receiver over different paths across the Internet.

Strict Source Routing
Bit sequence:

10001001	Length	Pointer	Route Data

The *Strict Source Routing* option differs in only one point from the *Loose Source Routing* option: The packet may pass exactly those routers specified in the Route Data list. If a packet arrives in a router not explicitly present in this list, then an ICMP message has to be generated and returned to the sender. Section 14.4 describes the *Internet Control Message Protocol* (ICMP).

As with the previous option, if fragmentation is required, then the Strict Source Routing option has to be copied in each single fragment, which means that One is in the first position of this option.

Record Route
Bit sequence:

00000111	Length	Pointer	Route Data

The *Record Route* option can be used to register the addresses of all intermediate systems an IP packet will pass on its way to the destination. The third byte includes a pointer to the field that is to accept the next address. The length of this option should never change; the sender specifies twice the available space, which is initially filled with zeros. These zeros are not treated as an *End of Option List*, because the length byte, Length, states the option's length. Each Internet node adds its address in a field specially provided for this purpose and increases the pointer by four [bytes] (corresponding to the length of an IP address). If no more space is available, then the IP packet is forwarded without storing the address. In this case, an ICMP message can be returned to the sender.

In contrast to the two previous packet options (i.e., *Loose Source Routing* and *Strict Source Routing*), this option appears only in the first fragment, if an IP packet has to be fragmented.

Stream Identifier
Bit sequence:

10001000	00000010	Stream ID

This option enables the transport of *SATNET Stream Identifiers* across the Internet. The *Stream Identifier* packet option is always 4 bytes long and has to be copied to all fragments, if fragmentation is used. However, this option currently has no practical use, and we list it here only for the sake of completeness.

Internet Timestamp
Bit sequence:

01000100	Length	Pointer	Counter	Flag
Address				
Timestamp				

The original RFC 791 includes the *Internet Timestamp* option as the only packet option of class 2 (i.e., debugging or measurement options). This option can be used to store time stamps of selected or all network nodes. A 4-bit flag determines the data to be stored here, and it can take either of the following values:

- 0—The option stores time stamps only.
- 1—The option stores all time stamps and addresses.
- 2—A router completes its timestamp only if its address is listed in this option.

Notice that the size of the *Internet Timestamp* option does not change, because the sender specifies it previously in the length field. For this reason, there is an additional (4-bit) `Counter` field, which includes the number of all routers for the time stamps of which there was no more space in the data field. The maximum length of this option is 40 bytes. The third byte points to the next four or eight bytes to be filled with an entry.

If fragmentation is required, this option appears in the first fragment only, and so the *Copy Flag* is set to 0.

14.3.2   Configuration

User Access   Each Linux user can use the `traceroute` command to track an IP packet on its way across the Internet to the destination node. This might suggest that the *Record Route* IP packet option is used in this case. Actually, this is not so; the `traceroute` command uses another method, for several reasons:

- Formerly, not all routers supported the *Record Route* packet option, which means that they wouldn't have been available for use.
- Record Route is normally intended for one-way use only—the receiver has to return an echo of the IP packet it received to the sender. This means that the recorded addresses would have to be duplicated.
- However, the main reason is lack of space: A maximum of nine IP addresses fits into the address list of the Option field. Formerly, this might have been sufficient, but today the average number of intermediate systems for a connection across the Internet is much higher.

For these reasons, `traceroute` uses the *Internet Control Message Protocol* (ICMP; see Section 14.4) and the *Time-to-Live* (TTL) field of the IP header, which stores the remaining lifetime of the packet. It sends consecutive ICMP packets with the same destination address and increments the value in the TTL field at each step. The first packet gets a lifetime of one (i.e., the first Internet node returns an ICMP message to the sender as soon as it receives the packet). The sender receives an ICMP message also from each of the next receivers, so that it can follow the path to the destination address. However, a trick has to be used at the destination address, because the receiver looks at the lifetime only if the packet is not delivered locally. For this purpose, the UDP port number is set to a meaningless value to cause the receiver to return the ICMP message *Port Unreachable*.

Notice, however, that this method works only because all IP packets from a sender normally take the same path through the Internet to reach the receiver in most cases. It was actually intended to let a user run the `traceroute` command to access the packet option *Strict Source Routing* or *Loose Source Routing*. When the first version of `traceroute` included this option, many system administrators found that it results in an excessive load on most routers. Consequently, to use these packet options today, we need a corresponding patch.

The following example uses the *Loose Source Routing* option:

```
# traceroute -g 129.13.92.254 rzstud1.rz.uni-karlsruhe.de
traceroute to rzstud1.rz.uni-karlsruhe.de (129.13.197.1), 30 hops max,
40 byte packets
1 rzasc01.rz.uni-karlsruhe.de (129.13.92.1) 20 ms 20 ms 20 ms
2 r-ascend-netz.rz.uni-karlsruhe.de (129.13.92.254) 20 ms 20 ms 20 ms
3 rzstud1.rz.uni-karlsruhe.de (129.13.197.1) 213 ms 22 ms 24 ms}
```

Because the traceroute command, which is normally installed in Linux, does not let a user access the IP packet options, another way to use it would be the ping command. ping is intended to verify that a host is reachable. For this purpose, it continually sends ICMP requests to the destination computer and expects a reply in the form of an ICMP message. Today, there are still ping implementations that allow you to use the packet options *Source Routing* and *Internet Timestamp*. For the same reasons as with traceroute, the *Internet Timestamp* option was removed from most implementations, which means that only the *Record Route* option remained. The following example shows how you can use ping with the *Record Route* packet option set. The route is output after the first request.

```
# ping -R rzstud1.rz.uni-karlsruhe.de
PING rzstud1.rz.uni-karlsruhe.de (129.13.197.1): 56 data bytes
64 bytes from 129.13.197.1: icmp_seq=0 ttl=253 time=235.977 ms
RR: isdn216-10.rz.uni-karlsruhe.de (129.13.216.10)
      rzasc01.rz.uni-karlsruhe.de (129.13.92.1)
      129.13.197.62
      rzstud1.rz.uni-karlsruhe.de (129.13.197.1)
      r-ascend-netz.rz.uni-karlsruhe.de (129.13.92.254)
      rzasc01.rz.uni-karlsruhe.de (129.13.92.1)
      isdn216-10.rz.uni-karlsruhe.de (129.13.216.10)
64 bytes from 129.13.197.1: icmp_seq=1 ttl=253 time=47.171 ms (same route)
64 bytes from 129.13.197.1: icmp_seq=2 ttl=253 time=48.728 ms (same route)
--- rzstud1.rz.uni-karlsruhe.de ping statistics ---
9 packets transmitted, 9 packets received, 0% packet loss
round-trip min/avg/max = 45.100/70.545/235.977 ms
```

If a user at the local computer has root rights, then the *verbose mode* of tcpdump lets the user additionally view the packet options of all IP packets. tcpdump monitors the data traffic at a network adapter. The following example uses tcpdump in verbose mode to monitor the previous ping example.

```
# tcpdump -v
User level filter, protocol ALL, datagram packet socket
tcpdump: listening on ippp0
15:37:56.025267 isdn216-10.rz.uni-karlsruhe.de > rzstud1.rz.uni-karlsruhe.de:
icmp: echo request (ttl 64, id 1284, optlen=40 RR{isdn216-10.rz.uni-
```

karlsruhe.de#0.0.0.0 0.0.0.0 0.0.0.0 0.0.0.0 0.0.0.0 0.0.0.0 0.0.0.0 0.0.0.0}
EOL)
15:37:56.261172 rzstud1.rz.uni-karlsruhe.de > isdn216-10.rz.uni-karlsruhe.de:
icmp: echo reply (ttl 253, id 28562, optlen=40 RR{isdn216-10.rz.uni-
karlsruhe.de rzasc01.rz.uni-karlsruhe.de 129.13.197.62 rzstud1.rz.uni-
karlsruhe.de r-ascend-netz.rz.uni-karlsruhe.de rzasc01.rz.uni-karlsruhe.de#
0.0.0.0 0.0.0.0 0.0.0.0} EOL)

Programming Access   We will use the ping program once more in another example to show you how IP packet options can be accessed during programming. This example uses Version 1.38. When ping starts, the first thing is to check the parameters passed. If they include -R, then the *Echo Request* packet has to include the *Record Route* IP option. For this purpose, ping uses the setsockopt() function to inform an existing socket about packet options.

The following example shows you how this function is invoked from within the source code of ping:

```
if (setsockopt (s, IPPROTO_IP, IP_OPTIONS, rspace, sizeof (rspace)) < 0)
      {
            perror (_("ping: record route"));
            exit(1);
      }
```

The specified options will then be set in each packet sent over this socket in the future. The IPPROTO_IP parameter means that the packet option to be set is an IP option. This does not necessarily mean that it is an IP option in the true sense. It could be present in another position within the IP header (e.g., IP_TTL also belongs to the IPPROTO_IP group). From the programming perspective, we always have to assume that the current kernel implementation does not support the desired IP option. In this case, setsockopt() returns the value 1 and outputs an error message. Subsequently, an arbitrary number of packets with the packet option set are sent over this socket.

Incoming ICMP packets sent by ping are checked for their options as follows: An option pointer that points to the first Option field in the protocol header is computed. The first option is processed, and the option pointer is incremented so that it points to the next option. For the *Record Route* packet option, the pointer has to point to a byte that includes the number "7". ping doesn't actually have to take care of this value; like all other option-specific constants, it is defined in <linux/ip.h>:

```
#define IPOPT_END (0 |IPOPT_CONTROL)
#define IPOPT_NOOP (1 |IPOPT_CONTROL)
#define IPOPT_SEC (2 |IPOPT_CONTROL|IPOPT_COPY)
#define IPOPT_LSRR (3 |IPOPT_CONTROL|IPOPT_COPY)
#define IPOPT_TIMESTAMP (4 |IPOPT_MEASUREMENT)
#define IPOPT_RR (7 |IPOPT_CONTROL)
#define IPOPT_SID (8 |IPOPT_CONTROL|IPOPT_COPY)
#define IPOPT_SSRR (9 |IPOPT_CONTROL|IPOPT_COPY)
#define IPOPT_RA (20|IPOPT_CONTROL|IPOPT_COPY)
```

If one of these packet options is found, then it is output.

14.3.3 The `ip_options` Class in the Linux Kernel

This section describes all functions of the `ip_options` class implemented in the Linux kernel. If options are passed to or from functions, then this is normally done by use of the `ip_options` data type. This type is defined in `<linux/ip.h>` and includes the variables, pointers, and constants required for all packet options.

`ip_options_build()`	net/ipv4/ip_options.c

This function takes the information about IP options from the socket object and creates the options part in the IP header.

The parameters passed here include a socket buffer, the packet options, the packet destination address, the routing table, and the `is_frag` variables. The socket buffer includes a datagram with a protocol header that is not yet complete. The passed packet options are copied to the end of the protocol header. If the option *Strict Source Routing* exists, then the destination address of the packet is written to the address list of the packet option. If the packet is not a fragment, and if the *Internet Timestamp* or *Record Route* option exists, then the required data is inserted into the corresponding lists. If the packet is a fragment and one of the two options exists, then these options are replaced by *No Operation*.

`ip_options_echo()`	net/ipv4/ip_options.c

The `ip_options_echo()` routine takes the options from an IP packet received and uses them to create an echo packet (i.e., a reply to the incoming message). This function is normally used to send a reply when packets with IP options have been received—for example, to invert a *Strict Source Routing* option. The parameters passed here are a socket buffer and the destination options.

`ip_options_fragment()`	net/ipv4/ip_options.c

This function takes the fragment that was passed as socket buffer and overwrites all packet options with the *No Operation* option, with the *Copy Flag* not set. As described in Section 14.3.1, this flag is not set for the *Internet Timestamp* and *Record Route* options. The replacement by *No Operation* has the advantage that the length of the protocol header does not change.

`ip_options_compile()`	net/ipv4/ip_options.c

This function compiles the Option field at the end of the IP header. `ip_options_build()` uses data structures readily prepared for packet options, but `ip_options_compile()` has to compile all options. The parameters passed here include the packet options and the socket buffer. This function works option by option until it reaches an *End-of-Option List* or the end of the protocol header. Any *No Operation* in the option list is skipped. If an error occurs in this procedure, then an ICMP message is returned to the sender.

`ip_options_undo()`   **net/ipv4/ip_options.c**

It can be necessary to delete the last entries in the packet options *Source Routing,
Record Route*, and *Internet Timestamp*. The function `ip_options_undo()` is responsible for this task. This function can follow once the `ip_options_echo()` was invoked,
for example. If an *Echo Request* with the *Record Route* option is sent to the local computer, then the function `ip_options_echo()` duplicates the options set in the incoming packet. These packet options are then used to return an *Echo Reply* packet. Unless
the `ip_options_undo()` function is invoked, the IP option would include two entries
for the local computer. The packet options represent the only parameter passed here.

`ip_options_get()`   **net/ipv4/ip_options.c**

This function checks on whether the IP options can be accessed when
`setsockopt()` is invoked. If so, then it returns 0; otherwise, it returns a negative error
code (error codes are defined in the file `<include/asm/errno.h>`).

`ip_forward_options()`   **net/ipv4/ip_options.c**

If necessary, this function adds all information required about the local IP node
to a packet that has to be forwarded. This information is added by the packet options
Record Route, Strict Source Route, and *Internet Timestamp*. The only parameter passed
here is the appropriate socket buffer.

`ip_options_rcv_srr()`   **net/ipv4/ip_options.c**

This function checks the IP options *Loose Source Routing* and *Strict Source Routing* in an incoming packet. For example, if the destination address in the protocol header is the local address, and if the address list has not yet been fully visited, the packet
may not be delivered locally. As with the previous function, the socket buffer is the
only parameter passed here.

14.3.4 IP Options in the IP Layer

Incoming Packets   There are several ways an IP packet can move across the IP layer.
It can enter either from the lower or from the higher layers (i.e., from the local Internet
module). Depending on whether it is intended for the local computer, the packet is
passed to the next higher or next lower layer. Figure 14–10 shows this relation and the
position within the packet-handling process where functions are invoked to handle IP
options in the Linux kernel.

If an IP packet enters the IP layer from a lower layer, then `ip_rcv()` is the first
function invoked. The packet is passed as socket buffer, and it first has to pass the
netfilters. Netfilters have the functionality of a firewall and can do address translations.
To translate addresses, `NK_HOOK()` with the `ip_rcv_finish()` parameter is invoked.
Chapter 19 describes how netfilters are handled and implemented. After this process,
`ip_rcv_finish()` is the function executed next. The only parameter passed to this
function is the socket buffer. It finds out the packet's path and checks its protocol

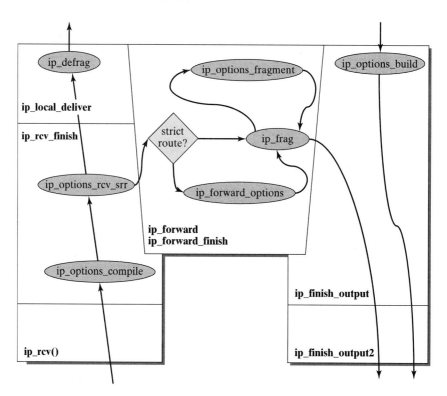

FIGURE 14–10
IP Options in the IP layer.

header. If the header length is greater than five (i.e., more than 5 * 32 bits) then the packet includes an option field that causes the function `ip_options_compile()` to be invoked. The packet options are separated and stored in the `opt` data structure. Normally, Boolean variables (e.g., `opt->is_strictroute`) are set at this point. Subsequently, the `opt->srr` pointer has to be tested. If this pointer is set to one, then the packet option *Loose Source Routing* or *Strict Source Routing* is specified, which means that the function `ip_options_rcv_srr()` has to be invoked.

The return value of the `ip_rcv_finish()` function is a pointer that points to either `ip_local_deliver()` or `ip_forward()`, depending on whether the packet has to be delivered locally or forwarded.

Local Packet Delivery   The function `ip_local_deliver()` is invoked if an IP packet has to be delivered to the local computer. This packet could be a fragment of a larger IP datagram, which has to be reassembled with the other fragments. This means that several things have to be checked—for example, whether all fragments have arrived, which is checked by the function `ip_defrag()`. Once all fragments have arrived, all options have to be removed from the first fragment to reassemble the fragments into the original datagram. The first fragment always includes all options that were copied when the datagram was fragmented. Next, the packet traverses the *netfilters* once more. The function `ip_local_deliver_finish()` completes a local packet delivery in the IP layer.

Forwarding Packets The function `ip_forward()` is invoked in the event that an IP packet has to be forwarded. (See the center part of Figure 14–10.) The packet is checked again, including a test for the *Strict Source Routing* option. If this option exists, and the local address is not in the option field, then an ICMP message is returned to inform the sender accordingly. In this case, neither *Strict Source Routing* nor *Loose Source Routing* may be specified in the option field to ensure that an *ICMP Redirect* message can be returned to the sender.

A backup copy of the IP packet (including all packet options) has to be created, because the packet could be changed in the further course. The value of the TTL variable is decremented by one. If the packet is too big and the *Don't-Fragment* bit is set in the IP packet header, then the complete packet is discarded. At the end, the *netfilter* is called again, but this time with the `ip_forward_finish()` parameter.

The function `ip_forward_finish()` checks the length of each IP packet options. If the length is not null, then the function `ip_forward_options()` handles the *Record Route* and *Source Routing* options, and `ip_send()` is invoked in either case. If the packet is too big and has to be fragmented, then `ip_send()` invokes the `ip_fragment()` function. Depending on whether the *Copy Flag* is set, only some of the packet options or only the first fragment have to be copied to all fragments. This function is extremely space- and time-saving. It also means that `ip_options_fragment()` is invoked only provided that the content of the socket buffer is the first or only fragment.

The next function is `ip_finish_output()`, which completes the packet-forwarding process.

Handling Packets Created Locally A packet created locally can take either of two paths across the IP layer:

- The function `ip_build_and_send_pkt()` is invoked. Though the passed socket buffer contains a datagram, it doesn't have a protocol header yet. In this case, packet options are passed as parameters, separately from the payload, and all pointers in the header structure are set. Depending on whether there are options, the header length, which was previously set to "5" [bytes], is corrected, and the function `ip_options_build()` is invoked, passing the socket buffer, the packet options, the destination address, and the routing table. Next, `ip_send_check()` verifies the checksum in the packet header, before the parameter `output_maybe_reroute()` invokes the *netfilters*. The IP options play no further role on the remaining path as the packet travels through the IP layer. At the end, the packet is passed to the lower layers or ARP (*Address Resolution Protocol*—see Chapter 15).
- The higher layers pass the IP packet as parameter of the function `ip_queue_xmit()` to the IP layer. Notice that the packet options are not directly passed as parameters to the function; `ip_queue_xmit()` can use a pointer referring to the socket to access them. The first step has to decide where the packet has to be sent to. If the *Source Routing* option is set, then the destination address of the packet is determined by the address specified next. This requires a check for whether the option `is_strictroute()` exists and for whether the destination address is unequal to the router registered in the local routing table. In this case, the IP packet

cannot be transmitted. If the route can be determined without problem, then the next step creates the remaining protocol header, as in the first way. The packet leaves the IP layer on the same path.

14.4   INTERNET CONTROL MESSAGE PROTOCOL (ICMP)

The *Internet Control Message Protocol* (*ICMP*) is the error-report mechanism for the IP layer, which also resides in the network layer. Though ICMP is based on IP, it doesn't make IP more reliable. Packets can be lost despite the use of ICMP, and IP or ICMP won't notice that packets are lost. The only purposes of this error-report mechanism are to report errors to other computers and to respond to such reports. It is mandatory for each IP implementation to implement ICMP. The ICMP implementation is defined in the following RFC documents:

- *RFC 792* [Post81b]: This is the basic definition, describing the packet types and their uses.
- *RFC 1122* [Brad89]: Definition of the requirements on terminal equipment (hosts) connected to the Internet.
- *RFC 1812* [Bake95]: This document describes the requirements for switching computers (routers) in the Internet.

However, RFC specifications often leave much room for flexible implementation. For some functions, it is even optional whether you implement them. For this reason, ICMP implementations and even configurations of the same implementation can differ considerably.

The most popular application of ICMP is error detection or error diagnostics. In more than ninety percent of all cases, the first information transmitted by a newly installed network adapter over an IP network will probably be that of the `ping` command, which is fully based on ICMP. This allows you to check the reachability of other computers easily and without noticeable load on the network. This procedure is often done in automated form (e.g., to monitor servers). Beyond simply checking the reachability of computers, the set of different error messages allow a network administrator (or a network-analysis tool) to obtain a detailed overview of the internal state of an IP network. For example, poorly selected local routing tables or wrongly set transmit options in individual computers can be detected. And finally, it is possible to use ICMP to synchronize computer clocks within a network, in addition to other—partly outdated—functions, which will be briefly discussed in this section.

14.4.1   Functional Principle of ICMP

ICMP sends and receives special IP packets representing error or information messages. Error messages occur whenever IP packets have not reached their destinations. All other cases create information messages, which can additionally include a request for reply. Notice that the ICMP functionality becomes active within the network implementation of the Linux kernel only provided that a problem situation occurs during another data traffic or when ICMP packets arrive from another computer. As mentioned earlier,

Version	IHL	TOS = **0x00**	Total Length	
Identification			Flags	Fragment Offset
TTL		Protocol = **0x01**	Header Checksum	
Source Address				
Destination Address				
Options (optional)			Padding	
Type		Code	Checksum	
ICMP data (variable)				

FIGURE 14–11
Structure of an IP packet containing an ICMP message.

ICMP transmits messages in IP packets. Figure 14–11 shows the general structure of ICMP messages (gray fields), which are transported in the payload of an IP packet. It is typical for the IP header of a packet containing an ICMP message that the *Type-of-Service* field is set to 0x00, which means that the packet is treated like a regular IP packet without priority. The protocol type in the IP header for ICMP messages is set to 0x01, as specified in RFC 790 [Post81a].

The 8-bit Type field in the ICMP part specifies the type of ICMP message. The Code field specifies the values an ICMP message can take. The original RFC 792 defines a total of eleven messages, but the current Linux implementation supports only some of them. These eleven messages are listed in Table 14–2. The 16-bit checksum extends over all fields starting from the ICMP type (i.e., over the entire part that IP treats as payload).

The following subsections describe the ICMP messages defined in RFC 791.

TABLE 14–2   ICMP packet types defined in RFC 792.

Type	Description
Destination Unreachable	The destination address cannot be reached.
Time Exceeded	A packet was discarded, because its TTL had expired.
Parameter Problem	Unknown or false options.
Source Quench	Informs the sender that IP packets were lost to overload.
Redirect	Enables path optimization.
Echo and Echo Reply	The data sent to the destination address is returned in a reply.
Timestamp and Timestamp Reply	The timestamp sent to the destination address is used to reply with the timestamp of the destination address.
Information Request und Information Reply	Request/reply used to find the network a computer connects to.

Destination Unreachable

The packet for a *Destination Unreachable* message includes the following fields:

Type–0x03	Code	Checksum
unused		
IP Header + 64 Bits of Original Data		

- ▦ Code = 0x00 (*Network Unreachable*): The network of an IP packet's receiver is not reachable. This can happen, for example, if the distance to the receiver's network is set to infinite in the routing table of a router.
- ▦ Code = 0x01 (*Host Unreachable*): The desired destination computer in the specified network cannot be reached.
- ▦ Code = 0x02 (*Protocol Unreachable*): This message can be generated if another protocol listens to the destination port specified in the TCP packet header. The message can be sent both by a router and by an end system.
- ▦ Code = 0x03 (*Port Unreachable*): The port address of the receiver specified in the TCP packet header is not reachable. The end system is "reachable" in this case, too, so both a router and an end system can generate this message.
- ▦ Code = 0x04 (*Fragmentation Needed*): This ICMP packet can be sent if an IP packet has to be fragmented in a router, but the *Don't-Fragment* flag is set in the packet header, so that the packet may not be fragmented. In this case, the router has to discard the IP packet.
- ▦ Code = 0x05 (*Source Route Failed*): If the IP packet option Source Routing is set and an error occurs, then this ICMP message is returned to the sender.

The IP header of the packet that caused the ICMP message, plus the first 64 data bits, are specified in the payload part of the ICMP message *Destination Unreachable*.

Source Quench

The packet of a *Source Quench* message is structured as follows:

Type–0x04	Code–0x00	Checksum
unused		
IP Header + 64 Bits of Original Data		

When the network load is high, it can happen that a router (or the receiver) discards IP packets because of a lack of resources (e.g., memory space or computing capacity). If this happens, then a *Source Quench* message can be transmitted to the sender. RFC 792 specifies that an ICMP implementation can generate such an ICMP message for each discarded packet. The sender should then respond by slowing down its transmission rate until no more *Source Quench* messages arrive. Subsequently, the sender can gradually increase its rate.

Instead of responding to discarded packets, routers, or end systems can send ICMP messages of the *Source Quench* type before they reach their capacity limits, to prevent the consequences of lost packets.

The only value defined for the Code field of a *Source Quench* message is 0x00. The payload part includes the IP header of the triggering IP packet and the first 64 bits of that packet's payload.

Redirect

The packet of a *Redirect* message is structured as follows:

Type–0x05	Code	Checksum
Router IP Address		
IP Header + 64 Bits of Original Data		

This ICMP message type is designed to optimize routing through the Internet. Assume that a router, R1, receives an IP packet of a sending end system, S, with receiver E. Based on a corresponding entry in the routing table of R1, this packet is forwarded to router R2. However, if R2 and S are in the same network (which can be determined based on the sender address), this route can be optimized by sending packets from S to receiver E directly to router R2 over R1, without detour. In this case, router R2 would send a *Redirect* message to end system S to announce that packets to receiver E will be sent directly to R2 in the future. Consequently, the field Router IP Address would contain the IP address of R2. The Code field would take either of the following values:

- Code = 0x00: Redirect IP packets that should be sent to the network that connects the receiver of these IP packets.
- Code = 0x01: Redirect all IP packets that should be sent to the specified receiver.
- Code = 0x02: Redirect all IP packets that should be sent to the receiver's network and have the same value in the TOS field as the IP packet that triggers the ICMP message.
- Code = 0x03: Redirect all IP packets that have the same receiver and the same TOS field as the IP packet that triggers the ICMP message.

Notice that no *Redirect* message is sent if the *Source Route* option is set in the IP packet options, even if there would be a shorter path to the receiver. The last field specifies the IP header and the first 64 data bits of the initiating packet.

Echo and Echo Reply

The packet of an *Echo* or *Echo Reply* message is structured as follows:

Type	Code–0x00	Checksum
Identifier		Sequence Number
Data . . .		

Echo and *Echo Reply* messages are normally used to verify the existence of an end system or intermediate system. To this end, an *Echo* message is sent to the desired system. The ICMP implementation in the receiver has to respond to this *Echo* request by sending an *Echo Reply* message. *Echo* and *Echo Reply* messages differ only in the Type field: 0x08 specifies an *Echo* message and 0x00 specifies an *Echo Reply* message. The Code value has to be set to 0x00 for both types. RFC 792 does not define explicit values for the other fields (i.e., Identifier, Sequence Number, and Data); therefore, the application can set these fields arbitrarily. The only thing the ICMP implementation has to ensure is that these three fields are copied from an *Echo* message to the *Echo Reply* message. The Data field can have an arbitrary length. For example, an ICMP application could use session numbers for the Identifier field and increment the sequence number for each *Echo* message it sends.

Time Exceeded

The packet of a *Time Exceeded* message is structured as follows:

Type–0x0B	Code	Checksum
unused		
IP Header + 64 Bits of Original Data		

An ICMP message of the type *Time Exceeded* is generated and returned to the sender if the lifetime of the IP packet has expired (i.e., its TTL value is 0) and the packet was discarded. There could occur either of the following two cases:

- Code = 0x00: A router sends this message if it discarded a packet because its TTL had expired.
- Code = 0x01: An end system sends a message with this code if it was unable to reassemble a fragmented IP message correctly within a certain time, because fragments were missing.

As in the *Destination Unreachable* message, the payload part in the *Time Exceeded* message includes the IP header of the packet that caused the ICMP message, plus the first 64 data bits from that packet.

Parameter Problem

The packet of a *Parameter Problem* message is structured as follows:

Type–0x0C	Code–0x00	Checksum
Pointer	unused	
IP Header + 64 Bits of Original Data		

If an error due to an invalid parameter in the IP header occurs while an IP packet is being handled in an intermediate node or end system, then this IP packet is discarded. For example, this can happen if there is a wrong argument in the IP packet options. In this case, the router or end system can generate an ICMP message of the type *Parameter Problem* and return it to the sender of the discarded IP packet. The Code field has to be set to 0x00 in all cases, which means that the Pointer field shows an error. More specifically, the pointer points to the octet in the original IP packet header where the problem occurred while the packet was being processed. For example, the value Pointer=0x01 means that the version number (i.e., the first field in the IP packet header; see Figure 14–11) is faulty.

The IP packet header of the discarded packet and the first 64 bits of its payload are attached to the ICMP message.

Timestamp and Timestamp Reply

The packet of an *Timestamp* or *Timestamp Reply* message is structured as follows:

Type	Code–0x00	Checksum
Identifier		Sequence Number
Originate Timestamp		
Receive Timestamp		
Transmit Timestamp		

These two ICMP message types are used to poll the current time from an intermediate or end system. The exchange is similar to the two previous message types, *Echo* and *Echo Reply*. The Type field is used to distinguish between *Timestamp* and *Timestamp Reply*: A value of 0x00 specifies a *Timestamp* message, and 0x0E denotes a *Timestamp Reply* message. The exclusive value for the Code field is 0x00. As for *Echo* and *Echo Reply*, the fields Identifier and Sequence Number are required by the sender to be able to allocate a *Timestamp Echo* message to a *Timestamp* message properly.

The payload part of these two ICMP messages consists of 32-bit timestamps. A timestamp is the time in milliseconds that has passed since midnight (GMT). The Originate Timestamp field defines the time when the transmitted ICMP message was last "touched" by the sender. Similarly, there is a Receive Timestamp specifying the time that the message arrived in the receiver. Transmit Timestamp stores the time at which the *Timestamp Reply* message was sent.

Information Request and Information Reply

The packet of an *Information Request* or *Information Reply* message is structured as follows:

Type	Code–0x00	Checksum
Identifier		Sequence Number

The way these two ICMP message types operate is similar to the *Echo* and *Echo Request* messages, except that they don't have a payload field. This message pair allows you to additionally identify the network that connects a computer. For this purpose, the value 0.0.0.0 is used as receiver address, which means that all computers in the local area network are addressed. The ICMP modules of these computers react to an *Information Request* by sending an *Information Reply*, where they state the LAN identifier instead of 0.0.0.0.

The Identifier and Sequence Number fields are used to allocate *Information Request* and *Information Reply* pairs, similarly to an *Echo* and *Echo Reply* pair. The Type field is defined as follows:

- Type = 0x0F: The message is an *Information Request*.
- Type = 0x10: The message is an *Information Reply*.

14.4.2   Configuring ICMP

The specified RFCs allow the local system administrator to control the behavior of some ICMP functions. The Linux implementation includes three cases where the sysctl() function can be used to control behavior at runtime:

- *Echo Replies*: The system manager can decide whether *Echo Replies* may be sent at all, for security reasons. This option is activated by default.
- *Echo Replies* to broadcast packets: The system manager can decide whether a reply should be sent to an *Echo Request* packet addressed to all computers in a LAN (i.e., destination address 0.0.0.0). This option is deactivated by default.
- *Monitoring illegal ICMP broadcast replies*: Faulty ICMP messages sent as a response to an IP broadcast can be ignored. (See RFC 1122 [Brad89].) This is not the case by default.

In addition, RFC 1812 [Bake95] specifies that the transmission rate of ICMP messages should be limited and that this limit should be configurable. The transmit function icmp_send() is limited accordingly, but the rate can be set only in the source code (in the xrlim_allow() function, XRLIM_BURST_FACTOR constant), which means that you have to recompile the Linux kernel.

14.4.3   ICMP in the Linux Kernel

The Linux implementation is done mainly in the file net/ipv4/icmp.c and in the associated header file include/linux/icmp.h. Each ICMP message type is defined as a constant with the type fields specified in RFC 792:

```
ICMP_ECHOREPLY = 0
ICMP_DEST_UNREACH = 3
ICMP_SOURCE_QUENCH = 4
ICMP_REDIRECT = 5
ICMP_ECHO = 8
ICMP_TIME_EXCEEDED = 11
ICMP_PARAMETERPROB = 12
ICMP_TIMESTAMP = 13
ICMP_TIMESTAMPREPLY = 14
```

```
ICMP_INFO_REQUEST = 15
ICMP_INFO_REPLY = 16
ICMP_ADDRESS = 17
ICMP_ADDRESSREPLY = 18
```

Almost all IP modules use the ICMP implementation to send ICMP messages.

`icmp_unit()`	**include/linux/icmp.h**

From the local perspective, the ICMP layer is stateless, except for a few internal statistics, but messages exchanged between two computers can include states. The ICMP socket is the only central structure included in the implementation. This socket can be reached exclusively with `root` privileges. This is the reason why, for example, the `ping` command requires `root` privileges. The initialization function `icmp_unit()` creates this socket.

The statistical information mentioned in the previous section is maintained in the data structure `icmp_statistics`. It includes the number of packets sent and received in total, the number of errors incurred, and the accumulated number of ICMP types.

The current contents from this statistics variable can be output from the pseudo file `/proc/net/snmp`. This file includes the meaning of the individual entries in the form of abbreviated ICMP types with leading "In" or "Out" for each packet and an additional row with values from the statistics array. The following listing is an example to show you what the contents of the `/proc/net/snmp` can look like:

```
> cat /proc/net/snmp
Ip: Forwarding DefaultTTL InReceives InHdrErrors InAddrErrors ForwDatagrams
InUnknownProtos InDiscards InDelivers OutRequests OutDiscards OutNoRoutes
ReasmTimeout ReasmReqds ReasmOKs ReasmFails FragOKs FragFails
FragCreates
Ip: 2 64 900 0 0 0 0 64 963 0 0 0 0 0 0 0 0
Icmp: InMsgs InErrors InDestUnreachs InTimeExcds InParmProbs InSrcQuenchs
InRedirects InEchos InEchoReps InTimestamps InTimestampReps InAddrMasks
InAddrMaskReps OutMsgs OutErrors OutDestUnreachs OutTimeExcds
OutParmProbs
OutSrcQuenchs OutRedirects OutEchos OutEchoReps OutTimestamps
OutTimestampReps OutAddrMasks OutAddrMaskReps
Icmp: 35 0 15 0 0 0 0 11 9 0 0 0 0 26 0 15 0 0 0 0 0 11 0 0 0 0
Tcp: RtoAlgorithm RtoMin RtoMax MaxConn ActiveOpens PassiveOpens
AttemptFails EstabResets CurrEstab InSegs OutSegs RetransSegs InErrs OutRsts
Tcp: 0 0 0 0 4 0 0 0 0 816 888 0 0 0
Udp: InDatagrams NoPorts InErrors OutDatagrams
Udp: 25 6 0 31
```

Sending ICMP Packets   You can send ICMP packets from outside of the ICMP implementation in the Linux kernel—for example, from within the ping program. This case is independent of the functions discussed below and will not be further discussed here.

`icmp_send()`	**include/linux/icmp.h**

Within the Linux kernel, an ICMP message is sent by the function `icmp_send()` in all cases where the message is not a reply to an ICMP message. This function gets all data from an ICMP message as call parameters, which means that it can send any ICMP type. In addition, to generate an ICMP packet correctly, this function is responsible for limiting the transmission rate of ICMP messages (see also the configuration options discussed in Section 14.4.2) and for catching cases where no ICMP messages may be sent. In this respect, two cases are possible:

- If the IP packet that initiated an ICMP message was an ICMP error message, then a reply to this error message could cause an infinite cycle of ICMP messages.
- If an IP packet was fragmented, then an ICMP message is sent for the first fragment only to avoid loading the network unnecessarily with redundant packets.

Table 14–3 shows the cases where Linux kernel modules send ICMP messages.

Handling Incoming ICMP Packets   The central structure used to handle ICMP packets that arrive in an end system or intermediate system is a function pointer array named `icmp_pointers`. This array is responsible for flow control and includes the function handling ICMP type n in position n. The major benefit of this method, compared to using a switch-case instruction to implement the same behavior, is that each function in the array includes context information in the form of statistics variables. These statistics variables are defined in relation to the respective ICMP handling function. This means that this array specifies the auxiliary function used to handle an ICMP message. These auxiliary functions can be divided into two groups: auxiliary functions for local changes only, and auxiliary functions that also send a new ICMP packet.

The most important functions used in the ICMP implementation in Linux will be described next.

`icmp_rcv()`	**include/linux/icmp.h**

TABLE 14–3   Generating ICMP messages from within the kernel modules.

Type	Module	Reason
Time Exceeded	Forward and defragment packets	A packet was discarded because it's TTL expired.
Parameter Problem	Detect packet options	Unknown or false options
Redirect	Packet routing	Obvious potential for optimization
Destination Unreachable	All modules that send, forward, or deliver IP packets	Inability to deliver a packet

This function is responsible for processing incoming ICMP packets, including a preprocessing process that drops noncompliant packets. While the internal statistics are being updated when an ICMP message arrives, the packet is also checked for correct length. In addition, the checksum is computed over the packet header, and the ICMP type is checked for a valid number. If the user has not set options in `sysctl`, then incoming broadcast packets of the types *ICMP Echo, ICMP Timestamp, ICMP Information Request*, and *ICMP Information Reply* are discarded.

The following functions are invoked from within the `icmp_rcv()` function for incoming ICMP packets:

`icmp_reply()`	**include/linux/icmp.h**

The function `icmp_reply()` is generally used to reply to ICMP request packets. Before a reply is sent, the internal statistics variables are updated first; then the TOS field is taken from Request, and the IP addresses of the sender and the receiver are swapped. Next, the packet is returned to the sender, including the payload passed as argument (corresponding to the ICMP reply packet). `icmp_reply()` is used by two functions, `icmp_echo()` and `icmp_timestamp()`, to reply to *Echo Request* and *Timestamp Request*, respectively.

`icmp_redirect()`	**include/linux/icmp.h**

This function updates the routing table when an end system receives an ICMP message of the type *Redirect*.

`icmp_unreach()`	**include/linux/icmp.h**

This function handles three ICMP message types: *Destination Unreachable, Source Quench*, and *Time Exceeded*. After a number of tests for packet validity, this function passes the error message to the service of the next higher layer belonging to the initiating packet. Error messages as a result of ICMP messages are similar to the error codes defined in Section 14.4.1. In the case of *Source Quench*, the receiving computer is expected to reduce its sending rate, which will be handled by the protocol in the transport layer above IP.

`icmp_echo()`, `icmp_timestamp()`	**include/linux/icmp.h**

A new ICMP packet has to be sent to handle ICMP messages of the types *Echo Request* and *Timestamp Request*. The basic function `icmp_reply()` is used in either case. The transmission is based on the rules discussed in Section 14.4.3. For `icmp_echo()`, only the ICMP type is changed, to `ICMP_ECHOREPLY`, then the payload part is copied from the Echo packet, and finally `icmp_reply()` returns the packet to the sender.

The function `icmp_timestamp()` responds to incoming *Timestamp* requests. Initially, it checks the length of packets previously received and finds out the current time. The payload is removed from the original ICMP packet and put into the reply packet, and the time is added to the Receive Timestamp and Transmit Timestamp fields. This means that the two time values in Receive Timestamp and Transmit Timestamp are always identical. Once the packet type has been changed to ICMP_TIMESTAMPREPLY, the function icmp_reply() returns the packet.

icmp_address(), icmp_address_reply()	include/linux/icmp.h

The standard actually specifies that these two functions be implemented. However, this functionality is not supported by the Linux kernel, because the designers found inconsistencies in the standards and thought that an implementation would not be meaningful at this time. When icmp_address() is invoked, only a kernel message is output. When a Linux computer receives an *ICMP Information Reply* packet, then it checks this packet for correct network mask (and complains by outputting a kernel message if it finds an inconsistency).

Another thing specific to the Linux implementation is that no reply is sent to packet types not discussed in this chapter.

Deviations from the Standard   Several ICMP functionalities originally specified in RFCs were not included in the ICMP implementation of Linux. The following properties are missing:

- The use of a *Source Route* specified in the IP options is not supported. If an IP packet that initiates an ICMP message is to use a specified route, then the ICMP packet would actually have to follow the same path back. This property is currently missing, but will presumably be implemented later.
- Sending *Source Quench* messages: The ICMP implementation in Linux sends no *Source Quench* packets. Today, it is considered pointless to send such packets, because they generate additional network load in an overload situation. (See RFC 1812 [Bake95].)
- *Information Request/Reply*: These packet types were originally designed for tasks that have more recently been handled by other protocols (e.g., allocating of IP addresses to booting computers without persistent memory). Currently, this problem is solved by RARP. For this reason, these packets are simply ignored. In addition, the use of these ICMP packet types was found to cause problems, because these two ICMP messages cannot be correctly applied in all cases. (See RFC 1812.) Though this functionality is still specified in this RFC, the Linux designers decided not to implement it. The only thing done is that a local error message is output when the computer receives an *Information Reply* message.

Address Resolution Protocol (ARP)

The conversion of addresses between different protocol layers represents an important task for unique identification of resources in a computer network. Such a conversion is required at the transition between two neighbouring layers within a reference model, because each layer uses its own address types, depending on its functionality (IP, MAC, ATM addresses, etc.). For example, the destination computer is specified in the form of an IP address if a packet is sent over the Internet Protocol. This address is valid only within the IP layer. In the data-link layer, both the service used by the Internet Protocol to transport its data and different LAN technologies (e.g., Ethernet, token ring, ATM), each with its own address formats, can be used. The network adapters of a LAN are generally identified by 48-bit addresses, so-called *MAC addresses*. A MAC address identifies a unique network adapter within a local area network.

To be able to send a packet to the IP instance in the destination computer or to the next router, the MAC address of the destination station has to be determined in the sending protocol instance. The problem is now to do a unique resolution of the mapping between a MAC address and an IP address. What we need is a mapping of network-layer addresses to MAC addresses, because the sending IP instance has to pass the MAC address of the next station in the form of interface control information (ICI) to the lower MAC instance. (See Section 3.2.1.) At the advent of the Internet, this mapping was implemented by static tables that maintained the mapping of IP addresses to MAC addresses in each computer. However, this method turned out to be inflexible as the ARPANET grew, and it meant an extremely high cost when changes were necessary. For this reason, RFC 826 introduced the *Address Resolution Protocol* (*ARP*) to convert address formats.

Though the TCP/IP protocol suite has become the leading standard for almost all computer networks, it is interesting to note that ARP was not designed specifically for mapping between IP and MAC addresses. ARP is a generic protocol that finds a mapping between ordered pairs (P, A) and arbitrary physical addresses, where P is a network-layer protocol and A is an address of this protocol P. At the time at which ARP was developed, different protocols, such as CHAOS and Decnet, had been used in the network layer. The ARP instance of a system can be extended so that the required addresses can be resolved for each of the above combinations, which means that no new protocol is necessary. The most common method to allocate addresses between different layers maps the tuple (*Internet Protocol, IP address*) to 48-bit MAC addresses.

15.1 USING THE ADDRESS RESOLUTION PROTOCOL

As mentioned above, the Address Resolution Protocol (ARP) is a decentralized protocol to resolve address mappings between layer-3 addresses and layer-2 addresses in local area networks. Figure 15–1 shows how ARP works. When computer A wants to send a packet to router R in the same LAN, then it needs the layer-2 address, in addition to the IP address, to be able to tell the data link layer which computer is supposed to get this packet. For this purpose, computer A sends an *ARP Request* to all computers connected to the LAN. This request is generally sent in a MAC broadcast message by using the MAC broadcast address (FF:FF:FF:FF:FF:FF). The intended computer can see from the destination IP address in the ARP PDU that this request is for itself, so this computer returns a reply to the requesting computer, A, including its MAC address. Computer A now learns the MAC address of R and can instruct its data-link layer to deliver the packet.

To avoid having to request the MAC address again for subsequent packets, A stores the MAC address of R in a local table—the ARP cache. (See Section 15.3.) Computer R can also extract the MAC address of A from A's request and store that in its own ARP cache. It can be seen from A's request that A and R will communicate soon, which means that the MAC address of A will be needed. In this case, we avoid one ARP request, because the mapping will have been previously stored.

15.1.1 The Structure of ARP Protocol Data Units

Figure 15–2 shows how an ARP PDU is structured; this PDU is used for the two protocol data units defined in the ARP protocol, *ARP Request* and *ARP Reply*. The only difference between these two types is in the *Operation* field.

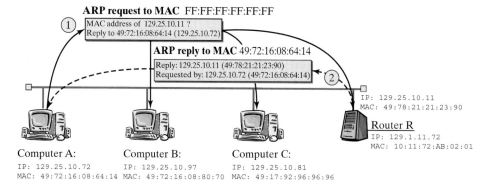

FIGURE 15–1
Example showing how ARP resolves addresses.

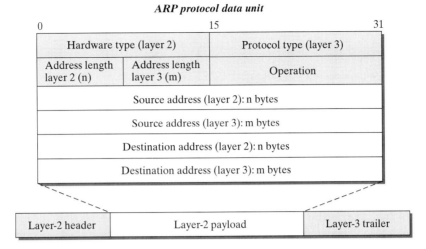

FIGURE 15–2
Format of the ARP Request and ARP Reply PDUs.

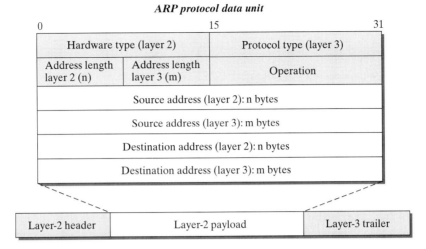

FIGURE 15–3
Example with values in the ARP Request and ARP Reply PDUs from Figure 15–1 (not considering the network byte order).

Figure 15–3 uses the above example to show how values can be assigned to the two PDUs. Computer A sends a request to router R, as shown in Figure 15–1, asking for that computer's 48-bit MAC address (say `129.25.10.11`) in the local Ethernet segment.

The fields of an ARP PDU and their meanings are as follows:

- ARP packets are transported in the payload field of MAC protocols. The identification as an ARP PDU is done specifically by the MAC protocol (e.g., in the *Protocol* field for Ethernet or by an appropriate identifier in the SNAP header).
- *Hardware Type* specifies the layer-2 protocol used (e.g., 1 for an Ethernet network).
- *Protocol Type* specifies the layer-3 protocol used (e.g., 0x0800 for the Internet Protocol).
- *Layer-2 Address Length:* n specifies the length of the layer-2 address used (in bytes). This field takes the value 6 for an 48-bit MAC address. Specifying the address length enables the use of different protocols with specific address formats.

▨ *Layer-3 Address Length:* m specifies the length of the layer-3 address. The field takes the value 4 for 32-bit Internet addresses.

▨ The *Operation* field specifies the type of ARP PDU—1 for *ARP Request*, 2 for *ARP Reply*. In addition, the PDU types *RARP Request* (3) and *RARP Reply* (4) were defined for RARP [FMMT84]).

▨ The fields *Layer-2 Sender Address* and *Layer-2 Destination Address* consist of n bytes and include the appropriate layer-2 addresses.

▨ The fields *Layer-3 Sender Address* and *Layer-3 Destination Address* have the length m bytes and include the layer-3 addresses of the requesting and the receiving station.

15.1.2   Receiving an ARP Packet and Replying

As was mentioned earlier, *ARP Request* and *ARP Reply* PDUs have the same packet format; they differ only in their *Operation* fields. An *ARP Request* packet also differs from a subsequent reply by the missing layer-2 address of the destination, so that it is easy to create a reply to a request. When receiving a request packet, in which the desired station finds its layer-3 address, the following steps are completed:

▨ The layer-2 address of the network adapter is inserted in the field *Layer-2 Destination Address*.

▨ The two address fields for the sender and the destination are swapped.

▨ The *Operation* field takes value 2 to mark the PDU as *ARP Reply*.

▨ Finally, the reply packet is sent.

An ARP request includes a valid mapping between the layer-3 address and the layer-2 address of the request initiator, in addition to the layer-3 address looked for, so one entry for the initiator is created in the ARP cache when the request is received.

15.2   THE ARP COMMAND

The arp command can be used to output the ARP table (ARP cache) of a computer. It can also be used to manipulate the ARP table (e.g., to create permanent entries or delete entries).

The following options are available for the arp command:

▨ *Display the ARP table:* you can use option -a when running the arp command to view the ARP table of a computer:

```
root@tux # arp -a
IP address HW type HW address
129.25.10.97 10Mbit/s Ethernet 49:72:16:08:80:70
129.25.10.72 10Mbit/s Ethernet 49:72:16:08:64:14
129.25. 10.81 10Mbit/s Ethernet 49:17:92:96:96:96
```

The first column shows the IP address of the destination computer; the second column shows the LAN category (e.g., 10-mbps Ethernet); the last column shows the layer-2 address of the network adapter.

If the word `incomplete` appears in an entry in the last column upon repeated calls, then this means that the network device specified by the entry has failed or is defective.

▓ *Address format:* In addition to Ethernet, ARP is also used in other broadcast-enabled LAN technologies (e.g., AX.25 amateur radio networks and token ring) for address resolution. These network technologies may use different address formats. `arp` shows the address format used in the second column. Notice that `arp` shows only the entries for Ethernet addresses, by default. To view a list of AX.25 addresses, you have to use the `-t` option with the command: `arp -a -t ax25`.

▓ *Deleting ARP entries:* You can use `arp` with the option `-d computer` to remove the entry of that computer. This forces a new ARP request upon the next request for the layer-2 address of the specified computer. Deleting an ARP address mapping can be useful when a computer's configuration is wrong or when the layer-2 address has changed—for example, when a network adapter has been replaced.

To avoid this case, ARP entries are automatically declared invalid after a certain period of time. This period is in the range of a few minutes, so that the replacement of a network adapter should actually not cause any problem.

▓ *Setting ARP entries:* It can sometimes be useful to add an entry manually to the ARP table. The option `-s computer layer-2-address` is available for such cases. It can also be used when ARP requests to a specific computer are not answered, because of faulty or missing ARP instances. The option -s can also be useful when a second computer in the same LAN identifies itself erroneously with the same IP address and replies sooner to the ARP request. The following command adds the computer `tux` having layer-2 address `49:72:16:08:64:14` to the ARP table: arp `-s tux 49:72:16:08:64:14`.

In contrast to entries determined automatically in the ARP cache, entries created with the option `-s` are not removed after a certain period; they remain in the ARP cache until the computer restarts (static entry).

15.3   IMPLEMENTING THE ARP INSTANCE IN THE LINUX KERNEL

In theory, ARP would have to run an address resolution for each outgoing IP packet before transmitting it. However, this would significantly increase the required bandwidth. For this reason, address mappings are stored in a table—the so-called *ARP cache*—as the protocol learns them. We have mentioned the ARP cache several times before. This section describes how the ARP cache and the ARP instance are implemented in the Linux kernel.

Though the Address Resolution Protocol was designed for relatively generic use, to map addresses for different layers, it is not used by all layer-3 protocols. For example, the new Internet Protocol (IPv6) uses the *Neighbor Discovery* (*ND*) address resolution to map IPv6 addresses to layer-2 addresses. Though the operation of the two protocols (ARP and ND) is similar, they are actually two separate protocol instances. The Linux kernel designers wanted to utilize the similarity between the two protocols and implemented a generic support for address resolution protocols in LANs, the so-called `neighbour` management.

A `neighbour` represents a computer that is reachable over layer-2 services (i.e., directly over the LAN). Using the `neighbour` interface and the available functions, you can implement special properties of either of the two protocols (ARP and Neighbour Discovery). The following sections introduce the **neighbour** interface and discuss the ARP functions. Chapter 23 describes how Neighbor Discovery is implemented.

15.3.1 Managing Reachable Computers in the ARP Cache

As was mentioned earlier, computers that can be reached directly (over layer 2) are called *neighbor stations* in Linux. Figure 15–4 shows that they are represented by instances of the neighbour structure.

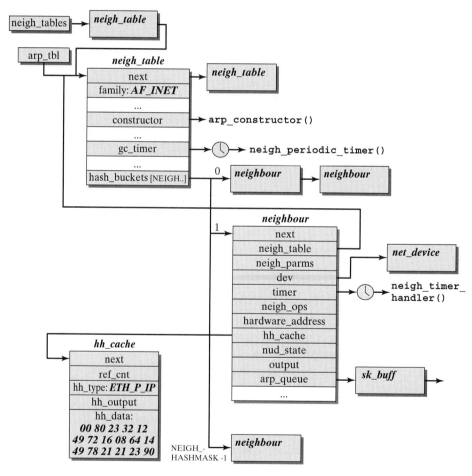

FIGURE 15–4

Structure of the ARP cache and its neighbor elements.

The set of reachable computers is managed in the ARP cache, which is organized in a hash table. The hash function `arp_hash()` can be used to map `neighbour` structures to rows in the hash table. A linear collision resolution occurs if several structures fall on the same hash row. The basic functions of the ARP hash table are handled by the *neighbour* management. This means that the ARP hash table is only an instance of the more general `neigh_table` structure.

The structures of the *neighbour* management and its linking are introduced below.

`struct neighbour`	include/net/neighbour.h

The `neighbour` structure is the representation of a computer that can be reached directly over the data-link layer. The ARP instance creates a `neighbour` structure as soon as a layer-3 protocol (normally, the Internet Protocol) asks for the layer-2 address of a computer in the LAN. This means that the ARP cache contains all reachable stations and, additionally, the addresses of stations that are currently being determined. To prevent the cache from growing endlessly, entries with layer-2 addresses that have not been requested are deleted after a certain time. The neighbour structure has the following parameters:

- `next`: Because neighbor stations are organized in hash tables, and collisions are resolved by the *chaining* strategy (linear linking), the **next** field references the next neighbor structure in a hash row.
- `tbl`: This pointer points to the `neigh_table` structure that belongs to this `neighbour` and manages the current entry.
- `parms`: The `neigh_parms` structure includes several parameters about a `neighbour` computer (e.g., a reference to the associated timer and the maximum number of probes. (See `neigh_timer_handler()` function, below.)
- `dev`: This is a pointer to the corresponding network device.
- `timer`: This is a pointer to a timer used to initiate the handling routine `neigh_timer_handler()`.
- `opts`: Neighbor options define several functions used to send packets to this `neighbour`. The functions actually used depend on the properties of the underlying medium (i.e., on the type of network device). Figure 15–5 shows the

	generic	direct	hh	broken
destructor	-	-	-	-
solicit	arp_solicit	-	arp_solicit	arp_solicit
error_report	arp_error_report	-	arp_error_report	arp_error_report
output	neigh_resolve_output	dev_queue_xmit	neigh_resolve_output	neigh_compat_output
connected_output	neigh_connected_output	dev_queue_xmit	neigh_resolve_output	neigh_compat_output
hh_output	dev_queue_xmit	dev_queue_xmit	dev_queue_xmit	dev_queue_xmit
queue_xmit	dev_queue_xmit	dev_queue_xmit	dev_queue_xmit	dev_queue_xmit

FIGURE 15–5
Available neighbor options.

neigh_opts variants. For example, the hh options are used when the network device needs an address to be resolved and supports a cache for layer-2 headers, and **direct** is used for network devices that do not need address resolution, such as point-to-point connections. The functions available in a neigh_opts variant are used for different tasks involved in the address-resolution process (e.g., resolve an address (solicit()) or send a packet to a reachable neighboring computer (connected_output()).

▨ hardware_address: This array stores the physical address of the neighboring computer.

▨ hh: This field refers to the cache entry for the layer-2 protocol of this neighbour computer. For example, an Ethernet packet header consists of the sender address, the destination address, and the ethertype field. It is not necessary to fill these fields every time; it is much more efficient to have them computed and readily stored, so that they need only be copied.

▨ nud_state: This parameter manages the state (i.e., valid, currently unreachable, etc.) of the neighboring station. Figure 15–5 shows all states a neighbor can possibly take. These states will be discussed in more detail in the course of this chapter.

▨ output(): This function pointer points to one of the functions in the neigh_ops structure. The value depends on the current state (nud_state) of the neighbour entry and the type of network device used. Figure 15–5 shows the possible combinations. The output() function is used to send packets to this neighboring station. If a function pointer is used, then the state of a packet does not have to be checked when it is sent. Should this state ever change, then we can simply set a new pointer.

▨ arp_queue: The ARP instance collects in this queue all packets to be sent for neighbour entries in the NUD_INCOMPLETE state (i.e., the neighboring computer currently cannot be reached). This means that they don't have to be discarded, but can be sent as soon as an address has been successfully resolved.

struct neigh_table	include/net/neighbour.h

A neigh_table structure manages the neighbour structures of an address-resolution protocol (see Figure 15–4), and several tables like this can exist in one single computer. We describe only the special case with an ARP table here. The neigh_table instance of the ARP protocol can be reached either over the linked list in the neigh_table structures or directly over the arp_tbl pointer.

The most important fields in a neighbour hash table are as follows:

▨ next: As mentioned earlier, a separate neigh_table instance is created for each protocol, and these instances are linearly linked. This is the purpose of the next pointer. The neigh_tables variable points to the beginning of the list.

▨ family: This field stores the address family of *neighbour* entries. The ARP cache contains IP addresses, so this field takes the value AF_INET.

▨ constructor(): This function pointer is used to generate a new neighbour entry. Depending on the protocol instance, different tasks may be required to generate such an entry. This is the reason why each protocol should have a special constructor. In the `arp_tbl` structure, this pointer references the function `arp_constructor()`, which will be described later.

▨ `gc_timer`: A *garbage collection* (GC) timer is created for each `neigh_table` cache. This timer checks the state of each entry and updates these states periodically. The handling routine used by this timer is `neigh_periodic_timer()`.

▨ `hash_buckets[NEIGH_HASHMASK+1]`: This table includes the pointers to the hash rows that link the `neighbour` entries linearly. The `arp_hash()` function is used to compute hash values.

▨ `phash_buckets[PNEIGH_HASHMASK+1]`: This second hash table manages the neighbour structures entered when the computer is used as an ARP proxy.

`struct neigh_ops`	**include/net/neighbour.h**

The `ops` field of each `neighbour` structure includes a pointer to a `neigh_ops` structure. The available options define different types of neighbors and include several functions belonging to a `neighbour` type (`connected_output()`, `hh_output()`, etc.). For example, the functions needed to send packets to a neighboring computer are defined in the `neighbour` options. The following four types are available for entries in the ARP cache: `generic`, `direct`, `hh`, and `broken`.

The respective functions of these types are shown in Figure 15–5. Depending on the type of network device used, the `ops` fields for new `neighbour` structures in the `arp_constructor()` function are set to one of the following four options:

▨ `arp_direct_ops()` is used when the existing network device does not include hardware headers (`dev->hard_header == NULL`). These stations are directly reachable, and no layer-2 packet header is required (e.g., for PPP).

▨ `arp_broken_ops()` is reserved for special network devices (ROSE, AX25, and NETROM).

▨ `arp_hh_ops()` is set when the network device used has a cache for layer-2 packet headers (`dev->hard_header_cache`). In this case, the `ops` field is set to `arp_hh_ops`.

▨ `arp_generic_ops()` is used when none of the above cases exists.

The `output()` functions of the `neigh_ops` structure are particularly important. Each neighbour structure includes an `output()` pointer that points to a function used to send data packets to a neighboring station. For ARP cache entries in the `NUD_REACHABLE`, `NUD_PERMANENT`, or `NUD_NOARP` state, the `output()` pointer references the function `connected_output()` of the `neigh_ops` structure; it is the fastest of all. `connected_output()` assumes that the neighboring computer is reachable, because these three states mean either that the reachability was confirmed recently or that no confirmation is required (permanent entry or point-to-point).

For `neighbour` stations in other states, the `output()` pointer references the `output()` function, which is slower and more careful. Direct reachability is doubted, so an initial attempt is made to obtain a confirmation of the neighboring computer's reachability (*probe*).

Possible States for neighbour Entries It is theoretically possible to leave the entries for all neighboring stations ever learned in the ARP cache. However, there are several reasons why these entries are valid for a limited period of time. First, it would mean memory wasted to maintain entries for all these computers, especially if there is little or no data exchange with them. Second, we have to keep these entries consistent. For example, there can be a situation when the network adapter in a computer is replaced and so this computer will have a different layer-2 address. This computer could no longer be reached with the old mapping. Therefore, it is assumed that the mapping stored for a computer is no longer valid if that computer has not sent anything for some time.

In practice, the size of the ARP cache is limited (normally to 512 entries), and old or rarely used entries are periodically removed by a kind of *garbage collection*. On the other hand, it could well be that a computer does not communicate over a lengthy time, which means that its table is empty. In fact, this was not possible up to kernel Version 2.4, because the size of a neigh_table structure was also limited downwards: No garbage collection was done when the table included fewer than gc_thresh1 values, which normally meant 128 entries. This bottom limit no longer exists in kernel Version 2.4 and higher. You can use the arp command (see Section 15.2) to view the contents of the ARP cache.

Each neighbour entry in the ARP cache has a state, which is stored in the nud_state field of the corresponding neighbour structure. Figure 15–6 shows all possible states and the most important state transitions. There are other transitions, but

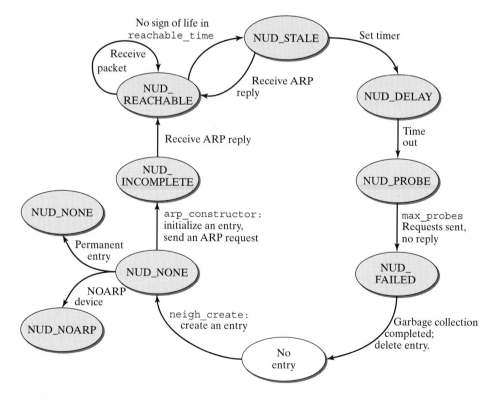

FIGURE 15–6
State transition diagram for neighbour entries in neighbour caches.

they hardly ever occur. We left them out for the sake of keeping the figure easy to understand. The states and state transitions are described below.

- NUD_NONE: This entry is invalid. A neighbor normally is in this state only temporarily. New entries for the ARP cache are created by the neigh_alloc() function, but this state is changed immediately.

- NUD_NOARP, NUD_PERMANENT: No address resolution is done for entries in these two states. NUD_NOARP are neighbors that do not require address resolution (e.g., PPP). Entries with the NUD_PERMANENT state were permanently set by the administrator and are not deleted by the garbage collection.

- NUD_INCOMPLETE: This state means that there is no address mapping for this neighbor yet, but that it is being processed. This means that an ARP request has been sent, and the protocol is waiting for a reply.

- NUD_REACHABLE: neighbour structures in this state are reachable with the fastest output() function (neigh_ops->connected_output()). An ARP reply packet from this neighbor was received, and its maximum age is neigh->parms->reachable_time time units. This interval is restarted when a normal data packet is received.

- NUD_STALE: This state is taken when an entry has been REACHABLE, but reachable_time time units have expired. For this reason, it is no longer certain that the neighbouring computer can still be reached with the address mapping currently stored. For this reason, rather than using connected_output() to send packets to this neighbour, the slower neigh_ops->output() is used.

- NUD_DELAY: If a packet needs to be sent to a station in the NUD_STALE state, then the NUD_DELAY state is set. It is between the NUD_STALE und NUD_PROBE states only temporarily. Of course, if the address mapping is confirmed once again, then the entry changes to the NUD_REACHABLE state.

- NUD_PROBE: The entry in the ARP cache is in the *probing phase*: Consecutive ARP request packets are sent in an attempt to obtain the layer-2 address of this computer.

- NUD_FAILED: The address mapping cannot be resolved for entries in this state. ARP tries to solve the problem by sending neigh_max_probes request packets. If it still doesn't get replies to these packets, then the state of the neighbour entry is set to NUD_FAILED. Subsequently, the garbage collection deletes all entries in this state from the ARP cache.

To understand the states better, we summarize three additional state combinations below:

- NUD_IN_TIMER = (NUD_INCOMPLETE | NUD_DELAY | NUD_PROBE): An attempt is currently being made to resolve the address.

- NUD_VALID = (NUD_PERMANENT | NUD_NOARP | NUD_REACHABLE | NUD_PROBE | NUD_STALE | NUD_DELAY): The neighbour entry includes an address mapping, which has been valid.

- NUD_CONNECTED = (NUD_PERMANENT | NUD_NOARP | NUD_REACHABLE): The neighbour entry is valid and the neighboring computer can be reached.

15.3.2 Operation of the Address Resolution Protocol (ARP)

Given that the ARP cache and other neighbour tables have been built as discussed in the previous section, this section describes how the Address Resolution Protocol (ARP) in the Linux kernel operates. We first discuss the routes different ARP packets take across the kernel and how the ARP instance operates. Figure 15–7 shows the routes of ARP request and ARP reply packets.

Incoming ARP PDUs arp_rcv() handles incoming ARP packets on layer 3. ARP packets are packed directly in layer-2 PDUs, so a separate layer-3 protocol definition (arp_packet_type) was created for the Address Resolution Protocol. This information and the protocol identifier ETH_P_ARP from the LLC header are used to identify that the packet is an ARP PDU and to treat it as such.

arp_rcv()	net/Ipv4/arp.c

Once a computer has received it, an ARP PDU is passed to the ARP handling routine by the *NET_RX* software interrupt (net_rx_action). arp_rcv() first checks the packet for correctness, verifying the following criteria—the packet is dropped if one of these conditions is true:

■ Is the net_device structure a correct network device (in_dev == NULL)?
■ Are the ARP PDU length and the addresses it contains correct (arp->ar_hln != dev->addr_len)?

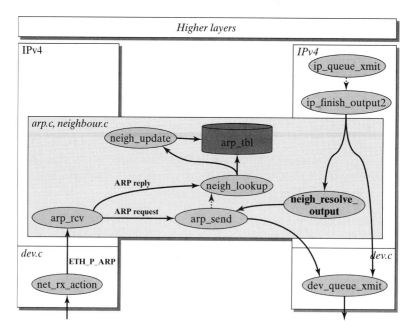

FIGURE 15–7
ARP requests and ARP replies traveling through the ARP instance.

- Does the network device used require the ARP protocol at all (dev->flags & IFF_NOARP)?
- Is the packet directed to another computer (PACKET_OTHERHOST) or intended for the LOOPBACK device?
- The arp_plen field should have value 4. Otherwise, the packet does not originate from a request for the layer-2 address of an IP address or a reply, respectively. Currently, the Linux kernel supports only address resolutions based on the Internet Protocol.

The packet is dropped if one the these conditions (in brackets) is true. If the ARP packet is correct, it is checked to see whether the MAC type specified in the packet complies with the network device. For example, if the ARP packet arrived in an Ethernet card, then the protocol type in the ARP packet should be either ARPHRD_ETHER or ARPHRD_IEEE802. Interestingly, the Ethernet hardware identifier is also used for token ring and FDDI network devices.

Subsequently, all packets are filtered, if they are neither ARP request nor ARP reply PDUs or if they probe for the layer-2 address of a loopback address (127.x.x.x) or a multicast IP address.

Further handling of a packet differs only slightly for an ARP request or ARP reply. Both types are entered in the ARP cache, or neigh_lookup() updates an existing entry.

An additional step for ARP requests returns a reply PDU to the requesting computer. To this end, the arp_send() function is used to compose an ARP reply packet (as shown below). One particularity here is that the computer can act as ARP proxy for other computers, in addition to listening to ARP requests with its own address. For example, this is necessary when the computer acts as firewall, and the firewall does not admit ARP requests. Consequently, this computer has to accept packets for other computers without the senders' knowledge. The computer acting as a firewall identifies itself to the ARP mechanism as these other computers. The work of the ARP proxy is done by arpd (ARP daemon).

neigh_lookup()	net/core/neighbour.c

This function is required to search the ARP cache for specific entries. If the neighbor we look for is found in the hash table, then a pointer to the neighbour structure is returned, and the reference counter of that ARP entry is incremented by one.

arp_send()	net/ipv4/arp.c

The arp_send() function includes all parameters to be set as arguments in an ARP PDU. It uses them to build an ARP packet with all fields properly set. The Hardware Type field and the layer-2 address are set in relation to the corresponding network device. The Internet Protocol is the only layer-3 protocol supported, so the fields for the layer-3 protocol type and the length of a layer-3 address always have the same values. Finally, the layer-2 packet header is appended, and the complete packet is sent by dev_queue_xmit().

neigh_update()	net/core/neighbour.c

The function `neigh_update(state)` is used to set a new state (`new_state`). This has no effect for `neighbour` entries in the NUD_PERMANENT and NUD_NOARP states, because no state transitions are allowed from these states to another state. (See Figure 15–6.)

If the state should be NUD_CONNECTED, then `neigh_connect()` is invoked to set the `output()` function to `neigh_connected_ouput()`. If this is not the case, the function `neigh_suspect()` has to be invoked to obtain the opposite effect.

If the old state was invalid (if (`!old & NUD_VALID`)), there might be packets waiting for this neighbor in the ARP queue. As long as the entry remains in the NUD_VALID state, and packets are still waiting in the queue, these will now be sent to the destination station.

Handling Unresolved IP Packets   So far, we have looked only at the case where an ARP PDU arrived in the computer and some action was taken in response. This section discusses how and when the Address Resolution Protocol resolves addresses. We know from Chapter 14 that an IP packet is generally sent by the `ip_finish_output()` function. The netfilter hook POST_ROUTING handles the last steps of this function in `ip_finish_output2()`. In the latter, the function pointer `hh_output()` is invoked for packets to a destination present in the layer-2 header cache. In contrast, the function pointer `dst->neighbour->output()` is used for network devices without layer-2 header cache. The function pointers `hh_output()` and `output()` of the `neigh_ops` options hide behind these two pointers. If the ARP entry is valid, then the pointers normally point to `dev_queue_xmit()`. (See Figure 15–5.) If there is no address resolution, then the `output()` pointer of the `neighbour` options is normally used; it points to `neigh_resolve_output()`. Of course, the IP packet can be sent immediately if the network device does not use ARP, so the pointer also points to `dev_queue_xmit()`.

The benefits of function pointers become obvious at this point again. The protocol status—the entry in the ARP cache, in this case—does not have to be checked every time; instead, we simply invoke the `output()` method. This means that the fast transmit function is invoked, or the address resolution method is used, depending on the entry's state. In summary, function pointers represent an elegant method of implementing stateful protocols.

neigh_resolve_output()	net/core/neighbour.c

`neigh_resolve_output(skb)` is the second function that can be referenced by the `output()` function pointer. In contrast to `neigh_connected_output()`, it cannot be assumed in this case that the stored address resolution is valid. For this reason, `neigh_event_send()` is used first to check the state the `neighbour` entry is in and whether the packet specified by `skb` can be sent to the destination station without prior address resolution. If so, then `dev->hard_header()` creates a layer-2 PDU, and `neigh->ops->queue_xmit()` sends the packet. If the network device supports a layer-2 header cache, and no entry yet exists for this receiver, then `neigh_hh_init()` creates this entry.

If the packet cannot yet be sent—for example, because the `neighbour` entry is in the NUD_STALE or NUD_INCOMPLETE states—then `neigh_send_event()` stores the packet in the `arp_queue` of the `neighbour` entry.

neigh_event_send()	**net/core/neighbour.h**

The return value of neigh_event_send(neigh, skb) is a Boolean value showing whether the packet specified by skb can be sent to the destination station (return value 0) or the address resolution is currently invalid (1), which means that the packet should not be sent. The value 0 is returned immediately for neighboring computers in the NUD_NOARP, NUD_PERMANENT, and NUD_REACHABLE states; otherwise, the function __neigh_event_send() is invoked, which does the following actions for the other states:

- NUD_NONE: New neighbor entries in this state are initially set to NUD_INCOMPLETE. Next, the timer of this neighbour is set, and neigh->ops->solicit() starts the first attempt to resolve the address.
- NUD_FAILED: A value of 1 is returned immediately, because the attempt to resolve the address of this station failed. No packets can be sent to this station.
- NUD_INCOMPLETE: Packets intended for computers in the NUD_INCOMPLETE state are stored in the arp_queue of the neighbour entry. Subsequently, the value 1 is returned to prevent the packet from being sent. The packet is temporarily stored in the queue of that neighbour entry until the neighboring station can be reached or the attempt to transmit is considered to have failed.
- NUD_STALE: In this case, the neighbour entry's state changes to NUD_DELAY, and the timer is set to expires = now + delay_probe_time. The timer's handling routine, neigh_timer_handler(), will then check the state of this entry as soon as the specified time has expired.

The function returns 1 if none of the above states is applicable.

neigh_connected_output()	**net/core/neighbour.c**

This function is the fastest possibility for neigh->output() to use without sending a stored layer-2 header. It is used only by neighbors in the NUD_REACHABLE state and for network devices that do not support hardware header caches. First, dev->hard_header() is invoked to create the layer-2 PDU; then, neigh->ops->queue_xmit() sends this PDU.

arp_solicit()	**net/ipv4/arp.c**

arp_solicit() is the actual function used to obtain the MAC address of a neighboring computer. It is used to send *ARP Request* packets.

The probes parameter in the neighbour structure stores the number of requests sent so far (i.e., the number of unsuccessful attempts since the neighbour entry was in the NUD_REACHABLE state).

arp_solicit() checks for how many ARP requests have been sent. If the specified limit has not yet been exceeded, then an ARP request is sent by the arp_send() function. The ARP_REQUEST parameter specifies the packet type.

If the MAC address of an interested computer is already known—for example, from an earlier request—then an attempt is first made to send the ARP request in a unicast packet to directly the neighboring station. This means that a simple check is done to see whether this computer is still reachable at this address, without disturbing other computers in the same LAN. Notice that a maximum of `neigh->parms->ucast_probes` are sent. Additional requests are then broadcast to all computers in the LAN. If the maximum number (`neigh->max_probes`) is exceeded again, then no more requests will be sent.

`neigh_timer_handler()`	**net/core/neighbour.c**

This is a handling routine invoked by the timer of a `neighbour` entry in the ARP cache. In contrast to `neigh_periodic_timer()`, the timer calls at intervals specified in the `neighbour` entry, rather than continually.

The timer is set when an ARP request PDU is sent, among other events. The triggering time is set to `expires = now + retrans_time` to check for whether a reply has arrived for this request, when this time has expired.

One of the following actions is performed, depending on the current state of the `neighbour` entry:

▪ NUD_VALID: The state of the ARP entry has changed to NUD_VALID since the time when the timer was set and the handling routine was executed. The corresponding computer is reachable, and its state is now set to NUD_REACHABLE.

The `neigh_connect(neigh)` function ensures that the correct functions of a reachable computer are executed. For example, it sets the `output()` functions to `neigh->ops->connected_output()`.

▪ NUD_DELAY: In this case, the state of the `neighbour` entry is changed to NUD_PROBE. The number of probes is set to `null`, which means that the entry starts the *probing phase*.

▪ NUD_PROBE: The entry in the ARP cache is in the probing phase; successive *ARP request* packets are sent in an attempt to resolve the computer's address.

When the number of sent requests (probes) has exceeded the maximum number (`neigh_max_probes(probes)`), it is assumed that the computer is not reachable, and its state changes to NUD_FAILED. If there are still packets for this computer in the queue of this `neighbour` entry, then the `error_report()` routine is invoked for each socket buffer, and finally the `arp_queue` is deleted.

If the maximum number of probes has not yet been exceeded, the `neigh->ops->solicit()` routine is invoked to send an ARP request. Before this request is sent, the timer is reinitialized, so that the timer handler will be invoked again as soon as `neigh->parms->retrans_time` time units (*jiffies*) have expired.

`neigh_connect()`	**net/core/neighbour.c**

`neigh_connect(neigh)` is invoked when the `neighbour` entry changes its state to NUD_CONNECTED. The `output()` function of this entry is set to `connected_output()`. If a hardware header exists, then the procedure to send a packet at the network device interface (hh->hh_output()) is set to neigh->ops->hh_output(), to be able to use the stored hardware header.

neigh_suspect()	net/core/neighbour.c

The neigh->output() functions are changed to neigh->ops->output(). This means that, if the fast way over the hardware header cache was previously used, it is no longer used now, so that, when the next packet is ready to be sent, a probe for the MAC address will be started (neighbor solicitation by neigh_resolve_output()).

neigh_destroy()	net/core/neighbour.c

A neighbour entry is deleted from the ARP cache, and its structures are released. Entries in the hardware header cache are also released. neigh_release() invokes neigh_destroy(). It first checks for whether there are still other pointers to this neighbour (if (atomic_dec_and_test(&neigh->refcnt))) and for whether the entry has already been marked as unused (if (neigh->dead)). Both conditions must be true before the neighbor may be deleted.

neigh_sync()	net/core/neighbour.c

This function has no effect for permanent neighbour entries (NUD_PERMANENT) or for network devices without ARP support (NUD_NOARP), and it returns immediately. Otherwise, the following actions are taken, depending on the entry's state:

- NUD_REACHABLE: If an entry is in this state and a certain time (neigh->reach-able_time) has expired since the last acknowledgement was received from the neighboring computer, either by an incoming packet or an explicit ARP request or ARP reply, then the entry is marked as NUD_STALE. This means that no sign of life has come from this computer over a certain period of time and so it probably no longer exists. The function neigh_suspect() is used to verify this situation; it tries to update that computer's state.
- NUD_VALID: If the computer is known and an acknowledgement has arrived before the normal lifetime of the entry (neigh->reachable_time) expired, then its state is set to NUD_REACHABLE, and neigh_connect(neigh) is invoked.

neigh_sync() is invoked by neigh_update() before the new state is entered in the neighbour structure. The intention is to ensure that the current state be updated before state transitions occur.

neigh_periodic_timer()	net/core/neighbour.c

This function initializes a timer for each neighbour cache. This timer periodically checks and updates the states of cache entries (i.e., it runs a so-called *garbage collection*).

The relevant handling routine is the function `neigh_periodic_timer()`. It visits each entry in the cache and does one of the following actions, depending on the entry's state:

- NUD_PERMANENT: This is a permanent entry; nothing in its state has to be changed.

- IN_TIMER: An attempt is currently being made to reach the specified computer by sending an ARP request packet. This also means that the timer of the neighbour entry is set, and the handling routine `neigh_timer_handler()` will run soon. In this case, the entry's state is updated at the same time, so that `neigh_periodic_timer()` changes nothing in the state of this entry.

- NUD_FAILED: If a neighbour entry is in the NUD_FAILED state, or if the time `neigh->ops->staletime` has expired, the computer is considered no longer reachable, and `neigh_release()` deletes this entry from the ARP cache.

- NUD_REACHABLE: If an entry is marked as reachable, but `neigh->ops->reachable_time` jiffies have already passed since the last acknowledgment, then it is classified as old (NUD_STALE), and `neigh_suspect()` (described earlier) attempts to update this entry.

The function `neigh_periodic_timer()` runs as an independent tasklet in multiprocessor systems.

Creating and Managing `neighbour` Instances

`neigh_create()`	**net/core/neighbour.c**

This function is responsible for creating a new `neighbour` entry and entering it in the respective `neighbour` cache. `neigh_create()` is normally invoked by the `arp_bind_neighbour()` function when `neigh_lookup()` was unsuccessful at finding the ARP entry of the interested computer. Accordingly, it creates a new entry.

To create a new `neighbour` entry, the function first initializes a `neighbour` structure in the appropriate `neighbour` instance (`neigh_alloc()`). If a constructor was defined for the entries in this table, then it is invoked now.

Before it adds a `neighbour` to the table, the function first checks for whether such an entry already exists. If not, then the entry is added as the first element of the hash row that references `pkey`. A new entry is added at the beginning of the hash row, because the probability is high that it will be accessed next. The return value is a pointer to the new entry in the ARP cache.

`neigh_alloc()`	**net/core/neighbour.c**

`neigh_alloc(tbl)` creates a new `neighbour` structure for a specific `neighbour` table (tbl). This table is specified additionally, because it includes some information required for the new entry. In addition, before the `neighbour` structure is created, the function first checks on whether the current table is full. `tbl->gc_thresh3` is the absolute upper limit of the table. This limit must not be exceeded. `gc_thresh2` is a threshold value that should be exceeded only briefly. The garbage collector allows you to exceed this limit for a maximum of five seconds. When this time expires, it runs a garbage collection. The following query tests for these two conditions:

```
if (tbl->entries > tbl->gc_thresh3 ||
    (tbl->entries > tbl->gc_thresh2 && now - tbl->last_flush > 5*HZ)).
```

If this is the case, then `neigh_forced_gc()` runs a garbage collection and checks for whether sufficient space was freed in the table. If the space freed is insufficient, the function returns `NULL` and doesn't create a new `neighbour` structure.

If the table can accommodate the new entry, a new `neighbour` structure is taken from the memory cache `tbl->kmem_cachep` and added to the table. The state of the new entry is set to `NUD_NONE`, and a pointer to the new `neighbour` structure is returned.

neigh_forced_gc()	net/core/neighbour.c

If a `neighbour` table is full (see `neigh_alloc()`), the garbage collector runs `neigh_force_gc()` immediately. This function is invoked by `neigh_alloc()` to free memory space for new `neighbour` structures. Entries that meet the following conditions are deleted from the cache:

- There is no longer any reference to the structure (`n->refcnt == 1`).
- The `neighbour` is not permanent (`n->nud_state != NUD_PERMANENT`).
- For an empty `NUD_INCOMPLETE` entry, the structure has to have been in the cache for at least `retrans_time` to avoid unnecessary duplication of request packets: (`n->nud_state != NUD_INCOMPLETE || jiffies - n->used >n->parms->retrans_time`).

The number of deleted entries is output as soon as this function has finished checking all `neighbour` entries.

arp_constructor()	net/ipv4/arp.c

Once `neigh_create()` has invoked the `neigh_alloc()` function to initialize a new `neighbour` structure, it invokes the appropriate constructor function for the specified `neigh_table`—for example, the `arp_constructor()` method for the ARP cache.

In the first step, `arp_constructor()` checks for whether the network device used requires the ARP protocol. If this is not the case, then the state of this entry is set to `NUD_NOARP`. Next, it checks for whether the `hard_header_cache` includes an entry for this network device. If so, then the `neigh_ops` field of this `neighbour` structure is set to `arp_hh_ops`. Otherwise, this `neighbour` entry uses the methods of the `arp_generic_ops` options. Finally, when the entry has reached the `NUD_VALID` state, the `connected_output()` function can be used to communicate with the neighbouring computer. Otherwise, the normal `output()` function will be used again.

`neigh_table_init()`	**net/core/neighbour.c**

`neigh_table_init()` takes the following steps to initialize a new `neigh_table` structure:

- It obtains memory for the `neighbour` cache (`tbl->kmem_cachep = kmem_cache_create()`).
- It initializes a timer (`tbl->gc_timer()`) and sets the expiry time to `now + tbl->gc_interval + tbl->reachable_time`. This timer calls `neigh_periodic_timer()` periodically.
- It inserts the new table into a singly linked list, `neigh_tables`.

`arp_hash()`	**net/ipv4/arp.c**

The `arp_tabl()` function uses this function as a method for computing the hash function. The hash value is computed on the basis of the IP address (`primary_key`), using modulo NEIGH_HASHMASK (ARP table size).

C H A P T E R   1 6

IP Routing

16.1   INTRODUCTION

One of the most important functions of the IP layer (the network layer of the TCP/IP protocol architecture) is to forward packets between communicating end systems across a number of intermediate systems. (See Figure 16–1.) The determination of the route that packets will take across the Internet and the forwarding of packets towards their destination is called *routing*.

16.1.1   Networks and Routers

As was mentioned in Chapter 14, the Internet represents a network of networks. The physical subnetworks built by use of different layer-2 transmission technologies, such as Ethernet, can include a different number of nodes each—for example just two nodes connected over a point-to-point link. The IP layer interconnects these subnetworks to form a global network having millions of nodes.

Special nodes, which are integrated in all subnetworks that are connected in one place, are used to link these subnetworks; these nodes are called *routers*. Figure 16–2 shows an example with five local area networks, connected through three routers. Router A also connects the network to the rest of the Internet. The network layer abstracts from

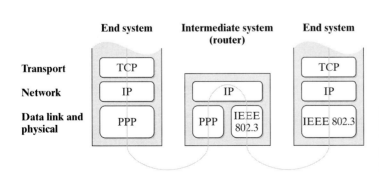

FIGURE 16–1
Routing within the IP layer in the TCP/IP protocol architecture (protocols in the other layers are examples).

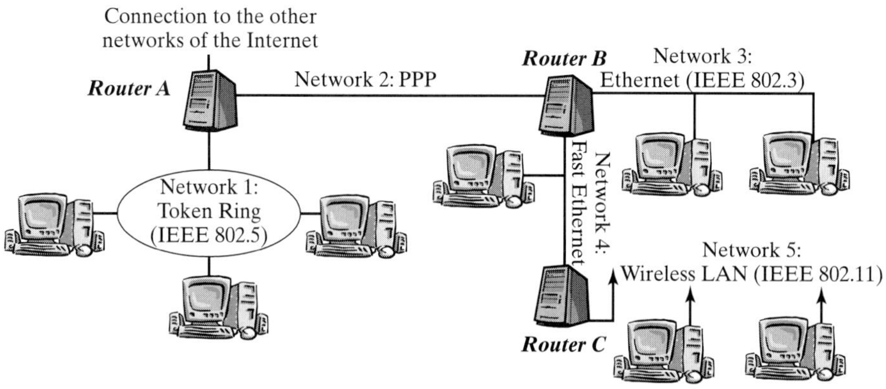

FIGURE 16–2
Routers interconnect networks.

lower layers, so it is irrelevant for the communication implemented over IP that the end systems are connected to different LAN types.

Routers are used both to link local area networks and to connect local area networks to the Internet. In addition, networks in the "core" of the Internet, which normally have a much larger geographic reach, are interconnected and linked to access networks through routers, or even built of direct links between routers ("two-node networks").

Routers are often especially designed for this purpose—so-called "dedicated routing devices." However, the Linux kernel also offers the required functionality to let you use a Linux system as a router.

16.1.2 Forwarding and Routing

Routers forward IP packets from one physical network to another, where the second network is normally "closer" to the destination network (not necessarily in the sense of geographic distance, but rather from a network-topology view) than the first network. To decide in what direction each packet has to be forwarded, the router requires a certain amount of information about the Internet topology, which it stores locally.

This topological knowledge—also called *forwarding information* in the rest of this course—can be managed manually for small networks like the example in Figure 16–2, because there is little of it and it changes only if the LAN topology changes. For example, all router B actually needs to know is the end systems in networks 3, 4, and 5. It can send all packets not addressed to end systems in these networks globally towards router A, because the "rest of the Internet" is behind router A.

In the core area of the Internet, the situation is not that simple. Rather than a small LAN, there is a large area of the entire Internet behind a network interface of a router. The knowledge required to be able to forward IP packets with arbitrary addresses in the correct direction is much more extensive. In addition, it has to be adapted continually: when new paths are added, when old ones fail or are overloaded, and when the network topology in remote places changes. For these reasons, a network the size of the global Internet requires automatic methods to continually update the topology information and determine suitable routes.

These methods to determine forwarding information in each router are also commonly called "routing." This means that we can identify two different functions that, together, form the entire IP routing mechanism, and which have to be clearly distinguished:

- *Forwarding* of IP packets in routers, which is based on given forwarding information. A router has to look up a database and make a decision for each packet that passes through this router on its way through the Internet.
- *Routing*: determining the best routes over which to transport each packet between networks, and deriving forwarding information from information about topologies and states exchanged regularly between routers within the entire network.

Forwarding is implemented in the Linux kernel, because it is a task of the IP layer. In contrast, routing is handled on higher layers: The *routing protocols* used to distribute information about network topologies and states normally build on top of transport-layer protocols, and the pertinent programs (*routing daemons*) are user-space processes running in Linux systems.

The interface between the two parts is built by a database, in which a routing daemon stores its forwarding information, and which the IP layer uses as a basis for its decisions when packets have to be forwarded.

As mentioned earlier, forwarding information in small networks at the "outskirts" of the Internet is rather static and so can be managed manually—you don't necessarily have to use a routing daemon. In this case, the system administrator can use tools like those discussed in Section 16.2.3 to add forwarding information manually to the database. This method is called *static routing*, in contrast to *dynamic routing*, which is based on routing protocols.

Routing is not done in the Linux kernel, so it is not discussed in detail in this book. Instead, we refer interested readers to general books about internetworking (e.g., [Come00]). This chapter focuses on forwarding in the IP layer and the forwarding-information database, which is also implemented in the Linux kernel.

16.1.3 IP Addresses

To be able to send packets to arbitrary end systems in the Internet, we need a means of unique identification of end systems. We know from a previous section that this is accomplished by using IP addresses, which are 32 bits in length and normally are represented by four single-byte values in dotted decimal notation for IP Version 4.

Network Addresses and End-System Identifiers   In addition to identifying network nodes, IP addresses have another important function involved in the finding of nodes. In fact, if IP addresses were randomly distributed (but unique) values, they could still serve as identifiers, but it would be hard to forward packets to a specific destination, because each router would have to know the forwarding direction for each possible destination IP address in the Internet. Considering the enormous number of end systems connected to the Internet, this would obviously be very expensive with regard to memory requirement and search time.

To allow for the forwarding direction to be determined efficiently, IP addresses are structured hierarchically, and consist of two different parts: a *network address* and an *end-system identifier*. The network address is identical for all end systems in one subnetwork; the end-system identifier distinguishes end systems in a specific subnetwork. During forwarding of packets, the end-system identifier can be totally ignored until the packet arrives in the correct subnetwork. This means that routers do not need to know end-system identifiers; in this way, the division of IP addresses into two parts dramatically reduces the amount of information routers have to store.

Because it always forms the beginning of an IP address, the network-address part of an IP address is also called *network prefix*.

Address Classes and Classless Addressing   The next question we have to answer is about the sizes of the network part and the end-system identifier part in an IP address. Three different variants were defined when addressing in the Internet was specified [Post81c]: The address classes A, B, and C, having 7, 14, and 21 bits for the network part and 24, 16, and 8 bits for the end-system identifier. The class an address belongs to is determined by the first (leftmost) bits of the address. Figure 16–3, which was also used in Chapter 14, illustrates this scheme. We will not go into detail about the two additional classes, D and E, which are reserved for special purposes, or into other reserved network prefixes and end-system identifiers again at this point; see Section 14.1.5 for this.

This addressing scheme was originally designed by assuming that each physical network could actually have a network identifier from one of the three classes mentioned above (depending on the size of the physical network). However, it was soon observed that this approach would quickly exhaust all available network prefixes. In addition, the existing classes proved often to be inappropriate: A class-A network could contain almost 2^{24} or 16777216 end systems, a number that even the largest organizations would hardly need, apart from the fact that no known physical network technology can handle that number of end systems. In contrast, class-C networks are much more numerous, but cannot hold more than 254 end systems, which is not enough in many cases.

These limitations motivated the development of technologies to better utilize the existing address space. The basic idea was to have the boundary between the network prefix and the end-system identifier at an arbitrary bit position, instead of only at the three positions dictated by the A, B, and C address classes.

For example, a class-A network can be divided in two networks with half the size each by using the first bit of the end-system identifier for division: All end systems with a zero at this position fall into one network, and all systems with a one

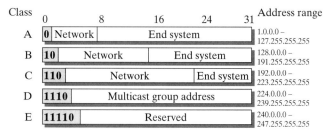

FIGURE 16–3

IP address classes with different division of network and end-system parts.

fall into the other network. This means that the network prefix has become longer by one bit inside of the new subnetworks, from the end systems' view.

This new division of addresses is totally transparent to the outside; it plays no role for routing outside the networks directly concerned: Only the router that connects the two new networks to the rest of the world has to know and consider this new division. This scheme basically allows us to divide an address space several times. The length of the valid network prefix grows then in line with the depth of the hierarchy formed by this scheme.

▓ Similarly, when working in the opposite direction, we could group a block of class-C addresses into a larger address space—for example, if they belong to a single organization (e.g., an Internet Service Provider). This corresponds to shortening the network prefix, forming a larger address space, which can be divided again, if necessary.

In this case, it is not necessarily meaningful to have the new division transparent to the outside, because it would require many unnecessary routing entries. For example, if an organization had a block of 256 class-C addresses instead of one single class-B address, then 256 routing entries instead of a single one would have to be published globally.

Today, the Internet uses *Classless Inter-Domain Routing* (*CIDR*) [ReLi93, FLYV93], which virtually ignores the "old" class division of IP addresses: Network prefixes can have an arbitrary length. However, the information about the actual length of the network identifier of a specific network can no longer be seen from the first address bits, in contrast with the method seen in the classful scheme. Consequently, this information has to be passed on and stored with each network address. There are two common notations:

▓ In the first notation, the number of bits belonging to the network prefix is denoted in decimal form, with a slash separating it from the address. For example, 192.168.152.0/21 denotes a network with its prefix consisting of the first 21 bits of the IP address 192.168.152.0.

▓ The second notation denotes a bit mask in addition to the IP address; the bit mask has the same length as the IP address. It is called a *network mask* and has all bits corresponding to the positions of the network prefix in the IP address set to one. The network mentioned above would look as follows in this notation: 192.168.152.0/255.255.248.0.

Router Addresses   Routers have their own IP addresses, as do all network nodes in TCP/IP networks. Because an IP address also identifies the network it belongs to, as we know from the previous sections, and because a router has to be connected to more than one network to be able to mediate between networks, it is obvious that a router has more than one IP address. More precisely, each network interface in a router has its own IP address.

Figure 16–4 shows the sample networks from Figure 16–2 again to illustrate this concept, denoting IP addresses for all end systems and all network interfaces of each router.

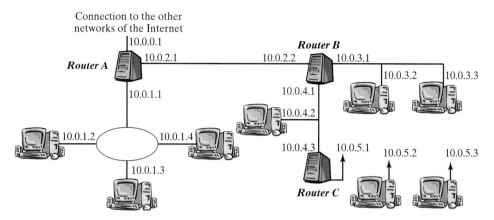

FIGURE 16–4
Assigning IP addresses to end systems and network interfaces in routers (example).

16.1.4 Forwarding Procedure

For a router, an IP packet received over a network interface falls into one of three categories, depending on its destination address:

- *The packet is addressed to the router*: In this case, the packet is not forwarded, but passed to a protocol instance of the transport layer in the router.
- *The packet is addressed to an end system in a neighboring network:* Packets addressed to an end system in a network that is connected directly to the router over a network interface can be forwarded directly to this end system. When the packet is passed to the data-link layer, the physical address of the destination system, which might previously have been discovered by the ARP protocol, is used.
- *The packet is addressed to an end system in a remote network*: If the destination system is not in a neighboring network, then the packet has to be forwarded over an additional router. This router is identified from the forwarding information, and its physical address is used as destination towards the physical layer.

The first case is characterized by the fact that the IP destination address belongs to an internal network interface. The second case can be detected by AND-combining the destination address with the network masks of neighboring networks. If the result of this operation matches the network prefix of the respective network, then the destination system is in this network. The third case applies when none of the two previous conditions is true.

In practice, the second case can be conveniently covered by the mechanism used to identify the next router in the third case, and "rule-based routing" is implemented in the recent kernel versions of Linux, so that the first case is also handled in this way. (See Section 16.1.6.)

The exact procedure involved in identifying the next router for the third case is strongly linked to the data structure used to store the forwarding information in the router. This data structure will be discussed in the next section.

Routing Table   The structure of forwarding information can be thought of as a table, where each row describes a specific address range, which is defined by a network prefix. This *routing table* specifies the network interface or the next router to be used for forwarding of packets having their destinations in the specified address range.

Figure 16–5 uses an example to show what a routing table for router B from Figure 16–4 could look like. We use designations common in Linux to name network interfaces. In practice, routing tables often include additional information in each row (e.g., describing the quality or the cost of a path, which help in selecting one of several routes to the same destination).

The example shows clearly how the second and third cases from the previous section can be distinguished: If the routing table includes an entry for a next router, then the packet has to be forwarded to that router. Otherwise, it can be sent over the specified network interface directly to the destination system.

An entry in a routing table is also called a *route* in the following discussion, to simplify matters.

Longest Prefix   Denoting a network address and a network mask means that the network prefixes entered in a routing table can have an arbitrary length. They don't even have to describe a single network that actually exists, but can instead group several networks in neighboring address spaces to reduce the size of the routing table. The most extreme example for this is an entry having its prefix length zero or its network mask 0.0.0.0. Such an entry represents *all* destination networks and is actually valid. It supplies a *default route*—the route packets should take when no specific entry exists for their destination address.

Naturally, a clear regulation has to be found for conflicting cases where several matching prefixes exist for one destination address. For example, such a conflict happens when the routing table includes a default route and additional entries. The problem is solved by selecting the entry with the longest prefix from all entries with matching prefixes. This means that more specific information in the routing table has priority over less specific information.

16.1.5 Routing Cache

The search for an entry with the longest matching prefix is the most time-critical operation in the forwarding procedure: It is used frequently, so its implementation should be efficient.

Destination	Network Mask	Router	Interface
10.0.3.0	255.255.255.0	—	eth0
10.0.4.0	255.255.255.0	—	eth1
10.0.5.0	255.255.255.0	10.0.4.3	eth1
10.0.2.0	255.255.255.0	—	ppp0
0.0.0.0	0.0.0.0	10.0.2.1	ppp0

FIGURE 16–5
Simple routing table for router B in Figure 16–4.

In Linux, all routing-table entries are sorted by prefix length, and the table is searched successively by descending prefix length. This method is not always efficient, especially when the table includes many different prefixes.

Rather than using different data structures to speed up the search process, Linux uses a *routing cache* to reduce the number of search processes. This cache stores the table entries used last and uses a hashing method that operates on the source address and destination address of packets to be forwarded, for accessing entries very fast. The routing table has to be consulted only for new address combinations not yet stored in the routing cache.

This method represents a good solution for end systems with a relatively limited number of concurrent communication partners; it is probably less suitable in the core area of the Internet.

16.1.6 Rule-based Routing

One routing particularity in Linux Version 2.4 and higher is that it lets you use several routing tables, instead of a single one. An additional set of rules is then used to select which table should be used for what packets. This method is called *rule-based routing* or *policy routing* and allows you to include other criteria (e.g., the source address) in the routing decision, in addition to the destination address, whereas routing decisions taken from one single routing table are always based only on the destination address and the destination-network prefix specified in that one table.

Rules   Each rule has a selector and a type. The selector chooses the packets to which the rule can be applied, and the type determines what should happen with a packet when the selector matches (e.g., that a specific routing table should be used or that a packet should be dropped). These rules are applied by priority values in ascending order. A unique priority value has to be assigned to each rule when it is defined. If a suitable route is found based on a rule, then the process is aborted, and the packet is forwarded. Otherwise, the process continues with the next rule.

The selector can contain the source address, the destination address, and the network interface at which the packet to be forwarded arrived. In addition, you can use the TOS field (which has more recently been called *codepoint*—see Section 14.1.2) or the `iptables` marking (see Section 19.3.5), which is called `fwmark` in the following discussion. Indirectly, the latter option lets you use additional packet properties (e.g., transport-protocol ports) for selection. All fields not explicitly stated in the selector are always considered to match.

There are five types of rules: `unicast`, `blackhole`, `unreachable`, `prohibit`, and `nat`. The "normal case" is the `unicast` type: A specific routing table stated in the rule is searched for a route. The `blackhole`, `unreachable`, and `prohibit` types cause the packet to be discarded when the rule is applied. They differ only in the type of feedback to the sender: `blackhole` creates no feedback, `unreachable` reports that the destination network is unreachable, and `prohibit` reports that the communication is not permitted. The last rule type, `nat`, can be used for static network-address translation (NAT). It is designed for special routing applications and not for the purpose of using one single IP address for several computers. This mechanism would be unsuitable for this purpose, because it is stateless. We will see in Chapter 21 that the masquerading mechanism of `iptables` is suitable for such cases. The `nat` routing rules are discussed in more detail in the work of Alexey Kuznetsov [Kuzn99].

Default Settings By default, the Linux kernel specifies three rules of the unicast type, with a selector each matching all packets. The priorities and identifiers for routing tables used for each type are defined as follows:

Priority	Table Name	Table Number
0	`local`	255
32766	`main`	254
32767	`default`	253

The three routing tables, `local`, `main`, and `default`, which are searched according to the above rules in this order for matching routes, are also created automatically. The latter two are initially empty, and the system administrator has to add entries (or use suitable scripts to fill them with entries) when the system boots. The `main` table is intended for "normal" routing entries; the `default` table is suitable for lower-priority backup solutions. The rules belonging to the `main` and `default` tables can also be deleted or modified.

In contrast to the second and third rules, the first rule is fixed, and the associated routing table is managed by the kernel itself. This table includes entries describing the addresses of local network interfaces. This realizes a very elegant approach to the categorizing of incoming packets, which was mentioned at the beginning of Section 16.1.4: Using just one procedure for all incoming packets, consult the set of rules and then the associated routing tables for each packet; if an entry is found in the `local` table, the packet is delivered locally—otherwise, it has to be forwarded.

Notice that only two tables, `local` and `main`, are searched in this order when rule-based routing is disabled in the kernel configuration.

16.2 CONFIGURATION

This section describes the options available to configure routing in Linux. First, this concerns the kernel configuration, which is used, for example, to determine whether advanced features, such as rule-based routing, should be integrated into the kernel. The options available for this configuration are described in Section 16.2.1. Second, you can also modify some routing parameters while the system is running. The setting options available for this in the `proc` file system are discussed in Section 16.2.2. Third, you have to add entries to routing tables and rule lists. The `ip` command, which is described in Section 16.2.3, is a good tool to manage such entries.

16.2.1 Configuring the Kernel

Some routing options can be set when you configure the Linux kernel, before it is compiled. All of them are in the networking options section and will be described briefly in this section below. In addition to the name of the preprocessor constant, which is defined when an option is activated, the label shown in the kernel configurator is given in double quotes. A prerequisite to being able to activate some of these options is that CONFIG_INET ("TCP/IP networking") should be enabled; without that, routing makes no sense, anyway.

▨ CONFIG_NETLINK   "Kernel/User netlink socket"

Rather than directly influencing the routing mechanism, this option activates the bidirectional netlink interface between the kernel and the user-address space, which is implemented with datagram sockets of the new protocol family, PF_NETLINK, and can be used to communicate with different kernel areas. The respective area is selected by an identifier, which is given instead of a protocol when you open the socket. Section 26.3.3 describes more details.

In connection with routing, the NETLINK_ROUTE "protocol identifier" is important, and it can be used by activating the following option. This option is available only provided that CONFIG_NETLINK is active:

▶ CONFIG_RTNETLINK   "Routing messages"

Routing rules and routing tables can be modified by using sockets of the PF_NETLINK protocol family and the NETLINK_ROUTE "protocol." This interface, which will also be called *RT netlink interface* below, is used in the ip configuration tool described in Section 16.2.3. Besides, by reading an RT netlink socket, you can "eavesdrop" on changes made to routing tables by other processes.

▨ CONFIG_IP_ADVANCED_ROUTER   "IP: advanced router"

This option has no direct effect; it represents a switch that allows you to select a number of additional options can be used to obtain much more control over the routing procedure. The options CONFIG_NETLINK and CONFIG_RTNETLINK are activated automatically when you select CONFIG_IP_ADVANCED_ROUTER.

▶ CONFIG_IP_MULTIPLE_TABLES   "IP: policy routing"

This option links the file fib_rules.o into the kernel and enables the rule-based routing described in Section 16.1.6. If this option is disabled, then the kernel creates only two routing tables, local and main, and searches them in this order.

The following additional options are available in connection with rule-based routing:

• CONFIG_IP_ROUTE_FWMARK   "IP: use netfilter MARK value as routing key"

This option allows you to include the fwmark, which can be added to certain packets by using packet filter rules (see Section 19.3.5), in the forwarding decision (i.e., you can specify different routes for packets with different packet filter marks). For example, you can make the route selection indirectly dependent on transport-protocol attributes (e.g., ports). CONFIG_NETFILTER ("network packet filtering") has to be active to be able to select CONFIG_IP_ROUTE_FWMARK.

- CONFIG_IP_ROUTE_NAT   "IP: fast network address translation"

When this option is active, you can use special routing entries to translate addresses (*Network Address Translation—NAT*). This functionality complements the NAT rules mentioned in Section 16.1.6; see [Kuzn99] for a description of how you can configure this rarely used option.

   Activating CONFIG_IP_ROUTE_NAT causes ip_nat_dumb.o to be linked into the kernel.

▷ CONFIG_IP_ROUTE_MULTIPATH   "IP: equal cost multipath"

If the routing table includes several equal-ranking entries to a specific destination, then Linux traditionally selects the first. This behavior cannot be used meaningfully, because the order in which the entries are found cannot be seen or influenced from outside of the kernel. You can use the option CONFIG_IP_ROUTE_MULTIPATH to enable special entries that specify several equal routes, and then have one of these routes selected randomly.

▷ CONFIG_IP_ROUTE_TOS   "IP: use TOS value as routing key"

When enabled, this option causes the value of the Differentiated Services Codepoint field from the IP packet header to be included in the routing decision. (This field was formerly called Type of Service, which is the reason it is still referred to as the TOS field in the kernel and in this chapter.) You can assign values for this field in routing-table entries, which means that these entries will be used only for packets with matching values in the TOS field.

▷ CONFIG_IP_ROUTE_VERBOSE   "IP: verbose route monitoring"

If this option is enabled, then messages are written to the system log when certain error situations occur during the routing process—normally ones caused by attacks or faulty configurations.

▷ CONFIG_IP_ROUTE_LARGE_TABLES   "IP: large routing tables"

The hash tables used to manage routing table entries normally have a fixed size. The size of these tables is increased automatically when CONFIG_IP_ROUTE_LARGE_TABLES is activated, so that the access speed doesn't drop when they include many entries.

CONFIG_IP_MROUTE   "IP: multicast routing"

This option activates multicast routing and links the ipmr.o file into the kernel. Multicast routing is discussed in Chapter 17.

▨ CONFIG_WAN_ROUTER   "WAN router"

This option has no effect on the routing procedure. It includes the general management functionality for special network interfaces used to build *Wide Area Networks
(WANs)*. This special hardware allows you to use a Linux computer as WAN router.

▨ CONFIG_NET_FASTROUTE   "Fast switching"

If the input and output interfaces of a forwarded packet are different, then you
can accelerate the copying process required in some cases by special hardware
support directly from network card to network card. CONFIG_NET_FASTROUTE
has to be enabled to be able to use this option. The only effect on the routing procedure is that a mark is set in situations suitable for fast copying. This can be handled by the drivers of network cards, if the required hardware is available.

▨ CONFIG_NET_SCHED   "QoS and/or fair queuing"

This option allows you to activate the options for traffic control, described in
Chapter 18. We include this option here only because routing rules and routing-
table entries can be used to classify packets. Notice that this requires the suboption CONFIG_NET_CLS ("Packet classifier API") and its suboption
CONFIG_NET_CLS_ROUTE4 to be activated. As a consequence, the symbol
CONFIG_NET_CLS_ROUTE is defined additionally. This symbol can be configured
nowhere else, and it causes the data structures for routing rules and routing-table
entries to be extended by an element required for classification.

16.2.2 Files in the proc File System

Some entries in the proc directory tree can be used to probe and manipulate data
structures and routing properties. You find such entries in two different directories,
/proc/net and /proc/sys/net/ipv4.

The /proc/net Directory   The /proc/net directory includes files that reflect extensive routing-related data structures in the kernel, namely the routing table main in
route and the routing cache in rt_cache. In rt_acct, you might additionally be able
to read statistics about the number of packets or bytes that used a specific route except
that it is not yet used and so this file is always empty. All files mentioned here have
read access only.

The /proc/sys/net/ipv4 Directory   The entries underneath /proc/sys are created by a relatively new uniform mechanism. Each of them describes a configurable parameter of the kernel. They can be probed and modified—either by reading from or
writing to a file, or by using the system call _sysctl() and the sysctl command. Entries for parameters of the IPv4 implementation, some of which are related to routing,
are located underneath /proc/sys/net/ipv4:

▨ ip_forward: This entry represents a switch for the forwarding functionality; the
system acts as a router whenever this entry is set to one. If it is set to zero, then all
packets received and not addressed to the local system are discarded.

▧ route subdirectory: The files in the route subdirectory reflect numeric or Boolean values, with one exception; they are used by the kernel to manage the routing cache, amongst others. The directory entries and their variables in the kernel normally have the same names, with an ip_rt_ prefix for the variables. The exact meanings of these entries will not be discussed here, apart from the one single exception: Writing to the flush entry causes the routing cache to be deleted.

▧ conf/*device* subdirectories: /proc/sys/net/ipv4/conf includes a number of subdirectories—namely, one for each registered network interface (lo, eth0, ...), one named default, and one named all. All directories include the same entries, which refer to the interface with the same name. In addition, the entries in the all directory are global for all interfaces, and the entries in the default directory represent default values for any interfaces registered in the future. The following entries are of interest for the routing mechanism:

▷ forwarding: Like the entry in /proc/sys/net/ipv4/ip_forward, the entry in forwarding represents a switch for the forwarding mechanism. The entry in the all directory even reflects exactly the same value. The entries in the interface directories apply only to the forwarding of packets that arrived via specific interfaces. Each time that the switch value (except the default value) is changed, the routing cache is automatically deleted. The all value (and accordingly also the value in /proc/sys/net/ipv4/ip_forward) has particular semantics: When it is written, then all interface entries and the default entry are automatically set to the same new value.

▷ log_martians: If the all entry or the entry of an interface is set to 1, then so-called "Martians"—illegal address values (e.g., values that are incorrect with respect to the configuration of the interface that received this packet)—are shown in the system log.

▷ rp_filter: If the all entry and the entry of an interface are active, then packets arriving over this interface are subject to *Reverse-Path Filtering*, which means that a check tests whether a packet with exchanged source and destination addresses, according to the routing tables, would be sent over the interface which actually received this packet. If this test fails, then the packet is discarded. Reverse-Path Filtering is a sensible security measure against packets with forged (or spoofed) source address. However, it can sometimes be useful to use different interfaces for different directions intentionally, so this measure can cause problems and therefore is allowed to be disabled.

16.2.3 Configuration on System Level

Before a Linux system can send IP packets, or act as a router and forward IP packets for other systems, we have to add appropriate entries to routing tables. Unless we are using a routing daemon for automatic routing based on a routing protocol, a capability hardly needed at the "outskirts" of the Internet, the system administrator has to either add static entries manually or use scripts upon system start or when new interfaces are added (e.g., when a PPP connection is established).

The "traditional" Unix command to manage routing tables is route. However, it does not support the relatively new rule-based routing, and all it allows you to do is modify the main table and read from the routing cache. It uses the ioctl() system call to interface to the kernel.

Alexey Kuznetsov, one of the major contributors to the development of the routing implementation in the Linux kernel, also proposed a tool that uses the more recent RT netlink interface to the kernel. It can be used to manipulate not only routing tables, but also a number of other parameters of the network configuration. The command is called ip, and it expects that the first parameter will always be an area to be configured. Table 16–1 shows an overview of all possible areas.

The syntax of this command is relatively uniform for different areas: The area identifier normally is followed by an action identifier (e.g., show, add, delete, help), followed by area-specific parameters, which are denoted by a leading keyword. The action identifier help always supplies a syntax description. For example, ip route help shows the syntax of commands used to manipulate and query routing tables.

The following subsections describe only those two variants of the ip command that are used to manipulate routing rules and routing tables: ip rule, and ip route. More information about the other variants is included in the ip tool documentation [Kuzn99].

The ip rule Command   The ip rule variant of the ip command serves to output, add, or delete routing rules in the kernel database by using ip rule show, ip rule add, and ip rule delete. ip rule show outputs all rules; the other two commands require additional parameters to describe a rule. These parameters are denoted by a leading keyword, as shown in Table 16–2; see also Section 16.1.6 for a description of the meaning of these parameters.

If mandatory parameters are not stated, then default values are used. The type used then is unicast with a reference to the main table, and the priority value immediately below the smallest number used (except for the value null, which is always present) is assigned. The priority numbers should be unique, but notice that this is not

TABLE 16–1   Variants of the ip command.

Command	Function
ip link	Configures network interfaces (see also ifconfig).
ip address	Manages additional addresses of network interfaces.
ip neighbour	Manages the ARP table (see arp).
ip route	Manages routing tables (see route).
ip rule	Manages the routing rules database.
ip maddress	Manages multicast address entries in network cards.
ip mroute	Shows multicast routes.
ip tunnel	Manages tunnels.
ip monitor	Monitors the RT netlink interface.

TABLE 16–2   Parameters for `ip rule add` and `ip rule delete`.

Keyword	Parameter
type	Rule type (`unicast`, `blackhole`, `unreachable`, `prohibit`, `nat`).
from	Source address prefix (prefix length separated by /).
to	Destination address prefix.
iif	Name of the input interface.
tos	Value in the TOS field of the IP packet.
fwmark	Value of the `fwmark`.
priority	Unique priority value for the rule.
table	Name or number of a routing table for `unicast` rules.
realms	Class identifier of a queuing discipline.
nat	First address of a NAT source address range for `nat` rules.

checked. The names of routing tables are translated to table numbers by using the information from the configuration file `/etc/iproute2/rt_tables`, and so names can also be assigned to tables other than default tables.

For example, to use a special routing table (in this case number 99) for IP packets with source address matching the 16-bit prefix 192.168 and received over the `eth1` interface, we could use the following command to insert the rule at position 1000:

```
root@tux # ip rule add prio 1000 from 192.168/16 iif eth1 table 99
```

The rule type (unicast) can be omitted, because it coincides with the default value. Next, we can use `ip rule show` to output the existing set of rules, together with the default rules:

```
root@tux # ip rule show
0:         from all lookup local
1000:      from 192.168.0.0/16 iif eth1 lookup 99
32766:     from all lookup main
32767:     from all lookup default
```

Of course, the table mentioned above—99—should also exist; otherwise, the rule would have no effect. We can create a new table implicitly by using `ip route add` to add entries to it.

The `ip route` Command   You can use `ip route add` to add, `ip route change` or `ip route replace` to modify, `ip route show` to output, and `ip route delete` (for single entries) or `ip route flush` (for several entries at once) to delete entries in routing tables. In addition, you can use `ip route get` to simulate a forwarding procedure, where the route found is output and stored in the routing cache.

TABLE 16–3   The most important parameters for `ip route`.

Keyword	Parameter
`table`	name/number of the routing table to be manipulated
`to`	type and destination address prefix
`tos`	value for the TOS field of the IP packet
`metric`	route quality (the higher, the worse)
`dev`	output interface
`via`	address of the next router

Routing table entries have a large number of attributes, which can be set with appropriate parameters when you create them. For viewing or deleting of tables, parameters stated act as selectors to limit the number of entries output or deleted. Table 16–3 shows only the most important parameters. We have divided them into three groups, by their meaning:

■ The `table` parameter is actually a command attribute rather than a route attribute. It specifies the routing table this command refers to. Here, too, either numbers or the names defined in `/etc/iproute2/rt_tables` can be used for tables. If the `table` parameter is not stated, then it is assumed that the command refers to the `main` table.

For `ip route show`, you can also use `all` or `cache` together with `table` to display all tables or the routing cache.

■ The `to` parameter to specify a network prefix and the `tos` parameter to specify the TOS value of IP packets, which may use this entry, supply the key to search a routing table for a forwarding entry: For an IP packet to be forwarded, the search algorithm first looks for the entry with the longest matching network prefix and then checks for whether the TOS value matches, if set in the entry. If the TOS value does not match, then the search continues with shorter prefixes.

The keyword `to` does not have to be stated, because the destination network prefix actually represents the default parameter for commands to manage routing entries. For a network prefix with length zero you can state the `default` keyword.

Between the `to` keyword and the network prefix, you can optionally state a type for the entry you look for. Entries describing routes to other networks and end systems are normally of the type `unicast`, which is also assumed by default. The `local` table, which is maintained automatically by the kernel, can additionally use the types `local` and `broadcast`, which describe addresses of local network interfaces. Such entries are used to see whether incoming packets are meant for the local system. In addition, there are other entry types that virtually never occur. (See [Kuzn99].)

The quality information, which can be set by the `metric` parameter, plays a role when several entries exist that otherwise match equally well. In this case, the entry with the smallest `metric` value is selected.

▨ The result of a search in a routing table is essentially a network interface, which should be used to forward the current packet, and the next router, if the destination system is not in the network directly connected over this interface. The `dev` parameter can be used to specify a network interface. The next router is specified by the `via` parameter, if required.

A next router can be specified only provided that it is known how this router can be reached. This means that another entry describing the subnetwork of this router has to exist; naturally, the next router always has to be in a directly connected subnetwork. The network interface used to reach this router can be determined from this entry. For this reason, when using `via` to specify a router when you create an entry, you don't have to use `dev` to specify a network interface.

There are a number of additional attributes you can assign to a routing entry (e.g., a set of TCP parameters—see Chapter 24), which will be used when the entry is assigned to a TCP connection.[1]

The following example shows the commands used to build the `main` routing table for router B from Figure 16–4:

```
root@tux # ip route add 10.0.3/24 dev eth0
root@tux # ip route add 10.0.4/24 dev eth1
root@tux # ip route add 10.0.5/24 via 10.0.4.3
root@tux # ip route add 10.0.2.1 dev ppp0
root@tux # ip route add default via 10.0.2.1
```

However, the last two entries would normally be created not manually, but automatically by the PPP daemon as soon as a PPP connection is established. `ip route show` can be used to obtain the table shown in Figure 16–5 (in a slightly different format):

```
root@tux # ip route show
10.0.2.1 dev ppp0 scope link
10.0.4.0/24 dev eth1 scope link
10.0.5.0/24 via 10.0.4.3 dev eth1
10.0.3.0/24 dev eth0 scope link
default via 10.0.2.1 dev ppp0
```

16.3 IMPLEMENTATION

The following discussion divides the routing implementation in Linux into three functional units:

▨ As described in Section 14.2, `ip_route_input()` and `ip_route_output()` are the two functions invoked when IP packets are handled to run routing-specific

---

[1]For efficiency reasons, rather than doing a routing request for each single IP packet created by TCP, there is only one single routing request when a connection is established.

tasks; they will be described in Section 16.3.4. These functions are also called "forwarding functions" in the following discussion.

▧ Routing rules and routing tables together form the so-called *forwarding-information base (FIB)*. Whenever necessary, forwarding functions query the forwarding-information base; this action is also called a *forwarding query* or *FIB request* in the following discussion. An FIB request is initiated by calling the fib_lookup() function. The implementation of routing rules is strongly encapsulated within the FIB, so routing rules and routing tables will be discussed separately in Sections 16.3.1 and 16.3.2.

▧ Because consulting the FIB for each single IP packet received or sent would require too much time, there is an additional *routing cache* that stores the table entries used the most recently and allows fast access to these entries. Section 16.3.3 describes how this routing cache is implemented.

16.3.1 Routing Rules

As we described in Section 16.1.6, rule-based routing uses a set of rules to decide which routing tables should be searched in which sequence for a suitable entry to forward a packet and whether the packet may be forwarded at all. The rules are processed successively by ascending priority value until a decision can be made.

The entire implementation of the rules-processing method, including the data types used, is included in the fib_rules.c file. The rather narrow interface is described by some function prototypes and inline functions in a common header file, ip_fib.h. If rule-based routing was disabled in the kernel configuration (CONFIG_IP_MULTIPLE_TABLES option; see Section 16.2.1), then fib_rules.c is not compiled. In this case, the "replacement functionality" (use of the two routing tables local and main, in this sequence) is fully handled by the inline functions in ip_fib.h.

Data Structures   The set of rules is represented in the kernel by a linear list of fib_rule structures, sorted in ascending order by priority value and hooked into the static fib_rules variable. Initially, this list contains three entries: the fib_rule structures default_rule, main_rule, and local_rule, which are statically defined. Figure 16–6 shows this initial state of the rules list. A read-write spinlock called fib_rules_lock is used to regulate access to the list.

struct fib_rule	net/ipv4/fib_rule.c

The fib_rule structure, to begin with, contains two management fields, a link pointer, struct fib_rule *r_next, and a reference counter, atomic_t r_clntref. The latter specifies the number of references to a specific instance of the structure. This counter is incremented by atomic_inc() when new rules are added, and especially when a reference to a rule is returned in a result for a forwarding request. A call to atomic_dec_and_test() in the interface function fib_rule_put(), which frees fib_rule instances, decrements the reference counter. The memory is actually freed when this counter reaches a value of zero. In this situation, the function additionally checks for whether the entry int r_dead was set to one by explicitly deleting the rule

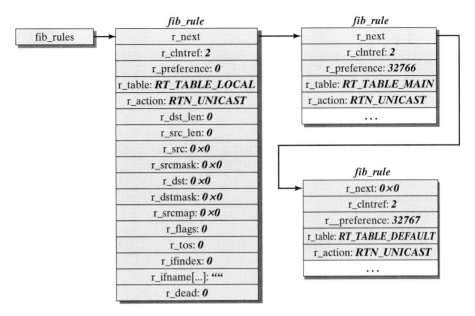

FIGURE 16–6
List with routing rules (initial state). Optional structure entries are not shown.

(by `inet_rtm_delrule()`; see further below). If this is not the case, then there must be an implementation error, which is written to the system log for the user's attention.

Next within the structure follows some information about the described rule: the priority value `u32 r_preference`, the `unsigned char r_table` identifier for a routing table to be used, and the field `unsigned char r_action`, which specifies the action that should run if the rule's selector matches the packet currently being processed. The five rule types mentioned in Section 16.1.6 can be coded with the values RTN_UNICAST, RTN_BLACKHOLE, RTN_UNREACHABLE, RTN_PROHIBIT, and RTN_NAT, which are declared in `include/linux/netlink.h`. Additional attributes for the action are the `u32 r_srcmap` und `__u32 r_tclassid` entries. The first of these two entries includes the new source address for static address translation. The second entry is present only if the kernel was configured with the CONFIG_NET_CLS_ROUTE option. (See Section 16.2.1.) It contains a class identifier for a queuing discipline that is assigned to packets, if the routing table entry we select later does not itself contain a class identifier.

The rule's selector is represented by an address prefix and a corresponding network mask for the packet's source and destination addresses (`u32 r_src`, `r_srcmask`, `r_dst`, `r_dstmask`), by the network interface index (`int r_ifindex`), by the content in the TOS field (`u8 r_tos`), and additionally by the fwmark (`u32 r_fwmark`), if activated in CONFIG_IP_ROUTE_FWMARK. Moreover, the structure includes the lengths of the address prefixes (`unsigned char r_src_len`, `r_dst_len`) and the network interface name (`char r_ifname[IFNAMSIZ]`). These attributes are used only when rules are inserted, deleted, and displayed at the RT netlink interface. In contrast, forwarding decisions use only the address masks and the much faster integer index for the network interface.

Though the u8 r_flags entry is accepted from the RT netlink interface, it has no meaning in rules processing.

Initialization and Internal Functions   The initialization function fib_rules_init(), which is invoked (from within ip_fib_init(), which, in turn, is invoked by ip_rt_init()) when the routing is initialized during system start, does not have to initialize the rules list, because its initial entries are already statically linked and anchored. However, it registers the callback function fib_rules_export() in the notification chain for state changes to network devices. (See Section 5.2.4.) If changes occur, fib_rules_event() is invoked, which branches to fib_rules_attach() when a new network device is registered, but to fib_rules_detach() when a network device is unregistered. These two functions visit all existing rules and correct the ifindex entry, which is meaningful for registered devices only and should otherwise be set to −1.

As was mentioned in connection with the r_clntref reference counter, the fib_rule_put() function is used to release references that point to fib_rule structures. This function is also declared in ip_fib.h, because it is invoked not only internally, but also when structures are released that were returned as replies to forwarding requests and contain a reference to the rule that led to the selection of a route from a routing table.

RT Netlink Interface   The RT netlink interface represents the only way to manage routing   rules.   For   this   purpose,   the   table   inet_rtnetlink_table[] (net/ipv4/devinet.c) has pointers for the message types RTM_NEWRULE, RTM_DEL-RULE,   and   RTM_GETRULE   that   point   to   the   functions   inet_rtm_newrule(), inet_rtm_delrule(), and inet_dump_rules(), so that these functions are invoked to handle the corresponding RT netlink messages.

A large part of the implementation of these functions consists in converting between the data structures of RT netlink messages and the fib_rule structure. In addition, when new rules are added, the values entered are checked for whether or not they are valid and consistent. If a rule is added without stating a required routing table, then the function fib_empty_table() is invoked and searches for a table not yet used.[2] If no priority is stated, then a new rule is added to the rules list before all other rules with a nonzero priority. When rules are polled (message type RTM_GETRULE), the auxiliary function inet_fill_rule() is used; it appends the information of a single rule to the RT netlink reply message currently being built.

Interface to Forwarding Functions   The rules database represents the access point to the FIB virtually, because rules have to be used to identify a suitable routing table for each forwarding request. For this reason, the "central" request function, fib_lookup(), is also implemented in fib_rules.c (or in ip_fib.h, if rule-based routing is disabled). However, it handles only a small part of the work involved; important parts are handled by invoking functions from other FIB parts, as we will see later.

---

[2]If you invoke ip rule add without stating a table number, then it automatically uses the table main. To create an RT netlink message with unspecified table, you have to use the table 0 option specifically with ip rule add.

In addition to these FIB interface functions, there are several functions that access specific elements of the `fib_rule` structure. This structure is not visible outside the `fib_rule.c` file.

▨ `fib_rules_tclass()` simply returns the queuing discipline's class identifier assigned to a rule.

▨ `fib_rules_policy()` transforms the source address as specified by a rule, if applicable.

▨ `fib_rules_map_destination()` transforms the destination address for NAT routes. (See Section 16.1.6.)

`fib_lookup()`	**net/ipv4/fib_rules.c**

This function, which represents the most commonly used FIB interface, returns a matching routing-table entry for a key passed as argument. The key is passed as pointer to an `rt_key` structure (declared in `route.h`). This structure contains the source and destination addresses (`src` and `dst`), the input and output network interface indices (`iif` and `oif`), the TOS value (`tos`), and the `fwmark` (?) for the packet to be forwarded, if applicable:

```
struct rt_key
{
            __u32          dst;
            __u32          src;
            int            iif;
            int            oif;
#ifdef CONFIG_IP_ROUTE_FWMARK
            __u32          fwmark;
#endif
            __u8           tos;
            __u8           scope;
};
```

The scope information (`scope`) can be used to limit the search range. For this, each entry in a routing table includes a scope identifier, and only entries with equal or smaller scopes are returned for a request (but smaller scopes have bigger identifiers). The following scopes are predefined:

Symbol	Value	Scope
RT_SCOPE_UNIVERSE	0	any destination
RT_SCOPE_LINK	253	destination in the same physical network
RT_SCOPE_HOST	254	destination in the local system
RT_SCOPE_NOWHERE	255	destination does not exist

To handle a request, the rules list is visited in the order of ascending priority value, and the action corresponding to the rule type runs for each rule with a selector that matches the key passed. Rules of the types unreachable, blackhole, and prohibit cause the function to be aborted and to return an appropriate error value. For unicast and nat rules, the routing table identified by the r_table entry of the rule is consulted.

Section 16.3.2 discusses the data structures used to represent routing tables and how these structures are searched. The interface for this is the function pointer tb_lookup() in the fib_table structure representing the root of a routing table. If a table search is successful, then the result supplied by tb_lookup() is returned; otherwise, fib_lookup() continues with the next rule.

fib_select_default()   net/ipv4/fib_rules.c

This function serves to select a route from several default routes; it is invoked whenever a previous FIB request returns a routing-table entry with a network prefix of length null. It obtains the request key and the request result as parameters. The default route is actually selected by the function pointer tb_select_default(), which is included in the fib_table structure.

16.3.2 Routing Tables

In the Linux kernel, routing tables are represented by rather complex data structures, which manage entries by using a number of hash tables for different prefix lengths.

Data Structures   A fib_table structure forms the basis for a routing table. This structure includes a pointer to an fn_zone structure for each potential prefix length (0 to 32 bits). All routing table entries with the same prefix length are allocated to a specific fn_zone structure. The fn_zone structure uses an additional hash table to store the individual entries, each represented by a fib_node structure. The hash function used for this purpose also uses the entry's network prefix. If several routing-table entries have the same hash value, then the corresponding fib_node structures are linked in a linear list. Ultimately, the actual data of an entry is not in the fib_node structure itself, but in a fib_info structure referenced in the former structure.

There are up to 255 different routing tables when rule-based routing is used. The associated fib_table structures are managed by using the array variable struct fib_table * fib_tables[RT_TABLE_MAX+1]. Their positions within the array correspond to the table numbers, which are used in routing rules to identify routing tables. Only position null is not used; at the interfaces, identifier null denotes an unspecified table and normally is mapped to the main table. If rule-based routing is not used, there are only two routing tables, each referenced by a global variable: local_table and main_table.

Figure 16–7 shows a possible instance of fib_table and fn_zone structures, where the routing table with number 254 (RT_TABLE_MAIN) includes entries with three different prefix lengths: 0 (default route), 16, and 24. The hash tables used to reference the respective routing-table entries are shown on the right-hand side of the figure. They have different sizes: For prefix length null, the hash function will always yield the same value, which is the reason why one single entry is sufficient here, while 16 entries

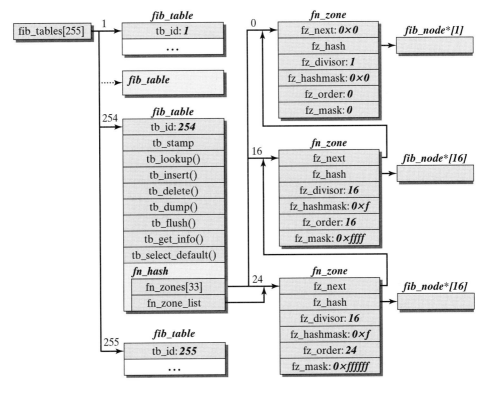

FIGURE 16–7
The fib_table structure with references to zones of different prefix lengths.

are allocated for other prefix lengths. The hash tables grow automatically when they fill up, if the option CONFIG_IP_ROUTE_LARGE_TABLES is active.

The fib_node and fib_info structures belonging to the routing-table entries are not shown in Figure 16–7, because of limited space. They are shown in Figure 16–8, which is described further along.

struct fib_table	include/net/ip_fib.h

In addition to its number, tb_id, and an unused element by the name of tb_stamp, the fib_table structure includes a number of function pointers, forming the interface to manage the entries stored in the table:

- tb_insert() and tb_delete() serve to insert and delete entries; they are used in net/ipv4/fib_frontend.c to handle RT netlink messages and ioctl() and kernel-internal calls.
- tb_dump() serves to output entries over RT netlink, and tb_get_info() serves to output entries in the /proc/net/route format.

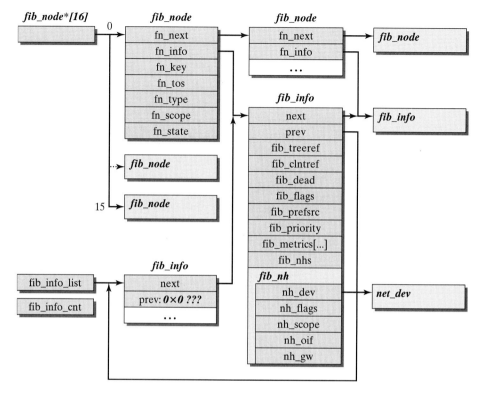

FIGURE 16–8
Hash table of a zone with fib_node and fib_info structures.

▨ tb_lookup() searches the table for an entry matching a key; it is used by the main query function, fib_lookup().

▨ tb_flush() frees all entries in the table that previously have been marked as deleted.

▨ tb_select_default() serves to select one route from several existing default routes.

These function pointers are set to functions in fib_hash.c, with names matching those of the pointers, except for the prefix (fn_hash_ instead of tb_), when a new fib_table structure is created by a call to fib_new_table() (include/net/ip_fib.h and net/ipv4/fib_frontend.c). This initialization is accomplished by the function fib_hash_init() (net/ipv4/fib_hash.c), invoked from within fib_new_table().

These function pointers are the only way to access internal routing table data structures; their implementation is fully encapsulated. The "core" structures fn_zone and fib_node are defined exclusively in the file net/ipv4/fib_hash.c. Also, the fn_hash structure, which is physically part of the fib_table structure, is declared "anonymously" as unsigned char tb_data[0] in include/net/ip_fib.h; it is actually used only within net/ipv4/fib_hash.c. The fib_info structure, which includes information about individual entries, is the only structure visible to the outside.

struct fn_zone	**net/ipv4/fib_hash.c**

An fn_zone structure manages all entries with the same prefix length by use of a hash table. The fixed prefix length is noted in the fz_order element, and fz_mask includes an appropriate network mask. The hash table consists of an array of fib_node structures, which are referenced by the fz_hash pointer. The array size is specified by fz_divisor. fz_hashmask holds a bit mask used to mask the hash value to the range permitted for indexing in the array in its last computation step.

An fn_zone structure for a specific prefix length exists only provided that entries with this prefix length actually exist. All fn_zone structures of a table are linked in a linear list in the order of descending prefix length (by using the fz_next element), which is hooked into the fn_zone_list element of the fn_hash structure at the bottom of the fib_table structure. This list forms the basis of search for an entry with the longest network prefix matching a specific destination address.

struct fib_node	**net/ipv4/fib_hash.c**

Each single entry in a routing table is represented by a fib_node structure. In its fn_key element, this structure contains the destination network prefix (with an identical length for all entries of one zone), and its fn_tos elements includes a TOS value, which is also part of the key used to search a routing table. The type and scope of an entry are coded in fn_type and fn_scope, and the fn_state element stores two flags used to manage the structure.

All additional information in a routing-table entry, which is not required for searching an entry, but represents merely part of the search results,[3] is located in the fib_info structure, which can be reached over fn_info.

struct fib_info	**include/net/ip_fib.h**

The fib_info structure represents information about the result of an FIB query, including the output interface to be used and the next hop along the route to the destination system, if necessary. This information is included in a fib_nh structure in the element fib_nh of the fib_info structure. The fib_nh element is an array to represent the situation where several equivalent routes lead to the same destination in the FIB. This array is declared with size null, and sufficient space is reserved for new entries that all stated routes can be stored. The number of these routes is then stored in the fib_nhs element of the fib_info structure.

The fib_nh structure is declared in ip_fib.h and contains the output interface to be used in the form of its index (nh_oif); as a pointer to the net_device structure (nh_dev), it also includes the IP address of the next router (nh_gw).

---

[3]Though quality information (metric) plays a role in searching, it is not explicitly used. The reason is that it already influences an entry's position in the fib_node list when the entry is inserted, so that entries with lower metric values are automatically found earlier.

The `fib_info` structure does not contain any backward references to its position within the routing-table data structures. Instead, the `fib_next` and `fib_prev` pointers serve to arrange all existing `fib_info` structures to form a doubly linked list, which is hooked into a global variable, `fib_info_list`. When creating a new entry, the function `fib_create_info()`, which is invoked by `tb_insert()`, first checks for whether an identical entry exists in the list. Rather than duplicating such an entry, it would merely increment the reference counter `fib_clntref`. This means that several `fib_node` structures can reference one single `fib_info` structure. When a `fib_node` is freed, then the `fib_info` structure is also freed, if the reference counter has reached null.

In contrast to `fn_zone` and `fib_node`, the `fib_info` structure becomes visible to the outside again: It is declared in `include/net/ip_fib.h`, and its contents are read directly in some places (e.g., in `net/ipv4/route.c`). All operations to manage `fib_info` structures that go beyond the plain reading of a data element are implemented in the file `net/ipv4/fib_semantics.s`, however.

Managing and Initializing Memory   The FIB implementation is initialized in `ip_fib_init()` (`net/ipv4/fib_frontend.c`). If rule-based routing is not used, then the function `fib_hash_init()` is invoked directly for the two tables `table_local` and `table_main` held in global variables. This function occupies memory for a `fib_table` structure and sets the enclosed function pointers to the `fn_hash_` functions. The substructure of the type `fn_hash`, which contains the zone hash table, is initialized to null.

In contrast, if rule-based routing is used, routing tables are not previously initialized. The global array that references the tables is created as a memory area initialized to null when the kernel is loaded. Whenever a routing table is accessed via an element of the array, then it is checked whether the table already exists, and, if this is not the case, it is created by `fib_hash_init()`.

The function `fib_hash_init()` also ensures that a slab cache (see Section 2.6.2) called "`ip_fib_hash`" exists. This slab cache supplies memory for `fib_node` structures, which are allocated in the function `fn_hash_insert()` to create new entries when needed.

Managing Hash Structures   The functions that access `fn_zone` and `fib_node` structures, which are used internally to manage routing-table entries by using hash tables, are collected in the file `net/ipv4/fib_hash.c`. They are invoked by all other FIB functions to access `fn_zone` and `fib_node` structures.

Encapsulation of these internal structures allows them to be reimplemented, if necessary, by using other data structures offering a more efficient search process, without the need to effect changes in other places.

The most important functions in `net/ipv4/fib_hash.c` are as follows:

- `fn_rehash_zone()` enlarges the hash tables, if necessary.
- `fn_new_zone()` creates a new `fn_zone` structure and sorts it into the zone list based on its prefix length.
- `fn_hash_lookup()` handles the main task in an FIB query: The `fn_zone` structures in a routing table are walked through in the sequence of descending prefix length, and the hash table is searched for an entry matching the key passed as an argument.

- ▓ fn_hash_select_default() selects one out of several default routes, considering whether the intermediate system specified as the next router is currently reachable.
- ▓ fn_hash_insert(), fn_hash_delete(), and fn_hash_dump() serve to insert, delete, and display entries over the RT netlink interface.
- ▓ fn_hash_flush() removes all fib_info structures of a zone that were previously marked as invalid.
- ▓ fn_hash_get_info() serves to display routing table entries over the proc file system.

Interfaces to the User-Address Space From within the user-address space, you can manage routing tables both over the traditional ioctl() interface and over RT netlink.

For the RT netlink interface, the functions inet_rtm_newroute(), inet_rtm_delroute(), and inet_dump_fib() from net/ipv4/fib_frontend.c are registered in the table inet_rtnetlink_table[] in net/ipv4/devinet.c, so that they can be invoked to add, delete, or output a routing table entry and handle corresponding messages.

ioctl() system calls are handled by ip_rt_ioctl() (net/ipv4/fib_frontend.c), which is invoked in af_inet.c by the general routine that handles ioctl() calls at PF_INET sockets. (See Chapter 26.) The parameters for the call are converted into an RT netlink message by fib_convert_rtentry() and passed to inet_rtm_newroute() or inet_rtm_delroute() for further handling.

proc File System The contents of the pseudo file /proc/net/route, which can be used to view the main routing table, are created by the function fib_get_procinfo() (net/ipv4/fib_frontend.c), which is registered by ip_fib_init(), using proc_net_create(), for this purpose. The function creates a header line and uses the function pointer tb_get_info() from the main table, which normally points to fn_hash_get_info() (ipv4/net/fib_hash.c), to output the data. There, all fib_node structures in fn_zone_list are visited, and the appropriate data is eventually output by fib_node_get_info() (net/ipv4/fib_semantics.c).

Reacting to Changes in Network Interfaces The functions fib_inetaddr_event() and fib_netdev_event() (net/ipv4/fib_frontend.c) are registered in two notification chains for state changes to network interfaces or changes to their IP addresses when ip_fib_init() initializes the FIB.

As soon as a network device obtains an IP address or when it is reactivated after it had addresses and was deactivated previously, then fib_add_ifaddr() (invoked by fib_inetaddr_event() or fib_netdev_event()) creates entries for local and broadcast routes in the local table. When addresses are removed, these entries are deleted accordingly by fib_del_ifaddr(). In addition, during removal of addresses, all routing entries that use the removed address as their preferred source address have to be deactivated. This is handled by the function fib_sync_down() from net/ipv4/fib_semantics.c.

When deactivating or deleting a network interface (and also when the last address of an interface was removed), fib_netdev_event() invokes the function fib_disable_ip() which, in turn, uses fib_sync_down() (parametrized differently) to declare all those fib_nh structures, that use the interface as their forwarding-output interface as invalid. Subsequently, the routing cache is deleted, and, finally, fib_disable_ip() invokes arp_ifdown() to inform the ARP implementation that the interface disappeared.

Interfaces to the Forwarding Functions   This section describes several operations in addition to those discussed in Section 16.3.1, which are used by the functions in net/ipv4/route.c to access the FIB.

fib_validate_source()	net/ipv4/fib_frontend.c

The function fib_validate_source() serves to check the source addresses of IP packets within a forwarding process. This check can be implemented elegantly by an FIB query, using fib_lookup() for the opposite direction (i.e., with source and destination addresses swapped): If the entry found is not of the type RTN_UNICAST (but RTN_LOCAL, for example, which means that the address is assigned to a local interface), then this address is not a valid source address for an incoming packet.

If the output interface noted in an inverted FIB query matches the actual input interface, then the validation is completed successfully. This is the only acceptable result when reverse-path filtering is active.

If the actual input device does not currently have an address, then the above check is considered successful, even if the FIB query returns no result at all. If the output device found does not match the actual input device, then another FIB query is done with the actual input device specified as a fixed output device. If this query supplies either a result of the type RTN_UNICAST or no result at all, the check is considered to have been successful.

fib_select_multipath()	net/ipv4/fib_semantics.c

When a routing-table entry with several routes is used in a forwarding process, the function fib_select_multipath() is invoked to select one of these routes. This decision is made randomly (the jiffies counter is used rather than a "real" random number generator), taking weights assigned to each of these routes into account.

ip_dev_find()	net/ipv4/fib_frontend.c

To find the network interface that belongs to an IP address passed as parameter, ip_dev_find() uses the function pointer tb_lookup() to search the local table. The result has to be an entry of the type RTN_LOCAL, and a reference to the wanted net_device structure can be taken from the entry.

inet_addr_type()	net/ipv4/fib_frontend.c

inet_addr_type() is another function that searches the local table for a specific address, but the address type is the result looked for in this case. The semantics is slightly different and is characterized by the specific requirements of the functions that invoke `inet_addr_type()`: Formally invalid addresses are previously filtered and then yield the `RTN_MULTICAST` result, and an address is treated as `RTN_UNICAST`, even if no entry is found in the `local` table.

16.3.3 The Routing Cache

Though the FIB data structures offer relatively fast queries, the cost to run such a query for each single IP packet would be altogether excessive. For this reason, the Linux kernel has a cache, in addition to the FIB, that stores the results of the forwarding queries used most recently allowing them to be accessed quickly. Each forwarding operation first consults the routing cache, and the FIB is queried only if no matching entry exists in the cache. The result of the FIB query is then used to create a new cache entry immediately.

The routing cache is based on a relatively simple data structure. One single hash table includes the cache entries, which are linearly linked when the hash value is identical. The hash function processes the source and destination addresses for packets to be forwarded, plus their TOS values. Each cache entry contains all information required to forward a packet.

Figure 16–9 shows the hash table (left-hand side), organized as an array of `rt_hash_bucket` structures. The pointer `struct rt_hash_bucket *rt_hash_table`

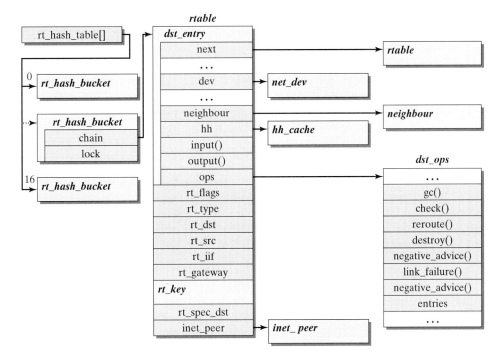

FIGURE 16–9
Data structures of the routing cache.

references this array. Within each `rt_hash_bucket` structure, the `chain` element forms the anchoring point for a list of `rtable` structures, representing the cache entries. Access to this list is controlled by the read–write spinlock `lock` in the `rt_hash_bucket` structure. The size of the hash table is defined according to the main memory size when the routing code is initialized and remains unchanged afterwards.

`struct rtable`	**include/net/route.h**

The `rtable` structure is rather extensive, and Figure 16–9 shows only an excerpt. In addition, we somewhat simplified the representation of its first element. Actually, the first element of the `rtable` structure is a `union` structure, u, which contains a `dst_entry` structure and an `rtable` pointer:

```
union {
    struct dst_entry dst;
    struct rtable *rt_next;
} u;
```

Both elements of u are used concurrently, without representing a problem, because the first element of the `dst_entry` structure is the `dst_entry` pointer `next`, and `dst_entry` structures occur only within `rtable` structures. This means that `u.dst.next` and `u.rt_next` are two different names for the same pointer; based on their types, the total object or only part of it are referenced.

The `rt_src` and `rt_dst` elements specify the source and destination addresses for IP packets handled by this entry. `rt_gateway` stores the address of the next router—or the destination address again, if no router is required. The interface identifier in `iif` can denote the output or input interface.

The `rt_key` structure integrated as element `key` is used as the key in searching the routing cache. The values stored there do not necessarily have to match those outside. For example, in searching for an entry of a packet that was created locally and should be sent now, normally no source address is specified, which means that `rt_key.src` in the cache entry is null. However, the source address to be assigned to the new packet is stored in `rt_src`.

`struct dst_entry`	**include/net/dst.h**

The `dst_entry` structure contains a large number of information elements. The most important elements are introduced below by origin and purpose:

- Some pointers refer to other data structures required when forwarding IP packets and so they are available there without additional effort—the `net_device` structure of the output interface, the `neighbour` structure to the next router or the destination system (corresponding to the `rt_gateway` element in the `rtable` structure), and the `hh_cache` structure, which includes a packet header of the data-link layer that just has to be copied.
- Function pointers to operations for further processing when receiving (`input()`) or transmitting (`output()`) an IP packet that matches the cache entry are simply

invoked at the appropriate positions within the IP protocol procedure, to result in the packet's being handled appropriately. The input() pointer in entries that can be used for incoming packets refers to ip_local_deliver() (unicast packets to be delivered locally), to ip_mr_input() (multicast packets), to ip_forward() (packets to be forwarded), or to ip_error() (forwarding impossible because destination is unreachable). The output() pointer refers to ip_output() (unicast packets) or ip_mc_output() (multicast packets).

▪ A reference to a dst_ops structure for IPv4 entries always points to the globally defined structure ipv4_dst_ops. It contains several function pointers, and users of routing-cache entries (e.g., TCP or ARP) can use them to supply feedback to the routing cache (e.g., about connection failures). In addition, the dst_ops structure holds a counter for occupied cache entries and stores a threshold value which, when exceeded, causes the cache garbage collection to start (as described later).

▪ The usage counter, __use, is incremented whenever the cache entry is used. The time of the last use is also stored in the lastuse element.

▪ Various parameters for transport protocols are copied from the fib_info structure.

Some functions to manage dst_entry structures are defined in the files include/net/dst.h and net/core/dst.c.

Interface to Forwarding Functions The implementation of the routing cache is hardly encapsulated against the other program logic used for forwarding; you find both in the file net/ipv4/route.c. For example, there is no separate function that searches for a cache entry. Each search operates directly on the cache data structure in both main interface functions for IP packet processing (ip_route_input() and ip_route_output()—see Section 16.3.4). Part of the creation of new cache entries is done there as well.

Nevertheless, there are a few methods that are used by the forwarding functions, yet clearly belong to the routing cache. The most important such methods are described below.

rt_hash_code()	net/ipv4/route.c

rt_hash_code() is used to calculate the hash value from the source and destination addresses and the TOS value passed as parameters. This hash value serves as index in the hash table of the routing cache.

rt_intern_hash()	net/ipv4/route.c

The forwarding functions use the rt_intern_hash() function to insert an almost complete rtable structure into the hash table of the routing cache. New entries are always inserted in the first position in a potential collision-resolution list. If an entry with identical key exists in the list, then this entry is moved to the front, and the new entry is discarded.

In addition to inserting entries, rt_intern_hash() procures the pointer to a neighbour structure matching the next router or destination system from the rtable structure.

Initialization   The initialization function `ip_rt_init()` allocates memory for the routing cache array, once an appropriate size has been computed. Subsequently, each element of the array is initialized. In addition, the slab cache "ip_dst_cache" that serves to hold `rtable` structures is initialized. The initialization functions of the IP interface management and FIB are invoked, the timer for cache garbage collection is started (see below), and finally, `proc` entries are created (see below).

Cache Garbage Collection   An entry is added to the routing cache for each new communication partner in the Internet, so we have to ensure that old entries that are no longer needed are deleted occasionally to limit the memory requirement and to keep cache searches fast in the long run.

First, a timer called `rt_periodic_timer`, which is initially started by `add_timer()` (see Section 2.7.1) in the initialization function `ip_rt_init()`, invokes the function `rt_check_expire()` at regular intervals. This timer is restarted in `rt_check_expire()`, where the interval (measured in 1/HZ seconds) is specified by the global configuration variable `ip_rt_gc_interval` (which can be set by `sysctl()` or by a `proc` directory entry called /proc/sys/net/ipv4/route/gc_interval).

Second, whenever the number of entries in the cache exceeds a threshold value, the function `rt_garbage_collect()` is invoked to delete old entries also. A call to `rt_garbage_collect()` is also made when an attempt to allocate a `neighbour` structure has failed. This is done because it is then assumed that the corresponding tables are full, because some `neighbour` entries are referenced by routing cache entries and therefore they cannot be deleted. Old routing cache entries are deleted to remedy this problem.

`rt_check_expire()`	**net/ipv4/route.c**

The function `rt_check_expire()` successively checks cache-entry lists anchored in the elements of the array `rt_hash_table[]`. If the element `u.dst.expires` of an entry specifies an expiry time, this entry is deleted if this time has been exceeded. If no expiry time is specified, then `rt_may_expire()` is invoked to check on whether this entry should be deleted nevertheless.

First of all, `rt_may_expire()` refuses to delete referenced entries (`u.dst_refcnt != 0`). Otherwise, it determines how long an entry has not been used and compares this "age" with two threshold values passed as arguments. Three types of entries are distinguished:

▨ Low-value entries: This includes broadcast and multicast entries, which are additionally not in the last position in a collision resolution list. Such entries are always deleted immediately.

▨ "Normal" entries: These entries are deleted if their age exceeds the first threshold.

▨ High-value entries: These are entries created by ICMP redirect messages. They are deleted only if their age exceeds the second threshold.

The first threshold passed by `rt_check_expire()` varies according to the entry's position in the collision-resolution list: Starting with a value identical to that of the second threshold, which comes from the configuration variable `ip_rt_gc_timeout`, it decreases by half in each step.

rt_check_expire() interrupts its work after a number of steps, depending on the configuration variables ip_rt_gc_interval and ip_rt_gc_timeout (by default, after one-fifth of the entire array has been processed), but at the latest when the jiffies counter changes its value. The next call continues processing from the same position in the array.

---

rt_garbage_collect()   **net/ipv4/route.c**

The approach taken by rt_garbage_collect() to deleting cache entries is similar to that of rt_check_expire(), except for the following points:

- Instead of checking a fixed number of array elements for old entries, rt_garbage_collect() sets a specific target with regard to the number of entries to be deleted. It stops once this target has been reached (where the time is limited to the interval between two jiffies changes as well).
- The second time threshold passed to rt_may_expire() is also specified dynamically; it reduces by half after each passage across the entire array until the target has been reached.
- The number of entries to be deleted is computed on the basis of the number used in the last call, at the beginning of rt_garbage_collect(). The computation tries to find a state of equilibrium, where about as many entries are being deleted as are being newly created.

rt_garbage_collect() is a very labor-intensive function, so there must be at least the time distance defined in the configuration variable ip_rt_gc_min_interval between each two calls, except when there is acute lack of space. If this is not the case, then the function returns immediately.

RT Netlink Interface   Routing-cache entries can be read via the RT netlink interface. The corresponding messages are created by ip_rt_dump(), which is invoked by inet_dump_fib() (see above) when cache entries are requested.

In addition, you can simulate a forwarding process (by using the ip route get command) over the RT netlink interface. More specifically, this procedure invokes ip_route_input() or ip_route_output() and returns a result, with the side effect being to create an entry in the routing cache. The corresponding RT netlink message is processed by inet_rtm_getroute() from net/ipv4/route.c, registered in the table inet_rtnetlink_table[] in net/ipv4/devinet.c.

The Proc File System   Some configuration variables, including variables to control the behavior of the cache garbage collection, are mapped to files in the /proc/sys/net/ipv4/route directory. Except for the missing ip_rt_ prefix, the file names correspond to those of the variables. The only exception is the flush file, which causes the routing cache to be deleted when it is accessed.

The files are defined by the control structure ctl_table ipv4_route_table[] in net/ipv4/route.c; the function ipv4_sysctl_rtcache_flush(), which handles access to the flush file, is also registered there. The ctl_table structure ipv4_table[] in net/ipv4/sysctl_net_ipv4.c includes a reference to ipv4_route_table[]. This structure is embedded in the central sysctl() tree over net_table[] in net/sysctl.net.c and root_table[] in kernel/sysctl.c.

The file /proc/net/rt_cache lets you read the content of the entire routing cache. The content is formatted by the function rt_cache_get_info() from net/ipv4/route.c, which is registered using proc_net_create() when the routing is initialized in ip_rt_init().

16.3.4   The Forwarding Process

Section 14.2.1 discussed how a forwarding query is embedded into the processing of in-coming IP packets: ip_rcv_finish() invokes ip_route_input() to find a dst_entry structure to determine the packet's further route. Section 14.2.2 discussed outgoing packets: their routing decision is made in ip_route_output(), which is in-voked by, for example, ip_queue_xmit().

ip_route_input()	net/ipv4/route.c

The function ip_route_input() is invoked for each IP packet arriving over a network interface. The parameters are a pointer to the socket-buffer structure, the des-tination and source addresses, the TOS value, and a pointer to the net_device struc-ture of the receiving network interface.[4]

First, rt_hash_code() is used on the addresses and the TOS value to compute an index in the hash table of the routing cache. If necessary, the list anchored in the chain element is walked through to find a cache entry matching addresses, input inter-face, TOS value, and fwmark, if present. If this search is successful, then a pointer to the entry is placed as dst in the sk_buff structure, and the task is complete.

If no matching cache entry is found, then either of the two following functions is responsible for further handling:

- ip_route_input_mc() is invoked if the destination address is a multicast address. Another prerequisite is that the input interface either belongs to that multicast group or has been configured for multicast routing. The packet can be discarded if this is not the case. The function ip_route_input_mc() will be discussed later in the chapter about IP multicast (Section 17.4). What is done there is similar to the procedure for local-destination addresses described below, the only difference being that the packet is always delivered to the local machine rather than causing an FIB query.

- ip_route_input_slow() serves to handle "normal" destination addresses and is described next.

Both functions take the same parameters as ip_route_input() itself.

---

[4]The last four parameters could, alternatively, be worked out from the first. However, because they are passed separately, knowledge about their representation in the socket-buffer structure does not have to be present in ip_route_input(). Though the socket buffer structure is still not entirely treated as an encapsu-lated "black box," at least only few data elements especially present for routing are accessed.

`ip_route_input_slow()`	**net/ipv4/route.c**

To begin with, an `rt_key` structure is filled with the parameters passed. However, before it is used to run an FIB query, the addresses are checked for invalid values—multicast source addresses, and addresses moving a network prefix beginning with null. Such packets are dropped, and, if verbose messages are configured with `CONFIG_IP_ROUTE_VERBOSE`, they are registered in the system log. The use of `0.0.0.0` as source and destination addresses in the sense of limited broadcast is explicitly allowed as an exception, for this is occasionally used for automatic network configuration.

Next, the FIB query is started by calling `fib_lookup()`. If no matching entry is found, then `ip_route_input_slow()` also aborts processing and returns an error code, which subsequently causes `ip_rcv_finish()` (from where `ip_route_input_slow()` was invoked) to discard the packet.

If the routing NAT mentioned in Section 16.1.6 is active, the next step transforms the source address according to the information in the routing rule used (or the destination address, if the route found is an `nat` route). However, the new addresses are added only to the `rt_key` structure; the old addresses are maintained in the call parameters of the function and are available for other operations. Once the destination address has been transformed, `fib_lookup()` has to be invoked once more to find a regular routing entry (no other transformations are permitted) to the new destination address.

Among other things, the result from the FIB query also shows whether the destination address is a local address, which means that the packet is intended for the local system. This case is handled separately in the further process.

- *Local destination address:* A new cache entry is created once the source address has been checked by the calling of `fib_validate_source()`. The function pointer `output()` gets the `ip_rt_bug()` value, because the packet is not allowed to leave the system. Next, the `input()` pointer is set to `ip_local_deliver()`, to cause the packet to be delivered to the local machine. Because there is no next router, the `rt_gateway` element of the cache entry is set to the destination address.

  Broadcast addresses, such as the `0.0.0.0` address mentioned above as source and destination or the normally limited broadcast to `255.255.255.255` are detected in the address validation at the beginning and handled identically to local destination addresses. However, `fib_validate_source()` is not called for `0.0.0.0` addresses.

- *Nonlocal destination address:* Nonlocal destination addresses have to be handled only if the forwarding function for the input interface is enabled, so this is checked first.

  If the routing-table entry found describes several output routes, then `fib_select_multipath()` is called to select one of those routes. Subsequently, the source address is checked by the function `fib_validate_source()`, which can also consider the output network interface found in this case.

  `ip_forward()` and `ip_output()` are set in the new cache entry for the `input()` and `output()` function pointers. The function `rt_set_nexthop()` does the necessary assignment to `rt_gateway` and also fills in other elements of the `dst_entry` structure that are of interest for forwarded packets only.

`rt_intern_hash()` is used to integrate the `rtable` structure, which is almost complete, into the hash table of the routing cache. It also supplies the return value of `ip_route_input_slow()`, which then is complete.

`ip_route_output()`	**include/net/route.h**

According to a comment in the `route.h` header file, where it is implemented as an inline function, the function `ip_route_output()` is going to be replaced by `ip_route_output_key()`. Actually, however, it is invoked in many different positions within the network implementation as the main routing interface (e.g., by the IP transmit function `ip_queue_xmit()` [see Section 14.2.2] or by `udp_sendmsg()` [see Section 25.3.1] for packets created by UDP).

Its only function currently is to create an `rt_key` structure with the source and destination addresses, the TOS value, and the output device from the passed parameters and to subsequently invoke the function `ip_route_output_key()`, which will be described next. The last parameter is the pointer `struct rtable **rp`, which serves to return the result; it is also passed to `ip_route_output_key()`.

`ip_route_output_key()`	**net/ipv4/route.c**

The task of `ip_route_output_key()` is to determine a routing entry for the `rt_key` structure passed. The procedure is similar to that of `ip_route_input()`; the routing cache is searched for a matching entry, and the process branches to `ip_route_output_slow()` only if no such entry is found. Rather than the input interface, the output interface is used for hash computation and comparisons.

`ip_route_output_slow()`	**net/ipv4/route.c**

`ip_route_output_slow()` is invoked if no entry for the destination of a locally created IP packet exists in the routing cache. This function runs an FIB query, enters the result in the routing cache, and returns the new entry. In addition, it handles several special cases for which `fib_lookup()` alone is not sufficient.

As with `ip_route_output_key()`, the only input parameter is an `rt_key` structure. This structure initially is copied to a new structure of the same type, which can then be modified without losing the information passed. The `iif` and `scope` information is not considered; instead, the loopback device is always assumed for `iif`, and `scope` is set to either `RT_SCOPE_LINK` or `RT_SCOPE_UNIVERSE`, depending on the `RTO_ONLINK` flag in the `tos` element.

The input parameters are first checked for errors or special cases. For example, for multicast destination addresses, a route is created immediately without FIB query if a valid source address is specified, which can be used to identify a usable output device. This special handling simplifies the transmission of multicast packets (and some multicast tools that traditionally utilize this possibility continue to work). For a specified output interface, a matching source address is found, and `127.0.0.1` is used for the destination address, if none is specified.

An FIB query is started once all preparations have been completed. Notice that the process can, in some cases, continue even if this query returns a negative result. In fact, if an output interface was specified during the call, then this interface is used by simply assuming that the destination is in the adjacent network.

The query result can be used to distinguish between local and nonlocal destination addresses. The loopback device is always the output interface used for local addresses, but `fib_select_multipath()` might have to select one out of several routes, or `fib_select_default()` might have to choose from several default routes for nonlocal addresses.

Again, `ip_route_output_slow()` completes the job by filling a new `rtable` structure, where the function `rt_set_nexthop()` is used, similarly to `ip_route_input_slow()`. The `output()` function pointer is set to `ip_output()`, and the `input()` pointer is set to `ip_local_deliver()`, if the destination address is in the local system. `rt_intern_hash()` is used to add the cache entry to the hash table and also yields the return value for `ip_route_output_slow()`.

IP Multicast for Group Communication

The history of telecommunication was characterized mainly by two technologies in the past hundred years (before the Internet era began): telephony, and radio and television broadcasting. These two technologies cover two fundamentally different communication areas or needs:

- *Individual* communication (unicast): Connections between two communication partners, where the direction of data exchange can be unidirectional (simplex) or bidirectional (duplex).
- *Mass* communication (broadcast): One station sends data to all stations reachable over a medium, where data distribution is normally unidirectional.

After these two technologies, the Internet followed as the third communication technology, changing the telecommunication world. Though the Internet was initially designed for individual communication, the protocols and mechanisms added at the beginning of the nineties introduced a new communication form: *group* communication (multicast). Multicast makes possible an efficient data distribution to several receivers. By contrast with the mass communication of (radio) broadcasting, where data is distributed to all participants within one single transmission medium, group communication delivers data units only to those receivers explicitly interested in this data. In addition, group communication in the Internet (IP multicast) enables each Internet computer to send data directly to the members of a multicast group.

Consequently, in the designing of mechanisms and protocols, two specific tasks can be deduced for the functionality of group communication in Internet systems:

- managing memberships in communication groups; and
- efficient distribution of data packets to all members of a group.

The first task is solved by the Internet Group Management Protocol (IGMP), which has to be supported by each multicast-capable Internet computer. Section 17.3 introduces IGMP and its implementation in Linux systems. For the second task, we have to distinguish between end system and forwarding systems. Section 17.4 will discuss how both types are supported in Linux. As with Internet routing, group communication also separates clearly between forwarding and routing. There are different multicast routing algorithms, including the Distance Vector Multicast Routing Protocol (DVMRP), which will be introduced in Section 17.5.2 as a representative example for these algorithms, using the `mrouted` daemon.

17.1   GROUP COMMUNICATION

Before we introduce the details of IP multicast in Linux, the following sections give a brief summary of the three communication forms: *unicast, broadcast*, and *multicast*.

17.1.1 Unicast

Unicast is the classic form of communication between two partners—point to point. In the context of this book, this means that two computers communicate with each other only. When a unicast communication service is used to transmit data to several receivers, then this has to be done independently of one another in several transmit processes. This means that the cost for the data transport increases in proportion to the number of receivers, as shown in Figure 17–1.

Naturally, if there is a large number of receivers, this cost leads to an extreme load on the network, and so this technique is unsuitable for the distribution of large data volumes, such as multimedia data. Broadcast communication represents a better solution in some cases.

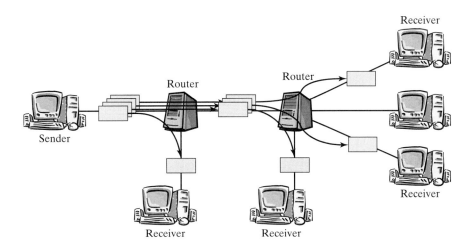

FIGURE 17–1
In unicast communication, the packet is sent to each receiver separately.

17.1.2 Broadcast

Broadcasting means that all participants in a communication network that can be reached over a specific medium receive the distributed data packets, regardless of whether they are interested in it. Examples for broadcast communication include the broadcasting of television and radio broadcasting programs, and advertisements in the mailboxes of homes.

At first sight, broadcast communication looks expensive. However, a closer look reveals that it is supported by the network technologies, especially in local area networks (LANs). In fact, each communication is a broadcast communication in local area networks, because the local network technologies (Ethernet, token ring, etc.) are broadcast media, where data packets are distributed to all stations. When a packet is received, the MAC destination address is checked to see whether the packet should be further handled by that station. This means that broadcast communication is very easy in local area networks. In fact, it is sufficient to send a packet to the network, so that all stations can receive it.

However, as with advertisements in mailboxes, not everybody will want to receive a broadcast packet they are not interested in. For this reason, though it is simple to broadcast data to a group, this approach is a burden for stations not interested in this data and reduces their performance. This holds also true for wide area network (WAN) traffic: Where point-to-point connections prevail, the benefit of the simplicity of broadcasting can easily turn into a heavy burden for the networks [Tan97].

17.1.3 Multicast

Multicast communication offers a solution to the problem described in the previous section. It enables a targeted transmission of data packets, in contrast to *n* single transmissions in unicast, yet it prevents the uncontrolled copying of data packets done in broadcast. In the Internet, this is implemented by defining groups, and each Internet

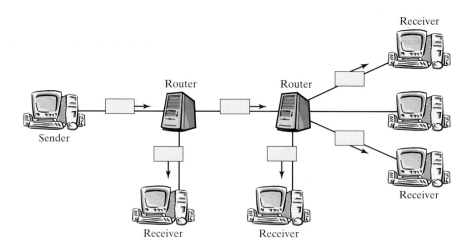

FIGURE 17–2
In multicast communication, the packets are first replicated in the network.

computer can subscribe to groups. Once a system has demonstrated its interest in participating in a multicast group, it will receive packets addressed to this group. In addition, an attempt is made to transport packets across the network so that as few network resources as possible are consumed. With multicast, data packets are not transmitted separately for each receiver. Instead, they are transmitted once and then replicated in the appropriate branching points and delivered to the receivers. (See Figure 17–2.) In contrast to broadcast, only stations that are members of that group receive data packets (with a few minor limitations, as we will see in Section 17.4.1).

In any event, IP multicast forwards data packets selectively to the subnetworks that really connect members of the corresponding multicast group. This approach reduces the network load considerably, compared to the distribution of packets in unicast and broadcast.

17.2   IP MULTICAST

IP multicast extends the unicast service of the Internet Protocol to the capability of sending IP packets to a group of Internet computers. This is realized more effectively than sending single unicast packets to the members of a group. The sender addresses the members of a group by a group address, the so-called IP multicast address. (See Section 17.2.1.) Normally, the sender doesn't know who is currently a member of a group, how many members are subscribed to a group, or where these members are located. IP multicast is one of the few implementations of the principle of group communication. Another network technology that also supports group communication is ATM. Figure 17–3 shows the IP multicast scenario in the Internet.

We basically have to distinguish between multicast communication on the MAC layer and those on the network layer (Internet Protocol). In local area networks, multicast is normally supported by the underlying technology. In this case, multicast packets are

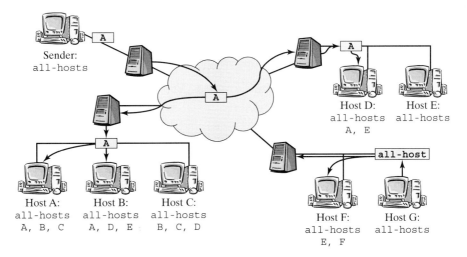

FIGURE 17–3
IP multicast scenario in the Internet.

transmitted over a broadcast-enabled network, and the connected computers use the group address to decide whether they want to receive the data. Section 17.4.1 describes in detail how multicast is supported in local area networks. In contrast, multicast communication on the IP layer (i.e., between the routers in the Internet) is much harder to implement. One of the most important functions is provided by multicast routing protocols, which organize the efficient distribution of data.

The separation between multicast in the local domain and in the routed network domain can be seen not only in how data are forwarded (data path), but also in how groups are managed. Joining and leaving groups is handled by the *Internet Group Management Protocol (IGMP)*; routers distribute their group information over multicast routing protocols. An end system tells its local multicast router only the IP address of the group it wants to join. The router will then have to find out how it can get the multicast data from the Internet. Joining and leaving of groups for computers in a local area network are handled by the *Internet Group Management Protocol*, which will be introduced in Section 17.3.

So-called *multicast distribution trees* are built to distribute multicast packets between routers across the entire network. The data packets are then distributed along these trees to the individual receivers and local area networks. These distribution trees are built by multicast routing protocols (e.g., the *Distance Vector Routing Protocol (DVMRP)* and *Multicast OSPF (MOSPF)*).

As in routing in the Internet, the control path and the data path are also separated here, as can be clearly seen in the implementation under Linux. The data path (i.e., forwarding and replicating of multicast packets) is defined by the information in the multicast routing table. The information in the routing table is procured over the control path, by the multicast routing protocols and IGMP. In addition to better structuring, another benefit of keeping the two mechanisms separate is that we can use different routing protocols. In fact, several protocols are currently available in Linux. Section 17.5.2 uses the DVMRP protocol and its implementation in the `mrouted` daemon as a representative example.

Before we take a closer look at the data and control paths of IP multicast, we will discuss important elements—multicast groups and their addresses—in the next section.

17.2.1 Addresses for Multicast Groups

The address range of the Internet Protocol (Version 4) was introduced in Section 14.1.5. (See Figure 14–3.) The classes A, B, and C are reserved for unicast communication; class E is reserved for future use. The address range of class D is reserved for multicast communication. This means that it is characterized so that the upper four bits of the 32-bit IP address begin with 1110 and take the range from 224.0.0.0 to 239.255.255.255 in the address space. The remaining 28 bits make available 2^{28} multicast groups.

One particularity of group communication is that the sender does normally not know who it is sending its packets to. The group address merely denotes a specific group and does not give information about the current members of this group. It could well be that there are no members at all in the multicast group, or that it has thousand or even millions of receivers. Each multicast-capable participant can join a group. A host that is not wanted in a group cannot be prevented from joining. The only barrier is to cipher the packet contents and to distribute the deciphering key to desired members only.

Multicast group addresses should generally be unique on a worldwide level, because nobody knows which computers join what groups. However, there is a way to limit the reach of a multicast packet, which normally is useful and is actually used by many programs. For this purpose, the *TTL* field in the IP packet is set to a specific value, which means that it will be discarded after the specified number of hops. (See also Section 17.2.3.)

Reserved Multicast Groups   In addition to user-specific multicast groups, a special range of group addresses is reserved for special applications. It is in the range between the addresses from 224.0.0.0 to 224.0.0.255 and from 239.0.0.0 to 239.255.255.255. Only some of these addresses are actually used at present. The following list shows some examples:

- *All hosts* (224.0.0.1): This group automatically includes each multicast-capable IP computer. It is also possible to leave this group. It is used, among other purposes, to determine the number of active groups within a local area network. (See Section 17.3.)
- *All routers* (244.0.0.2): Each multicast router has to belong to the *all-routers* group. It is used for multicast routing purposes.
- *DVMRP routing* (224.0.0.4): This group is used by the Distance Vector Multicast Routing Protocol (DVMRP) to exchange routing information.
- *RIP V2 routing* (224.0.0.9): This group is used by the Routing Information Protocol, Version 2, to exchange routing information.

The ping command can be used to find the computers belonging to a specific group within the local area network. For example, the command ping 224.0.0.1 shows all multicast-capable hosts. (See Figure 17–4.)

17.2.2   Configuring IP Multicast in Linux

To support IP multicast, we have to activate the option "IP: multicasting" when configuring the kernel. This integrates the IGMP protocol, and the computer is now capable of joining a multicast group and receiving its packets.

If we want our Linux computer to additionally act as multicast router, we also have to select the options "IP: multicast routing" and "IP: tunneling" (if IP tunneling is used to connect to a multicast-capable network).

```
klaus@tux # ping 224.0.0.1
PING 224.0.0.1 (224.0.0.1): 56 data bytes
64 bytes from 129.13.42.117: icmp_seq=0 ttl=255 time=0.184 ms
64 bytes from 129.13.42.28: icmp_seq=0 ttl=255 time=0.769 ms (DUP!)
64 bytes from 129.13.42.152: icmp_seq=0 ttl=255 time=1.427 ms (DUP!)
64 bytes from 129.13.42.11: icmp_seq=0 ttl=255 time=1.803 ms (DUP!)
64 bytes from 129.13.42.230: icmp_seq=0 ttl=64 time=2.111 ms (DUP!)
64 bytes from 129.13.42.64: icmp_seq=0 ttl=255 time=2.458 ms (DUP!)
```

FIGURE 17–4
Pinging all multicast-capable computers in the same LAN.

Once we have created and started the new kernel, the computer is able to receive multicast packets. To send packets to multicast groups (which capability, by the way, doesn't require multicast support in the kernel), we need a default route to be able to route multicast packets. In computers not acting as multicast routers, we normally add one route for all multicast groups—namely, to the complete 224.0.0.0 network. The command used for this purpose looks as follows, if eth0 is the computer's network card:

```
route add 224.0.0.0 netmask 240.0.0.0 dev eth0
```

In multicast routers, the routing daemon (e.g., mrouted) is responsible for setting the routes.

If the computer supports the **proc** file system, we can check the virtual file /proc/net/igmp to see the groups in which the computer is currently a member.

17.2.3 Multicast Programming

This section describes how you can integrate multicast communication into applications that you develop yourself. Berkeley sockets (see Chapter 27) are normally used to program applications with network functionality. Berkeley sockets let the programmer access network protocols to run the desired communication over these protocols. Also, socket options can be used to influence the properties of some protocols.

IP multicast is an extension of the Internet Protocol, which is the reason why the multicast options are accommodated in the options of the IP layer. Linux offers the following socket options for multicast:

- IP_MULTICAST_IF defines the network device you want to use to send multicast packets over the socket.
- IP_MULTICAST_TTL sets the *TTL* (Time To Live) value for multicast packets you send.
- IP_MULTICAST_LOOP defines whether multicast packets you send should be received over the *loopback* device.
- IP_ADD_MEMBERSHIP is used to join an IP multicast group.
- IP_DROP_MEMBERSHIP is used to leave an IP multicast group.

The socket options for IP multicast listed above will be described in the following subsections. In general, we need the following getsockopt() and setsockopt() functions to set and get socket options:

- int getsockopt(int socket, int opt_level, int opt_name, void* opt_val, int* opt_len)
- int setsockopt(int socket, int opt_level, int opt_name, const void* opt_val, int opt_len)

The two functions we use to set and get socket options have the following parameters:

- socket is the descriptor of the socket for which we change or get options. For IP multicasting, the socket has to belong to the AF_INET family. Because we can only use either UDP or Raw-IP for multicast communication, the socket will be of the type SOCK_DGRAM or SOCK_RAW.

▦ opt_level identifies the network layer that will handle the option: SOL_SOCKET (socket layer), IPPROTO_UDP (UDP), or IPPROTO_IP for the IP layer. For IP multicasting options, level should always be set to IPPROTO_IP.

▦ opt_len specifies the size of the data structure to which the opt_val pointer refers.

▦ Both getsockopt() and setsockopt() return 0 if successful, but −1 in case an error occurs.

The IP_MULTICAST_IF Socket Option   The kernel normally uses the default network device to send multicast data packets. A programmer can overwrite this behavior and define a specific output network device. The network device is identified by its IP address (if_addr):

```
struct in_addr if_addr;
setsockopt(socket, IPPROTO_IP, IP_MULTICAST_IF, &if_addr, sizeof(if_addr));
```

From now on, the entire multicast traffic created in this socket is transported over the specified network device. To undo this behavior (i.e., to use the network device selected by the system administrator again), we have only to call setsockopt() once more and set the device address to INADDR_ANY.

The IP_MULTICAST_TTL Socket Option   In the multicasting context, the TTL (Time To Live) field in the IP packet header has a dual meaning. First, it controls the lifetime of a packet, to keep the packet from traveling infinitely across the network. Each router decrements the TTL value by one and eventually discards it.

Second, the TTL field has the meaning of a threshold value. We have to avoid multicast packets from being routed out of the local area network or routing range. Otherwise, parts of the Internet could be loaded with undesired multicast packets. This is why we split the potential reach of a multicast packet into different zones. These zones are controlled by the *TTL* value specified in the packets. If a multicast packet exceeds a zone, it has to have a sufficient residual *lifetime* to overcome this hurdle.

▦ 0: limits the reach to the local system. The packet is not output on a physical network device.

▦ 1: The packet can spread only within the subnetwork. It is not forwarded by any router.

▦ <32: Local domain, organization, or department.

▦ <64: Region, country, national corporate intranet.

▦ <128: Continent.

▦ <255: Worldwide.

If a router's threshold value is larger than or equal to the TTL value of a multicast packet, then this packet is discarded. The default value of the TTL field in a multicast packet is one. This means that an application programmer has to set the TTL value explicitly to make it possible for a multicast packet to be transported beyond the local subnetwork. Notice that the TTL value of nonmulticast packets is larger than one for IP. The socket option `IP_MULTICAST_TTL` can be used to change the default value:

```
int ttl = NEW_TTL;
setsockopt(socket, IPPROTO_IP, IP_MULTICAST_TTL, &ttl, sizeof(ttl));
```

The `IP_MULTICAST_LOOP` Socket Option   There is a special network device, called the *loopback* device, to enable applications in the local computer to communicate. This device works at minimal cost and behaves like a physical network device. This is the reason it is often used to test network applications locally or to design them so that there will be no difference between situations where the communication partner is reachable locally or remotely over the network. One example is the X-Windows system. The loopback device in Linux is denoted `lo` and has the reserved IP address `127.0.0.1`.

The socket option `IP_MULTICAST_LOOP` can now be used to define whether multicast packets to be sent should be replicated over the loopback device to local sockets. For example, this could be useful for the video part in a videoconference, so that the users can receive their own images for control purposes. In contrast, this is not desirable for audio data, because it would cause interferences.

When setting the `IP_MULTICAST_LOOP`, we have to make sure that `opt_val` is a pointer to a variable specifying the Boolean value for enabled (1) or disabled (0). For example, the compiler would not accept the following call:

```
setsockopt(socket, IPPROTO_IP, IP_MULTICAST_LOOP, 0, 1)
```

The correct call looks like this:

```
int loop = 1;
setsockopt(socket, IPPROTO_IP, IP_MULTICAST_LOOP, &loop, sizeof(loop));
```

The `IP_ADD_MEMBERSHIP` Socket Option   The socket option (`IP_ADD_MEMBERSHIP`) is available on application level to join an IP multicast group. In the kernel, the call results in the function `ip_mc_join_group()`. The kernel is instructed to use IGMP, unless it is already used, to join the desired group, and to forward the data to the application. Notice that more than one application in one single computer can be members of a group.

For example, the code sequence to join group `233.25.10.72` looks like this:

```
/* struct ip_mreq {
 *      struct in_addr imr_multiaddr;   // multicast group to join
 *      struct in_addr imr_interface;   // interface to join on */

struct ip_mreq imr;

imr.imr_multiaddr.s_addr = inet_addr("233.25.10.72");
imr.imr_interface.s_addr = htonl("129.13.42.110");

setsockopt(socket, IPPROTO_IP, IP_ADD_MEMBERSHIP, (void *) &imr,
           sizeof(struct ip_mreq));
```

The `IP_LEAVE_MEMBERSHIP` Socket Option   This option is invoked to denote that a socket or application is no longer interested in receiving data from that multicast group. Internally, the option is implemented by `ip_mc_leave_group()`. However, this does not automatically mean that the computer won't receive any more packets for the multicast group. The computer's membership in the group is terminated only when no application is any longer interested in the group. Packets for groups that the computer is no longer interested in are simply ignored by the kernel.

The computer in the above example could leave the group as follows:

```
setsockopt(socket, IPPROTO_IP, IP_DROP_MEMBERSHIP, &imr, sizeof(imr));
```

17.3   INTERNET GROUP MANAGEMENT PROTOCOL (IGMP)

The *Internet Group Management Protocol (IGMP)* is used to manage group memberships in local area networks. A multicast router should know all groups having members in the local area network. Accordingly, the Multicast Routing Protocol subscribes packets for these groups. The router does not have to know exactly who in the local area network belongs to a group. It is sufficient for the router to know that there is at least one receiver. The reason is that, when the router transports a packet to the local area network, all stations subscribed to this group receive it automatically.

To avoid unnecessary data transmissions, the router checks periodically for multicast groups that are still desired. For this purpose, it sends a *membership query* to all local computers (i.e., to the *all-hosts* group) within a specific time interval (approximately every two minutes). Each computer currently interested in a group should then return a reply for each of its groups to the router. As was mentioned earlier, the router is not interested in knowing who exactly is a member of a group; it is interested only in knowing whether there is at least one member in the LAN. For this reason, and to prevent all computers from replying at the same time, each computer specifies a random delay time, and it will reply when this time expires. The first computer to reply sends its message to the router *and* to all other local computers of the specified group. Cleverly, it uses the multicast group address for this message. This means that the other computers learn that the router has been informed, so that they don't have to reply. The router has to continue forwarding data for this group from the Internet to the local area network.

Naturally, if a computer wants to join a group, it does not have to wait for a membership query; it can inform the router immediately about the group it wants to join. Section 17.3.3 describes how exactly the IGMP protocol works.

In addition to the tasks discussed above, IGMP is used for other things. The following list summarizes everything the IGMP is used for:

- Query a multicast router for groups desired in a LAN.
- Join and leave a multicast group.
- Exchange membership information with neighboring or higher-layer multicast routers.

17.3.1 Formatting and Transporting IGMP Packets

IGMP messages are transported in the payload field of IP packets, and the number 2 in the Protocol field of the IP packet header identifies them as IGMP messages. They are always sent with the TTL value one, which means that they cannot leave the area of a subnetwork and so means that IGMP manages group memberships only within a subnetwork. To distribute this information beyond these limits, we have to use multicast routing protocols.

Figure 17–5 shows the format of IGMP packets; it includes the following fields:

- *Version*: Number of the IGMP version used.
- *Type*: Type of the IGMP message.
- *Max. Response Time*: This field is used differently, depending on the IGMP version. (See Section 17.3.2.)
- *Checksum*: Checksum of the IGMP message.

The information in an IGMP packet is managed internally by the `igmphdr` structure in the Linux kernel. Consequently, it corresponds to an IGMP packet, also shown in Figure 17–5.

17.3.2 Different Versions

The Internet Group Management Protocol comes in three different versions: *IGMPv0*, *IGMPv1*, and *IGMPv2*. The first version (IGMPv0) is outdated [Deer86] and no longer used, so we won't discuss it here.

The successor version (IGMPv1) is specified in RFC 1112 and fully implemented in the Linux kernel. This version defines two protocol messages, which can be distinguished by the contents of the Type field:

- 0×11: A multicast router directs a query (`IGMP_HOST_MEMBERSHIP_QUERY`) for desired multicast groups to all computers in the LAN.
- 0×12: There is a reply to such a query (`IGMP_HOST_MEMBERSHIP_REPORT`).

The field *Max. Response Time* is set to null in this IGMP version when a packet is sent, and it is ignored by the receiver.

Version 2 of the Internet Group Management Protocol was specified in [Fenn97]. In this version, the field *Type* can take any of four values, and the field *Max. Response Time* plays a more important role.

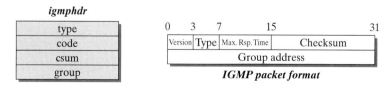

FIGURE 17–5
The IGMP packet format and its representation in the Linux kernel.

- 0×11: Query sent by a router (IGMP_HOST_MEMBERSHIP_QUERY)
- 0×12: Reply sent by an end system (IGMP_HOST_MEMBERSHIP_REPORT)
- 0×16: Reply of type 2 (IGMP_HOST_NEW_MEMBERSHIP_REPORT)
- 0×17: Request to leave a group (IGMP_HOST_LEAVE_MESSAGE)

The value in the field *Max. Response Time* is specified in tenth-second units. It specifies an interval within which a computer may not send a reply. Once this interval has expired, a reply is sent after a random time.

17.3.3   Operation of the IGMP Protocol

Now that we explained how an IGMP message is structured and how it is transmitted, this section will discuss group management, including the differences between IGMPv1 and IGMPv2.

Multicast routers send group membership queries (IGMP_HOST_MEMBERSHIP_QUERY) to the *all-hosts* group members with group address 224.0.0.1 periodically, at an interval of a few minutes (125 seconds is recommended). Each multicast-capable computer is a member of this group, so all multicast systems receive these queries. (See Figure 17–6.)

Notice that, in these queries, the router sets the TTL value to 1 to ensure that its query packets travel only within the local area network. Next, each computer belonging to one or more multicast groups starts a timer with a random value for each group. (See Figure 17–7.)

Next, as soon as the timer for one of these groups in one computer expires, this computer sends, a report (IGMP_HOST_MEMBERSHIP_REPORT) addressed to the multicast group. In addition, the value of the TTL field is set to one in this case. All members of the group receive this report and stop their timers. The effect is that only one computer sends a report, and thus a flood of reports is prevented. The router also receives the report. This reply is sufficient for the router to learn that at least one computer interested in receiving group data is in its local area network. Consequently, the router will subscribe packets of this group via the multicast routing protocol and forward them in the LAN.

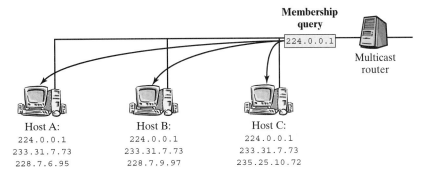

FIGURE 17–6
A multicast router sends a membership query to all multicast computers in the local area network (224.0.0.1).

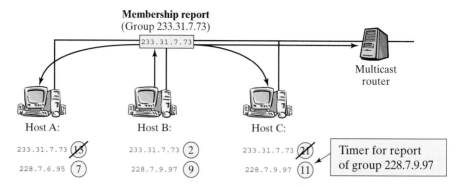

FIGURE 17–7
Membership report of a group by the participant with the smallest timer value in that group.

If the router does not receive reports for a specific group over a certain period of time, it assumes that there are no more interested computers, and deletes this group from its list. If a computer wants to join a group, it can explicitly request this in IGMPv2 by sending a *New Membership Report* packet. In older protocols, the computer may have had to wait a few minutes until the router sends a query message.

When IGMPv2 routers send their queries, they write a specific value to the *Max Resp Time* field. A value larger than null tells the computers that this is an IGMPv2 router. This means that IGMPv2 computers can send version-2 reports (IGMP_HOST_NEW_MEMBERSHIP_REPORT).

In addition, IGMPv2-enabled computers can leave a specific group by sending an IGMP_HOST_LEAVE_MESSAGE to the *all-routers* group. The group to be left is identified in the group address field. Early notification of a station to leave a group can help to reduce the load in the local area network. However, each group member's request to leave a group are sent to the local area network not when it is no longer interested in this data, but only if the group member was the *reporter*—the computer that originally sent the membership report for that group. This approach avoids a large number of *Leave* packets. If the reporter was the only group member, then the router can stop delivering packets of this group in any event. If there are members other than the reporter in the local area network, then these members can react to a *Leave* message immediately by sending a report to the router telling it that there is still an interest in this data.

A conflict can arise if there is more than one multicast-capable router in one local area network. In such a situation, two routers could transport redundant multicast packets to the LAN. The question is: Who decides which router will serve which group? The problem is solved by a simple mechanism known from other protocols: The router with the smallest IP address assumes the role of a *coordinator*. The other routers just listen to the traffic until the coordinator fails. In this case, the router with the next smaller address assumes the role of the multicast router. A good indicator that a multicast router has failed occurs when no more group queries arrive.

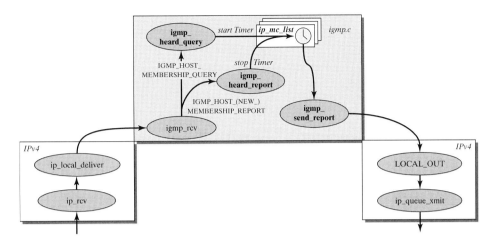

FIGURE 17–8
Implementing IGMP in the Linux kernel.

17.3.4   Implementing IGMP

This section describes how the Internet Group Management Protocol (IGMP) is implemented in the Linux kernel. Among other things, we will explain how entries for multicast groups are stored and how an IGMP query is handled in the kernel.

We saw how a packet is handled in the Linux kernel in Figure 14–4, and we learned that a packet can travel over different paths. The processing of IGMP packets begins at the multiplex point of IP: the point where the mechanism branches to the handling routine of the respective layer-4 protocol. The further path that an IGMP packet takes (see Figure 17–8) will be explained in the section that describes the igmp_rcv() function.

igmp_rcv()	net/ipv4/igmp.c

The starting point of the IP multicast control path is in igmp_rcv(). Once an IGMP packet has passed the lower layers and arrived in the IP layer, its protocol type is checked and the appropriate protocol-handling routine is invoked. For IGMP messages (protocol identifier 2), this is the function igmp_rcv(skb, len). The function involves the following steps:

```
int igmp_rcv(struct sk_buff *skb, unsigned short len)
{
        struct igmphdr *ih = skb->h.igmph;

        switch (ih->type) {
                case IGMP_HOST_MEMBERSHIP_QUERY:                     //0x11
                        igmp_heard_query(in_dev, ih->code, ih->group);
                        break;
                case IGMP_HOST_MEMBERSHIP_REPORT:                   //0x12
                case IGMP_HOST_NEW_MEMBERSHIP_REPORT:               //0x16
```

```
                  igmp_heard_report(in_dev, ih->group);
                  break;
          case IGMP_HOST_LEAVE_MESSAGE:                          //0x17
                  break;
                  ...
}
```

In this function, the type of the IGMP packet is extracted, and, once the IGMP packet has been checked for correctness, the function branches to the corresponding routine. If the message type is IGMP_HOST_LEAVE_MESSAGE, then the packet is ignored in a simple computer. For queries arriving from a router, further handling of the message is started by igmp_heard_query(). If the message is a report from another system, then it is handled by igmp_heard_report(). All other packet types are ignored.

igmp_heard_query()	net/ipv4/igmp.c

The function igmp_heard_query is invoked for IGMP queries arriving from a router (IGMP_HOST_MEMBERSHIP_QUERY). In this case, the function walks through the list of all active IP multicast groups to which the computer with the network card that received the query belongs. This list is managed in the structure dev->ip_ptr->in_device->mc_list. Next, igmp_mod_timer is used to start a timer or update a running timer for every group except the *all-hosts* group.

Notice that each computer belongs to the *all-hosts* group and that no timer is started for this group, for performance reasons. The requesting router assumes that, in addition to itself, at least one active multicast computer is connected to each local area network.

igmp_heard_report()	net/ipv4/igmp.c

If another computer responds to a query, it directs its reply to the appropriate group, and all other members of this group will receive this reply. The IGMP message type is either IGMP_HOST_MEMBERSHIP_REPORT or IGMP_HOST_NEW_MEMBERSHIP_REPORT, depending on the version used to send the message. As a response to an incoming query report, each other computer in the local area network can stop its timer for the group concerned. In the Linux kernel, this task is handled by igmp_heard_report. For this purpose, the list of active multicast groups of the network device that received the report is walked through. This list is managed in the structure dev->ip_ptr->in_device->mc_list. The timer of this group is stopped (igmp_stop_timer()), and the variable reporter records that this computer has not replied for this group (reporter = 0;).

igmp_send_report()	net/ipv4/igmp.c

Once a query message has been sent, a timer is started for each multicast group in each computer. The computer with the timer expiring first sends a query report. This is done by the function igmp_send_report, which was started by the timer handler (`igmp_timer_expire()`) for this group (`timer` in the `ip_mc_list` structure). In addition, the variable `reporter` in the function `igmp_timer_expire()` remembers that this station replied to the query. This information may be required later to tell the router that the computer wants to leave that group.

However, `igmp_send_report()` serves not only to send *query reports*; it can also be used to generate packets to announce that a computer wants to leave a group (*leave messages*). The actions required are identical in both cases; only the destination address and the IGMP message type are different. In case of a report, the packet is sent to the corresponding group; in the case of a leave message, all multicast routers in the LAN (*all-routers*) are addressed. Notice that the value of the TTL field has to be set to 1 to ensure that the response will spread only within the LAN. Next, the IP packet is built, and the IGMP fields are set accordingly. Finally, the packet is shipped out over the LOCAL_OUT hook.

`ip_check_mc()`	**net/ipv4/igmp.c**

`ip_check_mc(in_dev, mc_addr)` is actually not part of the IGMP protocol; it is used for IP routing. More specifically, `ip_check_mc()` checks on whether the local computer is currently a member of the multicast group `mc_addr`. For this purpose, the list of active groups of the network device's IP instance (`mc_list` in the `in_device` structure) is checked and compared against the group address passed. If a match is found, then one is returned; otherwise, **null** is returned.

`ip_check_mc()` is also used in the function `ip_route_input()` to learn whether the packet should be delivered locally. If this is the case (as is always true for multicast routers), then the packet is passed to `ip_route_input_mc()`. If the computer does not act as a multicast router, and if the packet does not belong to any group of the input network device, then it will be discarded. This actually means that rather few packets are discarded, because most undesired multicast packets are normally filtered out by the hardware filter in the network card. (See Section 17.4.1.)

17.4   MULTICAST DATA PATH IN THE LINUX KERNEL

This section describes how multicast data packets are processed in the Linux kernel. To get a good insight into matters, we will first explain the path a multicast packet takes across the kernel, then discuss different aspects of the data path. We will begin on the MAC layer, to see how multicasting is supported in local area networks and to introduce the following IP multicast concepts:

- virtual network devices,
- multicast routing tables, and
- replicating of data packets.

As we introduce the implementation, we will emphasize differences between multicast-capable end systems and multicast routers.

17.4.1 Multicast Support on the MAC Layer

In general, IEEE-802.x LANs are broadcast-enabled: each data packet is sent to each participant. Each network adapter looks at the MAC destination address to decide whether it will accept and process a packet. This process normally is handled by the network adapter and doesn't interfere with the central processor's work. The central processor is stopped by an interrupt only when the adapter decides that a packet has to be forwarded to the higher layers. This means that the filtering of packets in the network adapter take load off the CPU and ensures that it will receive only packets that are actually addressed to the local computer.

Filtering undesired MAC frames works well in the case of unicast packets, because each adapter should know its MAC address. However, how can the card know whether the computer is interested in the data of a group when a multicast packet arrives? In case of doubt, the adapter accepts the packet and passes it on to the higher-layer protocols, which should know all subscribed groups. The next question is whether multicast packets use the MAC address at all. The MAC format supports group addresses, but how are they structured?

There is a clever solution for IP multicast groups to solve the problems described above. On the one hand, this solution prevents broadcasting of multicast packets; on the other hand, it concurrently filters IP groups on the MAC layer. The method, described here, is simple, and it relieves the central processing unit from too many unnecessary interrupts.

IP multicast packets are packed in MAC frames before they are sent to the local area network, and they contain a MAC group address. The MAC address is selected so that it gives a clue about which multicast group the packet could belong to. Figure 17–9 shows how this address is structured; it contains the following elements:

▪ The first 25 bits of the MAC address identify the group address for IP multicast. The first byte (0x01) shows that the address is a group MAC address, where the

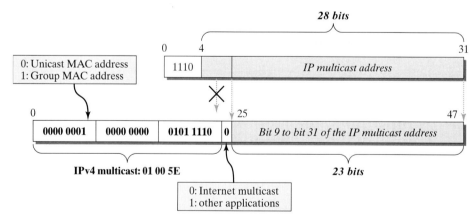

FIGURE 17–9
Mapping an IP multicast group address to an IEEE-802 MAC address.

last bit is decisive. Notice that the address shown in Figure 17–9 is represented in the network byte order.

The next 17 bits (0x005E) state that the MAC packet carries an IP multicast packet. The identifier here would be different for other layer-3 protocols.

▒ The last 23 bits carry the last 23 bits of the IP multicast address.

We can easily see that this is not a reversible mapping between an IP multicast address and a MAC address. For each multicast MAC address, there are $2^5 = 32$ possible IP multicast groups matching this MAC address. This means that the network adapters cannot filter exactly. Instead, they pass all matching multicast groups to IP. In any event, this filtering takes a lot of load off the central processing unit, because only multicast packets actually subscribed are normally delivered to IP.

We still have to answer one question: How can the network adapter know to which groups IP subscribed? To solve this problem, each network adapter manages a list with multicast group addresses that should be received on this adapter. If the network adapter can support hardware filtering of multicast packets from the technical perspective, then a driver method transfers this list to the adapter (set_multicast_list()). The adapter can then filter without disturbing the central processing unit.

The active multicast groups of a network device's IP instance are maintained in the mc_list of the in_device structure. When an application joins an IP multicast group, the IP group address and some other information are recorded in this list. In addition, ip_eth_mc_map() computes the appropriate MAC group address (for Ethernet networks) and adds it to the list dev->mc_list. Once set_multicast_list() has updated the card, the network adapter should be able to receive packets for this group. Figure 17–10 shows schematically how groups are managed in the IP instance and in the network device.

struct ip_mc_list	include/linux/igmp.h

▒ multiaddr is the multicast address of the subscribed group.

▒ interface points to the net_device structure of the network adapter.

▒ next points to the next entry in the list.

▒ timer is a timer used by IGMP to delay membership reports.

▒ tm_running shows whether or not the timer is currently active.

▒ reporter contains the value 1, if this computer sent the last membership report for this group to the multicast router. If another computer was faster, then reporter is set to 0. This information is required to send leave messages, which are transmitted exclusively by the reporter.

▒ users counts the number of sockets that subscribed this group. During closing of one of these sockets, a leave message is sent over IGMPv2 only when no more users exist.

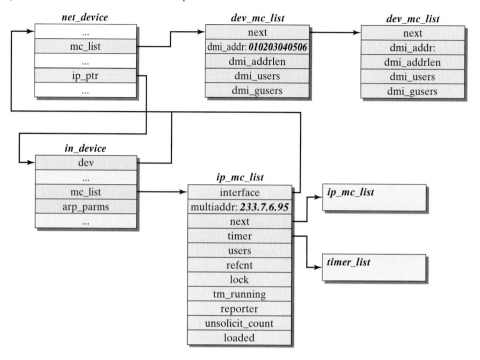

FIGURE 17–10
Managing multicast groups or addresses in an IP instance and in a network device.

dev->mc_list	include/linux/netdevice.h

- next points to the next entry in the list.
- dmi_addr[MAX_ADDR_LEN]: This is the layer-2 address of the group the packets of which should be received.
- dmi_addrlen specifies the length of the layer-2 address in dmi_addr.

17.4.2 Multicast Data Path in the Internet Protocol

Now that we have described how multicasting is supported on the MAC layer, this section explains how IP multicast packets are processed in the Linux implementation of the Internet Protocol. We will first look at end systems and multicast routers.

However, before we discuss the details of the processes involved, we want to introduce two important components of the multicast implementation: virtual network devices, which abstract from the two possible transmission types for multicast packets (i.e., LAN adapter card or IP tunnel), and the multicast routing table (multicast forwarding cache).

Virtual Network Devices Multicast packets can be received and sent in either of two different ways: either directly over the network adapter in a LAN, or packed inside a second unicast IP packet and transported through a *tunnel*. To prevent having to distinguish these two cases in the entire multicast implementation, an abstraction—the so-called *virtual network device* or virtual interface (VIF)—was introduced for both types.

struct vif_device	**include/linux/mroute.h**

In the Linux kernel, virtual network devices are represented by the vif_device structure. A *virtual interface* describes either a physical network device of the type net_device or an IP-IP tunnel. A flag is used to distinguish these two methods.

```
struct vif_device {
        struct net_device *dev;           /* Device we are using */
        unsigned long      bytes_in,bytes_out;
        unsigned long      pkt_in,pkt_out;    /* Statistics */
        unsigned long      rate_limit;        /* Traffic shaping (NI) */
        unsigned char      threshold;         /* TTL threshold */
        unsigned short     flags;             /* Control flags */
        __u32              local,remote;      /* Addresses(remote for
                                                  tunnels)*/
        int                link;              /* Physical interface index */
};
```

- dev: a pointer to the network device (net_device), which may be used
- bytes_in, bytes_out: statistical information about the transported bytes
- pkt_in, pkt_out: number of packets handled
- threshold: threshold value for packets that should be sent over this virtual network device (as in Section 17.2.3)
- flags: Flags to specify, for example, whether the VIF represents a tunnel (VIFF_TUNNEL).
- local and remote: either (a) the IP addresses of the tunnel starting point and the tunnel end point, or (b) the IP address of the network device
- link: Index of the physical network device.

Figure 17–11 shows how the vif_device structure is structured and embedded in its environment. Virtual network devices are stored in the table (array) vif_table. It can maintain a maximum of MAXVIFS entries for each computer. The maximum number is 32, and this number cannot be increased in current personal computers, to fit the variable vifc_map (net/ipv4/ipmr.c). Each bit of vifc_map marks whether the virtual network device with the index corresponding to the bit index had already been created. The maximum number, 32 VIFs for a 32-bit architecture, results from the data type, unsigned long, of this variable. Consequently, this number can be limited (but not extended) by MAXVIFS. This limitation results in the fact that a multicast router can be directly connected to a maximum of MAXVIFS other multicast routers.

Each entry in the array represents either a physical network device or a tunnel. The entries are set and removed by the multicast routing daemon (e.g., mrouted) by use of the socket options MRT_ADD_VIF and MRT_DEL_VIF. The parameters of the vif_device structure are passed in a vifctl structure (VIF control). Section 17.5.2 discusses how virtual network devices are configured.

Multicast Forwarding Cache   The multicast forwarding cache (MFC) is the central structure used to store information about how often incoming multicast packets have to

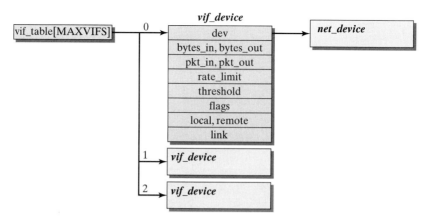

FIGURE 17–11
The vif_table of a virtual network device.

be replicated and where they have to be forwarded to. This means that the MFC implements the multicast routing table. The MFC is built in the form of a hash table, as we can easily see from the `mfc_cache` structure. All entries with the same hash value are linearly linked with the respective cache rows (singly linked list). All cache rows are grouped in the field `mfc_cache_array` to form an MFC hash table with a size specified by `MFC_LINES` (`include/linux/mroute.h`). By standard, the multicast forwarding cache comprises 64 rows or lines. Figure 17–12 shows schematically how the MFC is structured.

When additional routes should be found for an incoming multicast packet, then the multicast forwarding cache has to be searched for a matching entry. To find a matching entry, `mfc_hash` is initially used to determine the correct cache line. The input network device and the multicast group address are used as parameters. Next, the linked list in the cache line is processed until a matching entry is found. The entries in the MFC are of the `mfc_cache` data type.

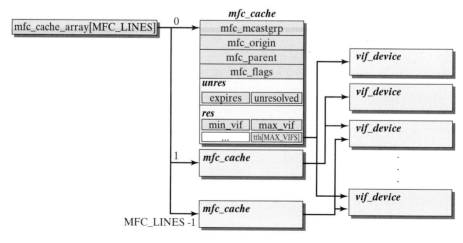

FIGURE 17–12
Structure of the multicast forwarding cache (`mfc_cache`).

The `ttls` field includes information about virtual network devices that can be used to forward the packet. A TTL entry smaller than 255 means that the virtual network device with an index identical to the index in the `ttls` array should forward these packets. The `ttls` array is processed sequentially. To optimize this process, `minvif` and `maxvif` store the minimum and maximum VIF indexes that should receive the packet.

struct mfc_cache	include/linux/include/mroute.h

```
struct mfc_cache
{
        struct    mfc_cache *next;              /* Next entry on cache line
                                                 */
        __u32     mfc_mcastgrp;                 /* Group, entry belongs to
                                                 */
        __u32     mfc_origin;                   /* Source of packet */
        vifi_t    mfc_parent;                   /* Source interface */
        int       mfc_flags;                    /* Flags on line */

        union
        {
                struct
                {
                    unsigned long expires;
                    struct sk_buff_head unresolved; /* Unres. buffers */
                } unres;
                struct
                {
                    unsigned long last_assert;
                    int minvif, maxvif;
                    unsigned long bytes;
                    unsigned long pkt;
                    unsigned long wrong_if;
                    unsigned char ttls[MAXVIFS];  /* TTL thresholds */
                } res;
        } mfc_un;
};
```

- **next** points to the next entry in the multicast forwarding cache. The cache lines are organized in singly linked lists. A NULL pointer in this field marks the end of a cache line.
- **mfc_mcastgrp** and **mfc_origin** together form the key for an entry in the multicast forwarding cache. **mfc_origin** is the IP address of the sending computer, and **mfc_mcastgrp** specifies the multicast group for a multicast packet, the route of which is represented by this entry.
- **mfc_parent** is the index of the virtual network device in the **vif_table**, over which packets of this MFC entry should arrive.
- The **mfc_un** structure is a *union* structure: It is either an **unres** structure or a **res** structure. The two structures are defined per union, because either one structure or the other is required, but never both.

■ unres is used for entries in the multicast forwarding cache when the multicast routing daemon has not yet finalized the routing selection. The entry for the mfc_cache structure is created in the MFC as soon as a packet for it arrives.

▷ unresolved is a queue for socket buffers that store packets for this routing entry until the multicast routing daemon has selected a route.

▷ expires specifies the time by which the daemon should have selected a route.

■ res is used in the mfc_un union when the multicast routing daemon has specified the routes for this entry.

▷ minvif and maxvif are indexes to elements in the ttls list of the MFC entry. They limit the range currently used by virtual network devices, which are used to send packets of this MFC entry. Stating this indexes saves computing time required to duplicate multicast packets. The maxvif index is limited by the MAXVIFS constant.

▷ ttls[MAXVIFS] is an array with MAXVIFS entries, where each entry specifies whether a packet should be forwarded over the virtual network device in the vif_table list with the corresponding index. This is the case when a value less than 255 exists. The value 0 cannot occur, because it is mapped to the value 255 when the table is built. However, an entry less than 255 is not sufficient to forward a packet; the TTL value of a packet has to be at least equal to the TTL value in the ttls array. This is the method used to create the threshold value for multicast packets described in Section 17.2.3.

Paths of a Multicast Packet Through the Linux Kernel   Figure 17–13 shows the paths a multicast packet can take to travel through the Linux kernel. Like any other IP packet,

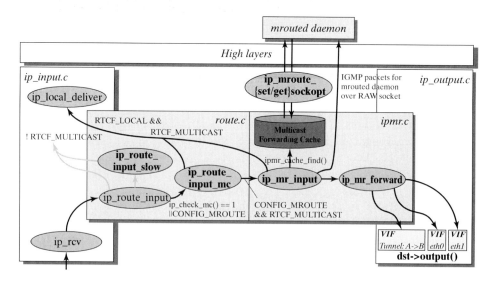

FIGURE 17–13
Overview of how a multicast packet can travel through the Linux kernel.

a multicast packet is received by ip_rcv(). The routing cache is normally asked for further packet-forwarding instructions in ip_route_input() (see Chapter 16), and multicast packets are no exception. In the case of an end system, ip_check_mc() checks on whether the multicast group is required in the computer at all. This means that all undesired multicast packets (i.e., packets passed upwards by the network card, either because of an unclear mapping of IP multicast addresses to MAC addresses, or because of an adapter without hardware filter, or by the promiscuous mode) are discarded. If a socket desires a packet, then the flag RTCF_LOCAL is attached to the packet at this point. In general, the flag RTCF_MULTICAST is also set in multicast packets.

If the packet is accepted (i.e., if the group is desired or the station is a multicast router, which accepts all packets), then the multicast packet continues its path in ip_route_input_mc(), where paths go in different directions, depending on whether the station is an end system or a multicast router. In end systems, *local* packets are passed to the function ip_local_deliver(), which forwards them to the application layer.

In multicast routers, all packets (including local packets) are first handled by ip_mr_input(). The most important task of this function is to use ipmr_cache_find() to find the entry in the MFC. Local packets are passed to ip_local_deliver(), and packets with other destinations are transported to ip_mr_forward(), where they will eventually be replicated. The details of each of these functions are described next.

ip_route_input_mc()	net/ipv4/route.c

ip_route_input() invokes ip_route_input_mc(skb, daddr, saddr, tos, dev, our) if the incoming packet is a multicast packet. First, the function checks the source and destination addresses (saddr, daddr) and returns an error, if present. Also, packets originating from the same computer should not arrive over this input routine for several reasons, including protection against spoofing. Once the sender address has been checked in the forwarding information base, memory space is allocated for a new entry in the routing cache. The route is entered in the cache, and the flag RTCF_MULTICAST is added. Subsequently, the packet is handled in ip_local_deliver() (for end systems) or ip_mr_input() (for multicast routers), and the computed hash value is returned.

ip_mr_input()	net/ipv4/ipmr.c

ip_rcv_finish() invokes ip_mr_input(skb) by use of the function pointer dst->input(), which is set to ip_mr_input() in ip_route_input_mc(), if the computer was configured as a multicast router. The first thing to be checked is whether the packet is an IGMP packet for the multicast routing daemon. If so, the packet is delivered to this daemon over the *raw* socket. Subsequently, the function ipmr_cache_find searches the multicast forwarding cache for a matching entry for the skb packet. If no matching entry can be found, then a local packet (RTCF_LOCAL) is passed to ip_local_deliver(), and packets that have to be forwarded are added to the queue for incomplete routing entries (unresolved queue in the mfc_cache structure). As soon as the routing daemon has determined the route, these packets are forwarded by ip_mr_forward().

If a valid entry was found in the multicast forwarding cache, then ip_mr_input() passes a pointer to this routing entry to the function ip_mr_forward, which duplicates and forwards the packet. Finally, packets marked local (RTCF_LOCAL) are passed upwards by `ip_local_deliver`.

`ip_mr_forward()`	**net/ipv4/ipmr.c**

`ipmr_cache_find(origin,mcastgrp)` searches the multicast forwarding cache (see above) for a specific entry. The source address of the packet and the multicast group address together are used as search key. An MFC entry found includes all virtual network devices (VIFs), which should be used to forward packets. The result is returned in an `mfc_cache` structure (see above).

`ip_mr_forward()`	**net/ipv4/ipmr.c**

`ip_mr_input(skb, mfc, local)` obtains the `mfc` pointer from `ip_mr_input()`, which points to the entry of the `skb` packet in the multicast forwarding cache and then duplicates the packet for each virtual network device that should be used to forward duplicates:

```
for (ct = cache->mfc_un.res.maxvif-1; ct >= cache->mfc_un.res.minvif; ct-)
{
        if (skb->nh.iph->ttl > cache->mfc_un.res.ttls[ct])
        {
                if (psend !=-1)
                        ipmr_queue_xmit(skb, cache, psend, 0);
        psend=ct;
        }
}
```

The actual replication of multicast packets is done in the `for` loop, which checks all array entries in the `ttls` field of the `mfc` structure from `maxvif-1` to `minvif`. However, the copies of socket buffers are not directly created by `ip_mr_forward()`. They are created later by the function `ipmr_queue_xmit()`, which is invoked if the multicast packet has sufficient lifetime (TTL) left to be sent over the current virtual network device. It passes the entire MFC structure and an index to each VIF that should receive the packet to `ipmr_queue_xmit` for each VIF.

Before a packet is replicated, `ip_mr_forward()` checks on whether the packet has arrived in the expected network device and on whether it was discarded, if applicable. One reason for this check will be discussed in Section 17.5.3. A conflict situation can occur if a computer acts as multicast router and runs multicast applications at the same time. If multicast packets are transported across the loopback network device, then the input network device can deviate from the default multicast route for these packets, and these packets will be discarded.

`ipmr_queue_xmit()`	**net/ipv4/ipmr.c**

`ip_mr_forward` invokes `ipmr_queue_xmit(skb, mfc, vifi, last)` to transmit the multicast packet `skb`. If the packet is not exclusively available (for example, because there are several references to the packet payload (`cloned`)), or if the packet is not the last of all of its replicates, then a clone of the socket buffer is created. In addition, a decision has to be made for the packet as to whether it should be transported through a tunnel or through a regular network device. In either case, `ip_route_output` with the respective parameters is invoked. For a tunneled packet, the variables `local` and `remote` from the pertaining VIF structure are passed; otherwise, the destination IP address from the socket buffer's structure is sufficient. In both cases, the variable `link` from the VIF structure passes an index to the relevant physical network device. Subsequently, the netfilter hook `NF_IP_FORWARD` is invoked. If it does not have to be fragmented, the packet is sent over the function pointer `dst-> output()`; otherwise it is sent over `ip_fragment(skb, dst->output)`.

17.5 MULTICASTING IN TODAY'S INTERNET

Multicasting was a thing unheard of at the advent of the Internet, and neither group addresses nor protocols to manage groups or multicast routing were available. In fact, the most important prerequisites to implementing an efficient group communication service were missing. The Internet was a pure unicast network.

Several proposals in this field were made [Deer91] when the Internet community had started to think that such a service was necessary, at the beginning of the nineties. Eventually, IP multicast was born when the Internet Group Management Protocol and the address class D were standardized. In addition, multicast routing protocols were proposed, so that nothing was actually impeding the introducing of the new communication form. However, though the Internet had evolved into an enormous global network during the last twenty years, it was still a unicast network, and gradually each system connected to the Internet would have had to be extended to IP multicast support. This change would certainly have taken several years to complete. In addition, the new technology had not yet been tested extensively. Consequently, a decision was made to build a multicast test network within the unicast Internet, the so-called *MBone* (Multicast Backbone On the Internet), rather than converting to multicast from scratch.

17.5.1 The Multicast Backbone (MBone)

The Internet Engineering Task Force (IETF) ran a pilot transmission session to officially introduce MBone in March 1992. Since then, more than 10,000 subnetworks have been connected to this network worldwide. MBone enables the connected multicast-enhanced subnetworks to run IP multicasting over the existing Internet, even though the Internet itself is not multicast capable.

The solution offered by MBone is relatively simple: It builds a virtual multicast network over the conventional Internet, which understands only unicasting, and connected systems communicate over multicast-capable routers (multicast routers). As soon as there is a nonmulticast network between them, multicast routers bridge this situation by a so-called IP-in-IP tunnel. This tunnel consists of a unicast connection used to transport multicast traffic. For this purpose, the multicast router packs a multicast packet into another IP packet at the beginning of the tunnel and sends it as a normal unicast IP packet over the network to the tunnel output. The multicast router at that end of the tunnel removes the outer unicast packet and sends the multicast packet to the multicast-capable network.

This method led to the formation of many multicast-capable islands interconnected by tunnels over the conventional Internet. Figure 17–14 shows an example for the basic MBone architecture. Technically, MBone is a virtual overlay network on top of the Internet. Similar overlay networks have been built to study other Internet technologies, including 6Bone (Six-Bone) for IPv6 and QBone to study quality of service (QoS) mechanisms.

17.5.2   Accessing MBone Over the mrouted Daemon

The mrouted daemon is a tool you can use to connect to MBone. It enables you to build tunnels to other MBone nodes and ensure connectivity. In addition, this daemon enables multicast routing for multicast packets within or at the boundaries of a multicast network. The standard implementation of mrouted in UNIX uses the *Distant Vector Multicast Routing Protocol* (*DVMRP*; see Section 17.5.3).

Like all daemons, mrouted operates in the user-address space and can be started and stopped at system runtime. It communicates with the kernel over specific interfaces, which will be introduced in the course of this chapter. The mrouted daemon can be exchanged at runtime, so we can implement different routing algorithms. The mrouted daemon is not the only multicast routing daemon for Linux, but it is the most popular and the most frequently used today.

How mrouted Operates   Multicast packet forwarding is separate from selecting of forwarding routes; the kernel is responsible for forwarding, and the routing daemon determines the routes. Again, this shows a known principle, the separating of the data path from the control path. To determine routes, the mrouted daemon obtains information about all incoming multicast packets, including their destination and origin. Using this information, it computes the multicast routing tables and passes them to the kernel over a specific interface. This means that the daemon tells the kernel how it should forward packets from a specific sender to a specific group. The paths or routes for multicast packets are stated in the form of virtual network devices, which were introduced in Section 17.4.2.

Interface Between the Multicast Routing Daemon and the Kernel   The mrouted daemon communicates with the Linux kernel over a special socket. The kernel obtains routing information for multicast packets by setsockopt() calls over a raw socket. mrouted uses the IPPROTO_IGMP protocol to open this socket a head of time. Within the kernel, a reference to the socket used by mrouted to communicate with the kernel

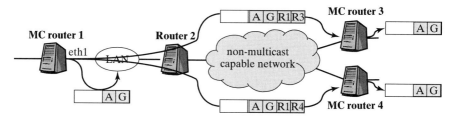

FIGURE 17–14
MBone consists of multicast islands connected by tunnels.

is stored in the variable mroute_socket. If mroute_socket contains the value NULL, then no instance of the mrouted daemon is running yet; otherwise, an instance is already active, and the socket is denied. This allows you to check for whether an attempt is made to create a second instance of the daemon and to ensure that the commands to manipulate multicast routing information in the kernel originate from the correct mrouted socket.

The options available to change the multicast routing table are handled by the function ip_mroute_setsockopt() (defined in net/ipv4/ipmr.c). MRT_INIT has to be the first option or the first command we send to the socket. All other commands (MRT_DONE, MRT_ADD_VIF, MRT_DEL_VIF, MRT_ADD_MFC, MRT_DEL_MFC, and MRT_ASSERT) are ignored; they return the result -EACCESS if the socket was not previously reserved by MRT_INIT.

The following subsections describe the most important functions and structures available in the Linux kernel for tasks handled by the multicast routing daemon. These functions and structures are declared primarily in the file net/ipv4/mroute.c. Subsequently, we use a few examples to show how the daemon and the kernel exchange data by use of ioctl() commands and socket options.

Kernel Functions Used by mrouted

ip_mroute_setsockopt()	**net/ipv4/ipmr.c**

ip_mroute_setsockopt(sk,opt_name,opt_val,opt_len) accepts commands from the mrouted daemon and processes them, including, for example, the creating and deleting of virtual network devices (VIFs) and entries in the multicast routing table (MFC). ip_mroute_setsockopt() is invoked by ip_setsockopt() in net/ipv4/ip_sockglue.c, because these are socket options.

In addition to the sk socket and the actual command, opt_name, this function can accept other parameters, including additional information (opt_val), if required for the command, and the length of this information (opt_len). In summary, this function can accept the following commands and additional information:

▨ MRT_INIT: This command sets the variable mroute_socket. It takes the value unequal NULL by default, and it returns an -EADDRINUSE error if another instance of mrouted (or another multicast routing daemon) is already running. Otherwise, mroute_socket obtains a pointer to the socket used to send MRT_INIT. This command has to be the first command for mrouted, because all other commands check on whether they originate from the socket specified in mroute_socket. If an error occurs, then -EACCESS is returned, and the command is not executed.

Before we can use a socket, we have to run the protocol option IPPROTO_IGMP to create the socket. Otherwise, an -ENOPNOTSUPP error is returned. opt_val has to point to an integer value with the value one; otherwise, the result will again be an error (this time, -ENOPROTOOPT).

▨ MRT_ADD_VIF: This command instructs the kernel to create a new virtual network device (VIF). The additional information this command takes is a pointer to a `vifctl` structure (see Section 17.5.2) in `opt_val`, which is passed to the kernel because it includes all parameters required. These parameters include an index of the virtual network device, the address of the physical network device, and tunnel information. Another important thing is the flag that states whether this virtual network device is a tunnel (`VIFF_TUNNEL`). If this is the case, then the kernel uses the function `ipmr_new_tunnel()` to create a new tunnel. Otherwise, `ip_dev_find()` is used to search for the corresponding network device. If `MRT_ADD_VIF` is sent before `MRT_INIT` initialized the socket, then `-EACCESS` is returned. This is also the case when `MRT_ADD_VIF` was invoked by another socket.

Other errors that can potentially occur are `-EINVAL`, `-EFAULT`, `-ENFILE`, and `-EADDRINUSE`—if `opt_val` is an invalid structure, if the structure cannot be copied from the user address space, if the VIF index is outside the valid range, or if the virtual network device already exists, respectively.

In the creating of a new virtual network device, a new `vif_device` structure is added to its list (`vif_table`), and the information relevant for this entry is taken from the `vifctl` structure.

- MRT_DEL_VIF: This command is used to remove the entry for a virtual network device from the list of virtual network devices (`vif_table`). The parameters used here are identical to those used in `MRT_ADD_VIF`. However, only the VIF index is evaluated.

- MRT_ADD_MFC: This command instructs the kernel to add a new entry in its multicast routing table (multicast forwarding cache) or, if an entry matching the specified search key exists, to update this entry. For this purpose, an `mfcctl` structure (see below) is additionally passed in `opt_val`. Once the validity check of the structure (error: `-EINVAL`) has been completed, `ipmr_cache_find()` (see below) checks the MFC cache to see whether a corresponding entry exists. If this is the case, then this entry is adapted to the new values; otherwise, a new entry is created. When a new cache entry is created, an `mfc_cache` structure is allocated at the same time, and all relevant information is taken from the `mfcctl` structure and transmitted. In this case, the entries in the field `mfc_ttls` having the value **null** are mapped to 255. The reason is that the validation process need only test whether the value is smaller than 255 to see whether a packet is to be routed to a VIF.

- MRT_DEL_MFC: This command instructs the kernel to remove an entry from the MFC. The kernel uses the function `ipmr_mfc_delete()` to delete an entry from the MFC.

`ip_mroute_getsockopt()`	**net/ipv4/ipmr.c**

The function `ip_mroute_getsockopt(sk,opt_name,opt_val,opt_len)` normally is used to poll the version number (0x0305). For this purpose, `MRT_VERSION` should be specified in `ip_getsockopt()`. `net/ipv4/ip_sockglue.c` invokes `opt_val`. `ip_mroute_getsockopt()`. We can use `ioctl()` queries to poll additional status information for multicast forwarding.

ipmr_ioctl()   **net/ipv4/ipmr.c**

ipmr_ioctl(sk,cmd,arg) can be used to poll various status information. If cmd has the value SIOCGETVIFCNT, then a pointer to a sioc_vif_req structure (see below) in arg is expected. It includes the index to the virtual network device for which information is to be queried (e.g., how many packets and what data volumes have been received and sent over this device). The result is added to the passed sioc_vif_req structure.

If cmd is equal SIOCGETSGCNT, then a pointer to a sioc_sg_req structure in arg is expected. The corresponding information about the matching entry in the multicast forwarding cache is determined.

ipmr_ioctl() is entered in inet_create() (in net/ipv4/af_inet.c) as ioctl() handling routing in the proto structure for *raw* sockets.

ip_mr_init()   **net/ipv4/ipmr.c**

ip_mr_init(void) initializes the multicast routing functions in the kernel; it is invoked when inet_proto_init() (in net/ipv4/af_inet.c) starts.

ipmr_get_route()   **net/ipv4/ipmr.c**

ipmr_get_route(skm,rtm,nowait) determines the route for a packet from a specific source for a specific group. This function is used for informative purposes only. The result is packed into a packet to send it to other routers (e.g., so that these routers can exchange routing information). The route for the actual routing of multicast packets is specified directly in ip_mr_forward().

ipmr_cache_find()   **net/ipv4/ipmr.c**

ipmr_cache_find(origin,mcastgrp) searches the multicast forwarding cache (see Section 17.4.2) for a specific entry. The packet's source address and the multicast group address serve as search keys. If an MFC entry is found, it includes all virtual network devices (VIFs) that can be used to forward the packet. The result is returned in the form of a pointer to an mfc_cache structure.

ipmr_new_tunnel()   **net/ipv4/ipmr.c**

ipmr_new_tunnel(v) is responsible for creating a new tunnel. All information required toward this end is passed, together with the vifctl structure (v). The function gets the tunnel network device, tun10, and tries to create a tunnel to the destination specified in v. If it is successful, then this *new* virtual network device is returned; otherwise an error message (null) is returned.

ipmr_cache_unresolved()   **net/ipv4/ipmr.c**

ipmr_cache_unresolved(cache,vifi,skb) is invoked by ip_mr_input() and ipmr_get_route(), if a specific entry was polled from the multicast forwarding cache, and if this entry either does not exist or has not been filled yet, though it was requested by mrouted. ipmr_cache_unresolved creates a new entry in the multicast forwarding cache and sets its status to MFC_QUEUED, which means that the route specified in this entry has not yet been entered by mrouted.

Subsequently, the timer is activated, and ipmr_cache_report is invoked to ask mrouted for the required route. The timer causes the entry to be deleted from the cache at a certain time, if mrouted cannot determine the route before this time.

ipmr_cache_report()	net/ipv4/ipmr.c

ipmr_cache_report(pkt,vifi,assert) asks mrouted to create an entry in the multicast forwarding cache (MFC) for a specific packet—its origin and multicast group—to determine the route. For this purpose, a packet is created, and sock_queue_rcv_skb() is used to send it to mrouted.

ipmr_cache_timer()	net/ipv4/ipmr.c

ipmr_cache_timer(data) deletes an entry from the MFC, if the mrouted daemon was requested to determine the route, and if it was unable to do this within a specific time. ipmr_cache_timer() is the timer-handling routine for mfc_timer defined in the mfc_cache structure.

ipmr_cache_alloc()	net/ipv4/ipmr.c

ipmr_cache_alloc(priority) creates a new mfc_cache structure and adds a few initial values, including the timer data and handling routine and information stating that the route does not exist yet. ipmr_cache_alloc() does *not* write the created structure to the multicast forwarding cache; ipmr_cache_insert() has to be invoked separately for that purpose.

ipmr_mfc_modify()	net/ipv4/ipmr.c

ipmr_mfc_modify(action,mfc) is invoked when the mrouted daemon uses MRT_ADD_MFC or MRT_DEL_MFC to manipulate an MFC entry over setsockopt(). In addition to this action, the function checks for whether this is a new entry or the entry already exists and just has to be filled. If the latter is the case, and if the MFC entry is set to the MFC_QUEUED status, then ipmr_cache_resolve() is invoked to send waiting packets.

ipmr_cache_resolve()	net/ipv4/ipmr.c

ipmr_cache_resolve(cache) is invoked by ipmr_mfc_modify() when the route is set in an MFC entry and packets are waiting to be sent. The timer (see above) is deleted, and ip_mr_forward() sends the waiting packets.

Data Exchange Between the mrouted Daemon and the Kernel   This section explains the most important structures exchanged between the Linux kernel and the mrouted daemon. The daemon passes data to the kernel as shown below. We use the example of a query of the virtual network device and an MFC entry to better explain the procedure:

Initially, the mrouted daemon allocates memory space for a sioc_vif_req structure and writes the index of the desired virtual network device to the vifi field. Calling of the ioctl() command SIOCGETVIFCNT makes the appropriate part be executed in ipmr_ioctl. The argument for the ioctl() command is the address by which the daemon has created this structure. Then it is checked whether the vifi index points to a valid virtual network device. If this is the case, then the referenced structure is filled with the appropriate values and copied back to the user address space by copy_to_user(). The structure used to pass the data of a virtual network device is as follows:

struct sioc_vif_req	include/linux/mroute.h

```
sioc_vif_req {
        vifi_t              vifi;        /* Which iface */
        unsigned long       icount;      /* In packets */
        unsigned long       ocount;      /* Out packets */
        unsigned long       ibytes;      * In bytes */
        unsigned long       obytes;      /* Out bytes */
};
```

- vifi: This is the index of the virtual network device specified in the vif_table: the VIF used to request information.
- icount, ocount: This is the number of packets received or sent, respectively, over this VIF.
- ibytes, obytes: This is the sum of bytes included in the packets received or sent.

The procedure involved in querying an entry in the multicast forwarding cache is identical, except that the sioc_sg_req structure and the ioctl() command SIOCGETSGCNT are used:

struct sioc_sg_req	include/linux/mroute.h

```
struct sioc_sg_req
{
        struct              in_addr src;
        struct              in_addr grp;
        unsigned long       pktcnt;
        unsigned long       bytecnt;
        unsigned long       wrong_if;
};
```

The elements of the sioc_sg_req structure handle the following tasks:

- src: This is the sender address; it is part of the key for the MFC entry.
- grp: This is the multicast group address; it is the second part of the key for the MFC entry.

▓ pktcnt: This is the number of packets sent over the desired MFC entry.

▓ bytecnt: This is the number of bytes forwarded over the MFC entry.

Because multicast packets can be received and sent both over physical network adapters and through tunnels, we use an abstraction of virtual network devices (VIFs). The mrouted daemon passes vifctl structures to the kernel. These structures define virtual network devices, including whether a VIF is a physical network device or a tunnel. The multicast routing table of the kernel is influenced by mfcctl (*multicast forwarding cache entries*—MFCs) structures. They represent routing entries used by the kernel to learn how to forward multicast packets.

struct vifctl	include/linux/mroute.h

```
struct vifctl {
        vifi_t            vifc_vifi;        /* Index of VIF */
        unsigned char     vifc_flags;       /* VIFF_ flags */
        unsigned char     vifc_threshold;   /* ttl limit */
        unsigned int      vifc_rate_limit;  /* Rate limiter values (NI) */
        struct in_addr    vifc_lcl_addr;    /* Our address */
        struct in_addr    vifc_rmt_addr;    /* IPIP tunnel addr */
};
```

▓ vifc_vifi: This is the index of this virtual network device in the array vif_table, which stores all VIFs (0 - vifc_vifi < MAXVIFS).

▓ vifc_flags: This part can be used to set options (i.e., VIFF_TUNNEL, if you want to use a tunnel).

▓ vifc_lcl_addr: This is the local address of the network device. For a tunnel, this address represents the entry point into the tunnel virtually.

▓ vifc_rmt_addr: This part includes the destination address of the tunnel, if the VIF is a tunnel.

struct mfcctl	include/linux/mroute.h

```
struct mfcctl {
        struct in_addr    mfcc_origin;          /* Origin of mcast */
        struct in_addr    mfcc_mcastgrp;        /* Group in question */
        vifi_t            mfcc_parent;          /* Where it arrived */
        unsigned char     mfcc_ttls[MAXVIFS];   /* Where it is going */
        unsigned int      mfcc_pkt_cnt;         /* pkt count for src-grp */
        unsigned int      mfcc_byte_cnt;
        unsigned int      mfcc_wrong_if;
        int               mfcc_expire;
};
```

▓ mfcc_origin: This is the packet's source address (i.e., the address of the computer that originally sent the packet).

▓ mfcc_mcastgrp: This identifies the multicast group that should receive the packet.

- `mfcc_parent`: This identifies the VIF that received the packet.
- `mfc_ttls`: This field specifies the VIFs a packet should be routed to. The field includes one entry for each potential VIF. A value of 0 or 255 means that the VIF with the corresponding index in the `vif_table` is *not* interested in the packet.

17.5.3 The DVMRP Routing Algorithm

The *Distance Vector Multicast Routing Protocol (DVMRP)* is the oldest multicast routing protocol; it was defined initially in [WaPD88] and extended later [Pusa00]. DVMRP was the multicast routing protocol used as basis to build MBone, and it has since remained the most popular multicast routing protocol. DVMRP uses a distance vector routing algorithm, which determines the shortest path to the sender. This means that it extends the principles of the RIP distance vector unicast routing protocol [Malk98] to multicasting capabilities.

DVMRP supports both physical network devices and tunnels as potential routes to forward multicast packets, mainly because these capabilities were required when MBone was introduced. This section briefly explains the approach of DVMRP, including a practical example.

How DVMRP Works   To build a distribution tree, DVMRP in its current version uses a principle called *Reverse Path Multicasting*. The shortest path to the sender is learned when a multicast router receives a multicast packet in a network adapter. If this route leads over the network device that received the packet, then it is forwarded to all neighboring multicast routers except for the interface that received the packet. Otherwise, the multicast packet is discarded, because it didn't arrive on an optimal route, which means that it is assumed that it does not originate from the direct path to the sender. More specifically, it is assumed to be a duplicate that might previously have been received. A multicast router is not able to see whether it has already received a packet or the packet is arriving for the first time. This is the reason why packets are accepted only if it can be assumed that they originate directly from the sender. This approach avoids a large number of duplicates—those created by a routing principle called flooding. Figure 17–15 shows how DVMRP works.

A unicast routing protocol is used to determine the shortest path back to the sender. In this respect, the `mrouted` daemon does not use the kernel's unicast routing table, but instead builds separate tables. The routing information stored in these tables is then exchanged between DVMRP routers in the network.

Though the Reverse Path Multicasting principle enables multicast packets to be distributed across the entire network without creating duplicates, it doesn't consider whether a specific subtree in the multicast routing tree is interested in the packets of a group. Packets are simply distributed, which means that they load the network with undesired packets. This is the reason why the method was extended to *pruning*. When the subnetwork of a router does not want to receive data for a specific multicast group, then the router can return a *prune* message to the higher-layer multicast router in the multicast routing tree. If this router doesn't have interested computers for that group, it can also send a *prune* message to a higher-level router. This method prevents an excessive number of packets from being forwarded in networks where there are no receivers. In addition, *graft* messages can be used to include a router or subnetwork in the

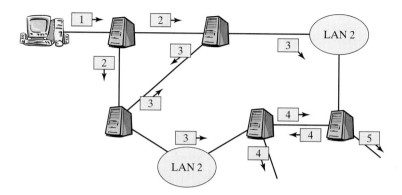

FIGURE 17–15
Schematic representation of how the Distance Vector Multicast Routing Protocol
(DVMRP) works.

distribution tree dynamically. To prevent a router from having to continually learn the
prune state for each network device and each group, it can use a timeout mechanism.
The status is discarded and the subnetwork is included in the multicast tree again as
soon as the time interval expires.

DVMRP belongs to the class of *dense-mode* routing protocols. Initial flooding
causes this method to work best in scenarios where the group members in the network
infrastructure are geographically close, so that flooding won't limit the bandwidth ex-
cessively until pruning has built the multicast routing tree. Other multicast routing protocols are Multicast-OSPF and Protocol Independent Multicast (PIM) in sparse mode
(PIM-SM) or dense mode (PIM-DM).

17.6   MULTICAST TRANSPORT PROTOCOLS

So far, we have actually discussed only unreliable and connectionless multicast transmissions based on UDP. This type of transmission is generally the most frequently used
application of multicast, mainly because it is much easier to handle. Nevertheless, there
are application cases for connection-oriented and reliable multicast communication,
and so extensive interesting research work is undertaken in this field.

Because the tasks involved in the reliable and connection-oriented transmission
of multicast data correspond mainly to the tasks of a transport protocol and these work
on top of the *IP Multicast*, a layer-3 service, the protocols developed so far are normally
called multicast transport protocols. The most important tasks of a transport protocol,
including connection management, flow control, error correction, and congestion control, are relatively complex and expensive for unicast communication, and point-to-mul-
tipoint communication adds special problems to this situation. For example, consider the
sender implosion problem, which occurs when many receivers return acknowledgements
for received data packets to the sender, overloading the sender with an enormous data
volume.

We will not discuss multicast transport protocols any further at this point, because there is currently no protocol used as a standard under Linux. We do list a few

protocols and research projects here. Some of these protocols have been implemented and evaluated. However, none of these protocols is especially suited for all multicast applications; each one has specific benefits and drawbacks.

- *Real-Time Transport Protocol (RTP)*—for real-time and multimedia applications.
- *Scalable Reliable Multicast (SRM)*—is currently used by the White Board tool.
- *Uniform Reliable Group Communication Protocol (URGC)*—supports reliable and in-order communication.
- *Muse*—an application-specific protocol for multicast news.
- *Multicast File Transfer Protocol (MFTP)*—works much like the File Transfer Protocol (*FTP*).
- *Local Group Concept (LGC)*—uses a hierarchy of local groups to prevent sender implosion.

Using Traffic Control to Support Quality of Service (QoS)

18.1 INTRODUCTION

In the Linux world, the term *traffic control* represents all the possibilities to influence incoming and outgoing network traffic in one way or another. In this context, we normally distinguish between two definitions, although it is often difficult to draw a clear line between the two:

- *Policing*: "Policing" means that data streams are monitored and that packets not admitted by a specified strategy (policy) are discarded. Within a networked computer, this can happen in two places: when it is receiving packets from the network (ingress policing) and when it is sending packets to the network.
- *Traffic shaping*: "Traffic shaping" refers to a targeted influence on mostly outgoing traffic. This includes, for example, buffering of outgoing data to stay within a specified rate, setting priorities for outgoing data streams, and marking packets for specific service classes.

    The traffic-control framework developed for the Linux operating system creates a universal environment, which integrates totally different elements for policing and traffic shaping that can be interconnected. These elements can even be dynamically loaded and unloaded as a module during active operation. We describe this framework in detail below, but limit the discussion of the implementation of elements in this framework to a single example. Subsequently, we will describe configuration options in the user space.

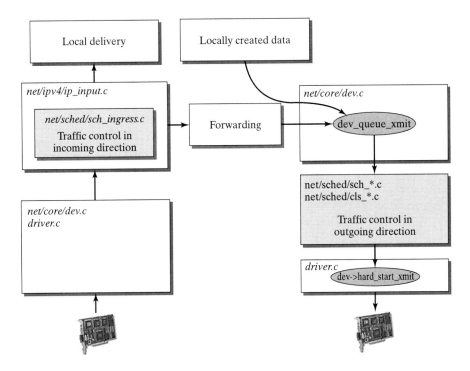

FIGURE 18-1
Traffic control in the Linux kernel.

18.2 BASIC STRUCTURE OF TRAFFIC CONTROL IN LINUX

Figure 18–1 shows where traffic control is arranged in the Linux kernel. Traffic control in the incoming direction is handled by the functions from the file net/sch/sch_ingress.c before incoming packets are passed to higher protocol layers or forwarded over other network cards within the kernel.

The largest part of traffic control in Linux occurs in outgoing direction. Here, we can use and interlink different elements for policing and traffic shaping.

18.3 TRAFFIC CONTROL IN THE OUTGOING DIRECTION

The traffic-control framework defines three basic elements:

> *Queuing discipline*: Each network device is allocated to a queuing discipline. In general, packets to be sent are passed to a queuing discipline and sorted within this queue by specific rules. During a search for packets ready to be sent, these packets can be removed no earlier than when the queuing discipline has marked them as ready for transmission. The algorithm used within a queuing discipline remains invisible to the outside. Examples for queuing disciplines include simple FIFO buffers

and token buckets. More elaborate queuing disciplines can also manage several queues. Queuing disciplines are defined in files with names beginning with sch_ (in the net/sched directory).

▨ *Classes*: Queuing disciplines can have several interfaces, and these interfaces are used to insert packets in the queue management. This allows us to distinguish packets by classes. Within one single queue discipline, we could allocate packets to different classes (e.g., to handle them with different priorities). Classes are defined within the queuing discipline (i.e., also in files with names beginning with sch_).

▨ *Filters*: Filters are generally used to allocate outgoing packets to classes within a queuing discipline. Filters are defined in files with names beginning with cls_.

Much as with a construction kit, single elements can be connected, even recursively: Other queuing disciplines, with their corresponding classes and filters, can be used within one single queuing discipline.

Figure 18–2 shows an example for the resulting traffic-control tree. On the outside, we first see only the enqueue and dequeue functions of the upper queuing discipline. In this example, packets passed via the function enqueue() are checked one after another by the filter rules and allocated to the class visited by the filter for the first time. If none of the filter rules matches, then a default filter can be used to define an allocation system. Behind the classes there are other queuing disciplines. Because this is a tree, we also speak of the *parent* of a queuing discipline. For example, the queuing discipline 1:0 is a so-called outer queuing discipline and the parent of the classes 1:1 and 1:2. The queuing disciplines 2:0 and 3:0 are also called inner queuing disciplines.

Packets are removed recursively from this tree for transmission: When the dequeue() function of the outer queuing discipline is invoked, the function searches the queuing disciplines of the respective classes recursively for packets ready to be sent, depending on the type of queuing discipline.

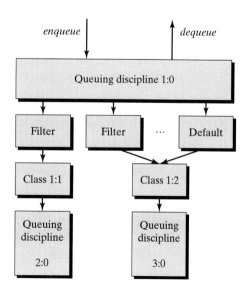

FIGURE 18–2

Example for a tree consisting of queuing disciplines, classes, and filters.

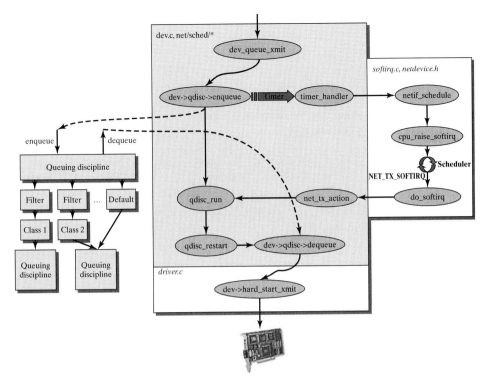

FIGURE 18–3
Inserting the traffic-control tree in the transmission process in the Linux kernel.

The path a packet takes through the kernel was described in detail in Chapter 6. Figure 18–3 shows how the traffic-control example relates to the transmission process shown in Figure 6–4. Rather than one single FIFO queue, we now insert a more extensive and configurable tree to handle transmit data streams; no other changes to the functions of the transmission process are required.

The following sections describe the interfaces of queuing disciplines, classes, and filters.

18.4 KERNEL STRUCTURES AND INTERFACES

The interfaces available for queuing disciplines and filters are mostly independent of the functionality available within an element.

18.4.1 Handles

All elements within the traffic-control tree can be addressed by 32-bit identifiers called handles. For example, the instances of the queuing disciplines discussed further below are marked with 32-bit identifiers, divided into a major number and a minor number. However, these numbers have nothing to do with the major and minor numbers for device files. These identifiers are unique for each network device, but they can occur more than once for several network devices.

In contrast, the minor number for a queue discipline is always null, except for input queuing discipline number ffff:fff1   TC_H_INGRESS (in include/linux/pkt_sched.h) and the top queue of output queuing discipline number ffff:ffff TC_H_ROOT. Major numbers are assigned by the user and are in the range from 0x0001 to 0x7fff. If the user specifies major number 0, then the kernel allocates a major number between 0x8000 und 0xffff.

For classes, the major number corresponds to the associated queuing discipline, while the minor number specifies the class within that queuing discipline. In this case, the minor number can be in the range from 0x0 to 0xffff. Minor numbers are unique only within all classes of a queuing discipline.

include/linux/pkt_sched.h defines several macros you can use to mask major and minor numbers.

18.4.2   Queuing Disciplines

The functions supplied by a queuing discipline are defined in the Qdisc_ops structure in include/net/pkt_sched.h:

```
struct Qdisc_ops {
        struct Qdisc_ops        *next;
        struct Qdisc_class_ops  *cl_ops;
        char                    id[IFNAMSIZ];
        int                     priv_size;

        int                     (*enqueue)(struct sk_buff *, struct Qdisc *);
        struct sk_buff *        (*dequeue)(struct Qdisc *);
        int                     (*requeue)(struct sk_buff *, struct Qdisc *);
        int                     (*drop)(struct Qdisc *);

        int                     (*init)(struct Qdisc *, struct rtattr *arg);
        void                    (*reset)(struct Qdisc *);
        void                    (*destroy)(struct Qdisc *);
        int                     (*change)(struct Qdisc *, struct rtattr *arg);

        int                     (*dump)(struct Qdisc *, struct sk_buff *);
};
```

The first four entries are a link to a list (struct Qdisc_ops *next;), a reference to the class-related operations (struct Qdisc_class_ops *cl_ops), which will be described later. They represent an identifier (char id [IFNAMSIZ]) and values used internally.

The following functions are available externally:

enqueue()	include/net/pkt_sched.h

The function enqueue() is used to pass packets to a queuing discipline. The return value is null (NET_XMIT_SUCCESS, see include/linux/netdevice.h), if the packet is accepted by the queuing discipline. If this or another packet is discarded when ordering packets, then the return value is unequal null:

- NET_XMIT_DROP: The packet just passed was discarded.
- NET_XMIT_CN: A packet was discarded—for example, because of buffer overflow (CN stands for "congestion").
- NET_XMIT_POLICED: A packet was discarded because the policing mechanism detected violation of a rule (e.g., the admissible rate was exceeded).
- NET_XMIT_BYPASS: The passed packet was accepted, but won't leave the queuing discipline over the regular dequeue() function.

dequeue()	include/net/pkt_sched.h

When the function dequeue() is invoked, the queuing discipline returns a pointer to a packet (skb), which may be sent next. The return value **null** doesn't mean that there are no more packets waiting in the queuing discipline; it means only that there are no packets ready to be sent at the time of the call. The total number of packets waiting in a queuing discipline is stated in struct Qdisc* q->q.len. This value should be valid when a queuing discipline manages more than one queue.

requeue()	include/net/pkt_sched.h

The requeue() function puts a previously removed packet back into the queue. In contrast to enqueue(), however, the packet should be arranged at the position in the queuing discipline where it had been before, and the counter of packets running through this queuing discipline should not be increased. This function is intended for cases where a packet was removed by dequeue() to send it, but eventually it couldn't be sent, for an unexpected cause.

drop()	include/net/pkt_sched.h

This function removes a packet from the queue and discards it.

reset()	include/net/pkt_sched.h

The reset() function sets a queuing discipline back into the initial state (empty queues, reset counters, delete timers, etc.). If this queuing discipline manages other queuing disciplines, then their reset() functions will also be invoked.

init()	include/net/pkt_sched.h

The init() function is used to initialize a new, instantiated queuing discipline.

destroy()	include/net/pkt_sched.h

The destroy() function frees the resources that had been reserved during the initialization and runtime of the queuing discipline.

change()	include/net/pkt_sched.h

The change() function can be used to change parameters of a queuing discipline.

dump()	include/net/pkt_sched.h

The dump() function serves to output configuration parameters and statistics of a queuing discipline.

The central structure of each queuing discipline, which is referred to by all functions introduced so far, is the structure struct Qdisc (include/net/pkt_sched.h), printed as follows:

```
struct Qdisc {
      int                     (*enqueue)(struct sk_buff *skb, struct Qdisc
*dev);
      struct sk_buff *        (*dequeue)(struct Qdisc *dev);
      unsigned                flags;
#define TCQ_F_BUILTIN 1
#define TCQ_F_THROTTLED 2
#define TCQ_F_INGRES 4
      struct Qdisc_ops        *ops;
      struct Qdisc            *next;
      u32                     handle;
      atomic_t                refcnt;
      struct sk_buff_head q;
      struct net_device       *dev;
      struct tc_stats         stats;
      int                     (*reshape_fail)(struct sk_buff *skb, struct Qdis
c *q);

      /* This field is deprecated, but it is still used by CBQ
       * and it will live until better solution will be invented.
       */
      struct Qdisc            *__parent;
      char                    data[0];
};
```

In addition to a reference to the Qdisc_ops structure, there is a pointer to link Qdisc structures and a handle for unique marking of an instance of the structure within the kernel. For a simple queuing discipline with only one queue, the entry struct sk_buff_head q; represents the header of this queue. Each queuing discipline is always allocated to exactly one network device, which is referred to by struct net_device *dev.

The function reshape_fail() can be used to implement more complex traffic-shaping mechanisms. When an outer queue passes a packet to an inner queue, then it can happen that the packet has to be discarded—for example, when there is no buffer space available. If the outer queuing discipline implements the callback function reshape_fail(), then it can be invoked by the inner queuing discipline in this case. Subsequently, the outer queuing discipline can select a different class.

The structure `struct tc_stats` contained in `struct Qdisc` (`include/linux/pkt_sched.h`) serves to carry along statistics (in addition to the `q.qlen` entry described earlier for the number of packets to be ordered). The following counters exist in the structure `tc_stats`:

```
__u64  bytes:         /* Number of enqueued bytes */
__u32  packets;       /* Number of enqueued packets */
__u32  drops;         /* Packets dropped because of lack of re-
                         sources */
__u32  overlimits;    /* Number of throttle events when
                         this flow goes out of allocated bandwidth */
__u32  bps;           /* Current flow byte rate */
__u32  pps;           /* Current flow packet rate */
__u32  qlen;
__u32  backlog;
```

These statistics can have certain inaccuracies if a queuing discipline manages additional inner queuing disciplines. This is the case, for example, when a packet was dropped in an inner queuing discipline, because the number of ordered `bytes` can then deviate from the real value. If a queuing discipline has several classes, then separate statistics can be maintained for each class.

A queuing discipline can be added in either of the following two ways:

`pktsched_init()`	**net/sched/sch_api.c**

This function is used when a queuing discipline is permanently compiled in the kernel. In this case, the RT-NETLINK interface, which will be introduced later, is initialized, and the function `register_qdisc()` is invoked. Unless additional queuing disciplines were selected when the kernel was configured, only the `bfifo` and `pfifo` queuing disciplines (defined in `net/sched/sch_fifo.c`) are selected here.

`register_qdisc()`	**net/sched/sch_api.c**

This function is invoked either by the above described function, `pktsched_init()`, or by `init_module()`, if we want to include the queuing discipline as a module. Initially, this function checks for whether a queuing discipline with the same identification—`id[IFNAMSIZ]`—of the `Qdisc_ops` structure already exists. If this is not the case, then the new queuing discipline is appended to the end of the list, and the functions are allocated.

18.4.3 Classes

Classes can be thought of as logically independent elements, but they relate closely to queuing disciplines as far as the implementation is concerned. Rather than independent files that implement classes, classes are always offered by queuing disciplines. In addition, notice that the classification (i.e., allocation of packets to a class) is handled by the filters described later (packet classifiers), which are logically separate from classes.

Unique class identifiers, similarly to queuing disciplines, are used to be able to address a class within the kernel. However, there are two identifying options for classes: The `classid` of type `u32` serves primarily to identify a class by the user and the configuration tools in the user space; this option will be discussed in Section 18.7. In addition, there is an internal identification of the type `unsigned long`, which can be used for general identification of a class within the kernel. In this case, various `classids` can be mapped from the user space onto an internal identification, if other filter information play a role (e.g., specific fields of the `skb` structure).

Queuing disciplines that supply classes offer various functions, including functions to bind queues to classes and functions to change or dump a class configuration. The functions introduced below are defined in the `sch_*` files and exported over the structure `Qdisc_ops` (`include/net/pkt_sched.h`) (except for the `qdisc_graft()` function, which builds on top of the former):

`graft()`	**include/net/pkt_sched.h**

The `graft()` function serves to bind a queuing discipline to a class. The return value is the queuing discipline that was previously bound to that class.

`get()`	**include/net/pkt_sched.h**

The `get()` function maps the `classid` to the internal identification; this is its return value. If a usage counter exists within the class, then `get()` increments this counter by one.

`put()`	**include/net/pkt_sched.h**

In contrast to `get()`, the `put()` function decrements the usage counter. If this causes the usage counter to reach null, then `put()` can remove the class.

`qdisc_graft()`	**net/sched/sch_api.c**

This function is used in all cases where a new queuing discipline should be attached to the traffic-control tree. It initially checks on whether there is a `parent` or the queuing discipline itself should form the root of the traffic control tree. In the latter case, the function `dev_graft_qdisc()` from `net/sched/sch_api.c` is invoked. If a `parent` is present, then the `get()` function is invoked first to map the classid to the internal identification. Subsequently, the `graft()` function is invoked to bind the new queuing discipline to the classes. Finally, `put()` is invoked to decrement the reference counter of the old class.

`leaf()`	**include/net/pkt_sched.h**

This function returns a pointer to the queuing discipline currently bound to that class.

change()   **include/net/pkt_sched.h**

The change() function is used to change class parameters or create new classes, provided that the queuing discipline allows this.

delete()   **include/net/pkt_sched.h**

This function checks on whether the class is still referenced, and it deletes the class if this holds true.

walk()   **include/net/pkt_sched.h**

This function walks through the linked list of all the classes of a queuing discipline and, if it is implemented, invokes a callback function to fetch configuration data and statistical parameters.

tcf_chain()   **include/net/pkt_sched.h**

Figure 18–2 shows that each class is bound to at least one filter. The function tcf_chain() returns a pointer to the beginning of a linked list for the filter bound to that class.

bind_tcf()   **include/net/pkt_sched.h**

This function tells the queuing discipline that a filter is going to be bound to the class. This means that the function is similar to the get() function, but can be used in some cases where we have to run additional checks.

unbind_tcf()   **include/net/pkt_sched.h**

This function is the counterpart of the previous function, bind_tcf(), which means that it represents an extension of the put() function.

dump_class()   **include/net/pkt_sched.h**

Like the dump() function for queuing disciplines, the function dump_class() serves to output configuration parameters and statistical data for a class.

18.4.4 Filters

The class packets that passed by the enqueue() function in a queuing discipline belong to is decided by filters.

To make this decision, a filter uses the `classify()` function. This function and other filter functions, which will be described below, are exported over the `tcf_proto_ops` (`include/net/pkt_cls.h`) structure:

`classify()`	**include/net/pkt_cls.h**

This function classifies a packet (i.e., the filter checks for whether there is a filtering rule that could be applied to the packet). The following return values are possible (as for `include/linux/pkt_cls.h`):

- TC_POLICE_OK: The packet was accepted by the filter.
- TC_POLICE_RECLASSIFY: The packet violates agreed parameters (e.g., a maximum rate) and should be allocated to a different class. However, the packet is not dropped yet, to enable the queuing discipline to transport the packet over a different class.
- TC_POLICE_SHOT: The packet was accepted by the filter, but the filter dropped it, because it violated agreed parameters.
- TC_POLICE_UNSPEC: The rule applied by the filter doesn't match the packet, and it should be passed to the next filter or filter element.

In addition, the `classify()` function in the structure `tcf_result` (`include/net/pkt_cls.h`) returns the `classid` and, if present, the internal identification of the pertaining class. The internal identification can then simply be made available, if a separate instance of the filter exists for each class. If the internal identification is not written to the result structure, then the `classid` has to be mapped to the internal identification in the queuing discipline (normally by use of a linear search). In some cases, the filter can be informed about the internal identification while binding to a class, so that no mapping cost occurs.

`init()`	**include/net/pkt_cls.h**

This function initializes a filter.

`destroy()`	**include/net/pkt_cls.h**

The `destroy()` function removes a filter. To remove bindings to a class, it will have to invoke `unbind_tcf()`.

`get()`	**include/net/pkt_cls.h**

Again, the `get()` function is used to map identifiers—in this case, to map a handle of a filter element to an internal filter identification.

`put()`	**include/net/pkt_cls.h**

The `put()` function is invoked to unreference a filter.

change()	include/net/pkt_cls.h

This function serves to configure a new filter or change the configuration of an existing filter. `bind_tcf()` is used to bind new filters to classes.

delete()	include/net/pkt_cls.h

In contrast to the `destroy()` function, this function is used to delete one single element of a filter. The difference between a filter and a filter element will be discussed later.

walk()	include/net/pkt_cls.h

As with classes, the `walk()` function walks through all elements and invokes callback functions to get configuration data and statistical parameters.

dump()	include/net/pkt_cls.h

The `dump()` function serves to output configuration parameters and statistical data of a filter or filter elements.

Next, when a packet is passed to a queuing discipline with several classes, then the latter invokes the function `tc_classify()` from `include/net/pkt_cls.h`. This function checks on whether the filter accepts the protocol specified in `skb->protocol` and then invokes the filter's `classify()` function. The return values are identical to those of the `classify()` function.

The central structure of filters within Linux traffic control is struct `tcf_proto` in `include/net/pkt_cls.h`. The entry `struct tcf_proto *next` can be used to link several filters to a list. In addition, there are entries for the accepted protocol, for the `classid` of the appropriate class, and for a priority. The priority can be used to order filters that can be applied to the same protocol. For this purpose, the filters are walked through from `prio` variables with small values towards larger values, and a packet is allocated to the filter with rules matching first.

In addition, a filter can be split internally into filter elements, and `handles` of the type `u32` are allocated to these internal elements. How filters are split and managed (i.e., in linear lists or in more efficient data structures such as hash tables) depends on the implementation.

As in queuing disciplines, there are two functions available to add new filters. The function `tc_filter_init()` (`net/sched/cls_api.c`) is used when a filter is permanently compiled in the kernel. From within this function, the function `register_tcf_proto_ops()` (`net/sched/cls_api.c`) is invoked, including the case where we want to embed the filter as a module. This function initially checks for whether a filter of the same type (`kind` element in the `tcf_proto_ops` structure) already exists. If this is not the case, then the new filter is appended to the end of the filter list, and functions are allocated.

18.5   INGRESS POLICING

The file `net/sched/sch_ingress.c` implements a queuing discipline designed for ingress policing. Its structure is similar to that of other queuing disciplines, and the exported functions are similar to the functions described in the previous section.

However, rather than buffering packets, this queuing discipline classifies packets to decide whether a packet will be accepted or discarded. This means that the queuing discipline actually assumes a firewall or Netfilter functionality. This functionality also reflects in the return values of the `enqueue()` function, which are converted to Netfilter return values, as shown in the following excerpt from the function `ingress_enqueue()` (`net/sched/sch_ingress.c`):

```
case TC_POLICE_SHOT:
    result = NF_DROP;
    break;
case TC_POLICE_RECLASSIFY: /* DSCP remarking here ? */
case TC_POLICE_OK:
case TC_POLICE_UNSPEC:
default:
    result = NF_ACCEPT;
    break;
```

First, the function `register_qdisc()` registers the functions of the queuing discipline with the network device. Subsequently, the function `nf_register_hook()` hooks them into the hook `NF_IP_PRE_ROUTING`.

Next, additional filters can be appended to this particular queuing discipline. These filters can access functions from `net/sched/police.c` to check on whether a data stream complies with a token bucket.

18.6   IMPLEMENTING A QUEUING DISCIPLINE

This section describes how we can implement a queuing discipline. We will use the token-bucket filter as an example, because it represents a fundamental element of many traffic-shaping approaches.

18.6.1   The Token-Bucket Filter

A token-bucket filter is used to control and limit the rate and burst (when a specified data rate is briefly exceeded) of data streams. Figure 18–4 illustrates the basic idea of a token bucket. In this model, the determining parameters are the rate, R, at which a token bucket is filled with tokens, and the maximum number of tokens, B, this token bucket can hold. Each token represents a byte that may be sent. Subsequently, the token bucket declares a packet to comply with the rate and burst parameters, if the number of tokens in the token bucket corresponds at least to the length of the packet in bytes.

If a packet is compliant, it may be sent. Subsequently, the number of tokens in the token bucket is reduced by a number corresponding to the packet length. If a

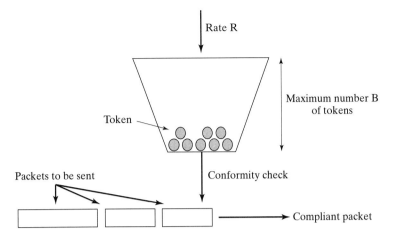

FIGURE 18-4
Model of a token bucket.

noncompliant packet is deleted immediately, then the token bucket runs a traffic-policing process. In contrast, if the packet is held back until sufficient tokens have accumulated in the token bucket, we talk of traffic shaping.

A real-world implementation will realize this model differently, so that the computing cost is less, though the result is the same. It would not make sense to increment a counter representing the number of tokens several times per second, even when there is no packet to send. Instead, computations are made only provided that a packet is ready to be sent and waiting at the input of the token bucket. In this case, we can compute how many tokens have to be present in the token bucket at that point in time. To do this computation, we need to know when the last packet was sent and what the filling level of the token bucket was after that. The current number of available tokens is calculated from the sum of tokens available after the last transmission, plus the tokens arrived in the meantime (i.e., plus the interval, multiplied by the rate, R). Notice that the number of available tokens can never be larger than B. If the number of tokens computed in this way corresponds to at least the length of the waiting packet, then this packet may be sent. Otherwise, instead of sending the packet, a timer is started. This timer expires when more packets can be sent as a sufficient number of tokens has arrived. The timer has to be initialized to an appropriate interval, which can be easily calculated from the number of tokens still missing and the rate, R, at which the bucket is filled with more tokens.

Such a token-bucket filter is implemented within the traffic-control framework in the file `net/sched/sch_tbf.c`. However, this is an extension (i.e., a dual token bucket). More specifically, two token buckets are arranged back to back, in a frequently used arrangement, to guarantee a mean rate and limit bursts. The first token bucket is set to a rate, R, corresponding to the desired mean data rate, and the second token bucket is set to the peak rate and a significantly smaller number of tokens, B. However, B corresponds at least to the maximum size of one maximum transmission unit (MTU).

To be able to store states between single transmit processes, the token-bucket implementation uses the `tbf_sched_data` structure:

```
struct tbf_sched_data{
/*Parameters*/
u32          limit;        /*Maximal length of backlog: bytes*/
u32          buffer;       /*Token Bucket depth/rate: MUST Be >= MTU/B */
u32          mtu;
u32          max_size;
struct qdisc_rate_table *R_tab;
struct qdisc_rate_table *P_tab;
/* Variables */
long         tokens;       /* Current number of B tokens */
long         ptokens;      /* Current number of P tokens */
psched_time_t t_c;         /* Time check-point */
struct timer_list wd_timer; /*Watchdog timer */
};
```

The `limit` field specifies the number of bytes in the queue used to buffer packets that cannot be sent immediately. The `buffer` field shows that the byte-to-rate ratio (i.e., times) is used rather than bytes and rates for computations in most places within the implementation. This means that a packet with a specific length takes some transmit time from the token bucket, the available transmit time of which is calculated from the current number of tokens to the rate R ratio. The variables `tokens` and `ptokens` store the number of tokens in the respective token bucket. The time at which the last packet was transmitted is written to the `t_c` entry, and the `wd_timer` field is needed when a timer has to be started for a packet's delayed transmission. Two pointers, `R_tab` and `P_tab`, point to the structure `qdisc_rate_table`, which stores the allocations of packet lengths to transmit times to avoid divisions during each transmission process. This table is created by the function `qdisc_get_rtab()` when `tbf_change()` (`net/sched/sch_tbf.c`) initializes the token-bucket filter. However, the actual computation is done in the user space by use of the `tc_calc_rtable()` function in `iproute2/tc/tc_core.c`.

We will now introduce and explain additional functions of the token-bucket filter.

`tbf_init()`	**net/sched/sch_tbf.c**

Initialization of the token bucket means merely that the start time has to be defined to initialize the timer. The macro PSCHED_GET_TIME (`include/net/pkt_sched.h`) is used to establish the start time. This macro accesses the TSC register described in Chapter 2, if it is present. A structure containing a pointer to private data and a pointer to the `tbf_watchdog()` function are passed to the timer. The `tbf_watchdog()` function has to be invoked when the timer expires.

`tbf_enqueue()`	**netsched/sch_tbf.c**

This function serves to accept packets and to append them to the end of the queue. Also, a number of statistics are updated, and error cases are handled.

tbf_dequeue()	netsched/sch_tbf.c

This function handles the actual traffic-shaping work. First, PSCHED_GET_TIME(now) is used to learn the current time. Subsequently, the number of available tokens is computed from the old value (q->ptokens or q->tokens) and the time elapsed. Next, qdisc_rate_table is used to compute the number of tokens required by the packet, and the difference between existing and required tokens is calculated. However, notice that a token stands for an interval rather than for a byte. If the number of tokens in both token buckets is sufficient, then tbf_dequeue() returns the top skb from the queue; otherwise, a timer is started. The inaccuracies of the standard Linux timers, described in Chapter 2, can cause a value of null to result from the conversion of the interval into jiffies. In this case, a minimum delay of one jiffie is selected, to ensure that a packet is never sent too early.

tbf_watchdog()	netsched/sch_tbf.c

The tbf_watchdog function is invoked when the timer for a packet expires. Within this function, only the netif_schedule() function is invoked, which eventually invokes the function dev->qdisc->dequeue() once computing time has been allocated, as shown in Figure 18–3. In the simplest case, this happens without multiple queues in the traffic-control tree tbf_dequeue().

18.7 CONFIGURATION

This section describes how the traffic-control elements are configured from within the user space. To configure traffic-control elements, the tc tools are used. This toolset is a command-line configuration program (available in [Kuzn01] as part of the iproute2 package). In addition, the RT netlink interface is used to pass configuration information to the kernel.

18.7.1 The RT Netlink Interface

The RT netlink interface is fully described in Chapter 26. For the purposes of this section, it is sufficient to know that the RT netlink interface is used to pass a pointer to the rtattr (in include/linux/rtnetlink.h) structure to the init() or change() functions of the traffic-control framework. The function rtattr_parse (net/core/rtnetlink.c) can be used to structure the data passed, and various macros, including RTA_PAYLOAD und RTA_DATA (include/linux/rtnetlink.h), can be used to print this information. The tcmsg (include/linux/rtnetlink.h) structure defines traffic-control messages that can be sent over the RT netlink interface from within the user space.

18.7.2 The User Interface

The tc program provides a command-line user interface to configure the Linux traffic control. This tool is available from [Kuzn01].

The tc tool enables you to set up and configure all elements of the traffic-control framework discussed here, such as queuing disciplines, filters, and classes. To be able to

use the Differentiated Services support in Linux, we first have to set the entry
TC_CONFIG_DIFFSERV=y in the Config file in the iproutes/tc directory. If the kernel
version and the version of your tc tool match, then calling make in the same directory
should enable you to compile successfully.

Depending on the element we want to configure, we now have to select the appropriate element, together with additional options:

```
Usage: tc [ OPTIONS ] OBJECT { COMMAND | help } where OBJECT :=
{ qdisc | class | filter }
       OPTIONS := { -s[tatistics] | -d[etails] | -r[aw] | -b[atch] file }
```

A detailed description of all additional options would go beyond the scope and
volume of this book. You can use the help command (e.g., tc qdisc add tbf help)
to easily obtain information. In addition, you can find an overview of ongoing work in
the field of more comfortable user interfaces in [Alme01].

CHAPTER 19

Packet Filters and Firewalls

19.1 INTRODUCTION

Each network packet handled by a Linux computer passes a number of distinctive points within the network implementation on its way through the Linux kernel before it either is delivered to a local process or leaves the computer for further routing. Direct access to the packet stream in the kernel opens up a large number of ways to manipulate packets, which are also suitable for implementing a security strategy in the network. For example, functions were built into the routing code early in the course of the Linux development. These functions allow the system administrator to influence how packets are handled, depending on their source and destination addresses. In addition to the pure filtering function, which lets you drop certain packets completely, this also includes more complex manipulations, including address-conversion mechanisms (*Network Address Translation—NAT*) or the support of transparent proxies. After its introduction in the form of ipfwadm in Linux Version 1.2, this packet-filter code later underwent two complete revisions to ensure better manageability, extension of the control options, and better integration of additional functionality (e.g., NAT). This chapter discusses the differences between the packet-filter architecture of the current Linux Version 2.4 and that of the previous Linux Version 2.2.

19.1.1 The Functional Principle of a Firewall

In its original meaning, the term *firewall* denotes a fire-resistant wall constructed to prevent the spread of fire. In connection with computer networks, a firewall is a protection mechanism used in a specific and exactly limited network (e.g., a corporate intranet) at a transition point from a neighboring network (generally to the Internet) to protect the intranet against dangers from the outside.

A firewall consists normally of two types of components:

  ▩ *Packet filters* are normally implemented in routers and monitor the entire network traffic flowing through these routers. These routers use a well-defined set of

383

rules (e.g., address information contained in a packet header) to decide which packets can pass and which will be dropped.

In the case of IP networks, packet-filter rules normally refer at least to the IP source and destination addresses, the transport protocol (TCP or UDP), the TCP or UDP source and destination ports, and some TCP flags (for TCP; particularly the SYN flag, which can be used to see whether a packet is a connection-establishment request).

■ *Application gateways* or *proxies* (e.g., mail relays and HTTP proxies) act as mediators between the communicating application processes and can implement fine-grained, application-specific access control.

A complete firewall configuration (see Figure 19–1) normally consists of an inner router with packet-filtering functionality, which forms the transition to the network to be protected; an outer router with packet-filtering functionality, which forms the transition to the external network; and a number of application gateways located in an independent local area network between these routers. This network within the firewall is normally called a *demilitarized zone* (*DMZ*) or *screened subnet*. If gateways are available for all required application protocols, then the packet filters can be configured so that no packets are forwarded directly between the internal and the external networks. Instead, exclusive communication is between the internal network and the DMZ and between the external network and the DMZ.

In the most frequent case, that in which the network to be protected has only this single connection to the Internet and so represents an edge network from the topological view, the most fundamental firewall functionality is to limit packet forwarding to packets with topologically correct addresses. This means that only packets with a source address outside of the network and a destination address within the network are permitted into the network (so-called *ingress filtering*). In opposite direction, for a packet to be able to leave the network, the packet's source address has to be within the network and its destination address has to be outside the network (*egress filtering*). If all edge networks would strictly implement this functionality, this would effectively

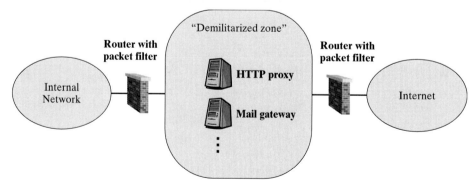

FIGURE 19–1
Structure of a firewall.

protect computers against attacks where hackers use falsified source addresses to hide their origin. This is the reason why the IETF explicitly recommends this approach in RFC 2827 [FeSe00].

Because the number of available IP addresses is extremely limited in IP Version 4, many firewalls in networks implement the *Network Address Translation* (*NAT*) mechanism. In this case, the internal network uses private addresses not visible from the outside. Chapter 21 discusses the NAT implementation in Linux 2.4.

19.1.2 Protocol-specific Particularities: TCP, FTP, and others

In practice, it often is insufficient to filter individual packets exclusively by addresses, protocol numbers, and port numbers. For example, the connection-oriented TCP transport protocol groups many IP packets to a logical connection. If we want to implement address translation (NAT), these packets have to be seen as a group, of course, and they have to be handled equally. The connection-tracking mechanism discussed in Chapter 20 is responsible for this task.

Special treatment of some packets is not only important for NAT, but it is also important for a pure filter functionality. For example, it often is desirable to permit only outgoing connections on specific TCP ports. To achieve this, we can utilize the fact that the SYN flag is set and the ACK flag is cleared in the TCP header of the first packet only in a TCP connection (connection-establishment request). To block TCP connections incoming on a specific port, all we have to do is to filter out all incoming packets that have the SYN flag set and the ACK flag cleared in their headers.

More serious problems arise in connection with some application protocols that use dynamically assigned port numbers. One of the best known examples is the *File Transfer Protocol* (*FTP*). In FTP, the client initially establishes a control connection to TCP port 21 in the server, and then uses this connection to transmit FTP commands and replies. As soon as a file has to be transmitted or a directory has to be displayed, FTP opens an additional data connection in the "reverse direction": from TCP port 20 in the server to a dynamically selected client port, where the client-side port number is sent over the control connection.

For a firewall that wants to permit outgoing FTP sessions only, either it would have to accept all incoming connections originating from TCP port 20 or a *stateful filter* would have to be installed to eavesdrop on and analyze all commands and replies from the FTP control connection and then permit only selected incoming FTP data connections. The first method is not optimal from the security perspective, and the second method causes considerable additional cost.

However, to solve these problems for the FTP protocol, there is an additional method that prevents firewall problems by selecting the "passive" mode of operation. Unfortunately, this operation mode, which establishes data connections from a client to a server, is not supported in all FTP implementations. The problem is even more difficult when filtering is used for some other protocols (e.g., the H.323 multimedia conference protocol, which is used in many applications, including the popular Microsoft NetMeeting; a number of control and data connections with dynamically assigned TCP and UDP port numbers belong to one single H.323 session, so that a stateful filter would become very complex).

Independent of the application protocol, we cannot use stateful filters when the control connections are encrypted. In this case, the only feasible method is to employ specially adapted client and server software that uses an appropriate protocol, such as SOCKS [LGLK+96], to let the firewall dynamically and selectively permit traffic on specific ports.

19.1.3   Quality Criteria for Packet-Filter Implementations

To be able to evaluate the quality of a packet-filter architecture, [ChBe94] formulates the following criteria:

1. Filtering is done both for incoming and for outgoing packets.
2. There is an option to distinguish connection-establishment requests from other packets within one single connection.
3. Filter options for protocols other than IP, TCP, and UDP either are available or can be added easily.
4. There are filter options for arbitrary bit patterns within packets.
5. There are filter options for routing information at both the input and the output.
6. There is an option to reject data packets, if the destination address of these packets was changed by source routing.
7. The set of rules is clearly represented, and there is an option to control the sequence in which rules are applied to a packet.
8. Dropped data packets can be logged.

We will see in our discussion in the following sections that the new netfilter architecture of Linux Version 2.4 meets all those criteria.

19.1.4   Limits of the Firewall Principle

Though a properly configured firewall is an important component for protecting a network, we have to understand that a firewall can never be a panacea. All packet filters operate on the basis of information contained in the protocol headers of incoming data packets. This information can be tampered with easily. For example, an adapted TCP/IP implementation makes it very easy for an intruder to send IP packets whose source address in the IP header is not the address of the actual sender (so-called *IP spoofing*).

To achieve tamper-proof identification of a packet's origin as a prerequisite for effective filtering of incoming data traffic, it is recommended that one use cryptographic mechanisms (e.g., the IP security architecture of IPsec). In Linux, we can use FreeS/WAN, which is an IPsec implementation.

19.2   THE IPCHAINS ARCHITECTURE OF LINUX 2.2

`ipchains` is a packet-filtering architecture consisting of an infrastructure in the Linux kernel and a user-space program to manage rules lists, like all packet-filtering architectures currently implemented in Linux. In Linux 2.2, this product is called `ipchains`.

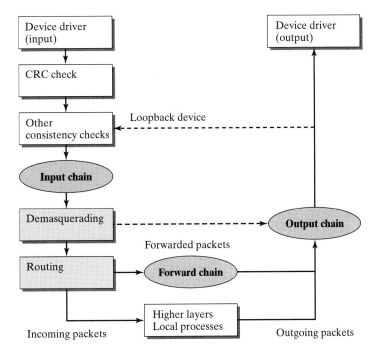

FIGURE 19–2
The packet-filtering architecture in Linux 2.2 (`ipchains`).

(See Figure 19–2.) Section 19.2.1 will discuss its invocation syntax and how we can define rules.

The filtering mechanisms implemented in Linux kernel Version 2.2 divide all data packets into the following three classes, depending on their source and destination addresses:

1. incoming packets—those addressed to the local computer;
2. packets to be forwarded and leaving the local computer over a different network interface based on a routing decision;
3. outgoing packets created in the local computer.

For each of these classes, the network stack of the respective protocol includes a prominent position, and each packet of the corresponding class has to pass it. In each of these positions, there is a *hook*, where a linked rules list (*chain*) is hooked, hence the name `ipchains`.

According to the packet class they are allocated to, the rules lists are called *input chain, forward chain*, and *output chain*. These chains are organized so that they are processed sequentially, beginning from the first defined rule. If a rule accepts an incoming packet, then this packet is handled according to the branch destination defined in the rule, where Linux Version 2.2 introduced the support of user-defined rules lists. This means that, in addition to the linear processing of rules lists, we can also implement branching. Other possible branch destinations are the following:

- ACCEPT—completes processing of the rules list and releases the packet for further handling.
- DENY—drops the packet.
- REJECT—discards the packet and returns an ICMP message of the "destination unreachable" type to the sender.
- REDIRECT—(an item new with Linux 2.2) makes sense only for the input chain and directs the packet to another local port. This is useful, for example, to implement transparent proxies, where all HTTP requests are redirected from port 80 to the port of a local HTTP proxy.

This means that, if a TCP/IP packet is addressed to the local computer, then it first has to undergo the usual verifications of the checksum field and the packet length before it arrives in the input chain, where it is handled according to this rule list.

Packets belonging to the second class (addressed to computers in a different network) visit all three rules chains hooked into the kernel in ipchains. As mentioned above, they first arrive in the input chain. The destination address is not in the local computer, so the packet is passed to the forward chain. Before this step, the packet is checked to see whether it is a packet masked by NAT. If this is the case, the packet is first unmasked and then passed directly to the output chain, bypassing the forward chain. If the forward chain accepts the packet, then a final step checks it in the output chain, before it leaves the router. Outgoing packets created in the local computer are handled exclusively by the output chain.

Each rules list has options to log the network traffic it handles. The counters of these functions have been 64 bits wide since Linux Version 2.2; this much finer granularity, as compared with that of the 32-bit predecessor versions, prevents overflow. In addition to the core functionality covered by ipchains, the packet-filtering architecture of Linux 2.2 uses additional modules to support more complex protocols, including active FTP (see Section 19.2.1), RealAudio or CUSeeMe, which are controlled over additional management tools (e.g., ipmasqadm). The entire core functionality is managed in the ipchains program, which is described in more detail below.

19.2.1 The ipchains Rule Syntax

This section describes the ipchains program, which is used to manage rules lists.

The basic structure of a rule definition is given by the following form: ipchains -<operation> <chain> <criterion> -j <branch destination>. Table 19–1 shows command-line options of ipchains and iptables, before we describe the options in detail.

- *Operation*: We can use one of the keywords listed in Table 19–1 to specify how we want the existing rules list to be manipulated. We use APPEND to build a list, which means that the new rule we just defined is appended to the end of a list. To generate a user-defined rules list, we use NEW. User-defined rules lists behave like subfunctions of the respective lists. This means that, when they are reached, they

TABLE 19–1   Command-line options of ipchains and iptables

Option	ipchains	iptables
Standard rules lists:		
	input	INPUT
	output	OUTPUT
	forward	FORWARD
Branch destinations:		
Accept packet	-j ACCEPT	-j ACCEPT
Drop packet	-j DENY	-j DROP
Reject packet	-j REJECT	-j REJECT
Convert/mask address	-j MASQ	-j MASQUERADE
Redirect to other port	-j REDIRECT	-j <Port>
Return from rules list	-j RETURN	-j RETURN
Log packet (*log*)	-j <branch destination>	-j LOG
	-l	
Criteria for filter rules:		
IP source address (*source*)	-s [!] <address>	-s [!] <address>
IP destination address (*destination*)	-d [!] <address>	-d [!] <address>
Source address and source port	-s [!] <address>	-s [!] <address>
	[!] <port>	—sport [!] <port>
Destination address and destination port	-d [!] <address>	-d [!] <address>
	[!] <port>	-dport [!] <port>
Transport protocol	-p <protocol>	-p <protocol>
Network device (*interface*)	-i [!] <device>	-i [!] <device>
TCP-SYN flag set	[!] -y	[!] -y
Fragments (consecutive packets)	[!] -f	[!] -f

are evaluated with regard to the current packet and then this packet is returned to the calling rules list, if none of the other rules applies to the packet.

▪ *Chain*: This is the rules list (input, output, forward, or a user-defined list) that the operation should run on.

▪ *Criterion*: This is the most complex part of the definition; it specifies packets that this rule should be applied on. First, the protocol (-p <protocol>) and ranges for the source and destination addresses (-s <address(es)> and -d <address(es)>, respectively) are defined.

In addition, we can limit the validity range for the TCP and UDP protocols to specific port numbers (-s <address(es)> <port(s)> and -d <address(es)> <port(s)>, respectively).

The criterion -i <interface> can be used to select only packets that arrive at or leave from a specific interface.

For the TCP protocol, we can use -y to specify that only packets with the SYN flag set and the ACK flag cleared should be considered. (See Section 19.1.2.)

We can use -f to specify that the rule should apply only to the second and all consecutive fragments of a fragmented IP packet. This criterion can be thought of as a simpler predecessor of the netfilter introduced in Chapter 20, which implements stateful connection tracking. Only the first fragment includes the transport protocol header, so we cannot specify port numbers together with this criterion.

All criteria can be negated by a leading exclamation sign—-s ! 127.0.0.1 would select all packets with a source address unequal 127.0.0.1.

▦ *Branch destination*: This parameter specifies what should happen to packets subject to these rules. ACCEPT lets these packet pass; DENY discards the packets silently; REJECT returns an ICMP error message of the type "Destination Unreachable" to the sender before it drops them. The branch destination RETURN is used for a conditioned return from a rules chain. This is particularly interesting during handling of user-defined rules lists, because it allows us to return to the calling rules lists.

Packets can be logged by the syslog mechanism by stating -l (log), in addition to one of the above branch destinations. This allows us, for example, to better detect and trace attempts of attacks (which means that one of the criteria described in Section 19.1.3 is met) or to monitor the traffic volume at a specific network interface.

19.2.2 Drawbacks of the ipchains Architecture

Design flaws were observed soon after the introduction of ipchains in Linux 2.2. The most important problems are as follows:

▦ ipchains had no uniform programming interface that would have enabled us to embed new rules lists into the kernel without having to consider network implementation details. For this reason, adding new rules lists was tiresome and extremely error-prone.

▦ In contrast, the netfilter architecture supplies a framework that minimizes direct interventions in the network code and allows us to append additional code in the form of modules for *packet mangling* into the kernel by using the regular interface.

▦ The integration of code for transparent proxies was expensive in ipchains and was connected to many interventions in the Linux kernel.

▦ In ipchains, rules were necessarily bound to a network address in general, which made the creation of rule sets much too complicated, because the address was the only way to distinguish packets generated locally from packets to be forwarded.

▦ ipchains implemented "masquerading" (a simple NAT variant) and the packet filter code in one piece, which made the code harder to read and unnecessarily complex.

19.3   THE NETFILTER ARCHITECTURE OF LINUX 2.4

Linux Version 2.4 divides the packet-filtering functionality into two large blocks: The so-called *netfilter hooks* offer a comfortable way to catch and manipulate processed IP packets at different positions on their way through the Linux kernel. Building on this background, the `iptables` module implements three rules lists to filter incoming, forwarded, and outgoing IP packets. These lists correspond roughly to the rules lists used by `ipchains`. In addition, similar modules are available for other network protocols (e.g., `ip6tables` for IP Version 6).

19.3.1   Netfilter Hooks in the Linux Kernel

As was mentioned briefly in Section 19.2.2, the netfilter architecture includes a uniform interface, reducing the cost involved to implement new functions. It is called *netfilter hook*, which means that it provides a hook for packet-filter code. This section discusses the components of this architecture and its implementation in the Linux kernel. Actually, this section supplies brief instructions to facilitate your writing your own netfilter modules.

Netfilter modules can be loaded into the Linux kernel at runtime, so we need hooks in the actual routing code to enable dynamic hooking of functions. An integer identifier is allocated to each of these netfilter hooks. The identifiers of all hooks for each supported protocol are defined in the protocol-specific header file (`<linux/netfilter_ipv4.h>` or `<linux/netfilter_ipv6.h>`). The following five hooks are defined for IP Version 4 in `<linux/netfilter_ipv4.h>`:

- `NF_IP_PRE_ROUTING` (0): Incoming packets pass this hook in the `ip_rcv()` function (see Section 14.2.1) before they are processed by the routing code. Prior to that, only a few simple consistency checks with regard to the version, length, and checksum fields in the IP header are done.

  Meaningful opportunities to use this hook result whenever incoming packets should be caught before they are processed—for example, to detect certain types of denial-of-service attacks that operate on poorly built IP packets, or for address-translation mechanisms (NAT), or for accounting functions (counting of incoming packets).

- `NF_IP_LOCAL_IN` (1): All incoming packets addressed to the local computer pass this hook in the function `ip_local_deliver()`. At this point, the `iptables` module hooks the INPUT rules list into place to filter incoming data packets. This corresponds to the input rules list in `ipchains`.

- `NF_IP_FORWARD` (2): All incoming packets not addressed to the local computer pass this hook in the function `ip_forward()`—that is, packets to be forwarded and leaving the computer over a different network interface.

  This includes any packet the address of which was modified by NAT. At this point, the `iptables` module hooks the FORWARD rules list into place to filter forwarded data packets. This corresponds to the forward rules list in `ipchains`.

- `NF_IP_LOCAL_OUT` (3): All outgoing packets created in the local computer pass this hook in the function `ip_build_and_send_pkt()`. At this point, the `iptables` module hooks the OUTPUT rules list into place to filter outgoing data packets. This corresponds to the output rules list in `ipchains`.

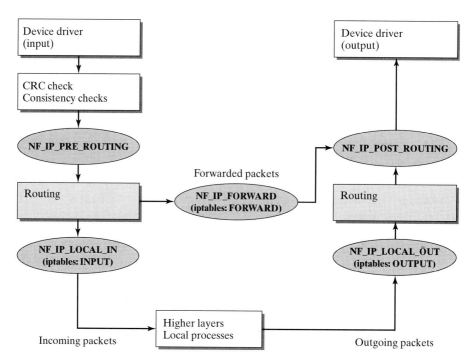

FIGURE 19–3
The packet filtering architecture of Linux 2.4 (netfilter).

NF_IP_POST_ROUTING (4): This hook in the `ip_finish_output()` function represents the last chance to access all outgoing (forwarded or locally created) packets before they leave the computer over a network device. Like the NF_IP_PRE_ROUTING hook, this is a good place to integrate accounting functions.

Figure 19–3 shows data packets traveling through different hooks.

NF_HOOK()   **include/linux/netfilter.h**

Calling the NF_HOOK macro causes the routing code to process the filter functions hooked into a netfilter hook. This macro is defined in `<linux/netfilter.h>` as follows:

```
#define NF_HOOK(pf, hook, skb, indev, outdev, okfn)            \
(list_empty(&nf_hooks[(pf)][(hook)])                          \
  ? (okfn)(skb)                                               \
  : nf_hook_slow((pf), (hook), (skb), (indev), (outdev), (okfn)))
```

The following fragment from net/ipv4/ip_output.c (at the end of the ip_build_and_send_pkt() function) serves as an example to see how we can use the NF_HOOK macro:

```
/* Send it out. */
return NF_HOOK(PF_INET, NF_IP_LOCAL_OUT, skb, NULL, rt->u.dst.dev,
               output_maybe_reroute);
```

In this example, rather than calling the function `output_maybe_reroute()` immediately, the packet-filtering functions registered with the hook `NF_IP_LOCAL_OUT` are processed first to send an IP packet. The values that filter functions can return are defined in `<linux/netfilter.h>`. If all functions return the value `NF_ACCEPT`, then the "okay" function `okfn()` at this hook (i.e., `output_maybe_reroute()` in this case) is invoked. If, however one of the filter functions returns `NF_DROP`, then the packet is dropped, and `okfn()` is not invoked.

More specifically, the `NF_HOOK` macro has the following arguments:

- `pf` (*protocol family*): This is the identifier of the protocol family: `PF_INET` for IP Version 4, `PF_INET6` for IP Version 6.
- `hook`: This is the hook identifier. All valid identifiers for each protocol family are defined in a header file (e.g., `<linux/netfilter_ipv4.h>`).
- `skb`: This is a pointer to the `sk_buff` structure with the packet to be handled.
- `indev` (*input device*): This is a pointer to the `net_device` structure of the network device that received the packet. It is set to `NULL` in the above example, because the packet is an outgoing packet.
- `outdev` (*output device*): This is a pointer to the `net_device` structure of the network device that should be used by the packet to leave the local computer. In the above example, the device used has to be determined first by use of the routing table (`rt`).
- `okfn()` (*okay function*): This function is invoked when all filter functions registered with this hook returned `NF_ACCEPT`, thereby okaying the packet's transit.

19.3.2 Registering and Unregistering Packet-Filter Functions

The packet-filter functions that are actually hooked into the netfilter hooks are so-called *hook functions* of the type `nf_hookfn`. The signature of a hook function is defined in `<linux/netfilter.h>` as follows:

```
typedef unsigned int nf_hookfn(unsigned int hooknum,
                               struct sk_buff **skb,
                               const struct net_device *in,
                               const struct net_device *out,
                               int (*okfn)(struct sk_buff *));
```

The parameters (except for the protocol family identifier) correspond exactly to those of the `NF_HOOK` macro (see Section 19.3.1), and they are passed by this macro to the packet-filter functions. [Russ00d] includes a simple example showing how a packet-filter function is implemented, with detailed explanations.

The return value of a packet-filter function specifies what should happen to the packet. It is of the type `unsigned int` and can take any of the following values, defined in `<linux/netfilter.h>`:

- `NF_DROP` (0): The active rules list processing is stopped, and the packet is dropped.
- `NF_ACCEPT` (1): The packet is passed to the next packet filter function in the rules list. Once the end of the list has been reached, the packet is released by `okfn()` for further processing.

▓ NF_STOLEN (2): The packet filter function withholds the packet for further processing, so that the active rules list processing is stopped. In contrast to NF_DROP, however, the packet does not have to be explicitly dropped.

▓ NF_QUEUE (3): The function nf_queue() (net/core/netfilter.c) puts the packet in a queue from which it can be removed and processed (e.g., by a user space program). Subsequently, nf_reinject() has to be invoked to return the packet to the Linux kernel for further processing by netfilter.

▓ NF_REPEAT (4): In contrast to NF_ACCEPT, rather than a continuation of processing at the next packet-filter function, the current filter function is invoked again.

nf_register_hook(), nf_unregister_hook()	net/core/netfilter.c

This function registers or unregisters a packet-filter function with the Linux kernel. The parameter passed is a nf_hook_ops structure, which includes all information required.

struct nf_hook_ops	linux/netfilter.h

To register a new packet-filter function with the Linux kernel, we first have to initialize a structure of the type nf_hook_ops with all of the management information required:

```
struct nf_hook_ops
{
        struct list_head list;

        /* User fills in from here down. */
        nf_hookfn *hook;
        int pf;
        int hooknum;
        /* Hooks are ordered in ascending priority. */
        int priority;
};
```

The fields of this structure have the following meaning:

▓ list: The nf_hook_ops structures are maintained in a linked list within the Linux kernel.

▓ hook(): This is a pointer to the actual packet-filter function of the type nf_hookfn.

▓ pf, hooknum: The protocol family identifier (e.g., PF_INET or PF_INET6) and the hook identifier (e.g., NF_IP_INPUT) are used to determine the hook for this packet-filter function.

▓ priority: Packet-filter functions within the rules list of a hook are sorted by the priority field in ascending order, so that they will be invoked in this order

when a packet transits. Priority values are defined as follows, e.g., in
`<linux/netfilter_ipv4.h>`:

```
enum nf_ip_hook_priorities {
        NF_IP_PRI_FIRST = INT_MIN,
        NF_IP_PRI_CONNTRACK = -200,
        NF_IP_PRI_MANGLE = -150,
        NF_IP_PRI_NAT_DST = -100,
        NF_IP_PRI_FILTER = 0,
        NF_IP_PRI_NAT_SRC = 100,
        NF_IP_PRI_LAST = INT_MAX,
};
```

19.3.3 Comparing `iptables` and `ipchains`

The most important differences between netfilter and the old `ipchains` architecture are doubtless that the flaws mentioned in Section 19.2.2 were removed: New packet-filter functions can easily be integrated into the Linux kernel by use of the programming interface introduced in Section 19.3.2. In addition, more complex functions, such as the support of transparent proxies or of address-translation mechanisms (NAT), are now implemented as independent modules with clearly defined interfaces. The changes to the existing network code to integrate a new hook for packet-filter functions are limited to one single call of the NF_HOOK macro in the netfilter architecture. (See Section 19.3.1.)

Moreover, the netfilter architecture changed the path different packet streams take across the kernel. In contrast to `ipchains`, `iptables` now handles each packet based on exactly one of the three rules lists used: INPUT, FORWARD, or OUTPUT. The routing decision is made early, before the transit through the INPUT or FORWARD hook, so that forwarded packets do not have to traverse all three hooks. (See Figure 19.3.) In `ipchains` (Figure 19.2), all packets had to traverse the input list before a routing decision was made; given this decision, packets were then redirected to a local process or to the forward list. This modification simplifies the rules-lists handling, because no undesired dependencies between them can occur, and it reduces the processing cost in the kernel, so that packets are handled faster.

And, finally, there was a slight change to the syntax of the iptables command-line tool used to manage rules lists, compared to the older `ipchains`. Table 19.1 gives an overview of the most important changes. Most options and parameters are identical. However, `iptables` rules lists use uppercase letters; also, DENY was renamed in DROP, and MASQ replaces the former MASQUERADE.

19.3.4 The `iptables` Command-line Tool

The `ipchains` management tool is a direct counterpart of the `iptables` program used in netfilter. This tool can be used to manipulate the rule sets in different tables and the associated rules lists. We saw in Table 19–1 that the invocation syntax of `ipchains` and `iptables` is similar in many aspects, because the netfilter architecture uses some of the same concepts, such as linked rules lists.

One of the most important differences is the name-giving introduction of several filter tables, reflecting the modular structure of the netfilter architecture. This modular structure includes NAT and other packet-manipulating functions, in addition to the pure filter functions. This is considered in the invocation syntax by introducing a new parameter, `-t <table>`, which expresses the reference of a rule definition to a table associated with a specific module. Accordingly, this changes the basic structure of an invocation to

```
iptables -t <table> -<operation> <chain> -j <branch destination> <criterion>.
```

This new form extends `iptables`, so that users don't have to use different management tools (e.g., `ipmasqadm`) to address additional functions and protocols.

The following program segment shows a simple configuration for a communication server that can be used by a network with the private address space `192.168.1.0-192.168.1.255` [RMKG + 96] to access the Internet; it obtains a dynamic IP address from the Internet provider:

```
#!/bin/bash
## enable IP forwarding
echo 1 >/proc/sys/net/ipv4/ip_forward
## insert connection-tracking modules (not needed if built into kernel).
if [ ! -e /proc/net/ip_conntrack ] ; then
                insmod ip_tables
                insmod ip_conntrack
                insmod ip_conntrack_ftp
                insmod iptable_nat
                insmod ipt_MASQUERADE
                insmod ipt_LOG
fi

iptables -F ## clean up before calling new ruleset
iptables -A FORWARD -m unclean -j DROP
## enable routing (source and destination)
iptables -A FORWARD -s 192.168.1.0/24 -j ACCEPT
iptables -A FORWARD -d 192.168.1.0/24 -j ACCEPT
## do NAT for all outbound connections
iptables -t nat -A POSTROUTING -d ! 192.168.1.0/24 -j MASQUERADE
```

The `echo` command at the beginning activates the forwarding of IP packets in the Linux kernel.

The `if` branch following next loads the kernel modules required, unless they were already loaded. `ip_tables` and `ip_conntrack` are the basic modules of the netfilter architecture for IP Version 4. The `iptable_nat` and `ipt_MASQUERADE` modules enable masquerading (a simple sort of NAT).

When `iptables -F` is invoked, all existing rules are deleted, to prevent a rule from being loaded twice.

The rule `-m unclean -j DROP` causes all packets with faulty IP headers (e.g., like those in a teardrop attack) to be dropped.

The next two rules enable access to addresses in any other IP network from the internal network (`-s 192.168.1.0/24`) and let packets from this network through to internal computers (`-d 192.162.1.0/24`).

The last rule activates the masquerading process, if the destination computer is not in the internal network.

19.3.5 The Netfilter Standard Modules

With the new netfilter architecture, we now have both the standard functionality and extensions (e.g., NAT) in the form of kernel modules. This section introduces some important netfilter modules:

- *Stateful connection tracking*: The `ip_conntrack.o` module, which includes additional protocol-specific helper modules (e.g., `ip_conntrack_ftp.o`), allows us to assign specific states to the packets of a TCP connection, where four different states are available:

    - NEW: The connection is currently being established, and no reply packet has yet been received for the first packet of this connection.
    - ESTABLISHED: The packets belong to an existing TCP connection.
    - RELATED: The packets are in relation to an existing connection, but not an integral part of that connection.
    - INVALID: All packets that cannot be classified (packets that cannot be assigned to any named connection and that do not initiate connection establishments) fall into this category.

    In addition, the connection-tracking module lets you limit the packet quantities directed over a network interface. This can be used to prevent denial-of-service attacks, where an intruder tries to flood the network with IP packets. For example, an exceptionally fast increase of the packet traffic can be intercepted as follows:

```
iptables -A INVALID-DROP -m limit -limit 5/hour --limit-burst 3 --limit
LOG
```

   Chapter 20 discusses the connection-tracking functionality in detail.

- *Address translation* (*NAT*): The new implementation of the NAT functionality (`iptable_nat.o` module, including protocol-specific helper modules, such as `ip_nat_ftp.o`) is much better performing than the "masquerading" of Linux 2.2. It is addressed from the nat table and implements various operating modes for address translation. The following four operating modes are currently available:

    - *Source NAT* changes the source address of an incoming packet before it is forwarded. This function is addressed by the SNAT option in `iptables`. This mode lets computers access Internet services from a network with private IP addresses, where the actual source address is hidden from the outside and replaced by the address of the firewall computer. A typical rule definition for source NAT is as follows:

```
iptables -t nat -A POSTROUTING -j SNAT --to-source <firewall address>
```

    - The second operating mode is a special version of source NAT, one especially used in communication servers for *masquerading*. It is designed for interplay with dynamically allocated IP addresses. For this reason, all old connection data yielded by the connection-tracking module is dropped whenever the connection is interrupted. A typical rule definition looks like this:

```
iptables -t nat -A POSTROUTING -j MASQUERADE -o ppp0
```

This definition causes the source address of all packets leaving the router over the first PPP interface to be set to the address of this interface.

▶ The *destination NAT* functionality is new in netfilter. It can be used to redirect packets to a different destination address exactly in line with the source NAT. For this purpose, the destination address in the IP header has to be changed before the packet passes the router, so that destination NAT is hooked in the netfilter hook NF_IP_PRE_ROUTING.

For example, destination NAT can be used to implement transparent proxies. The following rule definition directs all HTTP packets (TCP port 80) arriving over the second Ethernet interface to port 8080 of the HTTP proxy with address 192.168.1.2:

```
iptables -t nat -A PREROUTING -j DNAT \
    --to-destination 192.168.1.2:8080 -p tcp --dport 80 -i eth1
```

A special case of the destination NAT functionality is the REDIRECT branch destination. It redirects packets to a specific port in the local computer, so that transparent proxies can be easily included, if present in the local computer:

```
iptables -t nat -A PREROUTING -j REDIRECT \
    --to-port 8080 -i eth1 -p tcp --dport 80
```

▦ *Other possibilities for manipulating packets:*

Additional options that manipulate packets are available in the mangle tables. For example, we could mark specific packets to recognize them within the scope of a security concept or allocate packets to a specific queue in connection with the ip_queue.o module. For this purpose, we use the MARK branch destination. For example, the following call marks all TCP packets with the value 0x0a:

```
iptables -t mangle -A PREROUTING -j MARK --set-mark 0x0a -p
```

If packets are treated differently in the network, depending on the TOS or DS field (*type of service / differentiated services*) in the IP header, then this field can be changed by use of the TOS option, for example, to handle SSH packets in a special way:

```
iptables -t mangle -A PREROUTING -j TOS --set-tos 0x10
    -p tcp --dport ssh
```

▦ *Compatibility modules for* ipchains *and* ipfwadm:

The ipchains.o and ipfwadm.o compatibility modules ensure a soft transition from old Linux versions to Linux 2.4, because the old configuration files and scripts for ipchains (Linux 2.2) and ipfwadm (Linux 2.0) can be reused during a transition period. Because they exist solely for compatibility reasons, they will not be further developed in the future.

Connection Tracking

20.1 INTRODUCTION

This chapter discusses the *connection-tracking* module, which forms the basis for extended packet-filter functions, particularly for network address translation (NAT—see Chapter 21) in Linux 2.4.

The connection-tracking module manages individual connections (particularly TCP connections, but also UDP associations) and serves to allocate incoming, outgoing, and forwarded IP packets to existing connections. A new connection entry is generated as soon as the connection-tracking module registers a connection-establishment packet. From then on, each packet belonging to this connection is uniquely assigned to this connection. For example, this enables the NAT implementation to figure out exactly whether an incoming packet needs a free IP address and port number or one of the addresses and port numbers previously assigned can be used. The connection is deleted after a certain period of time has elapsed without traffic (timeout), which depends on the transport protocol used (i.e., TCP, UDP, or ICMP). Subsequently, the NAT module can reuse the address and port number that have become available.

The connection-tracking module is not limited to transport protocols; it can basically also support complex application protocols. For example, a stateful filter and an address-translation mechanism for active FTP (see Section 19.1.2) can be implemented. For this purpose, the connection-tracking module has to be able to associate newly established data connections with an existing control connection.

20.1.1 Using the Connection-Tracking Module

Two functions can be invoked to access connection entries: `ip_conntrack_get()` and `ip_conntrack_put()`. The `ip_conntrack_get()` function returns a connection entry for an IP packet passed as an `sk_buff` structure and automatically increments the reference counter for this connection. The `ip_conntrack_put()` function informs the connection-tracking module that the previously requested connection is no longer needed and decrements the reference counter.

To find a connection entry, we can use a so-called *tuple* (see Section 20.2.2) instead of an sk_buff structure with a complete IP packet. Such a tuple contains only the source and destination addresses and additional protocol information. The ip_conntrack_find_get() is used for this purpose.

20.2 IMPLEMENTATION

The module interface of the connection-tracking module is located in the file net/ipv4/netfilter/ip_conntrack_standalone.c. The file net/ipv4/netfilter/ip_conntrack_core.c contains the actual connection-tracking functionality.

20.2.1 Basic Structure

The connection-tracking module hooks itself into the netfilter hooks NF_IP_PRE_ROUTING and NF_IP_LOCAL_OUT (see Section 19.3.1 and Figure 20–1) with very high priority (the NF_IP_PRI_CONNTRACK is set to −200 in <linux/netfilter_ipv4.h>). This means that each incoming packet is first passed to the connection-tracking module. Subsequently, other modules also hooked into these hooks, but with lower priority, get their turns.

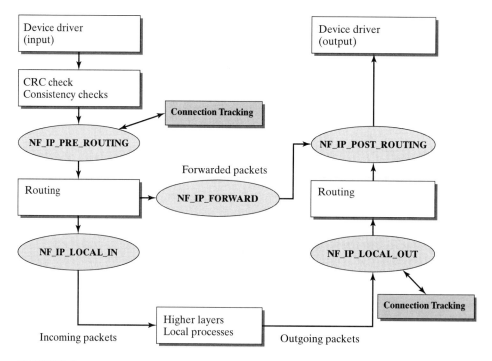

FIGURE 20–1
Netfilter hooks used by the connection-tracking module.

20.2.2 Connection Entries

struct ip_conntrack	linux/netfilter_ipv4/ip_conntrack.h

A connection entry is represented in the Linux kernel by an ip_conntrack structure, consisting of the following fields:

- A structure of the type nf_conntrack (defined in <linux/skbuff.h>), which includes a reference counter (use) that counts the number of open references to this connection entry.
- Two tuples for forward and reverse direction (tuplehash[0], tuplehash[1]), consisting of address and protocol information, which can be used to reference this entry.
- A status field (status), containing a bit vector with the following bits:

  - IPS_EXPECTED: The connection was expected.
  - IPS_SEEN_REPLY: Packets have already occurred in both directions.
  - IPS_ASSURED: The connection entry should never be deleted prematurely, not even when the timeout expires.

- A pointer (timeout) to a function that is invoked as soon as the timeout of this connection expires (i.e., when this connection has not been used over a lengthy period of time).
- A data structure of the type ip_conntrack_expect, which can be used to allocate expected connections (e.g., FTP data connections after a command was sent over the control connection) to existing connections (in this case to the control connection).
- Several structures of the type nf_ct_info, each belonging to a specific state. A pointer to the entry that matches an IP packet is entered in the nfct field of the pertaining sk_buff structure. The enumeration type ip_conntrack_info (defined in <linux/netfilter_ipv4/ip_conntrack.h>), which can take any of the following values, is used as index in the table that contains the nf_ct_info structures:

  - IP_CT_ESTABLISHED: The packet belongs to a fully established connection.
  - IP_CT_RELATED: The packet belongs to a new connection, which, however, refers to an existing connection (i.e., an expected connection).
  - IP_CT_NEW: The packet belongs to a new connection.
  - IP_CT_IS_REPLY: The packet belongs to the reverse direction of a connection.

- A pointer to an optional *helper* module to extend the connection-tracking functionality. (See Section 20.2.4.)

Connection entries are managed in a hash table, where a linked list is used to resolve collisions. An entry in this hash table is of the type ip_conntrack_tuple_hash and contains a reverse pointer to the ip_conntrack structure of that connection, in addition to the actual address information (tuple) (i.e., source and destination addresses) and protocol-specific information (e.g., port numbers). As is shown in Figure 20–2, this pointer is required to access the connection status or to check for whether the entry represents a tuple for the forward or reverse direction of a connection.

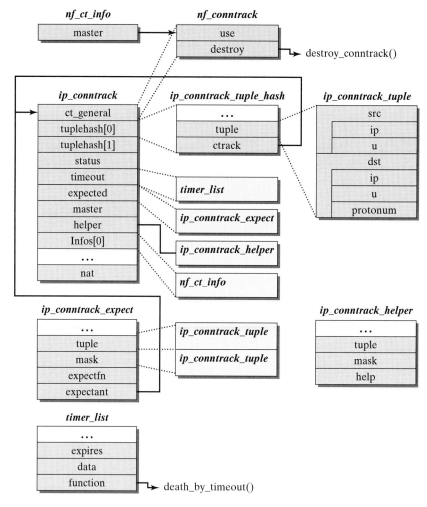

FIGURE 20–2
Data structures of the connection-tracking module.

| `struct ip_conntrack_tuple` | **linux/netfilter_ipv4/ip_conntrack_tuple.h** |

An `ip_conntrack_tuple` is divided into a manipulable part, for the source address and perhaps the source port (`ip_conntrack_manip`), and a nonmanipulable part for destination address, protocol, and perhaps destination port. This division facilitates the use of connection entries by the NAT module.

20.2.3   Transport Protocols

| `struct ip_conntrack_protocol` | **linux/netfilter_ipv4/ip_conntrack_protocol.h** |

To enable use of different transport protocols, there is a global list with these protocols (`protocol_list`). A protocol is represented by a structure of the type `ip_conntrack_protocol`. The two functions `ip_conntrack_protocol_register()` and `ip_conntrack_protocol_unregister()` are used to add a protocol to or remove one from the list of supported protocols in the form of modules at runtime. Notice that, when you delete a protocol from the list, all connections currently using this protocol are also deleted.

To support a specific protocol, such a module has to contain the following functions:

- Functions to output specific details about a connection in clear text (used by the proc file system).
- Helper functions to invert tuples (i.e., to swap source and destination addresses) and to extract a tuple from an `sk_buff` structure.
- Its own protocol-specific processing functions (e.g., functions to track the current state of the TCP protocol automaton, in the case of the TCP protocol).
- Update functions for the timeout timer to ensure that a connection entry can be deleted, if it hasn't been used over a lengthy period of time.

20.2.4   Helper Modules

| `struct ip_conntrack_helper` | **linux/netfilter_ipv4/ip_conntrack_helper.h** |

The so-called *helper modules* provide an interface to extend the connection-tracking functionality. The functions `ip_conntrack_helper_register()` and `ip_conntrack_helper_unregister()` are used to add or remove a structure of the type `ip_conntrack_helper` to or from a linked list (`helpers`). Each packet that traverses one of the connection-tracking hooks is passed to each of the registered helper modules.

This enables us to support active FTP, where the associated helper module, `ip_conntrack_ftp.o`, updates the list of expected connections as soon as it detects a GET or PUT command while listening to the control connection. This means that it can assign data connections arriving from the outside to existing control connections.

20.2.5 Global Variables

The following global variables are important for the connection-tracking functionality:

- ip_conntrack_hash, the hash tables with all connection entries—see Section 20.2.2 for details;
- expect_list, the list of expected connections. A connection is expected, for example, when a file transfer is started over an FTP control connection. This functionality is currently used by the FTP protocol only;
- protocol_list, the list of registered transport protocols. TCP, UDP, ICMP, and a generic transport protocol module with minimum functionality, which is used when no matching protocol is found, are currently implemented;
- helpers, the list of registered helper modules—see Section 20.2.4.

20.2.6 Functions

print_tuple()	net/ipv4/netfilter/ip_conntrack_standalone.c

This function is invoked by print_conntrack() and outputs a single tuple for a connection (forward and reverse directions) in text form:

src=129.13.65.4 dst=168.42.17.1 sport=8080 dport=80

print_expect()	net/ipv4/netfilter/ip_conntrack_standalone.c

This function outputs a single tuple from the list of expected connections in text form:

EXPECTING: proto=23 src=129.13.65.4 dst=168.42.17.1 sport=8080 dport=80

print_conntrack()	net/ipv4/netfilter/ip_conntrack_standalone.c

This function outputs the connection entry for an entire connection (forward and reverse directions) in text form. In addition to the two tuples, this includes their status and the states of their timeout timers.

conntrack_iterate()	net/ipv4/netfilter/ip_conntrack_standalone.c

This is a helper function used to walk through all connections; it is invoked by list_conntracks().

list_conntracks()	net/ipv4/netfilter/ip_conntrack_standalone.c

This function outputs the connection entries of all connections, both those currently active and those expected. It is required to generate an entry for the proc file system.

| init(), fini(), init_or_ cleanup() | **net/ipv4/netfilter/ip_conntrack_standalone.c** |

The init() and fini() functions are invoked to initialize or remove the connection-tracking module, and they, in turn, invoke the function init_or_cleanup() with the parameter 1 (initialize) or 0 (remove).

During the initialization, the actual connection-tracking functionality is initialized first by the calling of ip_conntrack_init(). Subsequently, the entry in the proc file system is generated, and the functions ip_conntrack_in() and ip_conntrack_local() are hooked into the appropriate netfilter hooks. Inversely, these functions are unhooked when the module is removed, the entry is deleted from the proc file system, and, finally, the function ip_conntrack_cleanup() is invoked.

| ip_conntrack_init() | **net/ipv4/netfilter/ip_conntrack_core.c** |

This is the initialization routine for the actual connection-tracking functionality. It adds the three standard protocols—TCP, UDP, and ICMP—to the protocol list and initializes the ip_conntrack_hash hash table.

| ip_conntrack_cleanup() | **net/ipv4/netfilter/ip_conntrack_core.c** |

This function prepares for a removal of the connection-tracking module. More specifically, a locking mechanism is used to ensure that all IP packets currently handled are properly completed. Subsequently, a few reserved memory locations are released.

| hash_conntrack() | **net/ipv4/netfilter/ip_conntrack_core.c** |

This helper function computes the hash value for a data structure of the type ip_conntrack_tuple.

| get_tuple() | **net/ipv4/netfilter/ip_conntrack_core.c** |

This function uses the protocol data passed from an IP packet to create a matching data structure of the type ip_conntrack_tuple. First, the IP source and destination addresses and the transport protocol are taken, and then the pkt_to_tuple function of the matching transport protocol module is invoked.

| invert_tuple(), invert_tuplepr() | **net/ipv4/netfilter/ip_conntrack_core.c** |

These functions invert an ip_conntrack_tuple structure by swapping the IP source and destination addresses. In addition, the function invert_tuple() of the matching transport protocol module is invoked—for example, to swap the source and destination ports for TCP or UDP.

For `invert_tuple()`, a pointer to the `ip_conntrack_protocol` structure of the transport protocol has to be passed as parameter; `invert_tuplepr()` determines this itself from the passed `ip_conntrack_tuple` structure.

`ip_conntrack_alter_reply()`	**net/ipv4/netfilter/ip_conntrack_core.c**

This function replaces the tuple in a connection entry for the reverse direction by the value passed in `newreply`.

`ip_conntrack_find_get()`	**net/ipv4/netfilter/ip_conntrack_core.c**

This function uses the `__ip_conntrack_find()` function to search the `ip_conntrack_hash` hash table for a connection entry matching an `ip_conntrack_tuple` structure, where the parameter `ignored_conntrack` can be used to exclude a specific connection from the search explicitly. If the entry exists, then it is returned, and the `ct_general.use` reference counter is incremented by one. Otherwise, the function returns NULL.

`ip_conntrack_get()`	**net/ipv4/netfilter/ip_conntrack_core.c**

This function gets the connection entry and the connection status matching a passed `sk_buff` structure. The information required are simply extracted from the `nfct` field in the `sk_buff` structure.

`ip_conntrack_put()`	**net/ipv4/netfilter/ip_conntrack_core.c**

This function decrements the reference counter of a connection entry by one. For this purpose, it invokes the inline function `nf_conntrack_put()` defined in `<linux/skbuff.h>`, which uses `atomic_dec_and_test()` to decrement the reference counter. If this action causes the counter to reach 0 (i.e., there are no more references to this connection), then the function pointer `destroy()` is invoked to delete this connection entry. This pointer normally points to the function `destroy_conntrack()`.

`resolve_normal_ct()`	**net/ipv4/netfilter/ip_conntrack_core.c**

This function tries to find a connection entry matching a passed `sk_buff` structure or creates such an entry, if it doesn't exist. First, it uses `get_tuple()` to create a structure of the type `ip_conntrack_tuple` from the packet's protocol data. Next, `ip_conntrack_find_get()` is used to find a matching connection entry. If no matching tuple is found, then `init_conntrack()` is invoked to create a new connection entry. Finally, the connection entry status is determined, and this status is used to set the `nfct` field of the passed `sk_buff` structure.

init_conntrack()   **net/ipv4/netfilter/ip_conntrack_core.c**

This function creates a new connection entry. First, it creates a structure of the type ip_conntrack. This structure consists of the passed tuple for the forward direction and its inversion (created by invert_tuple) for the reverse direction. Next, atomic_set() sets the reference counter ct_general.use to value 1. The only reference that exists initially is owned by the timeout timer, which is also initialized, and its timeout function pointer is set to the function death_by_timeout(). Previously, the relevant protocol module was initialized by calling its new() function. The function pointer ct_general.destroy(), which is invoked to delete a connection entry, is set to the function destroy_conntrack(). In addition, a helper is entered, if one was registered for the protocol used.

As soon as all data structures have been initialized, the next step checks on whether the connection to be entered was expected (i.e., whether it exists in the expect_list). If so, it is deleted from this list and set to the IPS_EXPECTED status.

ip_conntrack_in()   **net/ipv4/netfilter/ip_conntrack_core.c**

This function is hooked into the netfilter hook NF_IP_PRE_ROUTING; it is invoked for each packet arriving from the outside. It is also used by ip_conntrack_local(), because the only difference is in how fragmented IP packets are handled.

IP packets have to be defragmented before they can be assigned to a connection; fragments that have already arrived are collected by the function ip_ct_gather_frags(), which, in turn, uses the ip_defrag() function. When the last fragment of a fragmented packet is received, or if the packet was not fragmented, then an attempt is made to assign the packet to a connection.

First, find_proto() is used to determine the connection-tracking module for the transport protocol used. Next, the packet is checked to see whether it is an ICMP packet. If so, it is first passed to the function icmp_error_track(). If successful, this function returns one, and the packet is accepted by returning NF_ACCEPT.

In contrast, if icmp_error_track() returns null, the packet is further handled like any other packet. resolve_normal_ct() chooses the correct connection entry (or creates one, if none exists). Subsequently, the packet() function of the associated transport protocol module is invoked, and then the help() functions of all registered helper modules are invoked. If one of these functions fails, then nf_conntrack_put() releases this connection entry.

ip_conntrack_local()   **net/ipv4/netfilter/ip_conntrack_standalone.c**

This function is hooked into the netfilter hook NF_IP_LOCAL_OUT; accordingly, it is invoked for each IP packet originating from a local process. The only difference from how incoming packets are handled in ip_conntrack_in() is that fragmented packets are not handled by the connection-tracking module. All other packets are simply passed to ip_conntrack_in().

`icmp_error_track()`	**net/ipv4/netfilter/ip_conntrack_core.c**

This function serves to handle ICMP packets. First, some consistency checks are done with regard to the length field, the ICMP message type, and the ICMP checksum. More detailed handling is done for the following ICMP message types, each of which refers to a specific IP packet—one where the payload field in the header contains the ICMP message (described in Section 21.1.4):

```
ICMP_DEST_UNREACH
ICMP_SOURCE_QUENCH
ICMP_TIME_EXCEEDED
ICMP_PARAMETERPROB
ICMP_REDIRECT
```

`ip_conntrack_find_get()` finds a connection entry for the original packet header, which is also sent by this function, where the function `invert_tuple()` is used first, because the packet's source and destination addresses have to be swapped. If the function finds the entry, then a pointer to the appropriate `ct_info` structure is entered in the `nfct` field of the passed `sk_buff` structure.

`destroy_conntrack()`	**net/ipv4/netfilter/ip_conntrack_core.c**

Normally, this function is invoked over the function pointer `ct_general.destroy()` in the `ip_conntrack` structure to delete a connection entry. If this entry is linked to a "master" entry, then its reference counter is decremented by `nf_conntrack_put()`. Subsequently, a cleanup function hooked into the function pointer `ip_conntrack_destroyed()` is invoked, if present. Finally, `atomic_dec()` decrements the counter `ip_conntrack_count` to the number of existing connection entries.

`death_by_timeout()`	**net/ipv4/netfilter/ip_conntrack_core.c**

This function is invoked as soon as the timeout timer for a connection expires. Initially, `clean_from_lists()` (also defined in `net/ipv4/netfilter/ip_conntrack_core.c`) removes the connection entry from the list of active connections. Subsequently, `ip_conntrack_put()` decrements the reference counter. This deletes the connection, if there are no other references.

`ip_conntrack_protocol_` `register()`	**net/ipv4/netfilter/ip_conntrack_standalone.c**

This function registers a module for a transport protocol. The protocol is added to the `protocol_list`, if it is not yet present.

| `ip_conntrack_protocol_`
`unregister()` | **net/ipv4/netfilter/ip_conntrack_standalone.c** |

This function unregisters a module for a transport protocol; it is currently (in Linux Version 2.4.8) still empty.

| `find_proto()` | **net/ipv4/netfilter/ip_conntrack_core.c** |

This function searches the `protocol_list` for a protocol and returns the appropriate entry, if successful. If the function doesn't find a matching entry, then the generic protocol is returned. First, READ_LOCK locks the management data of the connection-tracking module for reading, before the helper function __`find_proto()` is invoked for the actual search.

| `ip_conntrack_helper_register()` | **net/ipv4/netfilter/ip_conntrack_core.c** |

This function registers a helper module by adding it to the `helpers` list, if note is not yet present.

| `ip_conntrack_helper_unregister()` | **net/ipv4/netfilter/ip_conntrack_core.c** |

This function unregisters a helper module by deleting it from the `helpers` list. For this purpose, it searches all connection entries that point to this helper module. Subsequently, the function `unhelp()` sets the `helper` pointer for each such connection to NULL. If a connection occurs in the `expect_list`, then this instance is deleted.

Currently, the most important application for connection tracking—and the reason why connection tracking was initially developed—is the so-called *network address translation* (*NAT*), which will be discussed in the next chapter.

Network Address Translation (NAT)

21.1 INTRODUCTION

The *Network Address Translation (NAT)* mechanism deals generally with the translation of IP addresses. It represents an effective way to encounter the exhaustion of free IP addresses (Version 4) in view of the explosive growth of the Internet. However, transition to IP Version 6 with its much larger address space progresses only slowly, because it was found extremely difficult to convert a decentralized network like the global Internet to a new protocol at one shot. Exactly this is where NAT comes in useful: For example, it allows all users in a local area network to access the Internet and its services, even though there is only one single official IP address available, and only private IP addresses (according to RFC 1918 [RMKG + 96]) are used within the local area network. A router accessible to the network, used by the users to connect to the global Internet, handles the required address mapping.

The NAT implementation in Linux 2.4 consists of two parts: *connection tracking*, and the actual NAT. Chapter 20 described how the connection-tracking mechanism is implemented.

21.1.1 Important Terminology

One of the most important technical terms in the NAT area is the so-called *session flow*. A session flow is a set of IP packets, exchanged between two instances and forming a unit in that they are treated equally by a NAT router. Such a session flow is directed to the direction the first packet was sent. For this reason, we speak of original and reverse directions in the following discussion. One good example is a telnet session: The corresponding TCP connection is initiated by the terminal computer, so the original direction of the relevant session flow points from the terminal to the server. TCP/UDP-based session flows can be described uniquely by an {IP source address, source port, IP destination address, destination port} tuple. Similarly, an ICMP session flow can be identified by an {IP source address, IP destination address, ICMP type, ICMP ID} tuple.

[SrHo99] describes three characteristic requirements that should be met by all NAT variants:

- transparent address allocation;
- transparent routing; and
- correct handling of ICMP packets.

The following sections explain each of these requirements and what they mean.

21.1.2   Transparent Address Allocation

Because we can use NAT to connect networks with different address spaces, these addresses from the respective address spaces have to be allocated among them. This allocation can be either static or dynamic. If we use static allocation, the allocations are maintained during the entire operation of a NAT router. Static allocations simplify the address translation, because no state information about specific session flows has to be maintained. In dynamic allocation, the allocation is specified at the time that a session flow is opened. This allocation remains valid until the session is terminated. In some cases, the allocation rule can be extended beyond the IP addresses to include the transport protocol ports. (See Section 21.1.6.) In any event, address allocation should be transparent: The mechanisms should be hidden from the applications in end systems.

21.1.3   Transparent Routing

We use the term "transparent routing" in the following discussion to distinguish the routing functionality of a NAT router from the functionality of a normal router. Transparent routing differs from normal routing in that packets are forwarded between two different address spaces by changing the address information in IP packets and routing to match these modified addresses.

Transparent routing can be divided into three phases: address binding, address translation, and releasing of the address binding.

- *Address binding*: This phase permanently binds two addresses from the two address spaces to be bound. This should not be confused with the address allocation mentioned above—the address allocation only determines valid bindings. These bindings will then actually exist only after the address binding. In connections with static address allocation, address binding is also static, but dynamic binding occurs at the beginning of a session flow and is released as soon as this session ends. If we want to map internal network addresses to global, external addresses, then we should bind each additional session flow originating from the same end system to the same address.
- *Address translation*: Once an address has been bound, each IP packet of that session flow has to be manipulated. This manipulation can be limited to the IP addresses, but it could also extend to TCP/UDP ports. (See Section 21.1.6.) Notice that the checksum in the IP header, or in the UDP/TCP header, has to be recomputed.

■ *Releasing address binding*: An address binding has to be released as soon as the last associated session flow ends, if we use dynamic binding, to ensure that the external address can be reused. In contrast, the binding is maintained if we use static binding.

21.1.4 Correct Handling of ICMP Packets

ICMP error messages normally require special handling (except for ICMP Redirect messages), because the payload (PDU) of these messages includes the header of the IP packet that caused the error. To achieve total transparency, this inner packet header has to be properly manipulated.

21.1.5 Differences from Masquerading in Linux 2.2

A simple NAT implementation, called "masquerading," had been an integral part of the Linux kernel (Linux 2.0 and 2.2). Later, the NAT functionality was moved to an external module in the course of converting to the netfilter architecture. The NAT support was heavily extended, so that now masquerading represents only a special case of the general address-translation functionality.

In contrast to the old masquerading, we now have a way to map more than one public IP address to the internal network. In addition, we can map a public IP address to several internal computers to implement *load sharing*.

The problems of the old masquerading included a close involvement of the packet-filter code, which meant extremely complex rule sets in firewall computers. This problem becomes clear from looking at the different hooks for "IP chains" (see Section 19.2): In the *input chain*, a packet arriving from the outside appears to be intended for the firewall itself; in the *forward chain*, the previously unmasked packet is not recognized, because its destination address has changed; and, finally, in the *output chain*, the packet appears to originate from the firewall itself.

In Linux 2.4, the NAT functionality was divided into two main parts: connection tracking, and actual translation. The connection-tracking module manages connections in the transport and application layers; the NAT module actually translates addresses. Both modules can be loaded into the Linux kernel at runtime, to strongly improve maintainability.

21.1.6 NAT Variants

We will be using the sample topology shown in Figure 21–1 in the following discussion to better understand the different NAT flavors and their main differences. The local class-C network with two end systems, A and B, uses the private address space 192.168.1.0–192.168.1.255; it connects to the Internet over a NAT router. This NAT router has the internal network address 192.168.1.254 and a reserve of global addresses, which can be mapped to the internal addresses (it could also consist of one single address—199.10.42.1 in this example). A server with the address 100.1.1.1 is the communication partner of end systems A and B in this example.

■ *Traditional NAT*: Traditional NAT is generally used (1) to connect a local area network using private addresses, as specified in RFC 1918, to an external network and (2) to allow the internal end systems to access the external network transparently. Traditional NAT is unidirectional: An address can be bound in one direction only

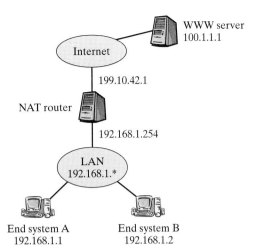

FIGURE 21–1
Example of a network using NAT.

(normally, when a session flow is established from the internal network towards the external network). In addition, you can translate either the source address (*source NAT*) or the destination address (*destination NAT*) of a session flow, but never both addresses at the same time.

▷ *Basic NAT*: This NAT variant is used to map internal IP address to one or several external IP addresses. To understand it better, let's assume that there is a (dynamic) allocation between the end system A (internal address 192.168.1.1) and a global address from the address space reserved for NAT (e.g., 199.10.42.1 in the sample network of Figure 21–1). Let's further assume that a WWW browser in end system A establishes a TCP connection from its port 1200 to port 80 in the WWW server 100.1.1.1. The NAT router binds the internal address 192.168.1.1 to the global address 199.10.42.1 for this session flow. However, this binding is valid for this single session flow only, and a new binding (to the same address) has to be done for each additional, secondary session flow.

▷ *Network Address and Port Translation (NAPT)*: This NAT variant represents an extension of Basic NAT. NAPT can translate IP addresses and additionally TCP or UDP port numbers. It is used to map various session flows from different internal end systems to one global IP address. (If only one single global address is available, then this corresponds to the "masquerading" of Linux 2.2.) This means that, in our above example, we could establish a TCP connection from port 1200 of end system B to the same port 80 of the same server by translating port number 1200 (e.g., into 1201) in addition to the IP address. In this case, we would obtain the following bindings:

· 192.168.1.1:1200 → 199.10.42.1:1200
· 192.168.1.2:1200 → 199.10.42.1:1201

Notice that, for mapping of source port numbers, port numbers from the privileged range (ports 1-1023) are mapped again to the privileged range. For transforming of the destination address, the ports should not be changed at all.

▶ *Bidirectional NAT and Twice NAT*: These two NAT variants are listed here only for the sake of completeness. In contrast to traditional NAT, bidirectional NAT lets you bind addresses during the establishment of session flows in both directions. Twice NAT removes the limitation of traditional NAT that we can transform either only the destination address or only the source address, but never both.

21.1.7 Problems

One general problem in address translation is application-layer protocols, where applications exchange address information. One good example is the File Transfer Protocol (FTP—see [Stev94a]). If an FTP client accesses an FTP server, then TCP first establishes a control connection to exchange FTP commands, such as GET or PUT. Now, if it wants to obtain data from the server, the client uses the PORT command to send an IP address and a port number. The client opens this port passively (see Chapter 27) and waits for the data connection, which is established by the server to the address it obtained earlier, to transmit payload.

The problems arising in the above case are similar to those known from packet filters. (See Section 19.1.2.) One major problem is that, if there is a NAT router somewhere between the client and the server, this router maps the client's source IP address transparently to another address, whereas the client sends its internal address in the PORT command, and this address is invalid from the server's view. To ensure that the PORT command can operate correctly, the NAT router has to also translate the address transported in the PORT command; it has to be able to intervene in the FTP protocol on the application layer.

Another major problem occurs in NAPT and relates to IP packet fragmenting. When IP packets are fragmented, only the first fragment contains the transport-protocol header with the port numbers of the source and the destination; but NAPT relies on this information when mapping addresses, so this means that the other fragments of the same packet cannot be handled properly. Consequently, we have to ensure that fragmented packets are reassembled before an attempt is made to translate addresses.

21.2   CONFIGURING NAT IN LINUX

The `iptable _nat.o` module implements the unidirectional NAPT variant described in Section 21.1.6. Like the Twice NAT variant, it can change the source and destination addresses of a session flow simultaneously.

To intercept and process packets, NAT uses the infrastructure supplied by the netfilter architecture. (See Section 19.3.1.) Figure 21–2 shows that it hooks itself into the netfilter hooks NF_IP_PRE_ROUTING, NF_IP_POST_ROUTING, and NF_IP_LOCAL_OUT for this purpose. The NAT module is invoked as soon as a packet traverses the appropriate hook, and a pointer to the `sk_buff` structure is passed, together with the packet. For configuration purposes, it is important that the source address be translated at the NF_IP_POST_ROUTING hook while the destination address is being translated in one of the other two hooks.

The first, preliminary versions of the new netfilter architecture allowed you to configure NAT by using an independent tool called `ipnatctl`. More recently, this

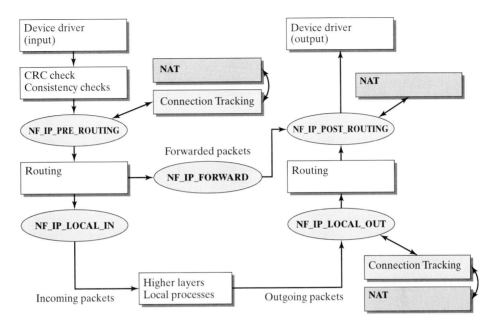

FIGURE 21–2
Netfilter hooks used by the NAT module.

functionality was fully integrated in the iptables tool. iptables can be used to specify rules that control the behavior of the NAT module. As was described in Section 19.2.1, a rule consists of a set of criteria to select session flows (*matching rule*) and a second part specifying how a session flow should be transformed (*binding type* or *mapping type*).

Criteria identical to packet-filter rules are available to select session flows: the IP source and destination addresses, the transport protocol, the port numbers, and the protocol-specific flags. The second part of a NAT rule defines how a session flow should be transformed. To this end, there are additional branch destinations, which are valid in the nat table only. We can use -j SNAT to activate the translation of the source address (*source NAT*) and -j DNAT to translate the destination address (*destination NAT*). In addition, we have to use --to-source or --to-destination to specify a range of IP addresses and port numbers, if present, for the address-translation process.

The selection criteria of the source NAT rule are applied to the original packet-address information in the event that both a source NAT and a destination NAT rule apply to the packet, though the destination address has already been changed by the destination NAT at that point. There are additional branch destinations (e.g., -j MAS-QUERADE for masquerading in the Linux 2.2 style) for special cases.

In the example discussed in Section 21.1.6, where source NAT is used to map the internal addresses from the private address range 192.168.1.0–192.168.1.255 to the global address 199.10.42.1, the corresponding iptables invocation would have the following form:

```
iptables -t nat -A POSTROUTING -s 192.168.1.0/24 \
         -j SNAT --to-source 199.10.42.1
```

21.3   IMPLEMENTING THE NAT MODULE

This section first introduces important data structures to manage session flows, allocations, and address bindings. Subsequently, it will explain the functions used to establish and tear down address bindings, to actually translate addresses, and to handle ICMP error messages.

21.3.1   Important Data Structures

All session flows are completely managed by the connection-tracking module described in Chapter 20. A structure of the type `ip_conntrack` is stored for each session flow. (See Section 20.2.2.) This structure includes two data structures of the type `ip_conntrack_tuple_hash`, representing the forward and reverse directions of a session flow. If a session flow is translated by the NAT module, then the `ip_conntrack_tuple_hash` structure for the reverse direction is adapted so that reply packets can be allocated to it properly.

In the example discussed in Section 21.1.6, where the internal address 192.168.1.1 is translated into the global address 199.10.42.1, a connection from port 1200 to port 80 in the WWW server 100.1.1.1 would be represented by the following entries:

- Forward: 192.168.1.1:1200 → 100.1.1.1:80
- Reverse: 100.1.1.1:80 → 199.10.42.1:1200

The connection-tracking module stores a pointer to the relevant data structure of the type `ip_conntrack` in the `sk_buff` of each packet. If the NAT module wants to allocate an IP packet to a session flow, it invokes its own `ip_conntrack_get()` function, which returns the matching `ip_conntrack` structure.

`struct ip_nat_expect`	`linux/netfilter_ipv4/ip_nat_rule.h`

The NAT module has an ordered list, `nat_expect_list`, with data structures of the type `ip_nat_expect`, to enable protocol-specific NAT modules (e.g., for FTP—see Section 21.1.7) to decide when a new session flow was expected, so that it requires special handling. Each of these structures consists essentially of a pointer to a function that actually makes that decision:

```
struct ip_nat_expect
{
struct list_head list;

    /* Returns 1 (and sets verdict) if it has setup NAT for this
       connection */
    int (*expect)(struct sk_buff **pskb,
                  unsigned int hooknum,
                  struct ip_conntrack *ct,
                  struct ip_nat_info *info,
                  struct ip_conntrack *master,
                  struct ip_nat_info *masterinfo,
                  unsigned int *verdict);
};
```

struct ip_nat_multi_range	**linux/netfilter_ipv4/ip_nat.h**

The `ip_nat_multi_range` structure is used mainly to specify the set of addresses available for address translation. It contains one or several structures of the type `ip_nat_range`, each specifying a continuous IP address range, and a `rangesize` field that takes the number of contained `ip_nat_range` structures:

```
struct ip_nat_multi_range
{
        unsigned int rangesize;

        /* hangs off end. */
        struct ip_nat_range range[1];
};
```

struct ip_nat_range	**linux/netfilter_ipv4/ip_nat.h**

The `ip_nat_range` structure serves to represent a continuous IP address range; the range boundaries are specified in the `min_ip` and `max_ip` fields:

```
/* Single range specification. */
struct ip_nat_range
{
                /* Set to OR of flags above. */
                unsigned int flags;

                /* Inclusive: network order. */
                u_int32_t min_ip, max_ip;

                /* Inclusive: network order */
                union ip_conntrack_manip_proto min, max;
};
```

If the flags bit vector contains the value `IP_NAT_RANGE_PROTO_SPECIFIED`, then the `min` and `max` fields additionally specify a protocol-specific address range: a port-number range for TCP and UDP, a value range from the ICMP ID field for ICMP.

NAT fully relies on the means offered by the netfilter architecture to manage the selection rules needed to specify packets requiring an address translation. For this purpose, two new branch destinations, SNAT and DNAT, are defined with the functions `ipt_snat_target()` and `ipt_dnat_target()`, which do the actual address-translation work. A multipurpose parameter, `targinfo`, is used to pass the address range available for translation to these functions in the form of an `ip_nat_multi_range` structure.

struct ip_nat_info	**linux/netfilter_ipv4/ip_nat.h**

As was explained in Chapter 20, the connection-tracking module creates a data structure of the type `ip_conntrack` for each session flow, to store all relevant information. If the NAT functionality was activated in the Linux kernel (`CONFIG_IP_NAT_NEEDED`), then this structure additionally contains a nat substructure, and the info field of that substructure contains a structure of the type ip_nat_info:

```
struct ip_conntrack
{
...
#ifdef CONFIG_IP_NF_NAT_NEEDED
        struct {
                struct ip_nat_info info;
...
        } nat;
#endif /* CONFIG_IP_NF_NAT_NEEDED */
};
```

The ip_nat_info structure stores the address bindings of a session flow:

```
struct ip_nat_info
{
        /* Set to zero when conntrack created: bitmask of maniptypes */
        int initialized;

        unsigned int num_manips;

        /* Manipulations to be done on this conntrack. */
        struct ip_nat_info_manip manips[IP_NAT_MAX_MANIPS];

        /* The mapping type which created us (NULL for null mapping). */
        const struct ip_nat_mapping_type *mtype;

        struct ip_nat_hash bysource, byipsproto;

        /* Helper (NULL if none). */
        struct ip_nat_helper *helper;
};
```

The initialized bit vector specifies whether the address binding for the source address (bit 0) or the destination address (bit 1), or both, was initialized.

The num_manips field specifies the number of executable manipulations stored in the manips vector. Manipulations are counted separately at different hooks and for different directions. Each of these manipulations is represented by a structure of the type ip_nat_info_manip.

The bysource and byipsproto fields include hash values used to sort the structure in the two hash tables described below, and helper is a pointer to an optional helper module. (See Section 21.4.2.)

struct ip_nat_info_manip	linux/netfilter_ipv4/ip_nat.h

```
struct ip_nat_info_manip
{
        /* The direction. */
        u_int8_t direction;

        /* Which hook the manipulation happens on. */
        u_int8_t hooknum;
```

```
/* The manipulation type. */
u_int8_t maniptype;

/* Manipulations to occur at each conntrack in this dirn. */
struct ip_conntrack_manip manip;
};
```

The `ip_nat_info_manip` structure represents a manipulation or address binding. It contains the direction (`IP_CT_DIR_ORIGINAL` for the forward direction, `IP_CT_DIR_REPLY` for the reverse direction), the netfilter hook number, and the address translation type (`IP_NAT_MANIP_SRC` for source NAT, `IP_NAT_MANIP_DST` for destination NAT), and its `ip_conntrack_manip` structure includes the IP address and port number to which the former address should be mapped.

To manage address bindings, the NAT module uses two hash tables, `bysource` and `byipsproto`, where collisions are resolved by linear lists. The `byipsproto` table is used to account for mappings done, to ensure that no two mappings to the same IP address exist. The keys are the transport protocol number and the IP source and destination addresses of the session flow after the address translation.

The keys for the `bysource` table are the transport protocol, the IP source address, and the source port before the address translation. This table is used by the `find_appropriate_src()` function to detect existing session flows. (See Section 21.3.4.)

21.3.2 Initializing and Uninitializing the NAT Module

The two functions `init()` and `fini()` are used to initialize and uninitialize the NAT module. In turn, these two functions invoke the `init_or_cleanup()` function with parameter 1 (initialize) or 0 (uninitialize).

`init_or_cleanup()`	**net/ipv4/netfilter/ip_nat_standalone.c**

The `init_or_cleanup()` function serves to initialize or uninitialize the NAT module, depending on the value of the init parameter.

To initialize the NAT module, the `ip_nat_rule_init()` function (from `net/ipv4/netfilter/ip_nat_rule.c`) is invoked first. This function uses `ipt_register_table()` to create the new netfilter table, `nat`. Subsequently, it uses `ipt_register_target()` to register the new branch destinations, SNAT and DNAT, with the handling functions `ipt_snat_target()` and `ipt_dnat_target()`. Next, the `ip_nat_init()` function (from `net/ipv4/netfilter/ip_nat_core.c`) initializes the standard protocols—TCP, UDP, and ICMP—and the two hash tables—bysource and byipsproto. Finally, the functions `ip_nat_fn()`, `ip_nat_local_fn()`, and `ip_nat_out()` are registered with the appropriate hooks, and the usage counter of the connection-tracking module is incremented.

To uninitialize the NAT module, the cleanup work is done in reverse order: First, the usage counter of the connection tracking module is decremented; then, the NAT functions are removed from the hooks; next, `ip_nat_cleanup()` deletes the hash tables and the transport protocol modules; and, finally, `ip_nat_rule_cleanup()` releases the NAT branch destinations and the NAT table.

21.3.3 How an IP Packet Travels Through the NAT Module

An IP packet that traverses the system is handed over to the NAT module twice:

▨ When it enters the system at the netfilter hook NF_IP_PRE_ROUTING. At this point, the packet is handled by the ip_nat_fn() function.

▨ Once it has been created by a local process—at the netfilter hook NF_IP_LOCAL_OUT. Notice that fragmented packets slip past NAT, and ip_nat_fn() is invoked for all other packets.

▨ At netfilter hook NF_IP_POST_ROUTING, when the packet leaves the system. The appropriate function is ip_nat_out(); it first reassembles fragmented packets, if present, and then invokes ip_nat_fn(). As was described in Section 20.2.6, although fragmented packets are reassembled by the connection-tracking module (ip_conntrack_in() function), these packets might have been fragmented again by the routing code in the meantime.

ip_nat_fn()	net/ipv4/netfilter/ip_nat_standalone.c

This function is invoked for each packet (not only for packets subject to address translation). The parameters it takes include the number of the netfilter hook where it was invoked and a pointer to an sk_buff structure, together with the packet.

First, the HOOK2MANIP macro is used to select the NAT variant to be used from the hook number. At netfilter hook NF_IP_POST_ROUTING, the source address (IP_NAT_MANIP_SRC) should be changed; otherwise, the destination address (IP_NAT_MANIP_DST) has to be changed. Subsequently, the ip_conntrack_get() function is invoked from the connection-tracking module to discover the associated connection entry and its state. The further approach differs, depending on this state:

▨ *Expected connection* (IP_CT_RELATED): If the packet is an ICMP message, then the function icmp_reply_translation() is invoked, which does the actual address translation. Otherwise, the packet is handled exactly as in the IP_CT_NEW case.

▨ *New connection* (IP_CT_NEW): The ip_nat_info structure in the connection entry is checked to see whether the address allocation has already been initialized. (This can happen, for example, when a connection establishment packet is retransmitted after a timeout.) If this is not the case, then the function ip_nat_rule_find() initiates the nat netfilter table processing. If the new connection requires address translation, netfilter invokes one of the branch destination functions, ipt_snat_target() or ipt_dnat_target(), to initialize a new address binding. Finally, place_in_hashes() adds the new address to the two hash tables, byipsproto and bysource.

▨ *Other cases*: No new address binding has to be created in any other case. Instead, only the ip_nat_info structure is read from the connection entry, to see whether any address binding applies.

Finally, the last step invokes do_bindings (see Section 21.3.5), which handles the actual address translation; the return value (normally NF_ACCEPT) is passed to the calling function.

21.3.4 Initializing an Address-Binding Process

`ipt_snat_target()`, `ip_dnat_target()`	**net/ipv4/netfilter/ip_nat_rule.c**

The `ipt_snat_target()` and `ipt_dnat_target()` functions are registered branch destinations for the netfilter table, `nat`. This table is processed only if the first packet of a new session flow was registered in `ipt_nat_fn()`. The table uses its rules list to identify session flows subject to source NAT or destination NAT.

Initially, either of the two functions uses `ip_conntrack_get()` to find the corresponding connection entry of the connection-tracking module and then invokes the `ip_nat_setup_info()` function to do a new address binding. The result of this invocation, the address information of the newly assigned binding, is passed to the calling function.

`ip_nat_setup_info()`	**net/ipv4/netfilter/ip_nat_core.c**

This function is invoked by the handling functions for the SNAT and DNAT branch destinations and does essentially three things:

- When the `get_unique_tuple()` (see below) is invoked, it searches for a free address available to do the address translation. If no free address is available, then the value NF_DROP is returned and the packet is dropped.

  To take other address translations into account, the entry for the reverse direction inverted by `invert_tuplepr()` is used as the basis rather than the connection-tracking address entry for the forward direction of the session flow, because the reverse direction entry already includes the translated addresses, in contrast to the forward direction.

- Invoking the `ip_conntrack_alter_reply()` function causes the reverse direction of a connection entry to be altered so that reply packets can be allocated properly to the correct connection, despite its translated address.
- Finally, the new address binding is added to the substructure of the `ip_nat_info` connection entry. The mapping rules (e.g., transformation of source address and source port) result from comparing the original `ip_conntrack_tuple` structure with the new structure, supplied by `get_unique_tuple`.

`get_unique_tuple()`	**net/ipv4/netfilter/ip_nat_core.c**

This function is invoked by `ip_nat_setup_info()` to search for a free address within a specified address range (represented by a structure of the type `ip_nat_multi_range`).

If the function is invoked at the NF_IP_POST_ROUTING hook (i.e., to map the source address), then invoking the function `find_appropriate_src()` checks for whether an address binding exists for the source address (IP address, protocol number, and protocol-specific part) in the `bysource` hash table for that packet. If this binding is within the specified address range, it is returned as a new address entry.

In all other cases, the combination of IP address and protocol number least used within the specified address range is determined by the function find_best_ips_proto_fast(). This function iterates over all possible IP addresses in the address range and uses the byipsproto hash table to check the number of bindings existing at this IP address. If it finds an appropriate IP address, it lets the function ip_nat_used_tuple() check on whether this address is unique and, if the IP_NAT_RANGE_PROTO_SPECIFIED flag is set, whether the protocol-specific part is within the address range (with the help of the protocol-specific function, proto->in_range). If this is the case, then the tuple is returned. If this is not the case, both the new address and the address range are passed to the protocol-specific function, proto->unique_tuple(). Now, this function attempts to vary the protocol-specific part (e.g., TCP port number or ICMP ID) to find a unique combination. If this attempt is unsuccessful, the function uses find_best_ips_proto_fast() to select the next best IP address, and the checking process starts over again. Eventually, if no combination can be found, value 1 is returned, and the packet is dropped.

21.3.5 The Actual Address Translation

do_bindings()	net/ipv4/netfilter/ip_nat_core.c

This function applies the address bindings specified in the ip_nat_info structure to a packet. To this end, it searches the info->manips list for all bindings that belong to the matching direction and the matching hook. Next, it invokes the manip_pkt function to do the appropriate transformations. This function transforms the IP addresses, recalculates the checksum in the IP header, and invokes the proto->manip_pkt() function for the protocol-specific part, which does the actual translation and computes checksums, if present.

Finally, do_bindings() invokes a helper module, if present (e.g., for correct FTP handling—see Section 21.1.7).

21.4 INTERFACES TO EXTEND THE NAT MODULE

The NAT module offers various extension options. These extensions are actually independent modules that can use the registration functions of the NAT module to register and unregister themselves. The following extensions are possible:

- *Transport protocols* (e.g., TCP): To use a new protocol, we have to write two extension modules—one for connection tracking and one for NAT.
- *Helper modules* (helpers): To be able to handle application protocols, such as FTP (see Section 21.1.7), properly, we can register helper modules. Again, this requires one helper each for connection tracking and NAT.
- *Configuration-tool extensions*: In addition, the iptables configuration tool has to be extended by the corresponding command-line parameters for each new protocol and each new helper module. We will not discuss this issue any further.

21.4.1 Transport Protocols

The functions ip_nat_protocol_register() and ip_nat_protocol_unregister() can be used to register a new transport protocol or to unregister an existing protocol. When registering a new protocol, we have to pass a pointer to a structure of the type ip_nat_protocol as a parameter.

struct_ip_nat_protocol	linux/netfilter_ipv4/ip_nat_protocol.h

```
struct_ip_nat_protocol
{
        struct list_head list;

        /* Protocol name */
        const char *name;

        /* Protocol number. */
        unsigned int protonum;

        /* Do a packet translation according to the ip_nat_proto_manip
        * and manip type. */
        void (*manip_pkt)(struct iphdr *iph, size_t len,
                const struct ip_conntrack_manip *manip,
                enum ip_nat_manip_type maniptype);
        /* Is the manipable part of the tuple between min and max incl? */
        int (*in_range)(const struct ip_conntrack_tuple *tuple,
                enum ip_nat_manip_type maniptype,
                const union ip_conntrack_manip_proto *min,
                const union ip_conntrack_manip_proto *max);


        /* Alter the per-proto part of the tuple (depending on
        maniptype), to give a unique tuple in the given range if
        possible; return false if not. Per-protocol part of tuple
        is initialized to the incoming packet. */
        int (*unique_tuple)(struct ip_conntrack_tuple *tuple,
                const struct ip_nat_range *range,
                enum ip_nat_manip_type maniptype,
                const struct ip_conntrack *conntrack);
        unsigned int (*print)(char *buffer,
                const struct ip_conntrack_tuple *match,
                const struct ip_conntrack_tuple *mask);

        unsigned int (*print_range)(char *buffer,
                const struct ip_nat_range *range);
};
```

The list header required to manage the protocol list contains pointers to predecessors and successors and is initially set to {NULL,NULL}.

name is a character string containing the name of the protocol.

protonum is the protocol number that will be entered in the IP header. A list of protocol numbers is normally available in the /etc/protocols file.

manip_pkt is a pointer to a function invoked by the manip_pkt function of the NAT module to manipulate the protocol-specific part of a packet according to the manip parameter. (See Section 21.3.5.)

in_range is a pointer to a function that checks for whether the protocol-specific part of án address (e.g., the TCP port) is within the specified interval [min,max]. Whether the source or destination address will have to be checked is specified of the value of the maniptype parameter (IP_NAT_MANIP_SRC or IP_NAT_MANIP_DST). The function returns value 1 if the condition is met, otherwise 0.

unique_tuple is a pointer to the module's "core function." It is invoked within get_unique_tuple() (see Section 21.3.4) to obtain a unique address by altering the protocol-specific part. The value of the manip type shows whether the source or destination address should change; the respective protocol-specific part of tuple is set to the value of the original tuple.

The protocol-specific part generally is altered according to a simple scheme (e.g., by incrementing the port number for TCP). Subsequently, the function ip_nat_used_tuple() is used to see whether the new address is still free. If so, then the function returns 1; otherwise, it has to return the value 0. If the flag IP_NAT_RANGE_PROTO_SPECIFIED is set, then range also contains information about the range in which the protocol-specific part of the tuple should be. Naturally, this information has to be taken into account.

The two function pointers, print() and print_range(), are invoked when the protocol-specific information in match and mask or range should be output in text form. This informative text should be written to the buffer passed, and the number of output characters should be returned. For example, TCP would invoke this function to output the port numbers.

21.4.2 Helper Modules

A *helper* is a function invoked by the NAT module from within the do_bindings() function, once an address binding has been added (see Section 21.3.5). This allows us to verify the payload of a packet and to modify address transmitted in that packet—for example, to detect PORT commands over an FTP control connection. (See Section 21.1.7.) A helper module is registered by ip_nat_helper_register(), and the only parameter it takes is a data structure of the type ip_nat_helper.

struct ip_nat_helper	linux/netfilter_ipv4/ip_nat_helper.h

```
struct ip_nat_helper
{
        /* Internal use */
        struct list_head list;

        /* Mask of things we will help: vs. tuple from server */
```

```
    struct ip_conntrack_tuple tuple;
    struct ip_conntrack_tuple mask;

    /* Helper function: returns verdict */
    unsigned int (*help)(struct ip_conntrack *ct,
        struct ip_nat_info *info,
        enum ip_conntrack_info ctinfo,
        unsigned int hooknum,
        struct sk_buff **pskb);

    const char *name;
};
```

help is a pointer to the main function of the helper module, which is invoked by do_bindings(), as was mentioned previously.

CHAPTER 22

Extending the Linux Network Architecture Functionality— KIDS

This chapter deals with the introduction of new, dynamically extendable functionalities in the Linux network architecture or in the Linux kernel. We will first show the usual approach to manage dynamically extendable functionalities and the operations generally involved in this approach.

Subsequently, we will use Linux KIDS, the implementation of a construction system to support network services, to show how a dynamically extendable functionality can be managed. Another interesting aspect of Linux KIDS is how its object-oriented concept is implemented in the Linux kernel, considering that the Linux kernel was not designed with object orientation in mind.

In addition, we will explain how the KIDS components can be embedded into the processes of protocol instances over existing interfaces, which means that you can use the functionality of Linux KIDS without having to change the kernel source code. Finally, this chapter describes how you can use a character-oriented device to configure the KIDS construction system, allowing you to easily configure this functionality in the kernel.

22.1 MANAGING DYNAMICALLY EXTENDABLE FUNCTIONALITIES

The Linux network architecture is continually extended by new functions and protocol instances. In most cases, such an extension can even be dynamic (i.e., at runtime), as we saw in earlier chapters: network-layer protocols (Section 6.3), transport-layer protocols (Section 14.2.5), and packet filters (Section 19.3).

All we need to implement such a dynamic extendibility are an appropriate interface and structures that manage the registered functionality. Functions like register_*functionality*() and unregister_*functionality*() can be used to register new functionalities with the kernel or remove existing functionalities.

These registering and unregistering functions execute all initialization or cleanup steps required. For example, when removing a functionality, we have to ensure that it is no longer used in any other location of the kernel. This means that it has to use a reference counter (*use counter*) and check this counter (`use_counter == 0?`) before unregistering a functionality.

The following operations are some of those normally executed in the registration function of an interface and undone, accordingly, in the unregistering functions:

- storing the new functionality of its management structure in a list, hash table, or another data structure;
- reserving memory for the required data structures or procuring other resources (IRQ, DMA, timer, etc.);
- incrementing reference counters;
- creating entries in the proc directory;
- using `printk()` to output status messages.

A new functionality (e.g., a new network-layer protocol or a new network device) normally takes many parameters. It would be difficult the pass all of these parameters individually in the registration function, mainly because they are required while the functionality is being used, which is normally outside the registration function. For this reason, a structure to manage the functionality is normally created. When registering a new functionality, this structure can be entered in a list, hash table, or similar management structures. This method ensures that we can access these functionalities and their parameters after the registration. Earlier chapters introduced a large number of such management structures, including the `net_device` structure for network devices and the `packet_type` structure for network-layer protocols.

Such a management structure is filled with the parameters required before it is registered. Subsequently, a pointer to this management structure is passed to the registration function. The elements of these management structures assume two different tasks:

- *Configuration data* is set before a functionality is registered and passed as (configuration) parameter within the structure. In the `packet_type` structure (Chapter 6), for example, these parameters include the `type` and `func` variables.
- *Runtime variables* are not explicitly set before a functionality is registered. They are needed later when the functionality is used (e.g., `next` to link structures, or a use counter to count references).

After a registration, of course, we can also use configuration variables as runtime variables, if the initial value is no longer needed.

After this brief overview of the principles of how to manage functionalities registered dynamically, the sections following discuss how the KIDS framework is implemented in the Linux kernel 2.4 (Linux KIDS). This framework relies heavily on the concept of dynamically extendable functionalities, as shown in our Linux KIDS example further below. Another interesting point is that the components and their instances are based on the object-oriented concept, and this approach could probably be adopted for other software projects in the Linux kernel. The next section begins with an introduction of its basics to better understand how the KIDS construction system works.

22.2   STRUCTURE OF THE KIDS CONSTRUCTION SYSTEM

KIDS stands for *Karlsruhe Implementation architecture of Differentiated Services* and was developed for the design, evaluation, and use of quality-of-service (QoS) mechanisms in networks [Wehr01b]. KIDS is an abstract model describing the structure and interaction of quality-of-service mechanisms, and it allows you to define individual QoS behavior in a flexible way. The KIDS framework was implemented on various platforms, including Linux (kernel Version 2.4) and the OMNeT++ simulation tool. Though Linux already supports some QoS features (see Chapter 18), KIDS introduces several important benefits, as we will see in the further course of this chapter. The next two sections will introduce the general structure of the KIDS framework; however, we will leave out a few details to keep things short—see [Wehr01a] for details.

22.2.1   Elementary QoS Components

KIDS was designed to create a flexible, extendable, and modular framework for implementing individual QoS mechanisms. It is based on the use of components that implement the elementary QoS mechanisms, and so it is easy to combine them to more complex QoS mechanisms. Simple combination of components and ensuring all potential degrees of freedom and easy extendability were the most important factors in the design of the KIDS framework.

KIDS can be thought of as a construction kit, similarly to the popular Lego system, consisting of components that have different interfaces. Components with similar interfaces can be connected (almost arbitrarily) to form complex constructions (in this case QoS mechanisms).

We can distinguish two different interfaces in the components of the KIDS framework (as seen in Figure 22–1):

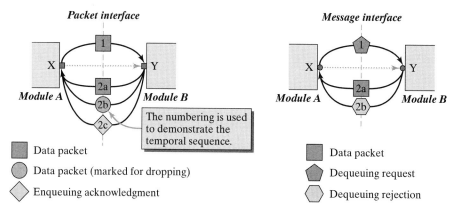

FIGURE 22–1
Interactions at the interfaces between two KIDS components.

▨ At a *packet interface* (□), a component, A, uses packet output X to pass a data packet it received at its input to the successor component, B. By convention, a KIDS component has but a single input.

▨ At a *message interface* (○), component A uses message output X to pass a message to component B, requesting the latter for a packet.

By using these two interface types, we can distinguish five component classes, as shown in Figure 22–2. Each QoS mechanism can be assigned to one of these classes:

▨ *Operative components* (BHVR) operate on packets: They receive a packet and operate their algorithm on this packet. The algorithm implemented in a component either changes the packet (active operative component) or studies its output to forward the packet (passive operative component).

Examples: Token Bucket, Shaper, Marker, Dropper, Classifier, Random Early Detection (RED).

▨ *Queue components* (QUEUE) are data structures used by components to enqueue or dequeue packets.

Examples: FIFO Queue, Earliest-Deadline-First-Queue.

▨ *Enqueuing components* (ENQ_BHVR) enqueue packets in queues based on special methods, which is the reason why they have no outputs.

Examples: Head-Enqueue, Tail-Enqueue, EDF-Enqueue.

▨ *Dequeuing components* (DEQ_BHVR) dequeue packets from a queue based on a special method. They receive a dequeue request on their message input and subsequently try to dequeue a packet from the queue. If successful, the packet is transported from the packet output; otherwise, a negative message is returned.

Examples: Head-Dequeue, Tail-Dequeue.

▨ *Strategic components* (DEQ_DISC) implement special strategies that can be combined in a flexible way to serve queues. This means that they decide on the route for dequeue requests to dequeue components, which eventually serve the queue.

Examples: Priority Queuing, Weighted Fair Queuing, Round Robin.

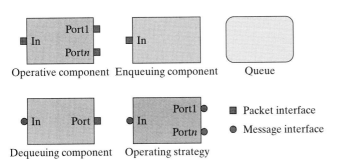

Operative component Enqueuing component Queue

Dequeuing component Operating strategy

■ Packet interface

● Message interface

FIGURE 22–2
Five different KIDS component classes.

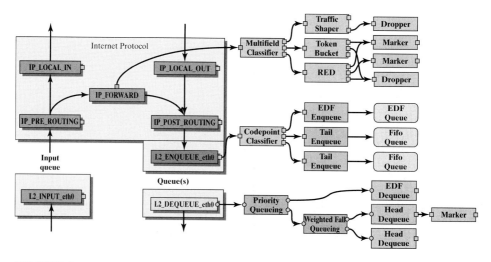

FIGURE 22–3
Example of a KIDS configuration.

By observing relatively simple rules to link components (see [Wehr01a]), we can design complex configurations. Figure 22–3 shows an example for such a configuration; it implements a router that distinguishes three service classes.

22.2.2 Hooks

QoS mechanisms extend the behavior of a protocol instance to enable us to handle packets in a differentiated way and obtain different qualities of service. Though the five component classes of the KIDS framework supply a construction system for flexible linking of QoS components to combine QoS mechanisms, we still don't know how a newly designed QoS mechanism can be integrated into the process of a conventional protocol instance. One of the most important factors is to select a location for the extension of a protocol instance, because we achieve a different set of packets, depending on these locations.

KIDS implements the concept of hooking points—*hooks*, for short—representing a defined extension of existing protocol instances to bind components of the KIDS framework. Figure 22–3 shows five strategic positions in the IP protocol and three in the data link layer, where hooks were integrated to subsequently hook in KIDS components at those points. Section 22.3.4 describes how these hooks were implemented on the basis of different interfaces in the Linux network architecture.

We define three types of hooks:

- *Packet hooks* are used at positions where a packet normally passes without differentiated handling (e.g., IP_FORWARD is passed by all packets to be forwarded).
- *Enqueuing and Dequeuing hooks* are used at positions where we would normally use a FIFO queue (e.g., the output queues of network devices on the data-link layer).

22.3 USING THE KIDS EXAMPLE TO EXTEND THE LINUX NETWORK ARCHITECTURE

Now that we have given a brief overview of the elements in the KIDS framework, this section will discuss its implementation in the Linux kernel as an example of how the functionality of the Linux network architecture can be extended. We focus our discussion on the design and management of the components: how and why they were designed, and how they are introduced to the kernel at runtime. In addition, we will see how hooks are implemented on the basis of different existing kernel interfaces, which means that we don't have to change the kernel to be able to use KIDS. Finally, we use the `kidsd` daemon as an example to show how components and hooks are configured and how they interact between the kernel and the user level.

22.3.1 Components and Their Instances

The KIDS framework offers different types of components that can be used to implement different QoS mechanisms (e.g., token buckets—see Section 18.6.1). A component can occur more than once within a component chain, and each of these occurrences can have different parameters. This means that we should be able to create an arbitrary number of instances from a component, but still try to keep the memory required by these instances low. This principle reminds us strongly of the object-orientation concept that lets you create an arbitrary number of object instances from a class. Although all of these classes exist independently, they have the same behavior, because they use the same methods.

This means that the component concept of Linux KIDS has an object-oriented character, though it was written in C, a programming language that doesn't support object orientation. The component concept of Linux KIDS consists of the following two parts:

- *Components* are QoS mechanisms implementing a specific behavior. They are managed in the `bhvr_type` structure of Linux KIDS. This structure contains all properties of a component (e.g., its behavior in the form of pointers to corresponding methods—shown below). These methods are used by several instances of that component concurrently, so they have to be *reentrant*. Components correspond to the principle of classes in the object-oriented model.
- *Component instances* are created when we need an instance of a component. To this end, we create a data structure of the type `bhvr`. It stores all information about this component instance—mainly, its individual parameter configuration. The instance should have the component's behavior, so reference is made to the information stored in the `bhvr_type` structure of the component. Component instances correspond to objects (or object instances) in the object-oriented model.

The following discussion introduces how these two structures are built and what the parameters mean. Subsequently, we will see how components can be registered or unregistered dynamically.

`struct bhvr_type`   **kids/kids_bhvr.h**

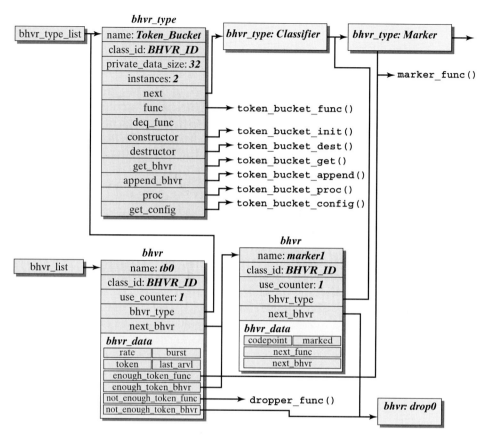

FIGURE 22–4
The bhvr_type and bhvr structures manage components and their instances.

Figure 22–4 shows how components and their instances interact. The bhvr_type structure of the token bucket stores general component information.

```
struct bhvr_type
{
    char                name[STRLEN];
    unsigned int        bhvr_class_id;
    unsigned long       private_data_size;
    unsigned int        instances;
    struct bhvr_type    *next;
    int                 (*func)(struct bhvr *, struct sk_buff *);
    struct sk_buff*     (*deq_func)(struct bhvr *);
    int                 (*constructor)(struct bhvr *bhvr, char * data, int flag);
    int                 (*destructor)(struct bhvr *bhvr);
    struct bhvr*        (*get_bhvr)(struct bhvr *bhvr, char * port);
```

```
int                (*append_bhvr)(struct bhvr *new_bhvr, struct bhvr
                       *old_bhvr, char *port);
int                (*proc)(struct bhvr *bhvr, char *ptr, int layer);
int                (*get_config)(struct bhvr *bhvr, char *ptr);
};
```

The fields have the following meaning:

- name is the name of the component (e.g., Token_Bucket).
- bhvr_class_id contains the component's class. (see Section 22.2.1.) Possible values are BHVR_ID, ENQ_BHVR_ID, DEQ_BHVR_ID, DEQ_DISC_ID, and QUEUE_ID.
- private_data_size specifies the size of the private data structure used in the bhvr structure for each instance of a component. Preferably, a separate private structure should be defined here (e.g., tb_data—see below), and a sizeof instruction to specify the size of this structure should be inserted in this position.
- instances manages the number of instances created from a component. This variable is managed by Linux KIDS. It should show a value of 0 when a component is removed from the kernel.
- next is also used internally, namely to link bhvr_type structures in the bhvr_type_list. (See Figure 22–4.)

The following elements of the bhvr_type structure are function pointers that specify the behavior of a component and are used to managing it.

- func(bhvr, skb) refers to a function that is invoked when a packet (or a socket buffer, skb) is passed to an instance (bhvr) of this component. It implements the functionality of this component type. A socket buffer is passed when func() is invoked. This means that this function corresponds to the implementation of a packet interface and is used only for operative components and enqueuing components. Section 22.3.5 uses an example introducing the func() method of the Token-Bucket component.

  The bhvr parameter contains a pointer to the bhvr structure of the component instance, which is passed to the socket buffer, skb, when the func() function is invoked. Because the func() method is used for all instances of the Token_Bucket component, the pointer to the instance-specific information also has to be passed. Otherwise, it would be impossible to see which instances, with what parameter or variable assignments, is meant.

- deq_func(bhvr) is used for dequeuing and strategic components. It corresponds to the implementation of a message interface and is invoked when a packet is requested from an instance (bhvr) of this component. A component implements only one of two functions, either func() or deq_func(), depending on whether its input has a packet interface or a message interface.

- constructor(bhvr, data, flag) is invoked when a bhvr instance of this component is initialized or when its configuration changed. This method takes the character-string data with the component's private data to be configured as parameters. The `flag` parameter shows whether this is the first initialization of this instance (`INIT_BHVR`) or it is a change to its parameters at runtime, where only the information passed should be altered.

- `destructor(bhvr)` is invoked to destroy the `bhvr` instance of the component. All cleanup work required (e.g., free memory or deactivate timer) should be done at this point.

- `get_bhvr(bhvr, port)` is invoked by KIDS to obtain a pointer to the `bhvr` structure of the component instance appended to the output, `port`. The number and names of a component's outputs are individual, so we have to implement a component-specific function.

- `append_bhvr(new_bhvr, old_bhvr, port)` connects the `new_bhvr` component instance to the output, `port`, of the existing component instance, `old_bhvr`. Again, we have to implement separate functions for the individual outputs of a component.

- `proc(bhvr, ptr, layer)` creates information about the `bhvr` component instance. This information can be output from `proc` files. The `layer` parameter specifies the distance from the component instance to the hook; this is required for indenting within the output. The `ptr` pointer specifies the buffer space this output should be written to. (See Section 2.8.)

- `get_config(bhvr, ptr)` is invoked by KIDS to write the configuration of the `bhvr` component instance to the `ptr` buffer space, based on the KIDS configuration syntax (see Section 22.3.6).

`struct bhvr`	`kids/kids_bhvr.h`

Each of the `bhvr` structures representing the specific instances of a component manages the information of a component instance (e.g., name on number of references). The `bhvr` data structure is built as follows:

```
struct bhvr
{
        char                    name[STRLEN];
        unsigned int            use_counter;
        struct bhvr             *next_bhvr;
        struct bhvr_type        *bhvr_type;
        char                    bhvr_data[0];
};
```

The fields have the following meaning:

- `name`: The name of this instance (e.g., `tb0` or `marker1`);

- `use_counter` specifies the number of direct predecessors of this component instance—the number of references to this `bhvr` structure.

- `next_bhvr` is used to link the individual `bhvr` data structures in the `bhvr_list`. This list is managed by KIDS and used to search for a component by its name (`get_bhvr_by_name()`).

■ bhvr_type points to the relevant bhvr_type structure, representing the type of this component instance. This means that this pointer specifies the behavior of the component instance, which is registered in the bhvr_type structure.

■ bhvr_data is a placeholder for the private information of this component instance (as is shown later). No type can be specified, because the structure of each component's information is individual. A *type cast* is required before each access—for example,

struct tb_data *data = (struct tb_data *) &(tb_bhvr->bhvr_data);}

The private information space is directly adjacent to the bhvr structure. The length of private information is taken into account for reserving the memory of the bhvr structure. As was mentioned earlier, it is managed in the bhvr_type structure.

Using the Token-Bucket Component as an Example for a Private Data Structure   The data structure containing private information (bhvr_data) is of particular importance. Its structure depends on the respective component, because it stores that component's parameters and runtime variables. Because all instances of a component have the same variables, though with different assignments, this data structure is stored in the instances (i.e., in the bhvr structures), and its length (which is identical for all instances of a component) is stored in the bhvr_type structure.

This tells us clearly that all information concerning the state or configuration of a special component instance is managed in the instance itself in the private data structure of the bhvr structure.

The following example represents the private data structure of the Token_Bucket component:

```
struct tb_data
{
    unsigned int    rate, bucket_size;
    unsigned long   token, packets_arvd, packets_in, packets_out;
    CPU_STAMP       last_arvl, cycles_per_byte;
    struct bhvr     *enough_token_bhvr;
    struct bhvr     *not_enough_token_bhvr;
    int             (*enough_token_func)(struct bhvr *, struct sk_buff *);
    int             (*not_enough_token_func)(struct bhvr *, struct sk_buff *);
};
```

The meaning of each of the variables in such a private data structure can be divided into three groups:

■ The parameter and runtime variables of a component are individual in that the component implements a special algorithm. This is the reason why they are managed in a private data structure of the component, which exists separately in each of that component's instances. Examples for parameter and runtime variables include the rate and bucket_size variables in the Token-Bucket component.

▓ In addition, private information manages the following two elements for *each component output*, because the number of outputs is also individual to the respective component and so it cannot be accommodated in the bhvr_type structure:

▷ The first element is a *function pointer* to the func() function (for a packet interface) or deq_func() (for a message interface) in the subsequent component instance. This means that a component instance stores a reference to the handling routine for the component instance appended to this output.

▷ The second element is a *reference* to the bhvr_structure of the subsequent component instance at this output. This pointer is used eventually to link the component instances.

The reference to the handling routine of the subsequent component instance is actually not required, because it can be identified over the bhvr_type pointer from the corresponding structure of the successor. However, this double unreferencing method is saved at the cost of an additional pointer, for performance reasons. If no component instance is appended to an output, then the two variables take the value NULL, and a packet to be forwarded is recursively returned to the hook. (See Section 22.3.5.)

22.3.2 Registering and Managing Components

Before we can use Linux KIDS to implement the desired QoS mechanisms, we have to tell the kernel which components are currently available. To this end, Linux KIDS maintains a list, bhvr_type_list, to manage all registered components. This list is based on simple linking of the respective bhvr_type data structures that store the entire information about components. (see Figure 22–4.) Linking of the data structures into a list corresponds to the normal approach to manage functionalities in the Linux kernel. (see Section 22.1.)

We can use the function register_bhvr_type(bhvr_type) to register a component represented by a bhvr_type structure. (See Figure 22–5.) More specifically, the bhvr_type structure is entered in the bhvr_type_list. (See Figure 22–4.) From then on, this component is known in the kernel, and we can create instances of that component. To remove a component from the list, we can invoke unregister_bhvr_type(bhvr_type). Of course, we have to ensure that there are no instances of the component left before we remove it, which is the reason why the instances variable has to be checked first.

In addition to the list of component categories, Linux KIDS has two other elements that can be used to register or unregister functionalities dynamically. To prevent this chapter from getting too long, we will discuss these two elements only briefly. They are managed similarly to the previous elements:

▓ *Hooks* are represented by the hook data structure; they are registered by register_hook(hook) and unregistered by unregister_hook(hook). If a protocol instance wants to supply a hook, it simulates a packet interface or message interface,

```
struct bhvr_type token_bucket_element = {
    "Token_Bucket",                         /* name                */
    BHVR_ID,                                /* class               */
    sizeof(struct token_bucket_data),       /* private data size   */
    0,                                      /* instances           */
    NULL,                                   /* next                */
    token_bucket_func,                      /* packet interface    */
    NULL,                                   /* message interface   */
    token_bucket_init,                      /* constructor         */
    NULL,                                   /* destructor          */
    token_bucket_get,                       /* get bhvr of a port  */
    token_bucket_append,                    /* append bhvr on a port */
    token_bucket_proc,                      /* proc output routine */
    token_bucket_config                     /* get config of a bhvr */
};


int init_module(void) {
    register_bhvr_type(&token_bucket_element);
}


void cleanup_module(void) {
    unregister_bhvr_type(&token_bucket_element);
}
```

FIGURE 22–5

builds an appropriate hook data structure, and registers the hook. Subsequently, components can be appended to this hook. The files `kids/layer2_hooks.c` and `kids/nf_hooks.c` include examples for hooks based on the TC or netfilter interface.

Different *queue categories* are managed by the `kids_queue_type` data structure; we can use `register_queue_type()` to register or `unregister_queue_type()` to unregister them. An instance of a queue variant is represented by a `kids_queue` structure. The management of queues is almost identical to that of component categories, but components and queues are different, so it was found necessary to manage them separately.

22.3.3   Managing Component Instances

The previous section described how we can register and manage components in Linux KIDS; this section discusses how we can manage instances of components—how component instances are created, deleted, and linked. A special syntax was developed to keep the managing of the QoS mechanisms as simple as possible. Section 22.3.6 will introduce this syntax. A character-oriented device, /dev/kids, is used to pass configuration commands to Linux KIDS and to invoke one of the methods introduced below.

create_bhvr()	kids/kids_bhvr.c

`create_bhvr(type, name, data, id)` creates an instance of the `type` component designated by `name`. For creating this instance, that component has to be present in the list of registered components (`bhvr_type_list`).

Initially, storage space is reserved for the data of the new component instance. This memory space consists of a `bhvr` structure that is identical for all components and a private data structure that is individual to each component. Subsequently, the `bhvr` structure is initialized, and the constructor of the component occupying this private data with this component's configuration parameters is invoked. These configuration parameters were extracted from the `CREATE` command and passed in the `data` character string. Once it has been created, the component is no longer connected to any other component. Finally, it is added to the `bhvr_list`.

`remove_bhvr()`	**kids/kids_bhvr.c**

`remove_bhvr(name, force)` deletes the component instance designated by `name` and removes it from the `bhvr_list`. `force` can be specified to state that the `use_counter` of that instance should be ignored, as normally should not be the case, because there could still be references to this data structure. Before the data structure is released, the component's destructor is invoked to free resources, if present.

`change_bhvr()`	**kids/kids_bhvr.c**

`change_bhvr(name, data)` can be used to alter the private data of a component instance at runtime. All that happens here, however, is that the `data` character string holding the information to be changed invokes the constructor. The `INIT_BHVR` flag is not set; thus, the constructor knows that only the parameters specified have to be altered. Otherwise, the entire component instance would be reset.

22.3.4 Implementing Hooks

Hooks are extensions of existing protocol instances allowing us to easily embed QoS components based on the rules of the KIDS framework [Wehr01a]. One of the most important factors is the position we want to extend by a hook—and thus by QoS mechanisms—within the process of a protocol instance. The reason is that we can always address a certain number of packets at specific positions (e.g., all packets to be forwarded, at the `IP_FORWARD` hook, or all packets of the IP instance to be delivered locally, at the `IP_LOCAL_DELIVER` hook).

Thanks to its set of different interfaces, the Linux network architecture offers an inherent way to extend a protocol instance by a functionality. These interfaces have been utilized in the KIDS framework, and so the hooks shown in Figure 22–3 could be implemented without the need to change the source code of the Linux kernel. The hooks for the IP instance are based on the netfilter interface (see Section 19.3); the data-link layer hooks are based on the Traffic Control interface.

The following example represents the netfilter handling method of the `IP_FORWARD` hook. It merely checks for whether a component instance is appended and invokes that instance, if present:

```
unsigned int ip_forward_hook_fn(unsigned int hooknum, struct sk_buff **skb, ...)
{
    if (ip_forward_hook && ip_forward_hook->bhvr && ip_forward_hook->func)
            return ip_forward_hook->func(ip_forward_hook->bhvr, skb[0]);
    else
            return NF_ACCEPT;
};
```

Additional hooks can be integrated easily, even at runtime. To integrate a hook, we have to store the information required about the hook in a hook data structure and use the `register_hook()` method to register it. The protocol instance we want to extend is then simply extended by a function call, structured similarly to the above example with the `IP_FORWARD` hook. You can find additional information about the concept of hooks in [Wehr01a].

22.3.5   How a Component Works

Once we have registered all components of the KIDS framework with the kernel and created a component chain and appended it to a hook, we need a description of how such a component should operate. The following example uses a packet in the `Token_Bucket` component to describe how this component operates:

`token_bucket_func()`	**kids/std_bhvr.c**

```
int token_bucket_func(struct bhvr *tb_bhvr, struct sk_buff *skb)
{
    struct tb_data  *data = (struct tb_data *) &(tb_bhvr->bhvr_data);
    CPU_STAMP       now;

    data->packets_arvd++;
    TAKE_TIME(now);
     /* calcs the tokens, that are produced since the last packet arrival */
    (unsigned long) data->token += (((unsigned long) (now - data->last_arvl)) /
                                (unsigned long) data->cycles_per_byte);

    /* check, if the bucket is overflood */
    if (data->token > data->bucket_size)
        data->token = data->bucket_size;
    data->last_arvl = now;

    /* check, if there are enough tokens to send the packet */
    if (data->token < skb->len)
```

```
{   /* not enough tokens -> out of profile */
    data->packets_out++;
    /* forward the packet to the next behavior (out-of-profile) */
    if ((data->not_enough_token_bhvr) && (data->not_enough_token_func))
        return data->not_enough_token_func(data->not_enough_token_bhvr, skb);
}
else
{   /* enough tokens -> in profile */
    data->token -= skb->len;
    data->packets_in++;
    /* forward the packet to the next behavior (in-profile) */
    if ((data->enough_token_bhvr ) && (data->enough_token_func))
        return data->enough_token_func(data->enough_token_bhvr, skb);
}
return KIDS_ACCEPT; /* Do not discard packet, when no behavior is attached */
}
```

The Token_Bucket component belongs to the operative component class, which means that it has a packet input and up to *n* packet outputs. In this example, these are the Conform and Non_Conform outputs.

When an instance of the Token_Bucket component receives a packet, the corresponding func() handling routine is invoked, as shown in the example. The parameters it gets include the socket buffer, skb, and a pointer to the data in the component instance (bhvr). At the very beginning, a pointer to the instance's private data is set from within this pointer, which requires a *type cast*. Since the function has to be fully reentrant, it must operate only on its own private data or local variables.

Subsequently, computations according to the token bucket algorithm (see Section 18.6.1) are done, and statistic variables are updated. The result from these computations determines the output that should be used to forward the socket buffer (i.e., the kind of handling to follow). If no instance is appended to the corresponding output, the function returns the KIDS_ACCEPT result, which means that the packet was processed and should now be forwarded to the hook. The counterpart is KIDS_DROP; it tells the hook that it should drop the socket buffer.

However, if a component instance follows at the desired output (data->..._bhvr != NULL), then that instance's handling routine is invoked (data->..._func()), and a pointer to the data of the subsequent instance is passed to this handling routine, in addition to the socket buffer. The return value of the subsequent component instance is used immediately for the return value of the token-bucket component.[1]

Linux KIDS handles packets in component chains via these nested function calls. Figure 22–6 shows this once more schematically. A description of the enqueuing and dequeuing hooks would go beyond the scope and volume of this chapter. We refer our readers to [Wehr01a].

---

[1]Of course, as an alternative, the token bucket could evaluate the call's result, however, this is not implemented yet. In the case of a packet marked to be dropped (KIDS_DROP), for example, it could put the tokens used by this packet back into the bucket.

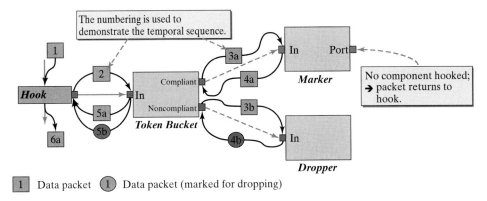

1 Data packet   (1) Data packet (marked for dropping)

FIGURE 22–6
Component instances interacting at a packet hook.

22.3.6 Configuring KIDS Components

This section briefly introduces how component chains are configured in Linux KIDS. The first question we have to answer is how configuration information gets from the user to the appropriate positions in the kernel. Various methods are available, including new system calls and special socket interfaces. Linux KIDS uses a different and very simple method, one based on a character-oriented device. (See Section 2.5.)

First, we create a character-oriented device, /dev/kids. On the user level, this device is explained in [RuCo01].

To configure Linux KIDS, we use the following commands, which can either be written directly into /dev/kids or sent to the KIDS daemon, kidsd, over a TCP connection. This daemon will then pass our commands on to the kernel.

- CREATE *bhvr_class bhvr_type bhvr_name* DATA *private data** END

  creates an instance of the *bhvr_type* component (e.g., Token_Bucket) and initializes this instance with the private data specified in the command. Possible component classes (*bhvr_class*) include BHVR, QUEUE, ENQ_BHVR, DEQ_BHVR, and DEQ_DISC—for example,

  CREATE BHVR Token_Bucket tb1 DATA Rate 64000 Bucket_Size 5000 END

- REMOVE *bhvr_class bhvr_name* END

  removes the specified component, if it has no successors.

- CHANGE *bhvr_class bhvr_name* DATA *private data* END

  changes the specified data of the component instance, *bhvr_name*. This command changes nothing to the existing structure; it merely accesses the private data of the specified instance.

▨ CONNECT *bhvr_class* *bhvr_name* TO *bhvr_class* *bhvr_name* port | HOOK *hook_name* END

connects the input of the *bhvr_name* instance to the output, *port*, of the specified instance following next, or to the specified hook, *hook_name*. One single instance can be connected to several outputs or hooks. However, only one single component instance can be appended to each output or hook.

▨ DISCONNECT *bhvr_class* *bhvr_name* port END

deletes the connection on the specified output. The REMOVE command can delete a component instance only provided that all links have been deleted.

IPv6—Internet Protocol Version 6

23.1 INTRODUCTION

Several years have passed since RFC 791 for IPv4 was published. During this time, the requirements on the IP version used in the Internet have changed considerably. For example, the address space for 32-bit IPv4 addresses is almost depleted, in particularly because each mobile device, or even each household device, is expected to get its own IP address. In addition, the transmission technologies in fixed networks have so matured that packet errors have virtually been eradicated. These facts were motivation for further development beyond IPv4 to the protocol for the future Internet, resulting in IPv6. Since 1998, several standards have been introduced for IPv6, and the bases for these standards are the following RFCs:

- RFC 2460 [HiDe98a] specifies IPv6.
- RFC 2373 [HiDe98b] describes the architecture for IPv6 addressing.

23.2 IPv6 FEATURES

The new IP version was improved in many important points, but this protocol has been used in the real world only to a limited extent. One of the reasons is that existing applications cannot run directly on top of IPv6. The most important changes from IPv4 are the following:

- *Extended address size*: Instead of 32 bits, each IPv6 address contains 128 bits, enabling several hierarchical levels and addressing a much larger number of nodes. In addition, the IPv6 address of each node can be configured automatically. The support of multicast routing has been improved. Moreover, a new address type, the *anycast address*, was defined, which allows you to send a packet to an arbitrary node from within a group.

    Simplified header format: Some of the IPv4 packet-header fields are no longer supported, or are now optional, to reduce the cost involved in processing IPv6 packets.

    Extension headers: The way IPv6 encodes information is completely different from that in IPv4, enabling more efficient forwarding, less strict limitations with regard to the length of options, and more flexibility for new, future packet options.

    Flow labeling: IPv6 is able to mark packets that belong to a specific stream. This allows the sender to request special handling of these packets, enabling a much better support of service qualities, such as priority handling or real-time services.

    Authentication and data protection: IPv6 specifies extensions to support authentication, integrity, and confidentiality of data.

23.2.1 Addressing

The address space, extended from 2^{32} (IPv4) to 2^{128} (IPv6) addresses, requires a new address notation. The preferred and abbreviated notation is the hexadecimal notation (e.g., FEDC:BA98:7654:3210:FEDC:BA98:7654:3120). Each group (i.e., one block between two colons, or between the beginning/end and a colon) represents 16 bits. Leading zeros can be omitted, so one group can consist of one to four hexadecimal numbers. In addition, it is assumed that many consecutive blocks consist of zeros, so a compressed notation was introduced: Each address may contain at most one occurrence of two consecutive colons. In between, as many zeros as necessary are used to reach the full length of an address. The following examples show this notation (the meaning of each of these addresses will be discussed further below):

    A "loopback" address:

        ::1 or 0:0:0:0:0:0:0:1 = 0000:0000:0000:0000:0000:0000:0000:0001

    A normal address:

        F83:5::12 or F83:5:0:0:0:0:0:12
        = 0F83:0005:0000:0000:0000:0000:0000:0012

Alternatively, addresses can be represented in mixed form, composed of the new hexadecimal notation and the decimal IPv4 notation. The format is then x:x:x:x:x:x:d.d.d.d, where x represents the hexadecimal groups of IPv6 and d stands for the decimal IPv4 convention. One example would be 0:0:0:0:0:FFFF:129.13.64.5 (or ::FFFF:129.13.64.5 in the abbreviated form). How useful this is becomes obvious if you think of embedding IPv4 in IPv6.

As does IPv4, IPv6 supports unicast and multicast addresses. A new form of communication introduced in IPv6 is *anycast*. Anycast is a mixture of unicast and multicast: A packet is sent to *one* computer in a multicast group, where the network itself decides which computer this is. The "broadcast" address of IPv4 (255.255.255.255) doesn't exist in IPv6. This functionality, which was used mainly by ARP (*Address Resolution Protocol*) to resolve IP addresses, is achieved by use of multicast addresses in IPv6.

ARP is no longer supported in IPv6. It was replaced by *Neighbor Discovery*, which was integrated into ICMPv6.

The structuring of the IPv6 address space is implemented by *prefixes*. A prefix is a sort of logical interconnection of a network, similarly to the subnetworks known from IPv4. A prefix virtually groups all IPv6 nodes with addresses beginning in the same way. For example, almost all IPv4 addresses of the Karlsruhe University begin with 129.13, using the notation 129.13.0.0/16. Subnetworks in IPv6 are denoted accordingly. The number of leading bits denoting the network are written after the complete IPv6 address and a slash. For example, the University of Münster, Germany, has the 6bone prefix 3FFE:400:10::/48. Normally, the bits in an address not belonging to the prefix are set to null; however, stating a complete address denotes the IPv6 address of a computer connected to the subnetwork specified by the prefix. In this representation, it is important to note that the compressed notation is also extended to 128 bits, rather than to the prefix length. This means that 3::16/64 is the subnetwork with prefix 0003:0000:0000:0000 and not prefix 0003:0000:0000:0016.

We can basically distinguish between multicast addresses and "other" addresses. Multicast addresses begin with eight ones (= FF:). All other addresses are unicast or anycast addresses, and which of the two is the case cannot be told from the address itself. The lower 64 bits of all (nonmulticast) addresses not beginning with the bit string 000 must have an interface identifier corresponding to the *EUI-64 format*; for Ethernet, this would be the MAC address of the network card.

Like IPv4, IPv6 uses special addresses required for specific purposes:

* *Unspecified* (:: = 0:0:0:0:0:0:0:0)

   This address, entirely consisting of zeros, does not stand for a real address, but for the absence of it. It must be selected only for source addresses and is used, for example, to configure the address of a computer automatically.

* *Loopback* (::1)

   Similarly, the loopback address does not stand for an actual network address either; it is used by a computer to send packets to itself. For this reason, it is inadmissible to send packets with the source or destination address set to ::1 to other computers. In addition, it would not be meaningful to use this address for a network interface. IPv6-capable routers have to drop such packets.

* IPv4-compatible addresses (::d.d.d.d)

   To be able to dynamically tunnel IPv6 packets over an existing IPv4 infrastructure, special IPv4-compatible IPv6 unicast addresses are assigned to the computers involved. These IPv6 addresses contain the IPv4 address in the lower 32 bits of their address; the remaining bits are set to null.

* Embedded IPv4 addresses (::FFFF:d.d.d.d)

   On the IPv6 side, an embedded IPv4 address is assigned to all computers actually supporting IPv4 only, so that these computers can be addressed by IPv6 computers. This addressing type is also called *IPv4 mapped IPv6 Address*; it consists of 80 zeros, 16 ones, and finally the 32-bit IPv4 address.

▓ Local addresses (FE80::x:x:x:x, FEA0::x:x:x:x)

▶ *Link-local addresses* (FE80::x:x:x:x)

A link-local address is uniquely allocated to an interface directly connected to the network. Its prefix is FE80::/64, and the remaining bits hold an EUI-64-compliant address. The link-local address can be used exclusively for this interface and in the connected network. It serves primarily for automatic address configuration, for neighbor discovery, and for networks without routers.

▶ *Site-local addresses* (FEA0::x:x:x:x)

Site-local addresses are designed for networks that do not require a global prefix, which means that they are not reachable from the outside. The format for these addresses has an EUI-64-compliant address in the lower 64 bits, and a 16-bit wide subnetwork number between the prefix, FEA0::, and the EUI-64-compliant address. Routers may not transport packets with local source or destination addresses beyond the corresponding network.

23.2.2 IPv6 Packet Header

The IPv6 packet header includes 40 bytes in total, as shown in Figure 23–1. It is interesting that an IPv6 packet header fewer less fields than a comparable IPv4 packet header, which includes twelve fields in its 20 bytes, excluding packet options. The slimmer packet header in IPv6 reduces the cost involved in handling IPv6 packets in routers.

The Version field defines the version of the IP protocol used; it is set to Version = 0x06 for IPv6. The TOS (Type Of Service) field known from IPv4 is called Traffic Class in IPv6. It is used to identify different classes or priorities of IPv6 packets and is set to

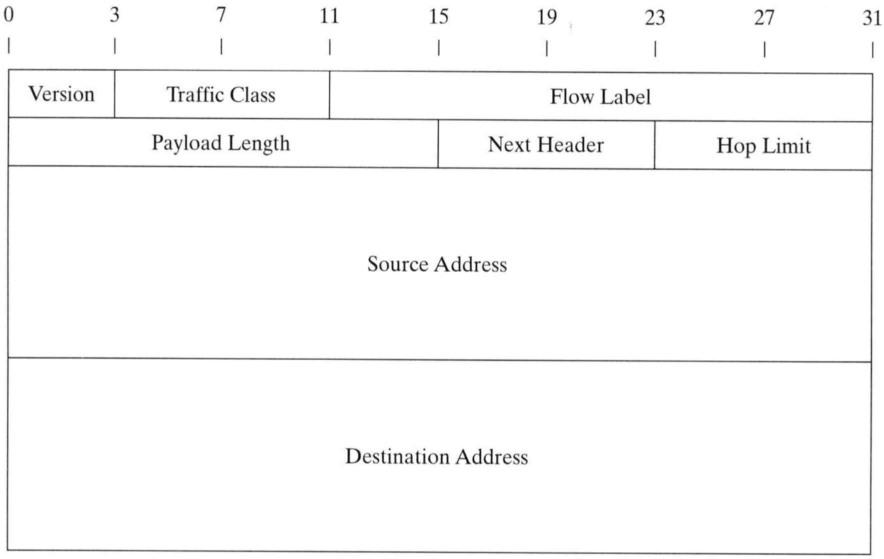

```
0      3      7      11     15     19     23     27     31
|      |      |      |      |      |      |      |      |

┌──────────┬──────────────┬──────────────────────────────────┐
│ Version  │ Traffic Class│            Flow Label             │
├──────────┴──────────┬───┴──────────────────┬───────────────┤
│   Payload Length    │      Next Header      │   Hop Limit   │
├─────────────────────┴──────────────────────┴───────────────┤
│                                                             │
│                                                             │
│                     Source Address                          │
│                                                             │
│                                                             │
├─────────────────────────────────────────────────────────────┤
│                                                             │
│                                                             │
│                   Destination Address                       │
│                                                             │
│                                                             │
└─────────────────────────────────────────────────────────────┘
```

FIGURE 23–1
The IPv6 packet header.

0x00 by default. The semantics of this field corresponds to the TOS field: *codepoints* in the Differentiated Services architecture are equally mapped to the TOS and the Traffic Class fields. The Flow Label field can be used to mark a related stream of IPv6 packets. These packets are then treated accordingly in the routers on their way to the receiver. This means that we can support QoS for individual packet streams (e.g., to support real-time services in a network). RFC 2460 does not specify the semantics of this field in detail. The Payload Length field is 16 bits wide and specifies the length of a packet (in bytes), excluding the packet header. It takes packet-header extensions into account, if present. The Next Header field specifies the type of "data" following after the IPv6 packet header: This can be either a packet-header extension (see next section) or pure payload specified by the higher-layer transport protocol (e.g., TCP). In this case, the values of the Protocol field known from IPv4 are used. (See RFC 1700 [RePo94].) The TTL (Time To Live) field in the IPv4 packet header corresponds to the Hop Limit field in IPv6, which serves a similar purpose: Each IPv6 router decrements the Hop Limit field. Once it has reached the value 0, the IPv6 packet is dropped, and an ICMPv6 error message is returned to the sender. Finally, the IPv6 packet header includes two 128-bit fields for the sender (Source Address) and receiver (Destination Address) addresses.

23.2.3   Packet-Header Extensions

IPv6 encodes optional information of the Internet layer in separate packet-header extensions, placed between the IPv6 packet header and the payload. The set of different packet-header extensions used is designated by different Next-Header values.

An IPv6 packet can have several extension headers, each determined by the Next Header field of the previous packet header or the previous packet-header extension. This is the reason why this field exists in each packet-header extension. Figure 23–2 shows how packet-header extensions are used. The length of each packet-header extension has to be a multiple of 8 bytes.

Packet-header extensions are processed in the sequence of their occurrence and only in the destination host, except for the *Hop-by-Hop* packet-header extension. For this reason, the *Hop-by-Hop* packet-header extension must be at the first position, if present. A full IPv6 implementation has to include the following packet-header extensions: *Hop-by-Hop Options, Destination Options, Routing, Fragment, Authentication Header*, and *Encapsulating Security Payload*. Except for the last two, all of these packet-header extensions will be discussed below.

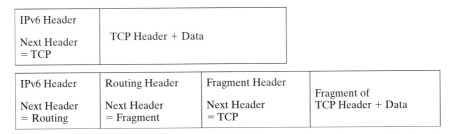

FIGURE 23–2
Examples of using IPv6 packet-header extensions.

Hop-by-Hop Options and Destination Options   The *Hop-by-Hop Options* and *Destination Options* packet-header extensions hold optional information relevant for the nodes on the way to the receiver. The *Hop-by-Hop Options* are processed in each IPv6 router along the delivery path; the *Destination Options* are processed in the receiver of an IPv6 packet. Both header extensions have the same format; they differ only in the Next Header field of the previous packet-header extension. The following values are defined for this Next Header field:

- Hop-by-Hop Options: 0x00
- Destination Options: 0x3C

Both packet-header extensions have the following format:

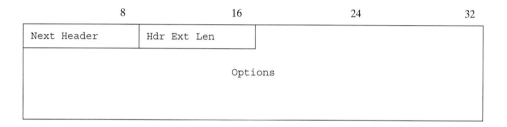

The length of these packet header extensions can be variable, so Hdr Ext Len specifies the length of a packet-header extension, in 8-byte blocks (excluding the first 8 bytes). The Options block includes one or several encoded option(s). The original specification of IPv6 (RFC 2460) defines two options used essentially for data *padding* to align subsequent packet-header extensions accordingly. One of these options, PAD1, corresponds to a sequence of eight zeros (i.e., 0x00); the second option (PADN) pads to an arbitrary length (in bytes) and is composed of three : 0x01 to designate PADN, the length of padded data (1 byte; includes the length without the first two bytes), and the subsequent "padding data."

Routing   The *Routing* packet-header extension is used to specify a number of nodes (routers) that a packet has to visit along the way to its final destination. This corresponds to the *Source Routing* option in IPv4. The *Routing* packet header extension is identified by the Next Header value 0×2B (in the previous packet-header extension) and has the following format:

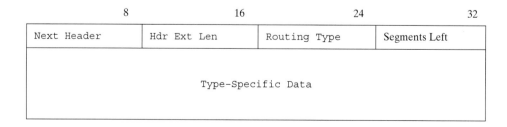

Again, the Hdr Ext Len field specifies the length of this packet-header extension in 8-byte blocks, excluding the first 8 bytes. Routing Type specifies the variant of the Routing packet-header extension. RFC 2460 standardizes only *Loose Source Routing* (known from IPv4) to Routing Type = 0×00. The Segments Left parameter holds the number of explicitly defined nodes a packet still has to visit. The last field holds type-specific information: the addresses of nodes left along the path (in addition to four reserved bytes, in the case of *Loose Source Routing*).

How an IPv6 packet that includes the Routing packet-header extension is forwarded can best be explained by a simple practical example. Assume that an IPv6 packet should be transported from the sender, S, over nodes R1 and R2 to the receiver, R. These nodes are addressed directly in the IPv6 packet header, and the Routing packet-header extension specifies the previous and subsequent destinations, including the end system. Each addressed node replaces the IPv6 receiver address by an entry for the next hop, and then replaces this entry by its IPv6 address. In this example, the IPv6 packet would be composed as follows in the respective stations:

- *Node S*: Source = S, Destination = R1, Segments Left = 2, Address[1] = R2, Address[2] = R.
- *Node R1*: Source = S, Destination = R2, Segments Left = 1, Address[1] = R1, Address[2] = R.
- *Node R2*: Source = S, Destination = R, Segments Left = 0, Address[1] = R1, Address[2] = R2.
- *Node R*: Source = S, Destination = R, Segments Left = 0, Address[1] = R1, Address[2] = R2.

Fragment The *Fragment* packet-header extension is required for sending an IPv6 packet to a receiver when its size is larger than the maximum packet size (*Maximum Transfer Unit—MTU*) of a connection on the route used. In contrast to IPv4, an IPv6 packet is fragmented by the sender only, never in the routers it traverses along the way. The *Fragment* packet-header extension is specified by the Next Header value 0x2C and looks like this:

8	16	29	31	32
Next Header	Reserved	Fragment Offset	Res	M
Identification				

Each of the two reserved fields has to be initialized to null. The 13-bit Fragment Offset specifies the offset (in 8-byte units) of the data following this packet-header extension in relation to the fragmentable part of the original packet. The M bit specifies whether more fragments are to follow (M = 1) or this is the last fragment of an IPv6 packet (M = 0). This corresponds to the segmenting and reassembling in IPv4. The Identification field identifies packets belonging together by a unique number. This number must be assigned only once for each sender/receiver relationship during a packet's lifetime, to avoid confusion with other fragmented IPv6 packets. The details are left to the implementation.

A simple example will help us better understand how fragmenting in IPv6 works. Assume that an IPv6 packet consists of a nonfragmentable part and a fragmentable part. The nonfragmentable part includes the IPv6 packet header and all packet-header extensions that will have to be processed by each node along the route (i.e., all extensions but the Routing header extension). The fragmentable part of this IPv6 packet is decomposed into fragments. Each of these fragments, except the last fragment (bit M = 0), is a multiple of 8 bytes. The resulting fragments will then look like this:

IPv6 Header + Hdr Ext	Fragment Header	First Fragment

IPv6 Header + Hdr Ext	Fragment Header	Second Fragment

...

IPv6 Header + Hdr Ext	Fragment Header	Last Fragment

Sequence of Packet-Header Extensions   In general, an IPv6-capable node has to be able to process packet-header extensions in any arbitrary sequence, even in case of multiple occurrence. One exception is the packet-header extension of the type *Hop-by-Hop Options*. However, RFC 2460 recommends the following sequence:

1. IPv6 packet header
2. *Hop-by-Hop Options*
3. *Routing* packet header extension
4. *Fragment* packet header extension
5. *Destination Options*
6. *Authentication Header*
7. *Encapsulating Security Payload*
8. Payload/packet headers of higher layers.

In addition, the standard requires that none of the packet-header extensions, except *Destination Options*, occur more than once. The last two packet-header extensions, *Authentication Header* and *Encapsulating Security Payload Header*, are also packet-header extensions, but they serve for seamless integration of IPSec in IPv6. For this reason, we will not discuss them any further here. A detailed description of IPSec is included in the following standardized RFCs:

- RFC 2401: Architecture of IPSec
- RFC 2402: Authentication Header
- RFC 2406: Encapsulating Security Payload

23.3 IPv6 IMPLEMENTATION

The implementation of IPv6 in the Linux kernel is in the net/ipv6 directory and in the header file <include/net/ipv6.h>. The code of IPv4 formed the basis for the

IPv6 implementation, so that most things are similar. As in IPv4, packets can reach the IPv6 layer in either of three possible ways. Figure 23–3 shows how a packet travels across the Linux kernel. Packets received by the network card are passed by the function `ipv6_rcv(sbk, dev, pt)` to the data-link layer, and `ip6_xmit(skb)` sends packets created by higher layers or protocols (e.g., UDP or TCP). Finally, special commands, such as `icmpv6_send()`, can be used to create IPv6 packets in the IP layer.

23.3.1 Incoming Packets

The `ipv6_rcv()` function accepts IPv6 packets incoming from the lower layer. If an incoming packet is addressed to a different computer, it is dropped immediately by `ipv6_rcv()`. If an IPv6 packet is addressed to the local computer, then the first things

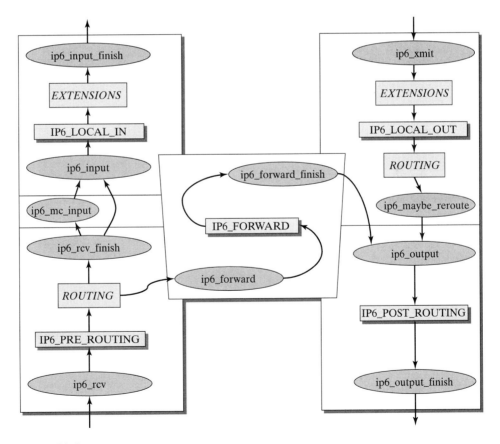

FIGURE 23–3
IPv6 implementation in the Linux kernel.

to do are to check the IPv6 packet header and the packet length and to use the skb_trim() function to correct things, if necessary. If a packet-header extension of the type *Hop-by-Hop Options* follows next, this extension is processed by the function ipv6_parse_hopopts(). Subsequently, the NETFILTER call NF_IP6_PRE_ROUTING passes the IPv6 packet to the ip6_rcv_finish() function, which invokes one of these three functions: ip6_input(), ip6_mc_input(), ip6_forward().

23.3.2 Forwarding Packets

ip6_forward()	**include/net/ipv6.h**

ip6_forward_finish()	**net/ipv6/ip6_output.c**

The ip6_rcv_finish() function invokes ip6_forward() when an IPv6 packet has to be forwarded. The latter checks first to see whether forwarding is enabled; otherwise, the packet could simply get dropped. Subsequently, the packet's lifetime is checked, and, if the value in the Hop Limit field is smaller than or equal to one, the packet is actually dropped, and an ICMPv6 message is sent to the corresponding node. If the IPv6 packet is not explicitly sent over this computer on its way to the destination, (which means that the address of the local node is in the *Routing* packet-header extension), and if the packet would leave the computer over the same interface on which it arrived in the local node, then an ICMPv6 message of the type *Redirect* is returned to the sender. IPv6 packets with a *Link-Local, Multicast* or *Loopback* source address will also be dropped. The final check is to see whether the length of the new MTU is exceeded and, if so, to send an ICMPV6_PKT_TOOBIG message to the sender. Finally, the NETFILTER call NF_IP6_FORWARD passes the IPv6 packet to the ip6_forward_finish() function, which, in turn, invokes ip6_output().

23.3.3 Packets Delivered Locally

ip6_xmit()	**include/net/ipv6.h**

ip6_output()	**include/net/ipv6.h**

ip6_output_finish()	**net/ipv6/ip6_output.c**

Packets that have to be delivered locally are taken by the ip6_rcv_finish() function and passed either to ip6_mc_input() or directly to ip6_input(). However, ip6_mc_input() merely checks to find out whether the multicast packet is addressed to this computer and, if so, passes it to ip6_input(). In turn, ip6_input() invokes the ip6_input_finish() function over a NF_IP6_LOCAL_IN netfilter call and assumes further processing. Initially, ip6_input_finish() checks to see whether the next packet-header extension is of the type *Hop-by-Hop Options*; if this is true, this extension will be skipped. If the next header extension is either a TCP header or a UDP header, then all further packet-header extensions are processed by the ip6_parse_extheaders() function. Figure 23–3 shows this process in the Extensions box. If the IPv6 packet is not for a RAW IPv6 socket, then the next step determines the transport protocol. Similarly to IPv4, the IPv6 implementation uses a hash function over the maximum number of protocols (MAX_INET_PROTOS - 1). Subsequently, the IPv6 packet is passed to the function in charge, which processes the payload. If no transport protocol was identified, the IPv6 packet is passed to the matching RAW IPv6 socket (if present); otherwise, the packet will be dropped and an ICMPV6_UNK_NEXTHDR message returned to the sender.

23.3.4 Transport-Layer Packets

Packets created by the transport layer can be sent via several different functions; one example is the function ip6_xmit(). This function accepts a packet—for example, from the TCPv6 implementation—and then uses the function skb_realloc_headroom() to first create free storage before the packet arrives, if the available storage is too small. Subsequently, the individual parameters for the IPv6 packet header are set, and the packet is passed to the function ip6_maybe_reroute() via the NETFILTER call NF_IP6_LOCAL_OUT, if it does not exceed the MTU. The function ip6_maybe_reroute(), in turn, ensures that an alternative route is found, if an entry in the routing table is no longer up to date. Next, ip6_maybe_reroute() passes the packet to the function ip6_output(), which filters multicast packets again before it sends the packet. Via the NETFILTER call NF_IP6_POST_ROUTING, the IPv6 packet eventually reaches ip6_output_finish(). This latter function uses Neighbour Discovery to figure out the further route for the IPv6 packet and then passes the packet to the transmit functions of the lower layer, from which the IPv6 packet leaves the local computer.

Layer IV—Transport Layer

Transmission Control Protocol (TCP)

The *Transmission Control Protocol* (*TCP*) offers a reliable, byte-oriented, connection-oriented transport service, in contrast to the unreliable datagram service used by the Internet Protocol (IP). Providing these abilities makes the TCP transport protocol very complex. A large number of protocol mechanisms are required to achieve the expected service. This chapter introduces these protocol mechanisms and describes how they were implemented in the Linux kernel.

The TCP protocol belongs to the transport layer and can be used as an alternative to the *User Datagram Protocol* (*UDP*), which offers a connectionless transport service. (See Chapter 25.) The transport layer is immediately below the application layer. Consumers using the service of the protocol are applications, and they reach the services of the TCP protocol instance over the socket interface introduced in Chapters 26 and 27. To implement the transport service, the TCP layer uses the *Internet Protocol* (*IP*). It provides an unreliable, connectionless datagram service, as described in Chapter 14.

24.1 OVERVIEW

The protocol units that exchange TCP instances in this way are called *segments*, and the protocol units of the IP protocol instances are called *IP packets* or *datagrams*.

24.1.1 Requirements on TCP

The TCP protocol was developed in the beginning of the eighties to run on top of the IP protocol and provide a byte-oriented, reliable, connection-oriented transport service. The requirements on such a protocol are as follows [Pete00]:

- to guarantee transmission of byte streams;
- to maintain the transmission order when delivering byte streams;

- to deliver not more than one single copy of each data unit passed for transmission;
- to transport data for an arbitrary length;
- to support synchronization between sender and receiver;
- to support flow control at the receiver's end; and
- to support several application processes in one system.

To meet these requirements, the TCP protocol provides a reliable, connection-oriented, byte-oriented full-duplex transport service allowing two applications to set up a connection, to send data in both directions reliably, and to finally close this connection. Each TCP connection is set up and terminated gracefully, and all data are delivered before a connection is torn down, provided that the IP protocol behaves in a service-compliant way. From an application's view, the TCP service can be divided into the following properties [Pete00, Come00]:

- *Connection orientation*: TCP provides connection-oriented service where an application must first request a connection to a destination and then use the connection to transfer data.
- *Peer-to-peer communication*: Each TCP connection has exactly two endpoints.
- *Complete reliability*: TCP guarantees that the data sent across a connection will be delivered exactly as sent, with no data missing or out of order.
- *Full-duplex communication*: A TCP connection allows data to flow in either direction and allows either application program to send data at any time. TCP can buffer outgoing and incoming data in both directions, making it possible for an application to send data and then to continue computation while the data is being transferred.
- *Byte-stream interface*: We say that TCP provides a stream interface in which an application sends a continuous sequence of octets across a connection. That is, TCP does not provide a notion of records, and does not guarantee that data will be delivered to the receiving application in pieces of the same size in which it was transferred by the sending application.
- *Reliable connection startup*: TCP requires that, when two applications create a connection, both must agree to the new connection; duplicate packets used in previous connections will not appear to be valid responses or otherwise interfere with the new connection.
- *Graceful connection shutdown*: An application program can open a connection, send arbitrary amounts of data, and then request that the connection be shut down. TCP guarantees to deliver all the data reliably before closing the connection.

24.1.2   The TCP Packet Format

Figure 24–1 shows how a TCP segment is structured. TCP groups data from higher layers and adds a header, as will be described below:

- The 16-bit SOURCE PORT (SRC PORT) field identifies a process in the sending end system.

Source Port	Destination Port	
Sequence Number		
Acknowledgement Number		
Length	Reserved	Control Flags	Window Size
Checksum		Urgent Pointer
Options (optional)		
Data (optional)		

FIGURE 24–1
The TCP segment format.

- The 16-bit DESTINATION PORT (DEST PORT) field identifies a process in the end system of the communication partner.
- The 32-bit SEQUENCE NUMBER (SEQ) field identifies the sequence number of the first data byte in this segment.
- The 32-bit ACKNOWLEDGEMENT NUMBER (ACK) field means that, if the ACK control bit is set, then this value includes the next sequence number expected by the sender.
- The DATA OFFSET field is 4 bits wide and specifies the number of 32-bit words in the TCP data header. This field is required, because the Options field has a variable size.
- RESERVED (6 bits) is reserved for future use and has to be set to null.
- CONTROL FLAGS are divided into the following flags:

  - URG (Urgent Pointer) points to important data that have to be forwarded immediately.
  - SYN is used to establish connections. SYN = 1 denotes a connection request.
  - ACK shows that the ACKNOWLEDGEMENT NUMBER field includes relevant data.
  - RST can request a connection to be reset. RST = 1 denotes a request to reset a connection.
  - PSH means that, if this bit is set, the TCP instance must immediately pass the data received to the higher layers.
  - FIN means that, if this bit is set, the connection is to be torn down.

- The 16-bit WINDOW (WNDW) field specifies how much additional buffer space is available for more data.
- The 16-bit CHECKSUM field contains a checksum that covers the TCP segment header and the data. As in UDP, a pseudo header is computed. (See Chapter 25.)
- The 16-bit URGENT POINTER (URGPTR) field points to the last byte of important data.
- The OPTIONS field is variable and can contain, for example, the maximum segment size.

24.2 IMPLEMENTING THE TCP PROTOCOL INSTANCE

The protocol instance of the Transmission Control Protocol is one of the most complex parts in the Linux network architecture. The protocol uses a large number of algorithms and features that require extensive mechanisms to implement them. This section explains how these mechanisms are implemented and how they interact in the TCP implementation.

First, we will have a look at "normal" receive and transmit processes in the TCP instance, where we will leave out many details. Too much detail would make it difficult at this point to understand the entire process in the TCP instance and the features of each of the TCP algorithms.

Section 24.3 discusses connection management—how TCP connections are established and torn down; Section 24.4 discusses each of the algorithms used to exchange data (e.g., congestion control and window scaling). Finally, Section 24.5 will introduce the tasks of the TCP protocol instance and how its timers are managed.

The TCP protocol instance is extremely complex. It consists of a large number of functions, inline functions, structures, and macros. In addition, the large number of algorithms used within the TCP protocol makes its description rather difficult. For this reason, we will begin with a general overview of the process involved when receiving, and then when sending, a TCP segment. A detailed discussion of the large number of algorithms used in TCP will follow in Section 24.4. In addition, this section assumes that data is exchanged over an existing connection. The complex management of TCP connections is dealt with in Section 24.3.

24.2.1 Handling Incoming TCP Segments

The transport protocol for an incoming packet is selected early, by the time it is needed in the IP layer, to be able to pass the packet to the appropriate protocol-handling routine in the transport layer. (See Section 14.2.5.) In the TCP instance, this task is handled by the tcp_v4_rcv() function (net/ipv4/tcp_ipv4.c).

Figure 24–2 shows how packets are processed in the TCP instance, and Figure 24–3 gives an overview of what happens when the TCP instance receives a segment.

tcp_v4_rcv()	net/ipv4/tcp_ipv4.c

tcp_v4_rcv(skb, len) checks for whether the packet in the form of the socket buffer, skb, is really addressed to this computer (skb->pkt_type == PACKET_HOST). If so, then the IP packet header is removed, and the protocol processing continues; otherwise, the socket buffer is dropped.

tcp_v4_lookup() searches the hash table of the active socket for the socket or sock structure. The IP addresses and the ports of the two communication partners and the network device index, skb->dst->rt_iif at which this segment arrived are the parameters used. If a socket with these addresses and ports can be found, the tcp_v4_do_rcv() function continues with an appropriate handling routine, depending on the connection state. If no socket can be found, then tcp_send_reset() sends a RESET segment.

tcp_v4_do_rcv()	net/ipv4/tcp_ipv4.c

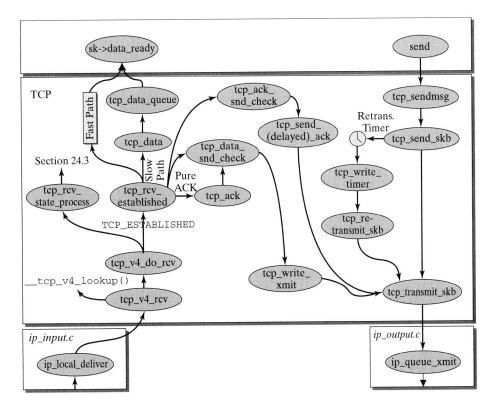

FIGURE 24–2
Partial representation of how packets are handled in the TCP instance.

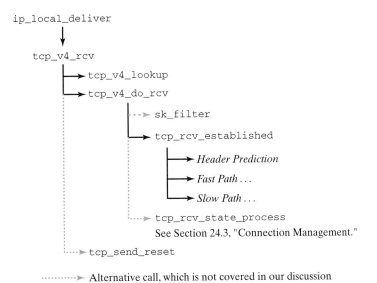

FIGURE 24–3
Overview of the process for receiving a segment in the TCP instance.

First, if socket filters are activated, the `sk_filter()` function checks the socket buffer. If the result is negative, the packet is dropped. Otherwise, the process continues with either of the following functions, depending on the TCP connection state (`sk->state`):

- TCP_ESTABLISHED: With a connection established, the socket buffer is further processed in `tcp_rcv_established()` (as is shown later).
- If the socket is in one of the *other states*, the function `tcp_rcv_state_process()` processes the socket buffer. This function is described in Section 24.3.

The latter cases—how all packets not arriving in the TCP_ESTABLISHED are handled—are introduced in Section 24.3. This section will explain how the TCP *finite state machine* was implemented. As we can already see at this point, the implementation of the TCP instance in the Linux kernel deviates from the usual concept of such an implementation. In educational operating systems, the state machine would probably be implemented with a central `case` statement to branch, depending on the state. However, real-world systems often prefer a "fast" over an "elegant" implementation for performance reasons.

At this point, let's return to the `tcp_rcv_established()` function and how it handles packets as they arrive. Receiving packets over an established connection is the most common case, but we will not discuss it in detail for lack of space. The TCP protocol has a large number of algorithms, which are discussed in Section 24.4 rather than in this section. This approach allows us to concentrate on the path a packet takes through the TCP instance without having to discuss each algorithm. Section 24.4 describes the features of these algorithms and how they were implemented.

`tcp_rcv_established()`	**net/ipv4/tcp_input.c**

`tcp_rcv_established(sk, skb, th, len)` handles TCP packets incoming over an established connection (i.e., in the data-exchange phase (TCP_ESTABLISHED)). Once again, this function is a good example of the intended objective: to achieve efficient protocol handling. In fact, `tcp_rcv_established()` distinguishes between two paths for packet-handling purposes:

- *Fast Path* is used to handled the ideal case of an incoming packet. The most common cases occurring in a normal TCP connection should be detected as fast as possible and processed optimally, without having to test for marginal cases, which normally won't occur in this situation.
- *Slow Path* is used for all packets not corresponding to the ideal case and requiring some special handling. For example, if a packet had to be manipulated to deal with a transmission error, or if it is a retransmitted packet, it is processed in Slow Path by appropriate error-correction mechanisms.

Fast Path and Slow Path are not distinguished specifically in the Linux kernel. It fact, this differentiation was proposed by Van Jacobson [Jaco90a] at the beginning of the nineties, and it was implemented in BSD UNIX in a similar form. A study in [Stev94b] showed that Fast Path was applied in from 97% to 100% of all packets incoming over a

TCP connection within a local area network and in from 83% to 99% of all cases in a WAN connection. Though these results are not necessarily representative and depend on the actual load of the networks, they show that it appears useful to differentiate between Slow Path and Fast Path.

Packets are processed in Fast Path in the following two situations:

- The segment received is a pure ACK segment for the data sent last (no *duplicate ACK*).
- The segment received includes data expected next, so that they are consecutive with the data received until then.

Fast Path is not accessed in the following situations (and so a detailed protocol-handling process is performed in Slow Path):

- *Unexpected TCP flags*: The process continues in Slow Path if a SYN, URG, FIN, or RST flag is set. These cases are detected by the *Header Prediction* described later.
- If the sequence number of an incoming segment does not correspond to the sequence number expected next (tp->rcv_nxt), then the segment is either a retransmitted segment or an out-of-order segment.
- *Both communication partners exchange data*: Fast Path cannot be used except in situations where the relevant TCP instance either only sends or only receives (i.e., where either the sequence number or the acknowledgement number remains constant).
- The current TCP instance sent a *Zero Window* (i.e., no transmit credit can currently be granted to the communication partner).
- *Unexpected TCP options* are processed in Slow Path. The Timestamp option is the only option that can be handled in Fast Path.

To make the differentiation between Fast Path and Slow Path worthwhile, Fast Path has to be detected quickly and reliably. Most of the cases mentioned above can be detected by the so-called *Header Prediction*, which uses a simple comparative operation on the Header Length, Flags, and Window Size fields and a predicted value to decide whether the Fast Path can be used:

```
/* pred_flags is 0xS?10 << 16 + snd_wnd
 * if header_prediction is to be made
 * 'S' will always be tp->tcp_header_len >> 2
 * '?' will be 0 for the fast path, otherwise pred_flags is 0 to
 *       turn it off (when there are holes in the receive space
 *       for instance), PSH flag is ignored.
 */

if ((tcp_flag_word(th) & TCP_HP_BITS) == tp->pred_flags &&
        TCP_SKB_CB(skb)->seq == tp->rcv_nxt)
{ (...FAST PATH...) }
else
{ (...SLOW PATH...) }
```

The comparative value (tp->pred_flags) is computed in the tcp_fast_path_on() function in advance, which means that it activates processing over the Fast Path (if the packets meet the preconditions):

```
static __inline__ void __tcp_fast_path_on(struct tcp_opt *tp, u32 snd_wnd)
{
        tp->pred_flags = htonl((tp->tcp_header_len << 26) |
                               ntohl(TCP_FLAG_ACK) |
                               snd_wnd);
}
static __inline__ void tcp_fast_path_on(struct tcp_opt *tp)
{
        __tcp_fast_path_on(tp, tp->snd_wnd>>tp->snd_wscale);
}
```

Should it ever happen that the TCP connection gets into a situation where Fast Path cannot be used, then the problem is solved by simply writing a null to the comparative operator of the Header Prediction—for example, much like what is done when sending a Zero Window in tcp_select_window().

Fast Path Once an incoming segment has successfully passed the Header Prediction, its processing in the Fast Path begins, where the following operations are done:

- The sequence number is checked to filter out-of-order packets (TCP_SKB_CB(skb)->seq == tp->rcv_nxt).
- The Timestamp option is checked, but only by evaluating the length of the packet header. All other options fail the Header Prediction, which means that a simple check of the packet-header length is sufficient. Subsequently, the Timestamp values, TSval and TSecr, are read directly. (See Section 24.4.1.) If the subsequent PAWS check fails, then the process continues in Slow Path; otherwise, the segment is all right. If the condition to update the tp->ts_recent timestamp is met, it is accepted by tcp_store_ts_recent().
- Subsequently, the packet-header length is compared with the segment length to distinguish pure acknowledgement packets from payload packets, and segments that are too short are dropped.

    - *ACK segment*: The acknowledgement number, if present, in a packet that contains no payload is processed in tcp_ack. Subsequently, __kfree_skb() releases the socket buffer, which completes the process of handling this segment. Finally, tcp_data_snd_check() checks for whether local packets can be sent.
    - *Data segment*: In this case, the segment contains the data expected next (was previously checked).

    At this point, the only thing tested is whether the payload can be copied directly into the user-address space:

    - If the payload can be copied directly into the user-address space, then the statistics of this connection are updated, the relevant process is informed, the payload is copied into the receive memory of the process, the TCP packet header is removed, and, finally, the variable with the sequence number expected next is updated.

* If the payload cannot be directly copied into the user-address space, then the availability of buffer memory in the socket is checked, statistical information is updated, the TCP packet header is removed, the packet is added to the end of the socket's receive queue, and, finally, the sequence number expected next is set.

▷ All management tasks arising from the receipt of a payload segment are completed in the `tcp_event_data_rcv()` function.

▷ If the segment's acknowledgement number confirms data not yet acknowledged, then the actions required are done in `tcp_ack()`. Subsequently, `tcp_data_snd_check()` initiates the transmission of waiting data that may be sent now that the acknowledgement was received.

▷ Finally, the process checks whether an acknowledgement has to be sent as response to the receipt of this segment, in the form of either *Delayed ACK* or *Quick ACK*.

Slow Path   A packet is processed in Slow Path if the prerequisites for Fast Path are not met or the Header Prediction fails. Slow Path processing considers all possibilities of a segment received over an established connection. The following operations are done consecutively:

▪ The checksum is verified.

▪ The Timestamp option is checked in `tcp_fast_parse_options()`, and the PAWS check works out whether the packet has to be dropped (`tcp_paws_discard()`).

▪ Using the sequence number, `tcp_sequence()` checks for whether the packet arrived out of order (OfO). If it is an OfO packet, then the *QuickAck* mode is activated to send acknowledgements as fast as possible.

▪ If the RST flag is set, `tcp_reset()` resets the connection (changes connection state and deactivates timer), and the socket buffer is freed.

▪ If the TCP packet header contains a Timestamp option, then `tcp_replace_ts_recent()` updates the *recent timestamp* stored locally.

▪ If the SYN flag is set to signal an error case in an established connection, then `tcp_reset()` resets the connection.

▪ If the ACK flag is set, the `tcp_ack()` function processes the acknowledgement.

▪ If the URG flag denotes that the packet contains priority data, then this data is processed in `tcp_urg()`.

▪ `tcp_data()` and `tcp_data_queue()` process the payload. Among other things, this includes a check for sufficient space in the receive buffer and insertion of the socket buffer into the receive queue or the out-of-order queue.

▪ Finally, two methods, `tcp_data_snd_check()` and `tcp_ack_snd_check()`, are invoked to check on whether data or acknowledgements waiting can be sent.

These actions complete the process of handling a received TCP segment. This section is only an overview of the rough process involved in handling incoming segments. At some point, we mentioned functions invoked in Fast Path or Slow Path, but we didn't explain them in detail. For this reason, we will briefly describe these functions in the following subsection.

Helper Functions to Handle Incoming TCP Segments

`tcp_ack()`	net/ipv4/tcp_input.c

`tcp_ack(sk, th, ack_seq, ack, len)` handles all tasks involved in receiving an acknowledgement packet or a data packet with valid ACK number (*piggybacking*):

- Adapt the receive window (`tcp_ack_update_window()`).
- Delete acknowledged packets from the *retransmission* queue (`tcp_clean_rtx_queue()`).
- Check for *Zero Window Probing* acknowledgement.
- Adapt the congestion window (`tcp_may_raise_cwnd()`).
- Update the packet round-trip time (*RTT*) and the timeout for packet retransmissions (*Retransmission TimeOut—RTO*).
- Retransmit packets and update the retransmission timer.
- Activate the Fast Retransmit mode, if necessary.

`tcp_event_data_recv()`	net/ipv4/tcp_input.c

`tcp_event_data_recv(tp, skb)` handles all management work required for receiving of payload. This includes updating the maximum segment size, the timestamp, and the timer for delayed acknowledgements (*Acknowledgement Timeout—ATO*).

`tcp_data_snd_check()`	net/ipv4/tcp_input.c

`tcp_data_snd_check(sk)` checks on whether data is ready and waiting in the transmit queue, and it starts the transmission, if permitted by the transmit window of the sliding-window mechanism and the congestion-control window. The actual transmission is initiated by `tcp_write_xmit()`:

```
static __inline__ void tcp_data_snd_check(struct sock *sk) {
    struct sk_buff *skb = sk->tp_pinfo.af_tcp.send_head;
    struct tcp_opt *tp = &(sk->tp_pinfo.af_tcp);

    if (skb != NULL)
    {
    if (after(TCP_SKB_CB(skb)->end_seq, tp->snd_una + tp->snd_wnd) ||
            tcp_packets_in_flight(tp) >= tp->snd_cwnd ||
            tcp_write_xmit(sk))
                    tcp_check_probe_timer(sk, tp);
    }
    tcp_check_space(sk);
}
```

tcp_ack_snd_check()   **net/ipv4/tcp_input.c**

`tcp_ack_snd_check(sk, ofo_possible)` checks for various cases where acknowledgements can be sent. Also, it checks the type of acknowledgement (i.e., whether it should be quick or delayed):

```
static __inline__ void tcp_ack_snd_check(struct sock *sk) {
    struct tcp_opt *tp = &(sk->tp_pinfo.af_tcp);
    if (!tcp_ack_scheduled(tp)) {
            /* We sent a data segment already. */
            return;
    }
            /* More than one full frame received... */
    if ((((tp->rcv_nxt - tp->rcv_wup) > tp->ack.rcv_mss
            /* ... and right edge of window advances far enough.
             * (tcp_recvmsg() will send ACK otherwise). Or...*/
        && __tcp_select_window(sk) >= tp->rcv_wnd) ||
            /* We ACK each frame or... */
        tcp_in_quickack_mode(tp) ||
            /* We have out of order data. */
        (skb_peek(&tp->out_of_order_queue) != NULL)
    {
        tcp_send_ack(sk); /* Then ack it now */
    }else
    {
        tcp_send_delayed_ack(sk); /* Else, send delayed ack. */
    }
}
```

tcp_fast_parse_options()   **net/ipv4/tcp_input.c**

`tcp_fast_parse_options(sk, th, tp)` handles the Timestamp option in the TCP packet header. (See Section 24.4.1.) `tcp_parse_options()` is invoked if the packet header contains several options.

Handling Incoming Packets in Other States

tcp_rcv_state_process()   **net/ipv4/tcp_input.c**

The `tcp_rcv_state_process()` function processes incoming segments when the TCP connection is not in the ESTABLISHED state. It mainly handles state transitions and management work for the connection. The detailed process is described in Section 24.3.

24.2.2 Sending TCP Segments

This section describes how payload is sent over a TCP instance (i.e., how TCP segments containing payload are transmitted). The transmission of acknowledgements (ACKs) is initiated by incoming TCP segments or by the *Delayed ACK* timer. (See Sections 24.2.1 and 24.5.)

A TCP instance uses the send() system call to send payload. The send() system call causes the tcp_sendmsg() function to be invoked. This function is present as a handling routine for this system call in the tcp_prot structure (net/ipv4/tcp_ipv4.c). Figure 24–4 shows the invocation hierarchy during the process of sending payload over the TCP instance.

`tcp_sendmsg()`	**net/ipv4/tcp.c**

tcp_sendmsg(sock, msg, size) copies payload from the user-address space into the kernel and starts sending this data in the form of TCP segments. Before it starts sending, however, it checks on whether the connection has already been established and on whether it is in the TCP_ESTABLISHED state. If no connection has been established yet, the system call waits in wait_for_tcp_connect() for a connection.

The next step computes the maximum segment size (tcp_current_mss) and starts copying the data from the user-address space. First, it checks for whether a "half empty" segment is present at the end of the socket's transmit queue (tp->write_queue), which could be used to pack data. Subsequently, or if no small segment was available, tcp_alloc_skb() creates new socket buffers. The data to be sent is copied from the user-address space into the socket buffers, and tcp_send_skb() is invoked to order data within the socket's transmit queue.

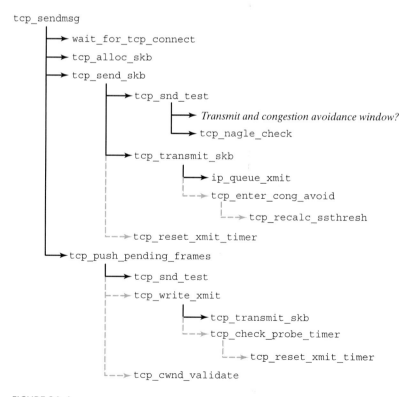

FIGURE 24–4
Sending payload in the TCP protocol instance.

Finally, the __tcp_push_pending_frames() routine takes TCP segments from the socket transmit queue (tp->write_queue) and starts sending them.

tcp_send_skb()	net/ipv4/tcp_output.c

tcp_send_skb(sk, skb, force_queue, cur_mss) adds the socket buffer, skb, to the socket transmit queue (sk->write_queue) and decides whether transmission can be started or it has to wait in the queue. It uses the tcp_snd_test() routine to make this decision. If the result is negative, the socket buffer remains in the transmit queue.

If the result is positive, it starts sending the present segment, that is, it uses the tcp_transmit_skb() function to complete the TCP packet header and pass the segment to the IP instance. As shown in Figure 24–2, the latter function is also used in other places within the TCP instance for this purpose.

The timer for automatic retransmission is started automatically in tcp_reset_xmit_timer(), if the transmit process was successful. This timer is initiated if no acknowledgement for this packet arrived after a specific time.

tcp_snd_test()	include/net/tcp.h

tcp_snd_test(tp, skb, cur_mss, nonagle)() is an inline method that checks on whether the TCP segment, skb, may be sent at the time of invocation. It verifies the criteria specified in RFC 1122 to ensure standard-compliant behavior and, mainly, that there is sufficient space in the transmit and congestion-control windows and what the Nagle algorithm says with regard to sending this packet. The behavior of the participating algorithms is described in Section 24.4.

```
/* This checks if the data bearing packet SKB (usually tp->send_head)
 * should be put on the wire right now.
 */
static __inline__ int tcp_snd_test(struct tcp_opt *tp, struct sk_buff *skb,
                    unsigned cur_mss, int nonagle)
{       /*      RFC 1122 - Section 4.2.3.4:
         *      We must queue if
         *      a) The right edge of this frame exceeds the window
         *      b) There are packets in flight and we have a small segment
         *         [SWS avoidance and Nagle algorithm]
         *         (part of SWS is done on packetization)
         *         Minshall version sounds: there are no _small_
         *         segments in flight. (tcp_nagle_check)
         *      c) We have too many packets 'in flight'
         *
         *      Don't use the nagle rule for urgent data (or
         *      for the final FIN -DaveM).
         */
return ((nonagle==1 || tp->urg_mode
        || !tcp_nagle_check(tp, skb, cur_mss, nonagle)) &&
        ((tcp_packets_in_flight(tp) < tp->snd_cwnd) ||
        (TCP_SKB_CB(skb)->flags & TCPCB_FLAG_FIN)) &&
        !after(TCP_SKB_CB(skb)->end_seq, tp->snd_una + tp->snd_wnd));
}
```

`tcp_transmit_skb()`	**include/linux/tcp_output.c**

`tcp_transmit_skb(sk, skb)` is responsible for completing the TCP segment in the socket buffer, `skb`, and for subsequently sending it over the Internet Protocol. To this end, it first fills the TCP packet header with the appropriate values from the opt structure—for example, much like an explicit transmit credit specified by `tcp_select_window()`. `tcp_syn_build_options()` registers the TCP options for SYN packets, and `tcp_build_and_update_options()` registers the options for all other packets.

Subsequently, all actions required to send a payload-carrying segment or a segment with its ACK flag set are executed:

  ▒ If the ACK flag is set, the number of permitted Quick ACK packets is decremented in the `tcp_event_ack_sent()` method (provided that the connection is in the Quick ACK mode). Subsequently, the timer for delayed ACKs is stopped, because the next step sends an acknowledgement.

  ▒ If the segment to be sent carries payload, we first have to check for whether an interval corresponding to the retransmission timeout has elapsed since the last data segment (stored in `tp->lsntime`) was sent. If this is the case, then the congestion window, `snd_cwnd`, is set to the minimum value (`tcp_cwnd_restart`), as specified in RFC 2861.

Subsequently, the function pointer `tp->af_specific->queue_xmit()`, which references the corresponding transmit function—depending on the Internet Protocol version (e.g., `ip_queue_xmit()` for IPv4)—passes the socket buffer to the IP layer for transmission.

Finally, the `tcp_enter_cwr()` method adapts the threshold value for the slow-start algorithm. This completes the transmit process for the TCP segment within the TCP instance, unless no acknowledgement arrives for this packet during the retransmission timeout, so that it would have to be retransmitted; see details in Section 24.5.

`tcp_push_pending_frames()`	**include/net/tcp.h**

`tcp_push_pending_frames` checks for whether there are segments ready for transmission that couldn't be sent during the regular transmission attempt. If this is the case, then `tcp_write_xmit()` initiates the transmission of these segments, if the `tcp_snd_test()` function agrees:

```
struct sk_buff *skb = tp->send_head;
if (skb)
{
if (!tcp_skb_is_last(sk, skb))
        nonagle = 1;
if (!tcp_snd_test(tp, skb, cur_mss, nonagle) ||
        tcp_write_xmit(sk))
```

```
            tcp_check_probe_timer(sk, tp);
}
tcp_cwnd_validate(sk, tp);
```

| tcp_write_xmit() | net/ipv4/tcp_output.c |

tcp_write_xmit(sk) continues to send segments from the transmit queue of the socket, sk, as long as it is allowed to do so by tcp_snd_test(). It checks for whether the conditions of TCP algorithms (e.g., slow-start method and congestion-control algorithm) are maintained. Data segments can also be fragmented (tcp_fragment()) before the maximum segment size is exceeded. tcp_transmit_skb() handles the final completion of the TCP packet and passes it to the Internet Protocol.

| tcp_retransmit_skb() | include/linux/tcp_output.c |

tcp_retransmit_skb(sk, skb) retransmits a TCP segment. The segment may have to be fragmented (tcp_fragment()), or it might be joined with the next segment (tcp_retrans_try_collapse()).

| tcp_send_ack() | include/linux/tcp_output.c |

tcp_send_ack(sk) is responsible for building and sending ACK packets. For this purpose, it requests a socket buffer and assigns the corresponding values to this buffer. Subsequently, it uses tcp_transmit_skb() to send an ACK segment.

24.2.3 Data Structures of the TCP Instance

| struct tcp_opt | include/net/sock.h |

The tcp_opt structure contains all variables of the TCP algorithms for a TCP connection. The names of these variables were adopted from RFCs 793 and 1122 for the sake of better understanding (except for uppercase and lowercase). This facilitates reading the source text and comparing with the TCP standard.

The tcp_opt structure is very complex, which shouldn't come as a surprise considering the complexity of the TCP protocol and the large number of its algorithms. A detailed description of the tcp_opt structure would go beyond the scope and volume of this chapter, especially because they are well documented and because the variable names correspond to the TCP standard. Nevertheless, we will list the variables and their tasks, to facilitate quick references when reading the following sections.

Among other things, the tcp_opt structure consists of variables for the following algorithms or protocol mechanisms:

- sequence and acknowledgement numbers;
- flow-control information;
- packet round-trip time;

- congestion control and congestion handling;
- timers;
- TCP options in the packet header; and
- automatic and selective packet retransmission.

```
struct tcp_opt
{
  int  tcp_header_len;    /* Bytes of tcp header to send               */

  /* Header prediction flags * 0x5?10 << 16 + snd_wnd in net byte order  */
  __u32 pred_flags;

  __u32 rcv_nxt;          /* What we want to receive next              */
  __u32 snd_nxt;          /* Next sequence we send                     */
  __u32 snd_una;          /* First byte we want an ack for             */
  __u32 snd_sml;          /* Last byte of most recently xmitted small packet */
  __u32 rcv_tstamp;       /* timestamp of last received ACK (for keepalives) */
  __u32 lsndtime;         /* timestamp of last sent data packet (for restart
                                    window)                            */
  /* Delayed ACK control data */
  struct
  {
      __u8 pending;          /* ACK is pending                         */
      __u8 quick;            /* Scheduled number of quick acks         */
      __u8 pingpong;         /* The session is interactive             */
      __u8 blocked;          /* Delayed ACK was blocked by socket lock */
      __u32 ato;             /* Predicted tick of soft clock           */
      unsigned long timeout; /* Currently scheduled timeout            */
      __u32 lrcvtime;        /* timestamp of last received data packet */
      __u16 last_seg_size;   /* Size of last incoming segment          */
      __u16 rcv_mss;         /* MSS used for delayed ACK decisions     */
  } ack;
  __u32 snd_wl1;          /* Sequence for window update                */
  __u32 snd_wnd;          /* The window we expect to receive           */
  __u32 max_window;       /* Maximal window ever seen from peer        */
  __u32 pmtu_cookie;      /* Last pmtu seen by socket */
  __u16 mss_cache;        /* Cached effective mss, not including SACKS */
  __u16 mss_clamp;        /* Maximal mss, negotiated at connection setup */
  __u16 ext_header_len;   /* Network protocol overhead (IP/IPv6 options) */
  __u8 ca_state;          /* State of fast-retransmit machine          */
  __u8 retransmits;       /* Number of unrecovered RTO timeouts.       */
  __u8 reordering;        /* Packet reordering metric. */
  __u8 queue_shrunk;      /* Write queue has been shrunk recently.     */
  __u8 defer_accept;      /* User waits for some data after accept     */

  /* RTT measurement */
  __u8 backoff;           /* backoff                                   */
```

```
__u32 srtt;                    /* smoothed round trip time << 3          */
__u32 mdev;                    /* medium deviation                       */
__u32 mdev_max;                /* maximal mdev for the last rtt period   */
__u32 rttvar;                  /* smoothed mdev_max                      */
__u32 rtt_seq;                 /* sequence number to update rttvar       */
__u32 rto;                     /* retransmit timeout                     */
__u32 packets_out;             /* Packets which are "in flight"          */
__u32 left_out;                /* Packets which leaved network           */
__u32 retrans_out;             /* Retransmitted packets out */

/* Slow start and congestion control (see also Nagle and Karn & Part.)   */
__u32 snd_ssthresh;            /* Slow start size threshold              */
__u32 snd_cwnd;                /* Sending congestion window              */
__u16 snd_cwnd_cnt;            /* Linear increase counter                */
__u16 snd_cwnd_clamp;          /* Do not allow snd_cwnd to grow above this */
__u32 snd_cwnd_used;
__u32 snd_cwnd_stamp;

/* Two commonly used timers in both sender and receiver paths.           */
unsigned long          timeout;
struct timer_list      retransmit_timer;    /* Resend (no ack)           */
struct timer_list      delack_timer;        /* Ack delay                 */
struct sk_buff_head out_of_order_queue;     /* Out of order segments go
                                               here */
struct tcp_func *af_specific;    /* AF_INET{4,6} specific operations     */
struct sk_buff  *send_head;      /* Front of stuff to transmit           */
__u32 rcv_wnd;                 /* Current receiver window                */
__u32 rcv_wup;                 /* rcv_nxt on last window update sent      */
__u32 write_seq;               /* Tail(+1) of data held in tcp send buffer */
__u32 pushed_seq;              /* Last pushed seq, required to talk to windows */
__u32 copied_seq;              /* Head of yet unread data                */
/* Options received (usually on last packet, some only on SYN packets)   */
char       tstamp_ok,          /* TIMESTAMP seen on SYN packet           */
           wscale_ok,          /* Wscale seen on SYN packet              */
           sack_ok;            /* SACK seen on SYN packet                */
char       saw_tstamp;         /* Saw TIMESTAMP on last packet           */
__u8       snd_wscale;         /* Window scaling received from sender    */
__u8       rcv_wscale;         /* Window scaling to send to receiver     */
__u8       nonagle;            /* Disable Nagle algorithm?               */
__u8       keepalive_probes;   /* num of allowed keep alive probes       */

/* PAWS/RTTM data */
__u32      rcv_tsval;          /* Time stamp value                       */
__u32      rcv_tsecr;          /* Time stamp echo reply                  */
__u32      ts_recent;          /* Time stamp to echo next                */
long       ts_recent_stamp;    /* Time we stored ts_recent (for aging)   */

/* SACKs data */
__u16      user_mss;           /* mss requested by user in ioctl         */
```

```
__u8        dsack;          /* D-SACK is scheduled                     */
__u8        eff_sacks;      /* Size of SACK array to send with next packet */
struct tcp_sack_block duplicate_sack[1]; /* D-SACK block               */
struct tcp_sack_block selective_acks[4]; /* The SACKS themselves       */

__u32       window_clamp;   /* Maximal window to advertise             */
__u32       rcv_ssthresh;   /* Current window clamp                    */
__u8        probes_out;     /* unanswered 0 window probes              */
__u8        num_sacks;      /* Number of SACK blocks                   */
__u16       advmss;         /* Advertised MSS                          */
__u8        syn_retries;    /* num of allowed syn retries              */
__u8        ecn_flags;      /* ECN status bits.                        */
__u16       prior_ssthresh; /* ssthresh saved at recovery start        */
__u32       ost_out;        /* Lost packets                            */
__u32       sacked_out;     /* SACK'd packets                          */
__u32       fackets_out;    /* FACK'd packets                          */
__u32       high_seq;       /* snd_nxt at onset of congestion          */
__u32       retrans_stamp;  /* Timestamp of the last retransmit, also used in
                               SYN-SENT to remember stamp of the first SYN */
__u32       undo_marker;    /* tracking retrans started here.          */
int   undo_retrans;   /* number of undoable retransmissions.           */
__u32       syn_seq;   /* Seq of received SYN.                          */
__u32       fin_seq;   /* Seq of received FIN.                          */
__u32       urg_seq;   /* Seq of received urgent pointer                */
__u16       urg_data;  /* Saved octet of OOB data and control flags     */
__u8        pending;   /* Scheduled timer event                         */
__u8        urg_mode;  /* In urgent mode                                */
__u32       snd_up;    /* Urgent pointer                                */
        /* The syn_wait_lock is necessary only to avoid tcp_get_info having
         * to grab the main lock sock while browsing the listening hash
         * (otherwise it's deadlock prone).                            */
rwlock_t                syn_wait_lock;
struct tcp_listen_opt   *listen_opt;
        /* FIFO of established children */
struct open_request     *accept_queue;
struct open_request     *accept_queue_tail;
int         write_pending;       /* A write to socket waits to start. */
unsigned int keepalive_time;     /* time before keep alive takes place */
unsigned int keepalive_intvl;    /* interval between keep alive probes */
int         linger2;
};
```

struct tcp_skb_cb	include/net/tcp.h

```
struct tcp_skb_cb {
        ...
        __u32           seq;            /* Starting sequence number*/
```

```
        __u32          end_seq;        /* SEQ + FIN + SYN + datalen*/
        __u32          when;           /* used to compute rtt's*/
        __u8           flags;          /* TCP header flags*/

        #define TCPCB_FLAG_FIN         0x01
        #define TCPCB_FLAG_SYN         0x02
        #define TCPCB_FLAG_RST         0x04
        #define TCPCB_FLAG_PSH         0x08
        #define TCPCB_FLAG_ACK         0x10
        #define TCPCB_FLAG_URG         0x20
        #define TCPCB_FLAG_ECE         0x40
        #define TCPCB_FLAG_CWR         0x80

        __u8           sacked;         /* State flags for SACK/FACK*/
        #define TCPCB_SACKED_ACKED     0x01 /* SKB ACK'd by a SACK
                                         block*/
        #define TCPCB_SACKED_RETRANS   0x02 /* SKB retransmitted*/

        __u16          urg_ptr;        /* Valid w/URG flags is set*/
        __u32          ack_seq;        /* Sequence number ACK'd*/
};
```

The preceding structure represents the control block of a packet. This type of structure is included in each packet.

struct tcphdr	include/linux/tcp.h

```
struct tcphdr {
        __u16          source;
        __u16          dest;
        __u32          seq;
        __u32          ack_seq;
#if defined(__LITTLE_ENDIAN_BITFIELD)
        __u16          res1:4, doff:4, fin:1, syn:1, rst:1,
                       psh:1, ack:1, urg:1, ece:1, cwr:1;
#elif defined(__BIG_ENDIAN_BITFIELD)
        __u16          doff:4, res1:4, cwr:1, ece:1, urg:1,
                       ack:1, psh:1, rst:1, syn:1, fin:1;
#else
#error "Adjust your <asm/byteorder.h> defines"
#endif
        __u16          window;
        __u16          check;
        __u16          urg_ptr;
};
```

Section 24.1.2 introduced the protocol header. The tcphdr structure maps this header, depending on the memory sequence.

24.3 CONNECTION MANAGEMENT

Being a connection-oriented protocol that supports a number of additional mechanisms, such as packet transmission in the correct order or urgent data, the TCP protocol is extremely complex. The protocol machine shown in Figure 24–5 is characterized by a total of twelve states. This complexity calls for extensive management of the current state of active connections.

24.3.1 The TCP State Machine

A TCP connection's state is stored in the state field of the associated sock structure. The response to the receipt of packets is different, depending on the state, so this state has to be polled for each incoming packet. There are three phases: the connection-establishment

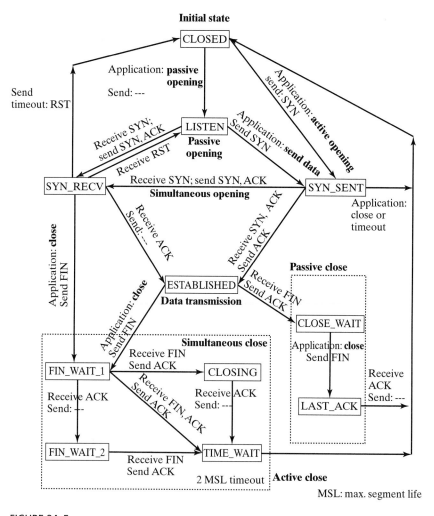

FIGURE 24–5
The TCP state automaton.

phase, the data-transmission phase, and the connection-teardown phase. Section 24.4 describes the protocol mechanisms of the data-transmission phase in detail. This section discusses the connection-establishment and connection-teardown phases.

As shown in Section 24.2, `tcp_rcv_state_process()` (`net/ipv4/tcp_input.c`) is the most important function for connection management, as long as the connection has not yet been established. Packets in the `TIME_WAIT` state are the only packets handled earlier in the `tcp_v4_rcv()` function.

`tcp_rcv_state_process()`	**net/ipv4/tcp_input.c**

The `tcp_rcv_state_process()` function handles mainly state transitions and the management work for the connection. Depending on the connection state, there are different actions when a packet is received:

- In the `CLOSED` state: The packet is dropped.
- In the `LISTEN` state: If ACK or SYN flags are set, then the connection establishment is registered, and data is ignored.
- In the `SYN_SENT` state: `tcp_rcv_synsent_state_process()` checks for correct connection establishment, and the connection is moved to the `ESTABLISHED` state. If this fails, then the remaining flags are processed.
- If the PAWS check finds an error, then a DUPACK is returned, and the function is exited.
- Subsequently, the sequence number is checked, and if a packet arrived out of order, then a DUPACK is returned and the packet is dropped.
- If the RST flag is active, the connection is reset and the packet is dropped.
- If a timestamp is present in the segment header, the `recent timestamp` stored locally is updated.
- If the SYN flag is set, but invalid due to the sequence number, the connection is reset and the packet is dropped.
- If the ACK flag is active, the next action is different, depending on the state:

  - In the `SYN_RCVD` state: The connection state changes to `ESTABLISHED`, and the acknowledgement is processed.
  - In the `FIN_WAIT_1` state: The connection state changes to `FIN-WAIT2` and the `TIMEWAIT` timer is set.
  - In the `CLOSING` state: Transition to the `TIMEWAIT` state occurs, if the packet is not out of order.
  - In the `LAST_ACK` state: The socket is reset, and the state changes to the `CLOSED` state, if the packet is not out of order.

- If the URG flag is active, then the urgent data is processed (by the `tcp_urg()` function).
- If the packet contains payload, then this data is processed or dropped, or an RST packet is sent, depending on the connection state.
- The packet is deleted in all other cases.

24.3.2 Establishing a Connection

A connection to the partner instance has to be established before a TCP instance can send payload. A connection is established on the basis of the so-called *three-way hand-shake* to reduce the probability of establishing a wrong connection. This could happen, for example, if a connection is established more than once, because of timeouts, or when a connection is established between two TCP protocol instances before an existing connection is reset.

To begin establishing a connection, both TCP protocol instances define an initial value for the sequence number (Initial Sequence Number—ISN). These initial values are exchanged and acknowledged between the participating TCP protocol instances in the three-way handshake.

The connection diagram shown in Figure 24–5 has the following states for the connection establishment phase:

- LISTEN: After passive opening, the local TCP waits for a SYN as a request to establish a connection.
- SYN_SENT: After sending a SYN, the local TCP waits for a connection establishment by the TCP instance of the communication partner.
- SYN_RECV: The local TCP waits for an acknowledgement that the connection has been established (ACK to SYN).
- ESTABLISHED: The connection is established, and the two communicating partners can exchange data; the connection-establishment phase was exited.

The most interesting functions during the establishment of a connection are those to initialize the sock structure, to set options before transmitting data, and to request a connection.

`tcp_v4_init_sock()`	**net/ipv4/tcp_ipv4.c**

This function runs various initialization actions: initialize queues and timers, initialize variables for slow start and maximum segment size, and set the appropriate state (TCP_CLOSE) and the pointer for PF_INET-specific routines.

`tcp_setsockopt()`	**net/ipv4/tcp.c**

This function sets the options selected by the service consumer for the TCP protocol: TCP_MAXSEG, TCP_NODELAY, TCP_CORK, TCP_KEEPIDLE, TCP_KEEPINTVL, TCP_KEEPCNT, TCP_SYNCNT, TCP_LINGER2, TCP_DEFER_ACCEPT, and TCP_WINDOW_CLAMP. The following options are important for the throughput of the TCP protocol:

- TCP_MAXSEG: This option specifies the maximum segment length stored in the user_mss variable of the tcp_opt data structure.
- TCP_NODELAY: This option deactivates the load-control function by setting a suitable value for the nonagle variable in the tcp_opt data structure. (See Section 24.4.3.)

`tcp_connect()`	**net/ipv4/tcp_output.c**

This function initializes an outgoing connection: It reserves memory for the data unit headers in the `sk_buff` structures, initializes the sliding-window variables, sets the maximum segment length (taking the service consumer options into account), sets the TCP header (including the SYN flag), sets the appropriate TCP state, initializes the timers and control variables for retransmission, and finally passes a copy of the initialized segment to the `tcp_transmit_skb()` routine to send and, subsequently, set the timer for retransmission of the connection-establishment segment.

Transition from CLOSED to SYN_SENT To establish the connection, the client sends a packet with the SYN flag set, and then changes from the CLOSED state to the SYN_SENT state. This happens in the `tcp_connect()` method, which is invoked by `tcp_v4_connect()` (see Figure 24–6). The `tcp_v4_connect()` function is invoked when the client application calls `connect()` at the socket interface.

`tcp_connect()` (`net/ipv4/tcp_output.c`) changes the state to SYN_SENT: `tcp_set_state(sk, TCP_SYN_SENT);`.

Transition from LISTEN to SYN_RECV The LISTEN state is assumed by the server's TCP when the server application activates the `listen()` invocation at the socket interface. When the TCP in the server receives the SYN character in the LISTEN state, it changes to the SYN_RECV state. This happens in the `tcp_create_openreq_child()()` function with the `newsk->state = TCP_SYN_RECV;` assignment. The left path in Figure 24–7 shows how this method is invoked. Subsequently, the `tcp_rcv_state_process()` function assumes

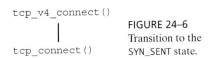

FIGURE 24–6
Transition to the
SYN_SENT state.

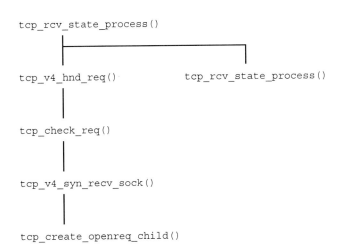

FIGURE 24–7
Transition from LISTEN to the
SYN_RECEIVED and ESTABLISHED states.

further handling. This function uses the function pointer `tcp->af_specific->conn_request()` to invoke the `tcp_v4_conn_request()` function (`net/ipv4/tcp_ipv4.c`), which specifies the initial sequence number. Finally, the `tcp_v4_send_synack()` function is used to send a reply with the SYN and ACK flags set.

Transition from SYN_SENT to ESTABLISHED After it has received a packet with the SYN and ACK flags set, the client TCP sends an ACK to the server and changes from the SYN_SENT state into the ESTABLISHED state.

`tcp_rcv_synsent_state_process()`	`net/ipv4/tcp_input.c`

The appropriate part of this function checks on whether the ACK and SYN flags were set and then returns a packet with the ACK flag set. The TCP changes into the ESTABLISHED state:

```
if (th->ack) {
        (...)
        if (!th->syn)
                goto discard;
        (...)
        tcp_set_state(sk, TCP_ESTABLISHED);
        (...)
        tcp_schedule_ack(tp);
        (...)
}
```

Transition from SYN_SENT to SYN_RECEIVED If the client TCP is in SYN_SENT state and receives only one packet with the SYN flag set, it returns a packet with the SYN and ACK flags set to the server and changes into the SYN_RECEIVED state. This happens when both TCP protocol instances start establishing a connection simultaneously.

`tcp_rcv_synsent_state_process()`	`net/ipv4/tcp_input.c`

TCP changes into the SYN_RECEIVED state:

```
if (th->syn) {
        tcp_set_state(sk, TCP_SYN_RECV);
        (...)
        tcp_send_synack(sk);
        (...)
}
```

Transition from SYN_RECEIVED to ESTABLISHED From the SYN_RECEIVED state, the server switches to the ESTABLISHED state as soon as it receives an ACK character (ACK to SYN).

| `tcp_rcv_state_process()` | **net/ipv4/tcp_input.c** |

TCP changes into the ESTABLISHED state:

```
if (th->ack) {
            switch(sk->state) {
            case TCP_SYN_RECV:
                (...)
                tcp_set_state(sk, TCP_ESTABLISHED);
            }
}
```

Now the connection is established and the communication partners can exchange data.

24.3.3 Tearing Down a Connection

A connection between two communicating partners can be terminated in either of two different ways: graceful close and abort.

- *Graceful close*: The higher-layer protocols of both computers start tearing down the connection either simultaneously or consecutively. TCP monitors this process and ensures that the connection is not disestablished unless all data has finally been transmitted.
- *Abort*: A higher-layer protocol forces the establishment to be torn down. In this case, the process of tearing down a connection is not monitored, and so data can be lost.

The state-transition diagram includes the following states for the connection-closing phase:

- *FINWait 1*: The local TCP initiated the connection teardown process and is waiting for a FIN or ACK to the FIN sent by the remote TCP.
- *FINWait 2*: The local TCP received an ACK to the FIN sent by the remote TCP and is now waiting for the connection to be closed by the remote TCP (FIN).
- *Closing*: Once a FIN has been sent and received, the local TCP waits for the final ACK.
- *TimeWait*: Once it has received the connection-closing ACK from the remote TCP, the local TCP has to wait until it is sure that the remote TCP has received the final ACK.
- *CloseWait*: A request to close the connection (FIN) has been received.
- *Last ACK*: Having sent a FIN to acknowledge the connection teardown, the local TCP is now waiting for the final ACK.
- *Closed*: The connection was closed.

Transition from ESTABLISHED to FIN_WAIT_1 Like the connection-establishment phase, the connection-teardown phase also uses a kind of three-way handshake. In this case, it is assumed that both communication partners are in the ESTABLISHED state. Specifically, a computer, A, initiates the connection closing by sending a packet with the FIN flag set to computer B and then switches to the FIN_WAIT_1 state. (See Figure 24–8.)

```
tcp_close()
    |
tcp_close_state()
```

FIGURE 24–8
Transition from
FIN_WAIT_1 to LAST_ACK.

tcp_close_state()   net/ipv4/tcp.c

This function switches the TCP to the next state, FIN_WAIT_1:

```
/* ns: next state (FIN wait 1) */ tcp_set_state(sk, ns);
```

Transition from ESTABLISHED to CLOSE_WAIT   When computer B receives the packet with the FIN flag set, it sends an ACK character to computer A and switches from the ESTABLISHED state into the CLOSE_WAIT state. (See left path in Figure 24–9.)

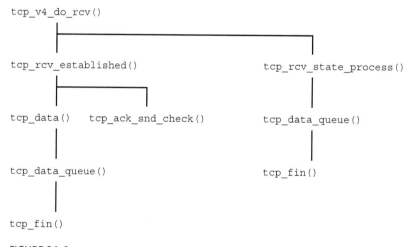

FIGURE 24–9
Transition from CLOSE_WAIT to FIN_WAIT_2 to TIME_WAIT and finally to CLOSING.

tcp_fin()   net/ipv4/tcp_input.c

This function is invoked if the FIN flag is set in the packet received, and TCP is switched to the CLOSE_WAIT state:

```
switch(sk->state) {
        case TCP_SYN_RECV:
        case TCP_ESTABLISHED:
            /* Move to CLOSE_WAIT */
            tcp_set_state(sk, TCP_CLOSE_WAIT);
```

```
            if (th->rst)
                    sk->shutdown = SHUTDOWN_MASK;
            break;
        (...)
}
```
`tcp_ack_snd_check()` (`net/ipv4/tcp_input.c`) sends a packet with the ACK flag set: `tcp_send_ack(sk);`.

Transition from CLOSE_WAIT to LAST_ACK While in the CLOSE_WAIT state, TCP tries to pass all data from the receive buffer to the higher-layer protocol as quickly as possible. TCP sends a FIN character to the TCP in computer A only if the local application in computer B has no more data to send. This confirms the connection teardown process, and the TCP in computer B switches to the LAST_ACK state. (See Figure 24–8.)

`tcp_close_state()`	net/ipv4/tcp.c

TCP switches to the LAST_ACK state as follows:

`/* ns: next state (Last ACK) */ tcp_set_state(sk, ns);`

For the TCP in the FIN_WAIT_1 state in computer A, there are different ways to tear down the connection, depending on how computer B responds.

Transition from FIN_WAIT_1 to FIN_WAIT_2 When the user at computer B sends data ready for transmission, after the FIN character was received, then computer B acknowledges the FIN character by sending an ACK character. Subsequently, it will send the FIN character after all data has been sent. In this case, the TCP in computer A switches to the FIN_WAIT_2 state once it has received the ACK character. (See right-hand path in Figure 2–49.)

`tcp_rcv_state_process()`	net/ipv4/tcp_input.c

This switches TCP into the FIN_WAIT_2 state:

```
if (th->ack) {
      switch(sk->state) {
             (...)
             case TCP_FIN_WAIT1:
                  (...)
                  tcp_set_state(sk, TCP_FIN_WAIT2);
                  (...)
             (...)
      }
}
```

Transition from FIN_WAIT_2 to TIME_WAIT As soon as the TCP in the FIN_WAIT_2 state in computer A receives a FIN character from computer B, it sends an ACK and switches into the TIME_WAIT state (right-hand path in Figure 24–9).

```
tcp_fin()                                              net/ipv4/tcp_input.c
```

```
switch(sk->state) {
    (...)
    case TCP_FIN_WAIT2:
        /* Received a FIN - send ACK and enter TIME_WAIT */
        tcp_send_ack(sk);
        tcp_time_wait(sk, TCP_TIME_WAIT, 0);
        break;
    (...)
}
```

Transition from FIN_WAIT_1 to TIME_WAIT   When computer A in the FIN_WAIT_1 state receives an ACK and a FIN character as a response to its FIN character, then it sends an ACK to acknowledge the connection-closing process, then switches to the FIN_WAIT_2 state:

```
tcp_rcv_state_process()                                net/ipv4/tcp_input.c
```

This function causes TCP to switch into the FIN_WAIT_2 state. If the FIN flag was set, then the transition from FIN_WAIT_2 to TIME_WAIT described above is initiated:

```
switch(sk->state) {
    (...)
    case TCP_FIN_WAIT1:
        (...)
        tcp_set_state(sk, TCP_FIN_WAIT2);
        (...)
        sk->state_change(sk);
    (...)
}
```

Immediately afterwards, the function `tcp_rcv_state_process()` uses `tcp_data_queue()` to invoke the `tcp_fin()` function, if a FIN was set additionally. (See Figure 24–9.) Next, an ACK is sent from within the `tcp_fin()` function, and the state is moved to TIME_WAIT:

```
switch(sk->state) {
    (...)
    case TCP_FIN_WAIT2:
        /* Received a FIN -- send ACK and enter TIME_WAIT. */
        tcp_send_ack(sk);
        tcp_time_wait(sk, TCP_TIME_WAIT, 0);
        break;
    (...)
}
```

Transition from the FIN_WAIT_1 State to CLOSING   If computer A in the FIN_WAIT_1 state initially receives a FIN character, then it switches into the CLOSING state. (See Figure 24–9.)

`tcp_fin()`	**net/ipv4/tcp_input.c**

This function switches the TCP into the CLOSING state and sends a packet with the ACK flag set:

```
switch(sk->state) {
      (...)
      case TCP_FIN_WAIT1:
            tcp_send_ack(sk);
            tcp_set_state(sk, TCP_CLOSING);
      (...)
}
```

Transition from CLOSING to TIME_WAIT   While in the CLOSING state, TCP waits until it receives an ACK character. Subsequently, it switches into the TIME_WAIT state. (See Figure 24–9.)

`tcp_rcv_state_process()`	**net/ipv4/tcp_input.c**

```
if (th->ack) {
      switch(sk->state) {
            (...)
            case TCP_CLOSING:
                  (...)
                  tcp_time_wait(sk, TCP_TIME_WAIT, 0
                  (...)
            (...)
      }
}
```

The TIME_WAIT State   The three different ways to tear down a connection all converge in the TIME_WAIT state. Computer A has to wait a specific period of time (twice the maximum segment lifecycle) before the connection is finally closed.

Additional functions are required to handle the TIME_WAIT state, and the special cases that can occur in this state, correctly.

`_tcp_time_wait()`	**net/ipv4/tcp_minisocks.c**

This function activates the TIME_WAIT state by initializing the `tcp_tw_bucket` structure and entering it in a hash table. As described earlier, this function is invoked by `tcp_fin()` when a connection changes to the TIME_WAIT state.

`_tcp_tw_hashdance()`	**net/ipv4/tcp_minisocks.c**

This function is a helper function of the `tcp_time_wait` function. It adds the `tcp_tw_bucket` structure to a hash table.

`tcp_timewait_kill()`	**net/ipv4/tcp_minisocks.c**

This function deletes a connection, or its representation in the form of a `tcp_tw_bucket` structure, from the hash table for `established` connections.

The receipt of packets for a connection currently in the TIME_WAIT state is separated in the function `tcp_v4_do_rcv()` and taken over by the function `tcp_timewait_state_process()` for further handling.

`tcp_timewait_state_process()`	**net/ipv4/tcp_minisocks.c**

This function processes a packet in the TIME_WAIT state, a state in which packets can be received only under specific conditions. Specifically, in relation to the `tcp_v4_rcv()` function, the following three cases are handled: receiving of a SYN packet, of a SYN-ACK packet, and of an RST packet. The connection is reestablished when an SYN packet arrives under certain conditions. Also, an ACK is sent as a response to a SYN-ACK packet under certain conditions. In contrast, an RST packet is normally sent as a response to an RST packet.

24.4   PROTOCOL MECHANISMS FOR DATA EXCHANGE

The following subsections introduce several protocol mechanisms of the TCP protocol. However, the TCP protocol uses a large number of algorithms; a detailed description of all of these mechanisms would go beyond the scope and volume of this chapter, but we will discuss selected parts of the TCP instance here.

To begin with, Section 24.4.1 will discuss flow control by use of the sliding-window method. In addition to flow control, we will have a look at the methods for window scaling, zero-window probing, and the PAWS mechanism, including the timestamp option. Subsequently, Section 24.4.2 will discuss methods for detection, handling, and avoidance of congestions: slow-start, congestion-avoidance, fast-retransmit, and fast-recovery methods. Finally, Section 24.4.3 covers methods for load avoidance, concentrating on the Nagle algorithm and the transmission of delayed acknowledgements.

The different timers used by a TCP instance and their management will be discussed in Section 24.5.

24.4.1   Flow Control

The TCP protocol uses flow control to regulate the data flow—the data volume exchanged between a sender and a receiver—on a per-time-unit basis.[1] Flow control limits the number of bytes sent in one communication direction to prevent buffer overflows in

---

[1]This section considers flow control in only one direction of a TCP connection and treats the two TCP instances as a sender and a receiver. In bidirectional data exchange, the flow is controlled separately for each direction, where each instance assumes both the role of a sender and the role of a receiver.

the receiving TCP instance and to meet the service consumer requirements. Reasons to limit the data flow by the receiving TCP instance include the following:

▩ The computing performance of the sending TCP instance can be higher than that of the receiving instance. This means that the sender creates segments faster than the receiving TCP instance can process them. In such a situation, the receive buffer at the receiver's end over flows, causing segments to be discarded.

▩ An application removes data from the socket receive buffer at specific intervals, which means that this buffer empties only occasionally. Examples include applications that output multimedia contents, receiving contents faster than their playback rate.

Consequently, flow control can be used to prevent the receive buffer of a receiving TCP instance from overflowing, which would cause additional incoming packets to be dropped. To implement flow control, the TCP protocol uses the *sliding-window mechanism*. This mechanism is based on the assignment of *explicit transmit credits* by the receiver [Pete00]. We will introduce it in the following section.

The Sliding-Window Mechanism The sliding-window protocol mechanism is used commonly in transport protocols or connection-oriented protocols, because it provides for three important tasks:

▩ The original order of a set of data segmented and sent in several packets can be restored in the receiver.

▩ Missing or duplicate packets can be identified by ordering of packets. Together with additional packet-retransmission methods, this enables us to guarantee reliable data transport.

▩ The data flow between two TCP instances can be controlled by assigning transmit credits. Specifically, it is distinguished between a fixed credit quantity (e.g., in HDLC) and explicit credit assignment (e.g., in TCP).

The following elements are added to the protocol header (using the TCP protocol as our example) to handle these tasks:

▩ All data is numbered consecutively by *sequence numbers*. The sequence numbers of the first payload byte in a data packet is carried in the packet header and denotes the sequence number of this segment. The `tp->snd_nxt` variable in the `tcp_opt` structure stores the sequence number of the packet to be sent next.

▩ Together with each segment, a TCP instance informs its communication partner about the number of bytes it can still receive in the *Window* field of the packet header. This is an explicit transmit credit granted to the partner. When a segment is sent, this value is specified by the `tcp_select_window()` function (described later).

▩ Together with each segment, the other TCP instance is informed about the sequence number up to which data has been received correctly (accumulative acknowledgement). More specifically, this value is higher by one, because the sequence number of the data set expected next is specified, so that all data from this sequence number on are implicitly acknowledged (ACK).

Example: Figure 24–10 shows how the sliding-window mechanism is used to implement flow control [Stev94a]. This example uses a simplified version of the slow-start algorithm. The figure shows a scenario where a fast sender ships 8192 bytes to a slow receiver.

In this example, the segments 1 through 3 belong to the connection-establishment phase. In this phase, the receiver grants the sender an initial transmit credit of 4096 bytes in segment 2 (in the win field). Together with the segments 4 through 7, instance A sends 4096 bytes, exhausting its transmit credit. It may not send more segments and has to wait for an acknowledgement from instance B, which actually grants it a new transmit credit. Together with segment 8, all 4096 bytes sent are acknowledged.

However, because it has not yet been able to empty its buffer, the slow receiver does not grant transmit credit to the sender (passing a value of 0 in the win field). Later, an acknowledgement arrives at TCP instance A, together with segment 9, granting it an additional credit of 4096 bytes. Subsequently, the source instance can send its remaining data (segments 10 through 13), arriving again at the situation described above, which results in the transmission of segments 14 and 15. Segments 16 and 17 refer to the connection-teardown phase.

In order for the sender to keep control over all bytes with regard to error handling and flow control, it has to take a certain view on the data. The view of the sending

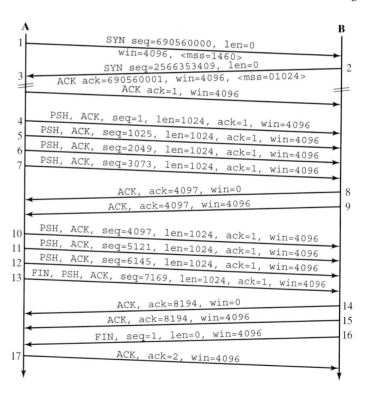

FIGURE 24–10
A fast sender transmits 8192 bytes to a slow receiver.

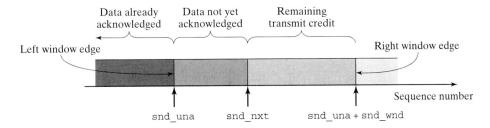

FIGURE 24–11
Byte-sequence range from the sender's view.

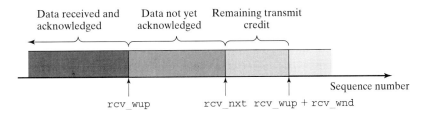

FIGURE 24–12
Byte-sequence range from the receiver's view.

TCP instance on the sliding-window mechanism is shown in Figure 24–11. The receiver's view on the sliding-window mechanism is shown in Figure 24–12.

Notice that the byte sequence range between the segment received last and the right-hand window margin corresponds to the remaining free buffer space. When the receiving TCP instance receives a segment that moves the byte-sequence number of the data byte received last to the right-hand receive window margin, then the buffer of this instance is full, and all segments arriving later cause a buffer overflow, until the right-hand window margin is moved further to the right, so that buffer capacity is available again.

Specifying the Transmit Credit   The flow-control mechanism is effective in many places within a TCP instance. A detailed description of all of these situations would go beyond the scope and volume of this chapter, especially because Section 24.2 discussed several flow-control aspects. This section explains how the explicit transmit credit for a partner instance can be specified in each TCP segment sent.

`tcp_select_window()`	**net/ipv4/tcp_output.c**

```
static __inline__ u16 tcp_select_window(struct sock *sk)
{
        struct tcp_opt *tp = &(sk->tp_pinfo.af_tcp);
        u32 cur_win = tcp_receive_window(tp);
        u32 new_win = __tcp_select_window(sk);
```

```
        /* Never shrink the offered window */
        if(new_win < cur_win)
        {
                new_win = cur_win;
        }
        tp->rcv_wnd = new_win;
        tp->rcv_wup = tp->rcv_nxt;

        /* RFC1323 scaling applied */
        new_win >>= tp->rcv_wscale;
        (...)
        return new_win;
}
```

tcp_select_window(sk) is invoked in the tcp_transmit_skb() method when a TCP segment is sent (except for SYN and SYN-ACK segments) to specify the size of the transmit credit (i.e., the *advertised window*). The current advertised window size is initially specified by the tcp_receive_window(). Subsequently, the __tcp_select_window() function is used to see how much buffer space is available in the computer. This forms the basis for determining the new transmit credit offered to the partner instance. However, as specified in RFC 793, care should be taken not to reduce a previously granted credit.

Once the new advertised window has been computed, the credit is stored in the tcp_opt structure of the connection (tp->rcv_wnd). Also, the tp->rcv_wup is adapted; it stores the current value of the tp->rcv_nxt variable when computing and sending the new credit, known as *window update*. The reason is that each segment arriving after the advertised window has been sent has to be charged against the credit granted, just as happens in the tcp_receive_window() function.

In addition, another TCP algorithm is used in this method, namely an algorithm known as *window scaling*, which will be introduced in the next section. This algorithm had to be introduced to make it possible to work meaningfully with a 16-bit number for the transmit and receive windows. This *scaling factor* was introduced for this reason; it specifies the number of bits to move the window size to the left. With the value F in tp->rcv_wscale, this corresponds to an advertised window increase by factor 2^F.

tcp_receive_window()	including/net/tcp.4

```
/* Compute the actual receive window we are currently
 * advertising. Rcv_nxt can be after the window if the sending
 * peer pushes more data than the offered window.
 */
static __inline__ u32 tcp_receive_window(struct tcp_opt *tp)
{
        s32 win = tp->rcv_wup + tp->rcv_wnd - tp->rcv_nxt;
        if (win < 0)
                win = 0;
        return (u32) win;
}
```

This method calculates how much is left of the transmit credit granted in the last segment, taking the quantity of data received since then into account. Slightly rewriting the equation, we can clearly identify the objective of this computation:

```
s32 win = tp->rcv_wnd - (tp->rcv_nxt - tp->rcv_wup);
```

The difference in brackets is the data quantity received since the last window update was sent: the sequence number expected at the beginning of the next packet, minus the sequence number of the packet expected next when sending the credit, which was stored in the `tp->rcv_wnd` variable. This means that the resulting value, `win`, is the data quantity that can now be received against the credit granted last, corresponding to the actual size of the receive window.

`__tcp_select_window()`	**net/ipv4/tcp_output.c**

```
u32 __tcp_select_window(struct sock *sk)
{
    // free_space is being computed
    free_space = tcp_space(sk);
    (...)
    if (free_space < tp->ack.rcv_mss)
            return 0;

    window = tp->rcv_wnd;
    if (((((int) window) <= (free_space - ((int) mss))) ||
            (((int) window) > free_space))
            window = (((unsigned int) free_space)/mss)*mss;

    return window;
}
```

The `__tcp_select_window()` method is used to check how much memory of this connection is available for the receive buffer and what size can be selected for the receive window.

In the first step, `tcp_space()` determines how much buffer memory is available. After a few adaptations of the determined buffer space, it finally checks on whether there is enough buffer space for a TCP segment with maximum size (`tp->ack.rcv_mss`). If this is not the case, then this would mean that a *Silly Window Syndrome* (*SWS*) [Stev94a] has occurred. To avoid SWS, no credit smaller than the negotiated maximum segment size is granted in such a case.

If the available buffer space is larger than the maximum segment size, then the computation of the new receive window is continued. The `window` variable is set to the value of the credit last granted (`tp->rcv_wnd`). If the old credit is larger, or smaller by more than one segment size, than the available buffer, `window`, is set to the next smaller multiple of a maximum segment size (MSS) of the free buffer space (`free_space`). The value for `window` calculated in this way is returned as a recommendation for the new receive credit.

The Window-Scaling Option   This option can be used to increase the value range for the flow-control transmit window from 2^{16} to $2^{16} \cdot 2^F$, where F is the exponent specified by this option. The window-based flow-control method used in the TCP protocol uses the 16-bit Window field in the TCP header. This field is used to grant transmit credits of up to 65535 bytes (the basic unit of the Window field is 1 byte, excluding window scaling). However, connections with a large path capacity (bandwidth times packet round-trip time) require a larger transmit credit to be able to send data continually. For example, if you consider a connection having transmission rate 10 Mbps and round-trip time 100 ms, then a constant data flow requires a transmit window of at least $10 \ Mbps \cdot 100 \ ms = 125000 \ bytes$.

The *window-scaling* TCP option was introduced in [JaBB92] to solve this problem. Window scaling enlarges the TCP window by from 16 to 30 bits. To ensure backward compatibility, the size of the Window field remains 16 bits; instead, the option changes the basic unit of the Window field to 2^F. Figure 24–13 shows the packet-header format of the window-scaling option used by the TCP instances to negotiate the F parameter [Stev94a]. The Shift Count[2] field includes the scaling factor for the receive window. If the F value of the Shift Count field is unequal to zero, then the basic unit used to compute the receive window is 2^F rather than 1 byte.

The window-scaling option can be sent only in a SYN or SYN–ACK segment in the connection establishment phase—see Section 24.3:

▓ In a SYN segment, it assumes two tasks [JaBB92]: It shows that the TCP protocol instance can use window scaling both when sending and receiving, and it outputs the scaling factor for the receive window of this TCP instance.

▓ In a SYN–ACK segment, this option may be used only if it was specified in the SYN segment. To enable the use of window scaling, both TCP instances have to have the window-scaling option set in their SYN segments during the connection-establishment phase. This ensures that window scaling is used only provided that both instances are actually able to do so.

The maximum scaling factor is limited to 2^{14}, and the maximum byte sequence number is limited to $2^{16} \cdot 2^{14} = 2^{30} < 2^{31}$ to prevent byte-sequence-number overflow. The negotiated window-scaling value is stored in the `tp->rcv_wscale` variable.

Zero-Window Probing   No minimum size for the advertised window is guaranteed, so it can happen that the sender has fully used up its advertised window while the receiver has no more new buffer space available. The consequence is that the sender receives

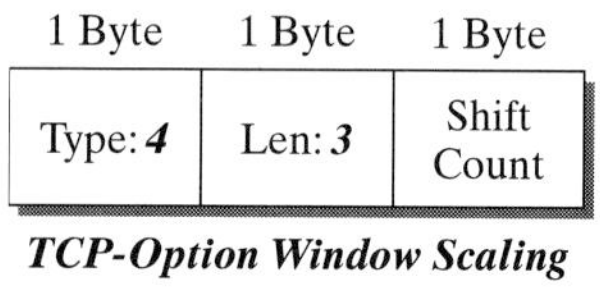

1 Byte	1 Byte	1 Byte
Type: *4*	Len: *3*	Shift Count

TCP-Option Window Scaling

FIGURE 24–13
Format of the window-scaling TCP option.

---

[2]Field name as used in [JaBB92].

an acknowledgement with a new advertising window having size **null**, which means that it must not send more data.

The problem is now that it can receive a new window size (i.e., a new transmit credit) only together with a new packet. There is no additional acknowledgement, because it cannot send more data, which means that the sender now depends on whether the other end sends data. If the receiver does not have data to send, or if it was also granted a window having size **null**, then the two communicating partners would wait eternally to be able to continue sending data.

To solve this problem, the Transmission Control Protocol includes a mechanism known as *zero-window probing*. This mechanism is based on an additional timer, the *probe timer*. When this timer expires, a TCP packet is sent even the advertising window has size **null**. This packet consists only of a packet header; it does not carry payload, because data must not be transmitted in this situation.

The communication peer acknowledges this packet, and, if the other end was able to remove its congestion, at least to some extent, in the meantime, then a window larger than **null** is granted together with this acknowledgement, so that the transmission of data can be resumed. If the window size **null** occurs again, then the communication peers have to wait until the probe timer expires to send another probing packet.

tcp_probe_timer()	net/ipv4/tcp_timer.c

```
static void tcp_probe_timer(struct sock *sk)
{
        (...)
        if (tp->probes_out > max_probes) {
                tcp_write_err(sk);
        } else {
                /* Only send another probe if we didn't close things
                   up. */
                tcp_send_probe0(sk);
        }
}
```

tcp_probe_timer(sk) is the handling routine for the zero-window probe timer, if it leads to a timeout. The routine initially checks on whether the peer has offered a meaningful transmit window over a lengthy period. If several (more than max_probes[3]) window probes were sent unsuccessfully, then an error message is output to announce that there are serious problems in the TCP connection (tcp_write_err()) and to close this connection by tcp_done().

If the maximum number of window probes has not yet been reached, tcp_send_probe0() sends a TCP segment without payload, and the acknowledgment segment will then, it is hoped, grant a credit (advertised window) larger than **null**.

tcp_send_probe0()	net/ipv4/tcp_output.c

---

[3]The value for max_probes is initialized to 15 and can be set in the proc file /proc/sys/net/ipv4/tcp_retries2.

```
void tcp_send_probe0(struct sock *sk)
{
        struct tcp_opt *tp = &(sk->tp_pinfo.af_tcp);
        int err;

        err = tcp_write_wakeup(sk);

        if (tp->packets_out || !tp->send_head) {
                /* Cancel probe timer, if it is not required. */
                tp->probes_out = 0;
                tp->backoff = 0;
                return;
        }
        if (err <= 0) {
                tp->backoff++;
                tp->probes_out++;
                tcp_reset_xmit_timer(sk, TCP_TIME_PROBE0,
                                min(tp->rto << tp->backoff, TCP_RTO_MAX));
        } else { (...) }
}
```

tcp_send_probe0(sk)() uses tcp_write_wakeup(sk)() to generate and send a zero-window probe packet. If the probe timer is no longer needed, as can be seen from the fact that there is currently nothing to be sent (tp->send_head == NULL), or if there are still packets currently under way and their ACKs could contain new credits, then it is not restarted, and the probes_out and backoff parameters are reset.

Otherwise, these parameters are incremented after a probe packet has been sent, and the zero-window probe timer is restarted, so that it expires again after some time. This time is tp->rto*2$^{\text{tp->backoff}}$ or a maximum of TCP_RTO_MAX (120 seconds).

tcp_write_wakeup()	net/ipv4/tcp_output.c

```
int tcp_write_wakeup(struct sock *sk)
{
        (...)
        if ((skb = tp->send_head) != NULL &&
                before(TCP_SKB_CB(skb)->seq, tp->snd_una+tp->snd_wnd))
        {
                (...)
                /* We are probing the opening of a window
                * but the window size is != 0
                * must have been a result SWS avoidance ( sender )
                */
                (...)
                err = tcp_transmit_skb(sk, skb_clone(skb, GFP_ATOMIC));
                (...)
        }
        else
        {
                return tcp_xmit_probe_skb(sk);
```

```
        }
                    (...)
}
```

tcp_write_wakeup(sk) checks for whether the transmit window is of size null and for whether the beginning of the data segment in skb is still within the transmit window range (snd_una + snd_wnd). In the case of a zero-window problem discussed so far, the transmit window has null size, so the tcp_xmit_probe_skb() method is invoked in the else branch. It generates the desired zero-window probe packet.

However, if the above condition is met, and if there is at least one packet in the transmit queue that is within the transmit window range, then we probably have a *silly window syndrome* situation. A packet that corresponds to the requirements of the current transmit window is generated and sent by tcp_transmit_skb().

tcp_xmit_probe_skb()	net/ipv4/tcp_output.c

```c
/* This routine sends a packet with an out of date sequence
 * number. It assumes the other end will try to ack it.
 */
static int tcp_xmit_probe_skb(struct sock *sk, int urgent)
{
        (...)
        skb = alloc_skb(MAX_TCP_HEADER, GFP_ATOMIC);
        (...)
        /* Reserve space for headers and set control bits. */
        skb_reserve(skb, MAX_TCP_HEADER);
        skb->csum = 0;
        TCP_SKB_CB(skb)->flags = TCPCB_FLAG_ACK;
        TCP_SKB_CB(skb)->sacked = urgent;
        /* Use a previous sequence. This should cause the other
         * end to send an ack. Don't queue or clone SKB, just send it.
         */
        TCP_SKB_CB(skb)->seq = urgent ? tp->snd_una : tp->snd_una - 1;
        TCP_SKB_CB(skb)->end_seq = TCP_SKB_CB(skb)->seq;
        TCP_SKB_CB(skb)->when = tcp_time_stamp;
        return tcp_transmit_skb(sk, skb);
}
```

tcp_xmit_probe_skb(sk, urgent) creates a TCP segment without payload, because the transmit window has size **null**, and data currently must not be sent. alloc_skb() procures a socket buffer having length MAX_TCP_HEADER. As mentioned above, no payload is sent, and the packet consists only of the TCP packet header.

The trick of this routine utilizes the fact that an old sequence number (i.e., a previously acknowledged sequence number) is written to the packet. tp->snd_una holds the first, so far unacknowledged sequence number, which means that tp->snd_una - 1 meets this purpose. The old sequence number causes the counterpart to send an acknowledgement. Together with this ACK, it also sends the current transmit window size, which is now, it is hoped, larger than **null**.

In the next line, the last sequence number is set to the first sequence number of this packet, which results in the payload size end_seq - seq = 0. Subsequently, a timestamp is added to the segment, and the segment is sent by `tcp_transmit_skb()`.

`tcp_ack_probe()`	`net/ipv4/tcp_input.c`

```
static void tcp_ack_probe(struct sock *sk)
{
        struct tcp_opt *tp = &(sk->tp_pinfo.af_tcp);

        /* Was it a usable window open? */
        if (!after(TCP_SKB_CB(tp->send_head)->end_seq, tp->snd_una +
                        tp->snd_wnd)) {
                tp->backoff = 0;
                tcp_clear_xmit_timer(sk, TCP_TIME_PROBE0);
                /* Socket must be waked up by subsequent tcp_data_snd_check().
                 * This function is not for random using!
                 */
        } else {
                tcp_reset_xmit_timer(sk, TCP_TIME_PROBE0,
                                min(tp->rto << tp->backoff, TCP_RTO_MAX));
        }
}
```

`tcp_ack_probe(sk, ack)` is invoked in `tcp_ack()` when a TCP segment with the ACK flag set is received and if it is suspected to be a reply to a zero-window probe segment. Depending on whether the segment opens the receive window (the first packet in the transmit queue affects the transmit window), `tcp_clear_xmit_timer()` stops the zero-window probe timer or `tcp_reset_xmit_timer()` restarts this timer.

Protection Against Wrapped Sequence Numbers (PAWS) The PAWS mechanism prevents a byte-sequence-number overflow, which would lead to inconsistencies, from occurring in connections with too large a bandwidth/delay product (i.e., when there is an excessive amount of data "in the pipe").

The byte-sequence numbers of a TCP connection are of length 32 bits. With a sufficient transmission rate and an accordingly large packet round-trip time, byte-sequence numbers can reach the end of the byte-sequence-number range within the time that a segment is delayed in router queues and thereby cause a byte-sequence-number overflow. In this case, the byte-sequence numbers take the initial values of the byte-sequence-number range. In this situation, the TCP protocol cannot identify delayed segment duplicates if their byte-sequence numbers are within the receive window and consequently cannot drop these duplicates.

The PAWS mechanism was introduced to solve this problem. It uses the Timestamp option, to protect the TCP protocol within a connection from problems caused by several segments' having the same byte-sequence numbers. The PAWS mechanism operates basically by attaching timestamps to TCP segments and dropping a segment as a duplicate if its timestamp is smaller than the timestamp of the segment received last, which cause the receive window to move forward. (See Section 24.4.1.)

All segments arriving over an established connection are subject to the following checks by the PAWS algorithm [JaBB92]:

- The RST flag should not be set.
- The TCP partner instance should have received a valid Timestamp option (i.e., the `tp->ts_recent` variable contains a valid value).
- If an incoming segment contains the Timestamp option, and if its timestamp, `tp->rcv_tsval`, is actually smaller than the timestamp stored last, `tp->ts_recent`, then this segment should be dropped. This check is done in the `tcp_paws_discard()` function shown below, which is invoked in Slow Path in the `tcp_rcv_established()` function. (See Section 24.2.1.)

```
extern __inline__ int tcp_paws_discard(struct tcp_opt *tp, struct sk_buff
  *skb)
{
  return ((s32)(tp->ts_recent - tp->rcv_tsval) > TCP_PAWS_WINDOW &&
        xtime.tv_sec < tp->ts_recent_stamp + TCP_PAWS_24DAYS &&
        !tcp_disordered_ack(tp, skb));
}
```

The second condition checks the validity of the `tp->ts_recent` timestamp. There is a very small probability that an extremely long time has passed since the time when the timestamp was taken from a received segment, which is stored in the `tp->ts_recent_stamp` variable. This means that, if more than 24 days have passed since this time, the `ts_recent` timestamp is considered invalid. [Stev94b] includes an example for such a situation.

If the TCP connection is not in the ESTABLISHED state, then the PAWS check on incoming packets is done in the `tcp_paws_check()` method (`net/ipv4/tcp_input.c`).

The *PAWS* mechanism requires the use of the *timestamp* option and the timestamp property as monotonically increasing values. In addition, it requires that the timestamp increase at least once per window and that the time in which it repeatedly takes the same value is greater than the maximum segment lifecycle.

The *timestamp* option is a prerequisite for the PAWS algorithm and additionally is used to determine the packet round-trip time and the *retransmission timeout*; we will introduce it next.

The Timestamp Option   This option offers TCP instances a way to continually probe and adapt the packet *round-trip time (RTT)* of a connection. The timestamp option allows you to set a timestamp in each segment. The receiver returns this timestamp in the acknowledgement segment, allowing the sender to compute the round-trip time for each acknowledgement received. A timestamp is a monotonically increasing value taken from a timer. Figure 24–14 shows the format of the *timestamp* option in the TCP packet header [JaBB92].

The *timestamp* option was introduced to make possible a more exact measurement of the packet round-trip time. When setting a segment, the sender sets the current

1 Byte	1 Byte	4 Bytes	4 Bytes
Type: *8*	Len: *10*	Timestamp value (TSval)	Value of timestamp received (TSecr)

FIGURE 24–14
Format of the timestamp option in the
TCP packet header.

TCP Timestamp Option

timestamp in the TSval field. The receiver returns this timestamp in the TSecr field of the ACK segment, together with the timestamp it set. Because the receiver returns the timestamp it received together with the acknowledgement for data it accepted to the sender without considering the timestamp's value, the timestamp unit is not relevant for the receiver. In particular, no timer synchronization between the communicating TCP instances is required [Stev94a]. This means that the sender can compute the packet round-trip time for each acknowledgement it received; this calculation is done in the method tcp_rtt_estimator() method of the TCP instance in the Linux kernel.

Notice that only a single timestamp variable per connection is used, to minimize the number of states the communicating TCP instances have to maintain. The value of this variable is updated by the following algorithm:

▦ TCP holds the value for the timestamp to be sent in the next acknowledgement in the tp->ts_recent parameter.

▦ When an incoming TCP segment with the *timestamp* option set in the tcp_rcv_established() method is handled, then the routine tcp_ts_replace_recent() checks on whether the tp->rcv_tsval timestamp contained in the tp->ts_recent variable should be accepted. If so, this is done by the tcp_store_ts_recent() method. In *fast path*, acceptance of the timestamp is checked directly.

▦ Whenever a TCP segment with the timestamp option should be sent, the value of the timestamp received is copied from the tp->ts_recent variable to the TSecr field when the packet header is assembled in tcp_transmit_skb().

The above algorithm shows the following behavior when segments are delayed or lost:

▦ When acknowledgements are delayed by the receiver, the timestamp in the acknowledgement refers to the first of the segments being acknowledged.

▦ When an incoming segment belongs to the current window, but arrives out of order (which implies that an earlier segment was lost), the timestamp of the earlier segment is returned as soon as it arrives, rather than the timestamp of the segment that arrived out of order.

Figure 24–15 shows an example for the use of the *timestamp* option [JaBB92]. The *timestamp* option can be negotiated by the same principle used for the *window scaling* option during the connection-establishment phase. A TCP instance can set the *timestamp* option in the initial SYN segment (i.e., in a segment with the SYN bit set and

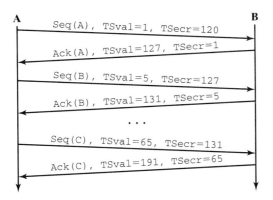

FIGURE 24–15
Example using the timestamp option.

the ACK bit not set), and it may set this option in other segments only provided that it received them in the initial SYN segment for this connection.

24.4.2 Detecting, Avoiding, and Handling Congestions

The flow-control mechanisms introduced in Section 24.4.1 ensure that only that amount of data is sent to a receiving TCP instance that this instance can accommodate, to avoid packet losses in the receiving end system. However, buffer overflows can occur in the forwarding systems—more specifically, in the queues of the Internet Protocol—when they are not emptied fast enough and more data arrives than can be sent over a network adapter. This situation is called *congestion*.

Detecting a Congestion   Congestions occur mainly in the IP instances in forwarding systems. The question is now how a loss by the TCP instances in the end systems can be detected. The reason is that the TCP instances suffer from such a congestion, and have to retransmit their data. In addition, they have to reduce their transmission rates, initially to resolve the congestion and then to avoid additional congestions. Unfortunately, the Internet Protocol does not respond to congestions.

This means that recognizing a congestion is a basic prerequisite for using the congestion-handling and -prevention methods. The TCP protocol has several mechanisms to detect congestions and uses various algorithms to respond to a congestion:

- A *retransmission timer* waits for a certain period of time for an acknowledgement once a packet has been sent. If no acknowledgement arrives, it is assumed that a congestion caused the packet to be lost. The initial response to a lost packet is the slow-start phase, which, from a certain point on, is replaced by the congestion-avoidance algorithm. Both methods will be introduced in the following section.

- The *receipt of duplicate acknowledgements (dupacks)* is an indication that a data segment was lost, because, although subsequent segments arrive, they cannot be acknowledged, because of cumulative ACK segments. In this case, it is normally not assumed that a serious congestion occurred, because subsequent segments were actually received. For this reason, the more recent TCP versions (TCP Reno, TCP New Reno) do not respond to a loss by means of the slow-start phase, but instead by means of the *fast retransmit* and *fast recovery* methods, which will be introduced further along.

Slow-Start and Congestion Avoidance   The slow-start algorithm is used once a connection has been initialized and the retransmission timer has expired. It serves for stepwise approximation of the transmitted data volume to the transmission capacity available in this connection. The slow-start algorithm is normally implemented together with the congestion-avoidance algorithm.

At the beginning of a connection, or after a congestion, the minimum transmission capacity is assumed; subsequently, it is increased exponentially until segments are lost or a threshold value is reached, representing an approximate measure for the available capacity. The following parameters are defined:

- The *congestion window* (snd_cwnd) denotes the number of bytes that may be under way at a certain point in time (without acknowledgement). This means that, in addition to the normal transmission window of the sliding-window mechanism, it defines a second credit, which also has to be available and sufficient to be able to send data.

  The congestion window is initialized to at most one segment at the beginning of the slow-start phase (i.e., only one segment, and that of minimum size, can be sent). Subsequently, the congestion window is increased by one byte for each arriving acknowledgement of a byte. This corresponds to doubling the congestion window when the data volume of the entire window has been fully sent and acknowledged.

- The *slow-start threshold* (ssthresh) limits the exponential growth of the slow-start phase when the available transmission capacity is approximately known. At the beginning of a connection, the threshold is set to the maximum value, to ensure that the slow-start phase will be able to test for the available capacity. If a packet loss occurs, then the threshold value is set to half the size of the current congestion window, to limit the exponential growth of the slow-start phase.

The *congestion avoidance* algorithm starts once the threshold value for the congestion window has been reached in the slow-start phase. This algorithm represents a measure for the available transmission capacity. For this reason, the congestion window still increases linearly during the congestion-avoidance phase, as shown in Figure 24–16. This value increases by one once n acknowledgements have arrived, where n corresponds to the size of the current congestion window. This means that the TCP instance increases its transmission rate only slowly, but still in a strictly monotone way. Naturally, the total data volume that can be sent corresponds to the minimum from the transmission window of the sliding-window algorithm and the congestion window, whichever is less.

Figure 24–16 also shows how the two mechanisms cooperate. The slow-start algorithm operates at the beginning of a data transmission. It terminates its exponential growth as soon as a congestion occurs, which is detected by the fact that the retransmission timer expires. According to the approach described above, the slow-start threshold, snd_ssthresh, is set to half of the current congestion window (i.e., 20 segments, in the above figure). Consequently, snd_cwnd takes the value 1 (2, in the Linux kernel), because the congestion was identified by the expiration of the retransmission timer. Next,

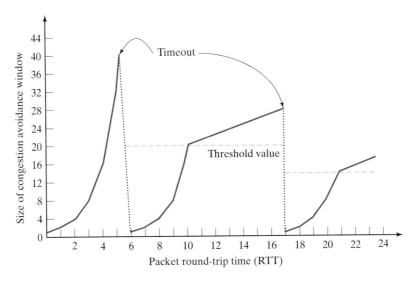

FIGURE 24–16
Operation of the slow-start and congestion avoidance mechanisms.

the TCP instance returns to the slow-start phase, which continues until snd_cwnd reaches the value snd_ssthresh. Subsequently, the congestion-avoidance algorithm is used until another congestion occurs at a window size of 28 segments; finally, this congestion is handled by the same approach.

The following example shows how the two mechanisms described above are implemented in the TCP instance of the Linux kernel:

`tcp_v4_init_sock()`	**net/ipv4/tcp_ipv4.c**

```
static int tcp_v4_init_sock(struct sock *sk)
{
        struct tcp_opt *tp = &(sk->tp_pinfo.af_tcp);
        (...)
        /* So many TCP implementations out there (incorrectly) count the
         * initial SYN frame in their delayed-ACK and congestion control
         * algorithms that we must have the following bandaid to talk
         * efficiently to them. -DaveM
         */
        tp->snd_cwnd = 2;

        /* See draft-stevens-tcpca-spec-01 for discussion of the
         * initialization of these values.
         */
        tp->snd_ssthresh = 0x7fffffff; /* Infinity */
        tp->snd_cwnd_clamp = ~0;
        tp->mss_cache = 536;
        (...)
}
```

Parameters for a TCP connection are initialized in the `tcp_v4_init_sock()` method, which is defined as an `init()` function of the `proto` structure. The most important parameters for congestion control are as follows:

- The size of the initial congestion window (`tp->snd_cwnd`) is set to the value two.
- The threshold value for the exponential growth (`tp->snd_ssthresh`) is set to "infinite" (the largest value that can be represented by an `int` variable).

The reason why the congestion window size is initialized to two and not to one (as by default) is as follows (as in many other places in the source text):

- This is an efficient way to avoid *errors in the TCP implementations of other operating systems*, ensuring smooth operation. In this case, some TCP instances count the SYN packet, even though the slow-start algorithm should not become active before the connection has been successfully established (as with all congestion avoidance and flow-control algorithms).

The following source-code fragment of the TCP instance shows how the congestion window grows exponentially during the slow-start phase and how the subsequent linear increase during the congestion-avoidance phase is implemented in the Linux kernel.

`tcp_cong_avoid()`	**net/ipv4/tcp_input.c**

```c
/* This is Jacobson's slow start and congestion avoidance.
* SIGCOMM '88, p. 328.
*/
static __inline__ void tcp_cong_avoid(struct tcp_opt *tp)
{
        if (tp->snd_cwnd <= tp->snd_ssthresh)
        { /* In 'safe' area, increase. */
          if (tp->snd_cwnd < tp->snd_cwnd_clamp)
             tp->snd_cwnd++;
        }
        else
        { /* In dangerous area, increase slowly.
          * In theory this is tp->snd_cwnd += 1 / tp->snd_cwnd
          */
        if (tp->snd_cwnd_cnt >= tp->snd_cwnd)
        {
                if (tp->snd_cwnd < tp->snd_cwnd_clamp)
                        tp->snd_cwnd++;
                tp->snd_cwnd_cnt=0;
        }
        else
                tp->snd_cwnd_cnt++;
        }
}
```

`tcp_cong_avoid(tp)` implements the congestion window growth in the slow-start and congestion-avoidance algorithms. `tcp_cong_avoid()` is invoked when an incoming TCP segment with valid acknowledgement (ACK) is handled in `tcp_ack()`. (See Section 24.2.1.)

Initially, the code checks for whether the TCP connection is still in the slow-start phase or is already in the congestion-avoidance phase:

▓ The congestion window is increased by one in the *slow-start phase* (i.e., when the current value of the congestion window `tp->snd_cwnd` is not yet bigger than the current threshold value `tp->snd_ssthresh`). However, it must not exceed the upper limit value, `tp->snd_cwnd_clamp`. This means that, in this phase, the congestion window is increased by one upon each incoming acknowledgement. In practice, this means that the amount of data that can be sent doubles each time. This behavior corresponds to the exponential growth shown in Figure 24–16.

▓ In the *congestion-avoidance phase*, the congestion window will be increased by one only if *n* acknowledgements have been previously received, where *n* corresponds to the current congestion-window value.

To implement this behavior, the additional variable `tp->snd_cwnd_cnt` is introduced; it is incremented by one upon each incoming acknowledgement (i.e., upon each call of `tcp_cong_avoid()` in the congestion-avoidance phase). Next, when the congestion-window value `tp->snd_cwnd` is reached, `tp->snd_cwnd` can finally be increased by one, and `tp->snd_cwnd_cnt` is reset. This method makes linear growth achievable.

In summary: There is initially an exponential increase of the congestion window, but, once the threshold value has been reached, there is only a linear growth, as shown in Figure 24–16. Notice at this point that the congestion window increases continually in `tcp_cong_avoid()`. It increases until the criteria for a congestion are met, which will then cause it to reduce in the function described next.

`tcp_enter_loss()`	**net/ipv4/tcp_input.c**

```
void tcp_enter_loss(struct sock *sk, int how)
{
        struct tcp_opt *tp = &sk->tp_pinfo.af_tcp;
        (...)
        /* Reduce ssthresh if it has not yet been
            made inside this window. */
        if ((tp->ca_state <= TCP_CA_Disorder)
                    || (tp->snd_una == tp->high_seq)
                    || (tp->ca_state == TCP_CA_Loss && !tp->retransmits))
        {
            tp->prior_ssthresh = tcp_current_ssthresh(tp);
            tp->snd_ssthresh = tcp_recalc_ssthresh(tp);
        }
```

```
tp->snd_cwnd = 1;
tp->snd_cwnd_cnt = 0;
tp->snd_cwnd_stamp = tcp_time_stamp;
(...)
```

tcp_enter_loss(sk,   how) is invoked in the handling routine of the *retransmission* timer (tcp_retransmit_timer). This timer triggers whenever a transmitted data segment has not been acknowledged by the time the *retransmission time-out (RTO)* expires. It is assumed that the data segment or its acknowledgement was lost. In modern networks, except wireless networks, packet losses occur only in congestion situations, and packets have to be discarded in forwarding systems to handle buffer overflows.

In such a situation, which is detected either because no acknowledgement arrives or because duplicate acknowledgements arrive, the TCP congestion-handling routine has to ensure that the data flow of the TCP connection involved is reduced.

Initially, the threshold value for exponential growth in the slow-start phase is set to a new value, which is computed by the tcp_recalc_ssthresh() method. Before this value is computed, the current threshold value is stored in the tp->prior_ssthresh variable. Subsequently, the other congestion-control variables—primarily the congestion window—are reset. tp->snd_cwnd is set to a maximum segment, which causes the TCP connection to start the next transmission in the slow-start phase again.

tcp_recalc_ssthresh()	include/net/tcp.h

```
/* Recalculate snd_ssthresh, we want to set it to:
 *
 * one-half the current congestion window, but no
 * less than two segments
 */
static inline __u32 tcp_recalc_ssthresh(struct tcp_opt *tp)
{
        return max(tp->snd_cwnd>>1, 2);
}
```

The threshold value for the exponential growth in the slow-start phase is recalculated in tcp_recalc_ssthresh(tp) as soon as a congestion situation is detected. Consequently, the current size of the congestion window, tp->snd_cwnd, is reduced to half as soon as the congestion is detected and is returned as the new threshold value. However, care is taken only that the threshold value not be smaller than two.

Fast Retransmit and Fast Recovery   The fast-retransmit algorithm was integrated in the TCP protocol for fast detection of single packet losses. Previously, the only way to detect packet losses was the expiry of the retransmit timer, and TCP responded to this by reducing the transmission rate in the slow-start phase.

The new fast-retransmit algorithm enables TCP to detect a packet loss before the retransmit timer expires—that is, when a single segment out of a series of many segments is lost. The receiver responds to incoming segments with one segment missing by

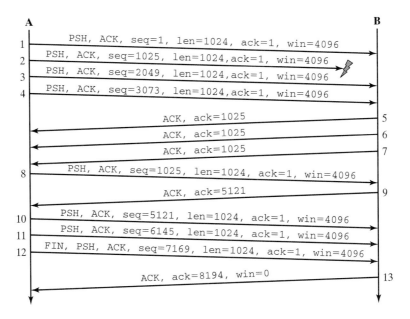

FIGURE 24–17
Detecting a single packet loss by duplicate acknowledgements (segments 5 to 7) and handling by fast retransmit.

sending duplicate acknowledgements, because it is now receiving packets out of order. Figure 24–17 shows such a situation.

The sender can see from the duplicate acknowledgements it received that a segment must have been lost, but that other segments still made their way to the receiver. This means that a massive congestion is very unlikely. The sender retransmits the data segment that follows the sequence number of the duplicate acknowledgements without waiting for the retransmission timer to trigger.

A new slow-start phase would be the normal response to a packet loss; that reaction would significantly reduce the transmission rate. Given duplicate acknowledgements, however, TCP detects that there is no serious congestion. For this reason, the fast-recovery method was introduced as an extension of the fast-retransmit algorithm. After a fast retransmit, the congestion window is not set to a minimum value, but instead cut in half, and, subsequently, increased linearly directly in the congestion-avoidance phase.

We will next describe how these two algorithms cooperate in the TCP instance of the Linux kernel[4]:

▦ When three acknowledgement duplicates are received, the variable `tp->snd_ssthresh` is set to half of the current transmit window. The missing segment is retransmitted, and the congestion window `tp->snd_cwnd` takes the value `tp->ssthresh + 3 * MSS`, where *MSS* denotes the maximum segment size.

---

[4]We will keep our discussion short, because the implementation of these two algorithms is extensive and is distributed over many positions within the TCP instance.

░ Each time that a duplicate acknowledgement is received, the congestion window `tp->snd_cwnd` increases by the value of the maximum segment size, and an additional segment is sent (if permitted by the transmit window size).

░ When the first acknowledgment of new data arrives, then `tp->snd_cwnd` takes the original value of `tp->snd_ssthresh`, which was stored in `tp->prior_ssthresh`. This acknowledgement should acknowledge the data segment that was originally lost. In addition, it should acknowledge all segments sent between the lost packet and the third acknowledgement duplicate.

24.4.3 Congestion Avoidance

The TCP protocol could produce considerable load, even when a relatively small amount of data is sent. This effect is due to the size of the TCP packet header, which comprises 20 bytes. If we add the IP packet header and an Ethernet packet header to this, the protocol-control information sent with each packet adds up to more than fifty bytes. With scarcely filled data packets or frequent acknowledgement packets (consisting of packet headers only), a large amount of bandwidth is wasted on packet headers. The two methods described below are aimed at minimizing these circumstances.

Delayed Acknowledgements   The principle of *delayed acks* enables the TCP protocol to delay an acknowledgement for a segment. The acknowledgement is delayed so as to eventually be sent together with the data (which is also called *piggybacking*) and so as to enable TCP to accumulate several acknowledgements. The delayed transmission of acknowledgements is implemented by using the *delack* timer, which will be introduced in Section 24.5.

Nagle Algorithm   John Nagle's algorithm, also known by the name *small-packet-avoidance algorithm*, serves to avoid excessive network load due to a large number of small TCP packets. For this purpose, the data to be sent is held back as long as possible, because two complete TCP packets would have to be sent for each payload byte in the worst case: the first packet to transport the data, and the second packet, which is sent by the receiver, to acknowledge the first one.

   This worst case occurs when data to be sent accumulate more slowly than they can be sent (e.g., in a Telnet connection, where the data to be transmitted is transported very slowly—a few characters per second—to the TCP instance. The TCP instance would pack each character in a packet and send these packets separately. The packet-header overhead created by this approach was described above.

   To avoid high loads in the network due to these many small segments, ones smaller than the negotiated maximum segment length (MSS), the Nagle algorithm [Nagl84] introduces the limitation that at most one segment in a connection may be unacknowledged before other segments are sent. The algorithm says that small segments should be retained pending arrival of an acknowledgement in the case of sent and unacknowledged segments. The data contained in these small segments are grouped into a larger segment. However, if an application (e.g., Telnet) wants to avoid packet delays, for some specific reason, then it can use the socket option `TCP_NODELAY` to disable the Nagle algorithm.

The following fragment shows the complete source text of the Nagle algorithm. These few lines are sufficient to achieve the behavior discussed above.

| `tcp_nagle_check()` | **include/net/tcp.h** |

```
static __inline__ int tcp_nagle_check(struct tcp_opt *tp,
                    struct sk_buff *skb, unsigned mss_now)
{
    return (skb->len < mss_now &&
        !(TCP_SKB_CB(skb)->flags & (TCPCB_FLAG_URG|TCPCB_FLAG_FIN))
        && (tp->nonagle == 2 ||
            (!tp->nonagle &&
            tp->packets_out &&
            tcp_minshall_check(tp))));
}
```

The Nagle algorithm (i.e., the `tcp_nagle_check()` method) is asked in `tcp_snd_test()` whether the existing segment may be sent. If it wants to prevent the segment from being sent at this time, then `tcp_nagle_check()` returns the value `true`. If there are reasons for immediate transmission of this data, then it returns `false`.

The first check is for whether there is a sufficient amount of data to fill a complete segment. If this is the case, then there is no reason to delay its transmission further. Consequently, the segment length (`skb->len`) collaborates with `mss_now` to determine the amount of data than can be sent at once.

The next check is to see whether there are particularly important control packets (e.g., FIN or URG packets). These packets have to be sent immediately, and Nagle's algorithm must not delay them.

The next line checks for whether the socket option TCP_CORK was activated (`tp-nonagle == 2`). It forces that only complete packets will be sent.

If all checks done so far have resulted in `false`, the next step checks for whether the Nagle algorithm has been disabled by the socket option TCP_NODELAY. If so, then `tp->nonagle` would have the value one, and `tcp_nagle_check()` would return `false`, which means that the segment can be sent.

However, if the Nagle algorithm is still active, then `tcp_minshall_check()` (described later) checks for whether small and incompletely filled packets are on their way (i.e., packets that have not yet been acknowledged). If there are no small and unacknowledged packets in the connection, this data packet may be sent; otherwise, it has to be delayed.

The previous line checks for whether any acknowledgements for packets are still missing. Only one variable has to be checked here, so this query is much faster than the method call in the next line (`tcp_minshall_check(tp)`). *Lazy evaluation* saves time, because the slower method has to be invoked only if the fast query has not yet returned a result.

| `tcp_minshall_check()` | **include/net/tcp.h** |

```
static __inline__ int tcp_minshall_check(struct tcp_opt *tp)
{
        return after(tp->snd_sml,tp->snd_una) &&
                !after(tp->snd_sml, tp->snd_nxt);
}
```

24.5   TIMER MANAGEMENT IN TCP

In closing, this section briefly discusses how timers are managed in TCP. Timers are used in different positions within the TCP protocol to control retransmissions and to limit the hold time for missing packets.

24.5.1 Data Structures

struct timer_list	include/linux/timer.h

```
struct timer_list {
        struct list_head list;
        unsigned long expires;
        unsigned long data;
        void (*function)(unsigned long);
        volatile int running;
};
```

The basis for each timer is the `jiffies` variable. As described in Chapter 2, it is updated by Linux every 10 ms.

A timer structure includes a function pointers that takes a behavior function when initialized. This function is invoked when the timer expires. The time at which it expires depends on the `expires` field. This field takes an offset (in the `jiffies` unit) for the current time (also in the `jiffies` unit). The behavior function is invoked when this value is reached.

TCP maintains seven timers for each connection:

▧ SYNACK timer This timer is used when a TCP instance changes its state from LISTEN to SYN_RECV. The TCP instance of the server initially waits three seconds for an ACK. If no ACK arrives within this time, then the connection request is considered outdated.

▧ Retransmit timer Because the TCP protocol uses only positive acknowledgements, the sending TCP instance has to see for itself whether a segment was lost. It does this by use of the `retransmit` timer, the expiry of which indicates that a segment could have been lost, causing its retransmission.

The exponential backoff method assumes that retransmissions are caused by a congestion. When segments are retransmitted, the timer value is increased exponentially so as to be able to detect segment losses.

The `retransmit` timer determines when packets have to be retransmitted during a data transmission phase. This value depends on the round-trip time and normally is within the range from 200 ms to two minutes.

This timer is also used during the establishment of a connection. It is initialized to three seconds. Upon expiry of this time, the backoff mechanism is used five times.

- Delayed ACK timer This timer delays the transmission of ACK packets. The value is smaller than 200 ms.

- Keepalive timer This timer is used to test whether a connection is still up. It is invoked for the first time after nine hours. Subsequently, nine probes are sent every 75 seconds. If all probes fail, the connection is reset.

- Probe timer This timer is used to test for a defined time interval, to see whether the zero window still applies. The value depends on the round-trip time.

- FinWait2 timer The expiry of this timer switches the connection from the FIN_WAIT2 state into the CLOSED state, if no FIN packet from the partner arrives.

- TWKill timer This timer manages the interval in the TIME_WAIT state. The value is twice the maximum segment lifecycle, which is 60 seconds.

24.5.2 Functions

This section first introduces all general timer functions.

`tcp_init_xmit_timers()`	**net/ipv4/tcp_timer.c**

`tcp_init_xmit_timers(sk)` initializes the set of various timers. The `timer_list` structures are hooked, and the function pointers are converted to the respective behavior functions.

`tcp_reset_xmit_timer()`	**include/net/tcp.h**

The function `tcp_reset_xmit_timer(sk, what, when)` sets the timer specified in `what` to the time `when` (i.e., to the time `jiffies + when`).

`tcp_clear_xmit_timer()`	**include/net/tcp.h**

The function `tcp_clear_xmit_timer(sk)` removes all timers set for a connection from the linked list of `timer_list` structures.

SYNACK Timer The actions of the SYNACK timer are implemented in the function `tcp_synack_timer(sk)` (`include/linux/tcp_timer.c`). This timer walks through a list of all connections with unacknowledged SYNACK packets and deletes all connections for which the timeout value `min ((TCP_TIMEOUT_INIT << req->re-trans), TCP_RTO_MAX)`, has expired. Subsequently, the `keepalive` timer is started for a new connection and initialized by `TCP_SYNQ_INTERVAL`.

There are various functions to manage the keepalive timer:

`tcp_delete_keepalive_timer()`	**net/ipv4/tcp_timer.c**

The function `tcp_delete_keepalive_timer(sk)` removes the keepalive timer from the list of `timer_list` structures.

`tcp_reset_keepalive_timer()`	**net/ipv4/tcp_timer.c**

The function `tcp_reset_keepalive_timer(sk, len)` sets the timer to the value `jiffies + len`.

`tcp_keepalive_timer()`	**net/ipv4/tcp_timer.c**

The function `tcp_keepalive_timer(data)` is the behavior function for the keepalive timer. When this function is invoked, the state of the connection is checked to decide whether this connection should be terminated. This function implements various logically separated TCP timers. In addition to the SYNACK timer described here, it implements the timeout in the FIN_WAIT_2 state and the actual keepalive timer.

Retransmit Timer The client's TCP instance sends a SYN packet to the server and waits for an answer (with SYN and ACK set) while the connection-establishment phase is active. At the same time, `tcp_connect()` (in `net/ipv4/tcp_output.c`) and the function `tcp_reset_xmit_timer(sk, TCP_TIME_RETRANS, tp->rto)` are used to set the retransmit timer to the value `TCP_TIMEOUT_INIT`. `TCP_TIMEOUT_INIT` is set to the value 3*HZ in the file `include/net/tcp.h`.

The retransmit timer is also used when the connection is established and running. The duration of the timeout is doubled, in the `tcp_retransmit_timer()` function (`net/ipv4/tcp_timer.c`), upon each retransmission, until it has arrived at the maximum and the connection is reset:

```
tp->rto = min(tp->rto << 1, TCP_RTO_MAX);
     tcp_reset_xmit_timer(sk, TCP_TIME_RETRANS, tp->rto);
     if (tp->retransmits > sysctl_tcp_retries1)
           __sk_dst_reset(sk);
```

The retransmit timer is initialized to the retransmission timeout (RTO), which is recalculated by use of various helper functions:

`tcp_set_rto()`	**net/ipv4/tcp_input.c**

This function computes the RTO (retransmission timeout) from the round-trip time values.

`tcp_bound_rto()`	**net/ipv4/tcp_input.c**

The function `tcp_bound_rto(tp)` limits the value range for RTO to a fixed interval.

`tcp_ack_saw_tstamp()`	**net/ipv4/tcp_input.c**

The function `tcp_ack_saw_tstamp(sk, tp, seq, ack, flag)` computes and sets the RTO and terminates the retransmission mode, if applicable.

`tcp_ack_packets_out()`	**net/ipv4/tcp_input.c**

In the retransmission mode, the function `tcp_ack_packets_out(sk, tp)` continues to send packets from the retransmission queue and updates the `retransmit` timer.

Delayed ACK Timer The `Delayed` ACK timer is implemented in the function `tcp_delack_timer()`.

`tcp_delack_timer()`	**net/ipv4/tcp_timer.c**

This function is invoked when the `TCP_TIME_DACK` timer expires. It resets the `Delayed` ACK timer and sends an ACK packet.

`tcp_send_delayed_ack()`	**net/ipv4/tcp_output.c**

This function is invoked by `tcp_ack_snd_check()` (`include/linux/tcp_input.c`) when an incoming packet should be acknowledged and when no direct ACK is required.

The function `tcp_send_delayed_ack()` uses the `mod_timer` (`&tp->delack_timer, timeout`) call to set the Delayed ACK timer. When this timer expires, the function `tcp_send_delayed_ack(sk)` sends a delayed ACK packet, and the Delayed ACK timer restarts.

Keepalive Timer The actual keepalive timer is implemented in the function `tcp_keepalive_timer()`, which serves to test a connection that has not been used over a lengthy period of time. When this timer expires, the function `tcp_write_wakeup(sk)` uses the function `tcp_xmit_probe_skb()` (both in `net/ipv4/tcp_output.c`) to send a probe packet. Subsequently, the variable `tp->probes_out` is incremented until the maximum number of probes, defined in `sysctl_tcp_keepalive_probes`, is reached.

Probe Timer Zero-window probing was described in Section 24.4.1; we mention it here only for the sake of completeness.

FinWait2 Timer   The keepalive timer is also used to implement the timeout when waiting for a FIN packet in the FIN_WAIT2 state. In this case, it is used to compute the timeout duration. During calling of the function `tcp_time_wait()`, the connection state changes to TIME_WAIT. The connection is closed when the timeout expires, at the latest.

TWKill Timer   The timeout in the TIME_WAIT state is implemented by the function `tcp_tw_schedule()` (net/ipv4/tcp minisocks.c), which is invoked by the function `tcp_time_wait()` when the connection is torn down.

24.5.3 Configuration

To be able to use the TCP/IP support, we have to activate the option TCP/IP networking in the kernel-configuration menu.

In addition, when creating a socket, you can use optional settings to influence the behavior. These settings are defined as constants in the file `/include/linux/tcp.h`. All available settings are listed in Table 24–1.

TABLE 24–1   Socket options for the Transmission Control Protocol.

Socket Options	
TCP_NODELAY	Disables the Nagle algorithm.
TCP_MAXSEG	Limits the maximum segment size.
TCP_CORK	Only segments with max. size are sent.
TCP_KEEPIDLE	Initial value for keepalive probes.
TCP_KEEPINTV	Interval between keepalive probes.
TCP_KEEPCNT	Number of keepalives.
TCP_SYNCNT	Number of SYN retransmissions.
TCP_LINGER2	Timeout duration in the FIN_WAIT2 state.
TCP_DEFER_ACCEPT	Notify only when data is received.
TCP_WINDOW_CLAMP	Limit the receive window.
TCP_INFO	Information about the current connection.
TCP_QUICKACK	Activate or deactivate Quick ACKs.
TCP_OPT_TIMESTAMPS	Activate or deactivate the timestamp option.
TCP_OPT_WSCALE	Activate or deactivate the window scaling option.
TCP_OPT_ECN	Activate or deactivate the ECN (Explicit Congestion Notification).

C H A P T E R   2 5

User Datagram Protocol (UDP)

25.1 INTRODUCTION

The *User Datagram Protocol* (*UDP*) is described in RFC 768 [Post80] and represents a minimal transport protocol. It runs on top of the Internet Protocol (IP) and essentially offers the same functionality as IP itself: an unreliable, connectionless datagram service. In this case, unreliable means that there are no mechanisms to detect and handle lost or duplicate packets. However, packets can be optionally protected against bit errors by using a checksum, which covers both the packet header and the payload of each packet, in contrast to IP. Otherwise, there is only one additional option, compared to IP: Port numbers can be used to address different applications in a specific end system.

On the one hand, UDP is used for transaction-oriented applications, such as the *Domain Name System* (*DNS*), where only one request and the relevant reply have to be transmitted, so that it is not worthwhile establishing a connection context, which would mean, for example in TCP, that three additional messages for the establishment and four messages for the tear-down were required. On the other hand, UDP is also used where the reliability of a transmission plays a secondary role, because one is primarily interested in transmitting data easily and quickly. For example, it is normally not a problem if some packets are lost when audio streams are transmitted in small packets. On the contrary, an automatic flow and error control with retransmission of lost packets would often be disturbing to the smooth playback of the stream.

25.1.1 Packet Format

Figure 25–1 shows the format of UDP packets. The header fields are briefly described below.

■ *Source port*: The source port is the port number used by the sending process, in the range from 1 to 65535; normally, the receiver of a request sent over UDP will

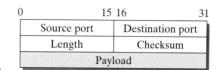

FIGURE 25–1
UPD packet format.

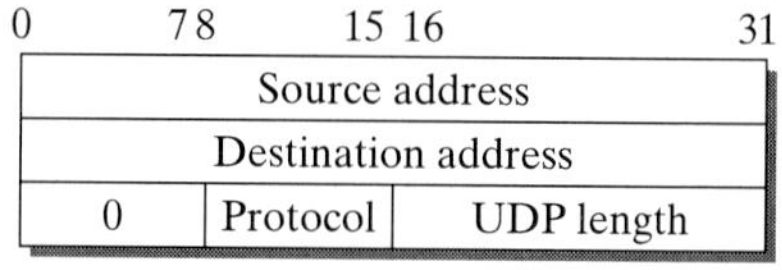

FIGURE 25–2
Pseudo header format for checksum calculation.

direct its reply to this port. RFC 768 specifies that giving the source port number is optional, and the field can have the value zero, if it is not used. However, for UDP over the socket programming interface in Linux (see Chapters 26 and 27), this is not possible, because a port number different from zero is automatically assigned to each socket, if the user does not state one.

■ *Destination port*: The destination port is used to address the application in the destination system that is to receive a UDP packet.

■ *Length*: The length is specified in octets and refers to the entire UDP packet, consisting of packet header and payload. The smallest possible length is therefore eight octets, and the largest possible UDP packet can transport $65535 - 8 = 65527$ payload octets.

■ *Checksum*: As in TCP, the calculation of the checksum includes a pseudo header, in addition to the packet header and the payload. The format of this pseudo header is shown in Figure 25–2. It includes the IP source and destination addresses, the UDP protocol identifier (17), and the length of the UDP packet. The checksum is computed as a 16-bit ones complement of the ones-complement sum over the data mentioned above, where a zero octet is appended if the octet number is uneven. This method can be implemented efficiently for all processor types (as described in RFCs 1071, 1141, and 1624 [BrBP88, MaKu90, Rijs94]). If the computation results in the checksum zero, the all-1-bit value is transmitted instead, which is equivalent in ones-complement arithmetic. A zero in the checksum field means that the sender has not computed a checksum.

25.2   DATA STRUCTURES

The implementation of UDP in the Linux kernel does not require any additional or particularly complex data structures. This section describes the data structure used to pass payload at the socket interface, the UDP datagram itself, which is included in the general socket buffer structure, and the data structure instances used to integrate the protocol into the network architecture.

25.2.1   Passing the Payload

The payload is given for the sendmsg() system call at the socket interface in the form of an msghdr structure, which is checked by the socket interface and copied into the kernel (except for the actual payload that initially remains in the user address space). Otherwise, the structure is passed, as is, to the udp_sendmsg() function for sending UDP packets.

struct msghdr	include/linux/socket.h

```
struct msghdr {
        void                    *msg_name;
        int                     msg_namelen;
        struct iovec            *msg_iov;
        __kernel_size_t         msg_iovlen;
        void                    *msg_control;
        __kernel_size_t         msg_controllen;
        unsigned                msg_flags;
};
```

For sending of UDP packets, msg_name is not really a name, but a pointer to a sockaddr_in structure (see Section 27.1.1), which contains an IP address and a port number; msg_namelen describes the length of this structure. The msg_iov pointer refers to an array of iovec structures, which reference the payload. This means that this payload can be present in a series of individual blocks, where each block is denoted in an iovec structure by its initial address (iov_base) and its length (iov_len):

```
struct iovec
{
        void                    *iov_base;
        __kernel_size_t         iov_len;
};
```

The buffer specified by msg_control and msg_controllen can be used to pass protocol-specific control messages. We will not discuss the format of these messages; see detailed information in the recv() system call manpage.

The msg_flags element can be used to pass different flags both from the user process to the kernel and in the opposite direction. For example, the kernel evaluates the following flags:

- MSG_DONTROUTE specifies that the destination must be in the local area network and that, for this reason, the datagram should not be sent over a router to its destination.
- MSG_DONTWAIT prevents the system call from blocking if, for example, there are no data to be received.
- MSG_ERRQUEUE means that no packet should be fetched, but instead a detailed error message, which might be available at the socket.

The following flag is an example of flags returned by the kernel to the user process:

- MSG_TRUNC indicates that the buffer space provided for receiving was insufficient, so that some of the packet data were lost.

The flags discussed above are only some examples; we will not describe all possible flags and their meanings here. Readers can find more information in the system calls' manpages.

25.2.2 The UDP Datagram

`struct udphdr`	**include/linux/udp.h**

The union element h of the sk_buff structure includes a pointer, struct udphdr *uh, which references the UDP header within the packet data. The udphdr structure is declared as follows, based on the packet format shown in Figure 25–1:

```
struct udphdr {
        __u16 source;
        __u16 dest;
        __u16 len;
        __u16 check;
};
```

`struct udpfakehdr`	**net/ipv4/udp.c**

When sending a packet and computing the checksum, as required, the data structure used is somewhat more complex. In addition to a udphdr structure, where the packet header is built, and from which it is copied into the packet later, it also includes the other data required to create the pseudo IP packet header:

```
struct udpfakehdr
{
        struct udphdr uh;
        u32 saddr;
        u32 daddr;
        struct iovec *iov;
        u32 wcheck;
};
```

The IP source and destination addresses are stored in saddr and daddr, the payload can be reached over the iovec structure, and the checksum is computed in wcheck during the sending.

25.2.3 Integration of UDP into the Network Architecture

As a transport protocol, UDP has two interfaces: one "downwards" to the network layer (the Internet Protocol) and one "upwards" to the application layer. The latter is formed by the sockets described in Chapter 26—more specifically, by the sockets of the PF_INET protocol family. (See Section 26.3.1.)

Interface to the Application Layer   The socket implementation uses the `proto` structure, which is defined in `net/ipv4/udp.c` for UDP, to access the functionality of transport protocols:

```
struct proto udp_prot = {
        name:                "UDP",
        close:               udp_close,
        connect:             udp_connect,
        disconnect:          udp_disconnect,
        ioctl:               udp_ioctl,
        setsockopt:          ip_setsockopt,
        getsockopt:          ip_getsockopt,
        sendmsg:             udp_sendmsg,
        recvmsg:             udp_recvmsg,
        backlog_rcv:         udp_queue_rcv_skb,
        hash:                udp_v4_hash,
        unhash:              udp_v4_unhash,
        get_port:            udp_v4_get_port,
};
```

The elements missing here (e.g., `bind` and `accept`), compared to the complete `proto`
structure shown in Section 26.3.1, are initialized to zero, which means that no transport-
protocol-specific handling of the corresponding events is done.

Socket-state information is stored in the `sock` data structure mentioned in
Section 26.3.1. The simplicity of UDP means that no protocol-specific additional data
is required, so there is no UDP-specific part of the `tp_pinfo` field.

Most of the functions referenced in the `proto` structure are not very complex, so
we will discuss them here only briefly:

- `udp_close()`: During the closing of a UDP socket, only the function
  `inet_sock_release()` (`net/ipv4/af_inet.c`), which is the same for all
  PF_INET sockets, is invoked to release the socket data structure. From there,
  `udp_v4_unhash()` is invoked (as described later).

- `udp_connect()`: UDP is a connectionless protocol, so the `connect()` system call
  at the application layer interface, which is used in connection-oriented protocols
  to establish a connection, has a slightly different meaning: It can be used to define
  the destination of all UDP packets subsequently sent over a socket, so that it
  doesn't have to be specified each time. Accordingly, the destination address and
  destination port are stored in the `sock` data structure within `udp_connect()`.
  The fact that this optional definition has taken place is registered by entering the
  state identifier TCP_ESTABLISHED, which is "borrowed" from TCP, in the `state`
  field of the `sock` structure. In addition, a routing cache entry is constructed by
  using `ip_route_connect()` and stored in the `sock` structure. This entry is used
  when packets are being sent, so that some overhead is avoided.

- `udp_disconnect()`: The state is set to TCP_CLOSE, the destination address and
  destination port are deleted, and a stored routing cache entry is released.

- **udp_ioctl()**: The `ioctl()` system call can be used here to poll the lengths of transmit and receive queues.
- **ip_setsockopt()** and **ip_getsockopt()**: There are no socket options on the UDP level, so these two entries refer directly to the general handling routines of the IP level. (See also man `setsockopt`.)
- **udp_sendmsg()** and **udp_recvmsg()**: These two functions implement the sending and receiving of UDP packets. Section 25.3 will discuss them in more detail.
- **udp_queue_rcv_skb()**: This function will be discussed together with the description of `udp_recvmsg()` in Section 25.3.2.
- **udp_v4_hash()**: During the receiving of UDP packets, a decision must be made about which socket these packets should be assigned to, so that they can be placed in that socket's receive queue to be fetched by the user process later. To facilitate this assignment to a socket, the `sock` structures of all UDP sockets are registered in a hash table, `struct sock *udp_hash[UDP_HTABLE_SIZE]`. The port number modulo `UDP_HTABLE_SIZE` is used as hash value.

  Within the `proto` structure, the `hash` entry could actually reference a function that enters a socket into the hash table. However, the socket had already been entered into the table by `udp_v4_get_port()` (described later) when the port number was assigned in UDP, so `udp_v4_hash()` actually is not needed and is never used.

- **udp_v4_unhash()**: This function is invoked when a socket is released, to remove the `sock` structure from the hash table.
- **udp_v4_get_port()**: This function is invoked by the `PF_INET` implementation in `net/ipv4/af_inet.c` whenever a local port number has to be assigned to a socket. The desired port number passed here can also be zero. In this case, a free port is selected, with a position in the hash table where as few sockets as possible are linked.

Interface to IP The interface used to accept UDP packets received by the IP layer is defined by the `inet_protocol` structure described in Section 14.2.5 in connection with the function `inet_add_protocol()` and shown in Figure 14–5. It is contained in `net/ipv4/protocol.c` for UDP and all protocols running directly on top of IP, appearing as follows:

```
static struct inet_protocol udp_protocol = {
        handler:            udp_rcv,
        err_handler:        udp_err,
        next:               IPPROTO_PREVIOUS,
        protocol:           IPPROTO_UDP,
        name:               "UDP"
};
```

The function `udp_rcv()` serves to receive incoming packets; Section 25.3.2 will discuss it in more detail. `udp_err()` handles ICMP error messages communicated by the IP layer.

To send packets over IP, UDP uses the function `ip_build_xmit()` from `net/ipv4/ip_output.c`. In contrast to `ip_queue_xmit()`, this function does not take the complete IP payload as parameter, but instead a callback function, which it can use to request this data. In addition, it uses a routing cache entry, also provided as a parameter, instead of handling the routing itself.

25.3 SENDING AND RECEIVING UDP DATAGRAMS

The sending of UDP packets, starting from the system call at the socket interface and running all the way until the completed packet is added to the output queue of the network interface, is handled in just one pass, but the receiving of UDP packets requires two separate steps: Once a packet has been received, udp_rcv() first allocates it to a socket in bottom-half context and places it into that socket's receive queue. From there, the packet is fetched via system call of a user process, which is mapped to udp_recvmsg().

Sending UDP Datagrams

udp_sendmsg()	net/ipv4/udp.c

The function udp_sendmsg() is invoked over the socket interface whenever a UDP packet has to be sent: The different kinds of systems calls all lead to this single function's being called. Its parameters are a sock structure with the state of the sending PF_INET socket, a pointer to a msg structure that specifies the receiver and payload, and the payload length in octets.

First, a locally created udpfakehdr structure takes the destination address and the destination port from the msg_name element of the msg structure. The destination doesn't have to be specified explicitly only if a default destination address has previously been assigned to this socket via udp_connect(). In this case, the information from the sock structure is used instead. The source address and the source port always derive from the sock structure. Additionally, they are stored in an ipcm_cookie structure. This structure, which we will not describe here in detail, serves later on to pass the addresses, the device identifier, and the IP options (if applicable) to the Internet Protocol.

Any control messages in the msg_control element of the msghdr structure are processed by calling the function ip_cmsg_send(), and the results are registered in the ipcm_cookie structure. Control messages can be used to modify the source address or to pass IP options, which will then also be registered in the ipcm_cookie structure. If no IP options are specified, then the IP options stored in the sock structure, if applicable, will be used.

A routing cache entry has to be procured, so it is also necessary to handle the source routing IP options beforehand; the address of the first intermediate station might need to be used instead of the destination address.

If the socket had previously obtained a routing cache entry by udp_connect(), and if the corresponding destination address has not yet been changed in the process of udp_sendmsg(), then this routing cache entry is now checked. If this check produces a negative result, or if the destination address was changed, then ip_route_output() is used to procure a new routing cache entry (which is then stored in the sock structure).

Eventually, the transmission of data is initiated by calling ip_build_xmit(), where either udp_getfrag() or udp_getfrag_nosum() is provided as the callback function for getting data, depending on whether the checksum in the packet header should include the payload.[1] The parameters used here also include the udpfakehdr and ipcm structures, the routing cache entry, the flags from the msghdr structure, and the total length of the UDP packet.

The following discussion considers only udp_getfrag(), because udp_getfrag_nosum() provides the same functionality, but is simpler for omitting the checksum calculation.

udp_getfrag()	net/ipv4/udp.c

For each IP fragment it generates, ip_build_xmit() invokes the callback function udp_getfrag() to get the required payload. A pointer to the udpfakehdr structure filled by udp_sendmsg() is one of the parameters passed here, in addition to the desired destination address, the fragment offset, and the desired data quantity.

The actual bulk of the work is done by the function csum_partial_copy_fromiovecend(), defined in net/core/iovec.c. This function not only copies the data referenced by the iovec structure directly from the user-address space to the desired location, but also computes the checksum. The result of the checksum calculation is stored in the wcheck element of the updfakehdr structure in each such step. The next step uses this intermediate result as a starting value, so that the checksum eventually extends over the entire data.

The first fragment has to be created last, because it contains the UDP header with the checksum. It is left to ip_build_xmit() to ensure the correct order; udp_getfrag() recognizes the first fragment only by the offset value zero. It extends the checksum calculation to the packet header and the IP pseudo header, and eventually it completes the packet header by inserting the checksum, before it finally copies it to the beginning of the packet.

Receiving UDP Datagrams

udp_rcv()	net/ipv4/udp.c

Once IP has received a UDP packet, it passes this packet in the form of an sk_buff pointer to udp_rcv() for further processing. After the packet length has been checked and the checksum has been computed over the pseudo IP header (if the packet header includes no checksum, or if the checksum was previously computed by the interface hardware, this is registered in the sk_buff), udp_rcv() directly forwards multicast and broadcast packets to udp_mcast_deliver(), which is described further later on.

The most important task is now to allocate the packet to a socket, so that it can be placed into that socket's queue until it is fetched by the user. This task is handled by the function udp_v4_lookup() (or udp_v4_lookup_longway()) invoked by udp_rcv(). This function looks up the udp_hash table and selects the socket with the most specific

---

[1] A checksum is computed if the flag no_check in the sock structure is null, which is the case by default. This flag can be set via the socket option SO_NO_CHECK on the SOL_SOCKET level.

information with regard to addresses, destination port, and input interface from the sockets linked in the entry and matching the packet.

When a socket has been found, then `udp_queue_rcv_skb()` is called and in turn invokes `sock_queue_rcv_skb()`, which inserts the packet into that socket's receive queue. Otherwise, an ICMP error message is generated, provided that the checksum calculation can be completed successfully. No ICMP messages are generated for packets with faulty checksums.

`udp_mcast_deliver()`	net/ipv4/udp.c

Like `udp_v4_lookup()`, `udp_mcast_deliver()` searches for a matching receiver socket. However, it does not select the single socket matching best, but all sockets with a matching destination port and—if this information is included—with matching addresses and input interface and correspond to the packet. All these sockets receive a copy of the packet. The copies are created by using `skb_clone()` and delivered as in `udp_rcv()` by `udp_queue_rcv_skb()`.

`udp_recvmsg()`	net/ipv4/udp.c

If a user process uses one of the system calls to receive packets, then the socket interface maps it to a call of the function `udp_recvmsg()`. This function removes an `sk_buff` structure from the receive queue of the socket passed as a parameter, interprets it as UDP packet, and returns the payload contained (and information from the packet header, if necessary) in the form of an entry in an `msghdr` structure passed by reference. If the receive queue is currently empty, then either the process has to be set to waiting state, or the call has to be terminated with an appropriate feedback, depending on the specification.

The process of fetching `sk_buff` structures from receive queues, of waiting for their arrival, and of copying the data are part of not only the UDP, are also required in several other places. Therefore, the file `net/core/datagram.c` contains generic functions for these purposes, which are used by `udp_recv_msg()`:

- `skb_recv_datagram()` serves to fetch an `sk_buff`. This is done by using `skb_dequeue()` (or `skb_peek()`, if the provided flags show that the packet should merely be read, but not be removed). If an `sk_buff` is actually available, then it is returned; otherwise, if blocking is permitted, the function `wait_for_packet()` implemented in the same file is invoked. It registers the process as a waiting process with the socket and finally invokes `schedule()` to temporarily obtain control.

- `skb_copy_datagram_iovec()` or `skb_copy_and_csum_datagram_iovec()` are invoked by `udp_recvmsg()` to copy the payload from the packet into the `msg_iov` element of the `msghdr` structure and to compute and verify the checksum in the process, if applicable.

- `skb_free_datagram()` is used to release the `sk_buff` structure after the address information has been copied in `udp_recvmsg()` and, for example, IP options have been taken over into a control message (by calling the function `ip_cmsg_recv()`).

CHAPTER 26

The Concept of Sockets

26.1 INTRODUCTION

The abstraction of sockets was introduced (based on the BSD version of UNIX, where this interface was used for the first time; also called BSD sockets) to facilitate programming of networked applications. An application can use this uniform interface to send or receive data over a network. This interface looks alike for all protocols, and the desired protocol is selected to match three parameters: family, type, and protocol. Chapter 27 gives a complete overview of all available protocol families (family). It also discusses how applications can use the socket interface. In contrast, this chapter gives an overview of the socket implementation in the Linux kernel.

Figure 26–1 gives an overview of how the socket support is integrated into the protocol implementations in the Linux kernel. The BSD socket interface provides a uniform interface upwards to the applications; underneath the interface, however, different protocol families are distinguished by protocol-specific sockets. Currently, one of the most important protocol families, PF_INET (protocol family internet) will be described in the following section. In addition, PF_PACKET sockets in more recent Linux versions provide an elegant way to send data packets by directly accessing a network device. For example, the use of the packet socket was introduced in Chapter 9. Section 26.3.2 describes the packet socket in more detail. In contrast, the Netlink sockets do not serve for data transmission over a network, but to configure various parts of the Linux network architecture. The part to be configured is selected over the parameters NETLINK_* of the socket's protocol variable, as shown in Figure 26–1. The third part of this chapter describes the PF_NETLINK sockets.

26.2 BSD SOCKETS

The Linux kernel offers exactly one socket-related system call, and all socket calls of applications are mapped to this system call. The function asmlinkage long sys_socketcall(int call, unsigned long *args) is defined in net/socket.c. Moreover, a

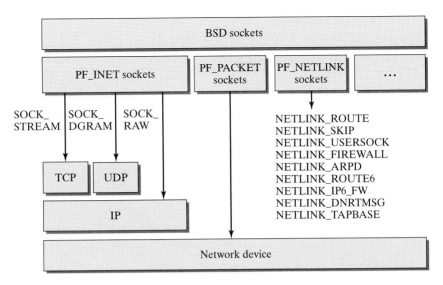

FIGURE 26–1
Structure of the socket support in the Linux kernel.

number is assigned in include/asm/unistd.h (#define __NR_socketcall 102) and added to a table with system calls in arch/i386/kernel/entry.S. The socket function to be addressed can be stated in the call parameter of a call. The admissible parameters are defined in include/linux/net.h: SYS_SOCKET, SYS_BIND, SYS_CONNECT, SYS_LISTEN, SYS_ACCEPT, SYS_GETSOCKNAME, SYS_GETPEERNAME, SYS_SOCKET-PAIR, SYS_SEND, SYS_RECV, SYS_SENDTO, SYS_RECVFROM, SYS_SHUTDOWN, SYS_SETSOCKOPT, SYS_GETSOCKOPT, SYS_SENDMSG, SYS_RECVMSG. From within libraries in the user space, the sys_socketcall() call with a specific parameter is mapped to an independent function (e.g., sys_socketcall(SYS_SOCKET,...) becomes the call socket(...)).

sys_socketcall()	net/socket.c

The function to be called is selected in the kernel by using a switch command in the function sys_socketcall(), and the command copy_from_user() is used to first copy the function's arguments into a vector, unsigned long a[6]:

```
...
if copy_from_user(a, args, nargs[call]))
        return -EFAULT;

a0=a[0];
a1=a[1];

switch(call)
      {
      case SYS_SOCKET:
            err = sys_socket(a0,a1,a[2]);
            break;
```

```
    case SYS_BIND:
        err = sys_bind(a0,(struct sockaddr *)a1, a[2]);
        break;
    case SYS_CONNECT:
        err = sys_connect(a0, (struct sockaddr *)a1, a[2]);
        break;
    case SYS_LISTEN:
        err = sys_listen(a0,a1);
        break;
    ...
    }
...
```

The most important structure within the BSD socket support is struct socket. It is defined in include/linux/net.h:

```
struct socket {
        socket_state            state;
        unsigned long           flags;
        struct proto_ops        *ops;
        struct inode            *inode;
        struct fasync_struct    *fasync_list; /* Asynchronous wakeup list*/
        struct file             *file;        /* File back pointer for gc*/
        struct sock             *sk;
        wait_queue_head_t       wait;

        short                   type;
        unsigned char           passcred;
};
```

This structure is slightly reduced, compared to that in earlier kernel versions. The socket state stored in state can take the following values (include/linux/net.h): SS_FREE (not busy), SS_UNCONNECTED (not connected), SS_CONNECTING (currently being connected), SS_CONNECTED (connected), SS_DISCONNECTING (currently being disconnected). The flags are required to synchronize accesses. The ops pointer references the protocol operation of the connected protocol (e.g., TCP or UDP) after the initialization. Just as there is an inode for each file in Linux, an inode is assigned to each BSD socket. A pointer to the file structure is stored in file; this structure is connected to the socket and can also be used to address it. If any process is waiting for events at this file, then that process can be reached over fasync_list.

A matching sock structure can be used via the sk pointer. However, this structure is initialized by protocol-specific sockets underneath the BSD sockets (e.g., PF_INET sockets) and connected to this pointer. The wait entry serves to implement synchronous (blocking) receipt. The type field serves to store the second parameter by the same name of the socket call in the user space. The admissible parameters are defined in include/asm/socket.h: SOCK_STREAM, SOCK_DGRAM, SOCK_RAW, SOCK_RDM, SOCK_SEQPACKET, and SOCK_PACKET. (The last should no longer be used.)

Now let's see how all of this works in the Linux kernel when socket() is invoked by an application. As was mentioned, this call is passed within the function sys_socketcall() in net/socket.c by invoking the function sys_socket().

sys_socket()	net/socket.c

This function initializes the socket structure and allocates an inode and a file descriptor by calling the functions sock_create() and sock_map_fd().

sock_create()	net/socket.c

In this function, the first step checks on whether the protocol family specified in the family parameter is available. An attempt may be made to load the corresponding module. Subsequently, the type field of the socket structure is described, and two additional functions are invoked: sock_alloc(), to provide a socket, and net_families[family]->create(). The function sock_alloc() is described further later on. net_families[family]->create() executes the create() function of the lower-layer socket. For this purpose, the respective protocols register themselves with the vector static struct net_proto_family *net_families[NPROTO] when the system starts or when the appropriate module is loaded by the sock_register() function (net/socket.c). They also pass the name of the protocol family and a pointer to the create() function. In case of the PF_INET socket, for example, this is done by the sock_register(&inet_family_ops) (net/ipv4/af_inet.c) call, which exports the inet_create() function. The control flow leaves the BSD socket area and is passed to the implementation of the lower-layer socket.

sock_alloc()	net/socket.c

This function is initially invoked by sock_create(); it reserves a new inode and allocates a socket structure. The fields of the socket structure are initialized to null, or state is initialized to SS_UNCONNECTED.

sock_map_fd()	net/socket.c

This function uses a number of helper functions to allocate a file descriptor to the socket, which is used to address this socket. It is also called a socket descriptor, but there is no difference from other file descriptors. This is the reason why you can also use the read() and write() I/O calls to read or write over a socket. The file entry for the socket structure is also set in the sock_map_fd() function.

The create() function of the lower-layer socket, which is invoked by net_families[family]->create()—as described above—now has to fill the other fields of the socket structure with entries—in particular, the ops pointer, which references the proto_ops (include/linux/net.h) structure. This structure serves to supply the BSD socket with the functions of a lower-layer socket. It includes a variable, which is stored in the socket family, and a number of function pointers:

```
struct proto_ops {
int          family;
int          (*release)        (...);
int          (*bind)           (...);
int          (*connect)        (...);
```

```
int         (*socketpair)   (...);
int         (*accept)       (...);
int         (*getname)      (...);
unsigned int (*poll)        (...);
int         (*ioctl)        (...);
int         (*listen)       (...);
int         (*shutdown)     (...);
int         (*setsockopt)   (...);
int         (*getsockopt)   (...);
int         (*sendmsg)      (...);
int         (*recvmsg)      (...);
int         (*mmap)         (...);
ssize_t     (*sendpage)     (...);
};
```

Notice that not all of these functions have to be fully implemented; in such a case, however, an error message should be returned.

This also makes the sending of data over a BSD socket easily understandable: For example, when an application sends data over the sendto() socket call, then the function sys_socketcall() executes sys_sendto() in net/socket.c. There, a message consisting of the transmit data, the address, and control fields is composed. Finally, the function sock_sendmsg() uses sock->ops->sendmsg() to invoke the transmit function of the respective lower-layer protocol-specific socket.

BSD sockets support many different protocols, so a general address structure, sockaddr (include/linux/socket.h), was defined. It consists of a protocol-family identifier and the corresponding address:

```
struct sockaddr {
        sa_family_t     sa_family;      /* address family, AF_xxx */
        char            sa_data[14];    /* 14 bytes of protocol address */
};
```

26.3   PROTOCOL-SPECIFIC SOCKETS

The central structure of all protocol-specific sockets underneath the BSD sockets is struct sock. This structure was oriented to TCP/UDP and IP in earlier kernel versions. Along with the addition of other protocols (e.g., ATM), the sock structure was extended, and other entries were partially removed from the structure. Initially, this created an extremely unclear construction having a number of entries needed for only a few protocols. Together with the introduction of the three union structures (net_pinfo, tp_pinfo, and protinfo), each of which contains a reference to protocol options of the matching layer, this situation should gradually improve, and the structure should become easier to understand. The structure is still rather extensive, but we will introduce only the entries of interest in the following sections.

26.3.1   PF_INET Sockets

This section describes the initialization on the level of PF_INET sockets when an application uses a socket() call.

As has been mentioned, this function is invoked by the function `sock_create()` to initialize the `sock` structure. Initially, the state of the BSD socket is set to SS_UNCONNECTED, and then the function `sk_alloc()`, which was described in Chapter 4, allocates a `sock` structure. The protocol family can only be PF_INET at this point, but we still have to distinguish by `type` and `protocol`. This is now done by comparing against the information in a list, `struct inet_protosw inetsw_array`, which is created by `inet_register_protosw()` (net/ipv4/af_inet.c) when the kernel starts.

Next, the `ops` field of the BSD socket structure can be filled. The `sk` pointer connects the BSD socket to the new `sock` structure, and the latter is connected to the BSD socket by the `socket` pointer. (See `sock_init_data()` in net/core/sock.c.) Similarly to the `proto_ops` structure, the `proto` structure supplies the functions of the lower-layer protocols:

```
struct proto {
void            (*close)            (...);
int             (*connect)          (...);
int             (*disconnect)       (...);
struct sock*    (*accept)           (...);
int             (*ioctl)            (...);
int             (*init)             (...);
int             (*destroy)          (...);
void            (*shutdown)         (...);
int             (*setsockopt)       (...);
int             (*getsockopt)       (...);
int             (*sendmsg)          (...);
int             (*recvmsg)          (...);
int             (*bind)             (...);
int             (*backlog_rcv)      (...);
void            (*hash)             (...);
void            (*unhash)           (...);
int             (*get_port)         (...);
char            name[32];
                struct {
                        int inuse;
                        u8 __pad[SMP_CACHE_BYTES - sizeof(int)];
                } stats[NR_CPUS];
};
```

Consequently, the `proto` structure represents the interface from the socket layer to the transport protocols. The `hash()` and `unhash()` functions serve to position or find a `sock` structure in a hash table.

Finally, `inet_create()` invokes the `inet()` function for the identified protocol from the `proto` structure, if it exists. For example, this would be the function `tcp_v4_init_sock()` (net/ipv4/tcp_ipv4.c) in case of TCP. A similar function exists in net/ipv4/raw.c for direct access to IP (SOCK_RAW). The other protocol functions are now available over the `sock` structure in these `init()` functions.

In TCP, the structure `tcp_func` (defined in `include/net/tcp.h` in `net/ipv4/tcp_ipv4.c`) is filled with TCP-specific functions and made available to the `sock` structure over the entry `tp_pinfo.af_tcp.af_specific`.

The transmit function of TCP (`tcp_transmit_skb()`—see Chapter 24) accesses the transmit function `ip_build_xmit()` (described in Chapter 14) available from the IP layer (network layer). However, this approach is not uniform (e.g., UDP does not implement an `init()` function, but accesses `ip_build_xmit()` directly).

26.3.2 PF_PACKET Sockets

The PF_PACKET sockets represent a type of socket created to allow applications to access a network device directly. The basic idea was to let an application state a packet type at a PF_PACKET socket (e.g., PPPoE connection-management packets with the type ETH_P_PPP_DISC). This means that all incoming packets of this type are delivered directly to this socket; and, vice versa, all packets sent over this socket are sent directly over the specified network device. Consequently, no protocol processing occurs within the kernel, so you can implement network protocols in the user space. At the socket interface, the application sets the family field to PF_PACKET. Formerly, PF_INET had to be selected, and the type SOCK_PACKET had to be specified.

As for PF_INET sockets, a `create()` function is exported when the PF_PACKET support starts (the function `packet_create()` (`net/packet/af_packet.c`), in this case). This function registers the functions of the PF_PACKET socket with the BSD socket. In addition, the functions `register_netdevice_notifier()` and `packet_notifier()` are used to invoke the function `dev_add_pack()` (`net/core/dev.c`) for all packet types registered with the PF_PACKET socket. This means that a handler is installed in the specified network device for all incoming packets of the desired packet type. This handler forwards the packets to the `packet_rcv()` function for processing, as was described in Chapter 5.

In the following, we will briefly introduce the transmit and receive functions.

`packet_sendmsg()`	**net/packet/af_packet.c**

Pointers to the `sock` structure and the message to be sent are passed to this function. Next, the network device that should be used for this transmission has to be selected. This can be done by using the source address specified at the socket, unless the device had already been added to the field `protinfo.af_packet->ifindex` of the `sock` structure as a consequence of a previous `bind()` call. Subsequently, the message is copied to an skb and directly sent to the network device by the function `dev_queue_xmit()`, without using protocols underneath the PF_PACKET socket.

`packet_rcv()`	**net/packet/af_packet.c**

When data of the registered packet type is received, the network device passes a pointer to the `sk_buff` that contains the receive data to the `packet_rcv()` function. The next step fills other fields of the `sk_buff` structure. Subsequently, the function `__skb_queue_tail()` inserts sk_buff in the receive queue of the associated sock structure. Next, the process waiting for a packet at the socket has to be notified. This is done by the function pointer `data_ready()` of the `sock` structure, which was bound to the function `sock_def_readable()` when the structure was initialized.

`sock_def_readable()`	**net/core/sock.c**

This function informs a process that data have been received. For this purpose, two cases have to be distinguished: If the application is in blocking wait at the socket, `wake_up_interruptible()` is used to add the relevant process to the list of executable processes. In case of nonblocking wait, the field of the descriptor that probes the relevant process has to be converted. This is done by the function `sk_wake_async()` (`include/net/sock.h`), which accesses the `fasync_list` of the BSD socket, as mentioned earlier.

26.3.3 PF_NETLINK Sockets

PF_NETLINK sockets are used to exchange data between parts of the kernel and the user space. The protocol family to be stated here is PF_NETLINK, and the type is SOCK_RAW or SOCK_DGRAM. The protocol can be selected from among a number of options (see `include/linux/netlink.h`): NETLINK_ROUTE (interface to the routing and the network), NETLINK_USERSOCK (reserved for protocols that run in the user space), NETLINK_FIREWALL (interface to the firewall functionality), NETLINK_ARPD (management of the ARP table), NETLINK_ROUTE6 (IPv6 routing), NETLINK_IP6_FW (IPv6 firewall), and others.

A header containing information about the length and content of the message is appended to data to be sent from the user space to the kernel. The format of this header is defined as `struct nlmsghdr` (`include/linux/netlink.h`):

```
struct nlmsghdr {
        __u32           nlmsg_len;      /* Length of message including header */
        __u16           nlmsg_type;     /* Message content */
        __u16           nlmsg_flags;    /* Additional flags */
        __u32           nlmsg_seq;      /* Sequence number */
        __u32           nlmsg_pid;      /* Sending process PID */
};
```

The field `nlmsg_type` can take any of three values: NLMSG_NOOP, NLMSG_ERROR, and NLMSG_DONE. Other valid values for `nlmsg_flags` are also available in `include/linux/netlink.h`.

This general Netlink interface is now used for communication between the user space and different parts of the kernel. For further adaptation to the respective application purpose, additional values for `nlsmg_type` were defined (e.g., for NETLINK_ROUTE6 in `include/linux/ipv6_route.h` and for NETLINK_ROUTE in `include/linux/rtnetlink.h`).

In addition to the PF_NETLINK sockets, there is another Netlink interface over a character device (see `net/netlink/netlink_dev.c`), but it is still included for reasons of backward compatibility only. We will mainly discuss the so-called RT Netlink interface below. RT Netlink sockets are actually `PF_NETLINK` sockets with the `NETLINK_ROUTE` protocol option set. These are currently the most interesting for network implementation, so we will continue describing the `PF_NETLINK` sockets with emphasis on this type.

PF_NETLINK sockets reside underneath the BSD sockets, where they register themselves exactly as do `PF_INET` sockets. For registering `PF_NETLINK` sockets over the function `sock_register(&netlink_family_ops)`, the function `netlink_create()` (both in `net/netlink/af_netlink.c`) is first registered as `create()` function with the BSD socket. The latter function handles all initializations required and registers the `proto_ops` structure.

Now, when data is sent to the kernel over a `PF_NETLINK` socket, the function `netlink_sendmsg()` (`net/netlink/af_netlink.c`) invokes the function `netlink_unicast()`. The vector `struct sock *nl_table[MAX_LINKS]` serves to manage `sock` structures that use a common `protocol` (e.g., `NETLINK_ROUTE` `sock` structures having the same `protocol` are distinguished by the process ID of the requesting application, which is copied into the `protinfo.af_netlink->pid` field of the `sock` structure).

`netlink_unicast()`	**net/netlink/af_netlink.c**

This function uses the function `netlink_lookup()` to access the `sock` structure that contains the desired value in its `protocol` field (e.g., NETLINK_ROUTE) and belongs to the requesting process. Subsequently, it has to wait until the field `protinfo.af_netlink->state` is deleted (access synchronization). Next, the `sk_buff` structure is positioned in the receive queue of the `sock` structure, and, finally, `sk->data_ready()` is used to access the respective `input()` function.

In the case of RT Netlink sockets, the function `rtnetlink_rcv()` is invoked here. This function was loaded by `rtnetlink_init()` (`net/core/rtnetlink.c`) when the system started: `rtnetlink_init()` uses `rtnetlink_kernel_create()` to set the function pointer `data_ready()` of the `sock` structure for NETLINK_ROUTE to the function `netlink_data_ready()` (`net/netlink/af_netlink.c`) and the entry `protinfo.af_netlink->data_ready()` to the function `rtnetlink_rcv()` (`net/core/rtnetlink.c`). At first sight, the naming convention of this function is confusing, because it is used for transmission, from the socket's view, but it serves to receive data from the user space, from the kernel's view.

On the basis of the values defined for `nlmsg_type` in `include/linux/rtnetlink.h`, the elements to be addressed within the kernel are now selected. Once again, we distinguish by `family` and `type`. `type` is identical to the type specified at the BSD socket (as mentioned above, RT_NETLINK defines additional types, which are exported from `include/linux/rtnetlink.h`); the RT_NETLINK support defines new, peculiar message formats and allocates them to a family (e.g., `rtm_family` to manage the routing table, `tcm_family` for traffic control messages). Each of these families defines its own structure, which determines the format of messages. These RT_NETLINK messages are within the data range of a PF_NETLINK message, which means that they are transparent for a PF_NETLINK socket.

A vector, `static struct rtnetlink_link link_rtnetlink_table[RTM_MAX-RTM_BASE+1]`, is used to enable kernel elements, such as the traffic control element, to allocate functions to messages of their families. The structure `rtnetlink_link` (in-clude/linux/rtnetlink.h) has two entries:

```
int (*dolt)(struct sk_buff*, struct nlmsghdr*, void *attr);
int (*dumpit)(struck sk_buff*, struct netlink_callback *cb);
```

An appropriate function can be allocated to each function pointer. The function `doit()` passes a command; the function `dumpit()` is used to read an existing configuration. For example, the following allocation is done for traffic control (`net/sched/sch_api.c`), among other things:

```
link_p[RTM_GETQDISC-RTM_BASE].dolt = tc_get_qdisc;
link_p[RTM_GETQDISC-RTM_BASE].dumpit = tc_dump_qdisc
```

As was mentioned earlier, the function `rtnetlink_rcv()` is used as an `input()` function. It invokes the function `rtnetlink_rcv_skb()` for each `skb`. The latter function uses the function `rtnetlink_rcv_msg()` (all in `net/core/rtnetlink.c`) to discover the type of a Netlink message and the family of the RT Netlink message and eventually invokes either `doit()` or `dumpit()`.

Layer V—Application Layer

C H A P T E R   2 7

Network Programming with Sockets

27.1   INTRODUCTION

An application programming interface (API) is required to enable application programmers to access the network functionality implemented in the operating system. One of the most common interfaces to access transport protocols in the UNIX domain is *Berkeley sockets* or *BSD sockets*, which obtained their names from the UNIX variant *Berkeley Software Distribution*, where they were implemented for the first time.

The design of Berkeley sockets (in the following discussion called sockets for short) follows the UNIX paradigm: Ideally, map all objects that are read or write accessed to files, so that they can be processed by use of the regular file write and read operations. Sending or receiving in a communication relationship can be easily mapped to write and read operations. The objects manipulated by such operations in the context of transport protocols are the endpoints of a communication relationship; these are represented by sockets.

27.1.1   Socket Addresses

A communication endpoint in the transport layer is described by three parameters in the Internet: the protocol used, an IP address, and a port number. These parameters therefore have to be allocated to a socket, before it can be used for communication. In building a communication relationship, we additionally have to specify the communication partner's endpoint address.

struct sockaddr	/usr/include/sys/socket.h

The data structure used to represent socket addresses was kept quite general, because the socket interface can also support other protocols, in addition to Internet protocols:

```
typedef unsigned short sa_family_t;

struct sockaddr
{
        sa_family_t           sa_family;
        char                  sa_data[14];
};
```

The `sa_family` element registers the address family (e.g., AF_INET for the family of Internet protocols). The exact address format is not yet defined in detail in the general `sockaddr` structure. For this reason, there is a more specific variant for Internet addresses, called `sockaddr_in`.

struct sockaddr_in	/usr/include/netinet/in.h

```
struct in_addr {
                __u32 s_addr;
};

struct sockaddr_in {
  sa_family_t           sin_family;     /* Address family: AF_INET    */
  unsigned short int    sin_port;       /* Port number                */
  struct in_addr        sin_addr;       /* Internet address           */

  /* Pad to size of 'struct sockaddr'. */
  unsigned char sin_zero[sizeof (struct sockaddr) -
                    sizeof (sa_family_t) -
                    sizeof (uint16_t) -
                    sizeof (struct in_addr)];
};
```

The address family is at the same position as above, and the IP address is stored as a 32-bit number in the element `sin_addr.s_addr`. The 16-bit port number is in the `sin_port` element. The remaining free space is not used. Notice that the addresses and port numbers have to be specified in the *network byte order*; see Section 27.2.3.

27.1.2 Socket Operations

Sockets are represented by normal file descriptors at the programming interface. These file descriptors can be used to perform write and read operations. However, the establishment of a communication relationship is different from opening a file, so, from the application's view, additional system calls are available for sockets.

Figure 27–1 shows the system calls employed during use of a socket—and their order. We distinguish between the client role (left) and the server role (right). This distinction does not refer to the payload transfer, but merely to the establishment of a communication relationship: A client actively initiates the establishment of a communication

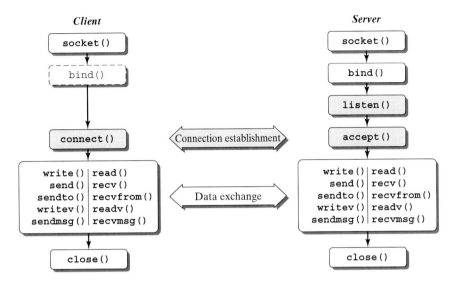

FIGURE 27-1
System calls at the socket interface; grayed calls are not required for connectionless protocols (e.g., UDP).

relationship, but a server initially remains passive, waiting for incoming communication requests.

We will briefly explain the meaning of each of these calls below:

- A new socket is initially created by the socket() system call, which requires information about the protocol to be used (TCP or UDP in the Internet). The result of this operation is a file descriptor, which is used in the further course to identify the socket and which has to be specified in all subsequent calls.

- bind() is used to allocate a local address to the socket. For Internet sockets, this address consists of the IP address of a network interface of the local system and a port number. Clients can do without bind() call, because their exact address often does not play any role; an address is then allocated to them automatically.

- The listen() call is used by a server to inform the operating system that connections should be accepted at the socket. This is meaningful only for connection-oriented protocols (currently, for TCP only, where it causes transition of the protocol state machine into the LISTEN state—see Section 24.3).

- An active connection establishment (e.g., in TCP) to an address passed as parameter is initiated by the connect() call. For connectionless protocols (e.g., UDP), connect() can be used to specify a destination address for all packets subsequently transmitted.

- accept() is used by a server to accept a connection, provided that it had previously received a connection request. Otherwise, the call will block until a connection request has been received.

The socket is copied when a connection is accepted: The original socket remains in the LISTEN state, but the new socket is in the CONNECTED state. A new file descriptor for the second socket is returned by the accept() call. This duplication of sockets during the accepting of a connection allows a server application to continue accepting new connections without having first to close previous connections.
Notice that accept() is not used by sockets for connectionless protocols.

▨ Now that a communication relationship has been established, data can be transmitted. If a connection exists, or if connect() defined the destination address for a connectionless protocol, then the write() and read() file operations are applicable. Otherwise, the functions sendto() and recvfrom() can be used, which require a destination address to be specified for each data unit to be sent or supply a source address for each data unit received.

▨ When a socket is no longer needed, then the descriptor can be released by close(). This function also closes the connection, if one is still open.

The following section discusses each of these system calls for the socket interface in more detail.

27.2   FUNCTIONS OF THE SOCKET API

This section gives an overview of the most important functions for the socket application programming interface. The original TCP/IP implementation of the BSD UNIX version, which the socket API is derived from, used only the six system calls of the input and output interface for file operations to communicate over networks. Only the next version added the whole number of additional operations that will be discussed below.

27.2.1   Functions for Connection Management

The functions described in this section serve to manage communication relationships: to create and delete sockets, to open and close connections, and so on.

```
int socket (int family, int type, int protocol)
```

Berkeley sockets, or sockets for short, are the basis for communication relationships over the socket interface. A socket represents the endpoint of a communication relationship in an end system and forms the interface between the network protocols and applications. This means that, in a communication using the TCP protocol, the two sockets in the two communicating end systems form the endpoints for this communication. In a multicast communication, more than two sockets normally participate in a communication.
An application can use the socket() system call to cause the operating system to create a socket, always the first step in communicating over networks. In the creating of a socket, the required resources are reserved in the operating system, and the type of communication protocol to be used is determined (e.g., TCP or UDP).
The result of a socket() system call consists of the socket descriptor—an integer number that uniquely identifies the socket. This descriptor has to be used in all subsequent system calls to identify the socket.

The following parameters are passed with the `socket()` system call:

▨ `int family` denotes the protocol family used and thus, mainly, the address type used. Constants for the following address families (`AF_...`) are defined:

  ▷ `AF_UNIX`: Sockets for interprocess communication in the local computer.
  ▷ `AF_INET`: Sockets of the TCP/IP protocol family based on the Internet Protocol Version 4.
  ▷ `AF_INET6`: TCP/IP protocol family based on the new Internet Protocol, Version 6. (See Chapter 23.)
  ▷ `AF_IPX`: IPX protocol family.

▨ `int type` denotes the type of the desired communication relationship. Within the TCP/IP protocol family, we mainly distinguish the following three types:

  ▷ `SOCK_STREAM` (*stream socket*) specifies a stream-oriented, reliable, in-order full duplex connection between two sockets.
  ▷ `SOCK_DGRAM` (*datagram socket*) specifies a connectionless, unreliable datagram service, where packets may be transported out of order.
  ▷ `SOCK_RAW` (*raw socket*).

▨ `int protocol` selects a protocol for the specified socket type, if several protocols with the specified type properties are available. In the `AF_INET` address family, TCP is always selected for the `SOCK_STREAM` socket type, and UDP is always used as the transport protocol for `SOCK_DGRAM`.

If the socket type in itself uniquely identifies a protocol, then the protocol argument in the `socket()` system call can be set to zero.

Application Example: A TCP socket should be set up. The first parameter is set to `AF_INET`, the second to `SOCK_STREAM`. The third parameter is not required; therefore, it is initialized to 0.

```
#include <sys/types.h>
#include <sys/socket.h>
int        sockfd;

sockfd = socket(AF_INET, SOCK_STREAM, 0);
if (sockfd < 0)
       printf("ERROR: Error when creating the socket.");
```

`int close (int sockfd)`

The normal UNIX system call `close()` is used to close a socket. When the socket is closed, the system has to ensure that data waiting in kernel buffers ready to be sent (be acknowledged) is actually sent (acknowledged). Normally, the system returns immediately after a `close()` system call, while the kernel still tries to handle data waiting in the queues.

The only parameter of the `close()` function is the following:

▨ `int sockfd` is the descriptor of the socket that should be closed. A process that terminates and releases all open sockets automatically.

Application Example:

```
#include <sys/socket.h>
int    sockfd;

/* Creating a socket. */

/* Communication operations. */
close(sockfd);
```

> `int bind(int sockfd, struct sockaddr *mAddress, int AddrLength)`

A newly created socket has no allocation to local addresses or port numbers. On the client side, user programs do not necessarily have to care about the local addresses they use, because they can be allocated automatically. In contrast, server processes have to specify the port they are working at, because this port is used to address the corresponding service. This means that the server has to bind a new socket to a local address and a port; this binding is the task of the `bind()` system call.

The `bind()` system call requires the following parameters:

▨ `int sockfd` is a socket descriptor.

▨ `struct sockaddr *mAddress` is a pointer to a structure with the address the socket is to be bound to.

▨ `int AddrLength` specifies the size of the address structure provided in the second parameter. The size of the address structure has to be specified, because different address families use different address formats.

The `bind()` system call is used in three cases:

▨ Servers register their own addresses within the system. They inform the system about the kind of packets to be forwarded at this socket, e.g., packets with a specific port number. Server applications use special globally defined port numbers, the so-called *well-known ports*. They are assigned by IANA upon request and listed in the file `/etc/services`.

▨ A client itself can store a specific address.

▨ A connectionless client has to ensure that the system creates an individual address for it, so that the other end of the communication relationship has a valid return address for replies.

Application Example: A TCP server registers its own address (IP address and port number) and declares itself ready to receive arbitrary client requests. The constant INADDR_ANY is used for the IP address, which tells the system that an appropriate local IP address should be used. This 32-bit value has to be brought into the network byte order (see Section 27.2.3) by htonl(). The port number should be a value higher than 1024, to avoid collisions with well-known ports. The port number is a 16 bits in size, so it is initially brought into the network byte order by htons(). Notice that it is a good idea to have previously initialized the entire address structure with zero values.

```
#include <sys/types.h>
#include <sys/socket.h>

#define SERVER_TCP_PORT 2001

int sockfd;
struct sockaddr_in serv_addr;

/*  Initialize address area. */
memset(&serv_addr, 0, sizeof(serv_addr));
serv_addr.sin_family = AF_INET;
serv_addr.sin_addr.s_addr = htonl(INADDR_ANY);
serv_addr.sin_port = htons(SERVER_TCP_PORT);

/*  Since a sockaddr_in structure was used above for the address,
    it has to be transformed to the more general sockaddr
    before using it as second parameter of the bind call. */
bind(sockfd, (struct sockaddr*) &serv_addr, sizeof(serv_addr));
```

---

int listen(int sockfd, int backlog)

The listen() system call enables a server to prepare a socket for incoming connections. The socket is switched into a passive mode and is then ready to accept connections. In addition, the operating system is informed that the protocol instance should order incoming requests in a queue.

listen() is normally used after the socket() and the bind() system calls and immediately before accept(). listen() is suitable only for connection-oriented socket types (e.g., SOCK_STREAM).

The listen() system call takes two parameters:

- int sockfd is a socket descriptor.
- int backlog denotes the number of possible connection requests (the maximum number of connection requests that can be placed in the queue). This is done while the system is waiting for the accept() call to be executed by the server process. This value is normally given as 5, corresponding to the current maximum value. Requests beyond this value are denied.

Application Example: A server process calls the `listen()` routine after it has used `bind()` to announce the port number it uses:

```
#include <sys/socket.h>

/* Create a socket and bind it to an address. */

listen(sockfd, 5);
```

```
int accept(int sockfd, struct sockaddr *Peer, int *AddrLength)
```

Once a connection-oriented server process has executed the `listen()` call described above, the server has to wait for a connection, using the `accept()` call. It blocks the process until a connection request arrives.

As soon as a connection request arrives, the address of the requesting client is stored in the data structure named `Peer`. The length of this address is stored in `AddrLength`. Subsequently, the system creates a new socket, which is connected to the client, and returns the descriptor of this socket as result of the `accept()` system call. A negative value is returned if an error occurs.

The `accept()` call takes the following parameters:

- `int sockfd` is a descriptor of the ready-to-receive socket.
- `struct sockaddr *Peer` is a pointer to a previously reserved memory space for the address of the communication partner. This address is entered in this structure when a connection request arrives.
- `int *AddrLength` specifies the length of the reserved memory space in bytes before the call. Once `accept()` has returned, this parameter shows the actual address length (in bytes).

Application Example: A successful `accept()` call has returned, and the server starts a child process to continue communication with the client in this new process. The parent process can close the new socket or wait for other client connection requests.

```
#include <sys/types.h>
#include <sys/socket.h>

int newsockfd, clilen;
struct sockaddr_in cli_addr;
clilen = sizeof(cli_addr);

/* socket, bind, listen, ... */

newsockfd = accept(sockfd, (struct sockaddr *) &cli_addr, &clilen);
if (newsockfd < 0)
        printf("ERROR: Creating new socket");
```

```
if (childpid = fork()) < 0)
        printf("ERROR: Creating child process");
else if (childpid == 0)
{
            /* Child process */
        close(sockfd);              /* Parent socket */
        doit(newsockfd);            /* Handle client request */
        exit(0);
}
close(newsockfd);                   /* Parent closes the new socket */
```

---

int connect(int sockfd, struct sockaddr *ServAddr, int AddrLength)

A newly created socket is not connected (i.e., it is not associated with a destination address or a communication partner). However, a user program has to establish a connection before data can be sent over a reliable connection. Once a connection has been successfully established, no destination address needs to be specified to transmit data in a connection-oriented communication (e.g., SOCK_STREAM). Sockets for connectionless datagram services don't have to be connected; they can transmit directly.

For the connection-oriented TCP protocol, the connect() system call results in the actual setup of a connection from the local system to a (remote) communication partner.

The following parameters are required to open a connection:

- int sockfd: Socket descriptor.
- struct sockaddr *ServAddr: Pointer to a structure that specifies the destination address to which the socket should be connected.
- int AddrLength: Length of the address structure in bytes.

Application Example: Once it has opened a socket, the client fills the data structure for the server address. If the IP address is available in dotted decimal notation, it can be converted by the inet_addr function. The port number of the server is brought into network byte order by the htons() routine. Again, it is useful to first initialize the entire address memory.

```
#include <sys/types.h>
#include <sys/socket.h>

#define SERVER_TCP_PORT 2001
#define SERVER_HOST_ADDR "129.13.35.77"

struct sockaddr_in serv_addr;

/* A sockfd was already created ... */
/* Initialize data space. */
memset(&serv_addr, 0, sizeof(serv_addr));
```

```
/* Enter address family in address structure. */
serv_addr.sin_family = AF_INET;

/* Set IP address. */
serv_addr.sin_addr.s_addr = inet_addr(SERVER_HOST_ADDR);

/* Set port number. */
serv_addr.sin_port = htons(SERVER_TCP_PORT);

/* Establish connection to server. */
connect(sockfd, (struct sockaddr*) &serv_addr, sizeof(serv_addr));

/* Transmit data ... */
```

27.2.2 Functions for Data Transmission

`write(), send(), sendto()`

The following are some of the system calls available for transmitting data over a socket:

- `size_t write(sockfd, buffer, length)`
- `int send(sockfd, buffer, length, flags)`
- `int sendto(sockfd, buffer, length, flags, destaddr, addrlen)`

`send()` and `write()` can be invoked only when a socket is in the connected state; `sendto()` can be invoked at any time.

These calls take the following parameters:

- `int sockfd`: socket descriptor.
- `void *buffer`: starting address of a buffer, which contains a sequence of bytes that should be sent.
- `size_t length`: length of the byte sequence to be sent in the buffer (in bytes).
- `int flags`: transmission control. (See details in [Come00].)
- `struct sockaddr *destaddr`: pointer to a `sockaddr` structure with the destination address.
- `int addrlen`: length of the destination address structure.

All four functions return the length of the data that was actually sent.

`read(), recv(), recvfrom()`

In analogy to the transmit functions described above, the following functions are available for receiving data:

- `size_t read(sockfd, buffer, length)`
- `int recv(sockfd, buffer, length, flags)`
- `int recvfrom (sockfd, buffer, length, flags, fromaddr, addrlen)`

The parameters these functions take are similar to those for transmit operations. All three functions return the length of data received.

`readv(), writev(), sendmsg(), recvmsg()`

As their arguments, the transmit and receive functions discussed so far each took a pointer to a single memory area that had to be transmitted or was to take in the data received, respectively. This is different with the following functions:

- `int readv(int sockfd, const struct iovec *vector, size_t count)`
- `int writev(int sockfd, const struct iovec *vector, size_t count)`
- `int sendmsg(int sockfd, const struct msghdr *msg, int flags)`
- `int recvmsg(int sockfd, struct msghdr *msg, int flags)`

The `vector` pointer in the `readv` and `writev` system calls (that otherwise behave like `read` and `write`) references an array of `iovec` structures. In turn, each of these structures references a memory location (`iov_base`) and specifies its length (`iov_len`):

```
struct iovec {
        void *iov_base;     /* Starting address */
        size_t iov_len;     /* Number of bytes */
};
```

The specified memory locations are used one after the other for sending or receiving data. The benefits of this behavior can be used when messages are composed of several parts.

The `sendmsg` and `recvmsg` system calls receive a reference to a `msghdr` structure, which also contains an `iovec` pointer. In addition, this structure can accommodate addresses for communication over unconnected sockets, and it makes possible the delivery of specific control messages to the transport protocol instance. (See also Section 25.2.1.)

27.2.3 Byte Ordering Methods

Unfortunately, not all computer architectures store the individual bytes of multibyte values in the same order. We distinguish between *little-endian* and *big-endian* orders. (See Figure 27–2.)

For this reason, we have to define a fixed byte order to ensure correct communication. In the TCP/IP protocol family, this is the big-endian format for 16-bit and 32-bit integer values. (The protocols handle only integer sizes.) The protocol has no influence on and no control of the format of data transmitted by an application over the network. The protocol defines the format only for the fields it manages itself.

`htonl(), htons(), ntohl(), ntohs()`

To enable computers with different byte orders (big endian or little endian) to communicate, the so-called *network byte order* (big endian) was defined for transmissions in

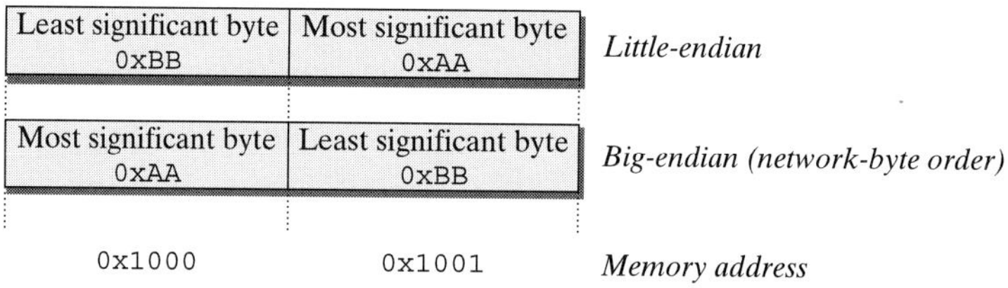

| Least significant byte 0xBB | Most significant byte 0xAA | *Little-endian* |

| Most significant byte 0xAA | Least significant byte 0xBB | *Big-endian (network-byte order)* |

| 0x1000 | 0x1001 | *Memory address* |

FIGURE 27–2
Little-endian and big-endian orders of 16-bit structures, using the number 0xAA BB as an example.

the Internet. The following functions are available to convert 16-bit and 32-bit values from the local format (*host byte order*) into the network byte order and vice versa:

- ▦ unsigned long htonl(unsigned long hostlong): host → network (32 bits)
- ▦ unsigned short htons(unsigned short hostshort): host → network (16 bits)
- ▦ unsigned long ntohl(unsigned long netlong): network → host (32 bits)
- ▦ unsigned short ntohs(unsigned short netshort): network → host (16 bits)

27.2.4 Functions to Handle Internet Addresses

Because the socket interface also supports protocol families, other than TCP/IP (e.g., the ISO/OSI protocols), handling IP addresses and DNS names is not as simple as it might seem. The most frequently needed functions are introduced below.

To handle 32-bit IPv4 addresses or socket addresses (IP address plus TCP/UDP port), the socket-programming interface defines the data structures described in Section 27.1.1, struct sockaddr and struct sockaddr_in.

All socket functions expect address information as parameters in the form of a generic sockaddr structure. However, this structure serves merely as a placeholder for one of the protocol-specific address formats (e.g., sockaddr_in, sockaddr_x25). This is the reason why a type conversion is normally required when calling these functions:

```
struct sockaddr_in *localaddr;

error = bind (sockfd,(struct sockaddr*)localaddr,addrlen)
```

inet_addr(), inet_aton(), inet_ntoa(), inet_ntop(), inet_pton()

IPv4 addresses are normally written in dotted decimal notation, e.g., 192.25.10.72. The following functions can be used to convert formatted character strings into in_addr structures and vice versa. The parameters are actually self-explanatory:

- ▦ int inet_aton(const char *cp, struct in_addr *inp)
- ▦ char *inet_ntoa(struct in_addr in);
- ▦ unsigned long int inet_addr(const char *cp)

The following two functions can be used instead of inet_ntoa() and inet_aton(). Their benefit is that they support several address families, mainly AF_INET and AF_INET6. It is, therefore, recommended to use inet_ntop() and inet_pton().

- int inet_pton(int af, const char *src, void *dst)
- const char *inet_ntop(int af, const void *src, char *dst, size_t cnt)

int getpeername(int sockfd, struct sockaddr *name. int *namelen)

The function getpeername() serves to find out the IP address of the communication partner with a connected socket. The following parameters are passed:

- int sockfd: Socket descriptor.
- struct sockaddr *name: Pointer to a previously reserved memory location for the communication partner's address.
- int *namelen contains the length of the reserved memory location in bytes before the call. After the call, namelen shows the address length in bytes.

If an error occurs, the functions do not return a value called "unequal null," but some integer value that is not equal to φ (the exact value is determined by the type of error. If everything went okay, then the functions return φ.

int gethostname(char *name, size_t len)

The function gethostname() serves to find out the DNS name (*not* the IP address) of the local computer:

- char *name: Pointer to a previously reserved memory location for the name.
- size_t len: Length of the reserved memory location. The call fails if the length is insufficient.

If an error occurs, then the value *unequal null* is returned.

struct hostent *gethostbyname(const char *name)

If the name of the communication partner is known, the function gethostbyname() can find its address. The name of the computer it looks for is passed in the name parameter.

gethostbyname() supplies a pointer to a hostent structure, which is defined in the header file <netdb.h>:

```
struct hostent {
    char    *h_name;        /* Official name of host. */
    char    **h_aliases;    /* Alias list. */
    int     h_addrtype;     /* Host address type. */
    int     h_length;       /* Length of address. */
```

```
char      **h_addr_list;        /* List of addresses from name server. */
#define   h_addr h_addr_list[0]  /* Address, for backward compatibility. */
};
```

The field h_addr_list contains a list with valid addresses, where the end of this list is denoted by an entry consisting of all zero bits. For IPv4, the list contains IP addresses in the form of 32-bit binary values, which can be copied into a data structure of the type in_addr—for example, by the memcopy() function.

27.3   EXAMPLES

The source text for a complete small sample application, where a client and a server communicate over TCP, is included in Appendix G. A much more detailed description of network programming in UNIX operating systems, including many examples, is found in, for example, [Stev90].

Appendices

The LXR Source-Code Browser

The Linux kernel in Version 2.4.9 consisted of 9,837 files, totaling to approximately 3,857,319 lines of source code. Even modifications from one version to the next comprise several megabytes. This volume of Linux source code makes it difficult to navigate to the desired place right away.

To facilitate working with the source code of the Linux kernel, the University of Oslo developed the LXR source-code browser[1] (http://lxr.linux.no). This browser is Web-based and represents the source code of the Linux kernel in HTML (HyperText Markup Language). The benefit of HTML, compared to normal source code, is the possibility of integrating hyperlinks that let you reference further information at specific positions, so that navigation between related source-code sections becomes very easy.

A.1   FUNCTIONALITY

The LXR source-code browser creates a reference file for existing C/C++ source texts. This reference file stores links between different parts of the source code. For initializing of the LXR, the source files are searched for certain keywords, and an index of these keywords is created. The following elements of a C program are recognized as keywords, and their functions are interpreted accordingly:

- Functions and function prototypes;
- global variables;
- type definitions (typedef);
- structure definitions (struct);
- variant definitions (union);
- enumeration types (enum); and
- preprocessor macros and definitions (#define).

---

[1]LXR is short for Linux Cross (X) Reference.

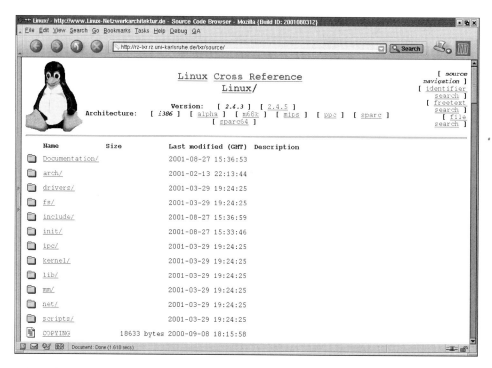

FIGURE A–1
Browsing the Linux kernel in the LXR source-code browser.

Subsequently, all keywords occurring in the source code are stored in an index file.

When a Web browser requests one of the source files, a Web page consisting of the original source-code file with all keywords emphasized by hyperlinks (see Figure A–2) is created. By clicking one of the links, another page is generated, which shows all information about this keyword. (See Figure A–3.) When a function is called, for example, the location (file and line number) of the function declaration, the actual function itself, and all locations where this function is invoked are displayed. Hyperlinks offer an easy way to jump to these locations. Figure A–2 uses the `ip_rcv()` function as an example, to show how this works.

Consequently, rather than creating static HTML pages, the LXR source-code browser generates the pages anew upon each request. Though this approach is somewhat slower than static pages, it does not modify the source code. In addition, the volume of static pages would probably be too big and take too much memory space.

We will briefly describe the possibilities of the LXR source-code browser below. Readers who want to use the LXR source-code browser can find both the source code of the current kernel versions and the LXR packet for installation at `http://lxr.linux.no`. You can also easily install the LXR source-code browser on your local computer, if you have a Web server and Perl.

The functionality of LXR is currently under revision. Reference information should no longer be stored in one single file in the future, but in a database (e.g., `mySQL`).

FIGURE A–2
Browsing the Linux kernel in the LXR source-code browser, using the `ip_rcv()` function as example.

Information about the current development in the beta stage is available at `http://lxr.sourceforge.org`.

A.1.1   Navigation through the source code

The entry point into the LXR source-code browser is shown in Figure A–1. This is the root directory for source files of the Linux kernel. From this page, you have the following possibilities:

- *Browsing to a specific file of the kernel sources*: You can click your way to a desired file by clicking the corresponding directories. If you know the file path, you can abbreviate it by directly typing the path in the URL. The path of the desired file is simply written after `/source/` in the URL. Figure A–2 shows this by the example of the file `net/ipv4/ip_input.c`.

- *Searching for a file*: If you don't know the name of the desired file, you can search for it on the `file search` page.

- *Searching for a keyword*: When working with the Linux source code, we are mainly interested in functions and data structures (i.e., what was defined as keywords above).

  Keywords are stored in the reference file of the LXR source-code browser. This file also includes all information about the use of a keyword. Clicking a keyword emphasized as hyperlink or explicitly searching for a keyword on the `identifier`

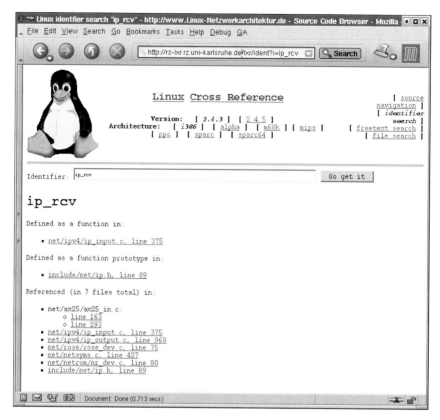

FIGURE A–3
Showing information stored for the keyword `ip_rcv`.

`search` page causes a Web page similar to the one shown in Figure A–3 to be displayed. For example, the stored information shown in Figure A–3 is output for the `ip_rcv()` function:

▷ *Definition of the function*: The location (file and line) of the `ip_rcv()` function, including statements, in the source code.

▷ *Definition of the function prototype*: The location where `ip_rcv()`, including its header file, was defined as function prototype. This information helps, for example, when searching for a header file to be included when you want to use this function.

▷ *Calls of the function*: All positions where either the `ip_rcv()` function is invoked or its address is assigned are displayed.

Naturally, this page with stored information varies, depending on the type of keyword. For examples, no prototype definition is shown for variables.

This information can be used to navigate easily through the kernel. Relations and processes can easily be tracked and analyzed.

    Various architectures: The particularities of various architecture-specific parts of the kernel are considered in the creating of the index. Selection of the desired architecture (top of the Web page) causes the respective source code parts to be displayed.

    Various source-code versions: You can use the LXR source-code browser to index several kernel versions or several software projects concurrently. Selection of the version or project (top of the Web page) causes the source code of the corresponding project to be displayed.

A.2   INSTALLATION

Installing the LXR source-code browser is relatively easy for an experienced Linux user. Problems or suggestions for improvement can be published in a mailing list. The following components are required to install the LXR source-code browser:

    The *LXR package* with the scripts to generate the source-code index and the HTML pages. The version currently most stable is `lxr-0.3`. It can be downloaded from `http://lxr.sourceforge.org`.

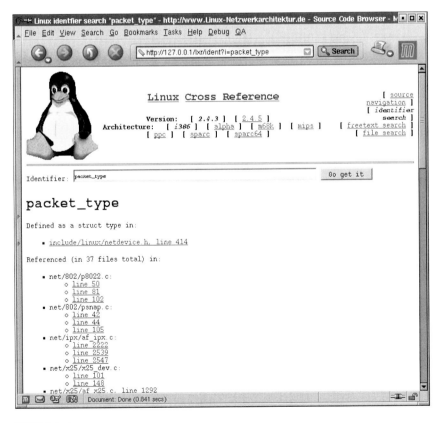

FIGURE A–4
Information stored for the C structure `packet_type`.

- A *Web server* that can work with CGI (Common Gateway Interface) scripts. We recommend the Apache Web server (`http://www.apache.org`).

- Perl is required to run the scripts. Mainly, the possibilities of regular expressions in Perl are used for the functionality of the LXR source-code browser.

- Glimpse can be used to extend the functionality of the LXR source-code browser. It allows you to search the entire source code of the Linux kernel for full-text search. This is useful mainly when one is searching for certain source-code identifiers the LXR parser was unable to identify. In addition, when you are searching for full text, Glimpse lets you display the corresponding lines of the source code, thereby simplifying and accelerating your search.

- A *Web browser* (e.g., Mozilla, Netscape, Konqueror) is needed for navigation through the pages generated by LXR.

- Finally, you need the *source code of the Linux kernel*. Notice that you can index several kernel versions or source texts of other programs concurrently.

Once you have installed the LXR scripts by the attached `Makefile` (read the `INSTALL` instruction included in the package), you first have to edit the configuration file `lxr.conf`. This file stores most settings of the LXR source-code browser. You also find details about the configuration of `lxr.conf` in the `INSTALL` instruction, included in the LXR package.

Subsequently, you have to create the source-code index for various kernel versions or other software projects. To create such an index, you use the Perl script `genrefx`, which is *very* time-consuming. Finally, you have to configure the Web server so that it recognizes and executes the Perl scripts in the directory `$(LXR-INSTALL)/http`. Experience has shown that this is the most delicate point in the LXR installation. Please also consult the literature for the Web server you use.

Naturally, readers who don't want to bother with the installation of the LXR source-code browser can easily access the pages of Oslo University at `http://lxr.linux.no`.

APPENDIX B

Debugging in the Linux Kernel

Debugging is a helpful step when writing reliable software. This is normally not a big problem when one writes simple applications. There are appropriate tools, such as the gdb debugger and its graphic variant, ddd, and other useful tools (e.g., `strace`), to track system calls.

However, the prerequisites are different for debugging an operating-system kernel. Remember that it is the very task of an operating system to provide a sufficient environment to run applications and to catch as many exceptions as possible to ensure that the work of other applications is not at risk. Probably the best known error in programs is a `NULL` pointer that references the memory position `NULL` rather than a valid memory address. When an application wants to access this page or run the statement at this location, the operating system should catch this error and output a message (i.e., `segmentation fault` or `memory protection violation`). The faulty application can then be checked step by step in a debugger to find the faulty places in the source code.

Unfortunately, it's not so easy to check an operating itself for errors. The reason is that, when a `NULL` pointer occurs in the system itself, there is no way to stop the computer from crashing. It is often impossible to find the exact location of an error or even the faulty component. Despite these circumstances, this chapter introduces several ways to track the process of a component in the kernel to discover potential sources of error.

In addition to prevent `NULL` pointer dereferences, it is also important to obtain information about the functionality of algorithms and kernel components at runtime, to be able to check for correct operation. In the selecting of an operating system, its correct operation is as important as its stability.

B.1 LOG OUTPUTS FROM THE LINUX KERNEL

One of the most common debugging techniques is the output of certain messages at strategic program positions—meaningful screen outputs are simply inserted (ideally before and after) at potential sources of error. This helps us to track the kernel's behavior and how it progresses. Of course, we could also output variable values and similar useful things.

Though this rather simple but useful fault-tracing variant often helps, there can be cases where an error in the operating-system kernel causes the entire computer to crash, leaving no way to store or read log information. These cases often occur when function pointers are wrongly initialized or are due to accesses beyond array boundaries. Some of these errors can be caught with the well-known "kernel Ooops," but some lead inevitably to a crash.

The following sections introduce several helpful methods to create outputs from the kernel and make them visible to the programmer or user.

B.1.1   Using printk() to Create Log Outputs

The `printf()` function is normally used in conventional writing of C programs—and the Linux kernel is actually not different—to output messages at a text console. `printf()` is a function of the standard input/output library (`<stdio.h>`), which is not available in the Linux kernel. For this reason, the Linux developers simply simulated `printf()` and integrated it into the kernel as the `printk()` function. Other functions borrowed from the standard libraries help the handling of character strings (`lib/string.c`):

`printk()`	**kernel/printk.c**

`printk()` offers almost the same functionality as `printf()` and has a similar syntax. A special property of `printk()` is the classification of messages to be output, by different debugging levels. The `syslogd` and `klogd` daemons can be used to store and output kernel messages or send them to specific addresses.

Altogether, there are eight debugging levels, from KERN_DEBUG, which is the lowest level (normal debugging messages) to KERN_EMERG—the highest level (system unusable). These debugging levels are defined in `<linux/kernel.h>`. Depending on the DEFAULT_CONSOLE_LOGLEVEL variable, messages are output on the current console. The administrator can use the command `syslogd -c` to modify the value appropriately.

`printk()` itself uses the `printf()` function to generate the output string. This is the reason why the syntax of the two functions and parametrizing of the variables to be output are identical. `sprintf()` will be introduced in Section B.2.

B.1.2   The syslogd Daemon

While the operating system is running, there are often situations where programs have to log error messages or specific information. An application in text mode outputs these messages simply at the console (`stdout` or `stderr`). A popup window is normally created for window-based applications (X11). The operating system kernel and processes working directly for it, such as daemons or child processes of the `init` process, have no direct allocation to a console.

Now, where should error and log messages be output? The standard output (`stdout`) of these processes uses the `/dev/console` console. In the X-Windows system, this is the `xconsole` window.

This approach can cause problems in a multiuser environment. On the one hand, messages can be read by anyone; on the other hand, the person in charge (normally the administrator) might be looking at something else and not pay attention to the message window. Another problem is that these screen outputs cannot easily be stored, which means that they are very volatile.

To solve these problems, we use the `syslogd` daemon. Daemons or other system programs outside the kernel have the possibility to generate messages for `syslogd`, which receives these messages over the `/dev/log` device and processes them. Within the kernel, log messages are simply created by the `printk()` function. If you additionally have started the `klogd` daemon, then the messages are also forwarded to `syslogd`. Section B.1.1 described how `printk()` works.

The messages mentioned above are accepted automatically after `syslogd` has started. The file `/etc/syslog.conf` defines how these messages should be further handled (i.e., in what files and by what criteria they should be stored).

The syslogd Configuration File /etc/syslog.conf   This file defines the rules for the processing of log messages by the `syslogd` daemon. If this file needs to be modified, then we first have to terminate the daemon and restart it afterwards.

`syslog` messages are distinguished by two criteria: by their *creator* and by their *priority*.

Priorities for `syslog` messages: There are eight different priorities. These are identical to the priorities defined for `printk` in `linux/kernel.h` (i.e., `emerg` corresponds to `KERN_EMERG`). The following priorities are sorted in descending order by urgency:

- `emerg`: System unusable—crash.
- `alert`: Serious error that has to be dealt with immediately.
- `crit`: Critical situation.
- `err`: Error notification.
- `warning`: Warning.
- `notice`: Special-situation notification.
- `info`: Regular messages within routine operation.
- `debug`: Fault-tracing messages.

Origin of `syslog` messages: Messages for `syslogd` can be generated by the following areas:

- `kern`: Messages from the kernel (`printk()`).
- `auth`: Messages from the area of security, authentication (`login`, ...).
- `mail`: Messages from the mail system.
- `news`: Messages from the news system.
- `lpr`: Messages from the print daemon.
- `cron`: Messages from the cron daemon.
- `syslog`: Messages from the syslog daemon.
- `daemon`: Messages from any daemon.
- `user`: Messages from application programs.
- `local0-7`: Message areas that can be freely assigned.

Processing messages: There are various ways to store and to deliver messages, which can be configured depending on the priority and origin of messages. The file /etc/syslog.conf always defines actions to be done in the following syntax:

origin.priority{;origin.priority}* action*

Each line outputs a processing rule, consisting of a sequence of message types (origin.priority), separated by a semicolon, and an action. Both the origin and the priority of a message type can be replaced by a wildcard (*). The following actions are possible:

- The message can be written to a file. To write a message to a file, we state the file name with the absolute path (starts always with a "/").
- The message can be sent to one or several users. The user names (login names) have to be stated in a list (separated by commas). The message is displayed only for those users who are logged in at the time of the event. You can use a wildcard (*) to send a message to all users currently logged in.
- A message can be sent to the syslog daemon of another computer, which is specified with a leading "at" character (e.g., @tux.icsi.Berkeley.edu).

Example for a syslogd configuration file—comments begin with #:

```
# /etc/syslog.conf - Configuration file for syslogd(8)
#
# print most on tty10
kern.warn;*.err;authpriv.none /dev/tty10
*.emerg                         *
#
# all email messages in one file
#
mail.*                          -/var/log/mail
#
# all news messages
news.crit                       -/var/log/news/news.crit
news.err                        -/var/log/news/news.err
news.notice                     -/var/log/news/news.notice
# enable this, if you want to keep all news messages
# in one file
#news.*                         -/var/log/news.all
#
# Warnings in one file
*.warn                          /var/log/warn
#
# save the rest in one file
#
*.*;mail.none;news.none         /var/log/messages
#
# All messages with priority emerg and higher will be sent to the
# users, who are logged in. They will also be sent to syslogd on
# host tux.icsi.Berkeley.edu.
*.emerg                         *
```

```
*.emerg                              @ tux.icsi.Berkeley.edu
# All messages with priority alert and higher will be sent to the
# administrator, if he/she is logged in.
*.alert                              root
```

B.1.3   Using console_print() for direct outputs

There can always be situations where the kernel gets stuck and no more output is possible. This is usually the case when `printk()` has written a message to the buffer, but `klogd` hasn't been invoked by the scheduler yet. In such cases, it is recommended to use the `console_print()` function for outputs. It outputs a specific string immediately at the current console.

`console_print()`	**kernel/printk.c**

In contrast to `printk()`, `console_print()` merely outputs a string, but does not convert variables into characters. In such cases, the output string should have been created previously by `sprintf()`. Naturally, we first have to reserve a byte array.

The use of `console_print()` is extremely helpful, but only provided that it is absolutely required to always output to the current console. This is conceivable only for temporary debugging or really important exceptions. Otherwise, unexpected outputs at the console can be disturbing and confusing for the regular user.

B.2   CREATING STRINGS IN THE KERNEL

This section introduces several useful functions to create debugging messages. As was mentioned earlier, they are somewhat similar to the functions provided by standard C libraries.

`sprint()`	**lib/vsprintf.c**

`sprintf(buffer, str, arg1, ...)` is a function very useful for converting certain variable types into strings. Its functionality is almost identical to that of the `sprintf()` function in the C library `<stdio.h>`. `sprintf()` also supports the formatting options known from `printf()`.

The character string `str` consists of regular characters and control characters, if present. Instead of control characters that begin with a % sign and end with a type descriptor (`c`, `s`, `p`, `n`, `o`, `x`, `X`, `d`, `i`, `u`), variable values are inserted according to the formatting specification. The *n*th formatting specification refers to the *n*th argument in the `str` string. The created string is written to the `buffer`, and the set of written characters (including the closing null byte) is returned as the result.

The formatting options of `sprintf()` are as follows: A format specification begins with the % sign and ends with one of the type descriptors mentioned. Between these two characters, there may be the following format specifications (in this order):

- `Blank`—No leading plus sign is used for a positive number, but instead a blank. A minus sign is inserted for negative numbers. This enables positive and negative numbers to appear aligned (if they have the same length).

▨ –—This argument is inserted left-justified in the string.

▨ +—A plus sign is inserted if the argument is positive.

▨ #—If the octal system (o) was selected as the output form, then a leading null is added to the argument; 0x or 0X are inserted for the hexadecimal system (x or X).

▨ min, max—The numbers min and max specify the minimum or maximum length of an output. min or max can be omitted if the respective option is not desired. If min begins with a null, then the output is padded with zeros to the minimum format length.

▨ h, l, or L—denote that a variable is of short or long type.

▨ type—A formatting specification ends with the type of variable to be output. The following types are available:

   ▷ c (*character*)—The character arg is output.

   ▷ s (*string*)—The string arg is output to the first null byte (unless limited by the maximum format length).

   ▷ p (*pointer*)—The pointer address is output in hexadecimal system.

   ▷ o (*integer*)—The number arg is output in octal system.

   ▷ x, X (*integer*)—The number arg is output in hexadecimal system.

   ▷ d, i (*integer*)—The leading sign for the number arg should be considered in the output.

   ▷ u (*integer*)—The number arg is considered to be an unsigned number.

The formatting options described correspond to the options of printk(), because printk() itself uses sprintf() to format an output string. However, sprintf() is useful not only in connection with printk(), but also to generate outputs in the proc directory.

As was described in Section 2.8, the output is recreated upon each read operation on the proc directory. This is not different from a string that includes output data. We can use sprintf() to output not only fixed text blocks, but also formatted contents of variables and memory addresses.

String Operations   **lib/string.c**

The Linux kernel has several functions for simple (and familiar) work with strings. These functions are similar to the string operations of the C library. We will briefly introduce them here:

▨ *Copying strings*

   ▷ strcpy(dest, src) copies the string src, including the closing null byte, to the address dest. strcpy() returns the dest pointer.

   ▷ strncpy(dest, src, count) copies a maximum of count bytes from the src string to the address dest. If the original string was longer than count bytes, then no closing null byte is appended. dest is also returned here.

▷ `strcat(s1, src)` extends the string `s1` by the string `s2`, which is appended to the end of `s1`.

▷ `strncat(s1, s2, count)` works like `strcat`, but copies a maximum of `count` bytes.

■ *Comparing strings*

▷ `strcmp(s1, s2)` compares two strings and returns 0 if the strings are equal. Otherwise, it returns a positive value if `s1` is lexicographically larger than `s2`, but a negative value if `s1` is lexicographically smaller than `s2`.

▷ `strncmp(s1, s2, count)` compares a maximum of `count` bytes of two strings. The return values correspond to those of the `strcmp()` function.

▷ `strnicmp(s1, s2, count)` also compares the first `count` characters of two strings, `s1` and `s2`, but ignores lowercase and uppercase.

■ *Searching in strings*

▷ `strchr(str, ch)` searches for the first occurrence of the character `ch` in the string `str`. If it was successful, it returns the memory location of the first occurrence; otherwise, `null`.

▷ `strrchr(str, ch)` searches for the last occurrence of the character `ch` in the string `str`. If it was successful, it returns the memory location of the last occurrence; otherwise, `null`.

▷ `strpbrk(str, ch_str)` finds the first occurrence of a character from the string `ch_str` in the string `str`.

▷ `strtok(str, tok_str)` returns the first string from `str` that does not contain any character from the string `tok_str`.

■ *Length of strings*

▷ `strlen(str)` returns the length of the string `str` (excluding null bytes).

▷ `strnlen(str, count)` returns the length of the string `str` or `count`, if the string is longer than `count`.

▷ `strspn(str, ch_str)` computes the length of that initial part of the string `str` in which only characters from the string `ch_str` occur, beginning from the first character in `str`.

■ *Functions for memory locations*

▷ `memset(ptr, ch, count)` fills `count` bytes of memory (starting from the `ptr` location) with the value of the `ch` parameter.

▷ `memcpy(dest, src, count)` copies `count` bytes from the memory location `src` to the memory location `dest`.

▷ `memcmp(ptr1, ptr2, count)` compares `count` bytes of two memory locations, `prt1` and `prt2`. The return values correspond to those of the `strcmp` function.

B.3   INFORMATION IN THE /PROC DIRECTORY

As was mentioned earlier, the files in the /proc directory serve to make current information about certain system components available to the user. They are regenerated upon each read access.

The /proc directory and its subdirectories include a large number of files that reflect the current system state. The meaning of each of these files should be known. Some information about the meaning of file contents and their—partially cryptic—syntax are in the Documentation directory in the kernel source text.

B.3.1   Entries in the /proc Directory

Initially, a separate subdirectory is created in the /proc directory for each process, named by the process ID. Each such subdirectory includes process-specific information. However, they are of minor interest for the Linux network architecture, so we will not discuss them any further here. Within the scope of this book, we are mainly interested in the /proc/net and /proc/sys/net directories, which contain information about and parameters of protocol instances and network devices, some of which can even be configured.

The /proc directory itself holds the following files of general interest:

- meminfo shows information about free and occupied memory in the system.
- kmsg: During reading of this file, the buffer with the last kernel messages is output and emptied. These messages are normally read by the klogd daemon and further processed by the syslogd daemon. (See Section B.1.2.)
- kcore returns a copy of the kernel. The file size corresponds to the size of the kernel in main memory, including the page size. This allows you to debug the kernel at runtime:

```
root@tux # gdb /usr/src/linux/vmlinux /proc/kcore
```

Section B.4 includes more detailed information.

- modules shows information about the modules currently loaded and their dependencies. The contents correspond to the output of lsmod.
- devices holds information about registered device drivers and their major numbers. The file distinguishes between character-oriented and block-oriented drivers. As was described in Chapter 5, network drivers represent a separate class of drivers; therefore, they are not listed in /proc/devices.
- interrupts lists all instances (character-oriented, block-oriented, and network devices) that occupy interrupts. Specifically, the interrupt number, the total number of interrupts (per processor), and the device name are listed. A look in this file often helps when controlling to see whether a device's driver works. You can see this by the presence of a device and by an increasing number of interrupts. Linux supports more than one device's using the same interrupt. In this case, only the actual number of the corresponding interrupts is shown; they are not itemized by device.

- ksyms shows the symbols exported by the kernel and their memory addresses in the kernel. This table is important for supporting kernel modules. (See Section 2.4.)
- dma and ioports show the occupied DMA channels and I/O ports, plus the instances that reserved them.
- slabinfo: This file holds information about the memory caches used in the kernel. (See Section 2.6.2.) Of interest for the network part are mainly skb_head_cache and the caches for the TCP transport protocol. To display information about a cache, you have to write a corresponding entry in the file mm/slab.c.

Entries in the /proc/net Directory   The entries in the /proc/net directory are listed below. Some of these entries are visible only provided that the appropriate functionality was embedded in the kernel (e.g., IP Chains). In addition, there is a separate version for the new Internet Protocol Version 6 for many entries that refer to the Internet Protocol Version 4. These entries can be identified by the 6 at the end, e.g., raw6 or igmp6.

- arp outputs the content of the kernel ARP table. (See Chapter 15.)
- dev shows all registered network devices and their statistical data.
- dev_mcast lists those layer-2 multicast groups to which a network device listens (*index, device name, number of references, number of bound addresses*).
- igmp lists those IP multicast groups to which the computer is subscribed. (See Chapter 17.)
- ip_fwchains contains rules for IP Chains. (See Chapter 19.)
- ip_fwnames holds firewall lists.
- ip_masq holds the masquerading tables.
- ip_masquerade holds the main masquerading table.
- ip_mr_vifs lists the virtual network devices for multicast (VIF).
- ip_mr_cache holds the multicast routing cache. (See Chapter 17.)
- netstat shows detailed network statistics (for SNMP purposes).
- raw shows statistics for Raw sockets.
- route shows the kernel routing table.
- rpc is the directory with RPC information.
- rt_cache holds routing cache information. (See Chapter 16.)
- snmp holds the Management Information Base (MIB)—data for SNMP.
- sockstat holds socket statistics.
- tcp holds information about TCP sockets.
- tr_rif shows the token ring RIF routing table.
- udp holds information about UDP sockets.
- unix holds information about UNIX domain sockets.
- wireless shows information about wireless LANs (e.g., IEEE 802.11).
- psched holds parameters for the packet scheduler.
- netlink is a list of PF_NETLINK sockets.

Entries in the /proc/sys/net/core Directory

- `rmem_default`: Default value for the memory space used for incoming socket buffers (in bytes).
- `rmem_max`: Maximum size for incoming socket buffers (in bytes).
- `wmem_max`: Maximum size for outgoing socket buffers (in bytes).
- `message_burst`: Parameters limiting the number of warning or log messages created by the network implementation (number of messages per second). This is necessary to limit the consequences of denial-of-service attacks.

Entries in /proc/sys/net/ipv4/ This directory holds the most important information and configuration options for the TCP/IP protocols. Most of these entries work as switches. Specifically, if a 1 is written to the file, then a specific functionality is enabled; if a 0 is written to the file, this functionality is disabled.

- `icmp_echo_ignore_all` or `icmp_echo_ignore_broadcasts`, respectively, suppresses a reply to all *echo requests* directed to the host or to multicast/broadcast addresses.
- `icmp_` ... can be used to specify, for various ICMP message types, how often at most an ICMP packet may be sent. This value is stated in packets per second.
- `ip_autoconfig` shows whether the computer should be configured automatically (e.g., by RARP, BOOTP, DHCP, or similar mechanisms).
- `ip_dynaddr` specifies whether IP addresses may be dynamically allocated.
- `ip_forward` enables or disables packet forwarding: 1 means that packets will be forwarded and that the computer behaves like a router; 0 means that the computer behaves like a *host*. "Toggling" this switch sets the default parameters as specified in RFC 1122 (for hosts) and RFC 1812 (for routers).
- `ip_default_ttl` holds the default value for the Time-To-Live (TTL) field in the IP packet header. This parameter normally is initialized to 64.
- `ip_mask_debug` enables or disables debugging messages in masquerading.
- `ip_no_pmtu_disc` disables the path MTU discovery mechanism.
- `ipfrag_high_thresh` specifies the maximum memory used for IP packet defragmenting. If this threshold value is exceeded, then the kernel starts dropping fragments until the bottom threshold value, `ipfrag_low_thresh`, is reached. (See Chapter 14.)
- `ipfrag_low_thresh`—see `ipfrag_high_thresh`.
- `ipfrag_time` is the interval (in seconds) an IP fragment is held in memory. If the rest of the fragmented packet does not arrive by the time this interval expires, then the fragment is dropped.

The following parameters concern the TCP transport protocol only:

- `tcp_syn_retries`: Number of attempts to establish a TCP connection (sending the initial SYNs). This value should not be greater than 255.
- `tcp_keepalive_time` specifies how long keepalive packets are sent, if keepalive is active.

- `tcp_keepalive_probes`: Number of *KeepAlive probes* sent by TCP before the connection is declared to have failed.
- `tcp_retries1`: Number of acknowledgements for a packet before it is given up.
- `tcp_retries2`: Maximum number of attempts to send a packet.
- `tcp_fin_timeout`: The wait time for the acknowledgement of a connection-tear-down request before the connection is aborted.
- `tcp_max_syn_backlog`: Number of TCP connection-establishment requests to be buffered for a socket.
- `tcp_window_scaling` enables or disables the scaling of TCP windows (as specified in RFC 1323).
- `tcp_timestamps` enables or disables the *TCP timestamp* (as specified in RFC 1323).
- `tcp_sack`: Switch for *select acknowledgements* (TCP ACK).
- `tcp_sturg`: Enables *urgent* priority data, as specified in RFC 793.
- `tcp_retrans_collapse`: Several TCP stacks in printers are faulty. You can activate this option to work around this problem.
- `ip_local_port_range` specifies the range for local ports of the TCP and UDP protocols. The first number specifies the beginning of the interval, the second specifies the end.

/proc/sys/net/ipv4/conf   The `/proc/sys/net/ipv4/` directory is subdivided; let's first look at the `conf` subdirectory. It contains, in turn, several subdirectories: one each for each registered network device, and one named `all`. All of these directories include the same entries, which are introduced here:

- `accept_redirects` shows whether *ICMP redirects* are accepted. This option is disabled by default in routers, but enabled in end systems.
- `accept_source_route` enables or disables accepting of source-route packets. This option normally is enabled in routers, but disabled in end systems.
- `forwarding` enables or disables the forwarding of packets on this network device.
- `log_martians` enables or disables the logging of "impossible" addresses (including class-E addresses in IP).
- `mc_forwarding` enables or disables multicast routing. If activated, the `CONFIG_MROUTE` option should additionally be compiled for the kernel, and a multicast routing daemon should be installed.
- `proxy_arp`: Support for an ARP proxy.
- `rp_filter`: Checking the sender IP address can be disabled.
- `secure_redirects` enables or disables the option that *ICMP redirect* messages are accepted only by routers present in the default gateways list.

/proc/sys/net/ipv4/route

- `error_burst`, `error_cost`: These parameters are used to limit the log messages of the routing code in the kernel. The larger that `error_cost` is, the earlier that log messages will be created. `error_burst` limits the rejection of warning messages.

- ush: Accessing this file causes the routing cache to be deleted.
- gc_elastic, gc_interval, gc_min_interval, gc_thresh, gc_timeout: These parameters control the automatic *garbage collection* of the routing table (i.e., how soon and how strictly old entries will be removed from the table.
- max_size specifies the size of the routing cache. Older entries are removed as soon as this size is reached.
- max_delay, min_delay: Delays for deleting the entire routing cache.
- redirect_load, redirect_number: These factors specify how many ICMP redirect packets may be sent. No more redirects are sent as soon as redirect_load or redirect_number is exceeded.
- redirect_silence is the timeout value for redirect packets. Once this interval expires, redirect packets that have not yet been acknowledged are retransmitted. This process runs even when redirects were disabled because redirect_load or redirect_number was exceeded.
- max_size: Maximum number of entries in the routing cache. If this number is exceeded, the least-used entries are overwritten.

/proc/sys/net/ipv4/neigh/[net dev]   The following parameters denote the immediate *network neighbors*; they are located in the /proc/sys/net/ipv4/neigh/[net dev] directory of the respective network device:

- base_reachable_time: A value used to compute the *random reachable time*. (See RFC 2461.)
- retrans_time: The time between two consecutive *neighbor solicitation* packets, used for address resolution and for checking the reachability of a local computer. This time is specified in ticks.
- unres_qlen: Specifies the maximum queue length for (higher-layer) packets waiting for the resolution of a specific address. (See Chapter 15.)
- ucast_solicit: Maximum number of packets sent to resolve a unicast address.
- mcast_solicit: Maximum number of attempts to resolve a multicast address.
- delay_first_probe_time: Wait time, after the expiry of which a valid *neighbor* entry is checked again. (See gc_stale_time.)
- locktime: An entry in an ARP/neighbor table will be replaced by a new one provided that the old entry is locktime ticks old.
- proxy_delay: The maximum wait time for the reply to an ARP request, which has an entry in the ARP proxy.
- proxy_qlen: Maximum length of the queue for a delayed ARP proxy timer. (See proxy_delay.)
- arp_solicit: Specifies the number of requests sent to the ARP daemon (on user level).
- gc_scale_time: Specifies the intervals in which the ARP table is checked for old entries (state = NUD_STALE). If an entry is in the NUD_STALE state, then an initial attempt is made to check it directly (by using a unicast packet). If this attempt fails, and if mcast_solicit > 0, a broadcast ARP request is used to find the computer.

B.4   USING A DEBUGGER WITH THE LINUX KERNEL

A debugger is a tool that allows you to stop a program under development during its execution and to execute it step by step to monitor the program state—the values of variables and the contents of memory locations—and to modify it, if necessary. A debugger can also be used for development in the Linux kernel. However, there is no way of stopping or stepwise running, because stopping the kernel would immediately cause the entire system to become unusable. Reading global variables and other memory locations is possible while the kernel is running, and it can often be helpful for better understanding active processes.

Interface Between Kernel and Debugger   Debuggers normally offer a way to edit a so-called core file instead of a running program. Such a file can be created automatically when a program is terminated by an illegal memory access. It contains a copy of the memory locations occupied by this program. We can use a debugger, after reading a core file, to check the program state when the crash happened.

The core file, as interface between the debugger and the program state, can also be used to monitor the Linux kernel. To this end, the file /proc/kcore maps the entire main memory of the system to the format of a core file. So, if we give this file to a debugger as a core file, we can use the debugger tools to check the current state of the entire system.

Compiler Options   In addition to a core file, a debugger requires a file with the executable program. In case of the Linux kernel, this file is available under the name vmlinux in the directory in which the kernel was compiled. When compiling a program to be debugged, the compiler should have been instructed to embed debugging information (e.g., the full names of variables in text form and references to the relevant places in the source code). If this information is available, the debugger lets you (for example) query variables by their names.

The C compiler gcc lets you use the -g option to embed debugging information during compilation. This option has to be entered in a make file at the appropriate position to ensure that it will be used when the Linux kernel is compiled. If we want to achieve this for the entire kernel, we can add this option to the definition of the CFLAGS variable in the main make file in the top directory of the source-code tree. If we want to check only limited kernel areas in the debugger, it is sufficient to add one EXTRA_CFLAGS = -g line each to the make files in the directories that contain the files for each of these areas. For example, this would be net/ip4/Makefile if we were to check routing.

gdb and ddd   One of the most popular debuggers in the UNIX world is the gdb debugger, developed under the auspices of the Free Software Foundation (FSF). gdb offers only a text interface to the user, so it is universal, but not comfortable to use. More recently, several front ends have been developed to remove this drawback (e.g., by offering a graphical user interface). Two representatives of this kind were also developed by FSF: the Data Display Debugger, ddd, and the Grand Unified Debugger (gud) mode of the emacs text editor. ddd has options for graphic representation of data structures, which make it suitable particularly to check such data structures in the Linux kernel.

A detailed description of how these tools work would go beyond the scope and volume of this book. Detailed instructions are included in each of the distribution packages.

Example   Figure B–1 shows an example for the graphic representation of data structures in ddd. This example uses a fragment from a concrete variant of data structures to represent some of the routing tables described in Chapter 16.

The entry point is a global array, `fig_tables`, the 254th element of which is the `fib_table` structure of the routing table `main`. The `fn_hash` structure (reachable as `*` `(struct fn_hash *) fib_tables[254]->tb_data`) is appended to the `main` table. The `fn_hash` structure has a number of pointers to `fn_zone` structures for prefix lengths 0 through 31 in its `fn_zones` array. The figure represents the data structure for the zone with prefix length 8. An explicit type conversion is required to display the hash table referenced there, because the hash table size cannot be derived from the pointer type, `fz_hash`. Specifically, we have to give the expression that describes this pointer a leading `(struct fib_node *[16])` `*` to make the hash table visible, as shown in the figure. The eighth element of the hash table is unequal null and refers to a `fib_node` structure for the prefix 10.0.0.0/8 (where the prefix length can be derived from the `fn_zone` structure further up). The figure also represents the associated `fib_info` structure, and the `fib_prefsrc` element of that structure contains the source address 10.0.0.1 in hexadecimal representation (in network byte order) and the hooked `fib_nh` structure.

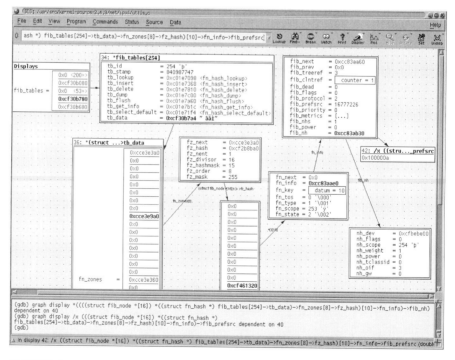

FIGURE B–1
Example using ddd: Checking routing-table data structures. (See Chapter 16.)

To use ddd in this example, we inserted the mentioned line, EXTRA_CFLAGS = -g, in the file net/ipv4/Makefile before compiling the Linux kernel. Next, we installed the kernel prepared in this way; then we used the command ddd /usr/src/linux/vmlinux /proc/kcore to start ddd.

Notice that gdb, upon which ddd is based, cannot see later modifications to the data structures itself, because such modifications normally do not occur in core files. We can use the gdb command core /proc/kcore to make the debugger reread the core file, so that the displayed values are updated.

APPENDIX C

Tools and Commands for Network Operation

The sections of this appendix introduce tools and commands to manage, configure, and control the network functionality in Linux. We will explain the most important operations and their parameters for each command. More detailed information about the exact syntax of a command and additional options are described in the respective man pages.

C.1   USING ifconfig TO MANAGE NETWORK DEVICES

The command ifconfig is available in Linux to configure a network device. It serves mainly to activate, deactivate, and configure a network device and its physical adapters. This tool lets you modify both protocol-specific parameters (address, subnet mask, etc.) and interface-specific parameters (I/O port, interrupts, etc.). ifconfig can also be used to modify the flags of a registered network device (ARP, PROMISC, etc.).

To be able to use it, a network device has to first be activated in ifconfig. To this end, the adapter has to be known to the kernel and be present in the list of network devices. (See Chapter 5.)

Syntax

```
ifconfig      [-a] [-i] [-v] interface [[family] address]
              [add address[/prefixlen]] [del address[/prefixlen]]
              [tunnel aa.bb.cc.dd] [[-]broadcast [aa.bb.cc.dd]]
              [[-]pointopoint [aa.bb.cc.dd]]
              [netmask aa.bb.cc.dd] [dstaddr aa.bb.cc.dd]
              [hw class address][metric NN] [mtu NN]
              [[-]trailers] [[-]arp] [[-]allmulti] [[-]promisc]
              [multicast] [mem_start NN] [io_addr NN] [irq NN]
              [media type] [up] [down]
```

- `interface` denotes the network device to be configured (e.g., `eth0`, `ppp1`).
- `family` denotes the protocol family of the network-layer protocol used. Depending on the address family, the addresses specified here have different address formats (e.g., `inet` (TCP/IPv4 protocols), `inet6` (TCP/IPv6 protocols), `ax25` (Packet Radio), `ddp` (Apple), `ipx` (Novell)). `inet` is the default choice, so it does not have to be selected.
- `address` is the address of the network device in the address format of the address family. IP addresses are written in the usual dotted decimal notation, `a.b.c.d`.

If `ifconfig` is started with the name of a network device, then only the configuration of this interface is output on the console. If you start it without parameters, it lists all currently configured interfaces. The option -a can be used to additionally display network devices known to the kernel, but not yet activated.

Example

```
root@tux # ifconfig
eth0    Link encap:Ethernet HWaddr 00:90:27:44:D9:89
        inet addr:129.13.25.10 Bcast:129.13.25.255 Mask:255.255.255.0
        UP BROADCAST RUNNING MTU:1500 Metric:1
        RX packets:879876 errors:1 dropped:0 overruns:0 frame:11
        TX packets:706287 errors:0 dropped:0 overruns:0 carrier:0
        collisions:45793 txqueuelen:100
        Interrupt:11 Base address:0xe800

lo      Link encap:Local Loopback
        inet addr:127.0.0.1 Mask:255.0.0.0
        UP LOOPBACK RUNNING MTU:3924 Metric:1
        RX packets:130 errors:0 dropped:0 overruns:0 frame:0
        TX packets:130 errors:0 dropped:0 overruns:0 carrier:0
        collisions:0 txqueuelen:0
```

- The fields `MTU` and `Metric` show the current values for Maximum Transfer Unit (MTU) and the metrics of the interface. The metrics can be used by routing protocols to make a choice when several routes having the same cost lead over two different network devices.
- The flags displayed by `ifconfig` correspond more or less to the names of command parameters and will later be explained further.
- The RX (Receive) and TX (Transmit) information shows how many packets have been received or sent over the network device.
- `errors` gives the number of errors that occurred.
- `overruns` shows the number of faulty packets. Among other reasons, errors can occur that are due to an overrun of the receive queue. An *overrun* occurs in a computer when more packets arrive than the kernel can process. The input queues reach their maximum (`max_backlog`), and all packets arriving additionally will be dropped. (See Chapter 6.)

The following list describes the parameters of the `ifconfig` command (with the names of the relevant flags in brackets). Some of these parameters enable certain modes of the network device (e.g., the ARP capability). These modes can be disabled by a leading minus ($-$) sign.

- up activates a network device. When you use this command to state an address, then up is taken as the default option. If up is called without additional parameters, `ifconfig` initializes the network adapter to the default values (e.g., the IP address to 0.0.0.0, which won't make much sense). The up option sets the flags UP and RUNNING.

- down deactivates a network device. However, this device remains in the list of registered network devices, so that it can be reactivated later. At the same time, all routes in which this network device participated are removed from the routing table.

- netmask *mask* assigns a subnet mask to the network device.

- pointopoint *address* is used for a point-to-point connection that directly connects two computers. Examples include SLIP and PLIP network connections. This parameter is used to set the IP address of the peer system. `ifconfig` shows the presence of a point-to-point peer by the flag POINTOPOINT.

- broadcast *address* sets the broadcast address of the network device. It normally is built from the network address and the appropriate address class. All bits of the host part are set to one. However, the broadcast address can also be set explicitly. The presence of a broadcast address is shown by the flag BROADCAST.

- mtu *bytes* sets the Maximum Transfer Unit (MTU) (i.e., the maximum size of a MAC frame) to the specified size. The default value is 1500 bytes for Ethernet adapters, 296 bytes for SLIP connections.

- arp enables the Address Resolution Protocol for network devices that use broadcast technologies (Ethernet, token ring, etc.) to allocate logical layer-3 addresses to physical MAC addresses. This option is set by default for broadcast networks. `ifconfig` shows the flag NOARP if ARP was deactivated.

- -arp disables the use of the Address Resolution Protocol and sets the NOARP flag.

- promisc moves the network adapter into the *promiscuous* mode. For broadcast-capable networks, this mode causes all packets to be received by the network interface and to be forwarded to the higher layers, regardless of whether they are addressed to this computer. This allows us to monitor the network traffic in a local area network. Of course, this mode should be used for analysis purposes only, which is often extremely useful. The `tcpdump` tool uses the promiscuous mode to analyze the traffic in a local area network. The promiscuous mode is shown by the flag PROMISC.

- -promisc disables the promiscuous mode.

- multicast enables the receipt of multicast packets addressed to groups at which the computer is registered as a member.

- -multicast disables the receipt of multicast packets.

- allmulti enables the receipt of all multicast packets, including multicast packets from groups of which the computer is not a member. This mode is used by multicast routers, among others.

- -allmulti disables the *allmulti* mode.
- irq, io_addr, and mem_start set the number of the interrupt, the I/O address, and the memory address of a network adapter.

C.2   USING ping TO TEST THE REACHABILITY

ping is the first tool generally used when a computer is not reachable, to check the network connection. ping sends an ECHO_REQUEST packet to the specified computer and expects an ECHO_REPLY. (See Section 24.4.) In addition, ping outputs statistical values about the connection. It is also possible to use the IP option *record route* to track the route of packets.

Syntax

```
ping [-DdfLnqRrv] [-c number] [-I address] [-i time]
       [-l number] [-p pattern] [-s size] [-t ttl] [-w time]
       computer
```

ping has the following options:

- -c *number*: ping sends only number packets, then terminates. Normally, ping runs forever until the process is stopped.
- -f runs a so-called *flood ping*. This means that ping sends as many packets as it received replies, or at least a hundred per second. This option can be used to check the behavior of a network or end system under high load.
- -I *address* specifies the network device (by the IP address) that should be used to send echo packets.
- -i *time* specifies the wait time between two sent *echo request* packets. This value is normally one second.
- -l *number* sends number packets at maximum speed. Subsequently, ping switches into the normal transmit mode.
- -n prevents the resolution and output of DNS names. IP addresses are written in dotted decimal notation.
- -p *pattern* fills sent *echo* packets with the specified pattern. This allows you to check the behavior of packets with certain contents.
- -q is the *quiet* mode, which outputs statistics only when the program is closed.
- -R enables the IP option *record route*. (See Section 14.4.) It outputs all routers visited, if these routers support the *record route* option.
- -s *size* sets the ICMP packet to size bytes. Normally, an echo packet is of size 56 bytes. Together with the ICMP header (8 bytes), the size is then 64 bytes.
- -t *ttl* sets the value of the Time-To-Live field in the packet header to ttl, which allows you to limit the reach of an *echo request*.
- -w *time* sets the maximum wait time for a reply to an *echo request* to time seconds. The normal wait time for an outstanding reply to an *echo request* is ten seconds.

Example

```
root@tux # ping www.Linux-netzwerkarchitektur.de
PING www.Linux-netzwerkarchitektur.de (192.67.198.52): 56 data bytes
64 bytes from 192.67.198.52: icmp_seq=0 ttl=246 time=4.589 ms
64 bytes from 192.67.198.52: icmp_seq=1 ttl=246 time=3.481 ms
64 bytes from 192.67.198.52: icmp_seq=2 ttl=246 time=3.271 ms
64 bytes from 192.67.198.52: icmp_seq=3 ttl=246 time=3.785 ms
--- www.Linux-netzwerkarchitektur.de ping statistics ---
4 packets transmitted, 4 packets received, 0% packet loss
round trip min/avg/max = 3.271/3.781/4.589 ms
```

C.3   USING netstat TO VIEW THE NETWORK STATE

netstat is an extensive tool for viewing the network state. For example, you can use netstat to display the routing table and the state of the socket currently created.

Displaying routing tables   If you start it with the -r option, netstat outputs the routing tables of the kernel. This corresponds broadly to the result of the route command. The option -n is used to output the IP addresses of computers instead of their DNS names.

```
root@tux # netstat -nr
Kernel routing table
  Destination    Gateway        Genmask        Flags MSS Window Use Iface
  129.13.42.0    0.0.0.0        255.255.255.0  U     0   0      478 eth0
  127.0.0.0      0.0.0.0        255.0.0.0      U     0   0      50  lo
  0.0.0.0        129.13.42.233  0.0.0.0        UG    0   0      238 eth0
```

The first column of this output shows the route destination. The column *Flags* shows the type of destination (i.e., *Gateway* (G) or *Host* (H)), to better explicate the entry in the first column.

If the destination is a gateway (router), the second column shows the IP address of that router (or, more exactly, the IP address of the adapter where the packet arrives in that router). If the route does not lead across a gateway, then the second column shows the value 0.0.0.0.

The third column shows the *reach* of a route. In routes with a (sub)network as the destination, the entry in the third column corresponds to the network mask; the value 255.255.255.255 is output for routes to computers (H). The default route has the mask 0.0.0.0.

All entries in the routing table are sorted so that the more special routes (long network masks) are listed before the more general routes (short network masks). When searching for a matching route, the kernel takes the bit-by-bit AND of the destination address and the network mask and compares the result with the route's destination.

The fourth column shows various flags that provide more information about a route. As has been mentioned, these flags specify the type of destination (gateway or host), among other things:

- G: The next hop is a router (gateway). This means that the packet is sent with the router's MAC address.
- U shows that the network device is enabled (UP).
- H: The next hop is an end system, addressed directly by its MAC address in the MAC layer.
- D: This entry was created dynamically, either by an *ICMP redirect* packet or by a routing protocol.
- M: The route was modified by an *ICMP redirect*.

The last column shows the output interface for a route.

Viewing Interface Statistics   We can start `netstat` with `-i` to output current statistics about active network devices. This option can be used together with the option `-a` to show inactive network devices in addition to active network devices. The output from `netstat` `-i` looks like an output of the `ifconfig` command and uses the same parameters.

Active Connections and Sockets   `netstat` supports a number of options we can use to list active and passive sockets. The arguments `-t`, `-u`, `-w`, and `-x` show active TCP, UDP, RAW, and UNIX sockets. We can additionally use the option `-a` to list all sockets currently waiting for an incoming connection. This shows all open server sockets.

```
root@tux # netstat -ta
Active Internet connections (including servers)
Proto Recv-Q Send-Q  Local Address        Foreign Address      (state)
tcp        0      0  localhost.4261       localhost.sunrpc     TIME_WAIT
tcp        0      0  sioux.1023           cocopah.1017         ESTABLISHED
tcp        0    280  sioux.22             tpc17.telemat.873    ESTABLISHED
tcp        0      0  localhost.4254       localhost.2301       TIME_WAIT
tcp        0      0  localhost.4255       localhost.2301       TIME_WAIT
tcp        0    217  tmnis.domain         tmins.4263           ESTABLISHED
tcp        0      0  sioux.4257           tlps17.print-sr      SYN_SENT
tcp        0      0  sioux.4259           tlps17.print-sr      SYN_SENT
tcp        0      0  *.printer            *.*                  LISTEN
tcp        0      0  *.dnacml             *.*                  LISTEN
tcp        0      0  *.1027               *.*                  LISTEN
udp        0      0  sioux.domain         *.*
udp        0      0  *.908                *.*
udp        0      0  *.987                *.*
udp        0      0  *.1017               *.*
```

This example of a `netstat -ta` output shows that most sockets either are in the LISTEN state (waiting for incoming connections) or already have an existing TCP connection (ESTABLISHED). Previously closed connections remain in the TIME_WAIT state for a little while before the sockets are deleted and so can be reused. (See Chapter 24.)

The first two columns of the output show the current number of packets in the input queue (Recv-Queue) and the output queue (Send-Queue). The fourth and fifth columns show the socket addresses (IP address / DNS name, and port) of the two communication peers. An asterisk next to connections that don't yet exist means that there is no communication peer yet, so that no address can be specified. `*:ssh` means that the computer waits for connections incoming at port `ssh`. The allocation of port addresses to protocols is defined in `/etc/services`.

C.4   USING route FOR ROUTING INFORMATION

The `route` command serves to set and manage routing information in a computer. The `route` command knows exactly two options; one to set, and one to delete, static routes. Dynamic routes are set by routing protocols.

Syntax

```
route add [-A family] [-net|-host] address [gw gateway] [netmask mask]
          [mss MSS] [dev interface]
route del address
```

- `-A family` specifies the address family (`inet`, `inet6`, etc.).
- `-n` shows addresses in dotted decimal notation and does not attempt to resolve them into DNS names.
- `-e` specifies the routing table in `netstat` format.
- `-ee` shows all information of the routing table.
- `-net` means that the specified address denotes a (sub)network and not a computer.
- `-host` shows that the address denotes a computer.
- `-F` shows the *Forwarding Information Base* (routing table). The options `-e` and `-ee` can be used to specify a format for the output.
- `-C` shows the current routing cache of the kernel.
- `del` deletes the specified route.
- `add` adds a route to the routing table.
- `address` specifies the route destination. This can be a (sub)network or a computer. The address can be written in dotted decimal notation or as a DNS name.
- `netmask mask` is the network mask for the new route.
- `gw gateway` specifies a gateway (router). All packets on this route are sent over this router, which knows the further path. Before it can be used as gateway for some destination, a computer has to know the route to it; either we must previously have set a static route, or the destination should be reachable over the default route.
- `metric metric` sets the metrics for this entry in the routing table.
- `mss MSS` sets the maximum segment size of TCP to MSS bytes. The default value is 536 bytes.
- `dev interface` specifies that packets on this route should always be output over the specified network device. If no device is specified, then the kernel attempts to find a network device to be used from other routes.
- `default` denotes the default route for all routes that do not have a matching entry in the routing table.

The output of the route command corresponds largely to the output of netstat. (See Section C.3.)

Examples

- root@tux # route add -net 127.0.0.0

  sets the entry for the loopback network device. Because no network mask was specified, the default network mask for a class-A network is assumed (255.0.0.0).

- root@tux # route add -net 129.13.42.0 netmask 255.255.255.0 dev eth0

  forwards the route for all addresses in network 129.13.42.0 to the network eth0. Packets are sent directly to the computers in network 129.13.42, not over a router.

- root@tux # route add default gw router-icsi.Berkeley.edu

  sets the default route to router router-icsi. All packets that have no matching route in the routing table are sent over this gateway. In IP computers, a default gateway should always be specified, because no computer stores the routes to all computers in the Internet.

C.5 USING tcpdump FOR NETWORK ANALYSIS

tcpdump is a high-performing tool for monitoring the packet streams in local area networks. tcpdump -i *interface* can be used to log and output all activities in a LAN. The actions of the local area network can be fully logged only provided that it is a broadcast-capable medium, such as Ethernet or token ring, and that the network card supports the promiscuous mode. In switched LANs, we cannot log packets that are not actually sent to the adapter.

Syntax

```
tcpdump    [ -deflnNOpqStvx ] [ -c <counter>] [ -F <file> ]
           [ -i <interface> ] [ -r <file>] [ -s <length> ]
           [ -w <file> ] [<expression>]
```

If tcpdump is started without specifying options, it outputs all packets received by the specified network device. This is normally a large number of packets; hence, the output can become unclear. For this reason, we can specify a logical <expression> to limit the number of logged packets. This logical printout helps make the output more clear.

We can use tcpdump for extremely useful studies. On the other hand, it can be misused by intruders to eavesdrop on communication in a LAN. For example, an intruder could log and evaluate the contents of communication connections. The intruder could then easily filter passwords transmitted in cleartext in Telnet or Rlogin sessions. For this reason, tcpdump can be executed only by administrators (root).

Parameters

- -c *counter*: The analysis of tcpdump ends after receipt of counter packets.
- -d *expression*: The expression is evaluated and output, and the program is terminated.
- -e: The MAC header is output explicitly for each packet (i.e., the MAC sender address, the MAC destination address, and the protocol type).
- -f disables the DNS name resolution. If computers are not listed in /etc/hosts, their IP addresses will not be resolved.
- -F *file*: The logical expression (see option -d) is read from file, and expressions in the command line are ignored.
- -i *interface* specifies the network device for which the packets should be logged. Without this option, tcpdump always selects the first element from the internal list of active network adapters (except the loopback network device).
- -l buffers the output line by line. Without this option, each character is output immediately.
- -n disables the name resolution. IP addresses are not converted into DNS names; similarly with the allocation of ports.
- -N omits the domain names in addresses (i.e., www instead of www.linuxnetzwerkarchitektur.de).
- -O disables the internal optimization of the qualification expression.
- -p means that tcpdump does not activate the promiscuous mode. However, a network device may be in this mode for other reasons, so there is no guarantee that the promiscuous mode is disabled.
- -q outputs abbreviated messages and less protocol information.
- -r *file* reads the packets to be checked from the specified file. The file should previously have been created by tcpdump, as is achieved by using the option -w.
- -s *length* sets the number of bytes that tcpdump handles as protocol header at the beginning of a packet. Normally, these are 68 bytes, which is sufficient for IP, ICMP, TCP, and UDP. For NFS and DNS packets, this value may truncate information.
- -S outputs absolute instead of relative TCP sequence numbers.
- -t suppresses the timestamp output.
- -tt outputs the timestamp in unformatted form. This enables faster processing, because the time information does not have to be converted. However, the readability of the output suffers.
- -v enables more detailed outputs. For example, this option additionally outputs the *TTL* values and the *TOS* field values of IP packets.
- -vv enables outputs that are even more detailed.
- -w *file* causes unprocessed packet information to be written to the specified file. Subsequently, you can use the option -r to edit and analyze this information. This option is recommended when tcpdump has problems handling a large number of packets.

-x causes each packet (except the LLC header) to be output in hexadecimal form. The number of output bytes can be defined by the option -s (default = 68). You can use an expression to output only packets of the LAN that meet this expression.

Expressions   Expressions consist of one or several primitives. A primitive, in turn, is built from a qualification parameter and a value (name or number).

There are three types of qualification parameters:

Types define the type to be qualified. Three types are available: host, net, and port; host is the default if no type is specified.

The *direction* defines the transmit direction of the packet to be analyzed. The direction can be either src, dst, src or dst, and src and dst. src stands for incoming packets and dst for transmitted packets. src or dst is assumed if nothing is specified.

The *protocol* specifies that only packets of a specific protocol type should be analyzed. Some of the protocols that can be specified are ether, fddi, ip, arp, rarp, tcp, and udp.

If several protocols should be analyzed, then the types can be OR-linked. If no special protocol is specified, then all protocols matching the specified type are analyzed.

Examples

src tux: All packets from computer tux.

(src tux) and (ip or arp): All packets from tux, but only IP or ARP packets.

port 80: All packets of the TCP or UDP protocols where the port is equal 80.

Notice that keywords and arithmetic expressions can be used in addition to this syntax. Complex conditions are achieved by AND, OR, and NOT linking (e.g., host tux AND NOT port 80 AND NOT port 21).

Other Conditions

less *length*: Only packets with the a maximum of the specified length are considered.

greater *length*: Only packets with at least the specified length are considered.

broadcast: The packet must be a broadcast message.

multicast: The packet must be a multicast message.

Arithmetic Conditions

Expression RelOp expression: The expression is an arithmetic integer expression and may include one of the following three operators:

▷ Binary operators (as in the programming language C: + − * / & |).

▶ If a *length operator* len occurs, then it is replaced by the packet length.

▶ An *access operator*, which can be used to access data in a packet.

Data in a packet is accessed as follows:

Protocol [offset : length]

The [and] characters must be stated; they are not used for optional specifications here.

Protocol is one of the keywords ether, fddi, ip, arp, rarp, tcp, udp, or icmp and denotes the network protocol. Offset can be one of the valid arithmetic expressions. Length is optional; it denotes the field size. Possible values are 1 (byte), 2 (short integer), and 4 (long integer), where 1 is the default when nothing is specified.

Examples

▦ ether[0] & 1 != 0 analyzes all of the multicast traffic.

▦ ip[0] & 0xf != 5 intercepts all IP packets with options.

Primitives can be grouped within brackets. The complete expression might have to be written between exclamation signs or be otherwise marked to prevent the shell from interpreting the information. Grouped or single expressions can be negated and logically AND or OR linked:

▦ ! or not: Negation.

▦ && or and: logical AND.

▦ || or or: Logical OR.

If a value is specified without qualification parameter, then the last of the specified keywords is assumed. For example, not host A and B is identical with not host A and host B, and should not be confused with not (host A or B).

The outputs of tcpdump are extremely complex and require a detailed explanation of the network protocols, in addition to a detailed description, which would go far beyond a regular syntax description.

C.6 USING traceroute TO TRACE PACKETS

traceroute can be used to trace the route of IP packets through the Internet. traceroute not only outputs a list with IP nodes (routers or end systems); it also determines the quality of the connection to each of these nodes by measuring the time to reach these routers.

Syntax

```
traceroute    [-m maxttl] [-n] [-p port] [-q query] [-r] [-s hostadr]
              [-t tos] [-w delay] host [packet size]
```

You can use `traceroute` to identify the route that packets actually take to the specified computer (host). Within local area networks, the path is only one hop, because the communication peer itself can be within this LAN—it is simply the next hop. In contrast, the communication relationships in larger networks (e.g., in the Internet) use much larger routes (as in the accompanying example).

Another benefit of `traceroute` is that it is suitable for analyzing connection problems. For example, if a computer in the Internet is not reachable, you can use `traceroute` to list all reachable routers on the path to this computer. If one of the intermediate systems does not respond, then it is easy to find the source of error.

To identify a router on the way to the desired destination computer, `traceroute` applies a trick rather than using the IP option *record route*. Specifically, it creates IP packets with the destination address of the specified computer and sends these packets to that computer. The trick is that the TTL value in the IP packet header is initially set to one. This means that the packet, on its way to the destination computer, has to be dropped in the first router, because its maximum time to live (TTL) has expired. According to the IP standard, the router has to return an ICMP message to the sender. From this ICMP message, the sender learns the IP address of the router and so can identify the first switching node. This method is repeated—each time with a TTL value larger by one—until the destination computer is reached.

Example: Connection in a LAN—Directly Connected Station

```
root@tux # traceroute www
    traceroute to www.Linux-netzwerkarchitektur.de (129.13.42.100),
    30 hops max, 40-byte packets

    1 www.Linux-netzwerkarchitektur.de (129.13.42.100) 13 ms 9 ms 9 ms
```

Example: Connection in the Internet

```
root@tuc # traceroute www.tux.org
 traceroute to www.tux.org (207.96.122.8), 30 hops max. 40 Byte packets

 1  router1. linux-netzwerkarchitektur.de (129.13.42.244) 10 ms 20 ms 20 ms
 2  141.3.1.1 (141.3.1.1) 10 ms 10 ms 10 ms
 3  Karlsruhe1.BelWue.de (129.143.167.5) 10 ms 10 ms 10 ms
 4  ZR-Karlsruhe1.WiN-IP.DFN.DE (188.1.174.1) 10 ms 10 ms 10 ms
 5  ZR-Hannover1.WiN-IP.DFN.DE (188.1.144.177) 30 ms 30 ms 30 ms
 6  IR-New-York1.WiN-IP.DFN.DE (188.1.144.86) 280 ms 130 ms 290 ms
 7  dfn.ny1.ny.dante.net (212.1.200.65) 260 ms 120 ms 270 ms
 8  * * *
 9  501.ATM3-0.XR2.NYC4.ALTER.NET (152.63.22.6) 280 ms 270 ms 120 ms
10  192.ATM2-0-0.BR1.EWR1.ALTER.NET (146.188.176.53) 260 ms 280 ms 290 ms
11  UUNET-EWR-1-PEER.cw.net (137.39.23.66) 280 ms 140 ms 130 ms
12  corerouter1.WestOrange.cw.net (204.70.9.138) 290 ms 130 ms 130 ms
13  core4.Washington.cw.net (204.70.4.105) 280 ms 290 ms 290 ms
14  fe0-1-0.gw1.spg.va.rcn.net (207.172.0.5) 140 ms 300 ms 270 ms
15  gwyn.tux.org (207.96.122.8) 160 ms 270 ms 270 ms
```

When traceroute doesn't receive a reply from the queried systems, it outputs *. If no connection to this system can be established, then several * signs appear, and traceroute eventually aborts. This gives one reason to assume that the famous digger cut a cable, or the cleaning person arranged the cables by color :-). If you do get a reply from the queried system despite several asterisks, this could mean that the system or the connected links are under heavy load.

If no parameters are specified, traceroute sends data packets having length 38 bytes to the destination computer. At most 30 stations are addressed by packets with limited TTL values before it is assumed that a packet has not arrived. Traceroute uses the port range between 33,434 and 33,434 + max stations - 1 (i.e., 33,434 to 33,463 in the normal case). For each station, at most three attempts are made to get a reply, and each attempt waits at most three seconds for a reply.

Parameters

- host is the DNS name or the IP address of the computer to which the route should be identified. The usual DNS mechanisms for name resolution are used.
- -m maxttl sets the maximum TTL value of request packets to maxttl, which means that a maximum of maxttl stations will be checked.
- -l specifies the remaining time to live (TTL) of each packet.
- -n specifies addresses in dotted decimal notation (i.e., no name resolution is done).
- -p port sets the basic port (i.e., the port number from which test packets should be sent). The default is 33,434. The port range depends on the number of participating stations.
- -q queries is the number of attempts to obtain a reply (default 3).
- -r means that routing tables will be ignored. A locally connected computer is addressed directly. An error is output, if the computer is a computer not locally reachable. This option can be used to test the routing situation or a computer without the existence of a route.
- -s hostadr uses the specified IP address as the sender address for packets for computers with several IP addresses.
- -t tos sets the value of the TOS field in the IP packet header.
- -w delay is the wait time in seconds for each attempt to address a computer (default 3).
- -s packet size specifies a different size for data packets (default 38 bytes).

C.7 OTHER TOOLS

In addition to the tools introduced in the previous sections, which have been available since the early days of Linux, there are several new programs that can be used to check and monitor networks. We will introduce three of these tools. Detailed information about these tools is found in the relevant manual pages or URLs.

░ bing is a tool to identify the bandwidth currently available between two computers. bing uses ICMP packets with different sizes and tries to work out the current bandwidth from identified packet round trips.

bing uses numerous options, which are described in the manual page (man bing). The following example shows how a 54-kbps modem line can be measured.

```
root@tux # bing 213.7.6.95 141.25.10.72
BING     www.linux-netwerkarchitektur.de (213.7.6.95)
         and 1701d.tm.uka.de (141.25.10.72)
         44 and 108 data bytes
1024 bits in 0.000ms
1024 bits in 20.123ms: 50887bps. 0.019651ms per bit
1024 bits in 10.103ms: 101356bps. 0.009866ms per bit
1024 bits in 10.138ms: 101006bps. 0.009900ms per bit
1024 bits in 10.557ms: 96997bps. 0.010310ms per bit
1024 bits in 19.966ms: 51287bps. 0.019498ms per bit
1024 bits in 19.174ms: 53406bps. 0.018725ms per bit
1024 bits in 19.314ms: 53019bps. 0.018861ms per bit
1024 bits in 19.510ms: 52486bps. 0.019053ms per bit

--  213.7.6.95 statistics --
bytes   out    in   dup  loss   rtt (ms): min        avg        max
   44    51    51         0%               0.049      0.053      0.078
  108    51    51         0%               0.023      0.024      0.025

--  141.25.10.72 statistics --
bytes   out    in   dup  loss   rtt (ms): min        avg        max
   44    51    50         1%              99.644    112.260    147.178
  108    50    50         0%             119.154    127.578    199.999

--  estimated link characteristics --
    warning: rtt big host1 0.023ms < rtt small host2 0.049ms
    estimated throughput 52486bps
    minimum delay per packet 86.182ms (4523 bits)

    average statistics (experimental):
    packet loss: small 1%, big 0%, total 0%
    warning: rtt big host1 0.024ms < rtt small host2 0.053ms
    average throughput 66849bps
    average delay per packet 98.793ms (5185 bits)
    weighted average throughput 66188bps
```

░ ntop shows information about the current utilization of connected networks. It logs all packets received over the network adapters and creates various statistics. Figure C–1 shows an example of the current distribution of the protocols used. We can see that ntop is browser-based (i.e., it represents its information in the form of Web pages). There is also a text-based version, which is similar to the top tool used to display current processes and their computing load.

Information about the use of `ntop` is available in the manual page or at `http://www.ntop.org`.

▪ `ethereal` is another tool for studying the data traffic in local area networks. In contrast to `ntop`, which is more suitable for creating statistics and studying the load distribution in local area networks, `ethereal` is used for detailed analysis of certain data streams. It captures the current data streams in a local area network and interprets the packet contents or the relevant protocol processes. Figure C–2 shows an example of how ethereal captures an HTTP request to a Web server, `http://www.tux.org`.

Information about `ethereal` is available in the manual page (`man ethereal`) or at `http://www.ethereal.com`.

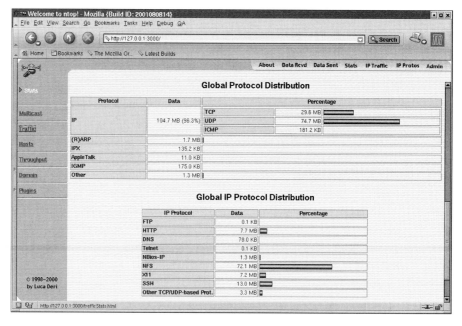

FIGURE C–1
Using ntop to analyze the network traffic in local area networks.

FIGURE C–2
Using ethereal to analyze data streams.

Example for a Kernel Module

```
/************************************************************
 * Example of a kernel module
 * Compile:
 * gcc -I/lib/modules/'uname -r'/build/include -c module.c
 ************************************************************/
#ifndef __KERNEL__
#define __KERNEL__
#endif
#ifndef MODULE
#define MODULE
#endif
#ifndef EXPORT_SYMTAB
#define EXPORT_SYMTAB
#endif

#include <linux/module.h>
#include <linux/kernel.h>
#include <linux/init.h>
#include <linux/proc_fs.h>

MODULE_AUTHOR("Test Author (klaus@Linux-netzwerkarchitektur.de)");
MODULE_DESCRIPTION("This is an example module for the book
          Linux Network Architecture.");

/*****************************************/
/* Example variables for module parameters */
/*****************************************/

unsigned int variable1;
unsigned long variable2[3] = {0,1,2};

/* Example function; will be exported as symbol. */

void methode1(int test1, char *test2)
{
     // do anything
}
```

```
EXPORT_SYMBOL (variable1);
EXPORT_SYMBOL (variable2);
EXPORT_SYMBOL (methode1);

MODULE_PARM (variable1, "i");
MODULE_PARM_DESC (variable1, "Description for the integer");

MODULE_PARM (variable2, "1-3l");
MODULE_PARM_DESC (variable2, "Description for the array of longs");
/*********************************************************/
/* Function to create the output from proc files. */
/*********************************************************/

#ifdef CONFIG_PROC_FS
struct proc_dir_entry *test_dir, *entry;

int test_proc_get_info(char *buf, char **start, off_t offset, int len)
{
        len = sprintf(buf, "\n This is a test module\n\n");
        len += sprintf(buf+len, " Integer: %u\n", variable1);
        len += sprintf(buf+len, " Long[0]: %lu\n", variable2[0]);
        len += sprintf(buf+len, " Long[1]: %lu\n", variable2[1]);
        len += sprintf(buf+len, " Long[2]: %lu\n", variable2[2]);
        return len;
}

int test_proc_read(char *buf, char **start, off_t off, int count, \
                        int *eof, void *data)
{
        unsigned int        *ptr_var1 = data;

        return sprintf(buf, "%u\n", *ptr_var1);
}

int test_proc_write(struct file *file, const char *buffer, \
                        unsigned long count, void *data)
{
        unsigned int        *ptr_var1 = data;

        printk(KERN_DEBUG "TEST: variable1 set to: %s", buffer);

        *ptr_var1 = simple_strtoul(buffer, NULL, 10);
        return count;
}

register_proc_files()
{
        test_dir = proc_mkdir("test_dir", &proc_root);
        if (!create_proc_info_entry("test", 0444, test_dir, test_proc_get_info))
        printk(KERN_DEBUG "TEST: Error creating /proc/test.");

        entry = create_proc_entry("test_rw", 0644, test_dir);

        entry->nlink = 1;
        entry->data = (void *) &variable1;
```

```
        entry->read_proc = test_proc_read;
        entry->write_proc = test_proc_write;
}

unregister_proc_files()
{
        remove_proc_entry("test", test_dir);
        remove_proc_entry("test_rw", test_dir);

        remove_proc_entry("test_dir", NULL);
}
#endif /* CONFIG_PROC_FS */

/**************************************/
/* Initialization function of the module */
/**************************************/

int skull_init(void)
{
        /* Register the functionality of the module, */
        /* e.g., register_netdevice, inet_add_protocol, dev_add_pack, etc. */

        #ifdef CONFIG_PROC_FS
        register_proc_files();
        #endif /* CONFIG_PROC_FS */

        return 0;
}

/*****************************************/
/* Function to clean up the module context */
/*****************************************/

void skull_cleanup(void)
{
        /* Unregister the functionality of the module, */
        /* e.g., unregister_netdevice, inet_del_protocol, dev_remove_pack, etc. */

        #ifdef CONFIG_PROC_FS
        unregister_proc_files();
        #endif /* CONFIG_PROC_FS */
}

/* Alternative function names for init_module() and cleanup_module() */

module_init(skull_init);
module_exit(skull_cleanup);
```

Example for a Network-Layer Protocol

```
/**************************************************************
 * Example for a network-layer protocol
 * Compile:
 * gcc -I/lib/modules/'uname -r'/build/include -c file.c
 **************************************************************/

#ifndef __KERNEL__
#define __KERNEL__
#endif
#ifndef MODULE
#define MODULE
#endif

#include <linux/module.h>
#include <linux/version.h>
#include <linux/kernel.h>
#include <linux/init.h>
#include <linux/skbuff.h>
#include <linux/in.h>
#include <linux/netdevice.h>

MODULE_AUTHOR("Test Author (fixme@Linux-netzwerkarchitektur.de)");
MODULE_DESCRIPTION("Module with a layer-3 test protocol");

#define TEST_PROTO_ID 0x1234

int test_pack_rcv(struct sk_buff *skb, struct net_device *dev, struct
  packet_type *pt);

static struct packet_type test_protocol =
{
        __constant_htons(TEST_PROTO_ID),
        NULL,
        test_pack_rcv,
```

```
        (void *) 1,
        NULL
};

int test_pack_rcv(struct sk_buff *skb, struct net_device *dev, struct
  packet_type *pt)
{
        printk(KERN_DEBUG "Test protocol: Packet Received with length: %u\n",
                skb->len);
        return skb->len;
}

int init_module(void)
{
        dev_add_pack(&test_protocol);
        return 0;
}

void cleanup_module(void)
{
        dev_remove_pack(&test_protocol);
}
```

Example for a Transport Protocol

```
/************************************************************
 * Example for a transport protocol
 * Compile:
 * gcc -I/lib/modules/'uname -r'/build/include -c file.c
 ************************************************************/

#ifndef __KERNEL__
#define __KERNEL__
#endif
#ifndef MODULE
#define MODULE
#endif

#include <linux/module.h>
#include <linux/version.h>
#include <linux/kernel.h>
#include <linux/init.h>
#include <linux/skbuff.h>
#include <linux/in.h>
#include <net/protocol.h>

MODULE_AUTHOR("Test Author (fixme@Linux-netzwerkarchitektur.de)");
MODULE_DESCRIPTION("Module with a layer-4 test protocol");

int test_proto_rcv(struct sk_buff *skb);

static struct inet_protocol test_protocol =
{
        &test_proto_rcv,      /* protocol handler */
        NULL,                 /* error control */
        NULL,                 /* next */
        IPPROTO_TCP,          /* protocol ID */
```

```
        0,                      /* copy */
        NULL,                   /* data */
        "Test_Protocol"         /* name */
};

int test_proto_rcv(struct sk_buff *skb)
{
        printk(KERN_DEBUG "Test protocol: Packet Received with length: %u\n",
               skb->len);
        return skb->len;
}
int init_module(void)
{
        inet_add_protocol(&test_protocol);
        return 0;
}
void cleanup_module(void)
{
        inet_del_protocol(&test_protocol);
}
```

Example for Communication over Sockets

G.1   SERVER

```
/********************************************************************
* Socket example: Chat application, server component comm_s.c
*
* Compilation: gcc -o comm_s comm_s.c
*
* comm_s <port> is used to start a server on each end system,
* and comm_c <destination system> <port> is used to start an
* arbitrary number of clients.
* All messages written in the client are displayed at the respective
* destination server.
********************************************************************/

#include <stdio.h>
#include <sys/types.h>
#include <sys/socket.h>
#include <netinet/in.h>
#include <signal.h>
#include <string.h>

/* Macro for easier output of IP addresses with printf() */
#define NIPQUAD(addr) \
          ((unsigned char *)&addr)[0], \
          ((unsigned char *)&addr)[1], \
          ((unsigned char *)&addr)[2], \
          ((unsigned char *)&addr)[3]

#define BUFSIZE 1024
char buf[BUFSIZE + 1];
```

```c
/* Signal handler to accept the SIGCHLD signal when terminating
 * child processes; otherwise, these zombie processes would remain.
 */
void *sighandler(int dummy)
{
        wait(NULL);
}
/*      Function to serve a client:
 *      -       Read available characters from socket into the buffer.
 *      -       Search for end-of-line character; if found, or if buffer full:
 *              output message, move the rest forward, and repeat.
 *      -       Abort, if error, or connection closed.
 */
void serve(int s, struct sockaddr_in *peer)
{
        int space, n;
        char *p, *q;
        q = p = buf; space = BUFSIZE;
        while (1) {
                if ((n = read(s, p, space)) <= 0) break;
                p += n; space -= n;
                while ((q < p) && (*q != '\n')) q++;
                while ((q < p) || !space) {
                        *q = 0;
                        printf("message from %d.%d.%d.%d %d: %s\n",
                        NIPQUAD(peer->sin_addr.s_addr), ntohs(peer->sin_port), buf);
                        if (q < p) q++;
                        memmove(buf, q, p - q);
                        n = q - buf; // Number of characters "done"
                        p -= n; space += n;
                        q = buf;
                        while ((q < p) && (*q != '\n')) q++;
                }
        }
        if (n < 0) perror("read");
        else if (p > buf) { // Output rest
                *p = 0;
                printf("message from %d.%d.%d.%d %d: %s\n",
                        NIPQUAD(peer->sin_addr.s_addr), ntohs(peer->sin_port), buf);
        }
}

/* Main program:
 * -    Process arguments
 * -    Open socket and wait for connections
 * -    Start separate process for each new connection
 */
int main(int argc, char *argv[])
{
```

```
        int s;
        struct sockaddr_in myaddr;
        int optval;

        if (argc != 2) {
                fprintf(stderr, "Usage: %s <port>\n", argv[0]); exit(1);
        }
        if ((s = socket(AF_INET, SOCK_STREAM, 0)) < 0) {
                perror("socket"); exit(1);
        }
/*      Socket option SO_REUSEADDR: Allow bind(), even when old
        protocol instances are still using the address. */
optval = 1;
if (setsockopt(s, SOL_SOCKET, SO_REUSEADDR, &optval, sizeof(optval))) {
        perror("setsockopt"); exit(1);
}

memset(&myaddr, 0, sizeof(myaddr));
myaddr.sin_family = AF_INET;
myaddr.sin_port = htons(atoi(argv[1]));
myaddr.sin_addr.s_addr = INADDR_ANY;

if (bind(s, (struct sockaddr *) &myaddr, sizeof(myaddr))) {
        perror("bind"); exit(1);
}

if (listen(s, SOMAXCONN)) {
        perror("listen"); exit(1);
}

/* Install signal handler for SIGCHLD signal */
if (signal(SIGCHLD, (sig_t) sighandler) == SIG_ERR) {
        perror("signal"); exit(1);
}

while (1) {
        int new_s;
        struct sockaddr_in claddr;
        int claddrlen;

        claddrlen = sizeof(claddr);
        if ((new_s = accept(s, (struct sockaddr *) &claddr, &claddrlen)) < 0) {
                perror("accept"); continue;
        }

        if (fork()) { /* Parent process */
                close(new_s); /* New socket is used by child process only. */
        }
        else { /* Child process */
                close(s); /* Old socket is used by parent process only. */
                printf("connection from %d.%d.%d.%d %d\n",
```

```
                    NIPQUAD(claddr.sin_addr.s_addr), ntohs(claddr.sin_port));
            serve(new_s, &claddr);
            printf("connection from %d.%d.%d.%d %d closed\n",
                    NIPQUAD(claddr.sin_addr.s_addr), ntohs(claddr.sin_port));
            exit(0);
            }
        }
}
```

G.2   CLIENT

```
/*********************************************************************
* Socket example: Chat application, client component comm_c.c
*
* Compilation: gcc -o comm_c comm_c.c
*********************************************************************/
#include <stdio.h>
#include <sys/types.h>
#include <sys/socket.h>
#include <netinet/in.h>
#include <string.h>

#define BUFSIZE 1024
char buf[BUFSIZE+1];

/* Main program:
*  -    Process arguments.
*  -    Open socket and establish connection to server.
*  -    Read text line by line and send it over this connection.
*  -    Close connection at end of entry (Ctrl-D).
*/
int main(int argc, char *argv[])
{
        int s;
        struct sockaddr_in addr;
        char *p;

if (argc != 3) {
        fprintf(stderr, "Usage: %s <address> <port>\n", argv[0]); exit(1);
}
memset(&addr, 0, sizeof(addr));
addr.sin_family = AF_INET;
addr.sin_port = htons(atoi(argv[2]));
addr.sin_addr.s_addr = inet_addr(argv[1]);

if ((s = socket(AF_INET, SOCK_STREAM, 0)) < 0) {
        perror("socket"); exit(1);
}
```

```
if (connect(s, (struct sockaddr *) &addr, sizeof(addr))) {
       perror("connect"); exit(1);
}

buf[BUFSIZE] = 0;
while (fgets(buf, BUFSIZE, stdin) != NULL) {
      if (write(s, buf, strlen(buf)) == 0) {
              perror("write"); break;
      }
}
close(s);
exit(0);
}
```

Bibliography

[Alme01]   Werner Almesberger. *Traffic Control: Next Generation.*
             http://tcng.sourceforge.net. (Visited on December 23, 2003.)

[Bake95]   Fred Baker. *Requirements for IP Version 4 Routers*, Internet Engineering
             Task Force (IETF), Requests for Comments (RFC) document series,
             RCF 1812, June 1995. *http://www.faqs.org/rfcs/rfc1812.html.* (Visited on
             December 23, 2003.)

[BBDK+01]   Michael Beck, Harald Böhme, Mirko Dziadzka, Ulrich Kunitz et al.
             Linux Kernel Programming. Boston: Addison-Wesley, 3d ed., 2002.

[BoBu01]   Uwe Böhme and Lennert Buytenhenk. *Linux BRIDGE-STP-HOWTO.*
             http://www.tldp.org/HOWTO/BRIDGE-STP-HOWTO. (Visited on
             December 23, 2003.)

[BlAl01]   Mitchell Blank, Werner Almesberger et al. "Project: ATM on Linux:
             Summary," *SourceForge.net. http://sourceforge.net/projects/linux-atm.*
             (Visited on January 9, 2003.)

[BoCe00]   Daniel P. Bovet and Marco Cesati. *Understanding the Linux Kernel.*
             Beijing and Cambridge, MA: O'Reilly, 2000.

[Brad89]   R. Braden. *Requirements for Internet Hosts—Communication Layers*,
             Internet Engineering Task Force (IETF), Requests for Comments
             (RFC) document series, RCF 1122, October 1989.
             http://www.faqs.org/rfcs/rfc1122.html. (Visited on December 23, 2003.)

[BrBP88]   R. Braden, D. Borman, and C. Partridge. *Computing the Internet
             Checksum*, Internet Engineering Task Force (IETF), Requests for
             Comments (RFC) document series, RCF 1071, September 1988.
             http://www.faqs.org/rfcs/rfc1071.html. (Visited on December 23, 2003.)

[Buyt01]   Lennert Buytenhenk. *Linux Bridge Utilities.* Sources at
             http://bridge.sourceforge.net, 2001. (Visited January 9, 2004.)

[ChBe94]   William R. Cheswick and Steven M. Bellovin. *Firewalls and Internet
             Security: Repelling the Wiley Hacker.* Reading, MA: Addison-Wesley,
             1994.

[Come00]   Douglas E. Comer. *Principles, Protocols, and Architecture*, vol. 1 of
             Internetworking with TCP/IP. Upper Saddle River: Prentice Hall, 4th
             ed., 2000.

[Deer86]   Stephen E. Deering. *Host Extensions for IP Multicasting*, Internet En-
             gineering Task Force (IETF), Requests for Comments (RFC) docu-
             ment series, RCF 988, July 1986.
             http://www.faqs.org/rfcs/rfc988.html. (Visited on December 23, 2003.)

[Deer91]   Stephen E. Deering. Multicast Routing in a Datagram Network. PhD dissertation, Stanford University, Palo Alto, CA, December 1991.

[Drak00]   Joshua Drake. *Networking Howto. http://www.linuxdoc.org/HOWTO /Net-HOWTO.* (Visited on December 23, 2003.)

[Fenn97]   W. Fenner. *Internet Group Management Protocol, Version 2,* Internet Engineering Task Force (IETF), Requests for Comments (RFC) document series, RCF 2236, November 1997. *http://www.faqs.org/rfcs/rfc2236.html.* (Visited on December 23, 2003.)

[FeSe00]   Paul Ferguson and Daniel Senie. *Network Ingress Filtering: Defeating Denial of Service Attacks which Employ IP Source Address Spoofing,* Internet Engineering Task Force (IETF), Requests for Comments (RFC) document series, RCF 2827, May 2000. *http://www.faqs.org/rfcs/rfc2827.html.* (Visited on December 23, 2003.)

[FLYV93]   Vince Fuller, Tony Li, Jessica Yu, and Kannan Varadhan. *Classless Inter-Domain Routing (CIDR): An Address Assignment and Aggregation Strategy,* Internet Engineering Task Force (IETF), Requests for Comments (RFC) document series, RCF 1519, September 1993. *http://www.faqs.org/rfcs/rfc1519.html.* (Visited on December 23, 2003.)

[FMMT84]   R. Finlayson, T. Mann, J. C. Mogul, and M. Theimer. *Reverse Address Resolution Protocol,* Internet Engineering Task Force (IETF), Requests for Comments (RFC) document series, RCF 903, June 1984. *http://www.faqs.org/rfcs/rfc903.html.* (Visited on December 23, 2003.)

[Foru95]   ATM Forum. The ATM Forum Technical Committee, *LAN Emulation over ATM Specification, Version 2.* AF-LANE-0084.000. *ftp://ftp.atmforum.com/pub/approved-specs/af-lane-0084.000.pdf.* (Visited on December 23, 2003.)

[Gren00]   Mark Grennan. *Firewall and Proxy Server HOWTO v0.83. http://www.grennan.com/Firewall-HOWTO.html.* (Visited on December 23, 2003.)

[Grou01]   Bluetooth Special Interest Group. *The Official Bluetooth Membership Site. http://www.bluetooth.org.* (Visited on December 23, 2003.)

[Hase97]   Michael Hasenstein. IP Network Address Translation. Undergraduate thesis, Technical University at Chemnitz, Germany, 1997. *http://www.suse.de/~mha/HyperNews/get/linux-ip-nat.html.*

[Hein93]   Juha Heinanen. *Multiprotocol Encapsulation over ATM Adaptation Layer 5,* Internet Engineering Task Force (IETF), Requests for Comments (RFC) document series, RCF 1483, July 1993. *http://www.faqs.org/rfcs/rfc1483.html.* (Visited on December 23, 2003.)

[HiDe98a]   R. Hinden and S. Deering. *Internet Protocol, Version 6 (IPv6) Specification,* Internet Engineering Task Force (IETF), Requests for Comments (RFC) document series, RCF 2460, December 1998. *http://www.faqs.org/rfcs/rfc2460.html.* (Visited on December 23, 2003.)

[HiDe98b]   R. Hinden and S. Deering. *IP Version 6 Addressing Architecture*, Internet Engineering Task Force (IETF), Requests for Comments (RFC) document series, RCF 2373, July 1998. *http://www.faqs.org/rfcs/rfc2373.html*. (Visited on December 23, 2003.)

[ISO93]   International Organization for Standardization. Information Technology—Telecommunications and Information Exchange between Systems—High-Level Data Link Control (HDLC) Procedures. ISO/IEC 13239:2003

[ITU-94]   ITU-T. Information Technology—Open Systems Interconnection—Basic Reference Model: The Basic Model. ISO/IEC 7498-1:1994

[JaBB92]   V. Jacobson, R. Braden, and D. Borman. *TCP Extensions for High Performance*, Internet Engineering Task Force (IETF), Requests for Comments (RFC) document series, RCF 1323, May 1992. *http://www.faqs.org/rfcs/rfc1323.html*. (Visited on January 8, 2004.)

[Jaco90a]   Van Jacobson. "4BSD TCP Header Prediction." *Computer Communications Review* 20(2), 1990.

[Jaco90b]   Van Jacobson. *Compressing TCP/IP Headers for Low-Speed Serial Links*, Internet Engineering Task Force (IETF), Requests for Comments (RFC) document series, RCF 1144, February 1990. *http://www.faqs.org/rfcs/rfc1144.html*. (Visited on January 8, 2004.)

[Kuzn99]   Alexey N. Kuznetsov. *IP Command Reference*. *http://linux-ip.net/gl/ip-cref*. (Visited on January 10, 2004.)

[Kuzn01]   Alexey Kuznetsov. IProute2 and the tc tools. *http://tcng.sourceforge.net/*

[Laub94]   M. Laubach. *Classical IP and ARP over ATM*, Internet Engineering Task Force (IETF), Requests for Comments (RFC) document series, RCF 1577, January 1994. *http://www.faqs.org/rfcs/rfc1577.html*. (Visited on January 8, 2004.)

[LGLK+96]   M. Leech, M. Ganis, Y. Lee, R. Kuris, D. Koblas, and L. Jones. *SOCKS Protocol Version 5*, Internet Engineering Task Force (IETF), Requests for Comments (RFC) document series, RCF 1928, March 1996. *http://www.faqs.org/rfcs/rfc1928.html*. (Visited on January 8, 2004.)

[MaKu90]   T. Mallory and A. Kullberg. *Incremental Updating of the Internet Checksum*, Internet Engineering Task Force (IETF), Requests for Comments (RFC) document series, RCF 1928, January 1990. *http://www.faqs.org/rfcs/rfc1928.html*. (Visited on January 8, 2004.)

[Malk98]   Gary S. Malkin. *RIP Version 2*, Internet Engineering Task Force (IETF), Requests for Comments (RFC) document series, RCF 2453, November 1998. *http://www.faqs.org/rfcs/rfc2453.html*. (Visited on January 8, 2004.)

[McSp95]   D. E. McDysan and D. L. Spohn. *ATM Theory and Application*. New York: McGraw-Hill. 1995.

[MLEC+99]   L. Mamakos, K. Lidl, J. Evarts, D. Carrel, D. Simone, and R. Wheeler. *A Method for Transmitting PPP over Ethernet (PPPoE)*, Internet

Engineering Task Force (IETF), Requests for Comments (RFC) document series, RCF 2516, February 1999. *http://www.faqs.org/rfcs/rfc2516.html*. (Visited on January 8, 2004.)

[Nagl84]   John Nagle. *Congestion Control in TCP/IP Networks*, Internet Engineering Task Force (IETF), Requests for Comments (RFC) document series, RFC 896, January 1984. *http://www.faqs.org/rfcs/rfc896.html*. (Visited on January 8, 2004.)

[NBBB98]   K. Nichols, S. Blake, F. Baker, and D. Black. *Definition of the Differentiated Services Field (DS Field) in the IPv4 and IPv6 Headers*, Internet Engineering Task Force (IETF), Requests for Comments (RFC) document series, RFC 2474, December 1998. *http://www.faqs.org/rfcs/rfc2474.html*. (Visited on January 8, 2004.)

[ObWe01]   Vincent Oberle and Klaus Wehrle. A High Resolution Programmable Timer for the Linux OS. *http://www.oberle.org/apic_timer.html*

[Ostr01]   Michael Ostrowski. PPPoE for Linux 2.4. *http://www.roaringpenguin.com/pppoe/*

[OtWi96]   Thomas Ottmann and Peter Widmayer. *Algorithmen und Datenstrukturen*. Springer Publishing, Heidelber, Germany 1996.

[Pete00]   Larry L. Peterson and Bruce S. Davie. *Computer Network: A Systems Approach*. San Francisco: Morgan Kaufmann Publishers. 2000.

[Post80]   Jon Postel. *User Datagram Protocol*. Internet Engineering Task Force (IETF), Requests for Comments (RFC) document series, RCF 768, August 1980. *http://www.faqs.org/rfcs/rfc768.html*. (Visited on January 10, 2004.)

[Post81a]   Jon Postel. *Assigned Numbers*, Internet Engineering Task Force (IETF), Requests for Comments (RFC) document series, RCF 790, September 1981. *http://www.faqs.org/rfcs/rfc790.html*. (Visited on January 10, 2004.)

[Post81b]   Jon Postel. *Internet Control Message Protocol*, Internet Engineering Task Force (IETF), Requests for Comments (RFC) document series, RCF 792, September 1981. *http://www.faqs.org/rfcs/rfc792.html*. (Visited on January 10, 2004.)

[Post81c]   Jon Postel. *Internet Protocol DARPA Internet Program Protocol Specification*, Internet Engineering Task Force (IETF), Requests for Comments (RFC) document series, RCF 791, September 1981. *http://www.faqs.org/rfcs/rfc791.html*. (Visited on January 10, 2004.)

[Pusa00]   T. Pusateri. *Distance Vector Multicast Routing Protocol Specification,* Internet Draft, draft-ietf-idmr-dvmrp-v3-10.txt (work in progress*). http://www1.ietf.org/mail-archive/ietf-announce/Current/msg08997.html*

[ReLi93]   Yakov Rekhter and Tony Li. *An Architecture for IP Address Allocation with CIDR*, Internet Engineering Task Force (IETF), Requests for Comments (RFC) document series, RCF 1518, September 1993. *http://www.faqs.org/rfcs/rfc1518.html*. (Visited on January 10, 2004.)

[RePo94]   J. Reynolds and J. *Postel. Assigned Numbers*, Internet Engineering Task Force (IETF), Requests for Comments (RFC) document series, RCF 1700, October 1994. *http://www.faqs.org/rfcs/rfc1700.html.* (Visited on January 10, 2004.)

[Rijs94]   Anil Rijsinghani. *Computation of the Internet Checksum via Incremental Update*, Internet Engineering Task Force (IETF), Requests for Comments (RFC) document series, RCF 1624, May 1994. *http://www.faqs.org/rfcs/rfc1624.html.* (Visited on January 10, 2004.)

[RMKG+96]   Yakov Rekhter, Robert G. Moskowitz, Daniel Karrenberg, Geert Jan de Groot, and Eliot Lear. *Address Allocation for Private Internets*, Internet Engineering Task Force (IETF), Requests for Comments (RFC) document series, RCF 1918, February 1996. *http://www.faqs.org/rfcs/rfc1918.html.* (Visited on January 10, 2004.)

[Roar01]   Roaring Penguin Software, Inc. *Roaring Penguins PPPoE Software.* *http://www.roaringpenguin.com/products/rp-pppoe/index.php.* (Visited January 10, 2004.)

[Romk88]   J. Romkey. *A Nonstandard for Transmission of IP Datagrams over Serial Lines: SLIP*, Internet Engineering Task Force (IETF), Requests for Comments (RFC) document series, RCF 1055, June 1998. *http://www.faqs.org/rfcs/rfc1055.html.* (Visited on January 10, 2004.)

[RuCo01]   Alessandro Rubini and Jonathan Corbet. *Linux Device Drivers.* Sebastopol, CA: O'Reilly & Associates, 2d ed., 2001. Online version at *http://www.oreilly.com/catalog/linuxdrive2/index.html.* (Visited on January 10, 2004.)

[Russ00a]   Paul "Rusty" Russell. *Linux IPCHAINS-HOWTO v1.0.8.* *http://www.tldp.org/HOWTO/IPCHAINS-HOWTO.html.* (Visited January 13, 2004.)

[Russ00b]   Paul "Rusty" Russell. Linux Kernel Locking HOWTO, March 2000. *http://www.kernel.org/pub/linux/kernel/people/rusty/kernel-locking/*

[Russ00c]   Paul "Rusty" Russell. *Unreliable Guide to Hacking the Linux Kernel.* *http://netfilter.gnumonks.org/unreliable-guides/kernel-hacking/lk-hacking-guide.html.* (Visited on January 13, 2004.)

[Russ00d]   Paul "Rusty" Russell. "Writing a Module for Netfilter." *Linux Magazine* (6), June 2000.

[Russ01a]   Paul "Rusty" Russell. *Linux 2.4 NAT HOWTO v1.18.* *http://www.netfilter.org/documentation/HOWTO/NAT-HOWTO.html.* (Visited on January 13, 2004.)

[Russ01b]   Paul "Rusty" *Russell. Linux 2.4 Packet Filtering HOWTO v1.26.* *http://www.netfilter.org/documentation/HOWTO/packet-filtering-HOWTO.html.* (Visited on January 13, 2004.)

[Simp94a]   William Allen Simpson. *The Point-to-Point Protocol (PPP)*, Internet Engineering Task Force (IETF), Requests for Comments (RFC) document series, RCF 1661, July 1994. *http://www.faqs.org/rfcs/rfc1661.html.* (Visited on January 13, 2004.)

[Simp94b]   William Allen Simpson. *PPP in HDLC-like Framing*, Internet Engineering Task Force (IETF), Requests for Comments (RFC) document series, RCF 1662, July 1994. *http://www.faqs.org/rfcs/rfc1662.html*. (Visited on January 13, 2004.)

[SrHo99]   Pyda Srisuresh and Matt Holdrege. *IP Network Address Translator (NAT) Terminology and Considerations*, Internet Engineering Task Force (IETF), Requests for Comments (RFC) document series, RCF 2663, August 1999. *http://www.faqs.org/rfcs/rfc2663.html*. (Visited on January 13, 2004.)

[Stal98]   William Stallings. *Cryptography and Network Security: Principles and Practice*. Upper Saddle River, NJ: Prentice Hall, 2d ed., 1998.

[Stev90]   W. Richard Stevens. *UNIX Network Programming*. Upper Saddle River, NJ: Prentice Hall, 1990.

[Stev94a]   W. Richard Stevens. *The Protocols*, vol. 1 of *TCP/IP Illustrated.* Reading, MA: Addison-Wesley, 1994.

[Stev94b]   W. Richard Stevens. *The Implementation* , vol. 2 of *TCP/IP Illustrated.* Reading, MA: Addison-Wesley, 1994.

[Tane95]   Andrew S. Tanenbaum. *Modern Operating Systems*. Upper Saddle River, NJ: Prentice Hall, 1995, 2001 (2d ed.)

[Tane97]   Andrew S. Tanenbaum. *Computer Networks*. Upper Saddle River, N.J: Prentice Hall, 3d ed., 1997.

[WaPD88]   D. Waitzman, C. Partridge, and S. Deering. *Distance-Vector Multicast Routing Protocol*, Internet Engineering Task Force (IETF), Requests for Comments (RFC) document series, RCF 1075, November 1998. *http://www.faqs.org/rfcs/rfc1075.html*. (Visited on January 13, 2004.)

[Wehr01b]   Klaus Wehrle. "An open Architecture for Evaluating Arbitrary Quality of Service Mechanisms in Software Routers,". in *Proceedings of IEEE International Conference on Networking (ICN 2001)*, Colmar, France, June 2001

[WeRi00]   Klaus Wehrle and Hartmut Ritter. "Traffic Shaping in ATM and IP Networks Using Standard End Systems," in *Proceedings of Conference on High Performance Switching & Routing, Joint IEEE/ATM Workshop 2000 and 3d International Conference on ATM*, Heidelberg, Germany, May 2000.

[WeRW01]   Klaus Wehrle, Hartmut Ritter and Lars Wolf. "Improving the Performance of TCP on Guaranteed Bandwidth Connections," in *Tagungsband der Konferenz KiVS 2001 (Kommunikation in verteilten Systemen)*, Hamburg, Germany, February 2001

Index